THE ACTIONS OF GODS

BOOK FOUR OF THE SPARK CITY CYCLE

ROBERT J POWER

THE ACTIONS OF GODS
First published in Ireland by DePaor Press in 2024.
ISBN 978-1-8382765-8-4

Copyright © Robert J Power 2024

All characters, names and events in this publication are fictitious and the work of the author's imagination. Any resemblance to real persons, living or dead, events or localities is purely coincidental.

The right of Robert J Power to be identified as the author of this work has been asserted in accordance with the Copyright and Related Rights Act, 2000.
All rights reserved.

No part of this publication may be reproduced, stored in a retrieval system, or transmitted in any form or by any means, electronic, mechanical, photocopying, recording or otherwise, without the prior permission of the
publisher.

Available in eBook, Audiobook, Paperback and Hardback.

www.RobertJPower.com

For Rights and Permissions contact:
Hello@DePaorPress.com

CONTENTS

1. After the Fall	1
2. Visitor	10
3. Sisters in Arms	21
4. Galvanised	29
5. Filling in the Blanks	41
6. Tragedy of the Healer	49
7. Behemoth	56
8. Lillium	65
9. Drahir	71
10. Wretched Legend	84
11. Wynn	95
12. For the Love of the Absent Gods, Won't Somebody Think of the Children?	101
13. Cordelia the Lost	107
14. Uden the Woodin Man	114
15. Boat Town	121
16. Born in Blood	129
17. The Road to Ruin	135
18. The Road to Rule	140
19. Routines	146
20. Great Escape	162
21. The Pub	170
22. Day in the Life	180
23. Feast in Ruins	186
24. Excerpts From the Desks of Weasels	201
25. Worst Day of His Life	206
26. The Misadventures of Brin the Wistful	212
27. Aimee	220
28. Palace	229
29. Middle o' Nowhere	235
30. Unleashed and Rabid	246
31. Captives of the Nest	252
32. Sesh at the King's Gaf	259
33. Broken Ranger	264
34. The Witching Hours	271
35. After the Breaking	281
36. The Player	288
37. God Lover	298

38. Slap Heard Around the World	306
39. The Finding of Friends	314
40. Killing What's Left Behind	319
41. Once Upon a Time, There Was a Caged Little Cub	325
42. Till Death	331
43. Among Snapping Teeth	340
44. Your Carriage Awaits	348
45. Life Aboard A Sinking Ships	355
46. Erroh the Wrath	363
47. It's Just a Little Trust	368
48. Demons	375
49. Emir's Last Day	382
50. Passing the Rubicon	391
51. Among Generals	400
52. Unless	408
53. Calming the Herd	418
54. The Politician	423
55. Army of One	431
56. Words Between Brothers	437
57. Valhal	444
58. The Pragmatist	451
59. More Excerpts from the Desks of Weasels	462
60. Engaging the Storm	470
61. Day One	474
62. The Next Day	487
63. Gauntlet	492
64. Into the Forest	509
65. The Forest	516
66. King of the Isles	524
67. At Last	535
68. Happy Families	545
69. Queen of Adawan	552
70. Blinding Storm	558
71. Assault on Adawan	565
72. Rare Old Times	575
73. Desperate Hours	582
74. Sailing Towards a Storm	590
75. After Party	598
76. Needful Lies	606
77. It's Not You	613
78. Drunken Ramblings and Revelations	621
79. Needless Honour	631
80. The Growing Legends of Demons	647
81. The Coming of Savages	653

82. Swift Goodbye	673
83. Edging the Siege	679
84. Violent Reunion	695
85. Wedded Day	701
86. Choose a Side	707
87. Choose It Good	714
88. Gathering of Too Few	721
89. Long Goodbye	732
90. Claimed	742
91. Come Out and Fight	749
92. Cordelia's Defiance	754
93. Quiet Times by the Flames	762
94. Committing the Greatest Sin, a Little Taste of Vengeful Scorning, and Visits from New Friends	768
95. The Making of Thunder	775
96. Respite of the Guilty	780
97. Stirring of a God	788
98. Final Excerpts from the Desks of Weasels	793
99. The Battle for Spark City	801
100. Final Fight	808
101. The Fall of Lea	855
102. After the End of It All	865
103. Kingly Ways	889
104. Vote	895
105. Second-Last Day	900
106. Broken Girl	904
107. Better Musings	910
108. Oh, Erroh	917
109. Recapping Lesser Leaders, an Unexpected Revelation, a Wonderful Moment and the Sudden End to Something Beautiful	925
110. Here We Go Again	932
111. The Boar	941
112. Breaking Hearts	949
113. Ambushed	955
114. Goodbye for Now	962
115. Cleansing Waters	967
116. Muck Ridge	973
117. The Long March	982
118. All Things Must End	988
119. Epilogue	1002

A note from the Author	1007
Exclusive Free Book From Robert J Power	1008
Also by Robert J Power	1009
Acknowledgments	1010
About the Author	1012

*To Jan, my one for life from the moment we met.
You were right, we got there in the end.
Let's keep going, beo.*

1

AFTER THE FALL

F*ailure.*
Pain.
Fire.
Anguish.
Failure. Failure. Failure.

The sound of hooves thundered in his ears. So fast. The world alongside was a blur of greens and browns. Erroh, atop his mount, terrified and determined, went with the charge. No longer could he hear the flames as they destroyed the eternal structure, but they were there. Still burning. He was a failure, and the world had ended.

Fuken failure. He'd met Uden and faced him atop the walls of Spark City. Met him with confidence—nay, arrogance—and almost died for his missteps. Beaten, battered, before he'd even believed he could do it.

I can never beat him.

His mind was awash with horror and terror. He was a man without a plan. An Outcast without land or banner. Everything was lost, and it was all his fault.

"Keep going, girl," he challenged, and his magnificent beast answered. She didn't fail. She didn't let him down. She found him when he needed her most. He, though, was broken and lost among the fires and smoke, too beaten to rise. Too damaged to be defiant.

He shuddered in the saddle as Highwind bounded over unforgiving terrain, and his body ached further with every jolting step.

Save me, girl. He didn't dare calm her charge, and she dared not slow. Only when they were clear of the city, of the scattered forces hiding among the eternal green, would she curb her pace. For there were many. Those not ordered to charge. Those who waited with beady eyes, seeking a fleeing failure of a warrior with the silhouette of humanity's desolation billowing up behind him in plumes of black and spark-filled smoke.

I am alone and lost; this is the end of it all.

Erroh's hammering heart was like lead in his chest. A terrible heaviness took hold and seeped through his body. He drew upon dwindling reserves of energy, and wasn't sure he could take any more than the gods asked of him. He'd endured too much. Too much pain. Too much loss and regret.

Betrayer. Cruel murderer.
Failure, failure, fuken failure.
You failed the world, Erroh. Again.

He gripped the reins, dug his feet in against the impressive beast's ribs and felt the agony in his ankle. Always the fuken left, he thought miserably, and shook unhelpful thoughts away. Those thoughts led to despair. The last thing he needed in a terrified flight from a fallen city was despair. It led to a lessening of the charge. A surrendering of the soul. He gripped the reins again with shaking hands, stealing what determination he could. He dared not look behind for fear of what pursued him. He imagined a smouldering army screeching outrage at his defiance. He imagined Uden upon a divine chariot of gold and blood. Too quick. Too fierce for a little cub upon a terrified mount.

You lost, and the world will burn.
As Uden said it would.

The air kept him alive. Brought reason to his spinning mind. Its rushing force took his smoky breath and infused him. He deserved little of this relief, but as he had often done during his short life, he took it, gorged himself upon it, regardless of his deserving.

Below, the hammering thunder softened as Highwind's hooves touched the softer ground, and he leaned lower and kicked her forward. He knew his miraculous escape would not go unpunished. Could not be ignored. The farther he travelled, the more he imagined a garrison of Riders in pursuit. An entire army of them, at least. All chanting their victorious god's name, all bent on finishing this ruined cub and being done with the matter.

The world saw you fall. The world watched you fail.
Again.

As the canopy of green closed in around him, he held in a scream of agony. Of relief. Of fuken desolation. Oh, that scream wanted to release itself from his lips. A lone rider upon a charging mount might remain concealed in the green well enough, but a screaming idiot too foolish to hold in his panic would offer an easy beacon for a hunting pack. So he kept that scream in, gripped the reins tighter, and hated himself in silence. He hated his vanquisher a little too. It was all he could do. It wasn't enough.

Get home to them. He kept that thought in his mind. It was all he could hold. All he could hope for. "You are so brave, Highwind. Just go a little farther, girl," he hissed again, and she did.

When the miles between the fallen city of Spark and the Outcast grew, he finally listened to his mount's laboured breathing and eased his assault upon her. As he hushed her, she gratefully answered his calming demands and lessened her charge. Stroking her mane, he told her he loved her, and she did not appear to care. And that was fine, for he was exhausted, and weariness came upon him as though held in an absent god's invisible glove. Tightening, crushing, everlasting.

Deserving.

"Fuk you all," he hissed in a croaky, broken voice, and it was a weak threat to those behind, or those ahead, or those surrounding him, or any of those who had him in a concealed arrow's sights—as though words thrown angrily could halt their charge. "To the fires with you," he added, and realised the stench of smoke no longer tormented him. He should have felt relief, but he felt only exhausted and broken. More so than usual, too.

He stayed upon the beast, reassuring himself that they might rest awhile once they came upon a suitable site. Really, though, he knew he would try to continue moving until he could ride no more. Until he reached Raven Rock. Until he found his nerve once again.

Further miles drew on and went by until, eventually, exhaustion and thirst pulled him from his horse. Painfully so. Hearing the call of water's delicate rush, he brought Highwind through thick undergrowth until he came upon a small river. Slipping off the mount and forgetting his shattered foot, Erroh dropped painfully to the ground.

"Fuk it," he cried, rolling awkwardly into a patch of bushes with nothing but stinging agony to break his landing. He spat dryly and lay for a moment. "Fuk it all."

Failure, failure, fuken failure.

"Maybe we rest a little while here?" It was a good suggestion, but Highwind thought little on the matter. She blinked at him, and shook her head free of a few buzzing insects before drinking from the water's edge.

"Save some for me," he whispered, scrambling beside her to drink from the cool flow. "I did most of the work escaping, anyway," he jested weakly. He hoped the water might revitalise him and strengthen his weary bones, but he felt no better. He drank deeply until the pain left his throat, until the dizziness left his vision. Until his belly filled and ached. Then he dipped his head to wash the city, the blood and ash, from his face.

This, strangely, gave him a little energy. Enough to climb to his feet again and discover, to his horror, the broken bolt plunged deep into his beast's rump.

"You poor thing," he cried, momentarily forgetting his own miseries and failures. The bolt had struck deep and snapped off sometime during their desperate escape. "It never slowed you down, did it?" he said softly. He lay his forehead against hers and loved her more so.

As he examine the wound, Highwind reared a few times but mercifully did not bolt away. He took no further chances, though, and, securing her to a tree, pulled a dagger free and went to task operating on the offending projectile. The bleeding from the wound had slowed, but the beast's agony was terrible. He felt her every cry of suffering; he lamented every act of clumsiness as he dug in, removing the piece.

"You don't deserve this," he said after a time. The dagger shook in his quivering fingers, for he was no drunken healer. "I'm trying," he whispered, hoping she would understand. He persevered and finally removed the bloody piece, dropping it on the ground before sealing the wound with a salve of mud and leaves. He tried to remember Garrick's further treatments for such things, but his fractured mind couldn't gather the memories needed. Gently, he faced the beast, placed his forehead against hers, and rubbed her gently again. "I will never speak ill of you ever again, my beauty," he pledged, and for a moment, he wondered if the beast understood him. If she did, she gave no sign. She was still upset. Slowly, she dipped her head and bit him on the shoulder. It was a fine bite, for she had all her teeth. She bit deep and drew blood.

"Bitch!"

Pulling away, she snorted her dissatisfaction a few more times before deciding the bite was enough. Perhaps she no longer felt the piece as before. Regardless, she snorted a second time and then went back to grazing. He left her to it, for he had more urgent, horrible matters to attend to.

Carefully removing his boot, he was dismayed to discover how badly his shattered foot had swelled in the saddle. "Fuk it," he cursed softly. Sitting by the river's edge, he allowed the cool water to cover his limb and felt relief for the first time in hours. Prodding around the injury and wincing at his own touch, Erroh began making a splint. A difficult task with few materials to call upon. He ripped his shirt, broke a few thick branches, and laid them side by side.

He hated the next part. Hated it because it involved a lot of pain without guaranteeing success. Gripping his injured foot tightly, he twisted it back and forth. He felt jagged pain shoot up his leg as he manoeuvred his ankle into different positions, hoping to ease the agony. He took the pain and did not cry out. That was their way. Above him, the sun moved across the sky as he massaged the ruined limb, hoping for success, but found nothing more but further pain. There were loud clicks, a few crunches, and he might have felt bones slide ever so beneath his touch. Eventually, when he neared crying out, he dropped his leg back into the cool water and wedged the mangled foot tightly between a couple of rocks.

"Take it," he whispered. A warning, a plea, a mantra. "Take the pain."

He tried to take it. He really did. Turning his body so that the immobilised ankle bent at an unnatural angle, he leaned into it and felt creaking, shattering torture. It took him now, overcame his mind. He'd never endured this kind of agony before. His mouth opened and gasped, and his eyes betrayed him as they let loose their deluge of sorrow.

"Take it because you failed the world, and everyone will die," he groaned between clenched teeth.

The world went dark, and he fell unconscious.

He did not scream.

Darkness.

He woke with a start and found himself among the shadows of a thousand ungodly things, and they reached for him. They loomed all around him, but he could not see. He was blind but for the shattered moon above.

Where am I?

He tried to rise, but a demon held his foot tight in its monstrous mouth, and he shrieked in horror.

I'm in hell, where it's hot as hell.

He hated the dark. The gods knew he hated the dark. That's why they'd brought him to this place. He gasped, pulled himself along the mossy ground, and wrenched himself from the demon's grip. Something in the monster's easy relinquishing of edible things grounded his frantic thoughts, and visions of a burning city roused him from the stupor. A one-eyed god took his angelic wings, spoken of in the ancient tales and beliefs, sending him into fire. Only then did he recover his senses. Hell might have been warmer. Hell might have been quieter too.

Fuk.

There was movement, loud and crashing. Pulling closer in the dark and marching, seeking, hunting. It was like thunder around him, closing in. "Oh, please, no," he moaned, dragging himself away from the stream's edge. His foot was frozen and numb. Whatever damage he'd inflicted upon himself had allowed some swelling to go down, but it was a ruin, and he had failed the world, and he was as lame as a heroic mount with an arrow in its rear, and he wanted to cry, and it was all fuken shit.

"Fuk."

Shivering again, he felt around for his boot and, holding back another scream, dug his foot back into it. He wrapped the torn pieces of fabric tightly around the leather before rising carefully, slowly, supporting his weight with the few sturdy twigs, and felt a little relief. He caught his breath in the moonlight and felt the cold mostly in his numb fingers. He felt alone and, for a moment, almost stopped. Almost gave up like the frozen South.

I have failed.

More thunder.

Move, Erroh.

The thundering roar of the marching Hunt filled his ears and caused him to panic anew. He thought it typical to escape with his life against impossible odds, only to fall asleep and get caught unawares. *One of these days, luck will desert me completely*, he thought miserably, testing his foot's strength and finding further success. He could not sprint, but he could fight.

Show me the Woodin Man so that I might have a second go at him.

Settling his nerves, he shuffled towards the distressed figure of Highwind. Patting her gently and offering words about shielding each other, he climbed atop her and brought her from the river. He saw them again through the forest, a line of fire marking their progress as they trundled through the undergrowth, marching down upon him—or just marching.

Kicking his beast forward, he fled the line of pursuers, hoping their tracking skills in the night were worse than they were in the day. Highwind still suffered from her injury, so the pace was slower than he'd have liked. Without speed to call upon, he chose unforgiving terrain instead and slowly distanced himself from the chasing pack. But it never felt enough. He peered down the moonlit path ahead, and his heart hammered with every thump of Highwind's hooves upon the mud.

Don't hear us, don't see us. Don't pursue us.

His prayers remained unanswered, for they continued their pursuit, deeper into the Wastes than he thought possible. Always thunder in his ears as they came ever closer to striking him down.

For hours more, he raced his weakening mount. She never faltered, and somehow, he never fell from the saddle or relinquished his grip. Yet still, the Hunt's Riders followed.

Eventually, the path opened up, the grass and twigs having been crushed by some other wandering convoy. Opting for speed over concealment now, he broke forth, away from the pursuing pack. Though exhausted and injured, Highwind relished the faster pace. The thundering sound of her hooves increased as she charged into the darkness, but tragically, within a few breaths, he heard the Riders following.

He imagined them. Upon fresher mounts, waving torches manically, seeking easy prey. He imagined his back a fine target. Even in the low light. Imagined the click of a crossbow and the *thunk* of a bolt through flesh.

"Faster, Highwind," he cried, and she could not answer. Instead, she weakened at his request, and his heart fell. He feared she might die upon this charge, yet he could not relinquish his urging. No, he demanded more, because he was a cruel failure of a legend, savouring his breath above that of all others.

Perhaps you'll save us if they shoot you in the rear again.

"Errrrrrrrr......... oooooooh!"

He spun around as the Riders called out in unison, but could barely see them as they closed the distance behind him. They, however, could see him. A moment later, they called him again, and he caught the gasp in his throat lest it turn to a whimper.

"Errrrrrrrr......... oooooooh!" they cried again, and more joined along, their cries building into a terrible chant as they hunted him down. He had failed the world, and none of this was fair.

Fuk, fuk, fuk.

He kicked his horse one last time and willed her to outrun this savage pack, but he knew his fate. He considered dropping from his beast, dipping into the treeline, and searching for a bush. Any bush. Even a big rock to hide behind. Instead, he gripped the reins, continued to charge, and listened to their chanting as they hunted him down.

He knew their bloodlust was at its zenith when they chanted his name even more loudly, more powerfully. It was a wall of noise. As one, they took few breaths and filled the night anew with their horror, and he was terrified. It was the war horns tenfold, for they played for him alone.

And then… ahead lay salvation.

But he saw it as damnation, for it was a Southern camp.

He saw the banners first, as he had a thousand times before. This particular Finger did not march; instead, they lazed and waited for night to pass. Light filled the darkness. The sight of the campfires and torches, and the crisp smell of their smoke, brought forth the memory of his desperate flight. Highwind found a last gasp of energy. She charged towards the campsite, seeking a respite, unaware she carried her master into certain doom. Unable to stop her outright, Erroh coerced her away from the camp and back into the unforgiving forest before the Southerners could rouse themselves and fill them full of bolts.

Beneath the cover of the leaves, he finally allowed her to slow. The race was done. There was no saving himself from this. The last thing he desired was her death on his conscience.

Concealed somewhere between the hunting Southerners and the settled Southerners, Erroh waited. Carefully, he dropped to the ground and released Highwind to enjoy these last few moments free. Perhaps as they gutted him, he thought unhappily, she might bite one or two of them and take flight.

"Errrrrrrrr……… oooooooh!" the Riders called again as they neared him.

Drawing his swords, he looked down to the camp, which was now rousing itself. "Fuk it," he said, deciding these were fine-fitting last words.

The hammering hooves of the Riders' Northern mounts pounded in his ears as they thundered towards him. He almost stepped out from the treeline. Almost leapt upon the leading Rider, hoping to take him from the saddle.

Instead, he dropped his shoulders and waited.

And they came upon him at terrible speed.

Screaming, hating, hunting, killing.

And then they charged past him, roaring their violent and hate-filled fury, towards the Southern camp.

What the fuk?

They charge towards their own kind?

The ground shook, and the air filled with war cries from both sides as the settled Southerners realised they were facing invasion. He lost count as the Riders stampeded past him, hundreds of them, only a dozen feet from where he stood concealed within the green. Each hoofbeat reverberated in his chest, and he was a failure. They screamed his name. They eyed the path ahead. They raised their swords and broke apart into formation and drove down upon the unprepared Southerners.

They went to war. They did it in his name.

Seriously, what the fuk?

2

VISITOR

Her name was Aurora, and she liked to kill. Tonight, she intended to do exactly that. Once she'd outstayed her welcome. Once she'd earned her visit. She was excited. It had been so long—far too long—since she'd slain.

Beneath her feet, the path was difficult. She trudged awkwardly through the open field, following the wind's gale like a goddess. And why not? She was a goddess. A goddess of murder and death, for she had been chosen. By her god, her only god. All hail her love.

Even in the wind. Even in the hail.

Her long leather dress dragged out behind her as she raced through this dreary night. Each step made it catch in the long grass; the hem was a ruin. Soaked and ripped and heavier from the wet. This was no night for midnight running, yet here she was, Aurora of the South. Free to kill, to do his deeds.

Hunting them all.

The gale concealed her raucous dash; her stumbles, too, which was fine. Stumbling was fine. Falling was not. Not even in a storm. It blew wildly, buffeting her and all those following behind. Miles behind. When they arrived, she would take care of matters; they knew her orders and were godly.

Delicious and godly.

She sidestepped a branch. It slapped her as she passed, and that was fine too. The branch was doing its part to protect. To slow her. Everything was a challenge. Everything was sent to slow her down, but she was a tempest in a gale. She was the light in the sky. She knew this because her god whispered it in her mind.

Good, Aurora Borealis. Very good.

She knew her actions to come. This was no rare hunt. Oh, no. She was quite skilled in the art of the hunt. Deceit, too. She slowed and listened for threats, knowing few would be out this miserable night.

"Time to play," she said softly, chuckling.

Play was also fine. Uden approved of play when hunting, she reassured herself, although she knew he would prefer the deed done cleanly. Nothing in the wind suggested a change of tactics for this assassination. It was boredom on her part. She was no fan of the practices of tediousness. So, instead of scaling a few walls, creeping in through an unassuming window, stealing towards the sounds of snores and mutterings with a blade in excited fingers, Aurora chose entertainment this evening. Sometimes a girl just needed a challenge. Sometimes a girl needed to murder, all personal like—not merely going to task like a skilled assassin in the witching hour.

She reached a cobblestone wall and took a moment to compose herself, catch her breath and thoroughly dishevel her hair so she appeared rightly pathetic. Above, the shattered moon's glow offered a hazy glare through the hailing storm, just enough to light her way. She could see lights, but the path from here to there was precarious.

"A nasty trip and a sprained ankle might well complete the illusion," she said to the night, and cursed Ealis to silence. Suppressing the lesser part of her, Aurora reached the outer wall without incident or clumsiness. Ducking low from the wind, she cleared her throat and repeated the words without the Southern taint to her voice. She needed to be more skilled with her Northern accent, but the Western accent came naturally. Ironic that it was a dead form of speech. Or as close to entirely dead as could be.

"Dead speech, dead lands… Colo."

"Coloooooh."

Perfect, Aurora. They'll never suspect a thing.

"And if they suspect a thing? I'll be dead in moments," she moaned to herself and bit her upper lip in pleasure.

Far better than simple assassination.

She watched the house for a while, taking a last moment to change tactics. To memorise her tale of woe. To prepare herself for a dance upon a cracking lake of ice. Perfect and precarious. She knew her prey. Knew their lineage, for they were elite and fierce. This family were an interesting read. A hunter needed to know these things when presenting themselves as an ally. Before snapping at the offered hospitality.

"Co... lo." She coughed again and once more repeated the name of the dead city from the dead lands and the father's place of birth. She'd never been, but she might visit after the world ended. After the world burned and Uden left her with a screaming child in her belly.

That's what he promised, and I am not scared.
I am not scared at all.
Definitely not.

The wind caught her hair, and she shivered in its hold. Being born a second time in the South did not grant her immunity from this chilling grasp. She could have worn a heavy cloak, but needed to sell her weariness openly. A slight shivering, a little freezing to death, would show it nicely.

"When I'm in Colo, I'll think of you all," she pledged in a whisper, and the words flowed freely as though in a river. Or from a swine's throat. Or the torn flesh of a fat girl. Or even a cat.

No, not a cat.

Satisfied with her accent, Aurora scrambled over the wall before sprinting towards the stronghold as though her life depended on it. It didn't at all.

The last of her dress's elegance was lost in the muddy, furrowed field, and its ruined state pleased her as she examined it in the dim light. Only a true brute would deny her shelter this night. On either side, she heard the many differing calls of farm beasts, locked in from the storm behind heavy barn doors. They were the smarter ones, she thought, wiping biting cold sleet from her frozen cheeks as she moved along a cobbled footpath lit by the glow of the moon and a welcoming flame burning near a familiar front door.

"Home," she whispered, and her accent was natural and perfect.

It was an impressive door—old and oak, built to hold out assassins and fiends up to no good, with only a cold brass knocker as decoration. She grasped it and knocked twice upon the solid door with her quivering left hand. Two acceptable booming requests for entrance. She swiftly switched hands and knocked twice more with her right, which was perfect. They would hear, and they would come, and she would earn shelter, and they would die.

And on to Raven Rock afterwards with my friends.

She dared not knock again lest she die for breaking the natural way of things. Thankfully, she needed to take no unnecessary risk; behind this impressive door, she heard shuffling steps and then saw, wonderfully, a glow from beneath her feet.

She also heard a few curses, and terror struck her. Not for her safety, for she had killed so very many Alphas before. Not all of them. Not yet. Oh no, this was the fear of her choice and the realisation that her actions might displease her god.

"Why play, Aurora?"
Because it's too cold to dance.

The door shunted and creaked open, and she stared at her victim, who was perfect. He was dishevelled and unimpressive in his appearance. She was almost disappointed. She wondered whether it was the late hour or the bitter aroma of silken wine on his breath that suggested his lesser threat. She wondered was it the lack of fire in his eyes. His lack of interest in a late caller was a telling thing indeed.

"Thank you, sir," she cried, bowing her head most pitifully. He must have found it an acceptable bow, worthy of his legend, for he bade her enter, and immediately the warmth took hold, and she was grateful for the reprieve from the awful night.

"What is a little waif doing out on such an awful night?"
Killing you.

"Bandits left me stranded," Ealis lied and bowed again as the tears rolled down her cheeks from the trauma endured. She leapt upon him, wrapping her arms around his neck, and the heavyset older man allowed her. "Took my horse, took everything I own," she gasped, and he hushed her shaking form.

"Lyanne," he called, and held her a few moments more. "Help this little one," her victim cried, and Ealis shook perfectly. "There, there, little one," he told her. "You are safe." He had a kind voice. Kind eyes too. From the wrinkles on his face, it seemed he was inclined to smile a great deal. A girl was inclined to notice these things. She knew little of his stature besides his exploits with the great betrayer Magnus. She'd heard he could tell tales. Little else, but enough to prey upon.

He embraced her once more and then eased her from his plumpness with an unexpectedly sturdy grasp as he took her indoors. He was old and killable, but those fists could beat her to death no problem. Little dark strands grew on each misshapen knuckle, too, and she thought it delightful. The first punch could stun her. The second would be the telling blow. He could hammer down with those fists, and if she dodged neither they might break through her skull. Then he could batter her.

"I ran from them," she said tearfully.

"Did they hurt you?" A very kind, trusting voice.

"I ran from them," she repeated, allowing her lower lip to quiver.

Perfect.

"You are safe here, little one," he said, and his face darkened, and his tone turned to a killer's. "Whoever they were, they will pay."

Distantly, she heard the thumping of footsteps on the stairs. She gazed at the steep stairway beyond, leading to a few floors above, no doubt, with a dozen bedrooms—a fine, impressive mansion. As remarkable as her god's domain, it was; such wealth disgusted her. They had no right. They needed to burn.

I need to take them from the fight to come.

"What is happening, Marvel?" a woman's voice called. She sounded worried. Aurora thought this fine instinct. Whoever she was, she would soon die. In blood. All over the place.

Wonderful.

Lyanne, his mate, trundled down the stairs in a sleeping gown. She was as thin as Aurora, though taller, with piercing eyes full of concern and confusion. They softened as Marvel, master of the house, presented Aurora for the older woman to gaze upon.

"Oh, you poor dear. You are indeed safe here," she said in such comforting tones that Aurora was inclined to believe her.

"She needs a drink," Marvel declared, and it was a welcome suggestion.

"Of course, you'd say that," Lyanne argued, leading the quaking girl from the gloom of the doorway toward the kitchen and its comforting, crackling fire. The aromatic leftovers of their evening meal reached Aurora's nostrils, and her stomach rumbled ever so. She could have eaten, but playing the part demanded accuracy.

"Ah, whisht, woman, will you?" Marvel snapped, as only an old married husband was inclined to do, having been slighted in the presence of a goddess.

It took Aurora only a short time to earn their trust. Sitting upon a comfy chair before their crackling fire, she regaled them with her tale of misery once more. A perfect tale, with enough details to convince and set both listeners at ease. With her cloak hung near the mantelpiece to dry, she allowed her body to ease its quivering—a hard thing considering the excitement coursing through her body in anticipation of future events.

The Actions of Gods

She accepted the towel and glass of sweet wine offered and matched Marvel's steady draining of his own goblet. She could sense by his loose tongue, his clumsy thoughts and actions, that he'd drunk heartily before her arrival. This disappointed her, but nothing in life was perfect, apart from counting.

Lyanne sat across from Aurora and stared with gentleness as only a mothering hen could. She said little, for Marvel spoke loud enough for them both, but her soft sigh was sufficient for all to hear every time she refilled her glass with a shaky hand. It took no fool to recognise she'd come upon them mid-argument. She wondered if they hadn't been shouting at each other until her knocks upon the door disturbed their battle.

Strangely, Aurora hoped they would share a few kinder words between them before the end. It was a small matter, regardless. They were excellent hosts, and she was grateful for their naïve goodness. She gladly accepted the invitation of a bed for the night. Moreover, she received Marvel's pledge that, come dawn, a hunting party would be dispatched.

Lastly, they offered her warm food, which she gratefully declined. Her stomach ached and burned with acid and hunger, but she deserved no satisfaction until her deeds were done.

Eventually, when the hour was past midnight, Lyanne declared she would prepare the waif a bed, and Aurora was grateful. A foolish thing it seemed to attack these two older warriors, for though they appeared decrepit, there was a threat to them both. They were impressive, but a warrior held a particular stride, and both walked well.

"I'll sit up and have one more," Marvel whispered, eyeing the flames through the crystal red of his filled goblet, and Lyanne muttered a curse under her breath before rolling her eyes and leading Aurora from the dimness of the dying flames.

Aurora did not like the stairs. Not one little bit. They were carpeted in a dark blue, and that was pleasing, but they were uneven. Fifteen in total, and this displeased her terribly. She'd have preferred one step more or one step less. She hated them silently as she followed the older woman to her room.

"You can stay in our son's room," Lyanne offered, gesturing to a door at the far end of the hall. "Don't worry, little one; Wynn left us long ago." She patted Aurora's arm comfortingly before stepping into the small bedroom to light a few candles.

"Thank you," Ealis said weakly, as though gestures of kindness were

15

too much. Truthfully, kindness fascinated Aurora greatly. She watched her prey go to work in the flickering candles, stripping the bedclothes as though it was a natural act. Perhaps it was. Perhaps that was all heroic Alphalines could master after the call of war had ended and the bearing of children overtook all else.

"I'm no fool, Ealis." She turned, and Aurora's heart hammered. "There's little chance a girl like you will sleep soundly tonight, having endured such troubles. Having only met us this awful night." She smiled, and it was a kind smile. "Little one, you are safe; there's a lock on the inside of the door lest you fear midnight visits from a drunken oaf."

She laughed, and Aurora laughed with her. "You are a welcoming family. Thank you."

Lyanne spun back to her duties, her voice wistful and warm. "My Marvel is an oaf, but he'd never harm a soul. A kind drunken heart, he has. Probably why I put up with his foolishness."

"He seems a lovely man," agreed Aurora, watching the older woman slip and tauten the under-sheets nice and snugly. A little waif could get rightly cosy within that bedding.

"Aye, he is."

Aurora slipped close to Lyanne, taking hold of the outer sheets as though helping, for that is what grateful guests did. And Lyanne smiled one last time. Even as the small bedside stool collided with the side of her head, knocking her senseless.

Easy.

Lyanne stumbled against the wall, but mercifully did not fall and arouse any eager ears. Taking advantage of the dazed woman, Aurora slung the sheets around her neck, twisted and pulled.

She gasped; it was beautiful. Her eyes bulged in knowing terror, and Aurora enjoyed the kill. It was a fabulous murder. She could have slit her throat, but such a woman deserved a unique death, and Aurora would honour her. Lyanne gasped and fought, for she was incredible, and Aurora wrapped her legs around her body, squeezing the last of her air from her lungs.

It's time to go.

When Lyanne fell, it was against the bed, and then they were upon the bedding, squirming and wriggling as though at play, until, with a last gasp, Aurora stole her breath and watched her die, which was exquisite.

She lay beside the dead woman for a moment, gasping in satisfaction. She hadn't strangled another in quite a time. It was a sacred act, and she was better for it. Tragically, though, Aurora's task was not yet done, so haste drew her from the warm cadaver. She eased away, left the woman to eternal sleep in her son's bed, and, extinguishing the candles, closed the door behind her.

She heard Marvel below by the fire, and she took a moment to calm her stirring heart, fix her bedraggled hair, and check for smudges in her makeup. Leaping the last two steps to calm her mind, Aurora glided back into the dark room with excitement fluttering in her heart. Her stomach growled loudly, and Marvel looked up from his imaginings in the flames and offered a drunken smile.

"Ha. I thought you were Lyanne, returning with a fresh bottle and a twinkle in her beautiful eye. I was forming the words of apology for my drunkenness..."

"I thought I might join you for another drink, as my heart still races," Aurora whispered, standing over the charming older man.

"We fought, you see."

I knew it.

Aurora nodded and sat across from him, watching him with grateful eyes. His voice was slurred. She was happy to wait a time. There was little rush to grant him peace.

"I never go to bed arguing. I should go to her. I heard something up there. Perhaps she tripped. She's been doing that these last few months. A dreadful thing, getting old."

He wiped his eyes and grinned, and Aurora was eternally grateful she'd taken this stronghold before her companions raided. It wasn't every day a girl could sharpen her wits at a game of concealment among the enemy. She was learning the art.

"Your accent is familiar; what part of the West did you say you hailed from?" the widower asked, draining his glass and looking around for a refill. Though it was not her place, she took the crimson bottle from beside the fire and poured them both a measure.

"Colo, though I haven't been there in a time," she said, knowing this revelation would please him. There weren't many settlements in the dead lands of the west, but Colo held its own against the slow decline of humanity.

"Aye, your accent is tainted, all right."

Tainted.

She fought her anger and caught it swiftly. "Where is your son?"

"Ah, that little fuk is walking the Wastes like a good little Alpha male."

"You are an Alphaline family?" she said, pretending surprise. "How long has he been wandering?"

"A few seasons or so. He'll be back soon enough, with the shiniest bride, no doubt. You would like him. He is prettier than me. Not as charismatic, mind."

She laughed and found Marvel even more charming. Settling back in her chair, she continued drinking with him until he fell asleep by the fire. A quick blade through the heart would do the deed swiftly, and she would have another Alphaline pelt by her hand alone.

His death makes it sixty.

No other Southerner can claim that high a number.

There was a beauty to that number. Nice and even. It was a better thing his son wasn't here this evening. Sixty-one was less pleasing, after all. If his son appeared with his new bride, though, she could make it even again. This, too, pleased her.

Until she heard the distant rumble, and she cursed under her breath. They were early. Or worse, impatient. Desperate to add to their own tally.

Despite the drunkenness, his eyes opened.

"I hear thunder," she mumbled, hoping the sound of her marching Finger could be mistaken. If only for a little time more. She was enjoying herself.

"Aye, thunder," he agreed, but she saw the alertness struggling through the veneer of cosy drunkenness.

Very well.

She stretched in her seat and slid the dagger free from her pocket. He sighed once more and gazed at his goblet. "I miss my son."

She did not strike his heart. Fuk him, but his reflexes were impressive. He caught the blow from the side as she leapt across, and for a tremendous moment, Aurora imagined him taking hold of her petite frame and shoving her into the fire.

Take my eyes first.

The blade punctured his shoulder with enough force to send him reeling away from her. Quick as a cat, she slid her second dagger free and leapt upon him, seeking his throat and only puncturing the side of his neck. A painful strike, no doubt, but his flabby skin took some of the blow. A salty stream of blood struck her, and she stood frozen in ecstasy before leaping at him again, seeking the quicker killing blow.

She knew him to be a legendary warrior, and he did not disappoint. Pulling the blade from his shoulder, he fought her off with the last of his will, and he was impressive. Fighting for his life, he attacked and almost killed her in the first few frenzied blows. The blade hissed close to her face, chest and throat. Swinging wildly, she ducked away from each strike as he chased her across the room, until he swung too carelessly, and she slipped up beside him and struck him three times deeply into his lungs.

"It's all right, Marvel," she insisted, but he thought differently, which was fine too.

"Lyanne," he sobbed as he fell to his knees, and she was on him again, holding her blade above his heart. She smiled and thought about kissing his blood-covered lips.

"She's waiting for you in the fires of the tainted," Aurora insisted, and plunged the dagger deep. He looked past her to something beyond and shuddered and died, and she collapsed to her knees, watching him fade. Two astounding kills, unique and intimate, and her task was worth the extra effort.

She removed the cleaver from its place upon the wall and dug through bone and incredible things until his head was severed, falling free with a delicate *thunk* upon the floor. In death, he looked peaceful, and she carried him out into the stormy night. He was warm against the breeze, and she hugged him tightly.

"It was a good fight," she reassured him, and he nodded in agreement with her help. Out here, she could hear the nearing army and spat in disgust. A savage thing they couldn't allow their leader a little time to herself. She knew they'd settle and send a scout to seek word of success, and she obliged.

"This won't hurt," she promised, and lanced his head upon the end of a farmer's pike at the front of the stronghold.

As though knowing the murder in the air, the many dozens of beasts bleated and howled against the storm's thunder in their holdings, and she smiled. They would fall silent soon enough and serve their purpose in the bellies of her kin.

She waited with Marvel's head for a while until hunger reared its head again. So to speak. Wiping his features a few times in the light rain and heavy snowdrops, she was satisfied with his appearance and left him to his welcoming duties.

———

She chose thick slices over thin from the honey loaf she found in the pantry. Denser bread allowed less spillage, and such things mattered when eating a victorious meal. She lathered each slice with soft butter and placed a thin piece of cheese on each side. She ignored the tomatoes, for she was no fan of such vegetables. She liked them cooked in a spitting pan but found them distasteful when eaten raw. Mercifully, there was fresh lettuce, and, trying a mouthful, she was delighted with its crunch. Adding two rich green strips on either side, her mouth watered. Next came the salted swine meat, for every fool knew the meat belonged at the centre of every creation. She nodded to the skilled preparer who'd slathered it in clove and maple only a day before. It added to the flavour, and she pledged to take the remaining chunks with her when she left. She added two more thin slices, inhaled the tantalising scent of her growing creation, and was pleased. After investigating, she found a jar of bitter mustard hiding on a shelf at the back of the pantry. With just enough to make a perfect balance, she added a little pepper and, careful not to cause herself to sneeze, cut the sandwich in half before sitting back in her chair and biting ravenously into it. She didn't mind the blood spatter as it rubbed off her fingers onto the brown bread. It merely added to the meal.

Licking her grubby fingers clean, she burped gently in honour of the fine feast and drank the last of her wine as the first footsteps of her scavenging force were heard in the courtyard beyond.

She wondered had her Uden watched her as she went to kill this warrior of the Faction Wars. She wondered how he might repay her for her deeds. She had sinned with many men these last few months, but taking Marvel's head was her gift. As would be the taking of Raven Rock.

She wondered if they would be enough to avoid his wrath.

She hoped it wasn't. She was ready to die at his hands.

I want to die.

3

SISTERS IN ARMS

"You are talking too much again. Far too much. You could shut up. That would be nice."

Lea did not reply to Nomi's words. She could hear the humour in her voice, and she welcomed it. If nothing else, Nomi was mastering the art of wit these last few days. No small skill in the middle of a rainstorm, in the middle of a forest with nothing but mocking to stave off thoughts of desolation. Spread out before them was an endless green expanse. Miserable and ancient. Unforgiving and vast. Miles stretched out in front of them through the murky woods to come. Behind them the same, but for a few scuffs in the ground where they had plodded. Scuffs that could remain forever in the dirt, never seen by another set of human eyes. An eternity from civilisation. An eternity from safety. An eternity away from everything they'd ever cherished. They were alone. They were lost. They were desolate.

"Stop complaining. Mounts never complain," Lea countered, shifting her hip ever so. Nomi loosened her grip in silence as she did. She merely gasped a few breaths and marched onwards. "Mounts know their place in the world."

Nomi snorted as a mount might and countered. "Aw... for a few breaths, you shut up. That was nice. I prefer the forest without your mumbling. Peaceful. Almost forget I'm carrying a boulder." At this, Lea smiled and allowed her success. Nomi seemed to enjoy her rambling mocking. They were a wonderful distraction from the efforts, and Lea would not deny her by showing offence or offering surrender. It was all she could do. The blonde girl stumbled, and Lea felt the strain along her legs where Nomi gripped her most tightly. Lea wrapped her arms tighter around the girl's neck, where she held on—just a gentle squeeze before easing her grasp.

"Whoa, there, horse. Watch your step."

Nomi grunted and, shifting Lea as though she were an awkward satchel upon her back, continued to trudge through the endless slippery mud. "You overeat. When you aren't talking, you are eating."

"Hey!"

Nomi giggled and stopped for a breath as it held in her throat. Lea was about to taunt her again, but she caught sight of the perspiration upon her mount's forehead and the strain in her features. The girl showed exhaustion only sporadically, so Lea held her words. It was all she could do, and after a few breaths, Nomi continued to carry her. Each footfall was assured, as if she knew her route despite having no compass or map. Around them, each hill rising above the canopy was similarly covered in evergreen trees. Nothing but green around them. Not even a river to follow. They marched north, hoping to meet the outskirts of the city. Or a friendly face. Or anything good. One of these days.

It wasn't the soundest plan, but it was all they could think of.

Three days now, they had travelled as sisters of the road. Most of the time, their pace was dreadfully slow as Lea sometimes insisted on walking herself. She hobbled painfully through the undergrowth with her ankle in a simple splint and leaning upon a long branch. Nomi took her weight with an Alpha's determination the rest of the time.

Making terrible time with no place to go.

They could have rested, they needed rest, but it felt foolish hesitating without suitable shelter. The pain had been awful today, and Lea despaired. She needed time away from the march. She needed to recover from her injuries. She needed to sit around and think about the dreadful revelation of her lineage. To discover her place in the world. To steel herself for the harrowing days to come. Mostly, she needed to find Erroh and leave him.

She meant it this time.

Some things couldn't be recovered.

Things were fated to end this way.

I don't know where you are, my beo, but this is the end.

"Are you all right, oh loyal horse?" Lea asked after a time, and Nomi whimpered before nodding her head. The path was slippery. Rain poured down upon their heads like a gushing stream; it made the going this evening that little bit more terrible.

The Actions of Gods

"One more mile," she gasped, and Lea watched the sky and the growing darkness of the surrounding trees. The night was welcome, but it was a different, more precarious experience. This was Northern land, but they were still in hostile territory. They faced no demented followers as they had when first escaping Raven Rock. Pursuers determined to seek their prey, no matter the distance. They faced only half-hearted trackers now and then from wandering patrols eager to break the monotony of a march. Those pursuits usually took only a couple of hours to escape. It became a typical task of each day while slipping through the disorganised Southern lines. Lea had experience with this constant threat, this constant terror. Nomi less so, but she was improving. She panicked less now at the hum of followers. She had adapted to exhaustion and weariness and depthless sorrow at their fortune. She was built for the road, as Lea and Erroh were. Lea hadn't seen it before, but she saw it now.

As dusk set in, she frequently drove them farther into the forests, eager to be done with this march. Anxious to be free of her responsibility, more like, Lea thought, and chastised herself. Nomi was better than that.

"One more mile, heavy sister."

One more mile would turn into three, and Lea atop her fading shoulders would allow her. Why? Because were she able to carry Nomi, she would do the same. At the best of times, sisters did this. Worst of times too. She could no longer hate this girl.

"Fair enough. Could you pick up the pace? I'm getting hungry."

Nomi laughed and kept going, her chest heaving as though taken with heavy lung, her powerful arms letting Lea's legs slip ever so as she trundled onward. "Could Lea... ugh... could you talk?"

"Oh, so I'm allowed to speak now?"

"Please speak. Tell me of things. Tell me again about the first boy you kissed. Funny story."

"I can't believe I told you that. As you wish, Nomi."

Nomi lasted only another hour before she began to falter, and Lea ended her torture. "Let me go; we're done," she said, squirming from her hold. Nomi did not fight the reprieve and carefully set her on her feet before collapsing in the mud. In the times before, while living in Raven Rock, Lea might have suggested in an even tone that Nomi belonged in such a state, but loyalty was a potent sauce, and Nomi had earned hers.

Sisters to the grisly end.

Nomi did not move; she stretched out, for this was part of their new routine, earned through three days of trusting each other. "Difficult today," she whispered, closing her eyes against the rain. Neither female had endured anything as comforting as dryness during this pilgrimage. This awful feeling of dampness reached into their bones, sucking away their wellness, happiness and fuken warmth.

Carefully, Lea hobbled over to an ancient oak tree and, beneath its thickest bough, hung with clustered rain-spattering leaves, went to task stealing a little warmth for them both for the night ahead.

"I can't move. Wish *I'd* hurt my ankle," Nomi said wistfully. Lea could hear the strain in her voice. She imagined the bruising around her body. Still, she carried Lea as best she could and was incredible. "But you have weak arms. Couldn't even carry me."

"I'd just drag you through the undergrowth. It would probably improve your appearance," Lea countered, gathering her twigs and rocks and erecting a little promising tower, all willing to be lit against the growing darkness. Nomi opened her eyes for a moment to shrug indifferently.

The wood took little time to catch, and only when the smoke gave way to a few crackling sparks and a little dancing flame did Nomi, upon her elbows and panting with exhaustion, slither beneath the tree bough to catch a little warmth for herself.

"I am a goddess of fire," Lea proclaimed, reaching into her pack for the fresh strips of quail she'd caught at dawn.

"Aye, heavy goddess, but goddess," Nomi agreed. She looked around the forest as though seeing it for the first time. There was reassurance in its stillness. The girl was still wary of fire. She'd never lit a fire thirty feet from a travelling Finger in the middle of a snowstorm. Lea had, but this was something else entirely.

"We should be safe out here, deep in the middle of nothing."

"Aye," Nomi agreed half-heartedly.

"I doubt any fool would be out in this dreariness tonight," Lea said, gripping her shoulder.

Carefully, Lea slid a skewer through the soft strips of flesh and laid them out over the dancing fire.

"Don't overeat," warned Nomi.

"Anything I eat, I'll replace in the morning."

"Not what I meant."

Lea was awakened abruptly long before dawn. She heard the hunters first. The subtle cracking of branches breaking the stillness. The low clamour of armour clinking in the darkness from clumsy steps taken swiftly. And then, from that dreaded darkened place, she spotted torches —a dozen or more. Surrounding them, drawing near, and they without cover or preparedness.

Not again.

Not at night.

She tugged at the sleeping Nomi only once before the girl shot awake with a start, already reaching for her weapon and belongings. Within a breath, she was on her feet, dragging Lea up as she rose. Her hair whipped out in panic, and Lea knew their glowing fire had drawn the hunters near. She stamped the dying embers to nothing, spitting once into their smoky remains for luck as she did. They had chosen warmth, sleep and a little food over practicality. There was no snow to conceal them. No hollowed-out log to squirm inside. No rock to hide behind. Their scent was there for all to smell.

Without words, despite her fatigue, Nomi dropped to shaky knees as any trained mount might do in a competition of equestrian grandeur before taking centre stage. She tensed and awaited the heavyweight. Even heavier, now, with last night's second helping.

"Go, go, Lea," she hissed when her rider resisted momentarily, taking a moment to count the torches. To summon the will to draw a sword and stop this dreadful fleeing.

To demand they take me to my father.

"We can fight."

"We would die," Nomi whispered, and made no move.

Cursing, Lea climbed upon the girl as the clamour became careful footsteps in the waving orange glow around them.

Nomi took off from their breached camp at pace. With little light to guide their way, she was far from silent. It didn't matter. She plunged onward, and Lea bounced helplessly in her grasp. To feel this helpless was no small matter, and with every yelp as a tree branch slapped Nomi's face or a gnarled root in the ground almost tripped her, Lea felt worse.

"Are they following?" Nomi asked.

"I cannot see."

Lea didn't know how long or how far they travelled, only that she caught sight of tears streaming down Nomi's face as she panted forward

—terrible, silent tears shed by a legend defying utter defeat despite the inevitable.

"Leave me here," Lea cried, knowing her doom.

"No."

"If I die, Erroh is all yours," Lea argued, and Nomi charged faster as though such a thought disgusted her. Perhaps it did. Perhaps Lea had judged her too harshly. Perhaps Nomi understood the significance of love. Even broken-hearted love.

Shattered forever without recovery.

"Damn you. Let me drop. You can still escape, Nomi," Lea cried. A finer hero might have struggled in Nomi's grasp. Might have kicked out and forced salvation upon the honourable girl and sent her on her way while standing fast and delaying their pursuers. Nomi would run for half a day without resting. Lea had only to give up. However, Lea wouldn't sacrifice herself if the girl was willing to carry her.

"I will not lose another sister." It was a fair reply, and despite herself, Lea loved Nomi as Erroh did. All it took was inhuman feats of determination and honour to sway her jealousy.

Their race ended in a river. Nomi cursed as the water's edge appeared from nowhere and took them both. Lea's world spun as though she'd been beaten in a sparring match; the dark water took hold and shook the life from her. Awful coldness, worse than three days' downpour, took Lea's breath as she slipped from Nomi's terrified grasp. She fought the pull beneath its frozen surface. They both did, and it was an awful battle.

"Too loud," gasped Nomi, reaching for the riverbank, missing and splashing below the water, and Lea, better used to near-drowning moments and better for it, took hold, calmed her, showed her the shallowness of the river and eased them both to its edge.

In truth, it was no river but a little pool with barely a trickling stream feeding its depths. Gripping some reeds, they clambered ashore and found themselves in a small glade with nothing but the awful cutting wind to worsen their coldness.

Nomi dropped to a knee to get her breath and carry Lea again, but her body shook with fatigue. Her hands gripped the dirt as though dragging energy from the soil itself, such was her panic. She was about to break, and she fought the inevitable. They had reached the end. There was no race left in her. Lea thought of hiding among the reeds, but then, all around them, she heard the pursuing enemy, and Lea almost gave up with her. Almost, but not quite.

"We must keep going, Nomi," Lea muttered, but Nomi crumpled into the grass. "We must find a place to hide."

"I can't. Leave me be."

"Please, Nomi, for me—get up and walk a little more," pleaded Lea, dragging the broken girl to her shaking feet. Above, the rain spat hate, splattering their faces in the wind's icy chill. "This is no place to die. Not yet, at least." They were uplifting words spoken through a liar's grimace, but Nomi nodded weakly. Lea dragged Nomi away from the reeds and misery, through the meadow, hoping to find a hiding place.

"Fuk it anyway," she hissed, realising this place had no cover. The trees were too thin and sparse to conceal themselves in. The long grass was barely tall enough to hide a pair of forsaken boots. No chance of a dark cave where the air was clear and welcoming. Not even a fuken bush.

Behind them, the chasing brutes neared, and desperation drew the last of Lea's energy. They followed, no doubt chasing the embedded steps of an exhausted mount too weak to charge one last time.

They shouldn't be out marching at this late hour. Gripping Nomi's hand tightly, she set off painfully through the darkness once more, seeking a gift from the absent gods. She would have taken anything.

What she found was a rock.

It was a very nice rock because it was the only object large enough to block out the chilling wind and some of the waves of rain. Its size was not what pleased her most, however. Upon this rock were the remnants of a terribly built shack. Held together with rotting wood and rope and layers and layers of long-dead branches, it was an excellent tool for concealment.

Kicking away the supports and dragging the roof to the ground, Lea laid the ruin out flat in the long grass and was rather pleased with its bush-like appearance.

"That won't work," Nomi argued as Lea dragged her beneath the painfully prickly covering, but Lea knew it *would* work, for she knew this rock. She remembered his tale. She remembered his sketches on his map. She knew exactly where she was.

It was his last gift to her. Given before they ever met. Ever clashed. Ever fell in love. A fine first gift for a courtship. Better than a bow. "Whisht, mount. You've earned a reprieve," Lea said, lying beside the quivering, broken girl. "It will work."

She felt the absent gods' presence for the first time in an age and offered a prayer to them as the dozen Southerners appeared from beyond the treeline. They chatted merrily as they marched—all casual, all terrifying. As though hunting two elite wanderers of the road was no matter. She felt Nomi tense, but Lea felt no fear, knowing they would pass, knew her hammering heartbeat would not alert them to her presence.

Thank you, Erroh.

The Southerners marched past the little pool without a second glance or a careless step, and Lea smiled in triumph as they veered away, waving their torches in the night as though they might scare some easy prey from its den.

Cordelia, the fox, would not emerge, though.

The moment held. She counted at least a dozen. They passed beyond the meadow, their footsteps becoming firmer as they reached another beaten path, and Lea understood this as a gift as the torches disappeared into the night.

"This is a healing place," Lea whispered, and Nomi nodded.

The gods must have understood Lea's intentions. Their gift of this place was well appreciated, but it would not quell her anger towards Erroh. Perhaps it was a reminder of his importance in her life. If that were so, she would bow to their greater knowledge and leave it at that. She wrapped her arms around the exhausted Nomi and reassured her.

"I am scared, Lea."

"Sleep, Nomi," Lea whispered. "We face no threat here."

4

GALVANISED

Their cries filled the night. Manic and cruel. Piercing and mesmerising. They screamed his name as they charged, which was a terrible, glorious thing. Erroh, from the cover of his hiding place, watched the two factions go to war, and he was utterly confused. If he thought about it, confusion was a fairly frequent ailment. This was truly perplexing.

What the fuk is going on?

"Erroh, Erroh!" the Riders screamed, and the settled camp shouted in reply. Their cries became more of a shocked and terrified outburst as allies became aggressors. How many Southern camps had faced an assault from their own kind in the middle of the night, Erroh wondered.

They must think I'm in that camp.

Their thundering beasts were a fantastical sight, to an observer at least. To those facing the charge, less so. Like a wave of muscle, hooves and whinnying cries of impending doom, they sped towards the heart of the camp, relying on surprise to take their enemy off guard. They charged down the defenders in a long line led by three or four fierce, careless attackers. Glimmering deadly blades of all shapes and sizes rose into the night, preceding them. Those at the front carried long pikes to plunge deep into their victims. Those at the back swung heavy battle axes wildly from side to side as the fury of war drew forth their bloodthirsty cries. In the middle, Erroh saw rapiers, hammers and even daggers slice the air, seeking opponents. And oh, the thunder of war was terrifying.

Without time to prepare, the defenders grabbed what weapons they could and charged defiantly towards the terrifying Riders, knowing those who charged first would meet an impressive, bloody end.

For a moment, Erroh respected their grim defiance. A similar unprepared group of soldiers might have fled. The moment turned from respect to horror as they finally clashed.

Swiftly, the attackers cut through the first line of struggling defenders, killing mercilessly. Men, women, and children barely old enough to raise a sword were felled as the driving army charged through them. The hundred swinging blades cut down those on either side, while those unfortunate to meet the attack head-on met a grisly, crunching end. Their panicked screams matched the yells of the attackers, and it was ruthless and wonderful. Erroh, however, was disgusted by the brutality and for not knowing his place on either side.

Not all Riders carried blades or hammers, however. Those few spun away from the long line racing around the massive camp in a great arc, but their threat was no less, for they each carried archers' bows and two quivers of arrows on either side of their waist. These were no doubt cut carelessly from nearby trees, with hands unfamiliar to such tasks; their weapons lacked the grace of Lea's Baby. Yet, still, atop their horses, they were an impressive sight. Where their tools lacked finesse, they made up for it in quantity. They sent wave after wave upon their scattering victims, and they aimed to fire every projectile. These were good tactics for inadequately armed warriors.

"*Erroh, Erroh!*"

The mad cries rang out, unrelenting, as so many astonished Southerners met their end, emerging from their tents to the piercing cries of the enemy and the low hiss of arrows that thudded into their unprotected bodies. It was swift slaughter, and Erroh climbed upon Highwind to bring himself closer to see the devastation. He did not know why.

"Just a look is all, girl," he whispered reassuringly. He didn't want to join this battle. Not really. Why would he? He was a failure in war. They'd have to scream his name a lot fuken louder to stir his heart. Still, he brought Highwind through the trees to get a clearer look at the hundreds of shadows at war, illuminated by the camp's night fires.

Just a little closer, is all.

Perhaps, were the numbers even, the attackers might have won victory in a few moments; however, this was no small Finger. They were a larger settled force than he'd ever seen. At least thrice the size of the group that had taken Keri. On a clear day, the defenders would have held these attackers easily. But at night, and using surprise as their ally, the battle could go either way. For whatever reasons the Riders attacked, those odds were enough.

The ruckus brought yet more of them from their tents, stumbling sleepily out into the battle. Many, without adequate armour, died within a breath of poking their bewildered heads out from behind their canvas door-flaps. But, soon enough, it became clear that one swift, brutal charge could never be enough to vanquish them. Though their bodies still fell—punctured, pierced or crushed—many more defenders appeared, clad in heavy armour, bearing polished steel and dull shields, ready to face this onslaught. The great defence had begun, and Erroh peered into the night, watching with interest.

He chose those who called his name aloud as his favoured victims. It wasn't about victory, though; it was about numbers. Southerners killing Southerners was very good for their war effort. Every dead Southerner was one fewer they needed to contend with. Two factions of the same region killing each other was a beautiful thing.

Losing less than a dozen in the first offensive, the attacking Riders reached the edge of the camp and set upon their next target, the long wooden gate of a livestock holding pen. Inside it, terrified and ready to escape from the tumult, the camps' mounts were prepared to bolt, and bolt they did once the gate was crushed in a splintering act of liberation. Slapping the beasts, the attackers directed them back towards the battle through the devastating path they'd blazed. Another shrewd move on the attackers' part, mused Erroh, bringing Highwind ever nearer. Turning the mounts into weapons themselves was a desperate, brilliant tactic. Erroh knew the reverence each Rider had for their horse. It would be a hard and terrible thing to strike down one's cherished beast. Even if it was to save someone.

In all his time studying the Southerners while he was in chains, he had noted that upon the battlefield, they'd never displayed a nuance of battle aptitude. They chose numbers and brave sacrifice over steady tactics and planning. Now, Erroh watched in wonder as the freed mounts trampled dozens more in their terrifying stampede. Some good tactics, indeed.

"Erroh, Erroh, Erroh!"

His own name reverberated in his mind. In his fractured body. In his faded soul. There was a frenzy to the chant. He neared the edge of concealment and kept trotting forward slowly, for he recognised a few familiar faces among the devastation. How had he missed it before? Had he not spent weeks under their imprisoned gaze while he recovered among the Wolves? Then he saw their leader—a small Southerner who looked out of place without his little waving white flag. He barked orders like a frenzied zealot from the front of the charging attackers, and they followed and charged anew. Waving their bloody weapons, they waded deep into the camp again, trampling and killing as they went. He imagined that the fear of the defenders probably matched the terror he'd witnessed in the many towns and settlements that had faced such similar assaults, and strangely, this pleased Erroh. He thought it fine justice, and swiftly steered his mount clear of the treeline and back onto the path. Highwind whinnied in agitation, and he patted her gently.

"No one will notice us here," he said, feeling his heart quicken. Nothing much, just a little stirring from seeing such a brutal skirmish. It was the Alphaline in him and nothing more. He was sure of it.

"Erroh, Erroh, Erroh!"

He thought the attackers were incredible. These wretched few were without proper leadership, without land to call home, without a god to fear to obey, and they chose a different calling. They sought war.

In my name.

"Erroh, Erroh, Erroh!" they yelled as they did battle, and he suddenly understood the tool they could be. They wore their allegiance openly and went to war without his blessings. Without his knowledge. He tightened his grip and willed the absent gods to grant them victory as the bow-wielding Riders charged a second time around the camp. Their shots were less accurate than before, but they were still effective enough, as they had many arrows to call upon. They threw everything into battle without regard for themselves.

Training and leadership are all they need.

Erroh watched for a few tense breaths more before he felt the change in the tide. He'd sensed such tides before. Like a coldness running down the back, as exhilaration gave way to terror in the flicker of the eye.

Like a few raindrops over a burning blockade in a defiant town.

"It's about to turn," Erroh muttered, and Highwind must have agreed. She trotted forward, drawn by violence. "They're rousing themselves for the counter." Highwind whinnied approvingly.

As one, the defenders, buoyed on by roared orders, manoeuvred across the battlefield into a defensive formation. Like serpents tucking in close before unleashing a terrible bite, they formed close to each other, raising their shields in one impressive wall and holding the charge.

That's a good idea.

The dull *thunk* of swords upon shields filled the air. A moment later, a hundred arrows embedded themselves in the phalanx of thick wood, fur and steel shields, and a chorus of defiant cries filled the night as the defenders stood their ground.

"*Uden, Uden, Uden!*" some voices roared, and swiftly, the defending crowd joined in, and Erroh felt his body turn cold. Deathly cold. His fingers twitched. His arm itched. His eyes narrowed as he peered through the devastation, through the panic and the horror. Beyond the terror, beyond the pleading, beyond the rage. He sought the instrument of defiance. The bringer of galvanisation.

He listened to the world and beyond.

Where are you?

He listened, and everything slowed down. Every voice became a whisper. Every cry, a song of misery for another's ears. He listened, he heard, and he saw.

That same fuken coldness came upon Erroh tenfold, and he held Highwind's approach for a breath. And why wouldn't he? He'd seen this brute once before. A lifetime ago, upon a frozen mountain's stronghold, beneath a flickering flame, just like tonight. This cur had watched Erroh fight Uden. He'd called for Erroh's head.

"I know you," Erroh hissed, and it was a warning. It stirred the soul as well. He tasted Uden's gelatinous eyeball in his mouth, and he licked his lips. He studied this brute of a general as he appeared among the defenders, his voice chanting loudest, his frame dwarfing most of the others.

He might have been Uden's son, such was his imposing physique. His face was gruff and young and cruel. A general's face. He sneered, and Erroh wanted to wipe that fuken sneer right off.

A wounded failure ready to bite.

The general barked out orders, and the defenders found strength in his authority, and Erroh thought this no good. The huge man stood impressively in thick steel armour, impossibly heavy and flawless. His open helm looked too heavy to wear, yet he moved as though unburdened.

"Hold tight," he roared in Southern speak, and the defenders dug into their stances and avoided further strikes from Riders as they drove by, screaming in frustration, knowing the battle had turned. One particular Rider recognised his threat immediately, for she drew upon him, sacrificing herself to deliver a killing blow and driving her robust mount towards the wall of stubborn shields, firing three arrows in quick succession. She was more accurate than most others. Twice she struck his chest and once his helm, but her blows did little more than bounce harmlessly off the unyielding armour.

She died well. She leapt from her mount as it reared against the wall of shield and defiance—an exemplary display of agility and stubborn foolishness. Erroh approved of such behaviour. She cleared the wall and fell upon the massive man, attempting to stab him with a humble dagger. She was no match for him.

In each hand, he carried two long battle axes. Adorned with jewels and shimmering strong steel, they looked like they belonged upon a wall in a god's stronghold. In the general's hands, they were terrifying. She swung, but he was quick for one his size. Slipping beneath her blade's tip, he struck her across the ribs, just one blow, but it was a devastating one. The weapon's edge held fast inside her, but she swung once more, even though her doom was already sealed. Her dying swing came short, and she gasped, falling to her knees, dropping her arms. Casually, he sent his axe through her head before pulling both blades from her corpse.

Seeing her vanquisher roar in victory over her broken body was a hammer blow to the attackers. Those circling the camp slowed and hesitated as though seeing enormous pikes upon a battlefield. Those attacking through the heart of the base faced likely defeat.

"Flee while you can," Erroh hissed, for he watched the defenders hold their formation as they marched out to meet the faltering attackers.

"*Uden, Uden, Uden!*" they chorused, and Erroh's anger stirred to a furnace. They fought, and now they died in his name.

And I am a dangerous failure.

"Fuken flee," he cried out, but their backs were to the insignificant failure of a man upon the saddle beneath the shadows of the treeline.

"Flee before they wipe you out," he cried again.

They did not flee. They died for him instead.

"Fuk it."

Both his blades were in his hands. He'd no memory of drawing them, yet he was here seeking battle. Why? Because he was an idiot.

"Fuk it all."

Erroh knew he would die in the moments ahead, but couldn't help himself. Couldn't walk away from this fight. He wondered whether it was a futile attempt at redemption or a finer end to his failure in this savage war. He felt tired in his soul. Meeting the false god the first time, Erroh had stolen away with his eye, but Uden had taken something far

The Actions of Gods

more precious upon the top of Spark City's walls. In defeat, Erroh had lost his own spark, his fire, and his fuken will to win.

"Once more, Highwind, unto death."

It was a fair request, and the beast responded to his gentle persuasions. He felt her body tense as her powerful legs kicked forward. Before, she'd carried him from burning calamity. Now she willingly carried him back into the fires. Perhaps she was tired like him.

She wasn't.

Neither group noticed his appearance on the battlefield, perhaps adding to his mystique. He charged along the outskirts as the Riders had before. Gripping Highwind with aching lags, he balanced in his saddle upon the beast and swung at all who neared him.

Erroh counted the numbers under his breath as he killed, for he desired the tally upon his tongue at the end. He hoped for a hundred more, but would be satisfied with one cruel, imposing general. He roared as he charged. A primal roar, born in Keri, mastered upon the field of battle. His victims screamed as he felled them, and his anguish mingled with theirs in a thunderous roar that was heard across the camp.

He awaited the moment when a pike would appear from the darkness and lance his heart right through, or when a sudden battle axe, sharpened for this defining moment, would emerge from the mass of struggling Southerners below as he smote their vileness.

Better to die here than face the failure I brought upon myself.

He hoped Elise waited for him. And his fallen friends too. He hoped there was wine and a place at a table. He could almost hear the comforting whispers from the smoky depths of death's tavern.

"Kill me, you bastards!" he challenged fiercely, riding along the outskirts towards the hesitant attackers. With aching, shaking hands, he struck and killed and never met a vanquisher's unforgiving tip. Before he knew it, he reached the panicked Riders and charged through them, his roars rousing them from their hesitation, stirring their dampening appetites for mayhem.

He glanced at their faces in the light from the flickering firelight and the dim, shattered moon above as he charged through them. They all were dumbstruck, as though they'd sat at a table with the ghost of a long-lost friend. Were they friends, he wondered?

Aye, perhaps in this final charge, they were. Regardless of friendship, he howled his killing intent, and they understood and swept aside and allowed him to race towards the general hidden behind his wall of defenders. In his ears, their chants returned with tenfold the passion. And why wouldn't they? Their muse had gifted them a second breath, had come from nowhere and dared to turn the tale of battle. The numbers of the dead were plenty upon his lips. He was Alpha; he was legend for a few breaths more.

They followed his lead, firing arrows back into the masses. Buoyed on by his presence, they were more accurate than before. Dozens fell in the first volley; the rest met the charging Riders screaming his name with equal vigour from the other flank.

I have an army.

They do not know I have failed.

"On me," he cried in their tongue, and they formed up swiftly. Erroh charged around the camp's outskirts once more so all could see his presence. He remembered his defiance in Keri and held it close. He remembered donning a wild skin to meet his doom bravely, and he held this memory closer. Visions of a ruined, beaten warrior threatening, cajoling an entire army and somehow coming off better struck his mind. He remembered laughing wildly in the face of almost certain death, which brought tears to his eyes. This felt like Keri. This felt like the end, and he accepted it openly.

His behaviour was insanity back then. So he tried it again. He began laughing maniacally, and fuk it, but it felt grand. He dredged up all his pain, woe and misery and let it loose. He laughed for the horrors he'd faced and still survived, for the triumph he'd endured despite achieving no success, and he thought it tremendous. And bitter and cruel too. So bitter, so fuken cruel that any sane brute would surrender to madness. Instead, he laughed at his misfortune, and it, too, was tremendous.

His laughter bellowed across the battlefield, and strangely enough, the defenders fell silent. Their surprise matched that of his allies. The last few echoes of Uden's name disappeared as he thundered along the outskirts with army in tow, and it was quite the impressive sight. He wondered if Uden could see it from his ill-gotten perch atop the walls of Samara. It was a small matter. To those at war, he had appeared from nowhere to stake a claim upon this battle. Such an unlikely feat was sure to give anyone pause, he imagined, and then laughed a little more.

The general barked further orders of charging, but the defenders made no move. Their eyes were upon the deity on the battlefield. Their stillness was contagious, and Erroh sensed the drawing near of advantage. Truthfully, he'd expected to be lying in the damp grass bleeding dry by now. Every moment beyond was a blessing.

The clashing of steel fell still as the defenders retreated away from the charging Riders. Those not part of the great defensive wall dropped to their knees in possible allegiance. Seeing their brethren withdraw, the *thunk* of arrows upon shield soon silenced, and the sounds of night resumed, broken only by the sound of rushing Riders and demonic laughter.

Sensing an opportunity, Erroh brought Highwind to a slow. Those enemies below her stepped away in panic, their weapons clattering in the mud, their desperate mutterings sounding zealous and terrified.

Did Mish sound like that when Uden took his head?

"Do you yield?" he roared in their tongue, and behind him, he heard his name whispered in excited breaths. His new allies certainly believed they did. He struck his swords against his armour and challenged them again to bow down to Uden's mortal enemy.

Give up, give up, give up!

"You are a foolish… god," the general spat, pushing aside his defenders to face Erroh. He'd seen the false god humbled, and his own god face to face, too. The small matter of Erroh's stunning appearance meant little to him. Dropping down and somehow stopping himself from shrieking in pain, Erroh faced him.

"A foolish god?"

They call me a god? Why not? I could be a god.

The brute marched forward, trusting his grandeur to keep steady any eager archer seeking an easy kill.

He was impressive. Each step was vast, taken with sturdy legs built to charge and support the weight of his massive upper body. However, it wasn't his body that intimidated Erroh. It was the enormous weapons he held out in front of him. Long and fully half the width of a set of Clieve, every strike from these axes was potential death, as the female Rider had discovered to her gruesome detriment. He'd never fought a brute with two battle axes. Ankle injury or no, crushing doubt or no, he had the beating of this brute. He knew this because he did not fear him as he did Uden.

"A false god," the general hissed in Erroh's tongue, and Erroh shrugged indifferently. He held out his blades and, for only a moment, worried such strength might shatter his sword if he caught an attack incorrectly.

Don't let him hit you, so.

It was a plan. A simple plan. It didn't work.

Around them, the crowd gathered in a massive circle. Enemies stood side by side—an uneasy truce, dependent on this simple duel of leaders.

Why always me?

Gone were the chants now, replaced by the crackling flames of torches flickering in the midnight wind and the drumming in his ears from his stuttering heart as he stood only a blade's distance from his opponent.

"I remember you," Erroh whispered, and the general nodded.

Aye, he remembers too.

Images of desperate clawing hands flashed in Erroh's mind, and the taste of a god's flesh. He was careful with his ankle, and his opponent peered at his bandaging.

"I remember your falseness, Erroh of the Spark," the general warned, and Erroh glanced around at their audience before raising an eyebrow.

As long as you know my title.

"I don't even know your name," Erroh said. His heart settled, and his adrenalin pulsed. His arm itched something awful. "So, I'll not remember you at all."

Suddenly the behemoth thrust himself forward and brandished the sharpened dague at the top, his axe held forward like a small dagger blade.

Erroh wasn't ready for such a simple manoeuvre. The sharpened tip was only a tiny dagger in terms of width, but it sank deep into his left shoulder, severing skin and muscle as though they were nothing. Erroh fell back and narrowly missed a second strike that should have taken his head, and his opponent laughed. It might have been a forced laugh.

Mocking my strategy?

"A fine blow," admitted Erroh, ignoring the sudden weakness and spinning his blades, should the beast move in for an easy victory. He felt warm crimson stream down his shoulder and cursed his complacency. "You'll get no other," he warned.

"You are not worthy," his opponent declared, and a few watchers agreed. Only a few. "You bleed like any human."

Feigning confidence, Erroh dropped his blades. "If you yield, I will allow you to live." He turned to the rest of the crowd. "I will let you all live." It was a sound ruse taken by a fool without a hand to play. Still, though, it was worth the effort.

"You will die this night, Erroh, as will your bastard followers."

"As you wish." With jagged daggers shooting up his leg and across his shoulder to his chest, he swallowed the pain, cursed it to the fires of hell, and launched himself as though to challenge the agony outright in a game of wits. Their weapons met, and Erroh surrendered himself to the battle. For anything else would end in death.

Drahir could see that the strapping upon Erroh's leg was inadequate to support such a skirmish. The smaller boy was skilled, but he only had to keep his distance and keep him from his favoured foot.

Admittedly, he was unnerved at Erroh's appearance in the middle of such a battle, but catching him off guard with the lunge had convinced Drahir of his shortcomings. Gods were never caught unawares.

This is my moment.
It is my time to claim it all.
I have waited long enough.
I alone can bring about peace for my motherless people.

Victory and acquiescence through battle were the ways of the South. Taming Erroh was an acceptable way to stamp his authority upon a creaking leader. God or no, Drahir knew well that Uden was getting older. Slower, too. Some said he couldn't fight anymore. Only a fool challenged another before the end of a campaign. Better to wait until boredom set itself upon the generals as wretched peace spread across the lands. Was this not how Uden had risen to power before Drahir was old enough to question his ways?

Drahir was a patient little cub even as he came into his prime. While Uden stretched his influence across the Four Factions, Drahir had marched alongside, playing the loyal general. But patience couldn't conceal his aptitude for warfare. Nor could it stop the whispers of challenges growing throughout the armies. It was the cruellest and shrewdest of decisions by Uden to deny him battle at the city gates. Uden had little intention of his followers gazing upon such a beast of war. A wise move, sure to hold back Drahir's rising star, he supposed.

Come dawn, when Drahir appeared at the fallen gates with Erroh's head upon a pike, his achievements would stir the beginnings of rebellion. This, too, was the Southern way.

All hail, Drahir. Gods killer.

He roared as he launched the next salvo, knocking at his opponent's defences before retreating from the counter—a lazy, weak and human counter.

Do you see his human ability?

"We can have peace," Erroh cried again, falling away, and Drahir sneered.

"Your time is done." He leapt upon the injured little cub, hoping to cleave his head clear off in one swift strike and raise it for all to see, but there was a blur of movement and his prey was gone, spinning away upon an injured, weakened leg, slicing out with his blades as he did.

Too fast.

He saw the crimson spray before he felt the pain. Before he could cry out, he felt Erroh behind him and, suddenly, the axes became heavy in his grip.

Godly speed.

He collapsed to his knees but did not die. Not yet. He felt the blade on his neck, and he understood his failure. "Kill me," he cried desperately. His bladder released in fear, and darkness took him.

"Do you all yield?" Erroh cried, and all around him fell to their knees, wailing his name aloud as though he were a god. His young opponent was heavy in his grasp, but he held him upright lest he lose the significance of his achievement. "Do you desire mercy?" His arm ached from where he'd struck the brute with his pommel, and he felt a terrible weakness overcome him.

"I am Erroh, line of Magnus, line of Elise. Do you follow me?"

They did not hesitate; they cheered, they cried his name, he heard the word "god" uttered among the many others, and he grinned maniacally. Those who'd challenged him moments ago now bowed before his magnificence. Those who'd fought each other were now embracing as kin. It was strange. It was unexpected. Yet, it felt natural.

Releasing the unconscious brute, he fell to a knee as the fatigue overcame him.

"Erroh," a voice cried. He recognised the tiny warrior, who looked terrified.

"Where's your white flag, friend?" Erroh gasped, and sudden darkness filled his vision. He touched his shoulder where the axe had pierced him and allowed the pain to take him. Around him, he heard the wailing of the injured, of the mourners. He listened to the braying of beast and baby.

I've been here before.

Hands took him as he fell. They held him aloft and carried him. His body swayed ever so as he fell unconscious. His last thoughts were of Lea, and a terrible coldness came upon him.

5

FILLING IN THE BLANKS

Her name was Aurora, and she liked to kill. Her name was Aurora, and she was made to kill. Her name was Aurora. Aurora. She needed to kill.

Need to kill.

Need to kill.

Aurora rocked back and forth. A masterful skill she accomplished by wrapping her arms around her knees and rocking upon muscled hindquarters worthy of a vile, brutal, beautiful killer. The early afternoon wind caught her hair, and she allowed it. Her lover was not looking at her; how she appeared mattered little.

Lover.

Lovers.

Beside her lay a plate of cherries. She couldn't remember them being left there, but they were meant for her—delicious, juicy, soft cherries. There were seven of them in all. Seven fuken mocking pieces of fruit just laughing in her face, in her mind.

"Fuken cherries."

Nobody could hear her up here. She was above the peasants and kings, so to speak, as the world did its terrible turning, and she did her rocking. She remembered sitting up here with Roja.

No, no. Don't go there yet. That is no path.

She rocked for a few breaths more and hated those damned cherries. She would have preferred eight. Or six. Or anything else. She felt a terrible pressure in her head where she stored her different minds. Her horrors. Her creeping memories. She didn't want to remember. Didn't want to forget, either. So she rocked and hated the vile servant who'd placed the fruit beside her.

"Seven fuken cherries." Nothing good came of the number seven. A vile number, to be sure. She hated that number. She held her rocking for a breath and, with quivering fingers, flicked one away. Six. It should have made her feel better, but it didn't. It made her feel desolate. And alone and in agony. And lost. And afraid. So fuken afraid. Shaking her head and rocking some more, she wondered if she would ever feel better again. Did she deserve to feel better? Now, that was a finer question.

Not with the red hair below.

"No, not yet," she whispered, knowing nobody could hear her. They were too busy dying, fleeing, giving up, or succeeding. She wiped some tears from her eyes and looked across to the gentle behemoth, entrapped and awaiting death, and the weight of guilt tugged at her shapely chest—crushing and killing.

I'm so sorry for this.

Wrek sat where they had chained him, and he was a brutalised ruin. She could see dried blood covering him. Down his front, where Uden's fists struck, were splotches of deep crimson. There were other smears of her Southern comrades splashed across his body from where his fabulous flashing blades had brought the fight, and she liked those stains just fine. But the deep blotches of drying claret covering most of his broken body were most upsetting. He hadn't wailed as she'd thought he would when he awoke beside the dead, seeping body of Stefan. He hadn't wiped the stains away, either. Instead, he'd sat up and accepted the chain around his waist. He had dropped his head when they attached him to the post.

Chained like the Ranger Jeroen.

When Jeroen was chained beside him, he might stir a little. That would be welcomed. She needed warriors with a spark in their eyes. She did not need wilted, ruined captives without any fight.

Or dead queen bitches from the city.

She shook her head, looked at the fuken cherries, and rocked more. She gazed upon a true horror and felt wretched, powerless to distract herself from her guilt. A few Azier warriors surrounded the gathering of flesh, bone, muscle, skin, blood, soul, and blond hair, lying motionless no more than a dozen feet away. Aurora moaned and began rocking wildly, until her god below hesitated for a breath to gaze at her sudden mania as though day had suddenly turned to night and lit itself in unnatural colours. She didn't care. She loved that gathering of wasted meat and blood; her agony would not be denied this awful afternoon.

The Actions of Gods

Four people carried him. Each one taking a limb, they hoisted her dead Stefan into the air and carried him away. His eyes were closed. His mouth was still agape. His jaw forever clenched in a deathly, grimacing grin. His matted, bloody hair dragged in the dust as they marched away, and she wanted dearly to see his heart. To whisper lovingly to it and hold it close to her own.

It's not fair.

"I did this."

They carried him to a house, and she wiped more tears away. The sun was burning her eyes. She had seen the glare and wilted beneath its gaze. She belonged in the dark, where nobody watched her. Where blood never flowed. Where night never came alive in beautiful colour.

She took two cherries, chewed eight times, and spat the remains over the edge of the wall. They fell to the dusty ground as though struck down by two bolts, and she clenched her body, remembering the awful sound of condemning deeds. It was a long drop. Longer when already slain.

Stop it, stop it, fuken stop it.

She wondered what became of Wynn and Lillium as they dropped over the edge. An agile Alpha might have landed smoothly and rolled into the nearest bush. That's what she would have done. Perhaps they kept rolling. They looked like fiends capable of a little rolling over the arth. She marvelled at the dead attackers they left behind them, for there were many. She'd seen them—through the mania of a shattered mind, a little betrayal and the killing of a lover—delivering some fine killing upon her people. And then they had been gone, and she had told no one.

I lied to Uden.

He never noticed.

Uden had looked away, and that was fine. She no longer commanded his desires. She knew this now. Perhaps she'd always known.

Mostly when among comrades.

She had called Wynn and Lillium comrades for a while. Comrades of war, death, and other such essential things, and perhaps she had called them friends. She respected their brutality, their threat. Her heart skipped a beat in excitement. They would fight again. They would be hunted. She could track them, she thought desperately, and felt the awfulness take its hold.

You die this very night.

"So be it," she whispered to the wind, and such a thought terrified her. She was terrified because it was her Outcast comrades who deserved to kill her and not an enraged bastard god. Below her, she heard a gasp, and she looked away.

No, no, no, no.

She wondered what had become of her little Tye. All brave and foolish and full of killing. She hoped he had dropped into the dark tunnel when the fighting began and fled far from here.

She smiled as she rocked and imagined the little one, Lexi, in his grasp. Dragged through the darkness by brave little Tye. Away from the monsters. Away from Aurora. Ooh, she imagined Lexi would be rather grateful for such daring. She wondered what a little amorous Alpha female might do to reward him. She imagined their furrowing a thousand miles from here, and such was her hope that she forgot her misery for a breath. Shiny little Alphas in love might do well to hide away from this awfulness; she imagined and hoped. She prayed on her god's will, too, and knew it to be a futile prayer.

Still, though.

Make her moan like Stefan made me moan, and all will be well.

Confident her little Tye was away from this place and living a charmed and happy life, Aurora stood up and gazed across the devastation she'd brought. A betrayal she'd delivered long before she'd known them. Before Fyre had scratched at the door.

Betrayer.

Abruptly, panic retook her. She wondered if it was the cherries. She suddenly imagined herself in the sights of the goddess Lea. She prayed an arrow was already notched and close to release. She closed her eyes and hoped the silent projectile would take flight and tear her heart apart —right where Uden had clawed and torn and reshaped it to do his bidding. She opened her arms wide as though crucified and waited for death. Dying at the hands of a vengeful Outcast was not terrifying at all.

"Shoot me through the heart, then through each eye," she ordered, wondering if Lea understood. She patted her chest and waited more and almost wailed.

Betray.

Betrayal.

Betrayer.

"Kill me, Lea," she whispered, and no arrow came, and she was distraught. "Just do it."

She imagined Lea had slipped away, killing dozens on her way. She wondered did Nomi slither away after her? Hoping to trip her up on the way out of town. Hoping to leave her to die and claim Erroh for her own.

"Taking this town hurts more this time," she said, and nobody was listening to little old Aurora Borealis. She remembered the similar nightmare. If the first taking of this town had begun her cracking of the mind, this betrayal today had broken her in two. She remembered her final kill that day. A good kill too. Worthy of her greatness.

"My name is Aurora, and I like to kill," she said as though Uden spoke through her, and she felt that terrible pressure once more.

I lie.

And I lied to Uden.

He probably knew she lied. His wrath would be devastating. She knew this because her birth depended only on truth, love, fear, and needing to kill.

Covered in blood.

Blood covered her, and it gave her little relief. Little reward either. She brought her fingers to her lips and tasted Roja's blood, and it was bitter and awful, and she was a betrayer of her people.

I have no people.

She stared at the cherries and hated them. More than that, she faced them and dared to defy their purpose of torment.

Do it.

Do it.

She did it. She took one and, rubbing it in her fingers, flicked it away into nothing. They were uneven again. Uneven by her hand. And she had lied to Uden; her name was Aurora, and sometimes she didn't like to kill. Sometimes.

It's a start.

Snatching the plate, she tossed it deep into the Wastes. It might have smashed. It was a small matter. What mattered was the cherries had been uneven at her shaking hand.

So much blood.
Too much blood.
Alder's blood.
Stefan's blood.
Roja.

She wanted to clean herself of Roja's stench. She wanted to dive into the nearest frozen river and never resurface. She would be cleaner then.

"Save her, healer," Uden spat, and Aurora gazed down at him now. He was impressive. A giant. Terrifying. Beautiful. Around them, the Hunt went to task ravaging the town, but Uden didn't seem to care, nor seem to notice either. Better for them, she imagined. He had the look of threat about him. Pacing back and forth like a caged hound ready to kill, he stopped only to threaten the wretched, drunken healer who continued to defy the darkness and return her to life. "Or you will die this very day."

Emir didn't take any notice of this threat. Aurora was not surprised. She knew his passion was depthless, and the small matter of working upon his lover offered him enough incentive. She could tell Uden, but she might start screaming at him until her soul and mind were empty. Until he finally heard her.

Emir's fingers were a blur as he delved through Roja's innards. Cutting, cleaning, removing and sewing. A fine thing to hold life and death in the balance, Aurora imagined, as the healer wiped his forehead with a stained hand. The offending bolts lay discarded in the dust beside him, and Aurora considered recovering them. To keep a souvenir of her terrible crime. She fought the bile churning in her stomach, seeking release.

The rest of Roja was partly sealed. She remembered Emir screaming that were she moved, she would surely die en route. So, with nothing but his trusty healer's bag, a few basins of clean water and no shortage of cleansing alcohol, he had fought to save her. Under the watchful eye of a god. A false god. A cruel bastard. A killer of innocents.

Like Fyre.

Roja's eyes shot open, and Aurora hated this moment.

"Shush, my love," Emir cried as the girl screamed in agony, and her wails were terrible. They echoed across the town. Like the howls of a mother losing their child, or a girl losing her soul in blood. Such violent screams they were that carrion birds took flight from their meals in the dust, tearing Aurora apart.

I did this.

"Save your energy for the fight," he begged, reaching into his bag to recover the foul rag. "Please, Roja," he cried, and, dousing the rag with a vile-smelling potion, he held it over her screaming mouth and took her consciousness swiftly. Aurora knew what would happen next. So did Emir. He eyed the bastard lying piece of shit false god.

"Fuken cur," roared Uden. "Save her," he demanded, and there was an unusual desperation in his tone. Aurora had never heard such a thing. She'd never deceived him either.

"I heard you the first time," Emir murmured, and it was a fine petulant retort, sure to enrage the god wonderfully. She remembered craving that anger. Remembered hoping Uden would dash her head against the nearest wall a dozen times until her skull shattered into a thousand pieces.

Those were the days.

Roja shook in her slumber as the poison went to task, killing her from the inside. Emir dropped beside her and checked her breath, then her pulse. All the while, Uden paced. Usually, by now, he would have taken hold of Emir and shaken him mercilessly. Perhaps now, with his one eye, he could finally see Emir's effort.

"Save her, healer," Uden demanded, more softly now, and Emir shook his head. He took a deep breath.

"She's fading away. Not long now," he warned after a moment, and awaited the assault. For reasons unbeknownst to Aurora, Roja's hurt caused Uden depthless anguish.

As much as Stefan's death had?

"If she dies, you will die too, healer," Uden repeated, as he had done so many times before. Such mania was no good look for the bastard false god.

"I do not fear you, Uden. Save your threats," Emir said, sitting back in the dust as though at rest in the middle of a warmer season. Aye, he appeared relaxed, but he faced the god without blinking. His voice was cold and steady—a pleasing tone for a healer. "A vile potion torments her wounds when she is near dry, faded almost to nothing. Still, I try to steal back her life."

Uden could contain himself no more. "Know this," he shouted, pulling the healer to his feet. He thrashed him thrice across the face. Not enough to knock him unconscious but enough to remind him of the possibility of his future demise. "If you do anything but treat her with—"

It was a fine strike, even from a wretched healer. Emir's fist shot out, struck Uden across the chin, and broke his hold. He followed with one open-handed slap across Uden's godly face, and Aurora knew his breaths were nearing their end. "I'll do all I can," Emir shouted, slipping away from the god and dropping beside Roja to tend to her.

Aurora almost leapt from her ledge to kill him but caught herself. Those Southerners currently ransacking the town of supplies hesitated, but the moment passed, and they resumed their duties.

"Save her, healer. And you will earn my grace," Uden said coldly.

"I do not know what that means," Emir countered. Aurora knew what his grace felt like. It was a wondrous thing. She fought the primal urge rising inside her, craving it. Craving him. Craving all the killing. All the blood too. She bit her lip, rocked a few times and hated the bastard.

"What do you propose, healer?" Uden asked, dropping to a knee beside Emir. Aurora waited and watched to see what his next move would be. Waited for his powerful hands to reach around and strangle the life from her comrade, her noble enemy, her friend. Instead, Emir spoke of intricate medical things Aurora had little knowledge of. Uden nodded in silence, learning of the girl's fate, learning of the healer's deep understanding of healing, learning more of the tools created by the ancients.

Aurora knew Emir lied. And why wouldn't he lie? She had lied, and Uden hadn't noticed. Such things were terrible and precarious. She looked at the fading Roja and smiled, thinking her march would soon be done. She would sleep eternally, and such peace was beautiful. Aurora would follow soon after, and that was fine. These were pleasant thoughts to console Aurora as the world she knew shattered all around her.

6

TRAGEDY OF THE HEALER

He was close now. Real fuken close to breaking, and nothing was stopping him. Emir wiped away some stains from the girl's porcelain face with eerily still fingers and dared not weep. Not yet. Only when the deed was done. Not until he was ready to climb into the night and never return.

Perhaps tonight.

Waking up was a misery, but it was something he did throughout the night. Every time he woke, this room seemed colder, darker. Less hopeful too. His body was weary tonight. Wearier than it had ever been. He had believed himself exhausted before, but this was something else entirely. He felt like he'd emerged from a week of heavy drinking and been commanded to climb a mile-high mountain. His head thumped unmercifully, and he wondered if he hadn't pushed himself too far this time. Giving himself to her, in body, soul and blood. Too much blood. A candle flickered in the evening breeze, casting shadows around the room.

Room of the Dead.

It was a fine room for the dead and dying. It was drearily lit by a few flickering candles and nothing much else. There might have been a light switch, but the bulbs above his head were long since shattered. The many windows were covered over with thick, stained curtains. All for privacy, no doubt, creating a place where merry drinkers in better times could hide from the day. Blearily, he remembered searching merrily for signs of alcohol in this old tavern when they first arrived in Raven Rock. That was a lifetime ago. Back when he thought his path was difficult.

Back when he thought he'd tasted the hell of what his life was. Back when he didn't believe he'd find a use for the sawdust on the floor.

He ran his finger along her skin and loved her with all he had. Deep down, though, love wasn't enough. It had never been. It never would be again. He wanted to weep now, but he held firm. Falling apart before the deed was done was a poor use of his time. There would be time to give up and die come the morrow. Until then, he would stand firm, albeit from a sitting position.

Her breath was weak, but it was a breath. Her face was deathly pale. He hated that colour. Good things never came from that colour. He watched her momentarily and wondered if checking her pulse would make any difference at this late hour. Probably not. So he leaned back in his chair and concentrated on his exhaustion.

Being bled dry drains you.

He wished he'd chosen a more comfortable chair, or found a cushion for it at least, or a blanket to stave off the chill in the night air. He stared beyond her sleeping body to his tools and willed them to work their miracles. They were stained with his blood, these ancient rubber and glass pieces. Some considered the blood-sharing process a vile practice (especially in the city), but he would roll the dice where desperation played its hand. If Roja survived this terrible night and those beyond, he would gladly take her spiteful condemnation for his actions.

"My blood is yours, my love," he whispered, and she made no reply, and her silence crushed him. The world was ended, and only now, with barely any energy, could he think of the day's horrors. His arm ached where he'd pierced himself, allowing his heart to pump into her. "I am alone, and I need you tonight."

She didn't reply, but he didn't mind. Breathing was enough for now. Breathing and fighting off infection, invasion and poison was bound to take a lot out of her. He had played his wretched part; the rest was upon her. The stitching would leave mild scarring upon her perfect skin, and he would cherish those marks every time he gazed upon them. He pledged this to himself and hoped it was a good pledge.

He wanted to drink. He'd never wanted to drink as badly as he did now. Not even his learning of Aireys falling beside Quig had demanded such a quenching as this. However, he would deny himself any release from sobriety in this room of the dead. He reached for his glass and drained it before pouring another. Cool, ordinary, life-giving water was his beverage this evening. He'd need to refill his body with blood if she needed another few pints in the days ahead. He would keep giving, no matter the awfulness.

"I'll even stay sober for you, Roja," he whispered, smiling, loving her, all the while fighting sleep himself. She didn't reply, and that was fine. She'd never had an issue with his drinking, anyway.

Here it comes.

He felt it now. A sorrow without depth, and he knew he could no longer fight its draw. So he took it and used it. He could feel no worse than he already did. His task required sobriety and only a partly fractured mind.

It is time.

"I'll be with you now, friend," he said into the chilly darkness, waiting for an unlikely reply.

Despite himself, despite his terrible exhaustion, he climbed to unsteady feet and shuffled to the other body lying across the tavern's countertop. They'd left him here to serve as a warning of failure, which was cruelty on Uden's part.

As if he's been anything but.

"You fuked up, Stefan," Emir told his friend.

I know, he imagined Stefan replying. For a terrible moment, he imagined Stefan standing over them both. Dressed in his finest wear, his hair tied up with a red silken ribbon. Half his golden sword along his waist. His full-toothed smile.

Emir was alone.

The body's face was frozen, but his eyes were mercifully closed. Blood covered everything. He had soiled himself, too, and Emir lamented for his friend's pride.

I trusted her, Emir, he imagined Stefan whispering, and though it was a comfort, it was also soul-crushing to believe his friend was still nearby. Outside. At the fire with everyone else. Anywhere but atop this death slab, stretched out and needing tending to.

"Oh, Stefan. It is all right, brother." He wondered if this was how a man turned to Primary murder. A few imaginings? A few conversations with the dead? A fuk-load of guilt? "You did well at the end. You had comrades; you had honour; you had redemption." He thought them great words. He knew the grief his best friend had endured for the sins of his lesser life. As deaths went, there were worse, he supposed. He hoped Stefan had known this too. Saying you loved someone in your stolen final breath was rare and wonderful. Even if one's untimely demise was a whore's fault.

Truthfully, he knew no imagined voice in his head spoke of deathly matters now, and Emir felt lesser for it.

With aching, weary limbs, bruised and battered, he went to task with cloth and water. It was all he could think to do. It would be barbaric to send a dead man to his grave in such a state. Emir had mastered his art in the city as a fledgling apprentice; this deed would be no rare act. He started with the blood on his comrade's face and moved on to the hair afterwards. It was scrubbing his trousers and beneath that took the longest.

Add some eucalyptus too... That voice again.

"Aye, I know what to do," Emir mumbled as he finished the grim work by sprinkling the body with eucalyptus oil. "Nicely seasoned," he jested, and fought the sorrow, the tears more so. He wondered what had become of Stefan's mind. Had he gone to the darkness? Was he in an eternal dream? Was he already in the mind of an infant as it freed itself from its mother's womb?

"Are you with Aireys and Quig?"

I am.

"You left me behind, brother," Emir muttered, drawing away from his dead friend. "I'll never see you again."

He imagined no reply. Instead, he thought about a beautiful tavern where all his friends were drinking, singing, dancing, laughing and loving, and he wanted to be outside its welcoming door, about to step through. He wondered if that was where happiness lay. He wondered if it was warm. It was so close that he could almost taste it, and he wanted to escape to this wondrous place.

"Soon enough, I will," he whispered, sitting back in his seat to while away the hours in tense silence. Closing his eyes, he hoped for the end. "Soon enough," he repeated, and it was a fine pledge.

He did not know what drew him from sleep, only that he woke in alarm. It was still not dawn. The room felt cold, empty and lonely. He scrambled from his chair to tend to Roja and almost collapsed as he did, such was the weariness in his fragile body. She still took breaths, and he allowed himself a deep sigh of relief and offered a nod to the absent gods. Miles to go, but the hours were kind. If her body accepted his blood, there was hope.

"How are you?" he asked, knowing she would not wake. And she did not stir. To an innocent onlooker, she appeared almost at peace. Her face was no longer clenched in an agonised grimace, and her forehead was no longer covered in a veneer of sweat, and he took these as fair omens of good things. He ran his fingers through her hair, kissed her once on the cheek, and sat beside her. His service as healer was done, and now he played the doting, worried mate rather than the commanding healer overseeing life and death. He was no fan of this fate.

"How is my friend?" Aurora asked from across the room where Stefan lay, and he recoiled in fright. She looked like a wraith, covered in crimson and sweat, and he'd never found her more terrifying. "Is she alive?"

He gripped a scalpel and held it up to her. It was no impressive blade, but he was done with this life. Were they not all waiting for him? Did they not play his favourite song? She gazed back at Stefan, and he knew a quick few steps and a swift slice could end the bitch's life. An outstanding vengeance that would render his resulting death a worthy one. He gripped that blade real fuken tightly for a few breaths.

Not until Roja's fate is decided, Stefan's voice whispered, and he knew it was his mind swaying him from the edge. She moved closer and ran her stained fingers down Stefan's ruined face as though caressing a lover in bed.

Killer.

Betrayer.

Whore.

"You cleaned my boy," she whimpered, her voice wretched and broken. He thought it an acceptable act. He wanted to swing that blade, Stefan be damned, because she had damned Stefan. Her two blades lay upon a table behind her, and for a moment, Emir wondered if he could close the distance before she drew them.

"He deserved more than he received. It was the least I could do," Emir snapped. She leaned over and kissed the fatal wound, and this tore at Emir's will. He could feel himself breaking more and slipping further from this world's sanity. He wanted death. He wanted his friends. He didn't want to be alone anymore. It wasn't fair.

"He was so beautiful, and I loved him so," she said, and he knew it was a lie because she was a great betrayer and none of this was fair, and he suddenly wasn't sure his own friend's imagined voice would be enough to stop him leaping upon her and slitting her neck.

"You betrayed us."

"I did."

"Fuk you," he hissed, dropping the scalpel. Some things were more important than vengeance.

She finally faced Emir, and tears streamed down her cheeks. "Will Roja live?" she asked, and turned to the healing tools he'd used for the operation. He wanted to stop her, but he knew if he touched her he might draw a fist and never stop striking her. She tugged gently at the rubber tubing as though it was a fascinating toy before touching her finger to the impossibly sharp needle attached to its end. "Uden told me of your actions." She lifted the needle and held it over her heart, moved it to her jugular vein and then to her lips. Whatever thoughts stirred in her mind were lost in her unreadable expression. Without warning, she brought the needle to her arm and dug it into her flesh. "Is this what you did?" she asked, watching the tubing for blood, and Emir grasped her hand.

"Take out that needle."

"I want to give her my blood too," she said, and her words came in a rush. "I have adequate blood. Worthy of her. She should not be lying here. She should be on her feet. It would be better if she were on her feet. Better. Much better."

"It doesn't work like that, Aurora," he snapped, roughly pulling the needle from her arm. A few droplets of crimson came with it, and she flinched at the pain and his actions. He wondered if he could shove that needle through one of her eyes, into her brain, and kill her there and then. After a breath, he stepped away and regretted the disinfecting he'd need to do again. "Blood isn't usually compatible. I took a chance with mine; I shall not use another's."

"Blood is blood," she cried desperately, and her act of contrite wretch truly disgusted him. "Take my blood, please. I offer it all." She produced a knife from nowhere, and he took a step back in horror as she sliced into her arm and allowed a stream of blood to run free.

If truth be told, he was tempted to allow her to pump her blood free of her body, into a nice jar. Truly, she'd be none the wiser. He could allow her to empty herself, all in the name of some false healing, which would be justice.

"You do not know what you speak of, witch."

She clutched her head as though struck and gasped. "Don't call me that, not today."

He didn't care. He threw her a rag of bandaging. "Stop bleeding all over the floor."

Denied the gift of blood, she was crestfallen. She wrapped her arm and left the knife by Stefan, and he wondered about taking that knife and…

"Spark is taken."

It's over now.

Everything is finished.

Nothing else matters.

Why were three words so powerful? He felt as though he had been struck by a fist. No, far worse than any strike. It was a bludgeoning to his heart, his mind, his soul. Emir collapsed back into his seat. He felt everything spin, and once more, he felt his mind separate, and it was too much.

Far too much.

I want to die.

What of Erroh?

He heard her words from a distance. She wept as he did. A liar's stream of tears as she told him of Uden's words of Spark's great defences falling in no time at all. He asked after Erroh, and she was distraught and silent, and Emir knew. He fell from his seat and sought air and found nothing. He heard the clatter of his utensils as they fell around him, but their melody faded, leaving him with nothing but his agony. He wailed like a braying beast of slaughter, for this life had finally become too much. He heard Stefan's whispers in his mind and reached for familiarity. Reached for anything as the world shattered.

Emir finally let go and lost himself completely.

And then the world exploded.

7

BEHEMOTH

Magnus had a plan. A simple plan. But the sea on all sides, rushing wild, was doing all in its magnificent power to get in its way.

"It'll never work," he whispered, knowing his voice would be lost to the roar. There was no one else around to hear him anyway. They were too distracted, listening to their own screams, to pay him any heed, and that was fine by him. Near the front, where no wise fiend would wait, he stood listlessly, his eyes upon the swirling waves on all sides.

He growled under his breath. It was his habit when facing impossible odds and relying on nerve and good luck to carry him through, keep him afloat, stay alive another day, follow through with a well-thought-out plan. His growl warned the sea and the storm not to worsen. He growled, for only strength would serve him this terrible night. Would comfort him as the waves tempested around him and bellowed their challenge to let go and play in her deep waters evermore.

The barge creaked loudly beneath the strain of the violent sea. A terrifying hint at bending wood, ready to snap, separate, and sink away. He didn't like those creaking sounds, not one little bit. His hand remained tightly gripped around the cage release. He held that grip taut for many hours against arthritis and bitter biting cold, but he would not release the hold. Pain could be controlled.

This is nothing to what will come.

His other hand held tightly against the edge of the sea barge. He had a good grip despite the cold, his gnarled hand hooked tightly against the guardrail like a talon. Enough to keep him steady and upright. As the world rose, fell, shuddered and lurched, the barge threatened to spin upon itself, capsize into the darkness and kill everyone aboard.

Not tonight. He refused to give in to terror this nauseous night. Or back down from any trial, for that matter. For that was all a storm was— a fuken trial of the nerve. Besides, it was a strange thing to accept powerlessness in fate's grip. He just needed to stay where he was. Pain be damned to the fires of hell or the depths of the oceans. Or to whatever gods most people believed in.

"Take the pain." These words he demanded, and he cared little whether they carried in the night. They were adequate words. Words to live by when searching for inspiration, when composing poetry and meaningfulness. Or just trying to survive a nightmare. Three simple words that could change the world. No one ever knew how much pain they could take once they realised pain was unavoidable. His master had taught him that too.

Take the pain.
Survive longer.

The rest of his body was in pain too. He had not stepped from this precarious edge, despite the captain's warnings, despite the force of water as it broke against the vessel's bow. He'd stood at attention two days and two nights, chased by this roaring storm, while most others upon this faltering barge wavered and stumbled.

He looked to the sky and the massive sails. He thought it a small blessing the wind was at their back, watching it catch and drag them ever closer to his death. The days before were rough, but tonight was fiercest. They might very well die this night, but they were making excellent time doing it. He looked off into the darkness towards an unseen coast. They'd reach the shores faster than he'd ever expected if they survived a few miles more. It was the small things.

He took a breath and softly hummed a few notes. It was a fine distraction against this awful channel crossing. "No mortal man, or woman, can swim to ground; we all fall down alone." His melody was lost in the blowing squall, and it was a small matter. He had no remarkable singing voice, and besides, singing about the sinking of ships by storm and monster was unlikely to find a willing audience aboard the *Grand Cantus* on its ten thousandth or so crossing. The soft, damp wood smelling of mould and varnish along the vessel's edge suggested a great age, as did the patched and stained sails and the mismatched oaks upon the ruined deck. This fine vessel had likely tasted many similar nights afloat, he imagined. Sometimes experience was essential. Sometimes a barge had a set number of storms she would devour in her grand charge across the near never-ending ocean before she took a deep breath and dipped her head below the surface.

He thought of the next line, ignoring any premise of fear or superstition. But before he could sing, the vessel's tip rose high above the massive waves a few feet before him, holding sickeningly in mid-air before dropping to the surface again with a thunderous boom, covering him and his most valuable treasures. The rush of spray and wave was awful. His ears stung at the attack, and he gripped the barge's edge tighter and found the words to the following line.

"Oh, god. These seas…" he sang at the storm, showing no fear on his weathered face. There were likely fifty other souls aboard praying to their gods—those absent, those ancient, and those more recent. At least one lost soul needed to show some nerve and challenge the way of natural things. "… All hope is gone. Who sails these seas?"

He gripped the cage lever, seized the barge's edge tightly and felt his stomach lurch as they dipped much farther and crashed deeper, and the freezing waves drenched him through. He thought he'd become accustomed to each drenching, but how could anyone become used to a thousand needles striking simultaneously and think little of it? The cold took his breath, squeezed the air right out, and his body shook something terrible. But his hands remained at task. They were fine, ruined hands indeed.

He stared beyond the waves and sought light in the distance, but found little sign of land. Probably a good thing too. Many ship captains chased a landfall and then lost their nerve, dooming many a barge upon the rocky coast. Water was water, and rock was rock. Hard to tell the difference, though, when blinded by terror. Daring a glance away from the oncoming waves and mustering what readiness he could for himself, he gazed down the deck of commotion to the captain working the wheel. He'd thought him a grizzled old soul and given him barely a glance of recognition as he came aboard, but there was a sturdiness to the plump old seafarer. Watching the wheel spin, he saw there was an assurance. A knowing. That was enough. Until the mast snapped and the boat floundered, of course. Then, Magnus would regret his decision to make this voyage home so inconspicuously, choosing a small, charming barge instead of a larger vessel. Still, nothing to be done about it now, he supposed, and looked to the clear night as a thin trailing cloud raced across the sky, buffeted by the unforgiving gale. The shattered moon was dimmed for a moment before its glow returned to light the sea and her victims a little more. A small blessing: the night was clear. Small blessing indeed.

Beside him, the cages rattled as one of his treasures shuddered in the barge's sway. Only then did he look at them, and they met his gaze with terrified, unblinking eyes. "I'm sorry, my boys."

At this, the nearest of his fierce war hounds crawled forward from the mass of shivering fur and teeth and licked his fingers. A desperate, silent plea to set them free from this horror. "Only that I could." He would never have locked up such proud beasts, but he could not have left them behind, either, as he marched to his doom. He had brought them partly for their protection, but also because no man could ever enjoy walking his last steps alone.

As long as those steps aren't wet and upon no stable ground.

His hound pleaded once more in silence before another wave took them both, and the beast scampered backwards towards the rest of his brethren and nestled in to recover what heat he could. Magnus's heart was heavy watching his boys brought so low. He must have apologised a hundred times since he'd banished them into the cage when the first winds blew. Locking them in was a cruel kindness, and although the barge's bow was no place for any fool this night, he would not leave them to fret alone. The only thing worse than the piercing cry of a gale was the desolate wail of a dozen hounds alone. Besides, if the barge flipped, he'd pull that fuken lever right quick and give them a fighting chance to swim ashore.

It won't flip.

Aye, standing in the wake of every breaking wave was no place for any fool this dreadful night, but at least he wasn't down in the middle deck where a few braver passengers were busy throwing their dinners over the side.

"Should just find a bucket down below, fools," Magnus said to nobody while gazing down at the horror unfolding there.

In the wind, the lantern flames waved as wildly as the spray but somehow stayed alight against the storm, and it was a small blessing. In the flickering light, Magnus caught sight of a child. No older than Erroh had been upon his first march across the Wastes, the boy was diminutive and unimpressive. Careful to hold his stomach as barrels and bodies rolled across the deck, unable to find any balance, he approached Magnus like a sailor seeking a beacon in a tempest. He did not know just how precarious his path was, and finally, for the first time in days, Magnus chuckled aloud.

Magnus could not hear the retching against the turmoil. Nor did he hear the silent streams of spittle and vomit given flight from sickened mouths. He did, however, hear the cries of horror from the boy as the wet surges and rancid projectiles struck him from all sides. A host of arrows might have caused less mess, and the boy's screams were ungodly. As was his slithering shuffle across the middle of the deck, where no other fools dared to tread lest they slip in the mixture of stomach waste and seaweed and salty pools of water and probably a few other vile things as well.

Climbing the steps below where Magnus stood, the boy wiped what vomit he could from his clothes, face, mouth and hair, and Magnus returned to his watching of the sea lest the ruined child approach him.

"Did you see what those fuks did to me?"

Magnus did. "Bad place to walk, little one." It was good advice and delivered with enough coldness that the child wisely shifted his gaze to the cage with its shivering hounds and moved a little farther on.

"My friends call me Padir."

I'm no friend.

Magnus sighed in reply. If the boat sank, he'd desire no company on the way.

Padir did. "I'm rightly covered in all manner of shit… Smells bad… That looks like carrot… didn't know there was carrot in our soup. It was nice soup."

At this, Magnus snorted and offered the boy a nod. A "You can leave with a jest" nod. The child took it as something different. Of course he did. He climbed the last few steps and dropped to his knees beside the cage.

"They're well behaved."

Oh, for fuk's sake.

"Not if I let them loose." As he spoke, a wave struck the boat, rising and covering them both, and Padir nearly slipped back down the steps to the ill-fated middle deck. Tragically, the boy returned and stood beside the legend, gripping the barge's edge tightly.

"If you fell into that water, my king…" He dipped his head slowly. He smelled of three days' sailing and a bucket of vomit. "…I'd leap in after you." Magnus finally faced the child as any king would with his subjects. The boy wasn't done, and fuk him, but there was a charm to his behaviour. It was an act—a ploy to win him over. Magnus respected a cunning little shrew at the best of times. The worst of times too.

The Actions of Gods

"Would that earn me grace at your side upon your... um... triumphant return home?" the child asked.

"You play a pleasing, honourable friend. Are you to be trusted?" It was an invitation to truth.

"No, my king. I merely wish to ally myself with the fiercest... um..." He looked around for inspiration. "... hound in the cage. And I can be useful to royalty returning to our savage lands without an army to protect him."

"How do you know who I am?"

"I know your legacy. I've seen the art. You are hard to miss. Truthfully, word is easily spread in the east. I had my eyes upon you and took a chance when you boarded. Wasn't until tonight I had the nerve to approach."

Magnus cursed. He thought he'd escaped his beloved East Faction unnoticed, but for a kind serving girl who'd cared for him for a few days in his estate. Every night she'd come to his bed and left unsatisfied. Until Magnus knew Elise's fate, he would spend himself in no other. Still, she'd been warm and comforting. There were worse things when preparing for the end of his life. Aye, she'd left unsated and eager, with a pledge of secrecy on her supple lips. He doubted she would betray him. But this boy was proof that his movements were observed, and he had delayed too long. He thought he'd passed through the port at Calas without incident or recognition, but the boy was proof to the contrary. Who knew what messages were already in flight upon a swifter vessel, or in the hands of a desperate rider? Too many, most likely.

"If we sink this awful night, I would like to see the wave that takes our king. Such a thing would be beautiful and terrifying," Padir said strangely, and Magnus shivered despite himself. He eyed the massive surrounding waves and recovered his nerve. Worry profited man nothing, after all. Also, he liked the boy's poetic darkness. It was refreshingly savage. It had been a few years since he'd spoken with a soul from his homelands. He would be a fine companion to have when a wave took them all.

"We won't die this night, little one," Magnus said gruffly. This appeared to please his new companion greatly. "But where I'm going will be dark indeed. Best you go upon your way; I won't be the strongest hound in the cage for long."

"I'll carry your bags until you are bested, sire." The boy reached for the massive pack at Magnus's foot. It was half his height and twice his weight. Why he even reached for it was a mystery, given they were upon a barge so close to sinking, and Magnus released his hold on the boat's edge and gripped the boy, halting him, lest he somehow discover the crown wrapped among his belongings. As strange as it was to walk the halls and acres of his estate without Elise's presence nearby, it had been another thing entirely removing his crown from its case. He'd be glad to be rid of it as long as they pledged one last march for their detested king.

"Not today, little one."

Padir left the bag and leaned back over the ocean as another wave overcame them. He wiped water from his hair with shivering fingers and, with it, some of the vomit. Any fool introducing themselves to royalty in this state was a man of nerve. Or idiocy. Magnus suspected both, and that was fine. Was the legend Erroh not similar at his age? Before life got in the way, at least. Padir might yet grow into something impressive. He might find his calling as Magnus's servant. And Magnus? It was no evil deed to pass on knowledge to the youth, even if their paths crossed only this once.

Neither one said anything for a time. They merely stood and waited for death, or the first sign of the coast, and a gale picked up, and the flapping of the sails was thunderous as they fought an invisible god's hand dragging them farther and faster across the ocean. After a while, Padir coughed and cleared his throat. He rapped his hands along the wooden edge, and Magnus saw the worry of silence had gotten the best of the boy.

"Will the barge hold tonight?" Padir asked.

"Look to the captain. What do you see?"

"He's swinging the… wheel thing. He looks scared. I think he's praying."

"Listen to his words, young one."

"Wait—I think… I think he's… singing."

"Strange way to pray."

"A good sign?"

"Aye, Padir, a singing captain is always a good sign."

The child shuddered a little, though in the flickering flames and the light of the shattered moon his pale skin appeared to find a little colour. "Still, I fancy my chances. I'm a skut of a thing, but I can swim for days. Even in this swell."

Magnus laughed, but when he spoke, his tone was serious. Knowing. Instructive. Like a master's. "Look to the bow and the route."

"Aye, through endless waves doing all they can to stem our flow."

"Now look to the clear night above."

"I see the stars and the shattered moon."

"If it were a cloudy night, we'd be rightly fuked. As it is, follow the stars. A strong swimmer could swim the wrong way for eternity. Better a fine swimmer with a path in the water."

"I see."

Magnus smirked. "Spread your hand wide and look up. That's the distance they'll travel across the sky at night. So, when we tip and the barge goes under, follow that route with the stars until you reach the shore."

The boy didn't seem to understand, and that was a small matter. This was no night for teaching simple navigation, and for all Magnus knew, Padir might have believed the little shimmering lights above were the absent gods themselves, watching from their diamond palaces. It was not Magnus's place to disagree with the boy's beliefs. In the end, they were this close to death and needed only a few more buckets of sea water in their lower hull to drag them down. It would be rude to criticise his ideology. He didn't know why anyone needed to argue such things, anyway.

"When we tip?" Padir asked wearily.

"If we tip."

It was hardly a landing worthy of a king, but Magnus didn't mind. He braced himself as the barge lurched forward beneath the overcast sky upon a heavy wave and, with a shudder, came to a smooth stop upon the wet sand. Only then did Magnus pull the lever, and his hounds shot out from the cage, hissing and snapping as though ready to rip the throat of some unfortunate foolish enough to be in their way.

"Go," Magnus barked, and not one beast hesitated as they leapt clear of the barge and dropped into the shallow, retreating water below. They howled in ecstasy at the prospect of solid ground and perhaps a little prey. They darted through the waves, barking and snapping at each other as the few days of frustration were lost to the excitement of the sprint. Magnus watched them for a moment and marvelled. The beasts did not notice the sailors unloading the cargo from the vessel as they raced against the tide's return. He offered a gentle nod to the captain, who took a moment from shouting orders to provide a deep bow. A fine thing the captain had never approached him seeking opportunity. A finer thing he hadn't spoken loudly to entice other different-minded fools desiring opportunity with a wandering, savage royal. Giving silent thanks for the companionship and stability, Magnus tapped the barge's edge one last time before hoisting his bag over aching shoulders and dropping to the sea below.

The water was freezing, and he loved it. He dug his head beneath the surface and kissed the sandy ground as the receding surf soaked him anew.

"So I may walk with you, Magnus of the three clans?" the boy said, still close behind him.

"It is a free land. So you are free to follow whomever you choose. Until you follow someone with a brighter star, that is." Magnus dug a handful of sand from beneath the water and held it tightly in aching hands. He rubbed the grains across his forehead and then placed another fistful against his heart before kissing what remained and letting it fall back into the water. Above, the clouds wept in his honour, and he smiled. He knew he would meet his end upon these isles, yet still, he loved them with all his heart.

They belonged to him.

For now.

8

LILLIUM

She lunged with the blade and snapped her wrist sideways, and felt the innards give under the twist. *Perfect.* She pulled the sword out, took some of him with her and kicked the dying man from the wall, letting him fall soundlessly to the ground far below. No brute followed him, and she took a breath and screamed triumphantly. Dreams were made of this. Vile, killable brutes were all around her, and she delivered what vengeance she could. She wondered if she would awaken from this sleep, wrapped up in Wynn's arms or her sweaty bedclothes. She hoped not. She wanted this. Wanted to die this way.

Perfect.

Beside her, Wynn appeared, and he was glorious. Killing was an excellent look to him. With hair whipping left and right, his cloak catching in the breeze, and his face grim and controlled, he appeared godly, like nothing she'd ever seen. His sword was bloody, quivering and divine, for he had killed as many as she, which pleased her greatly. They'd walked some awful miles together, but these last few steps into the darkness would be beautiful. She was ready for death. Dying among good company was a great fate indeed. She gazed down at Wrek and Stefan below, fighting an entire army, and thought them brave and elite. No greater compliment. She assessed the distance and stepped over the edge to drop down among them—a worthy reason to sacrifice the higher ground.

But instead of dropping, she was held fast for a moment as Wynn rushed her from behind. Screaming in frustrated terror, she felt herself go over the wall's edge, felt arms wrap themselves around her, felt him nearby. She could smell his scent. Knew his cowardice.

Falling.

Spinning.

Some crashing too.

They landed among the bushes, rolling as the ground painfully met them. They lost the screaming roar of war among the bushes, and for a bleak moment, Lillium wondered whether skulking away might be the smarter move on their part.

"We must move," Wynn cried.

Fuk that.

He released her, and she stumbled to unsteady feet as he returned one of her fallen blades to her. Looking around in desperation for the second, she suddenly realised how damp she had become. From head to toe, she was covered in their blood. She wondered if a fiery lick of crimson paint running through her hair would be a good look to her. Shaking her head to gather her senses and recover her nerve, she raised her sword in challenge, but once more, Wynn was too quick and denied her. With a fierce grip, he pulled her from the wall and honourable death, and she could only let him.

Running away is survival.

She knew this. But knew it was wrong. Around them, the forest was thick and inviting. Alphalines, hand in hand, could run for miles. He tugged her roughly as he led her, and her eyes could only settle on his pack bouncing on his shoulders. He had a fine run. Perhaps it was because he was running away from destiny. From an exquisite and grisly fate too.

The trees passed on either side of them, one after the other, each one concealing their retreat, and she felt the stirring of anger. Her weary, clumsy feet found their assuredness on the muddy ground, and suddenly, like climbing free of a sweaty lover's embrace, she found her wits again.

"No, Wynn, no—stop."

"Hush, my Lillium," he cried, even as she fought the pull. Beyond, in the distance to her left, she could make out the alarming numbers through the trees. They lined up, awaiting their moment to breach the open gates. So close… Just a few steps away. Countless dozens, spreading out, surrounding the fallen town, and she knew that all was lost. This was the end. And her lover was dragging her from the fight.

"Stop it," she demanded, pulling free.

He spun around in panic. "The town has fallen; we cannot save them. They're dead. They're all dead. It's just us, Lillium, just us."

"I will not run," she roared, loud enough for all to hear. She didn't care who heard, as long as Wynn heard. And understood his betrayal once more. How dare he defy her wishes? How dare he deny her the chance to fall with her comrades? Her friends. She wanted to kill everyone. Kill until she, too, was slain. Why couldn't he understand this? Why couldn't he, just once in his wretched, pathetic life, be the Alphaline male she thought he was?

"There is no choice," he said, slipping beside her and touching her mouth. His eyes darted back and forth in terror. She wanted to scream again. To bring their doom upon them. She stared at those eyes and hated him. And placed the tip of her sword to his chest so he would allow her to speak.

"Release me, Wynn."

He saw the frenzy in her eyes, and that was fine. She cared for little in this moment, apart from killing. "We can still fight, Lillium. Just not here. We need better ground."

She could see through his lie, and she spat in his face, pushing him away with the tip of her blade. He raised his hands in defeat, and she faced the treeline in silent challenge. She willed them to come a dozen at a time: a threat and a prayer to the absent gods.

"Very well. If you choose madness, I will stand with you," he whispered and, loosening his bag, he dropped to the ground and began rummaging. Beyond, she saw a few bastard Southern attackers spot their escape, and she smiled, gripping her sword tightly.

"These are our last moments. Let me give you one last gift," Wynn said, pulling a large metal sheet from his bag. "I... should have... um... given this to you sooner," he admitted, tossing it over to her.

It is the most beautiful thing I've ever seen.

It was a mask of heavy black iron, cut, moulded and shaped by unskilled hands. She'd never cared for head guards or for anything that obstructed her vision or movement. She'd always wondered why some Black Guards and Rangers covered their entire heads in heavy shielding when good vision was more beneficial in a melee. But this was a masterpiece. She loved this face guard at first sight.

He pulled a second piece from the pack, and she noticed he did not wipe the spittle from his face as he donned the armour. His faceplate was as crudely cut as hers, but it had a strange impressiveness. Perhaps it was the thin layer of faded white he'd applied to the surface. Around the eyes, he'd painted a little red. Around the mouth as well. It looked like a sneering killer's face had been sliced, dried and placed upon a wet skull. She loved it.

Her piece was less decorated, but it was smooth and impressive. It had once been painted a light green, and she immediately imagined repainting it to her desire. He'd taken the time to line the inside in soft material and, placing it against her face, she strapped the leather buckle tightly. Strangely enough, it fit perfectly. "A pleasing last gift."

"I cut the shape to your face," Wynn said, drawing his blade and facing the oncoming Hunt as they charged them down.

She offered a bow and marvelled at the precision with which he'd ensured she lost no vision. Admittedly, they would not see her smile as they struck her down, but behind this mask, she felt safer than before. Felt calmer despite her beating heart.

"Let's kill them all!" he howled.

Perfect.

It wasn't the entire invading army who saw them, which was a small grace. Rather, it was a platoon, driving through the forest seeking easy kills, that met two of the fiercest warriors to walk the Four Factions. They came in groups of three and it was easy. More than that, it was magnificent. Their attackers were laboured and careless—and easy prey. She leapt upon each fiend as they broke through the treeline, unaware they were to meet their end. They swung with deadly intent, but she was too quick. The world slowed, and she saw everything around her. This was no sparring ring. No deathly struggle in the lonely darkness either.

But it was close to being both.

She heard their roars more clearly than she had upon the wall, all defiant and guttural, as they determined to end her. She hissed in reply and killed. It became routine. One after the other, she met each warrior's initial strike. One swift block after that, and then her sword delivered a killing blow through the heart, face, stomach, whatever. Then, kicking forward and ducking beneath the next in line, she delivered the next strike and was a goddess. And she was happy.

"To the fires with you!" Wynn roared from beside her. He leapt into death willingly, and for once she was proud. He carried only one blade, yet killed almost as efficiently as she. Flanking her and taking whoever was wise enough to avoid her attacks, he met their challenge and ended their lives quickly enough. "Aye... and you," he added, taking another life, and she felt tears of joy and relief streaming down her hidden face. An acceptable way to die after an unimpressive life. He reached for a fallen shield and appeared heartened as he batted back any brutes who broke through his defence and attempted to attack from behind. He roared with every strike, and they fell at his feet. She thought them both perfect. Two divine Alphas going into the darkness, screeching defiance.

Once more, she lost count of the bodies at their feet. She understood their true devastation only when Wynn pulled at her suddenly.

"Retreat to better ground," he cried, and he was alluring even behind the mask. Such unnatural beauty, with eyes alive and burning with terror and excitement. Exhilaration, as well. "We can kill more on better ground," he screamed, and it was no lie. There was no terror in his voice. From behind the iron mask, his voice was calm and cold. A killer's voice. She wanted a killer at her side. Not a snivelling wretch, in love with misery. She liked that tone. She could trust that tone.

"As you wish, Wynn."

I trust you for the next few steps.

He tugged gently, and she followed. Stumbling over the many warm bodies still leaking into the wet soil, they sprinted deeper into the forest. Lover beside lover. Seeking a better killing ground. With brutes giving chase, they were calm, composed and collected. In unison, they raced death and murder, and she loved every step. After a time, they found a hollow. Thick and surrounded by clustered trees, with a nice little stream running through it. He slowed and drew his blade, and she liked that too.

"This would have been a fine place to camp," he noted thoughtfully. Behind them, the roar of terrible things grew, and it was the end, and it was divine, and she was happy. This wasn't dying with her comrades, but it was dying covered in their vanquishers' blood, which was fine too. "A better place to kill them all," he added. She loved this most of all.

She leaned close to him and clasped his collar in a trembling fist. Placed her forehead against his with a delicate *thunk* of metal. "Until they kill us both."

"Race you into the darkness," Wynn whispered, and drew away to meet the first unfortunate Hunt breaking into their little hollow. She watched him for a moment with mouth agape and thought his step appealing. He killed the first with a strike across the neck and hammered the body as it sprayed blood all over him in its last moments. He killed the next just as smoothly, catching the brute's swinging blow on his shield before sending the blade into flesh.

Only then did she join him.

He blocked the third attacker's blow, and she finished with a lunging stab through the chest. She heard his shrieks of agony, and it was pleasing listening as he fell away from them both.

A half-dozen more came charging through the forest, and with adrenaline coursing through her and a skip in her step, she leapt ahead and met them. Charging them, dodging blows, ducking blades and delivering devastation of her own. She spun through them, with their cries of horror in her ear, and she feared nothing, for this was the end. She giggled, cried and howled, and her stomach churned in misery.

And then an axe appeared from beside her, and the world was slow, and she was in motion, and she hated them with all her rage and all her heart. With every part of her.

"No!" she heard Wynn scream, and it was all right. It was perfect, and she was happy. She spun to meet the swinging axe, knowing this was the end. She did not flinch or beg. Nor did she imagine a better ending for her life. She took the strike in the head and slipped ahead of Wynn into the darkness, with a tear upon her cheek and a beating heart unprepared for the end.

9

DRAHIR

"I'm sorry, Lea."

Drahir froze again hearing the slurred words. He held his breath, daring not to think about this painful name for too long. A shiver ran down his back; he shuddered and licked his dry lips. This was torment most harsh, imagined by those who had taken him, no doubt, in revenge for his lineage, and made real by their god's unnatural gifts.

"Lea, please…"

He had heard similar words repeated these last few days during his cart-mate's wild ravings of misery and anguish as his wounds were tended to; each time, they quietened after he was given a taste of dream syrup. He spoke nonsense most of the time. Much of it meant little to Drahir, but when Lea was mentioned, Drahir knew it was for him and him alone. Drahir *was* sorry, too. Lea wouldn't know how sorry he was.

Drahir looked at his sleeping vanquisher, who was little more than a boy. He had seemed like a boy that terrible night too. A decade younger than Drahir, small, weak and mediocre. Perhaps that was simply part of his illusion. Underneath his youth lay a squall of violence, a thunderstorm of cruel impressiveness. Yet still, a boy.

"Forgive me," the boy slurred, and Drahir squirmed in his uncomfortable seat. The chains clinked loudly, and he winced in pain. This was no end for any warrior.

Shut up, Erroh.

Please shut up.

The cart shuddered on a bump in the path, and he lurched forwards. As did the supine body at the front of the cart. A god and a prisoner, gathered together before the end. Above, he could hear the rain spatter down upon the roof, and this, too, was a torment worse than the bindings that held and bruised his arms. This was defeat; this was his lowest moment, and a sleeping demon still tormented him with whispered words.

"… Lea."

Shut up, shut up, shut up, fiend!

He shook his head and feared more about Erroh's invasion of his thoughts. He knew his name for her. What else might he know? Might he understand his grief? His regret? His cowardice?

Just a boy.

Oh, to slither his fingers out of the bindings, leap upon the sleeping brute and rip his fuken throat out. It wasn't a very impressive throat for a false god at all.

Do you read these thoughts, Erroh?

Are you hearing me now?

It isn't enough that you vanquished me, but now you violate thoughts I hold most precious.

To the fires with you, cur.

Had he the spittle to waste, he would have spat upon the sleeping boy. A futile act of defiance. Had he room to manoeuvre, he might even have relieved himself upon him. That would have been satisfying too. Alas, he was as dry as a dog's gnawed bone. He concentrated on the rain above. It was getting heavier too. Each delicate wet splash was a wonderful and awful distraction from the god's actions. Pathetically, he dropped his head, and his stomach growled as though commanded. He'd steal any bone from a hound, and any chunks of meat attached while he was at it. A fine bone could make a decent soup if needed. Add a little bread, and one had a feast for a prisoner. Or a king. Or a god. Or a murderer. Or a failed warrior.

Stay out of my mind, Erroh.

In reply, Erroh whimpered from the depths of his dream syrup sleep.

A drip of water rolled off the cart's edge and met its death upon Drahir's stained fingers. He watched another and moaned. He knew he couldn't reach it, yet still, he could not stop himself. He heaved, the chains rattled, and his other arm, attached to the far side of the cart, ached and shifted. Just a little more, he thought, fooling himself cruelly as the drip disappeared through his fingers. He'd never known thirst like this. It was an ache, a desire. Hunger could be controlled, but a man might give up everything he knew to take away this longing for a few drops of glistening, pure water. To ease the ache in his head like a chisel upon pristine marble. Beating and shaping and ruining. He knew he was ready to—

"Arrrrrgh!" he screamed when his shoulder nearly popped free of its socket, and he, a pitiful wretch, was still too far from the edge. He pulled once more and slumped. Had he tears, he might have wept. Instead, he moaned a few more times in misery.

He heard voices outside from a few of his keepers. The cart travelled as fast as the march. It took time. He'd begged for water every time they tended to Erroh's injuries, and each time, they left him thirsty. For two fuken days now.

Vengeance for your lineage.
You will probably die this day, too.

"We're nearly there now, Drahir. Are you ready to kneel before him?" a voice muttered from somewhere out along the cart.

"Is that you, Gunter?"

"It is, old friend. You know what I ask." Gunter was no real friend of his. They were comrades. Had been under the same banner for a time, though. He'd been a passionate zealot of his father's, once upon a time. Drahir had been surprised to see the rodent of a man charging into battle with Erroh's name on his lips and a shimmering blade in his hand. He'd always thought him more of a diplomat.

"And I ask for water. Please, old friend."

There was a thoughtful silence. Drahir imagined the popping of a cork. The quick unlocking of the cart's door and a gesture of eternal friendship soon after. "I'm sorry. We will not tend to you until the god of Spark decrees it."

Drahir stared at his sleeping companion and almost moaned again.

"Unless you kneel to him, brother. Offer allegiance as we all have."

"Leave me to my dying misery," Drahir snapped, kicking at the doorway. He caught the latch with his toe, and shards of pain shot through his leg. "Bastard," he shouted to the door, to his comrade, but neither took notice.

"Fuk your allegiance!" he shouted again, but Gunter spoke no more, leaving Drahir to his misery and sore toe.

"Fuk your allegiance," he whispered to his sleeping cart-mate.
Allegiance.

His people were in dreadful pain. They always had been. They needed a queen. A mother, to watch over and love them. Sooth them back to sense, to joy. In peace, or in war. Instead, they had a tyrant of a father in Uden. A tyrant who took advantage of their ways.

His people valued their allegiance, cherished it as though they were drops in the rain. He licked his lips again and swallowed painfully. Oh, to be out in the rain throwing around his allegiance for sustenance. He alone refused to take a knee. He alone knew his destiny was decided the moment he admitted defeat. One simply didn't surrender to the false god. No matter how terrible the thirst.

Rivers of allegiance can be yours for the price of your soul and lineage.

"Cowards," he rasped, and swallowed painfully. He decided that this death was not for him. Burning in a pyre was a less cruel murder.

Though this, too, is murder.

The false god stirred in his sleep, and Drahir wondered if he would ask for a drink when he next came invading his mind. When he next came whispering of Cordelia.

My little lost Lea queen.

Leave her memory to me, alone, Erroh.

Visions of the battle they had fought two nights previously came to mind, and he cursed under his breath and swallowed painfully again. A thousand times, the result would be the same. Even injured, the child had been fierce. He'd defeated Drahir more quickly than he'd taken his father as well.

And showed mercy. Such behaviours had spurred further whispers among the Southerners, he imagined. Perhaps it was no surprise his comrades had dropped to their knees so willingly.

"I'm not ready to serve you, Erroh." He coughed and hacked, and Erroh stirred again, and he hated him and hated himself a little too.

Unless I get a drink of water.

Unless I can learn to fight like you.

Distantly, he heard the drawing nearer of civilisation and, craning his neck, looked through a crack in the cart's wall into the lessening darkness. He peered further through the lines of trees until the signs of a camp appeared. A few flickering lights in the distance. The well-worn pathways throughout. The stumps of trees felled to make space for soldiers. Plenty of soldiers. He listened intently for the hum of songs and chatter, the braying of beasts of burden. The gathering of warriors. Plenty of warriors.

Erroh must have heard it too. He shot awake with bleary, drunken eyes, and Drahir recoiled painfully.

The Actions of Gods

"What the fuk?" It was an excellent, confused question, and Drahir said nothing. Instead, he eyed the water bottle sitting alluringly beside Erroh. He could almost smell the water within. He licked his lips and almost wailed.

"Where am I?" demanded Erroh, sitting up fully now. The effort took more than he'd expected. He spun and fell back among the straw littering the floor of their shared cart. For a moment, Drahir gazed at the straw and lamented his exhaustion. He'd earned a few bleary moments of unconsciousness these last few days, but every time the cart rattled or shunted, his arms and back had caused him no end of agony.

"Where's my dad? Was everyone taken by hounds in the night?" Erroh demanded, leaning near Drahir. Close enough to kick out at. To strike with an unforgiving forehead.

Though the rest of him was unimpressive, his eyes burned with unnatural fierceness, and Drahir looked away. He would yield to the boy only if he could find an advantage to it.

"Fuken hounds, with fuken teeth... Am I a captive?" Erroh asked, looking around the cart. His voice was slurred. "Who took me? Was it Uden? Where is everyone?" Perhaps he looked for his blades. Perhaps he believed he could take on the entire Finger alone. Perhaps he could. Another cold shiver ran down Drahir's spine. Erroh could reach into his mind and read his longings for forgiveness, his pleas to a long-lost child, but he couldn't tell he was meeting his own army.

Erroh leapt up and placed a hand against the door along one side. The bottle of water rolled free, and Drahir listened to its sloshing, which was the purest agony. Erroh pushed, testing the door's sturdiness, and against his wishes, Drahir shook his head. "Not a captive... a god."

As if seeing him for the first time, Erroh looked at Drahir. "Where are we going?" he asked drunkenly. He reached for the water bottle, but missed by a clear foot before focusing enough to take that delicious water in his hands. Daring a careless inspection of the contents, he shrugged and drank deeply, and Drahir hated him as though it was he who'd set alight the fire that terrible night, killing his sister. He hadn't felt this rage in a while, but Erroh's simple whispered words tore at his soul.

Like any gods.

"You have nothing to fear, vanquisher. They are bringing their god to his disciples," Drahir muttered, and Erroh stopped drinking and wiped his mouth as though the water were the finest ambrosia.

Don't ask, and don't accept.

"What the fuk is going on? Did Uden capture me?" Erroh whispered. Then, unexpectedly, he leaned close and held the bottle to Drahir's lips, and, mercifully poured water into his mouth.

Erroh's head spun terribly. His words were slurred. He felt he was in a hazy dream. He'd felt like this before, sometime after some arrows had gone through his chest. He looked to his companion and was confused as to who he was. The man said nothing. He merely licked his lips as though tasting the finest ale, and truthfully, Erroh recognised that grateful satisfaction. He offered the water again. It was a struggle to keep his hand steady. He inspected the cleaned wound in his shoulder and discovered it had been tended to as though Emir himself had been in charge of the surgery.

"My name is Erroh," he offered, gingerly twisting his arm and feeling slight pain. It would hurt in time, but plenty of parts of him were in pain. Just another ache to suffer. It was a small matter. He was in a wonderful mood all of a sudden. That crushing feeling that everything was wrong was long gone. He didn't know where he was, but he was thoroughly glad to be here. He gazed at his companion and offered the water again.

That's a general.
Oh good.
I think we had a sparring session.
I think we fought to the death.
I think we are friends now.
But I'm not quite sure.

His opponent had been striking and fierce. To slay him would have been a dreadful waste. This he did remember. His father had always said, "Mercy is a good ally and a better way to make allies. Unless you need none, of course."

His cart comrade muttered something under his breath. Erroh didn't catch it, but he imagined it was a small matter and a smaller cutting remark. He wondered about cutting remarks. And dancing hounds. Out in the night.

Wait, what?

"Fine. Don't talk, so," Erroh suggested, shaking the bleariness from his mind and failing. So he took to looking around his cage again. Still small and still bumpy. A small lantern swayed easily in the cart's sway. He stared at this for a few breaths, mesmerised. He could feel syrup working its fingers through his mind. Reluctantly, he drew his gaze away from the light to the thick wood walls with no windows but a small door.

"I don't like doors like that." It wasn't a constructive statement on his part, but his tongue felt like some exercise.

He focused on something apart from the unlikeable door. Leaning against the panels of their sealed cage, he could see through each slatted piece of wood to the world outside. It was dark, and it made him dizzy.

Clear your thoughts, idiot.

He knelt in the straw and strained his eyes to discover their route. Only then did he notice the strange, hard shell upon his leg where he'd been injured. It resembled a clay pot: dark, rough, cold, its surface hard to the touch. Strangely, the throbbing pain he'd felt before was lost now beneath this encasement. He tapped the shell several times where his leg had once hurt most and felt little. More than that, he wondered if he could walk on his foot. Or go dancing with hounds in the night.

Concentrate.

He started to beat a rhythm with his foot and this pleased him ever so. He hoped his companion would join in. He didn't. That was fine. He was getting bored of the rhythm anyway.

Distantly, he could hear the hum of a settlement, and it distracted him from the shell holding tight his injury. The sound was both reassuring and unsettling. Perhaps he was no prisoner, but he'd be wary until he was free of the cart.

"I am Drahir of the South. You have shamed me," said Drahir, shamed Southerner of the South, startling him from his reverie.

"Oh." Erroh turned to him. "Sorry about that."

"It would have been a good death." His words were smooth and comfortable. He was Southern, yet spoke Erroh's words like his own.

"Are there such things as good deaths?" Erroh asked, and thought of standing upon a mountain or the edge of a city wall, dashing a blade into a demented god and killing him before he fell forever to the ground below. He suddenly jumped as though falling.

Did that happen?

Drahir of the South shrugged. Erroh offered the water a third time. It was something to do while making a friend. Or worsening an enemy. Or finding a dance partner for the hounds on the other side of their cage, waiting for the music to kick in.

You were doing well for a moment.
Be quiet, absent god.

Erroh shook his head a few times, and Drahir drank his fill and leaned back in his chains. "If I knelt to you, I would earn my release, but I cannot serve you, Erroh. I am bound by my father, by bloodline."

"I wasn't even asking," Erroh countered, watching the man. He was around a decade older than him. Who knew? He was shirtless, and Erroh could see the scars of a thousand beatings. Old imperfections and wear upon young skin now turned to leather. His eyes were old and hard. There was madness in them. They were familiar, though. He held that thought and tried to sober his mind.

"Why are you staring at me? Are you trying to invade my thoughts again?"

What? Can I do that?

Of course I can.

"Of course I am," Erroh said. And why not confess? "It's just one of my many gifts. Now, you go and tell Uden to fuk off, or I'll climb into his mind and tear it apart."

"I'll never see my father again."

"Father?"

Drahir shrugged. "Someone would have told you, eventually. He is my blood, but we differ in our beliefs."

Erroh thought this very interesting. He appreciated the honesty. Such things mattered between friends, and something about sitting in a caged cart in the middle of the night made him talkative, even if it was to argue horrors. "Like burning females alive? Is that a belief you can't fathom?"

Drahir shrugged and turned away. "It is war most foul... but it is war."

Erroh didn't know what he meant, precisely, nor whether the man condoned the act, but he thought on those words and sought clarity of the mind. He drank from the bottle again and wondered did such water recover his senses.

Was I dreaming about hounds?

Somewhere beyond, the sounds of chanting grew, and Drahir sighed again. He was a man of limited gestures, Erroh decided. "Word has reached their tainted ears." It was Erroh's name now, just as before, chanted over and over, and every rumble of the cart brought them nearer.

After a few more moments, which drew out longer than Erroh imagined possible, Drahir leaned forward. "Why did you cry out for Lea? As if anyone was worthy of such forgiveness?"

Oh, Lea, my darling love.

Erroh's stomach dropped. The crushing guilt, squashed by his awakening in the cart, returned tenfold. So, even in sleep, he had spoken aloud his sorrow. "She is my mate." He didn't know why he told Drahir, but it didn't matter. He felt like talking. He had things to say. Opinions to declare, points to make.

"Are you not mated to the whore called Nomi?"

"She is no whore. She is a friend—a comrade of the road and little more. Lea is my one for life. And I left her behind to meet Uden upon the city walls." He thought on this and remembered a little more. Flashes of the previous days. Terrible days, really.

Drahir's face was a menacing grimace suddenly, and Erroh decided he didn't want to say another word to him lest he use it against him or, worse, her. Erroh slapped himself, and his vision cleared for a breath. And then he smiled stupidly at Drahir.

"You met Uden upon the wall?" Drahir asked. He sounded panicked. "Did you kill him?"

"I failed."

"Again?"

"Aye, again." Erroh now realised why he found him so familiar. A boy would likely remember the last few faces who watched him as a god felled him. Were he not poisoned by dream syrup, he might have remembered as he had before.

"I know you. Don't I? You were there that night when I took Uden's eye. You are one of his generals." Before Erroh could stop himself, he leapt up and struck him across the face, drawing blood and a pained yelp. Though he didn't know why, he felt guilt. More than that, his mind settled as though the haze was slipping away.

Not friends after all.

He caught visions of their melee, of his mercy.

The cart rolled to a halt, and Drahir faced him. "I will die soon. Let me know of Lea, as a final request? Tell me of her. Is she a wanderer? Was she in the city? What became of her? Tell me of her, Erroh of the Spark; I can hear the crowd so close. No doubt, they will take me aside this night and slit my throat."

"Unless you yield to me?"

"Unless I yield to you."

Erroh didn't like the man's look. Not one little bit. Nor why he desired to know of his mate's life. He shut his mouth as though to say nothing. And then opened it again and started talking. It seemed like the thing to do. "Well, she has black hair, long and beautiful. She has pale skin. Pale like snow, but warm. Oh, she has a cutting wit and a kind heart. She's shit at cards. Really, really shit. Is that enough, dead man?"

"Tell me of her eyes?"

"Dark and beautiful."

Say no more, idiot. He will use this against you.

No he won't. We are friends.

Voices rose above the chanting from beyond. "Does she have no brothers or sisters?"

"They died in a fire… I think. She doesn't remember. She was a child."

Drahir shook as though stabbed through the heart. Erroh shook as though realising his error in revealing such things.

"A fire," Drahir gasped and began to weep, and Erroh could only sit and watch a while. Long enough that he drained his water and felt the comforts of some sobriety return, shaking its unwelcome head. And in the haze of pain, memory began to return. He said nothing for a time.

Finally, Drahir's eyes blinked thoughtfully, and he recovered himself. "I'm sorry, Erroh. I am scared to die."

It was an acceptable reaction to death, Erroh supposed. Few people ever met their end with confidence. Those of Keri had, though. Theirs might have been good deaths indeed.

Without warning the little doorway snapped open, and Erroh jumped in fright. After a breath, he moved clumsily towards it, manoeuvring his encased leg with some difficulty. He wasn't at all ready for what awaited him.

Climbing out to massive fanfare was unnerving, and somehow, he didn't stumble and fall. Probably not what the delighted, chanting crowd would have appreciated. He was certain he would throw up, collapse, go limping into the night, but instead he calmed himself and played the sober legend as best he could.

They were too many to count, of every age from child to elder and every year in between. They stood applauding, cheering, and calling his name loud enough that even Uden atop his wall might have heard their joyfulness. These were his people, and they were without a region to call their own. Just like him.

Welcome home, Erroh.

He dropped from the cart to face the manic clapping of a diminutive Southerner who had once borne a flag of peace. His clothes were dishevelled now and covered in dark brown stains. Probably blood or mud. Possibly both. He still held the same zealous gaze as before, when he had brazenly marched through the battered camp. But his gaze was upon the beaten Erroh now, and less on a demented false god. He knew how to pick his leaders.

"Erroh of Spirk, we proud," he cried, clasping Erroh's arm and squeezing it. The crowd roared anew, and Erroh shuddered from the attention. He wanted to evade their sight. To be far away in the arms of his beautiful mate. Surrounded by his friends in the safety of Raven Rock.

They had the good grace not to swarm around and smother him. At least that was something. He'd never seen a gathering of Southerners this great either. He could have counted, but it would have taken the night and he probably would have fallen asleep halfway through. Regardless, they were many.

A hidden army.

Deep within the forest, they were concealed from the world; he could tell from the treeline surrounding them on all sides. Far away from the war and the city, waiting for their god to march and offer his grace. There were countless carts overturned, lying side by side around the camp. A fine discouraging barricade against any surprise attack from Riders in the middle of the night. He wondered how many bandits and Fingers had been taken to earn such materials. The tents erected within the barricade were tatty and weathered. At least a hundred little campfires flickered throughout the area, lighting away the dark—but alerting any hunting eyes.

"You have been busy," Erroh offered, gesturing to the camp as he scanned the watching faces, demented and hopeful. True vagrants of war. He'd released less than fifty Southerners. Now there were many hundreds, spread out across the camp.

"Building army," the man cried above the crowd's cheering.

Erroh waved at the crowd, and this spurred them to action. In no time at all, a gathering was underway. Some pulled out instruments and began to play music. Eerie music, melodic and slow. But beautiful. He'd heard only a few similar pieces on his chained march into madness so long ago. Shivers ran down his back as the wailing notes erupted through the chanting.

Not in chains.

Unsure of what to do next, he bowed, and received a few hundred similar gestures in return. They laughed, they cheered, they believed he was something special. They didn't know him at all. After a time, he felt he looked foolish, standing before them like this. He offered as respectful a dismissive gesture as he could in the hope they would turn their eyes upon someone else for a time. Few did, but they all went about celebrating, which was something.

It was a strange gathering and a stranger evening, even as the last of the dream syrup slipped from his system. The diminutive man stuck beside him the entire time. Perhaps meeting Erroh before had earned him a little grace. At least he spoke slowly enough that Erroh understood most of his words.

"Celebrate in honour of Erroh," he declared, loudly demanding wine and food and many celebratory things from his compatriots. Though Erroh's head still spun, he offered no objection. He merely wanted a few moments to let matters sink in.

Gunter, as the little man called himself, was a nervous, unlikeable little skut of a thing but a fine drinking companion. He had also led this great gathering of Southerners and charged under Erroh's name, so there was that to respect about him. They sat at a long makeshift table, and Erroh was glad of so few companions. His mind still reeled, his vision doubly so.

"Where did so many come from, Gunter?" Erroh asked, accepting a second goblet of a strange, silky liquor that tasted of almonds. It made the dizziness worse, but it was a small matter. It infused him with much-needed confidence, false as it was. He needed some fire in his blood, for he had yet to march through the camp to meet with his disciples. It was a feeble act on his part. Hiding away from those who'd gathered around him, forsaken their people, offered their loyalty in honour of him. In his defence, he had an injured ankle. Besides, although he sat upon a seat beneath the pouring rain, away from the revelries, many crept near and bowed before scuttling away. Others defied Gunter's disapproving glare and stood fast, jabbering swiftly in Southern tongue. Catching every second or third word, Erroh offered game smiles and knowing nods. So far, he was still determining what they demanded of him as their leader.

"We war in your name. Many kneel when we attack. Not all worship Uden. Not since great fire of Conlon," Gunter whispered, leaning into Erroh's ear as though he spoke a shameful secret.

"I don't know what that means. I was staring at those hounds over there. They look to be listening to the music intently."

"Hounds?"

Gunter was befuddled again at Erroh's words, so the god drank deeply and tried not to focus on the hounds, no matter what trouble they were stirring. He needed his mind, needed his wits. Also, he needed to stop thinking about matters and let his problems slip away into the night.

The Actions of Gods

For a time, he did, until eventually he turned at the sound of a voice from within the cart. It cried out sagely in their tongue, barking orders and issuing threats until a few of Erroh's new subjects went to task, removing the prisoner and leading him over to kneel in front of Erroh. He looked as though he'd been crying. Seeing a warrior as fierce as he, broken, was no pleasing sight, and Erroh stood to face him.

"He will not yield," Gunter yelled, and this was met with much disapproval around the encampment. The music softened and stopped. The joyousness fell silent, and Drahir dropped his head where they held him.

"Every warrior has the right to defiance," Erroh said, then cursed himself and tried to translate it into their tongue. Gunter spoke over him, interpreting his words, and this was met with many heads nodding their approval. Gunter took the hint. He took a dagger from his scabbard, tapped Drahir's neck, and then his heart.

After a moment's pause, Drahir raised his head and tipped it back, inviting the blade.

"Wait," demanded Erroh. "Surely there are alternatives to murder." The crowd did not appreciate this, but as Gunter translated, they held their tongues. Mostly.

"If he does not kneel at your feet, he must die. This is our way, Erroh," Gunter said, and the crowd agreed. He held the blade to Erroh's cart-mate's throat. With a pained expression, he took his hair, and Erroh dared not to look. He dared not look away. A god would watch murder like this.

"I yield," whispered Drahir suddenly, as the blade touched his throat.

At this, the crowd erupted, and they freed Drahir immediately. The chains fell away loudly, and the music resumed. Placing a knee forward, Drahir held his hand to his heart.

"I will follow you... my god." His tone unsettled Erroh. Gone was the frantic gaze he'd seen in the cart.

Just the dream syrup playing tricks, no doubt.

Taking Drahir's hand, he pulled him to his feet. "Can I trust you?" he whispered, and slowly, Drahir shook his head.

"Can you trust any of us?"

It was a fair question. Most terrifying questions were.

"Can I trust you tonight?"

"Aye, for tonight you can, brother."

That was enough for now, Erroh thought.

10

WRETCHED LEGEND

Elise dropped her bindings, spitting on them where they fell. She no longer needed them. Truth was, she'd have been out of the bindings by day's end anyway, but having a comrade offering help was always welcome. Kaya bowed, and this pleased the older female. Nothing was more pleasing than a few confident words earning her some grace and a little loyalty.

"I am restless," she confessed to the younger girl. Many times, a sensible head served her best. Other times, a little wildness was required. After many years asleep, Elise was feeling wild. Perhaps it was her terror for her family. All of them. She felt sudden panic rise and quelled it immediately. Being mated to Magnus had taught her the art of control when a storm erupted all around them. She could have lost herself in uninformed imaginings. Instead, she endured, and called upon her own pragmatism. Whatever happened had happened. A terrible, cutting truth —and one that should have taken her breath. She closed her eyes for a moment and swallowed the fear she had for her family, for the world, for fuken everything. She needed to escape this place, and after that, she aimed to march once more.

"I wish to leave this prison. This very day, Kaya," Elise said to her carer. Her captor. Her healer. Her comrade? She calmed her breathing and her panic. She slid into the mind of her legend. She became the elite female whose rage the world feared. She bit the inside of her cheek and focused her mind on the simple task of discovering what she could and earning the girl's trust outright.

I am Elise, and I will rise to the top and burn every fuk who gets in my way.

It felt fantastic to engage her rage. Her bloodlust. She calmed her mind, became merely a cold watcher of events.

"This is no prison," Kaya said, "but you cannot leave. At least, not yet."

Elise eyed the girl carefully in the dim light and grunted in dissatisfaction, and Kaya appeared very unhappy with this. The girl had cut her bindings; what had she expected of a legend as renowned as Elise? A tentative approach? What was the fun in carefulness, anyway?

"I can show you the way, but I don't think you'll like it." The girl was cautious in her words, and Elise watched her recover the bindings. Perhaps she was saving them for later use. It was a small matter. Kaya wasn't entirely unaware of Elise's abhorrence of chains and holding. That would become crystal clear soon enough.

"Tell me of this place," she demanded, stretching her slim body, shaking the stiffness away, breathing deeply with stronger lungs. Oh, she felt fine this day. Felt ready to tear the world apart. Felt prepared to go to war with her mate. She looked forward to gazing into his beautiful eyes and challenging him to stir a brew of trouble with her. "Tell me, so I may know all that faces me." There were no locked gates or bars surrounding her bedside. This suggested carelessness. Or overconfidence. Things she could take advantage of. Even in a dark prison.

Kaya shrugged uncomfortably in the flickering light. "This is Adawan, our home. For the bandit clans, I mean," she whispered.

Without a word, Elise rose from her bedding and slipped out through a wide-open doorway cut in the stone. On the other side was a dark chamber. Kaya followed and stood beside her.

Adawan? She imagined Magnus's fury at such a prison. Elise, however, was curious. "Ever since I was a girl, I was told Adawan was a wasteland. A dreadful place where fires burned brightest," Elise said, looking around the dimness. Outside the chambers, her voice echoed strangely, as though deadened by some strange heaviness. It was a place where voices died. Perhaps she wasn't used to hearing her voice echo, she mused, listening to the hum of the chamber. The sounds seemed to resonate far above her, a deep, far-off drumming in her ears, filling her mind as though she listened with blankets upon her weary head. Wherever they were, answers and adventure were up there with the humming.

"Adawan is an unforgiving sea of parched death. That's why we took it for our own," Kaya whispered. She began to move, her steps swift and silent. A thief's step, if truth be told. "That is why we hide here now."

Elise kept pace with her strange companion. Away from the flickering light, there first was darkness, but in the gloom, Elise's eyes made out shapes, subtle shades of darkened colour. She spotted a path—perhaps it led to those humming undertakings?

Blessed with beautiful dark skin, Kaya was more difficult to see in this dimness. The girl was likely a master of concealment when out at banditry, Elise thought. Kaya gestured for Elise to follow the path away from the safety of her room, and Elise was eager. She touched the walls as she passed, and it was cold and dusty in places. Instinctively, she dug her nails in as she walked, then drew them back and discovered a whiteness upon her fingers.

"What is this place?"

"A salt mine," Kaya offered as they reached a thin set of steps cut into the wall and leading upwards. Elise gasped with wonderful lungs and marvelled at the value in these walls alone. Whoever ran this mine had enough salt to rule the world. Sine made the city spin, but salt could dry out the world as a whole. One Faction at a time. They had fought wars over lesser treasures. Her mind raced at Adawan's potential. And at how best she could take advantage. Suddenly, the urgency of escaping this prison lessened. Only a little, though.

Kaya, leading the way, suddenly spun around on the third step and faced Elise. Her voice was low and guarded, as though to evade eager ears. "It's our bastion against the night. I've seen what marches across this land."

"Terrifying things," Elise said, sniffing and licking her lips. She'd never been a huge fan of salt, but there was something to the salty taste in her breath. "Cowering and hiding from threats is not in my blood."

The breathable air was a thousand miles from the stuffiness of her previous bedchambers. Visions of Silvia's attack sprang into her mind, and her fists clenched. She tried to recall anything before the dream syrup and could remember only a few days in and out of sleep upon a moving cart, and her temper rose. "I should be dead. In chains. Swinging from a fuken tree. Why am I here?"

"I don't know your crimes. I only know you have friends in high places," Kaya offered. Her black hair was more apparent now, and Elise realised they were coming upon a dim glow from somewhere in the world above. The hum lessened, but it remained. Humming in her ear. In her head. In her very being. Awful, unnatural vibrations threatening to make her heart skip a few beats. She wanted to stumble forward more quickly, but instead turned to painful questions.

"Did my daughter come with me? Is Lexi well?"

"..."

"Is she dead?"

"You came with guards, alone," Kaya said after a moment, causing Elise to fret mid-step. She fought the panic, the sadness again. An awful, lonely battle that threatened to spill over into her heart and her actions. She focused on practicality once more. The Wolves couldn't slay Lexi, not without good reason. Lexi was mostly innocent of all matters involving disloyalty to the city. Mostly. Still, she knew Silvia wasn't stupid enough to kill her daughter while allowing Elise to live.

Calm yourself.

She fell silent, ceased musing on her daughter and all she loved and, instead, focused on the steps leading upwards, and as they climbed, there came further signs of life in this place. Their path brought them onto a level surface, with many paths leading away in every direction. Upon these paths Elise saw countless wretched bandit maidens and brutes, similarly dressed like Kaya, wandering up and down like ants in a hive.

An underground settlement outside of the world.

"How far are we from the surface?"

"Only a half-mile in steps from here," Kaya said warily, and terrible dizziness came upon Elise. She'd never known herself to be claustrophobic, but knowing how far down she was from the sun was a sudden, sobering horror. She stumbled against the wall and waved away Kaya's attempts to support her.

"Just catching my breath, friend."

Let me out, let me out, let me out.

"Shit, you weren't ready to walk. I shouldn't have released you yet," Kaya cried, catching the attention of a bandit wandering by carrying a sack of something that looked suspiciously like rock salt.

"I'm fine. I'm glad you never told me how far down I was when chained."

The bandit watched the women for a few moments before shrugging and continuing swiftly upwards towards further light. (A half-mile away, no doubt.) "We need to get you to bed."

"I've slept long enough, friend." She shook the dizziness away, ground her teeth and began walking with Kaya again.

At least an hour passed. She kept walking, despite the hard going, and did not falter even when their steps brought them through communities living beneath the ground, all of them wretched and broken—bandit families, hidden away in little chambers similar to hers. The mine hummed loudly with their footsteps and voices. Most were females, doing their best to care for their children. They laughed, chatted, argued and existed in this gloomy place, and Elise wanted nothing to do with Adawan mines anymore. Still, they climbed, and with each step, Kaya appeared more and more uneasy with her choice of actions. Elise wanted to take her aside and reassure her she'd chosen the righteous path, but she said nothing, instead focusing on steadying her breath in the face of such exertions.

Eventually, unfiltered sunlight touched her face. She stood a moment, panting, covered in perspiration. The air was thinner above ground, more challenging to breathe, but infinitely better than the wet breathing she'd suffered these last five years.

"Welcome to Adawan," Kaya said as they cleared the slope of the mine's mouth and met the wretched stench of human waste.

Elise had seen mining settlements throughout her life, and this one was no different. It was larger than most, but these types of habitations were similar throughout the Wastes. She looked above the closely packed structures to the mine's great natural surrounding wall. How strange, Elise thought, that such a place could remain concealed from the city's eyes, yet here it stood.

Unless they've always known.

"Take me to whoever rules, so I might convince them I wish to leave," she said, and with a subtle shake of the head, Kaya pointed to a large building at the far end of the settlement.

Elise followed her gaze. She knew little of Adawan, but was now suspecting she could never leave. She tried to calm her growing unease. The wiser manoeuvre would be playing this game slowly, seeking power in this place and learning the rules.

In Elise's defence, she shared many traits with her firstborn. A lack of patience was one of them. Her body was burning with energy. She felt she could march right out of here should she flex her muscles a little. It wasn't the most ingenious plan, but she'd been here long enough with no knowledge.

Few bandits took notice of them as they glided through the crowds. She counted absently the many packed buildings they passed. Like the horrid cave below, they, too, housed families. She wondered if these were the richer bandits, with a better view and pure, wet air to breathe. Or were they the peasants, shunted upwards to endure the harsh desert nights? It was a small matter. They all shared the same gaunt expressions with the denizens below ground. Perhaps they had tasted the horrors of war and were grateful for any port in the storm. Most carried a weapon, and all wore a black sash on one arm.

"How many live here?" she asked, and Kaya shrugged.

"When I arrived, there were only a couple hundred. Now, though, there are at least two thousand more. And every day more arrive." Such numbers were a potent mix for mayhem against the Southerners, Elise thought bitterly.

"So when all have fought and died," Elise said, and looked around in disgust, "only the cowering rats will remain."

"We've wanted no part of your city… female," Kaya retorted. "It's a finer plan than fighting against the Southerners in open warfare."

"Would you not fight?" Elise snapped, and Kaya stopped, frozen. There was a flash of depthless sorrow on the younger woman's face. There was rage too. An extraordinary rage that Elise recognised well. Had she herself not worn such an expression the day she'd met the Wolves in the rain?

"I lost everything."

"So you lost the will for vengeance?"

"I never said I wouldn't fight."

"Who won't fight, then?"

At this, Kaya pointed to a brute of a man sitting casually in front of the largest building. Elise recognised the tavern for what it was and grinned. No settlement was complete without a tavern to fuk things up. She looked to the sky and frowned at how early it was. Better to discuss precarious things with a careless drunken brute with sloppy reflexes than with a hungover brute with a headache, a nasty mood and normal reflexes.

She marched through the crowds, all the while ignoring the raised voices from nearby stalls as customers and stallholders bartered loudly. She saw very few treasures among the stalls as she passed. Mostly, they held slabs of salted meats and dried fruit. Some carried little pouches of tobacco weed or cofe, the sad signs of rampant poverty. Typical that in a place of wealth, most people struggled. This place had that in common with the Spark.

"Ulrik is a fine man," Kaya said, drawing Elise from her thoughts of the city's hovels. "Though a little cautious. He gathers everyone in these mines, in an effort to eke out some survival. Be wary; there's quite a threat to him," she added.

"And I am but a fragile old legend," countered Elise, stirring her nerve again. She quickened her pace, and Kaya followed. Two innocent females up to no good.

"Let me introduce you," Kaya said, but Elise had little interest in formality. She knew her value in this place. She'd known it the moment she'd woken and found herself away from the city. Whoever had ensured her imprisonment here knew well her importance. Ulrik would know this as well. It was like playing a game of cards, and she had every intention of throwing everything in with the first deal. Erroh would have been so proud.

Show nothing but grandness and greatness. Then swallow them all.

"I am Elise of the city, and I seek freedom," she called and, grinning, marched through the last of the gathering crowd, who fell silent in her wake. And why wouldn't they? She was a goddess.

Grandness and greatness.

Ulrik rose from his chair holding a goblet of wine and dropped from his stoop to meet her, as though facing a challenge was the most natural thing in the world. Perhaps it was. She did not understand the customs or beliefs of bandits, but she imagined strength was appreciated.

"You are property and little more, woman. Get back in your cage," he mocked as a few guards stepped between them. She counted three. Only three? That was insulting. She didn't stop. She was at war. They just didn't know it yet. Walking at this pace was too enjoyable. Breathing deeply was as pleasurable as drunkenness. And starting a fight felt like the best move.

"Stop right there," one guard called, and his roar silenced the stalls behind her and every watcher in between. She didn't stop. Stopping was for careful fools, those too afraid to claim greatness. This might have been a shitty little mine in the desert, but when Elise marched through it, it would become part of her legend.

He did not reach for a blade; none of them did. Knowing her value for certain settled her. All that remained was the violence. He reached for her as though dealing with an aggrieved woman struggling with a newborn and bitter about her rations. She met the hand as it touched her shoulder. Gripping and spinning, she pulled him off balance while twisting his arm. He screeched as she felt a snap. His screams were silenced as she spun him to the ground and, still holding his arm, placed her foot upon his neck.

He'd have died that moment if this were war, but there were no blades. There was nothing wrong with a few broken bones, either.

Releasing the beaten man, who immediately resumed screaming, she set upon the second. He was twice her size and half her age, and it was hardly fair. He swung wildly, and she sidestepped and leapt upon him. With her powerful thighs wrapped around his chest, she struck him with both fists and sent him sprawling back. She could not match him for strength, but her fists were a stinging blur, and as she squeezed the breath from him, she pummelled his face until he collapsed, arms raised, trying to stem the onslaught. She released him from his shameful defeat and faced the third.

"No, no, Reuben, hold off. She'll just kill you," Ulrik called, dragging his last guard away from the melee. He held his arms up to hold her charge. The third guard appeared relieved and offered no argument.

"I was just playing with them," she said mockingly.

He looked to her companion. His face was a mix of humour and resignation. "You didn't tell me she was so spry, Kaya."

At this, Kaya shrugged, but Elise could see her cower at his words. She almost spun on the girl to reassure her of her decisions, but instead she stood fast and stared Ulrik down.

"Some females just can't be chained," Elise countered, eyeing the brute and suddenly noticing his casualness. The hairs on her neck stood up as he approached her. He spared a muttered curse for the two fiends she'd battered and little more. She suddenly wondered if she should have simply spoken to him instead of announcing herself so spectacularly.

I've spent too long being a feeble ghost of myself.

"And if you agree to stay here, you will remain unchained," he told her. "You will be… a guest." It was a fine counterargument, and delivered courteously. Observing her, he drained his wine goblet and tossed it away.

"I have places to be," she said, and bowed. It was a nice touch. She was just as calm, but the fiend watched her with his beady, scrutinising eyes. He knew her threat. He was also confident. That was never good.

I am Elise, and all should bow.

He stretched a few muscles in his neck before slapping his face a few times as though fighting drunkenness. Still, his tone was courteous. "Silvia paid a fortune for your stay. Such funds help our efforts," he said. His eyes hardened, and his smile faltered. His tone became cold. "I don't want to kill you. But I will."

He'd spent a lifetime playing cards, she imagined. Her bravado had little effect. His guards were humbled, but he was something else entirely. She drew her own cards close and bowed again. "Whatever that whore paid for me, I will cover thrice over." Around her, the crowd were circling closer, their eyes alive with delight at this unexpected display of violence. She aimed to please.

"Whore?" He looked around, playing to the crowd. "Be careful what you say of the future leader of Spark." At this, Elise's stomach lurched. She dropped her head. What else didn't she know? "Anyone who paid what she did certainly holds you in high esteem. And I aim to honour her wishes, for now."

At this, he unclasped his sword from his waist and dropped it in the mud. "But if you wish to challenge my position, you can fight me for it. All fair, like." The crowd cheered as though this was terrific news. And perhaps it was. He pulled his shirt open, revealing a robust body, then wrapped his sash tightly around impossibly thick biceps. She felt her heart flutter in anticipation of the skirmish.

That was easy. She had fought Magnus with fists; she could take this behemoth. Couldn't she?

"Don't fight him; you'll earn nothing from it," whispered Kaya, and Elise shrugged her away.

"I'm not one to hold my punches, legend," Ulrik snarled. Gone now was any warmth or humour, and Elise grinned in anticipation. He was rugged and likely earned everything he had through violence. Built like a wall and just as sturdy. And she? Well, she had played this game many times before.

I am Elise, and I have slept too long.

"Only one of us may challenge. You need a sash," he hissed, tapping his own swath of black fabric. He looked around for a willing volunteer. Within a breath, a sash was torn free from an arm and cast at her feet. It was Reuben's. She did not know these traditions, but she would follow them willingly if they desired her to play the part. Snatching the sash, nodding gratefully, she began wrapping it around her arm. Ulrik stepped closer, and that's when it all went wrong.

She missed the first strike but felt an open slap across the face from nowhere, impossibly fast. She almost tripped in her hasty retreat. The blow wasn't enough to injure, but it stung like a bitch. She spun away, angry with herself for dropping her guard with a dishonourable bastard like him, and he was upon her. With fists raining down, she blocked what she could, but soon suffered nasty strikes to her face and head. Each strike was fiercer than the one before, as though his fury grew with every blow, and his speed and strength were incredible.

"I expected more," he taunted, gripping her loose hair and driving his

The Actions of Gods

knee into her face. She fell backwards into the whooping crowd and felt a thousand unwanted hands take hold, pull her to her feet and shove her back into the fight.

Do better, girl.

She wasn't used to this manhandling. Not even from Magnus at play. She saw double, swung wildly for one brute, and received a hearty blow to the stomach from another, stealing her breath. With this, she collapsed to her knees. She felt no shame. This wasn't the first time she had been bested with fists. It just made things complicated.

"Do you yield?"

She'd have preferred another blow, knocking her out, rather than accepting defeat. So she hawked a mouthful of bloody spittle at him and missed him by a foot.

Fuk.

"Such an old pretty face," he declared slapping her again. This time she collapsed fully onto her back in the mud. He stood over her, grasped her head, and held a fist before her battered face. "Just yield," he whispered, and he was kinder now. Perhaps he valued his payment over an all-encompassing victory. She was swift despite her faintness, and she felt her strength return. She spun and twisted in his grasp, allowing a few strands of hair to rip free, before wrapping herself across his shoulder, pulling his arm out straight and bending it against the joint.

The crowd gasped. A few even cheered, and he grunted as he fought her manoeuvres.

"Yield," she gasped, and ducked away from his free hand as he attempted to fight her off like a boar would a pack of hounds.

He did not yield; he fought her, for he was brutish, stubborn and worthy of his title of leader.

"I have you," she grunted. She did. She was sure she did.

He bent low, trying to squirm away, and she torqued his arm again, awaiting a pop. He was a master of the fist, but a hold could devastate unless he somehow regained his feet.... Which he did, and she was lesser for it.

She didn't know where he had mustered the strength to perform such a feat, but he rose and took her with him without warning. With one arm entrapped by a goddess, he pulled her from the mud. Roaring defiantly in her ear, he dragged her high into the air, and she knew her own momentum was lost. Brutally, he drove her back to the ground, where she fell free and knew this battle was done all too quickly.

He did not ask her to yield a third time. Instead, he pulled her skyward again like a rag doll before slamming her down upon the nearest stall, shattering it beneath her weight.

She heard the crowd cheer in ecstasy as she fell into a ruin among the debris, and then his fists were upon her. He pinned her with heavy knees and punched her thrice in the face, spilling blood and knocking the sense from her.

She allowed him, unable to defend herself. Then hands came between them, and she was vanquished.

"Take her back to the hole," he roared, and those same hands picked her up and prepared to carry her back towards the endless darkness. The horrible depths of this world. She felt him undo the sash from her arm, and her eyes opened in panic.

"No, that is mine," she cried, and he studied her for a moment before grinning in understanding. She was not broken; she was not finished. This challenge was done.

For today.

"See to her, Kaya," he ordered before turning to the crowd. "Welcome to Adawan," he roared, and the onlookers agreed and chanted their own, similar welcomes.

"Welcome to Adawan," they cried, and the world darkened as she was dragged from the light back down into the dimness, where the air was heavy with salt, and fuk it if Elise wasn't altogether intrigued with this new world.

11

WYNN

Killing was easier with the remnants of his first victims' armour upon him. Torched, melted and put to a grander use. Wynn was no skilled smith or elite armourer with the golden touch, but somewhere among the furnace, the whetstones, the hammers and anvils, he had smelted and reshaped his victim's pieces and found a tiny part of himself again. At first, he'd considered making a dagger, but such a brutal tradition did not need to continue. And besides, both he and Lillium had adequate blades already. It had felt right to shape them into masks. As though taken by an absent god's hand, he'd cut and made some beautiful hideous things. He'd imagined presenting her steel mask to her as well, probably on some special occasion. Something grand and memorable. He had wondered if she would tend to her mask as he had his own, painting and decorating, placing all the horrors he held within upon its surface. Truthfully, he'd been wary she would reject the gift. As it was, gifting the piece in the hour of their deaths was a grand enough gesture, he supposed. In the end, at the end, it was accepted. That was enough for him. A fallen mate could ask for little else.

Donning his own mask now and trapping himself behind the protective shield, he felt different. With the feel of the metal against his face, his sword felt lighter; his stomach settled. Perhaps it was the concealment of his real bastard deeds behind this mask of horror and metal that freed him ever so. He wondered if she might feel the same. Or better, might she discover restraint and caution behind this last gift of love? As it was, the guard was a good look to her, and she was a tempest of wrath as she leapt into battle and he only a step behind. And they were elite. Perfect, divine warriors bringing a fight to an entire army and winning. For a time.

Thunk.

Wynn spun around like a deer would, spotting an arrow moving swiftly towards him. The world slowed to nothing, and he saw Lillium struck down. He heard screaming and realised it wasn't her voice, but his. A terrible, agonised wail, piercing and definite and knowing. Her hair flashed crimson immediately, waving outward as her head shot back in muted, deathly silence. The axe did not lodge itself in her. She fell away from it, and a stream of blood followed in an awful, glistening arc.

Dead, gone, lost, forever.

Her vanquished body dropped pathetically into the leaves and mud. It was a terrible thing to receive a final kiss, a worse thing to see a lover struck down dead in front of him. Her arms spread out; her swords fell free. That's how he knew she was dead. He imagined her determination alone would have made her hold those swords tightly, even unconscious. Probably would have made her kept killing, too.

She might not be dead.

His attacker showed no interest in her felling. He continued to battle Wynn, blissfully unaware of his opponent's agony. Swinging a smaller hatchet, he roared defiantly and knocked Wynn back a few feet, then charged forward to finish him. Wynn's limbs suddenly felt heavy, and he sensed the Hunt gather around him. He imagined a thousand sets of eyes from the trees, all staring at their Alphaline finale. Their hands would appear next, he supposed, gripping and brutal and ready to tear him apart.

His opponent fell upon him, screaming brutish words, and Wynn was neither interested in nor intimidated by his passion, for a deep, aching hollowness had come upon him. The constant anxiety he'd endured since he and Lillium had mated was absent after so long. Instead, this emptiness reassured him, and he became blessedly numb. He prayed to the gods. He offered everything he had that he might be the one felled and she the one standing above him, broken and grief-stricken but alive.

"Take me," he cried to the absent gods, knocking his opponent away, but he knew they weren't interested in his words. Not in these brutal days, when every fool bartered for a loved one's lost soul.

Kill them all.

The Actions of Gods

He looked past his attacker to the brute raising his axe to remove her head and cursed him. From beneath the hollowness came a little fire of hate, and he fanned it. Meeting his attacker's strike, he sidestepped, thrusting his blade into flesh. The dying man's screams were louder than his own, and he held that thought and fanned his fire a little more.

For her.

It was a fine mantra, and he played it in his head a few times as he swung his shield fiercely and knocked the axe free of its wielder. Kicking aside his victim's struggling body, he charged upon Lillium's killer. He did it for her.

He was not swift in his killing. Nor did he care even a modicum for any fiends who sneaked up behind him. None of that mattered. He leapt forward and pierced her killer's shoulder. He screamed and swung wildly, and Wynn plunged his blade low through the fiend's knee. He howled, and Wynn swung with all his power down upon the man's gripped fist and sliced his hand free of his arm. Around him, he heard shrieks of horror, and these, too, were louder than his own, and he fanned that flame to a bonfire now. The man stumbled backward, away from Wynn, clutching his spurting stump, and it was a delicate, pathetic last act.

"To the fires with you," Wynn roared, sending his blade through the man's groin. This brought the loudest scream yet, and Wynn matched it with his own roar, and the rest of the Hunt charged in and fell upon him.

Wynn swung now without fear or care, without thought, even without cruelty. He simply killed, and he killed many. They fell like humans to a vile god's will, and he slaughtered them with as much regret as a one-eyed god could muster. Always moving, always swinging as though within a sparring ring, unafraid of a stray blade or loose arrow, he stabbed, plunged, slashed and maimed. One by one he silenced their roars, for he was an Alphaline male and they were interlopers upon his territory. For his domain was beside her. It always would be. He tore into them, forsaking defence in favour of attack. One man against a hunting pack. It was hardly fair, and it was incredible. The world continued to turn wonderfully slow, and he was a deity among the movement. He gave himself to the fight and tore them apart.

He didn't know how long he fought, but at last he surfaced from this red haze of murder, chasing three Southerners back through the forest towards the town. It was a lucky thing the closest brute stumbled; he fell upon her, plunging his swords deep into her back. Her dying screams were different than the yells of the males. She was angrier, and as he placed his blade across her throat and ended her life, he finally slowed and stopped.

Be with Lillium.

Stumbling away from his murdering, he counted the number of kills absently, and they were many. Lillium would be proud, he told himself as he reached her side, sliding the mask from his face and discovering his stomach's need to remove the bile of battle from within once he did. Wiping his mouth, he tended to the tears as they streamed free and fell beside his love. He wanted the mask back on. He knew his sins would seem lesser this way, but he would not gaze upon her while concealed.

Blood flowed from her forehead, down the inside of her less-decorated mask to her neck, and he was horrified. Still, she drew breath and moaned weakly as he removed her face guard. The axe had struck her head, but the mask had taken some of the blow. The wound looked clean and far from deep. The mask itself was dented, and he begged the absent gods not to be so cruel as to tease him with these glimmers of life and then steal it away. He attempted what healing he could—listening to her heartbeat for signs of strength and weakness, applying some bandaging to her ruined head. The blood didn't flow as freely. He wasn't sure if it was a sign of hope or death.

"We have to move, Lillium," he whispered, but she did not rise. Only then did the fatigue of war strike him, and he collapsed beside her.

She would not like that.

She would want you to fight.

He listened for sign of attackers gathering their reinforcements, seeking a little revenge for his savagery.

Wynn listened hard for another moment, and then, hearing nothing, formed a plan. It was relatively simple. "Better than nothing," he said, though doubting it would work. He rose and scrambled through the forest, looking to gather some long, sturdy branches able to hold her weight. Once he found a suitable pair, he set them to one side and began the awful task of stripping some garments from the fallen. His brow was covered in sweat, his fingers in their blood, and as he worked, he was panicked lest the Southerners return. But he kept at it until he had finally attached enough strips of fabric to the wooden pieces. He carried his makeshift pallet back to where Lillium lay.

"I'm no suitable mount, but I will carry you far," he pledged, rolling her battered body onto the flimsy stretcher. She moaned again, but that was all right. He was fighting for her, and that was better than lying in the mud with her, waiting for their murderers. Only then did he fully acknowledge the dozens of broken bodies lying around them, and he felt the fire diminish away to the dreaded sorrow, and he cursed his weakness. Spitting once upon the nearest body, he slid his mask down upon his face and felt better.

"They had it coming," he snarled to the forest, his sleeping lover and the fuken wind, and his voice was cold and reassured. He liked this voice.

Wrapping some strips of clothing tightly around her chest to keep her steady, he placed their few belongings in alongside her before taking hold of one end of the crude stretcher and hoisting her up. She was light in his grip, but the pain and exhaustion would come; this he knew.

He walked a few steps away from the horrors, and then, distantly, heard the low sound of breaking branches. Without hesitation, he charged deep into the undergrowth, pulling Lillium behind him. Immediately, his body screamed in complaint, but he swallowed the effort and pain. He counted his steps in his mind, two at a time. He didn't know why, but he increased his pace every hundred steps. The effort made him gasp loudly, but he drove relentlessly forward and left the branches, the dead, the town and his comrades behind. Nothing mattered but Lillium's survival. He would offer few complaints if wrenching his arms from their sockets in a desperate charge ensured such a deed. Nor would he feel guilty for leaving their dead comrades behind. This was war, but also survival.

Before long, he was a mile deep into the forest and showed no sign of stopping. A mile deep became many more. The hours disappeared into nightfall, and still he dragged her, ignoring his fatigue every arm-shattering step of the way. Even when his body could not run, he still dragged her, through the undergrowth, down precarious slopes, over streams. Whatever the world presented, he bested. He never heard his pursuers, nor did he imagine them capable of following even such obvious tracks in the night.

"I will not stop," he hissed to himself when dizziness took his sight, fatigue clawed away at his resolve, and his will was tested to its limit. He did not check her condition beyond listening to her breath while gathering his own every few miles. He certainly didn't tend to his wounds either. He carried her until the effort took him from consciousness, near dawn the following morn.

"I will not..." he gasped, finally letting her drop before stumbling against a tree. "... fail you," he pledged as the world around him turned a sickly black. He gripped the tree as his efforts finally took their toll.

Painfully, he dropped to the ground. His eyes were watery and visions swam before him in the darkness. He tried to reach for her, then stopped and reached for his canteen. "Just some water," he said, and the simple process of popping the cork became too much.

"Not far enough," he whispered, collapsing in the dirt beside her.

12

FOR THE LOVE OF THE ABSENT GODS, WON'T SOMEBODY THINK OF THE CHILDREN?

He could feel it now in every part of his body. A tingling of worry. A deep knowing. His mind reeled against this horror, but his gut knew. Something was not right, and suddenly Tye, line of Mea and Jeroen, felt naked away from the town's protecting walls without a weapon.

"Whisht. It's nothing, little cub. Sure, it's as quiet as a dry tavern out there," Wrek insisted, stretching as they walked back towards the town.

Real fuken quiet.

Tye knew something was awry despite Wrek's calm complacency. His older comrade reassured him it was just his imagination or his paranoia. The older man was right. Perhaps the fear from a night's prolonged drinking was pulling him down.

Or else Wrek's senses are dull.

That's what happens to older people comfortable in their skins.

Tye knew his instincts were sharp. Always had been. A life lived in the forest had taught him the soundless language of the watchers. His mood turned now as though an invisible fiend tugged at his burgeoning chin-hairs. He knew something observed them. Watched their every step back towards the town, too. He looked into the green for the tenth time.

Watchers who hide expertly?

Lots of trees to hide behind.

"Come on—this foolishness is doing us no good," Wrek offered, and Tye began jogging back to the gate.

The gate.

"Why isn't the gate closed?" Wrek said suddenly, and Tye noticed his comrade jog alongside him, and heard the panic grow in his voice too.

Just the wind, Wrek?

See? See?

"Aurora was to close it behind us," the behemoth added, and perhaps any other day such a mishap might have been addressed, but these last few days since Erroh's fatal departure there had come a languidness among the comrades. A carelessness. And why not? Were they waiting for news of the war? Was the world not tranquil and silent while titans met in Spark City? Still though, first the forest, and now the gate.

Tye took no chances. If Wrek wouldn't believe, then he would take matters upon himself. He darted from the gate towards the town centre, away from his comrades lying by the fire enjoying the early morning sun. Part of him knew he overreacted, but that was fine. Answering the hairs at the back of your neck was fine too. He'd gladly follow his gut and accept the mocking consequences any season of the year. Behind him, Wrek slowed, no doubt finding calm behind the walls, open as the gates were.

Why the fuk isn't the gate closed?

He could have thought on this matter, but panic overcame him. He turned to sprinting and discovered his quarry where he spotted her most mornings, sitting alone outside the building belonging to Roja and herself. More recently, to Emir as well. This was part of Lexi's routine now. Every morning, after playing pretend that she was strong with her comrades she would slip away to sit on a stoop with her head in her hands, weeping away her misery. A pathetic sight, but Tye recognised strength in her actions. She cried so she could be brave all day. These precious few moments were for her alone. Her parents, Elise and Magnus, had abandoned her, and now her brother, Erroh, had as well. They had left her behind, all alone.

He had suffered similar stings, and had he the words to console her, he might have offered them. As it was, like a juvenile with too much time on his hands, he watched her from afar and kept his notions of advice to himself. He only stalked her out of duty, for Erroh demanded it. It wasn't a lot in life, but it was enough for him, and though it might well have been a phantom threat of wild imagination, she was still his first port of call. She always would be. Why? Because his idol told him to protect her. There were worse pledges to be made.

"You have a sword? Good," he called as he approached. He could feel the sweat running down his back. Could feel invisible arrows ready to be let loose. Any moment now. A hiss. A *thunk*. And then darkness. Running, he glanced back towards the gate, all open and inviting. Still nothing, but the stillness beyond was heavy. As though the carrion birds above fell silent as a predator entered the arena. He reached for her as she wiped the tears from her pretty eyes. "Come with me."

She looked at him in horror, angry at his intrusion. Sometimes a girl just needed a little time to shed a few tears, and he thoroughly agreed. He was a fan. When nobody was around, he was stronger after a little relief. It was something he could have said.

"Fuk off, Tye," she snapped, slapping his hand away. "You little shit."

He was taller than her, but now wasn't the time to argue. He felt his heart hammer in his chest, and he reached for her hand again. "If you want to live… please, come with me."

She must have appreciated his uneasy tone, for she took his hand. Hers was rough and calloused. Firm and without sweat. A good grip.

"What's wrong, Tye?"

He didn't quite know yet.

"I don't know."

"That's not a great answer, idiot. Where are you taking me?"

It was a fair question. Looking back at the gates, he dragged her down the road towards their escape route. "I…um… I just think we have to go."

She allowed him to pull her along the path as though they were mated Alphas pursued by a hunting pack. Perhaps she saw the panic in his face, or the cold, knowing sweat covering every part of his body. Or else, like him, she sensed the stillness. That terrible, deathly stillness that heralded very bad things.

Very bad things are coming.

The moment had arrived. He didn't know how, only that he felt it like a taste in the air. Suddenly he sprinted, and she followed, looking back as he did.

"What is it?" she said, mocking him. "Oh, Tye. Is this a jest?" She giggled, and his heart hammered further. He counted his breaths, wondering how many he would take before everything went wrong. "Tye," she suddenly snapped as they reached the tunnel of Wynn and he dropped to his knees, fumbling with clumsy fingers at its hatch.

"I'm scared," he hissed, freeing a little of the heavy lid. Just enough to grip and slide it across, revealing the dark hole beneath it. "Come on, you… fuken… thing." He felt it slide farther, and his head was dizzy with fright. His limbs buzzed with adrenalin; his body was ready to fight, and to run away. He couldn't get the lid free. He needed to slide the lid free. Everything would be fine if he got the lid free. He wished Wrek were here—he would get the cursed lid free with little effort. "Come on and slide free," he said through clenched teeth. His hands shook. His head spun a little more. His gut screamed, threatening to churn up bouts of hot bile. This was the end of the world, and all he desperately wanted was to hear Wrek and Lexi berate and belittle him at the fire later this night with a goblet of sine and a steaming bowl of soup.

That will never happen again.

And I can't get this fuken lid free.

She pressed her foot down on the lid and held it tight. It didn't help at all. Raising an eyebrow, she stared into his eyes. "Taking me into the dark, are we?" This was a good question; if she had removed her foot, he'd have been happy to answer.

"I'll put the lights on," he insisted, pushing her foot away.

"There are smoother ways of getting me all alone."

"I'm not trying to get your dress off," he snapped, and distantly he thought he heard a scream. It might have been the wind.

That wasn't the wind.

"Oh." She sounded put out, and he wasn't sure why, but he didn't care because the fuken lid slid free, and he spotted the rungs leading to salvation below. "Well, I shall not get in there."

"Please get in."

"Please fuk off."

He formed a compelling argument. He was a wordsmith like that. "Just get in the stupid fuken hole, you stupid fuken cow." It was a fine suggestion. He heard another trick of the wind and a rumble beyond that.

"Fuk off, Tye," Lexi countered expertly, but then, hearing the scream, she dropped down the ladder like a female born to climb ladders—and to stand at the top of one as a leader.

"They're coming," he cried, scrambling in after her. He turned and reached up to slide the stubborn lid back over their heads, plunging them into darkness before dropping down beside her.

Alone at last, pretty girl.

"What was that?" she whispered, and he knew her panic, for he was just as lost. Above their heads, the screaming increased. The thunder intensified. Raven Rock's vanquishers were drawing near.

"They found us," he hissed, stepping away from the ladder and the noise. He felt along the walls in the darkness, found a switch and flicked it. Behind him, farther away from the horrors above them, a few dim bulbs came to life. Not enough to reveal them, but enough to light their way.

Beyond them lay a strange tunnel. Its stonework was grey and unnatural, if truth be told. Smooth as ice, with strange, unfamiliar lettering painted upon the walls by an expert hand. Thin pipes ran along the sides of the tunnel, along with some wires giving the lights power. There was enough space for them to walk side by side. That was something.

"Our friends are up there," she gasped. The screams of war had begun, and he felt himself a terrible coward. Still, protecting Lexi was all that mattered. A good pledge. She stepped back to the ladder and climbed two rungs before falling still as a boot charged over the lid. She rose no more; instead, her hand tapped at the grip of her sword. "Dying."

He felt wretched.

She placed her head against a rung. She might have been crying, but she was silent. "They're already dead." It was no question. It was a truth, and carefully, she dropped beside him. Her face was as pale as that of a brute who'd been bled dry. He searched for words and found none. He wanted to declare that this was not cowardice. But it was. It really, really was.

"Come on, Tye," she said, getting to her feet, "lest they look down here."

Swiftly they shuffled through the tunnel of their now-fallen companion. Side by side, hand in hand, for support, for assurance alone. She led the way, and he was glad of it. If there was some Erroh cleverness in her, he hoped it came to the surface soon.

"Do you think they marched because Erroh is dead?" she asked.

"Aye, I do. I'm sorry, Lexi."

"Do you think the city has fallen?"

"Aye, that as well."

"I'm sorry too," she whispered, and he felt her hand squeeze his. It was too much, and he stopped and dropped to a knee.

"I just need a breath."

She did too. She wrapped her arms around him and wept with him. Somewhere above, their friends lay in ruin and horror. A little down the road, their hopes for victory and salvation had been lost with the falling of the Spark. Somewhere ahead, there was a brutal death to come, and it wasn't fair. He hugged her back and placed his head against hers. Bonded in tragedy. There were worse ways of finding eternal friendship.

He broke free first. Wiping away the tears, snot and shame, he took her hand and pulled her gently to her feet. Together, they continued their desperate pilgrimage towards unknown safety. He'd done this trek only once before, and that was among living comrades in a line, as Wynn proudly showed off his mastery in ensuring their escape was smooth and unnoticeable should an unlikely attack on the town occur.

The exit hatch was a great distance away from the fallen town. It creaked softly as it opened, and carefully, he slid out and helped her before sliding the lid closed again. Someone had perfectly concealed it beneath a bush on a crest high above the town. *A fuken bush.* It was a nice bush because the roots and leaves were solid, thick, and, well, bushy. The berries were rich red and prominent against the eternal green. Slowly they crawled along, hidden in the foliage, until they found a suitable spot to gape in horror at the tragedy below.

Tye held Lexi close for hours as she watched Emir attending to a dying Roja. He shed a tear for his friend Stefan, left alone in a pool of blood in the middle of the town. He had little hope for Wrek, who, dazed and beaten, was chained to a post where he was felled and destroyed. They watched as the sun set and the great god Uden walked through their town, and their sorrow and anger were depthless. They watched in puzzlement as Ealis walked freely among the vanquishers.

"We can't leave them like this, can we?" Lexi said after a time, and he agreed. His knuckles stung from clenching his fists. His lips were split and bloodied from chewing on them. This waiting around was killing him. Safe up here, there was nothing to do but think and regret. Up here, it was easier to reject a pledge.

"No, Lexi, we can't."

"We shouldn't have left them alone, should we?"

"No, Lexi, we shouldn't have."

"Will they expect two youths with blood on their minds sneaking back in and stirring up a brew of trouble?"

"No, Lexi, they won't."

13

CORDELIA THE LOST

The girl lies in bed, watching the darkness as sleep remains aloof. She doesn't remember the day. Only that she is tired and hungry; she is always hungry. She knows this because her father always says this. She can hear the wind at the window. It raps gently and carries with it the heavy snow. She would like to climb up to the window and catch sight of the monsters out in the night, but she cannot reach the sill. There is a chair in the room beyond, but her parents would hear her movements, and she knows she should have been sound asleep many hours ago.

Distantly, beneath the thump of the window and the wind's squeal, she can hear the voices as they shout. She hates nights like this, and they are many. She loves her father with all her heart. She loves to walk alongside him as he marches through the fields of their lands. He doesn't slow his step, for that would show weakness. She knows this, for he says it every time she falls behind, every time she hurts herself too. Her mother says she is the apple of his green eyes. She does not know what this means, but it makes her father smile; when he smiles, he is happy. Things are good when he is happy. Sometimes, though, she is afraid of her father.

Tonight, in bed, with a tummy rumbling, is one of those terrible times.

She tries to hum to herself. A song her mother sings when she is weary and sleepy from taking the bottles of bitter awfulness. The girl doesn't know the words, but she knows the tune. Sometimes, on nights not unlike this, she might hear her mother singing the song, and up here in bed, the girl might listen and hum along. Tonight, there is no singing, no smiling. There are only fighting voices.

The girl knows that lying on her belly might stop its rumbling. She thinks her brother told her this. She knows she has two brothers but cannot remember the older one. She knows that when her parents talk of him, they fight. They cry. They have nights like this. She rolls onto her side and feels no relief. There comes the sound of smashing glass from below and more words. She wishes it was later in the night. She wishes the voices would trail off to silence in their room, and that she could creep down and steal a midnight meal for herself.

She turns onto her back in the bed now, and the voices fall silent. She wonders whether breaking glass was enough to end the fighting voices. She hopes so. She regrets not finishing her dinner. She had eaten half her bowl of mush and spat out the last mouthful. Her father had laughed, and she had smiled. Her mother had not been happy. She wishes now she'd returned for food before the fighting broke out.

She wonders will there be excellent food in the city of light. Her mother assures her the world will be hers, but the girl doesn't understand what that means or how that will affect the food. Her father doesn't want her to go to the city, which pleases the girl. She would rather walk their lands beside him, making him smile, making him happy.

The stairs creak from the weight of her father's powerful stride, and the girl's heart leaps in excitement. Her mother will not be far behind. The girl sits up in bed and feels the cold immediately. She knows the importance of avoiding the cold in this season. She cannot light a fire yet, but her father likes that she sometimes tries to make a spark. She hears the lighter creak of her mother's stumbling step as she passes the room, and the girl rips her bedclothes free in excitement. She drops from her bed and, keeping the cold at bay, ties her slippers and wraps her cloak around her. She knows the kitchen stove will have burned out, and the wind will set it to freezing. She knows this because this is not the first time she has slipped from her bed to eat.

Carefully, she lifts the latch on her door and slips swiftly downstairs. With heart hammering and tummy rumbling, she steps carefully over the third step, for it creaks loudest, and sticks to the edges of each step as she moves silently towards the kitchen.

Without warning, the fighting voices suddenly erupt again from her parents' room, and she freezes at the last step. She doesn't want to see her father angry. He has struck her before; he will strike her again. The girl does not want to be struck. If she creeps back to bed, he will not attack her, but she will also be hungry. It is puzzling; she chooses a full belly over anything else. Besides, if she is struck, her father will be sorry in the morning. He will smile with her and hug her and tell her she is "the most important goddess in his life."

She passes the kitchen table. She can smell the bitter stench of bottles on its surface. Most empty. A few turned on their sides. She and her brother once stole a mouthful of the bubbly drink from the bottles. She spat it out, and her brother laughed, and she liked his laughter. She misses Drahir. She wishes he was home more, but he is working on the farm, though she does not know which one. There were fewer fights when he was home.

Above, the voices are raised again, and the girl fears her choice was the wrong one. She has left her bedroom door open, so if her father storms out, he might discover her intended thievery. Ignoring the thundering roars, she runs across to the pantry and unlocks the latch, slipping in. Inside she is safe. The girl likes the pantry. It is always full of wonderful-smelling things. Strange foods she doesn't understand that her mother loves to throw into the pot on the stove. She herself will not pour strange foods into the pot on the stove now, as she does not have time to make soup. She also doesn't know how to make soup, so she reaches for her favourites. The bread is always fresh. Her mother bakes loaves every second day, slicing each one neatly and hiding it beneath a cloth cover. It is the girl's favourite midnight stolen meal. She takes a thick slice of bread, and strikes further success when she finds a large wedge of cheese. Breaking a chunk free, she places it on the bread and dares a quick bite, even as her parents' bedroom door swings open and terrible screaming fills the house.

The girl knows she is in trouble. She quivers as she chews, and the food is not as enjoyable as it should have been. They are screaming now because they must have seen her bedroom door open, and the girl takes another bite and slides the pantry door closed. She bites again, chews, and tears come down her eyes because the screaming is getting louder, and she has never heard such cries. She is afraid of how much her father will strike her now. She frantically looks around for a hiding place but cannot lift the sacks of flour and grain to slip behind them. She puts her hood up and, biting again, looks out through the keyhole so she will know when her father will find her. She knows it is always better to be prepared for the strike.

She sees her mother first, and her mother is not well. She is holding her stomach. There is blood on her stomach, and she is screaming. She is afraid, and the girl knows how painful blood is. She also knows her father doesn't like her to cry when there is blood. She is worried her mother's screaming will make him strike her again.

The girl sees her father, and her body goes cold. He is walking down the creaking steps carrying his dagger, and the girl wonders why it is not in the cabinet that she is not allowed to open. He is roaring, and she cannot understand his voice. Her mother is at the table now. She screams in pain and anger, reaching for the kitchen lantern above her. The girl is terrified because this is worse than any typical night, and she wonders is it worse because they have discovered her out of bed. She wants to hide because her mother is beside the door and has taken the swinging lantern; she is shouting at her father, and the girl is terrified.

Her mother throws the lantern, but her father is quick. The girl knows this because he is a warrior, and warriors must be quick to fight wars. Only the fastest warriors win wars, too. Her father has been in many battles and was fast, just like now.

Straining to see through the keyhole, she sees the lantern swing and miss, then strike the wooden beam in the kitchen ceiling. Broken glass spreads out over the kitchen table. Her father runs around the table and grabs her mother, and the pantry door slams back and strikes the girl on the forehead as it opens ever so. Not enough for them to see her, though. She wants to cry out, but her parents are fighting. They are hitting each other. Her father is cutting her mother with the dagger, and the girl is terrified. She feels her bladder release, knowing her father will be furious. She holds the door, preventing it from opening, and does not know what to do. Suddenly, the door is wrenched from her grasp. It swings open, and the girl almost screams as her father and mother wrestle with each other, and the surrounding kitchen is on fire. Something wet is on the girl's face. In the light from the flames licking over the table, up the beam, she sees it is red. It is blood from her mother, and the girl knows something terrible is happening, and she should be in bed. She steps out into the kitchen, and the fire has caught on the stairs where the lantern landed and broke. She knows her mother fills that lantern with oil daily, and she fears her father will be furious.

"Lea!"

Farther away, her parents resume struggling. Her mother is kicking and punching. Her father is drunk; he is stumbling. His forehead is bleeding like her mother's. He is not screaming in pain. He is swinging the dagger again, and the girl is afraid now. She tries to go up to her bedroom, but the stairs are alight, and the fire is burning around her.

The Actions of Gods

She is still holding her bread. She cannot remember when she dropped the cheese. She wants to leave this place. She knows how dangerous her father can be. She doesn't want to be struck, so she runs to the front door and lifts the latch. It is almost too high for her, even on tippy-toes, but with every season, she is growing a little more. Her father says she will look like her mother when she grows older. Her mother is exquisite, but she herself is tiny. Still, she reaches for the latch and flicks it open.

The fire is growing, and she can no longer see her parents fighting; the wind takes hold of the girl, and she knows how dangerous the wind at night can be. She steps out into her courtyard and keeps going. Through the iron gate, the girl is desperate to find Drahir. She looks into the blizzard and fears for herself, but she knows Drahir will protect her. She runs from the glowing warmth into the freezing night and trusts her instincts. She's marched these lands with her father many times. Wrapping her cloak around her, she runs and follows the darkness. Behind her, her home is on fire, but every step takes her farther away. She thinks she knows the path, but every step in the deep snow is challenging, and her legs are not powerful like her father's.

"LEA!"

She is cold now. Colder than she's ever been in her life. Her cloak is not enough, and her hands are cold, still holding the bread. Finally, she drops the food, tucks her shivering fingers into her cloak, and, weeping in terror and sorrow, runs further into the snow, hoping to find Drahir, someone to look after her, keep her safe, and not strike her.

She wants to lie down. To sleep until the cold goes away. Her hair whips around her, stinging her eyes, and crying is a torment. She does not like this feeling, and she is sorry she left her bed this night. She sees a light, far ahead through the hazy snow, which stops her from lying down. She trudges forward, hoping to find Drahir, hoping to get warm. Hoping to...

"Lea, wake up," Nomi hissed, shaking Lea. Lea shot up and knocked the girl away. She almost swung, but Nomi was away, climbing from her bedding lest Lea take her dreams out on her. "You keep talking, whimpering. You'll tell them where we are," Nomi snapped.

Lea sat up, rubbing her hair. It was damp with sweat; her entire body was just as wet. She tried to remember the dream, which still set her heart racing, but with every breath, it was fading away. It had seemed important. She remembered the fire and little else.

Green eyes.

"Just some bad dreams," she countered, stretching and feeling at her ankle. Wincing, she twisted it until the pain shot up her leg. They had welcomed these last few days at Rock. Dreadfully boring but welcomed. Her days were little more than bathing her foot in the creek, wrapping it tight and spending hours beneath the cover of Erroh's shelter, elevating her leg. It had been Nomi's suggestion, and Lea was too tired to argue. So she lay and thought on her misery. Less of Erroh and more of her vile father. She could not bring herself to say his name aloud. Speaking it aloud would make it real. She'd felt like this before. Back when she was a child, taking shelter in a neighbour's homestead before her lonely transport to the city.

Fire.

She felt her mind was shattering. It began to shatter the day she'd returned to her homestead. Seeing her father had merely sped up her downfall. She had never remembered her dreams growing up, but these days she remembered far more. Only some things, but enough. That was something, she supposed.

"It's a little better today," Lea said, leaving her ankle to rest. This pleased Nomi, who tested it for herself. Roughly she massaged the affected area, and Lea grimaced in pain. With prodding fingers, she eased some stiffness from the injury.

Scowling, Nomi shook her head in agreement. "Aye, not ready."

The Southern female was probably right, but Lea's restlessness was getting the better of her. Oh, to wrap it up in a refined splint and walk the movement back into the bitch. Still, Nomi was skilled enough in her healing ways, so Lea offered little argument.

"Can you please scream less in your dreams?" Nomi said.

Lea could see the irritation on her companion's face. What good was concealment if one of them constantly cried out every night in their dreams?

"I'm sorry," Lea said weakly. Ignoring the trauma of her lineage and realising her entire life was a fuken lie was no little task. Harder, too, keeping it to herself. Perhaps were Erroh beside her, she might have spoken sooner, but Erroh had left her when she needed him most. If he lived, she could never forgive. Would never forgive.

"We should…" Nomi thought about the word. "… wrap your mouth at night? Safer."

It was a jest, but Lea nodded in agreement and bit the inside of her cheek. Controlled pain sometimes settled her spinning mind. It gave her something to master. She wanted to tell the girl about her sins. Release this gnawing torment from her soul and share the burden. She wanted to weep endlessly until dry and curse his name with such vitriol that the absent gods themselves would cover their ears in discomfort. And then she wanted to break something. Maybe her mate's jaw.

I can't do this.

Lea felt the wrench of a vile god take hold of her chest and squeeze, and she was too afraid to cry out or fight a moment longer. She wanted to close her eyes and never wake up. Never dream.

She reached for Nomi and grasped her hand, for this moment was awful, and she had never felt more alone. Even on the lonely march south. She feared the girl's judgement, feared her silent condemnation. She feared what might become of everything if she spoke the truth.

"What is it, Lea?"

Say nothing.

Lea saw Wiiden's green eyes as he was about to strike her. She felt the world darken as panic took her, and she fought this moment and gripped Nomi's hands tightly.

Take the horror.

"Lea!"

The world around her spun. She tried to focus on anything, anything at all, and faced Nomi. Looked into her caring eyes. They were terrified and pleading, and Lea fought the tears, the panic, the terror.

"My name was Cordelia."

Whisht, girl.

"It is a pretty name."

"Only my brother called me Lea. I do not know why." No, that was a lie, she thought. She felt it now. The current of truth edging closer to release. The pull was alluring, and the agony too great. She had not remembered much, but she remembered hating her name. She took a breath, and strangely, there was air to savour. Her heart settled for a moment, and she fell silent.

"Tell me of him, Lea."

Say nothing.

"No, not now."

14

UDEN THE WOODIN MAN

Uden rarely allowed himself the weakness of human emotions, yet here he was, being human all over this horrible place. He had no love for this town. This place had a particular nastiness, for he knew Raven Rock's history. From Aurora's excited tongue a few years previous, he had learned of their heroic downfall. She had regaled him with tales of its stubborn defiance in the face of destruction, a thing that had intrigued her. Such wasted heroism disgusted him. The town had fallen, and the fools had perished. Uden had little interest in Northerners succumbing to slaughter, no matter how highly Aurora thought of them. Anything that fascinated Aurora was always enjoyable, but not here. Perhaps this place had given birth to the defiant king's whispers of sedition. If a town could hold out so impressively against all odds, it could also spread hope contagiously through the mouths of those who lived to tell the tale. If Raven Rock had ignited the spark, Erroh of Keri was the furnace that had smelted away some of his grandness.

Erroh.

Fuken Erroh.

Fuken Raven Rock.

Truthfully, there should always have been an opponent worthy of his lore. And oh, how long he'd waited for another to challenge him. He'd expected Magnus to be his equal in this grand war, but that old fool had allowed other fates to decide their legend. Magnus would still die for his crimes, but Erroh was his equal in the people's eyes.

Grabbing his bald head a moment, Uden cursed aloud. A curse worthy of his stature. He was in no mood for conversation. Bedding the

The Actions of Gods

girl had exhausted him. She was small but energetic; he wasn't used to a challenge. Or else he was allowing his humanity to show that little more.

Or else I'm ageing like a man.

He left the blonde girl to sleep a while longer. She knew her place in all this. She would disappear away to her tent afterwards and await his call. It might never happen again, but it was a small matter. He liked her uneasy smile.

He marched away from his tent, through his gathered guard, out through the town's gates and towards the centre of the town, not knowing where to go but desiring to understand this town's dreariness and feel better about himself.

All around him, he could see the scars of battle from Aurora's great campaign, and in a way, he wished they had not taken this place so easily this time. A fair fight and fair massacre laid upon the defiant town might have sent the correct type of whispers abroad through his army's loose tongues.

His steps were heavy and loud on the stone surface as he walked between the buildings, marvelling at their age and their dreariness. The ancient stone structures brought no wonder from him. Nor was he affected by the lines of lights, burning without fire, illuminating his lonely way ever so.

He carried a blade at his waist. A fine weapon worthy of killing a false god. He thought about calling out to Erroh. Every room in every structure was thoroughly secured already, but he imagined the boy might have hidden for a few moments and waited for Uden to present himself.

Well, here I am, boy.

He felt the anger stir once more as he walked each path, following the walls across. He'd long waited to slay the child and had failed at the last moments. He tapped the sword's grip irritably. He had let the boy fall, and the little fuk had somehow survived. Through fire and falling, through a fuken marching army, he still fought, and were Uden to allow himself the imaginings of a man, he might have wondered if there wasn't something unique to the boy. He felt his hands turn to fists as he reached the far wall and began marching back towards the town's centre. He was losing control of himself. He needed to vent this wasted human emotion in some violence. An act or two of cruelty, with screams in his ears and bloody visions gazed upon with one godly eye. He could have bludgeoned one of his Azier guards, but he wanted a purer taste of violence this evening.

With every step he took, his anger grew. This wasn't how the world would be formed around him. He had failed at the city. He could see it now. Such things could overthrow a king. Could cause the downfall of a god. Bring an easier assassination upon a leader too.

And take away an ungrateful lover.

He stopped where he had killed the blond boy, and his fury took hold as he thought of Aurora's unusual behaviour. Too long she had been from his gaze, and cruelly, his reach was losing its strength. She was no longer with him. She was away from his influence, and this was worrying indeed. He stood over the scuff marks where he'd battered the tainted fools, and the memory of her screaming pleas for mercy stung him anew. He spat in the dirt and cursed his frustration in silence. He should have been above this.

He eyed the prisoner chained to the post and walked towards him, drawing the bloodied dagger, long since dry and flaking. He had not yet decided the brute's fate, and this indecision infuriated him. He'd granted him life in the brightness of day, but everything was inclined to change once darkness drew in. He spun the blemished blade in his fingers and considered making the prisoner a gift to her. All he asked for was her subservient devotion in reply. It was a fine blade. He'd made it himself. Sharp and true. Perfect for plucking out eyeballs, removing manhoods or killing vile, treacherous bastards.

He licked his lips and grinned in anticipation. He was justified in his torture. The hour was late. Despite that, Aurora had not knelt at his feet. Uden had even honoured her request to bring the prisoner from whatever camp she desired. Another fantastic gift, yet still, Uden walked the paths of his most dreaded foe alone, without her.

Do not seek her out.

"I need you," he whispered, looking into the night. She was silent, wherever she was among his soldiers, and this stung. He saw all, but not her betrayal. At least not yet. All beautiful things turned bitter and cruel, eventually.

Do not call out for her.

"I will always love you," he added after a time, and still she did not appear, with a grin on her face, a sparkle to her pious eyes and a want to her body. He'd waited long enough to spend himself in her. So he'd taken another. It was a godly thing.

Perhaps she's mad at me?

He would not beg, would not ask, would not wait, so he was allowed to cut a little flesh in reply.

He neared his unmoving quarry and thought again of how little she

The Actions of Gods

had spoken to him as they stood over his niece's convulsing body. Truthfully, he'd despised her in those awful moments. A lesser god might have stolen her life there and then, but Uden was a kind and forgiving god to those he loved. "And she treats me like this," he hissed into the cool air, and ahead, the chained behemoth looked up from his misery for a breath. He caught sight of the blade, and his face turned ever so pale in the shattered moon's glow. He suspected the god's intention, and that was all right. As Uden crouched near, he swiftly looked away, and Uden was unimpressed with his cowardice. He knew the behemoth's name. An uninteresting, unoriginal name, as well.

"Where is Erroh, Wrek?" he whispered, kneeling close to the beaten man. It was less a query and more a demand, and Wrek looked to the ground in reply. Uden could smell the wretchedness to him. Blood, sweat, desolation. All prisoners smelled the same, eventually. It was the human in them. "Tell me, and you will not die. At least not tonight." He lanced the blade into the ground at the prisoner's feet—a gift. Wrek laughed humourlessly at this pledge and spat at the god. A delicate, insolent act, and Uden was upon him before he could breathe again. Without warning, Uden wrapped his fingers around Wrek's throat and squeezed, and the man did not fight. Instead, he faced the god and hated him in brutal, silent defiance. This, too, impressed Uden. A far cry from the last man he'd strangled, who'd gasped and struggled and fought pathetically. Licking his lips and imagining some sweet cake, Uden allowed Wrek to gather his breath.

"Is Erroh alive?" he asked, squeezing tight again. He enjoyed strangling the life out of people. It was a wonderfully intimate act. The prisoner gasped but gave nothing away, and Uden wondered how well Aurora might behave should she discover Wrek dead in his chains. He'd allowed her one outburst. He had little desire to strangle her to death. He released Wrek, who coughed and heaved, and Uden wondered if he hadn't broken him with his godly touch.

"Oh, aye. Erroh is alive. He's impossible to fuken kill. He's going to finish off the second eye," Wrek hissed, and kicked out at Uden fiercely. It was a difficult angle, but his strike had a sting, and Uden stumbled ever so. It was another impressive display, and Uden patted the brute as he struggled in the chains.

"Impossible to kill? Wouldn't that be quite the tale?" He stood up, wiping the spittle from his cheek.

Leaving the blade behind, he turned and continued his march through the town and thought of Aimee. These last miles were most pleasurable.

The most challenging too. Aimee had fought his actions with every ounce of her will, but with the drums of war rumbling in her ears, she had finally surrendered herself to him. If Aurora was a beautiful creation he took as a lover, Tempest was a godly daughter worthy of his line.

My girl.

My little girl burned.

As it had these last few days since the feast in the city, his head spun for a few moments as he fought horrors too painful to acknowledge. His steps slowed, and he paused before the healer's doorway. He dared not knock, for that was a human thing, yet he also feared storming in unannounced as the skilled healer went to task, cutting into her, returning what health he could.

Roja the red.

He knew seeing his niece would stir terrible things within, and seeing her in such a state would be stirring. It would be tragically fitting to gaze upon the last of his bloodline after twenty years' absence, fitting that she be splayed out upon the dirt for all to see.

Like the last day he'd seen her with her parents.

Without warning, a sudden dread came upon him, a terrible feeling of awfulness, and his anger gave way to an agonising sorrow that pledged to swallow him whole should he allow it. He stared at the doorway as though it held some terrible secret, as though stepping through it and seeing her lifeless body might return to him a life he'd once lived decades ago. He was frozen there, and he felt more human than he had in years. He needed to see her. To look at her once more and love her as he had these many years.

Wiiden.

Uden the Woodin Man was terrified, and he cursed that name. He held the curse and forced back deep memories he dared not seek. He swallowed deeply and did not cry out. Did not weep. He rapped his fist upon the doorway three times and entered, regardless.

Within, he felt the suffocating air deep in his chest, and he fought panic. He did not like this room. Did not like the scent of death and hopelessness either. It was a wretched tavern and no place fit for a girl with blood as divine as hers or for gods as impressive as him. He tried to speak, but no words came. He felt like a child among adults as they tore and ripped at each other, and he could only watch and await the victor.

The healer did not quiver as Uden stood over her. The healer did not meet his eyes. He only sighed as Uden stroked her stunning red hair. Emir's grubby, naked arm was lying out flat, his hand gripping hers, and were Uden to allow himself, he might have thought their embrace beautiful. Instead, he watched the crimson flow from the boy through his machinations into her, and it fascinated him, even after learning of the healer's plan. She had been deathly pale before, but now there was a faint rosiness to her cheeks. Still, though, she whimpered now and then as she fought the vile serum coursing through her body. Uden had seen Aurora's eyes fill with horror as she whispered what she knew of the brew, and once again, his temper threatened to rise before he calmed himself. This was no room for anger and wrath. He knew this now, with the instincts of a fine hunting hound.

"Her colour has improved. Has the serum run through her yet?"

The healer shrugged, and that was fine. If a god of pain was ashamed of his creations, Uden would push him no further.

"Is your blood suitable for her?"

"Probably not, fiend, but it is taking, and I'll have no one else take the chance," snapped Emir. He eyed Uden momentarily, and Uden wondered if he wasn't fantasising about slitting his throat again. This, too, was fine if he did.

"Tell me she will survive, friend."

"Perhaps."

It was no guarantee, but, in that moment, Uden regretted having struck the boy as he first went to task healing her. Such emotion was human. It had no part in Uden's makeup. The god reached out and touched the swelling below Emir's eye. It would turn deep purple and black the following morn. The healer pulled his head away, and Uden remembered he had taken that strike well.

"I was harsh on you before, healer; I will not be again." He grasped the boy's shoulder and squeezed it. "What else do you need?"

"Nothing from you, cur."

He liked the healer's defiance. He respected it as he respected Wrek's pride. "Very well, healer," he whispered, and it was a godly reminder that he was in the healer's debt. Uden had never seen a human so close to death, brought back from the darkness. Such a miracle was to be revered. Knowing he held the recipe to a vile serum was even more of a reason to be in his good grace. This healer interested Uden.

Feeling better than he had, he left the hut without another word and walked from the town out through the gates down towards his gathered army, who were settling in for the night.

He casually walked through the temporary camp. For once, he eyed those most loyal to him and offered a bow, a few words; he even smiled at those he passed. Eventually, he found her along the outskirts of the camp, alone by a fire, looking out into the night. He sat beside her, at her level, endeavouring to understand his first creation as she struggled with her divinity.

"What do you want, my god?" she said after a time, and her greeting angered him ever so, but only briefly, for he accepted she was in turmoil, awash in a sea of confusion. These wretched outcasts had crawled into her thoughts and perverted her beautiful mind. He was a compassionate god, was he not?

"Oh, my beautiful Aurora, I want a great many things."

"What do you want of me?"

"I want to lie with you, hold you, struggle with you, tear you asunder and bring you to the light."

"What about your blonde whore?"

"She is little to me."

"Regardless, I am well here, by the fire," she whispered, and turned to face him, and she was beautiful, but he saw a terrible ugliness in her eyes and the tears she shed.

"Very well, my love, but there is someone I wish you to meet."

15

BOAT TOWN

Mea didn't know who had coined the term "Boat Town," but it was a fitting nickname for the wretched floating fortress of refugees sailing down the river, carrying a city's inhabitants still reeling from war. She stood upon the bow of her vessel and sipped her tea. It was something to do as the dawn's first light broke, bringing another wretched, painful new morning.

"Riders! Up along the banks. West side, west side," a voice cried from far above, and she could only nod in grim exhaustion. Of course they appeared from the west side. The Riders along the east had taken a right fuken battering an hour before. They were probably licking their wounds, replenishing their ranks. Taking a fuken nap, most likely. They'd return soon enough. In a few hours, probably. They'd either be silent and deadly, mounting an ambush, or else wild and intimidating as they thundered through the thicket. They might come from far ahead, or they might rear up from beneath the cover of shrubs and wastes. It didn't matter which one. They would return, and her boys would go to war, regardless.

Not the Alpha females, not yet.

"Shields!" a commanding voice cried, and she watched the burgeoning blue sky, streaked with reds and oranges, as the projectiles took flight. She sipped her tea, for that was what a true Mydame was inclined to do as bolts and arrows sailed over her territory, and she could not do a damned thing about it.

She tried not to recoil as the flaming arrows struck the edge of Boat Town's western flank with desperate accuracy. Holding a gulp of tea in her mouth for a few moments to enjoy the sting, she watched the battle unfold as it had a hundred times before. Swishing the tea now, she held that pain and enjoyed it sharpening her wits, waking her from the stupor, and shaking her from the delirium she'd found herself in these last few days.

"A second volley," the voice cried, and Mea dashed her fist upon the barge's balcony edge. More pain. More alertness. The second volley took flight and struck with more success than many before, and she wondered had their gathering of vessels neared the river's edge a little carelessly. Sailing these deep waters in a solitary galleon was a small matter, but clustered up close was something else entirely.

Closing her eyes for a breath, she heard the alarm in the voices of the captains of the hundred and more barges, boats and yachts, all playing the part of one monstrous ferry, carrying its weary cargo in the chosen direction. As they sailed from death and ruin towards probable death and ruin, their cries joined in a concert of panic and exhausted defiance as the men relayed orders down through the wind. Their voices boomed at last as one roar as they struggled together to survive the next few moments.

"We must pull left."

"All left."

"Left, left, you bitch."

She heard the creaking of a hundred river vessels fighting to turn away from the edge as the Riders along the bank raised their crossbows and fired burning bolts down upon them. She felt the current take hold and swiftly turned to the other bank, fearing another attack, and they sailed right into it.

The volleys of projectiles did their cruel damage as they had many times before. Damage, aye, but no arrow had pierced their hearts yet. That would come in time, no doubt. They only needed to slip free of this cursed river and into open water. Away from arrows, away from pursuers. They could take stock afterwards. Such thoughts reassured her.

She watched a large sail catch a flame three boats in, and she cursed aloud. An unimposing young man scaled the mast swiftly, as though it was a tree with a thousand footholds, and climbed nimbly out along the rigging before hacking the sail free as it smouldered in the early morning breeze. The burning fabric fell to the deck, where the fire eaters went to task putting it out. Mea smirked at her judgement of the boy. While many collapsed under this terrible strain, some rose to the challenge—and shimmied right up the fuken mast.

We will survive this.

"Come on, put out the fires, you lazy fuks," a barking voice demanded, and she could hear his anger, and she was grateful for his leadership. "And the rest of you, load and hold." There was a wave of motion along the edge of Boat Town, more potent than the river they sailed upon, as her boys lowered their shields and smoothly loaded their weapons.

This is the right thing to do.

She sipped her tea again, swallowed and allowed herself pleasure for a few breaths as the Wolves countered the attack. She liked this part. The violence in her whetted her appetite for a bit of death. These foul brutes had sacked and razed their city and chased them as they fled in terror. Her people would welcome a little vengeful bloodshed.

"Fuk them up!"

There were a few cheers as a volley of bolts shot off into the air, striking the riverbank and many of the Riders upon its muddy surface. It was the one time she allowed bloodlust to rule her intentions. Her master general was honour bound to kill as many as possible in each volley, and she insisted they show little mercy.

There weren't set targets with so many Riders. She watched them fall, some screaming and some silently, some from a lone arrow, others filled with a dozen bolts. Those latter ones never climbed back onto their mounts, which was most pleasing.

"Again, you wretched Wolf fuks," the voice roared, and those who had reloaded let loose a second volley that was just as devastating. Their horses reared, they fell in blood, and Boat Town moved a few more feet from range. "Did I say that was enough?" the owner of the voice roared. He stood impressive among them. Younger than his demeanour suggested. Doran the wild, Doran the dependable. He struck a Wolf hard upon the back as he struggled to reload a third time. Straining, Mea could barely make out the hissed abuse he aimed at the soldier. It was less cutting than the tongue-lashing she'd imagined. Perhaps he understood that embarrassing a comrade in front of the rest would not serve their cause.

We have this.

"Incoming from the other side," another voice yelled, and Mea suddenly felt a dreadful coldness take her. She'd believed this skirmish a success a breath too soon. Facing a second attack always spread them too thin.

Unless the females join the fight.

"Not yet—their battle will come," she muttered. She could imagine them now. Her fledgling army of Alphas deep below in the different holds, stretching their limbs, sharpening their blades, readying themselves for war. Only a breath from charging free of their holdings and declaring war on the Southerners themselves. Their wrath was excellent, and their spite a tonic. Managing the mood of those who spoke for the demoralised citizens was nothing compared to arguing the finer points of vengeance with a few hundred Alpha females denied a chance to defend their home.

She could take their vitriol; their frustrations too. They had not tasted blood yet, but they would. War would greet all of them who were old enough to swing a blade. Their blooding would come in open battle when they needed leaders most, and not here, in creaking, bobbing clashes where an innocuous arrow might pierce a general easily enough.

She was growing to admire her Wolves in the days since the city's fall, but they were mindless warriors with little education. The cruel truth of the matter was that they were expendable. Her Alphalines were not. At least not yet.

This was all I could do.

"Here they come!"

She caught sight of the Riders charging from a few hundred feet behind. Dozens, all frenzied and refreshed, aiming to sink her city.

With the newcomers nearing, those few remaining Southerners from the first attack launched another volley. A few dozen arrows, alight and deadly, took flight and struck.

They aimed for Boat Town's master general and nearly struck him down. Only Alpha reflexes saved Doran, who ducked below the barrage, and Mea gasped in terror. Though he wore the Wolfen attire, his value was as great as hers. As he dropped, he dragged a struggling Wolf away from the barrage, but the young warrior was the first to be killed. She watched Doran hold the man for a breath, staring at the arrow that had pierced his eye, and for a frozen moment, she wondered how Doran had not broken yet.

"Ah, fuk me," he cried in frustration, easing the fallen soldier to the deck floor. Climbing to his feet again and turning his back to the attackers, he stared off towards the real threat on the other side of the colossal floating fortress. "Finish that pack of rutting rat bastards while I'm gone," he roared to those alongside, and then began scrambling from one boat to the next, looking carefully about him as though judging his route.

Doran was swift. Having run from one massive edge of the fortress to the other many times in the last few days, he'd learned the art of quick traversal in this terrible place. Hopping over barrels, debris, stores and supplies, slipping beneath beams hanging loosely in the breeze, and scaling the web of rope bridges, he charged, and she wanted to charge with him. She wanted to pick up a bow and strike them dead for their actions. She wanted to war, for that was her calling, but she offered no such pledge. Not until they made the lake. Nothing mattered but the lake.

It can get no worse than this.

He leapt down to the deck of the nearest barge, cleared the next railing and leapt to the next barge beyond, where the route took him over larger galleons without as many obstacles. Upon this deck, he sprinted and was Alphaline male in all his glory. Within a few moments, he was halfway across, and he dared a glance as he passed her; she could see the sweat on his brow, the exhaustion on his face, and she held her hand to her chest and bowed. He grunted and nodded before leaping over the barge's edge to the galleon's deck beyond, narrowly avoiding a watery grave below. Behind him, his long line of soldiers followed his orders, picking off the remaining Southerners easily enough. As the last one fell, she knew they had earned a reprieve for now, while Doran's night would never end.

They will sing no songs of his bravery.

Of our misery.

But there will be songs.

"Line up, shields," he shouted, and she could see the labour in his movements and, if she could in that moment, she would have awarded him a medal for his dedication to violence.

She set down her mug of tea and followed Doran. Slowly though, for she too was tired, and no Primary should be seen running. Let the war wait for her, she thought grimly, and smiled at her foolish, tired mind as she leapt over the rushing water to the galleon. She was careful not to let Doran see, for it would displease him to discover her manoeuvring closer to the battle, but relocating herself just one ship closer to the edge of their sailing fortress was only a little deceiving on her part. No bolt could travel this far in, she imagined.

The ship she found herself on had an elevated rear, perfect for seeing the way ahead but also the battle beyond. She offered a curt nod to the barge captain, who was answering the calls to bring the boat back from the left. He grunted as he spun the wheel, but no swift turning could undo the damage already done. They would face two volleys this close, no doubt. Perhaps even three. Leaning against one of the many thousand ropes binding the vessels to one another, close enough that a legendary Alpha might charge from one side to the other in time to meet the attack of another Southern army, she watched them and worried about this newer clash unfolding.

She couldn't hear Doran's orders from this far away, not against the growing wind's rush, but his soldiers could. She watched the shields rise as the arrows struck deep into Boat Town's heart, and she grimaced. She wished she still had the tea to savour, but she had left her mug behind.

Flames suddenly erupted in rapid succession, as they had a dozen times in the last three days. Just as swiftly as they appeared, she watched the fire eaters go to task putting them out and thought each man and woman tending to the task to be a hero in their own right. Their duty was not the taking of lives, but they stood among the hail of arrows and tended to their mission, never knowing if their next breath would be their last. She had seen a few break in their duties and thought no less of them.

"What are you waiting for, you fuks?" Doran's voice rose above the rush, and she smiled. The arrows and bolts from hundreds of Wolves standing firm along the edge of Boat Town continued, killing indiscriminately, and she was proud of her boys. Aye, they were bastards, the lot of them, but they were keeping this wreck of a city afloat, and they did so without rest or complaint. Some without a hearty meal, either.

She watched in silence for a time, as she had done during every attack these last gruelling few days, and her people beat back the fiends, matching brutality with brutality, to give them thought for their next attack. The screams of anguish filled the air; the cries of triumph grew louder. The smoke billowed and died, and the boats kept sailing farther from the city, from the end of the world. And Mea, Primary of nothing yet still leading, watched it all and despaired.

This is our life now.

When the fires eventually settled, when the last Rider was sent fleeing, Doran shuffled back through the boats and climbed up to meet his Primary. She could see the exhaustion in his features. His bald head was drenched in sweat. He had no will to wipe it clear. His face was covered in ash and dried blood, his usual sneer lost now to a pained grin. Still, he was beautiful.

"Whoever called for the boats to pull left needs a flogging," he said, resting against the balcony beside her. She stood straight in his presence.

The Actions of Gods

Appearing regal, reminding him of his duty. It was all she could do without saying it aloud.

"They've driven us well; it was just a little panic, is all," she replied sternly. Too sternly. He was very close to breaking. To relinquishing his position in favour of doomed safety below deck. He nodded and looked beyond her to the coming of the day. Time was nothing in these moments. The attacks would continue. She placed her hand on his shoulder, and he nodded weakly. "This is a necessary evil," she said of their clustered vessels, and he nodded in agreement. It wasn't he who'd suggested they lash the hundred boats together, but he'd supported the idea.

"After three days without rest, we are all inclined to make mistakes," he said, looking past her, across a half-dozen boats to one of the few dead bodies on the deck. "I should be there when they pop him over… pop them all over," he said, and Mea could see now exactly how close to breaking he was. He'd accepted her demands, but his were the more significant efforts. He turned to leave, and she held him fast.

"It's not a master general's duties. Rest your eyes a little." She eased him to the edge of the balcony. It was no fantastic bedding of straw and silk or throne of comfort. It was a bench of hardened wood, but it would do for now. "I'll call for some food. It'll be a while before they gather their numbers." He nodded and lay on the hardwood, closing his eyes.

"That last one took my wind a little," he said softly, and she watched him fade into unconsciousness. Her stomach grumbled, but she could not eat a mouthful lest the bile erupt and sink the entire town. *It's better to eat when there's open water.*

"Shush, hero," she said softly. "You've done enough for now."

He didn't reply. He stretched out and snored softly, and she was grateful. Every moment he slept was a win for their cause. Were he to manage an entire hour, he might continue waging his defensive brutality for three more days. She faced the way ahead, looked through the masses of people upon the countless vessels, and feared for them all. Somewhere ahead lay the lake. A simple lake. Their only bastion of hope against annihilation.

Gently, she sat down and offered a smile to the watching barge captain as he stayed the course, just like his hundred and more comrades. He bowed deeply, and she wondered if he was one of the few who had argued against dragging the vessels together. Did he see little logic in moving at this agonising pace? Did he believe leaving the slower vessels behind was the crueller and saner option? Was he the type of man who could look at himself in the mirror after willingly condemning a thousand souls to death? She received no answers to any of these questions as sleep took her.

———

She did not know how long either she or Doran had slept, for the dawn was raging and beautiful as the terrible cry of warfare drew her from her sleep. Wearily, she climbed to her feet as, beside her, Doran shot up from his slumber, tightening his armour and looking towards each bank of the river.

"From the west edge, the west," a voice cried, and Doran muttered a curse under his breath.

His hands shook, his face was pale and his eyes were bloodshot and faded. He shook his head a few times, slapping his face. He faced her. "I don't care how curious you get, Mydame. You aren't to go farther than this vessel," he warned, grinning as though exhaustion and misery did not hold him in their unforgiving grip. Before she could reply, he leapt over the balcony, shouting orders as he did. Her Wolves followed his barking commands, and she could do little more than stand and watch the rushing Riders as they broke the treeline and hunted them down.

"We just need to reach the lake," she whispered, and it was a prayer to the absent gods.

16

BORN IN BLOOD

Her name was Aurora, and she killed those she believed were enemies. She draped her hair out over her face, covering her eyes, covering her panic. She counted her steps as they shuffled through the camp. Thrice already, she'd lost count; such was his influence. Her mind spun and fractured; she was a lost little girl, led to slaughter in chains.

I do not wish to meet your new lover.

"Her name is Tempest. I think you will like her," Uden insisted, and his voice was silk in her ears.

That is not her name.

Her mind flittered with thoughts of Stefan, humbled, and of herself soaked in ale. Of better times when she didn't care. She'd seen flashes of the girl in between tents. Aurora had a mind for faces, though it was fickle at times. But she knew this girl, and her name was not Tempest.

She tried to fight his hold on her mind, but he was her god, which was a torment. She wondered if he could sense how much her hand shook. His grip was firm, his fingers locked in hers like chains. She was in agony, helpless to do anything but to follow, and Ealis wailed deep within her mind as she faded away to nothingness. She wasn't interested in meeting the girl. Not now, not ever.

"Tell me of… Tempest, my god," Aurora whispered, and feigned dreaminess. Her free hand still shook, but it took hold of her blade, and she wondered how many strikes she might get before he or one of his guards struck her down. She imagined three. Her fingers touched the grip, and she was tempted because her name was Aurora, and she was born to kill.

He pulled her near, and she smelled his musk, and it enticed and enamoured her, and she wanted to die. She met his gaze and blinked a few times, and he kissed her, and it was beautiful, and she loved him, and she wanted to vomit and tear his eye out and eat his heart, and also she wanted to lie with him and writhe until they were sated.

And she also wanted to kill the girl.

I must die this night.

"You behaved unexpectedly," he whispered in those dulcet, thunderous tones, and she screamed inside. Deep down, where a soul once shone, a charcoal husk remained. Releasing her from his embrace, he kept his hand tight in hers. He wasn't ready to let her slip away just yet.

Lest I kill your whore and save her soul from your cruelty.

"I'm sorry, my love," she lied. She didn't love him at all. She wasn't sorry at all, either. But she was a goddess, and goddesses went to task with their godly acts. Sometimes it was deceit; sometimes it was complete surrender. "I was fond of the boy, and he had value. I was angry with you." She stroked his cheek and gazed deep into his depthless soul with her beautiful eyes, and she saw a thousand of her victims staring right back at her.

How many did I kill for him?
Why did I kill for him?
All those higherline families.

She knew the answers, for they were many, and she wanted him to see through her lies, tear her heart out, and leave it with Stefan's. That would be a glorious end. That would be an end worthy of a beautiful horror like her.

He laughed, and she recoiled inside, but with her lips she smiled despite the nausea. He was her quarry in that moment. And as he trained her, she adapted to his words and actions. It was an awful game she had mastered long ago. Win, lose; it was a small matter, she thought, and grinned, licking her lips before presenting her neck for him to cut into. "Do it, my love. Cover me in blood and send me to the next." She slipped her dagger free and offered the blade. A smooth move, sure either to end the game or progress them to the next move. It was how they always played; he would expect as much.

"Your neck is not mine to slit," he countered, and she purred in ecstasy as he pushed the blade away. She licked his cheek and smiled, and her deceitful eyes were alive and alluring, even if she was dead behind them. He smiled, and she knew he might furrow with her this

The Actions of Gods

night, and it would be awful, and she would moan, and it would not be fair, but it would be done until she played another move. "At least not tonight."

She took the reprieve and allowed him to lead her through the camp of her people towards a tent hardly fit for a god alone. This time, she did not look at her feet as she walked or hide her face from the watching Southerners. Instead, she marched and played the part of a girl who belonged in this god's shadow. She returned her dagger to the scabbard and ignored the wretchedness she felt within for not drawing a little blood.

The night is young.

And I do not wish to meet his lover.

"You will love my daughter of blood," he said suddenly, and her body recoiled against itself. She stumbled in his grip but played it off as clumsiness.

Daughter?

"Tell me of Tempest," she said again, careful to keep her voice smooth and even like Lea would when speaking with Nomi. Strangely, in the light of the shattered moon and the flapping torches, she caught sight of a genuine smile. Like that of a father. She feared this tale, for it would be horrid.

Uden claimed he had never taken a child. Oh, how long she had craved to deliver a child upon him, worthy of them both. Hearing that his legacy was now flesh and blood and bone and innards was a precarious thing. She felt the killer in her grind her teeth and wail in jealousy. Another part of her wailed for the misery she was to see.

This girl is not just a lover.

Something awful.

"She was younger than you when I took her from this world," he said, releasing her grip, and she saw that prideful face and her fingers tingled, hovering over the blade again. She felt her heart hammer and her stomach lurch. On the surface, she grinned in excitement. She played her god in this game of deceit, which was the hardest thing she'd ever done.

"So long ago."

"I am a greater being than I was the night I pulled you from darkness."

"And covered me in blood," she replied instinctively and screamed internally. She sought the colder part of her mind. The part that would have allowed her to survive these next few precarious moments. She frowned as he led her to the tent and invited her inside.

"She fought as hard as you, Fyre, but she slipped into divinity, just as you did," he whispered, and Aurora wanted to throw up as her eyes adjusted to the brightness within. She saw the chains hanging and remembered the killing, the meat, the blood, his taunting, his lessons. It was almost too much, and she slipped away from him, reached up and touched the chains. They clinked, and she wanted to relieve herself and slit the skin from her body until she died.

Beyond the chains, she saw the child and felt death push deep into her beating chest.

Tempest rose from her bedsheets. She wore a thin blouse, grubby white trousers, and little else. She moved slowly as though still asleep, and Aurora wanted to take the girl from this place and return her soul.

"You are Aurora," the girl said, and Aurora allowed tears to stream silently down her cheeks. This was not the girl she expected to greet her, but cruelly, she knew this girl as well. Knew her as the gift she had been to her god, which was a terrible thing. This girl's fate had been the worst of all the torments and cruelties she'd inflicted upon her victims.

"Aimee," she whispered, and behind her, Uden snorted in anger, and Aurora knew her misstep. This was no longer Aimee of Raven Rock but a child lost in a god's demented enchantments. "She has grown to become quite the lady," Aurora whispered, trying not to meet Tempest's seeking eyes lest she discover a lost soul. "Still, though, a little young?"

"She is not you, Aurora," Uden growled from behind her, and Aurora shook ever so; his sudden fury was mesmerising and terrifying. "I would not ruin her as I do you. I would not have her sullied for a human's pleasure." He paused for a breath, and she saw warmth in his eye.

His one solitary green eye.

"When she does take a lover, it will be her choice," he proclaimed, and Aurora knew her insinuation had horrified him, and she saw hope there that the girl had not endured the truly terrible. Part of her was relieved. Part of her pushed her petty jealousies away as well.

It was a small tent with little more than bedding and a roof, and Aurora wondered how lost the girl was. Her own last days as Fyre were a disturbing memory. She could see the fear, the confusion and the hatred in the young girl's face, in her stance, in the way every word spoken in her presence was a torment. She strode towards Aimee, intending to greet her as kin, for that was what she was, in a way.

Sisters of Blood.

Without warning, Aimee was upon her. The girl was swifter than she remembered, and Aurora almost died in the first swing. She'd seen the

The Actions of Gods

girl as she had wanted to appear: a waif, broken and terrified—and as cold a killer as Aurora herself. Removing the blade from the scabbard hanging beside the bed was quite the skill, and concealing it until Aurora stepped into range was something close to mastery. The blade nicked her chin as she leapt away, and a second slash tore her shirt open and sliced the flesh underneath. Suddenly the room was tiny, the hovering blade long and assured. Aurora rolled away from the strikes, drawing her dagger and sword, and met the attack while begrudgingly approving of Uden's newest creation.

"No, girls. Behave yourselves," Uden called, but there was cold humour rather than authority to the bastard's voice.

"We are just playing," Aurora countered as she met the younger girl's strikes, forcing her to retreat. The fight turned on its head despite the swift ambush.

That's right, you wonderful little bitch. I'm ready now.

"To the fires with you," screamed Aimee, and Aurora recognised that defiance. Their blades met and rattled loudly, and though it was a tempest she faced within the tent, Aurora was calm and clinical. Ruthless too. She remembered seeing this girl fight, and there was elegance to her manoeuvres even now. But the girl was too wild for these tight quarters, and battling within a tent was no last stand in a town as loved ones all around met their doom. She was restrained, and it was too easy.

"Oh, my girls," roared Uden, and suddenly, he was among them as they fought. Stepping through their manoeuvres, studying their actions, enjoying the encounter, his face ever close to the flickering blades. He was in range, Aurora realised, licking her lips. So very close. For a breath, she imagined swinging wildly and striking his eye. Or slicing clean through his throat and then plunging her dagger through his heart. He might die without screaming that way. While she was imagining these beautiful things, a blade struck her shoulder and stung like a wasp driven wild by fire. "Both of you—perfect," he said, grinning savagely.

"You took it all," screamed Tempest, forcing home her advantage, and a lesser warrior might have fallen. Instead, Aurora dropped her dagger and caught Tempest's wrist as she lunged carelessly. Swiftly, she twisted and knocked the blade free and controlled the girl. She could have ended her life. Tempest struggled and fell heavily as though accepting of death, and suddenly, Uden was upon Aurora, his green eye flashing in anger and brutality. He pulled the girls apart easily and then, wrapping his arms around Aurora, pulled her close.

"Whisht, you won this battle, little one," he insisted, and Aurora could smell his musk again. She was drunk on it and fought her desire as Tempest collapsed against the outer tent's flap and kept going.

"She runs again," Uden gasped, releasing Aurora and removing his scent from her. "With many eyes watching, she won't get far." Already beyond were a few raised voices, no doubt challenging a diminutive goddess fleeing their master's cavern.

"Let her run. When you have me, what else do you need?" It was a compelling argument. He smiled cruelly, and Aurora knew his answer, so she placed her hand in his. "Let me get my sister so that I might walk with her these last few… glorious miles," she whispered dreamily. She dropped her blades at his feet—a pleasing gesture.

"If you kill her, I will be most displeased."

17

THE ROAD TO RUIN

"You should all be bowing in the presence of His majesty," Padir cried in the tavern's rush, and Magnus clenched his teeth. "Look at him—our mighty king, all dressed as a pauper. Yet still mighty as fuk." The boy stood on the table, raising his voice above the din, and people began to turn and stare. So much for a quiet meal after a long day in the saddle, he thought miserably.

"Quiet, you," Magnus snapped, but he knew there was little point in requesting subtlety. Padir was in full flow, gathering attention from all who sat in the tavern this stormy evening. Every day, the young companion pushed his daring that little bit more with the Islanders, and Magnus, grand king of these Savage Isles, could not stop him. Looking around this dingy tavern, Magnus thought it ever so familiar. There was something to this place, but perhaps it was an after effect of visiting so many taverns. Avoiding meeting the eyes of the patrons gathered, he concentrated on the simple ornaments and hunting trophies hanging upon the walls. Traditionally, the Islanders were proud of their taverns and tastes, but not so here. He knew these trophy beasts; he'd hunted them often, but never had he once placed their heads upon a wall to add cheer or decoration. It was common in the Isle of Bawn. Less so here. He caught sight of a boar's head and grimaced—no beast of such magnificent threat deserved to be mounted upon a wall for eternity. A king could outlaw such practices, he imagined, and almost laughed at the notion. Any royal decree in these lands would not help him.

I'll be dethroned, regardless.

Looking beyond the countless trophies to the vast and crowded bar, he wondered if he had taken over this place some hazy night a decade before. Had the Rangers eaten heartily and merrily here on some fantastic night in better times? Probably. The march had taken a long time, and there had been plenty of taverns to commandeer along the way. Even when not at war. Even when merely visiting. He looked to the desperate servers and the tavern owner behind the bar as a hundred cries of orders filled the air, drowning out the small trio playing in a smoky corner. Any tavern owner in this part of the world was a wealthy fiend indeed. For all the false savagery his people were accused of, to say they could drink a lake dry were it filled with ale was a fairer criticism.

My people.

The people who weren't demanding ale at the bar sat at long tables. Their conversations were hushed, their expressions cutting. Magnus knew from their gazes precisely what they thought of his appearance, exactly what they thought of Padir's outbursts too.

"He demands ale. Your finest ale. Some food too." If the boy was aware of the nasty glares delivered his way, he gave no sign; he continued his pleading bravado uninterrupted. Aye, Magnus's pocket of pieces was lighter than he liked, but for a king to demand sustenance was a little uncivilised, even if it was his right.

"Get down from the table," Magnus hissed, but the boy wouldn't be silenced. He stood proud in his rags, puffing out his chest, demanding recognition of Magnus's grandness. He would have made quite an impression among the elite of the courts in years past. Perhaps he still would.

"Don't you, Magnus? Don't you demand the finest that this grand establishment offers?" It was a fair question, but Magnus had no intention of adding to the scene.

"You'll get us hanged, boy," Magnus hissed, dragging at his sleeve and nearly pulling the boy from his podium. It was a kingly act on his part, but Padir was far from thrilled. There was a slyness to the boy. A threat too. He played the jester part just fine, and as those around might laugh, his keen eye might seek opportunity.

"It's just you they'll hang. I'll be wrapping the rope around your neck," he countered, grinning, before righting himself, hopping down and sitting in the seat next to his king. At the bar, a tavern girl was busy pouring them the finest ales, and Padir seemed pleased with this result.

"Make sure you double knot the noose."

With Padir no longer scuffing the table's surface and informing the patrons that their reviled king had returned, the crowd returned to their

The Actions of Gods

conversation. Magnus could hear them muttering their distaste for royalty and how easily they could get away with nasty deeds. He wasn't afraid in this place, though. At most, they might curse his name under their breath as he passed, might even spit in his food, but no Isleman or Islewoman would dare put a grubby hand on him. Until the clans met, until tradition was followed. Until he returned the crown to the throne.

Then there'll be time for a good lynching.

A week inland, and he still didn't know where Padir's allegiance lay. Probably not the finest notion for a comrade of the road, but Magnus wouldn't complain. The boy knew the lands well. Claimed to know every soul they met on the march, too, and had a fantastical tale for every green hill, murky bog or eerie wood they passed along their way. He knew the people and spoke their silent language of gesture fluently, and Magnus had learned he could read a room right swiftly. His excited, youthful tongue was a clever disguise for his resounding intelligence. He played the jester just right. Sometimes it was amusing; sometimes it was practical. Sometimes, though, he pushed Magnus's temper to the limit.

For years, Magnus had received thorough reports from reliable comrades, and he understood the Islands' prosperity, but sometimes it took a fresher gaze from one less touched by the royal court to see that little bit more. Having one so close to the nation's mood was a fine thing. Padir was a little shit, but he welcomed it.

"Aye, then I'll take the crown for myself after," the boy hissed, but held his grin lest his jest go too far. Magnus merely grunted, and the child beamed in delight for his wit and the complimentary ales making their way to them through the swiftly parting crowd. Within a breath, an attractive serving girl placed them on their table.

"Thank you, my darling," the lad said grandly. "I'm Padir. I'm well endowed." The girl goggled and blushed as the apparently well-endowed boy broke from tradition and slid a copper piece across the table as a tip. She smiled with open eyes and returned the coin to him before slipping away.

"Ah, you are a dreadful man to attract women with, sire," Padir muttered, watching her glide effortlessly through the crowd. "She'd probably be too much for you anyway... king or no."

For a moment, Magnus was a thousand miles away. Thoughts of Rienna rushed through his mind like waves breaking against an unwelcoming shore, and his stomach turned. She wasn't Elise. She was something else entirely.

"Did you hear me, Magnus?"

Magnus heard him, but he was more interested watching the tavern girl glide away. She had a nice walk. Thin, fine hips, long flowing hair. Just like Rienna. He felt a stirring in his undergarments and smiled ruefully. Where had that urge been when she'd stripped herself of her garments and offered herself to him? He knew Elise wouldn't have minded, and his stomach turned again. Elise wouldn't have minded because she was dead now. His stomach churned horrid bile, and he gripped the pint of ale tightly in vice-like fingers and forbade the sadness from rising.

"Magnus?"

He thought of Rienna kissing his body delicately, hoping to stir some life into him. He remembered her taste, her touch. Exciting, fresh and new. Unwelcomed. For she was not his mate, his love for eternity, however long that might be.

She's waiting for me in the dark.

"My lord," Padir said, and there was a gentleness to his voice. It was low and careful, for the boy had likely picked up a thing or two about the king's moods. Walking the Wastes with a comrade who'd suffered such a defeat and lost everything close to him was no small thing. Padir took hold of his king's shoulder and shook him ever so. "I was jesting, is all, sire."

At this, Magnus nodded. He thought once more of Elise lost in the darkness and his dreadful fate to come, and he stored it away lest it break him again. "If I wanted that girl, I'd have her easily enough, young one," Magnus snarled, but his threat was empty. This the boy knew too.

"Of course, my liege. Who could resist the crown?"

As quickly as it appeared, the gentleness was gone. Instead, the easy mocking had returned, and that was fine. He welcomed it. Easier to mock and jest than admit weakness. "If I required a crown alone to take a woman to bed, I'd hardly be much of a man," Magnus countered, and his voice was witty, stronger, kinglier.

"I'm sure it helps, my liege."

"That's why you should find a worthy mate before you take the crown. Let her do the charming." Gently, he shoved the boy away from him and drank deeply.

As usual, the boy watched him intently. "Is it good?"

"Doesn't taste tainted. A little piss at most," Magnus offered, and, delighted, the boy drank from his own pint.

"Yeah, there doesn't seem to be any poison in mine either."

"I'm glad I could make the path safe for you, little one."

The Actions of Gods

For a time, they drank while listening to the driving rain as it dashed upon the roof above their heads. With his mind racing, Magnus might have preferred the solitude of a night's ride through the storm, but the wind was too cutting, and any fool knew a stubborn man could ride himself to freezing were he careless. A night like this, in a tavern near their destination, was a casual luxury.

I have missed these lands.

As the hours passed, more and more patrons donned their cloaks and hoods and marched out into the night in search of a warm, dry pillow beneath their heads. By midnight, there was scarcely a soul within, and Magnus, deciding the last round was his limit, placed a hefty bag of pieces in the tavern girl's hand. Padir was momentarily horrified at the gesture, for they could barely afford such a thing, but instead of voicing his disapproval, he immediately took credit for the act.

"It is true—he insisted," Magnus confirmed to the delighted girl, who took Padir's hand and pulled him up for one dance. It was a small lie, enough to earn the opportunity to charm her for a second dance. Perhaps more after that.

Sometimes, to be generous was kingly, Magnus supposed, watching the boy spin her around, and again he fought off his feelings of desolate loneliness. Oh, to be young. To be vibrant and hopeful. To have a future as well. To be a right fuker, tearing these isles apart in search of his master and taking everything himself.

"Nearly home," Magnus whispered to the empty table, and truthfully, it was fine company even if it offered no reassuring replies. "And I will be lesser for it," he added.

18

THE ROAD TO RULE

"Ah, fuk this. I think she gave me something. Actually, I'm rather sure of it. Filthy little tavern wench." Padir shifted in his saddle and continued scratching somewhere in his nether regions. He found only a little success and dug deeper. After a few breaths, he smiled in fleeting victory.

Thump.

"Perhaps if you bathed now and then, there wouldn't be an issue with the itch," Magnus offered. He'd told the child time and time again to bathe daily while they were on the road. For hunting, but for comfort too. The little shit never listened. He always believed himself to be knowledgeable and to have the perfect answer to every question. He was worse than Erroh. Magnus's knuckles were white as he gripped his reins tightly.

Fuken Erroh.

My regret.

My eternal pride.

Erroh had known certain lines were never to be crossed. Not even in a fight to the death. Unlike Magnus.

Giving himself up to the saddle's sway, he avoided the younger man's eyes lest he engage him in further discussion this miserable morning. The storm continued this day, and it had little respect for the king. The clouds above were heavy and generous. Rain poured down upon their weary heads, and the wind cut through their cloaks. It was a miserable day on the road, made worse by inane conversation.

They were close to the court of Risbeigh, and they travelled these last few miles apprehensively because, in his infinite wisdom and bravado, Padir had brazenly announced their arrival in every settlement during the first half of the march. Now, as they moved farther along the coast, word spread as swiftly as the rain upon the wind—talk of a king's arrival. Many a passing traveller might offer a bow as they trudged past, or a tiller upon a field might take a knee. Others stared coldly, with harsh words upon the tips of their tongues but little nerve to deliver them in person. Wasn't that the way with humanity? Brazen and brave and loud, oh, so fuken loud, until actually facing their foe. There was a special place in the netherworlds for snivelling cowards like these. Of this, Magnus was confident.

"Washing?" Padir said, returning to his earlier topic. "No lack of washing caused this. And besides, I wash enough as it is in this misery," he continued, looking pointedly up to the rain.

At this, Magnus sniggered. He'd never met an Isleman or Islewoman who wasn't obsessed with the weather and its peculiarities. These isles saw rain nearly every day, even in the warmer months, yet the inhabitants always seemed thrown by its arrival. Himself included.

"Fuk this rain," Padir mumbled, wrapping his scarf tight against his hood before scratching at his groin again. "Fuk her for giving me this affliction, too."

Thump.

"Perhaps, on our return journey, we should stop off at that tavern and see if you accidentally left something with her too?"

This time the boy grinned, tapping his head with a grubby finger. "I'm careful enough in my endeavours." After a moment, he coughed. "Perhaps though, when we... return... with your treasures... we should avoid that tavern. Just in case."

Thump.

Thump.

Magnus looked uneasily behind them, along the path they had taken. He was familiar with the tale of a woman in white at midnight. He also knew it was a fine place for an ambush, but he felt little fear. No one from these lands would ambush him. Nevertheless, habit had him examining the endless forest for a few breaths, listening to the wind, but he found little movement in the glistening leaves.

Nothing hunts me.

He knew humiliation would probably come. So, too, would bruises and blood. Not out here, though, where eyes couldn't see an assassination. Couldn't make a political move for the court. Still, he kept looking behind him and thinking back to fonder things, when not searching for threats. He imagined a few hundred Rangers marching behind him, their swords sharp and oiled, their armour secure and polished. All of them loyal and above the banner these two isles answered to. He wished he had them now, marching these last few days towards his kingdom. To listen to their cheer. To laugh at their jests. To accept their sage advice. To show a little muscle where paupers feared to tread.

Padir leaned across in his saddle. "Tell me, master. Why didn't you return home sooner?" The boy had a coldness in his tone now. It was a loaded question, no doubt, and not for the first time, Magnus wondered did the boy have his best interests at heart.

"You have a nerve to ask me that, boy," Magnus warned in an equally cold tone. It didn't matter that the boy had every right to query him. Was he not a fair king?

"These lands are without a ruler, my liege," countered Padir. He brought his horse alongside. The boy had begun to ask a little more about his plans every few days now. About his expectations. About his business. Never enough to aggravate, but enough to test Magnus's nerves. Enough to seem interested, but not enough to appear as a spy. And if he were a spy? Well, without army or endeavour, Magnus was hiding very little this final march. "Some might take offence if you leave us in the shadows and return only when you have little else."

Thump.

Thump.

Thump.

From Padir's clothes, accent and frequent vacant stare, Magnus imagined he'd endured a harsh enough life. Those who suffered difficult lives had a right to challenge leaders. Was that not why Magnus himself had dared to question, fight, and rule a handful of decades before?

"You don't remember the days before my rule, little one," Magnus said quietly, holding his temper and concealing any show of emotion. It was good practice for the upcoming clan discussions.

"Ah, yes. From the mouth of a decrepit elder. The days. The good old days."

Magnus shook his head and considered striking the boy. Just once. Not even with a closed fist. Just enough to knock sense into the little shit, who believed he knew the ways of the world from the few years he'd had opinions about it. Even though he'd been absent these last few years, Magnus understood the benefits of his empty throne better than the boy ever could. He knew the world; he knew his people.

"Do you know the Four Factions?"

Padir shrugged. "I go where I find employment." He found something interesting in the air to listen to; Magnus could hear it too. Had for a while. "I don't enjoy travelling in too far; I know the eastern coast. They are shit lands, Magnus, real fuken shit lands."

"Aye—exactly, my young friend. But these Savage Isles flourish."

"Ha! I would hardly call these lands flourishing."

"Do you know a fiend or friend who has starved to death?" Magnus said, eyeing the boy coldly. "Do you know a friend or fiend who died by a bandit's blade? You might see the brewing conflict if you ventured farther into the Four Factions. Might see the hungry too. War brings these things. But even in peacetime, unfortunate things were brewing throughout the Four Factions. Be glad of this absent king's nation. There will be war if someone else holds the throne. There will be true horror. There will be real things to worry about. Then, I wonder just how important your opinions and grievances with me are."

The boy nodded, but he didn't look in any way convinced. There were equal problems for those blessed with knowledge and ideals. But those who preferred their voices to be heard over those of decent folk were a plague upon humanity. Always had been, always would be.

Hard to be open minded when one only sees in black or white.

Magnus liked to think of himself as somewhere in between, where grey slipped in somewhere between the extremes. Magnus believed in his actions and the sacrifices he'd made for his island of birth, but even he, as king, was open to admitting a mistake now and then. A less frequently spoken truth was that Magnus's reign was the greatest in the Savage Isles' history. He was successful, paradoxically, because he played no part in leading. He allowed the lunatics to rule themselves, and they were better for it.

"Fair point, my wise and praiseworthy liege, but tell me, how prosperous might these lands have become with a king upon a throne?"

Another fine point from the boy's fine mind, and Magnus wanted to take him by the scruff of his neck and convince him of his errors. Many might believe that replacing a sitting king was the answer to everything and that all their problems could be waved away with a righteous decree. All a king in these savage lands could do was become a focus for much of their subjects' strife. These barbaric, beautiful lands would be wrought in conflict as much as the Four Factions had been, were Magnus sitting.

It was a small grace that his people followed the old ways. A small blessing too. He would march into court and demand one last kingly decree and be done with it. It was a foolish plan. This he knew and feared.

Thump.
Thump.
Thump.
Thump.

Magnus could hear it now from somewhere ahead in the road. He peered through the murk of the rainy, misty morning, expecting the Riders to reveal themselves, and after a moment, Padir noticed it too. He sat up straighter in his saddle. He even ceased scratching, and for a disturbing moment, Magnus wondered if he'd misplayed his hand. If the loud declarations of his arrival and their slow pace upon this march had allowed the dissent to grow to something malevolent. A little slaughter by the side of the road might be a perfect end to their absent king.

"Whisht, boys," Magnus warned his hounds, as their growls grew with the thunderous noise. After an anxious few breaths, perhaps a dozen Riders appeared, looking like vile, wretched pieces upon an ancient game board. They were exquisitely clad in metallic armour, painted a rich, dark green. Magnus cursed under his breath, for he knew these fiends.

Padir knew them too. "The Green Branch knights," he cried in delight. And why wouldn't he be impressed? They were the king's royal guard. Fierce and heroic. Unbeaten in war, unrivalled in brutality. Their pledge was to the king, no matter the clan they were attached to.

"Over here," cried Padir, waving wildly, lest these brutes upon their monstrous mounts somehow not see the lone figures upon the murky path.

They did not reply. They merely watched for a time and then, as one, thundered down towards them. Magnus caught sight of his clan's banner waving upon one rider's staff and felt a little pride—it was a good flag, with a puck's head upon a wave of black and white. There were more extravagant banners, but his was his own.

"Word must have spread of our arrival," Padir said, and Magnus grinned bitterly.

Indeed.

"They really should slow down," the boy gasped, and it was a fine suggestion.

"Perhaps they aren't best pleased to see us," Magnus countered as

The Actions of Gods

they loomed ever nearer. Though his instincts to attack surged, he dared not grip his blade nor send his hounds charging out to distract and destroy. He was a king and above such uneasiness.

The thunder filled the air above the beating of his heart, the neighing of his mount and the snapping and warning cries of his boys. They charged in a line, two Riders followed by the rest. He imagined the terror an assassin might have felt as they ran them down. They did not scream or raise a blade; they merely met their king at pace. When they were a few feet from colliding with his mount or a hound beneath, they separated spectacularly and surrounded man and boy swiftly. And then, as though it were tradition, they fell into formation around Magnus and his squire.

They could have bowed. They could have declared their allegiance to their king. They could have said hello. Instead, they simply began to march with them as though they had always been part of this royal entourage.

"Wonderful! A royal escort for the last few miles," Padir shouted. He smiled, but Magnus could see his hands shake as he gripped the reins. Aye, their approach had rattled him too. An untrusting king might think it a sign that the boy doubted his own allegiance. Feared what doom might fall upon him for supporting Magnus.

"If they take my head, I will say you are not loyal to me, little one," Magnus mumbled after a time, and one of their chaperones glanced over at him as though caught unawares in the wrong bed. "But I think we'll be fine," he added, furtively watching those around them.

They trotted as one across a ridge of muddy brown and wet grey. Magnus knew this last leg of the path well. So close to home, so close to the end of it all.

"Of course we will, your majesty," the boy replied.

A fresh bout of rain began to fall, taking the last warmth from Magnus's aching, tired body. Then, in the distance, beyond their entourage, through the hazy mist and the awfulness of the day, he caught sight of the far coast and the capital fortress of Risbeigh, and far off, he heard the first notes of horns and the beating of welcoming drums as they filled the wet morning air.

The journey was done. The king had returned.

And everything was about to take a terrible turn.

19

ROUTINES

On the second day, Erroh woke from a restless slumber with a start. His dreams of murder and misery were lost in the waking moments. He blinked in the gloomy light and wondered just where he was. He wondered if Lea was nearby, and the crashing certainty of his new life struck him anew. Sweat covered his body; his head spun with a hangover residue and the dream syrup's sluggish departure. Rolling free from his damp bedding of blanket and straw, he struggled to his feet, wincing in pain with every movement. Checking his foot first, he found more strength than before. He could even put half his weight upon the cursed thing. Dressing wearily, he crawled out from his ramshackle tent to face the day.

He saw nothing but greys and browns; such was the dreariness of this camp in the daytime. Smoke filled the air from a hundred burning fires throughout this place of desperation and desolation. Some of the inhabitants were cooking stews in copper battered pots, others burning arrow shafts into place, while many had simply lit their fires to stave off the wretched cold in the bitter morning. He almost recoiled at the smell of the smoky air. He recognised that stench of humans and their waste all too well. This was the march. It should have reminded him of his youth. Instead, it reminded him of sorrow and loss.

Strangely, Drahir waited for him outside. Erroh wondered about the man and shuddered. Perhaps it was the lack of trust he held for him. Perhaps it was the look in his eyes. Drahir attempted casualness, but there was a burning intensity behind that gaze. Nothing good came from such eyes. Truthfully, Erroh barely trusted any of the fiends in this muddy, grey place. Some had been determined to take his head a few days before. Now they served him? He did not understand the whorish nature of their loyalties.

Drahir offered a deep bow. He looked fresh from a decent night's sleep, while Erroh knew he appeared a ruin. Such things mattered to a god, he imagined. Bowing to the guards standing diligently at his doorway, he stretched, yawned and wandered out into the camp of his gathered army.

Just keep that fuk from slipping in as I sleep.
And don't slip in yourself, either.

He recognised one guard who had chanted his name. It wasn't much, but it was something, so, taking a breath and finding his thoughts, he decided to entrust his life to these former enemies.

"Think I'll take a walk," he said to Drahir and the silent guards, but primarily to no one.

These are your people, to wield as weapons or send away to hide in silence.

With no grand proclamations of his arrival and divinity, he found walking among his new followers easier without the weight of grandness burdening him. He was simply Erroh of the road, was he not? It might not help them to know his fallibility, but it made it easier for him to meet their gazes. He walked through the camp as before, and they bowed as he went. He shook his head and bade those who fully knelt to rise. They were embarrassed by his insistences, and he was embarrassed for his struggles with their language. It was one thing to practice with Nomi, but suddenly becoming entrenched in the guttural language was something else entirely. They muttered thoughtful, pleading, hopeful, desperate, joyous, wretched, brazen, frightened, nonsensical words at him, and he tried to understand them all, but their tongue was so swift, and his mind was still slow and drained. He caught every third or fourth word and offered a reassuring smile where possible.

When he was entirely lost, Drahir, who flanked his every step like a hunter would a calf, offered a gentle translation—and translated what Erroh provided in reply. Erroh never thanked him or engaged in conversation despite his constant presence. He kept his hand upon Mercy, strapped upon his waist for subtle preparedness.

Hours passed on this pilgrimage until he came upon a group of warriors training, which he found terrifying. In little muddy patches of grassland, away from the central part of the camp, at least fifty warriors took to striking fiercely at each other as though in real battle. They wielded sharpened blades of all shapes and sizes, and Erroh was amazed at their recklessness. And a little impressed. He'd never seen the Southerners train with their blades upon his long march to madness. He wondered if it was a decree from Uden that only sharpened, deadly blades be used when honing skills. Aye, the cream might rise to the top, but at what cost? He walked among them more carefully than before as they spun and struck, screaming as though they were upon the battlefield. He dared not speak aloud lest he inadvertently get a distracted warrior killed. Most of the time, their armour took the blows in even contests. However, in one bout he watched a warrior nearly lose an ear, a finger, and possibly his manhood in an unevenly fought skirmish. The man escaped with a cut down his face that bled enough for a healer to be called. Erroh offered the victor a bow and the bested youth a pat on the back. Both appeared equally pleased.

"This is our way. It teaches us not to fear battle," Drahir explained, reading Erroh's confusion at such perilous training regimes, and Erroh shook his head in bewilderment as he turned and strode away from the training grounds lest he see a fool be disembowelled in front of his eyes.

"Do you lose many to serious injury?" Erroh asked incredulously.

"A few," replied Drahir, snorting.

"It is mindless and foolish."

"It is our way, but you can change whatever does not please you."

"Perhaps I will."

More hours passed, and Erroh, succumbing to the pain in his shoulder and ankle, sought a place to rest. At a quiet order from his shadow for the day, word spread, and swiftly, a small group of men placed an unspectacular throne of barrels and cushions high above the camp on a valley slope and bade him sit and judge in silence their activities. Tired, and feeling a deep desire for a flavour he couldn't recognise, Erroh sat on the makeshift throne. Seeing him ensconced there, his army's generals immediately strode over to meet and speak with their leader. There were more than he'd imagined. A couple of dozen at least, and they stood around him, offering their thoughts in their basic tongue, and Erroh understood little. In return, they struggled with his own loose words and terrible pronunciation. Even with Drahir's translations, only a few understood what their god demanded. Thankfully, this was very little. Erroh had little loyalty to the group, and they? Well, they said they were his to command, but that may have been lost in translation. Those he recognised from their time as captives, or from the tribe he'd fought with, he instinctively engaged with, despite

The Actions of Gods

the creeping, suspicious feeling at the back of his mind that wouldn't quite disappear. The ever-present Drahir, playing the part of a loyal companion, unsettled him most.

Eventually, with darkness upon them, they brought him food, which was dreadful. Salted stew with awful lumps of charred meat and carrot. They offered a sliver of stale bread and, grimacing, he swallowed the awful mess and accepted no second helping. He did not eat alone. Around him, generals and labourers sat in the grass and ate merrily. He listened to their near-familiar words, picking up what he could, and it was the most enjoyable part of his day, despite the taste in his mouth.

Eventually, his healers attended to him upon his throne. They checked the stitching on his wounds and tested the strength in the carapace of dried mud holding his ankle in place. Though his mouth watered at their offer of more dream syrup, he ignored his desires and the spoonful placed before him. That was the least enjoyable part of his day.

His last night duty was to tend to Highwind in her recovery. Pleased to see her wounds cleaned, and she well fed and rested, he whispered in her ear a few times before touching his forehead to hers. She wanted to leave this place. He could tell it in the way she bit his shoulder. Leaving her to graze, he walked with Drahir back to his tent, where his guards granted him entrance.

"Why do you follow every step I take?" Erroh asked his companion.

"I wish to understand you better, brother," Drahir offered, then turned swiftly on his heels and stalked away.

"You are no brother of mine," countered Erroh in his tongue, but Drahir was already gone.

With exhaustion tugging at his every movement, he stripped off most of his garments, leaving them discarded on the ground. He heard the young, attractive female enter his tent only when she was standing in front of him.

"What the fuk?"

She smiled in reply, kneeling at his feet. At his waist. He didn't like that smile, not one little bit. That smile meant she was up to something. So did the kneeling. She said something in her native tongue, and it sounded like she wanted to do something with her tongue. She was beautiful and familiar. Something in the way she wore her long blonde hair, the unnatural sharpness to her features. She resembled Nomi just a little, which was far too much.

She gestured to the bed and suggested she was a gift, or he was a gift for her, or that bedding was a gift, and she smiled, and he was but a weak male, and they were alone, and nobody would know, and she would distract him from his worries, and she was removing her clothing, and it was almost too much.

"No, please, not tonight," he said suddenly, pulling away, staring at her and feeling lesser for it. She held herself proudly before asking him "Why?" in his tongue, and he explained, "One for life and Lea." She didn't understand, but he didn't care anymore, so he opened the buttons on his tent and gestured for her to leave. This she did in disappointed puzzlement, and after exchanging an equally puzzled gaze with his guards, Erroh returned to his privacy.

Using a long copper basin of cold water, he began half-heartedly scrubbing some grime from his battered body. It was something to do while despising his failures, lamenting for all he'd lost and praying silently to the absent gods that they would make the following day better than this one. Shivering and damp, he lay among the bedsheets and thought of his mate and their dreadful future before falling into a restless sleep.

———

On the third day, Erroh woke with a start. His bedsheets were damp from sweat; his head ached a little, his shoulder stung as though an insect had attacked it throughout the night, and his belly was sick from hunger, fatigue, or possible poisoning. More than that, his body shivered unusually, and his tongue desired a sweet taste he couldn't quite recognise. Gingerly, he rose and stretched his aching muscles, carefully twisting his immobilised ankle. There was more movement beneath the ankle mould, and the pain had lessened somewhat. He took it as a small victory and picked up his clothes from where he'd left them. Smelling the damp, marred material, he grimaced at their dreadful state. The day was too cold to scrub them and walk them dry, and without oils to cover the aroma, he would carry his scent loudly. Smelling them once more and discovering the scent had not improved in the moments past, he vowed to improve their appearance the following day. Certain he'd remember his vow come nightfall, he donned them swiftly and imagined his father shaking his head in disapproval. Hard to hunt in clothing that screamed warnings of a man-beast hiding in the long grass.

I am alone and lost and scared, and I sent you away.

As before, he emerged from his tent and met Drahir awaiting him. To be more precise, Drahir alone was waiting. Sitting with a little skillet over a small flame, cooking a few pieces of salted meat, he looked perfectly at ease with the early hour. Erroh welcomed the wonderful aroma after the stench of his tent, but when Drahir offered some of the food, Erroh shook his head despite his stomach growling.

"I would hardly poison you," Drahir muttered. He placed a few long strips onto a little plate for Erroh regardless before taking a few pieces for himself and sitting back in the dew-laden grass to enjoy his breakfast. It was just a little too tempting.

Fuk you, Drahir.

"What happened to my guards?" demanded Erroh, and his companion shrugged.

"You are among allies in this place. I sent them away. They looked… tired."

Erroh didn't like the tone in his voice. Not one little bit. The strips of meat still sizzled, and Erroh licked his lips—just one or two bites. Collapsing beside Drahir, Erroh bit, savoured and enjoyed, and his mistrust flittered away with every bite.

"See? Nothing to fear," insisted Drahir, chomping his pieces greedily.

"Thank you, Drahir."

"If I have poisoned you, it is a fine last meal."

As before, Erroh began his day walking down through the camp. There were still ominous dark clouds, but it was a clearer morning. He wondered whether the rain would hold off. Would the chill bother him all day? He could only hope not. He took in the camp with a more critical eye. While most of the Southerners were camped in a long line, ready to embark immediately, some were clustered tightly against the deep surrounding forest. It resembled the Rangers' camp he had grown up with. There was familiarity in it. Terrible sadness, too.

Unlike the Rangers' camp, though, it was clear how meagrely supplied this army was. The people were gaunt and desolate. He'd seen similar expressions among the wretches in the hovels outside the city. Humans had a knack for surviving on what scraps they could, and this army was the very picture of heartrending endeavour. They had taken what they could from every wandering Finger they liberated or slaughtered, but they were, in the end, a mishmash of nomads unsure of what they were. He remembered a few generals arguing over the construction of defences the previous evening; he'd had little to say to them then. Now, with a clearer mind, he saw that some Southerners kept their carts ready and supplied, while others along the outskirts had disassembled the large wagons and made an outer perimeter wall. They had completed a third of the barricade, but materials were sparse. That was the basis of the argument he remembered. With enough of them in agreement, though, they might sacrifice the rest of the carts to finish the job or even commit fully and tear down a few fuken trees on the outskirts while they were at it.

He wondered if he offered his thoughts on the matter, would that help or hinder? He thought this a self-sufficient, growing settlement. Why not keep it secure?

And to the fires with those who think elsewise.

He had no desire to treat them differently, but sometimes the masses didn't know better. Sometimes they needed a little telling what to do.

Is this how Uden lost his way?

Shuddering, he strolled among the people, trying to understand their ways a little more. He did not know why he cared or desired to display his lesser godliness, but he suspected it was for his ease of mind. He could be a leader. A fine leader. But not a god.

That's how all this madness began.

There was less fanfare this time as he padded among them. The Southerners did not bow as ardently as before, and he welcomed it. The words spoken by those compelled to approach were less ingratiating, too. They were pleased to see him, but there was less delirium than before. Perhaps it was the smell.

Hours passed with Drahir at his side, and strangely, as though learning the art of riding a mount again, he found that as the day went on, he understood their language a little more. He lost only every fourth or fifth word and, most of the time, he was able to engage where he could. More than that, he discovered his hand no longer fell upon the grip of his blade as often as before.

Trust—or foolishness?

As with any good afternoon, it turned to evening. Once more, he came upon the arenas of clashing blades. Again, many warriors were battling, but now he felt more confident. He watched their savagery for a while before taking two young warriors aside and watching them spar alone. As he did, the entire gathering fell still, and he shuddered again.

As both warriors danced around each other, no doubt unnerved by his scrutiny and the gathered crowd, Erroh found it easier to study their ruthless, yet flawed training. They were threatening in their movements to the untrained eye, charging in with menace and speed in all manoeuvres but the final strike. Then, seemingly unwilling to severely maim their opponent, they held back. It was, admittedly, a human touch to the violence, but it would be devastating to their cause.

"They need dampened blades," Erroh suggested, and the crowd listened.

"What is such a thing?" Drahir replied, speaking for the watching crowd.

"They need to practice killing without actually killing."

Drahir stared at Erroh as though he'd sprouted a second head and suggested they could bring down Uden with a few carefully chosen flowers in his afternoon tea.

"No, no, brother. This is our way. In battle, they will adapt. This is how Southerners train," Drahir countered.

"And you are all fiercely brave," Erroh said aloud to all who listened. His words of praise were well met. "However, battle should be instinctive, born from routine." He swung his own blade left and right several times, then closed his eyes. "If you hold back a thousand times, you might hold back a thousand and one upon the battlefield." With his eyes still closed, Erroh swung his blade at Drahir and, instead of a killing blow, struck the man in his arm. The crowd gasped at the unexpected attack and the show of mercy. Drahir's gasp was especially loud as he leapt away, clutching his arm where the flattened part of the blade had left a nasty sting. "Useless in the frenzy of war."

"What do you suggest?" Drahir asked, and Erroh had the perfect solution. With the help of Drahir to translate whatever words he missed, he had some of the trainees wrap their blades in thick cloth to numb the killing strikes. To others, he suggested they sheath their blades entirely and attack with the scabbard attached. The warriors did not take to the task warmly, but followed his orders regardless. With weapons hobbled they spread out across the area and went to false war with each other, and soon enough the dull thudding of safer violence filled the evening air.

"Killing blows!" demanded Drahir. Though not entirely trusting of Erroh's orders, they did their part and obeyed. Erroh watched the two young warriors closest to him, and though wary, they duly became more ferocious in their attacks. After a while, their stances changed altogether. They were freer in their movements, no longer concentrating on avoiding killing or being killed. They might still die on the battleground, but it would be a fairer fight.

Perhaps I'll suggest a second blade come the morning and double sessions for a year.

Content that he had brought something to their war effort, Erroh retreated from the battlefield, leaving the warriors to work on their skills. Fatigue was taking him once more. A long day. A better one, but long. He desired no more questions, no more silent, worshipping gazes of expectation. He wanted a little time to himself and his thoughts.

"What else can you teach us?" Drahir suddenly called after him, and Erroh spat in the dirt in annoyance.

I have little time to teach you much.

He had feared that, at some point, the people would turn to him with demands for salvation and genius, for that was what was expected of gods. Truthfully, though, what could he teach them in a short period that would bring them any benefit? He imagined some of his more impressive moves might be lost on warriors so inept. They were brave, but they were no Alphas. Although, of course, who knew what their potential might be when life was at stake? Why was it Alphalines alone who were allowed to master the blade? He suddenly thought of Jeroen, and thought those days had indeed been great.

"Have someone carve dozens of sparring blades," he told Drahir. "Have them compete with each other daily. They need to practice for hours on end. Until bruises and cuts cover them." It wasn't the finest advice, but it was advice.

"As you wish, brother."

"I'm no brother of yours," Erroh muttered, but Drahir merely shrugged.

A short time later, Erroh took his place on his throne and was grateful for the reprieve. Fatigue gripped his body, but the exhaustion was less than the day before. Who knew time away from the saddle would revive him? Strangely, the Southerners served him the same meal as before, stew that tasted a little too salty on his tongue. Still, his stomach growled, and this time he ate heartily. When they offered a second plate, he accepted.

Once more, with his meal finished, he sat, met with his generals, and listened to their thoughts. This time he recognised more words. Listening to their guttural tones reminded him of another time, not so long ago, when he had been in chains. He suggested they continue reinforcing their outer perimeter, and they met this with a split agreement. However, they fell in line immediately, rose, and went to work. A nauseous feeling stirred in Erroh's stomach as he watched them tear apart their carts. His heart hammered, and he felt a thin layer of sweat cover his body. Suddenly he wanted to flee this place, away from duty, war, death and leadership. Far from leadership. Instead, he scratched at his shoulder and tested his ankle a few times, appearing confident in his actions. As night drew in, a strange event occurred. A group of Southerners marched to the centre of the gathering and called for silence. Those watching, grateful for the break from monotony, looked on as the group gathered props and donned costumes.

"They have not practised long, but they intend to impress," Drahir said from behind the throne, and Erroh joined the crowd in clapping anticipation. Without a stage, it was far from a Keri performance, yet still, they stood before him, and Erroh thought it remarkable that in war and misery, there still bloomed creativity, albeit strange. A stranger performance, too, because it was about him.

With Drahir laughing and translating in his ear, he watched a group gather upon a wall of defiance as Southerners rushed and fell. The hero, a slightly taller version of himself, was fierce. He spat some wild fluid over a torch, causing flames to billow outward and giving the impression that Erroh blew fire into the gathering hordes and scorched them alive. Regardless, the crowd cheered. Erroh wished foolishly for a moment that he had that skill. Better than coughing in Uden's face.

After a reenactment of the tragic fall of Keri, though with no mention of a burning pyre, Erroh watched his younger self chained and frozen and taken in by a female resembling Nomi. The crowd cheered as he took her to bed in an exaggerated act of furrowing, and Erroh wasn't sure he remembered that incident.

Lines were forgotten and missed frequently, the actors stumbled and missed their cues, and although Erroh enjoyed the goings-on, he found his wariness growing despite the mirth. All he could do was clap along and laugh at the correct times as his double injured Uden by blowing fire in his face, then shouted some impressive line of defiance before leaping skywards towards freedom.

"I don't remember it happening that way."

"Nor I."

Then came the battle of the Open Plains. How Erroh singlehandedly tore his opponents all apart, bringing mocking from the crowd and a chorus of jeers between those who had fought that day and those who had never seen the god of 'Spirk' in full flow.

The liberation of the prisoners followed. Then the growth of the army. Then more frenzied furrowing between himself and Nomi. And then he met Uden upon the wall of the burning city, and the world slowed, and Erroh wanted to flee once more. After much fire had blown their former god's way, the young, taller Erroh had leapt skywards again and landed in the middle of another skirmish.

"I remember this one."

"As do I."

A pathetic, naked version of Drahir ran around the makeshift stage, and Drahir laughed loudly at this. Erroh met him in battle, and as Drahir fell, the crowd as one cheered, and despite himself Erroh stood and applauded with them, allowing his unease to slip away.

"I didn't put up such an impressive fight," Drahir said, laughing, and again, there was a familiarity to him. But he could not trust him. Not yet.

"Nor did I," Erroh said, rubbing his shoulder absently.

"Still, an enjoyable break from the monotony of misery," Drahir suggested, and Erroh faced him. He saw no malice in him and hardly imagined him being the same brute who had almost killed him a few days before.

"Why do you find yourself beside me these last few days?" he asked now. "I imagined an embittered, vanquished soul would earn little grace at my side."

"It is our way. Just because I knew defeat makes me no less of a leader. I am wiser for it. Once I pledged my allegiance, I recovered my place. A leader then. A leader still."

"Yet, I am the leader here," Erroh countered.

"Aye, you are."

The players, delighted with the reaction from Erroh and the crowd at large, bowed as one and then retired to their own gathering, one that none but the players were invited to. Erroh offered them a deep bow of respect for taking an ordinary evening and filling it with rambunctious deceit.

With the moon spitting shards down upon them, and upon the lands a thousand miles from this camp, he sat back upon his throne, allowing the healers to tend to his wounds. Satisfied with the clay shell's task, they gently shattered the cast leaving Erroh more movement than before. A little pain too admittedly, but nothing a few days ignoring couldn't take care of. Once again, he declined the dream syrup they offered, despite the want in the back of his mind and on the tip of his tongue.

When they had finished with him, he rose and walked towards his hut. His last stop was with Highwind. He brushed her down and reassured her that a charge was coming. In reply, she tried to kick him,

The Actions of Gods

but he knew she was merely offering her thoughts on this stillness. She was improving. Ready for a charge.

Drahir walked with him to his tent, and the two men shared a few words about the play, the state of the camp, the need to reinforce, the skill of swordplay and, last of all, the saltiness of their dinner. Erroh saw no guards at the entrance, and he hesitated.

"If you want these fools to trust you, you need to show your trust for them," Drahir said.

"How foolish would it be for me to trust any of you? Am I to rest unguarded? Who's stopping a bastard from creeping in and slitting my throat?"

"I'm the only brute here wanting that."

"So why not do it?"

With a flash of anger on his face, Drahir leapt upon him, gripping his neck and spinning him to the ground.

This is it.

This is the end.

Drahir held him for a breath beneath the shadow of his tent, where few would see. Erroh struggled, but the warrior was too heavy, too mighty. Too prepared. He pulled Erroh's sword from its sheath and stared at it in the moonlight.

Dying by my father's blade.

My blade.

The world slowed, and Erroh was powerless beneath his opponent's weight. How stupid to fall into this trap. A trap brought on by his own questions. Without warning, Drahir leapt free of his chest, and the crushing weight was gone as swiftly as it had appeared.

As Erroh coughed, Drahir reached down and, grasping his hand, pulled him to his feet. "I could have gutted you, dragged your body into your tent and slipped away into the night, and none could have tracked me through this forest. Truthfully, I could have killed you a thousand times before this moment, too. As, I'm sure, you could have killed me. Brother, I have no desire to best you. Not without facing you in a fair fight."

Erroh regarded him uncertainly.

Is this a clever ruse?

To kill me even harder?

"I'm not your—"

"Aye, brother," Drahir muttered. "Not my blood brother."

With that, he spun away, leaving Erroh shivering, confused, and somehow a little less terrified of betrayal.

Walking into his tent, he stripped his clothes free. His mind was elsewhere when he heard a sound and turned to see a pair of alluring women entering the tent. They had stripped their garments off before he had time to speak.

"What the fuk?" he stammered.

They were as attractive as the previous girl had been. But better than that, they were two. Their faces were richly painted and radiant with desire to please their king. Erroh stared at their nakedness longer than he meant to. He was but a hot-blooded Alpha male, was he not? With difficulty, he took a step backwards from the nearest raven-haired beauty. She was worthy of his godliness; they both were, if truth be told, for they were beautiful, they were radiant, they were welcoming, and he was a wretch. They whispered to him about essential, sensual things they intended to do, and it wasn't fair, and it was good to be the king.

He stepped farther away and deflected the first kiss before it landed on his lips. He held the girl at bay; she smiled dazzlingly, and the second one reached for his chest. Swiftly, he held their attack with slow words. He spoke their language, and as though his life depended on it, he spoke it well. Despite the cruelty of the absent gods, placing such temptation in his way, he battled them away with words of love and a mate. Of a girl called Lea and a pledge for her alone. Eventually, a little embarrassed, they recovered their garments and scurried out into the night.

Alone again, he embraced the cold water, relishing its calming effect. He scrubbed more thoroughly at his body with a bar of soap, before scouring his ruined clothes with a little brush and leaving them to dry in the fire's warmth. With exhaustion taking him, he lay down in the bedding and missed Lea for a time before falling into an uneasy sleep.

He slept well, and on the fourth day he woke feeling less weary than before. Stretching in the cool air, he washed himself a second time and found the water bracing and welcomed. Recovering his better-smelling clothing, he dressed and met Drahir outside by the fire. This time it was slices of lightly fried and salted potato, which he accepted gratefully.

The day was clear; the sky was blue with few clouds to mar the morning light, and it raised Erroh's mood ever so. His foot ached far less, and his stitching looked clean and adequate. To ward off the night's fatigue and the heavy breakfast, he stretched a few times, drew his blades free and swung them, practising a few techniques to warm himself up.

Drahir watched in silence, and Erroh imagined warriors falling at his feet with every strike, and mercifully, his foot held firm as he turned and lunged in the muddy grass.

"Save that for the sparring arenas," was all Drahir said, and it was a fine suggestion.

Summoning his will for his people, he walked among the warriors who'd lost their loyalty to him and felt more at ease than before. Only with the sun warming his face did he recognise community. Many of the larger groups held different coloured banners, and he wondered if each Finger had a different flag. The smarter manoeuvre would be for all to lower their banners, select a favourite and answer to that one alone, for that was how unity was born. But it was not his place to ask that of them now. Instead, he spent much of the day talking with each gathering in turn, asking for one warrior from every finger to represent their colours in training come dusk.

Drahir, ever beside him, queried this notion eventually, and Erroh shrugged as he led them to the arena.

"This is a dreary place. Nothing like a little competition to raise the mood, the desire and the skills." He recovered two seeping oak branches, carved thin to resemble sparring blades. There were a dozen sets so far, and Erroh inspected them. "A fine start," he said, spinning them despite their lack of balance.

He invited Drahir to enter an arena with him, and every soldier stopped their blunted efforts to watch this event. Swiftly the two men went to war, and it was awkward and unimpressive, for Drahir was unused to such weapons, and Erroh was still a shadow of the warrior he would be. Still, the crowd cheered as both warriors fought and scored blow after blow upon the other. Eventually, Drahir scored a clean three hits in a row, and Erroh yielded, much to the crowd's amazement.

"Well fought, friend," Erroh shouted, then turned to the onlookers. "Who will fight next?" he roared, conceding the arena to a bemused Drahir.

A few brave warriors reached for their blades, and Erroh invited the least impressive into the arena. "Which banner do you fight for?" Erroh asked, pointing to a blue and grey flag waving gently in the wind.

"Fir Erroh," he replied immediately.

"Aye, for Erroh and who?" he asked, pointing to another banner.

"Banner? Pride?" He looked at Drahir to correct his accent. To correct his meaning. Drahir didn't know what he meant, but the boy pointed to another banner.

"Fir Erroh and fir... um... Nediya."

"For Nediya!" Erroh roared, and there were boos. Quite a few boos. There were even a few from Drahir, but he saw one small gathering remain silent.

"Fir Nediya," the boy cried again, and Drahir thumped his blade against his chest in invitation.

They fought for a time, but the honour of Nediya was not spoken of again, for the youth was severely beaten. Still, the next in line screamed "Fir Erroh," but also "Fir Achar," and there was much mocking and jesting, and suddenly these skirmishes meant that little bit more.

"Fir Erroh, and fir Duse," was the cry for three more battles before Drahir finally met defeat, to much fanfare. Many clans cheered this unlikely victory, and for a moment, Erroh forgot the nightmare his life had become. It was enough. Sometimes moments such as these were all that mattered.

With the clatter of good-natured rivalries in his ear, Erroh retired from the arena with an impressed Drahir at his side.

He took the throne once more, knowing this would be his last night here. His heart ached for Lea, his companions, his duty. Hiding with this unimpressive army would do little for the world's fate. Nor for his own. He doubted word would have reached Raven Rock by now. Nevertheless, it was time to step back into the world.

He ate the evening's stew heartily and found it to his liking. He chewed and swallowed the stale bread and thought wonderfully of a prison break a lifetime ago. All the while, Drahir watched him. When he had finished his meal, Erroh declared to him and his generals, who discussed the new training routines, his intent to depart the following day. Only Drahir was pleased, and he reassured his comrades that this was no place for a god forming an army. Placated, they pledged to continue the fight, to resupply where they could, and to scout the lands to the best of their abilities. It wasn't much, but it was enough.

With the night growing late and a storm brewing, Erroh went to visit Highwind in her field, where, offering an apple, he pledged that battles and wrath were in their future soon. She did little for a time but stare coldly through him before suddenly attempting to knock him senseless with her snout, and he thought this a fine omen of her desire to war once more.

Drahir walked him to his tent once more and offered little more than a few pledges that the army would grow and train in his absence. It reassured Erroh.

Stripping off some of his clothes, he waited for any uninvited guests to enter. With only the sound of the wind blowing outside the tent flaps and no hint of footsteps, he relaxed, stripped fully naked, and began scrubbing his clothes again. With excited thoughts of Lea and his comrades to distract him, he didn't notice the attractive young man enter the tent and strip off his own clothes.

"Fir Erroh, and fir the South," he said smoothly, and Erroh leapt away in fright. Somehow, it was both easier and entirely harder to shun the attentions of such an imposing, virile warrior.

"What the fuk?"

It was a good question, one he'd asked many times these last few days without receiving a reply. The young man smirked and displayed his impressiveness, and Erroh looked at him longer than he probably should have before raising his hands in polite refusal.

"You fear the touch of a man? How Northern of you," his suitor mocked, and Erroh could only shrug.

"I am not ... built that way."

"You are built very well."

"Thank you very much."

The boy returned to his own tongue, suggesting the Southern way was more accepting of such persuasions. Erroh congratulated him and his people on their open-mindedness before telling the young man he had already made his love choice. And then he told him about his one for life and how much his heart burned for her, and the warrior smiled and declared he wished he had such a mate before bowing deeply, recovering his garments and strolling back out into the cool air in search of another lover for the night.

"May your search be fruitful," Erroh called before resuming scrubbing his garments until they were fully clean and he hung them to dry by the fire.

Trying not to think of how little the young warrior was affected by the cold air, Erroh dropped into bed, thought of Lea, and missed her for a time before blowing out the light and falling into a deep, peaceful sleep.

On the fifth day, Erroh left the camp.

20

GREAT ESCAPE

The shattered moon seemed to have taken a break from spitting its deadly shards into the distant lands. It remained hidden behind thick clouds, and thus the land was grim and dark and perfectly suitable for a good night's sleep—and for a daring assault with little chance of success.

Taking advantage of the thick shadows and knowing the signs to make haste, two figures slunk swiftly through the long grass, watching their step lest a careless stumble ruin their grand adventure. They had done little more than watch, seeking opportunity. Now, though, they had felt a sudden urgency to go to task. Around them, the night was alive with the rustling of the forest, and the hum of a settled army. The wind rushed past their ears, each gust shaking the canopy of leaves above their heads and disguising their steps as they neared the impregnable wall surrounding their fallen stronghold.

"Careful, idiot," Lexi murmured suddenly.

"Why did you stop?" Tye hissed.

"Whisper, don't shout… fuk's sake."

Lexi was just as loud as Tye, who shook his head in frustration. His unanswered question, as well as having to crouch at the foot of the wall, were both ample reasons for his irritation. They had discussed the terms of assault many times over; slowing and stopping and crouching had not been part of the plan. Both had agreed that a relentless pace of scaling and invading was the best way to begin this grand liberation. Get over the wall quick as spit. After that, they could take their sweet time creeping through Raven Rock in search of Wrek, Emir and perhaps Roja.

It was all the young legends could do during these ending times. It was that or continue hiding in the green, disappearing from this fight with nothing but their own sorry lives secure. There had been no discussion about it. Almost.

"I think I heard something above," Lexi whispered warily.

"Where?" exclaimed Tye, bending closer to her.

"Somewhere above. A light shuffling of feet. Or of wings."

"Like a bird startled?"

"Aye... perhaps," muttered Lexi.

"I hear nothing now."

"Nor I."

"..."

"..."

"Well... um..."

"..."

"Should we move?"

"Aye, maybe so. Probably just a bird."

They moved farther along the wall, all the while worrying how loud their steps were, fearing a keen listener or the watchful eye of a guard walking along the border. Beneath the shadow of a massive seeping oak, Lexi fell still again, and once more, unprepared, he bumped into her. This time his foot tangled in hers and he fell loudly into the thicket. The night erupted in cracking wood, rustling leaves and the thrashing of awkward youthful limbs.

"Shit," he cried, while somehow having the mindfulness to lie still lest some fiend glance their way seeking the source of the noise.

"For fuk's sake, Tye, will you be careful?"

"I landed in some thorns. It hurts." He waved his fingers at a spot where some thorns had broken his skin. A devastating injury, no doubt. "Fuk's sake, Lexi. Why do you keep stopping so suddenly?" It was a fair criticism, and she pointed to the wall above.

"Here is where we climb."

"That wasn't the plan."

"There's more cover beneath this tree than I thought. There are better ridges, too. The plan has changed."

"But we settled on the corner edge."

"The plan has changed."

"Of course it has."

He got to his feet and scrambled from the bush and briars, pulling thorns free, then slid low beneath the smooth wall. She pointed again to where he would climb, and at the ridges cut into the wall. Neither young Alphaline had spotted the easier footing earlier from their vantage point overlooking the town. Adapting to negatives and positives was the sign of swift thinking, albeit in a plan that would never work. Any young Alphalines destined for greatness needed to prepare for this sort of thing.

Lexi slid up beside him and hissed at him to be swift. And why wouldn't he be swift? They'd discussed this part meticulously, though practice might have helped. It was a small matter. Listening for movement above and hearing no flapping of birds or shuffling of feet, Lexi locked her fingers together. He stepped upon them and she launched him upwards, towards the top of the wall.

"Ow! Shit—fuk!" he yelped, informing her of his progress.

"Shut up, idiot," she snapped. This was going splendidly.

"Hang on... Nearly have it... almost... ow... fuken fingers... fuken wall."

With a colossal effort, he pulled himself up and stretched out along the top edge, gasping loudly. On any other night, to any watching guard, he might have stood out, but tonight, he was merely an indistinct outline against the heavy black. Below, Lexi stepped back a few paces and gauged her run-up. She needed little space—just a few steps and a leap. They'd argued for a time over this manoeuvre and decided that of the two of them, she was far more likely to reach the desired height unassisted. He had the strength to pull her up if necessary. Taking a last moment before committing fully, she listened and heard nothing but the rush of wind, the faint buzzing of insects and the faint murmur of the approaching army far off in the distance.

"Wait—hang on," Tye hissed.

"What is it?"

"Hush, little one."

"I'm a few seasons older than you!"

"I thought I heard something, but... um..." He paused, listening. "No, I think we are fine. Go for it."

"What did you hear?"

"Nothing. Go for it."

"Was it flapping wings?"

"Just go for it, would you?"

She went for it, sprinting as fiercely as she could towards impenetrable rock, then leaping high like a hawk catching a breeze. Or an excited frog. A pulse later, she was a young deity in flight. Her left foot, chosen for its assuredness, struck the top of the wall, slid, kicked off again, and drove her farther into the sky like a bat racing dawn. Her companion reached for her but never came close. And then failure. The absent gods might have winced had they seen her face connect with stone before she slid to the foot of the wall with a painful crash.

"You missed," he whispered. It was a fine observation.

"Fuk you."

"That's it. Up you get. Let's go again."

"Shut up, idiot."

"Perhaps take a few more steps back. Also, I think your face is bleeding."

"I'm aware. This time, reach for me."

"I did."

She went for it again. A goddess upon a flying mount. Racing wildly towards a wall of brick and stubbornness. Soaring high like an eagle with the wind at its back....or just a wretched cricket losing its way. She flew and careened painfully against the wall to the ground below.

"Oh, that looked like it hurt. So close," he said as she peeled herself off the ground.

"Shut up."

"Everything is all right. No one can hear us. There's not a soul in the streets below. If you came up, you could see it."

"Can you reach lower for me?"

"You are too heavy. You'll pull me off the ledge."

"Just fuken try. Ugh. One more time."

"You know, we should have stuck to the plan." He readied himself once more. "All right. You can do this. I believe in you. So do the absent gods."

They didn't.

She went for it. A divine being soaring higher than any mortal. Charging fiercely towards an imposing town wall pierced only twice before in eternity. Flying like a swallow from its nest. Or a young drunken Alpha's bottle as it took flight.

"I have you. Almost."

"Pull me up."

"I'm trying, Alexis."

"I cannot get a grip."

"You are so heavy."

"You are so weak."

Either she was lighter than he thought, or he was more potent than she claimed. Regardless, he pulled her up, and she scrabbled for a hold and then turned and sat on the edge with him, looking down into hostile territory. Both Alphalines had the sense to stop for a moment, calm their nervous chatter and settle upon their chosen route towards rescue. This time, Lexi went first. Dropping near silently to the ground below, it was her turn to trip on an unknown obstacle as she rolled away from the following Tye.

"What the fuk?" she exclaimed. The obstacle was a body, lying face down on the dusty ground.

"It's a body," he pointed out helpfully, leaning over it.

"Is he dead?"

Tye poked the corpse gingerly. "He's not conscious. Did you crush him with those thunderous thighs of yours?" It was a jest. He knew her thighs were perfectly shaped and slender, but he also knew the cutting power of such words.

"Something doesn't feel right," she said, ignoring him.

"Of course not. We shouldn't be here. While we are, we should check him for breath." He reached down again.

"Or else we should leave him."

"Aye, probably that."

"We have the luck of the absent gods tonight."

"Aye, it appears so."

They didn't.

Both young Alphalines slunk farther into the darkness, away from the fallen Southerner and the wall below which he had been felled. As they moved, they had better sense than to speak. Each step they took upon the grey stone was careful. Only a keen listener might have heard them as they glided through the streets towards their quarry.

All was well until, near the centre, where Wrek lay unmoving, they came upon two idle guards sitting upon barrels watching the embers of a glowing fire die away in the night. Tye and Lexi exchanged a glance. Their hands would not remain clean tonight. They'd discussed such an eventuality, and he gestured with a hand, and she shook her head. So he gestured with his other hand, and she agreed. They crept up on the oblivious guards from behind, silently drawing their blades. She waved her fingers for three, two and on one, they both leapt towards the left guard. Only reflexes saved their lives—or Tye's, to be exact. Realising his error, he sidestepped her and pounced on the right-hand guard. Lexi plunged her blade deep into the first man's back, taking his breath, holding his scream with a shaking, cupped hand. Tye's strike was a little less smooth. Diving upon the sitting brute, he dug the blade deep into the man's throat. The guard fought his last fight and fought it well, and Tye drove his face into the ground and plunged the blade into him a second and a third time before the man fell still and died in Tye's arms.

"What the fuk were you doing?" she hissed.

"I was going for the left. Like I said."

"*This* is the gesture for the left!" she snapped, gesturing left.

"You didn't do that."

"Yes, I did. You weren't paying attention."

"Well, it's a small matter now."

"Aye, they are dead."

"Aye. Dead."

"Check their pockets."

"Oh—that might help."

Lexi bent and rifled the dead man's clothing. Discovering a treasure of a little bronze key, she pocketed it and straightened once more. They stood side by side, gazing at their deeds and perhaps offering a silent prayer for the souls fallen before creeping through the darkness towards Wrek.

So far, so good.

Before slipping out into the open space, where any passing Southerner might see them, they stood in the shadows and rested momentarily. Without words, they strained their eyes against the inky darkness around them, watching for signs of the skulking enemy. A few moments later, the sound of a group of soldiers marching through the gate crushed their hopes.

"They're heading towards the fire. Fuk. We should have hidden the bodies," Tye growled.

"Hard to hide the blood with the mess you made of him," she whispered, panic rising in her voice.

"That wasn't my fault."

"Of course it wasn't."

"Well, what should we do?"

"We could run."

"Aye, we could, and leave our comrades behind."

"We could fight them?" It was a good suggestion.

"There are only... a few..." In fact, there were more than a few—more than they could handle.

"If we do it smoothly, maybe no one will come running."

"And if they do, we'll kill them all."

Choices made, they watched the brutes wandering back towards the fire, where their dead comrades awaited them with silent warnings of invasion. They drew their blades in preparedness, and each of them gestured—correctly this time—towards the group they chose to attack. Knowing this would be their doom, they stood out from the darkness. And from nowhere, there came a dreadful thunder of noise. Suddenly, the town erupted in movement as a dozen mounts charged from their place of holding towards the group of men.

"Shit—what the fuk?" Tye cried as the horses galloped frantically in amongst the new arrivals.

"Our old fuken mounts got loose!" Lexi said, her face suddenly alight with excitement.

"What the fuk will we do?"

"Fuken move, Tye! Go, get to Wrek."

"That wasn't the fuken plan!"

"Fuk the plan. We have the absent gods protecting us."

"Shit, fine. Fuk, fuk, fukety fuk. Let's fuken do it."

Throwing caution to the wind, they sprinted towards the bleary Wrek, who looked around in puzzlement, having been wakened by the commotion. Unprepared for such an unexpected twist of fate, he blinked stupidly as they pulled the battered warrior to unsteady feet, then offered a thankful prayer to their invisible collaborators. Lexi pulled the little bronze key from her pocket, shoved it into the lock and snapped his bindings open.

"Are you okay, Wrek?" she cried, taking his hands in hers and leading him away from the post.

He nodded, rubbing his wrists.

"You take him; I'll seek the others out," Tye said, sprinting towards the building where Emir had brought Roja the day before. Lexi had watched them carry Roja in, and she had not emerged again.

"Not alone, idiot," she cried, setting off after him with Wrek in tow. She kept up with Tye for a few breaths, but Wrek stumbled and collapsed, taking her with him. "It's all right, big man," she told him. "Let's get you out of here." She helped him back to his feet, and, to his credit, despite the bruising, looked lively and alert. "Can you make it over the wall?" she asked, leading him towards the nearest ladder. It wasn't part of the plan, but fuk the plan. Let Tye's good fortune carry him the last few steps and bear greater reward.

. . .

I have this, he thought, running towards the dark building and seeing the light within. A smarter move would be peering through the keyhole, but there was little time before the mounts were chased down and their victims' bodies discovered. He did not hesitate; he kicked the door open to find a vile, betraying killer waiting for him on the other side.

"Not you," he cried, and he was a young cub again, smitten with a beautiful damsel who wasn't a damsel but instead the killer of his comrades and ten times the swordsman he was. It didn't matter, though, because her crimes needed to be answered for. If he killed her, then perhaps it would do just a little to right the balance of good and evil in this awful world.

For Stefan.

He swung his sword impressively, and she caught it with her own blade, holding him easily like any master would an inept student. Perhaps this was precisely what she was doing. Her eyes were beautiful, dazzling, and alive with the fire of murder and victory, and he knew he could not beat her. He would die at her hands.

21

THE PUB

It became routine to be startled from slumber by thundering mounts charging down the pathways beyond their all-concealing green. It became customary to relinquish a killing strike on an unsuspecting quail as they ducked for cover at the sound of passing platoons. It became routine to huddle against rock as rolling carts and wandering Fingers drew nearer to the city, never knowing the precious treasure of a god's lost daughter lay just a few feet away. It became routine for Lea to stare blankly at the flickering flames of their small campfire, all the while thinking of a horror with green eyes. It also became routine for Nomi to ask her to release the burden of the demons that haunted her. And something about those flickering flames made Lea desire, over and over again, to reveal the truth of her legacy, which threatened to drag her into the depths of eternal misery.

"Tell me what ails you, Lea. Is it Erroh? Is it all we have lost at Raven Rock?" Nomi would ask as she sat beside her, studying her comrade as though she were a book of intriguing enigmas, only a handful of clues away from being revealed.

"I have lost everything I believed in, Nomi," Lea would answer, and say little more. At this, Nomi would nod in reluctant silence and stare into the fire. For this, Lea was grateful, for she desired to trust her, to reveal everything. To confess her horrors and seek redemption from a female who had no reason to offer these precious gifts. So Lea stared and saw green eyes and horror in silence, never knowing how close she was to releasing the horror to the world. To Nomi too.

They stayed another two days in this unsettling sanctuary before

Nomi finally agreed that returning to the march was the finer move. Grateful for a release from the monotony, Lea gladly packed what few belongings she still had and, after one last test of weight upon her injured ankle, summoned the warrior within and sought further for a plan.

She scraped her name upon the eternal rock, as far from Erroh's etchings as possible, and offered a delicate kiss to the enormous thing in honour of its shielding gift. Nomi took the dagger from her and carved her own name into the grey stone. While Lea's birth name was scribed in delicate strokes, Nomi attacked the boulder as though it owed her a pouch of pieces and refused to pay. Eventually, as pleased with her handiwork as those before her had been with their own, Nomi stood back, admiring the letters upon the surface, before grabbing her pack and following Lea through the treeline.

Having abandoned any thoughts of returning to Spark City, they marched along the path leading farther south. It wasn't much of a plan, but considering nearly every Southern cur who rode these last few days had been headed north, towards Samara, it took no tactical genius to choose the opposite direction and march until better fortune found them.

Using the path as their guide but keeping hidden beneath the evergreens a few feet in from the treeline, they made good time indeed. Lea's ankle took all she could throw, and it remained assured. They spoke little in the first few hours, their ears pricked, listening for any menacing sounds either before or behind them. Twice they faced Southern fiends. The first encounter began with humming in the ground somewhere ahead, at which they swiftly leapt farther into the green before the first Rider appeared. Concealing themselves behind dark tree trunks, they watched a couple of dozen Southern Riders pass them without notice. Within a few breaths, they had passed by, and the nomadic females continued their journey towards nowhere in particular.

The same low, familiar rumble heralded the second Southern encounter, and this time they hurried farther into the green, for it soon became apparent that this was a different threat entirely. The roar suggested a giant Finger, and they were correct. It was one thing to remain stuck and recover in a concealed bastion behind a rock where a fool could become used to the terrifying noise of many bad things, but it was different out on the road. Nomi dug in beside Lea as they hid behind a clump of ferns, deep in the darkened woods, and waited. This Finger was enormous, and, unlike the band of Riders before it, disinclined to rush itself. For a few moments, Lea was back in the South, frozen and terrified as the enemy neared, but never seeing her. She forced the thoughts away. She could never follow Erroh like that. Would not shiver for months on end waiting, either.

Nomi counted absently under her breath as they passed. After a few hundred souls she fell silent, no doubt feeling as disheartened as Lea.

The children brandish weapons too.

In times of war, all must fight. Both women knew this. In disgust, Lea sat in silence and reviled her father, her legacy, her entire life. She felt a terrible stirring of anguish and bit back a shriek of desperation with all her will. Now was not the time. The battlefield would be a finer place for that, with her father in her sights. It was these cold thoughts that settled her.

Like any good army making terrible time, the Finger eventually passed and the rumble faded into the distance, yet neither girl moved until the forest returned to its usual silence, overlaid with the reassuring hiss of insects. First peering up the path to ensure no sly hunting party followed, Lea and Nomi continued through the woods, searching for inspiration or signs of resistance still fighting against this indomitable threat.

A few hours before dusk, they came upon a crossroads and made a choice. Veering ever so slightly west, they found themselves on a route that was not as well defined but had fewer signs of marching threats. Reassured that few others had taken this path, they relaxed as the sun set around them. Basking in the silence and stillness for a time, Lea had the strange sensation that she was out in the wilds again, in the days before the world had ended. Before he had betrayed her.

The peacefulness and the easy walking were so pleasant that, instead of setting a camp early, they decided to march a few more miles. To their surprise, they rounded a bend in the path and came upon a very unusual building: a pub, which of course had no business being in the middle of the Wastes. It was as ancient as the walls of Spark City itself, yet nowhere near as pristine and tended to.

"What's a Rast?" Nomi asked as they stepped tentatively into the courtyard, and though the evening was warm, Lea felt a chill run down her back.

"It says 'Rat's Nest,'" Lea corrected her, wiping the grime from the painted sign.

They drew their weapons, though they knew the unlikeliness of a fiend concealing themselves behind the cracked windows, the layers of ivy and thick, dusty spiders' webs. This was a forgotten tavern, lost now to the endless Wastes. Weeds grew from its roof and along the walkway to the door, suggesting abandonment a long time before. Lea drew an arrow and allowed Nomi to lead with her club held out. Moving slowly and carefully, they silently scoured the outer courtyard in search of threat, regardless. Then, heaving her shoulder against the door, Nomi broke through it easily, and they glided into the interior of the tavern. With only the light from the doorway guiding their way, they crept about and found little but web-covered emptiness and a few scurrying rats.

Wonderful.

They found some wood and lit a fire in the hearth, then a few candles after that, and soon found themselves in a fine cosy room altogether. After so long fighting the season's chill, finding themselves in a snug, warm building without drafts was welcomed. More than that, Nomi broke through one more door in the courtyard to discover countless bottles of alcohol shimmering in the moonlight.

What could go wrong?

———

Sitting in front of the flames, Nomi sipped her glass of sine while Lea drained hers. Together, they looked over a collection of hand-drawn maps they'd found.

"They are all the same," Nomi whispered, and Lea ran her fingers across the scribblings. It wasn't unusual for taverns to scribe their maps for the area and sell them to desperate wanderers seeking a path. Whoever had created this piece had made quite the decent bartering off copies of it, she imagined, despite the familiar errors. She knew the maps. She also knew this place, for she remembered her mate's tales fondly. Mostly. Seeing the abandoned card table, she wondered if this was the last tavern Erroh had visited. For the second time now, she wondered if the absent gods were sending her a message.

A reminder?

A warning of things to come?

A goodbye?

Fuk Erroh, and fuk the absent gods, too.

Carelessly, Lea crumpled the parchment and threw it into the fireplace. Watching the flames take hold, brightening the room with her symbolic act, she immediately regretted her decision. Such maps gave travellers a slight advantage. They were flawed, but largely accurate. Stuffing the remaining maps into her pack, she poured another glass of sine and downed it immediately. The burn took her mood and softened her bite.

"Nice, after such a time outside," Nomi muttered, rooting in her bag.

"Aye, wonderful with a drink, too," Lea offered, watching the flame, thinking of a house burning, thinking of green, murderous eyes and trying desperately to remember bitter, awful things lost in years of regret and horror.

I want to remember so I can hate you more.

Still, the harder she tried, the further her memories flitted from her grasp.

"You stare at the fire again. Tell me of your brother?" Nomi asked. She held out a stick of dried, salted meat, which Lea declined. Tonight was no night for denying drunkenness. Tonight she would drink on an empty stomach and be glad of it.

"Tell me of the South," Lea countered, refilling her goblet and offering a top-up to her companion. She wondered if Nomi would be up for a game of cards later. Chips and cards were still lying where they had been left upon a card table. It was something to do instead of talking.

"I had a sister, beautiful like me. Older, smarter, better," Nomi said sadly, and Lea listened, for that is what drunken sisters did when hearing of another's torment. She spoke quietly of her youth, of her roving Finger, and her faded beliefs, and witnessing the consequences of family asking too many questions. She spoke of disappearances and lonely, silent tears; she told of concealing her grief should fiends come visiting a second time. Lea listened with a heavy heart, offering a caring hand when the silent tears returned. This time, however, Lea drew those dreadful tears out, for terrible memories like these needed to be purged, brought out into the open.

When Nomi could talk no more, and Lea could barely see anything beyond the fireplace, they embraced and wept together. Silence hung between the two women for a few moments, and Lea poured them each another drink, finishing the bottle with a top-up of her sister's goblet.

"My head is spinning," Nomi slurred, and Lea knew the horrifying hangover both would face come dawn, but somehow, it didn't matter. What mattered was finding another bottle and bringing her own sins alive.

"My true name was once Cordelia," she began. "Only Drahir called me Lea… So now, I am Lea."

Nomi nodded in understanding; her eyes were glazed, but she was determined to understand and assist. "Both are good names."

Lea took a deep breath and paused for a moment before speaking again. No time like the present.

"My father is Uden, the Woodin Man."

Lea climbed from her bedding and stumbled through the Rat's Nest tavern, gazing at the ruin she and Nomi had left it in the night before. She tried to remember her actions, but could only remember the screaming, hers and Nomi's. Her stomach turned as she spied the slivers of half-eaten dried meats strewn on the floor with the debris—so much glass and splintered wood. Visions of thrown chairs filled her mind, and she tried desperately to recall her actions. Her belly gave an ominous lurch, and she clutched her stomach as it fought her will. Stumbling through the doorway into a dreadfully bright morning, Lea made it three steps before throwing up. She didn't know why she tried to stop herself, but she did, making the moment far worse. A warm, sickly bile of chunks of carrot and ground-up bird meat spilled through her fingers and down her blouse, and the stench was vile.

"I am a ruin," she cried aloud, spitting grains of awfulness from her mouth. Strangely, even though her head thumped painfully, she felt lighter. The thought of the mayhem she and Nomi had created after her revelation suddenly made her smile. Who knew a few violent, crashing outbursts could ease a dour mood?

She began to walk now. Beyond the stables, where she sought a water source to wash away her unpleasantness, she discovered a dead body decayed to time and the elements. She knelt by the fallen man and wondered what sort of life he had led. What kind of person he had been. "Death must be good if your skull is grinning," she whispered, and considered burying him once her body felt a little settled. Maybe Nomi would help once she rose.

Any fool with knowledge of plantations and settlements might have known there almost always lay a water source nearby, and Lea was more than any fool. Wiping some drying bile from her lips, she wandered into the Wastes listening for a stream or a brook. It was an excellent way to distract herself from the worst hangover she'd ever had. In the shade beneath the forest canopy, all was quiet despite the warm day, and Lea was grateful for the calm. Listening to the satisfying crack of twigs underfoot, she wandered deeper in, concentrating solely on listening for the whisper of water, and soon enough, she found it. It was no elegant, rushing river or calm, depthless lake, but it was a satisfying little stream, perfect for washing the night before from her face, hair and clothes.

Listening to the glistening swish of the beautiful wet elixir, she knelt at its edge and dipped her face in the water. So absorbed was she that she did not hear her hunter steal up behind her. Suddenly, powerful hands gripped her neck and plunged her head fully beneath the surface.

———

Nomi stretched in the bedding and squirmed in her comfort. She could feel the hangover, but trusted the water she'd forced down her throat the bleary night before would work its magic. She'd tried to force some water down Lea, but the stubborn goddess had favoured clear sine instead. Her mild headache was little compared to the aching thunder her comrade was probably experiencing. Distantly, she heard footsteps in the courtyard and wondered how on arth Lea was up and rearing to go this awful dawn.

Stretching a second time, then rising and slipping into her clothing, she fought the growing hunger in her belly and fantasised about a warm meal for breakfast. Having a few eggs to gorge herself on would be marvellous.

Stepping from her bedroom into the main tavern, she grinned at the devastation they'd created. Any passing Southerners would have been very amused, or more likely fearful, at seeing them venting their aggression upon the unfortunate room. She wasn't sure who'd thrown the first empty bottle at the wall in frustration, but she had undoubtedly been the first to throw a full bottle through the far window before joining Lea in her screeching wails of delight, relief and regret. Of hatred, too.

The tables and chairs had been next, and with each act of destruction, the two of them screamed away that which burdened them. Only pure inebriation drew them to their beds at the late hour; indeed, the night had been decades in the making. She thought again on Lea's words and, as before, felt nothing but sadness for the awful life Lea had endured. And would still endure, cursed as she was with such a fate. She strode through the open door and, careful to avoid the little pool of vomit in her path, walked immediately into the dozen Southerners' trap.

They raised their crossbows and swords and encircled her silently, and Nomi fell to her knees in terror and in panic.

"I am Southern," she cried as they circled her. All looked ready to burn her at a pyre. "I am your kin," she lied, fearing their darkest intentions and knowing her fate. They hesitated momentarily, and she faced them each in turn as they surrounded her, lowering their blades, peering at her attire and enjoying her better features.

Play the Southern part.

"What are you doing here?" one asked. He was tall and gruff—usually her type of bed mate.

"Who are you?" another one asked, younger, without a full beard but possessing a strong jaw.

"Where is your Finger?" a third asked. He was heavyset and older, but a sparkle was in his eye.

All fair questions, and she nodded in panic. "They captured me," she offered, and it was a half-truth. "I've been trying to find my comrades," she added, feigning excitement, and that pleased them.

This is how it ends.
Not like this.
Oh, fuk me, please, not like this.

The water that had just moments ago resurrected her with its cool goodness now threatened to take her life. She struggled against her attacker's hold and felt the arms tighten around her neck, squeezing her as his elbows dug into her body. The brute was heavy and crushing, and she kicked out, screaming in terror and anger, which made it so much worse. Water flooded into her lungs, killing her, and this was the unimpressive end of Lea the unfortunate.

Fight.
Fuken fight.

She tried. She tried, but her killer had the advantage, the brutality. He dug in and forced her deeper into the stream as she pulled at his deathly grip. The water was a foot in depth now. Her head and shoulders were fully submerged, while her rear was as dry as a bone.

Please, no.
Mercy.
Mercy.

She tried to see, but the stream was a blurry brown rush in her stinging eyes. She felt a rock, embedded deeply in the mud, rub hard against her skin like an imperfect helmet, and it cut deep into her forehead, and she knew she bled. And oh, the crushing pain in her screaming lungs was maddening.

I cannot beat him.
He decides if I pass.

He pressed harder on her now. Strangling and drowning, she felt panic grip her more tightly than his physical hold, and she knew she was powerless in his brutish grip. She thought of Erroh and of drowning, and her anger was depthless. It wasn't fair. None of it was. To be undone by a vile fuk without conscience, without honour.

Not like this.
Please, not like this.
I am Alpha.

As though it were whispered to her by an absent god, Lea suddenly formed a plan, a simple plan.

She eased her struggle as the end came for her. She stopped battering at the iron grip of her assailant and, awaiting the dark as it stepped ever close, fought against reflex and fell deathly still. Still, he held her tight, and the pain was agonising. She felt the darkness descend upon her; it was cold, awful and silent.

She allowed her arms to fall away from his hold. Felt them splash alongside her limp body, and she allowed them to drift aimlessly beside her. She let her body be pushed farther into the stream by her stronger killer, and somehow, she resisted the urge to raise her head and swim. It was the worst moment of her life. Worse than Erroh drowning her before. Worse than seeing Uden. Worse than witnessing the fire. She held her body in a deathly pose, and she prayed to the absent gods, to nothing at all, to anything that listened, to deliver her this last bet.

I am dead.
Feel my dead body.

She allowed her bladder to release and felt little shame for the act, and still, he held her, but now his grip was lessened for a strangled breath. She fought the urge to rear up and take him off guard, knowing it would be folly.

Just a moment more is all.

Panic left her in favour of control. Even as he suddenly plunged her violently against the stream's bed, she did not react, but she vowed to remember the act. She pledged he would suffer for it.

I can do this.
I am Lea of the Road.
I am Alpha.

Suddenly, he released her and shoved her once, and still, she did not react, for she was sly little Cordelia, the fox. Instead, she held that fuken agony for a moment more and remained still as a corpse.

And then her victim was away. His weight was no longer upon her. And then she moved. With a mighty heave, she plunged herself fully into the water, pulled her feet under her, and on powerful legs rose above the surface, the embedded rock in her hand. She spun on him and struck him once across the face. Not enough to kill, not enough to daze, but enough to buy her a moment to struggle away from his clumsy grasp.

And she took that breath now, and her lungs sang in joy even as she hacked what water she could from her heaving chest.

Without breath, she remained controlled. "My turn," she yelled. And if he didn't understand? Well, soon, he would understand.

He charged in after her, and she did not hesitate. Leaning into him, she drove her foot into his groin. His scream was piercing, impressive. He could have been a singer, but she'd never have the pleasure of finding out. He gasped as he fell to his knees, and she struck him again with the rock, and his face exploded in a spray of crimson. He collapsed backward into the stream, and she fell upon him now, striking him over and over with brutal efficiency, and it was all too easy. Sitting on his chest, she punished him for his cowardly act, for no man, woman or child deserved what he had tried to do to her. She didn't know how long she battered him, but long after he fell still, she continued to drive the rock against his face, through skin, into bone and beyond. He might have relieved himself on her too. It was a small matter. Finally, gasping, she fell away from her kill. Only then did she see the Southern garb he was dressed in, and a great fury took her. Fury she hadn't felt in so long. Fury that might carry her a few steps more towards war. Towards finding her father. Towards taking his fuken head off.

She liked this anger. It was a gift.

22

DAY IN THE LIFE

"Shit. Fuk me. Fuk this. Fuken stupid…" Fine words, with just the proper urgency and fright to emphasise the panic. Around him, the wind rushed wildly and the trees passed in a blur. It was a rush, and he was terrified. Glancing frantically behind him, he searched for movement. He prayed for none. "Fuk you, Erroh… idiot." More fine words. Appropriate, too.

I am an idiot.

Rain was coming; he could tell by the dreary darkness of the morning sky. In the air's taste. He had felt it before leaving the Southern camp. Now, with every mile that passed, the clouds grew more ominous.

Too late to turn back, either way.

He thought it an awful thing to ride in the rain, a more challenging thing escaping a few dozen Riders in the deluge, too. A bitterly cold raindrop struck his cheek, and he knew it was merely a scout for the downpour to follow. So far, Erroh was having a rightly shitty day altogether.

Admittedly, departing the camp of his Southern comrades had been an excellent start to the day. Having suffered no assassination attempts while he had been their guest was a fine thing, but knowing that they awaited his return was reassuring, for he would need every soul available to pull together a fighting force for an attack on the city. They had pledged to continue their training and their "recruiting." Indeed, their numbers had risen from fifty to hundreds within a few months. It seemed to work, so who was he to stand in their way?

'God of Spirk'?

He might have laughed at his own wit, but the rumbling of hooves behind him drew him from his thoughts. "I have this," he growled through clenched teeth, knowing the lie for what it was. He didn't have it at all. Had he not brought this unimpressive pursuit upon himself? He could've read the path better. Could have listened to the wind more closely. He really should have seen the signs long before he stumbled upon the encamped Riders lazing by the river, probably after a long night burning women. For a frozen moment, it seemed ridiculous. Both parties stood stunned for a while, regarding one another in astonishment. In hindsight, Erroh thought ruefully, he probably shouldn't have raised his hand and said hello. That's when it all went wrong. That's when they had stirred to movement and pursuit.

Truthfully, it was Highwind who had this. Or so he hoped. If she didn't, this was the end.

"Faster, girl," he cried, and a few further raindrops fell upon his sweat-covered head. This race had only begun, yet his heart was a turmoil of wild beating, and adrenalin burned through his quaking body, demanding he either turn and fight or drop clear of his horse and sprint for himself. Adrenalin was no trusty advisor in some matters.

Highwind was warming up to the race. He could feel the power in her body as she thundered through the deep undergrowth, ever competent upon the uneven ground, gaining her stride with every length. He was panicked, but she was having a wonderful time of it. Having had only a gentle canter in the few hours since their departure, she'd gladly accepted his urging.

He could see them again—terrifying brutes upon monstrous mounts built for the cold and for heavy labour. Highwind, by contrast, was built to glide through the waste.

"That's it, my girl," he cried, kicking her ever so gently, easing her dash into a breakneck race as they left everything behind them. This was no terrified charge through a burning city with swords and arrows firing, though. This was a blessed release after many days chained.

Run like there's a dying girl's fate at stake.

She might have heard him, or might have sensed his terror. Whatever it was, she galloped harder. The world slowed but for their ride, and suddenly, he knew something had fated him to live another day. She thundered through the forest with no path to guide her way, with only his reflexes saving her from end after awful end as he steered her wide of tree trunks, boulders and sudden dips in the land.

Onwards she carried him, and soon they were away from the Hunt.

Farther back, out of sight, their pursuers halted or stopped, for behind him Erroh heard nothing but silence. The rain held off a little longer, and his beast of burden had once again saved foolish Erroh.

"I think we are clear," Erroh said after a time, easing Highwind to a slower trot. A short time later they came upon a shallow river, where he slid off her back and stepped into the freezing water. He led her far, following the current. To her stubborn credit, the horse walked on, likely grateful for a reprieve after the sudden sprint following the days of doing little more than eating and recovering. She carefully stepped after him over the mossy, slippery stones until they climbed ashore and stood listening to the world and its silence.

"We did it," he whispered in her ear as he clambered up the bank, and she snorted in reply as though she knew her value these last few panicked miles. "Fine—*you* did most of it."

After they had drunk their fill of the cool water, Erroh climbed back into his saddle. For a little while more, they raced through the forest, seeking to put further distance between themselves and their pursuers lest they be more stubborn than Erroh expected.

There came no following threat as it was, and only the absent gods knew their fate, bloody as it was.

Eventually, with many more miles covered and the sun setting, Erroh made a fine camp for himself deep within the endless green. Ensuring no further injuries had been accrued and no current ones reopened, Erroh left Highwind to graze for the night in a rich dell of long grass.

For himself, he set his bedding beneath an ancient seeping oak, suitable for concealment and protection from the cutting winds. He built himself a little fire, surrounded by the most prominent rocks he could find, and tended to duties he'd done happily a thousand times before.

He only lost a dozen arrows in the growing darkness while hunting, but he earned a kill. It was no fine boar or rich quail, but it would do. He stripped the feathers from a felled pigeon and tried not to think of the sinewy meal it would make. For a while, he watched the oily meat sizzle and burn upon the spit, and the smell was familiar and filled him with such nausea he almost kicked the offending piece into the Wastes forever. He eyed the stale loaf of hard bread he'd taken in case of such a turn of events, but instead, he finished charring the meat, then ripped off a few tasteless chunks to settle his grumbling stomach.

"Needs salt," he muttered to nobody in particular as he went to task. He did not throw it up, but he did suffer a few precarious moments as he forced the meal down. With the bird at last stripped bare and eaten, he took a few bites from the bread and was grateful to remove the awful flavour from his mouth, replacing it with a less disgusting taste. Sitting back, he longed for a glass of sine to help the meal go down, followed by a few solitary card games to ease the monotony of his thoughts as the night drew in. As he dug in his bags, seeking out his deck of cards, he found a curious thing he'd nearly forgotten about: a blade of gold, its shine hidden beneath a layer of concealing paint. He thought of Stefan in flight and chuckled for a time. At some point, Erroh had half-heartedly attempted to scrape the paint from the bright metal. He vowed to tend to the job and complete the piece. If nothing else, it would be a fine decoration for his mantelpiece in whatever home he took for his own. Taking a few moments for himself, he imagined wrapping the piece where the blade shattered and making a grip for a rather shabby, expensive and ineffectual dagger. He scraped gently at it with a rock and eased a little paint free. It was something to do while avoiding a far better use of his time. He didn't last long tending to the blade, but that wasn't to say he was ready to retire for the night.

Attempting a lonely routine he hadn't tried since a night in chains so long ago, Erroh, line of Magnus and Elise, stripped his shirt off and drew his blades from their scabbard. Carefully stretching already aching muscles, he stretched out his arms with a blade in each hand, remembering their balance, feeling their weight. Ensuring he was ready for foolish manoeuvres.

Uden is taking no night off.

Favouring his injured ankle and testing his shoulder a few times, he spun his swords in an impressive arc and turned on one foot, testing further his balance, technique and resilience. He spun each blade faster and faster until they were a blurring arc of death before moving in his unpredictable form. He was slow at first. He was hobbled, but would not allow such a weakness to slow his techniques.

Uden fought better with one eye.

His body responded eagerly to his demands, and soon he was cutting through the glade, away from the light and the comfort of stable grounds, and it felt strange, unsettling and devastating. He suppressed the desire for Lea to meet him in this act, matching his moves and countering. Instead, he envisioned countless enemies charging towards him in battle, and he slew them all without mercy. Those that didn't drop to an imaginary knee, of course.

Sooner than he would have liked, and without another warrior of equal skills to drive him beyond his limit, he collapsed in the grass, gasping and perspiring. His body ached, his mind was slow and exhausted, and sleep called, but he climbed to his feet and wandered down to the little brook that bubbled merrily in his ear. Stripping his garments off, he dropped into the stream and tended to his aching body. He gasped at the cold but took it. More than that, he controlled the grip on his chest as he dipped lower beneath the surface. After he had scrubbed away the day's sweat and grime from his skin, he turned his attention to his clothes and scrubbed them vigorously too. The following afternoon, he would be with Lea again; he imagined it might help to be respectable. His heart skipped a beat in anticipation.

Laying his damp garments by the crackling fire, he cast a log upon the flames before wrapping himself in bedding, just before the raindrops began to fall.

"Keep me sheltered," he asked of the oak with its thick clusters of countless leaves. He enveloped himself, bedding and all, in his long cloak lest the leaves betray him, and closed his eyes.

Perhaps it was the cutting breeze, the rustling of leaves or the heavy darkness as the shattered moon hid behind the clouds that unsettled him most, but he couldn't shake the awful feeling in the pit of his belly, nor could he fall into a restful sleep. Instead, he listened to the gentle patter of raindrops as they attempted to break his natural shield. It was something to do while he tossed and turned.

Silence.

"My Lea," he whispered, and it was a prayer, a pledge, and a declaration of his love. He shuddered when he thought of this day and the memory of wandering aimlessly along the road for a few years, avoiding such undesirable things as a mate and eternal comfort. "I was nothing without you." But there needed to be more than these simple words. He thought of his behaviour, and it stung him to think how much he might have hurt her. Lying there in the silence, he remembered his lonely, solitary life and how far from this solitude he desired to be. Suddenly, he almost shot up from his bedding to grab his damp clothing, biting wind be damned, to ride out into the night and get to her even earlier than he'd planned.

I'd have killed Uden with Lea at my side.

His body quivered from the cold, the loneliness and his knowledge of his actions. But he accepted the truth for what it was. He was nothing without her, and he would never betray her again—and would never leave her behind, either. He would be by her side always. Even at the end, when death was in the wind and nothing was left in either of them.

It was a fine pledge worthy of a legend, one that he would offer her when they met. Closing his eyes once more, he allowed sleep to take him, never knowing the following day would be the worst of his life.

23

FEAST IN RUINS

He watched the boy fall and collide, and he enjoyed every moment. And why not? It was a long plummet, an entire life in the making. It was a thing of beauty. A fine end. A worthy chapter in his legacy. But as Erroh fell from sight, lost beneath the cloudy veneer of smoke, Uden ground his teeth. He would have liked to see the end. He would have liked the boy's last vision upon this arth to be the sight of his vanquisher far above, cursing his last journey. Would have liked to see his head crack open and gush crimson upon the stone streets. That would have been nice.

"Not much of a god," he murmured, and his voice carried far. Farther across the city than any other's cry, even on the quietest of days. He allowed himself a moment more to lament not having seen the end, but consoled himself with the deliciousness of victory.

It's over.

It has just begun.

They watched from below, and through wet, smoke-filled eyes, they stared up at their god, and he gifted them a taste of his triumph. He could not hear their bellows, but as he raised his hand in victory, he spied many of them, through breaks in the smoke, saluting his success. And why not? They had all marched so far, as one fine, godly thing, to raze this kingdom, and it was a fine day to be Southern.

"So, this is Samara," he growled, dropping his arm and looking across the smouldering ruins. Truthfully, Uden had never set foot in the city of light, but in another life, he had loved this city. His head spun for a breath, and he dropped to a knee to settle himself.

Everything is burning.
And she is dead.

He honoured fire. Fire was a cleansing thing. From fire, there came redemption. And an end to wretched things. Gods stirred from beneath fire. Sometimes, though, in wavering moments, he remembered the heat, remembered the heartrending anguish.

"I am the Woodin Man. I am the Woodin Man," he hissed, and it was a good mantra. Wood was eternal, wise and sturdy, and would not shatter and break under strain or tragedy. Shaking away his thoughts, he stood, faced the fires below, and hated them passionately as much as he honoured them. A god could think like this. He felt that spinning again, and he suppressed it. He was Uden and would bow to nothing, especially when those below might watch his actions.

Rise and triumph.
That's what a god does.

With godly determination, he took a step forward and then another after that. Up here was a fine throne from which to observe the end of the world. No need to cower, he told himself, and felt that steel in his nerve. And the horrible memories of another life faded away.

Honour the flames.
Burn them all in her name.

The vision of a hundred sails upon the water shook him to sudden lucidity. He played his part by walking along the top of the wall, presenting himself as an inspiring conqueror. Sometimes it was about reminding both those who loved and those who doubted how impressive he was. A false god had summoned him to this height, after all. Having seen off the boy, he might as well show the world his victory.

As he walked across this monstrous, imposing city to where the great harbour gates lay open, he could see the fleeing vessels more clearly than before. They lay tranquil and effortless upon the still mirror of water, against the tumultuous backdrop of fire, smoke, death and ruin. A great fury overcame him, and all joy of victory was suddenly lost in this sight. Though the city had fallen and her significance dwindled, it would be a tragedy not to drain her blood dry before the end. Every soul that survived was a slap in the face of his decree. Angrily, he hacked at another rope bridge, similar to the one from which he'd cut the boy. It was a petulant and human thing to do, but sometimes a god needed to be human.

"To the fires," he screamed, hacking the thing free and watching it fall to the fires below. It wasn't beating a man to death with his hands, but it was enough.

Did I expect everything to fall into place in one attack?

He probably had, and shrugging, he cursed the defiance and the cowardice of the Northerners once more before looking back to the city below. He watched for a few breaths as the unlucky few who'd not fled with the armada battled bravely against impossible numbers. Where no cover of smoke marred his sight, he watched death, which was pleasing. He touched his hand to his chest and offered them a quick blessing. They were vile, but that didn't mean they needed no respect.

Above him, he saw the clouds thicken and gather, and he wondered would the rains come and douse these fires. He wondered if he would approve of such a thing, wondered whether he had called for the clouds himself.

I work in mysterious ways.

He stayed upon the wall's edge, gazing out at his devastation, until his personal guard approached. Cheery and triumphant, they said little but offered smiles, and he allowed it. They had all seen Erroh fall, too. They could hold that victory, and he would not begrudge them of that.

"I want the body," he said, and it was a good order. He did not know what he would do with the carcass, but cutting out its broken heart before a large audience was the type of godly thing expected of him. Then he cleared his throat, preparing to make a second proclamation, something he'd never believed he would attempt.

"Extinguish the flames," he said. Why allow a perfectly good stronghold to burn to an empty husk? He looked to the sky and wondered would the clouds assist his divine declaration. Strangely, he didn't believe it would rain when he'd woken this morning.

It was a small matter that Gemmil might disagree with his command.

He took the first step towards the smouldering streets, and strangely, his stomach rumbled in hunger. He didn't know why, but it made him smile. His lips became wet and his mouth watered for sustenance, for wine and meats. His tent was close by, but he desired the smell of ruin and victory in his nostrils this day. He wanted to raise his glass and eat in the middle of a burning city.

For this is what a god did.

Even as it rained around him.

. . .

The Actions of Gods

His victory march through the city was less triumphant than he'd hoped. The people did not bow or cheer; they went to fight the fires and the wretched Northerners who had been left behind. However, the first raindrops soon fell, and he took it as a fine omen of his might. The farther he marched, the more heavily the drizzle fell, and he expected they would accept the unlikely rainfall as a gift from him. And if they didn't? Well, he would let it be known.

He had memories of another life in the streets. A god allowed himself to recall these things. He welcomed some of them. However, the unexpected tears that flowed down his cheeks were an irritating reminder of the stirrings of humanity still within his mind. Fortunately, the air was thick with smoke, and many of the people he passed also had streaming eyes. Hiding his face behind a damp cloth, pretending to struggle to breathe, he watched comrades fall to their deaths from collapsing buildings as he passed, and for these burning souls, he offered a bow and a prayer for them alone.

It was the right thing to do, he thought.

A sacred gift at their end.

Near his journey's end, thunder cracked, the skies opened and a heavy downpour covered the smoking city. Uden smiled, for he knew this was his will. He brought fire, but he also brought the cooling rain. Those whispering against him would be wise to remember that.

Eventually, he reached Samara's heart, where few fires still burned. There, he arranged to meet his chosen few in the Cull, a famous room of dark and cold, for a fine feast in celebration of this historic day. When he declared his intention to dine in the Primary's domain, his guards swiftly provided a grand table and suitable chairs for such an extravagant event. As he strode into the chambers, he looked up at the illuminated podium. Spitting on the floor in disdain for the vile bitch, he took his place on the throne as the new king of the city and wished the fires of hell upon his predecessor. He didn't mind sitting in this room alone. Sitting in the cold was a tonic after the intense, sweaty heat of the pathways.

"This is how I celebrate victory," he snarled to the podium.

A few guards appeared from beyond bearing dishes and goblets and a bottle of the most decadent red wine. With a quick popping of the cork, a glass was poured for him, and the rest of the bottle was set aside for his guests, who had yet to arrive. It was grand, indeed.

"Warmed by the city's anguish," he added, snatching the bottle from his server and enjoying the warmth. Victory would taste divine once this vintage was allowed to breathe for a little time.

Sometimes, it took an army devastating another to change the tide of war. Other times, it was a defiant act that stirred the fires of dissent. As he drank and reflected, a messenger arrived with an update of an impressive Northern Rider racing through the burning streets, which sullied his good mood. Whispers suggested it was Erroh, and such a blatant lie was dangerous.

His better mood returned as the servants prepared the feast for his victorious friends. He even went as far as cracking a jest or two with his quiet servers, who appeared with delicacies liberated from the city and the camp beyond. Eventually, the table groaned under the weight of a lavish spread. Uden summoned the servers one last time and ordered them to leave him and his forthcoming party in peace. Uden was perfectly at ease with his own company, for there was plenty to think about.

"Enter only to deliver the dishes and refill our glasses," he said to the last server, who took the suggestion as the threat it was. When great minds convened in private for the first time in decades, he did not welcome eager ears. He was a god, but even a god had friends.

"Wiiden. We did it," Seth cried from the doorway. Uden wasn't used to seeing how old this man had become. Every time he gazed upon his comrade, he was reminded of the years that had passed. But, he wondered, wasn't regretting the years lost a human trait? Seth was less than he'd been. His hair was thinning, and his eyes had lost their wildness. He appeared hobbled, no doubt gelded into submission by the queen bitch of this city. He appreciated the man's sacrifice. But 'Wiiden'? Uden bristled at his friend's cavalier use of the dead term. Still, any anger he felt quickly evaporated, for he was a patient and forgiving god.

Uden rose to nobody but Gemmil, and when that man arrived he stood and met him in a warm embrace, and the memories flooded and faded, and he laughed in joy.

"That is not your god's name," Gemmil said quietly, referring to Seth's use of 'Wiiden.' Uden, seeing his worry, assured him that Seth would not suffer for the slip. They were all friends, were they not? The closest. How could one ever feel genuinely comfortable if one couldn't misstep comfortably?

The Actions of Gods

"My apologies, my lord," Seth said, coming forward. Uden clasped his hand tightly, causing Seth to gasp, and it was more than apology enough. Seth had his trust; he always had. He always would.

"A fine day, Uden," Gemmil said, pulling Seth away roughly and embracing Uden as a brother once more. And why not? They were closer than kin. After so much planning, they could display camaraderie openly without judgement.

Ushering his friends to their seats, Uden urged them to eat and drink deeply of the spoils of victory, and both men did.

Though the world beyond was a turmoil of fire and rain, suffering and strife, within the Cull, the mood was light, enthusiastic and welcomed. They spoke of years gone by, some joyful and exciting, some less so, and it was grand times indeed. They laughed, jested and reminisced, and pledged for a violent, brutal future. They cursed the North, the city and the savage cur that was Erroh. They toasted unity, the South and vengeance. Those swift few who delivered the dishes of steaming, salted meats and moist, buttery vegetables might have believed this was a simple gathering of decrepit mercenaries sharing boastful tales; such was their candour. They had no idea of the grandness of each man. Regardless, if this march had been arduous, this meal was a tonic.

When the three men were a few mouthfuls into their main course, there was a knock at the heavy door. Nobody stirred, and only when the door opened without invitation did Seth recognise the interloper and give a gentle curse under his breath. In the doorway, a diminutive figure paused, coughed once and, stepping into their sanctum with a careful grin, offered a deep bow. Uden knew the man. He did not like the man, not one little bit. Nor did he approve of his appearance at this elegant table.

"Well won, Uden," Sigi offered, still bowing as if bested in combat. Perhaps it was an attempt at complete submissiveness. Regardless, such obedience belonged among the soldiers or the worshippers as he gave sermons. Not at a feast of legends. The man didn't know Uden at all, did he?

Uden looked closer and saw that a blonde-haired woman stood with him. He did not mind that Sigi had brought company. He searched for her name, and it did not come immediately, and that was fine, for she was human, and he was a god. He liked her white dress. It was rare that a girl took his fancy as she did, but that, too, was part of his humanity. The matter of her being attached to Sigi was of little worry. He imagined she was the type of tainted girl who was attracted to power.

"My lord," she said, bowing as she entered, and he could see the terror on her face, which was intriguing. He'd like to see more of it. After he broke her in.

"Greetings, Sigi. We did not expect you this evening," Seth offered. He eyed Uden, who showed little but disdain for the interloper. An intelligent man might step out of the room. A more brilliant man might do so and leave his companion behind.

As ordered, two servers appeared at the table bearing a chair each. The table was large and long, ideally suited for guests, regardless of welcome. "Sit her beside me," Uden muttered, gesturing to the girl. There was always something intoxicating about sitting beside an attractive young lady. It was the human in him.

"As you wish, my lord," she said, giving him a dazzling smile capable of cracking mountains. She hid her fears behind that gorgeous smile, and she fascinated him. As she took her seat beside him, he inhaled her aroma of soap and rose oil, underlaid with a taste of charring.

Delicious.

If Sigi cared, he showed little on his dull, simpleton features. And Uden had even less respect for him. How dare he treat a goddess with indifference? Were he himself to sit with his lover at his side and another man showed an interest, Uden would have shown his teeth—and his blade a moment after that.

Instead of watching after his beauty, however, Sigi sat beside Seth, swiftly produced a burlap sack, and slid it across the table to the god. "Let me present an offering of peace and respect between our forces," the unimpressive man said, and Uden eyed his weak jawline, hiding beneath a trader's smile. He'd never met a smiling trader he liked. He always felt he was getting the lesser part of a deal. Taking the sack, he wondered what deal this smiling trader offered. Carelessly, he opened the bag and pulled out a bottle of clear alcohol. "It is from my first brew of the city," Sigi said. "Aged in an ale cask for four seasons. Each bottle is the price of a farmer's season wage."

It was a remarkable boast, or at least it sounded remarkable, and Uden popped the cork and sniffed indifferently. "Very nice," he offered, returning the cork to the bottle and the bottle to the sack. Sigi's eyes flickered in irritation as though Uden had propositioned his lover for the night. He hadn't, but he would, and she would accept. Sometimes, a god knew these things.

"A toast to the grand conquerors," Sigi offered, holding aloft his claret goblet. "May we all benefit from the fruits of war."

Uden raised his glass but did not drink his wine like the others. If Sigi noticed, again, he showed little on his irritating features.

Conversation returned to the table, though it was more strained than before. The servers moved among them, placing plates, utensils and many main courses in front of them. Uden immediately offered some warm honey bread to the blonde beside him. "This will taste good with the meat juices," he whispered, for he was a generous god and had known his way around a kitchen.

"Thank you, my lord," she said breathily, and her voice was a delicate tremor in his ear. And her name came to him: Silvia. He knew of her unsuccessful deeds during the taking of Samara, and she was blameless for the failures. It was Sigi alone who had failed to deliver the city. His pledge had been firm, but those cursed Wolves had broken free of their restraints, hadn't they? Held the city instead of opening the gates, hadn't they? Silvia had simply lost an election. Uden had little faith in such politics, anyway. They had never served the South. They never would.

"A fine day to see the city in such a state," Seth said, refilling Sigi's glass but addressing Uden. Seth pledged for the man. Swore to his importance in a city still flush with Wolven packs, and that had been fine. Now though, with the Wolves aboard a fleeing armada? Less so.

Gemmil picked at his plate with his eyes upon Sigi. No doubt he was as unimpressed with him as Uden was. "Now that the rains fall, the mood among the streets has turned jubilant. I suggest we let them celebrate a few days," he murmured.

"They have earned a reprieve," agreed Uden, knowing well the importance of morale. He also appreciated the need for reprieves when earned. "But there are barges to follow." They had won no war. They had walked through some smoke.

"We have Riders in pursuit. It was a clever tactic to flee upon the water, but they'll need to come ashore at some point, and we will wait them out," Gemmil argued, and it was a fair point. If Uden was a master of blades, Gemmil was a master of minds. And Seth was somewhere in between. Together, they were a fine trio with a fine, brutal legacy.

Sigi leaned forward and rightly ruined Uden's mood. "You know, they say it was Erroh who rode through the fires upon a steed of black." His simple eyes were unblinking; his tone was conversational. He took some bread and left it to soak up the juices, as Uden had suggested to his female companion. "Quite the feat and all. Surprised we didn't see him race past our tent as he went." At this, he laughed, and, bless her foolishness, Silvia laughed with him. Then she offered Uden the smile again, and she was lovely.

"Erroh fell from the wall into fire; it was not him," Uden said quietly. It was a warning. Tonight, they would not speak of the tainted cur who had taken his eye and fomented dissent among his people. Tonight they would talk of finer times earned and those to come.

"Oh no, it was him," Sigi persisted. "Several guards at the wall saw him; they swore by it. Small enough, with dark hair and dual blades upon his back. I'd say it was a fantastical thing—the actions of a god," he jested, and Uden held his fork tightly. His other hand scratched at his patch. He knew what soldiers swore in the heat of the battle. Soon they would say he flew thrice around the city, spitting arrows from his rear while laughing maniacally. He knew the damage the tales of a boy falling from a mountain had wrought upon his hold. Oh, aye, there had been quite the lies with that tale.

But Sigi wasn't done. Of course he wasn't. "I believe I met him once. Or at least I might have met him. I certainly met an Erroh walking to the city a time before. Charming little drunk, and generous in his trading. He left me some words from the past and all. Generosity is a thing to be remembered," he added, tapping his head knowingly, and Uden wanted to grab his fuken head and drive it through the table.

"I wouldn't call him a charming drunk," Silvia offered, and Uden thought her wonderful. He enjoyed when human desire took hold, and suddenly, he imagined writhing with her and how pleasurable it would be for a time.

"Enough of his vile name. He is dead; let us concentrate on better things," Seth said, and Gemmil struck the table twice in agreement, and Uden appreciated their attempt at ignoring the thorn in his side. Though he knew full well Uden was inclined to obsess over every detail until the boy's body was recovered.

"How would you know how charming he is?" Sigi asked in a tone suggesting he was blissfully unaware of how precarious his steps were. Another few comments, and he'd find out.

"I culled with him, did I not?" said Silvia.

At this, Uden leaned forward, finding great interest in her. The boy had culled? This meant the boy had a mate. Or, to be more precise, a widow now. Regardless, this was very interesting indeed.

"Whisht, little one. Tell us more of you," Gemmil said gently; he topped up her glass. He had taken a liking to her also. When Uden tired of her, he might offer her to him as a gift. Still, Gemmil took so few to his bed that it might be generous for Uden to step away altogether and allow him alone to bed her. Uden was a kind god, was he not?

But that godly smile.

Unsure of what to do, Silvia smiled and shrugged as though there was little to her, and Uden gazed at her beauty for a few breaths and challenged his own sense of generosity. He rather liked her. He was entitled to please himself, was he not? "I cannot imagine any fool not choosing you," Uden said. It was a smooth compliment, and she liked his words. Sigi chewed his juicy bread and left a few wet crumbs on his chin and Uden wanted to rip his throat out.

"It was I who walked away from him."

"A fine thing indeed," agreed Seth, who shuffled uncomfortably in his chair. Perhaps Seth, too, was as intrigued by the girl as he was. Uden stared at Sigi coldly. When he and Silvia had been guests of the Hunt, Uden had seen how arrogantly he had treated the girl in the few days before the invasion. A goddess was to be displayed and adored with reverence; a goddess like that was to be watched with a fiery gaze, lest another set their eye upon her. Sigi did neither. He treated her as property. As a notch on his belt, a prize to attend to when needs arose.

Fuk you, Sigi.

"And you have risen to greatness since," Seth agreed. At this, Gemmil nodded, his fingers ripping and tearing the meat on his plate. He smiled and appeared relaxed, but Uden could tell his agitation. Was it the girl? Was it Uden's shared interest? Sometimes even a god did not see all.

"We will make you queen of this city," Uden said, and she appreciated this greatly.

"We'll take Samara as our own?" Gemmil asked. His fingers relaxed.

"Aye, for now," Uden said, and his older comrades were pleased. Excitedly, they spoke of the potential in this place, and Uden almost forgot the manner of words they'd shared. Or at least moved on from them.

Sigi didn't. "I do not understand the rules of the Cull. Whom did Erroh choose... or who chose Erroh as his mate? Was there a fight?"

"He mated with a whore named Lea," Silvia offered, and her face scrunched up in annoyance.

Lea.

Visions of the fire stirred in Uden's mind. Terrible, heartbreaking fire. He thought of Drahir and little Lea, and his mood dropped.

"I hate that cow. To the fires with her," Silvia growled, and he found her less attractive when she frowned. He wanted her to smile at him. He needed her to. That might dissuade his memories of another life from breaching the surface.

"The girl was insipid," Seth said quickly. "A lesser family from the East, I think."

My little Cordelia.

"Didn't Roja also cull with Erroh?" Gemmil asked, and Uden smiled at his attempt to change the subject. Uden should have been mad at his comrade's attempt at manipulating the conversation, but perhaps Gemmil knew that Erroh's mate sharing the name of Wiiden's dead daughter might have soured his mood. Might have burned terribly in his mind like a sleeping child above an inferno.

All charred and burned away to ash.

"Aye, and she was treated terribly by Erroh and left as I did," Silvia said.

"To better choices," Seth said, raising a glass.

But Silvia wasn't done. She turned her attention to the topic of the unsuccessful Primary. "Don't talk of Roja and choices. She followed a childhood fantasy. A healer. Up to his elbows in blood and disease and failure. A drunk, too."

Uden was displeased. He wanted more for Wiiden's niece than a drunkard. His head spun, and he drained his glass of wine. He craved something more potent in that moment but would not honour Sigi by opening his unique blends of sine, no matter how badly he desired it.

"Well, she chose not to be in the city, so we might celebrate that," Gemmil decided, raising his goblet of shimmering crimson.

"I wonder what became of those who marched with Erroh," Sigi wondered, and Uden's knuckles turned white in frustration. He eyed Seth, who nodded in silent agreement. What goodwill the man had earned in destabilising the city was slipping away with every word spoken.

"We suspect they remain in Raven Rock, where we will tend to their fates," Gemmil muttered. His eyes were cold; he, too, was tiring of Sigi's words.

There suddenly came knocks on the door. Within a breath, one of Uden's generals marched in. His face was flushed; his body smelled of charred victory. He looked anything but joyous. "I bring word of Erroh," he whispered, dropping to a knee. He looked like a man delivering words that might cost him his life.

"Tell us," Seth said, and the general hesitated.

"Just tell us his body smoulders, and this will be the end," warned Gemmil.

He fell silent, and Uden felt his anger growing. "Tell me."

The general dipped his head lower. "We sought where he fell and found only a few bodies. None of which were Erroh's."

"He survived the fall? That is ungodly!" roared Uden, slamming his fist upon the table. His glass of wine toppled and spilled over the dress of the goddess beside him. She made no move and allowed his wrath, and for a strange moment, this infuriated him more. He thought about strangling her before Sigi and watching the light leave her eyes.

Slowly, she rolled the goblet away, and her hands did not shake. "I hate him," she muttered under her breath, and these words saved her in that moment.

"How?" Seth demanded, and it was a fair question. They knew the boy had a god's amount of luck, but surviving a fall from such a height was impossible.

Uden reached for his general. Aril was his name. He was young and careless and fierce. All things they themselves had been in their youth. Uden took him by the throat, and the general flinched for a breath before allowing Uden to hold him, which impressed the god. "Answer me."

He coughed once and began to speak. "A brother pledges he saw the false god fall, and it was no straight drop to the bottom." Uden eased the grip. "He fell hard, but was well enough to limp away."

Uden felt the room close in tight. Here he was, celebrating a victory over a husk of a city. All the while, his nemesis spat in his face again.

I lost no eye this time.

He cursed his actions, knowing he could have killed the boy outright had he been less impulsive. From nowhere, there came a phantom claw, and it took hold of his chest and squeezed. Leaving the general to live, he sat back in his chair and waited for this awful moment to pass. Around him, he heard them converse, but he couldn't follow their words; he could only gasp as though struck in the chest with a jagged blade, awaiting a decapitating second blow. He knew this panic well, though it had been decades since it had bubbled up from deep within. Some things could always be recalled. He watched Gemmil dismiss the general, and it was a fine thing, too; Uden was fit to kill, and better a useless sine merchant than a trusted general brave enough to deliver crushing news.

Why does this boy continue to torment me?
Because a god must face his equals in war.
A god must overcome.

He held that thought like a taut rope in a raging storm and drew himself ashore, allowing the anger to take him with every stroke. He would rise, tear that little fuk apart limb from limb, and slay his mate.

He felt the easing upon his chest and took a deep breath.

"If this is true, we will locate him," Gemmil said swiftly, and Uden nodded in agreement. Better to have a plan rather than give in to emotion.

"You might hate him, but it was a marvellous feat," suggested Sigi. And Uden wondered whether the cur was daring to mock him so openly. "If what Seth has told me about the South is true, he'll gather more support from that feat as well." He smiled absently as a server appeared and removed their plates before setting down fruits and sweet cake as dessert. "We have sent the Samarans fleeing, but that's not to say we cannot end this war peacefully." Sigi sniffed the sweet cake and grimaced before addressing his audience once more. "Uden, you need to win the support of those not of Southern blood. You need to show them you are a king worthy of followers."

He thought on this a moment, and Uden felt his pulse rise, felt his fists clench. He wanted to kill the man where he sat and spend the rest of the night ravaging his mate to complete the punishment.

"Hmm," Sigi said at last. "Perhaps if the Southerners did away with burning the women, those eager to fight to the death might lay down their swords willingly."

"Those who give life must burn, for that is—" Seth said, reciting his religious decree, and Uden raised a sacred hand to silence the cur. Inflicting such death was barbaric and cruel, but it was war. And messages were to be sent—messages to an old dead woman deaf to his savagery.

She burned.

So they must burn.

Sigi tasted his sweet cake, chewed and swallowed as though it was an affront that a man with his rising star was to endure such awfulness. "This dessert is no good at all. Is there any cream to be had?"

Uden shot him a glance. The cake was one of his favourite desserts upon the march, and only for this did he allow a rare taste of sugar pass his godly lips. Quietly, he took a bite and enjoyed the dry apple-honey concoction and the cinnamon aftertaste. Perhaps he was a barbarian at this table, but he had grace. Manners. Also, he'd had enough.

"What do you bring to this gathering, Sigi?" Uden asked.

"I bring sine," the man replied, pushing his plate away.

"What use do we have for sine anymore?" Uden asked.

"Very little," countered Gemmil before the unwanted guest could answer. It was a telling few words, and Uden approved. He looked to Seth, who was playing with his food, his shoulders slumped.

"I suppose so," his old comrade agreed. It was not permission; it was merely his thoughts on the matter.

"Sine controls the world." It was a nuanced answer from such a fiend, and Uden smiled.

Without warning, he stood up, hauled a surprised Sigi from his chair, and dragged him across the table.

"What are you doing?" the man cried, flapping and fighting as the god held him fast and decided how best to kill him. He looked beseechingly at Silvia, who leapt away from her seat and stood against the wall. Only then did he realise how badly he'd stained her dress.

"You come to my table and insult my food?" Uden roared, lifting the cur and slamming him hard against the table, almost breaking it in half. That would have been a tragedy. They had not finished eating. "You come to a place you have no right to be?" He struck the man fiercely, grabbed a lump of the delicious sweet cake, and shoved it into his gaping mouth. Tightening his grip around the man's throat, he squeezed, and Sigi coughed, wheezed, and fought pathetically in his godly grip. "What vile coward turns his back on his people for profit?"

It was a fair question, and Sigi tried to explain his actions, but choked on the clump of cake. Still holding his throat, Uden slid him from the table, where he crashed to the ground and prepared to die. He saw Silvia step nearer to see the murder, and he wondered might love cause her to take a knife to his throat and cut it.

She did not. Instead, with terrified, streaming eyes she silently watched her man die in a frenzy of spluttering, gagging and retching, which was all he deserved.

"No one will remember you," Uden whispered as Sigi's last few thrashes weakened and fell still. He gasped and hacked once more and then stared beyond Uden to the darkness above, and then he was gone. Careful not to fall for a clever ruse, Uden took hold of his throat once more and squeezed for a long time until he was confident the sine merchant and city betrayer was dead.

Feeling far better about himself, he recovered his fallen chair and hers and bade her sit down with him.

"What will you do with me?" Silvia whispered. She tried to smile, bless her, but her eyes were terrified, and he touched her shoulder tenderly. To reassure. A godly touch.

"You are very much safe, little one," he insisted, and with a quivering nod, she sat down next to him.

"Well, that could have been avoided," muttered Gemmil disapprovingly.

Beside him, Seth drained his glass and poured another. "A fool he was, but he was an agreeable means to the end of the city. I'll miss him," he said, raising a glass to the dead man.

Uden offered his own in honour of the fallen. Why not? He was an honourable god, even if his victim was insignificant.

"It needed to be done. It was only a matter of time before he attempted to climb even higher," muttered Gemmil, and Seth agreed. He looked at the body for a moment before returning to his dessert.

"You'll have to be wary of his guards," Silvia whispered. She did not toast to his death. Instead, she simply drank, and Uden wondered how soon he could tastefully invite her to bed with a god.

At least an hour more.

"They are skilled, vicious, but for the right price, we could convince them to fall in line," Seth added.

"How many in total?" Uden asked, offering his handkerchief to Silvia and pointing to the stains on her gown.

"A dozen are waiting outside the building, maybe ten more down at their tents."

"I don't rely on loyalty payments. I rule by adoration and strength... Just have them killed," he added, and Silvia froze momentarily before dabbing at the blotches of wine on her dress.

"It will be done, my god," Gemmil said. He rose from his chair and hopped over the carcass to knock on the servers' door to deliver the god's latest request. "Make sure it's done by the time we are finished," he hissed to the server tasked with arranging the clean-up. By the time he sat back down, Silvia had recovered her nerve, which was most impressive.

"Will you miss him?" Uden asked smoothly.

"Will you distract me?" she countered, leaving the crimson stains where they were to lean in and smile most wonderfully for him.

"I will do what I must."

24

EXCERPTS FROM THE DESKS OF WEASELS

Solstice 12th
    Dear Seth,
It has been quite a time. There is much to say, and more ink is needed. There isn't time to explain the horrors we have gone through. Do you see the splotches upon this parchment? I write this, and I weep. In sorrow, in anger. In absolute disgust. Oh, vilest comrade, a pox upon you and your kin. Why choose to betray us both now? To betray the rest of the South? I pray this will be my last letter to you. How easily dreams of the city of light took you in. Why, Seth? Why did you bow at her knees? Was it so you could undo her dress that little bit easier and serve her delight as she stood upon her podium with legs spread wide and proclaimed herself all-knowing queen bitch? You know her touch is a serpent's caress, do you not? Brother, I have tasted that old poison, and for this, I am happily a thousand miles from here.

Wiiden isn't aware of your stoop. The terrible things that have happened would be enough to break him. But not before he gathered what wretched soldiers we can call upon and come for your hide. I hear them roving outside my camp, and I can write no more, nor shall I, until you declare your allegiance to your brothers. Your true brothers. Do you remember? We have bent the world to our needs. We have taken fire to any who stepped to us. Have you forgotten? Or has the prison of light blinded your honour?

They play the horns as I scribe this. Around me, they pack up, and we must continue, though the hour is late and I have not slept. Do you sleep well in a feathered bed with silken sheets? Are you resting by an open fireplace as you read this? I am still marching for what is right, even though I can barely hold my quill.

I must leave now. Magnus is nearing; his pack have our scent. To the fires with you, cur. I hope this letter finds you, and finds you in dreadful times.

Gemmil

Equinox 110th

Oh, Gemmil, this is the fifth missive I have sent in as many months. I do not know if your stronghold still stands. Nor do I know your whereabouts, but I will continue to scribe my words until I die; such is my regret to be separated from both of you. More than that, it pains me to know you think my betrayal was by choice. I had none, but regardless, I defend my actions as I defend the free walls of Samara. You could not know the casualties we suffered on the last day, with Magnus and Elise storming through our ranks. No arrow could penetrate either of them; no blade could cut them down. They rallied their lesser numbers, and we were lesser for it.

I think back a thousand times about what Dia might have done; nevertheless, I see no counter to the ocean. We were a beaten force that day. We still are. What remains of our army is a farce. You have yet to see the full extent of the Rangers' savagery, and I pray you never do. It was an unlikely mercy offered by such a bastard, and we took it and spread open the gates of Spark City like Amelia's legs to any gangling brute in the colder seasons. Truthfully, Dia's decision to kneel at Magnus's feet was her only recourse, and the city is saved. For this, thousands more are saved as well.

I love Samara. You know I always have, but more than that, though you call her cruel and poisonous, I love Dia too, and I believe she loves me. I have never found love in my life; why deny something with your foul tone? Were you beside me right now, I would thrash you for such words. Not even Wiiden could stop me. But then, by the open fireplace, I would sit you down and weep for all you have lost and endured. We have all seen enough, and I am tired. Our kings are dead, and our lands have fallen to Magnus's cunning and Elise's cruelty. This war is over. Honestly, after the Ten Rivers battle, there was only one victor. Dia knows the importance of humanity's survival. The city must stand; the females of the city must reproduce. Dia understands the value of a strong *bloodline in this fuked-up world, and I see it too, even if I'm not regal enough for her taste. It is the way of things. Recovering the world after war means sacrifice. Fuken war. If this letter finds you with breath and wits, fade into the night. Find life in this terrifying new world. Forsake that cursed word, war, and be better for it.*

I weep as I write this, for I never have a night with dry eyes. My tears are for my two best friends. I hope these missives arrive safely. I hope you read them in safety, having thrown the savage mongrels off your scent. I hope this letter is not discarded by the remains of a smouldering ruin. (Or just beyond the gates of Samara.) I hope you cast this letter into your fireplace as tinder to warm your aching bones. I pray to the absent gods that you will return word of your survival. Until then, I will continue to write. I will continue to hope.

Yours,
Seth of Samara

———

Solstice 5th
Dearest Seth,

I have been longer now upon the road than I would care to be. I don't know why I write. Perhaps I do it for myself, to have something to imagine beyond my path. Your letters made some fine kindling—all of them. So, for that, I am grateful. I even read a few. You went to such lengths, with such dainty writing. You always had the daintiest writing. How many death warrants have you written in such a delicate script? Not nearly enough, brother, for that is your penance. Did you scribe mine upon parchment? Did you do the same with Wiiden's? Did you do it because Wiiden's vile mate asked you to? Ah, yes—a neutral topic to discuss between us both. At least in our hatred of Amelia, we can find something to agree on.

Did you hear the pleasing news? She is with a child. Again. Is this one Wiiden's, do you suppose? I wouldn't ask the man such a question. They are drawn to each other like oil and fire. Love is nothing but a foolish emotion that can burn the world. I learned that from Magnus and Elise. A pox upon them both and their kin. May they remain infertile.

Truthfully, Wiiden has been happier these past few months despite the awful grind. His line is growing more plentiful; I suppose that is something to comfort anyone in the frosty nights.

Once more, I hear the horns of departure calling, and I am tired now, but we've been driven back farther. The South is calling. I do not know how wise it is to step across their borders, but an enemy of an enemy might be welcomed on the march. Honestly, I do not understand why I remain in contact with you and ask about your whore. I do not know why I need to think of you at all.

Why do we send these messages? Are we not enemies? Are we not nomads without a banner? All the while, we are hunted by Magnus and the Wolves of the North. I stare at these words and wonder if I should even send this message. Should I set this letter alight for kindling for a few warm breaths? That might be a better use for it.

Gemmil

Equinox 23rd

Oh, Gemmil, my lost friend. I fear for you this past season, and your spiteful silence unsettles me, though I suspect the terrible truth. I have heard worrying things—word of a desperate last skirmish upon the shadows of the Southern mountains. When the South was crushed, I heard word the royals of Rodian and Inessa fell to the blades of Magnus and Elise. Tell me this is not true. I lament for all lives lost, but for friends even more. I thought they might have slipped away from the war when they brought little Roja into the world. Is that not what life is about? To bring life into this world?

Sitting in my palace of bitterness and warmth, I wonder if I scribe to a ghost. Are you a cadaver amid the Wastes, slain in honour and brutality? I pleaded with Dia to end the skirmishes. To leave the South to its stubborn ways, but she will not relent. She will not even listen to her better advisors anymore. Nor me and my quiet voice. A crown delivered by a barbarian upon her head has swayed her somewhat. Truthfully, to see him offer a false pledge to her sickened me to the core. And she, the fool, believed a brute like him would desire peace.

I do not know my place in Samara; things change with time. Little keeps me here anymore. This role was more than love; it was duty. I feel empty with Dia no longer warming my bed for a season now. Oh, aye, she claims to trust me and my judgements, but I know better now. I feel only anger. I see the truth at the end. My pledge was never about duty. And I was wrong, Gemmil, I was so fuken wrong. I know these words will never reach you, but still I must write them.

I hope you and Wiiden wait for me in the darkness. I want to earn a place at your table still.
Seth

Equinox 5th
Dearest Seth,
It has been a year now since last we spoke. At least. I worry what has become of you. Have you marched from the city, as you hinted? I hope not. There is little left in the world. For you, for me. For those who cannot forgive Magnus for his crimes. Wiiden has forsaken me. He has given up the warring, and our wretched little troop is lesser for it. His oldest, Breiga, still marches, but he is a shadow of his father, and I wonder if the same blood taints them, or is he the offspring of Amelia's many dalliances? Regardless, some soldiers have latched on to him out of desperation. He has no grit for this struggle, and I wonder if I shall slip farther into the Southern region and lose myself. I cannot decide if I should continue marching with this nomadic tribe, but I am too stubborn to give in. Truthfully, we are pursued by nothing more than a few scraps of soldiers with a thirst for vengeance for some distant transgressions I have no memory of.

You say you were wrong to choose love over a futile life, but I challenge such a confession. I have lost a dozen soldiers this week alone; some to the cold, some to an unfortunate skirmish, and a few more to infighting between the men. We ate a warm meal on the sixth day of the week. A good week. We fight for nothing now. We move in between factions, seeking something we can never have. There is no liberating. There is only discontent. No longer do the villagers take us in warmly. We can no longer comfortably steal back to our strongholds as before without discovering an ambush at the gates. This is the end of everything. Stay where you are. Fade away to nothing by that fireplace and scribe these missives until your hands become withered and old. I will write as long as I continue to return to my stronghold without receiving a blade to my throat.

Goodbye, old friend.
Gemmil

25

WORST DAY OF HIS LIFE

"On the first day,
    "I went out,
"and I found myself, far, far away,
"and my knees hurt…" Erroh felt the sun on his face, and he smiled despite the chill in the morning. He hummed a few more notes of the ancient song and fell silent. This morning, he was in a great mood, and the rolling line of curs nearing him would not bring him down. The oncoming rumble was loud enough to cover any false notes, and he had quite the hiding place beneath the clustered leaves of some evergreen bush. Beside him, Highwind was still, chomping on a rich clump of grass, indifferent to the passing army. His heart was settled, his mood excited.

"And it was natural," he continued as they appeared, patting Highwind gently, waiting as the Hunt marched. He had made no error this time in charging straight into their wanderings. He had learned his lesson, that these lands were no longer free to roam with no regard for a random ambush. There was little chance any keen-eyed cur would spot him through the trees, though. He calmed his breathing as they passed. He blinked less, too, taking them in, and he thought them different from the usual Fingers.

Aye, they marched with massive carts of supplies as any Finger, but they herded no animals of burden along their line. They were far fewer than their usual numbers, but more than a battalion of Riders. Their armour was a different shade of grey to the usual darker finish. He was interested in the carriage pulled along by the mounts. It was an unusually decorative one, in bright brown wood, intricately carved with a skilled hand and finished with embossed jewels at every edge. It was a godly carriage, and Erroh's body quivered coldly. For a colder moment, Erroh imagined Uden within the sealed, intricate doorway, no doubt nursing his regret at losing another chance at killing a little cub and sitting alone with nothing but his near-blind thoughts. For a moment, he wished his new comrades from the South were beside him, all willing to terrify the unaware army with chants of their new god before exploding through the forest and slaying all who defied them. And if Uden appeared humble and willing to fall at his feet, as was their way, Erroh would cut that fuker's head off and claim it was *his* way.

He's in there.
He's probably asleep.
He's unprepared.
Do it.
End the war today.

Erroh watched that carriage for a time, all the while breathing more and more quickly. Even if there was no god, whoever was within that carriage was significant.

A lover?
A child?
A target?
Do it, Erroh. End this war.

He thought about it longer than he should have. He almost drew his swords, imagining the surprise such a roving army would have, were a lunatic Alpha to emerge from the green, spitting bile and magnificence. He wondered if they would rear and flee in surprised terror. Might he make it to the cart's door? Would it be locked? How many blind plunges through the wood would it take to lance whoever sat within?

"And on the next day," he mumbled under his breath, and couldn't remember the words to the second verse. It did not matter. It was natural, and the moment passed. As did the carriage and its accompanying group of soldiers. He released his hold on Vengeance. Once more, a coldness came upon him, and for a terrible moment, he wondered if that had been his only opportunity to ambush the cur.

"It was natural," he sang, louder than before, leaving the words hanging in the air as he brought Highwind out from cover to watch the rear of the envoy as they marched on through the Wastes, not caring enough to look behind them. Sweat covered him. To his surprise, he tasted blood on his lips, where he'd chewed them in nervous excitement, and spat crimson onto the ground.

"Come on, girl, let's go home," he whispered, leading Highwind from the path towards Raven Rock.

Initially, he didn't notice it, for his mind was awash with excitement and relief. The sky had cleared, suggesting an unseasonably warm day. Beneath the canopy of green, he could feel the growing warmth, and it reminded him of a day a long time ago when he'd hidden in a little sanctuary until his world had come crashing down around him.

This was worse.

He saw the dark smoke through a break in the green, and though Highwind carried him farther, Erroh remained frozen in his seat. Releasing the reins, he held his chest as though struck by a phantom club in the gut, and all the while, he knew it was the end of the world when he saw the smoke.

"Oh, please, no," he begged the absent gods, but they knew better than to answer or comfort him. He raced the last mile and only then noticed that the route was freshly churned. They were all dead; he knew it. He would lose everything because he was a failure. Again, the absent gods dared not argue nor comfort him. "Please, anything but this."

He dropped from Highwind, taking only his swords with him. He did not lead her, nor look to see if she wandered. Only a lifetime under Magnus's teachings had him take some precautions. He scrambled through the undergrowth, still far from the impenetrable wall, seeking a higher ground where he could take in the devastation he suspected waited for him.

Lea is dead.
Lexi is dead.
They are all dead.

He shook the thoughts away, but he knew better. He'd been so confident his appearance in the city would end the war. He had been so sure. He had been so wrong.

The last few steps were the hardest. Twice he stumbled in the unforgiving terrain as he climbed for a better vantage point. This felt like the first town. This felt a thousand times worse. Near the hatch of Wynn's tunnel, Erroh sat upon a ridge overlooking the horror, and here he lost his mind. He could not stop the tears flowing. He could not look away. Nor would he.

They are all dead.

He'd only once seen Raven Rock this quiet, and that was the first time he'd seen the place. How fitting it would be that it would be the same on its last day. There were no corpses in the town. Everywhere he stared, he saw death, and it was too much. He threw up upon himself. The retching echoed loudly enough that any fiend still waiting in the shadows might hear him. He didn't care. He wanted to die. He wanted to wail. He wanted to kill.

Crumpling in the concealing grass, he lay there for a time, his body quivering and broken, his will burned away to nothing like a female in a burning pyre.

"I can take no more," he whispered. He lay staring at the dead town, knowing nothing in the world would be the same again.

It was Highwind who stirred him, as she usually did. Without a master to direct her, she rambled through the undergrowth, wandering downward, until the beacon of home drew her to Raven Rock as it had before. Her empty, echoing steps filled the dead town, and Erroh, broken upon the ledge, heard them and watched her for a while, and his heart broke for her. She had returned home and found absence. Only she wasn't smart enough to comprehend the terrible turn of events.

Summoning a strength he did not know himself capable of, he scrambled down through the undergrowth and marched through the town. The shadows of death were worse here. There was still energy in this place. He thought about the passing Southerners and cursed his lack of resolve. Might this discovery have been less crushing were Uden dead at his hands? How different might events have been had he left the Southern camp a day sooner? Or if he had ridden straight to Raven Rock that first painful day?

You failed everyone.

He felt eyes upon him as he walked through the streets. He imagined flashes of movement behind curtains in some of the buildings he passed. He might have drawn his sword and challenged his imaginings to a fight, but he was alone in this grisly place. This time was worse than before.

He faced only one horror at a time and saved the worst for last. Casting barely a glance at Nomi's little shack and its door, swinging in the morning breeze, he stepped into his own house and prepared himself for both a miraculous sign of life and the stark evidence of devastation.

He scrambled from room to room, searching for her body. Searching for signs of a struggle. To his horror, he found their bedroom door shattered to a thousand pieces, along with everything else within. "You put up a fight, didn't you?" he wailed, his voice breaking. "Even as they pulled you from your slumber." He tried not to imagine the terror she had endured, but it was too much. He fell against the wall and wept; his hands shook, and his vision darkened so that all he could see was the open window. He could see the smoke still rising.

The loneliest walk was to the pyre. He caught sight of Highwind. She was plodding uneasily through the stables, unsure where to find her comrades. She consoled herself by finding a bag of discarded feed, no doubt dropped during their plundering. For just a breath, he too wanted to be distracted by a fine meal. He wanted to be a thousand miles away.

He passed the long-extinguished campfire where the blood was most plentiful and wondered who had fallen in this place. Had they killed enough to walk into the darkness with pride? Each of his friends' faces came to mind, and he loved them all. He thought about his family, and it was too much.

Worse than Aireys.

He wept for Nomi, for Alexis and then for Lea. It was all he could do, falling to his knees in front of the great pyre in the centre of the town. A message from Uden, no doubt. Erroh had taken his eye, and Uden had replied with tenfold the cruelty.

He could see a body within the ashes. The shape and nothing else. She had been burned, and it was dreadful, and he sobbed into the ground. He thought about dousing the flames though the fires were massive. He thought better of it. Whoever burned to nothing would float forever in the air.

It is Lea who was burned here.

He wailed again, striking the ground, and nothing was left in him but senseless hatred for the unfairness of evil deeds. "Face me, you animals," he cried, knowing the town was long abandoned. His defiant words fell on nothing. His quarry was a hundred miles from here at least. He thought for a breath of hopping upon Highwind one last time, charging through the Wastes with swords raised and a red fury upon his vision, and hunting these murdering fuks down, but the agony of this awfulness was too much for a cub as little as he. He felt a cage beckoning in his mind, and it was a tempting invitation.

Just sleep and never get hurt again.
Sleep it all away.

Erroh would not sleep. Could not sleep. It was a fine thing, too, for of course he was not alone in this town at all. The raiders emerged from their hiding places. They spilled out by the dozen or so, their armour polished, their swords oiled and sharpened. From a handful of houses, they emerged with murder in their minds. Slowly, they surrounded him, and he could barely raise his head to face them.

But face them, he did, for his day could get no worse.

26

THE MISADVENTURES OF BRIN THE WISTFUL

Brin was no stranger to receiving orders; he'd spent most of his life doing just that. He'd always considered himself of higher stature within any given conflict. A child of battle, a man of skirmishes, and now an older veteran of swords, death and war. He was no hero, though. He'd never stood out in the haze of battle, nor in the legends about great warriors. He'd never once inspired others in a clash, but never once had he fled from battle. He knew his place within the ranks. A good soldier answered orders without question. And he had done so, especially in his younger years, before the clans gathered as one and began fighting outside of themselves. He had also followed orders of such brutality and tastelessness that their tales deserved to be forgotten at the bottom of a bottle of ale. Orders had made him the man he was, but now he was tired and broken. The orders he followed now were harder to take, for he knew his death would be this day. Or tomorrow. Or the day after. Whichever day. But soon, because these orders ensured his death. He knew it in his bones where they ached the most.

"It is freezing in here. Can we not set a light?" Freya asked from beside him. She was younger than he, enthusiastic, arrogant and careless in war. He knew this because he'd seen her struggle and thrash with some Northern curs when they took this town. He had hobbled in after her, watching her scale the wall with her brethren and nearly die for her efforts. While Brin was cautious about meeting more of these wild bastards in a fight, Freya had tenfold the eagerness. Some zealots desired the ultimate act of sacrifice. She had enlisted herself in the right unit.

"No, we remain here, all quiet, until Erroh comes wandering the arth to gaze upon his fallen home."

"He won't be along—not yet, at least," she countered, wrapping her arms around herself. It was cold even in the early sun. A fire in the little room overlooking the pyre would hardly be noticeable, but while there was a chance they could take the fiend by surprise, Brin would happily take the cold. Besides, he was a cold-blooded soldier, was he not? Even if he was hobbled.

"He'll be along. I feel it in my bones," Brin warned, and it was enough to silence his young comrade. Even talking or thinking of his aching bones was enough to send daggers of pain through his knees. Absently, he massaged them and leaned back in his chair. It was something to do while waiting for death.

She sat back away from the grubby window of the healer's surgery and picked up the bowl of cold, half-finished porridge. As she ate, she muttered to herself. No doubt, from her tone, she was most displeased with his decision to remain cold.

"Eat up," he mocked gently, and the muttering continued. He couldn't imagine eating in a miserable room with the smells of death, blood and antibiotics so prevalent, yet there she was, spooning the shit into her mouth like it was a bubbling boar stew. Why she had even cooked the concoction, using the pot by the long burned-out campfire, was another thing entirely, but Brin suspected her young life had been filled with similar hard choices. She had seen a store of raw oats not yet spoiled, so she had simply taken advantage and saved her own rations for another day.

Was I as dedicated to survival?

He smiled bitterly. He had never been that dedicated. Certainly was not anymore.

"Can you hear that?" she whispered suddenly. She began spooning the porridge into her mouth more quickly lest it go to waste before a fight. Before an ambush. He heard nothing, but then again, he was older, with ageing ears built more for sleeping and less for detecting fiends sneaking up on them, searching for a victim.

"There again—a mount's steps," she said, setting the bowl upon a slab marred with long-dried blood. She had a smudge of porridge on her grubby chin, and he thought about telling her before falling silent. She was good-looking enough. A piece of cold porridge would hardly make a difference. Might be ammunition for when she muttered a crude jest under her breath the next time she disagreed with him, too. Brin was old enough to be petty, especially if it was their last day.

He craned his neck and listened for a time until, finally, there came the gentle tapping of a nearing mount.

"Well, that is strange," Freya muttered. She had discovered the porridge and, wiping it away with a finger, looked cautiously out at the animal trotting through the town.

"Could be a trap," Brin whispered, watching the horse wander. He had little time for those mounts, small and delicate as they were. He preferred a Southern mount. For a moment, he lamented his own lost horse. Long gone it was, taken by Erroh in a frozen town in a different life. For weeks, he'd missed it. It was something to do while recovering from a false god's touch.

"We are the trap," Brin said, correcting himself, and Freya grinned. She did not know what force she faced, were the trap to be sprung and a false god to be assaulted. They hadn't enough soldiers, but Gemmil had insisted that was all they would spare. The rest of Uden's soldiers had delayed for days in the dead town waiting for Erroh to return. Nobody believed he would, but Brin certainly had. He had that type of luck. It was a shitty task led by a broken Rider, too unfortunate to ride another day.

"Let me gather the mount and see where it came from," she said.

Again, Brin shook his head. But he could feel it now like a whisper in his mind. He didn't know how, only that he knew.

After a time, Freya peered out the window. "Who is that?" she whispered. Brin was sitting in his chair, whispering prayers to his old gods. He had prayed when he heard movement besides a wandering mount in the streets beyond. Mostly, he'd heard grunts and cries of agony. "There's a man at the fire," she added gleefully.

Slowly Brin climbed to his feet. He heard the crunching in his bones as he shuffled over to the window. Heard it louder as he reached for his blade. Outside, he could see a figure.

"Is it him? When will we take him?" Freya said eagerly.

"Prepare yourself," whispered Brin, knowing this was the end. She brushed her hair back behind her ears, and he thought her fetching. He might have slept with her. There was bedding in the corner and everything. It would have helped to stave off boredom. In the first few months after his assault, he'd had many women come and bed him. Even with his battered knees, they had leapt upon him, and he'd been willing. He had told the tale he had delivered to Uden the Woodin Man, and they had listened and rewarded him. Thinking him blessed, believing him godly. Enduring his first march, he'd felt like a spry young man. Now, though, as the army's march drew on, women were less willing to lie with an older man. Less inclined to get pregnant lest they miss their god's call to battle. Though Freya had mocked him, he knew enough that she would take his touch and he hers—a fine last furrow.

"Is it him?" Freya gasped as the figure collapsed, and Brin felt deathly cold.

And I, the fool who survived one of Erroh's attacks and lived.

It was a shitty order and a shittier way to die. Brin had said as much. Gemmil had not argued. Merely offered a curt nod and kicked his horse on to leave the ambushers behind.

"Tell me, Brin. Is it him?" she asked again, strapping her chest plate tighter and taking hold of her steel sword. She already knew the answer, but he was the master of this group.

"When we charge on him, allow the others to attack first. He is as quick as fork lightning. Pick your moment," he pleaded, but her eyes were full of bloodlust. The eyes of a demented zealot with permission to slay a false god. He opened the door quietly, and she pushed past him. The rest of the doomed soldiers, hiding behind curtains and doors in the surrounding buildings, did as he did.

Outside in the morning heat, Brin shuffled forward as Erroh wailed and struck the ground in torment, and Brin thought this interesting.

"Erroh of Spark, drop your swords and bow your head," he cried, and Erroh didn't stir. Didn't even look up. Instead, he watched the fire for a few breaths. From all sides, they came to surround him, but Freya rushed ahead of the Southern circle and drew her blade.

"To the fires with you, cur," she screamed, and Erroh, who had fallen to his knees, finally looked up.

Brin had seen Erroh move with terrifying speed before, and it was no surprise to see the boy come alive now. His body was a blur of movement, and, as he had feared, Freya died before anyone else.

She managed a scream as Erroh slipped away from her strike, allowing his blade to trail out behind him as he did. Spinning, Erroh struck out with his second blade, giving her a gentle rap across her throat, and it was devastating. Brin watched the spray and knew immediately her wound was mortal. She had a strong heart. It pumped frantically as she stumbled away and collapsed against him. Her expression was not one of fear or sadness but a grimace of fury.

"He was quick," she whispered, and the tears poured down her cheeks. "Take him," she gasped, and died, and Brin held her momentarily as his other comrades began to die around him.

This was a terrible mistake.

The false god never stopped moving. His second kill was the solitary archer Dahl. The fool had charged forward with the others, despite Brin's instructions. Relying on human reflexes to win the day was no sound tactic against such a fiend. He managed one shot from his crossbow, and perhaps on any other day, against a lesser demon, the shot might have pierced Erroh's armour and taken his heart. But Erroh struck the bolt out of the air, splitting it and ducking as it passed—a miraculous shot worthy of a sonnet. Leaping upon the unfortunate crossbow wielder with swinging blades, Erroh soon ended his life.

"All at once," Brin cried, but his new comrades were not listening. Instead of charging in, grabbing Erroh, and suffering only a few losses, they engaged in swordplay and fell one after the other. First, Ebbe. A tall young warrior with a long sword. Ebbe had claimed the sword was his father's. Used to "kill a thousand Northerners in the Four Factions war," he'd boasted. It was a fine piece, indeed. He was dead before he got to swing it. Erroh, spotting the movement of his shoulders, leapt forward, sending his death blades through Ebbe's forehead. His body hung still for a moment as his impressive sword fell in the dirt. For a breath, he caught sight of Erroh marvelling at the blade before moving on to his next kill.

"Get around him! Take him from the back," Brin cried, but the eight remaining warriors were unprepared for the ferocious speed of their assailant. "Don't engage him," Brin added, moving towards the melee as it shuffled swifter from his reach.

Oh, to have legs so I could charge forward and flee swiftly.

Elgot tried to steal victory next. Sneaking in from the side as Erroh retreated away from the gathering blades, using the flames to cover his rear, it was a sound tactic. He came within range, gripping his daggers and ready to strike, but his steps were heavy, and he got in too near. In that frozen moment, he stepped way too near. Why did he step in so near? Truthfully, Elgot had heavy steps for such a diminutive young warrior. Stepping too close was simply asking for trouble. Erroh did not look; did not need to. Even as the young warrior's blades neared him, he blocked the strike carelessly with his left hand while his right spun his sword in an arc. Then he stopped mid-spin and plunged the blade deep into a thoroughly surprised Elgot. Brin couldn't tell if the young man died immediately, only that he dropped his weapons and, clutching his stomach, fell away from the melee, leaving the false god further room to manoeuvre.

Brin slowed his steps now, for his weak knees could not carry him far at pace. Using his sword for balance, he walked towards the skirmish, towards his death, and strangely, he was at peace with this. He had a child back home in Conlon. The mother was an unimpressive wench with a bitter tongue but fine hips. He had done his part for this war; he had done his part to keep his bloodline going. In this moment, he merely hoped that when Erroh killed the rest of his comrades, he took little time and fewer strikes to send him to Valhal.

The next to die in this skirmish was Anika, and she died worse than the others. Fitting, thought Brin. He had known her for most of this march and thought little of her nasty mind. There was a cruelty to her he had rarely seen in any warrior, and it was she who blocked the next counter from Erroh. She squealed in triumphant surprise, but her victory was short-lived: instead of retreating as before, Erroh suddenly charged into the clustered storm of swords, swiping, blocking, cutting, killing. He stepped among them as though dancing among blades and menace was no matter at all. He was a blur, and he was terrifying. Though she took his strike, she could not take his power, which sent her stumbling headfirst into the flames. At this terrible moment, the pyre shifted, and a heavy load fell upon her, trapping her for a few awful, burning breaths. Brin tried to rush to her aid, but the damage was done. The blaze took hold of her hair, clothing and skin. She screamed and struggled beneath the weight of the burning logs, and Brin thought no woman should endure such torment. No man, either. No matter how nasty. To his horror, instead of surrendering to her fate, she finally struggled free, rose, and lurched away in a wave of ashes, sparks and terrible flame. She ran blindly for a few moments, her body immolated, her eyes unseeing and scorched, her tongue screaming her torment for all to hear. She ran through the melee, causing havoc among the fighters as they fled from the human torch. Less so, Erroh, who looked on placidly at this new level of brutality.

Eskil was the only comrade who went to Anika's aid. Brin couldn't be sure if they were friends, lovers, or simply comrades, but she fell upon him and entangled him in her burning ruin. Brin wished they hadn't doused the burning pyre in so much lantern oil in that moment. He died to a blade while batting at the flames that engulfed them both. Perhaps in his last moments, doing a kindness guaranteed him a rightful seat at a Valhal table.

Brin watched on in horror as Erroh continued his assault upon the ambushers, and they were lesser for it. Bodies fell on either side of his two blades. Halden, a keen watcher of birds among the march, fought hard but failed. He was a strange brute who would stare for an hour at a bird going about its day, building a nest, gorging itself upon worms, or just whistling for threats or mates. Then Halden would kill it with a crossbow so he might eat. Brin preferred not to have any connection with prey, but Halden thrived on it. The brute might have fared better against Erroh with his crossbow from a distance, such were his inadequacies with the blade he carried. Brin watched it fall from the man's lifeless, crimson-soaked hands.

It might have been Donir who fell next, but he couldn't be sure in the crimson haze. He was there, upright, with thoughts in his mind, before disappearing into the flames from which Anika had risen. At least Donir did not wail. Donir had always wanted to die well, just like his mother. Brin thought she might have been proud when they met in the darkness beyond.

Kare put up a good fight. She met Erroh for a few strikes and managed a swiping blow across his chest, but drew little blood. Were the rest of her comrades aware or skilled enough, they might have taken advantage, but this was a terribly selected group of soldiers led by a hobbled, wretched man without acclaim. As it was, they scattered as her blade met their assailant. Erroh slowed for just a breath and slipped away from her next strike. He was slightly slower now, but still she could gain no advantage. She swung wildly, but he blocked her every strike, and Brin wondered if Erroh was taking a breath, deciding how best to kill her and the rest of the ambushers. Whatever went through Erroh's mind was swift, for without warning, he thrust himself forward, knocking her blade skyward. Without blinking, he plunged his blade through her heart and killed her. It was a fine killing blow. One moment she was swinging her blade; the next, she was nothing but reflexes and blank, unfocused eyes. Despite that, she caught him a second, final time as she collapsed. She drew no blood, but for a girl who had praised herself for being the finest blade master in their little troop, she had acquitted herself admirably. That was something, at least.

Eventually, exhaustion began to get the better of Erroh, for he fell upon the last ambusher with gasping breath and tore him asunder. Brin watched numbly and tried to remember the man's name. He wore a thick mask, and Brin found he couldn't remember the poor man's face either. He was barely skilled enough to match Erroh's lightning blades. Every time the unfortunate warrior attempted to attack, Erroh struck with both swords, knocking him back, step by step through the ruined battlefield.

Was it Gard? Brin wondered, and had visions of him playing cards surrounded by his comrades. He thought it was Gard. Gard would laugh his wonderful, deep laugh every time he played a victorious hand. This Gard was silent, though, as Erroh killed him. Perhaps it was bravery. Perhaps it was Erroh's demented screaming in his ugly tongue that stilled his booming voice.

It was time to end this battle, and Erroh ended it spectacularly. With a final clash of blades and a sudden spin of body and blade in a dreadful arc, Erroh sliced Gard's head from his body. His head rolled free, and a fountain of blood covered Erroh as he stood panting, looking over the destruction he'd wrought.

Brin had begun to hobble towards the battlefield, but now, as the last body fell, he halted his march. He wasn't afraid; he merely wanted this horror to end. He imagined his comrades waiting for him at a long table in Valhal. They would pour the first few goblets, and they would sing, and they would cheer, and they would laugh, and the pain of life would be done.

Brin raised his quivering blade, almost in salute, and waited for the vile, false god of fire to see him there and finish him. Within a breath, Erroh turned, and Brin felt a terrible, cold fear come upon him. In that moment, he knew he faced a god. And he knew his days upon the arth had at last come to an end.

27

AIMEE

No. Not Aimee. That was wrong. Her name was not Aimee. Her name was Tempest, and she believed she liked to kill. No, it was more than a belief. It was a certainty. *She liked to kill.* Aye, killing made the pain fade away. Made the screaming voices in her mind fall silent in delicious reverence as blood spilled around her and her belly grumbled for food. She was a good hound. She was beaten in. Like any good hound. Like the best hound. Uden's favourite hound. Uden's favourite.

"I will take her tongue," Aimee whispered, and shook her head. Not Aimee. Fuken Tempest. On a violent night, she was born into this world by the grace and touch of her beautiful god's will, and she was greater for it. Also, a thousand times worse. "I will take it and then her heart, and he will be pleased. Or angry." She was not sure. She could not think. She was not used to thinking. She remembered the act from a lifetime ago, but she had not thought for herself since the night she was born. When the pain was intense and he so fierce. "I will slit her throat," Aimee screamed, shaking her head as she charged through the camp. Those of the bastard Hunt who looked up from their duties dared not speak to her or take hold of her and shake the wits into her. Or from her. Whichever, really.

Aimee, of Raven Rock.

Fleeing from Aurora and her wickedness had taken her far from her tent. For hours she had hidden among the tents of her enforced comrades, hating them in silence. Hating herself even more. Eventually, like a pigeon drawn to its nest, she found herself at the outskirts of her home, and it was too much. It was too beautiful. She could feel it now, a glimmer of warmth beneath the screaming voices, and it tasted less like blood and death and more like ale and good cheer. Her feet carried her swiftly the last few steps. With most of the Southerners left behind now, she scampered through the gates, then stopped dead in horror.

Aimee is home.

She almost called out for Kaya, and such a thought hurt her, cut deeply into her heart and whispered that life would be better taken away. Like Kaya's life, like everyone else's. Without warning, she collapsed against the gate and remembered the last night, when Raven Rock had fallen. She remembered the screeching of metal most; the panic and the piercing cry of the world's end had silenced the demons within her mind as though she herself had been doing the killing.

"I like to kill," she lied, for it hurt less when she lied.

Her feet ached, and she looked down at them and grimaced, seeing the scrapes and grazes. A better warrior might have taken a moment to don a pair of shoes before she scampered away from her sister, her mother, her fuken precursor. Her Aurora.

My Aurora, for he demands it.

She imagined picking a shard of split, jagged rock from her soul, and she grinned at the pain. She loved pain. She did not know why. She remembered pain in her other life, which had not suited her. Nowadays, a little pain helped her swallow the misery a little.

"My name is Tempest; I like to kill," she whispered, and it felt heavy on her lips. Only the best lies felt heavy, so she bit her lip until she drew blood, which settled her thoughts for a breath. She remembered her last kill. It hadn't taken long: a little bravado from Uden, and she had delivered the girl to her doom with a few sweet kisses of the blade. He had been impressed, and why not? She would outdo Aurora, become ten times the warrior and, as Uden liked to say, "kill the last of the little Alphalines too fearful of rearing their heads." She had seen Alphas before; she knew their impressiveness and carelessness. For months, he had promised her plenty of Alphalines to kill in the city.

I must carry on where Aurora failed.

The girl Aimee held little love for Spark City. The goddess Tempest even less. Denying her the gift of walking Spark's smouldering streets with sword raised, all eager and excited, was a cruelty with far-reaching consequences. Instead of gifting her the freedom to kill, Uden had shepherded her back to her home, where Aimee's world had ended and Tempest's mind had shattered. Seeing this place had churned her mind.

I am Tempest; I like to kill.

Aimee climbed to unsteady feet and faced her home. Did Uden know she came from here? Was he tormenting her this one last time, hoping to burn away the last vestiges of humanity still hiding away in the darkest recesses of her tormented soul? She thought she would not see Raven Rock again. A girl had left, and a vile monster had returned in its place.

They would be so ashamed of me.

"Hello, Raven Rock," she whispered, wondering if the town recognised her beneath the horror she had become. "It's a beautiful, terrible thing to be home." She touched the gate and wandered through. It was quiet at this late hour without the hum of a day's natural melody to distract. There was nothing but the buzz of a gathered army. That and the gentle breeze. And perhaps something else.

I could run.

Her body convulsed; she felt her stomach lurch, and her body tingled in terror. She wanted to scream, cry, and keep thinking that thought, until it burned within her mind. He had said she was almost ready. He had said he trusted her with a taste of freedom. He had pledged she would never feel his love again were she to run.

She wondered how easy it would be to leave this fantastic prison. To escape his ever-loving gaze. For a strange moment, she imagined the sun on her face, the taste of salt on her lips—the feeling of freedom in her bones.

I am Tempest; I like to kill.

She felt his pull and his love, and it was potent, and she stumbled through the streets searching for a little crevice to hide in for a time. To gather her thoughts, to remember whom she loved. To summon the will to return to him as any dutiful daughter fearful of a raging inferno might do.

"I was Aimee. I wanted to be a runner."

Kaya knew I'd make a fine runner.

More thoughts flooded in and overcame the torment, and she allowed them. Her mind spun; she wanted to kill; she wanted to punish; she wanted to save; she wanted to die. All in the same moment. In Raven Rock, his voice wasn't as prevalent in her mind. In Raven Rock, she listened to her memories. Most were cruel and awful, but there were others that warmed and kept her. Tempest hid from these thoughts, and Aimee embraced them.

Because I am unfinished.
I am not yet his child.
I am myself.

It was the wall she sought first, and perhaps it was the wall that drew her from this nightmare of a split mind. Avoiding the few wandering guards patrolling a futile, dead town, she climbed a ladder and stood barefoot upon the top. She'd walked this wall a thousand times in her youth. Something was reassuring about its age. It would live on after her. After them all. After Uden. Without warning, tears spilled from her eyes and she defied her instincts to wipe them away lest he know of them and become enraged; she allowed them to spill free, which was beautiful. She had never cried during this new life. Truthfully, upon the wall with Kaya at her side, Aimee, facing horrors and inevitable death, had cried far less than most young warriors might have done. Kaya had approved, and she thought of Kaya, and it kept her from fleeing from the darkness into his all-embracing light.

A runner uses the dark.

She walked along the wall, a wraith of grace and silence, little more than a shuffling shadow against the night. That wasn't Tempest; these were Aimee's ways. She allowed her tears to flow, and each silent one was a memory reclaimed. Suddenly she no longer feared for her soul. Suddenly she saw the woodland beyond for the gift any runner would perceive it to be.

And then she saw something else.

To be accurate, she heard something first. A clumsy breaking of branches against the night's calm. Someone was moving slowly and clumsily, and they were beautiful. And then she could see them. A boy, a girl. Both her age, striking in their beauty, and she gazed upon their wandering, and it was a wonderful thing. Gone now was her panic, and her stuttering thoughts. Gone, too, were her miseries, replaced by idle curiosity. The two intruders were scaling this town's defences like foolish bandits, crazed by hunger and boredom. Ducking low, she lay flat along the wall only a dozen steps from where they tangled in the undergrowth.

They come to save their comrades.

She looked around the darkened town and wondered what luck would befall them for such marvellous stupidity. She wondered, were they Alphalines? All naïve and unprepared for the city. Even with no sign of wandering soldiers, she lay flat. Careful to keep her hair from streaming down the wall and catching in the low light, she became a hidden watcher, which was beautiful.

For only a breath, she considered calling for an alarm, or better, leaping from high with sword in hand and slaying them where they stood. It didn't matter that they likely were better fighters than she or that her sword remained in her tent.

Besides, she wished them success, though she didn't know why.

She was startled by the sudden appearance of a patrolling guard at the foot of the ladder. As he took a moment to relieve himself a few feet below, Aimee watched, and terror took her. Tempest fought from deep within; she put in a good fight.

Dropping silently beside him, Aimee gifted Tempest a little violence to quell her desires. Swiftly, she reached from behind and took his breath with a delicate swipe across the throat. Not deep enough to kill, though Tempest begged her. Instead, as the soldier struggled and tried to cry out, she wrapped herself around him and squeezed. With nothing but the memory of Kaya's instructions as her guide she felt success even in the dark. After a few tight breaths, he fought and gasped and fell to his knees, where she adjusted her grip to his neck alone.

"I bet I can snap his neck in two."

"Looks like a weak neck."

She quelled that voice and held him without killing and eased him to the ground. Above her, she heard arguing, and she winced at her failure. A runner was never caught unawares.

She saw an attractive boy's foot hanging above her as he climbed over the wall and then slipped a little farther down to a dark corner, where he ducked out of sight. After this, strangely, there came no other words, but she knew he was silently watching. She could see his face, and she liked it. And she knew to remain still until he looked past her. Despite the gloom, she could just make out his eyes, and she thought they were lovely. Kind. She wasn't used to kind. She imagined cutting them out and also kissing him. She wasn't used to such feelings. Had not felt such things in a long time. Not since before the killing. Not since before…

She scuttled away, for she was skilled at such things. Away from this boy. Away from the events she had no right playing a part in. Each barefoot step was silent as she moved through the dusty streets of her fallen home, and for a moment, she remembered its glory again. In reply to her memories, an invisible vice took her, held her by the throat and threatened to squeeze. It had a green eye, and it mocked and loved her. And she loved it back.

I hate him.

She stumbled, and the boy froze for a moment, listening, but did not notice her. She heard him mutter words as he began to move once more, and there was more movement as the beautiful girl appeared from the shadows and followed him. She stayed where she was. Their mission was not hers. She wanted no further part.

And then she saw the dozen guards in the fire's light, and she knew these beautiful Alphas could never slip by them and free the prisoner. Her eyes fell upon the broken ruin by the post, chained like a hound, fit for killing. She knew him from a lifetime ago. A kind man, a leader, and an Outcast too. They were supposed to shun him in Raven Rock, but Kaya had a big heart, and she had ruled the mood.

Beautiful, exotic Kaya of the deep north.

Other memories flooded her now, and she wanted to scream and fight their dreadful gift. Instead, she wandered to the warmth of the fire and stepped out into the light, revealing herself to the watching eyes. They knew her threat and lineage, for her delicious god had seen to such things. They fell silent as she approached, and she searched for the words—anything to distract herself from her thoughts.

They did not know how to address her, and this pleased her. Easier to set them to task if there was a slight uneasiness about them. She knew this because Uden had educated her. There were ways, and though she was a limpet in a greater saltwater pool, she was still godly.

"Good evening, comrades," she whispered, her voice firm. Firmer than she had expected, with such horrors playing in her mind. "Do we need so many guards attending to a chained wretch?"

One guard, an older fiend, heavy of face and fuller of belly, bowed and began offering, no doubt, a compelling argument, but the hour was late. She hadn't the time for courtesy or argument. She had places to be; she had beautiful people to help.

"They ordered us to—" he began.

"Whisht," she hissed, drawing near him, and she wondered about taking his tongue. She also wondered might any of his comrades come to his aid. She could slip in low, take his dagger, and slice and cut for a time. She knew the art of taking a tongue; she had hated learning it, and so had her victim. "With so much to prepare for, a god might presume you are taking an easy night while the rest work," she said, eyeing the man coldly. She observed the pathetic ruin of the prisoner. He looked broken and wretched. But if the beautiful Alphas sought his freedom, she would do what she must. She addressed the crowd now. "Leave two alone to watch the fire. The rest, assist your comrades."

There were mutterings but nothing as brazen as argument. The older fiend left the fire, taking his men with him and leaving her with two more placid curs. When the echoes of their footsteps disappeared into the melee of the unpacking camp, she considered killing both men, whose vacant stares suggested little threat.

Just a little killing.

Instead of succumbing to her urges, however, she slipped away from the fire and her potential victims. Her silent steps brought her to the broken figure attached to the post, and the sight of him finally shattered her. He was a little older, a little more wretched, but she almost bowed to the former leader of Adawan. She knew him, knew his fierceness, knew his beliefs too. Despite these valid reasons for fearing him, he had been a prosperous friend to Adawan in another life, even after his usurping. Raven Rock had mourned the passing of his rule, if not his archaic politics. Aimee knew it was all right to be a good person and also to be wrong. There were worse things. Few people agreed, though.

"Wrek," she whispered, and his beaten face rolled a little towards her. He stared with a swollen eye and she saw little recognition in it. And why would there be? She had been a little waif the last time they had met, scared of his stature. For a moment, she remembered her life completely. She remembered Adawan. That was the plan in the end: to run to Adawan should the gate collapse, and collapse it did.

Kaya's screams.
She left me.
I allowed her.
So I could die with the rest.
And I did.
A thousand times since.

Shaking the thoughts away, she caught sight of a dagger dug into the ground. Unsure of why such a blade stood just out of his reach, she pulled it free, examined its delicate beauty and slipped it into his belt. A stunning gift. He was, after all, Reckless of Adawan. Such a thing was a terror. She kissed his forehead and left him where he lay; it was all she would do. Could do. She was no Alpha; she was no Alpha hunter, either. But she was curious; each act now brought her closer to the gates and the forest beyond.

I cannot forsake his love.

Slipping away from the watching eyes by the fire, she slid into the shadows and scaled the wall gracefully. She had never had trouble as a child climbing this wall, and tonight was no different. She remembered the many nights she had spent upon this wall and the honour of the run and the watch. She allowed herself the anguished relief of a smile. With her head bowed so that nobody would see her.

He sees all.

"Fuk the Woodin Man," she whispered to the night, and felt more potent for it. She sat, and from this height, she saw more than her false god; her words of blasphemy were ambrosia. She gazed into the night, towards the dimly lit room where the healer attended to Uden's kin. She knew the building better as the Fighting Mongoose Tavern and her fists tightened, and she turned away and dropped her feet over the outer side of the wall.

"Drop and be gone," Aimee whispered, but Tempest held her leap. Looking back once more and preparing to surrender to sacrilegious escape, a strange thing happened: she caught sight of the killers in the darkness and her breath caught in her throat.

She knew their plan and could see it unfolding from this height, for she was a master of warfare—Uden had told her as much. She watched them steal up beside the unsuspecting guards and slaughter them. There was beauty in the killing, for it was vicious and silent. The boy left a little more blood than the girl, and this was delicious, and Tempest recoiled and licked her lips.

"Free him, you beauties," she whispered, and the false god Uden must have watched and influenced, for from nowhere a dozen guards appeared, and Tempest's heart sank, for their adventure was about to end. She wondered about leaping back down into the darkness, stealing up behind the guards and assisting her unfamiliar comrades, but she had no blade. She could only hope the Alphas were as devastating as their legend suggested.

And then she had an idea, a simple idea. Tempest doubted it would work, but Aimee believed.

Without hesitating or thinking better about her actions, she sprinted along the upper wall, caring little who saw her, before dropping into the pen that held the former inhabitants' mounts. Though she had little skill riding such magnificent horses, she could tell how impressive these beasts might have been with a gathering of Runners urging them through the forests in search of prey and fortune.

In another life.

She unwound their holdings, then slid the pen gate open, slapped their rears and sent them thundering into the night. It was all she could do for the interlopers, and she wished them the grandest fortune of the night. Then, slipping away from the chaos she had created, as the freed mounts rushed through the town towards the main gates, she walked casually around the rear of the building housing Uden's dying niece. She knew the back door was easy to break. More than that, she knew he had always left a key beneath a long-dead potted plant. Silently, for she was a skilled assassin, she unlocked the door, turned the old wooden handle and slipped into the old tavern's backroom with murder on her mind.

28

PALACE

Magnus was no stranger to this part of his country. No stranger, but it was not his home. It never had been. He had been born near here, but it was hard to love a place filled with such painful memories. This place had been his making. For that, he was grateful. His throne lay nestled within the keep of Risbeigh. Of all the strongholds he could have chosen, it was the least impressive, but since it faced the endless oceans of the east, he had thought this would be a fine first line in the unlikely event of an invasion from some unknown race, and that he would be part of it. That was what he had once believed. Not anymore.

"A grand welcome, it is," muttered Padir from beside him. From the moment they had stepped through the gates of his palace, he'd felt the eyes upon him. If his subjects had held onto their disdain for him for the time it had taken him to reach here, it seemed they could barely contain their disgust at his return.

I should have returned the crown while I had their good will.

"Just keep your wits about you, young one," Magnus whispered.

"Oh, I'll escape from here with my life. I'm no king." The boy laughed crazily for a few breaths, though not loud enough that he might break the enchantment that had fallen upon the watching crowd.

They stared in silence and judged, but at least there were no stones or rotting vegetables in their grubby grasps as they watched the parade. That was something, Magnus supposed. The icy stares aimed at them by the leader, Gregor, and his accompanying riders, probably helped. He had not recognised Gregor at first. It had taken a mile of silent riding for the memories to be jarred. The little shit he'd known as a stable boy had risen high in the ranks. Wasn't it the way with the most ruthless? Gregor did not meet Magnus's eyes once. Instead, he kept his gaze firmly on the road, honour and duty etched in his every movement. Gregor was a staunch believer in the ways of the Savage Isles and would allow no harm to befall the king if he kept his word.

How long will their loyalty last once I play my part?

"You could always compete for the title," Magnus growled, and Padir fell silent. He knew the boy wasn't foolish enough to compete for the crown. That honour belonged to the finest warriors of the Savage Isles with ideas above their station and recklessness on their side. Besides, he was without a clan to carry his name. Magnus understood that well enough. It was something he might face again. "The old ways," he muttered to himself.

"It's a fine enough settlement, I suppose," Padir stated, but his eyes were wide in terror. It was easy to show bravado out on the march, but walking delicately along the silken tendrils of a spider's web was something else entirely. Some things were never destined to end well, it seemed.

Risbeigh had stayed the same. The grand walls, standing now as they had always stood, remained untouched by war or skirmish. As high as a three-story building, they would impress most people, at least those who'd never visited Samara. The keep's guards still patrolled the top, marching in twos, looking out over a peaceful realm, their green cloaks flapping magnificently in the wind from the ocean, only a mile to the east. Behind the impenetrable walls, Magnus noticed that additional buildings had been added among the existing, clustered few. Each structure, old and new, was pristine. He thought this was the way of every capital.

Your chosen capital.
Not that of the masses.

He did not meet the eyes of the watchers passing through the main street before taking the gentle climb towards the keep, which towered above all other structures. He did not listen to their whispers and mutterings, either.

The king has returned.
To the fires with him.

"It seems they were expecting your arrival," Padir said quietly, gesturing. Along the long wooden arch of the keep's great doors hung banners from all the clans. Above them all was the royal banner. Magnus held his step for a breath and gazed at the plethora of colours waving in the morning breeze. Oh, aye, they were good, impressive designs, but they may as well have been dipped in crimson such was the bloodshed between them.

You have had your share of bloodshed too.

He had tried to avoid conflict with the factions by outlawing royalty. Allowing the Spark to rule. It had all been for nothing. The old ways had lasted because improvements weren't always required. The Four Factions continued to war, regardless. Perhaps it was simply in the nature of humanity to tear and kill for a grain of respect, for an ounce of dirt? Magnus almost smiled at the notion. He was responsible for more deaths than any other person. Perhaps, instead of reimagining society, then, he might have adapted what worked in the Savage Isles. He had tried to end wars, but he should have accepted wars were inevitable. There was a dignity to bloodshed in the Savage Isles. Battles were won and lost over matters, but they were fought between those willing to fight. The people of this country, by contrast, were happy for the fighting clans to do their region's business.

Let the peasants suffer the more challenging life of tilling upon a field.

"Aye, I wonder who spread the word," Magnus muttered, eyeing the boy and wondering about his careless tongue. Of course, they were prepared for his arrival. Of course, they would have speakers from every clan present. How else could they get this lynching done rightly swiftly? He licked his lips. He might like a fine ale before they took him.

"My liege," Gregor offered, and nothing more. His Green Branch knights fell away from them and led their mounts away from the keep's entrance down towards the stables. Their official task was ensuring his safe return to the throne, but Magnus imagined them joining the dissenting voices to come.

I could have done things better.

Aye, he could have, but these lands had known peace. They could still fight. It was in their blood.

Dropping to the ground, a handler immediately took his mount from him. His hounds would stay at his side for the duration, however. If nothing else, that might give him and his party a warning against an ambush.

"Greetings, my liege," boomed a heavyset woman, and this time Magnus did smile openly. He'd have known her voice anywhere.

"Edain, my old friend," he cried, wrapping his arms around her. She was as old as he was, and just as wide. He felt her meaty arms grip him fiercely, and his breath was taken.

"A brave man you are, returning in such a way," she whispered before releasing him and bowing. The warning was clear, and his hopes for peace evaporated. He could see the fear in her eyes, and what did he expect? She had supported his leadership. She had been his eyes and ears in court these last few years. She was cunning and wise, but more than that, she was brave and honest. There were worse subjects to call upon.

As the honoured greeter of the king, she led Magnus and his party through the iron and oak doors, and immediately Magnus sniffed the aroma of a sumptuous feast. Farther down the main hallway, he could see the grand ballroom was being prepared with festive decorations.

"A feast in honour of me? I was hoping to meet privately with some of my chosen," he protested, and she stopped in her tracks.

"Safer in public," she said, her voice low. "Not everyone resents your presence, but this is still a precarious time, Magnus." She gripped his shoulder tightly. He could see the concern in her face, a worry she could show only behind closed doors. She had her kin to care for. It wasn't unknown that the passing of a king's crown often resulted in bloodshed among the most zealous.

The old ways.

"Let's get you both rested and washed. The smell of the road upon you both is ungodly," she said. It was a fair point. Magnus desired to dip his head beneath the surface of a washbasin, and Padir, away from the public eye, was scratching again.

His hounds bounded along, sniffing excitedly at the new aromas throughout the king's domain; their claws clicked loudly on the marble floor, and he could see their excited confusion at their surroundings. This dwelling was more lavishly decorated than his own home, but still more subtle than previous royal domains he'd visited. According to tradition, the king always chose his own residence. This stronghold was far from the rest of the world. It was a long road to travel, just to kneel before the crown and complain. Magnus ran his fingers absently along the icy wall as they passed. Smooth as the floor and just as cold. Magnus liked the cold. He'd need to, once this evening's festivities were underway.

"Who is your little companion?" Edain asked, stopping outside an old oak door decorated with gems cut by a skilled pair of hands. Magnus couldn't remember the last time he and Elise had lain together in this room. A terrible sadness came upon him, and he forced it far away. He didn't need to think about her.

Elise is dead, and you are alone and far from home.

"This is Padir. He speaks for me," Magnus said, grinding his teeth, for he could not take his eyes from the wood and suddenly wanted to cry out. To cry for her and for losing everything he'd once held with an unforgiving grip. He was home, and this was not home. Magnus turned to Padir, who tried and failed to disguise his anger at Magnus's proclamation about his affiliation. It was no small thing being granted this title. Dangerous thing, too. But in this moment, Magnus cared little for Padir's annoyance. Let the little fuk throw his hat into the sparring ring already.

Edain turned the key and opened the door to a brightly lit room. "Very well. I will see to his pleasure. I shall take the hounds, too," she said, allowing Magnus to enter his chambers. His hounds followed, and he didn't stop them.

"They will remain by my side," he said, and she caught the door before he closed it.

"Did you bring it?" He had, but he said nothing, and she nodded. "It is your right and your right alone to carry a blade into the feast," she whispered, careful not to be overheard, and he closed the door without another word. Fine advice indeed, and an offer he might consider.

He listened to her footsteps disappear, then turned as he heard Padir's voice explode in excitement, likely over the matter of having a luxurious room to himself, and Magnus smiled again. Some responsibility was all the boy needed to encourage him to step into the precarious world of royals and entitlements. With such titles and responsibilities came advantage.

He tried not to see signs of Elise in the bedroom but could not close his eyes to the memories—in the glamorous gowns hanging from hooks in the wardrobe, in the embossed hairbrush by her bedside, in the discarded paints left upon a dressing table beneath the one small window in the room. She'd chosen such a place for the natural light.

She'll never return here.

Hoping to feel less wretched, he stripped his clothing off and slipped into the bath of steaming, soapy water that lay waiting for him on the far side of the room. He imagined they'd begun boiling the water for this massive porcelain tub the moment he'd appeared on the horizon and had only just fled the room moments ago, having emptied the last jug of water as he turned the final corner. He felt invigorated despite the scalding water turning his skin bright pink. He wondered, however, was it just the comfort of cleanliness that soothed him. Scrubbing the march from his aching body, he rested for a while and fought the temptation to close his eyes and sleep the evening away. Eventually, he climbed regretfully from the bath, dried himself, and applied sweet-smelling oils to his skin. In the wardrobe, he found fresh clothing for the nightmare ahead.

He chose robes of vibrant silken red—a fitting colour. Before he donned them, however, he shaved himself so that he might look like a more respectful royal. Examining himself in the long mirror, he thought himself rather fetching, and he wondered how aroused Elise might have been seeing him thus, even with threats at close hand.

"That's when you are at your best," he whispered, feeling that fuken sorrow come upon him once more. This time, he did not fight the pain. Instead, he extinguished the torches, lay back on his bed in the darkness and thought more of her and her terrible fate. His hounds stood beneath him, daring each other to climb up on the bedsheets and comfort their weeping master. He did not invite them. Instead, he cried himself dry, lamenting the miles marched and the agony in those that lay ahead.

He lay wiping his stinging eyes until exhaustion took him, and he fell asleep. He did not remember his dreams, which was a good thing, for the dreams suggested the pain to come and might have tested his resolve.

29

MIDDLE O' NOWHERE

"Ease off, boys; the fight's done for now."

"Wait, sir, there's one. Right there. Little shit, sneaking around in the bushes."

"I said ease off; there's little point. You. Hey, you. You, right fuken there. Put that arrow back in its quiver. "

"But sir, I have the shot!"

"You think you have the shot? You don't have a shot."

"I have the shot! I know I do."

"It's just a bush!"

"Sir—it's moving, sir! Look at it. The sneaking little Southern bush-fuker."

"I said it's a fuken bush," Doran shouted, ending the argument immediately as the young Wolf held his strike. In disgust, he spat over the barge's edge into the black water below. The offending bush skulked away from the foliage and lost itself in the green. It left behind a dozen similarly concealed Southerners along the bank. Their leaves were studded with arrows and tarnished with splatters of crimson. A clever ruse by the Hunt to sit and wait, but it was all for nothing. After so many days honing their nerve, the River Barge Wolves had made quick work of the ambushers. Doran was proud of his boys, prouder than he'd ever expected to be, considering the terrible blemish on their name. Who knew that all it would take was certain death for them to find their pride, snarl, and fuken bite?

"Could have added to my tally," the youth muttered, and Doran fought a smile. He didn't think Erroh's suggestion of counting their kills was much of a tactic, but it was improving morale among the defenders of Boat Town and was a fine distraction from the fact of their limited ammunition. Only the recovery of their attackers' spent arrows and bolts, embedded in the wood of the barges, bolstered their stores. Even those that had struck down their brethren were retrieved and used again.

"Was an easy shot as well," the Wolf said sullenly. He was disgusted, and Doran approved. It wasn't an easy shot; their abilities were clearly improving. On another day, he might have allowed the boy to take the shot. But it wasn't worth the expense of a miss. An Alpha would have made that strike, but an eager and incredibly fatigued raw soldier less so.

They're not completely raw anymore.

"Could have doubled your tally, you mean," some jester mocked, and the warrior gamely laughed with the rest. Doran listened to the banter, which was a tonic to the pain he felt. Pain of the body and most of the soul.

I have no soul left.

He patted the archer and leaned away from the barge's edge to rest against the far wall. Around him, dozens of arrows and bolts stuck out of the gunwales and walls, shot wildly in a desperate panic as the massive Boat Town sailed on by. Their enemy's results had not merited their clever tactics; he had heard a few screams from the watch guard who had faced the first volley and little more after that in the second. His boys had put them down before they'd drawn a third. He'd seen a few pass by the spot where he'd crouched, and he wondered if it was luck or a gut feeling or a whisper from an absent god that had driven him to take that moment to rest and warm his aching limbs.

"Sir, you took a blow," the archer said absently, pointing to his arm, and only then did Doran feel the tear in his flesh. It was funny; at the time, he remembered feeling the searing pain for a breath, but the wails of anger and the roaring of orders all around him had soon quelled whatever impact such an unimpressive injury could have. Still, he'd need a few stitches and a quick, burning clean of the wound lest it get infected. He looked up at the night sky and pledged he'd tend to such things at dawn.

We are so close.

He had told himself this many times these last few hours. The Southerners must have thought the same thing. Those sneaky fuks had positioned themself at the bank's edge for a long time in one final, desperate attempt to damage the floating convoy, but again, they had failed.

The Actions of Gods

Doran smiled and listened for a few breaths to the night's silence and the sound of the rushing water beneath. Though this monstrosity moved at a painstakingly slow pace, its hundred or so captains had doubtless sharpened their skills under the horrendous conditions. The ships were still slow, just not as slow. It wasn't much, but it made a difference and had saved lives, probably on both sides. The skirmishes had occurred more frequently over the last few days but had concluded far more swiftly too. In the blink of an eye, it seemed, the water had turned crimson, and Spark City had left death and ruin in its floating wake. Truthfully, the Southerners had done their fair share of damage, but Doran focused solely on the positives. If he thought more deeply about the tragedies he'd endured, he might drop beneath the platforms and plunge to his death below. So he focused on better things.

Peering back to Mea, who sat statuesque upon her throne near the middle of the gathering, he politely acknowledged her with a raised hand. She had led them this far, and Doran would carry whatever burden she demanded of him. Few people could achieve this kind of dedication. All it had taken was a war to help him find his way.

Mea was clearly wilting with fatigue, and he wondered about speaking with her for a while and convincing her to take another hour of rest. There was only so much anyone could take after nine days of battle. *Nine days.* He wondered if it was, indeed, nine days. It might have been. Then again, he had only ever been genuinely awake when blood was being spilled.

"Sir, I think we could be clear," a voice cried from far above in one of the crow's nests. Immediately, Doran snapped to attention. He looked down at the waves breaking along the lake's edge, watching the bank slip ever so slightly away from the borders of the massive barge. "Sir, I think... I think we *are* clear," the Wolf cried from the small platform far above.

Doran couldn't look up for long, lest his vision spin, but he could hear the man's excitement well enough. Soon after, there came excited chattering as the man's comrades agreed. He dared not believe it. Not yet. Yet still... Dropping to his knees and laying his forehead on the wooden deck, he fought a sob of relief. He dared not close his eyes. Doing so for even a moment brought on tears; he'd swiftly discovered this on the second night. Squeezing the bridge of his nose and finding relief, Doran shook his head and willed the tiredness away. Aye, Mea had pledged it might take only another day or so, but Doran hadn't dared imagine any future beyond the grind of this routine horror.

So long, Southern fuks. I'll see you again when we regroup.

"Nothing will reach us now," an excited voice cried out, and Doran desired to believe too. Instead, he watched the tail end of the colossal structure float farther away from the shore, away from the dying and dead ambushers, away from any further threat.

"Sir, you have not yet rested this night," one of his comrades said quietly, and a few heads nodded in agreement. He tried to think when last he'd stolen an hour of slumber among the swaying sails, and couldn't recall. Truthfully, his mind was numb beyond bearing. He felt almost drunk with exhaustion. He knew a few fiends who would pay a handsome piece for such delirium. Still, he would happily see each of his Wolves sleep a few hours before he dared drop the vigil himself. That's what leaders did; that's what Erroh would have done.

"I'll sleep at dawn. Meantime, I need a dozen of you to patrol these floating ramparts, monitoring those we protect. Order every Wolf you meet to get some sleep. Everyone else, get some food, and then get some sleep. A few of you might even find a bowl of water and soap." At this, they laughed, and he grinned. He didn't care who stood the extra few hours; let them work it out between themselves. For now, he would walk through the floating town, showing its inhabitants that there was still a hound marching these decks. Without the threat of sudden death, however, the problems of lowerlines had already started. The female Alphalines were already kicking up a storm. It wouldn't suit to have the rest of Samara joining in. Still, the Alpha females had their grievances. He could see why.

"I'm going to show my face among the citizens," he told them, and that was enough. They had learned he was a man of few words and less instruction. He didn't need to speak much, for they would listen. Turning from the grand defenders, he stepped from the edge of the floating city's defences and started towards the centre. Though he was as tired as any of the others, putting the Primary to bed first was still a priority. She was likely to be more stubborn than he. Her commitment to this sorry floating wretch of a city was nothing less than impressive.

Climbing one of the countless drooping, swinging ropes, he brought his aching frame up to the level above. With no need to sprint as arrows hailed down around him, he found the actual effort of traversing these barges tedious and clumsy. Still, to have wrapped all these vessels together was a miracle in itself. Constructing smooth walkways would have been another miracle entirely. Reaching the next level and taking a moment to choose his route to the Primary, Doran stood away from eager eyes and allowed himself to gasp a few times. It was all he could do instead of collapsing over the main deck in front of his warriors.

I did my best.

I did my best.

No matter how often he reassured himself, though, there was always the crushing knowledge that mistakes had been made and lives had been lost. He dared not ask for the numbers missing or fallen lest he sour his mood even more. Instead, he stared into the dark waters and hoped the attacks were over. He had never known such exhaustion as this. Few had, he'd wager. On top of lacking sleep, his body was bruised and battered. He looked at his useless hand and grinned. A strange thing that he'd taken no time these last few days to lament his injury. Perhaps, a little war and misery were all it took to keep his mind distracted. After all, what was one extra cut when his entire body pulsed with agony?

At least my hand doesn't bother me.

He looked at his hand in the shattered moon's glow for a few moments more, and when he looked up again he caught sight of a figure standing on a level across from him, looking out along the deck towards the lake water, and his heart sank.

Wasting no further time, he leapt over the gap between the two barges and landed beside the man. A young man. It was always a young man. The absent gods were cruel in their punishment, and they had one more punishment to inflict upon him this night.

At least one more.

The youth's eyes were glazed over. Yet still, he stood proud, and Doran hoped he was too far gone to know his fate. With his leader appearing at his side, the boy turned to look his way, then gasped loudly in desperation and horror. Doran carefully laid an arm across his shoulders.

"What's your name, boy?" he whispered in kindly tones. He recognised him, but he couldn't remember the name.

The boy gulped, closed his eyes and offered some name that Doran did not understand. It didn't matter. What mattered was how unfair this was. "It is a fine name," Doran lied smoothly. The boy would never know. The boy wouldn't need to know. "That name will be remembered," Doran lied again, and were the boy able to nod, he might have. Instead, he remained pinned and motionless, like a garment from a wealthy merchant being shaped to fit.

Pinned.

"You stood firm, you held the line, you helped us all," Doran whispered gently, then lowered his arm and took the boy's wet hands in his own. Doran wanted to cry out, to wail for the horrors the young man had experienced. Also, he wanted to remove the vision of this poor doomed warrior from his mind. He did not remember what it was to sleep, but he knew he would dream of this boy and many others. "The town owes you a debt."

The boy was fading. Just not swiftly enough. "I think it's time you lay down, warrior," Doran suggested, and for a moment, the boy's beautiful, dark eyes shot open again. For only a moment, though. He knew. They both knew. It was time. The arrows had pinned him and kept him on his feet. The shock did not kill him and it was a tragedy.

Distantly, Doran heard the voices of people approaching and knew he needed to act quickly. He desired to put this boy down in privacy. It wasn't the first; he hoped it would be the last.

"Close your eyes, little one. I've got this," Doran whispered, and the boy consented. He closed his eyes because his general told him to, and Doran reached for the first arrow.

The boy opened his eyes only once throughout the ordeal, and Doran hoped the removal of arrows was enough to let him bleed out quickly. It was no small thing to meet an entire wave of ambushing Southerners. It was another awful thing to face at least half a dozen arrows and take each fuken one bravely.

Not even Erroh could survive this.

He knew the danger of removing any embedded projectile: paradoxically, these arrows had kept the boy alive, each one staunching the flow of blood as he waited to die.

As Doran finally pulled away the arrow lodged in his throat, the boy released a whimper the projectile had denied him. The sound was melodic, tragic and definite. At last, the boy leaned forward, into the waiting, bloodied arms of his merciful killer and then slid down silently to the deck. Doran held him as the last of the boy's blood drained away, and then his Wolves appeared and gloved hands gently pulled the corpse away from his trembling frame.

"I think I'll take that rest after all," Doran said huskily.

Ricken was the boy's name, said those who delivered him to the water. They had been his friends. Doran smiled sadly, committing the name to memory as they slid the body over the edge. They held it in place for a moment before letting it fall to the dark waters below the moving city. The body floated, turning gently in the water's grasp for a drowned breath before sinking and disappearing forever.

I did my best.

He offered a gentle nod to Ricken's comrades before climbing wearily through the ramparts towards the civilisation of wretched vagrants. He saw Mea in the distance, leaning against a bulkhead, steaming brew in hand, engaged in conversation with one of the many civilians. For a moment, Doran considered following his original plan and tending to her rest, but Ricken's brave, strained features stung his mind, clung to it and tore at it. He needed something more than sorrow and strife tonight.

You've earned this.

He waved to Mea as he strode past, three barges apart. If she saw, she offered no reply, and that was fine. He was too tired to speak with her now on future matters, for Mea would have plans. Unlike most, she was thinking beyond the present, which suited Doran just fine. Truthfully, he was still pledged to Erroh's plans and to the Wolves they trained, but in Boat Town, Doran truly belonged, and he would be needed just as much if they were to survive the next little while.

Do it for Erroh.

Erroh.

Thinking of the boy, Doran stumbled in mid-step and leaned against a wall. He felt the sorrow in his chest, felt the desperation too. He knew Erroh better than those who condemned him, and he understood the little cub's importance. They said the boy had died in Samara, and Doran knew it to be true, but still, he would have no man speak of him as fallen. Doran had not seen him fall. He only saw him rise to the sky, seeking a fight while the rest fled. Aye, Doran had rescued the Primary, and such a feat was significant, but not a single hour had gone by since then that Doran didn't regret not scaling the wall with him. There was a burning fire in the unimpressive little shit that Doran was compelled to follow. He'd felt that same compulsion upon the open plains.

And I, the brute who tried to kill him in honour of a narrow-minded bitch queen of the city.

Still, a pledge was a pledge, and he was a Black Guard like his father before him.

The platform rose ever so as he trudged across the last few boats near the centre. Fewer torches were lit here, and fewer people wandered the decks. He knew where they were: all hiding below in the stores with all the supplies, no doubt pilfering whatever they could while their brethren died brutally for them above.

"Fuk it," Doran hissed, shaking away the anger. Calming himself, he reached for a rope ladder that led up to the side of the grandest and most considerable ship of them all.

Only the finest for the city's finest.

At the top of the ladder, he pulled himself aboard. The aroma of perfume immediately struck him, and he enjoyed it for a few breaths before setting off again. His heart quickened as he reached the door where the goddesses remained, all stewing in a frustrated furnace of finery. Stepping through the doorway, he entered another world. Gone was the stench of waste and wretchedness, replaced by the females' fine, sweet scent of spice and flowers.

Within, most of the remaining females were gathered in conversation, most holding cups of steaming tea or cofe. The smell of bread and honey suggested they knew how to care for themselves. And for each other. No male was allowed near these quarters, but Doran had been granted freedom of the city. The females were the first to declare it too and they welcomed him most. He had seen below decks of many other vessels, and most were wretched. Body after body, shoved against each other, fighting for scraps and water or the bucket of waste. He had seen too many of these below-deck prisons, which looked like the end of the world.

In the galleon of the Alphalines, the so-called prison was something else entirely. The inmates sat in open beds with room to stretch; some higherlines hid themselves between blankets hanging on either side of their cots. They were in prison like the rest, but they were royalty. While those on the other decks sang a terrible melody of weeping, arguing and fear, the females here chatted quietly and argued delicately; some amused themselves with songs or poetry. He even heard a few peals of laughter. Truthfully, they had been afforded the same amenities as those on the rest of the barges, but regiment and routine had won over here. They had made the best of this misery, and it was telling.

He caused a stir as he entered, but it was one of respect. While he might have feared their gazes before, now he acknowledged their respectful nods as he passed. A few reached for his hand and offered a squeeze, and it was strange to feel appreciated by them. Mea less so. They loved and adored Mea, but at this moment, she had denied them their right; in truth, they had reason to grievance.

Eventually, he reached the far end of the ship, where those with injuries remained. As he stepped into the healer's bay, he was assailed by the cool, bitter air, and his heart beat faster. A few of the beds were occupied, and he could see an assortment of jars brim-full of healing

The Actions of Gods

herbs and tonics. There was a solitary healer tending to the sick, an old man with greying hair. Upon seeing Doran, he smiled sadly and returned to wrapping a bandage onto a young Alphaline's wrist.

Celeste.

Doran reassured himself of the healer's pledges that Celeste would recover and that her coma was passing, that it was simply a mild side-effect of the trauma she had suffered. He had told Doran there was little to fear. He did not speak of the child struggling to live within, though he knew of her wondrous affliction.

There was one other in the room, another young Alphaline female, pretty and painted, with her hair in a tight bun, yet still stunning in a bright golden silk dress, unfit for such a place.

"How goes it out there?" Julli whispered to him. He had not known this girl before the violence, before the flight, but in the handful of times Doran had visited his unconscious lover, they'd shared enough words to be courteous. Julli was Celeste's best friend and had stayed by her side since they had delivered her sleeping body to the healer's bay.

"We are through the worst... with acceptable losses," he said, looking at Celeste. It wasn't love, it might never be love, but he cared for her greatly. Incredible pairings grew from less than that. Who knew what a child of theirs might bring to this world? Sitting down on a little wooden stool opposite, he reached over and stroked her hair. Her face reacted ever so, and he caught his breath. "We are sailing out into open waters. For now, we are safe enough."

Julli nodded. "Better news. She woke some time ago. She's flittered in and out of sleep since then, but she is well." She placed her hand on his shoulder, a strange, consoling gesture, and Doran smiled at her good news. "If you wait, she might wake again." Doran could only smile and nod as his emotions got the better of him. He fought the tears. Not just tears of relief for Celeste, but of sorrow for the days and nights of horror he'd endured.

"How is the mood in general?" he asked, and still she kept her hand upon his shoulder as though she were unable to speak of such terrible things.

Julli took a breath, held it, then breathed out again. "It is less than joyous. Our anger with Mea is simmering. You say we are safe for now, but there will be answers demanded."

He understood her frustration. She was a warrior like he was. All of them were. Being denied the ability to fight for their home was a dreadful thing. That order had been reasonable considering their lack of advantage, if truth be told, but denying them the opportunity to stand with the Wolves as they floated along through the barrages of bolts and arrows had been a step too far in the minds of the hot-blooded females. Mea had pledged that their chance to fight would come, but words would hold back these feminine legends only for so long. They were more than ready to bite into some Southern flesh. There were a couple of hundred of them, and Doran knew they would be a ferocious force to contend with. However, Mea was Primary, and the Primary decided the moment. So, until then, they remained hidden away without a kill to their name, while Doran and the Wolves went out and fought and died for them every few hours. This was the way; Doran was fine with it.

"Mea has guided us well these last few days," he said evenly.

"We want to kill."

"And you will. We can only run and hide for so long."

She seemed happy with that. Nearby, the healer coughed, scribbled something in a notebook and ambled away slowly, leaving the two alone to wait with the sleeping girl.

"You look ruined," Julli offered, and Doran smiled sadly. Aye, he fuken was. On another day, he might have snapped a retort, but he sensed a gentleness in Julli. Some Alphaline females were larger than life, boisterous and intimidating. Others were gentle, fragile enough to crack at a jest from a cutting tongue. "You should get some sleep."

It was a fair suggestion, and not the first one he'd heard this hour.

"Aye. Perhaps I'll find a bed to rest my head in." He considered rising and leaving Celeste to her sleep and recovery. Gently, he reached up to remove Julli's hand from his shoulder, but she took hold of his and squeezed. He turned to her and saw that her face was tragic now. He'd seen this look many a time. He caught his breath, she gulped, and he smiled.

"Is there something you need to say?" he asked her.

"Celeste bleeds now," she whispered, and placed his shaking fingers on Celeste's forehead. For a moment, he didn't understand what she meant, and then he realised, and he was crushed. At his side, Julli wept gently for her friend, her lost child and her friend's lover, whom she barely knew, but Doran was suddenly cold and empty. He rose to his feet, dropped his head and then, careful not to tangle his fingers in Celeste's hair, he stroked her forehead once more.

"I... have duties I must attend to," he whispered, straightening, and his voice was delicate and broken, and he hated the sound. He wanted to embrace Celeste, weep with her, and spill the contents of his belly onto the floor in rage and grief. He could feel his knees shaking, and summoned a last burst of strength.

I don't deserve this.

"I'm so, so sorry, Doran," Julli cried, and he could feel her sorrow for him and couldn't take it. He hadn't been expecting to be a father. He hadn't truthfully considered the idea of being a father, but this numbness was as bad as a dagger blow. He needed to leave, escape this horror, and resume his solitary march across these vessels as they sailed out into the middle of nowhere, seeking sanctuary.

"I… can't be here," he whispered, turning away and seeking an escape from this prison.

30

UNLEASHED AND RABID

It was warmer than he thought. At some point, the sun came out and blazed down upon him. It was not the season for such warmth, yet here he was sweating in its glare. He tried to catch his breath, but his body shook with every inhalation. He panted like a hound.

Around him, the bodies remained bleeding and burning, and it was all a vicious blur. He had not taken the time to savour each kill, and this was a terrible thing. Instead, he had allowed his body and limbs simply to follow instinct and had torn the group apart. He should have felt triumph or relief that he still lived. Instead, he only felt horror, anguish and a lack of fulfilment. Wiping his brow, he watched the last figure draw his sword and hobble forward pathetically. Erroh found his breath and, with it, his desire to punish, torture, maim, and fuken kill. He could feel the damp warmth of the dead upon him, and he was disgusted. He wanted a breeze to cool the fresh crimson covering his body. Their blood, not his. They hadn't come close, and he had taken them apart. It had been so easy.

"Who burned in the fire?" Erroh called to the approaching fiend, and gripped his blades. This skirmish was done, yet his opponent still dared to attack. The shuffling man said nothing, and that was fine. He brought his sword up to Erroh openly. He had no intent on answering questions. This was fine, too. Erroh had nothing left in him but cruelty.

They have taken everything else.

"I am Brin. You are Erroh. It is time to end this," the approaching Southerner jeered, and Erroh cared little for the threat in his voice. He merely spun his blades and met the sword's strike as it came at him. Brin was slow. Too slow to be pretending to be a talentless waif, all the while luring Erroh into another trap. Besides, he had both his eyes. He swung and shuffled forward, and Erroh met every strike and stepped backwards as though he were out for a stroll in the forest. With his mate. Who, perhaps, wasn't dead?

"Who burned in the fire?" Erroh demanded as he held and countered. A swift strike from his sword knocked his opponent's blade from his grip and sent it spiralling away to fall by the flames. With his other sword, Erroh lunged forward and gashed Brin's unprotected shoulder. A spray of blood took flight, and his opponent yelped. Erroh stepped away, smiling in satisfaction. "Answer me, cur."

The cur did not answer. He held his shoulder and shook a little, knowing he was doomed, before leaping back towards the fire to recover his blade. Erroh stalked lazily after the fuker as he retrieved his blade and retreated away from his vanquisher.

"You have killed my companions," Brin hissed, holding the blade out. Erroh invited him to attack, but the older warrior was shaken, ready to bolt, and this was most pleasurable. He deserved no mercy. None of them did. In the flicker of flames, he saw the devastation more clearly now: they had taken everything he loved. These bastards were the making of Erroh's ruin, and he remembered his first pledge and wanted to kill them all. He would start with Brin and his comrades. He would fill his emptiness with their screaming.

"Again," Brin howled, and he was desperate, which was wonderful. If Erroh had nothing else in the world, he would have his vengeance.

Kill them all.

"They will not miss your company for long," Erroh said. It was not a threat but merely a calm explanation, clarifying that Brin could expect there to be no living beyond this day.

The old man was far too slow, but he bravely fought the darkness, and perhaps on another day, Erroh might have admired him for it. But not today. Brin suddenly charged with blade out, legs shuffling as swiftly as they could carry him. Unfortunately for Brin, this wasn't swift at all. Erroh slipped past the strike, swung a kick and sent him crashing to the dirt. He was upon the man within a breath, holding him in a vice-like grip. A quiver of coldness took Erroh for a moment as he gazed at the old man's pained face, and he wondered, did he know this fiend? Had he torn his comrades apart in the open plains or in Keri?

"Tell me who burned, and I will show mercy," Erroh demanded in the Southern tongue, and the man hesitated. He shouldn't have hesitated.

Erroh took hold of his finger and snapped it out of place. An easy manoeuvre if you knew how to do it—and how to put it back. Erroh had little intention of putting it back. Brin's scream was so pleasing Erroh considered snapping a few more.

"I do not know who burned," Brin whimpered, ceasing his struggle to grab his hand and soothe the pain.

At this, Erroh leapt to his feet, spun his blades, and suddenly realised they were no longer alone in this town. Standing at the gates, staring at them in horror, was Drahir. He held his mount's reins in his hand, but said nothing, and Erroh hated him too. This fiend had tracked him so skilfully that Erroh never knew he'd been followed.

"Liar," Erroh roared, turning from Drahir back to his victim.

The hobbled and bleeding man climbed gamely back to unsteady feet and tightened his grip on his blade. Wiping fresh tears from his doomed eyes, he stepped towards Erroh, raised his sword and then lunged and missed him by a few feet.

"Liar!" Erroh repeated, striking him with a closed fist that sent him tumbling to the dust.

"I surrender to you, Erroh," Brin croaked, spitting blood, dust, and possibly a tooth from his quivering mouth. He sat up with difficulty, staring up at his vanquisher, and Erroh hated him with everything he had.

"Who burned?" Erroh said again through gritted teeth.

The man shook his head; whether his refusal was from lack of understanding or foolish pride, Erroh couldn't say, nor was he moved. Almost delicately, he plunged his blade through Brin's other shoulder and enjoyed the screams. And why not? The Southerners had come and destroyed the world, and the fact that this pathetic shit was sitting in the dust, snivelling for forgiveness, meant little to him, would not have moved any Alphaline male who had lost his mate.

Lea is dead.

Everyone is dead.

He could feel the horror rise in him once more, and he swallowed it back lest it take hold and drown him, leave him quivering beneath a blanket, shuffling senseless around a frozen lake, striking at the bars of a cage. Or simply accepting the end of it all.

Lea is dead, and he asks for mercy.

"Erroh!" Drahir roared, and Erroh barely heard him. Instead, he kicked Brin's fallen blade back over to his victim.

Take the blade and wait for death.

"Can you not see the horrors delivered by this cur?" Erroh cried to

Drahir, who, though pale and shaking, offered no excuse for the misery in this place. And what could he say? This was a sin committed by his people. A terrible sin inflicted upon the world, directed at the tremendous tainted cur known as Erroh.

Brin sobbed gently, but once again he climbed to his feet. With barely any strength, he raised his sword and held it out, inviting Erroh to attack. Eager to please, Erroh swung again, and once more, Brin's blade took flight and landed among the ashes of the fire.

"Mercy!" Brin begged weakly.

Erroh regarded him coldly. The fiend clearly had no intention of answering him; thus, there was little reason to push him further for answers. If this fuk gifted him no closure, then perhaps a little killing would be a tonic.

"To the fires with your mercy," Erroh said, drawing back his blade and preparing to swing it one final time. It would be a fine strike. Enough to take the fiend's head clean from its roots. He knew this because sometimes, when he had been as angry as he was now, this had been his chosen move. Lea had mocked him for it time and time again. She had also joked that taking Uden's head would have been a decisive manoeuvre. She had also suggested he be this angry when next they met in war. Perhaps, had he been as angry then, everything would be different now.

Anger is a gift.

He swung his sword, but instead of the chunk of his blade through flesh and bone, Erroh heard only the unsatisfying clang of steel on steel. Countering the strike, Drahir stayed Erroh's sword with his own before shoving Erroh away from the beaten man and standing between them.

"A Southerner called for mercy," Drahir shouted, though he lowered his blade and held out an appeasing hand to his leader, and Erroh's fury grew.

"How dare you!"

"He called for mercy. He is beaten; there is no honour in this," Drahir cried, and indeed, Brin looked rightly pathetic on his knees, bleeding and moaning miserably.

"Move out of my way... brother," Erroh said coldly. He was no longer Erroh of the road. He was nothing, perhaps less than nothing. He had only anger and cruelty left to him now. He thought of Lea, he thought of Lexi, he thought of Nomi. Of Roja and even Ealis too. He imagined them screaming in the flames, and he wanted to retch, to scream. Mostly, though, he wanted to kill their killers.

I am a failure, and I brought ruin to the world.
Again.

"I will not, Erroh," Drahir warned, setting his feet for the attack. His instincts were right. Erroh felt the anger come upon him, and he allowed it, welcomed it.

"I do not know who burned," Brin cried now. "I do not favour such things. Not all of us favour such practices."

For a moment, Erroh believed him, but it wasn't enough. Nothing would ever be enough. Erroh would burn the world, and it would never be enough.

Also, he's probably lying to save his soul.

Drahir raised his blade, and Erroh charged at him. The world slowed and bowed to his vengeful will, and Drahir immediately retreated. Brin scrambled to his feet and narrowly avoided decapitation as both warriors passed him. And then the old man was gone from Erroh's mind. Instead, all that remained was killing his comrade who served him.

A small matter of loyalty.

"Please," Drahir cried, retreating beneath the storm of swords, but Erroh simply focused his hate upon this new opponent and went to task, cutting through his defences, inflicting what pain he could.

Drahir offered some resistance, at least at first, unlike the rest of the other warriors he'd met that day. This was different from the night they'd met. The Erroh that night had been weak and broken. This day, Erroh was elite. Fuelled by depthless rage, he broke through every defensive tactic Drahir offered, and every strike became an attempted killing blow. They shuffled through the dust past the burning pyre, and Erroh grew stronger with every strike he delivered. All the while, Drahir retreated, forgoing all offence to save his wretched skin.

In Erroh's mind, he could hear panicked cries, could hear the agony of the dying, and he screamed with them, for he had let them all down. Breaking through Drahir's defence with a sudden ducking swipe, he caught an opening, and both warriors knew it. For a moment, the world slowed to a complete stop, and Erroh needed only to allow his body to finish the task. He met his victim's eyes and hated him. He heard his cries, pathetic and beaten, beneath his own. Drahir too cried for mercy now, but Erroh hated everyone, hated everything.

Kill him.
Kill them all.

It was a tantalising suggestion, and Erroh hesitated. Just enough for Drahir to spin away, still crying for mercy and—no, not crying at all. He was fierce. He *demanded* mercy, and Erroh felt the rage ignite within him again and he wanted to destroy him as he had before. He was tiring now, and with his limbs becoming heavy, Erroh continued to strike out, but there was less venom in his movements. Still, he advanced on the cur, who met every blow, each strike propelling them closer to the shade of a building where it wasn't so hot, where Erroh's eyes did not squint against the brightness, where the smell of dead, burning comrades wasn't assailing his nostrils.

"Please, Erroh."

"I must kill," Erroh cried, and continued to attack, but his strength was dwindling, his blows as feeble as the spurts from an emptying barrel. Soon enough, he was spent.

"This is not the way," Drahir said, panting.

It felt like the way. "I cannot."

Still, he swung, but his body was heavy, his breathing laboured, and fatigue was taking hold and crushing his will to destroy. He thought of Lea, and sorrow took him.

"Mercy, brother," whispered Drahir, and Erroh realised his strikes were barely pushing Drahir back. Instead, they were sliding harmlessly away. More than that, Drahir's hand was out as he attempted to take hold of him and embrace him. Tears sprang to Erroh's eyes, and he dared not allow them to fall; nor did he dare to stop them.

"Don't take away my anger," begged Erroh, dropping his blades. "Without it, I am nothing."

"I yield to you, Erroh," Drahir whispered, knocking both blades effortlessly from the broken Alpha's grip. Erroh allowed them to fall, and then, as Drahir embraced him, he fell to his knees, his body and spirit fully broken by this awfulness.

"Help me," Drahir called to Brin, and Erroh heard the sound of feet shuffling towards him, and he didn't care. He felt a flask placed to his lips and answered the command to drink. He felt himself go heavy as he collapsed in the dirt and he felt himself break completely. He knew she wouldn't have wanted him to break, but he couldn't help it. It was too much. Too many steps. One horror too many endured.

"I am done," said Erroh of the road.

31

CAPTIVES OF THE NEST

When his warriors first surrounded her, Nomi answered all their queries as best she could, and her smile carried her through the rest of the journey. She guiltily explained that no savage murder had occurred in this place the night before, merely a couple of girls releasing their anger to the night. She suggested that if the Riders had followed the noise, they would all have enjoyed a drunken night under the warmth of a roof instead of waiting outside until dawn.

When asked about the second girl, thinking quickly, she declared Lea also separated from their finger. When pressed, Nomi pondered her skittish companion might not have returned because she feared them to be roving packs of warriors in black, all bent on committing Northern atrocities. Nomi was quite confident Lea would not reappear anytime soon to out her lies. Strangely enough, the Southerners heard of similar attacks, and Nomi's heart hammered as each lie fell easily from her lips. She feared her lies would not carry, but they accepted her as their comrade and left her to her freedom. But not before asking her to accompany them to the "fallen, tainted settlement," where Uden waited.

According to his keepers, his name was Jeroen, and Uden demanded him. Nomi knew the name, and she knew the man. She knew Erroh's pledge to save him.

"Are you the father of Tye?" she whispered, bending down beside him in the shade, sheltering from the burning sun. A fine thing, too, for the afternoon's haze was a little harsh on her growing hangover. His keepers watched, but she figured it was mere interest in Uden's prize. She had praised the god, and they were satisfied with her devotion.

He looked coldly at her as she offered the water flask, and she could see the fire in his eyes. He was fierce, playing the part of a defiant prisoner.

She remembered Erroh being close to breaking at the mention of loved ones while he was in chains. "Though I do not know where he is, know this, I am a friend. I am his friend; I am friends with Erroh and Lea, too," she whispered, and this time he faced her, his unblinking eyes conveying his desperation to know more. "Who holds your keys?" she asked, and he gazed directly at their leader. Zarate, he had called himself. A tanned Southerner from their region, with a weak beard too. She nodded to Jeroen, and he took the water, and it was settled. She would not leave Jeroen. Not this time. This wasn't the frozen South, where stepping from a Finger mid-march was death. There were plentiful means of escape all around them. She need only pick her moment. Turning to Zarate, she placed her hands on her chest and offered an innocent smile.

Nomi had only begun charming Zarate when it all went wrong. With noon approaching, she went to task, earning his interest. It started with the offer of a steaming mug of tea; then she began giggling wonderfully at his jests as they sat alone, away from the rest of the Riders. She even touched his arm once, running her fingers down to his palms and muttering how strong and worn they were, before adding that she was without child and that it had been far too long since another had entertained her. He had touched her arm in reply, and strangely, she realised she'd missed the simple act of charming a lover. She also needed the touch of a man; it was like an itch unscratched for a year. There were only so many ways one could scratch before a pair of manly hands was needed to finish the job.

And it certainly won't be Erroh.

"You have a powerful jaw," she said, trying not to be distracted by the jingle of a key against armour at his waist. He was young and vibrant. A handful of years younger than she. He would desire to be swift, but if she played her part, she could keep him interested long into the night. She imagined she'd likely need to go the distance to put him fully at ease. And then rub his chest until he fell into a deep sleep.

Nomi had a plan. A simple plan. That never had a chance to work.

The screaming from the forest drew them from their privacy. Immediately, they took to arms, expecting a group of savage brutes in black, but instead they were met by a woman from their own group. Blood covered her hands, and she babbled wildly about having pulled her comrade from the stream, how his face had been destroyed, and Nomi felt the world closing in around her.

"The other killed him," the woman screamed, pointing Nomi's way, and in that moment the delicate weave of lies fell apart. "You all saw him follow the girl," the woman shrieked, and it was devastating testimony.

"What happened?" Zarate demanded, and he shoved Nomi away, lest her vileness rub off on him.

His loss, she thought wryly.

"He was bludgeoned and drowned," the woman went on, her eyes wild with trauma. She charged towards Nomi, and nobody stopped her. Why would they? There was no need for trial or justice. Nomi knew the flavour of a lynching. She had been there before. She froze. Terrified. A vision of Uden's manic grin formed in her mind. The crowd cheering. The taking of the child's head and the knowledge that it was her turn next.

"Run," Jeroen cried, and his voice cut through her shock. She ran, and this ended her. Perhaps had they given her a moment, she might have escaped with her life, with words of condemnation for the attacker, with suggestions that it wasn't her comrade after all. As it was, she turned and ran for the nearest break in the trees.

Don't look back.

She vaulted over the little wall cordoning off the expanding green of the arth and fled through the canopy of trees. Behind her, the screams continued, sounding less like shock and more like rage. She also heard their curses and orders for her head. And then all she heard was the rush of wind in her ears and her own panting breath as it escaped her throat.

Leave them all behind.

Terror drove her, and she initially believed she had the speed and skill to distance herself from her pursuers. Hope was light and also a crushing thing. Behind her, she heard the cries of excitement disappear, only to be replaced by the furious thump of horses' hooves.

Fuk, fuk, fuk.

Find me. Lea.

She veered from her chosen route towards rougher terrain, hoping the uneven ground would slow them. If she could just slip deeper into the trees… She sprinted faster and faster through the overgrowth, her breath coming in ragged gasps, desperate to leave them behind.

Run or hide?
Run or hide?
Fuk, fuk.

The Actions of Gods

She felt the going become tougher. Her body ached; her exhaustion came upon her violently and cruelly. Her body betrayed her as though death was not at stake, and she cursed her failures. She stumbled once, falling to a knee, and her own momentum dragged her forward a few more feet. Panic took hold; she had been here before. Gasping and swallowing a whimper, she stumbled and fell again a second time.

Close behind her, she heard their trampling thunder and she stood still, listening, trying to understand their route. There was no outrunning these curs, she realised; there was only concealment. She looked around, hoping to see a rock, cave or brook to hide herself in. She would have taken an attractive bush at that terrifying moment. She heard their voices, listened to their outrage, and she was no Alpha. No Alpha would be this terrified.

Get up, girl.

It sounded like Lea in her mind, and she followed its command. Taking a deep breath, she looked around and blinked in surprise. Ahead, standing starkly against the luscious green of eternal forest, was a lone bush. What caught her attention was its lack of living colour. Its deathly brown scraggle of withered leaves and dried branches was a strange sight among such vibrancy.

A dead bush in fertile ground makes no sense.

She tore her eyes away from the dead bush as the pursuing sounds came closer. The hunters' voices were frenzied, wild with the scent, and she knew this was the end.

Get up, girl! Run, hide, live.

Good advice, and she took it. Standing, she spotted a wide path and sprinted towards it. With a few stolen breaths, she dared to believe again. Her feet behaved as she demanded. Her mind swallowed the panic and granted her a swift pace. She charged past the brown bush, ignoring it in her desperation, and fate played a terrible jest on her.

Clank!

She turned and stared at it in puzzlement. Who expected the ground around a dead bush's roots to clink so loudly as she passed, yet here it did, and she recoiled at the noise.

"Loud. Too loud."

She staggered again but kept going, even as the roars intensified and the thunder of hooves appeared behind her.

Fuk you, bush!

It was Zarate who struck her, slamming into her from behind with the full speed of his mount driving him forward. It was a brutal blow, and she hit the ground violently. She wondered for a dizzying moment, might she take advantage of this? Trying to climb to her feet, she leapt towards him, hoping to catch him off guard and take his life, his keys, his horse and, soon after that, his prisoner. Tragically, her body was unsteady. More than that, she wasn't swift or graceful. She felt the world slow, felt herself unable to move as she desired, and he dodged around her strikes, countering every blow. She screamed in fury, terror, and a little anger too.

They struggled for a few more breaths before the woman who had first alerted them of their comrade's grisly fate appeared among the trees with murder in her eyes. Nomi knew that look, and she knew her fate. Terror took her again, and all strength left her. Dropping her raised fists in defeat, she collapsed to the ground as Zarate struck her fiercely in the stomach, taking her will and the last of her fight.

That wasn't enough for the woman. She was older than Nomi. Her accent was Southern but with a harsher tone. She was from one of the wilder clans, the last to join Uden, but the strongest of his supporters now. Wasn't that always the way?

She called for Nomi's head; she called for her body to be put to fire, and Nomi offered little fight as more hands appeared around her, took hold, and placed a noose around her neck. Only then did Nomi understand this was truly her end. Even if Lea was watching, hidden in the shadows, there was little chance she could wage war upon a dozen fiends without a blade.

Be brave.

She didn't want to be brave. She wanted to live. A few gloved fists from faceless aggressors struck her, and she lost the run of her mind. She begged for her life, and her killers relaxed their aggression and began to take joy in her horror. They cracked jests at her expense; they mocked her fading soul; they cursed her to the darkness without Valhal, and she hated them for it. Still, she argued for her life. She promised them her body for whatever acts they demanded. She pledged a life of servitude in exchange for her breath, and they laughed at her petty efforts.

The Rider holding the rope swung it high towards the branch of a tree and got the angle completely wrong, and it fell back down harmlessly onto the leafy ground. For this clumsiness, he was ridiculed, and Nomi's mind was numb.

Say it.
I can't.
I must.

Say it.

The most careless of notions came upon her, and she despised herself for it. Her life would pass without event, although, granted, it had been a life well spent. But in her lay words that could change everything. Words that could affect those she loved long after they left her to swing in this tree.

Simple, untruthful words.

"You cannot kill me," she told them, "for I am important."

They taunted her again. The disgraced Rider threw the rope into the air a second time. A better throw. Its end flew gracefully over the long, heavy branch and returned to his waiting hand. There were a few jesting congratulations, and Nomi wanted to cry, scream, attack, but they held her tightly, and they tightened the rope lest her little feminine head slip right out.

"This is a mistake."

Again, they ridiculed as a few took hold of the rope and pulled.

"You vile witch!" the woman screamed, and spat in Nomi's face, and Nomi gasped as the rope took her balance. Any moment she would hang, would swing, would relieve herself, and she would choke and be gone. "Burn in the darkness."

"I am Cordelia; I am the daughter of Uden," Nomi of the South lied, and for a breath, they heard her. They pulled again, though less fervently now, but still, her feet left the ground. She kicked and gasped, and nothing came, and she knew she was dying and she was a coward for giving up Lea's secret.

"Uden has no daughter," Zarate roared. He held the rope as she swung, and her toe caught a blessed root upon which she balanced, letting it hold some of her weight. Not a lot, but enough to breathe, to face her killer and answer.

"Lost in a fire, but I have risen above," she rasped. Her voice was calm, for she would not tremble at the end. Would not give them the satisfaction.

"She is a liar," the woman screamed, kicking Nomi from her stoop and killing her anew.

This is it.

Die well.

"Uden sees all," warned Nomi, screeching against the finality, raging against the coming dark. She fought, oh, she fought, but the rope swung, and one fiend pulled, and this was the end. She felt it now, the coldness of death, but more than that, she thought of her sister and her family beyond, and although she dove into the nothingness terrified, she sensed something waiting for her. She wept for everything she had been and everything she had become. She cried as she said goodbye to the world, and the rope swung, and she swung helplessly with it.

Let go, girl.

It was a fine suggestion, and she did.

And her body fell painfully to the ground, and the air and life surged back into her chest.

"She lies, she fuken lies," the woman bleated, and Nomi shook and coughed and sought her breath.

"Probably," said the Rider, "but I will not kill our god's daughter. More than that, I will not doom us, for Uden sees all."

Around her, Nomi heard a few agree, and she wept openly at the horror and unfairness of her miserable life.

32

SESH AT THE KING'S GAF

"Come on, Magnus, it's time to eat," cried the voice behind the door, and Magnus growled under his breath. His hounds did not. They were relaxed, lazing on the floor. They knew the voice well, and their journey had been so long. "The entire world is waiting for you, Your Highness," Padir mocked.

Magnus looked at himself one last time and hissed the hounds to immediate attention just as his comrade began knocking loudly upon his door for the third time. Carefully, he drew his crown from its hiding place in the sack, held it in the light, and hated this burden. The metal piece felt heavy in his hand, as it always had.

Heavier upon the head.

It was a perfectly adequate headpiece, without jewels or precious metals adorning it. And why should he wear such extravagant pieces as the kings of the factions did? Had the people benefitted from the beauty of their crowns? Had those lavish headpieces held off the killing blows when death had found them all?

As a younger cub, with viciousness as his ally and ambition as his warring comrade, all he had desired was to rule these savage, beautiful lands gallantly. This he had accomplished, but it was never a king's place to sit and rot upon a throne. It was better for a king to face the challenges and know his place as a servant of his people. This was the savage way. He ran his fingers along the grey metal and wondered what kind of life it might have been, ruling over all parts of the open world.

"One that would have ended by now, and ended badly," he whispered to reassure himself.

He opened the door to Edain and an impatient-looking Padir.

"I had a fine bath, and I'm not scratching nearly as much," the boy declared, offering a smile, and for a moment Magnus smiled with him. However, neither man's smile reached his eyes.

"It is time, my liege," Edain said, leading him from the bedroom towards the brightly lit hallways and the grand court of the king.

"It is long past time, Magnus—far too long. The feast will be over by the time we set foot inside," Padir muttered.

Magnus could already hear the notes of music flowing through the hallway, along with the hum of revellers. That revelry would die down soon enough, no doubt.

"I see you have the crown. A fine thing," Edain said with relief, eyeing the metal piece he held by his waist in a loose grip.

"So, will you retract your leadership?" Padir asked, grabbing Magnus by the shoulder. The boy had asked the same question a thousand times before, and asking it again here, standing mere steps from their destination, meant nothing.

Magnus could see servants strutting swiftly in and out of the grand banquet hall through a large archway. Within, he could barely make out the crowd gathered at long tables and benches laden gloriously with feastful things. Despite his trepidation, Magnus's stomach churned in hunger. This was a meal he would savour, for it could be his last.

He swatted the boy away, and with his hounds mirroring his every step, Magnus marched towards the king's court, his eyes upon the vacant throne sitting alone on an elevated platform a few steps in height. As with the crown, it was barely decorated. A reminder that the title of king, in these lands, was a transient one.

Unless they have the most feared warriors to call upon.

For a breath, he was hammered again by the loss of his Rangers and, selfishly, his sorrow was for himself. He would give anything to have made this journey with their support. Collectively, the clans could have wiped the Rangers out as swiftly as a betraying pack of Wolves. However, the clans rarely allied, and individually, no clan was fierce enough to go against Magnus and his army. And now, he was trying to gather them with nothing but words to stir their will for warfare.

I'm dead.

Such a morbid thought was strangely liberating. All at once, Magnus felt settled, holding at the archway and hearing the whispers of his imminent arrival for the first time in years. His heart relaxed, his instinct took over, and his mind became cold and calculating.

The Actions of Gods

"Announce your king," he snarled to Padir, who turned pale. And who wouldn't fear the repercussions of appearing to support a fading monarch when the knives came out? "Do it," Magnus commanded, and Padir scuttled through the archway as the cacophony faded away to silence.

"To all gathered, I, Padir of the Glohss, declare that…um… King Magnus has arrived," he intoned, and then shrugged and faded into the nearest corner, offering a subtle bow and a weak gesture to the arriving monarch.

It was a fine announcement if one was attempting to distance themselves from any hope of solidarity. It was also enough to silence the last whispers of the gathered crowd. Considering the impressive numbers present, it was a fine feat: the last time Magnus had gathered here, there had been fewer guests. Stepping through the archway now, however, and smelling the rich aromas of delicious foods and revelry, Magnus could see that all clans were present after all. Change of leadership was in the wind. Aye, there would be whispers of his chosen successor, outright arguments and perhaps even a little violence. That was their honourable way, and no clan would refuse to throw their hat into the sparring ring should it be needed.

Like any kingly throne room, it was a fine, impressive place, more than adequate for the numbers gathered. Against the growing dark of early evening, there flickered a thousand candles, fixed upon chandeliers and mounted at regular intervals along the walls. Together, they cast an almost unnatural glow high into the dark wooden rafters above. The grand fireplace running along one side of the room held a blaze large enough to burn an entire tree in one evening, and such was the heat, Magnus felt it on his face from the very centre of the room, where he strode along the crimson silk carpet towards his throne. Each clan's banner hung high, and together they waved delicately in the ocean breeze like strands of some ancient goddess's hair.

It was the smell of this place, though, that reminded him of the threat at hand. These great warriors, all seated at rows of trestle tables, were in their finest ceremonial garb, but they were still warriors of the road and built for war. To Magnus, it felt like being among the Rangers again. He avoided their eyes, and he tried not to limp as he marched towards the elevated throne. Once there, he placed the crown upon the stately iron and wood chair, to the sound of gasps of relief and murmurs of excitement from the gathering below. He was resigning his place, but not without a fight, not without a pledge from those coming after.

And if there be no pledge?
Well, that's when the trouble starts.

Spinning around, he faced his subjects, who eyed him curiously. The only allies around him were his intimidating hounds, who sat silently at his feet, their eyes glittering.

Who needs an army with hounds as loyal as these, anyway?

"We have gathered as friends this day, and I am glad to be back among my brethren," Magnus said. He stared down at the tables, laden with steaming platters of food. To his surprise, even though most of the warriors sat with mugs of ale, wine or mead, few had filled their plates and almost no one was eating. *They're waiting for me.* All but one table. Magnus had expected as much.

He met the eyes of Teaolor, and he blinked first. Why? Because she was the rightful heir to this throne. Her clan, Clan Cara, was pledged to take the throne, and few might argue such an appointment. Teaolor was as tall as Elise and nearly as striking, with a subtly threatening way about her. He had met her a few times before and was never far from being impressed with her nerve and her singlemindedness. Clan Cara were his allies for as long as they needed him, which was fine too. Were she to agree to his last action as king, she might have the sheer stubbornness to wrangle the rest of the clans into line.

Even Clan Dearg.

Teaolor wiped some grease from her sharp chin and burped loudly. Seated around her, her kin and comrades ate sparingly, but they ate, sending a fine message of defiance and warning, and he approved. She would be a fine king indeed.

The crowd watched with held breath as King Magnus left his crown and throne behind him, descended from the platform, and took his seat at the nearest long table. The others at the table offered polite nods as the serving men moved in and swiftly placed dishes before him. With a casual wave of his right hand, he signalled to the rest of the subjects that they might begin to feast in his honour. It was a welcome order, and the room filled once again with happy chatter and the clink of cutlery upon plates and bowls.

A steaming slab of meat was placed upon Magnus's plate, and, for only a moment, he imagined himself welcome. This couldn't be further from the truth, he knew, but he'd offered peace to the proceedings by acknowledging the need for his successor. By not challenging her rudeness. By claiming no table for his own. It was a fine art, playing the crowd's favour, and until he needed to, he would offer no festering anger to these proceedings.

Soon enough, music filled the air as a trio of troubadours near the corner began to play. Padir dropped into a chair beside him, raising a glass as Magnus raised his own.

Those at the table raised theirs in reply, and they resumed feasting as though they were allies.

Magnus tore into a leg of meat and chewed contentedly, savouring its rich flavour. The Savage Isles favoured vegetables over meats for most meals, but for special occasions like this one, they cooked meat, and the dishes were usually memorable. Padir waited for a time before tearing the other leg free and taking a bite himself.

"Ah, good. Was just making sure," he said, enjoying every morsel.

"Most poisons don't strike you down until a few hours after eating," Magnus offered, grinning. For an entire breath, Padir stopped chewing before shrugging and continuing.

"Sometimes, during exciting times such as these, it is nice to stop and take a moment or two to catch one's breath," Padir said. "To simply rest and not have something happen for a while."

"Aye. It's a good thing to rest before the true mayhem begins," Magnus agreed, dropping the bone from his meal to one of his hounds and turning to the steaming vegetables. Whenever the Savage Isles served vegetables, they, too, were a memorable thing.

"Don't waste those bones," he murmured to his dining companions, and a dozen bones from a dozen plates were dropped to the rest of the patient hounds gathered at his feet. It was good to be the king, thought Magnus, enjoying the last hours while he could.

33

BROKEN RANGER

He tried to forget his name. It was a laborious task given his rich heritage, filled with warm memories of love, life, hopes and dreams. The cruelty of memories was no friend to a broken man waiting for death. If he forgot his name, then perhaps he could forget the names of those he'd left behind, those he'd loved, those he'd honoured and served. Most of them would forget him, no doubt; this was no terrifying thing. He thought he would fear his name being lost in the ether. Forgotten as the world turned. But no; he didn't mind. All names were forgotten; all lives ended.

All things must end.

The forgotten Ranger sighed and fought the feelings of desolation that washed over him. He had done well these last months, taking the pain, swallowing it in dreadful mouthfuls, pretending he was lost from everything, knowing he could affect nothing. He did this because thinking anything else might have broken his sanity. He had once believed himself a heroic warrior, blessed with elite skill, bound for greatness; he had marched with a legend, after all. He wished nothing but good health for his master, his idol—the grandest legend in history. Jeroen, however, was nothing like that fiend. He was lesser, and he accepted this terrible truth. Legends broke chains to keep fighting, to survive and return to those they loved dearest, bringing with them fantastical tales of heroism and stories of superhuman feats. Jeroen himself was fallen, resigned, and lost in the tales, which was fine. A worthy end to any good character in any book. But with that chapter long completed, he now endured awfulness in the pages beyond the epilogue.

And so, he wanted to forget his name, his actions, and his terrible decisions that had led to this fate.

He dropped his head in the afternoon shade and stared at the long strands of hair that hung on each side of his face. It was something to do while fighting the memories stirred up by the female Nomi. It was all he could do, lest the spark of hope rear its unwelcome head and cause a stir in his fragile mind. He'd always liked his hair, but more than that, *she* had liked his hair, had enjoyed cutting it, enjoyed making him pretty and respectable. It would appal her how knotted his locks had become since his capture. He cursed under his breath, and the few remaining guards took little notice. Why would they? He was felled and broken, and he was alone. He had tried at first to attract their attention. A long time ago now, it seemed. He had even wrapped his ruined hands around a keeper's neck one night. That was before he'd lost most of the movement in his hand. Killing a jailor might have improved his life. It was the little things.

But you didn't kill again, did you?

He sighed again and watched the break in the trees where the female had fled. No, he hadn't killed, and they had beaten him for that and attached the chains to his hand. Only that strange female assassin had seen to ending that torment. He looked at the ruin of his misshapen hand and wondered would it ever recover. He remembered the pain, and sometimes it ached something awful. He could have gladly taken that pain again if it meant he could grip anything like a Southern neck once more, but no. His movement was limited now, his strength drained and broken.

Forgotten, useless warrior.

Distantly, he heard the screams and the beatings, but felt no tears form. He was too thirsty to cry. The girl had been generous with her water flask until they discovered her ruse. He licked his lips and fought the returning dryness.

Do not cry away her gift.

Her hushed words still burned in his mind. Foolish thoughts from a female new to adulthood. She'd pledged freedom, spoken of his friends and kin, gifted him life from a canister and then, in a cruel moment, she'd been gone, away into the thicket where death awaited her. Her words had left their indelible mark, though, and he was lesser for them. He wanted to forget his duty, hope, and thirst for vengeance. He wanted to forget what it was to rage against the unfairness of his lot, to demand violence at the end of his life. He thought of Erroh; he thought of Lea, and he hated. He hated the world; he hated those who roamed it. Mostly, though, he just hated that he still remembered what it was to be an Alphaline.

They carried her back through the green, and he knew the torment to come. They cast her still body onto the dirt, leaving her bleeding and silent. They attached the chains around her waist, and he lamented ever so for her. Were he capable, he might have crawled over and comforted her, but he would not face the heat any longer than needed. Nor would he show her any affection lest they turn such a thing against him. They were cruel, and he had seen enough horrors to know that hiding in the shade and emptying his mind was the shrewder tactic.

For a time, he watched them argue with each other about her fate and caught most of the words that they threw about. Knowing their language was an insignificant advantage, but it was something to do while he looked on, stricken with horror and sadness.

Satisfied that the girl would be no further trouble for now, the warriors turned their attention to sacking the old tavern. Jeroen watched and listened as they spoke of Uden's daughter and her eventual fate. Some called for burning, others for imprisonment. A couple even suggested freedom altogether lest the god become displeased.

A memorable man with a legacy to create might find this interesting. The broken Ranger did not. He merely sat in the shade, awaiting the call of the endless march.

He allowed himself a few solitary, stolen moments to think of her. A few breaths of love and regret before letting her go like a leaf in the wind. Although he would try to forget her, he knew he would be denied that, as much as he was denied the relief of forgetting his name. He thought of the boy, too, for a breath after, and his heart almost broke before he forced the pain deep down; only at the end of his life would he allow it to resurface. He did not think of their names. Like his own, they, too, must be forgotten.

This is all my doing.

After eating a scrap of bread and draining the solitary mug of water he was afforded every day, Jeroen stood up before one of the brutes rushed over to tug fiercely at his chains. He would stand of his own accord. He watched as they lifted the girl and placed her broken form upon the lap of the Rider to whose horse he was bound. Thus, the goddess would traverse the miles in relative comfort compared to the journey that awaited him. The Rider spurred his horse into motion, and, taking a deep breath as the chain rose out before him, Jeroen began jogging. Immediately, his body began to ache from the dull thumping of his feet upon the path and the strain in his wrists, but he had no choice but to keep moving. He had tried fighting this pull before, to no avail. At least they did not make him sprint, he told himself. The horse trotted ahead, and he followed along, partly dragged and partly trotting himself, always keeping up a delicate balance between the two. He felt his anger fester and burn away to nothing beneath the churning of bread, water and bile in his gut. He watched the ground and nothing more and fought the retching, the tears, the outcry of unfairness. He played a few words in his mind as company. Better that than dwelling on the promise of freedom that would be snatched away the moment they offered it.

This is my life. This is all I will ever be.
This is my life. I am nothing.
This is all my doing.

By late evening, his body trembled and his steps were clumsy. As darkness came in around them, the Riders slowed, and for this blessing he was grateful. For an hour more, they marched towards the town. He was desired there, it seemed, although he did not know why. Eventually, near a little stream, they stopped, and he fell to his knees and held his stomach and its terrible ache. Every night he almost broke anew, such was the exhaustion.

He knew their routine and, as usual, he argued little tonight as they attached his bindings to the nearest oak. A better Alphaline might have taken that moment to attempt freedom, but he wasn't even a Ranger anymore, let alone a fine warrior of legend. Instead, he curled up and watched his keepers chain Nomi's wrists.

Sleep didn't find him; the volume of the Riders as they drank and ate was too great. Swigging from bottles of sine, they sang and laughed and raised epic toasts to the South and their brutal false gods.

Strangely, his keeper sat down and offered a mouthful of sine to a semi-conscious Nomi. Unlike Jeroen, the girl still had fight to her. Spitting what he offered into his face, she leapt upon him, screaming and striking, and for a moment, Jeroen remembered the beauty of defiance, war, and many foolish notions. Her keepers believed this to be the finest act of hilarity and left her to her outrage. Instead, they turned to Jeroen, the forgotten Ranger without banner. Unlike Nomi, he was desperate for the drink. Greedily, he took the mouthful that was offered to him and a second one after that. He did not know why they offered him this gift, nor whether they had tainted the fluid, but he didn't care. For the swiftest moment, he was a free man again, at work in the ill-fated distillery, sampling a fine brew after barrelling. Again, he felt that familiar fire festering deep within him, and he allowed the burning liquid to feed its embers for a time.

I was someone once.

I was elite.

Holding that thought instead of pushing it deep down, he lay back, shivering in the cool air and wrapping his arms around himself, trying once more to seek sleep.

He did not hear the first kill, but he saw it. A strange thing it was to wake in freezing dew just as dawn broke, and to see a figure glide elegantly across the campsite. In among the many sleeping curs she went, and for a breath, he wondered if Nomi had broken free during the drunken night and made an escape.

No. You know this female.

There was something to her he couldn't remember. Couldn't believe. And then, like a rushing geyser, his memories came alive. He watched in astonishment as she leapt upon a guard standing watch, drew a dagger and plunged it into his back while holding a hand over his mouth. Jeroen, the Ranger, sat up and watched in disbelief as Lea held her victim, waiting as he bled out and died without sound. She left him where she'd killed him, sitting upright, leaning against his spear for support. Without taking a breath, she fell upon the other guard and slit his throat with equal efficiency. He managed a slight moan, and Jeroen froze in terror for her, for himself, for the entire world. Lea looked at her next victim, and Jeroen could contain himself no longer. Quietly, he raised his chains, and, hearing their gentle clinking, she silenced him with a swift finger to her lips. Of course, she would free him; of course, she would allow him to kill with her. He pointed to his keeper, and she nodded. As she made her way over towards Jeroen, she killed twice more, and her movements were smooth and beautiful, and deep down where there still lay hope, Jeroen felt a spark take light and catch a little fire.

Finally, she killed Zarate himself and then sat upon his body, rooting in his pockets for treasure, and Jeroen's mouth watered. He remembered this feeling of blood boiling and swords plunging deep into bastard flesh.

When she was finished seeking out her victim's riches, she changed course and went to the unconscious girl instead, and Jeroen was dismayed. More so when the bleary-eyed Nomi's chains fell loudly to the dirt; there was still so much silent killing to be done.

"Please," he gasped, hoping Lea recognised his voice beneath his scruffy, bearded face. Remembered his name. "Release me, Lea."

For a breath, she paused and peered into the early light. He stared at her, trying to find the words, but he was a fallen Ranger, broken and lost. All he had was vengeance. He saw the key in her hand and saw her hesitate before tossing it warily to him. It rose in a perfect arc and landed smartly in his hand. Around them, the stirrings of wakening came upon the remaining brutes, and he had no fear. Taking the key in his good hand, he pressed it into the lock.

"Jeroen?" she said, louder than either would have liked, and fuk him, but hearing his name spoken aloud after such a time fanned that flame into a furnace. He was Jeroen, broken but crawling. How long had he awaited this? How deeply had he doubted this would happen? It didn't matter. Nor did fearing for his life.

I will take more than one as I fall.
If I fall.
Click.

The chains fell away, and with them his anguish, misery and tragedy.

"Is that you?" Lea cried, oblivious to the Riders who stirred around them. Only Nomi acted. Leaping to her feet, she fell upon the nearest Rider, and began stabbing her with a fallen Rider's blade.

Within a flash, Lea was beside Jeroen, swords in her hand, screaming her version of anguish. With his heart pumping in a frenzy of excitement, Jeroen dove upon the nearest Rider, stealing the cur's blade and using it against him.

I was something.

Jeroen led the two women in the melee that followed. Screaming wildly with every strike, he was a god among insects; such was his indifference to their enemies' lives. He punished, hunted, and terrified; the slaughter had been a dreadful, chained lifetime in the making. They moved as one among the slower, still-drunk wretches and tore their lives from them as though it was a small matter. Next, wading through the undergrowth, Jeroen killed six more, most with a single strike. It was magnificent. For a breath, he was back on the battlefield with Magnus at his side, killing all who faced them. Turning to the last Southerner, who foolishly blocked his first strike, Jeroen took the man's eye before sidestepping around his panicked slashing and delivering the second blow through the other eye, driving his blade deep into the man's brain.

Watching the warrior fall, Jeroen laughed and cursed his journey into darkness before falling to a knee.

He heard Lea's voice but would not face her; could not look up from the anguish as the fervour of battle departed. He could only gaze at the spot where his discarded chains lay in the damp, crimson-stained grass. He could not stand, and Lea allowed him to take a moment. When he'd taken time enough, he felt her small arms encircle his shoulders and squeeze, and such affection was too much. He couldn't believe this moment had come. Couldn't believe this was no cruel dream, sent to take his sanity. He smelled the aroma of the road, overlaid with the perfume of sweet flowers. A female smell it was, and a welcome one. He wasn't used to another being so close to him. Not since he'd left Spark City.

"I've had a terrible time," she gasped, squeezing tighter, and he felt her sorrow matching his, and he feared the worst.

"So have I, little one," he whispered in a tone he used only for Tye. He wanted to know of his son. Of his mate.

Tye.

Mea.

"It is time to make them pay. Let's begin by standing up," she whispered, which was a fine idea.

"Aye, little one. Let us kill them all."

34

THE WITCHING HOURS

His name was Emir, and he liked to drink. He also liked to heal people, but drinking was his passion. He wanted to drink now. To curl up into a wretched ball of drunkenness and give up. Instead, he stared unblinkingly at Ealis—an easy thing to do from his place in the dust.

"Get up, brother."
But I am done. I am lost.
"Everything is about to change."

Even as he imagined Stefan's faded voice in his head, Emir knew it was no ghostly fiend from beyond the darkness. Emir created him to feel better. To feel less alone. When the right thing needed doing.

"Fine, I'll get up," he whispered, staggering to unsteady feet. She continued staring at him with unnerving eyes, and he hated her. "Why are you here, witch?" he asked. He'd hoped to sound determined, but he was little more than a broken prisoner waiting for the end.

She looked as though she were to protest, but instead caught her words and grimaced as though he were prey, before staring wistfully at Roja for a moment. Aurora was dishevelled, and dried blood covered her clothes. There was fresh blood upon her hands. A terrifying thing, and he wondered what evils she might have been doing with Uden while they were marching.

"I bring you gifts this evening, dear friend," she said.

"Friend? I see no friend."

"You are one of my closest friends, Emir. As is Roja. And Erroh. And Lea. And Stefan. And Lexi—"

"Get out of my surgery... Aurora," Emir shouted, taking an authoritative step towards her. His fingers were a whisker from the scalpel. She had nothing more than a dagger in her grasp.

"What will make Roja wake and rise?"

"Nothing, vile Southern whore."

"A whore perhaps, but not Southern, not really," she countered, slipping past him, twirling her dagger absently in her grubby fingers like the tail of a feline upon the hunt. "Please, allow Roja to rise from her deathly slumber. Time is of the essence. She should not be sleeping. No. Better she be awake for this."

Better than what?

"Why do you ask me these things? What does your master demand of her? I told him she needed rest," Emir snapped. He was terrified, without hope. So he relied on his dedication to healing. It trumped everything else. He knew they would slay him once she recovered. *If* she recovered. She had improved, but nothing was certain.

Aurora slipped away and began rooting through his open bag of healing tonics. She held them up, one by one, in the flickering light as though she understood their importance. "Which of these medicines will wake her? We only need her to walk a little." She shook a bottle of green fluid and then uncorked it. Without hesitation, she tipped the lip of the bottle to her tongue and recoiled at the poisonous taste. Antiseptic usually had that effect. Were it not the middle of the night and he not so exhausted by the small matter of the world ending, Emir might have smiled or even chuckled. As it was, he gazed at the scalpel, thought of Stefan, and almost threw caution to the wind.

"I have no potion to pull her from this healing sleep. Nor would I try. The girl is broken. You saw to that, witch. Right now, she needs the calming balm of sleep. Now fuk off, back to your master." He ground his teeth. His voice did not break. It didn't even tremble. For a strange moment, he was back among the wretches of the hovels, demanding respect and caring little for exhaustion, sadness or argument. He thought he'd been truly pitiful then. On reflection, though, they might have been the finest days of his unimpressive life.

In reply, she smashed the bottle on the ground and reached for another. She held it out, her eyes cold and determined. A killer's eyes, unused to not getting her way. "What about this one?"

"That's for a fever."

Smash!

She reached again, and he snatched the bag from her grasp.

Killer!
Betrayer!
Witch!

"Leave this place, Aurora. Before you make things much worse."

She did not strike him, although she certainly appeared to desire it. He'd seen that glare on the faces of many females in his time. Instead, she allowed him to recover his healing bag.

"Terrible things occurred. I will not be with Uden. I *cannot* be with Uden. I leave this place tonight and will bring you, Roja and Wrek," she told him.

He almost believed she was sincere, but instead he drew back his fist and struck her fiercely across the chin. It was a fine strike. Quig would have been proud. As would Stefan. Watching the bitch collapse in a heap, Emir felt alone in the world.

"To the fires with her."

"To the fires with you," he cried, and spat upon her. His mind raced. He thought about grabbing one of her swords. They were lying there, all innocent-like. A person like him could do fair damage with them, especially when she was distracted by a possible concussion. She moaned and dragged herself to her feet. The world slowed, and he imagined the satisfaction of killing her and screaming Roja's and Stefan's names as she died—a fitting end. Uden might take unkindly to him for killing his little spy, but it was a small matter. What mattered was taking that fuken blade and stabbing her in the back. All the way through.

"To the freedom with you," she whispered, and he never took his chance. She turned away from him, but not before he saw tears spilling from her eyes. "I give you my word. I will grant you safe passage. Some of my sins can be undone."

"Some sins might be forgiven. Not all, and most certainly not yours," he retorted.

"We can carry her. I can find a cart," she said desperately, and turned back to him, but her attention was caught by something else. Something behind him. He didn't care. His mind spun at the thoughts of freedom. Guilty thoughts, for he could not move Roja. Not even for the chance of them both living freely. He wasn't as brave as Erroh, denying Lea in her dying breaths. He wasn't as cruel, either.

"We cannot."

"We can... find a way," Aurora argued. Her eyes were on the darkness in the back area of the tavern. Without warning, a flicker of movement burst from the darkness. Aurora hissed like a feline in battle, and the female who charged upon her hissed similarly. Emir spun away as the females rounded on each other. They raced towards the swords, and the younger girl, no older than Tye, reached them first.

"Tempest, please," Aurora cried, but the girl hissed again and swung a blade at Aurora's unprotected skin.

"That is not my name," Tempest screeched, then stumbled as Aurora spun away from her swing, using her dagger impressively as a defence.

For a desperate moment, the small room came alive with the flash of clashing blades. The struggle was violent and pure, and Emir could only watch on in confused terror. He did not know this girl, did not know her motives, but while Aurora was careful in her blocking, she never once stabbed back at the younger girl. Instead, she appeared to favour defence over a kill. Having watched Ealis fight these last few weeks, he thought this was most peculiar. Even with a lesser blade, she was imposing.

"I know your name, your true name. I remember," Aurora roared. She spun away from the melee and stood beside the dead body of Stefan. She hesitated for a breath as she gathered her senses and resumed her stance. Spinning her dagger like a sword in a training arena, she circled the cold slab where Emir's friend lay, then bent and ran her fingers through his knotted hair. A strange thing during mortal combat. She looked back up at the girl. "Aimee of Raven Rock."

At this, Tempest, or Aimee of Raven Rock, lowered her blade, and Aurora dropped her dagger and gestured to the girl like a welcoming mother after a tantrum by a spoiled child.

"This was my home." The girl sounded feeble and broken. Perhaps she was. Perhaps Aurora had a hand in killing one of her friends this day. Maybe all of them.

"I know the nightmare you suffer. I know the way back, too," Aurora assured her, and Emir stood motionless, unsure what to do as these warring factions brokered peace. "Leave with us this very night. He will never find us."

Us?

"Uden sees all," Tempest of Raven Rock or something said warily. She shook her head as though irritated by an insect. He'd seen that look before. Seen it on the day of the tournament, from a Regulator he'd believed to be a friend. "I need him to see my last godly act in this place." She stepped back away from the gesturing Aurora. Her roar of violence had become a young girl's delicate shuffle. Only then did Emir see the youth and not the fierce warrior who'd stormed the building with death on her mind. She was young and unimpressive. She looked ready to bend and break. Her storm had blown out. He desired to know her intentions, yet still would not speak lest his presence cause another outbreak of fighting. He'd broken more than enough uneasy ceasefires in Keri.

"What are you doing, little one?" Aurora asked carefully. She stepped after the girl, who had moved towards Roja.

"He cares about this girl."

"No, little one. Do not."

"This pretty, sleeping whore."

Only then did Emir see her intentions, as she stood over the beautiful sleeping goddess. Saw it in the way she took hold of Roja's hair and placed her blade against the sleeping girl's throat. He was frozen, for he knew only words would bring her away. "Do not do this," he breathed, and kept his eyes on the blade in the flickering light.

"She is a friend," warned Aurora. She took a cautious step closer to Tempest. Again, she reached out as a mother would. Tempest still showed little interest. Instead, she gripped Roja's hair more tightly, and pulled her sleeping head close as though to make a swifter killing when the moment came. The moment took an eternity. And all Emir could do was watch his love's perfect hair waving back and forth in the young girl's grip. It wasn't fair. None of it was.

"Is that why you tried to kill her?" snapped Tempest. She pulled her blade away from Roja's neck and pointed it towards Aurora, who seized her chance in a blur of movement. She leapt towards the girl, slapping the tip of the blade away from her face, striking her as she did. The girl's head rocked back, and she fell away from Roja, collapsing to the floor. He supposed it was a motherly act, even from one as deranged as Aurora.

He grabbed the scalpel and, taking no chances, charged towards Tempest, prepared to end her life. He was crazed, furious, determined, and only the tip of Aurora's dagger held him at bay. She knelt over the girl, her eyes on Tempest alone. "You will leave this one," she ordered him. "She is no threat; she is no witch."

"Remove her and yourself from this room," he mumbled, and slowly, she nodded.

"As you wish, dear Emir."

She reached down and gently slapped Aimee across the face, hastening her back to consciousness. Cautiously, Emir produced a bottle of awful-smelling salts suitable for waking a dazed girl—less so a slumbering goddess. Taking the salts, Aurora revived her. Emir heard a quiet flurry of delicate reassurances, pledge after pledge of survival and vengeance, and after a time, Aimee nodded in agreement. A moment after that, she wept. A moment after that, Aurora Borealis cried with her. And a moment after that, the door crashed open and in stormed the legendary Tye, looking to stir mayhem.

As usual, Emir was thoroughly confused about what was occurring. Perhaps, were he drunk, he might have seen through this chaos. As it was, he feared for his friend, who set his eyes upon Aurora and raised his sword. An hour before, his only thoughts and worries had been about Roja's life. There was a beauty to singlemindedness. But now it seemed he wasn't alone in the world.

For a moment, Aurora said nothing. She stared through the boy, her eyes softer than before. Now, she seemed less a killer and more a companion. It took no healer to see that.

"Oh, fuk this," Tye screamed, breaking the moment. He did not hesitate. His body was a blur of aggressive, youthful motion. He swung at Aurora with deadly intent, and only instinct saved her. She matched his strike with her dagger and drew away, recovering the second sword before meeting his next flurry.

"Please, Tye," she cried, dodging his strikes, ducking away from his threat—and he *was* a threat. Emir had known him only as the young Alpha, standing in the shadows of extraordinary beings, but now there was a distinct energy in the boy. He was wildfire, spreading out across a gorse field, searching for destruction, death and a little vengeance. Emir had seen him fight a hundred times, but nothing had prepared him for this display of skill. Aurora, usually a match for him, fell away desperately, slashing and blocking for her life. The room became nothing but the flash of blades in the flickering light.

"I mean you no harm," she howled, suffering a cut on her shoulder. A glancing blow, admittedly, but a blow between friends was no small thing.

"I mean you plenty of harm."

Too loud.

They were screaming. To be more precise, Tye was screaming and driving forward, and the moment of victory was upon him. Emir had seen enough skirmishes to spot the signs. He'd seen no one apart from Erroh or Lea dominate her as Tye did now. Who knew betrayal was such a potent driving force?

"I bring mercy and escape tonight," she gasped, catching a block and giving him a stinging slap across his face to quell the savage child.

It did nothing but infuriate him.

He came at her again, cursing her for the death of Stefan, shouting Roja's name, condemning her betrayal of comrades, and she blocked as best she could. Still, he was either taken by a demon of the fires or held in hand by the absent gods, for he broke through, searching for the kill, and she was helpless to stop him until he struck her across the face himself with an open palm and followed up with a defence-splitting strike. It should have killed her, and would have but for a third blade entering the fray.

"Enough of this, pretty Alpha boy," Tempest of Raven Rock roared, blocking the fatal blow. For a moment, their eyes met. Hers were like those of a hound with a feral hare. His, like a lover's surprise at an interloper appearing suddenly from underneath the bed.

"Who the fuk are you?" he said in astonishment.

It was a fair question, allowing Aurora to slip out of range but not out of the fight. Not yet.

"I am not your enemy," Tempest of Raven Rock replied. Regardless, she held his blade in place for a few moments.

He didn't appreciate this at all. Delicately, he held his blade up to her. "Remove yourself, girl."

She, in turn, didn't appreciate *this* at all. Hissing, she struck at him, but he met her blow and knocked her aside as though she were nothing. She stumbled against the doorway from which Tye had appeared. At this, Aurora screeched like a beast in the night, and despite knowing he outmatched her, she leapt upon him, striking.

"I don't need you, sister," roared Tempest, turning towards Aurora.

"Sister?" cried Tye, spinning away from the onslaught towards Tempest, whose eyes were set upon Aurora, and Emir could only watch as the three figures chose and changed their victims. For a moment, they held their blades out, facing each other.

Everything went still. Blades quivered in outstretched hands. Three pairs of eyes darted from one face to the next. Swift gasps filled the air. No one knew what to do. No one wanted to make a move. A delicate, perfect moment of balance in a storm of swords.

"None of you should be here," Emir said.

He probably shouldn't have spoken. It broke the moment. Tye leapt forward, slashing at Tempest, who met the strike as Aurora slid up to him, attempting to get under his guard. A fine move, but he caught her intent, spun away, and slashed defensively out at her as he did. In a breath, all three separated again, and perhaps at that moment, they all realised another hunted them. Sensing the more significant threat, Tye turned back on Aurora, charging her. He roared vengeance. Tempest defended her, stepping forward again, trying to slice into him from the side. She cried for mercy while Aurora dodged Tye and knocked Tempest away, screaming foolishness.

There was uneasiness in the duel now. The three contestants circled the room, slashing at both prey and hunter, but there was a new carefulness in each strike. All knew a killing blow delivered on their part might allow a blow upon themselves. It was a battle that could never be won, only lost, and Emir finally found his nerve.

"You should not be here," he roared, knowing his voice was no more likely to alert their keepers than the noise of the skirmish. The three combatants hesitated for a tense breath, and he slid between all three blades, holding his hands up in the most calming gesture he could muster. It must have been influential, as one by one they lowered their swords: a silent, fragile treaty in the middle of the surgery, with Emir as peacemaker.

They didn't know him at all.

"I have made the path clear for you to escape this place," Tempest of Raven Rock said.

"Who are you? What are you doing here?" Tye asked.

"I am Aimee. I watched you come in. I am leaving this place. I am escaping the Woodin Man." She spat Uden's name, and Tye sheathed his blade. He looked at Emir for guidance, and Emir shrugged.

"She is like me, bound to do his vile bidding," Aurora offered. She stepped away, placing herself between the girl and Roja lest Aimee or Tempest or whatever she called herself now desired to punish Roja for Uden's crimes. "She will hurt nobody. Nor will I," Aurora muttered, eyeing Emir as though the attempted assassination of Roja was simply a sisterly thing.

"Oh, fuk this. I'm taking Emir, and we are getting out of here," Tye declared. He beckoned for Emir to follow. "We have Wrek as well."

"Who's out there? Is Wynn there? Is Lillium? Is... fuken Lea?"

"Just Lexi. Come on, brother; the hour is late. There is much running to do."

Aurora stepped forward, her blade sheathed now like his. "That's why I'm here. I came to free him. I have sinned; I have regrets." She sounded sincere, but Tye looked ready to attack her again.

Emir raised his calming hands again. *No need to fight. We are all equal threats here—nothing to worry about.* "I cannot leave without Roja. She's too weak to move."

"She's still alive?" Tye exclaimed, pushing past him to look at the girl. He had thought she was a corpse and that Emir was a prisoner watching over her. "Will she live?"

"We must move her. I will help," Aurora offered, and Aimee hissed under her breath.

"None of you can help. I will stay with her until she either dies or recovers," Emir stated, and they could not move him. Definitely not. Here until the end. For a breath, he imagined freedom, and his stomach turned with the shame.

Tye shook his head and looked around the ruin of the healer's surgery. "You must leave now! She would want you to live."

"She would want you to live."

I know.

It was tempting. He had heard tempting things in his life, most of which had involved alcohol and regrets. This, however, was a temptation of the soul. He looked to his lover and knew her chances would diminish a little with his absence, but if he were to leave with his comrades...

"I cannot leave her. I will not leave her."

"A brave sentiment."

"She's going to die, Emir; we need you now. Wrek needs you; he's not in a good way. We don't know where to go."

"You've freed Wrek?" Aimee asked. She looked pleased. "I know where we can go."

Tye stared at her momentarily before ignoring her and taking hold of Emir's cuff. "We have to leave. Let us go." He dragged Emir away from Roja, away from responsibility, away from guilt. And for a moment, Emir allowed him.

Aurora followed, as did Aimee of Raven Rock.

Out in the night, away from the thick stench of death and recovery, Emir breathed deeply. He stared at the streets as though seeing them for the first time, and his mind sharpened.

"Go on. I'll be just a moment," he said, releasing himself from Tye's desperate clutch.

The females charged into the night. Aimee appeared to know exactly where to go, and Aurora followed.

"We need you," the boy said, and his words were cutting. No longer was he the fierce storm who'd entered the room in search of heroism and bloodshed. Now he looked diminished and human again.

"Human—just better at it."

Emir stepped back to the doorway and looked to where his grisly fate awaited him. Within the room lay little more than the reward of Roja waking and his own death after that. "She needs me more," Emir said softly. He stepped in and slid the door shut, locking it behind him. He heard Tye on the other side. His words were desperate, tragic, pleading, and Emir could only turn his back to him as he stared at the sleeping goddess.

"Go now. While you can," Emir ordered and struck the door a few times. After a time, he heard the boy turn and begin to move away.

"Goodbye, Emir. May the wind be at your back."

"May the road rise up to meet you, little one."

Hearing the soft footsteps disappear, Emir recovered a glass and a jar one-quarter full of clear, burning liquid and sat down by his lover. No. Not a lover. She was more than that. She was his mate forever. His one for life. He would kill for her; he would die for her.

"Allow me just this poison, my darling," he whispered, pouring a glass of sine to start the terrible day. She made no move to indicate whether she heard him or understood his sacrifices from where she slept, and that was all right. She dreamt only of finer things, he told himself. Smiling wretchedly, he watched the first rays of sunrise climb from the darkness to sneak in and warm his face. Stroking her cheek gently, he thought this an acceptable way to start the last few days of his life.

The absent gods thought it a fine start too.

35

AFTER THE BREAKING

It was raining. Erroh knew this because his body shook at the touch of the cold droplets as they caught in the bitter wind. He also knew it because his vision suffered beneath the hazy downpour. Definitely rain. He couldn't remember when it had started. Or how he had climbed upon his mount. Closing his eyes, he tried to remember. Everything was a blur —a lazy gathering of memories since he'd collapsed before the fire and broken away to nothing. Around him, the trees swayed effortlessly in the breeze, and he watched their eerie, lonely dance. Everything he did would be lonely now, too. He knew this because she was gone. Dead. Lost forever. Little Erroh of the road was nothing without her, except a little wet. He didn't feel wet. His body was numb. He knew the stages of shock, and he was in its nasty grasp. He watched the raindrops in the water alongside him. Watching them ripple and disappear was usually calming, but nothing could ever settle Erroh again. The river was quiet here. No doubt deep enough that he could fling himself from Highwind's back and drop below the surface and never return. He wondered if Drahir would rescue him as Lea once had. Probably, and Erroh would hate him for it.

Do it.
Drop into the river.
Give up.

Drahir led the way through the dark forest, and he did so in silence. For a time, he had attempted to engage Erroh in conversation, but the effort of talking was too much. Erroh desired silence, and his companion respected his decision. Erroh had learned the art of conversation with

Lea as his sparring partner. Were he to survive this war, he would revert to tradition; and besides, talking was overrated anyway. Everyone was skilled at talking. It was deeds that were harder and deeds that were remembered.

He looked at the water again. He thought some more. Awful, empty thoughts that threatened to swallow him whole. Her beautiful eyes had gazed upon him, and her smile had warmed him as she whispered lovely sweet nothings as he'd smelled her perfume and tasted her breath. He had loved her with everything he had, and now she was ash. His stomach lurched, threatening to spill its contents over his wretched, wet armour.

"Can you hear that?" Drahir said quietly, bringing his horse to a stop. Erroh was uninterested, but he slowed regardless to listen to the soft murmur in the hazy forest ahead.

"Aye, something ahead."

He cared little for what lay ahead. He looked around and wondered about his victim. Visions of his grubby, shaking hands, assisting Erroh into the saddle, filled his mind. It had been sunny then. Or at least warm. He remembered he was gone now. Upon a horse, travelling south. Or to the city? Wherever. Erroh couldn't remember; he knew only that Drahir had forbidden the fiend from travelling with them. It must have been something he'd said. Or done. It didn't matter. What mattered was this living horror he found himself in.

"It's a patrol following the river," Drahir said. He dropped from his horse and rubbed his fingers in the mud, cursing. "They are charging."

Erroh didn't care.

Swiftly, Drahir dragged his mount from the muddy path along the river and pulled her in towards the treeline. Erroh knew this game well. It was a skill the hunted swiftly learned. He was tired of learning and of slipping out of the hunters' way. He heard them now, just as Drahir came rushing from cover, cursing him openly, grabbing Highwind's reins and pulling them both into shelter.

There was plenty of time to hide. The Riders took longer to appear than their hasty approach suggested. Eventually, a few dozen came galloping through the hazy mist along the riverbank. Erroh, concealed behind aged oak trees, watched dispassionately. He could feel Drahir's eyes burning through him as they passed, in case he charge out and start some shit. He didn't care enough. He only wanted to lie in the darkness and weep for her. When he had wept enough, he would weep for the rest. When he had no more tears to shed, he would take up his sword and kill a fuken deranged god. For now, though, he did not wish to be out in the rain upon a saddle. He wanted to feel something again.

"I will not give away our concealment," Erroh said after a time, and Drahir flinched in horror. It was no matter. The rumble of the mounts passing would cover his voice. Erroh had been this close to threat many times before. And if they heard? Well, some lesser part of Erroh that wanted to live might surface, take hold of his sword and deliver a little revenge.

"Whisht, Erroh. Why take a chance?"

At this, Erroh shrugged, and such was the effort, he added a sigh. It was a fine sigh; a casual watcher might have heard it and understood how broken this young warrior was. Finding little interest in the killers on the path, he stared at the concealing green leaves around them. The passing mounts set them shaking, sending sprays of fresh droplets upon their heads, and for a strange moment, Erroh felt his numbness subside a little as a freezing cold rivulet spilled down his back. He welcomed the awful chill for a breath and stared at the passing Riders, looking for a fight. He ground his teeth. Lea had loved the warmonger in him. When there was nothing else, there was the warrior that impressed her most. The warrior, free of a cage, who was to save her and kill them all. He thought of the snow and a frozen cell and fought the lure of violence. Lea had feared this terrible indifference of his, he knew. For a moment, his heart sank, considering how much she would disapprove of his behaviour. Again. He knew that were she in his position, she wouldn't stop fighting until their fate had been decided.

The Riders passed, their thunder becoming swiftly lost in the steady downpour, and Drahir climbed back upon his mount, but not before staring at Erroh's blade, held tightly in his fist. Following the man's gaze, Erroh looked down with surprise. He hadn't realised how tightly he'd held his sword's grip. The blade was halfway pulled from its scabbard, and Erroh had no memory of taking hold of it. Regretfully, he slipped the blade into its leather sheath, nudged Highwind forward, and followed. He thought on the sword for a time and felt the spark of fury stir deep within him. It wasn't much, but it was something. If there were little more than vengeful violence to guide his actions, he would live a short but bloody life before meeting her in the dark beyond.

They followed the path from where the Riders had emerged; it was now peaceful and silent. Erroh found his gaze falling not upon the route but upon the river alongside him once more. He didn't know why, only that his body ached numbly, and the freezing water was tantalising. The bubbles reminded him of a life lived well and painfully. He thought of Keri, and of his comrades falling in weather as dreary as this. He thought of the march to madness, and of the chains at his waist. He thought of Uden, and of his father's fingers around his neck. He thought of the lives he had taken, and of a little town where he and Lea had fallen in love.

There were other thoughts, too. Some were so wicked and vile that they belonged only in the cruellest of nightmares. Mostly, though, he thought of his numb body and his indifferent mind, imagined plummeting through the cold, welcoming water. It was no place for any leader's thoughts to roam, yet here he was.

Do it.

Drop into the river.

Give up.

He leapt silently from his mount towards the water's edge.

He'd been here before. The world spun and turned as he fell towards the water's surface. He wondered if he would hit rocks on the way down. Would his head be dashed and broken? Would his life be done? As his thoughts returned to the world around him, he noticed Highwind hesitating, confused that her burden was suddenly absent. He also caught sight of Drahir's back and hoped the man left him to it. Let him drown and disappear and be done.

He hung in the air. As he hit the water, instinctively and against his will, he spun and tucked himself, and his hands reached out, broke the surface first, softened his descent into the muddy darkness below.

Can't even allow the absent gods to choose my fate without getting involved, can you?

The water rushed up and covered him, and his body was no longer numb. It recoiled, and he gasped, and he drew himself upwards. As he broke the surface once more, the cold took him, and he ignored it. And why wouldn't he? He'd endured far worse. This was merely bracing.

"What are you doing?" Drahir exclaimed, wheeling his horse's head around and galloping to the water's edge. He dropped from his beast but stayed on dry land, watching Erroh closely. His master wasn't worth the cold dunking if he could avoid it.

The biting cold jarred Erroh back to his senses. "I fell, is all," he lied, and Drahir raised an eyebrow and reached out a hand.

He could have told Drahir of his fathomless sorrow, but speaking was an effort, as was hauling himself up the bank and climbing back atop his horse with such cold limbs. Gripping his reins was more difficult than before, but Drahir took off on his mount, and Erroh felt compelled to follow despite himself.

They set camp early that night. Deep in the forest, they rested their mounts in a grassy glade, and Erroh sat back, watching Drahir prepare a campfire. The warmth was welcomed, although holding his shaking hands out towards the flames brought back awful memories. His chest felt tight; his breathing became shallow and swift. He should have panicked, but he leaned against a tree and gasped for a time, willing himself to be still. He punished himself with visions of the horrors he'd endured, and the world around him darkened. As before, Drahir was beside him, hissing and dragging him back ashore, but Erroh had no interest. As the larger man took hold of his shoulders and began to shake him, Erroh did not fight his grasp or answer his pleas. Instead, he closed his eyes and collapsed to the ground.

"Erroh. Erroh—you must wake up."

Erroh didn't want to wake up. He wanted to lie here and die. Or drop into another river and allow it to drag him far from here. Far from responsibility, far from this life.

Suddenly, an awful strike across the cheek restored his senses, and he shot back awake.

"Erroh?"

"That hurt."

"Are you all right?"

"Let me lie here, Drahir."

"As you wish, brother." Drahir appeared relieved, and Erroh offered a weak smile, if for no other reason than to ensure he did not strike him a second time. If he did, Erroh might strike him back. It seemed like so much work. Propping himself up against the tree once more, Erroh gasped a little more but forced the horror from his mind. Allowing the fire's warmth to dry his clothes, Erroh closed his eyes again and fell asleep almost immediately.

His dreams were of Lea. She was alive. It was cruel.

Awaking to the crackling of a larger fire, Erroh shot awake again. Across from the fire, he saw Drahir weeping silently, and he thought this a strange thing. What fresh horrors had this brute endured that he would need to weep so openly, Erroh wondered. Looking to the sky, he realised it was dawn on another dreary day. Stretching his aching body, Erroh rose swiftly, as did Drahir, who wiped his eyes.

"We should ride," the Southerner mumbled, and Erroh shrugged. His mouth was dry, and his stomach churned with hunger, but any thoughts of eating or drinking were unwanted.

"If you say so," Erroh said.

For hours more, they rode in silence. Erroh scratched at a worn part of his reins to pass the time and keep himself from thinking of miserable things. He did not know why. It had started when he pulled away a loose flap of leather to reveal a softer layer beneath, and he had gone at it with his nails, scratching and cutting. It was something to do as the sun passed across the sky.

They neared the Southerners' camp as evening drew in, and Drahir called for them to rest awhile. Erroh thought this a strange thing. Having built another little fire, the man sat down opposite Erroh, scrutinising him thoughtfully. On another day, Erroh might have cared. As it was, he was indifferent, for, at that moment, his mind was awash with thoughts of Lea and his childhood. Both lost forever.

"Will you still lead us?" Drahir asked.

"Until I drag us to the depths of oblivion," Erroh muttered, gazing at the reins hanging down Highwind's withers. He could see the damage his fingernails had made. Could see the foolishness of his actions.

"Perhaps it would be better if you did not return," Drahir said after a long pause. "I should lead them. You can hide in the forest. Away from the coming violence."

"Perhaps, though I like violence."

She always thought I was good at it.

"Perhaps I should kill you where you sit, ruin that you are," he said coldly, and Erroh shrugged.

"You gave your word you would not."

"I spoke with a worthy leader at the time."

"Time... that is all I need, fiend. I am tired of this fight. Tired of this horror. I have lost everything in this world. Allow me time to grieve." Erroh felt his chest tightening as he spoke. He fought the urge to weep. That would come when he was alone.

"Time? If you return, I will grant you time, but you must play your part."

"I will play my part," lied Erroh.

Late in the night, Drahir roused him from sleep. The rain was pouring again, and the fire's light had dimmed to nothing. "Come on, we will travel now the rest of the way," Drahir said, pulling Erroh to unsteady feet.

"As you wish, brother," Erroh said mockingly, and for a moment, Drahir froze as though preparing to strike him. Erroh didn't care. His stomach burned with hunger; his mouth was parched and raw. He welcomed discomfort. If Drahir struck him? Well, that would be feeling something too.

They rode quietly the rest of the way to the camp. Erroh spent the time with his legs firm against Highwind's ribs while he went to task, tearing the offending reins. To his joy, he broke them free a few hours after midnight, just as they spotted the dim lights of the camp and, for a moment, he felt happy. He did not know why. He did not care. Nor did he care when the joy slipped away as swiftly as it had arrived, and he felt cold, empty and alone—feelings he deserved.

"Good to see you've returned, Erroh of Spark," a sentry whispered, bowing deeply.

Play the part.

"Glad I return," Erroh mumbled, feigning a smile before nodding at the two warriors standing watch over the camp's main entrance. In the few days he and Drahir had been away, the townspeople had filled in much of the perimeter with carts and logs. Amazing the effect a few loose words could have when one was the king.

"Try harder tomorrow," warned Drahir, and Erroh shrugged.

They walked their mounts through the sleeping camp, and suddenly Erroh was overcome with gratitude for Drahir's suggestion to return this late. Facing so many hopeful and happy subjects would have been too much.

"Perhaps tomorrow I will be improved," Erroh said, handing the broken reins to his companion.

"Sleep well, Erroh. Sleep better."

"Sleep well, brother."

"Not anymore," the man said, and led the horses away.

Slipping through the flaps of his tent, Erroh stripped, dropped into the cold bedding and wrapped himself up tightly away from the world and from horror. He was asleep before his body warmed. He dreamt of Lea; he dreamt of a cage creaking in the frozen night.

36

THE PLAYER

Sometime during the night, Elise opened her eyes and snapped awake. Stretching her limbs, she slipped swiftly from her bedding despite the near-complete darkness. She'd done this before. Many times. Lighting a little oil lamp, she yawned and enjoyed the deep breaths she took. For a few wonderful breaths more, she summoned her desire, her need, her strength to face whatever was to occur as she always did. This was the quietest moment of her day. She enjoyed it most. In these first few moments, before Kaya came to call on her, she could lament after her family and miss them. Down here in the dark, she could be wary of the coming day, the strength she'd need to show and the doubts she'd have to conceal from those who needed her most. Although her family was spread out across the Four Factions, this was where she needed to be. She was a mother first and lover second, but this place was her true purpose in this world.

Drinking from her tankard of water, she stretched, still breathing deeply and slowly. She caught her reflection in a standing mirror, a gift from Ulrik after the unfortunate event upon her arrival. That had been then. This was now. Things had very much changed since then. Things usually did. She was skilled at playing bandit. She enjoyed it. They enjoyed her participation. More than that, the prison in which she had first woken was a goddess's chambers. It was private, away from the rest of Adawan. It was also a sanctuary for Elise, and they had made her welcome. Her behaviour earned their respect and, with it, the finer things in life. Like freedom. Like a warm carpet beneath her feet. Silken bedding as delicate as her own in the east. On the wall, ancient pieces of art hung, reserved for those with a keener, richer eye. She took great pleasure in them.

Within this room she called her own, there was also an extensive wardrobe filled with enough gowns, corsets and paints to make a girl her age feel pretty. To have a room to herself was a rare privilege, she knew, especially with so many arriving in Adawan daily. However, she would not share, regardless of her charitable mind. A legend did not share. A legend took the finer things. A legend could sit in the dark alone, gathering the strength to face the world. And she was worthy of it all. It had taken only a few weeks for many to understand her legend. Picking a fight with the toughest hound in the lot was certainly one way of doing that.

Flexing in the mirror, she thought herself beautiful again. Her thin arms, once so fragile and wasted from heavy lung, were now tight and muscular. Not enough to make her a brute, for she still enjoyed her devious daintiness, but enough to carry a heavier burden. The heaviest burden would come soon enough. Not today, but soon.

Gazing at the tightness in her jaw, the flatness of her belly and her perfect, sturdy legs, she knew Magnus would desire her immensely, which was pleasing. She liked to be alluring, but knowing she was war ready was fantastic.

Stretching herself, she dropped to the ground and began doing push-ups. An excellent way to burn energy first thing in the morning. She hadn't exercised in years; such was her fragility. Breathing in the air of this place granted her life again. She wasn't willing to waste it, either. Switching to one arm, she drove down and up, enjoying the burn, feeling it in muscles freshly born after a decade of immobility. With her body covered in sweat, she continued her different routines until her body was taut and her chest heaved wonderfully in exhaustion.

That done, and panting lightly, she began wrapping her knuckles as she had done every morning these last few weeks, and this part she enjoyed most.

The large sack of sand waited for her, and she began striking it fiercely in the dim light of the flame. After a session of beating the ever-living shit out of the bag, she found it easier to face the world. She always began with simple combinations of right and left, each stinging strike denting and shaping the thing and sending it swinging wildly, and she moved with it. Always in motion, always balanced, always a threat. She envisioned dreadful things as she struck, and the bag took her frustrations, terrors and agonies. She worried about Magnus's fate,

Erroh's and Lexi's, and the world's. Each worry was driven deep into the bag of sand, and through clenched teeth, she screamed with every strike. Time would slow to nothing as the goddess moved around the room, constantly dipping and dodging away from the swinging weight, delivering rapid-fire blows as it passed, perfecting her strike, perfecting her defence. It was something to do in this dark hole, away from the burning skies above.

Eventually, knowing Kaya would likely be on the way down to call her for the exhausting day to come, Elise slowed and retreated away from the swinging sack, and only then did she realise how exhausted she was.

Not finished yet.

Stripping off her garments and catching sight of herself again in the mirror, she flexed once and was pleased with the older woman staring back. She was ancient but still divine. Beautiful things got their way as well. Taking a damp rag and wiping the grime of sweat, salt and dirt from her body, she hummed to herself awhile, an old song about the end of the world and the people beyond. It was a familiar tune, one she often used to prepare herself for the coming day.

She drizzled some sweet-smelling oils over her body, for she had much to do, and she desired to look and smell good doing it. Spending a few breaths applying the right amount of paint to her face, she dressed swiftly, for suddenly, the thundering of excited boots came from the darkness beyond.

Perfect timing.

"Elise? Are you decent?" a voice called, as Elise wrapped her long, damp hair up into a neat ponytail. She looked better with her hair down, but some things couldn't be helped.

"I am. Please enter," she called out to Kaya.

"Oh, thank the absent gods, you are finished," Kaya said, stepping into the room. Then she stopped and narrowed her eyes. "*Are* you finished? You have that look, Elise. Why are you smiling?"

Elise indeed smiled as she strapped her sandals tight. She looked good, she felt better, but she was a goddess who needed to push herself.

"Do you have the beating of me today?" Elise asked. She raised her eyebrows. It was not a question. The girl would accept the challenge even if she didn't want to compete—especially if she didn't want to compete. Kaya was learning under Elise's wing, even if that included besting a legend at a gentle race. Truthfully, it would be no peaceful race at all; more of a gruelling marathon guaranteed to take the breath and weaken the knees. But doing it enough benefitted the body just fine.

Elise wrapped the black sash around her thigh. This sash had been earned and she wore it proudly. That battle would come. Not today. Not until she was sure she could win. If she had only known then what she knew now of Ulrik's impressiveness, she might have done things differently.

Aye, but you wouldn't have earned your place here.

That was true. Sometimes defeat was everything. It was the last breath bloodily taken or the last strike before giving up a dream. A legend took defeat and learned from it. Without defeat, Elise might never have truly learned the ways of these fantastic, barbaric people. Might never have fallen for this place. Who knew Elise belonged down in the depths of nothingness? She ran her fingers along the black sash and loved it. It had been a gift from the young warrior bandit Reuben, who had been the first to turn to her side. He'd seen before most others.

"Oh, for fuk's sake, I thought we were taking today off. I just did my hair," muttered Kaya. Regardless, she began stretching, following the routines Elise had shown her. Kaya was a goddess like Elise and bested her now and then. Less so these days. Elise was getting better every day and getting stronger too. Nothing was wrong with merely existing in the world as it was, but attempting to improve was a wonderful thing, frustrating as it was at times.

"I'm just a delicate waif, you know," Elise said, jogging from the room, knocking Kaya roughly as she did. There was no start to their contest. There was just the run. Picking up speed, stepping upon the first flight of stairs from her palace to the world above, Elise picked up the pace, knowing the girl would be right behind.

"Typical cheater," growled Kaya, racing after her, her feet attacking the steps as swiftly as Elise's.

Upwards they ran, Elise a few steps ahead, Kaya hissing and cursing behind her. The first flights were easier after so many weeks of training. The muscles in Elise's calves felt like solid rock as she flew up the steps. She could only imagine how Kaya's were.

Both females charged upwards, and Kaya charged alongside, trying to barge Elise aside. A fool might slip from the edge and have a painful fall to the level below. A luckless fiend might slip off completely and meet an end at the bottom of the shaft, but neither Kaya nor Elise was clumsy enough to fall. Both women were graceful and determined.

"Don't fall, you bitch," gasped Kaya, kicking out at Elise, who rode the challenge. Other bandits slipped back into their less lavishly decorated hovels as the tradition of the race passed them by. A few cheered the pair on, calling out their support for one female or the other as they dashed past, and in a flash, they were gone, charging ever upwards to where the air was different, lighter somehow.

I am like a fish out of water, mused Elise. And perhaps that was true. She had been built for the depths.

Kaya took her at the last flight. She reached out, grabbed the older woman's collar, and shot forward as Elise gasped and surrendered the race—a cruel blow and perfectly acceptable. Elise wasn't foolish enough to believe anything in life was fair. She would merely be ready for it next time.

"That was easy," teased Kaya, collapsing against the mine entrance.

"Walk it off. Don't stop," hissed Elise, although stopping and collapsing against the wall looked appealing. Instead, she forced her screaming limbs to march onward, through the entrance, out into the grim grey of the day. "I will see you at the bar," she added, and Kaya, allowing herself one last breath, nodded and made her way back through the crowd of refugee bandits.

The people of Adawan watched Elise as she made her way towards the ramparts. Some offered a smile, some offered salutes, some bowed, and very few bore her ill will. Truthfully, though, it was the womenfolk who showed the most respect. Their smiles were most welcomed, and she took them all, held them close to her heart and marched with shoulders back and a determined gaze ahead. Not even Ulrik could diminish the fire that had been stirred up by her defiant behaviour. A lesser man might have seen to her disappearance, or forbidden her from leaving her cell. But as far as she knew, Ulrik was open to many things, including potent allies. Even if they wanted to claim his throne. *Especially* if they wanted to claim his throne. Elise would claim his throne, and few would find an argument. But she would do so only when the moment arose. Until then, there was plenty to do: tasks to be completed, defences to be erected, wars to be prepared for.

Adawan had become overly populated with bandits. In fact, these last few months their number had increased tenfold. And with their arrival, word of Southern dominance across the factions. Only a fool would ignore the potential of a warmonger lurking in their midst, and Ulrik had put her to work.

Sharing a few words with the line of busy chefs surrounded by bubbling cauldrons and stoves smelling of sweet and salted bread, she accepted a brew of mushroom soup as breakfast for the fifth day in a row. Afterwards, she climbed to the summit of Adawan's mine and into the green world beyond, and immediately felt the coolness of the shade. High above the roving mass of grey, beige and black, she could imagine she was out in the forests again, and she enjoyed a few pleasant, peaceful moments before she went off to her duties.

She passed through the crops and ran her fingers over the long stalks of grain. They had cut down half the forest above Adawan to make way for these crops. The area would take years to recover, but in time it would, and with the numerous mushroom farms in the mine and the crops coming into season up here, food was plentiful. Enough so, in fact, that she wondered about the possibility of establishing a few trade routes with the city. Such a thing would be suitable for Adawan's flourishing economy, and who knew how swiftly a trade route could improve relations between the settlements? After all, the people of Adawan were more than bandits, killing and plundering: they were survivors, and Spark, the light and capital of the world, certainly had its own gruesome histories.

Reaching the edge of the farmland, where the green met burning desert, she came upon a gruff-looking bandit at toil.

"Morning, Elise," he said.

"Ah, good morning, Frog," she answered. She did not know his actual name, and he looked like no frog she'd ever seen, yet still, the name suited him, although she could never say why. She knew him to be in charge of the felling of the trees, a job to which he'd taken well. He wasn't the only bandit up above the salt mine, either. There were dozens —all hacking and chopping at the larger trees. In just a few weeks, the gaps in her path had become more noticeable. At least they had the sense to replant saplings as the mature trees fell. This war would end, and it was foolish not to think of the next one.

Just over a week had passed since they had first seen the Southern scouts, all sneaky-like, viewing the goings-on from a distant vantage point. They had given chase, but the distance was too vast. Adawan had become a little tenser in the days since, yet there had been no further signs of a roving horde marching on them. Every day that an army that didn't appear on the horizon was a good day. And until that happened, Adawan would continue to work at protecting itself. Elise would see to that.

Farther out in the scorching sands where no shade could ever exist, Elise could see countless shirtless workers digging a long trench around the sanctuary, just wide enough that getting over it would be difficult. When stopping a charge was out of the question, sometimes it was about simply making it harder.

It's a start.

Every hundred feet, there stood tall platforms overlooking the trench. Each was high and wide enough for a dozen archers and fire carriers to settle within it, and Elise imagined they would cause any approaching attackers to think twice. Lining their defences, there also stood long anti-cavalry spikes, dug deeply and firmly into the sandy ground like little naked tree saplings. Every foot taken by an enemy would be earned with blood and tears. Elise knew well that no amount of defences could withstand an entire Southern army siege, but with an underground river to call upon and ample food and bodies to spare, Adawan might hold out long enough to persuade an army, parched with thirst beneath the sun's unforgiving rays, to retreat to more welcoming surroundings. Armies had collapsed under less harsh conditions.

And a savvy leader would counter a retreating army.

She gazed across the barricades that had been erected along the edge of the green, and she was pleased with the skeletal defensive structures the workers had dug into the ground. They weren't ready yet, but this sanctuary was becoming a rightly impressive fortress. Pleased with the night's advancements, she spoke with a few bandits as they worked. Despite the ominous feelings in the wind, their conversations were easy and light-hearted. When she spoke, they listened, and this was another sign of her importance in this place.

Walking along the border of the oasis, she was less pleased with the defences along its eastern parts. Delicately, she reprimanded the leader of that area, Gar, who argued that the major attack would come from the west. It was a compelling argument from a man who'd never seen a battle, never thought beyond what was in front of his nose. She listened and politely shut down each argument with gentle insistence, until, without a leg left to stand on, he agreed to her demands. More than that, he pledged to make the needed improvements by the day's end. With a smile, she bowed and left him to scream orders at his workers.

She climbed one of the watchtowers and took time to gaze at a large gathering of nomadic bandits nearing the outskirts of the defences. She welcomed such a sight. Her people were supplied and secure, and she almost welcomed the bandits to take up arms against them. She looked at their wretched, exhausted faces and wondered what strife they had suffered upon the march. She also wondered why they were travelling in such a large band; surely it was easier to remain unnoticed in smaller numbers, especially for people skilled in concealment, as these nomads doubtless were. Leading a few hundred people through precarious lands was no small thing. She watched their leader for a time as he argued for entry through the barricades, and she could see his threat in every move he made. This pleased her immensely.

Eventually, with the sun tiring her, she climbed down and returned to her adopted home. All who noticed her slipped out of her way as she passed, as though she were a king.

Up ahead, she saw Ulrik, the current leader of Adawan, perched at his table outside the mine's tavern, with Kaya in a chair beside him. Seeing Elise approach, he called for a refill for himself and a fresh beverage for her.

How times have changed.

"Good afternoon, legend," he declared, motioning her to a seat across the table. Gone were the bottles of wine, bags of pieces and tightly gripped cards. Instead, maps and notes from scouts littered the table, along with the two steaming cups of cofe. Kaya nodded a greeting to her, then returned to reading through the numbers, her brow creased in worry. It was the usual look to her.

"More coming in. Sizeable group, too," Elise said, flicking her chair around and leaning on its back to face the table. Unlike Magnus, she cared little for maps; she simply desired to know the enemy's location and when to fight.

Ulrik reached and moved a few figures across the map's edges; it was apparent there were more bandit locations she had yet to learn of. In time, she'd earn his trust fully on such matters. That was fine.

"There can't be many more groups slipping through the Southern net," Ulrik muttered. She peered more closely at the map, which showed the fresh numbers that had been reported flooding towards Spark, and a chill ran down her back.

The city will hold.
The city will take the brunt.
We can take the rest.

"If they need to get here, they'll get here. Whatever it takes," Kaya said dreamily. Elise knew that vacant stare well. Kaya was at the table, but really, she was back in Raven Rock, reliving terrors. Whenever they spoke of the roving beasts, Kaya's mind went back to her sieged home. Elise knew this because Kaya had admitted it. Briefly, Elise had worried it might become a distraction, but she trusted the woman just fine.

Anyone who stared a potential siege in the face and still desired to fight, as Kaya clearly did, would be indispensable.

"Every one of them a soldier too," Elise said, and Ulrik hammered the table once with his fist. He relished talking of fights and poring over maps while drinking cofe with his co-conspirators; it was a welcomed thing. Still, Elise knew well that this was about something other than a victory for Ulrik. It was about survival. This he'd admitted to Elise and a few other eager listeners at a late hour, over a bottle of sweet wine. She admired his courage and his nobility, but she had grander plans: survival in the first wave, counter-charging on the second. She caught sight of Ulrik's biceps as he struck the table and remembered the power of his strikes. He caught her staring and grinned.

"Are you coming for me today, Queen of Adawan?"

"Not today, my liege, but prepare yourself."

He laughed, and she laughed, and that was fine, for they each knew the other's threat. She knew his fierce strength, brilliant mind, and the experience he had garnered while holding his seat. He knew her power, even as a frail woman. Now she was swifter, sturdier, and looking ten years younger. More than that, she had passionate support throughout the settlement. Sometimes, a shrewd leader knew the winds of change were afoot. It didn't matter she was a newcomer to this place. Or that she'd never once been a runner on a job. This was no gang of thieves. This was a burgeoning civilisation at the end of the world. Any fool could see she had their best interests at heart. Any quick-witted person might also notice she had grandness in mind for this wretched hive of banditry.

"Oh, fuk me. You might have to wait in line for your throne," Kaya said suddenly.

They all turned and looked beyond the table: the newcomer nomads, who had no doubt convinced the sentries of their lineage and entitlements, were marching down the ramp now.

"Fuken Bison," growled Ulrik. He clenched his fists and gritted his teeth. His entire body became rigid, and Elise found this very interesting.

"Who is Bison?" she asked, gazing at the monster leading the pack.

Kaya leaned forward. "Before this war shit, Bison commanded the west regions. A right bastard, too. Strong as a giant as well." Kaya looked nervously intrigued, and Elise thought this wonderful. "He is a fine soldier but a terrible leader. He believes in the older ways, the more brutal, less open-minded ways of doing things. He'll fuken hate you, Elise. And he will reach for Ulrik's crown."

Ulrik was nodding his head in agreement. "And I must welcome the bastard in and play the part of gentle host until he does," he muttered. Getting to his feet, he stepped down from his perch and marched towards the big brute. They stood at similar heights, and as they embraced, Elise was sure she felt the ground shudder slightly.

"Can this Bison defeat Ulrik?" she whispered to Kaya.

"If Wrek couldn't beat Ulrik, I'm not sure anyone could," Kaya said weakly. "Although I would not wager on such things," she added.

"I am very much looking forward to speaking with this boy," Elise said, her mind racing.

"You have that look, Elise. Why are you smiling? I hate that smile."

37

GOD LOVER

Her name was Aurora, and she did not love her god anymore, but she did want to kill. She didn't know where to direct her wrath, but it was a small matter; looking around the camp, there was plenty to choose from. Her body was taut like a spring in a rich fiend's bedding, just moments from letting loose, tearing everything apart—as if she hadn't done enough damage as it was. She looked at her shaking hands and imagined the blood upon them. Too many lives had been lost by her deeds. A king, a prince, countless Alphalines. And children not yet of age. And Aimee of Raven Rock.

Tempest.

She shuddered and broke; her mind left her, and she became undone. But instead of falling to pieces, Ealis stood upright, catching her breath. The hour was late, and her sins were plenty. She looked out through the camp, following the route Aimee might have taken. She wondered how she would have behaved were she reborn in blood and meeting the goddess who came before. She might have acted as the girl did.

But I delivered her to this torment.

She shuddered again and marched away from Tempest's tent. The people all around her were busy, and they took no notice, and this was fine. She was hunting the girl. Hunting her redemption, too.

She glided through the camp, a wraith of stealth; she kept her face hidden beneath her hood, her godly eyes seeking a lost girl bent on assassination. All the while, her mind was awash with dreadful thoughts of her actions. Seeing Tempest was a step too far. In that moment, she could feel Fyre's skin, tormented and scourged by a cruel bastard.

"Too much. I can take no more," she whispered to nobody at all. She despised her weakness. Inside her mind, she heard her victims and felt the warmth of the blood, which was awful. She fled from the settled soldiers, her feet light and swift. Towards the woods, towards the silence of the green. She almost didn't stop. Every step away from the town made her feel better, until, eventually, she slowed and stopped as swiftly as she had started running. But then, as though compelled, she turned back around. Her heart hammered, and she knew Uden's hold was still upon her, and she hated him for it. Were she capable, she might have tried to kill him, but she knew the truth, knew her failures. She didn't even have the nerve to seek Tempest and save her from herself and him.

"I am nothing," she wailed, and turned back to the camp. And then, through the throngs of people, she saw the girl. The other fuken girl. That vile stunning blonde girl. Her eyes narrowed as a new hunt began.

She watched the stunning girl through the crowd. Marching as though she commanded the army. Perhaps through her whispered tongue, she did. A casual onlooker might have missed her in the camp's dimness, but Ealis caught her dazzling white dress beneath a cloak, and Aurora climbed to her feet and followed. The girl was oblivious, but Aurora never forgot a face; she wondered whether the girl would remember hers. Slipping into a tent reserved for her alone, Ealis stole up and waited for a few breaths.

Be swift, be devastating, be fuken ruthless.

She straightened, her mind filtering the anguish to her desire. The tent was fair and comfortable. A few decorations more than most soldiers'. A lavish bed but still far less extravagant than a god's. Nothing else stood out about the tent, nor why should it? She had likely had little time to pack many belongings since the fall of Spark. Slipping through the tent, the girl did not hear her approach, but she saw her in the reflected mirror. The mirror rested on a table covered in expensive paints and perfumes for allurement.

Aurora remembered the girl's name too. It was Silvia. It was a nasty, annoying name. She was a nasty, annoying person. The girl did not jump as Aurora approached nor yelp in surprise. She stared at the approaching Ealis and continued brushing her long blonde hair, and Aurora wanted to kill her.

"I know you," Silvia whispered suddenly, stopping the brushing to stare at her guest. "You were with Stefan the night he disappeared."

"I know you too."

"I am hard to forget." The girl smiled a dazzling smile that could topple mountains. *Or a wretched, beautiful man.* "Was he your lover? Did you warm his bed at the end? Before you betrayed him… Aurora?"

Aurora recoiled, realising this bitch knew her. Her hands became fists, and she wondered how best to tear her to pieces. Skin first. "I did my part for my god," Aurora whispered. She felt perspiration gather under her arms, and a solitary droplet rolled down her left arm. She suddenly needed a drip of sweat to roll down the other side. Her mind reeled. This tent felt wholly too small. And she, without a weapon.

"My betrayal was for the city's benefit," Silvia snarled. "Perhaps were matters more favourable, it would have been no betrayal."

She spun around, and Ealis could only marvel at the golden sheen of her hair. Like honey on a summer day. A small wonder Stefan was so taken with her. She thought of the girl's cruelty to her boy in their solitary meeting. She remembered the shame she had inflicted upon him and held the hate, which was a comfort.

"As it is," Silvia said coolly, "we landed on the correct side of this war."

The girl stood up and eyed Aurora curiously, and Ealis's mind shifted. She wanted to kill, to survive. To be merciful. To get revenge. She did not want to speak with this girl anymore. She did not want to know her victims anymore. She wanted to undo everything she'd ever done. She wanted so many things.

"We landed where we did," spluttered Ealis, stepping away from the girl. She wondered about leaving the tent and escaping into the Wastes. Disappearing forever and forgetting her awful lot in life. "At the expense of great things."

"I did all I could. I did better than most."

"I do not care for what you did," Aurora whispered. She did care, though. She wondered if this witch's actions had been worse than her own. Bitterly, Stefan had told her of her higher status within the Spark and how the world was to bow at her feet. Now, here she sat, alone among those who had felled the beast, and she, little more than an entitled lover of a cruel bastard. Such things did not happen easily. The more Ealis knew, the easier it was to understand her. To find a reason to spare her. Or else to kill her without remorse.

"As the city rotted, I tried to eliminate the festering infection. I did it for the city. Do not talk of great expenses. I sacrificed everything and received nothing." She held her tone, but Aurora could see that her anger had been stirred. She'd seen such uneasy gazes in people before, primarily those at their wits' end. Sometimes when she stood over them with a blade, they pledged the world for mercy.

Silvia began to brush her hair manically, which was unsettling. "I even saved her most precious daughter." At this, Silvia smiled sadly as though lost in thought. "If nothing else, I broke and saved a faded goddess." There was pride in her voice. Aurora did not like this. She wondered if Uden had manipulated her mind already, and then thought better of it. She was too old for such things.

Isn't she?

Silvia rubbed her eyes as though they were alight with wildfire, then blinked and addressed Aurora with a cruel glare. "I know what Uden thinks of you. Do you want to share his love? I would share his love. Would you share? Like we shared our love for Stefan? Beautiful, lovely Stefan. Beautiful, before you got him killed," Silvia almost sang, and Ealis wondered was the girl demented or drunk or as lost as she was.

Two swords were still in their scabbards by the bed, and for a moment, Ealis wondered about leaping for them and slaying the bitch who had struck her down with words. Besides, Aurora didn't want to share anything.

"I should not be here."

"Did Stefan suffer as he fell?"

"He was in love when he fell," Ealis whispered, and suddenly Silvia was beside her, staring into her eyes, cutting into her soul, and Aurora pushed her away. A delicate push. A warning. Uden would not want her bruised.

"No, little rat of the South. He loved me when he died, always loved me, and I loved him," she spat. Aurora was cold and reassured, and her vitriol was fine. "We are two rats of Spark, aren't we," Silvia added, which was fine. She turned back and resumed brushing her hair, and Ealis allowed her to. Aurora did not.

Silvia likely saw her approach but couldn't stop the violent strike. Gripping that fabulous hair, Aurora slammed her face down upon the table, shattering the mirror, taking one of her front teeth. She swiftly grabbed her again and drove her down a second time, and there was a pleasing crunch as the girl's nose split apart. Gasping, Silvia struggled away, and Aurora slipped forward and drove her fist beneath her chin, taking her voice in a fluid motion. It was a killing, silencing blow, and Silvia's desperate struggles ceased as she gasped for breath. Aurora thought of Stefan as she laid the girl out flat and, adjusting her foot over her face, drove down, taking her teeth and her fuken smile.

The girl convulsed, and it was pleasing, and she still did not die, for she was a higherline, and Aurora knew that meant a strong bloodline.

"He loved me at the end," Aurora whispered, taking hold of the dying girl's blade.

She pierced her chest with a full downward thrust, and Silvia of Spark City died within a few breaths. This was a shame, but Aurora didn't mind. Taking the second blade, she pried the witch's chest apart, grunting with the effort, to reveal the stunning treasure underneath. Sliding and cutting among the slippery innards, she freed the desired organ.

Looking at it in the light, she clenched her fingers a few times and watched the last of the warm blood bubble out, spilling over her fingers onto the floor below, and it was delicious.

"Not very impressive," she whispered, and dropped the empty heart beside the demented, grinning body. Then, she stamped down thrice upon it until it was little more than a mush of ruin.

A last gift for you, my love.

Only then, with her gift to Stefan crushed, did she understand that she had gone too far. She knew Uden barely cared for the girl beyond a quick furrowing, but she had belonged to him, and Aurora had spat in his eye for such a sin. "Mine now," she whispered, taking the girl's unimpressive swords.

Wrapping her cloak around her to cover the blood beneath, she had little on her mind beyond escape, but not before attempting to free those she cared for most in the world.

The night was cool; the wind was light, and her steps were lithe as she slipped inconspicuously through the camp towards Raven Rock. Her heart beat madly, her vision was dark, and she wondered if this was the end of her, but she marched onwards, regardless.

Too many sins.

She met the two guards at the healer's bay door and did not waver. "Both of you, come with me," she ordered, and blessings of a blind god upon them, they did not query her or hesitate, either. They followed her along the quiet streets. Not so far away that any casual watcher might notice, she caught sight of Wrek, alone and chained where they'd left him, and she vowed at that moment that her actions would be worthy of their forgiveness. She had one more task before setting them all free and escaping into the Wastes forever. After that, well, who knew what horrors might befall them all, and that was fine indeed.

She led the two guards through an open doorway into an abandoned, freshly sacked house. Inside, it was dark, and this was perfect.

"Aurora, what do you require of us?" one of them asked warily, fearful that she desired to lie with them both. Neither would survive the dawn were word to reach Uden of such an act. Neither would survive the night were they to turn her down.

"Silence and privacy," she replied, and it was no lie. Without warning, she spun around with both blades in her grubby hands and cut into them. The first fell away, clutching the remains of his bearded throat. The second ducked, taking a slice to the ear. He tried to scream, and she was upon him, burying her blade deep in his sternum. "Whisht," she cooed, drawing the sword from him and plunging it deeper a second time. Blood gushed over her hand like a rushing waterfall, and its flow warmed her. Looking closer at his contorting, pale face, she believed him to be only a couple of decades old. He would never see a third one. It was a bloody shame for one so young, but this was the way of the world at war. She would play her part.

The boy died at her hands, and she pounced on the second man, who was crawling on all fours out towards the dark street. She thought it was undignified but needful, and dragged him by the leg back into the house. He fought her every step, kicking, hissing without a voice, and she thought him brave. Rolling him over, she sat on his chest to watch him die. Despite her beating and his terrible wounds, he still struck out at her, and she thought this defiance was marvellous. She did not stop his struggles; she leaned in close and kissed his bloody lips.

Born in blood and delicious.

He passed with a few last moans, and she thought it an excellent passing. For a breath, she thought of an old Ranger, and she froze as her victim bled himself dry upon her. "Both of you endured good deaths," she assured the dead men, and slipped away from the blood-spattered room. Closing the door behind her, she glided through the night, playing the part of an innocent shadow as Uden had once trained her to do.

She did not knock as she entered the healer's surgery; instead, she glided noiselessly through the door and came upon her sleeping friends, who were beautiful. She caressed Roja's cheek as though she were a sister, and Aurora regretted her earlier actions. Watching her sleep, she imagined the proud girl already dead and, momentarily, imagined slitting her throat as a mercy.

Emir would not like that.

She nodded to herself and slipped over to brave, wretched little Emir, and she loved him too. She felt the tears on her lashes, but they weren't for him. Instead, she faced her lover, who was most beautiful.

She ran her fingers along his cold cheek, sending shivers down her spine. She leaned in and kissed the wound with which Uden had ended his life, and then kissed him thrice more upon his lips. His mouth was agape ever so, and she touched his tongue with hers, and although he was beautiful to touch and taste, it was no pleasurable thing kissing him this last time.

Too cold.
Too dead.
All are dead.
By my hand.
My sinful hands.

"I violated her for you," Aurora whispered, and she spoke to his ghost, for she sensed him in this place. "Is she in the dark with you? Are you both dancing? Is she keeping you warm? For me?"

He did not reply, nor did she expect him to. But telling him was enough. Death must have been a fine place, for none returned from it to tell the rest, she thought, and felt warmer despite his touch.

"I must do this," she said. His face was pristine, and she thought fondly of Emir, who had ensured that her man disappeared into the night looking his best. What he left behind was for those who desired. She desired. She lifted the sheeting covering his chest and discovered his garments were covered in dried dust and caked blood. She didn't care. She undid the buttons on his shirt and, stealing one of Emir's finer scalpels, cut deep into his belly. "I will leave you pretty," she ensured, cutting just deep enough and ripping into his stomach ever so. Enough to fit a pair of hands is all.

Her surgery did not take long, nor did she leave him ruined as she had her previous conquest. Working the scalpel with quiet determination, she cut through his innards, lacerated organs that would never work again, and neared her prize. When she discovered his heart, she yelped in joy. Not loud enough to wake either sleeping person, but loud enough, nonetheless.

Cutting and tearing, she liberated the organ from his chest and pulled it free. She did not mishandle this beautiful thing, however. She wiped the blood free, gazed at its size, and thought it was far more significant than Silvia's. "I knew it," she exclaimed in delight, running her finger along its surface before carefully placing it in a little empty satchel on a chair beside his bedding. "Oh, that is perfect," she whispered to it, buckling the sack and putting the strap over her head. This was a gift for her and her alone.

Carelessly, she stitched some of his stomach back together before buttoning his shirt up and again returning the sheet to its resting place. Covered in dark, aged blood, she felt calmer than before. Wiping her hands, she felt even better.

Emir suddenly stirred in his seat, and instinctively, she stepped away and wondered what this night might bring next.

38

SLAP HEARD AROUND THE WORLD

It was a fine meal, and he ate his share, as did most in the banquet hall. Eventually, there came a time in the evening for traditions. And for everything to go to shit. Wiping his beard clear of gravy and gristle, Magnus took a breath and stood to face the mob.

"It is time," he said quietly, and as though the entire room had awaited this proclamation, they all fell quiet mid-sentence, mid-bite, mid-fuken-breath. He rose and stepped towards the crown, and with him, there followed a gathering of suitable warriors selected by their clans for nomination. They leapt up from their chairs as much as drunkenness would allow and followed like good little hounds. The peaceful passing of the crown was a long-held tradition. Teaolor was the rightful choice. Had her clan not done their duty these past years? Were they not solid and popular? Would she not be a mighty king? Would the other clans not fawn around her, hoping to garner a place in her court until she passed the banner? This was whispered throughout the lands, and Magnus was no fool. She was the rightful recipient. These were dignified times. There would be no kingly trials.

I had it far harder in my day.

He took the crown in his hands, and there were a few eager mutterings among the crowd. The absent king was about to name his successor. All would be well in the kingdom. Celebrations would ring loudly throughout the lands; the people would be happy.

For a time.

He turned the crown roughly in his hands and thought its metal finish unimpressive, its weight heavy. He despised this piece, but it was a

The Actions of Gods

means to an end, and as the world was ending, he had the means to save it.

"I stand before you, an old, broken man without an army." It wasn't the strongest start, admittedly, but it was a foolish thing to invite a savage to the table with anything but brutal honesty. "The world beyond has fallen to ruin. A war has crept upon my adopted lands." He allowed the low chorus of booing, and that was fine. It was no wise move to speak of the Four Factions as a home while upon the throne. Truth was, his home was anywhere Elise strode. It always had been. It always would be. There were worse places to be, too.

"Spit on the Four Factions," a woman cried from somewhere among the revellers, and this was unappreciated. The perpetrator was swiftly hushed with a few choice strikes, and she quickly apologised for her outburst with a raised hand. Magnus didn't mind. Better someone voice their dissatisfaction. The Savage Isles had never been allies.

"The Four Factions are as we are. They want peace as we do." There were a few nods of agreement. Aye, they might not see similarities in many things, but there was a reason no Faction had invaded these rich lands, and these isles had little interest in spreading their territory. Begrudgingly, the savages would agree that humanity flourishing was a good thing. "But they cannot do this alone. As we speak, they die bravely as the Southern machine marches on." He eyed the crowd and knew he was losing their patience. Holding the crown above his head for all to see, he raised his voice, and despite his age and diminished strength, he was impressive. "I stand today and gaze upon the rulers of each clan and ask them to pledge themselves to the war in the Four Factions." A brave gambit, and the crowd hissed and jeered, and Magnus held his breath. It was one thing for him to live on foreign soil. It was another to ask them to join a fight they had no part of. It didn't matter that these isles would face an assault from Uden soon enough.

Of the five gathered chosen, Teaolor stepped forward, and the crowd fell silent. She was impressive. Her eyes were cold and unforgiving. Magnus knew a killer's gaze, and he knew a firm gaze, and she carried both. She dropped to a knee, and the crowd knew for certain who his choice would be. She did not smile, and that was fine. There would be plenty of smiles once she held the crown. Beside her, a second figure stepped forward. Magnus knew him as Sloan of Clan Dearg, and his face burned with rage. As young as Teaolor, he was powerfully built with jet-black hair cut tight to his skull. He wore no beard, and his silent snarl was easy to see as he stepped beside her but did not bend the knee.

Proclaiming his objection without words, he folded his arms like a petulant child, and Magnus stared through him and looked to the next clan leader, willing to shed blood for his cause. It was no small thing for him to deny support for the outgoing king's last order. And while the people challenged Magnus, the shame of Teaolor was a worry. There was always a clan that challenged.

I smell a trial in the air.

At least it'll bring the clans together.

The third to step forward was Brigid. A fierce warrior, tall and muscular with a striking face, she too did not bend the knee, suggesting her Clan Cullan, the largest of all the clans, would not fight for the future king. She looked to Teaolor in apology, and Magnus's stomach turned.

"Two cowards unwilling to honour tradition," he snarled, eying the remaining clan leaders.

Curroi of Clan Branach stepped forward. For a breath, he almost dropped to a knee, but then he folded his arms as Sloan had, and Magnus dropped his head in defeat. The crown felt heavier than ever. The world was ending, and everything was rightly fuked. Rian, of the relatively unimpressive Clan Seanan, dropped to his knees, but there was nothing to help Magnus save face. Magnus's popularity was diminished, but worse than that, his natural successor was embarrassed, and for a few breaths, he could only look around this room and remember his own coronation as one of triumph. Any coronation earned through the king's trials was worthy, he supposed.

Teaolor struck the ground in frustration and eyed Magnus with those killer eyes, and he understood her frustrations. She could argue that a silent agreement before the coronation might have helped them both, but silent agreements had a way of being forgotten once the king marched. Whoever took the crown would be living on borrowed time. Trials were in the wind. So he did what any desperate royal did when grasping power as the world burned to ash. He made a foolish, rash decision, hoping to save his skin and the world while he was at it.

"To the fires with your traditions. To the fires with your honour. To the spitting fires with your respect. You all have lost mine this day," he roared, and he was louder than ever. His voice echoed, and he marched towards Sloan, who stepped back. That was all it took. If the savages respected nothing like honour, loyalty and the tradition of a king's last request, they certainly respected courage. He shoved Sloan as though he were nothing, and the rest of the suitors stepped back; such was the fury in his actions. He was dimly aware of Gregor and his Green Branch knights appearing around the throne as though anticipating a riot. Technically, Magnus was still king, so who knew their loyalty?

Time to find out.

"I will not yield this crown to another this day, for I have the measure of you all, and you are less than I am," he bellowed, and he took that heavy fuken crown and placed it upon his head and hated himself for it. He caught sight of Padir spitting out a mouthful of his drink, of Edain blessing herself in the old god's ways, and of a hundred others reeling in bewildered confusion as the king chose himself as his successor.

In the back of his mind, he knew this act was folly. He knew he would probably be lynched immediately. Instead, the crowd fell silent as though unsure, and sometimes an intelligent politician could take that hesitation and spin themselves a few feet of hanging rope.

"You kneel and stand like petulant children hoping Father will bestow a gift upon you? To the fires with your expectations," he thundered, and he could have sworn he heard mutters of agreement, down the back where no one would see. Buoyed on by his active imagination, he turned from those he had condemned and marched back to his throne, playing the part of demented warmongering king just perfectly. "I demand your kingly tributes," he boomed, before sitting on the throne and confirming his coronation.

For a few breaths, nothing happened. And then something happened. It was Brigid who stepped forward. This time she dropped to a knee. Magnus could see her shocked face, and this pleased him. She removed a wristband of leather and pearl from her wrist and offered it as tribute.

"I offer a gift on this day," she whispered, but everyone listened, for the power in this room was turning. Magnus nodded dismissively.

He gestured to Sloan to approach now, and this the man did sheepishly. His grimacing face was flushed with rage, and Magnus laughed loudly as he came forward.

"Should have just agreed," Magnus whispered, and the man nodded and hated him.

"Peace has reigned under your rule," said Sloan. "I offer no argument as my tribute, but this will pass like water under a bridge," he warned.

"And you a lazy oak, just floating along with it?" Magnus challenged, but the man was already upon his feet, wiping the dust from his knees, and Magnus waved him away.

This is working.

"You should not have done this, my liege," Rian offered next. He did not drop to a knee; his knuckles were white, and, for a moment, Magnus wondered if Teaolor held his loyalty as Magnus should have held hers.

"You should offer your tribute," Magnus warned quietly, and the young warrior nodded.

"Very well. I offer you a warning as tribute. This bravado of yours will not last the night, my liege. You have merely slapped the senses from us, but we will recover. We will return to you this slight. Better you slip free from this place and surrender your leadership in a trial, and then you might survive the coming hours."

"A fine warning, boy, but I see no clan with the nerve to challenge. Now, away from me lest I put your warriors on the front line," he warned, and Rian's gaze was one of hate as well.

Curroi's clan could have been more impressive in their accomplishments given their vast size. If Magnus could choose a clan to call upon in war, he would have selected these fiends. To a man, they were large and desperate to impress. There were worse motivations in war. Curroi stepped forward, and he smiled with everything but his eyes. "I pledge that you will have my forces should you march on the Southern threat."

Any fool could see the lie for what it was. Although Magnus did not know why he lied, he nodded as though the man's words were gospel from an absent god. He waved Curroi away and turned to Teaolor, kneeling on the ground. Her face was red, her body was tense, and Magnus sensed a threat. Still, he bowed as she stood to face him.

"Do you have a tribute for your king?" he asked, and she recoiled at his words.

She leaned in close, real fuken close. "Why do this to me, Magnus? Was I not an obedient servant? Is this not my time to lead our people?"

"Would you have agreed to my final pledge?"

"Perhaps."

"The world is ending. I had no choice." It was the truth, and she nodded in frustration. Truthfully, denying her leadership suited his needs better than those of the Savage Isles. He may have earned soldiers for a time, but he had also denied the islands a potentially prominent leader.

She'll get over it.

"I offer justice as a tribute to the king," she thundered so all could hear her submission. She offered her hand, and he reached for it.

She was quicker than she looked. Far too quick. Erroh quick. Perhaps even faster and more devastating. Her extended hand became a fist, and she struck him fiercely across the chin. It was a perfect strike.

He knew this because he toppled from his throne and collapsed to the ground.

The crack was as loud as any he'd heard, and it echoed around the room, dying away to silence in the tall rafters above. He slumped on the ground, and the crowd came alive. Clans erupted in violence, ignited by an attack upon the king, and Magnus could only stare stupidly ahead as he tried to recover his senses. The world darkened, and footsteps surrounded him, and only then did he hear the howling of people and hounds, and he wondered where his dogs were.

"Where are my boys?" he said slowly, and nobody listened. He shuddered and found a little strength in his arms. With all his might, he tried to shuffle upright, but his body wouldn't move.

Am I dying?

He could only lie there, still looking ahead, as a fierce riot between clans surrounded him, fuelled by frustration and ale. Punches were thrown, and bodies were flung, and were he able to move, he might have smiled and leapt into the melee to deliver a little retribution to those he despised. He would start with Sloan, perhaps Teaolor after.

Suddenly, arms were upon him, and he could not fight them off. "Where are my dogs?" he whispered again, but once more nobody listened, and the great echoing clamour ringing in his ears cleared in a high-pitched, unnatural squeal.

Around him, the screaming was as loud as a battlefield, and he couldn't find words of his own to quell the turmoil. He thought of Rangers dying, and he almost broke anew. Instead, he fought the hands dragging him, pulling roughly, and he wondered if he was being taken to be hung. But he could only worry about his hounds.

"To the spitting fires, get your hands off me," he cried, and his voice was weak, and everything around him was loud and desperate. "Where are my hounds?" he shouted. Distantly, he heard someone curse.

Without warning, they hoisted him from his feet into the air and carried him. The warm brightness suddenly became darker, colder, and then without warning, he found himself out in the night, with only the desperate cries of a dozen warriors around him, carrying, ordering, ushering, and he was confused about his fate.

"Where are my hounds?" he cried, and still nobody listened. They merely barked their own words, and he felt the cold air on his face. He looked to the clear night sky and saw the stars, and wanted to count them as they said to.

They dropped him onto a pile of straw with a nasty heave, and he found movement returning to his limbs, but dreadfully slowly. Voices surrounded him. All talking at once. All arguing. All working towards one cause, and he was thoroughly confused.

"Get him in."

"He's in, secure."

"I see some people."

"Just a boy. His squire—he's shouting something."

"Get some armour on him."

They placed a shield over Magnus's upper body and head, and with strengthening arms, he pushed at it so he could count the stars.

"He's moving better."

"Is there a healer?"

"There's already one called."

"Let's stop this fuken delaying."

"Get three beside him, and we go."

Heavy, bulky things—warriors, maybe?—sat around him, and he felt the rumble and lurch of a cart as they rolled forward.

"Where are his hounds? He's asking about his hounds," someone said.

"Are they dead?"

"What? Did someone kill them? Did some fuk kill his fuken dogs? I will fuken kill them if they did. I don't give a fuk if they are royalty or not."

"Don't worry, Gregor. Nobody killed them. They're being chained up, the nasty bastards."

"That's fine, so. Let's go faster."

Magnus struggled a little more as his senses returned, but the fiends in dark emerald armour held him still, nestled safely in the straw, for at least an hour as they rumbled over rough terrain.

Eventually, he was allowed to sit up and was surprised to see the king's guard fulfilling their duty again. Leading the charge on a sturdy mount was Gregor. With a solitary torch, he led them through a deep forest. On either side of him rode knights, all alert, all ready to protect as though they'd spent years preparing for such an assault. Behind them, upon a bucking, foaming mount, rode Padir looking ready to throw up or collapse or both, and strangely, Magnus was grateful the boy had escaped the attack.

Hardly an assassination attempt.

Magnus felt his jaw and grinned at the memory of a girl half his size toppling him from his throne. It would make an excellent story, and such a tale might suit her legend, particularly if she attained the title someday.

'The girl who beat up a king' has a nice royal ring to it.

Time moved differently when one was concussed, but sometime later, the rhythmic roll of the cart slowed and they came upon a little hovel, deep in the forest, where the riders eased their charge.

"No one will find you out here," Gregor said, opening the cart's back for a more dignified exit. He moved swiftly, as though a fiend might appear from the night and come a-killing. Magnus wanted to tell him it had been a slap and little more, but he allowed his senses to recover slowly, leaving room for Gregor's men to do whatever they needed. It wasn't much of a plan, but keeping the crown wasn't much of a plan, either.

What the fuk have I done?

"We will remain here until peace resumes and you can make your next move. Whatever that may be, my liege," Gregor continued, but Magnus hadn't been listening. He'd begun counting the stars. There were quite a few.

"Well, this is something I'm far more used to," Padir said miserably, surveying their meagre lodgings. "Knew I should never have put my hat in with you," he added glumly.

"I want to know my hounds are safe and well," Magnus said, brushing straw from his trousers and hobbling slowly towards his new abode. He'd expected mayhem, but he had never expected to survive it. Perhaps Gregor, in his wisdom, had understood that removing the king while tempers flared was the smarter move for now.

Perhaps it *was* the smarter move, thought Magnus, feeling his chin for any breaks and trying to get his feet to answer his demands. He'd need them working properly for the days of torture to come.

39

THE FINDING OF FRIENDS

Lea eased through the forest in near silence. Despite her aching ankle, she did not disturb the early morning's serenity or the flow of natural things. The slow pace was a torment, shifting her weight from one foot to the other, but she was used to taking the pain. What was another pinch of agony? Around her, the forest was alive as dawn took its time to rear its head. The world was preparing for a new day, and Lea, soaked in sweat, with unkempt hair and thighs rubbed red from the slow ride, wished she could sleep the morning away.

The last days had been exhausting. Frustrating too. Jeroen had passionately insisted they seek the city, which had sent them careening into hostile territory. He usually led, for he knew these lands better than she, but it was an arduous, treacherous journey. Lea understood his desire to see his mate. Understood his recklessness too. Were things different, she might have behaved as he did. As it was, their march had a purpose now. Even if it was folly.

More and more Southerners had begun to appear along the paths. Wary of meeting a roving pack head on, she, Nomi and Jeroen kept their ears sharp and their mounts at a slow pace. At least a dozen times, they were nearly discovered before concealing themselves within the tree line. They all agreed travelling at night was the safer manoeuvre. It was tenfold the slog, with barely any light to guide their way, but the Hunt were easier to avoid. They had spent long nights travelling. The moments of light in between that and sleeping were hers.

Ahead, Lea sensed movement and held her step. Her body ached, and that was all right. She had little trouble exhausting herself before sleep.

The rising sun was burning her eyes, and she welcomed the tears that began to flow, easing the stinging from the dust and the many hours awake. For a time she stood motionless, and only her stomach's grumbling gave her away. Nothing moved, and she cursed under her breath. Regardless, she drew Baby from her back and tucked three arrows into the hand that held the bow's grip. Her drawing hand remained by her side for a breath.

Let's see if this works.

She enjoyed the hunt. She enjoyed the silence, and she really enjoyed the privacy. To be fair, Jeroen was a welcomed tonic to her sorrow. Although it was harder than she remembered, there was still kindness in his voice; sometimes, when he dropped the hollow gaze directed at nothing, he looked like himself. He was a man in love, still in love, and Lea couldn't think of anything better to do, so they travelled painfully slowly, following Sigi's map towards the city. It was something to do until inspiration struck her. Or until a Southern pack tracked them down.

Okay, don't rush this technique.

She pulled an arrow from her hand holding the bow, then notched it and drew it back in one swift motion. It was a strange manoeuvre that she had come up with during her many hours in the saddle—making a single action of reloading, to be precise. Any warrior might think it unnecessary, but Lea believed it might add to her prowess if it proved effective. She had no desire to spar with Nomi or Jeroen, but the desire to become a better killer was appealing.

That was slow but smooth.

Happy with her attempt, she released the arrow without letting it fly and returned it to her waiting hand. After a breath, she drew it again. This time she was quicker. She stepped forward through the green, repeating this manoeuvre. Most times, it felt awkward and unnatural. Frequently, she missed the reload entirely, and the arrow fell harmlessly to the pine-needle-covered ground. Sometimes, though, she notched and drew that arrow just right. Had she had an archery range and a few dozen arrows, she might have spent a wonderful few weeks grasping the technique before mastering the art. As it was, though, she had an arrow short of a dozen in her solitary quiver, and every projectile released was less effective once returned.

Better.

She moved further into the woods in the growing light of dawn, hoping to catch a little breakfast off guard. Or a late dinner. Whichever, really. Her companions were lazing by the camp half a mile back. They would be sound asleep when she returned. Better to avoid conversation, she thought bitterly. Every time Jeroen spoke of Erroh, she died a little inside. More than that, she grew colder towards her mate, and perhaps, deep down, she wasn't ready to hate him just yet.

That will come.

She ventured on for a time until she neared a path. Upon it were two quail, just lazing about, waiting to be slaughtered. Stepping gently and with just a tiny bit of pain, she moved closer, staying deep in cover; she drew an arrow and hesitated. They chirped at each other like an old couple complaining about the cost of wheat that season, and she wondered, were they mates? Were they little quail in love, all excited about their future hunting, their future little quails? She watched awhile, thinking of her misery.

"To the fires with you, fukers," she whispered, putting her new skills into action.

Taking a breath and enjoying the burning release with a quick closing of her eyes, she imagined the shots, hated the birds, and went to task killing.

The bird on the left looked lively. Lea went for him first. She nicknamed him Erroh, and swiftly she drew and released in one smooth action, and once the arrow was on its way, she immediately drew a second arrow from her grasp, drew back, and released it towards the fat little quail she called Lea.

"Ah, fuk me," she growled, watching both birds take flight and her arrows fly far from their targets. They would never know how close they'd come to death. They left behind a couple of discarded arrows, embedded in two trees opposite, and a solitary feather floating in the breeze.

Suddenly, the hammering of hooves upon ground reached her ears. It was coming from somewhere ahead. She leapt out from the trees to recover the arrows. Pulling them free and returning them to her quiver, she slipped behind a thick oak trunk and kept herself hidden as the rider approached. Any other morning, she might immediately have begun walking back to camp with an aching ankle and an empty belly, but today, she hesitated and glanced after the rider as he passed.

It can't be.

She recognised him immediately, and the world slowed to nothing. He was beautiful; he was impressive; he was a legend; he was the only man she had ever loved. Or would ever love. He looked drawn and desperate as he passed her, and she reached for him instinctively, although he was out of reach. To him, she likely appeared as little more than waving branches. Even when she called weakly for him, her voice was weakened by shock.

Is he a ghost?

Am I dead?

"Erroh," she cried, and for a moment, she loved him. Just a moment. Scrambling out from the cover of the trees, she waved after him, calling, wailing, and he never looked back or noticed her, nor could he, such was the pace at which Highwind carried him. She ran, watching his beautiful silhouette in the hazy morning as it disappeared among the dark trees ahead, and she was frantic. Waving and screaming, with Baby knocking wildly against her two swords, she sprinted with all her might, hoping to catch his attention, hoping the absent gods granted him the sense to look behind.

Look behind.

See me.

I beg you, my love.

She sprinted as fast as her sore ankle could carry her, and it was painfully far. Even with the thunder of his followers in her ears, she wouldn't relent. Instead, she wailed, and she was pitiful, and he had left her behind, and she was alone, and he brought forth disaster upon her again.

Like always.

"You left me again," she cried, but her eyes were dry. Instead, she felt only anger and resignation, and she accepted this for what it was. She slowed in a dense stand of trees where eager eyes might have watched and hunted. It was a small matter. Gasping and gathering her air, she turned to face his hunters and felt betrayed anew.

Of course.

She counted twenty at least, and she was not afraid. At a hundred feet, they charged her, and she knew the end as it rumbled down upon her. She cursed the absent gods and also thanked them for this knowledge. She was a wretched little female in love, and he was a burning star far too bright to be embraced.

"You leave me behind one last time? As you wish, my love," she whispered, and looked back once more to where he had disappeared, and she hated him, and a cold intent came upon her. She looked at her arrows, and then quickly notched and fired. She dared not try a new technique where murder was concerned.

Her first kill of the day went into the darkness screaming, and instead of enjoying the moment, she fired again. All the while, they stormed down upon her, and she took her time with each one. Again and again, she aimed and delivered, and still, they charged on. She was but a girl in love, after all, and they were still fifteen at least.

Each shot was a kill, and it was easy, and truly, had she a dozen more arrows, she might have killed them all, or at least sent them fleeing, but she fired and killed eleven before her quiver ran dry.

With nine brutes almost upon her, she drew her blades and readied herself. If she avoided the first trampling, she could tear through them. The world slowed. She heard their fierce war cries, and suddenly she was no longer alone. From either side, a wave of black emerged, bristling with crossbows and intent. All screaming, all wild. In a flash of howling crimson, the dawn turned for the better. Many brutes around her fell, and the newcomers hacked and crushed those not killed in the ambush with axe and hammer in a delicious show of violence. She stood among them and watched these Wolves from the forest kill efficiently, which was pleasurable. She almost forgot about Erroh. Almost.

In a few frenzied breaths, the murder was done, the twitching limbs fell still, and they had annihilated the Riders. From among the brutes marched the tall figure of Aymon. Unlike most others, he bore no bloodstains; his weapon was dry.

"Well, you certainly ruined our ambush," he mocked, offering her a bow.

"Where did you come from?" she gasped.

He shrugged happily, looking at the devastation. "Here I thought I'd get a good bit of experience for some of my greener boys—you know, get them a little killing and all. We nearly took out a solitary Rider, but the fuk was moving a little too quickly. Ah, well. Better luck next time." He nodded, gazing further up the road. "And then along comes you and just ruins everything."

"It is good to see a friendly face," she said, returning the bow.

"There aren't many of us left. The world has fallen, and there is nothing left to do but kill as many as we can," he said.

She looked back up the road that Erroh had taken, and for a moment, her heart skipped. Then she collected herself, focused on real things, like inexperienced soldiers needing some killing and friendly faces at the end of the world. She turned her back on Erroh and marched away with her new comrades, and felt fine about it.

40

KILLING WHAT'S LEFT BEHIND

It was no small thing to feel alone, for that was Emir's lot in life, and it was a miserable, lonely one. Today, though, it was worse. Of course, it was worse. It was always worse. It was reassuring to know that no matter what happened, it would get worse. Always. It was encouraging because he knew to take his blessed moments, the ones where he didn't feel so wretched, and cherish them. He sat over his sleeping goddess and loved this moment. Her breathing was steady, her colour was improving, and her brow was less sweaty than before.

He cherished his headache less. Muttering a curse, he drank water from a goblet and enjoyed its quenching. He had not drunk enough to merit this headache, but that too was his lot in life. Sitting alone, forgotten by fairness. Left behind like a discarded cloak in an after-hours tavern. It was fuken shit.

Truthfully, he'd brought it on himself. He shouldn't have drunk a glass, let alone five. Not with his body already drained of blood and she possibly still needing refilling, but sobriety was too hard to take in this miserable room.

When they'd come for him, there had been aggression. There were too many loud voices in a guttural language. He'd gently explained in his tongue the need for silence, and they had disagreed. Not one disgruntled guard had struck him or moved him from his seat, mind you, but he knew they spat in the food they offered him, which was fine. Food was food, and he was wretched.

The cries from the streets beyond had continued throughout the morning, and their fury was a tonic to his misery. Many Southern keepers had popped their heads round the doorway to see the diligent healer still attending to his solitary patient. A fool, they likely called him, one who forsook freedom in favour of duty, and he didn't mind. Trying to understand their mutterings was a fine distraction from imagining the taste of breaking his chains, fleeing from this place, and feeling the wet slap of branches against his face as he slipped through the Wastes, far away from imprisonment.

"And you, the fool, chose her."

"I did," he whispered to the lonely air, imagining his dead friend shaking his head in bewildered bemusement. "Perhaps I should have run with them, left the grouchy bitch behind," he added, smiling, knowing he didn't mean it. Sometimes it was nice to believe there were choices. He could hear Stefan's laughter in his mind, which was also a tonic. Enough tonics and he'd be just fine.

Turning from thoughts of dead friends, he stroked her hair as he had done a thousand times these last few days. It was oily and tangled, and he wondered how horrified she might have been to see herself in such a state.

"You smell, Roja," he whispered, and she made no reply.

"This is the longest I've seen you without a coat of paint upon your face."

She just breathed.

"You have more freckles than I ever imagined. I could count them. But I have much to do before sundown."

He craved her cutting tongue. Even her subtle blush as he put her in her place. He desired anything but the unmoving porcelain doll with a few freckles lying below him.

"You've let yourself go, my love," he said, caressing her cheek, and she stirred ever so. He prayed to the absent gods she would wake soon while she still had the strength to wake. "But I still like you," he added, just in case she could hear. "I've always liked you. Even when you beat me up."

She stirred again and, distantly, he heard further roars between Southerners outside, and he wondered what plans were afoot, what heads would roll, too, for the previous night's escapees? He wondered how far away his comrades were. For a dreadful moment, he imagined them nearby, waiting to come for him and Roja a second time.

"I will die for you, my love," he whispered, and kissed her lips, wanting to give her his life. Give his soul too. This was a different anguish to Aireys. Perhaps this was worse. He hated these thoughts.

The Actions of Gods

"You've caught up on your sleep; it's time to rise," he whispered, and of course, she did not stir. She breathed silently, and for a moment again, but only a moment, he wondered if he had chosen poorly.

The door opened behind him, and he awaited the grating voices of his conquerors, sent to disturb his lonely, left-behind solitude. Instead, he heard only the door closing quietly behind him.

"It is a bad morning for me, healer," Uden growled, and a shiver ran down Emir's spine. He turned to see the brute standing over him, and he was impressive. His face was a portrait of controlled fury, and Emir stood to face him. Sometimes it was best to stand clear of a charging bull; other times, it was best to face it head on.

"Have you seen anybody stand tall against a bull and survive?"

It was a fair question, and Emir didn't have time to answer his imagination, for Uden grabbed him by the scruff of the neck and drew him near. Emir could see fresh blood upon his keeper's clothes, and he squirmed in fear.

"Who caused such horrors to befall me?" Uden roared, and every word shook Emir to his marrow. It was no small thing standing up to a bull; it was something else entirely getting screamed at by a god. "Was it Erroh? Was that cur here last night?"

"I do not know what occurred," Emir cried, and was flung across the room for his trouble, colliding with his dead friend before tumbling in a heap upon the lonely, left-behind ground.

"Watch it, idiot."

"You fuken liar! You fuken liar!" the crazed god roared, storming across and taking Emir by the throat, pulling him to his feet and pinning him to the wall. "You have moments to live. Do not die with a lie upon your lips," he commanded, and it was a compelling argument. Emir struggled and gazed down upon Roja, who lay sleeping still, and he fought the panic, although not the brute's hold on him. He knew better. He could care less.

"I... don't... give... a... fuk," he gasped. He did. He really did, but he could see the frantic madness in his killer's eyes. No pleading or argument would stop the cur at his task. Better to feign bravery at the end. That's what they did in tales. That's what Aireys and Quig and Stefan would have done. He wanted to be brave like them. He missed them. He wanted them. He wanted to go to them. And Uden squeezed his throat, and his air disappeared, and just for a moment again, he regretted not leaving with them, and he hated Uden for crushing his valour, for taking his sacrifice at the end, for ruining him more than death alone could ever do.

"Who are you to sacrifice yourself?" demanded Uden, and Emir hated him. He looked to Roja and sought strength from her sleeping form. "Look at me," the brute howled. He struck him with an open palm across the face, and it was a hammer. The world darkened; he needed to relieve himself. He might have, all over his pants, all over a god. A pathetic, fitting end.

"Who would do that?" he roared.

Emir tried and failed to rasp out a reply.

"What was your true plan? What comes next? Will Erroh return?"

They were all fine questions, and Emir did not reply. Instead, he allowed the brute to hold and kill him while keeping his eyes on Roja, and she sustained him. There were worse ways to die. Looking at your true love at the end was one of the better ones.

"Tell me," demanded Uden, squeezing tighter, and the world went dark.

"Tell me!"

"Tell me!"

"Tell him!"

Emir would not, and, closing his eyes, he let himself die at the hands of a god.

———

"Wake up, damn you," roared Uden, battering the boy, who was limp in his hands. He slapped him twice more across the face, then picked him up, carried him across the room, and placed him upon a healer's slab, where he lay unmoving. "I command you, healer." He remembered that Emir was his name and shouted it aloud, almost showing him respect. *Almost.* Then, furious with his lot in life, he concentrated his anger upon the sleeping boy.

Not sleeping.

The boy was important. The boy carried the knowledge of a concoction so vile it tormented to madness those who tasted but a drop of it, then killed them horribly. Had he not seen the agony of Roja, who had been felled by this foul potion? An intelligent god could take advantage of such concoctions. There were stirrings throughout the arth, murmurs of things that needed to be quelled. The grand invasion hadn't been as easily handled as they had imagined, had not been the grand quest he'd pledged to his followers. Not in these parts, nor in the South, where dissent was rife. Dissent was like a cancer. Better to squash the resistance in one powerful swipe. Let terror take the last of their defiance. Also, if nothing else, he could provide quite the agonising end to a false god with such poisons. He wanted this concoction. Had wanted it from the moment Aurora had confirmed his suspicions of its existence.

Aurora Borealis.

He suddenly thought of Aurora standing over his niece, and he hesitated. Her eyes flashed in his mind, and with it came a dreadful sorrow he was unprepared for. It was such a human thing to feel this betrayed, this lonely. He looked upon the dead boy with distress and understood his misstep. Such was his frustration that he struck the boy across the chest. A divine punch, where the heart would sit. And at this, the boy stirred. His mouth opened for a weak, lifeless breath, and Uden struck him again with an open palm. Emir turned with the strike, and desperately, Uden slapped him again.

A god feels nothing in life, in death.

In storm, in snow.

In fire.

In regret.

"Please," he roared, and he was godly, touched by greatness; he knew this as truth. He had always known it. Even when tested, and fate had sorely tested him this day. He was alone, and this boy could return Roja to life. After that, Emir was free to die.

Suddenly, Emir shook, gasped, lurched, and fell from the table, and Uden's godly reflexes caught him.

"Ha!" he roared in triumph, and Emir struggled in his grip, his face red from strikes, his chest heaving, his whole body no doubt suffering the effects of a god's will.

I bring life.

I bring death.

I am a god.

"Release me," Emir gasped in a broken voice, and Uden laid him back upon the slab beside Roja.

"As you wish, healer," Uden whispered.

"Why am I here?"

"I was not done with you, little one. Nor is Roja."

Emir rolled onto his side and threw up, and Uden laughed heartily. A terrible morning, but a wonderful afternoon. From death, he had stolen life, and it was beautiful.

"To the fires of hell with you, fiend," Emir gasped, spitting bile upon the floor and himself. All the while, he shook, which was understandable. "I can barely breathe," he muttered, holding his neck, then his chest, and Uden placed his hand upon his shoulder, for that is what gods did with their disciples in extraordinary moments.

"You and I will understand each other. For you are blessed."

"Fuk you, Uden."

Again, Uden laughed and allowed the boy to recover his breathing. "You have earned my favour this day, boy. Do not test me."

The boy had plenty more to offer, but Roja took that moment to disturb their battle of wits. She convulsed violently, her voice rang out in a dreadful deathly shriek, and Uden's heart broke for her agony, for her lineage, for his miseries.

"Save her," he roared, but there was less anger in his words than before. Less desire to strike the boy so he would go to task quicker. Regardless, the boy went to task quickly. He pushed Uden aside and reached for her.

"It's okay, my love," he cried, and shot a look at Uden. "Pass me my transfusion utensils," he demanded, pointing to a strange apparatus of tubing, bottles and needles, strange things indeed to a god unfamiliar with ancient human implements. Regardless, he scooped them up as Emir began wiping her arm and then his own furiously with a sharp-smelling cloth.

"What can I do?" he asked, allowing the authority to sweep through his words, but Emir wasn't listening. He was tending to his niece, and that was fine.

"Shut up and allow me to see to her."

Uden watched the boy pierce his skin and then hers and slowly drain himself dry as he fed her his blood for a time, and it was a strange, marvellous thing.

"This one should do it," Emir whispered to the sleeping girl, and something in his voice reassured Uden.

41

ONCE UPON A TIME, THERE WAS A CAGED LITTLE CUB

Erroh rolled away from the light and ducked his head beneath the covers. It was dawn; it might have been noon. The sunlight streaming into his little haven burned his eyes; it didn't matter. Beneath the bedclothes, he could smell his body odours, and he was pungent. He wondered if the entire tent smelled as bad and doubted it. There was a strange integrity in allowing one's self to fall into this sort of disgrace. To lower one's self this far suggested an actual loss of the mind. This wasn't the snow of the South but something else entirely.

"Perhaps today you will rise," a voice murmured, and Erroh wrapped the sheets more tightly around his head. Beneath these coverings, he didn't have to think, act, fight or exist. Under here was a fine place to live and give up. He'd been to this place before, and it was all right to visit now and then. He was on his fifth day now, perhaps his twelfth. Nothing mattered beyond sleeping, hiding his thoughts and weeping until his eyes were dry.

He pondered the words and thought it a fine question, but Erroh knew well the answer. He would rise and wreak all hellfire upon those who had cast him into this torment, but not until he was empty of this all-encompassing grief. "It will not be today, friend," he muttered through a little break in the sheets. Any wise sleeper with their head beneath the blankets knew well to leave a similar gap for such occasions, and if nothing else, Erroh was a talented sleeper.

He heard the food placed down on his bedside table, and his stomach growled as the aroma of mushroom and mess soup filled his nostrils. He had been no huge fan of eating these last few days, but enduring torment was more manageable with a full belly. He had learned that too.

"No bacon?" Erroh asked, ripping the bedclothes free and sitting up. Drahir sat opposite on a little wooden stool as far from the aromatic Alphaline as possible.

"Stocks are low, but the bread is fresh." Drahir was his ever-constant companion, and Erroh still did not know how he felt about him. He owed him much. For one, he was in this bed with his honour intact. Erroh couldn't remember much of the assault now, but he knew he had almost murdered a fiend as he begged for mercy. It was no small thing to become a savage in war, and Erroh wasn't ready to be that. Not yet. "You eat better than most in this camp while doing little. The least you could do is eat what's given with some appreciation."

"No wine to drink today?" Erroh quipped, and Drahir shook his head, and that was fine. He had drunk deeply in silence for the first few days until the numbness took some of his pain. Not a lot, but enough. After a time, the wine had done nothing, but Erroh still drank, slept, ate and relieved himself. All without leaving the sanctuary of this tent.

"Not today. Stocks are low," Drahir said again. Erroh could see the irritation in his Southern shadow's face. Every day the misguided fool tended to Erroh, which was frustrating. He fed and talked with him and never once complained about Erroh's lack of enthusiasm. Never once ordered him to walk out amongst the Southerners, nor did he once suggest sparring with his new warriors. He did not invite the other generals to meet with their beaten leader either. Erroh wondered if he simply hadn't told anyone of his return.

Would that be so bad?

"Very well," Erroh said, dipping some bread into the soup. He ate slowly, which irritated Drahir, but Erroh didn't care. The food sustained his pilgrimage of mourning. He didn't need to make a glutton of himself. Truthfully, although the mushrooms were fresh, he would have liked a little less salt—or at least the option of some pepper to give it a little kick. When recovered, he might speak with the chef and offer advice. It was what any decent leader would do. Swallowing the slightly salted, mushroomy bread, he prepared to wrap the bedclothes around him again, making his intentions clear, and the cage in his mind clanked shut for a little longer.

"War brings nothing but misery, but we remember those we love, and we march on, brother," Drahir said with a sigh, and left Erroh to his recovery. Erroh might have explained his agony, but his words caught in his throat every time. Silence was easier. He watched the tent flap close over before wrapping himself back up in his bedding to think of his lost comrades, and when he slept, his dreams were a torment of snow, death, fire and a god with a green eye.

It was later that evening that Drahir stirred him from his horror. As before, his comrade appeared at sunset with a bowl of food, and Erroh showed little interest. At the time, he'd been mulling over the last words he'd shared with Wynn. Unimpressive words, for Erroh had done his best to conceal his real actions from Uden. The things one thought about were strange when one had nothing left.

"It is time to get up and go back into war," Drahir said, setting down the bowl of stew and recovering the half-eaten soup from earlier. Sitting upon the stool, he dipped the bread into the cold meal and ate greedily, and for a moment, Erroh felt a little shameful for the waste.

"I am still in mourning, friend," Erroh said, sitting up as before. He scratched his stubble and discovered it to be closer to a beard; it was a fine distraction from the stench in his bedding. Perhaps when he recovered his will, he'd regain his pride. After that, a little soap too.

"We are all mourning, brother," Drahir said between mouthfuls.

"I would have preferred bacon or some boar," Erroh said, spooning a little stew into his mouth. He might have preferred some bread with the meal, but Drahir had ended that.

"If it got you up and fighting, I'd have it for you."

"Do not bother yet," Erroh said, wishing he had some salt for the stew. The vegetables were juicy and fresh, but the meat was tough and chewy. Still, he ate and enjoyed feeling the pain in his stomach giving way to contentedness.

Drahir sighed again, his mind unreadable, but clearly worried. Erroh might have pried, but hadn't the passion to care. And then suddenly, he very much cared.

"Little Lea, poor little Lea," muttered his companion, placing the empty bowl back on the table. His face was grave, and Erroh felt a dangerous anger come upon him. Were Drahir to mock his fallen mate, he would not leave this tent alive.

Drahir must have read Erroh's intentions, for he raised a hand in a calming gesture. "Be still, Erroh, mate of little Lea."

Erroh didn't want to be still at all. The tiredness from doing nothing fell away from him. "You should watch your mouth, fiend," Erroh muttered. He felt a terrible coldness come upon him, and his arm began to itch.

"It pleases me to see that fire. Knowing how much you care for your fallen comrades also pleases me. Mostly, though, it pleases me to know little Lea had a mate worthy of her."

Erroh didn't like his tone. Didn't like his words either. He drew a fist and looked round for his blades on the far side of the room. He craved violence. He only had to convince his stubborn legs to carry him from the warmth of his cage.

Drahir leaned forward as though sitting over a campfire. As though his words were necessary. "Let me tell you a tale to help you sleep a little longer, little cub."

The swords were right over there.

"Choose your words carefully," Erroh warned, and Drahir smiled sadly.

He chose his words well, however, and Erroh listened in horror to the truth of his mate's legacy. The longer the tale went on, the worse it became, and Erroh felt a terrible grip upon his chest, but only for a time. Visions of Lea striking at the burned-out house stuck in his mind, but he could only listen silently as his world crashed around him. He tried to hate his brother for telling such a tale, but hate gave way to sorrow. Sorrow gave way to regret. Regret gave way to anger once more, not for Drahir but for the world and the Southern brute who terrorised it. He never knew his hatred for Uden could run deeper, but Drahir had found a way.

Anger is a gift.

With the tale told, neither warrior said anything for a time. It was Erroh who spoke first. "When you come for me at dawn, prepare for a long day."

Drahir smiled sadly once more, then bowed and left, leaving Erroh to his solitude. Sleep called. Healing sleep, where he could come to terms with Lea's betrayal. His mind spun as he thought of her lineage. Of her loyalty. And although she was dead, he hated her in that moment. For many a moment. He played her words over again in his mind and sought deceit in them. He found none, but the anger remained. He cursed her, he cursed Uden, he even cursed Drahir for whispering these cutting truths. He wailed and thrashed and spat his hatred for the unfairness of it all.

And then after a time, something changed. A spark of love simmered anew for his one for life, and he thought less of her unwitting betrayal and more of the goddess she was. He thought of fiends who no doubt despised Erroh because of his father's and mother's actions, long before he was born, and he thought of how helpless he was to them. He held that thought real fuken close.

She didn't know.
She couldn't have known.
She would have told me.

And although he didn't forgive the thing she had no part in committing, he accepted her tainted lineage. As she had his. It was his final gift to her after the end, but also to himself. Were he to agonise over it longer, who knew how easily he could slip into that cage.

At midnight, he climbed free of his bedding and gazed at himself in the mirror. He was a pitiful sight. The water bowl Drahir had brought was freezing and untouched, but the soap was soap, and who needed a heated bath anyway?

He scrubbed himself raw until his body shook, and only then began to feel like himself. Afterwards, he tended to his beard, which was more difficult than he thought. He tried and failed not to think of Lea scraping the whiskers free, and a furnace of anger came upon him, not for her, but for the unfairness of it all and the roads that had brought him to this place. He tended to his matted hair after scraping the last chin hair free. It was an easier job; he simply cut whatever unwanted locks drooped over his fringe. He somehow managed a style not entirely dissimilar to a respectable Alphaline on the eve of their second day's Culling.

Maybe some orange mead for the breath.

Last of all, he opened the tent flap to look out into the night. Count the stars and all that fuken shit. Also to clear the stench from his quarters.

Feeling lost and alone in the world, without any hope, he still managed a smile as he turned, leaving the tent flap slightly ajar, and dropped back into bed. His demented mind was sharp, unforgiving and cold. There was a level to the bloodshed he desired; before he could adequately honour her and all those he loved. He knew this now, just as Drahir, his brother, had known the exact words to stir him from his wretchedness.

"No more cage," Erroh whispered to the wind as the air filtered through the tent, delivering a most welcome freshness.

When Drahir came to wake him, Erroh was alert and eager for the day.

"Bacon and eggs," Drahir offered, placing the food down, and Erroh greeted him as family with a warm embrace.

"I still have family," Erroh declared.

"Is it time to go fight this war?" Drahir asked with an uneasy smile. Only then did Erroh recognise the same features in him. It was a sad, beautiful thing.

"No, brother. It is time to win this war."

42

TILL DEATH

The going was easier once Lillium needed no further tending to. Her injuries remained, but her mind returned to its usual sharpness after a day or so. Better still was her ability to walk, run, and fight if needed. She and Wynn became two lost souls searching for the road to Spark in the middle of nowhere. With masks drawn over their faces, they marched through the Wastes side by side, looking for trouble and hope and finding little of either.

Initially, they came upon small patrols and watched, hidden and shivering, from behind the treeline or beneath rustling bushes. Eventually, though, when daring took either one and the advantage of surprise was with them, they leapt upon their prey and almost always slaughtered whoever was unlucky enough to come upon them. And those they sent to flight left filled with terror of two humbled Alphalines, unsure of what to do with themselves.

But the rains came, and with them, the cold truth of their misery. Of the terrible luck that had befallen them. Their routine became one of silence and sorrow. Where once they had marched, each step now became a dreadful stumble of hopelessness. Lillium's thirst for vengeance faded in the hours of aimless wandering, seeking a path. Wynn's mood darkened to that of the eternal clouds above, and it was awful for the young pair. They had no map, but they had their wits, and they used the dimly shining sun to chart a way northward.

When they spoke, their conversations were disheartening. And why wouldn't they be? Were these two wanderers not the wretched survivors of a vanquished battalion? Had they not betrayed their comrades and fled? Wynn took the blame and admitted to it. Lillium shared the guilt; she said so and all, but Wynn still caught her resentful gaze now and then. He could have shared the torment he had suffered for dragging them away from the fight. He could have told her that living was the best revenge and that plenty of blood would be spilled. Instead, he allowed her resentment and continued trudging through the muddy, unforgiving terrain and missed his friends something awful.

On the third day, marching with nothing but cold and wetness as company, they came upon a small settlement. Careful of signs of ambush, they circled the town twice with drawn blades, seeking any sign of life or threat. Eventually, shivering in their soaked-through clothes, they rested atop a ridge overlooking the quiet settlement, watching as the rain fell upon the buildings and the surrounding trees.

"Abandoned," Lillium muttered. It might have been a question.

"Aye, it feels that way."

"Should we visit?"

"Aye, I reckon so."

"You lead, and I'll follow."

"Sounds like a plan."

It was their most cordial conversation in the last three days. Wynn had almost forgotten what it was to hear her voice without the cutting tone.

The few buildings in the settlement were widely spaced and as grey as the road they stepped on. Already suffering the wrath of time, each structure looked ready to crumble under a gale and long-ruined curtains waved gently in the windows suggesting desertion. Abandoned and forgotten. If nothing else, each hovel was a roof over its occupants' freezing heads.

Wynn and Lillium made their way across a small bridge above a rushing river, no doubt fuelled by the torrents of rain. They walked with swords raised, fearing very bad things, expecting worse. As they passed from the mud of the waste to the stone of the settlement's roadways, their footsteps echoed hollowly. Something in the air was tainted, as though some dreadful thing had occurred here. As though the ghosts still watched their every move, unable to tell their tale.

Warily, they walked the perimeter before daring to search the buildings within, long sacked. The only thing that caused them alarm was the faint outline of a familiar Southern warning upon a wall.

Fuk the Woodin Man.

"We are too late to do anything for this town," Lillium said, sheathing her blade.

"It can keep us dry, at least," he said.

They shared a room on the highest floor of the largest building. The staircase creaked loudly with age, and Wynn imagined plummeting down through it and meeting his splintered end at the bottom. A bad way to go—without honour, and unworthy of a tale. He wondered if Lillium would miss him and thought it a possibility. The window of their room provided a vantage point from which they could spot any sneaky ambush. It was cold and damp, with the stench of wet rot, but mercifully, there was fuel and a few dried logs, dusty and eaten through by insects, and Wynn went to task lighting a fireplace in the corner to bring some heat into the room.

"This will do," Lillium said, stripping herself naked. She hung her clothes by the fire to dry and sat down in its glow with an old blanket wrapped around her shivering form.

Shrugging and satisfied he would return to a warm room, Wynn left her to her privacy and went back downstairs, where he began scrounging for food. It was a fruitless task, as it were, as he found little success for a time, so he ventured outside and began to search the other buildings. Finally, in the depths of a basement in the last building where only a hidden brewery should have sat, he discovered a small cache of preserving jars with pickled vegetables within.

Braving the downpour, he dashed back to Lillium with the treasures.

"Quite the feast we'll have," she offered. "You took such a time, so I went scrounging and found this," she said, pointing to an opened bottle of red wine. Her glass was full, as was the one waiting for him, and he was grateful for the gesture. He popped open the first jar of preserves, and, taking turns delving into the pickled onions within, they dined greedily. For a time, it felt like a feast indeed.

Later, with the wind howling outside in the darkened night, they sat together beneath the blankets, naked and warm and with full bellies. Wynn leaned against the back wall and fought the sleep of the wretched, hunted fool. There was a bed on the far side of the room, but neither desired to leave the warmth of the fire.

When Wynn woke the following day, Lillium had already returned from bathing in the freezing river. He knew this because, in between bites of food the night before, she'd declared a dozen times how much she desired to clean the Southern filth from her body. She scraped the cold ashes from the fireplace, piled up more logs, and lit another fire to take the chill from the morning. Upon the fire, she boiled a brew of tea, and Wynn, feigning sleep, watched with squinted eyes. For a moment, he wondered what life might have been like had they taken better paths and lived a farming life together in such a hovel. She hummed to herself as she went about her morning, and he thought her beautiful, although he missed the blue in her hair. He dared not say anything. Instead, he just watched and enjoyed her peacefulness. The rain lashed down on the rooftop, and from the dark sky beyond the curtained window, he could see it would be another miserable day. Locked up in a warm bedroom with a belly full of food on such a day was an acceptable way to waste some time and make a slight recovery. It was the little things.

"I know you are awake, idiot," she said suddenly, and with eyes closed, he grinned.

"We might have slept better in the bed over there," he said, stretching the hardness from his muscles.

"We might not have slept at all then." She smiled lightly and went to task with her paints, concealing the marks from warfare upon her face. An easy enough task with a suitable powder. "Although it would have been a wretched experience, such was the state of us." She sniffed the air, and he took the hint.

"Anything for you, my dear."

Climbing down to the river with soap in his mind and steel in his gut, a very naked and freezing Wynn leapt into the rushing water and immediately regretted it. Yelping and rubbing his arms against the river's icy touch, he stood waist deep, allowing the less harsh rain to spatter upon his chest. As he scrubbed away the grime, his thoughts of torment distracted him from his actual suffering. Closing his eyes, he thought of his comrades left behind, and it was too much. Like the rushing water, the feelings of sorrow overcame him. For a breath, he accepted Lillium's rage as a fair assault.

"Don't cry," he warned, splashing in the raging water, scrubbing harder so the stench would disappear. The blood and mud too. "Don't you dare fall back to wretchedness," he warned, dipping his head under the roar, and the natural brute dragged a little sense into him. He could feel himself panic, feel himself give up. He could feel other things too, angry things, and he cursed the absent gods for their cruelty, and he was justified. His knees touched the bottom of the riverbed, and he thought about staying under there a little longer. Just until his thoughts cleared, until his desire to breathe mattered more than idle regret. It would be a dangerous thing, he knew, as the pull of the current was strong, but nonetheless, he relaxed his body, hated the world, and allowed the current to take him. A few feet at first, and then he was little more than driftwood, slowly being dragged from the one thing left in his life worth fighting for. Worth dying for.

Are you sure?

He thought of Lillium. He thought of her beauty. He thought of her behaviour. Before. And every day since. He thought of their first kiss. Their furrowing. He thought of Erroh. He thought of her touch and his passion. He felt anger, and he allowed it, for it cut him deep; sometimes an Alpha just needed to cut themselves deep or break a bone. Opening his eyes suddenly to the bubbling wash, he kicked up and was bemused to find he'd been dragged a great distance by the river.

"Could have dashed my head against a rock and all," he said to the river, and the river made no reply. It continued on its way, and Wynn felt less of a man than when he'd first climbed into its freezing embrace. He dragged himself to the riverbank's edge and lay gasping among the reeds for a time. He thought of many more things, and they did not help his mood. Eventually, the cold got the better of him, and, carrying his clothes in his arms, he returned to Lillium and her cold smile of acceptance.

As the morning rain gave way to a stormy afternoon, they agreed to stay in this place one more day. Wynn might have desired to spar with Lillium to burn off unwanted energy or put unwelcome thoughts to rest, but instead, they sat across from each other in the small room, thinking of any conversation to share.

―――

"You were brave when I fell," she said suddenly and only then did Wynn realise how much he desired compliments from her. For a moment he smiled, and then his mood darkened. She could have said it sooner. Should have said it sooner.

"I know. It was a shitty thing I had to do, but it was done, and yes, I was fuken brave, Lillium."

She smiled curiously. "It's the type of thing Erroh would do; I liked it. I like thinking of it now."

Don't say it.

"Erroh is dead, Lillium; it's just me here now."

For only a moment did she flinch. Then, she shook her head dismissively, her eyes alight with fire. "Our boy is very much alive. He'll be back; I feel it in my bones." Reassuring words, no doubt, and perhaps had Wynn not gone swimming and had terrible thoughts, he might have felt better. As it was, this was the end. He knew that in his bones too.

"When did you fall in love with Erroh?"

This time, she did not flinch; she raised an eyebrow thoughtfully. "I love the idea of him."

"When did you fall in love with him?"

She looked away. She sniffed the air absently. She tapped her finger on her knee. It was a very nice knee. She had very nice things. But this was the end. "I never did."

"Did Lea know you loved him?"

"Of course. I love him, but I never *loved* him."

"Will you go to him now that Lea is dead?"

"Lea is not dead. She escaped. I know her. Stop asking me questions." Lillium peered at the goblet of half-drunk wine like a prisoner would eye a glimmering key, and Wynn shook his head. Everything was more manageable with a glass in hand. But this was the end, and this would be sober.

"Was it the first day of the Cull?"

She flinched and wrapped her arms around her knees. "I loved him, Wynn; I'm sorry. I did. He was beautiful. He *is* beautiful. He is perfect."

"Why did you walk away?"

She would not meet his eyes even though he stared at her. "Sacrifice for a goddess. It was what any good sister would do. I was generous. Too generous." He didn't understand.

"I don't understand." Wynn felt sick in his stomach. The sickness that comes of knowing of a brutal inevitability. "Tell me."

"Do you need to hear this, Wynn? Are we better these last few months? Are we not falling into a somewhat good life?" He did, and they were, but it wasn't real, and it was the end.

"Why did you not choose Erroh?"

"I had many choices, but I chose you," she snapped, and he felt he had cut her. He did not understand what many of her choices had meant, but that was a small matter.

"You settled for me?"

She began to reply, but then caught her words. She took a breath, and her feet began to tap the floor. She had nice feet too. "Aye."

He was crestfallen, but that was fine. It made it easier to endure all this. "At least I know."

"Lea had it rough her entire life. She sought Erroh first, and I stood by my sister. But I thought you beautiful, Wynn. I still think you beautiful."

"Will you go to Erroh and grieve with him? Comfort him?"

She shrugged. "I do not love him now as I once did then. I did not love you then, as I love him now." She thought for a breath. "Perhaps, I do not know what love is, but I would love to know."

He didn't understand her. He played her words in his mind and became more and more confused. "You deserve to be loved. By him, or by someone beyond."

"I might need someone, Wynn. It would be best if you had someone too. We have each other for now, and that is enough for me."

"I cannot do this."

"I'm sorry, Wynn; you deserve something better than this."

"I need no apology. Not anymore."

They spoke no more for the rest of the day. Wynn found sanctuary in scrounging through every nook and cranny of the house, seeking treasure but also seeking distraction. It mattered little to him whether he was successful or not, but the absent gods, no doubt feeling guilty about his misery, delivered upon him a bottle of sine in an old undergarment cupboard, which was the highlight of his day.

Lillium, seeking distraction for herself, went hunting and returned as dusk fell with two quail and a grimace of regret on her face. As night drew in, they enjoyed a small banquet, and Wynn jested first about their terrible fates.

With the bottle of sine loosening their tongues, Wynn charmed Lillium as though it was their first night as a couple, and she laughed and smiled and was lovely, and for a breath, it didn't feel like the end of it all.

But it is.

Eventually, as the wind howled, the rain lashed, and the fire began to smoulder a luminous red, he took her hand and led her to the bed. Standing beside her, close as only mates should be, he whispered in her ear. "Tonight, you are Lillium, goddess of Spark, beautiful, blue-haired mate, and I am Erroh of the road."

"What? I don't understand." He took hold of her wrist, held her forcefully, and kissed her neck. "What are you doing, Wynn?"

"Whisht, goddess. That is not my name."

"Wynn, stop jesting," she snapped, and tilted her head as he kissed her neck and gently bit it, for that is what Erroh might have done. She stumbled in his grasp and he held her against the wall. A solitary candle flickered at the bedside, and, licking his fingers, he quenched it, and she gasped at his strength. "What is this?"

"A gift. Nobody will know. It's only you and me now. I've always wanted this. You have too."

She moaned ever so, and he kissed her as Erroh might have, and she was thirsty for him. Her eyes were closed in the dim glow of the fire's embers, and he knew her thoughts were elsewhere. "Oh, we shouldn't."

He dropped to his knees and ripped her undergarments free of her thighs, and she allowed him. More than that, she took hold of his head. "Erroh."

He went to task as a legend might have. He attacked her differently than he ever had before, and she was grateful. They writhed and became entangled, and he was rougher than foolish, forgotten Wynn ever was. He threw her upon the bed and delivered upon her ecstasies she could only have imagined, and oh, she called for Erroh loudly, and each time he attacked her more fiercely.

He did not cherish her pleasure as he had done since Raven Rock. He enjoyed her body more and took his own pleasure, and she devoured him hungrily, until, after many hours of furrowing, he finished his last and she hers.

Lying naked in bed with nothing but the storm outside and the sound of their desperate panting within, she turned and pulled his arms around her perfect form, and for a moment, Wynn was content.

"You were perfect, Lillium," he whispered, for any man should have said that after such a violent act of desire.

"Thank you, Erroh," she whispered, kissing his fingers and burrowing deep into his chest for warmth and comfort. This somehow broke Wynn more than he could have imagined.

They woke to the calling of birds and the suggestion of a sunny day. Stretching, they unravelled themselves from each other, and he took a moment to stare at her as she dressed.

"Why are you looking at me like that, Wynn?" she scolded.

"I want to gaze at your beauty one last time."

"I don't understand," she said, but she did. He could see it in her face. He beckoned her close, and she followed. He kissed her once upon the lips, and she knew it was the end too.

"This town has been good to us," she said sadly, and he agreed. He placed his forehead to hers and saw tears flowing down her cheeks. "A fine ending," she whispered.

Packing what few supplies they could carry, they slipped away from the town as little more than comrades of the road, each lost in their own thoughts. They knew they would never again be lovers, and, strangely, it hurt less than either thought it would.

43

AMONG SNAPPING TEETH

I should have chased him further.
   Should have followed him.
Should have found my horse and fuken hunted him down.
I did not.
Fuk me; I did not.
Green eyes.

Lea muttered a curse under her breath. For her thoughts and also for him. Her mind still reeled, but now, in this light of the day, she could doubt herself, which was terrible.

Ahead of her marched a Wolf. One behind her too. A few more after that. One line. One indistinguishable set of prints ruining the ground, making a mess, but making the numbers difficult to track. They were inexperienced at warfare, but they were doing some things right. It felt different being among the Wolves without Erroh. For one, the seething anger he stirred did not affect her as much. She felt more like Lea of the city and less like Lea of the road, mated to Erroh. Her mount walked with her, and behind them trailed the horses procured from the dead Southerners. They moved through the green as a unit, marching at the pace of the slowest foot soldier, but still as a deadly ambushing force. As Erroh had commanded them to be. He might have been proud had he waited around to see them at war. She suppressed the anger where it stirred and focused on the path ahead.

Conversation was low between the Wolves, but it was present. A promising sign and welcomed after any battle without fatalities. They were buoyant in their victory, but they were cautious. They whispered numbers among each other as though they were standing firm upon a wall in a dead town, and for a moment, Lea was back among those heroes on the better days. When the fires burned, the rain was tomorrow's problem. Many Wolves were older than she, but they looked young to her eyes. Perhaps she just felt old today. Perhaps that was the cost of living a life with Erroh. It was a fun, frustrating life, but it took its toll on the skin. And the eyes too.

A dozen paces ahead, the leading Wolf who played the part of the slowest foot soldier stumbled ever so but then continued masterfully. Watching him, she could see him favour his left foot in every step. He'd taken no blows in the melee but still marched injured. Sometimes, his grunts as he stumbled on a slope or gnarled root were loud enough for all to hear, but he did not ease the pace of his forced march, slow as it was, and they followed him. He was no longer the arrogant Alphaline she had judged him to be before.

Erroh trusted you.

They marched, leading their stolen mounts for a few miles until, at the forest's thickest, they came upon a sudden break and a sprawling community within.

It was impressive, and Lea was surprised at their endeavour. They had begun with less than fifty Wolves; now they massed hundreds. All tightly packed away in the middle of nowhere, doing nothing more than gathering strength. Every tree that had once stood in this part of the forest had been put to use. Barricades had been built, and large, crude gates would prevent any invading group of Riders from driving through. Hundreds of tents filled the open field, all neatly in rows, all delicately flapping in the morning air like white flags of submission. These fuks had little interest in compliance, however. Those not sleeping in their tents were tending to tasks. Some ladled soup from the many bubbling pots lined up at the centre of the camp; others underwent drills on the training fields. Yet others were wrapping their armour around themselves, gathering weapons and departing as Lea and her comrades entered. They nodded respectfully as they passed; a few touched knuckles as they passed and joked about "not getting anyone killed this time, or at least anyone important." There was laughter, and then they were gone, as though marching into the Wastes to hunt the enemy was no matter.

"You can say it, Lea. We've built something impressive here, haven't we?" Aymon said. He stepped from the line as his comrades broke rank and began to lead their mounts to a massive pen holding many similar horses. One of the outcast black guards took Lea's reins before she could argue and led her beast away with them. It was a small matter. She had little affinity for the beast. A horse was a horse.

Apart from Shera.

"Not too bad at all," she countered, noticing the pride on his face. She could see the strain there too. "What injury do you carry?" she asked before she could stop herself. It was not her place to ask such things of a leader, even if he was a general in her mate's army. Even if she was no Wolf.

He shrugged absently as Jeroen appeared beside her and allowed his mount to be taken from him. Like Erroh, she could sense his unrivalled hatred for the Wolves. It didn't matter that these gathered few were the braver group; they'd fought with him as the Rangers fell. Or that they answered to Erroh above all else. Like Erroh, he didn't trust them. Perhaps he had greater reason than most to harbour prejudices.

Nomi appeared beside her, like a fabled wraith from the marshes. She was quiet and nervous. A sister could tell these things, and Lea understood her fear. Nomi had likely noticed the glares, just as Lea had. Had they not parted ways on uncertain terms? Did they still believe her a traitor? There were too many males for one Southern girl to contend with.

She deserves to know of Erroh.

Aymon lowered his voice and leaned into Lea. "Worrying things have occurred these last few days," he said, gesturing to an open tent. Outside it were a handful of chairs and a general-like table covered with maps and totems of enemy positions.

"You may speak with both my companions as well," she told him.

"Some things are for generals alone," he replied, daring a subtle bow of respect. "There is a war upon us."

"Enough of this shit," Jeroen snapped, standing before Aymon and puffing out his chest. He was as tall as Jeroen. "Fuk this war. I need a safer passage through the ranks of Southerners, all the way to the city." Even now, his raspy voice was alien to her. It was unsettling. "Surely you have routes through the territory. Maps, like. All marked out with the places where Southerners don't tread. I need to travel to Spark, so that I might return to my mate." At this, Lea smiled.

"Your mate? In the city? Best you stay with us a while, hear of events," Aymon said gently, but his eyes were cold. He did not know he spoke to an Alpha. Did not know he spoke to a Ranger. Did not know he spoke to the mate of the Primary.

It was strange to tell Jeroen such a tale of the widowed Mea, rising above misery and heartbreak to rule the world, but Lea had, over the light of a morning fire, as they prepared to sleep. He had not taken it well; they had not spoken of it since.

"I demand to see Mea," Jeroen hissed.

"Are you... Jeroen?" Aymon gasped, peering at the wretched man, beaten by war, life and solitude. Lea could see the realisation on his face as Jeroen nodded, and Aymon cursed a few times under his breath. "We'll get you to her, but it won't be at Spark City." A coldness ran through Lea at his words. "Come, let us see to our wounds, and I will tell you all I know," he said.

Something was wrong. Lea could feel it. Raven Rock wasn't the only calamity to befall her. She did not know how she knew this. Her heart hammered like the iron training dummies enduring the strikes from the practising Wolves.

"Can any of you not swim, by chance?" Aymon asked.

A burning anger overcame Lea at hearing of a foolish warrior's sacrifice as a city burned. As its people fled, he had stayed behind, standing alone. *Of course, he did.* Hearing of a floating gathering of boats holding off a wave of attackers sounded improbable, yet Aymon swore he had seen the monstrosity in the middle of a vast lake many miles north of the Spark. Her anger turned towards Mea for abandoning their sacred home in cowardice, but she swallowed that with a bitter biting of the lip. She wondered if Erroh had escaped the city and sought out the floating town. She wondered was that why he had raced by so quickly.

Had not seen her. Had not looked behind to see her.

"We've had a few communications from Runners," Aymon told her. "The South hasn't a notion what the fuk to do. Truth is, those at Boat Town don't know what to do either," he muttered, scratching at his outstretched, miscoloured leg. A healer was unwrapping the bandaging, and the injured limb looked angry, enflamed, and rightly useless. It was a brave thing for him to lead with such a hindrance, but also foolish. "Fuken Doran has stayed with them and all. He's left me and Azel to batter these green bastards into place while he sleeps the days away with a city whore." A smile cracked through his grimace. Perhaps he was happy for his friend. Perhaps he was more content knowing the Wolves had a foot in Boat Town if needed. Unsteady as it might have been.

"Mea will have a plan," Jeroen said quietly. His pale face was almost as white now as the snows of the South. It was a terrible thing to know your mate ruled the world, and worse still to learn that her first act as leader had been to surrender the greatest fortress in the world and go… swimming?

"Well, she had better, for there is no one left to fight them," Aymon said, wincing as the last bandage came free. He'd said earlier that he'd never imagined the damage a solitary bolt could do. Lea knew, but she'd also had the world's finest surgeon working on her.

"Erroh will still fight them," Lea said quietly.

"I'm sorry, Lea. Erroh is dead, lost in the flames of Spark. But he died bravely." Aymon dared to reach for her, and she caught his hand in mid-air before he took her shoulder.

"Did you not see the rider? Before the Southerners set upon me?" she asked. It was a fair question.

"Aye, I saw a Rider riding like hellfire down the path, but you took my attention. And the fiends chasing you."

"They weren't chasing me."

Nomi gasped, startling Lea, who had almost forgotten she was here. Perhaps the girl deserved to know sooner, but Lea had intended to tell her when they were clear of him. Only Uden knew what that crazy bitch would do to find Erroh. Her Erroh. And everybody else's. After a breath, she mouthed a silent apology. Nomi might have been angry but for the stupid, incredulous grin on her face.

Aye, girl, I thought that would make you happy.
You can go and find him.

They did not hesitate to please their Primary. Or at least earn some favour by returning her broken mate. When night fell, Lea found herself alone, walking the camp, taking in the war in all its solemnness; its sounds and smells, too. She entered the place they called their armoury, and it was the only unimpressive area in their camp. She walked along the near-empty hanging racks of armour and weapons and gazed at the dark metal implements. Many of the pieces were recovered Southern ware, dyed and shined to weak imitations, but army colours were army colours. Among the items were pieces of genuine city guardian ware, and it was these she found most interesting. She was drawn to them, if truth be told. Lea needed something more than what she was. Lea had needed it the moment her one-eyed cur of a father had strode into her life and taken her heart. She stared at the armour and found the pieces wonderfully familiar. She could see the dents where they had been struck or slashed by blades. Mated to a Ranger's son and he a Ranger in the making, she had been cursed to hate all wolven things. True, their actions had been vile, but looking around this dreadful camp, she found this little makeshift armoury more comforting than anywhere else. Without Erroh, she was less; without her city, she was nothing. She wanted to be something again. Wanted to be more than a master general's unassuming mate, whispering in his ear.

And then she looked a little further to a gathering of mounts roaming free behind a crude fence. Walking among them was a slightly smaller horse. Built not for Southern charging or Northern hauling but for speed. Her heart skipped a beat, for she had not seen the beast in a lifetime, not since it had left with the Keri convoy and she left behind to die. Who knew what tales the beast might tell if it could speak, what trials it had endured to become a war mount of these Wolves? She saw it as a portentous thing.

"Well, look who it is," a voice called from behind her, drawing her from thoughts of her mount, Shera. It was Azel, one of the last surviving archers from the fall of Keri and a brother of war she felt akin to. He stood in finest black armour, although it had clearly suffered the wear of a long morning's amble. He looked as exhausted as she felt, but his eyes were excited, his smile warm. He ran to her, embraced her warmly, and it felt good to be embraced. "I heard about Raven Rock; I thought you had fallen." He didn't let go, and she didn't fight it. "Are you to fight with us?" he asked eagerly and released her with half a breath. As far as hugs went, it was a fine hug indeed.

She turned to look at the armour once more.

"Where is your mount? Where are your belongings?" Nomi asked when Lea did not mount up with them. They were surrounded by a dozen warriors clad in glittering black, rearing on their mounts, readying themselves for the perilous journey through the night. "We are to leave now?" she asked, and Lea, standing beside Aymon, dropped her eyes for a moment.

Jeroen, understanding her decision, shook his head in silent anguish. "War is not the way, little one. If I know Erroh, he is waiting for us all in Boat Town."

Exactly.

"Then send him my regards; this is my place here," she countered quietly, and he raised an eyebrow. He might have said more, but she was resolute, and mercifully, he said nothing more. Life among Alphalines was always a challenging thing. He would know that too.

Nomi, however, was outraged. She babbled some Southern words in a desperate, frantic outburst and began to climb down from her mount.

"No, my sister," Lea hissed, holding her firmly in the saddle. "This place will not be good for you or them," she whispered, and Nomi knew it too.

"Come with us?" Nomi whimpered desperately, with such terror and sadness that Lea almost acquiesced. They'd only just become sisters. Now was not the time to split their bond.

"You know why," Lea whispered, and Nomi nodded slowly, for her secret was sacred, and Lea was grateful.

"Will you come for us?" Tears streamed down Nomi's cheeks, and Lea started to weep too. For a breath, Lea remembered seeing the girl, battered and beaten at her hand, soothing her wounds by the river, and she grabbed Nomi's leg and hugged her. She wanted Nomi to stay. To bring war with her. To kill everyone. It would be great.

Until a foolish brute of a Wolf takes umbrage at her presence.

"She will come for you when we go to war as one," Aymon said and, unhappy with the emotional girls, nodded to the lead rider, who took off beneath the glow of a solitary torch. The rest followed until only Nomi remained behind, and the tears she shed cut Lea.

"I love you, sister," Nomi sniffed.

"I love you too, sister. Be safe. I will be along," she pledged, and then Nomi was gone, and Lea was separated that little bit more from what she called companionship, which was all right. This was the way. She could no longer look at those she loved, for she could see only his deathly green eyes. Could only want to kill. Watching them disappear into the night, Lea wiped her tears.

"Can't say I hate having a skilled warrior like you walking among us," Aymon said.

"You will hate me when I drive the fire into you tenfold," she warned, and he laughed.

"You sound like Doran barking out orders."

"I will need armour. I will need a banner to fight under," she said.

"Welcome to the Wolves, Lea of Spark City."

44

YOUR CARRIAGE AWAITS

Emir watched the two Southerners place the corpse awkwardly upon the flames. It should have been a simple task for four sturdy murderers: use a long slab of wood to keep her level and dignified, slide her upon the pyre, and let her burn to nothing. They did an awful job, however, for curs well versed in the burning of women. There was no ceremony or softness, no respect for their duty. Two murderers carried her from her chambers, where she had lain for longer than dignity deserved and Emir saw with dismay the ruin her dress had become. He could barely make out her face, for the damage was severe. He wondered had Uden killed the bitch and cared little what happened to her after? She was a traitor to the cause, and as goddesses of kindness and love were put to fire…

"So are traitorous witches."

He imagined what turmoil the real Stefan might have endured seeing her dumped into the flames, watching her hair catch light, seeing her bloodied hand, still wearing rings, slide and droop and hang lifelessly as the fire took hold.

"I suppose you brought this on yourself," he whispered, watching Silvia burn away towards nothing but memory. "To better days," he added, touching his lips and bowing lightly to her. He remembered happier moments in the wretched city with Stefan, Silvia and Roja as they all fell in love with each other. Well, as he and Roja began to fall in love, at least.

"It could have been love."

He hissed his imagination to silence and walked away from the pyre as the flames went to task, cooking her to seared meat and a husk of charcoal after. He did not return to Roja, however, for he had a second funeral to attend. This one would be far less impressive than the cremation of Uden's lover. He enjoyed being numb to her fate. She had lived a privileged life and met an end at the blade's edge where she had positioned herself.

"It was not love," he argued with his imagination.

Wandering through the streets, he cursed his luck and his fate. Today, he would leave this place, and no amount of goodwill he enjoyed from a demented god could delay their withdrawal. Before that, though, there were matters to attend to.

"Thank you."

He could see the marks in the dirt where they had dragged him, but it was a small matter. He was dead, gone, forever absent. Stefan would care little for their care of him now. As Emir had asked when they took the body, they had brought Stefan to a fine spot near the townspeople who had perished. Stefan would be a stranger to them, but he'd never found it challenging to make new friends.

For a time, at least.

The two Southerners were finishing digging the grave, and Emir sat in the grass and watched a while. Six feet down, he'd asked, and as many across. Wide enough to house his unimpressive broadness. It was a two-person job, and Emir was glad not to be doing it himself. Filling in the hole would be something else entirely.

When the hole was done, they muttered something incomprehensible and dropped their shovels in the dirt before strolling away, and Emir was alone for a time. He didn't mind. He liked the silence. Absently massaging his throat, he yawned in the early morning sunshine.

"It's time, brother," his imaginary Stefan whispered, and Emir wept. A regrettable thing, but he didn't want to bury him this morning. Not like this.

"Do you need help with your unpleasant task?" a deep voice asked, and Emir froze. A large shadow fell upon him, and a cold shudder ran down his body. He raised his fists—such was the freshness of his trauma, let alone the presence of Stefan's killer at the graveside.

"To the fires with you, cur," Emir snapped. He climbed to his feet and, taking the wrapped body of Stefan, began dragging him to the hole in the ground.

"Valhal awaits me, not fires," Uden growled. Much to Emir's dismay, he took hold of his friend's frozen legs and assisted the smaller wretch, and it was too much.

"Take his hands from me."

"Take your fuken hands from him!" Emir roared, and Uden did no such thing. He held the body's weight as Emir climbed into the grave and took the burden from below. "I need no help." But he did. If he wanted to save Stefan's dignity at the end, he needed help—even help from a killer.

"I'd rather be left in a crumpled heap than take his help."

"I know," shouted Emir, shaking his head, sniffing phlegm into his mouth, struggling with the body as he eased it to its resting place. "I fuken know." Uden looked at him in puzzlement but said nothing more, and within a breath, the gruesome task was done. Laying his comrade out flat, Emir kissed his fingers and placed them upon Stefan's shrouded forehead. He said goodbye, and it was awful. It felt like losing Quig, like losing Aireys.

"Tell me of your friend," Uden said, reaching down and pulling Emir up with barely any effort.

Emir wanted to strike the brute. He wanted to scream in his stern face and let him know the torment he had suffered. He wanted to grab one of the nearby spades, catch him unawares, maybe smash his brains free of his skull, bury him with Stefan, and claim innocence. But Emir would not do that, for he feared the madman and his actions. He also knew he would be unsuccessful; he knew it in his bones. He'd already died recently; he didn't want to die again.

At least not yet.

"He was not my friend, but he was my brother for a time."

"And I took him from you, so you hate me."

"Aye."

"What was his name again?"

"He was Stefan. Of all your nameless victims, I hope you remember his."

"He was brave. He put up a fight."

Emir turned away and began shovelling the dirt; he couldn't stand to speak more with the murderer. His silence was a suggestion for privacy, but Uden continued to stand close by. Ignoring him, Emir shovelled a load of dried mud upon the body, and his heart broke again. The tears continued to flow, and he allowed them.

To his horror, a second mound of dirt was dropped beside the first. A considerable amount too. "There is no need to cry for your brother, Emir.

A god buries him; he will dine in Valhal this night. Come on. If we work together, we'll be free of this place sooner."

Emir was horrified. For once, words couldn't form upon his lips. He simply worked a while with the god and they filled the hole nicely. When he'd patted the ground flat, Uden placed a large rock upon the grave. Then, with a small blade, he began scribing 'Stefan, a loyal brother' into its surface.

Forgoing any concern for his welfare, Emir leaned in close. "There is no Valhal, cur."

He expected wrath or a cutting strike. Instead, the larger man laughed heartily. "I like your defiance," Uden said. "But I will win you over."

With the deed done and the hour still early, they returned to the army who awaited their god. A large carriage was parked outside Emir's surgery, and six fiends were carefully loading Roja's body aboard. Emir darted up to help, but these brutes, no doubt threatened under penalty of death, were far more careful with her than they had been with Silvia. He offered suggestions as they slid her gracefully through the doors and rested her upon a bed of silk and straw at the centre of the large compartment. A foolish notion, Emir thought, watching them wrap her coverings around her fragile body. Silk made her sleep, and were they not trying to wake her?

"I know you are unhappy, dear Emir, but it needed doing," Uden warned.

The two men climbed into the carriage, and Emir shuddered at his carriage companion.

"You could have left me here with her," he said. "Could have kept a few guards watching us."

The god laughed again. He stroked Roja's cheek gently. "I will have her back in her palace." His voice had a strange gentleness, and once more, Emir feared the worst.

It was an impressive carriage, if truth be told. Sturdy wood with metal sheeting on the outside to stop any attempts at assassination. Within, the seats were bouncy and padded. Perfect for long-distance travelling. Even with a psychopathic murderer and a sleeping goddess as company.

As the carriage jerked forward, Emir looked out at the town and felt terrible sorrow. He gazed at the flames of the funeral pyre for a few breaths and then looked beyond them to the buildings he'd grown accustomed to. This had been a place of fear and unease, but, for a time, he had been happy here. Roja stirred in her bedding; he took her hand, loved her, and wanted everything in the world for her. Mostly he wanted anything but whatever Uden had planned for her. He could have asked about her importance and Uden's fondness for her, but feared what the answers to his questions might reveal. She settled, and Emir sat back in his seat. Uden pulled a wooden slat over the solitary window, and the carriage became darker and lonelier.

"You never know what fool might take a strike at a god as we pass through these lonely forests," he said, and there was eagerness in the man's voice. As though he very much desired some fool to come attacking him, and he a seething furnace of warmongering. Slowly, he bolted the carriage doorway and dared an "it's just you and me" grin, and Emir's stomach turned. If truth be told, no matter the misfortune that had fallen upon Emir throughout his miserable existence, he'd always believed himself capable of escaping any situation with his skin intact. But now, staring in uncomfortable silence at the brute across from him in this impressive carriage with its excellent cushioned seating, he was unsure what to do, and thought himself truly lost. Perhaps if Roja recovered, he might better plan his escape or death; whichever, really. Until then, he was lost. That feeling increased tenfold when Uden, reclining with his back to the fallen town and all its horror, produced Emir's notepad and flicked through a few pages as though it was an injured Alphaline's diary.

"This is an interesting read, healer."

It was. Emir knew this well. He'd written it believing in self-praise, even if nobody else did. He froze as though caught cheating at a game of cards by a large brute with a pointy sword. The mad god flicked through a few more pages, reading Emir's scribblings aloud under his breath for a while. Emir sought a distraction, sought anything but the vision of this man thumbing through his book of deadly concoctions. Truthfully, though, there was only one, and he'd concealed it well.

"Thank you," Emir said evenly. He wished he had the road beyond to look at. Anything but face the brute.

Uden must have read his mind, for he laughed aloud again, and in such close quarters, it was terrifying. "I skim through these pages looking for a vile serum that can end the war." He shook his head, tapping the old parchment pad. "But you hid it in here among so many different ingredients. Didn't you?"

This was true. It was a clever concealing trick on Emir's part. There were a thousand ingredients in there, each with many thousands of permutations. It would take a lifetime and a half for a stranger to stumble upon the horror he'd discovered. He'd never been a great fan of cyphers and puzzles, but concealing the authentic ingredients to such a vile tonic was an excellent puzzle in itself. He had yet to trust Magnus with the formula; he certainly wouldn't trust Uden. Still, though, despite the knowledge he'd scribed for those who came after, at this moment, he wished he'd had the foresight to cast the cursed thing into the fire as he stood vigil over Roja.

"I have read about the effects of this concoction, and of how to prepare it. Yet there are no ingredients written here, no beginnings to work upon," Uden growled. His eyes were wild, his grin dangerous. He leaned across Roja and tapped Emir on the temple. "But they *are* all locked in here, aren't they?"

"I don't understand."

The god laughed again. He sat back and cast the notebook across to Emir. "You will give it to me sooner than you believe. You have earned a little grace with me, boy, and I am a patient god, for now." He emphasised the last few words, and Emir could only nod in despair.

With a sigh, Uden spread his legs out wide and rested his head against the back of the carriage. His huge form rolled with every bump and shake. Closing his eyes, he folded his arms and eased himself to sleep, and Emir could only sit and stare for a time, too afraid to move, talk, or even think coherently.

Are you there, imaginary Stefan?

There came no reply, so Emir wrapped his arms around his chest, gazed at Roja and waited for the brute to wake and threaten him some more. It was something to do while waiting for his death.

"Look at her beauty," Uden said, and Emir woke to the dizzying outline of the Spark's shadow against the shattered moon's glow. His body was stiff, his mouth was dry, his head was aching and his stomach grumbled. Altogether the worst way to wake up when imprisoned beside a lunatic. "We will rebuild her... Roja will rebuild her," Uden added, leaning out through the opened window, and Emir wished for a stray arrow from a begrudging Southerner to strike him. As the carriage rolled on, he was shocked to see the numbers of soldiers camped on the city's outskirts.

Spark never had a chance, he thought miserably. *None of us did.*

Drawing his eyes away from the conquering army, Emir looked to the looming darkness of the walls drawing closer. He'd seen the city as dark as this before, but that had been from within a prison cell inside the city. As he had been then, he was petrified now, far too sober, and once again awaiting death. At least then he had been among friends with a sword in his shaking hands. And someone had a metal pipe, he recalled—still better circumstances.

Suddenly, Roja began to cough loudly, and Emir pulled himself away from the depressing sights to comfort her. Before he could, however, her eyes shot open, and she sat upright, coughing until her breath cleared, leaving her gently gasping. Emir took her hand in the dim light, and she squeezed it tight. She reached for him, and he held her close. Her face was pale but vibrant, better than before.

"Where am I, my love?"

"You are home, my dear," Uden whispered, and she recoiled in terror. "With those who love you most."

45

LIFE ABOARD A SINKING SHIPS

The ground beneath Mea's feet was unsteady. A trick of the light and the mind, no doubt. Every step she took upon these vessels was careful and calculated. Hardly the actions she'd taken since climbing to the highest tier of greatness. She swallowed her tea and grimaced at its cool temperature. She'd spent too long wandering among her people and not enough time just enjoying the revitalising. A small matter. She was getting better at walking these treacherous decks.

"Mydame," a Black Guard murmured as they met along the walkway. He stood aside on tiptoes to allow her to pass, and she offered a smile in gratitude, but he was already past her, no doubt marching the decks in search of peace and calm upon these troubled waters. He'd be walking for quite a time before this storm of people settled to the stillness, like the lake they floated upon.

She stepped over a barge's edge onto a smaller vessel and, taking a moment to pick her way across a hastily made rope bridge towards a higher level, continued her quiet pilgrimage through the transient town of her making.

She still felt the deck heave up and down. A phantom feeling that followed her throughout the day and the night beyond, born of the instability of any floating barge. Even when she managed to get a few hours of sleep, she dreamt of the rise and fall of the land. She looked into the night, and the world did not tilt as severely as her mind suggested. And why would it? Who knew how effective a hundred anchors could be when dug deep into the dark riverbed below? The same people who knew how solid a flotilla of vessels wrapped neatly together would be, she mused. This town rose and dropped, all right, but most inhabitants didn't notice it. And certainly not in any dreams.

Nightmares, either.

She continued to drink her beverage despite its unsatisfactory temperature. It was only a cup of tea, but it wouldn't look good for the current Primary to be seen wasting anything. Not with the shortages of all supplies creeping up on them at an alarming rate.

"People consume more during times of panic," Sigi had once told her, and she bit the inside of her cheek to drive away the memory. Wise words from a total bastard deserving of a sticky end. All would be well if she were granted just a few moments alone with him. For a few bloody breaths, at least.

Above her, on the rear of a galleon, she heard a young couple giggle and flirt and murmur about counting the stars, braving for better days, and seeking empty quarters for a time. For a moment, she listened and smiled. There was a beauty to love at the end of the world. Even if it would all fall to pieces in heartbreak and ruin, splinter apart like an unsecured barge in a tempest.

She drained her tea and slipped away to leave them to their privacy, for finding any privacy in Boat Town had been a rarity since emergence day. Let them enjoy the night where they could.

Further towards the centre of the gathered vessels, more and more people appeared. Some bowed to her, a few smiled, and others ignored her, which was fine with her. This place had become a furnace of activity since they'd docked out here. She had hoped there would be a sense of gratitude or triumph, given that most still took breath, but most of the citizens emerging from the holds accompanied their liberation with muttered curses or outright outrage.

She hopped over a sleeping man; beside him lay his mate and two children. Wrapped up in a blanket from the cold, they were just one family among countless families on the barges' surface now. Beneath the decks, they had waited, rested, moaned, and become dissatisfied. Up above, even with fresh air to improve their demeanours, they still behaved much the same as before, as they waited between feeding times for their meagre shares of rations.

A town of wretched wastrels, and she, the mayor of them all.

"Excuse me," she said, slipping by another group of homeless citizens blocking her path on the unsteady surface. They looked up and looked through her, expressionlessly. A lesser Primary might have taken offence at their indifference, Mea just marched onwards. There was little point in singling out anyone in particular. Collectively, the citizens of Spark City needed to adapt to the harsher life of survival.

Stopping at a newly placed gangplank secured over a deep drop, she tested the weight with one tentative foot and felt the swaying increase in her mind. "Lead by example," she whispered, and strolled across as though it were nothing. Every day, more and more similar gangplanks appeared throughout the floating city. She'd given no order, but apparently some saw the value of quicker traversal. Although there were still plenty of routes that ended in a watery drop, at least a few citizens were beginning to show their worth and engineer ways around these.

On the other side of the new walkway sat a long trough of freshly dug soil, placed snugly against the gunwales and close to the water's spray. It was only one of a few dozen she'd seen already this evening. The fresh sprouts of mushrooms had already appeared in the damp soil, planted, she knew, by those with the foresight to know the probability of hunger spreading throughout the settlement. She was both wary and hopeful of such thinking, for she knew of the meeting to come.

The farther she travelled, the more of these transient garden beds she saw. Every one reassured her somewhat that others besides her saw the value in this place—those few who were willing to work for their meals. Where the troughs were most plentiful, a few armed wretches sat watching over them. They may have appeared to laze, but their eyes were open and alert. Watching guard over mushroom growing was hardly challenging, but come the first pangs of real hunger among the citizens, she knew this place would become a trove.

In the distance, she could see the Wolves tending to war, and unlike the citizens here on the barges, the Wolves were going to task eagerly. And why not? They had tasted enough battles without payment and would continue to receive no payment, for they knew the value of survival.

Although the town was quiet enough at this late hour, aside from the usual hum of grubby people clustered too closely together, there came the reassuring sounds of hammers and metal clanking. Although she had failed to complete the ballistae before the attack on Samara, she had been wise enough to transport the tools and materials to continue their construction. How different might everything have been had they had an extra two weeks to counter the great war machines that ravaged the stony streets? Still, standing above them, watching the workers finishing the monstrous machines, she was grateful for what she had. A dozen of them were at task completing the beasts, all under the watchful eyes of Doran, who immediately straightened up when he saw her.

This grand workshop resembled a carpenter's bay, albeit far larger and out in the open. The craftsmen had taken charge of a large galleon and—likely earning the captain's ire—they had stripped the deck clear and cut into the underbelly, creating a somewhat efficient workplace with ample supplies just above the water's level. There was nearly everything here that the war effort could need, in addition to an adequate smith's workshop. She had heard arguments for and against a furnace being added, but so far, they had made do with clumsier tools at hand. She wasn't enthused at the thought of having such a fiery beast aboard a wooden town, but what did she know? She was happy to leave it to the dedicated workers who'd created this place in only a few days.

"I see progress," she offered, patting an upright piece of jutting wood as she passed. It was as thick as her arm, with a long arrow tip as large as her upper half. There were thirty such arrows, and she imagined the devastation each one could bring upon a roving horde. It would require a lot of work for just one shot, she knew, but it was a defence they could call upon, and one her advisors had suggested be completed swiftly.

Give me a year in this place, and it'll never fall.
Or sink.

"Not bad for a group of clumsy carpenters," Doran mocked, walking through the mayhem of tasks. She felt momentarily sorry for those who rested their heads in the nearby vessels, but then thought better of it. The more they stayed awake and gazed upon human endeavour, the better.

"Incredible work," she said, and though few, if any, looked up from their arduous tasks, she heard a few murmurs of gratitude. Some even smiled, and that was something. "Walk with me, friend," she said to Doran, and he did.

He walked more easily upon the deck than she. Those wretched few they met swiftly stepped aside as he drew near—his legend as Wolf captain was growing.

"You have not left us yet," she said quietly, and he laughed. A good start. She had grown fond of this young Alphaline. Half her age, yet he carried himself as old Dia had. That was the weight of responsibility. "More than that, you hold this place in order."

"Aye, Mydame, I do. It's no bother. Not these days."

This time she laughed, and he along with her. Their steps brought them towards the vessels reserved for the refugees that had never lived in Samara. Some of these had stepped inside her gates on only two occasions. They were the hated ones from the hovels—those most adept at and prepared for this life.

"I must speak with Holt," she said, and he spat over the edge into the water. He knew Holt and the fallen town he originally represented. It wasn't just the Keri wretches he spoke for now, however. Those at the hovels also allowed him to speak for them, and Mea was inclined to listen. Without the wretches, there would soon be a complete collapse of society.

It wasn't a challenging walk, but this part of Boat Town smelled the worst. No doubt the rest of the city would come to stink as severely over the next few weeks. However, it was likely to be the people of this quarter who discovered a way to eradicate the aroma first; such was their aptitude for life in the mud. Mea could only smile as two wretched guards stood outside Holt's room, forbidding them passage. They would have been beaten for insolence against the Primary in the city of light. Such an act would have abhorred Mea, but Wolves would be Wolves no matter what. For now, Doran merely ground his teeth irritably until a voice bade them both enter.

She liked Holt. There was a kindness to the man, and his eyes suggested wisdom matching the wrinkles on his face and the greyness of his hair. His abode was small. A boathouse, barely large enough for a half-dozen sailors. It was without decoration but for a small stove on which sat a boiling pot of water. The whitewash on the wall was freshly painted, though. A strange thing, she mused.

"Honey water?" he asked, and she offered her mug. Doran shook his head and refused a seat when offered, while Mea sat down opposite and enjoyed the bubbling delicacy and its burn.

"Now, why is it that the Primary is visiting me at this hour?" he asked, sitting back in his chair and sipping his brew. He appeared calm—too calm. No leader of any people should ever have felt this calm with her present. Still, she offered a faint smile. She needed his support. Or his approval. Whichever. She would take anything. The boat was rocking up and down, and she was glad to be seated.

"Your people seem to work best at night," she said. Although she was smiling, there was an edge to her voice. Any good negotiator was disinclined to climb into bed with the enemy immediately. There always needed to be a slight snapping of teeth first. Even when desperate.

He understood. "You have an issue with my Runners?"

She didn't at all. They were swiftly becoming the needful in this place. As the citizens had turned to lick their wounds during the first few days, Holt and those hailing from Keri had immediately set about earning their riches. By the first day's end, they had procured a dozen rowboats at the cost of much of their paltry funds they had collectively gathered. After that, they went after string. A shrewd move, for who knew the value of string would be triple the price of a pint of ale by the third day? Well, Holt certainly did. That string became netting rightly quickly.

Those boats and those nets became very valuable, for every day since then, the flood of fish into the city had been enough to keep mouths full as the rationed bread stores quickly diminished. In another week, fish would be the only sustainable food in this place, and Holt's people controlled the distribution. So far, they were charging little, but things would soon change, and Boat Town could not withstand a rise in prices like Sigi had inflicted anytime soon.

However, not satisfied with owning just the fishing market, Holt had commissioned the many miniature mushrooms farms throughout the decks. A man able to spot these opportunities and take advantage of them was probably the right man to lead, so the wretches entrusted him with city dealings. Thus, Mea needed to understand him that little more. Even Doran, who was outspoken on many issues, understood this man's sudden importance to this settlement's survival.

On the fourth day, Holt had commissioned a few wild characters who were clever enough to steal ashore and scrounge what supplies they could. They were called the Runners, a bandit term, but fitting, for they were reckless and daring. Everything good in humankind. These Runners had been slipping out across the lake, making landfall beneath the cover of darkness and returning, sometimes days later, with precious contraband. Most, but not all of them, returned for not even the most competent runner could slip past every patrol, every set of watching, hunting eyes, every single time. Mea desired to send some of her Wolves out on such adventures, but every sword was important.

"On the contrary, Holt, you are an important man; I want your friendship and help. I have no issue with your dealings, your Runners." It was honesty, and he shifted in his seat thoughtfully.

"I'm at your service, Mydame."

"No, Holt, you are not." He raised an eyebrow, and she shrugged. She had the numbers and the steel for now, but everything would change swiftly, and she wasn't brazen enough to believe a sharp blade and a sharper tongue would stop the masses from seeking full bellies. She had built this town, but it could easily slip from her fingers. It was no matter her losing power, but thousands aboard these unsteady decks needed saving. They weren't ready to fend for themselves. Holt knew that, and as Mea had set about defending the town and settling the growing dissatisfaction, he had gone and ensured their collective survival. At a potential price, no doubt. In truth, the Wolves had been bought off before; she didn't trust it wouldn't happen again. "I hold the Wolves, but they will turn."

Doran sighed under his breath and folded his arms. Perhaps he was insulted; perhaps he agreed. It was a fine thing that he showed emotion but said nothing after. As she did every day, she silently thanked him for his arrival and his lack of interest in returning to his own tribe deep in the woodland. Somewhere.

"I will give them no reason to starve, no reason to take their loyalty elsewhere; I follow different desires." He bowed deeply, and she took his words as a pledge.

"What do you follow?"

He smiled sadly, his old mind distant, and for a silent moment, she wondered had he gotten lost in his thoughts.

"For so long, I desired only to get inside those hallowed walls. And once we were in, it was time to leave. So, we moved along, and were forced to grind out a miserable life for ourselves." He sighed, and she wondered about his motives. She wanted to trust him. She wanted to find an ally.

He cleared his throat. His eyes lit up like a city on fire. "I see the people of Samara; I hear them bitch and moan about the world's unfairness. They are right to complain, for it is every person's right to complain. I have complained too. And I learned the value of a complaint to the masses." He held out an empty hand and smiled. "I do not hate those who demand better things, for they have fine, pretty words—and a fine point, too. But with such anger, such unfairness in this world, it is better to please one's self when our voices fall on silent ears." She wasn't following entirely, but there was a tender strength to his words. Sometimes it was the right move to listen to those who had lived before, those who had seen the actions of gods and humankind alike and lived through it. "I was a wealthy man until a storm came to Keri. I lost everything, and I complained. But little changed. I never expected a miracle to right such wrongs, but a glimmer of something is enough for one such as myself, burdened and toughened by life. Truly, someone like me should hold the riches of food at my fingertips. A man who has tasted the wretchedness of war, who has drunk of such horrors that a parched tongue was a blessing."

She found herself nodding along with his words. There was a decency to him she hadn't fully seen until now. For some strange reason, she felt less alone in the world.

"I know you, Mea. I know your actions. Although you think yourself alone upon these sinking, waving barges, know this: word of your actions has reached this old man's ears. I know you spoke for Emir; I know your allegiance to the young Alphaline Erroh, who sacrificed everything for my fallen brethren. You gathered us all up and planned the impossible. Near singlehandedly, you have led us to this point without complaint, without cruelty, without a hint of corruption." He reached across to her and took her hand. "I will not betray you or a solitary soul in this place. I do this not out of greed but for a desire to save others, as I have seen legends do. There is beauty in this life, Mea, even at the end of the world, and it is then that we must show compassion and kindness to those who scream against us with complaints. I give you my word that you have my complete support. You only need ask for what you desire, and you will have it."

Speechless, Mea swallowed her tea, and the burning was a fine tonic to the ball of emotion crawling up through her throat. Without warning, Doran, beside her, placed his hand on her shoulder. His eyes gleamed with tears, but he held fast against uttering encouraging words in this murky room.

"A fine gesture, Holt," Doran said gently, then sat beside her. "Perhaps there are ways my men can help you in your endeavours? Perhaps, somehow, we can find a way to survive all this."

Mea thought these fine words, too.

46

ERROH THE WRATH

Erroh strode briskly through the camp, with Drahir following behind him. A fire had ignited deep inside his stomach, and he needed to fuel it. To kill, to take some of this dreadfulness and inflict devastation upon the enemy. He felt like Erroh of Keri, spirited and driven wild by horror. He had no fear; his sorrow was drenched beneath a terrible rage. He was tired of life taking him aside and placing the cruellest curses upon him and him alone. His hands curled into fists, ready to strike like a startled, tormented serpent. His breath was calm, though, and his heart settled.

"Tell me how you hunt your comrades," he said as Drahir caught up with him. The Southerner was eyeing him optimistically. Erroh knew this because he grinned dangerously, his smile splitting his face from cheek to cheek.

"We have eyes throughout; we learn their routes, their numbers. Sometimes we send out a couple of dozen warriors to take care of a patrol. Sometimes…" He hesitated. "… we take full forces and attack a full Finger like they did with mine. They will offer mercy or death." This sounded easy enough.

"I wish to go hunting."

"If you take your horse, there isn't a warrior here that wouldn't follow. To fight with their god would be an honour, brother."

At this, Erroh flinched. For only a breath did his step hesitate. "I'm no god," he insisted. He might be many things, but he would not claim to be a god. Not anymore. Not if the cruelty of the absent gods was something to go by.

"Don't underestimate the power of a deity's word among us."

Erroh spun on Drahir. "You are aware I am no god, right?"

"Let us see if you are when this war is over, and we are counting those legends who survived, brother."

"I do not expect to live very long."

"Then neither will I."

They marched through the camp. It was still early in the day, and many still slept in their tents. Others lounged in the morning air, coming to terms with another day in this wretched, nomadic life, away from everything they'd ever known. That was the price of dissent, Erroh supposed. With conflict, sometimes there came significant change. Other times it was a life lived out in the cold as a blizzard flurried all around.

Those who gazed upon him dropped to a knee as before, and Erroh didn't try to stop them. Instead, he stared ahead and focused on the arena as it drew near. He could not stand to speak openly with those who followed him. Not today, not when his mate was dead, and her lineage was a lie, and he could barely think rational thoughts beyond murder and vengeance.

Away from the watching eyes of his followers, Erroh felt a little better. The sparring arenas had changed little in the few days since he'd seen them, but there were more sets of sparring blades on hand, and the ground was worn and more bloodied than before. Despite the early hour, there were already a few dozen gathered around the sparring rings. Some were in conversation; others were finishing their steaming morning beverages. Still others were practising their techniques, and this pleased him.

"Where are the rest?" he called out, and no doubt recognising his terrible accent, they swarmed around him as he marched towards the nearest arena, where he stopped and stared at those gathered. With hopeful gazes, they awaited wise words and instructions. "We will need more fighters." A few, desperate to please, disappeared in search of "the rest," and this too pleased Erroh. He had energy to burn and anger to diffuse.

"Who has been champion the last few days?" Erroh asked, and there were mutterings. Her name was Johann. She hid her shapely features under sturdy armour, but her smile of excitement was endearing and welcomed. She immediately reached for her sword, and Erroh pulled out a pair of his own.

The crowd watched, and more and more funnelled in from the camp now, eager to see their leader at war. Johann turned to begin and called out "Fir Vade." Erroh didn't know that particular Finger's name, nor did he care. He held his arms out to delay the start of the battle, and slowly began to stretch. After a few breaths, Johann copied his techniques, which pleased him. He wanted fury and brutality, but he also aimed to teach them. Sometimes the difference in battle came down to a stretched limb, lithe and swift and deadly. Many of the others began to copy his movements now, and Erroh approved.

When he completed his routines, the arena was crowded with eager spectators. There was an energy in the air, and although Erroh felt like dying, he felt a little better among these abandoned few.

"For me," he declared, and she raced towards him, arms flailing wildly, with just the right amount of skill to catch him off guard. For a few breaths, at least. They clashed, and she was fierce but no elite warrior. Not yet. She spun and thrust, and he caught every blow with a blade, and everyone watched and cheered raucously as their god attempted to take the title.

She lasted as long as he needed her to. At last, dipping beneath her strike, he lunged in with a killing blow and followed up with a strike that knocked her helmet free. She crumpled into the dirt, and he stood over her, gasping. Her smile was still upon her lips, and he bowed in respect.

"Not bad, friend," he offered, dragging her to her feet. "Who is next?" he roared, and many declared they wished to compete. He waited to catch his breath before selecting a large brute similar in size to Wrek. He was shirtless with much body hair, and he raised his blade in mock challenge, and Erroh had been here before. Battling Southerners, hoping to earn their respect. No, their awe. He had impressed before, but this morning, he was determined to show the depths he would go to in order to destroy, lead, and have vengeance too.

The man was older than Erroh by at least a decade and appeared to have spent every day of those additional years hoisting large boulders above his head. His sparring swords were impossibly small against his tree-trunk arms, but Erroh was far from intimidated. This was no test of pugilism. That said, were it a fistfight, the way Erroh was feeling, he would have defeated the man too.

They called out their banners and met in the centre of the arena, and the crowd gasped as Erroh met every blow the fiend offered and countered every strike, slipping past each one and drawing blood as though using a pail in a stream. With the jeering cries in his ears, the man fell swifter than Erroh expected. Gasping for air, he begged mercy, and Erroh shook his head impatiently.

"Very well, but next time take more punishment," their god declared, and although humiliated, the man nodded. Turning to the watching crowd, Erroh called for the finest warrior in the camp. His eyes fell on Drahir, brother of Lea.

This third fight was unlike their last. Drahir was just as deadly, moving swiftly, his shoulders relaxed, his blade probing for victory. Erroh, however, was like wildfire. He never stopped moving, allowing the world to slow; he owned this fight from the moment their blades clashed.

He took all his pain and focused it upon every delivered blow, and although Drahir was a near master, he had no chance, taking strike after strike before being repeatedly knocked to the ground, usually with a fresh welt or a stinging cut. As with Johann, Lea's brother appreciated the battle for what it was. Perhaps, also, he felt relieved that Erroh no longer lay desolate in his bedding.

It is no shack by a frozen lake.

The crowd watched Erroh spin the blades in a flurry of steel, and their gasps were audible. For almost an hour, the two combatants attacked each other, Erroh always drawing victory, but Drahir refusing to concede. Instead, he began to study Erroh's unpredictability and attempted to counter him. He was not as skilled as his younger sister, but his tactics were similar to hers, familiar, and for a very brief moment, Erroh felt less alone, less aggrieved and less broken.

The moment was fleeting, though. Soon after, Erroh would feel that crushing heartbreak come upon him. Instead of whimpering and hiding away, he hit harder, moved viciously, and the crowd were enthralled. Eventually, Drahir collapsed and sat bleeding on the trampled ground of the arena.

"No more," he gasped, and finally Erroh, looking fresh and reserved, dropped to a knee beside him, panting with exhaustion.

"All you who watch know the distance we will push for victory, even in training," Drahir called out, and Erroh agreed.

"Get fighting," Erroh roared, and the trainees found partners immediately. They, wrapped and deadened their blades, and swiftly, the camp was alive with the loud clatter of training.

"Who is next?" Erroh cried out, and Drahir looked up in amazement.

"You should rest, Erroh."

"I have only begun. Now, who will dethrone me?"

For the rest of the day, Erroh met and defeated every warrior he faced. As the hours took their toll, so did his speed, fury and ability. Yet

The Actions of Gods

still, none could beat him, and again, there came many more watchers as Erroh, covered in sweat, bruises, blood and mud, fought each challenger as though it were his life he fought for and any misstep would result in his death.

"I tire of this," he suddenly roared, knocking down a young warrior for the sixth time.

The youth, who had instantly regretted his steps into the battle, took the reprieve with a relieved smile. He'd met a god and had the bruises to show for it. Immediately an admiring crowd gathered around him.

Erroh could feel their burning eyes upon his battered, panting frame. "I seek a proper test, a proper hunt before this day is out," he said when he had caught his breath. They were acceptable fighting words, and he regretted them as soon he said them. Truthfully, he craved a slice of bread, a glass of ale and a few hours of sleep. Hearing their roars of approval was a tonic, however. He caught his breath slowly and forced his beating heart to calm ever so. He looked around for Drahir, who, having not spent the last few hours kicking the ever-living shit out of untried warriors, appeared refreshed and eager to answer his words.

"Who will ride with Erroh into battle this day?" Drahir called, and many Southern warriors cheered in excitement. They were a warring folk, were they not?

"Ride with me, brother? So we might spill some blood this fine day?" Erroh asked of Drahir alone.

Drahir placed his hand on Erroh's shoulder. "Of course, Erroh. Who else will find us the prey?"

Late in the afternoon, a hundred warriors took to their mounts, all following their new master, who'd shown them the level of strength he would demand of them in the coming battles. Following a suggested route in the hopes of coming upon a few battalions or, even better, a Finger flush with supplies like bacon and ale, Erroh rode out in search of his first victory at the head of these Southerners.

When they returned many hours later with rich supplies, bloodied blades and tales of impressive victory, the first tale in Erroh the Wrath was written. There would be more.

47

IT'S JUST A LITTLE TRUST

"How is the tea?" Gregor asked, and Magnus shrugged. It was tea. It was perfectly fine, he supposed. A bit bitter. He might have liked to add a bit of milk. Some honey too. Magnus could have said any of this, but instead, he shrugged. It was a fine reply. Gregor stirred the tea leaves in his own mug for a few quiet breaths and supped. "Needs some milk."

Having a cup of tea in this little shack was the level of entertainment offered to a king now, so when Gregor had asked, he'd said yes. For four days, he'd done little more than sit around and drink tea without milk or honey. Four fuken days without answers, without knowledge of what had occurred. Well, all of that was soon to change, what with his elite spy out in the world, stirring up trouble, no doubt, and hopefully discovering the fate of his hounds.

The kitchen he found himself in was deep down below the structure of the building. Deep and hidden, without any sunlight. Not that there was any sunlight in any other room in this miserable place, anyway.

A miserable shithole on the outside.

Miserable warmonger abode within.

Any passerby looking more closely at the shutters covering the outer windows might still not notice the thick bars of iron covering each thick pane of glass. It might take a man a month of hacking with an axe to break through such metal. However, the thickness of the heavy iron door was most impressive. A brute might find it easier to smash through the thick stone walls than to make even a dent in the grand entrance. It was a cleverly constructed fortress and a prison all in itself. Gregor had assured him the house was coated in thick, fire-retardant paint, so a cast torch would offer little more than a quick blaze of light before fizzling against the walls. Anyone attempting to besiege them would be wiser simply to wait out the residents within. Looking around this kitchen at the deep below of the fortress and the sacks of food and supplies, such an approach was likely to take an age. Indeed, this was the safest residence in the world, and Magnus venomously hated it.

"I miss my hounds," Magnus muttered, taking the heavy silence from the air. In the waking hours, there was rich conversation between the dozen guards who lived here. But their camaraderie was for themselves alone and did not include a savage, warmongering king. They ensured his protection and kept him locked away as the world went into turmoil, but regardless, Magnus felt that their easy conversation was a step too far.

He looked beyond the kitchen to the long hallway and their barracks beyond. The room was lined with three-tiered bunks, where the off-duty guards slept, lazed and waited. They passed the time playing cards, betting what little wealth they had, laughing and jesting. Magnus, however, just drank tea, hating this solitude, missing his dogs a while.

"Those hounds will be your death," warned Gregor.

"Those dogs have kept me alive. They've also kept me sane at testing times," Magnus argued, although he was grateful for the break in the silence.

"They are sacred beasts; no fool will touch them."

"If they do, they'll lose whatever limb was nearest for their efforts." Magnus sipped his tea and worried a little more about his boys. It was strange. At the end of the world, these innocent beasts did not know the world's rules, and he feared for them the most. As much as he missed them, they would miss him tenfold. He felt guilty for leaving them to such a fate. "But I wonder what those fuks would do to punish an old king too foolish to relinquish his crown."

For a moment, Gregor said nothing, which was fine with Magnus. Boredom and worry were not satisfactory topics for conversation. Finally, he replied. "Even an old broken-down king, who should have known better, will still receive the same respect. Your hounds will be taken, chained, walked and fed. I assure you of this, Your Highness."

It wasn't the first time Gregor had insisted on this, and truthfully, every time Magnus heard these words, he settled somewhat. It was no small thing to feel so helpless.

"Thank you, Gregor."

"Besides, I'm sure that idiot Padir will return with fine word of their welfare."

Again, Magnus felt better at this, but then his spirits fell once more: the boy should have returned sooner. He had been full of cockiness when he'd broached the topic of returning to the palace; truthfully, he was the logical spy for such an endeavour. All of the branch knights were well known in court; even dressed in rags, any of them would be spotted at once. Padir, however, was not of a clan; he was not really aligned with Magnus. He could easily slip in among the royalty with his clever, beady eyes and find "the lay of the land, the tension of the people, the boiling point of the stew," to quote the boy. And fuk it, but Magnus trusted him because, as confident as he was in the boy's ability to suit his greater needs, he also trusted him not to deliver a pack of infuriated savages to their sanctuary. And besides, surely there wasn't enough coin to buy him, to cause him to be known as a king betrayer. Even if it was Magnus the absent, he betrayed. Still, earning Magnus's ire was no good for anyone.

Watching the boy depart upon the charging horse the day before had been a worrying thing, and Magnus had been lesser for it, even without the young man's distracting words. So, since that time, he had done little more than share tea with Gregor and stare at the armoury's weapons.

The two men said nothing more for a time until Gregor, standing up, prepared to return to the barracks. "If it means anything, Magnus, I understand your actions. I understand the dangers of leaving the South untended. Were I to have faced you, I would have knelt."

"You would have sailed with the forces towards Spark?"

"Yes, Your Majesty, although I have lived a life of peace without war. Perhaps it's the savage in me." At this, he set off down the corridor to retire for the evening with his comrades, who joked and cheered loudly when he entered. These few warriors were a family in their own right, and Magnus once more thought of all he'd lost and fought the anguish as though it were a fresh trauma upon himself.

Will the pain ever end?

"When I die," he whispered, setting the empty mug on the table.

He would have preferred to be in the barracks among the rest of his guards throughout these lonely, tedious hours. He could have enjoyed their banter even if they hadn't conversed with him. It would have felt like sitting among his Rangers once more.

Instead, he had found himself in his solitary room, away from everyone else. Distantly, he could hear their laughter, their ease. He shut the door and lay down in his luxurious silken sheets. He could see the heavy lock on the door in the dim candlelight. If fiends stormed the castle, this was the room he would likely fall in. He blew out the candle and closed his eyes; he thought of Elise, Erroh and Lexi, his hounds, and he fell asleep.

By the sixth day, Magnus was beside himself with worry and frustration, as were the rest of his guardians. Time had come and gone that the boy should have returned. Gregor was already preparing a second envoy out into the world, both to discern the mood and to determine whether to offer surrender. Or at least that's what Magnus imagined from his place of solitude. Truth was, he had played his cards, and his bluff had been revealed to the rest of the table. He wasn't out of the game, but everyone knew they could bleed him dry until he conceded.

Unless.

There was always an unless. A word to live by in the darkest days. Here in this dark room, he was seeing pretty fuken darkly. Maybe if his hounds were beside him, he'd have felt better. He stood in the armoury, idly examining the weapons, as was his habit now. It was something to do, he supposed.

"Do you want some tea?" Gregor asked from the doorway, and Magnus spun around in fright.

"Aye, thank you, friend," Magnus said when his heart had calmed, taking the tea. It was his fifth of the day and, at this late hour, likely to keep him up half the night. Still, it was something to do when there was nothing to do.

"They are fine pieces," Gregor said, following Magnus's gaze to the weapons in their racks. "A little different to your beasts, but no less creative in their effectiveness." Sipping his tea, Gregor stepped past Magnus to gaze at the three sets of Clieve lined up side by side. Each piece was strikingly similar to Magnus's, but these were shaped for a different type of warmongering. With blades a foot shorter than his own and light shards of metal shielding each one along its side, they were an attempt at improving devastation. Strange, then, that they lay dormant in a little shack in the woods. "They are lighter too, more manoeuvrable," Gregor went on. "Probably easier to master by anyone proficient in dual-wielding skills. There's less need of a shield-bearer, too."

"That's exactly what the world has always needed," Magnus said, nodding. "Easier ways to kill. Still, they are beautiful. Who are these pieces for?"

"They are ours, set aside for pressing times." Gregor shrugged uncomfortably. "If it comes to that, we will not go into the darkness without taking many with us."

"These beasts should not be used on any Isle warriors, no matter the mood, no matter the war. But for the Southerners, they could be put to use."

Truthfully, Magnus had fallen in love with these mighty weapons the moment he had set eyes upon them. There were undoubtedly other impressive weapons in this cache, suitable for any battle, but these shiny, beautiful tools of brutality had a special place in his heart. He could only imagine the hours of work it might have taken to create each mechanism. Each foretold a different flavour of murder. Truthfully, the reason they remained concealed was likely him. And it was a good thing too. Were he still a Ranger, he might have taken them all for himself and claimed it a kingly fee. More than that, he might have had their creator brought to his domain and argued about the desire to have more of these war machines active in the Rangers. For only a breath, Magnus thought how different the battle with the Hunt might have been had there been a dozen more of these beautiful weapons of horror to call upon.

He ran his finger along the cold steel of one blade and imagined himself wrapping the straps around himself and wielding each blade one last time. A crushing sadness overtook him, though, as he remembered his knee and its stiffness. He could not bear the weight of these beasts. Not for long, at least. He let his hand fall to his side. This was no way for any warrior to feel.

Suddenly, a guard appeared at the door. "They have come for the king."

"Who has?" demanded Gregor, dropping his mug. It smashed loudly.

A waste of tea, thought Magnus, drinking the last of his own in a steaming, stinging gulp.

"Everyone."

It was no lie. Watching from behind the protected windows in grim silence, he counted hundreds of warriors under every clan banner surrounding the little fortress. They carried torches; they were dressed in armour. They came for a king, but would happily leave with a dead man and his followers. They called out for him, for his head, for a fight, for surrender too. They called for a lot of things. Mostly, they called for the doors to be unlocked lest they break through them or burn the place down altogether. Whichever, really. It had not taken long for the crowd to gather, and mercifully, they all stood watching instead of sacking the little hovel. Was it out of deference for his title, or fear of the shame of becoming known as king-slayers? Whatever the reason, they held for a time, but they had marched many miles; they could not simply stand and wait. It would take only one fool to cast their torch upon the house and the rest of the flock would follow. The house could take a dozen torches, but an army enraged and vengeful would find a way through, no doubt.

Around him, the Green Branch knights went to task arming themselves. Gregor barked out orders. Some of them involved donning those beautiful suits. Another was delivering Magnus back to his room and locking his door. There was desperation in those knights, but there was no panic or terror. There was acceptance, and he thought highly of them.

It did not hurt Magnus that the crowd had come for him. Nor did it bother him that in the days after the assault, there had been no calming of tensions. Strangely enough, what hurt most was seeing Padir, sitting atop his mount among them. He looked positively radiant, beaming with joy. There were no chains on his wrist or bruises on his face.

Betrayed.

He shouldn't have been surprised. Yet here he was, deceived by a snake who'd proclaimed anything but loyalty, and he was a trusting fool.

"Ease yourself, lads," Magnus said, stepping away from the window towards the doorway.

"No, sir, you must not," Gregor called, but Magnus was doing precisely what he must. Perhaps the resignation on the king's face had him step aside.

"Easy, lads," said Magnus again. "There is no fighting our way out of here. This country needs no fresh murder on its plate. I will offer myself, and it will be fine."

It won't.

Before any could offer suggestions or stand in his way, Magnus breached the doorway and stepped out into the cold night. The crowd fell silent, and Magnus marched out with his head raised. He managed six whole steps before they fell brutally upon him. He felt the blows from fists and feet. Everyone got in a lick. He blocked what he could, but at last he was felled and taken. Then suddenly his attackers paused as one.

"Leave him," roared a female voice, and through the throng of his once loyal subjects, he saw Teaolor drop from her mount. His assailants withdrew, and she stood over him. "Get the chains."

They dragged him to a cart and placed him upon his knees, then chained him in place with his arms stretched out to his sides. Magnus searched deep within for the strength needed to turn events on their head. He had come to a hostile land, seeking every possible path towards uniting the clans under one banner to serve the Four Factions and, ultimately, the Savage Isles. Every gambit he had attempted, every card he had played, had led to failure. He was almost beaten. Almost. He knew there was one more act in his play and one more piece to cast upon the table.

But was he strong enough to do the impossible?

Looking around at the other players who had come to this place this night, he sincerely doubted it.

"Your hounds are well," someone whispered from beside him. He turned and looked up to the figure of Padir upon his horse. "Chains are a good look to you, my liege," he added, and shrugged.

"You will pay for this, little one," Magnus hissed.

"Aye, probably, but tonight I'm free, with a full belly and good company." At that, he turned his horse and disappeared into the crowd, cloak flapping, leaving Magnus to his dark thoughts.

48

DEMONS

The Hunt called them demons. There were two of them. As vile as serpents, as swift as hawks, and deadlier than the night itself. In times of war, fables and legends were always spun by warriors, and the Hunt were no different. It took only a handful of tales for Erroh, the false fire god of Spark, to grow to myth. And now, it came time for the demons to spread fear. The tales of these abominable legends spread more quickly than most. A few weeks was all it took when whispered words were shared by so many in close quarters. Nobody could recall when the first tales had begun to spread, but soon the stories of the demons were heard around campsites throughout the Southern territories. Any wise general would have known that tales of resistance would be whispered, but this was something else entirely. Stories of Southern comrades discovered with slit throats began to pique the interest of all who heard them. In the beginning, it was small patrols discovered slain where they stood. But then the tales became more worrisome, recounting how, in the dead of night, phantoms slipped into the camps of the Hunt, killing many in their sleep. What was most terrifying was that they were all similar tales from separate voices, and as such they multiplied like viruses in a sickly old man. All of the stories spoke of two fierce killers, roving the arth, with fearsome expressions on their demented, metal-clad faces mocking life and everything holy. The more zealous of the listeners referred to them as demonic hunters, and the name stuck, and the legend grew.

Demons.

As time passed and whispers became spoken words, uttered with both confidence and terror, more and more eyewitnesses swore to waking with the rest of their Finger to the horror of nearby comrades slain and two figures dashing away into the forest, never to be seen again. As news of successes spread through the clustered groups of the Hunt, so too did the tales of terror, and of the two demons at the heart of it.

Some said their faces were concealed behind the stretched skins of their victims. That to view their proper forms was an invitation to madness. Others said that beneath their masks there lay such beauty that to gaze upon either beautiful beast was an invitation to enchantment.

But still the stories grew. Soon, the generals were ordered by Uden himself to snuff out each tale as swiftly as it appeared, but the demons' legacy would not be diminished so easily. Not when Uden was absent, no doubt playing with his new obsessions; not while the demons stalked those unfortunate few doomed to take the night watch or those few fools who slept a little too deeply.

"I saw them no less than eight days ago," the old warrior says, watching the flames, and those around him listen intently. "They vile brutes moved as a pair of dreadful serpents. Only by chance, I was away from the fire at the time." He pats his groin, and there is uneasy laughter. "As I relieved myself, I heard a scream. All bloody and wet." He looks at his groin again, shaking his head. He has told this story many times already. He knows the audience; he knows the pantomime. "Spilling the last of it all over myself, I crept forward with sword drawn, but it was already too late." He looks around, and the crowd is enthralled, clinging to every word, afraid to miss a beat but also terrified to hear everything. They will listen, believe, and congratulate him on his survival; they will offer him fine food and a bottle of burning alcohol, and he will take a fine lover this night for his troubles too. The redheaded woman who has hung on his every breath, most likely. She has a fine bosom and a shapely jaw. "Twelve of my comrades, down by the great bridge. All hacked up and spluttering their last. I saw the demons, no word of a lie." The crowd gasps; many will have heard a few excited tales, but few will have heard it from a man who has seen the act for himself.

"What did you do?" the redheaded woman asks. And he smiles warily.

"Trying my best to take them off guard, I crept down to the fire seeking vengeance, but as swiftly as they appeared from nothing in the forest, they soon disappeared again into the silence, and I was left alone without my brothers." At this, he dips his head and stares at the flames, for that memory cuts deep. He knows they are in Valhal, but it is dreadful to be left behind and, worse still, to not desire to follow one's comrades.

He takes a breath. He continues on bravely. Most of his tale is true, but not these last few moments. Truthfully, he'd stayed well hidden where he'd pissed himself and made no move once the screams of the dying filled the valley. From his hiding place in the trees, he'd seen the fiends tear apart his comrades, and they were inhuman in human form, their faces hidden behind demented masks of unnatural metals. He'd shuddered at their appearance. Upon finishing the last blow, they turned and stared deep into the forest where he had hidden. Only his prayers to Uden kept him concealed. He had always believed in gods. Now he believed in demons too. After both demonic creatures failed to discover him, he had sat hidden for no less than an hour until dawn arrived and, with it, the courage to venture out and look upon the aftermath of their gruesome deeds.

"Does Uden know of these fiends? Did you report it?" another listener asks, a younger boy in ill-fitting armour.

"Of course, he knows. I said it to him myself." This isn't true, either, and, worse, it doesn't sound truthful. He grinds his teeth in frustration. He will be prepared the next time. He will draw out the tale, which will be smooth and perfect. It will sound better than telling them of his cringing report to his general of the terrible deed, for which, in exchange, he was given the day to grieve and prepare the broken bodies for burial.

He leans away from the fire, for his story is done. The crowd relaxes, although the people are wary of the dark trees around them. Sleep will be less welcomed from now on.

The storyteller smiles as the redheaded woman slides up beside him. Lured by his brush with such a presence, she wants to know more, and he will tell her more once they are alone, lost in the throes of passion.

"Come with me," she whispers, and he gladly accepts.

"Fuk it," Lillium hissed, slitting the throat of the last fiend, whose screams lessened and fell to a waterlogged end. She squirmed and gasped for a few gurgled breaths, and Lillium considered another slash across her neck. A deeper cut. One to sever the right veins. She raised her knife, but the woman fell still, and Lillium was done. Her target was reached, at least for now. "That's a hundred to my blade," she whispered, and she was proud. She stared at the dead woman and committed her face to memory. She couldn't remember every victim, but a face appeared in her mind every now and then, and she held it there. She desired to remember this kill. Absent gods willing, she'd remember her thousandth kill as well.

"You still count?" Wynn murmured in disgust, and she flinched. It was an instinctive thing when a mate uttered harsh words. It was no small thing to free one's self of instinct.

I still count.

"Proudly, and I'll continue." She wiped the dagger on the woman's blouse.

He began to laugh, a strange sound coming from behind his face mask. "You crazy bitch."

At this, she laughed too. And why not? She was crazy. Demented. They both were. Their actions suggested as much. Crazy and happier these last few weeks than ever before. Why? Because they were killing indiscriminately.

He stood up from his own kill, sparing less than a breath to look at his deed. The victim rolled away, and he took a deep breath. "I don't keep account of my victims."

"You match me, give or take a dozen," she mocked. They stood over the bodies of six Southerners, all cut and silenced. Three apiece. Their actions had been swift and brutal, their enemies too slow to react. Fair-minded fiends might have frowned upon their murder, but she didn't care. They had killed many in the dead of night, creeping like wraiths into their tents, sometimes right into the centre of their camps as a hundred others around them slept. They were always swift: a few kills here and there and out into the darkness again before the fools could rouse their wits enough to catch them. Sometimes they pursued, and that was fine. Both Wynn and Lillium had become masters at moving swiftly in dim light. More than that, they moved silently, leaving few footprints to track. Sometimes they met the pursuers and sent them to the darkness like their fallen comrades. Other times, when pursued by particularly stubborn numbers, too many to slay, they slipped deep within the concealing bushes along the nearby paths. Lying beside or upon each other, holding their breaths, daring not to move and resisting the powerful urge to kill was a rush of blood she enjoyed, as was gazing at the nearby sets of boots, their owners unaware of how close they were to a successful hunt. Before, she might have felt uncomfortable this close to him. Feeling his warmth, sharing his breath, their limbs intertwined in this deadly game of catch the fiend. But not anymore; her stomach no longer lurched, her body no longer shook with anger. She no longer needed to scratch the itch of her desire, either. And she never found him stealing glances at her anymore. She appreciated this distance now. A wise fiend might believe they had become friends these last few weeks, and Lillium liked to think so too.

"I'm not even close to your tally, Lillium, but give me time," he said, and she could hear the horror in his voice, muffled though it was behind the beautiful, demented mask, and that was fine. He suffered for every murder, but he rose above it, which was admirable.

"Ah, fuk me," she said, scampering over to a pile of empty bedding and laying her hand upon it. It was still warm, and without blood upon it.

Wynn looked around the darkness and the thick cluster of trees. "Seven beds, six little fiends," he growled. "One must have slipped away on our way down from the ridge."

Excellent.

Hidden behind her own demented mask, which she'd cleverly named Muillil to mirror her beauty, her face was warm in the cool air, and she smiled. She had grown to love this last gift he had offered. After she'd placed her decoration upon it, of course, and made it her own. She appreciated the fear it instilled when she appeared above her victims, brandishing her blade. Or when she took a few moments to hone her swordplay as they fought desperately for their lives. Although she did not understand why, she felt somehow free when she was hidden behind this protection. Perhaps it was knowing few could see just how wide her smile grew when she killed. She wondered whether Wynn ever smiled behind his mask. Had they chosen to still bed with each other, she might have had him wear the piece as they furrowed. That might have been a sight, she mused.

She licked her lips and peered out into the night. Somewhere in the darkness where demons hunted, there hid a shaking brute. She wanted to go tracking, to add to her tally. "Tell me, Wynn," she said casually, "if you woke in the middle of the night and needed to piss something awful, where would you wander in this light?"

"Right there," he said, looking to a distant break in the trees. A fine path through and thick bushes to hide the stench in. "What about you?"

"I'd roll over and hold it a little longer," she mocked, but her eyes strained to see a little more; her ears pricked up for any sound of breaking twigs under the feet of a panicked Southerner fleeing certain death. She only saw darkness; she only heard the wind. Again, he laughed, and she enjoyed this time when conversation was more straightforward, and life was simply a matter of lunging from one kill to the next.

"We could be searching all night," he muttered, reading her eagerness, and he was right. They had enjoyed unbridled success these last few weeks, but not through luck or an absent god's fortune. They had stuck rigidly to a time limit. They'd stuck to their task each time, and when it was done, they were away like darkness fading after sunrise. Tonight it was already late, but there could be more camps to scout and assail.

Taking a moment to unbuckle the saddles and reins of their victims' mounts, she slapped the beasts firmly on the rear, and they took off into the night in search of a better life. All the while, he sifted through their belongings for whatever supplies were on hand. A short time later, laden with a bottle of sweet-smelling alcohol and a few loaves of bread, they slipped silently from the campsite in search of new prey.

This life could have crushed them, she knew. Discovering Spark had fallen should have driven her to death or madness, but it had not. Seeing the brutes scurry around the great city like ants upon a conquered hill had taken her breath and the strength from her shapely legs for a few moments. But instead of weeping, giving up, seeking out death as the world collapsed all around them, they two, alone, had gone to war.

Their lives were disciplined. Driven by Erroh's insistence that a few Alphas could do great things with the forest for cover, they had made waves among their enemy. Rarely using mounts, and moving stealthily so as not to draw notice, they rested for a few hours at sunset most days and glided silently through the Wastes for the rest of the night. They were always tired, hungry, and suffering bruises and pain, but neither one complained, for they two were elite warriors, waiting for the end but killing as many as possible until then.

They followed no marked routes and rarely took the same path twice. They struck when the need arose; they caused havoc wherever they could. They became so familiar with the sight of a hundred oblivious Southerners marching by that they barely worried any more. They were at home among the enemy, and for Lillium, for a time, it was beautiful to be free of responsibility, free of wondering about those she loved, already knowing their fate.

The Actions of Gods

The days and night passed thus until, as they moved along the Great Mother, they came upon a large army deep in the Wastes, camped and in preparation. Further along the river, they saw many crude rafts being constructed. Still farther on they slunk, watching as they went, and at length they came upon the same fiends building massive war machines. Curiosity drew both Alphas further along the river until it opened out into a vast lake, and across the water they gazed upon a grand monstrosity that seemed to be made of dozens of vessels lashed together. Unsure of what action to take, Wynn and Lillium spent a day and half a night watching this strange floating fortress for clues as to its purpose, while keeping an eye on the gathered army among the trees.

It was deep into the night, and they were still without a plan, when they spotted a handful of cursed Wolves on the other side of the river, skulking out of the forest. They recovered a hidden rowboat from a thick layer of branches along the black water's edge, climbed quietly in and pushed off from the bank, rowing across the lake towards the massive gathering of vessels. Only when they had faded to near invisibility against the dark waters did Lillium's heart leap in hope.

We are not entirely alone.

Realising that the gathering of vessels was a bastion, a fortress of sorts, they moved down to the water's edge, still under cover of darkness. No sooner had they dipped their feet into the cold water than a terrible roar shook them both. Suddenly, the night came alive in fire and horror. Above their heads flew a thousand deadly burning arrows. In the fire's light, they saw many rafts laden with Southern archers moving slowly across the lake—a terrifying sight. More than that, great boulders, flaming and fierce, were flung across the sky as though thrown by the absent gods themselves. The boat carrying the Wolves was struck with a hundred arrows, killing most aboard. Those few not pierced scrambled overboard, howling, and dove deep beneath the black water for escape. Screams filled the air, both of horror and triumph, and both Alphas stood watching helplessly as fires took hold of the strange floating monstrosity and the Hunt went to task sinking it.

"What can we do against such numbers?" she cried, gripping Wynn's arm.

"We can join this fight," Wynn snarled, and she agreed.

49

EMIR'S LAST DAY

When Emir woke that morning, he did not believe he would die that day, but he suspected it could happen. Truly, he had awoken to finer outlooks in his life. Scrambling out of the bedsheets, he stretched and immediately felt a pang of regret that it was not his lumpy bed in Raven Rock. That had felt like home. That had felt better than this. He looked around the room as though for the first time. The last time, too. It was a perfectly pleasant bedchamber, situated at the top floor of a fine house that had once been owned by wealthy traders in better times. The bed was a four-poster, and he had no idea why anybody would design a bed like this, but the rich desired to show their affluence with such things. It was the same in Keri as it was here. The bedroom was fitted with a large oak wardrobe, and for a sleepy moment he considered rifling through the outfits so he could look his best today.

"I'm not built for these," he said to no one as he slid the wardrobe open to reveal the silken garments within. He turned to look at himself in a full-length mirror and was satisfied with his rugged wretchedness. Stained shirt, ripped trousers. His usual attire. It didn't bother him. Long ago, he had turned away from wealth and niceties. Niceties like the plates hanging on the walls in this room. He did not know why the wealthy hung plates on walls. They were fine plates with decoration on their surfaces, but they were useless unless there were scrambled eggs upon them.

Scrambled eggs.

His stomach grumbled. These last few days he'd been in Samara as an entitled prisoner; he'd eaten well, but only this fine, depressing

The Actions of Gods

morning did he desire breakfast. He slipped from his room and then trod quietly past hers, and went down to the kitchen where stores of fresh ingredients were already waiting. His keepers did all they could to make his stay as artificially pleasant as possible.

He did not hesitate, for it was after dawn, and he desired to savour what quiet moments he could. Cracking six eggs into a ceramic bowl, he whisked them with a bit of butter, a little salt, and a fuk-load of pepper, and then a bit more butter. Tearing open a warm loaf of honey bread, he smeared a healthy amount of butter on two pieces and placed them butter side down on a pan where the flame was hottest. The room immediately filled with the hiss of beautiful things, but he had only begun. He was careful; he would not mess up this meal. Taking another pan he had warmed above the hot stove, he stirred the eggs into it until the bottom caught and the yellow deliciousness thickened. Angling the pan so only an edge was heated, he stirred the eggs with a spoon. A fork would break it up too much. Adding a little more butter, he checked the nice burn on the toasted bread and, satisfied they were suitably browned, he flipped them over and returned to the eggs.

"Ah, fuk," he muttered, discovering the eggs were thickening too swiftly. A skilled egg maker could handle this, though. He did not panic. He'd been here before. He'd never be here again. He'd do it right in the end. Removing the pan from the heat, he stirred the thick eggs to a perfect wet slush in a few breaths. Satisfied, he returned them to the heat. An arduous enough process, but for the perfect Emir eggs, it was a task worth doing right. Soon they began to dry and cook nicely, and this pleased him. He knew people added milk for consistency. They were lunatics. He could admit that now. Easing the frying pan from the heat, he plated the bread and set a pot of freshly brewed cofe on the stove's cooler edge. The aroma was as welcomed as a last sine at the end of a drunken night, and Emir grabbed two mugs and poured bubbling black liquid into them. He added a dash of milk to each and a half-spoon of honey to hers. It was how she liked it. He was a dutiful mate; it was the little things he hoped she remembered.

Churning the eggs again, he added more butter and then ladled a dollop onto each chunk of bread. The aroma made his mouth water, and he helped himself to a little bit that had fallen from her bread.

"Perfect."

Grabbing a tray, he loaded the food and drinks onto it, along with some cutlery, and glided upstairs, balancing the feast in shaking hands.

Dawn was breaking, and he stopped to gaze out through the landing window as the sun's rays reddened the sky, heralding the new day.

"Beautiful," he whispered, and the aroma of cofe and eggs struck his senses again; he did not want to mess up the meal, so he climbed the last steps, walked quietly down the hall, and stepped gently into her chambers.

"Good morning, my darling," he whispered, and she stirred, pushing her red hair to one side, and despite her drained look and pale skin, he thought her beautiful. Even the freckles. Especially the freckles.

She rolled away from the morning's light, pulling her silken sheets with her, and he walked to the other side of the bed. "It's time to get up, my Roja."

"No, it's not," she argued from beneath the bedding, and he loved her with everything he had, and his heart broke that he would break hers, but there was too much at stake in the world, and although he was a brave man, he, too, would be easy to break. It was easier to leave. Easier to escape. He had planned his route.

"Oh, very well," she muttered, rolling free of comfort and safety. Wincing, she sat up and as he passed her a cofe, he made a cursory inspection of her wounds and was happy with the stitching. Every day she was healing nicely, and although she was confined to bed rest, she'd be up and about any day now, for no Alpha could stay restful for very long. "I feel better, my love. I feel like getting up, facing this world."

Of course, she does.

"Let's see how you are without the dream syrup in your body for a time."

She grimaced. "Aye, I suppose so." She sipped her cofe and smiled. He'd gotten the mix just right. He sat beside her and offered the eggs, which she declined, and he was a little hurt. Perhaps it was a painful memory from a better time in their lives, when everything was awful but the city had been theirs to enjoy.

"You must eat; you need your strength," he said, and begrudgingly, she did. He appreciated this passive Roja, but the sooner she had the fire in her belly, the better. Not today, though, and probably not after he left. His stomach churned. Of all things, the guilt of leaving her was far worse than saving his soul. Were it just himself at risk, he'd have stayed with her until Uden flayed his skin from his body, but there was too much at stake, and he could not take a chance. He could not stay; he could not risk getting caught. A terrible thing, really, and were he alone, he might have wept for his misery and shitty decisions, but instead, he smiled and loved her and cherished these moments.

"Oh, these eggs are good," she said. Surprised, he turned to see her spooning a second and third mouthful, and his heart soared.

"Oh, it was nothing," he said, taking his own plate and a fork and enjoying his share of the buttery mess.

They sat for a time, and although she was ever so dreamy, her wit was improving, and she made for heartening company, and he could not help himself touching her more than usual. A casual stroke down her arm; the tucking of a few loose red locks behind her ear, taking her hand and kissing it. She smiled, ate, giggled, and listened and loved him in return. And it ended all too soon. Like battles. Like life. Like love.

As she recovered, so too did Uden's insistences. He was patient, but Emir knew the depths of his cruelty. The day she walked from these silken sheets was the day Emir would be punished. Was this not Uden's subtle promise?

He drew a spoonful of dream syrup from her bedside locker, and she took it gladly. He gave her less than he had the previous day, then left the bottle by her bedside as she settled back into the bed, squirming in comfort and savouring its sweet flavour. There was little more than a double dose left in the bottle. Hardly fatal if she took it in one go, but enough for a merry trip all the same.

"You are needed, healer," a voice from downstairs barked, and Emir sighed and looked longingly at Roja. She knew the routine. She would sleep, and he would return with fresh meals and delicate caregiving.

"Of course I am; I will be a moment." He committed the sight of her to his mind, for he would need it in the steps beyond. "Roja, I love you," he whispered, and with eyes closed, she drew him near and kissed him, and he savoured her.

"I have always loved you, Emir. Always."

"Goodbye."

"I will see you later, my love," she whispered, and she was asleep. He turned and left her, knowing she would never forgive him, and it was all right. This was the way.

The two Southern fukers walked him down through the dreary streets, and indeed, it was a pitiful place. Gone was the vibrant, disgusting cluster of bodies he'd once known. Instead of the fetid smell of humanity, there was nothing more than the stench of charring and dampness in the air. Instead of gazing at the ruined buildings or meeting the cruel eyes of any passing Hunt fuks, he kept his eyes to the ground, counting his steps to his healer's bay.

"Just get through today," he muttered as his companions left him to scrub and prepare himself for the horrors to come. His theatre was a large healing shack ten times the size of his tiny office in Keri. At least the doors worked fine. Within, there was every ingredient needed and every utensil a fierce young healer could ever require when battling death. All in front of an audience too. At least a dozen other healers were already there, preparing themselves for the day, bloody and educational as it would be.

From far and wide, they brought the injured, the dying, and the rightly fuked to meet with Emir. And this was the way of things now. His days had become a shining few moments with Roja followed by hours of the bloody torment of war surgery.

Teaching.

On better days, he might have felt pride in his actions. He was tasked with teaching those who were as old as he, some much older, in his practices, for the city leader believed him a creator of miracles. A destroyer of death. A guardian of the grievously wounded. Or whatever poetic shit the false god would proclaim to his zealots.

There were a hundred patients, if not more, and their many open wounds were tended to by his disciples. It shouldn't have mattered, but assisting the enemy stung him. Still, though, he walked dutifully from body to body, gazing calmly into their terrified Southern eyes, bringing hope as he went to work on them. And he was a god in this hell, where humanity's crimes were most apparent. He was real fuken good at saving these poor bastards, and, worse than that, he was a damn fine teacher too.

"You should always watch for infections," he murmured to his acolytes, and they scribbled notes and nodded their heads. A few carefully double-checked their gory work. "You are going to be fine," he whispered to a Southerner who didn't know what he said, but it didn't matter. The tone was reassuring. The truth was, the infection was too rampant, the patient's body too weak. The man would be dead by the end of the day—a small matter. Emir prescribed syrup to let him dream away the last few hours of his life. There were worse ways to go, he thought miserably.

He rarely rested, just ground his teeth and continued to walk among the properly fuked fiends, teaching and saving where he could. But as evening approached, he was filled with dread at the summons that he knew was coming. Scrubbing the last drop of blood from his body, he wiped his face dry as the two guards returned with a command from the false god. Of course, they did. Tentatively, Emir drew his students aside and suggested the last few treatments that were needed before he left. He might have felt relief or regret for leaving, but Emir's mind was resolute, set upon his actions and the escape to come. It was a simple enough plan, and it would work.

He knew the way, and the guards followed a few steps behind, always watching, never speaking, and that was fine with him; they were the enemy.

As always, Uden met him in the Cull. The fires in the city had done little to improve the warmth in this room; Emir's breath was visible in the faint light. As usual, Uden was already waiting with a steaming meal and a bottle of wine. Were it not such a ridiculous sight, Emir might have found it amusing. As it was, although Uden smiled and spoke warmly, his eyes were cold. He watched Emir's every move as though studying his body language for threat or concealment.

"There's my boy," he said, sliding a chair out for the smaller man. Every movement he made was calculated and unsettling. Not many people could offer a meal, some wine, even a fuken chair and yet terrify their guest with every move.

Fuk off, Uden.

"Full of the joys tonight, are we?" the god asked, and Emir shrugged. Truthfully, he was terrified of the brute. Even now, there was such strength in all he did. Every time he saw him, he imagined Stefan fading to nothing. "It's no matter; a god can eat with his own voice as comfort."

"Talk away, so," Emir said, sitting and staring at the food before him. Excellent meats, plenty of vegetables and a thick, peppery sauce that was drizzled across the plate. He thought of this morning's eggs and imagined the flavour on his lips. He would have liked Stefan's imaginary voice to be with him, to comfort him at the end, but the cur was away now. Emir was truly alone, and perhaps it was better that way. Uden raised an eyebrow at Emir's defiance but, thinking on this slight, decided that shrugging indifferently before reaching for some steaming slices of bread was a fine enough reply.

"In a mood tonight, are we?"

"I'm always in a mood."

The god dipped his bread in the pepper sauce and chewed quietly. As he did, he reached out and tapped a notebook that lay on the table between them. Three taps, and then he returned to eating. It was the same unspoken question he'd asked at every meal, although Emir suspected his patience was now growing thin.

"I will not."

The god finished his bread and poured them some wine, and Emir gratefully drained his own goblet. He would need to be drunk for his escape to work. Easier with a belly that was empty but for sloshing red wine.

"I visited Roja today," Uden said. "She is looking well. You did a fine job dragging her back from death."

"She has a strong heart."

"Like her father," he countered, and froze, deep in thought, for a breath.

Emir reached for the bottle and refilled his goblet. He kept the bottle nearby, knowing Uden wouldn't stop him. He was quite the host; he would be until the time came that he wouldn't be. Uden tapped the notepad a second time.

"When will she be able to walk around?"

"She should not be rushed, but she looks to be improving."

"Soon enough so?" There was an uneasy tone to the brute's voice.

"Aye, soon enough."

Emir missed his courage. He missed the days when he could spin on brutes and lash out. When he could stare a god in the face and laugh and mock. Now, though, with the threat of the world upon him, he was terrified. He needed to escape. He had to. He would. He didn't need to fear the steps he was about to take. So he drained his glass and reached for the bottle again.

"A healer like you brings much to this world that benefits my people. I know it is your mind. I know it is your hands too." He reached out and took Emir's hand. He held his fingers in an impossibly hard grip, squeezed absently, and twisted Emir's wrist so that he lurched in his seat and spilled a few drops of crimson wine.

"Release me," Emir demanded.

"I've killed in this room before," Uden mumbled, his eyes upon Emir's callused, shaking hand. He was not hurting him, but a little more pressure and everything would crack and shatter. This threat was new. Emir needed to escape. He wanted his hands. "It's a good room for cutting. Better to kill in here than outside where others might see."

Emir agreed. He nodded his head and all. He thought about leaping upon the god, taking that glass of wine and putting it through his godly eye. Instead, Emir whimpered, and Uden released him immediately.

"Oh, show heart, my boy. I will not kill you. I'll simply take your hands. You can do much without hands. Afterwards, though, the day after, I might need to take more. Would Roja forgive me for taking your manhood?" He laughed and shook his head. "How much would you care for her without desire blinding your vision?"

Emir wanted to cry. To scream. To attack and to flee. He did not want to escape, but there was no other choice.

"You are a cruel bastard, Uden," he muttered, and the god laughed.

"That I am, but I once tasted more horror in this world than any man should have. I have lost all. So, that gives me a right to be cruel, and tell me, little healer, who would deny me a little cruelty when I show such love?"

Emir began to quiver, for he was familiar with this sort of wild talk, and it was unsettling. No brute believed themselves mad, crazed or dangerous. They considered themselves the sanest, most justified of men. Or gods. Whatever. Emir knew there was no stirring from that path. What could shake a man to his bones so much that he would embrace madness? It certainly wasn't losing an eye.

"I'm glad you care for her. I'm glad you love her. And I am happy for you both." Uden tapped the notebook again. This time he kept his finger on its surface. Emir could feel his eyes burning into him, into his soul. If he still had one. "I would like to remain happy with you," he warned. "Tonight, drink well and think on your misgivings. Things will change, dearest drunken Emir. And I don't want things to change, but all things end, and she will forgive my actions."

"Until tomorrow, so," countered Emir, and Uden, dismissed by a wretch, merely smiled and stood before bowing to leave.

"Until tomorrow, friend. Enjoy the wine," the brute whispered, before disappearing out through the doorway into the recesses of the Alphaline tower, leaving Emir alone with his thoughts. He listened, waiting for the heavy steps to disappear. As he did, he drank deeply from the bottle. His stomach groaned, and the desire to pick at his meal caused a momentary hesitation. He could have escaped more easily from his home, but he dared not drag Roja into his horror. Instead, he would escape in this cold room.

"I have no fine memories from this place," he said to the room, and, understandably, received no reply. So he wept aloud, and only then was his escape threatened by his will. Draining his glass, he smashed it against the table.

"What are you doing?"

His imagination knew precisely what he did, what he was about to do. He was no master in the art, although he had learned that making a slit upon the wrist was a reliable way to drain one's self. Less painful than the throat, at least.

"If I had rope, it would have been much easier," he whispered, and then he sobbed, for this was the end, and he was so scared, and he didn't want to leave, and Roja would break, but so too could the world, so he drank again and, taking a shard of goblet glass, ran it up his wrist and cut as though he were in his surgery. To the fires with the fiend who'd said it would hurt less, for the pain was agony, and as the crimson spilled over his forearm, he dropped the glass and laid his arm out on the table so he could gaze upon his death.

"Fall asleep," he demanded of his body. With his good arm, he picked up the bottle again and drank deeply, and his warm wrist ached and bled, and he could not look, lest he lose his nerve and stem the flow like he'd done a thousand times before.

It did not take long at all. He felt the darkness, felt his dead comrades nearby, smiling and weeping. Emir fell from his chair, taking his plate and the wine with him. He thought it a fitting end as he lay among the rubble and the darkness closed in around him.

"I'll see you on the other side," he whispered to Roja, loving her with all his fading heart. As a tragic silence fell upon the room, like a thousand thundering boots had ceased to move, Emir, the wretched healer of Keri, gasped and died alone in a cold room.

50

PASSING THE RUBICON

Tye ran through the forest seeking out prey. He was swift and silent, for he had to be. They were in treacherous territory. A few feet to his left, Lexi kept pace with him. Like him, she was no king of the forest, but she was getting better, moving through its green undergrowth just fine.

In the beginning, in the first few days, they had clustered together for support. Safety in numbers, an enemy of an enemy, and so forth. Uneasy allies, at best. Vile, betraying bitches at worst. As they shuffled away from their bindings, they all argued—fine arguments with expletives and all. There were even threats. Blades were near drawn. Each voice was unsure, yet so righteous, louder than the next, until eventually, Wrek cut through them all, and Tye was first to listen. Lexi settled down soon after to hear him out. And finally, their vile companions on this ill-fated march fell silent. They could all see the world was getting smaller, every day, a mile at a time, as they wandered farther from Raven Rock, farther towards nothing. Any fool could see the Hunt was moving, roving, hunting, and even a king was likely to end up dead on his throne if he did not attempt to counter the oncoming wave. Or flee to dryer ground. Real fuken dry ground. So, onwards towards this place called Adawan.

Enjoy the green while you can.

"There's nothing here at all, Tye," Lexi hissed, and he agreed. It was a hard thing to hunt without a bow. Harder still in forests utterly devoid of life. "Fukers probably hunted it all," she added, and he could hear the gasps in her voice. A mile they'd charged from the path, away from those unsettling comrades. They just needed a little time to themselves. Just a little breath of fresh air before that became a distant memory.

"Aye, maybe so," he said, slowing and dropping to a knee beneath an incline leading into another glorious glade. This part of the forest was unusually warm. It was lush, but there was a dryness to the air. It probably meant they were nearing their destination. Or, more accurately, the dreaded path to their destination. She slunk up and sat down close beside him, closer than she had before Raven Rock. That was fine. He liked her closeness. Safer that way.

"I'm so fuken hungry," she muttered, leaning back against the incline. She dipped her head beneath the shade of some overhanging branches. Tye didn't recognise these types of trees at all. Perhaps, were he better skilled at such things, he might have known what he could eat here, and what would kill him.

"At least you'll fit your clothes a little better."

Slap.

He laughed, and so did she. Why not? When they were out in the forest away from their companions, they were more at ease with each other.

"Fuk me," she said, rolling away. "You could do with a bath, Tye."

He sniffed under his arm and shrugged. "It keeps *her* away, so I'll refrain from bathing anytime soon."

"She does have eyes for you."

"And for you."

"Reckon I'd best not bathe either, then."

"You look tired."

"Let me sleep here a while; the others will catch up."

There was a comfort in the girl. She was a comrade. Those they marched with were not comrades. They claimed there was no ill will between them. Claimed there would be no bloodshed, and truthfully, they had shown no wickedness these last few days, but still, both young Alphalines found it challenging to find any ease around them, particularly in the dark where slitting a throat was an easy enough task.

"Do you want me to rub your head?" he asked.

"I'm all right; I'm not suffering a headache today. Not yet, at least."

"Think you could rub mine for a while?" He laughed, but she was drifting away. Or else not listening. Regardless, she nuzzled her head against his chest. He had a fine chest. Perfect for a pillow.

"Are you listening?"

"No, idiot, I'm not. Will you fuk off and leave me to dream of bread, honey, cheese, beef, soup, and some wine."

"It's not too late, Lexi, not too late at all. We can just grab our packs—"

"Oh, for fuk's sake. Will you let me rest, Tye?"

He shrugged, and she opened her eyes, and only then did he realise how bloodshot they were. Perhaps he would rub her head. She deserved a rest.

"No one would know," he went on. "We'd just slip into the forest." She sighed, and he knew she was thinking of it. He knew because she'd suggested it the day before. They'd convinced themselves that Aimee's suggestion of marching to Adawan was the safer call, even with these fiends matching their steps. It wasn't much of a plan, but it was away from the city, away from war.

Into outlaw land.

He thought of those bandits marching through the Wastes, seeking a bastion in the burning sands. What would his father think? he wondered, and it stung.

Sorry, Father.

"I reckon if our... comrades wanted us dead, we would be dead. Adawan sounds safe, secure. It sounds like a fuken stronghold. We've lived in a bandit town for months. What's wrong with taking the next step?" She sounded so reassuring, but she was younger than he. And he was charged with protecting her. Not that she needed much protection. Regardless, he went wherever she went, and indeed, she would follow him wherever too. Sometimes a young cub knew these things.

"I've never been good in the heat; I'm wary of traipsing across the dunes," he mumbled, and she rested her head back on his chest. He liked when she did that. It made him feel warmer than not. Sometimes at the end of the world, all a young warrior needed was someone to hold.

"We'll drink plenty of water, drink more when we arrive," she whispered, and he could hear the exhaustion of sleepless nights falling upon her.

"It's a long walk."

"It will be fine, idiot. Wrek knows the place. I trust him. Have we not earned a little reprieve with their kind?" It sounded like a compelling argument, but her words were hollow. Particularly about Wrek: the nearer they drew to the edges of the sands, the more agitated he'd become. Tye had asked, but Wrek had never been one to share his thoughts.

"I just have a bad feeling." She grabbed his collar, and a strange comfort overcame him, and she smiled, and for an odd moment, he felt better. And then he thought about his fate, his life, all that he'd lost. "Get your hand off me, you craven trollop," he jested, and she did, but she did not laugh. She merely curled up, and he held her. "But you are *my* craven trollop."

She giggled and nestled in against his chest. "Asshole."

He let her sleep for a time, listening to her breath, enjoying the feel of her hair against his cheek. She moved once, took hold, and wonderfully, he could feel her chest against his. She had a fine chest, although usually, she hid it well beneath several layers. He'd told her so, enjoyed her blush, and laughed at her foul reply. A cad might have attempted to look down her top. Just a little peek to pass the time. It was right there, all tempting like. But shit like that ended with nasty things. He imagined kissing her and shunted that thought away right quickly. If they kissed for no better reason than lack of choice or boredom, they'd probably end up furrowing, and if they ended up furrowing, it would mess everything up. They enjoyed each other's company in this miserable slog. And besides, Erroh would kill him. Lexi moved again, and her chest slid away; he was lesser for it. With her warming his shoulder, he just sat and listened to the wind for a time.

―――

"I expect you did nothing to me as I slept," she chided, stretching her body. Her elbow struck the side of his head, and she laughed and continued her stretch regardless. It was a fine stretch. He'd always enjoyed watching her as she stretched. Less so an elbow to the head. Trying for a witty remark, he looked to the sky and realised the day was getting on. They would need to reach the edges of the sand by midnight. He knew this because Wrek and Aimee had insisted they were close now.

"I'm rather small, as you know, so you didn't feel anything," he countered. It was a fine, witty reply. Self-deprecating. He'd always believed the finest humour was at one's own expense. It took a confident, sly mind to be comfortable to paint one's self as a fool. Easier to catch people unaware that way too.

"I did feel that; I thought it was a twig scratching away at my underbits. You are getting much better at trying to sleep-please females. If you had a map, you'd know where to put everything."

"It was such a disaster down there I'd need a compass and all."

"I keep it like that to keep the rats out." She had mastered the art of wit too.

"Well, the rats have certainly cleared out. But there was something else down there. Something unsettling. Something I'd rather never speak of again."

She blushed, muttered something about teeth and blades, and he took the victory. "Come on, my dear. Let's return to our comrades of the road."

"Look at those fuken rats, all scurrying around like fuken vermin," Lexi muttered beside him. He nodded in agreement. It was a fine point. From their hiding place, they could see everything. And what they saw was worrying.

"We are rightly fuked."

"Aye, we really fuken are."

The sands leading to Adawan were worse than he could have ever believed. For three days, they'd shuffled along from late evening through the night, then stopped to take whatever paltry shade they could during the warmer daylight hours. His skin was covered in hardened mud, a strange tactic suggested by Wrek at the cost of part of their precious water supply. It was a strange thing to smell of dirt all day, but covering his face and hands with the solution was a tactic against the blazing sun. It wasn't a lot, but it was something. He gazed at his companions, similarly smeared in mud, marching in a solitary line towards a beacon in the distant nothingness; they were the definition of wretched solitude —until they discovered they weren't alone out here.

From their hiding place, upon a large mound of rock mostly covered by sweeping sands, Tye could see the bright glow of reddened skin upon every soldier and Rider. All ten thousand of them. At least ten thousand. It might have been more. Could have been less. He'd never seen ten thousand warriors lined up together, burning up in the sun, marching towards war.

"So much for finding a place untouched by war," muttered Lexi unhappily.

"We could turn around right this moment," Tye hissed, spitting mud from his lips. Distantly, he could see Wrek and Aurora settling down for a few hours' rest. Or they might have been sitting up having a feast. They could also have been dancing around, for, really, they appeared as specks on the horizon in this blazing heat. They were the clever ones resting, but Tye's curiosity got the best of him. Best of *them*.

"We've come this far, at least halfway," Lexi argued, staring back at their comrades with a mix of suspicion and fondness. Reading facial expressions through the layer of muck on her face was impossible. They had travelled far, driven on by Wrek's directions and Aimee's unsettling enthusiasm. Marching right back into the forest was an appealing thought.

"Beyond the point of no return," Tye said grimly.

"Long, long walk back towards shade," she said after a time. It was an hour before noon. Their long march for the night was done. Another two days or so and they would reach their bastion. She shook her water canister and grimaced; flakes of dried mud broke away from her face as she did. She absently wiped at the uncomfortable glaze but caught herself. Tye knew the desire to scratch too. A constant, awful need that would bring nothing but momentary comfort followed by sunburn for hours after.

"Three days in, and our water supply is near done. Could be a painful march to the Wastes."

"I wouldn't mind a little thirst if we turned back now. What if we come upon a hostile place? Wrek has been far from open about what we can expect. And now that we are here, out so far, I'm thinking the worst."

"Wrek is fine, Tye. The fight scrambled his thoughts. Emir told me sometimes it can take a few weeks to find your mind after a battering. He needs a break, is all."

"Fuk me, where did you come from?" Tye cried as Aimee dropped down beside him. Her face was as mud-laden as his, but somehow, she carried it better than he or Lexi did. Perhaps it was a bandit skill learned in her youth. Tye could have asked, but he didn't. She was unlikely to answer. When she spoke, it was out of absolute necessity. She slithered between them, her cold eyes calculating the numbers marching.

"You were hardly careful in your talking," she snapped. Her every movement appeared to be a threat, but she gazed upon Wrek as though she were a child lost in a forest and he the heroic parent. Wrek, for his part, looked upon her like a desperate father at a child he had long ago failed. She spoke most with Aurora, but listening to their unsettling conversations of blood and death, as though they were discussing the weather of the day or what tasty meals they favoured, unsettled Tye deep in his soul where hope and sanity still reigned.

"It was just us scouting," Lexi snapped, and Aimee gazed her way for a breath before breaking into a dazzling smile.

"I want to see my jailors up closer too." At this, she tilted her head respectfully, but it was a forced action. "I wish to know all I can before the siege. Sometimes knowing the smaller details can be the difference." She gazed back at the gathered army; her eyes followed the massive carts that had been repurposed as water carriers. They were as tall as a man upon a mount and trice the length, and each was dragged by eight horses. There were a dozen in all—not enough water for a long siege, but enough to allow the army to take an unprepared settlement.

Lexi narrowed her eyes. If there was a weakness to target, that was it. A siege wouldn't last long if a clever little fiend slipped through their defences and popped the corks on those huge tanks. "My... people will need to know what they face."

"They face death regardless," Tye replied.

She gritted her teeth before smiling through her deathly brown veneer. It was a fine smile, considering. "They will fight."

"The right sort of people," Tye muttered, and she was pleased with this. "Come on. I think we should get back to camp and get some rest. Shitty fuken day of marching to come."

"Lead the way, my pretty Tye," Aimee said, and Tye wasn't sure he felt altogether happy with Aimee marching behind them. Who knew what a girl like her could get up to? Especially one who appeared to favour his jawline, even under this muck. Beside him, he could swear he heard Lexi snigger.

"It's a bunch of trees," Lexi said in dismay. And from this distance, that was all it appeared to be. Tye agreed; it looked like a long strip of green against the burning yellow of the lifeless sands. No, that wasn't entirely accurate. There was plenty of life in these sands. Little shit lizards scampering all through this forsaken desert, climbing up his leg, seeking a place of shade where he rested. Not to mention a whole fuk-ton of rats following three days behind. Plenty of life in this shithole desert altogether, and he hated it all.

"Oh, my beautiful Lexi with the pretty eyes and rear. It's so much more than that; you'll see it when you get there," Aimee whispered. She sounded positively giddy. It was unsettling.

It had been no easy march. Every last mile they'd trodden on the scorching sand was difficult, every step painful to their aching limbs. They were dry to the bone and raw from sweat and the ceaseless rubbing of clothes and armour on damp skin. They'd run out of water entirely the evening before. These last few hours had been awful, and even the layers of mud could not stop the sun from blistering their skin.

"Lead us in, Aimee," Tye said, and the girl smiled wonderfully—a rare thing in the days she'd been marching with them. In that time, they'd not only marched together, but their duo had become a trio, and although she spoke little, there was a vulnerability to her that set Tye's nervousness at ease. She no longer looked at him as though he were a delicacy to eat. She now merely gazed at him with subtle adoration, which was fine. That was probably because of the mud on his face, he thought.

Regardless, he'd slept and rested easier these past few days since they'd left the Hunt behind, since Tye had shared his meagre rations with her, since Lexi had taken to tidying her hair with a comb before they set their heads to sleep. She was no friend, but who knew what camaraderie they might find in the time ahead.

Aurora still marched behind the trio. Only a few feet behind, no more, no less. Each painful step she took was controlled and rhythmic. She unsettled Tye more than Aimee did. He couldn't even see the beauty in her eyes anymore. He only saw Stefan's death, her betrayal of him, and each time he looked, a terrible fury overtook him. So he tried not to look at her despite her desperate attempts to win his favour. She had approached him three times when they were alone in the days since. Each time, she'd come bearing nothing more than a hopeful gaze and an offering from her canteen, but each time, he'd refused to speak to her. She had not tried today, though, and that was fine. Let her wallow in her guilt. Tye could have asked why she cared so much for the girl, but he couldn't bring himself to face her.

Wrek marched last, far behind them all, with hunched shoulders and his head low as though he'd been struck in the stomach. Upon seeing the sanctuary, he'd muttered a few words under his breath, then crossed himself in an archaic gesture of fear. A smarter little Alpha might have wondered if he didn't want to come to this place at all. Still, he'd marched onwards as though it were a small matter. Perhaps he feared what lay within the trees. Or who. Every bandit had a bloody history.

Plenty of regrets, too, Tye imagined. Tye suspected he marched because Aimee desired to march here too. Perhaps he felt compelled to get her to this place.

None of them believed they'd survive the last leg of their journey, such was the heat and dehydration. Tye had never known such a parched tongue, but complaining merely added to the misery.

As they neared the sanctuary, they caught sight of the defences, and they were impressive.

"It can't be," Lexi suddenly said, stumbling. She fell to a knee, her eyes upon the ramparts where a female was clearing the obstacles to reach them. "No, it can't be," she wailed, and stumbled again as all strength left her. She broke into a run, then, towards the woman drawing near, and Tye was thoroughly confused.

"Alexis!" the woman cried.

They had come for sanctuary. They had come with horrors weighing down their every step. For a moment, his shell cracked. He felt like a little cub returning home. He watched the two women embrace. Mother and daughter. He smiled. He felt relieved. He felt like weeping in joy. He had done his part. He had done good.

And then it all went terribly wrong.

51

AMONG GENERALS

Lea leapt forward, striking fiercely. She'd waited weeks for this moment; she could wait no more. Could barely contain her excitement, either. There were eyes upon her as she moved, and that was fine. She was the only female warrior among them all. The best of them all. A leader among generals.

"Fuk me," Aymon cried, retreating beneath her wave of violence. He had no chance. She knew it, and, as she stared into his rapidly blinking eyes, he did too. This was no unevenly matched melee in the dusty sands of Spark City's arena; this was no battle for a wretch's honour and life. No, this was far more pressing because Lea of the Spark was in control of her destiny for the first fuken time in her life.

"Easy," she jeered, but that was a lie. It wasn't easy at all. It would have been a tough contest, even on her best day and his worst. It wasn't easy, but it was inevitable. They struck back and forth, his solitary blade meeting and blocking her rhythmic battering from both sides. "You are too slow," she added, and this was a half-truth. The whole truth was that she was too fast for him.

"Shut your pretty mouth, girl," he mocked, blocking and retreating, favouring his better leg, his eyes seeking a path away from this inevitable loss. Around them, the crowd watched with bated breath, and Lea loved the performance. Away from the shadow of a legend, she could move freely, she could be great, and they would all see.

She was more than a vile brute's daughter.

She was more than a timid waif running through the streets, afraid of her shadow.

The Actions of Gods

She was more than Erroh, and she did not need him anymore.

Some of that was true.

She could see the frustration on Aymon's face. As they had gathered for sparring for weeks, Aymon had avoided meeting her in combat, as was his right. It wouldn't serve their cause for a recruit to come in and usurp the general in the first few days. So, she had been patient. She had played her part at being a Wolf, and she was enjoying it.

"Beat the bitch's rear," came an excited cry from the crowd. There was laughing and booing; there were grand jests all around, especially from those who would lose a pretty piece in the wagers upon this battle.

"Easy, now, or you will be next," Lea called, turning towards the heckler. All the while, she retreated from Aymon, her left blade pointed out in warning to him, her right low and tucked in defensively should he spring a trap while she engaged the crowd. She half expected such a ruse, but instead, he played along.

"I'm trying, boys," cried Aymon. "Fuk me, I'm trying, but the bitch won't keep still."

More laughter.

"Batter the bearded bastard," came another voice from the crowd, and Lea grinned. This pageantry was terrific for morale. Terrific for displaying the level each warrior could aspire to.

"Just slap her until she cries. No bother at all," came a third mocking voice.

"Kick him between the legs—he'll be fine," someone else shouted, and she was sure it was Azel, and she added to the laughter.

They charged each other again, and he was swifter. Favouring his injured limb, he caught her off guard for a breath, but he announced each strike with too-obvious manoeuvres, and she easily batted his attacks away. Still, he persisted, and she screamed in triumph, in excitement, in exhilaration as she met each blow and countered, and they became nothing more than a blur of blades in the centre of the arena. The crowd cheered louder, their mocking cries silenced, for the skill on show was breath taking to behold. They could see his desperation, his threat, and her cold, calculating pursuit of him as she danced in and around each strike, daring him to release his defence, slip, and rightly fuk up. The world slowed, and she had not thought of green eyes for an entire day, and Lea knew she was home.

At first, her comrades had issues with her presence, which was fine. She was a female, smaller than most, with less strength than a man. Perhaps her receiving a fallen Wolf brother's shimmering armour ahead of those more deserving hadn't helped. Or that she had received a sizeable private tent, when such things were invaluable among those less distinguished. It was simple resentment at first, and that was fine. She hadn't cared; she had taken the muffled criticism, the sly comments, the outright tasteless jests, on the chin. In the beginning, at least. But after her first few missions into the Wastes with a dozen other comrades, she had earned their respect. Perhaps it was her uncanny ability to return from every foray without a scratch on her shiny new armour, and with her comrades sporting a few dents on their own. She had not lost a Wolf on her watch either—no small feat when they were venturing out to cause mayhem.

She knew the lands better than the finest scout, not because her tracking skills were elite but more because of her ability to discover the finest hunting grounds, and to sniff out an ambush long before she and her comrades walked merrily into death. When she drew her swords, genuine respect came swiftly, though. They called her a killer to her face now, which was pleasing. When setting upon the enemy, she was terrifying. After a battle, when she was alone in her quarters with no one to see, she would gasp, retch and shiver, thinking of the lives she had taken. It was a small thing to relive the pain of battle from the safety of a bedcover. In a fight, however, she was alive, and her kill tally was steadily rising.

When Wolves of higher rank began requesting her presence in their marching units, Lea knew she had found acceptance. Initially, they had treated her as a mere talisman, and she took these jests good-naturedly. But soon enough, as they saw the destruction she could cause, she became essential.

Even now, no more than an hour after she'd returned from a fierce ambush on a few Riders patrolling a bridge they frequented, still covered in blood and a day's sweat, she had spotted Aymon in the sparring arena and challenged him openly.

There would be no change of leadership, and no challenge to his status either. It was simply a little reminder to those unknowing few that she was a star in the night sky; she was an Alphaline.

"All right, let's do this properly," Aymon roared, batting his sword against his chest, and those who had placed a wager on his victory were heartened.

"So, I should start trying then?" she said lazily, spinning her blades impressively as her mate might have done.

He drew his arms in close, held his blades low, and she did not strike. "You're going to hurt me badly, aren't you?" he said softly, so no one would hear.

She smiled with evil eyes and tore into him.

———

"Lea, did you have to keep striking my injury every few blows? Was it not enough that you outscored me so easily without punishing me?" Aymon muttered from his chair. A damp cloth was wrapped tightly around his knee.

It was a fine question. She had not needed to punish him, but it had been enjoyable.

"I thought it was a fair fight," said Azel, trying and failing to conceal the delight in his voice. It was a fair fight, and although there had been no yielding, she had not cast the killing blow. It was a small matter. The gathered crowd had witnessed a spectacle. A few wiser masters of the blade might have noticed she took it easier on their leader the longer the fight drew on. There was a time and a place for decency. Sometimes it could have been in a battle to the death in a stadium filled with vengeful citizens. Sometimes it was allowing a warrior to save face for the betterment of the army. She had played her part. Aymon knew the actual outcome.

"A fair fight? You weren't the one fighting," Aymon countered.

"You did all right," Azel said gently. He sat next to his lover, stroking his arm absently.

It was strange, thought Lea, to see such affections on public display, but clearly this place was a far cry from the city and Dia's ancient, misguided beliefs. Everything in this camp was done differently, it seemed, its inhabits of a different mindset altogether. No fool in this group of Wolves would have said a thing, even if they had an issue. Lea had never thought much of Dia's beliefs either way. It simply hadn't occurred to her. Seeing the two men openly showing their emotions beside her, she was surprised at her indifference. Their behaviour was normal here, but before, it had been something she was taught to distrust. To fear. To hate. To punish. These were, she realised now, an old woman's archaic notions about survival of the species, carrying on the next generation. Truly though, lust was lust. Love was love too. She'd experienced both. What business was it of hers, or anyone else's, who gazed with desire at whom? People would always furrow. Babies would always be born.

Let people be themselves, for fuk's sake.

"Aye, it was a fine fight," Lea agreed. She sipped her ale, and it was a welcomed tonic after so many exhausting hours of killing and performing. Her chest was heavy this evening, as though she'd caught a touch of heavy lung while out in the damp forest that day.

Or else it's the sins of my actions.

Lea drank again and felt a little better about the heaviness, the sadness and the agonised thoughts that consumed her most days.

"Ah, to the fires with you both," snapped Aymon, pulling his arm from Azel for a breath. He leaned forward and lowered his voice. "I thought you would take a little vengeance on me." Around them, the Wolves settled down for a night's earned rest. They sat away from the masses at the front of Aymon's grand tent, drinking ale, speaking in low tones as though they were upon a journey of leisure without a care in the world. Few recruits were invited to dine and drink with the generals, but Lea had sat with them many a night these last few weeks. Sometimes, they spoke of tactics; sometimes, they jested and laughed as though they were the closest of friends. Sometimes, after a harsh few days or after tending to the body of a fallen brother, they sat in silence, each lost within his own thoughts, each uninterested in disturbing the others. It was a strange, comforting ritual. Tonight, they jested and joked.

"Is that why you have been avoiding my challenges?" Lea asked.

"I was just waiting until I was healthier." He rubbed his knee absently and laughed, and although Lea had hated this man before, there was something more human in him than she'd realised. She was at ease around him more than she was with most males. His lack of interest in bedding her was a refreshing thing. "But also, I was wary."

"You are my general; it isn't my place. Besides, Erroh was happy to forgive you on the matter."

He laughed. "I asked for no forgiveness, but it's probably good that he and I are no longer at odds. Better yet, you and I are on better terms; you could have ruined me today. I'm no fool." Azel opened his mouth to defend his man, but Aymon silenced him with a casually raised hand. "For that, I am grateful. You are the greatest warrior I've ever seen. Better than Erroh, perhaps."

"Not yet, but I will be."

"He'll take that personally," Azel muttered.

She nodded. When she and Erroh met again, things would be different. Everything would be different. These Wolves were not her friends. Not yet. But they were comrades of war. Every day they went into battle against impossible numbers, hoping to make a little dent in the South's massive armour. The hours in between were spent recovering, resting and conversing. She had spoken aloud to them of Erroh and her anger. It was her right; she meant no discourtesy to his legend. Her words were merely fact. They knew well enough not to press the matter, for Erroh was their master general, but, these last few weeks, although she served Aymon first and Azel second, she was among brothers of war. She'd forgotten what it felt like to have brothers.

She shook away a distant, painful memory. There was no need to step onto that dark path this fine, victorious evening. "Let him take it however he desires," she said.

"What must you both have endured to become what you are," Aymon said, and although it was a throwaway comment, Lea was suddenly shaken. Indeed, she had suffered greatly for her crimes and the misery she had inflicted. She had endured quite a lot. Sometimes thinking of such things was an invitation to madness.

"Enough of this heavy shit," muttered Azel. He leaned in towards Lea, refilling her mug of ale. "I have a suggestion for you."

She didn't like his tone. She never liked that tone.

"You need to have another couple of these beverages," he said. "Get your head all nicely buzzing, and get yourself wonderfully furrowed by one of these rampant brutes."

She wasn't expecting that. Her hands shook. "What?"

"It'll do you good. Look at me and my boy here. Even knowing death's around the corner, we are rightly relaxed most of the time." Aymon started to laugh, and Lea gamely laughed with them. And then she drank some of her ale, and he offered a refill despite the paltry amount she'd consumed. Her heart began to hammer, although she had no idea why.

"Hey, it isn't just me trying to pervert your virtue," Azel cried, and Aymon begrudgingly agreed, and she shook her head wordlessly.

"I think I am fine," she said after a breath, but Azel wasn't close to dropping the suggestion.

"You'll feel better, and best do it tonight," he insisted. "Everything will change soon enough."

She shook her head and thought of Erroh, and the ale churned queasily in her belly. Visions of another man inside her filled her mind. Tasting every part of him. And he doing the same with her. Their breath mingling as they took their pleasure with each other. She hadn't mean to think of it at all. There were particular itches to scratch, but the idea revolted her. She did not want this. But she was becoming tired of protesting. "I'm not interested in another man."

"You think Erroh isn't furrowing any desperate damsel he can find?" mocked Azel. He was grinning at her reaction, at her frigidness.

"I couldn't care less."

But she did care. The idea of it abhorred her, and her own weakness enraged her. So, she drank and muttered a few curses under her breath at her companions, her behaviour, and a passing Wolf who she wished hadn't chosen that moment to be shirtless, revealing his finely carved chest muscles. She had always liked a man with a body like that. Like Erroh's.

Aymon smiled, but his tone was kind. "We joke, Lea, but truly, if there is someone you wish to bed, take them tonight."

"Why tonight? What are we doing come tomorrow?"

Azel giggled and refilled her drink. Again. "After this fuk here got promoted, he wouldn't sleep with me until I was promoted above recruit."

"And it's better that way, idiot. And you did get promoted," Aymon countered.

"Only when you couldn't hold out another lonely night. Slept my way to the top, I did," Azel said, winking at Lea.

"The point is, Lea," said Aymon, "I am promoting you to second general."

"Wait, that's above Azel," she gasped.

This time Azel turned severe. "It's better for the war effort. No one should be giving you orders. Better that you be the one leading us out into the Wastes."

Aymon nodded in agreement, and Lea was unsure what to say, how to act. Her head was spinning now, but for better reasons than before.

"So, to avoid a scandal, surely there are a few of the lads you'd spend tonight with," Azel added, losing his seriousness in a breath, and she could only smile. All thoughts of Erroh or any other man were lost in the moment. She had stayed in this camp out of desperation. Now she would flourish.

"I am honoured."

"Aye, you are. And now, you answer to me alone. Your banner is the Wolf."

Lea was silent for a moment. She craved none of these wonderful brutes. Not even for a night of passion and regret. But she did want every single one of them as her own. To command and to wage a terrible war with. She dropped to a knee and bowed in front of Aymon.

"Hey," cried Azel in mock alarm. "He's mine. Get your own."

52

UNLESS

It was a rainy morning. Of course, it was. The cruel, absent god, or gods, had seen to it that it rained this awful morning. It didn't matter that it usually rained in this part of the world. That didn't matter at all. As bad as the rain was, it was the cutting breeze that took his will. It may have been malevolence on the part of some hidden deity that controlled the weather this morning, but it was his own shitty timing at this shitty part of the year that had landed him here. Magnus's hair billowed in the cursed wind as it drew in from across the endless sea, and he shivered miserably in his bindings. The return had taken its toll on his tired body, but he hid his grimace behind his beard. It was all he could do on this miserable wet day. Although he had not enjoyed his return to the palace in any way this time, the people—his people—had taken great joy in his swift return. The silent glares they had offered in the days before had given way now to raucous cheering. It was a nasty thing too. His leadership did not really affect them, yet here they were, screaming bloody fuken murder as he passed through them. They demanded his head, his crown, his honour. They had no idea why, of course.

Idiots.

They had heard rumours in the wind from clans desperate for power. It was the way of the world, he supposed. They never looked beyond the fine things they had, which were better than anywhere else in the world. Instead, they believed him to be at fault for everything rightly shitty in their world. The victorious "army" followed behind his shame in single file, each warrior waving and cheering along with the crowds on either side of the path; they were triumphant and impressive. He ached for his Rangers; they would have beaten some manners into these fiends.

"To the fires with the king," he muttered under his breath, and had the people heard, they might have agreed. He had expected this treatment, this behaviour, but still, it caused him no end of shame and embarrassment to see their excessive mirth. He wondered should he continue stabbing the beast or fade away in defeat, become the reviled Magnus they thought him to be and escape with his tail between his legs.

Do not give in yet.

For the love of fuk, don't cry, either.

He would not cry. Not out here where everyone could see. He'd tasted worse moments in his life, he told himself, and he held his nerve against the misery and the unfairness of it all. It wasn't much of a plan, but his hands were tied, his bindings were tight. His options were down to nothing, however, unless...

Fuken unless.

Instead of weeping or raging, he quietly cursed the cart driver for the slow pace he was making through the busy street. The chains on each side of the cart held Magnus fast, and from his kneeling position, he tried and failed to hold his head up proudly. As the first tomato struck him, he tried to cower away.

How rich is your land that you can waste such food?

Misguided idiots.

You are all lost.

Unless I throw my last card down.

The Isle people had no fear of starvation, it seemed, and a second tomato was thrown. It struck his cheek, and he hissed at the attacker. A young girl, buoyed on by her older brothers, cheered wildly and tossed a third tomato at him. In truth, it was a fine throw. It cleared a few heads and arched up and down again to strike him. For a moment, Magnus considered roaring at her in his ungodly war tone. It might silence the crowd for a breath, give them a little scare, remind them that he was still potent. Instead, he played the defeated brute as yet more fresh vegetables and fruits were cast his way.

Tomatoes were the messiest, potatoes hurt the most, but lettuces had little effect. Thankfully, there mainly were lettuces, and he thanked the gods for the little things in life. Towards the end of the procession, when the crowd had grown even more frenzied at the entertainment, a few rocks were thrown. He expected a few of his keepers might have come to his aid, but none did, although the cart driver had the good sense to increase the pace now. Magnus took the blows stoically, for he had no choice. One jagged piece split his eyebrow open, and only then did he react. Dazed and spitting vitriol, he sought out the perpetrator, who had ducked back into the crowd.

When they arrived outside the palace, the cart, laden with bruised produce and a helping of stones, looked like a trader's store in a rich fiend's market. As they unhooked Magnus from his bindings, he could still hear the roars of dissatisfaction from his people, and it stung. He'd seen a king's lynching once in his life. There hadn't been rocks.

Children these days.

His keepers surrounded him and led him through the private entrance down to his palace. Every palace needed a prison cell, and Risbeigh was no different. They lit torches as they went deeper into the cold nothingness, and for a strange moment, Magnus wondered should he have enjoyed the rain while he could. Should he have embraced the freezing wind on his skin? Would he return? Was he too dangerous to be left alive?

I have one hand to play.

Unsurprisingly, these thoughts helped little with his unease. As they dragged him through the jail, shoved him into his cell, and attached his chains to the far wall, he fought the sudden grip of panic.

"Are my hounds alive? Can I see them?" he asked, but his jailors said little. They merely clicked the chains, locked the cell and bolted the door, and suddenly, Magnus, King of the Savage Isles, was all alone in the dark.

Time passed differently in chains. Magnus had a taste of such things, but now he found there was nothing as soul-destroying as pure darkness with only the clink of chains for comfort. He tried to move, but the effort was exhausting without food or water to fuel him. He tried to sleep away the hours, but all too frequently, his dreams were nothing but harrowing visions, and each time he shot awake and screamed into the darkness.

Alone, alone, a-fuken-lone.

He tried calling out to his jailors for the first dozen hours or so. Distantly, he could hear rumbles from the world far above as the palace staff went about the business of choosing his successor. Or better yet, the fiends who would compete for that honour.

Eventually, they came to him bearing gifts. Not very good gifts, but welcomed. They were little more than scraps and gravy, delivered every afternoon, but they were ambrosia against the gnawing pain in his stomach. Every night, an hour before sleep took him, a faceless guard would appear again, bearing a mug of lukewarm water, and he would greedily swallow it, bathing the burning, arid surface of his throat in bliss.

But mostly, he was left in silence, sitting alone in the dark while the world went along on its merry way without him. It was terrifying. Worse still was the fear of the war in the North Faction. Every moment he spent hunched up in here was a moment less upon the sea, racing desperately towards Samara before it fell.

He might have screamed out into the darkness until he was hoarse, might have dashed his fists against the wall until he could no longer move them; he might have wept until he died of thirst; he might have lain back in the dark and given up completely.

But he didn't, for he was Magnus and he had one last chance to play a part in this war. That one constant thought kept him sane in his more lucid hours.

He counted four days or so, blunted by darkness and boredom. Tired of sleeping, he'd begun stretching his body as per his old routines. More than that, he found that without vision to distract him, he could practice more complicated stretches that affected other parts of his body wonderfully. Every day he felt himself grow smoother, lither on his feet, and his knee hurt less and less. Who knew a little solitude could benefit him so much? When not stretching, he sat upright with legs crossed, resting his body as though asleep. It was an exercise his old comrade Garrick had gifted to him long before the old fool was lost forever, telling him it was a fine technique that required only practice and patience. With nobody else to talk to, it wasn't long before Magnus slipped into a near unconscious state, ever breathing, ever relaxing, ever discarding unhelpful thoughts.

There were worse ways to endure the nothingness, and although he was ever close to cracking beneath the strain and tedium of his circumstances, his body appreciated the stillness.

Within this trance, he saw his flaws, his mistakes, and, more than that, those he cared for through the eyes of truth and not through those of an overbearing father. In Elise's case, he knew now that he had suffocated her last few years with his worry when, instead, he might have let her live a better, more vibrant life even if it had meant she might have burned away sooner. He wished he could walk with her now through a lush forest where the damp air was at its freshest and proclaim his love for her just once more.

He thought of Lexi and realised her path was her own to walk without the threat of his judgement upon her. From what he knew of the little goddess, she was becoming quite a lady, and he might have done better to free her from her restraints a little more than he had. Just a little. A small amount. But enough. He wished he could have told her he trusted her choices. Trust was as important as love; he could see this now.

In the dark, he also thought deeply of Erroh, and although his anger with the boy still burned brightly, he also understood his actions. The boy was a better man than he. A softer, kinder man, which made both his heroism and his severity more impressive. He wished he could embrace the boy, tell him he loved him and admit the lessons he'd learned out walking the wastes were better than those he'd learned from his master.

All of these things would have been nice. A lesser man might have despaired at having such regrets, but it instilled in Magnus more determination. If they lived, he would offer his words of apology; he would sacrifice himself.

And if they were dead?

Well, if they were dead, he would see them on the other side.

Such thoughts comforted him as he sat in his peaceful pose, upright in his cage, until a flash of flickering fire against his closed eyes drew him back to the damp cell. He kept his eyes closed against the light for a moment, then opened them to see figures appearing before him. They were blurry at first, but he wiped his eyes, felt the sting, and brought them into focus. They stood watching him, judging him. Magnus stared at the lantern's flame until he could see them more clearly. For that is what a king did, even when he was a prisoner.

"You look a fuken ruin," Sloan hissed from outside the cage doors. Magnus wanted to shout the man down, draw him near and pummel him senseless. Instead, he merely shrugged as the light illuminated his squalid surroundings. He probably did look a ruin, but wasn't that always the way when one was reviled by the populace, when one had lost a war and been dumped in a dungeon?

"Where are my hounds?"

Beside Sloan and his waving flame was another figure; she unlocked the cage, stepped in and knelt beside him. He recognised her immediately and prepared himself for the inevitable strike to come, one that he would likely deserve.

The Actions of Gods

"They are chained and snapping, like any good savage pack," Teaolor replied. She offered him a mug of cool, fresh water, a far cry from the water he'd lived off these last few days. He drank deeply lest she rescind the offer too swiftly. "We will have trials, Magnus. Word has gone out. They will commence in three days."

Magnus sighed with relief. He had not been left behind as the world turned, after all.

"What will my fate be?"

Sloan chuckled. A cruel sound in this awful room, but a fitting sound from a classless cur. Overall, Magnus thought his chuckle suited him. "You will remain here until their conclusion, until the coronation," he said and sneered. Magnus wondered if the man realised that his voice and his behaviour resembled those of the villains in stories written for children. All he needed was a dark cloak, an oak cane and a few hounds to kick as he marched. And a dozen giggling children watching the spectacle. Magnus might have told him this and added that although they were on opposite sides, he bore the brute no ill will. They were of the same isle, were they not?

"Will you two enter these trials?" Magnus asked.

They looked uneasily at each other, and Magnus had his answer.

"Will you concede the crown for the trials, Magnus?" Sloan asked quietly. His eyes were on the door as though an entire kingdom waited beyond with word of surrender. Perhaps they did.

"Very well. I surrender my crown to the trials. I accept every entrant without question, for that is my word, and these are the old ways," Magnus proclaimed, and both were delighted with the card he had played. And why wouldn't they be happy? It was much less messy than killing the king, who was clinging to power longer than desired.

"Will you honour my last request?" Magnus asked, leaning forward. He asked the question to both, but as he spoke, he stared into Teaolor's eyes. She did not blink; she did not flinch. "Will either of you march with a shiny crown upon your head?"

"I will think on this matter," Teaolor whispered, and she took Magnus's hand and squeezed it. She begged him with those hopeful eyes to leave matters as they were. His time was done. There was only pathetic shame to be had should he play another hand in this loaded game of chance.

Unless.

"Should I win, Magnus, you will know your freedom by my hand.

More than that, I will consider this matter too. Marching into war would be a strong first kingly move indeed."

Magnus turned and stared at the younger man and wondered how committed he was. Was this a ruse to allay his fears? Or were these fools considering the more significant ramifications? What had they learned of the war? They sounded like right proper savages, and he grinned maniacally in the dark.

"This pleases me, young ones. Had such words been spoken sooner, we would not be in such a dreary place. As it is, knowing three warriors who might be king favour war is a pleasing thing. I do indeed look forward to resolving the trials."

Sloan understood before Teaolor. He rushed past her and took hold of Magnus. "You must not, you old bastard."

"Oh, but I must, for I am not done."

Teaolor took hold of him as well, desperation on her face. Perhaps she feared his potential. Perhaps she feared for his life. Losing a king in the trials would be shameful, especially if he died too soon. "Don't say it, please, Magnus."

"I wish to enter these trials, as it is my right."

"Ah, fuk me," she screamed, releasing him and shoving him away in disgust. The card was played. It was rare for a king to put himself through the brutal trials a second time. It was a legendary, magnificent pledge, though. And foolhardy for one so old. He could die, probably *would* die. At least it would show his commitment to these islands, and such acts went a long way. He hoped.

Sloan took it worse. He struck Magnus across the face, a fierce blow that took his senses. Magnus hadn't expected that and fought against the chain's hold before taking another strike in the stomach. "I'll fuken kill you," Sloan roared.

"Enough," Teaolor hissed, pulling his assailant from him. "Leave him to his foolishness; we can't have him competing with bruises covering his wrinkly old face."

"He just can't hide in the dark," Sloan shot back. "He can't just leave us to our customs. You fuker, Magnus. You complete fuker. You have no right," he roared, and fought her grip until he relented with a muttered "As he fuken wishes," before storming from the cell, leaving the room in darkness.

"You couldn't just show respect for those who will lead after?" she whispered, and it was a cutting jibe. Truthfully, he was behaving shamefully, but such was necessity. Let his name be worth shit if it brought these lands into war against true evil.

"We cannot hide in these islands anymore, little one," he countered, but she wasn't listening. She turned to leave.

"We will make arrangements," she hissed and left him to his silence.

It was a day and a night before his next guest arrived, and he was less than welcome.

"Hello, Your Majesty," Padir whispered from outside the open cage door. Magnus, resting cross-legged against the far wall, opened his eyes to the intruder, who stood with a bucket and rag in one hand, looking at him curiously. Behind the boy, and the open door he came from, shone the light of a warm season's day, and Magnus squinted against its sting. "I wasn't certain what you were doing there all silently. I thought you might have died. But you didn't."

Magnus exhaled slowly and wondered if he could reach the boy and drag him in with him, where he could exact a bit of vengeance. No one would notice; no one would even care.

"I know that look. I've seen it myself a thousand times," the betrayer warned, and pulled a key from his pocket. "Now, if you pledge not to kill me, I'll let you try this key in that lock over there."

He grinned in mock triumph. There was only a little fear behind those untrustworthy eyes.

"You had best not be in this place when the chains come free."

"*If* the chains come free—of course," he countered, and tossed the key to Magnus's waiting hand.

"I should kill you for your betrayal, you little shit."

"No, you have no right to attack me, Your Highness. I am of these lands, and even though I am but a wretch, I have still earned the right to criticise your ways and behaviour, and I probably know you better than anyone left in these isles."

The chains crashed to the ground, and Magnus was free to roam, to devastate. To fuken destroy. He leapt upon the boy, who offered no resistance. Magnus struck him once, but Padir merely grinned and spat away the blood from his lip.

"Look at you, brave Magnus. Attacking a boy for no great reason."

"I have my reasons."

"And I have mine," shouted the boy, who pushed away from his grip, climbed to his feet and stood over Magnus. "You know the ways of our people. You, Magnus, the greatest of us all. The warrior king of legend. Your place was ruling our lands."

Such was the passion in the younger man's voice that Magnus held off throttling him again. If only for a breath before the actual beating. Thing was, the boy's passion was winning him over.

"You said none of this on the road."

"I said fuken plenty, but you were too driven by your desires to listen. I would follow you to the ends of the world, but only if you were worthy. Instead, our king—our fuken king—hides away and answers to another from the golden city of light. You had no right to anything but the offering up of your crown."

Magnus climbed to his feet. The boy was screaming now. Such an outburst was impressive from someone facing certain death. "I was trying to ensure peace," Magnus said quietly. He felt diminished.

"Peace or war is irrelevant, my king. It is our ways that matter. You have no right to throw your might against everything our nation stands for because you alone believe yourself right. That is not our way."

For a time, the boy said nothing more, and Magnus leaned back against the walls of the cage. He suddenly felt weary. It had taken only a few days in this dreadful place, and now a daunting truth was being shoved in his face.

Magnus glared at him. "Why do you come to me now, boy?"

Padir reached into the bucket and pulled out a soapy rag, which he wrung out.

"You can hardly face the trials looking a ruin," he said. "I'm theoretically your squire, so I take this time to assist you." He took a step towards Magnus, who took a step back. "I'll clean your face, but that's it."

"No. Why do you serve me when my actions disgust you so deeply?"

For a breath, Padir thought on this and shrugged. "You are following the proper ways by surrendering your crown to the trials. For this, I respect you."

"I will enter. Does that shock you too?"

"No, my liege. It is an honourable thing and, truly, a way out of this awful business." He drew a sweet roll from his cloak and held it out. Magnus didn't hesitate; he snatched the creamy deliciousness, shoved it into his mouth and barely chewed before swallowing.

Padir watched him, smiling faintly. "Unless, of course, I'm lying, and I just laced that cake with poison that'll klll you in a few breaths. Or

The Actions of Gods

worse, have you shitting your pants for the next three days. Wouldn't that be funny? You, all brave, risking everything—and taking a shit at the same time." At this, he laughed, and Magnus licked his lips—a small matter.

"You think I will have a chance?" Magnus asked. He didn't need to know the answer. He didn't even believe it himself, but it was his last card, and although he'd competed decades before, experience would not count for much in a competition such as this. He'd told himself this for many a night, and it brought little reassurance. That he was the oldest man in the field meant nothing, too, he supposed, nor that he was the oldest king ever to attempt such a ludicrous challenge.

I'm so fuked.

"I doubt you'll live to see the end, my liege, but I will cheer you until you pass, or fail, or get eliminated, or get lost, or just whatever," the boy said, laughing merrily. "And then I'll continue with my march."

53

CALMING THE HERD

Mea left Holt's cabin to face Boat Town feeling a little easier, a bit lighter than before. She noticed Doran appeared lighter too. Who knew a little humanity was all it took to lighten the load? She imagined he felt relieved there was someone else to carry some of the weight in the days ahead. He smiled slightly for a time as they walked side by side through the inner veins of their fortress. His pace matched her own. Her step was assured for a moment, her shoulders a little less slumped, until their path brought them into the way of their dignified ambushers.

My angry sisters.

The women were all dressed in their finery, painted for allurement. This was the season's social event, and in the light from many burning torches they carried, they looked their best. She might have guessed there were a hundred of them, perhaps more. All silent, side by side, waiting and watching and readying themselves to voice their concerns. They did not come with sharpened blades or deadly intent, however, but with grievances. No Wolves dared approach them, but they were nearby should things take a nasty nautical turn. Against the gloomy midnight sky, they shimmered in the torchlight.

"My sisters," Mea began, and the crowd were telling in their silence. At the back of her mind, where she stored her worries, she had expected such an ambush. Still, she felt unprepared. She had been meeting with them daily, but it seemed that her appeasing words had not been enough. There always came a time when a gathered mass erupted in frustration. The pitchforks usually followed. She scanned the pretty female faces and saw no weapons on their persons. They were lethal enough without blades, hammers or pitchforks, but the lack of weapons was a hopeful sign. "You are out late this quiet night," she offered, seeking their leader. Anyone with authority beyond the usual bitching and complaints. Someone headstrong enough to spur these fantastic goddesses to action.

A tall girl in golden and white silk with long, flowing blonde hair stepped forward. She was of age, although perhaps had yet to cull. Mea knew her as Melinda. There was something in her pretty resting gaze that Mea found appealing. The girl spoke for them, but it was plain she was no leader. A mother could tell these things.

"We are displeased with matters, Mydame," Melinda warned, and Mea folded her arms. She'd always remembered Dia striking similar poses when challenged by an upstart. She added a cruel stare, but it was nowhere near as cutting as the looks her predecessor was capable of.

Give me a few more weeks alive, and I will perfect that too.

"My sisters, I know you are angry. I feel the strain as you do." Beyond this gathered mass of feminine mob, she could see out into the dark water, where a small rowboat bearing a beige banner drew near. She knew it to be a messenger from Aymon's Wolves, no doubt requesting Doran's return, delivering word of the land's current clashes, suggesting improbable strategies. One of these days, his scrolls would provide a little good news for once. One of these days, she was likely to hop aboard with them and sail away from responsibility altogether.

"We float here and slowly starve, and all the while those brutes tear our home asunder. We must fight Mydame; we were born for it," Melinda continued, and Mea agreed. The girl made fine points, but the truth was a harsh pill to swallow. "You keep us here as near prisoners, and there is a war to fight."

To lose, too.

Mea's stomach churned, for she could sense their growing agitation. The surface beneath her feet began to rise and fall ever so. She leaned lightly against a wooden beam beside her without changing her stance; she wished to appear nonchalant but also to stop herself tipping over. That wouldn't appear strong at all. Nor did having her leadership questioned out in the open. She thought back for a few moments; as the city fell and the flames grew, she wondered if she might have found a way to move the Cull's domineering podium aboard with the rest of the supplies they had taken. She could have created her own room of the Cull for such meetings. Could have painted the wooden walls in a similar black, made a right domineering vessel, all for her benefit. Was that not a Primary's finest ally? Was it worth a dozen souls left behind? Not at all. Life was precious at the end of the world too.

"Do you have no answer for us?" Melinda sneered, playing the vile challenger perfectly, and the other females were rightly stirred at her outrage. This was no good at all. Many great things had fallen apart under lesser things such as this.

She leaned away from the beam, and her feet felt impossibly light, as though she could float right over the nearest edge into the dark waters. "My sisters, the hour is late. We draw nearer to the end." She looked at all who faced her and imagined how she might have felt were she among them, blinded by grief and outrage as they were. They could only see what was in front of them. Of course, they would gladly choose blood over common sense. But she was a little wiser now; a little more bitter, too. She understood Dia far more now than she had ever imagined she could. Saw her good points and forgave her shortcomings. In turn, of course, for any of these wonderful warring females to see as she did would require them to see the world for what it was. To suffer the heartache she had endured. To make those cutting choices that reached down into the soul and tore it asunder. How could they see the distance they were from salvation?

Oh, what have I done?

Not for the first time, she questioned her decision to flee the burning city without any attempt at a counterattack. Every one of these goddesses would have joined the battle. Would have offered quite the fight, too. Her better sense served her when these darker thoughts took her. It would have been a fantastic defiance worthy of many a tale, and perhaps the perfect end to a well-lived life. She imagined that Uden, the bastard destroyer, would have stood upon a mound of Northern dead as high as Spark's walls, and that would have been that.

"We have only begun," snapped Melinda, and Mea stepped to her.

"Remember who you speak to," she warned coldly, and the girl nodded unconsciously. At that moment, Mea remembered herself. She remembered her resolve. "We draw nearer to the end, and we will fight. But know that this is no war, my sisters." Her voice was strong, and they listened. She placed her hand on Melinda's shoulder. "You crave murder and vengeance, and I do too, but heroism is for the dead. With such evil at our waterlogged gates, all we can do now is survive." Her words were truthful, and shocking even to her. This was no war they could win. Such thoughts were unfamiliar to any Alphaline, but a Primary accepted them well enough. Her pledge was to the survival of civilisation. "All we can do is live, for that is a fine vengeance."

"But, Mydame, we must stand up and fight against such things. Others, out there in the Wastes, fight as we hide."

"Every single one of you is free to leave, but until there is an advantage, until there is a war to be won, I will not sacrifice the best of us." That was it. They had made their feelings known, but she would not be swayed. No number of flaming torches would quell her doubts in this matter. They were alive this night. Every day was a step closer towards more extraordinary things. She needed only a moment, a spark of hope, and then they could be unleashed in all their fury.

Beyond, as though drawn like moths by the gathering of torches, she could see the boat drawing closer to the edge of Boat Town. A few Wolves greeted them wearily. She knew this, for there were raised voices, but nothing out of the ordinary. For a moment, she wondered could it be a group of Southerners dressed in the clothing of murdered Wolves, but she dismissed it outright. That's what passwords were for, right?

Right?

As she finished addressing the women, Doran stepped forward. His voice would carry weight with them. He had once said he had been an unappealing choice in the Cull, but she'd always thought him charming and decent looking. Now, though, even after the attentions of Celeste, any female would have battled tooth and nail for him as mate. More than that, they listened to him, respected him.

"You wonderful creatures know little of war," he began, "but you can learn. You can do more and be ready for when the time of war does come upon us." His tone was a master general's, and the ambushers faded under his bark. He was not cutting; he was simply himself, and a few of the women nodded as the appeal of Belinda's suggested mutiny seemed to disappear. "You spend your time below decks complaining of the unfairness. But I would welcome you all into action. War comes in more forms than blades." At this, they visibly diminished. "Put your energies into benefitting this miserable place instead of assailing your Primary at this ungodly hour." His tone was like Jeroen's when Tye had behaved unbearably over a foolish matter. She could have hugged him right here, in this place, such was her gratefulness.

But then, something caught her eye. A figure. Tall, imposing and impressive. But as he walked through the crowd, she could see he was a shambolic ruin, utterly reduced from the man she had last seen. Her heart broke and lifted all in a moment. Her stern face cracked into a disbelieving smile. She was a young female again, and she had just claimed him, and there was nothing but terrifying joy in the world.

"Oh, Jeroen," she gasped, and the females, no doubt perturbed by his presence as he pushed through their defiant little stand, separated so the mother of their city could reunite with her chosen love. There were gasps and excited cries as the whispered truths filtered through the crowd. In that moment, all talk of retribution faded as a perfect couple found themselves together again.

"My love," he whispered, looking tired beneath that shabby beard. He hobbled, swayed on the uneven deck, and she ran to him on feet that were suddenly lithe. No wavering at all.

"By the gods, you have returned to me," she wailed, and he embraced her, and she collapsed with him upon the deck, and there was no one else around but him. She wept openly, behaved as no Primary would, and couldn't care less. He held her, and she him, and he was so weak and ruined, and she loved him, and nothing else mattered.

"I will never leave you again," he pledged, and for once, it was a fine pledge. Her guards, unsure where to look or how to behave, disappeared quietly into the night. As did those whom Doran had shamed. The rest watched for a few breaths more, all dissent lost to the wonderful spectacle of two so old, still so loving, still so in love, for that was what they themselves wanted in mates.

Finally, Mea and Jeroen were alone, in the dark, upon their knees on the unsteady deck, holding each other, never daring to let go again.

"Wherever you march, I will follow," she promised him in return, and it was a fine pledge.

54

THE POLITICIAN

Elise sat opposite the brute and studied his body movements and his features. She could see the desire. That was the only part of himself he allowed to show openly, and that was fine. She could make use of that. "Tell me, what else can I do for your people?" she cooed. She sipped the glass of wine and swished the liquid around her mouth before swallowing. It wasn't pleasant, but one wasn't inclined to complain when enjoying grand enough things before the end. And it was the end; their scouts had determined the Southern fuks were not too far away.

It's time.
It's fuken time to rise.

"Nothing, my dear. You have done enough these last few days." He smiled. A rare thing from such a threatening brute. He had a nice smile. It made him appear handsome, open and kind. That was probably why he chose to grimace most days. The grimace was a pleasing, threatening look to him as well. "Not many have been so welcoming." It was true. She had done quite a lot since their arrival. At least for him and his kin. Truthfully, it wasn't too hard to manipulate a few extra luxuries, arrange better accommodations for his gathering of warrior bandits. She'd wasted a little favour of her own and owed a little in repayment, but ensuring Bison was pleased with her, valued her, and got to know her was most important. And he had.

"I aim to please, Bison," she whispered, stretching across his bedding. He was quite the gentleman. There were limited places to rest in this little hovel, but he had offered the bed willingly. Bison himself sat nearby upon a barrel, looking mightily impressive as he towered over her, and she felt like a delicate waif in comparison. Elise was no fool—she was twice his age—but he was an older-minded fool, entrenched in the old way of thinking where females knew their place. Men like him were frequently drawn to strong women, although they rarely knew why. And Bison was drawn to little old her. It didn't hurt that her body was firm in all the right places, that her rear was as tight as the waist belt she buckled, or that her jawline was as sharp as his steel. She was older than any childbearing girl, but any hot-blooded fool would take her to bed if given the offer.

"You please me just fine," he whispered, and he smiled, and he was trying to charm her, and it was easy.

She smiled back and spread her legs wide upon the bed. Hardly a womanly thing to do, but a brute like him would enjoy such a view. It didn't matter that a layer of silk and leather guarded her modesty. What mattered was her subtle offer of what lay in his future, so to speak.

"Not yet, but let us see how matters unfold." She played a part, and she played it well. He sipped his wine, no doubt thinking of smoother words, desperate words to remove her undergarments. Of furrowing her through the day, the night, even to the dawn beyond. Or perhaps he would be done with her after a swift slog. It could go any way with a man like him. She lay in the bedding, looking at the wooden ceiling above their heads. If they did furrow, everyone would hear. They would talk. That was the curse of the upper parts of Adawan: no privacy. At first, what she thought was a better life beneath the stars and fresh air, turned out to be a hovel fit for a hound. She lived in a palace far below.

"Deep in the heart of this salt mine where I rest my rear, a male and female could make all sorts of noises, and none would hear," she said. As though she had conjured them, a few passers-by muttered about the cost of market cheese in wartime, and she laughed as their voices filtered away into the growing mass of voices nearby. "I do find it strange that Ulrik would afford me such fine bedchambers, yet here you are, an entitled man, leader of so many, resigned to a wretched shack among the dregs of us." She could see his irritation at this notion. She was but a new bandit queen to their ranks. She did make a fine point about her quarters, though.

Regardless of insult, he did not rise to the bait. Instead, he focused on the problem at hand. Her virtue, to be exact. "I want you, Elise. I've not wanted to destroy a woman like you in quite a time. Take your clothes off."

Smooth.

She giggled. An alluring giggle. A charmed giggle. To keep him baited, but also distant.

"Of course you do. I'm incredible in the sack." She smiled, bit her lip, and looked around worriedly. "There's a lot of sacks in this... palace."

He dropped to his knees beside her. His hand reached out and rested on her thigh. "It is no palace for a woman like you, but when I'm in you, you won't care."

"I am a lady. And I do look forward to allowing you in me. But not among these sacks and listening to talk of cheese and shit. Besides, if I lie with you, Ulrik will not be best pleased."

"Ulrik does not lie with ladies."

"I am his named ally. I am his to command, and a lady like me has earned a bit of favour."

Bison slid his hand between her thighs, and she shook a little at the gentle invasion. There was little subtlety to this brute. He had powerful arms; she liked powerful arms. A man could do a lot with powerful arms. Magnus could. She couldn't take Magnus in a fistfight. But she could beat him if need be. With the smarter plan. With the proper leverage. Bison held his mighty hand there, and she exhaled slowly, pressing back ever so. Ever so. It had been a time since a man had touched her like this. She liked being handled there, just not at this cost.

"I'm not that type of lady," she warned, looking at his hand. She dared a sip of wine. "Among the many things you will claim when you take this haven, you will get all of me. Although perhaps in my quarters," she said, sniffing, and with a gentle squeeze that caused her a ripple of pleasure, he released his grip, and she sighed. "But not until you take the throne." She wasn't the only benefit that came with leadership, but she was a little incentive. Sometimes that was all it took.

He slipped his hand away completely, and his face turned serious. "With the enemy at the gate, such a grasp at power would be a foolish manoeuvre. Best we all stick together," he offered, and she did not like his tone, not one little bit. She knew he was neither a fool nor a fearful coward, but somewhere in between. She needed to twist him to her means. She just needed the proper leverage.

"It's never good to have two such hounds in the cage. The people speak of your prowess. Your threat. In truth, Ulrik is a good man. A very good man. But now, we need a warrior to lead us. More than that, we need the two of us together, saving us all." It was a risky manoeuvre on her part, but she'd spent many days working on this. She had tickled and teased him, playing his desires, just waiting to pounce. He was a brute, and rightfully feared Ulrik as much as Ulrik feared him. Both should have learned to fear more than the other man, but it was a small matter.

She slid beside him, took his hands and held them to her chest. Distantly, she heard passing voices discussing the outbreak of rats, and thoughts of a dreadful siege flittered into her mind. She'd seen the effect of a siege before; such a thing would be a colossal mistake in Adawan. Sometimes it took more than waiting the bastards out.

"You can beat him. More than that, I can intervene immediately should it turn."

"Intervene? Oh, yes—you talk about this violence as a small matter. What good can a lady like you do should I need assistance?"

She smiled and gripped his wrist; she allowed him a breath to understand her intentions. He smiled, and she twisted. His smile turned to a grimace of agony, and she rolled with his suffering, smooth and feminine like the goddess she was.

"Oh, fuk me," he cried, and she was upon him now, controlling and at ease. Had Ulrik offered such a target, she might have beaten him. She knew better, though.

"I will… when we win," she whispered in his quivering ear. "And what do you promise me when we win?"

"I'm no fool. There's no agreement needed. I would place our forces in your hands ten times above anything else," he promised, which pleased her. Her legend had clearly reached as far as Bison's ears; her aptitude for war, too. He might be a cruel bastard of a leader, but he was smart enough to play to her strengths. She eased, left him scrambling on the floor, and stood over him. She liked this angle.

"You crazy bitch," he snarled, but he wore the grin of an old-minded man impressed by a feminine touch. She offered her hand and pulled him to his feet. As she did, she grabbed his manhood through his breeches before kissing him on the lips. One good turn deserved another. He did not fight her; he merely enjoyed the assault, which pleased her.

You'd better hope Magnus never learns about you.

"When I warn you it is time, be ready. Be fuken fierce," she said and, squeezing him gently, released him before swiftly escaping his quarters, leaving him standing dumbly in the room with an aroused manhood and a goofy, idiotic grin upon his face.

. . .

"Did it go well?" Kaya asked from her seat outside. Elise raised a knowing eyebrow and beckoned her to follow. A politician's work was never done. It didn't matter the slime they crawled through or the acts they performed as long as they were justified in their actions.

Spitting in the dirt several times, she strode through the crowd. There was a terrible energy in the air this morning, and she was moments away from igniting a spark that could take them all.

To greatness or failure.

"Where is he?" she muttered to the girl matching her every step.

"Are you sure about all of this, Elise?"

Without warning, Elise stopped, grabbing Kaya by the shoulder as she did. "Again? You ask this? Again? I know you care for him, fuk, even I do too, but if we wish to survive this war, we must do this."

Kaya knocked her hand away, her eyes cold. "I'm with you, Elise. Do not test my loyalty, and I will not test yours."

The two women stared at each other for a breath, and the tension passed. It was natural on the cusp of a siege, a charge, a desperate leap towards greatness.

"Forgive me, little one. That fuker just brings out the worst in my behaviour."

Kaya leaned in close. "What did he say this time to rile you up so much that you try to start a fuken war in this place?"

"He was no worse than normal," Elise muttered, marching on but with less haste. She was flustered after the meeting. Best she play her part coldly. There was nothing worse than a fiery Alphaline with a flustered outlook. She began to count in her head.

One, two, three.
He grabbed me between the legs. Four, five, six.
It wasn't the worst.
Seven, eight, nine.
It's been so fuken long.
Fuken ten.

"It was just his grabby hands, a little more than normal."

"I can think of worse fates than getting bedded by that brute."

Ten, ten, fuken, ten.

Strangely, Kaya's smile made her feel better. "I trust you, little one, but I know the depths of betrayal." Instinctively, she took the girl in an embrace. This was her last card to play. She needed to play it well. The exotic girl beside her was a tonic to her fears and doubts.

"Come on. He's out by the first line, inspecting the defences and probably taking credit for your work."

"Our work."

They strolled through the green shade towards the burning sands, silent but for a few easy comments of the thick defensive lines cut into the ground that the Southerners would face when they came a-charging. Sooner rather than later was the opinion around the campfires most nights. At least seven or eight thousand in all, by their scout's estimates. A hefty number of Uden's savages, all for little old Adawan. It wasn't the first tactical mistake on Uden's part to send so many, either. It was only a shame he hadn't sent more. Enough that they could hold, not enough to be overrun. Just as Erroh's little defiance in the town of Keri had reverberated throughout the lands, so too would the unimportant sand pit of Adawan change the war.

As long as I control our forces.

Not so long ago, knowing of Bison's reluctance to challenge Ulrik's position a week before might have been a comfort at these trying times, but alas, as the Hunt drew nearer, the chance that Ulrik would not go on the offensive was too great a risk to take. She needed to make sure. Ulrik would get over it or hang for his stubbornness.

They climbed free of the shade and caught sight of the fantastic brute himself, standing at ease with his last line of defenders. Carrying a jug of water that he shared with any defender with a parched tongue, he walked among the warriors, watching the distant horizon and the gathering cloud of dust slowly rising into the flawless blue sky above.

"Well, look at the hero, coming to ensure his soldiers are wet," she called, and he laughed, as did his soldiers. Truthfully, she admired him: admired his assuredness, his grim determination. He would do anything to protect his flock. Even die. Such a thing was admirable, if not a little narrow-minded. A man like him should have stared at the sky and seen the potential.

Ulrik marched up to the waiting females, still offering water to any outstretched hand as he did, and there were many, for it was a blazing hot day. Truthfully, there was no shortage of water. Any of the warriors could have walked a few feet to drink from the nearest water barrel, freshly stocked, freshly cooled. It was the gesture, the principle of the matter.

"I just met with Bison," she warned, and his face darkened. "Aye, not good news, just as before," she added. She took the mug from him and poured it over her hair. Wonderful refreshing water covered her, and she squealed in delight. Looking off to the Southern idiots, marching towards them in the hottest hours of the day, she imagined what price any of them would pay for refreshment as cool as this.

It'll only get worse, fukers.

He was about to ask about the dreadful news and press her about the lies she spun him, but Kaya dropped to her knees, her hands cupping her face. "Oh, no, it can't be."

Ulrik turned, following her gaze out across the burning sands to the little group of haggard wanderers marching towards them. "It can't be..." he echoed.

For a breath, she wondered was it a Southern ploy to deceive, and then she recognised the hulking form of Wrek, the kind-hearted giant who had helped save her cub. And then she saw Tye, and her heart leapt for the boy and Mea.

And then she was running.

It was instinct.

She couldn't believe it. Wouldn't believe it. She refused to believe it. It was her.

"It can't be," the girl cried, staring across the burning sands at her. It was.

"It can't be," Elise cried as the tears fell, and she gazed at her daughter stumbling along with her haggard companions. "My daughter," she mumbled. "Alexis," she roared, and they met, and the world was right again; her will was restored. She wept as the girl wailed in her arms.

"Mom?"

"I'm here, my love; I have you now," she whimpered, and held the girl tightly lest she break and, with it, her mind. She heard soldiers thundering out to greet them, their voices loud and powerful. She held Lexi tight, though, and refused to let go, and the screaming worsened. Kaya was upon one of the females, attacking with her fists in wonderful combinations, taught to her by the Alphaline herself. The pretty girl with the mud on her brow and the stunning eyes was struck again and again, and she did not fight back, and Wrek was down on his knees with his hands upon his head. Soldiers were grabbing at him, roared on by Ulrik. Elise was too speechless to react, even when Tye was taken to the ground by three soldiers, charging him as though he were a Southerner. She caught sight of the last girl, as wretched as Lexi, pulling Kaya away from her victim only to scream shrilly and embrace Kaya like a sister before both girls collapsed upon their knees, weeping. She saw Tye chained and beaten, but it didn't seem real. She could only embrace Lexi, who saw none of this, for she was weeping into her chest, which was fine. For these wet moments, nothing else mattered.

Not even saving the fuken world.

55

ARMY OF ONE

Rasmuus had endured enough of this march. Of this war. Of all of it, really. He doubted he was alone in that, for this was no war. This was a half-hearted invasion with awful repercussions. As he rode atop his Southern mount, the sun burned his neck, flies kept sticking to his skin, his mouth was already parched, and his belly was sick from his paltry rations. He was done. Finished.

"How far?" a voice from behind called, and he sighed. As finished as he was with this war, he had little choice but to continue. "It's a little warm in the saddle today," the voice went on. It was his sister, Sara. The favoured child too. Different fathers but a dutiful mother, who was back home in the South, resting her old knees. He'd like to have relaxed his own knees a while. Instead, he was driving a Finger through a deep forest carrying supplies for a war he knew nothing of.

"I know how warm it is," he countered. It was supposed to be a cooler season, but now and then, when he wasn't prepared for it, the fuken sun blazed and burned, and he could only mutter under his breath and obey the will of their god. Although few said as much, he wasn't alone in his distaste for their leader. They were a nomadic race, and this gathering under one banner was becoming rightly frustrating. "It'll be cooler down at the water's edge." He knew that would silence her for a time. She was constantly questioning everything more than he. Perhaps that's why he led this Finger. Or rather, was cursed to lead this Finger. And she stuck by his side. He was one of Uden's youngest-ever generals, and Sara was two years younger than he was. She had all the time in the arth to become *the* youngest ever general, and

Rasmuus wouldn't deny her such an honour. That said, shunting supplies across the arth to support the actual fighters was hardly a task that would bring her much notoriety or add much glory to his own leadership.

Sara was already looking to the next concern she had with this march. She was always swift to complain and challenge his actions. Only in private, though. Out here in the saddle, leading a wretched convoy of at least two hundred swine, a dozen dozen herds of cattle, and thrice both numbers in poultry, they could meander along at a crawl, and she would speak her mind.

"We should have reached the bridge by now," she grumbled. "Those Riders should have returned sooner as well; I have a bad feeling about this day," she said, bringing her horse alongside his. On many matters, she was right. Without their entourage to escort them, their pace was inviting to any manner of murderers and bandits.

"Nonsense, girl, we have little to worry about. They've scouted the path ahead, and there is no sign or sound of menacing things in the forest," he replied confidently, and she nodded apprehensively. He couldn't help but notice her crossbow lay in her lap, already primed and loaded. A foolish thing, for she was useless with the weapon and likelier to shoot herself or the back of her unfortunate mount's head.

"More and more Fingers are disappearing in the Wastes with nothing but blood along the path they took."

"It is war, Sara, and those sorts of things occur on the outskirts." He looked around confidently; this was Hunt territory. Aye, he'd heard of Fingers and entire battalions being eradicated but there were plenty allies located a few miles along either stretch of the road. Despite his expectations, they'd survived this exhausting march north without incidents or banditry. They were not far from Samara, the cursed city of light. Only a lunatic would drag their army into such hostile land for the sake of a few supplies.

Enough supplies to feed a starving city.

Sara wasn't done. She was pale this morning, paler than usual. Rasmuus's mind immediately went to an extreme. He wondered was she with child. Brave, enthusiastic fools had dared his ire by attempting to bed her these last few weeks. It was a brother's prerogative to refuse them, especially if she had high ideas about her command.

"What about the demons?" she challenged, and blessed herself with the old god's signs, and he hissed at her to cease the practice lest those few hundred behind them catch sight of her. A thing like that could get back to their god, after all. Rasmuus didn't believe in an all-seeing eye, but he believed rightly in the value of a loose tongue.

"There are no demons. They are tales spoken by the fire, whispered and grown to nothing," he argued, but she knew he'd sat among those listeners and gasped at tales of the demons as she did. She blessed herself again, although this time with more subtlety. "Come on. Let us think on better matters, like why we two fools are running supplies instead of taking to war." It was an attempt to distract her from worrying thoughts of gathered forces surrounding them as they rolled slowly through this area perfect for an ambush spot.

"Ah, better things indeed," she muttered, but her eyes were on the surrounding forest.

For a time more, they followed the path their comrades would have taken until, hearing the reassuring hum of rushing water, they came upon the bridge they were to set down upon. As expected, all thirty of their mounted comrades had arrived at this spot long before.

And met their deaths.

"Oh no! Please, no," Sara cried. Her crossbow dropped from her saddle, but she held it in a weak hand. "No!"

He was well aware she knew some of the Riders better than he. Not too well, he hoped. She screamed at the sight of them all, lying in the sun upon their backs, all dead, cut and torn, staring into the darkness beyond. But it wasn't the bodies of the dead or the many mounts neatly hobbled along the bridge as though on parade that unsettled Rasmuus the most. It was the one soul who had survived this massacre.

"Who are you?" he demanded, but he already knew. The figure stood among the dead. He was covered in blood but carried no injury. He merely stood in silence as they approached.

"It's the demons," a voice cried from behind them. The loud rush, grind, creak and wail of carts and livestock drawing to a slow stop filled the air, but Sara brought her mount forward, and Rasmuus followed.

It is no demon.

It is far worse.

The figure stood and gazed at them from among the fruits of his impressive killing, and Rasmuus felt a shudder run through his body. Riders were fearless, devastating warriors, or at least that's what they'd have any lesser Southerners believe. And certainly, for one brute to have slain thirty warriors was terrifying and godly.

Beside him, Sara dropped from her horse, tears streaming down her face. Rasmuus could see her agony, but he was unmoved. He felt their loss as she did, though perhaps a little less. He saw beyond his own emotion, for he was a general, and she was not. And while she saw a solitary warrior fit for killing no more than thirty feet away, Rasmuus saw a god deciding their fate.

"Hold," he cried, but she didn't listen. She raised the crossbow, stumbled forward and fired. A loose shot, chest high. Erroh, as Rasmuus knew him to be, eased himself wide of the stray bolt, and it flew past harmlessly, embedding itself in one of the bridge's support beams. Erroh looked at the bolt with mild curiosity, then held his arm aloft as though holding back an invisible army, and Rasmuus did the same.

"Do not fire again," Rasmuus warned, and Sara dropped to her knees, weeping. She clutched her belly and threw up, and he dropped beside her. He did not raise a blade; he dared not challenge the watching god, who removed his blades from their scabbards and held them loosely along each blood-covered thigh.

"Do not try that again, or you will die at my hands," the god said, and he was terrifying. Those few remaining soldiers marching in behind Rasmuus and Sara gathered up around the front of the cart. Were there to be an ambush anywhere along the line of carts, the battle would be over in moments. Rasmuus did not fear another attack; he feared the god alone, who stood with swords drawn but not raised, not yet.

"I offer one mercy this day," Erroh intoned. "Those who will march with me may bow. Those still fighting their doomed fight for Uden may leave freely."

It was a trap—an offensive manoeuvre by a deceitful god. There were over a hundred of his comrades who might draw against him. At least two dozen crossbow wielders on top of that too. He looked back and considered for a breath the fate of this Finger, of his own faith and fate. And of his broken sister weeping in the dust.

Drahir watched from the edge of the treeline as the two groups exchanged words. For hours he'd waited in the shade while Erroh alone stood out, inviting an entire army to defeat him. Drahir's heart hammered, watching their leader take such a chance. Around him, dozens of comrades watched silently as their leader battled wits with the newcomers. "For mercy," Erroh had suggested as they stood over the bodies of the Riders, and he had grown to know well these weeks that such a word from this warmonger was a strange thing. If nothing else,

Erroh showed little mercy to those who raised a blade. There was something strange and cold in his eyes when he'd directed the rest of their comrades into cover. In truth, he'd looked a sight facing them down with nothing but a ploy as cover. It was marvellous and foolish. Terribly foolish. But whatever Erroh desired, they granted, and truthfully, Erroh had done more than enough to earn this obedience and trust.

Drahir watched them more closely as the girl wailed in the dust; truthfully, he felt for her loss. Seeing a friend or, worse, family lost was no small matter. He felt his heart grow heavy about how close he himself had come to discovering family once more before it was taken from him.

"Take the mercy, please," he whispered to the wind. For as foolish and brazen and careless as the plan Erroh had suggested was, to spare a few lives was an excellent reward. For days, they had scouted this fine convoy and its riches. A tempting target, no doubt bound for the city, this treasure would help their cause tenfold, but more than that, it would hurt the city's supply line. In a dreadful war without any hope of victory, these moments made it that little bit more bearable. He wished he could hear Erroh's words, but they were lost in the wind, as were those of the terrified Southerners. The sight of Erroh upon the bridge among the dead was as impressive as that of Uden upon a stage, taking a young boy's head from his shoulders.

There was movement among the challengers for a time as a few of them argued, but finally all but about a half-dozen of them began to drop to their knees. The rest stood with blades raised, but they made no charge, and a fine thing too. A half-dozen was fine for Erroh. He'd seen that for himself too.

There were further protests, and there was pleading, but in the end, the holdouts surrendered. Drahir might have had these fiends put to death, but the generous god of the bridge let them live. More than that, he offered them the mounts of the dead warriors. Whether this was a parting gift or simply to add credibility to the stories that would be told, Drahir would never know.

Tales of one warrior killing thirty Riders and staring down an army and not blinking first were worth six warriors returning to the fold. Worth some mercy too.

Only once the surrendered warriors had fled atop their mounts and the Finger was turning slowly towards their new base did Drahir and his comrades appear from the forest with clean blades and looks of disbelief.

They cheered their master, their leader, their god. They sang songs of certain victories to come. And Erroh, upon a mount of his own, was quiet in accepting the praise. His mind was on future things, his face grave.

"When that girl shot that bolt, I thought you were done for, thought I had allowed our fearless leader to fall over a foolish notion of mercy," Drahir said quietly, and Erroh nodded.

"Hardly fearless," he said. "In any case, she escaped, much to the dismay of…" He looked around at the Finger's leader. He was shaken; he looked as though the sight of his slain comrades had taken its toll. With a start, Drahir recognised him: a young general destined to wallow in Uden's army.

"I cannot remember his name; I should have remembered his name," Erroh said, following Drahir's gaze.

"He still draws breath; I'm sure he will not mind. I know him too. This was a fine mercy on our part."

"To the fires with mercy," Erroh spat. "I thought showing mercy might stir something within me, but truly, I struggle." He took a deep breath. "I almost called for you to kill them all. Right at the end. After hours of waiting in the fuken heat covered in dead Southern blood."

"But you didn't, and it is all the more impressive. Wars are won with such clever ploys."

"I dare say I will not try such foolishness again."

"Aye, perhaps so. But today, we have struck a blow to the belly of the Hunt, and such things can influence tides, stir dissent, and improve our chances in the next skirmish for all we know."

"I think I prefer an easy kill. More honour in less deceit. You say we struck a blow? I have a taste for something more, Drahir. We must do more than merely chip away at such daunting numbers. We need to cut deep."

"What do you suggest?"

"Something great. Something bigger. Something brutal."

"So… what do you suggest?"

For a moment, Erroh smiled. "We need to go to a little place called Adawan and gather some unwilling fighters for our cause."

56

WORDS BETWEEN BROTHERS

Wrek had regrets. Depthless regrets. Sometimes it seemed his entire life was just a heap of wretched, regrettable events. He'd failed as a leader; failed as a warrior too. He thought of Raven Rock, and as usual, his stomach clenched, and he tasted bile. He was only a handful of years older than the others, but strangely, he'd thought of them not only as friends and comrades but also as a father would his own children on the cusp of greatness. A failed father. He took the blame when no others would, and that was fine. He'd claimed to know people well, claimed to spot evil hidden beneath the façade of a careful grin. Deep down, though, where the regrets were living, he knew he should have seen the betrayal coming and the town's fall. He had fuked up. In truth, they had all fuked up.

Ealis.

Fuken Ealis.

She had claimed innocence. She'd begged for mercy. She'd claimed she was a changed person. Most people would not be fooled again, but Wrek sought the goodness in people more and more these days. Perhaps she could earn redemption. He sighed in the silence and gripped the bars, doing all he could to appear nonchalant—a fine attempt with the raging storm stirring within.

Don't give in to him.

He looked around his cage. It didn't take long. It was relatively small. Dimly lit too, by just a candle burning outside the doorway. The ceiling was barely high enough to hang a man from, and the depth was slightly more than Wrek's length. He frowned at the broken-up cot shoved against the grimy wall. Lying on it, a man like Wrek could reach out and touch both sides of the room should he try. Wrek didn't try. He just stared ahead in stony silence. He would not blink, would not turn away. He could barely breathe.

Don't say a fuken word.

Wrek wanted to run to the bars and thrash at them until they bent to his tremendous will, cursing them for denying his right to move. He wanted to attack the little bucket in the far corner and spread its contents all over the room. He wanted to do it all. Anything but think on regrets of a life wasted. Anything but stare at his brutish keeper. His bastard jailor. His oldest comrade. His greatest adversary. His big brother.

At least I'm not alone.

He almost blinked at that guilty thought. Although the cells suited his two comrades a little better, they were just as trapped as he. They were housed in the cells on either side of him, where they sat, stared or paced around, and his shame for their fate was dreadful.

I could have warned them.

"Oh, Wreckless," Ulrik whispered from the other side of the bars, and he despised that term now. That was an archaic term for a vicious beast. He was not Wreckless anymore. Hadn't been in a long, long time.

Since I fell?

It had been in Samara, the city of light, that Wrek found the measure of himself, found himself a little too. His better self. His true self.

Ulrik grinned dangerously. Wrek could have replied. He could have offered the bastard a piece of his mind, but instead, he fell silent. He would not be released, no matter his words, no matter whether or not he admitted his guilt. He had broken their laws in returning. It didn't matter that war was in the wind; every brute was worth his weight in armour, and Wreck was worth more than most, regardless of his recklessness.

I will die in here when Adawan falls.

"Why am I chained?" Tye, ever the furious Alpha, cried from the cell beside him. It was a brave fool who would allow that boy to go free when the time came. "I have done nothing but come with bearing of bad tidings. This is shit behaviour on your part."

Ulrik, still watching Wrek, was unmoved. This moment was slowing down to nothing. To an eternity.

"You stand with this fuker?" Ulrik growled. He did not face Tye. His eyes were only for Wrek. There was a grim smile on his lips; his eyes were cold. Wrek recognised those eyes well. He'd been at the short end of that glare before, right before his banishment.

"With Wrek? Of course, I do."

Wrong answer.

"Then you stay with him."

"I do not stand with him," Ealis said from the cell on the other side. "Can I come out? I will behave."

At this, Wrek smiled. He did not know Ealis as he'd believed he had. However, setting her free was likely to result in equal bloodshed. Perhaps at the hands of Kaya. He hadn't expected the dark-skinned goddess to show such viciousness, but as they had dragged the chains around him and Kaya had battered at Ealis, he'd been surprised at her violence. He'd known her for many a year. A fine bandit, wise and quick-witted. He thought she'd fallen in Raven Rock with the others. She had looked past him as she'd struggled with her prey. Had said nothing as they pinned him and Tye down. War changed everyone. Or else she was wary of the repercussions. Or else they weren't friends as he'd believed.

"By all means, let Aurora Borealis out. She does not speak or stand with me," Wrek said at last. He knew Ulrik wouldn't. Not until the fighting. Who knew after that?

Probably Ulrik.

"I've changed my mind. I don't stand with Wrek. Don't even know him at all," mocked Tye from beside him. Wrek could hear the boy grip the bars as he spoke, desperate for Ulrik to set him free. "Also, do you know who I am? I'm fuken important."

This was no lie, but Ulrik cared little. He struck the cage, and Tye yelped in fright. Tye was impressive, like any Alphaline, but Ulrik was a mountain of menace. It didn't matter who Tye was or what his lineage was. He would remain.

"Fuken asshole," muttered the young Alpha, stepping away from the bars. From the sound of crackling straw, it seemed Tye had lain down in his cot. His arguments had been disregarded; the boy was entitled to rest. Truthfully, Wrek hadn't been this tired in an age. His mouth was wet and quenched, but his body still suffered from the pace of the march across the desert. That bed sounded rightly enticing. He would lie down again on his own cot once Ulrik had told him if he would live or die.

"You shouldn't have returned," Ulrik said. He looked older than before. Somehow nastier. Somehow more brutal. And Wrek felt softer. He was undoubtedly wiser. One might say a more knowledgeable man. Aye, one with prejudice, but also with a greater understanding than the thug who had once ruled this place.

So unfairly?
Probably.

"War is in the wind," whispered Wrek after a time.

"Last I heard, you were making a fine name for yourself in the city. That's rightly fuked now, though, isn't it?"

"I did what I had to. I wasn't going to disappear into the night, never be heard from again."

Ulrik leaned forward. His eyes were still cold and cruel. Wrek knew that gaze was saved for his victims alone. "It would have been a finer choice on your part."

"Well, you didn't kill me then; you won't kill me now," taunted Wrek. He was partial to a battle of wits as long as no cheating was involved. With Ulrik, the only way to bet was aggressively.

"You think me merciful?" Ulrik asked in a strange voice. Wrek raised a sceptical eyebrow, and Ulrik smiled, a dangerous smile that would entice the victim to request more. Wrek didn't want to ask for anything more. Suddenly, he decided to play his cards close to his chest, but Ulrik was determined to drag more words from him. "You think me weak for allowing you to leave this place with your tail tucked between your rear cheeks?"

"You couldn't kill yer own blood. It's a small matter now." He wondered was Tye listening. Did he care? Was he enraged that Wrek had led him into a trap? If he was, he'd shown no anger in the hours they'd spent alone in these cells, away from the burning heat. Aye, he'd pressed for a reason, and Wrek had been honest with him. He'd been a leader, had failed as a leader, and his older brother had banished him from this place. That he deserved banishment was something else entirely. Wrek hadn't thought so at the time, but in the years since, with open eyes, broken-hearted and wiser, he'd seen things a little more clearly. It was hard to walk with a man like Emir and not question your values, as was fighting for scraps for the wretches in muddy hovels. As was seeing the treatment delivered upon the so-called lowerlines in times of strife by a Primary, whose beliefs he too had once followed. He had done so because his father had taught him thus, and for a time, Wrek had been a dutiful son. Even now, he struggled, but struggle was better than nothing.

Sometimes, Wrek wondered whether the world would be a better place without intolerance and stubbornness fuelling its fires. Or better yet, if people learned how to understand the views of others and cultivated forgiveness for others' narrowmindedness.

He thought of Dia's awful end and wondered pitifully if her actions hadn't brought doom down upon herself. Truthfully, everyone in the entire fuken city knew the predilections of her assassin. Knew his motives too. For Wrek, this should have reaffirmed his beliefs. His father's beliefs. Should have narrowed his mind to nothing but untainted hatred. Instead, it had offered a crack to look through. Just a little one, a hole that let in the light and had shown him a less hate-filled way of seeing the world. He was no shining example of tolerance, mind. Oh no. He still had to work on these things. For example, he was still uncomfortable at the thought of men at play. All furrowing and proud about it. The writhing, the sweating, the fuken noises. He tried not to think of the noises. He thought of Aymon. He thought of Azel. He thought them both fine humans. Worthy of life, strife, terrible times, and comfort too. And of lust. But also of love. Fuken love. His father had never told him that love might be involved. Certainly not when Ulrik revealed himself. And Wrek? Well, Wrek had been Wreckless, hadn't he?

He knew his condemnation of Ulrik was cruelty when he first took the throne from his withered father upon his deathbed. Ulrik had accepted his place in the pack for a time. More than that, he had been a fine second to the fierce one. Ulrik's only mistake had been confiding in his brother one drunken night about the truer part of him.

I deserve this.

It was Wrek who had banished Ulrik from their tribe at first, never thinking for a breath that Ulrik was well capable of gathering his supporters. Or of his taste for vengeance. Perhaps had Wrek had eyes more upon his actions than his potential fortune, bloodshed might have been avoided—namely, his own. Back then, the mine had been barely operational, but Wrek, with only his dim wits to guide him, had believed in Adawan's importance. It had taken only a handful of dealings with a few large settlements for the wealth to start rolling in by the barrel. If only he'd known the value of this mine or looked upon the world as Sigi once had, he could have controlled it all, or at least made it a little better.

Raven Rock might not have fallen.

But Ulrik and his clan had come a-calling, hadn't they? It had hardly been a fair fight, and Wrek, softened from his time out of the saddle, had suffered for it.

"When you left, we heard you could be found in the little town of Nioe," Ulrik whispered, and Wrek remembered the place well. He'd known a girl there for a time. She'd probably fallen with it. So many lost.

"What of that place?"

"I sent the two boys."

Wrek's heart sank, the type of drop that came only with news of the most profound betrayal. That could cut deep. Could shatter a man. "Smit and Fitz?" He shook his head in horror. But it made sense. A terrible sense. Why have enemies when friends were the finest assassins?

Steel and Leather.

"Seems they fell as the town did. Rightly lucky for you."

Those wild bastards had been good friends. More than good friends. Near brothers. Better brothers than he and Ulrik. Friends, aye, but still likely to slit your throat for the right price, the wrong price, or any price. Those two lunatics, with Wrek and Ulrik, had been the finest Runners in the lands. Destined for greatness until it all went wrong. He thought of them now, as he frequently did in quieter moments when regretful thoughts entered his mind. They could have left Adawan with him. Could have lent their influence to Ulrik's eventual damnation while they were at it. As it was, they'd watched Wrek toppled and offered little more than a bow as he shuffled from his kingdom.

"I would never have expected their blades." He dropped his head against the side of the cage.

Strangely, Ulrik rested his hand on his head for a moment—an overly protective, brotherly habit he'd had since their youth. "Well, it is no matter now, Wrek."

Wrek felt like weeping. A terrible guilt overcame him. How easy it would have been to find him under Sigi's wing. He was glad of their deaths for a horrible moment, as much as he was sorrowed to learn of their passing.

"What will become of my comrades?"

"Whatever becomes of you will become of them."

Wrek had questions; he had words of mercy to beg, too. If not for him, then for Tye and perhaps Ealis as well. Mostly Tye, though.

Suddenly, a goddess appeared in the doorway; she was elegant, familiar and fierce, and Wrek could feel her anger from where she stood. It took him a moment to realise it was Elise. He was never one to remember faces, but Elise was not a person anyone was likely to forget.

"It is time," she cried. She did not look into the cages. Did not acknowledge the prisoners at all. "If you wish to hold your throne, come with me now."

Ulrik, cursing, spun away and followed her into the cool darkness, and Wrek fell away from the bars and sat by the bed, his mind spinning, his heart heavy and broken. A terrible thing to return here in such a way, he thought miserably. A terrible thing to come all this way and not find the words that would give reason to his journey.

"What the fuk was all that about?" asked Tye from beside him. He did not wish to reply. He just dropped his head in his hands and regretted his decision to return. Regretted more the apology he had not delivered. The simple few words he could have offered. The brute deserved it more. And Wrek deserved to say them. Instead, he had found himself mute and pathetic. His father would have approved, and such a thing was harrowing.

"Who the fuk are you, Wrek?" Tye demanded.

"I am little more than a wretched, broken bastard seeking redemption, little one," he said after a time.

"Aren't we all," whispered Ealis from the cage on the other side.

57

VALHAL

The world was a blur. Everything was distorted, and Emir found himself sauntering forward. Each step seemed to take an eternity, as though his legs were weighed down with honey. He was not alone on his journey, either, but no other walked this path. He felt a comfort take hold. He wasn't used to feeling comfortable. He imagined it felt like being a young child cradled by its mother. If he understood what that sensation felt like. It also felt like being part of a gathering of family. Or of friends. Or of those he'd loved as much as life.

I do not feel alone.
I do not feel left behind.

He felt his heart beat weakly, and he desired no such awareness. That heartbeat was pain, loss and sorrow. He welcomed its impending absence, for this path was the place to be, in the blur where his mind could remember little. Gone were the cold, sadness, misery, hate and fear that had followed his every step these last few years.

Ahead he saw a massive building, and he was drawn to it with his slow-paced feet.

"So, you decided to come too?" a voice from beside him said, and it was silky and confident. He hadn't heard that tone in a time, and suddenly, the world around him cleared ever so.

"Brother," he cried, and Stefan shone a full-toothed grin upon him. Returned to him were his good looks; his face was no longer sallow and broken. There was also no hole in his forehead; it was a good look.

"You are walking so slowly, brother. You'll miss everything before it's time to go." Stefan walked slightly ahead, his eyes glistening in this hazy

light, and Emir hadn't seen him so at ease since his first day as grand champion of Puk.

"Don't leave me behind," Emir cried, but Stefan had already found his stride.

"I think I've delayed longer than I needed," his ethereal comrade countered and marched towards the massive building, and Emir was left behind in his wake, but that was fine because Emir was coming home. This he knew, and he was at peace. *"I want to go in first,"* Stefan called and, offering a gentle wave, left Emir behind on the path. Within a few steps, he was away in the distance, walking through the building's doors to its warm glow beyond. Emir could have hurried and forced his limbs to thrash against the pace, but he was assured there was no delay in his step. There were beautiful things to come, and he was in no rush. He looked from the path to the world on either side, and although he could not make out landmarks, mountains, forests or illuminated cities of light, he felt they were there. So close, but not prepared to reveal themselves to him. Still, though, peering with eager eyes through the misty blur of vision, he saw grand structures not of the world, nor of this time either, and although he felt the understanding of such things on the edges of his thoughts, he did not seek out answers, nor did he rush for knowledge. It would come when the time was right, when the faltering heart in his chest beat its last.

And then a girl with stunning black hair walked past him from nowhere. Beautiful and fierce and powerful, although he did not know how he knew this. She offered him barely a glance, and before he could greet her, she was gone, lost in the mist around him, and he was so very curious. He might have followed her, seeking answers, seeking something, but the draw was to the building ahead, and as swiftly as she had appeared, she was gone from his mind.

It might have been a moment, a breath, or a pulse of time, and then he reached the building. It might also have been an hour, a week, a day or a year. Somehow time was different in this place, and he smiled. The doors of the building resembled a tavern he had once known, a lifetime before the world turned to hell. He knew what awaited him, and for a moment, Emir smiled. The door opened and he stepped through. Within lay the promise of good times indeed, although he could not see them for himself, for his vision could not accept all the things around him now. Although he felt the presence of a thousand others, he could not see anything more than a blur of motion around him as though the world turned at a different pace than his mind. And perhaps it did, for although none of this made any sense, it also made perfect sense, and he was almost home. And he was no longer alone.

Distantly, he could hear chatter, hear music so sweet, and almost taste the ructions of the last night of the Puk, and his heart beat loudly in his chest. Such was his excitement that he held his arms across himself lest the heart escape its cage.

"I am home," he whispered, and everyone knew him, accepted him, and welcomed him. Still, his steps were slow, and although it should have upset or irritated him, he was calm now. He ventured deeper into the tavern and followed his instinct. His steps were many, and they carried him towards a table, and he felt his heart leap in joy. A joy he'd never endured his entire life. He could feel them near, those he cared for. Could almost hear them.

Beside the table stood Stefan. His eyes were alive with mischief. "I will chance my luck with her first," he whispered, and Emir did not understand. He did not care. His old dead friend gazed at the table, spoke to nothing, said some words not for Emir's ears, before stepping towards Emir and placing his hand upon his shoulder. "We did our best, didn't we, brother?"

"We did our best."

"I did not believe myself worthy of all this splendour," Stefan said, looking beyond Emir, looking around the room like a newborn with curious excitement.

"I cannot see it all. Tell me of it."

"You will, brother," Stefan said, and embraced Emir, who realised with a pang that this was goodbye for now, although he wasn't sure how he knew it.

Stefan's face changed suddenly as though a cloud had passed over it. "Well, now, I did not believe I would see her here; this will be an interesting exchange," he whispered, looking to another area deep beyond, and Emir could see nothing, for it was not for him, and that was fine, for this place was home. His heart beat in excitement, in wonderment, and Stefan slipped from sight. Faded to the blur of nothing and Emir could sense revelry in that deep, wondrous nothing.

Suddenly, Emir saw Quig, and his heart beat in excitement. Quig saw him too. He stood by the table, waiting patiently as the world around him slowly came alive in a blaze of colour and realism. "Oh Emir, whatever the fuk did you do?" he bellowed, and beaming, he took hold of Emir and lifted him from his treacle march as though he weighed nothing at all.

"You left without me," Emir cried, and tears spilled down his cheeks, for it had been so long. "You left me behind; I had to follow." It was no lie, and the stinging agony of torn flesh struck him. As swiftly as it appeared, it was gone, though.

"We both did," a voice said, and Emir could only cry, and they with him. Aireys appeared from below him as though getting up from a table. She fell upon him, kissing him on the cheek, once upon the lips—a delicate kiss between friends, between those who had once been in love.

"My love, I have missed you," Emir wailed, and his arms were free of the honey clutch. He hugged her tightly, knowing this was no dream. This was the end, after the end, and it was beautiful.

"And I, you, dear Emir," she said softly, and her silken voice was the sweetest song he'd ever heard. He could see past her perfect shape to the table, the cards that lay upon it and the game at play. There were other figures present. Figures he had no right to see. One of them appeared to reach up and rub at his dwindling hair and, for a cold moment, Emir remembered more of the life he had left behind. "Although you call me by the wrong title," Aireys whispered, and all thoughts of regrettable actions were forgotten; he turned to face her and thought her a most beautiful goddess.

"I do not understand," he whispered, and she smiled wonderfully as though she held no grudges, carried no grievances for his sins against her memory.

"You have left someone behind," she insisted, and he dared not recollect her name in Aireys's presence.

"Typical you would bring that up," chided Quig, and Aireys shrugged.

"If I approve of things, I say them," she insisted, and, from the table, she took a goblet of red wine.

"May I sit with you?" Emir asked, and she offered the glass to him, and he drank, and it was like no wine he had ever tasted.

Aireys stroked his cheek, and only then did she smile sadly. "There are moments, dearest Emir, where the absent gods reward us. This is such a moment."

Quig elbowed him playfully; in his hand appeared a glass of sine. "They must think highly of you," he said, and Emir could only smile, for he did not understand the giant's words.

"There is no place for you at the table," Aireys said, gesturing to the players whom Emir might or might not have recognised should he have tried.

"I will be alone?" Emir asked, and his heart beat gently now, for this was no place for the living.

"You were never alone," Quig declared, and he offered the wine and Emir desired to drink. He tried desperately to see the world for what it was, to ease himself into a seat at the table. "Sure, I kept an eye on you the whole time," Quig insisted, and strangely, it was no lie, although Emir didn't understand how.

"As did I," Aireys agreed, and Emir reached for her. He never wanted to leave, and indeed, he knew they desired him to see this place for himself, to play a few hands. To be home.

"You've become the right little hero, haven't you?" Quig mocked, and held the boy by the shoulder.

Aireys gripped his other shoulder, her face kind, beautiful, and a little sorrowful. "We will see you just moments from now, but may you live a life in between as the man I know you are." Emir felt a terrible force pulling him away from the table, from the dim vision of motion. He wanted to stay, sit with his friends, and silence the anguish he endured every day. "Live, and love, and more, my dearest Emir," she said, and this was goodbye for now, and Emir was sorrowful, as the world of the living called, as did the terrible pain.

"Go be a fuken hero," Quig said, and Emir's heart panged and beat stronger in dreadful sorrow, and he gasped, and it all filtered away.

And he stared with eyes open into the eye of a mad god. He could not move, could only lie in the brute's monstrous arms as he carried him through the freezing streets of Samara at an incredible pace, and the warmth that held Emir began to disappear and, with it, thoughts of old friends. Dead friends. Better times. Like the nights in Keri.

"Don't you fuken die on me," Uden roared, and it was terrifying, and Emir fought unconsciousness. "I command you." The world darkened, Uden gripped him, and he couldn't resist the coming sleep. "Please, Emir!"

Emir opened his eyes and felt people all around him, attacking the injury that had stolen his life. He tried to struggle, but he had no strength. He could hear the mad god shouting, threatening. Then he felt the warmth of a callused hand upon his forehead. "I see you will live. I will ensure it, too," Uden said, as though he were a doting father. Emir squirmed, but his bindings entrapped him. His arm was lying flat out. The tubing for transfusions was embedded in his skin, leading to the god who towered above him, and Emir fought for words, but he was so weak. "It is a gift."

"I do not need this," he gasped, for the risk of his blood becoming contaminated was too great. Now that he lived, he didn't want to die.

Dying isn't so bad.

Right?

"Shush," the god said, and Emir fell unconscious again.

"I give you my word, Emir, truly I do," Uden whispered, and each word tore through his body like a hammer into a carcass. Emir fought the weariness of waking to the sight of the mad god standing over him. "Truly, your bravery, your sacrifice... These are godly things indeed," the mad god insisted. Waking up a little more, Emir could see the notebook in his hands, and fear took him for a breath. "You are better alive, better safe," he said, placing the notebook beside Emir's broken body. "Just do not step into the night as before," he begged, and incredibly the mad god kissed Emir's hand as though he were royalty. "No harm, no torment will come to you, no matter how powerfully I desire the tonic. It is your recipe alone. I will ask for it no more."

Emir could only shake his head weakly, and the mad god was appeased. He smiled, a tear rolled down his cheek, and distantly, Emir thought of friends long dead and missed them, but they were gone. Lost in the ether forever. Emir was alone.

Am I, though?

I am.

"You have godly blood in you, and you are worthy. Sleep now, dear Emir. Come tomorrow, it will be better," Uden insisted, and Emir closed his eyes and fell asleep.

"You fuker! How dare you!" she wailed as Emir came to. He was no longer in the healer's bay as before. Instead, he was in his own bed. His body was stretched out, strapped tightly down to prevent him stirring up trouble. "I hate you, I fuken hate you," Roja wailed. She was upon his bed, sitting over him, her pale, beautiful face clenched in agony, and Emir, stirred by the dream syrup as it faded away, felt truly horrible.

"I'm sorry," he croaked, and she struck him across the face—a fine slap, one he richly deserved for his actions.

"You left me behind," she roared, and, putting a glass of water to his lips, allowed him to drink and soothe his parched throat. "I can't do this without you." He could see the wrapping on his injury. His students had tended to him expertly. *Fuk it anyway.* Closing his eyes, he tried to sleep and hide his shame from her, but she gripped his collar and shook him ever so, and he was helpless in her grasp. "Promise me," she demanded.

"Of course," he pledged, although he had no idea what he pledged. He thought of Aireys, Quig, the last night in Keri when they had played, and he wanted to weep.

"Promise me you will never leave me like that again," she demanded, and he snapped awake at her accusation.

"I will never leave you, my love," he pledged, and something in those words rang as truth. He suddenly desired to tear himself free of his bindings, embrace her, and pledge the entire world to her. "I'm sorry, my dearest Roja. I will never escape like that again."

She held his collar a little longer, and he thought her beautiful and terrifying. Eventually, weeping, she released him and then wrapped herself around his body. "You pledged your word, so you must stay honourable," she warned, bending to let him kiss the top of her head. "You must keep your word."

"As you wish," he said, and allowed her to embrace him tightly once more. "Could you undo the straps a little?" he asked after a time.

"Not a fuken chance," she hissed, and clung even more tightly to him lest he take flight and leave her behind again. "Not until I trust you again."

"As you wish," he whispered, and allowed sleep to take him properly this time.

Distantly, in the recesses of his mind, where absent gods delivered gifts of kindness, there played a song of defiance and revelry, sung by warrior comrades who watched in near silence with pride. Although Emir slept, his dreams were a little warmer than before.

58

THE PRAGMATIST

Elise was furious. She held Lexi in her arms for a bit longer, although her body shook with rage. Rage, but also the gratefulness of a mother reunited with her child. She took shallow breaths lest the girl wake and cause her to rethink her actions, for there were many to come. Elise's heart had broken ever so as they had led her down to their sanctuary, knowing the horrors the girl might have endured. Knowing the weight in every step she took. Sleeping, though, the girl looked more like herself.

She eased the sleeping girl from her lap and wrapped some bedsheets around her. That done, Elise slipped away and stood quietly, stretching in the low light. Her body creaked and groaned but answered her demands easily enough, and soon she was gasping deeply.

"What are you doing?" a tired, dreamy voice asked, and Elise smiled.

"Sleep, little one. You have little to worry about." This wasn't the entire truth, for an army was marching upon them. These next moments might change the whole war. She might have spoken more with Lexi and told her of matters in this place, but the child carried enough for now. Although Lexi's arrival was tinged with terror and sorrow for her son, Elise was heartened by the absent gods' favour. She took Tye and Wrek's imprisonment as a sign. They would be needed—especially the boy. Blood would be spilled, and she would call upon her best, most savage killers.

Watching Lexi wrap herself in the sheets and then hearing her breathing turn to snoring, Elise continued her routine until she was ready.

Creeping away from her quarters, she sought out Kaya and the child Aimee and discovered them in a similar position: the child was sleeping, and Kaya was seeing to her needs. Although Kaya had moved her quarters down into the deep near Elise's, the difference between their chambers was vast. Elise would see to this come victory, but it would have to do for now. She knocked quietly at the door of Kaya's tiny room, and Kaya opened it noiselessly.

"Who is this girl?" Elise asked, indicating the form in the bed, and Kaya wiped her eyes as though she'd slept deeply these last few hours.

"I cared for her in another life. Back then, she was just a child, although potentially a champion." She clearly had more to say, but she fell silent and stared back at the girl as a mother would. With no washbasin to call upon, as Elise had, the child was still caked in dry mud and had ruined her bedsheets. Kaya's clothes were ruined too, but the younger woman didn't care. "I do not know the horrors she has endured, but she is different from the starlet I once knew. For this, I will take flesh and a life, too, if offered."

"You speak of the other girl? The one you attacked out in the sands?"

At this, Kaya cursed. Her knuckles turned white. "That witch is one of the leaders from the South. I'll never forget her cruel eyes. She took my home, my kin, and everything else from me in Raven Rock."

"Then she will be made to pay."

Kaya merely nodded. Her thoughts were elsewhere—no doubt in Raven Rock. Elise knew the tales of that siege from her friend's mouth, knew the impressive measure of Kaya and those who had stood with her. It would be a terrible thing if a tale like theirs were to be lost in time and not celebrated in songs, poems or bards' tale for those after to remember, to acknowledge the heroism of which humanity was still capable. And the horrors too.

"Is it time?" Kaya asked, and there was a strength in her voice, as though being denied a kill by Ulrik had guaranteed her loyalty. That was fine. When twisted to your needs, anger was a gift and a fine ally.

"Go to him; you know what part to play. This is not the end of all things, Kaya, but this could be the war's turning." She gripped the girl and placed her forehead to her own. A quiet moment for the women before all hell broke loose and spilled all over the sands. "I can hear the drum of battle, and we'd best be ready."

"It will be done, my general," Kaya whispered, then bowed deeply before spinning away and taking to the stairs. She leapt up them three at a time and within a breath, she was gone from sight. Within a few more, she was out of earshot.

She thought of Lexi and the Rangers, and any trepidation she had gave way to festering anger. Just enough to buoy her steps, but not enough to cause her to misstep.

This must be done.

Swiftly, Elise marched through the darkness, headed deeper into the mine towards the cells, towards her destiny. She was Elise, legend of the Four Factions, but these moments ahead would define her legacy. She knew Adawan would survive this assault regardless of who held watch. It was never about survival, though. It was about the rest of the world.

Not far from Kaya's chambers, she came upon the cells keeping the prisoners. It was a strange thing, she thought, for bandits to require holding cells. As she moved closer, she saw that they were little more than caverns cut into the side of the salt walls. Thin bars and thinner doors were wedged tightly into the stone to keep naughty prisoners from escaping. Gazing at the structures, she imagined them easy enough to break with the proper leverage, with the right mind for such things. There were a dozen cells in all, but she knew she would find him at the far end of the corridor. She wondered would she earn her own place behind these rickety bars for her actions. Anything to put manners on her, she supposed. At least there would be company.

She listened for a time as Ulrik spoke to the monster Wrek, and she found this curious. She could have argued against Tye's imprisonment, she realised guiltily, but there was room for only one fight at a time.

At the sound of her footsteps, Ulrik turned to face her.

"It is time," she said simply. She'd never seen him nervous, but Wrek's appearance had clearly rattled him something terrible. This was pleasing, for she knew anything to unsettle him could benefit Bison in the skirmish to come.

"What? Now?" he roared, and she nodded gravely. She dared not gaze at Tye, lying in bed, or at Wrek, broken and lost. The girl, though, stared at her with inquisitive eyes. Fine eyes too. Magnus would very much like a girl with eyes like this.

"You look familiar," the girl whispered, and her words made Elise uneasy. However, that might well have been the battle in the air. The precarious hand she'd just played.

Ulrik marched past, and she hurried after him and drew up alongside, playing the part of ally as she claimed to be. It was no lie, for she respected the man, but her deceit was a means to an end. He thundered through the unimpressive prison and the wretched depths she'd once called her domain. A few guards nodded as he passed, but Ulrik was blind to their salutes. His face was a burning red like the sky on fire at dusk. It was a good, terrifying look to him, she admitted. She'd rarely seen him so angry before, not even when she'd challenged him. This was something different, and Elise imagined this emotion could benefit her cause. Or else it would get her killed in a fit of misplaced rage. In truth, it would be no battle to the death, for they were no fools weakening their ranks over petty jealousies. Elise could have overcome him with a blade, but fists were their way. It was hardly fair. A girl had to even the odds in any way she could.

"When it begins, take the strike well and play the part," Ulrik warned, and she nodded. Her heart fluttered in excitement; terror, too. A good feeling of adrenalin before a battle.

"I know what to do, Ulrik; just make sure you punish him before I need to get involved."

Ulrik muttered under his breath, then cursed loudly. He thundered swiftly up the stairs, and she could see him gasp for air while she breathed easily enough. "I can beat him; you are merely insurance." He shot her a glare. "Do not betray me," those eyes commanded.

She increased her pace, smiling as though thoughts of betraying him hadn't entered her head. Not once. Not ever. These last few weeks, she'd offered him no suggestion that she still held aspirations of ruling this wretched place. It wasn't hard, once he'd guaranteed her almost everything she desired to fall in line. Almost. But not entirely.

He matched her step now. She feigned a panicked breath, but indeed, after having raced this stretch daily for so long, this brisk march was more like a stroll. "As long as we agree on who controls the defences, Ulrik, I have no desire to betray you. Just ensure the strike looks fierce."

"Oh, it'll be fierce," he teased, and she felt a shudder run down her spine.

By the time they reached the surface of the mine, there was already an excited hum in the air. Kaya had done her part, for the market was abandoned. Instead, merchants and customers alike had gathered at the tavern to complete their business. A crowd of bandits awaited them, and they swiftly split as Elise and Ulrik walked forward.

"Looks like Bison has prepared the world," Ulrik growled. His face was pale now, and his fists were clenched tightly. He marched with his head held high, and Elise thought him menacing enough that were Bison to have challenged him openly, he might have second-guessed his decision.

"He must be confident that everyone has come to see," she suggested, thinking Kaya had done rather well to stir up the energy here. "Say little, Ulrik. Let your silence unnerve him." An acceptable ploy on her part. Keeping them separated these last few weeks made twisting them to her will that little bit easier, but it would take only a few words shared between the two men for them to discover her ruse.

The crowd stirred and roared as they approached the old tavern where the mass of bodies was tightly clustered. They had known this day was coming since the other large hound had entered the fray. Some believed in younger blood. Bison, for example, had faced the Wastes and survived. There was steel in such a man. Others believed in the wiliness of the elder. Ulrik beating Wrek for his throne? Was that not a tale of legend?

As they neared the edge of the crude arena, which was little more than a rough outline in the dust, Elise darted a few steps ahead. The last thing she needed was for Bison to open his mouth and spoil everything.

"Well, here I am, brute," Ulrik challenged the solitary male standing within the arena. "All passionate and shit."

Shut up, Ulrik.

Beside Bison stood a nervous Kaya. She was gasping, having roused the crowd, having stirred the brute, having cast her hat into the ring with her actions alone. Elise might be forgiven for her behaviour should the truth surface, but for Kaya, it was a cutting betrayal indeed. Elise might have felt guilty for ensuring the girl's culpability, but nothing mattered beyond the right outcome.

"You thought I'd cower at your challenge?" roared Bison, stepping forward to meet Ulrik. His shirtless chest glistened in the early sun. Every muscle was a stark reminder of the strength he could wield. Impressive scars ran up and down his body. This brute was built for savagery and suffering, and he'd clearly endured a life of strife. A fuker like that could hit like a hammer and take shots like a stone wall.

Oh, fuk me. Stop talking and fight.

"You overthink," countered Ulrik. If there was any fear in his voice, he hid it behind a terrible rage, no doubt brought upon him by the sight of his kin.

You've brought this upon us all.

This would be no controlled challenge of masters, no clash between Rangers and Wolves, no dignified debate over a chosen Primary. This would be a brutal, savage battle between right fuken bastards, and her heart beat in excitement, in nervousness, in relief.

"I seek to challenge," declared Elise, stepping away from Ulrik to face Bison. Those who called her an ally had expected such a reckless, desperate challenge. Those who disagreed knew this was no place for her, but to the fires with their opinions. She stripped to her undergarments, casting her outer clothes aside. Between such brutes, she appeared a waif. Looking more closely, one might see assuredness where there should have been trepidation. She didn't care. She was an afterthought in this grand skirmish, and she had her own little part to play, was all.

"I challenge too," Bison hissed. The crowd cheered, although there was a nervousness in the air. Perhaps they considered bickering to be a bad omen before a war. Perhaps they feared the battle itself would derail their best-laid plans of survival. Perhaps they were right. There was no ceremony, only a casual shrug from Ulrik, who welcomed all challengers. He raised his fists, and Elise wasted no time. Filling her lungs with deep and controlled breaths, she sprinted towards the king, screaming to gather his attention. Behind her, she heard Bison curse in shock, which was fine. He was no part of this. Not yet.

"Come on, so," demanded Ulrik, and she did, sprinting down upon him like a pigeon against a ferret, lifting her feet high in the air with her last step and leaping towards him. And he, twice her weight if not more. She swung and missed and felt his fist collide heavily with her chin. A fine strike, and one that would have knocked most unprepared warriors from their feet. She fell back from him, dazed despite her readiness for such a strike. "Down you fuken go," he roared, and she thought this was a fine idea.

Too hard.

She'd expected such a blow, but he'd held little back, and she was lesser for it. Falling backwards, away from her vanquisher, she stumbled to her wobbly feet, entreating them to carry her far from threat. And carry her they did, across the arena, where she collapsed in a heap away from the violence, away from the behemoths.

She kept an eye upon the skirmish as it slipped away from her grasp, and although she heard a few jests and curses from the gathered crowd at her expense, she made no move to counter, to put them in their place, to show any pride. Instead, she lay battered and beaten in the dust, and she knew deep in her heart this was precisely where she needed to be.

"Fuk it," hissed Bison, watching her fall. For a dreadful moment, he appeared as though he didn't want this fight. As though he'd walked into the arena unprepared to be the lone warrior standing. "I'll not go down so easily," he warned, less confidently than one might have expected from one so large. He rounded up on Ulrik, who was still shaking the sting from his wrist. Bison glanced once more at the battered goddess and frowned at her absence.

"I'll not hold back, so," growled the king.

Most traditional fights between skilled pugilists, using rules, respect and rest periods between rounds, were known to take over an hour. Usually, both combatants were careful in their approaches, stringent in their defence, and patient in their attacks. These bandit brutes, however, had no such interests. When a claim for power was contested through fists, these fights were swift, vicious and devastating. This would be one such skirmish. Without warning, Ulrik charged at Bison, who retreated beneath his blows. A fine thing, too, for they struck fiercely, battering heavily against his raised guard. As skilled as Alphas might be with blades, bandits matched this sort of violence with their hands. Bison countered the blows with a flurry. But instead of defending himself, Ulrik met each strike across the face with an attack of his own, and the crowd erupted with shouts loud enough that the marching Hunt might have worried the bandits were pleased with their invasion.

There was no break in the violence. Both men took turns measuring the other. Combination after combination was cast against the other. The slapping crack of gnarled fists on flesh filled the air. As did the grunts and snarls. The spitting disgust and the colourful curses—the many, many curses that accompanied most strikes. The types of curses that would put a hardened soldier to shame. The types of curses casually offered by battered bandits reaching for the crown.

Ulrik was dealt the first devastating blow—a crack across the nose from a fully extended right, snapping something snappable within. Ulrik was dazed and disfigured as he stumbled away, and the battle looked finished. A lesser man might have retreated fully, uttering a gasping plea or dropping to a knee to gather his breath, but as he fended off Bison's renewed attack, Ulrik gripped the bridge of his nose and, with a sickly twist, returned the appendage to a somewhat normal position. The stream of blood continued to flow down his beard, but it was a lesser stream. The crowd gasped; even Bison hesitated, perhaps out of curiosity, perhaps to change the attack and finish it off. Instead, he met a sudden straight across the bridge of his own nose for his efforts. The type of strike that broke breakable bones. And break they did.

"You bastard," he cried in shock as his blood gushed over the sand. To be fair, he took only a solitary step backwards to compose his jarred senses. Most would have collapsed, including Elise. Ulrik took the reprieve to gasp a little, bending over to get air into his lungs, likely wet with blood streaming down into them. "To the fires with you."

For a moment, both warriors wavered. Bison recovered first and charged upon the weary Ulrik, leaping upon the slightly smaller giant and pummelling him in the stomach with his powerful arms. Ulrik took the blows, then flexed his hands, took Bison in a mighty grip, and lifted him from his feet.

The crowd gasped as one, watching in horror and excitement as their leader hoisted the pretender and dropped him on his head upon the throne with a sickening thud. Then, bending over him, Ulrik began punching the dazed brute with the last of his energy. The crowd chanted as each strike landed, and it infused Ulrik with further energy, but Bison was younger, hardened by a life in the saddle. He squirmed from the brute's grip and, striking him once across the nose to stem his attacks, rolled backwards and leapt to his feet in a smooth motion as though Ulrik's attacks had little effect—and truly, perhaps they hadn't. He struck a pose for the crowd, flexed his arm muscles and, indeed, he was a terrifying sight as he grinned at his opponent.

Shaken, Ulrik rose unsteadily to one knee and could only look regretfully at the unconscious Elise lying ruined in the dirt.

"Yield," Bison growled, and Ulrik shook his head. The anger from before was slipping from his grasp; the fight had left him. He was a fine ruler, but all he had wasn't enough against Bison. "I will beat you until you take no further breath," Bison warned, spinning past his opponent before lunging back, clutching his neck and striking him fiercely across the face.

"Fuk you, animal," Ulrik whispered, although his voice was weak. Like any tough bull fighting for his life and pummelled by a thousand swipes, he was still impressive, but he was beginning to flounder.

"You are too old," Bison assured him as he wrapped his arms around the brute. "Sleep well."

Ulrik struggled; the crowd gasped in awe at his defiance. They cheered Bison on, for no fool wanted to lose the favour of their new leader. They roared their excitement, and Bison grinned.

Too late he realised they weren't cheering for him.

The kick to his head came from the right, slightly behind him. One sweet motion, perfectly angled. Weeks in the making. Months in training. Years in the mastering.

She had lain among the ruins as she'd said she would and watched with thin, slitted eyes as Bison and Ulrik went to battle, and it was far more gruesome than she could ever have expected. For a few deep, controlled breaths as she watched the brutes pummel each other senseless, she had thought herself lucky that Ulrik hadn't inflicted as much damage on her as he could have in their clash.

The crowd mostly forgot about little old Elise of Samara, sprawled out in ruin as the battle continued. As she lay there, she had resisted the urge to grip her chin where Ulrik had struck her. She'd agreed to such a blow with him long before, yet hadn't expected him to put his full force behind the impact—a small matter once her senses were returned to her.

She hadn't believed Ulrik would put up such a fight against the larger man, but he had been magnificent. However, as she had expected these last few weeks, Bison had overcome his doubts and bested the behemoth, despite her gentle insistence that Ulrik was the superior fighter.

Thrice, she almost leapt to her feet to ambush Bison, but her nerve kept her grounded, and the fight took a better turn for it. She watched unmoving, calming her breathing, steeling her nerve until the moment arrived. Then, with Ulrik weakened nearly to unconsciousness, she turned to her ally as Bison towered over him, ready to put him down.

She was swift; she rose to her feet in one fluid movement and reached him in three steps before the crowd realised the blur was, in fact, a freshly charged Alphaline in all her glory. She was no seasoned fighter, but one could hardly spend half a life in Magnus's company without understanding the finer acts of brutality, without conquering one's fears of a contest of the fists in such an arena. Or, come to that, in a tavern, which was where most fights broke out. For just a moment, she remembered standing back to back with her young lover as they waged war on a gathering of brutes in a little unknown tavern in the Wastes. She took that memory, the heartache, and threw it into a strike.

She knew the most devastating of strikes was the one a brute never saw coming. She had fine fists. Fantastic and toughened and built for striking. But not even a concealed strike would damage a brute strengthened by fury. So she threw everything into her kick.

She kicked him real fuken hard, right in the head.

It was enough to break his hold. He dropped to his knees in dull confusion, fighting the darkness no doubt clouding his vision. His eyes stared blearily in shock, and she could see the realisation of betrayal coming upon him. He swung weakly, and she struck again. This blow was a fair one that he could see coming. It caught him straight across the neck, and he gasped, and he was done. She took no chances; like a viper in the sands of Adawan, she struck out again and dislocated a finger as she did. Dislocated his already damaged nose again, too. The brute stumbled and fell unconscious. This was no illusion, nor an act on her part.

She could not enjoy her victory, however. As she spun around lest Ulrik take advantage, she finally hesitated and met his dazed eyes below her. He was a ruin, and for a breath, she felt guilt for her actions. For only a breath, though, and fortunately, in Adawan, she would have many more to give.

"I'm sorry."

Knowing victory was upon her, she was careful lest there be one more trick in this brute's armoury. He spat blood, then looked around ever so slowly as she danced away from his reach, came up behind him, and took hold of him. Wrapping herself around his arm and neck, she clutched tightly and held him fast. She began to twist and manoeuvre with the proper leverage, and despite his injuries, he fought her every move. This was different from their first battle, however. Bison had seen to that. Although he struck out at her, she took the blows as they landed and ducked her head away from the rest and, wonderfully, they began to weaken. The crowd's raucous cheering began to die away.

"You played me," he whispered from a bloodied mouth and in reply, she twisted more tightly and pulled his arm up, gripping him near its socket. He instinctively tried to rise, but he was not fresh, and she, well, she'd taken just one glancing blow to the chin. And she'd spent months running up and down those fuken steps in preparation for this moment.

"It's time, my friend," she hissed. She had more and could give more. She could twist another few angles and pop many things, but she held him, watching him bleed and fade.

And then his hand was upon her arm, tapping ever so delicately, and the crowd saw it too.

"I am spent. I yield my throne," he cried, and she released him without hesitation lest she kill the legend. Or worse, keep him from fighting for Adawan come the desperate hour.

Suddenly, there were arms around her, lifting her to her feet, lifting him too. And then Bison was dragged alongside, and although he was dazed, he shrugged off the help, determined to stand unaided.

The Actions of Gods

She raised her hands in victory, and the crowd suddenly dropped to their knees as the combatants faced each other once more.

"I hope you know what you have done," gasped Bison. He did not wait for a reply. He dropped to a knee in deference.

"I have saved us all," she declared.

"Aye, perhaps, you have, legend," Ulrik said, taking her hand before he, too, dropped to a knee.

59

MORE EXCERPTS FROM THE DESKS OF WEASELS

Solstice 5th
    Dearest Gemmil,
    I hear a hum. Can you hear it? All the way from your frozen bastion? All the way down there, where the wind is cutting and the blizzards are fierce? No, you cannot hear this hum at all. Few can, if any. This hum is eternal. And possibly internal. I hear it in the day, at night and every moment in between. A low hum. So low, my old friend, that even someone who stands beside me cannot hear this monster's purr. Sometimes, I hide beneath my silken sheets, pull the duvet over my head, and whimper and pray that this hum will lessen, will yield its terrible assault. But no, there is no peace for me. I hear it in the walls, in the streets, everywhere.
    Sometimes, when I stand upon the city wall's edge where the drop is fatal, I hear only stillness. It is a silent, deafening thing, and I might go mad trying to root out its source. Truthfully, if the hum is real, I suspect it is the lights of this once glorious city. Or the wires of their generators, which run along every path of this monstrous bastion. I suppose that long ago, I was deaf to their song until I listened once, and now I cannot forget it. I may be truly going mad. And why not? I have little in this world to keep me sane. I believed the world would be a finer place at peace. Perhaps I was wrong. Perhaps I was wrong about a great many things.
    It is late. I have not slept well these last few months. I barely dream either. My eyes water and my head feels like a log that's been split by an axe. My hand shakes ever so as I scribe these miserable words. I am sorry. I am ever so lost. You, out in the frozen wilderness searching for

scraps and meaning, must laugh loudly at my misfortune. Apart from scraps, have you found anything worthwhile? Has a lovely Southern lady taken your fancy? Have you adapted yourself to the frozen lands? Are you a barbarian now? Are there any hums to be heard down there?

I have written to Wiiden, but his last few replies have been less coherent, less passionate than they once were. He is ever so different. Perhaps we all are. Perhaps I could change more too. As I write this, though, it is a new year, and I have been waiting to hear from him for a time. If you see him, condemn his silence for me. And tell him I wish him a good retirement, and that Roja is doing well under Dia's gaze. More than that, I keep a watchful eye on her, as he asked.

Yours, Seth.

Equinox 75th

I hear no hum, dear Seth. Perhaps it is the stinging of your pride playing such a worrying melody. Perhaps the years in that cursed city of yours have finally become a growth in your mind, festering, reminding you of the terrible times gone by. There is a cure in it, too, brother, so fret not. That hum will flitter away to silence after the crumbling, and she will crumble someday. Those of us still fit and able will listen and cheer and enjoy the silence—all of us, that is, except Breiga, for all the fine gifts these magnificent lands have gifted me, they have granted Breiga also. The way that fool commands forces up and down these lands is a travesty. He has a grip on this region, and it is pathetic. If, truth be told, and I deliver only truths when we speak, without my desperate hand guiding his charge, he would still be shuffling through the first few settlements squandering more of our warriors than we can afford.

Forgive me. The hour is early, and I have not slept much these last few days. My words are harsh, trivial and unworthy of the boy. Honestly, he has a decent enough heart, a good chin and bravery. But there is a sin upon him I cannot forgive. He is not his father. Over the years, he has shown the measure of the man he could be. And though many would be satisfied with the few hundred under his grip, how far might Wiiden have dragged us? These scattered lands war between themselves like children over honey cakes. Were an exemplary leader in command, there are numbers here to challenge the mighty Savage Isles themselves.

It is a clear morning here, and I can see across these frozen mountains for miles. I can also see how easily things could be for the better. I miss Wiiden. I miss his brutality, brother. Could the actions of greater gods bring about change? Especially actions committed by blood-soaked hands. I speak wearily now. Warily too. I will rise, listen for a hum, and tend to my duties as an advisor this fine morning. Strangely, I miss the savagery of survival under Magnus's charge. Those were terrifying, heroic days. Be well, my friend.

Yours from the deep South,
Gemmil.

Solstice 25th

Dearest Gemmil,

I am in a terrible way. I cannot take this fuken city. I cannot accept that whore of a Primary. She condemns me to nothing. To irrelevance. I see it now. Tonight, I scribe here in the dark with another flickering bulb above me. I swear I have changed the fuker twice this month alone. Here at my desk in this darkened room with a terrible fuken chill taking me, I preside over Alphaline ancestry, Alphaline events. Alphaline matters. A vile task in this city of Dia, to tend to cubs as they cull, so they might fuk and make this world better with more little cubs. I do not know how I will endure another pompous conversation about my attentiveness with a whore leading her Cull, how I will bear another wretched conversation with an aroused male as he sniffs around seeking answers and advice, all the while proclaiming himself to be of regal bloodline. A pox upon every single one of those fuks. May their lines fester and become infertile. May Dia's grand designs fall dead upon her watch. The world will survive; we do not need her enforced rules and regulations.

Forgive me—I ramble. It is Culling season, and the scent of lust and desire permeates the city day and night. I am sure I have more to share, but I cannot help but regret the passage of time and the decisions we made. The hum pervades my waking hour, and it is regret. I know this now, just as I know it is from the unnatural turbines of this city. If Samara ever falls, let those cursed things be the first to be destroyed. Let the Alphalines burn in the moments after.

Yours regretfully,
Seth.

The Actions of Gods

Solstice 105th
  Dear Seth,
  How have these last few months treated you? I hope you are better-minded than in your previous few messages. We have been through so much, brother. Let no mere regrets take your will. Let no further ill tidings carry you closer to an early grave or, worse, to madness of a humming nature. I write this tongue in cheek, brother, for I seek distraction from my unenviable task. As I write this, I travel to Wiiden's estate with word of terrible things. Alas, even though he has chosen a life of silence and solitude and trusted his son to carry the banner of his kin, there has been a terrible event. Just terrible. As though the gods spied on our missives, so carelessly scribed in ink. Terrible things, indeed. Breiga, through no fault of his own, has fallen to a cowardly blade. A terrible death. A terrible thing. I had come to the camp too the night before. I discovered his body, and so violent were the wounds upon him that I was left shaken. He had been slit from ear to ear as he slept and bled to death in silence. Just terrible.
  We found the murderer—a vile young cur desperate to prove himself. We put him to a swift death that very day. We might have gifted his grieving father the opportunity to carry out this act, but this is the South, best to slay the young fool immediately, so that is what I did. Wiiden will understand, for a boy in chains upon the march, claiming innocence, was bound to garner favour as the miles passed. It was done painfully, though, so that will please Wiiden and his whore, no doubt.
  There is more, alas; I fear my words will bring you little solace. As though this terrible deed wasn't evil enough, in the weeks since, the clans who were beaten and gathered under Breiga's ill-fated rule are whispering of dissension. They talk of splintering. Were I capable or impressive enough, I might have attempted leadership. As we know, however, I was not born for such things. As I near this estate, I only hope the child Cordelia can take the pain from Wiiden. If a light is in our friend's eyes, it's for that little girl. She is but a few years old and already a right little miss. I have little warmth for children, but she has a spark in her eye. You will see it the day she arrives in Samara, likely during the coming year. Until then, she will have a duty these next few months. She must ease his spirits until he is strong, so that he is ready when he must claim leadership. They say a father's love for a daughter is the greatest thing in the world. I write this, and I feel a right old uncle from the war, doting on a child they barely know nor care for.

It is late, and I tire from a day in the saddle. I am sending this now, and I hope it finds you better than before.

Be strong, brother.
Yours,
Gemmil.

Equinox 143rd
Dear Gemmil,

I cannot stress how much these letters have comforted me. I'm sorry I have not written sooner. Months and seasons come and go, and I find myself beaten by this life, beaten by Dia. Beaten by the love I had for this city. I look in a mirror and see a shell with dead eyes staring back. Aye, I still have my jawline and my hair. I even have a firm belly. But honestly, I am less than I was. There is no fight left in me. I remember our trio, violent and desperate in our heyday. War was beautiful, and we were gods. In many ways, I feel akin to Wiiden, tiring of stunning savagery and retiring to the silence of peacetime. Like me, Wiiden has suffered for his acts. My suffering is of the soul, but his suffering is far deeper. Who knew we would end up like this?

It looked like good fortune smiled upon us all for a few days. I hear the hum, and I regret, and I read back upon some of your earlier messages, and I taste your anger and welcome it now. All those years ago, you were right. You still are. Indeed, you are the only one of us worthy of a crown. Had I the strength and an invitation, I might pack up this horrid life and come seeking you down in the South. But I know there is no invitation in the wind, nor do I deserve such a gesture. Regardless, please do not fret, my old friend.

How is Wiiden? I have written him many times since Breiga's passing, and he needs to write me back. He might spend time in Samara. A few days hunting the hum might distract him from awful things. Perhaps you might come, too. No fiend will call for your head; no jail will await you. I suspect I will receive a resounding silence on your part, which is also expected. It is late in the season; it feels like another Culling season is just over the hill. I don my mask, sit, and endure Dia's remarks again, and slowly give up to fate.

Be well, my friend.
Seth.

Solstice 33rd
Dear Seth,

I bring word of awful things indeed. When I spoke with Wiiden last and broke his heart, I believed him sane and robust enough to take such a devastating loss. But things have taken a horrible turn. And tragically, by his own hand. Not three nights ago, I learned that a deed most awful had come upon his house once more. Although I heard only from young Drahir's mouth the awfulness of the matter, it appears Wiiden has suffered another colossal heartbreak. The little one, Cordelia, has perished with her mother in a fire. The death of the whore is of little consequence to me, but the loss of the little one is a heartbreaking thing indeed.

I held Drahir for an hour as he cried deeply for little Lea. I have sought out Wiiden, but he is lost out in the wastes. Taken to flight in his horror. This "accidental" fire was set by his hand. I fear we have likely lost Wiiden forever. As I write this, I cry for my old friend. He, the greatest of us all, deserved more from life than this. He is dead. I feel it in my bones. I have sent what pathetic scouts I have to seek him out, although by now he may be little more than a corpse hanging in a tree. I do not know what will come of these events. I wonder should I have taken him south with me to bury Breiga instead of leaving him with his whore and so many bottles of ale. I had great hopes for him. For us all. I could tell he was getting restless for vengeance, brother, but now all is lost. I feel a hum in my mind, for I regret the world as you do, brother.

Yours,
Gemmil.

Solstice 97th
Dear Gemmil,

I write this hastily, for I hope word reaches you as swiftly as the riders rush. Have you found Wiiden? Have you discovered him alive? For once, it is I who am sending you words in the wind, and they are fine words indeed. When I learned the news not three hours ago, I swiftly scribed this missive. The child Cordelia is alive. Can you believe such a remarkable turn of events? She barely knows what has occurred— understandable in one so young.

I see the resemblance in her. I see his fire, although it is hidden beneath a sweet grimace. After the fire, she was taken in by the family Marteen. I know little of the details, save that they know her legacy and importance. The father of the household delivered her to the city. He fears Wiiden's outrage and fears for the girl's life. Surely our boy would never have attempted to murder the child as she slept? Regardless, they know how to keep silent their actions lest he come for her. I, too, will keep her secret, at least for now. The family are returning to their homestead. They have been generously rewarded for their deeds from my pocket—a small sacrifice.

I am sending this now in desperate hope you can swiftly spread word. If nothing else can return him to his senses, it might be this news of the child.

May this message find you swiftly.
Seth.

Equinox 54th
Dear Seth,
I have received these last five messages. Please forgive me for my silence. A blessing upon you for your silence regarding Cordelia. These past few months have been a trying time. I will say that I bring good word of Wiiden. He lives, although he is different from when we last spoke of him. He is torn asunder, and honestly, he is better for it. Gone now is the doting drunk we endured this last decade. He has forsaken everything, and I am at his side. Prepare yourself for this, my oldest friend. We ride into battle once more. Although he is still himself these last few months, there is the scarring of his life upon him. He talks of things. Holy things. He talks to himself a little more too. It is somewhat unsettling, but our brother is ten times the warrior he once was. That pain, that horrid, horrid pain, has lit a fire in him, and we have taken clans apart in the South, and it is glorious. In three months, he has gathered more followers than Breiga ever did in three years under his watch. Wiiden is a god among men, and I gladly glorify him, for that is what right-hand men will do if needed. I fear for him, though. I fear losing him again. There is no place in his heart for hope. Allow his furnace to burn. He sets his sights on the South. More than that, brother, he sets his sights on the city. This will be no swift march, though. Nor will we dare wake the slumbering savage in the east. At least not yet.

The Actions of Gods

There are things to be done. Acts to be played. I ask you, brother, are you with us? Will you play your part as I begged you all those years ago? I have seen to the silencing of the family Marteen. Necessary murder in truth. Such loose words might undo all that we can build. So, with that, I have one request. It is no sweet act nor a brave deed, but it is necessary. You must kill the little one, lest he eventually learn of her fate. Do it swiftly. Do not make her suffer.

May this message arrive swiftly. May it find you well. May it find you strong enough to commit terrible deeds.

Your friend,
Gemmil.

60

ENGAGING THE STORM

Mea shot awake and gasped in the darkness. Something was wrong, terribly wrong. She sat up and held her chest against her thumping heart. She couldn't remember where she was. She knew only that she shook and everything was wrong. She felt bedclothes around her, and her memory began to return.

Somewhere terrible.

In the light, everything was still. Eerily still. Mea pulled at the clothes, at the warm arm resting against her leg. Distantly, she could hear the wind, could hear a gentle snore. Could smell the acrid stench of damp humanity dashed against aged oak.

She slipped from the bedding and her mate and felt the chill in the air. Jeroen stirred, and she immediately felt reassured in his presence. Naked in the darkness, she felt her senses return as she edged the curtain aside to look into the night. She felt that terrible panic take her once more. She searched her mind for the remnants of the dreams and found little. She hadn't dreamt a great deal these past few weeks. Whatever thoughts had stirred her to rise just now weren't from any dream, though, and she wrapped her arms around her body to quell the shivering.

Something is wrong.

"What is it, Mea?" Jeroen whispered, and she jumped at the interruption.

Something dark and terrible is near, and I am terrified.

She wanted to tell him of her sudden fear. She wanted him to reassure her. But her better sense prevailed. Even in the low light, she could see his beautiful face scrunched up in mid-sleep worry. If nothing else, she would reassure him. "Nothing, my love. Go back to sleep."

"Of course, I will," he countered, but he was already slipping free of the covers. He knew her voice all too well. And for a breath, she was relieved he was awake too. Everything was easier when he was beside her, although she did not know why. "Fuk me, it is a blustery one out there," he added, sliding up beside her.

It was a blustery night and worthy of the season. Unlike most other inhabitants of Boat Town, she kept her chambers above ground, out where the air was fresher, out where she could hear the changing of the mood, the wind, the fuken tide. Out where she could look into the night and seek reassurance against terrible feelings. "I just woke with a start and could not shake it."

It's so dark out there.

"You've never been one to ignore a feeling," he said, and moved closer beside her. She felt his arousal against her naked skin, and she smiled. There were beautiful ways to distract from unfamiliar, bad feelings. He embraced her, cupping her breasts but looking over her shoulder, out beyond the curtain into the darkness. "It is dark out there tonight."

"Have you not had enough these last few weeks?" she asked, and he chuckled. A fine, hearty chuckle too, from deep within. She enjoyed this sound. He had not laughed a great deal since his return. Every day, he improved a little bit, she told herself. He was not the larger-than-life Jeroen she once knew, but he was something else. Something she still loved. Would always love. She spun around and kissed him as though it might be their last. She did not know why. She couldn't help herself. Ever since he had returned, their desire and passion had increased tenfold. To any other elder-mated couple, this would have been a miracle in itself. For herself and Jeroen, she suspected it was more than sex. It was their comforting way to endure the horrors they carried. It could also distract from the uneasy stillness of the world.

The Hunt were out there, preparing to attack in some way. And Boat Town? Well, Boat Town went about its routines of surviving under a siege. It was a strange thing to live on the edge; nothing had happened yet. A stillness had fallen upon both assailants and defenders. And those aboard this gathering of floating vessels were adapting somewhat to this dreadful life. It was the way of survival, she supposed. And most nights, she slept. Most nights she did not fear the end of the world until she woke with bleary eyes and her heart pounding in panic. It was easier facing death in the light of mornings.

But tonight is different.

She looked back out into the dark, and that strange feeling of dread came upon her once more. There were fewer torches lit along the edges of Boat Town. She wondered if the wind had been fierce enough that the flames had struggled, or if there had been a torrential downpour heavy enough to quench them as she slept? She looked to the sky and saw little but clouds and the dim light of the shattered moon trying to break through. A nasty night for slipping away from Jeroen's warmth and reassuring distractions, yet still, she began to dress. After a moment, so did he.

"What are we doing?" he asked kindly, and she did not want to alarm him with further dark thoughts of dread.

"Ah, it's probably nothing. Just a bad dream."

"Aye, probably," he agreed, strapping his belt tight.

"You should stay here."

"I should." He donned his boots swiftly. He bound his sword to his waist and draped his shield behind his back. He could not hold a second blade. Not yet. Perhaps not ever. He had wept over many things since his return, but not his feeble hand. A life less suited to duelling suited him just fine. She could see he was tired of this world, craving something more beyond warfare after drowning in it for too long without relief. "Wherever you go, I will be beside you."

"So you can protect me?"

"So you can protect *me*," he said, smiling.

When they came, they came swiftly. It was an acceptable tactic to delay for as long as they did. Any fool could see that the inhabitants of this floating monstrosity had slipped into a dangerous life of ease. As the Northerners passed their time fishing and slipping ashore, the Hunt had gone quietly to task preparing. They could not hide their great constructions or conceal a grand invasion, of course, so they had allowed the Samarans all the time in the world to rest and recover and become lazy in their tainted little haven. It took no master of tactics to devise a suitable first venture aboard the monstrosity. It took only a little sacrifice on their part, and all were willing to die for the greater good. They waited until the wind was at its fiercest, watching and studying the

The Actions of Gods

positions of every guard at any time before tasting the breeze and being satisfied with their plan.

Alas, it was the emergence of another force that drew their decision to attack that very night. And attack they did, and under the right conditions too.

It was a silent, deadly strike like a poisoned needle upon a king's throat as he slept. With the howling wind masking their movement, with heavy, dark clouds shielding their approach from casual eyes and no armour to weigh them down, the brutes, fifty in total, arranged in neat rows, slid silently into the dark water. Swift as otters, they eased themselves closer, ever closer, before separating into pairs as their gentle swimming strokes brought them to the edge of the floating sanctuary. They were told not to rush, not to make careless sounds, for there was time enough. They knew every foothold available, and where every guard might stand carelessly on watch. They slipped aboard silently, drew blades no bigger than their fists and glided through the walkways, looking for all the world like the rest of the damp peasants of the North aboard the floating town, out for a near-dawn stroll.

There were no more than a couple of dozen guards to tend to, and tend to them they did. A few startled brutes managed a squeal as their killers took them with a few swift plunges of the blades through their ribs, their necks or their groins, but they were overcome easily enough. Within a few moments after the invaders had climbed up out of the freezing water, the sanctuary of the tainted was at their mercy. And there was little mercy to be had.

Their next step was to cast all the torches over the edge to fizzle out in the black waters below. Nothing stirred more panic and ill-discipline in wartime than an inability to see one's killers. They moved along the edges as one terrible unit, killing any fools who were out too late. They did so in silence; they did so in darkness.

The extinguishing of the torches was the signal for the archers at the lakeside to begin their advancement. This would be no long battle; this would be brutal.

The Southern general raised his hand in a silent gesture as the boats drew near. Their targets were the dim glows of lanterns and cooking fires further within Boat Town. The incoming rafts and skips fell still upon the water's smooth surface as a hundred arrows and bolts were loaded.

"Now," the general hissed, his voice carrying like an arrow in a gust.

61

DAY ONE

Magnus felt out of place, a hard thing for a man with such arrogance in his makeup. Perhaps it was his height. Towering over all others like a grandfather among playful youth, he felt old, withered, unwelcomed, and truly out of place. Decades ago, such a thing would have served him well. Then, he had wanted to disappear among the competitors and become less of a target should the trials take a turn for the worse. Truthfully, he had little idea how today's events would go, for no trials were ever the same.

He expected certain things, of course, but ultimately it was all in the hands of the quiet few, absent from the king's court, who decided how each day would progress. He hoped the first day would not entail a grand, gathering battle. The tall brutes would be the first to be taken out in such a scuffle, so that the smaller competitors would have a greater chance—a sound tactic. He looked across the many bobbing heads and saw that few of the attendees were as tall as he. His attention was drawn to one huge brute on the far side. His arms were pikes of iron, his legs as sturdy as trees. This man would reign supreme if all the trials depended on strength alone.

Magnus leaned against the courtyard wall and bowed his head, attempting a little anonymity. There were over a hundred contenders gathered, and they were boisterous. They did not know the seriousness of this event, so they laughed, jeered and made outlandish boasts about their prowess. It was all too familiar, for he'd been here before and shared similar bravado. He'd joked and looked at the finer things instead of concentrating on the tasks ahead.

From an elevated platform, Edain in all her glory read from a long list of names. Any were welcome to attend this event, from the fiercest of every clan to the pauper and the farmer. It gave the impression of inclusion, and such things were good for people who were unsure of what they desired in a very unfair world. The crowd fell silent at her warnings about blood, strife, and perhaps death too, and Magnus's heart also sank a little. He had, after all, brought this event upon the unprepared, those most unfamiliar with the truest tests of might and will.

"I'm sorry," Magnus whispered to the excited crowd and those within it who might well die. "It is necessary," he added weakly, and knew such an excuse would be pathetic to the bereaved families the dead would leave behind.

Acceptable.

Come the following day or so, the majority would return to their unimpressive lives with little more than stories to tell and, hopefully, few regrets that they had tried to seek something great. There were others, though, like the behemoth on the other side of the courtyard, who had spent years preparing for this event. They would last longer.

For a moment, Magnus missed his hounds anew. He had hoped that, having been released from the chains, he might see them before the spectacle, but alas, he was denied even that comfort.

When I become king again, I will have them by my side.

But now was not the time to dwell on this. So, instead of fretting about his only allies in these lands, he focused on the many hundreds attending the event as spectators alone. They must have come from miles around, trudging along the paths, through the marshes and forests, along the eerily lit roads, all for a chance to watch the fiends who were willing to compete. All for immortality. All for glory. All for the tale to tell. Some of them were elderly, he saw, with weakened limbs and sticks to lean upon. Some were youthful and excitable, gathered in cheering groups and boisterously enjoying the entertainment. Others were here with lovers and young ones, eager to witness this historic occasion. He wondered how these rowdy spectators would feel as the event commenced, knowing they were unwilling to enter the fray themselves. Regardless, they cheered or booed loudly as every name was read out. Magnus, for his part, had deep admiration for every competitor. Were he able to, he would have shaken each hand, bowed deeply and expressed his respect, and then he would have thrown himself among them, eager to beat them all and win back the right to save the world, but also, he would carry whatever fiends he could and leave none behind. For that is what any king would do.

The trials were a simple thing. Every day, competitors would be eliminated, retire outright, or be unable to continue. It was a complicated yet worthy thing to find the finest servant of the people, and these trials were the way this most sacred of tasks was accomplished. It had been done thus for a hundred years before his arrival, and if the Savage Isles survived this war, it would be done thus for at least a hundred years after —or at least until these isles outgrew such foolishness as the monarchy.

More farmers' names were called, and their good humour was infectious. They and their friends were creating the stories of their lives, and Magnus smiled at their enthusiasm. They waved to the crowd, boasting and jesting and behaving as though they were without fear. That would change, Magnus knew. But it was a small matter. Their high spirits merely added to the occasion.

Brigid's name was met with outlandish cheering. And why not? She was one of the clan leaders, a warrior who had been tried and tested, and who was revered among her peers. Her face was a grim, determined canvas. She was smaller than most of the others, but strength was only sometimes required for such tests. Surrounded by sisters and brothers of her clan, she was a force to fear—or to end up bowing to.

Soon after, he saw the big brute stand proudly as his name was called, and Magnus became confident he would last until the final day— unless some shrewd combatant took him out sooner, of course. The behemoth was of no clan, but he was a warrior. The crowd knew him as Tusk. Whether that was an unfortunate name or a witty nickname, he appeared primarily human with a little animal thrown in. Such creatures made impressive opponents.

Tusk accepted the applause with a grand bow as more names were read. Beside him, Padir waved to no one at all when his name was called. Still, Magnus admired the boy for attempting to grasp the impossible.

Sloan's name soon followed, and the crowd cheered loudest for him, for they knew his potential. Although Magnus had no fondness for the man, he had to admit that he appeared striking, raising his hand to the many demanding his attention. He had the build and maybe the resolve to get to the final day, but all of it could be undone in one misstep, one sputtering of the will.

Strangely, when Teaolor's name was called, many voices called for her head, mocking her failures, and Magnus frowned at her shame. This was his doing, and had he met her steely glare, he might have offered an apology. As it was, he kept his eyes to the ground and waited to hear his own unpopular name.

As the list of names continued, Magnus noticed that Curroi of Clan Branach had not entered himself in the event. A strange thing, considering his legacy. Magnus thought little of him for the act he had committed, but it was no matter now. His absence meant one less combatant to overcome.

As though to make a point, to rightly leave a shitty taste in everyone's mouth, Magnus was summoned very last. He answered Edain with a gentle nod. The crowd booed, and although he had expected it, his stomach churned. They thought him unworthy and a betrayer for leaving these lands. A small matter. They would kneel and accept his reign when he took his crown outright.

If.

"I commend you all," Edain declared eventually, and the watching crowd erupted in excitement, with the exception of those who suddenly understood the weight of their endeavours to come. Even Magnus felt it in the pit of his stomach, in the slump of his shoulders.

"For the next few days, you will be tested by various means," Edain intoned. "All is fair in blood and battle, but those caught in underhanded deeds shall meet a cruel end," she warned, and Magnus nodded along, but honestly, he was no longer listening to her instructions. It was the same as before. They would be tested, each in their own way, until the final day, when the fiercest would prevail. Magnus leaned against the far wall, summoned his will, focused his breathing and began to stir himself for the trauma and exhaustion ahead. His breakfast sat uncomfortably in his belly, and for a terrible moment he worried he might throw it up. They would eat little over the next few days, which could be costly. Aye, there were strength and wits to be tested, and though Magnus recalled the strain of the testing from before, it was the gnawing hunger and dreadful exhaustion he never forgot.

Around him, the palace's courtyard suddenly bustled with excitement as Edain called out for the first march. Two carts full of bulging packs were dragged into the square, and Magnus's heart sank, for he understood this would be no real test. It was merely a funnel to sieve out the weakest from the litter before the real dangers appeared.

So it begins.

Stretching for the third time since dawn, Magnus fell to the back of the gathered combatants as they formed up into lines, each one eager to receive a pack from the men who stood atop the carts. The men were of no particular clan or banner. Most guards presiding over this event were as neutral as possible—all but one.

Magnus was ashamed to see Gregor, stripped of his royal garments, standing among them. The man had done little more than his duty and had been made to pay for the act. Although the other Green Branch knights were present, none had been punished like him.

"Combatants, when you have received your pack, move clear of this area immediately," Gregor called. He stood upon the cart, handing the packs carefully down to eager hands that reached up as though to receive rations of precious food. "Follow the Riders from this place," he added every few moments. Magnus shook his head sadly. A brave warrior deserved no demoting, yet here was Gregor, handing out bundles like any regular labourer called to serve the Crown. Magnus could not face the man, and lined up for the second cart instead.

"Take your time, little one," Magnus warned Padir, who had pushed through the crowd and come up alongside him. "It's not supplies they are providing for this event."

The first few to receive a pack had already begun following Gregor's instructions and marching out of the courtyard and onward through the settlement. Accompanied by a few Riders upon horses, they moved like cattle led to slaughter, and perhaps, in a way, they were.

Regardless of Magnus's words, Padir stepped along with him, though the cheeriness was gone from his face now. When they reached the front of the line, he almost dropped his pack as it was handed to him. Swiftly, he undid its straps and then cried out in horror at the collection of heavy rocks stacked up inside.

"What the fuk is this shit?"

"A reminder of the burden we must carry as leaders," Magnus insisted, taking his own pack with a grunt. He did not check its contents; he merely strapped it tightly to his back and began walking away with the rest. Immediately, his balance was thrown off as the rocks within it shifted position. It was no devastating weight, but it would weigh him down, and Magnus knew the agony they would all endure an hour from now.

"This is rightly shit," Padir muttered, marching past him. His pack was uneven, its straps tightened to leave a little space around the shoulders; it bounced ever so with each step he took. He wasn't the only one who had made this error, and for a breath, Magnus almost allowed him to continue on his merry way.

"Come here," he growled, stopping the boy and tightening the straps.

"That hurts, Your Highness."

Little shit.

"Trust me," Magnus murmured, giving the straps a final tug and setting him upright.

They walked beneath the arch of the palace leading into the town. They were far behind the rest of the marchers now, and there was only one Rider to monitor their progress. It was Gregor, and Magnus still would not face the man. Thankfully, Gregor had little interest in engaging in conversation either. Instead, he just watched with a blank face as they walked through the settlement. The crowd had thinned out now that the bulk of the parade had passed.

"It's so tight at the shoulders," Padir complained, and suddenly Magnus doubted the boy would even reach the ocean.

"It'll hurt a lot more this time tomorrow," Magnus said after a time. His eyes were upon the near fully erected structure on the outskirts of town, and his heart skipped a beat. The Gauntlet was the only thing he truly feared; the steps required to conquer it were perilous. He watched a dozen builders go to work with mallets and nails, testing the beast's gears, the swinging clubs, the fuken hammers. He'd hated those fuken things.

"You mean we'll be carrying these for the day?"

"If we are lucky, little one."

Padir did not reply. His face was grave now as he noticed the structure. Magnus could see the questions boiling over in his mind, but he lost his words every time he went to speak.

"Don't worry, Padir," he told him. "You'll probably have yielded long before you face that bitch."

"You promise?" Padir jested weakly.

———

To Magnus's surprise, the boy didn't quit. He kept up with Magnus and the rest of the gathered crowd just fine. However, his brow was covered in sweat, and Magnus could relate to the torment he was clearly feeling. The boisterous competitors, led by Tusk, had kept their bravado up for the first six or seven hours, but now, as the day drew on, heads were drooping, conversation was low. Every step had become agony, and Magnus's knee stung unmercifully with every movement. Still, he continued to march onwards with Padir at his side. He thought it humorous that he couldn't entirely rid himself of the little shit's presence. Misery loved company, he supposed.

A dozen competitors had already bowed out, most just dropping to the ground in front of the mounted soldiers. Gasping and muttering under their breath, they looked as broken as Magnus felt, and indeed, they were likelier the smarter ones. Magnus stared through them as he marched past. Seeing each one fall infused him with determination. It was more than just the fact that their yielding meant fewer numbers to compete with. It was knowing that, despite his age and ravaged body, his will was steel. He remembered that same determination from a lifetime before. It had carried him far once. He hoped it would continue to match his step in this contest.

Magnus dug deep into himself. He swallowed the pain and imagined his body young and capable and not so close to breaking. Truthfully, though, he was in torment most of the time. He just learned to take the pain and accept it. It was the Alpha influence in him.

"This is fuken awful," Padir gasped after a few hours' silence. It was the quietest he'd ever been in Magnus's company. When he spoke, he drew Magnus from his dark, painful thoughts.

"You know this is not even a trial."

"What does that mean?"

"This is just to weed out the dregs," Magnus said, and knew those around him listened and feared. They all knew of the trials. But nobody sang songs of the walk between ventures. Suddenly that pack felt a little heavier.

They marched along the jagged coast, this convoy of hunched warriors upon a narrow path, all in line, one following the other. With a cutting wind in their faces and little but the rush of cold air in their ears, they marched for hours, chasing the fading sun until night fell. With the darkness came orders to march down to a long beach as the tide drew in.

"First trial," Magnus muttered. He knew that there were any number of trials discussed and argued in the courts before such an event. These might have been decided long before talk of Magnus's defiance reached their ears. Had Magnus cared, he might have sought out what was planned and prepared himself for it. They probably wouldn't have told him anyway. The same "they" who knew of the Clieves. Besides, it was probably better to treat these trials like he would the Gauntlet. Worst thing anyone could do was try and prepare themselves for it. Better to trust one's instincts and take a leap of faith.

A few dozen warriors kept eyes on the combatants as they led them down to the beach, where the rush of the ocean was louder than the wind. Exhaustion took Magnus all of a sudden, and for a few breaths, he dropped to his knees in the sand and allowed the rest to march ahead.

"I don't think we can rest, Magnus," Padir said nervously. He pulled gently at his king lest the fatigue dethrone him completely.

"I'll rest every moment I can. You would be wise to do the same, young one," Magnus countered, but he knew this reprieve was short-lived. There was already a wide gap between themselves and the last competitor. "Fine—let's have a rightly shitty night," he muttered gloomily as Gregor drew up alongside them.

"Take your time, my liege," Gregor said softly. Although he appeared to carry no rank anymore, most other soldiers followed his word. "There are many hours left until the new day."

"It'll be a long night," Magnus countered, rising. Setting his pack on the sand, he began stripping his clothes away until he stood in only his undergarments.

"Shorter for some," argued Padir. After a breath, he too set down his pack and began to strip away his own outer clothing. He picked up his pack again, stepped towards the water and dipped a toe in. "Oh, fuk me—it's freezing. Couldn't you have returned to the isles in a warmer season?" He stepped gamely through the first wave and met the next at his knees. He immediately began rubbing his arms as though it would stem the coldness, but the nightmare was only beginning.

Behind him, Magnus gathered up his pack, arranged it on his shoulders once more and started towards the water. Biting back a yelp of surprise at the cold, he began trudging through the rushing waves out towards the darkness of the black sea. Beyond, a little further ahead, there were moans and gasps from the other competitors, who were already waist-deep in the breaking waves. Some of the soldiers abandoned their mounts and climbed aboard crude rafts, which bobbed lazily on the surface where they were anchored. Others remained mounted and watched, rested, ate, and stayed warm, while the rest stood with burning torches, looking out over the throngs of shivering bodies in the spray. They waved those warm flames and cast light over the whole strange spectacle. They could see just enough to keep a watchful eye, enough to save those who couldn't save themselves. They barked warnings and instructions, but few heard anything above the sound of their own chattering teeth.

"You cast away your pack, you walk right back ashore," Gregor called out. His mount fought the rush of the cold water, but he patted her to ease, then dropped down and waded towards one of the rafts. "You drown yourself, that's also a banishment from the tournament."

There was laughter from his comrades. Even a lowly soldier could be born to lead, and for a moment, Magnus regretted he wasn't chest-deep in the water with the rest of them. He had known Gregor many years, but only in the last few days did he recognise that the man was made of kingly things.

Padir, however, was not made from kingly things at all. He scrambled in the water, fighting the waves in panic, and Magnus grabbed his arm and took hold. "Be still, oh loyal comrade," he mocked, and Padir settled ever so. He appeared like a beast struck by the sparkle of a city's unnatural light. "Just move with the waves, find your footing; we'll be here until dawn."

It was no lie, and though the boy shook as Magnus did, he nodded and began to move with the waves as they struck against his chest.

They waded in farther until all the competitors stood in a grand cluster, each one leaping slightly as the waves crashed and dashed against them. Some stumbled and went under; others were dragged beneath the water by the weight of their pack. In the beginning, all who floundered rose gamely back out of the water again in a spluttering stumble, but Magnus imagined that as the hours wore on, fatigue would make rising without a pack attached seem mighty attractive. For his part, he allowed the numbness to overtake his body as swiftly as he could. He felt like dying in this awfulness, but short of his heart betraying him, he knew he had the will to survive this trial.

It did not take long for the first combatant to falter. All it took was losing his footing on the sandy bottom as a wave caught him unaware. Down he crashed beneath the tide, and Magnus could only watch from a distance as his pack kept him submerged, and his weakened body fought and gave in to panic. Stripping his burden free and leaving it where it lay, the man pulled himself back above the surface, cursing the trial and his own weakness. By the time he'd scrambled ashore, another three had followed after. All it took was a little crack in their wall, Magnus mused, and the waves flooded through.

"They have the right idea," muttered Padir unhappily as the disqualified combatants waded past him, free from their crushing weight. Still, though he was pale and shivering, he stayed firm, and though Magnus hated the little shit, he respected his grim determination. He was the smallest competitor in this event and as such, was feeling the rocks far worse than anyone else. "I bet they get fed when they go ashore."

The Actions of Gods

"I bet it's roast rack of boar," Sloan muttered from somewhere close by. His head hung low; his arms were wrapped around his chest as he tried desperately to preserve whatever warmth he could. Gone was his smug arrogance, replaced with a cold stare of concentration. Every wave took its toll on the man, but he held firm, and Magnus recognised another exemplary leader, even if he was a smug fuk who deserved a beating.

"I bet there's a creamy sauce with it," Teaolor added, and watched longingly as their competitors slipped from wet to dry land and a likely feast. Like Magnus, she too was feeling the strain, but there was steel in her voice, and at that moment, as though the absent gods had whispered in his ear, he knew she would be there on the last day.

"Boar with honey and onion is the only way," Brigid declared, and a few of the others nodded in agreement. Magnus did too. His son had once suggested such a thing, and Magnus was determined to try such a feast.

"Fools," shouted Tusk, who was farthest away. If the waves were testing his will, he did not show it. He merely looked at the shattered moon above as though in great thought. "Boar should be delicately slathered in pepper sauce, glazed in maple and finished off with cloves dug deep into the outer husk," he added, and Magnus imagined such a glorious gathering of flavour, and his belly growled.

"With some roasted potatoes and a fuk-load of buttered carrots," Padir said after a time, and they all nodded in agreement.

Were Curroi to have stood in the waters with them, he might have added his thoughts on the matter, but he was not present, and the conversation was lesser for it.

The hours passed, and with them, the slow trickle of defeated competitors. Every time a warrior dumped their pack in the wash and trudged ashore, Magnus took their failure as fuel for his desire. Although his knee ached and his back felt like a shard of jagged ice had lanced him right through, he thought himself to be enduring the torment rather impressively.

Among the rest, only Tusk was too stubborn to be defeated by the cold and the waves. For hours more, he faced every wave with a roar of defiance. Magnus wondered if it was a game he played to grate on the other competitors' nerves or simply his own way of enduring the cold. Regardless, his voice echoed across the spray, adding to the irritation of all within earshot. Eventually, a hardened old warrior spun on him, gripping his shoulders and shouting for his silence, and slapped him across the face. The crowd might have approved; they might have agreed. They might have said as much, too, until Tusk suddenly shoved his accoster's head below the surface and held him as he thrashed. Were Magnus close, he might have taken this moment to challenge the brute, but his knees were too fatigued, the distance too great. The soldiers roared and shouted warnings, but there was no stopping a Tusk in full flight. As the diminutive warrior weakened beneath the other man's massive weight, Tusk suddenly pulled him from the water and began ruthlessly thrashing him. By the fourth strike, the beaten man stopped struggling, and Tusk, perhaps fearing disqualification over the simple act of murder, slid the pack from the unconscious man's shoulders and dragged him to the nearest raft.

"He struck me first. You all saw it."

No one dared to contest this, and besides, he had indeed been struck first. No fool challenged the brute after that either.

An hour before dawn, Magnus first took notice of Padir's troubles. The boy had taken to a demented routine of floating, sinking and rising desperately again in time with the waves.

"Are you okay, boy?" Magnus hissed, nearing him.

"I've lost all feeling in my legs," Padir said quietly. It was no plea; there was no panic in his tone. It was grim acknowledgement of his woes. "Can't stay upright anymore." With this, a wave took him and dragged him under. He struggled to rise, spitting a mouthful of salt water from his quivering lips.

"I think it's time," Magnus said.

"I'd prefer to die rather than be beaten by my legs. Fuk that, I will rise," he argued, and Magnus wondered had he blinded himself with ideas of grandeur.

"You don't belong here," Magnus hissed. He took hold of the boy, who clutched him as though he were a floating log.

"Release me—I belong here. I'm just fine." With all his strength, he shoved Magnus away in one last attempt at defiance, but suddenly he stumbled back into the waves and did not rise, and Magnus was helpless to watch him kill himself. There was very little struggle as the boy hung suspended in the water. Gregor shone the light over the area where the annoying little shit had once stood, and Magnus saw a hand desperately clawing for the surface. Then the water stilled, and a few bubbles broke the surface as the boy no doubt cursed him with his last breath. It was no way to die, but it was a worthy thing to attempt greatness with a body so unprepared.

"Oh, fuk me," the king whispered, reaching down and pulling Padir back to the surface.

The boy fought for breath, his nose ran, he coughed and hacked, and although he was a burden, Magnus held him upright until he recovered his breathing.

"You should not be doing that," Brigit called. She was suffering now, as were most of the others. Her hair clung to her pale face, but she was defiant.

"Would you stop me saving a life? Would any of you?" Magnus called out, and strangely, Gregor, on the boat, turned away. With him went the light, and Magnus was alone with his soaked companion.

"I can do this," Padir groaned. His eyes were upon the land, and Magnus could see the desperation in his face. All he had to do was slip free and struggle ashore. There was no shame in it. He'd done better than most. "I cannot fail in the last hour."

"There's more than an hour; there's a half night yet to come," lied Magnus. He played no deceitful game. He reviled the little shit, but he was not ready to have him drown beside him on the off-chance he'd endure another hour.

"Release me. I'm feeling better now," lied Padir, and Magnus could take no more. He released him, and the boy fought his body's collapse. He did well too, splashing, yelping, sinking, and nearly drowning until Magnus took hold of him and ripped his pack open.

"Do not do this to me," the boy gasped.

"You will live this night and owe me," Magnus whispered, as though there was some deal to be made. Careful not to drop it, he undid his own pack and took a few rocks from Padir's, and a few more after that. With his bag soon filled to the brim, he hoisted it back onto his shoulders. Staggering a little under the weight, he released Padir, who floated easier in the water now. "Do not sink again," Magnus warned, and the boy, shaken, grateful, confused, and a little suspicious, nodded in agreement.

"That is against fair competition," cried Brigit, who had seen everything.

"There are no rules. The boy inspired me to save him. Surely that's a kingly thing on his part," argued Magnus, bracing himself against a heavy wave.

"I see no problem," Tusk cried, interrupting himself in mid-scream to chime in. "Perhaps you might carry a few of mine for the rest of the night?"

Magnus, sensing his threat, turned and faced him. With steel in his tone he wasn't confident he could support, he gestured to the larger man. "Come and gift them to me, and we'll see if I go down as easily as your last victim." Acceptable words; Tusk stared at him for a time, trying to understand whether he'd been threatened. Then, unsure, and unwilling to take a chance, he turned away and began attacking the waves once more with his cries, and Magnus sighed deeply. Beside him, Padir floated, testing his legs and finding some strength.

"I think I can take them back soon."

"Of course you can, little one."

62

THE NEXT DAY

Magnus had felt cold many times in his life. Terrible coldness, like a fruitless chase in the depths of the South. Dangerous cold that threatened to take his breath. This cold was different. This cold threatened to take his very soul. He wavered in the water but stayed upright despite the weariness in his bones and the ache throughout his body. The combatants had drawn near the shore during the night, drawn in by the current. Looking around, he could see that only fifty or so remained this harsh morning.

There might have been fifty-one had Curroi entered the event, but he had not. He probably lazed in silken sheets as his peers waged war on each other's discipline.

Among those whose discipline had been tested most, none had died this night, which was remarkable. He praised the work of the guards who had spent the night pulling exhausted, drowning competitors from the unforgiving waves with little rest. Theirs was a similarly nasty pilgrimage without reward.

He could have cried with relief when the first light flooded the sky in crimson, amber and blue. Despite himself, he imagined a world where every movement was taken freely, without awful frozen shards of pain. In desperation, he watched the soldiers as the morning sun lit the day and wondered if he would ever feel warmth in his body again. They did not stir for a time; they merely stood in the water, still as statues, until the flaming sphere lit up the lands and the first calls to end the event were given.

"A fine morning," bellowed Tusk, wading back towards the beach.

His impressive cries of defiance had dwindled away as the night drew on, but he charged inland as though he'd enjoyed a hearty night's sleep. Perhaps he was too stupid to realise his exhaustion. "Let us all get going to the next trial."

"Idiot," muttered Padir as he passed, and Tusk turned slightly and eyed his detractor before continuing on his way.

"You might pay for that one later," Sloan muttered, following the crowd.

"I have Magnus to protect me," countered the pale youth, who waded beside the king.

"I'll not do everything to get you the throne," Magnus grumbled, splashing through the relentless waves and struggling against the early wind as it cut through him.

"Thank you," Padir said quietly as they approached the shore. If Magnus didn't know better, he might have believed the boy.

Those who had foolishly not stripped off their garments met no reprieve from the cold, and Magnus felt sorry for them. The soldiers must have thought so, too, for they lit a few fires to warm the life back into them. The sodden combatants dropped down one by one in front of the flames, and indeed, Magnus was grateful for the fire, too. Stripping off his soaked undergarments, he lay down before the nearest blaze, rested his head on his dry clothes, using some to cover his shame and allowed the flames to fully dry him out and warm him up. His empty stomach was close to lurching, his mind was adrift with lesser thoughts and his eyes were burning against the morning's light. Around them, the first cheeriness returned to the competitors as the fires warmed their shaking bodies. There were jests, laughter, and even prayers to ancient gods, both absent and present, and for a moment, wrapping his arms around himself, Magnus smiled in relief.

"You can dry and rest for as long as you like, but you must return to Risbeigh by nightfall," Gregor announced, and there was a collective cry of disbelief. There were some dreadful curses thrown his way, too, but there was no convincing their keepers. "We will not wake you. We will not allow you to be assisted by either beast or man. But you may leave your packs behind."

Immediately, the gathered competitors rose once more on shaky legs. A few continued to warm themselves by the flames for a few breaths longer before they, too, trudged after the leading Rider on a miserable march back along the coast.

"I don't think I can walk another mile without some sleep," mumbled

Padir. He knelt at the flames, his knuckles white with anger and frustration, and Magnus felt the same. Even as sleep threatened to take him, he knew the precariousness of a delay. Even an hour undisturbed would have infused him with the will to continue this march, with the energy to keep pace, but he knew well that an hour of sleep led to many more when a body was this tired. However, he had a plan where he could rest a while and then get back to the event.

"Don't suppose I could trust you to stay awake and allow me a little rest?" he asked Gregor, who smiled ruefully while shaking his head. "Very well, friend. Do you have a spare canteen of water?"

Shrugging, Gregor extended the bottle, and Magnus took a few mighty gulps.

"I suppose we should leave, so," Padir muttered.

"Wait a moment, boy," Magnus said, grabbing his hand. "Let the rest march on without sleep. I'll wake us in no more than two hours," he whispered, and as the rest of the combatants, soaked and weary, began to move up the beach towards the path, Magnus continued to drink from Gregor's canister—a wonderful thing after spitting up sea salt all night.

"We really should move with them," Padir said. His eyes were watering; his face looked even more wretched than usual. Magnus knew he himself probably appeared ruined.

Not ruined. Not yet.

"I have a bladder the size of a shrew," Magnus said, finishing his water and lying back in the sand. "I'll wake up soon enough to relieve myself."

"Otherwise, you'll wake up this evening without a kingdom and a damp patch in your trousers," quipped Padir.

Magnus had a reply, but chose to let his mind rest. And soon enough, he was asleep.

It felt as though only moments had passed when he awoke, but he knew better. There was an awful, wonderful moment where he considered giving in once more to this delicious slumber, forgetting whatever deed he had to do once he woke. He'd dreamt of roast boar in those few wonderful moments and dearly wanted to return to that pepper gravy dream once more.

Get up.
Get dressed.

He did. The sun had moved ever so across the sky, and he knew this was important. Pulling himself to his feet, he moved down to the shore and relieved himself in the ocean. That done, he returned to the fire and the little sleeping shit of a cub sprawled out in the sand. His mind had returned somewhat in those first few moments, and the realisation of the massive task ahead of them had shaken him once more. For a moment, he considered leaving the boy behind, partly for his own good but also for a bit of retaliation on his part. "It's no way to lose such a contest," he said at last, as much to reaffirm his decision as anything else, and kicked the boy awake.

"One more hour, please," Padir cried.

"I'll not call you again," Magnus warned, and this time, the boy stirred and, against his better judgement, leapt to his feet and began dressing. "How very kingly of you."

They followed the path to the coast's top, and pausing there to scan the miles to the horizon, they saw no sign of their comrades. In the bushes nearby, however, they saw Gregor lazing by his mount, his breathing little more than a snore. Magnus strode over and took this moment to kick him awake too.

"Tell me this—we don't have to return by the same route we took to get here, do we?" Magnus asked as the man struggled to find his wits.

"As long as it is by foot, I have no issue."

They set off with Gregor behind them. The path was more manageable with a few hours' sleep under their belts. More than that, Magnus knew this coast, knew these lands well. They cut across the tops of peninsulas where the coastline followed a more jagged route, thus sometimes saving a few miles at a time. For a time, Magnus's mind was clear of thoughts, but occasionally, he imagined marching these miles with his hounds at his side, and a sadness came upon him. Not just for his boys but for everything he'd lost on the way. But instead of dwelling on such sorrow, he forced himself to take the next step and the one after. It was all he could do. It was just about enough.

Morning turned to afternoon, to evening, and truly, it was an exhausting slog over bog lands, sandy dunes, open grasslands and rocky coastline. As evening fell, they saw wanderers in the distance, some sticking to the path, some getting left behind, some even collapsing at the side of the road with limbs unwilling to carry them another mile, and Magnus respected them for getting this far. Still, though, he and Padir and Gregor came alongside them and then marched past; they were making fine time indeed.

The Actions of Gods

Eventually, far off in the distance, they caught sight of the settlement. This should have elicited euphoria, but instead, the trio were drawn to an encampment on the outskirts of the town where great torches blazed brightly against the night sky—and illuminated the terrifying next event.

"The fuken Gauntlet," Magnus muttered, and a chill like an ocean wave took hold of his flesh and wouldn't let go.

63

GAUNTLET

He had known this beast was coming. They all did. They'd even gazed upon her skeleton on the first day. Back then, there had been over a hundred challengers; now, just forty remained. Those forty were elite and hardened. The beast's glow had brought them all to this place like moths. They circled her in the flickering light from the hundred torches upon her surface. It was the one constant in all trials. Still, seeing this altered beast again in all her glory was dreadful.

Only Tusk and a few of his comrades had arrived before them, and that was no surprise. Tusk was asleep at the far end of the structure, no doubt saving his energy for the trauma to come. Padir was relieved to see him in this state of rest and was happy to avoid the man for as long as possible. A table of freshly baked honey bread awaited them, and such a feast was welcomed as much as the prospect of sleep.

Magnus and Padir sat below the ladder leading to the first platform, twenty feet up, and ate a few mouthfuls of bread. Padir argued for more, but Magnus was wary lest their guards had tainted the food in some awful way. It was a terrible enough thing to endure trials; it would be far worse with an aching belly spilling its contents every hour.

"That beast is terrifying," said Padir quietly, lying back in some long grass that had not been shorn to make way for the beast's assembly. Wrapping his cloak around his shoulders and closing his eyes, he appeared impossibly comfortable. "Wake me when it's time to die," he jested, and Magnus laughed.

He gazed out around the area and listened to the sounds of the night: the dull murmur of competitors, and the excited, muted chatter of their audience, who sat around waiting impatiently for events to unfold. He listened, too, to the flap of fire from the Gauntlet and only partly hoped the beast would catch fire and that they could move on to the next savage event. Soon, though, he closed his eyes, knowing sleep was as precious as gold in this dreadful event. Any fool could be challenging and fierce, but an exhausted mind was enough to bring any warrior to their knees. Sometimes it wasn't lack of skill that brought a competitor down. Sometimes it was the casual, ill-spent moments before that. Padir and Tusk had the right idea, he knew, and careful to fill his mouth with only one swallow of water, Magnus lay back and closed his eyes.

He slept deeply for all too brief a time, and indeed, it was a godsend. Awaking to the sound of the excited crowd who were discussing the events to come, Magnus took a moment to calm his nerves and settle himself for the coming nightmare. Although he ached from head to toe, his mind was far clearer than it had been on the morning in the sea.

"It is time," a voice cried.

"Just another hour," whispered Padir from beside him. He fought Magnus's gentle shoving like any child when a parent came to wake them at an ungodly hour.

"Come on, little one. It's time to get ourselves killed."

"My last wish is for more sleep. Grant a dying man this gift."

"Move yer rear, or I'll leave you behind."

This had the desired effect, and the boy sat up and rubbed his eyes. Magnus looked to the sky; he didn't know how long he had slept save that the shattered, spitting moon had moved across the sky. Were he to guess, it was after midnight. The voice that had woken him was Gregor's; the man looked as tired as Magnus felt. Gregor and his companions were walking through the gathering of victorious combatants, kicking awake those who slept, silencing those who had questions. He marched proudly despite his lack of regal attire, and Magnus again thought him an impressive man.

As though herding sleepy, argumentative sheep, Gregor directed the combatants to the front of the great machine where Edain stood upon a podium, looking like she'd rested and eaten well the last few days. If Magnus had squinted his aching eyes, he might have imagined it was Dia delivering addresses to an expectant crowd. She began to speak, and the public could barely contain themselves, even at this late hour.

She spoke words like honour, sacrifice, legend and tradition, and although the audience approved, the combatants barely listened, for above her, loud clangs and the grinding of metal filled the air as three men began rotating the levers to set the beast in motion.

Oh, fuk me.

It took little time, for like rocks rolling down a hill, once the wheels began to turn they continued moving of their own volition, gaining momentum as they went. The machine fully came to life as Edain offered proclamations of the Gauntlet's grandness—all automated, all rhythmic and all terrifying. Tragically for the contestants, the Gauntlet was never the same machine twice. Instead, each one was the creation of some skilled engineer who had been given the honour of building her. Magnus imagined the bastard at least a decade before, scribbling mechanism after mechanism upon a vast canvas as he sought to trick and maim those who would attempt to beat the beast. Great chains as long as the machine spun and carried the paddle, platform and hammer mechanisms. The beast reminded him of a stinging hive of honey wasps, and would be just about as safe to any clumsy, sweet-toothed thief. The ground shook, the crowd gasped, the flickering flames cast dancing shadows across the vast, open grassland where the Gauntlet waited, and despite his trepidations, Magnus walked towards the beast as though she were a mount to be bested or an entire army to be charged.

"Oh, fuk me," he breathed.

The crowd were lost to her, gaping at the machine, but Edain continued. "You brave few who have survived the previous tests must now stand upon these hallowed steps and prove yourselves once more." Magnus imagined her practising in a mirror and fuming that this grim machination of doom would overtake her delivery, no matter how grand. "If you fall, you are not destined for this throne," Edain continued, but Magnus already knew the rules of this beast. Climb up, get through the obstacles and climb back down on the other side. He would have preferred a shorter speech, but it was no matter, he supposed. Those of the court desired shows of pomp and circumstance, especially when advertising their skills to prospective employers.

"Oh, fuk me," cried Padir, and Magnus looked past him to the structure looming over them both. It hadn't changed substantially from the bare bones he'd seen when they had marched out on the first day. It was still just over twenty feet high, but should a fiend take a foolish fall, the drop could end their life. He could have sworn the Gauntlet he'd almost perished on, many years earlier, had been higher. He tried to remember how many injuries had been sustained that dreadful day, how many deaths there had been. More than enough to weed out those who were unprepared. He looked at Padir, who was gazing at the swinging paddles. He watched the boy move along to the hammers, then study the mechanism and its timing, and Magnus remembered almost making the same mistake when he was young.

"We should do this first," Magnus called, and the boy shook his head.

"Absolutely fuken not."

Magnus took hold of his collar and pulled him close. "Look around. Everyone watches in trepidation. Trepidation is fine. Trepidation will keep you swift and careful."

Padir nodded. "That sounds like a fine plan."

"Listen, you little shit. Things will occur on this platform. Things that will take that trepidation and turn it into crushing fear. Fear will get you killed up there. If that overtakes you, then I tired myself out with the rocks for nothing. Best we get this bitch cleared long before anyone else does."

"I wish to stay. I wish to study the route."

Magnus began to laugh, for he saw the boy was dead set on making the same youthful mistakes as he once had himself. "That's the first trick of the beast. She never displays herself in proper sequence. Those cogs will turn and chew at different timings, and anyone who falls for her deceptions will fall this night. Only fools believe they know the route, that they have discovered her secret. Trust me, those who go first can take their honey-sweet time, and no one will rush them. A rush upon this beast will be devastating."

Padir was unconvinced. Regardless, Magnus marched towards the platform, and the boy followed. Nobody followed after, and this reassured Magnus. For a breath, he was less the battered old king desperate to cling to power and more the adventurous wild legend who had taken these isles by the scruff of the neck and made them his own.

"This will never work," Padir cried, and Magnus grinned. It might not work, but this type of violence he was built for. Besides, if he did plummet to a grisly death, it was best to get it over and done with.

"The best of luck to you all," Edain shouted, and bowed to Magnus. "May you meet no brutal death upon these mechanisms of torment."

Thanks very much!

Magnus stilled his nerve with a few happier thoughts of hounds, comrades, family and mates, then took a breath and began climbing towards certain doom. He couldn't remember if the beast had shaken as violently before. Perhaps his legs were betraying him at the worst possible moment. Regardless, it was the hardest climb up a ladder he'd ever endured, and all too soon, he reached the end, and the real test began.

The platform he stood upon was ancient oak, polished and smooth and just wide enough for two foolish legends to stand and gather their wits, formulate plans, and regret their decisions. Below him, Padir scrambled up, gripping each rung lest his feet betray him on the way.

"Fuk me, it's higher up here than it appeared," he cried, dropping to a knee lest a gust of wind blow him to the grassy ground below. From here, there were two ways down: the ladder at the far end of the structure's walkway, at least a hundred feet across, or a drop anywhere between here and there. "After you, Your Highness," he added, gripping a solitary handrail at the edge.

Up here, the sound of the killing mechanisms driving the beast lessened in volume. Now, all Magnus could hear was the hiss of paddles swinging left and right across the walkway to the next platform. Three platforms in all. Each thirty feet wide, give or take. He stepped out towards the edge and walked a few feet along, and hesitated as the nearest paddle whooshed past, clearing the footway by a hand's width.

Fuk me.

He turned and foolishly glanced down to his comrades below, watching in grim terror and the faint hope that he would be taken out swiftly. It was a small matter, he supposed. The thought that death would be swift was scant reassurance, and he slipped by the next paddle as it swished by. Then, as though the absent gods were stirring a brew of trouble for their amusement, the behemoth was shaken by a nasty gust of wind and the beginnings of rainfall.

"Ah, fuk me," Magnus cried again, bracing himself against the wind and the cold spatter of freezing rain. He only narrowly avoided the next paddle as it swung real fuken near and tried to take his fuken head off. "Fuk this!" he hissed and slipped forward, moving past the next paddle and onto the next platform in the same treacherous leap. With just the last platform to reach, he stopped to calm his beating heart and secure his footing.

"Why are you stopping?" cried a voice from behind him. Real close. Too close. He dared a glance behind him and saw Padir balancing where he'd just stepped. "Keep going."

Truly, there were better places to have a conversation. It was an unspoken rule between competitors to avoid needless chatter, especially

The Actions of Gods

in precarious places like this. Nevertheless. "What the fuk are you doing?" Magnus demanded.

"Wherever you step, I'm right behind you, Your Highness. Now get me home," the boy cried as paddles swung between them. He dared a positive gesture with his thumbs and even offered a smile as though he knew exactly what he was doing.

"Em… all right."

This was probably a fine time to end the conversation, Magnus reasoned, and that was precisely what he did. He slipped past the last paddle and reached the platform beyond it. A moment after, Padir leapt across into the waiting arms of his king, who resisted the urge to batter him. The urge to beat him was lost in the relief that they'd reached the next platform.

"That was easy," a shaken Padir declared, dropping to a knee to save his energy for the next pathway.

Magnus well knew that luck and caution would save their lives, and perhaps those of most of the others, as they navigated the next obstacles. Here, instead of paddles, massive hammers swung back and forth across the way to the last platform. Each hammer was the width of an ancient seeping oak trunk, and each was designed to smash anything in its path. Magnus stood watching, reading the speed of the first swinging hammer as it flew past and struck out into the night before returning almost lazily. Once he'd figured out the rhythm of the thing, Magnus relaxed.

"This appears easier," Padir said, and his words made Magnus suspicious.

Dropping to a knee, he went against his better judgement and watched the mechanisms for a few breaths more. "Aye, it appears like that," he said at length. "How about you lead this part and let an old man rest." It was a fine, compelling argument, but Padir laughed at the notion.

Magnus watched the hammer swing past one last time, then stepped out carefully onto the walkway. Instantly, his feet betrayed him as though he were a drunk attempting to assault a steep flight of stairs. He stepped forward again, trying to regain his balance, and his other foot betrayed him, and suddenly, he saw the hammer returning on its merry way directly towards him. Leaping backwards, he narrowly avoided being struck and tumbled back against Padir, almost knocking him clear.

"Wrong way, Magnus," Padir said, grunting and steadying himself.

Magnus scrambled away from the boy and bent low, placing one hand on the spot where the hammer almost touched the smooth wooden walkway on the lowest part of its swing. He pounded his palm against the surface and immediately, with a loud crack, the panel dipped slightly lower, while the next one shuddered upwards like a trader's weighing scales. Every piece of the platform after that arced and dropped similarly, rippling one after the other, until the wave settled at the far end of the last platform. Magnus removed his hand from the platform and the panels dropped back into position, settling themselves into a deceiving flat walkway once more.

"What the fuk is that?" said Padir breathlessly.

Magnus had seen nothing like this in his life. He had no answer either.

"Do not follow me just yet," warned Magnus, stepping back out as the hammer shot by. Bracing himself as he waited for the platform to betray him, he took another tentative step. He wobbled but held his balance before stepping forward again. This time he struggled under the sudden jerk, nearly lost his footing, and leapt back to cower beside a terrified and thoroughly confused Padir. Magnus stood regarding the platform and the hammers once more. He thought hard about this. He could easily make it across the path without the hammers swinging if the pathway itself weren't rigged to buck under his feet, but given his age and his weight, he knew he was unlikely to time each dodge properly. Perhaps dodging wasn't the answer, then. He turned to Padir.

"I think I have it. Pay attention to the timing of these hammers, but ignore the floor. I'll go first and show you how it's done. When I give you the signal, charge as I do. But don't fuken attempt to cross until I'm through, or else we'll both get killed." He shook Padir so he knew not to attempt any foolishness.

With a quick nod, Padir acquiesced, and Magnus turned, eyed the hammers one last time, and then ran like the wind. Fortunately, the deadly gusts were at his back, allowing him more speed. A good thing, too, for as soon as he hit the first panel and leapt towards the next, he was already falling. Fortunately, Magnus was prepared to fall—as long as he fell with momentum.

I'm so dead.

Tripping, flailing and imploring his body not to give in to this reckless stumble, he kept running, meeting every panel as it rose to trip him, but somehow not losing his balance and tumbling over the edge.

The world slowed as he ran-fell towards the platform, and hammers filled his vision on every side, but when he hit the ground, it was upon the platform on the other side. Collapsing against the edge, he gathered his breath, turned and held out a hand to Padir, signalling him to hold his approach. Magnus could give him the route, but the boy needed to trust himself. He just needed a push. And if a stray hammer shoved him over into the grass below, well, so be it.

"Don't fall when you hit the panels. Just keep moving, and you'll be fine," Magnus assured him. "You can do this, little one."

"I really can't," the boy screamed, and Magnus gestured at him to begin his run-fall. Padir gave him one last desperate look and began to sprint. He took that first panel well. And then the next, and wonderfully, the hammers swung harmlessly past him, one after the other, and he leapt gracefully across the platform as though it was no matter.

"That's it, boy," Magnus cried encouragingly, and the boy ignored him. A fine thing too. He kept running, almost flying over the dancing ground beneath him, and then a sneaky fuk of a hammer struck him just a foot from the platform and Magnus's waiting hand.

Oh no!

The boy did not fall. Rather, he was batted upwards, away from the platform and the walkway, into the night. He managed a scream, and his leg kicked out where it had been hit, and by some chance, it passed in front of Magnus's face.

He knew the chances of catching the boy were slim to none. As was avoiding getting dragged away by his weight. Regardless, Magnus leapt for him and took hold of the boy's leg with both hands, even as his own legs wrapped themselves around a support beam on the platform. He landed heavily on his belly, knocking the wind out of himself, and almost released the thrashing limb. Magnus gasped and felt every bone in his body dislocate momentarily as the screaming Padir swung below him, dangling by one foot.

"Fuk, me, shit. Fuk, help! Oh fuk, where am I? Fuk, help. Please. Fuken anyone," Padir howled, suggesting he wasn't aware Magnus was already following these suggestions.

"I can't hold you long. Find something to grab onto," Magnus yelled, feeling his knees shudder under the weight. Then, realising his fate was not yet sealed, Padir roused himself and began to move with a sudden agility. Bending at the waist and gripping his own leg in both hands, he hauled himself up like a spider, as though rising slowly from slumber. He hoisted himself to where Magnus's arms held him and, gripping the larger man's shoulders, kicked his leg free and climbed back to the platform, using Magnus as his ladder.

"Close one, that," he gasped, ruefully checking his ankle. "Just grazed me, is all. Did you see how far I flew upwards?" he added, testing the weight on his feet and being very happy that he suffered only minor pain. On the other hand, Magnus was sure he'd ruptured every organ in his body and yanked every bone out of its socket.

"I saw, little one. I saw," he said, massaging his shoulder.

"Well, thanks for that."

"Fuk off."

With the hammer platform behind them, they now faced the final ledge, and after examining it closely, Magnus determined that there was no concealed trick to halt their progress. In place of hammers or paddles, thick wooden axes swung back and forth. A terrifying sight, for there were a dozen of them, each one the size of a small man and likely as heavy. But it was not the axes themselves but rather the shifting path, constructed of a dozen platforms held together by thin chains and swinging as wildly as the axes, that gave them pause. Magnus found himself weaving from side to side as he watched both platforms and axes, seeking a rhythm he could follow, but such was the genius of this monster's creator that there was no timing to master and no beat to follow. Each long step he took would be out over a gap, beneath which was a steep drop to the ground. Each step would need to be swift and careful and taken from a swinging position. For a moment, he remembered himself as a child swinging from a rope out across a deep river on a warm day. He remembered his friend attaching another rope to a tree leaning out across the river on the other side, and both idiots attempting to propel themselves from one rope to the other in a death-defying leap of hilarious fate. His friend had made it twice, if he recalled correctly, though no one else had been there to witness the feat. Magnus had never come close to completing the dare. This felt just as likely to be a success.

Everyone look away, and I'll say I did it.

Well, no time like the present. He stepped out and began to move. Padir watched as Magnus went and shook his head in horror.

"What do you think?" Magnus called out, raising his voice, for as close as the boy was, such was the clanking of chain and mechanism that his voice was nearly lost.

"I think I should have let you drop me," Padir said shakily, but nonetheless, he too began to move.

"Step where the platform will be," called Magnus, thinking again of the swinging rope.

"I don't understand."

"Follow its trajectory to where it will be."

"Oh, that makes no sense, but I'll trust you."

Far below, the crowd were gathered, and a comforting thought occurred to Magnus: in the event that he fell, they'd provide quite the soft landing. To one side, he could see the other competitors, craning their necks, watching Magnus and Padir anxiously. In these contests, no competitor dared climb the Gauntlet until the first competitors had faced her tricks.

He looked beyond them at the stars now. The night was young, with plenty of hours left to get the task completed. This was a good thing; he'd prefer to avoid tackling this beast at pace. Rushing her would be fatal.

The first few steps in the last section were the worst, Magnus knew from previous experience, so he didn't take them. Instead, he hesitated and tested his nerves. He couldn't concentrate on a route or focus on anything but the many swinging axes and shifting platforms. The first platform swung right by him, and he suddenly felt too slow, too old for this. Suddenly, he felt like a failure, felt pathetic standing among the youth.

"Just step out," Padir said from behind him. The little shit looked far too calm. Truthfully, though, it was fine advice. He only needed to let go, trust his instincts and reach the end.

No fuken problem.

"Just give me a moment," he countered.

"I've got this," Padir said, slipping past him smoothly. And fuk it, but he clung onto a chain as it swung by, let it hold him aloft, and allowed the platform to swing out wide before returning. The first axe shot past, and instantly, the boy stepped out to nothing and met the wooden platform as it came back and caught him. Without hesitation, he hopped to the next before spinning back around. "You were right—step where it *will* be." He beamed a dazzling smile and gestured for Magnus to follow. "I'll not wait for you, Your Majesty," he said and leapt to the next platform as though it was nothing, and before Magnus realised it, he was following the cub. Leaping across to nothing, he met solid ground. Ahead he could see the axe nearing; it flashed in his vision, and from the other side came another piece of solid ground. The axe shot past, and suddenly he was less wary, more focused, and across to the next. Within a few breaths, he heard Padir cry out in triumph, and suddenly Magnus was himself again, slipping through the obstacles, clearing each step with an entire breath to spare.

"That's it," cried Padir as Magnus cleared the last obstacle and leapt to safety. There was no cheering from below, not from the competitors or the gathered crowd, which had grown significantly. From this height, they could see the numbers lining up for their turn to climb; they'd seen the path they had to follow, but truly, nothing could prepare them for what was to come.

For hours more, Magnus and Padir sat and watched those unfortunate few attempting to best the colossus. Many times, a combatant was knocked clear of the Gauntlet. They heard bones break some of the time, but most suffered little more than a few bruises and a shattered dream. It was fine entertainment. And it was a fine relief that no deaths were on Magnus's shoulders.

Brigid met her unfortunate end on the first step in the final section. She took it carelessly, which was her downfall: she stepped upon the platform, and as she stood planning her route, she missed the swaying platform completely. She yelped once, and instinctively, Magnus felt the urge to reach out for her despite the great distance he'd need to sprint in less than a breath. Fortunately, there were more than enough of her supporters below to catch her.

She spun away from the gathered group, cursing her luck, her face red with embarrassment and rage, before storming off to the palace, no doubt to discuss the event with Curroi. He himself had not entered this tournament at all, but he likely had opinions on what tactics might have worked had he been present. As it was, few spoke with her as she blustered past, or dared to offer their thoughts. Few things were more intimidating than a clan leader enraged.

"They need to increase the pace," said Gregor, coming up beside Magnus. He looked exhausted. He gazed at the shuffling few still left below the ladder of the first platform. "Dawn isn't far out," he added.

"Perhaps you should tell them," Magnus argued, but the warrior shrugged.

"It's nothing to do with me." He wandered off again, keeping an eye on the competitors squirming across the platforms above.

"Go insist they increase the pace, little one," Magnus whispered to Padir. Running out of time was no way to be eliminated.

"It'll be good if fewer qualify for the next event," Padir suggested.

"Not necessarily, and besides, could you live with missing out on such a thing because those ahead of you took too long?"

They both looked up now as Tusk took to the platform. He moved swiftly, his body unsettlingly agile even at that height, and once more, Magnus was wary of this brute's chances. Magnus wanted nobody to fall, but were there one to do so, he hoped it would be Tusk. He attacked the platforms easily enough and gave a mighty roar as he reached the last one without breaking a sweat.

"That ugly fuk just destroyed it as though it was a stroll," grumbled Padir in displeasure.

"Small matter. Something will get him."

"Maybe so. Probably not me, though."

"I think you should warn them of the coming dawn, little one," Magnus reminded him.

"Why don't you warn them?"

"They're more likely to slow down even more if their king suggests anything."

The boy muttered a few curses before strolling over to the ladder and the few remaining competitors. As Magnus expected, there was a sudden eruption of movement as they all scrambled atop the beam to beat the race to dawn.

Teaolor was one of the last to attack the platforms, and Magnus marvelled at her grace upon the obstacles. While others shuffled, she danced, leaping as though upon a training beam with no one watching. She glided across the final barrier with an impressive flip at the end, displaying bravado and confidence, and truly put Magnus's accomplishments to shame.

"Is it wrong that I feel a stirring in my nether regions watching her move?" Padir said quietly.

"Aye, she moves well," agreed Magnus, watching her slide down the ladder, puffing out her impressive chest in triumph.

As dawn neared, fewer and fewer survived the obstacles without injury. With haste making them careless, many took direct blows from swinging menaces and ended up in a messy heap in the grass below. Thankfully, there were more than enough healers to deal with the savage blows they took, and as the light broke across the horizon, the numbers had dwindled to just over twenty combatants.

All but three remained upon the Gauntlet now, and for some reason, Sloan was one of the last. He shuffled along with his comrades in tow, and they talked their way through the machine as they worked. They made a fine unit, and Magnus nodded approvingly as they reached the last section without incident.

"They're a step from home. I was hoping Sloan would fall. He's a ratty fuk; I wouldn't want him on the throne," Padir said quietly.

"There are worse men to lead the islands," countered Magnus. He, too, did not like him, but he knew the man was a born leader.

"Like you?"

"Probably."

"Like me?"

"Probably not."

"I agree."

The land lit up as the sun began to peer over the horizon. Around them, those who could rested and slept. Those too infused with adrenaline watched on giddily, their heads filled with thoughts of their successes. Even Magnus smiled at how far he'd progressed. It didn't matter that he felt as though he'd spent a day fighting in the Clieve or that his body ached as though he'd taken a battering from a dozen pugilists.

I'm still here.

"Oh, fuk. He took that wrong," cried Padir suddenly, drawing Magnus's attention back to Sloan or, more accurately, the comrade behind Sloan, who found himself stuck between two platforms. "He's panicking. Look at him." The competitor was gripping tightly to the chain, swinging back and forth. Behind him, their third companion screamed at him to hurry up, while Sloan did the opposite, trying to coax the man from his platform. "He's frozen. Like you were."

"Shut up, little one."

The world slowed, and Magnus could see it happening before he could shout out a warning. The young man leapt mindlessly towards Sloan and met a swinging axe as he did. His body jolted sickeningly as though he had received a death blow, and he fell from the platform, only to catch his leg in one of the chains. He hung upside down for a time, unmoving. Unconscious and upside down was certain death, Magnus knew. He couldn't watch. He couldn't turn away either. Unlike with Brigid before, there was no gathered crowd ready and willing to catch the man. Sloan saw this too, so he leapt back towards the platform and gripped the boy's leg. As luck would have it, he took a blow to the knee from a passing axe, and there was a sickening howl.

"Sloan is fuked as well," said Padir, watching raptly, but Magnus was already charging towards the platforms, bellowing for those nearby to gather beneath the swinging Gauntlet. A small cluster of combatants roused themselves, although far too slowly. Looking up, Magnus could see Sloan faltering beneath the weight of the unconscious man.

"Hold him," Magnus roared, and the crowd drew in close. The axe swung back around, and Sloan, unable to shift himself, took another glancing blow as it passed. There was a sound of ripping fabric, but mercifully, no limb was severed. Seizing her opportunity, the final competitor took a chance. Leaping clear across to where Sloan lay, injured and holding his precious weight, she wasted little time skipping past them to the next platform. And why not. Neither man was of any use to her now.

Eventually, when he could hold him no more, Sloan released the unconscious man to the many hands below, who caught and saved him like midwives catching a newborn. For a wonderful moment, Magnus thought it an extraordinary act of humanity. He thought of the bloodthirsty atmosphere of his previous trials, and realised that as a people, they had grown to respect and love others a little more in peacetime.

Sloan watched from above, and then tried desperately to climb to his feet. A difficult enough thing with two able legs, but as it was, he was hobbled and likely to fail now.

A terrible thing.

He tried to rise and move, but his bleeding knee betrayed him. He rose, buckled, and fell, but kept trying, and Magnus thought him courageous. Clinging to the chain, Sloan, a beaten man, watched the axes and platforms rush by. He waited for the sun to come up signalling an unfair defeat.

A terrible, terrible thing.

He didn't know why he did it. When asked afterwards, he would merely shrug in reply. Suddenly, Magnus was upon the ladder's first rung before his senses got the better of his actions. That didn't stop him, though, because it was rare to do the right thing in this world, especially from an elevated position where the stakes were so much higher. If nothing else, though, Magnus would always do the right thing, even if it was the stupidest possible thing to do.

"What the fuk are you doing, you idiot?" cried a voice eerily similar to Padir's.

What the fuk am *I doing?*

He caught the beams of sunlight upon the rungs and charged upwards lest they turn to grease before he reached the top. He did not hesitate to move across the first platform. Perhaps it was adrenalin; perhaps it was the madness that took him. Regardless, he was not scared, not even nervous. Instead, he was determined to save the man. Why? Because he had taken the blows from the evil machine even as he held a defenceless man in his grasp. That was a kingly thing. Magnus dashed across the first section, avoiding the paddles like Teaolor putting on a show.

He did not hesitate on the second, either. He merely picked his spot, leapt with each pivot of the platform, and glided across to the other side. He could see the dawn was fully upon them, though, and feared the sudden slowing of the axes and platforms.

Don't you fuks stop this machine until I have completed this deed.

Ahead, he could see Sloan slumped in defeat. Yet still, he massaged his knee, stemming the flow of blood, hoping to pop it back into place. Magnus called out to him.

"Move to the side, friend," he cried, and Sloan, too shocked to question his sudden appearance, shuffled to the edge. Magnus leapt across each platform as though he were Tusk, challenging each axe to ruin him and fearing none of it.

"What the fuk are you doing, cur?" Sloan hissed as Magnus landed beside him and, truthfully, almost knocked him clear to the crowd below, who watched in silent awe. It was a fair question under the circumstances.

"Helping you."

"I need no help. I merely need to pop my knee back into place."

"I can do that too, but there is no time left. Look to the sun. Look to the brutes down below, hovering over the levers of this bitch."

"I will not take your help. I will not carry that with me."

"You don't deserve to meet defeat this way," Magnus countered. They both swung wildly, undoubtedly adding to their momentum. Truthfully, he hadn't fully thought out exactly what he'd do to help the man, and now that he was here, that sun was getting awfully warm.

"Of course I don't, but it is shameful to accept help from you. I'm not like the boy. You don't need to save me from drowning."

"Would you have allowed a friend to drown?" Magnus asked desperately.

"You call that betrayer a friend?" Sloan challenged. It was a fair question.

"Well, I don't have many friends anymore."

They swung for a moment more, and suddenly Magnus understood what to do. "I cannot help you across these platforms without getting us both battered, but climb upon my back, and I'll carry you across." At this, he dropped to a knee and gripped the chain for support. "Don't fuken hesitate; just do it." Far below, Gregor held his hands up to those attending to the mechanisms. Magnus willed him to belay his order for a few breaths more. Just long enough for this fiend to come to his senses.

Sloan leaned in close. His voice broke. "I cannot rule and have it known that the old king carried my weight. Our lands deserve someone better than that. Please understand this, Magnus... though... I am grateful for your sacrifice."

"Any fool knows we are not friends. Not comrades. Not even true allies. But Sloan, know this. I kneel to serve you now. Surely the fact that you inspire me to such an act is evidence enough of your kingly nature."

For a few breaths more, Sloan did nothing, and then finally, with a terrible sigh, he wrapped his arms around Magnus's neck. With the man's grip nearly strangling him, Magnus climbed to his feet.

"After all this, I hope you don't drop me now," Sloan growled into his ear.

"Wouldn't that be a funny thing? To behave like this, and then have us both drop off the edge in front of the watching world." Magnus summoned all his remaining strength and stepped out. Sloan gripped tighter lest he slip, and Magnus shunted himself forward to the next platform and the one after that. In no time at all they were across, and, panting, Magnus collapsed against the ladder. From far below came the roar of cheering, and it was a strange thing to Magnus in these lands.

Sloan slid down the ladder first. Magnus struggled down after, his body reminding him of the many years he had marched. By the time they were both on solid ground again, the levers running the Gauntlet were bringing the behemoth to a slow. As the roar of the mechanism eased off, the crowd's appreciation for Magnus's theatrics could be heard clearly. They chanted his name a few times, and he bowed before disappearing away from the beast to catch his breath and prepare himself for the next nightmare event to come. Only Padir walked with him, his face pale. His incredulous gaze was both horrified and proud.

"That is the most impressive thing I've ever seen, my king," he whispered, patting Magnus on the back.

"That is the sacrifice any king should offer to his people," Magnus gasped, dropping to a knee. The world became dark and he was afraid he would faint, but he held a point in the grass ahead and gazed at it until his vision returned.

"I fear I may have misjudged you, Magnus," the boy said, dropping to a knee beside him, offering water.

64

INTO THE FOREST

Magnus rubbed at his knee as though it would take away some of the pain. It didn't, but he was distracted for a few breaths from the pulsing shards of agony shooting through his thigh and beyond. These last few weeks, he'd felt stronger on his injured knee, but his fingers shook uncontrollably, and he dearly wanted to stretch out in a bed of silk or even straw and soothe those aches with a long rest in peace and darkness. Instead, he was counting down the moments before marching once more.

And then a strange thing happened. The absent gods took pity on him for a breath; there came the low rumble of carts from the settlement—four in total, all driven by four large mounts. The carts themselves were empty but for two long benches at each edge. They were the types of carts used for transporting workers to work on a massive machine of doom.

Workers... and foolish legends seeking immortality.

Edain was not present this early in the morning. No doubt she was sleeping off the long night before.

"Fine warriors, all of you," Gregor called out. He was back upon his mount with the sun behind him, and gazing upon him caused Magnus's eyes to water and sting. Gregor looked as tired as the rest of his comrades and the rest of the competitors. The new king would do well to reward them all for their diligence in tormenting them. Such dedication was a rarity. They had lasted while most others had faltered. "You have earned a reprieve. I suggest you take what rest you can," continued

Gregor as the carts rolled up close and drew to a halt. A weary guard opened the back of each one and invited all aboard.

Magnus wasted no time. He sprinted to the furthest cart, leapt in, and slid up to the front, where he dropped his head into his hands, suddenly overcome by fatigue. He'd tried and failed to fall asleep in the hour or so since the event had ended, such was the adrenaline pumping through his body. Immediately, his shadow sat down beside him. Unlike Magnus, Padir had slept the hour right through. He looked far fresher than the rest of the competitors climbing aboard. Following him was Sloan. Like Padir, he'd spent the previous hour wisely. There was strapping around his knee, and though he could probably walk unaided, he carried a makeshift crutch and leaned on it heavily as he took a seat beside the woman sitting opposite Magnus. A strange thing, thought Magnus, that Sloan had left his supporters behind to take this place. Perhaps his injuries had led them to believe his star was dwindling to nothing. Or perhaps he desired to be protected by Magnus in the trials ahead. Perhaps he just fancied that particular seat. Regardless, he dropped his head into his hands as Magnus had, his mind, no doubt, consumed by regret and bitterness.

"How's the knee?" Magnus asked, as the remaining competitors climbed aboard the carts.

"I'll not last much longer, but for now, I can walk."

"Maybe that'll be all we'll have to do," jested Padir, leaning back and resting his head against the cart's edge. He couldn't have been comfortable, but the boy yawned and immediately fell asleep. He was the type of fool who did well in battles, Magnus thought suddenly. Some people were gifted with undeniable luck, and the boy embodied good fortune. He had no right to be this far into the contest, yet there he was, lazing as though he had all the time and pleasure in the world.

"I'll keep up," Sloan mumbled, massaging his knee as Magnus did his own. The drivers urged the beasts onwards, and the carts began to lurch forward. There was less camaraderie than before. Everyone's face was drawn with exhaustion and apprehension. Magnus knew there was only a day or two left in this wretched event. The lesser wheat had been threshed. The cream had risen.

"I'll not leave you behind either," Magnus replied. This close to the end, alliances were earned through little more than kindness or the offering of advice. Although only one could stand victorious, this competition was a fine venue for the beaten to earn a place in the new court. For Magnus, his only hope was that the victor would honour the fallen king's final request. That was all that mattered.

To the fires with the throne.

The carts rumbled down the path towards the burning sun as it climbed steadily into the sky. Such was the rhythmic bump and roll of their stubborn progress that Magnus finally felt sleep calling. Their cart led the convoy, and those behind were as quiet as his. The other occupants of the cart were also restrained. Including Tusk. The big man hung over the edge lazily, staring at the path beneath, scrutinising every rock they passed. The energy of maintaining such an aggressive act appeared to be taking its toll, for he held himself upright with difficulty. Perhaps having come this far without proper supplies or sleep had taken his nerve. Magnus had seen such things occur at the strangest times. Without warning, Tusk looked up and met the eyes of Magnus. He looked scared and broken for a breath, but anger swiftly swallowed the vulnerability. He snarled an incomprehensible warning before rolling back into his seat, and Magnus felt that familiar coldness run through him. When a brute was infused with nothing but hate, they either burned out or burned brighter than the sun.

He sought out Teaolor, but she was alone in the rear-most cart, stretched out, sleeping. He once more fought the regret of knowing he'd denied these isles a fine king.

She'll become great when she wins.

If.

He looked around in search of Curroi, but the seat where his place might have been was empty. Were he there, the fiend might have been sleeping like the rest. Magnus yawned, sat back and closed his eyes, willing his dreams be rich and distracting. More than that, healing, for his body was heavy and his will was cracking. Magnus had only love and sorrow now to infuse his steps. Such fuels were sparse and short-lived, he knew, and for the first time in this horrible event, Magnus realised he could not win this crown. And he was right.

"I'll get through this last day, though," he pledged.

It was no smooth trip through the lands that day. The path became unforgiving, and the bouncing jarred their tired bones. For hours they passed through a deep forest where the canopy hid the carts from the unforgiving sun, and Magnus's apprehension grew. Eventually, deep in the woods with evening drawing in and his belly grumbling, there came the sound of hounds barking, and for a moment, Magnus thought it was his boys. Sitting up, he could see the gathering of a great camp far ahead. Flames illuminated the suffocating shade, and the smell of rich meat filled the air.

"Looks like we've arrived," Padir said in mock excitement.

"And they've prepared quite the feast, too," Sloan said. As he had done on and off over the last few hours, he tested his knee once more and grimaced as it popped loudly.

"I hope there's boar," muttered Tusk from the cart alongside. He clung to the edge with powerful arms, looking less angry than before; less lost too. The grim determination had returned, and Magnus considered this a terrible omen.

"I could use a hard drink," Teaolor offered from the cart behind theirs, and there were hearty nods of agreement. She looked exhausted despite the day off her feet, and Magnus wondered whether his face looked as drawn as hers. Whether he looked ready to drop to a knee and give up.

As the carts approached, the barking increased in volume, and Magnus's heart dropped as he thought of his absent boys. Eventually, the dogs came into view. There were a few dozen, at least, all chained in their hunting packs of four or five apiece. They took umbrage at the incoming competitors, and barking savagely, they let them know it. Thankfully, they were on the edge of the camp, as far from the competitors as possible. A few of their keepers stood around talking to each other as though this was nothing but a usual hunt.

"There are quite a few of those fuks," noted Padir, and Magnus understood the threat to come. He looked at Sloan's knee. The man noticed this and read Magnus's fears; he'd need to do a great deal more than keep up.

"How far?" Sloan asked, eyeing the growing gloom of night, wondering about the distance out of this forest.

"At least until dawn," Magnus offered, shrugging.

"You know our trial?" Padir asked, his hopeful eyes begging Magnus to suggest that the hounds were merely here to observe the event and certainly not take part. And not take part of his rear, either.

The carts slowed, and immediately Teaolor dropped to the ground, her hair tied and braided, her shirt tucked tightly into her trousers. She knew the ordeal to come too. She looked nervous, though, and eyed the many hounds warily. She remained close to the cart, lest the beasts break free and tear her asunder. *Foolish Teaolor,* Magnus thought. That would come later.

Only Tusk appeared nonchalant; his earlier fears had been replaced by his usual bravado after a day's bumpy rest. He stretched and readied himself for the chase he would lead. Magnus imagined there wasn't an ounce of fat upon him. The fuker could run all night, which he would likely have to do.

And Curroi was still not present. As before, he had not entered this competition either, and was likely better for it.

"Do I need to tell you all the dangers of this trial to come?" Gregor called out, and a few listened eagerly, hoping to learn their fate wouldn't be as brutal as they feared. "They probably won't kill you when they catch you." He hesitated to allow that to sink in. "Well, as long as you lie still and take the savaging until a keeper finds you," he offered, and though his remark was light-hearted, Magnus knew the truth behind his words. A fine thing that these Savage Isles hounds were as well trained as they were. "Play dead, friends, and all will be well." Gregor gestured around the camp, where a number of campfires were burning merrily, each with a spit on top. Beside each fire rested a freshly seared slab of boar meat, ready to be roasted, and for a moment, Magnus's mouth watered enough that drool escaped his lips.

They don't normally feed us this much.

He thought hard on this.

"Fuk me, is that boar? I could murder something for that," Padir cried in excitement.

Of the competitors remaining, they were last to charge towards the meat. Padir arrived before Magnus did and set their portion of meat over the fire to cook, and soon, the air was filled with the aroma of charred flesh and the promise of succulent flavours to come. A while later, satisfied the meat was cooked through, Padir went to tear a chunk free, but Magnus stayed his hand.

Long ago, when he himself had been fit and healthy, he had been able to handle himself with the beasts during this part of the challenge. But now, he wasn't sure his body could muster the pace required to stay ahead of the pack once they were released. More than that, unless Sloan surrendered his place, he would likely be savaged this night. He also feared Padir wasn't smart enough to escape the forest unaided, and was confident that this was the test.

"I wouldn't eat any of that meat just yet," Magnus said, taking the meat for his own. Looking around the camp, he saw that all the others were feasting but for Tusk, who suspected similar tricks involving tainted meat.

"They wouldn't poison us?" cried Padir miserably, although he did not attempt to recover the meat. Only Sloan, sitting opposite, nodded his head and muttered a curse under his breath in frustration.

"It was one thing to offer some bread," the big man said, "but this seems overly generous."

Then Magnus formed a little plan in his head. It wasn't much of a plan, but it was enough to build on. "Our bellies might not be able to take the meat, but there's little point in a dead beast going to waste," he said, climbing to his feet and discovering the task to be more difficult than he'd have liked.

Taking the meat, he marched towards the nearest pack of hounds. He wasn't foolish enough to believe he could win their favour, but that wasn't to say offering them a little meat wouldn't hurt. If Magnus understood anything about hounds, he understood their memory, nature and amiability under the right circumstances. He also knew that whether this meat was tainted or not, they wouldn't suffer sick bellies as humans would.

The keepers watched him approach without argument. Tearing a strip free, Magnus approached the pack, who had risen to their feet and stood growling in low tones. Their pack leader, the largest hound, stepped forward. It was held only by a chain looped around its thick, muscular neck.

"Look at you," Magnus challenged, dropping to a knee, and the rest of the hounds fell silent as their alpha tensed, ready to tear apart this trespasser. "You want to take my neck, don't you, beautiful?"

The beast did; he bared his teeth in warning. And Magnus leaned on all fours in front of him and, ever so gently, growled in reply. The beast hated this; he began snapping and snarling. The chain holding him pulled taut, and he fought to free himself. Still, Magnus growled and edged closer, and still, the keepers did nothing, which was fine. The beast had a thin stripe of white upon his head, stretching down through his grey back to his tail. As big as any one of Magnus's beasts, he was terrifying, and despite Magnus's trepidation, he felt oddly calm as he crept towards the snapping brute.

"Whisht," he hissed, and the beast really fuken hated the suggestion. Especially when Magnus held the roasted deliciousness out in front of him. After a breath, Magnus demanded he settle, but the dog reared up on his back legs, seeking a way to tear at Magnus's throat. Magnus barked loudly and demanded he drop down again. Still, the beast fought against his bindings. For a while more, though time moved more slowly when one was eye to eye with a killer, Magnus spoke to the hound with different commands that he'd once used on his own pack, or commands his master had once used, or commands his comrades had used throughout the many years he'd trained and observed the art of managing such beasts. Magnus's heritage was very much entrenched in these practices, and though any fool watching might have believed him to be simply tormenting another creature, a proper trainer might have recognised his attempts to get through the savage behaviour.

Eventually, using a term taught to him by a comrade from the southernmost part of the Isle of Glaws, he saw that the hound hesitated for a breath, and Magnus challenged him. The beast turned his head sideways for a moment before snapping again, and Magnus thought him a superbly trained specimen. He gifted the animal a morsel of the meat, which, after sniffing it for a beat, it swallowed in two swift bites. Then the hound began barking again, as did the three other members of his pack, and Magnus stood up over it. Stamping his foot loudly, he roared at the hound before spinning away back towards the fire and returning to his comrades, who were watching him open-mouthed with astonishment.

"Well, I would imagine that hound will now be hunting you above all others," Sloan mocked. In his hands was another cooked piece of meat, though he had not yet taken a bite of it.

"Let us hope so, brother. He's a fine beast, worthy of dethroning a king." At this, Magnus reached out his hand, and Sloan offered him the meat.

"Keep cooking," Magnus instructed him. "I have a few more hounds to introduce myself to." With that, he set off towards the second pack, seeking out the leader. Padir scampered along with him.

"Can I do anything here apart from lusting after a little boar?"

Magnus grabbed the boy close. "You are a swift little fuk, aren't ya?"

"I am."

"Sniff around the camp and find me some lengths of rope if you can. Long ones, that won't break but thin enough that I could strangle you with it."

Padir smiled, no doubt wondering what plan his king might have conjured up. Were he to know the truth, his smile might have faltered. "No problem at all, my liege."

65

THE FOREST

It was a daunting forest, and had Magnus paid attention to the road a little longer, he might have guessed the distance they'd travelled, or indeed, sought out landmarks in the land—a high rise here, a rushing river there… Anything, really, to help them follow their own trail home. As it was, he'd taken the reprieve and was suffering the consequences now under this suffocating canopy of green and shade.

Knowing the hour was late and the time for departure neared, his hands went to work tearing the cloth sacks at his feet. A few competitors had asked why he had desired the empty meat sacks, but Magnus had shrugged and hobbled back to the fire carrying a handful of them. Already he had over a dozen thin strips of durable cloth in front of him. He'd have preferred leather strips, but such hasty, terribly conceived plans meant one must do with what was at hand. He tore off another long piece and ripped it down through the middle, but the fabric had rotted away. Cursing under his breath, he threw the offending piece into the flames and began tearing off another. It was something to do while waiting for this final trial to begin. The final trial. It felt like the final trial. He believed it was the final trial. He hoped it was the final trial. His body was desperate for it to be the final trial.

Until the battle.

"You must reach the town by dawn," Gregor called out. His eyes were sunken in their sockets; his face was gaunt, as though he'd not rested in a year. Although he spoke loudly to the mostly sated competitors, each word took quite an effort. He wiped the sweat from his forehead; it had beaded there from the exertion of the simple act of standing, and it was an exhausting thing to gaze upon. "It's a casual walk, and even the most hobbled among you should be able do it," he added, offering Sloan a sideward glance. "Of course, you'll have company on the trip." He did not need to point out the two dozen hounds barking at his words. "A head start of an hour or so to stay ahead of the pack should be enough," he said, and the younger part of Magnus, who remembered what it was to run for hours, knew well the advantage of fitness.

Magnus gazed at Tusk, who had already begun stretching, his eyes wide in excitement. Magnus could see him plotting his route. Follow the moon and aim for home. A brute like that would likely allow nothing to get in his way. He kept his gaze on the nearest path into the forest, and Magnus could see his body twitching in excitement. Beside him, those few who could keep up with his pace were stretching as he did. Mimicking and preparing, like good little future comrades of court. Probably not a confident, challenging thought between the lot of them, though. Magnus frowned, thinking that if this brute won, he would choose these simple-minded friends as advisors, and the Isles would suffer.

Tusk will probably desire to prove himself in war, though.

Magnus spat on the ground and fretted about such short-sightedness. That type of thinking wouldn't serve the Isles after this war ended, and this war would end.

He looked to Teaolor, and was unnerved by her appearance. Hunched against a cart, she held her stomach like it would betray her. Strands of her long, braided hair hung loosely down over her face, and he wondered whether this trial was one step too many for her.

He might have sought out Curroi among the gathering of pale, wretched competitors slowly climbing to their feet to prepare for the midnight stroll, but he hadn't entered the contest. Instead, he was probably dining upon fine wines, fresh fruits and buttered boar at that moment, and making plans with far-reaching consequences.

Last of all, he looked at Sloan, who was agonising over a sliver of meat, uncooked and unwanted by a cluster of nearby hounds. At length, with a hearty grunt, the younger man climbed to his feet and tested his weight on the crutch. Of all those who had entered, he was favourite to fall first. Magnus imagined many a warrior surrendering at that moment, but instead, Sloan turned to face the pathway farthest from the one by which they'd entered, and Magnus thought it a shrewd move.

"Couldn't just ask us a whole lot of questions and eliminate everyone as they go?" Padir grumbled, climbing to his feet. He stretched in preparation for the hours ahead after a brief scratch in a sensitive place.

"Boy, you should run ahead of us both and be well clear of the pack," Sloan said to Padir. "As should you, Magnus, though from your injuries, I'm not sure you'll be more than a dozen feet ahead."

"Then we'll be mangled together; it should be quite the event." Sloan laughed, and Magnus took hold of Padir for a breath. "Sloan is right, little one. Of all the events, this one suits your shitty little legs perfectly."

"If it's all the same, I'll stick with you, Your Highness."

When Gregor gave the order to depart the camp soon after, there began a great scramble through the forest as exhausted but sated competitors fled from the safety of the firelight into the depthless forest. Magnus was the last to leave. Glancing once more at the barking hounds, he set off into the night, taking a path headed north towards Risbeigh. He was not alone, for Sloan marched along with him, his crutch striking the ground forcefully with every stride, his breath a gruff gasp with every effort. Behind them strolled Padir, examining each tree as he passed for branches within easy reach. Once he reached them, he tore a few leaves free and left them where they fell. It was something to do, Magnus supposed.

They walked cautiously through the night, silent but for the clinking chain around Magnus's waist. It was a discarded choke chain belonging to one of the keepers. It was not rope Padir had found, but far more than Magnus could have wished for—a delicate treasure delivered by the little shit. For at least an hour or so, they walked their route, all the while listening for the release of the beasts behind them. They followed the stars; they followed the moon. They made fine time, but this walk was never about arriving before dawn. It was about survival. Despite Sloan's arguments, they avoided rivers and streams. On any other day, with healthy limbs fit for running, they might have been able to conceal their scent by moving quickly, but that only worked for so long when walking. The hounds would quickly pick up their scent now, even with their head start. This was fine with Magnus. Although he hadn't terrified his comrades with the truth, he actually desired the beasts to pick up his scent.

Walking into an open dell, Magnus halted beneath an enormous seeping oak. "This is where we should take a rest for a time."

Both comrades were astonished. Padir, believing it a jest, walked on for a few feet before slowing.

"The night is young, Magnus. Surely your bones can travel a few more hours?" challenged Sloan, eyeing the shattered moon through the tree canopy as it spat its deadly shards from the heavens above.

"You are up to something, aren't ya?" Padir said after a breath. He grinned, and Magnus nodded. "What do we do?"

It was a simple plan. It would never work, argued Padir, but he followed Magnus's instructions regardless. As did Sloan, who began gathering fallen twigs and dried branches for kindling and then spreading them out in a wide arc beyond where the lowest tree branches touched the ground. Padir went to task stripping chunks of bark from whichever trees were willing to give up their veneers so easily.

Magnus too went to task, strapping the pieces of bark around his most vulnerable parts with the strips of sacking he'd brought with him.

Sloan lit each of the piles of kindling, then stood away from the catching fires and began adding larger logs, hoping to build the fires into something to terrify the hunting pack. Not enough to stop the beasts from charging; just enough to give them pause and make them direct themselves towards a more enticing feed. Then he took out the remains of the meat from the camp and set the raw strips to roast over the fires. In no time at all, there was the welcoming aroma of a feast to welcome any interlopers.

Suddenly, the distant call of horns was heard, along with the baying of hounds and the shouts of the keepers as they followed and warned and terrified their hounds' prey. As the hounds drew steadily closer, Magnus could hear the snapping jaws of the killers, and for a moment, he imagined himself as a fox or a boar hearing this calamity charging towards him, and he felt a pang of compassion and regret for the fear he'd delivered upon many a beast he'd hunted. If nothing else, he pledged never to attend nor arrange a grand hunt again. He was old, and it was late in the day, but he supposed it was better than nothing.

"They'll be upon us soon," Sloan said. Strapped around his and Padir's arms were thick paddings of bark, but there wasn't enough time for further precautions. Magnus, however, resembled a bulky tree as he stood with arms, legs, groin and neck covered over with bark. It was no impressive steel armour, but it was light and sturdy. If he required the bark to hold against a bite for more than a few breaths, however, it wouldn't matter what armour he wore. The beasts would have him.

Padir had suggested a faceguard, but most faceguards were not intimidating, and he wanted the beasts to see him. To appreciate their prey. To appreciate their challenger.

Nearby, there came a sudden, piercing cry that might have been human. "Light the branches," Magnus shouted, and both Sloan and Padir lit thick branches heavy with dried brown leaves—makeshift torches perfect for distracting any beast wary of fire. The branches took light, and not a moment too soon, for out from the forest treeline sprinted a figure covered in mud and leaves, pursued by fur-covered killers.

"To us," Magnus roared, and, realised it was Teaolor who sprinted down upon them, bringing death with her. Desperately, she veered and sprinted towards the trio. Through the mud caking her face, he could read her expression of utter confusion, mixed with gratitude for their presence here.

It's always nicer to be savaged in company.

"Come on, you fuks!" demanded Magnus as Teaolor sprinted past him through the one break in the fire arc. He heard Sloan order her to climb the tree. Whether she did or didn't meant little to Magnus though, for the chasing pack charged through the treeline and then drew up short at the appearance of fire and a walking tree. At least, at first.

For the hounds were well trained.

Barking and snapping, their pack leader charged first, and Magnus recognised him as the first beast he had "charmed."

Magnus met the charge, roaring as only a seasoned warmonger could, and it was terrifying to see him sprint up towards the creature and it's pack.

I'm so dead.

The animal went for his arm, and that was fine. Magnus held it out and felt the dreadful, crushing grip. His whole body shuddered under it's weight as it jerked and twisted and attempted to neutralise its victim. Magnus, however, had had a lifetime of training these exquisite hounds and was prepared for the assault. It was frenzied, ripping at the thick bark, searching for blood and bone to ravage. Magnus felt only a faint touch of the violence, like looking through a pane of glass as a storm raged around. In that first moment, he could have killed the creature. Could have dropped his weight upon it, twisted and snapped its neck. Such a thought abhorred him, though, for he was no animal. And besides, in the time it took to kill the beast, the rest would finish him off. As it was, each of the remaining three hounds following Teaolor into Magnus's trap were but a moment from attacking.

With all his strength, he lifted the hound aloft and struck him once across the head. As he did, he roared out a call for the beast to submit. The strike and the command, even uttered by its enemy, was enough to distract the animal. He dropped, and Magnus kicked him away. Not hard enough to injure him, but to deliver the message that there was no easy prey to be had here. By the time it recovered and turned to reattach itself, Magnus was already away, leaping towards the next hound. This one, too, he struck with an open palm, then howled another demand for allegiance. The beast fell back, howling in fright and surprise. And then Magnus felt the last hound take hold of his thigh and pull fiercely.

Clever boy.

He fell to one knee, and only reflexes saved him. Taking hold of the creature, he rolled in the dirt towards the flames, taking the beast with him. He felt its teeth snapping at him, claws raking him, and with all his strength, he threw the animal towards the flames and the two figures waving the burning branches, screaming in primal rage.

Scrambling onto all fours again, the first hound came upon him once more, biting into his shoulder and breaking the skin. Magnus's scream was piercing, but despite weakened legs, he somehow stood and began to move towards the fires again, with the animal clinging to him every step of the way. For a moment, at least. And this moment saved him. Saved them all. Believing it hadn't caused enough harm, the hound released itself and sought another hold—only to meet Magnus's powerful double slap across its nose before it was lifted high above the ground as though it were a pup.

"You aren't my boys," roared Magnus, throwing the animal as far from him as he could. It wasn't far. His shoulder was fuked; his knees were jarred. His lower back felt as though a thousand needles were dug into it. It didn't matter; the hound howled in shock, and the other three hesitated for a breath. Magnus didn't. He charged the nearest one, gripping it tightly and flinging it further than the first. Unprepared for such violence, the hounds began once again searching for weakness, and Magnus countered them again. Swinging a kick at the ribs of the nearest circling creature, he sent it scuttling away, then turned to the last one. Slapping it fiercely across the back, the face and the rump, he sent it yelping away to seek sanctuary with the rest of its dazed pack.

Only the leader remained. "Is this it?" demanded Magnus, dropping to a knee in front of the hound as it stood defiantly before him. It was savage and dangerous, but there was a wariness now that wasn't there before. It didn't need to know how exhausted Magnus felt or how weak his body had become. "Come," he roared, and struck the ground. He beat his chest, and the hound's growl turned to a low rumble, but Magnus knew the threat was very much still there. The beast was eyeing his throat, having decided Magnus needed to die. And that was fine. Magnus dropped his arms and presented his throat, ready for it to attack.

Neither man nor hound moved for a breath.

"Fuk me, this is working," cried Padir, and Magnus hissed him to silence. The creature turned and eyed the boy for a long moment before Magnus jerked forward to catch his attention.

"Only me, little one," he called to the animal, bidding him take his chance and attack one last time.

And then it did. Suddenly, it leapt and was upon Magnus. He felt the pressure on the bark as the hound bit down, heard the bark crunching as it bit with all its might, hoping to break through this unexplainable shield covering its prey. He met the hound's eyes, and neither blinked. Instead, Magnus stared into the animal's soul and silently asserted his dominance, and the beast watched and listened, even as Magnus's arms wrapped themselves around him and squeezed. For a breath, Magnus thought of Erroh, and, grinning, he squeezed tighter, and the growls grew loud in desperation. And then Magnus was squirming around the fur-covered body, seeking leverage, and soon enough, he had it.

"Go on, bite my fuken face off," Magnus mocked, knowing its instincts would not serve it well. Magnus's face was unprotected, but a bite to the face wasn't a killing blow, after all. Magnus rolled over and pinned the hound, but still it growled and snapped at him, still hoping to kill. Magnus's total weight was upon it, and suddenly the creature released its grip, but Magnus did not. Instead, he gripped the animal like a master and continued to pin him down. The hound writhed and struggled as Magnus hissed commands, demanding its submission. And finally, with a groan, it relented.

Looking to the rest of the pack, who cowered from the flames and watched the defeat of their pack leader, Magnus climbed to his feet and pulled the chain from his waist.

"Whisht," he warned, and slipped the chain around the subdued hound's neck before pulling tightly and slightly choking it for a breath. Then, he released the hold and stared down into its eyes, asserting his dominance over it. He held the hound in place for a few breaths more before stepping away and dragging on the chain again. The great animal yelped and fought, but then fell to a sitting position. "There we go, boy," Magnus whispered. Still holding the chain, he leaned over and patted him gently, bringing the animal to stubborn surrender. Then, he pulled some meat from his pocket and offered it a treat for "good behaviour." After a breath, the hound, no doubt humbled, aching and grateful for the reprieve, ate the piece, and then a second one, before wagging its tail. Just once. But it was better than nothing.

The rest of the confused pack slowly edged closer, and Magnus roared them to silence and to distance. With their leader under a new master, the three remaining hounds growled and complained, but they, too, fell to sitting poses, and all of them in turn received a treat for their better behaviour.

"That is a kingly thing I have just witnessed," Sloan said as Magnus approached with hounds in tow.

"That was just a simple plan that worked, friend," Magnus countered, though truthfully; with the frenzy of battle fading away, the effort it had taken was beginning to take its toll. He stumbled and dropped to a knee, for just one desperate breath.

Slowly, Teaolor slipped down from the safety of the branches. She looked worse than before; she, too, dropped to a knee and muttered a few curses. Magnus imagined he heard a 'thank you' somewhere in between the obscenities. It was a small matter. What mattered was the moon overhead and the hours until dawn.

"So now what?" asked Padir, looking at the hounds and at Teaolor and taking a side step away from both.

"We enjoy the rest of our walk," said Magnus. Taking hold of the chain, he climbed to unsteady feet and led his little entourage back into the dark forest.

66

KING OF THE ISLES

As one group, they marched through the night towards dawn, towards Risbeigh, towards the final battle. Towards the last day. Magnus led the pack, or rather, technically, "Stripe," his war hound, led the pack. The beast marched through the undergrowth, panting and groaning as though out on a hunt. The hunt was over for the animal this night, but Magnus wouldn't tell him that. Instead, he directed him, and the creature was glad of a purpose. On either side of them, the rest of the pack marched through the woods without restraint. If their leader was satisfied with this turn of events, so were they. That wasn't to say they didn't react every time there was a scream or a frenzy of loud barking every hour or so. Grimly, Magnus hissed each animal onwards towards the path, all the while worrying about the health of whoever had met a grisly fate at the jaws of the furry fiends.

Let it be nothing more than a bite in the rear.

Sloan and Padir marched behind, side by side, with torches illuminating their way. Although the conversation was muted, Sloan tolerated Padir's inane comments better than he'd thought he would. They matched each other's steps while watching the shadows surrounding them. It wasn't they who commanded the will of the beasts, after all, and every time there was a breaking of twigs, or the low growl of hunters, each stuck by the other as they had at the fires earlier. Safety in numbers, Magnus supposed. That said, only twice did another hound appear ahead on the path, but, seeing the marching pack, both decided Magnus and his companions were either keepers of the beasts or prey not worth assailing and darted off into the darkness.

It was only Teaolor who lagged. It wasn't her fault entirely, for her body betrayed her, as had the bodies of most of the others this night, thanks to the tainted meat. Thankfully, by midnight she no longer needed to squat and relieve herself a few times every hour. It was a terrible, cruel act by their keepers that both debilitated them and attracted hunters with a keen nose for the stench. Frequently, appearing from the trees, tightening her belt and seeming far lighter than before, she cursed Gregor's name passionately and vowed miserable revenge when she took the crown.

Magnus wondered what he might have done had his desire to sate himself been greater than his gut feelings that the meat had been tampered with. Teaolor, however, had realised the poisoning quicker than most.

Her plan to conceal herself in a mudded riverbank until the affliction cleared itself, before chancing a desperate dart towards the town, was likely a better plan than most others. It was terrible luck the hounds came upon her so swiftly. It was, however, smart to charge towards the burning light. Which is exactly what she did.

And likely survived because of it.

She still hadn't thanked him for saving her, which was fine. It was a kingly thing to remain proud. Had he shown a little less humbleness these last few days, he might be merrily floating towards the Four Factions, preparing for war and his likely end.

Though Magnus appeared in control, his face taut in concentration and determination, deep down he was anything but. His heart hammered out of time, his chest ached, and he feared collapsing in a deathly heap at every step. His bruised body felt the ache of the last few days, and though Magnus feared no death, he was wary of the trip. He had a dark feeling that, this time, his body wouldn't be able to take this strain. He might have enjoyed conversation and taken the distraction as a respite against the weakness in his arms, knees, and even his fuken breath, but he was too tired to talk. This felt like an old man's end. Still, he continued the slog through the undergrowth, over uneven ground, through valleys and glades, but mainly through forest as suffocating as his breath in his weakened chest. Not a terrible way to go; at least he'd have few worries about the war's outcome if he were dead, he mused, and these sad thoughts were oddly comforting. He'd come close to death many times through the years, but now he had an uneasy certainty that this would be his last dawn.

"If I die before the end, will you all march in my honour to the Spark?" he asked suddenly.

Nobody said a word for a time, and Magnus's steps became slower and weaker. He ached to release the hound and collapse into the dirt. That impossibly comfortable-looking dirt.

Padir was the first to reply. "When I become king, I will gladly honour your request, Your Majesty," he said. He even patted Magnus on the back in genuine affection and respect—or else it was simply a distraction as he searched his pockets for a few spare pieces. Regardless, Magnus could have gripped the boy's arm and wept in gratitude. Instead, he grunted and continued on his way.

"I will honour you should you fall... should you fail to take the throne," Sloan mumbled. Magnus caught his frown. He wondered whether the man regretted the strike in prison. It, too, was a small matter. "More than that, I will travel back with you to the Spark; it is a debt I would likely pay sooner than later," he added, and his words moved Magnus. Perhaps he'd bring some of his clan with him.

"You won't fall," Teaolor said after a time. "I'd wager a year's ale that you will find a way to win this event outright."

"I would happily take that bet. You can repay it to my widow," Magnus said, fighting a pang of sorrow for his mate.

"A man like you will never die," Padir said, and then one of the hounds beside him growled at some unseen threat in the dark. After a breath, they left the danger behind and continued.

I live to march another mile.

That mile turned to another mile and many miles after that, and they marched like legends through the darkness. Until eventually, they recognised landmarks long before dawn. Better than that, just before the first burning rays of sun lit up the sky, they cleared the last treeline and followed the path down towards the settlement. And for a moment or two, Magnus allowed himself a little relief. Looking around at the comrades who'd accompanied him, those he'd grasped roughly to him in dire straits, and at the hound pulling him forward with every step, he thought he recognised the familiar hallmarks of a Ranger march. All he needed was the gruff, low tones of Garrick in his ear, suggesting this particular route was flawed. But Garrick was gone. He was alone and, with another day to endure, Magnus's heart felt heavy. More than that, it began to beat more quickly now, tripping over itself every few beats, and again, he worried about his fate.

Pushed myself too far.

As before, the area immediately outside Risbeigh had been altered to suit the needs of the trials, and Magnus was pleased with what awaited them. There was a hastily created arena where the Gauntlet had once stood. Truthfully, it was no more than a vast, open space, its grass flattened and covered in sand. The sand was for bravado, for exhibition, and why not? This was the end, no doubt. A few dozen posts had been sunk deep around the great ring of flattened sand, and a makeshift fence of rope and chain encircled the entire arena. A fine thing, too, for behind the low-hanging barriers stood the hundreds of spectators. Ten times more than had attended the first event. They had come from every creek and crack around, no doubt surrendering a day toiling in the field or labouring over lumber to watch the final battle take place. To be able to say they were there when a new king was crowned.

Or an old one?

As they approached the arena, Magnus's new hounds began to bark excitedly as their true master appeared with a leash and an expression of shocked embarrassment. All the other hounds were leashed, and all other competitors had returned as well. Releasing Stripe and patting the beast once upon the rear, Magnus cried, "Go now!" and the pack returned to their rightful place.

Good boys.

"Is this the end?" Padir asked. He looked as broken as any other competitor. Magnus began counting those remaining. Only eight more still stood, uninjured, by the entrance to the arena.

"This is the end."

The crowd began to cheer loudly as they approached, and strangely, he heard his name chanted loudly above the applause, which was humbling. Straightening his back, he marched proudly, his last few steps as fresh as the day, as though the previous days' events hadn't come close to killing him.

"It appears you have some fans," Sloan said, not unkindly, from beside him. "Word must have spread of your feats in the trials." He still limped, but he had either found a slight recovery or merely adapted to a shuffling life of agony. Either way, he looked better than he had.

"Or of the acts of humanity you've shown," Teaolor added. Although her face was still deathly pale, she sounded less exhausted than before. As the hours had passed and she had begun to regain her strength, she looked less the mud-covered fiend scrambling towards a fire and sanctuary and more the burning, energetic clan leader who had struck him from his seat.

"Kingly acts," Padir said, and patted Magnus's aching shoulder. "Oh, shit—sorry, my liege," he said as Magnus recoiled. The broken king wasn't sure if the boy jested, if any of them were truthful in their words, or if his deeds had indeed inspired the crowd. What mattered was putting one foot in front of the other and reaching the arena where it would all end. Then, finally, he would be able to rest.

The crowd parted, and again, it was Gregor who approached. Looking far better rested than before, he offered a deep bow for Magnus and Magnus alone, before inviting them into the arena to face the end of it all.

"You should have arrived here by dawn," he said quietly, and for a terrible moment, Magnus's heart sank. Sloan stared coldly towards the man as though he'd defecated in his favourite soup dish. Teaolor shoved past him towards the rest of the gathered competitors, who sat on an extended bench beneath a flapping tarp at the arena's edges, away from the crowd.

"Only a brave man would deny the king his last stand," Padir offered, though he looked crestfallen. Likely the boy was reflecting that he should have jogged the last mile to get ahead of the first rays of dawn.

"Aye, I'm no fool. And after such an impressive entrance, the crowd would lynch me for denying them a spectacle," Gregor agreed, looking past them towards Teaolor, who stomped across the arena as though each sand-filled step was an affront to her name. "I've just tended to your hounds, Magnus; they'll be glad to see you after this," he said, and then, leaning in close, whispered, "No competitor died this night. I thought that would please you."

Magnus almost broke with relief at that moment. Gregor spun away, gesturing for them to enter the arena, and the roaring increased as they marched across the sand towards the seated competitors.

Some still carried the stench of upset bowels and soiled clothing. Those poor few who had ingested the tainted meat looked exactly as Magnus felt, and, wrinkling his nose, he took a seat on one of the benches opposite a fuming Teaolor. On either side, a space swiftly appeared for his comrades who sat with him, and the relief of rest was unimaginable.

Outside, Gregor surrendered the control of the crowd to Edain, who took to her podium as before and began calling out the names of each competitor remaining. The crowd reacted to every name, and Magnus hung his head as fatigue took him, as his body betrayed him completely.

Too much.

"This is it, comrades," Tusk mumbled. Unlike the rest of the resting competitors, he stood away from the benches, staring wearily at the rack of weapons in front of him. "Once more for glory."

To Magnus, it felt like the first trial, with all of them knowing rest was days away. As on the first day, the people were watching them, but none was part of their group. No one knew what thoughts they had, what fears they hid. This tournament was the making of legends and the measuring of all who stood proud.

"It's been the hardest thing I've ever done," Tusk added, all bravado gone. Instead, he showed a humility Magnus had not seen before.

Magnus wondered whether time and contemplation had brought a little sentiment to the brute. Was he as bonded to those around him as Magnus was? As Magnus had once been in the first trials he'd endured so long ago. That event had been different altogether, with a different type of savagery and heartbreak.

"I did not think I would survive the forest," a competitor said, and a few people agreed.

"These weapons are heavy and blunted. A terrible thing to die from such a blow," another said after a time.

At this, Tusk picked up one of the dozen similar weapons. One for each remaining competitor. "I will try to batter with every blow. My aim will be to defeat, not to kill."

"Don't aim for me," mocked Padir, and Magnus's senses were stirred. There was another energy in the air. It felt like a death was at hand. Perhaps Tusk felt it too. Perhaps they all did.

"Perhaps if we aim only for the chest, the arms, the legs?" Teaolor offered, and Magnus's heart was lifted ever so by their words. This was more than victory. This was behaviour befitting leaders. He might have applauded, but his limbs were so heavy.

"I agree, but in a battle for victory, who's to say accidents do not occur?" Sloan said. He hobbled over to the weapons and felt their weight. "Very heavy," he agreed.

All things must end.
It is time.

Edain began reciting the rules to those many hundreds listening, to all but the broken warriors.

"I do not want any of you to die," Tusk said, and there were many nods from those upon the benches. The crowd was cheering, and Magnus admired every warrior who had made it this far. But his joy at knowing none had lost their lives soon faded to a grim sense of foreboding.

They were calling for the competitors, exhorting them to batter each other to a pulp for the crowd's amusement. For the stories to be told for years to come. This battle, however, was not to the death but merely to yielding or unconsciousness, although of course accidents did happen, usually where the crown was involved. Magnus had barely a breath left in him, scarcely the energy to move, and he wondered whether his heart would last the first skirmish. The wiser part of him whispered he should sit this one out. Merely drop to a knee when the victor turned to him.

"Have you got anything left, my liege?" Padir asked. He looked nervous but determined. Padir would not sit this battle out, even when he was pitted against Tusk the indomitable.

For a moment, he wondered might his terror be merely the absence of peace in his soul and rest in his knees. Had the trials exhausted him enough that he couldn't think clearly? He watched as Tusk lifted his club, his eyes cold and calculating. Kind words were one thing, but taking the crown was another.

There was a roar as the crowd demanded the competitors appear beneath the canopy and wave to their followers and fans.

"Wait, brother," Magnus called, rising and standing taller than he felt. "Do not step out there with a weapon." At this, Magnus hobbled over, sucking air deeply as he did, and hoisted a cumbersome club. He spun it as his son would have when attempting bravado and trying to gain the onlookers' attention. "I will carry no such weapon into this battle but these shivering beasts," he said, raising his fists. Then, he stepped out onto the sands of war and accepted the rapturous applause from those awaiting fine drama. It was a brave, foolish move, but it was all he had left, and amazingly, Sloan followed a breath after, hobbling slightly, without either crutch or club. He grinned at Magnus and stood beside him as the crowd declared their appreciation. Only Edain appeared confused, and that was fine.

Padir appeared, and stood next to Teaolor. Both were without clubs as well, and Magnus was proud to stand with these legends.

And then Tusk appeared. In his hands were two clubs, held ready for violence. He roared his name and dropped the clubs in the dirt before

The Actions of Gods

charging into the sand as far from Magnus as possible. Truthfully, with fists as his only weapon, Tusk had the grander advantage, but he'd never faced a collapsing Magnus, had he?

Only one loss to my name, and that was kin.

The remaining competitors charged out into the sands. Some alone, some aligned with Tusk. Some might have aligned with Curroi, but he was not in the arena. He was not even present for the event. And he was hardly missed.

"You fine legends—to the defeat!" Edain roared, and each warrior tensed, assuming a combative stance.

Magnus and Tusk faced each other across the sand. The last day was upon them. The final skirmish was to occur, and Magnus's heart began to beat against the adrenalin, the terror, the excitement.

"Oh, fuk me," muttered Sloan.

"I regret not slipping a club beneath my shirt for such a moment," Padir hissed, scratching nervously. He was poised and ready to attack, but he was the smallest and most unimpressive of the lot.

Magnus gazed up at the crown, which lay upon the podium in front of Edain. It rested on a green silken pillow, but instead of inspiration, Magnus felt only deflation. His body felt heavier than before, his vision darkened, and he dropped to a knee as though in prayer.

"My king," cried Sloane, grunting as he dropped beside him. He gripped his shoulder and squeezed, and Magnus was so tired, so alone, so regretful of his actions and the effort still to come.

"Gather in close and let the others defeat each other," Magnus advised under his breath. He dropped his hand to the sand, and his stomach churned loudly with hunger, with wretchedness. "Stick together until it's only you three who remain."

Teaolor stood beside him. Her face was grim and determined, a fine look, and he would not meet her eyes. So she reached down and took his hand. "Rise and lead us, king," she hissed. Distantly, he heard Edain declare this battle a righteous thing before crying aloud for its commencement. At that moment, the crowd cheered and called a dozen different names. There followed the shuffling of feet, and Magnus expected a strike to his head to finish him off. Instead, Teaolor pulled him to his feet and, with a slap across the face, she screamed in his ear.

"Lead us."

Tusk waited no longer. He charged upon the nearest challenger, a young woman heavier than most with muscly arms and short-cut hair. She swung once, and in response Tusk displayed terrifying speed of fist and body. He struck her three times. Once across the throat, once upon the stomach and once upon the chin. The woman collapsed, gasping for air, the fight taken from her swiftly.

"I come for the king," he roared, and those with sense left him to it. As bodies scrambled and struggled, swinging and kicking at each other, he strolled through the melee towards Magnus and his comrades.

"Damn you, Magnus, show us one more moment," Padir cried before spinning towards Tusk, ready to defend his ailing master, and in that moment, Magnus loved the little shit. Sloan turned with him and Teaolor with them. For a moment, Magnus imagined the trio taking the fight to the fiend. Were they better trained in hand combat, were Sloan not so weak, and were Padir effective, they might have bested him. As it was, Tusk roared, knowing victory was upon him. As would the crown be.

If they had clubs, the odds would be better balanced.

And then Magnus was charging, rushing through the weak defensive line of his ill-prepared trio. He did not stop, and Tusk met him. They clashed in the centre of the arena, and for the few breaths that Magnus heard them, the crowd were rapturous. And then all he heard was the cracking of fist on flesh and the louder buzzing of a head jarred by a couple of brutal strikes.

"Show me the great master," Tusk roared, breaking Magnus's defence, delivering a few stinging blows, and Magnus was sent reeling. As he stumbled, Magnus watched his companions fall upon Tusk's few remaining allies with wondrous violence and brutal skills. They fell as one unit, digging in, protecting each other, and had another fist not knocked Magnus to the ground, he might have appreciated their tactics. As it was, he stumbled in the sand, spitting blood from a swelling mouth.

Tusk circled him, answering each cry with swift combinations, and Magnus quickly recognised his technique. It was a devastating technique, one that dictated the fighter never throw a solitary strike. Instead, it was built on combinations to break through defences; most warriors would easily fall to such skill. Most, but not all. Magnus had a plan. A simple plan. And like the others, it had to work.

I have one chance.

Rising to one knee, Magnus dropped his defences, playing the beaten monarch to a tee. His nose bled, his mouth hung open and his hair clung limply to a beaten head. A wary warrior might have offered mercy, which is precisely what Tusk offered.

"Will you yield, great one?"

Magnus shook his head, and the effort appeared to take his breath.

"You know what must be done."

Tusk leapt in, swinging with his favoured devastating left, but Magnus was ready. And for the next blow too. Forming a fist with gnarled, arthritic fingers, he threw everything into a counterblow. It was a fine strike. He watched his opponent's shoulder and guessed the trajectory—a delicate skill he'd learned a lifetime ago, and he was desperate enough to attempt it.

The crack was louder than the loudest strike in the arena as Magnus's fist met Tusk's. Before Tusk realised the devastation wrought upon his hand, his momentum and counterblow followed through and similarly met Magnus's other defending fist. Again, the snap echoed out across the arena, and there were hisses and winces from the crowd, who recognised the pain Magnus had inflicted. Knowing the strike was coming and tightening his fist a moment before Tusk could, Magnus suffered only a broken knuckle on his right hand. The left looked less dented and disjointed, and that was fine.

Tusk screamed out and stood away from the kneeling man, cradling his hands in shock; the fight was over before it had truly begun. Leaping forward and wrapping his arms around Tusk's less injured hand, Magnus head-butted the brute across the nose three times before knocking him to his knees. Then, with his left hand, he delivered blow after blow upon the dazed man's face, taking his fight, taking his breath, taking his consciousness after a time too. Leaving him to fall, Magnus stood unsteadily to face whoever was next.

To his surprise, Teaolor, Sloan and Padir remained alone. All three were covered in blood and swelling, and were likely to be covered in bruises come the following day. Again, Magnus dropped to a knee, only now appreciating the importance of the tasks. All the others remained on the ground. Some were unconscious; others were merely huddled over, holding their injuries, beaten but worthy.

The noise of the crowd dwindled to silence as they began to grasp the drama unfolding before them and watched allegiance falling to the fires. All three remaining competitors stared at Magnus as though he were their last challenge, and they were right. The more intelligent move was turning on him and taking him from the fight before he could recover his breath. Instead, Padir strode forward, a rueful grin on his face.

"I pledge myself to you," he declared, dropping to a knee.

Beside him, Sloan dropped too, planting his fists in the sand. "You are worthy to lead us for a lifetime more," he cried.

Teaolor was last to drop, though drop she did, and the crowd erupted in delight. They chanted Magnus's name, declared his title worthy, and demanded King Magnus lead them for years to come.

"I will march a hundred thousand miles for you, for a lifetime and beyond," Teaolor declared, bowing her head.

"Magnus, Magnus, Magnus!" the crowd cried, and all hatred was forgotten in the moment by the people. His people. He was no grand king, adored by the many, but the tales of his determination, kindness and honour during the trials were legendary and worthy of their respect. For a breath, Magnus could only raise his hand weakly; around him, the rest of the competitors regained their awareness or swallowed their pain, or both. One by one, they, too, bent a knee, and the crowd, unable to contain themselves any longer, rushed the crude fences to show their appreciation.

Suddenly, glittering green silk filled Magnus's vision as the crown was placed upon his head by a beaming Edain, who knew her place once more.

Even Gregor dared a smile as Tusk and a few others hoisted the king upon their shoulders and carried him through the settlement, towards the throne, towards celebration, towards some fuken food and a little rest after, perhaps. Magnus felt less alone than he had in a lifetime. He felt like a Ranger.

Without warning his many hounds appeared at his feet, barking wildly, and desperately, he dropped to greet them. They showered him in kingly adoration, and for a wonderful moment Magnus smiled, took deep, calming breaths and felt the claw of strain leave his chest. It would return, he knew, for there were great things to come. Great and terrible things that would likely kill many, if not all, of those here today. There would need to be swift planning; there were swords to sharpen and supplies to store aboard an armada before sailing up the coast towards open ocean and onwards to war.

But for now, there were warriors just itching to answer a new king's requests for battle. All of this could wait until tomorrow, however. Tonight belonged to the once-shamed King Magnus, who had once fallen, but who now returned ten times stronger.

Perhaps, were Curroi present to see such things, all things might have differed in the years to come during the significant fracturing of the Isles. However, he was not present. He was upon a horse, racing towards the coast, racing towards his own goals.

67

AT LAST

Erroh was wet. No, that wasn't entirely accurate: drenched right fuken through was more accurate. Hunkering down in the saddle, wrapping his arms more tightly around his ribs, he brought Highwind down a gentle slope and felt her slide, and the rain lashed against his uncovered face. For a breath, he was back among his comrades in Raven Rock, about to ruin himself and all their supplies. Highwind must have remembered too. She adjusted and allowed her powerful hooves to gather stability. Good thing, too, for to fall now would be death to her rider. However, this was far from the precarious slope near Raven Rock, and swiftly, rider and mount found level ground and charged through the rain. As they did, Erroh waved at his fleeing comrades to follow.

Erroh hated many things in this world. Getting drenched in miserable conditions was one of them. Another was driving his mount down slippery slopes. Mostly, he hated being chased by a fuk-load of pursuing Riders. Even in the rain, the wind and loud the spattering of leaves, he could hear the rumbling, drawing ever closer.

"Quicker, Highwind," he commanded, gripping his reins tightly lest the leather slip free from the pace. Highwind answered his demands and snorted against the splashing rain and the biting wind; it was a dreadful day to ride, a worse day for escape.

This is all my fault.

Drahir charged up alongside, pushing his beast to a frenzied pace to match Erroh's. "They can't keep up this pace," he cried. Unlike Erroh's leaner mount, built for speed and grace, Drahir's was a Southern animal;

sturdy and robust, and terrible for this type of race. "Nor can I," he roared.

Behind both riders were twenty of their comrades, all gathered up, all similarly racing for their lives and losing. Unlike Drahir and Erroh, who were comfortable upon these massive charging mounts, the rest of his riders were inept at such efforts. Their pursuers, however, were used to this pace and galloped along with no problem at all.

With his mind racing, Erroh led them further into the deep forest. He dared a look behind his comrades to the Riders gathering at their rear—at least seventy of them, and closing fast. They had been galloping like this for an hour, but the Riders were steadily shortening the distance between them. Now, it seemed, was the time for some form of brilliance on their leader's part. But without the advantage of surprise, Erroh saw no escape.

Idiot.

He'd brought this upon himself, upon them all. Not content with merely murdering and pillaging and slowly chipping away at Uden's vast army patiently, he had arrogantly sought more significant numbers for this mayhem. A shrewder warrior might have been content, but Erroh's desire for destruction had finally brought his luck to its knees. He'd been sure he was right. He'd believed he could entice the bandits to join their cause. Not even when Drahir had argued vehemently against such an unlikely alliance had he thought differently. He'd brought twenty Riders with him, even after Drahir had suggested just three or four upon their wildest steeds was the best move. Appearing with a show of force had seemed like a good idea at the time. It hadn't taken long for the Southerners to pick up their slow, rambling scent, and now all was lost.

"You can go on without us," Drahir called from behind, and indeed, it was an honourable suggestion. Highwind would easily outrun their pursuers, but leaving comrades behind was unthinkable. Or was it? He looked to the uneven path ahead, and it became mighty tempting to kick her forward and disappear. Who would know? Apart from himself, that is.

"Aye," Erroh agreed, and slowed his pace to join with his comrades.
I will not leave them.
Time to be a hero.

Lea felt it in the air today. She didn't know what *it* was, but it was ever-present. Perhaps today was the day she would come upon an unprepared Uden and do what her mate had failed to do on two separate occasions. Or else, today might be the day she took a blade through the heart and slipped away. That would be fine as long as she was killing when she fell. Regardless of what *it* was, she'd lived long enough in the Wastes to know when something was afoot. Something great and terrible. Something.

"What is it?" a man's voice asked from behind, and she hissed him to silence. Closing her eyes in the dreadful deluge, she listened to the forest, the crack of twigs, the rustle of shrubbery, the thunder of cavalry, the hiss of rain and the patter of droplets on leaves.

Wait, what?

The thunder of cavalry.

"There's something ahead," she whispered, and her comrades fell silent, although their mounts whinnied and snorted, such was their disapproval of their masters standing in a downpour. She imagined they would be sprinting soon enough. She strained her ears for the rumble of hooves beyond the natural sounds. *There*. Distant. A mile, perhaps less. Heavy numbers, at a great pace. "Coming our way."

Behind her, a fresh noise disturbed her: the gathering of thirty warriors preparing themselves for a charge, always towards the enemy, never away. Cordelia, the fox of the Wastes, had a reputation to uphold. Blood was in the air, death too, and the touch of steel was only a hurried race away.

For just a breath, Lea remembered a young Alphaline watching her brutish mate go through her bags, removing her needful things. Just a handful of seasons ago. Half as many years, if one were to count the days. They had travelled many miles since, endured pain, glorious victories, horror, and triumph. If she could, she might have warned that hesitant female that things would change. She would no longer feel lost, hopeless, broken. Things would both improve and get so much worse.

Gripping her reins, she kicked Shera forward, and the magnificent animal obeyed, breaking first into a trot, then a sprint. Across the deep terrain they charged, and Lea listened to the wind and the rain, seeking prey. It didn't matter how many. They would fall to her and her boys. Her pack followed her in a line, the better to hide their numbers, eyes wide in terror and excitement. Her elite legion, her snapping Wolves—no one else's. Only hers. She gestured their route and signalled them to ambush, all from her saddle. They didn't question or argue; they trusted their Alpha queen, who was magnificent.

With the wind against them, their enemies' thunder lessened. The rain did the rest. Lea and her legion came at the offending thunder from an angle. Staying ahead of them and seeking their path was easy, once they'd discovered an appealing open glade. Then, Lea of the Wolves raised her fist, and her boys answered. Distantly, she could see birds rising, aggrieved to face the rain at this early hour, and the rolling of distant undergrowth as the thundering beasts charged through. With eager eyes, she sought their leader, calculated their numbers. Sounded like a dozen, she thought, but soon the numbers grew, and her heart beat in excitement.

More.

Loads more.

Too many.

She calmed herself lest her nerve take her. And her boys, for that matter. She had ambushed over thirty Riders without a scratch so far. What was double that, anyway?

Double the kills.

She watched her boys line up with crossbows on the far side of the dell, awaiting her order. If their quarry travelled through, there would be blood. If they veered off on another path, no blood would spill. Especially their own. It wouldn't be the first time a perfectly placed ambush was lost to an unexpected twist in a quarry's path. On those occasions, they laughed and drank and commiserated about what could have been. It was good being a queen of the forest with her boys.

As they neared, she could taste the battle, could feel it once more.

It.

The same surge she'd felt at the moment she'd gazed upon a lost little Alpha male in the city. Like that night in the South when she'd pulled him from the river. She was no believer in gods easing her moves, but she trusted in her feelings. So she pulled her bow from her back, gripped six arrows, and prepared to draw. Her record was four kills in half as many breaths before she shot wide. Perhaps she would reach the half-dozen killing shots today. That would be significant too. That could be *it,* she decided, and knew better.

The Riders thundered into the opening just short of the perfect ambush spot, and she held her hand up to hold her men's joint strike. And then she froze.

It can't be.

"Hold," she screamed, and if those who were ambushed as they dropped from their mounts heard her, they didn't react. They had deadlier things to contend with. "They are not the quarry," she cried, and willed no fingers to release their bowstrings, let alone hers. "They are not to be struck!"

They broke into a clearing. Erroh noted how effective the tree canopies might have made as an ambush point. They might have found out for certain if they'd had longer to prepare. But they had no time. So they did the only thing they could do: drop from their mounts, cluster together and hope for the best. If good fortune followed and they caused a little disarray, so much the better. Erroh knew battles were won on lesser things.

"Drop down on me," he roared, and those last few, grateful not to be left behind, thundered into the opening just in time to realise his counter. Dropping to the sodden ground, he gathered his warriors into position. "Raise shields," he roared, though he held no shield himself. Instead, he trusted luck and reflexes to save his neck should the Riders slow their charge and draw their crossbows. "Tighter," he ordered, and his comrades clustered around him, holding up their shields like a barrier to cover themselves and their companions. All around them, mounts, no doubt sensing death and carnage in the air, sprinted wide of the little gathering of defenders. They took refuge in the treeline as the Southern Riders strode into the opening and met a small, huddled group of defiant warriors ready to give them a fight.

This is it.
This is the end.
No one here gets out alive.
I'm on my way, Lea.

He'd had a bad feeling all morning. He had a bad feeling every morning, but today there was merit in worry. He realised that now, even as his brave brethren clustered around him. He felt it in his gut, even as he drew his swords. It was the same sickening feeling he had when things were about to take a terrible turn. Like consuming a god's eye. Like watching the rain fall upon a wall of fire. Like walking into a Cull to face a group of nasty bitches—or agreeing to share a life with one. Aye, he had a terrible feeling.

Unprepared for their sudden dismount, the Southerners channelled through the path into the green towards the gathered defenders without raising their weapons. It was only a moment's hesitation on their part, and the world slowed, and Erroh decided to take the fight to the bastards.

He thought it an acceptable way to die. Noble and gloriously foolish. As his comrades knelt low and huddled against each other for support, bracing themselves against the thrashing strike they would face from the passing mounts, Erroh, in the middle, stood upright and alone. Even Drahir, cursing in his ear, dared not rise from the makeshift defensive shield.

"Don't worry, brother. I have this," Erroh said calmly. And why wouldn't he be calm? He'd been here many times before. This would either work or not. He climbed through his Southern brothers towards the rushing Riders, then stepped upon the shoulder of his nearest comrade, and, with all his energy, kicked high towards the leading attacker.

Flying.

Colliding.

A little bit of killing.

The Rider was unprepared for such an assault and did what any surprised Southerner would have done then. He took the left blade through the throat and bled all over Erroh. Landing awkwardly, Erroh spun the right blade and lunged towards the second Rider, who took the strike masterfully through the belly. His was the more painful death, for he fell, breaking bones, bleeding everywhere and writhing in agony beside his dead comrade. He called for somebody to help him stem the flow, and hold him as he shivered and died. Perhaps, were his companions capable, they might have helped his passing. But they were too distracted by the business of getting torn apart by a solitary warrior who appeared to fire bolts and arrows with his very screams.

The world slowed to nothing, and Lea watched her mate go to war and thought him impressive. Impressiveness had never been the problem, though. He leapt upon the nearest Rider, and he was a legend. She heard his name uttered by her comrades, who held their fire by the grace of some absent gods.

"Take the ones upon the mounts," she cried finally, and they released, and it was glorious. She thought of Keri, thought of his foolishness, thought of his recklessness, thought of his beauty, thought of him alone, turning the course of a battle with one magnificent counterattack. And she was far above, covering him with shot after shot. She also remembered love, his warmth, his touch and also his pledge. "Again," she roared, but they were already releasing the shots of their own volition, and that was fine. They were hardened and experienced. They would not miss. They would not kill Erroh either. Besides, she had her own killing to do.

Green eyes.

The Riders who were not taken by the first blows or waves of arrows charged past the shell of protection, unsure of their direction or their orders. Lea leapt from Shera, firing at them as she did. These were no quail, all skittish and careful; these were great lumbering brutes upon hesitant mounts, unsure in the chaos. It was easy. Drawing arrows, notching and releasing in a series of smooth motions, she fired all of them in a blistering few breaths and broke her record for kills. Six fell in silence, some still atop their wild mounts, seeking an escape from this sudden violent charge.

Aim for a dozen next time.

The shell of defenders erupted in a haze of violence and attacked the Riders who were left, and who were clumsy and off balance atop their beasts. They took the weak strikes upon their shields and punished the Riders. The clatter of blade on blade was lost to the squeals of the dying and the roars of the victorious. The frenetic voice of Erroh was loudest, and Lea was drawn to it. Not out of love, for love did nothing but tear her apart.

I hate that I love you.
I hate you so much.

He did not know why he still drew breath, only that he was grateful for every gulp of air after the first strike. He saw arrows erupt from the forest, but with so much blood filling his vision, he could only focus on the victims as he charged through them, wounding, killing, and defeating. He lost himself to the frenzy of battle. Mounts reared in terror, bodies fell to the ground on either side of him, and still, he pushed on through the wave of Southern black, never stopping, never delaying, always awaiting the defining blow from the corner of his eye that would take him. It was a fine way to go, he decided. A tale worthy of his apparent legend. He wondered briefly about those he loved. He felt them near, felt *her* near, and it was a reassuring thing.

"I'm coming, Lea," he whispered mid-roar. It was a prayer and a pledge, and as warriors died around him, he thought it a fine pledge. She would have liked his killing, he thought. He never stopped spinning, cutting, ducking, and all too soon, his body tired, and he knew it was the end. He wondered whether his comrades were free of their shell. Were they attacking as he was? If not, it was a shame to put this charge to waste. He might have turned around, but there were mounts to slip past, Southern Riders to gut, and sins to put upon his already tarnished soul along the way.

The long grass was slippery from the rain and the blood. Nevertheless, he strode through it, swinging both blades. Suddenly, a Southerner spun towards him with a mighty battle axe. Erroh blocked, but such was the force that his guard was broken. He stumbled, and the axe drew high to finish him.

I love you, Lea.
I forgive your lineage.
It wasn't your fault.
Here I come.

Suddenly, three arrows struck the brute, all within a breath of each other. One through the axe-wielding arm, another through his unprotected throat and a third through his heart. Dropping the axe before he could swing, the man slumped in the saddle and died without a word, and Erroh, ever confused, ever relieved, thanked the absent gods and recovered his breath to face the next warrior, for there were many more. At least for a time. A short time. He drove forward until the last mount passed, until he recovered the breath in his lungs.

And then she was beside him.

A female, hardened and fierce and crimson and ruined. She moved through the mayhem as smoothly as a girl he'd once known, and for a moment, he wondered had he taken a blow without him knowing after all? Was this warrior his love? Coming to him, bringing him to the darkness beyond? Was she another of Uden's lost daughters? But then he saw that this goddess wasn't alone, and through the bewildered haze, Erroh saw Wolves from all sides giving the fight to the remaining Hunt.

And then it was done. The day was won, and Erroh still lived. He knew this from the sting of grazes from passing blades, from the sickly churn in his stomach, from the rawness in his throat and the terrible weariness in all his limbs. Dropping to a knee for breath, he gazed at the girl, covered in blood and glory, and he thought her beautiful. She stood away from him, staring at her last victim and watching the wary Southerners who had charged with Erroh. She would not look at Erroh, and the truth of the turning world struck him.

Lea.

My Lea.

Nobody else's.

Only mine.

Tears streamed from his eyes, and he almost collapsed. Instead, he felt his heartbeat in his chest, each one dedicated to her. He had never thought her more enchanting, more perfect, more welcomed. All his wretchedness left him. The days and weeks of torment and harrowing sadness were replaced with a deep sense of wellness. Knowing all would be perfect; all would be right.

"My beo," he cried, and he dropped his blades. He wanted her and none other. Wanted to take her in his arms and be done with this war. To ride away into the forest and leave their legend upon this rainy battlefield.

As though in reply, the absent gods delivered a break in the clouds; a shimmer of sunlight broke through and shone upon them both. For them and only them. At last. Together again and ready for war. It was perfect. Were a bard to strike a few notes together and describe this moment with any accuracy, they would have heard the greatest love song of all time, and still, it would not come close to expressing the love he felt for her, the gratitude for the events that had led them to this moment.

Upon hearing his voice, a few Wolves rushed to him, but he had no time for them. They dropped to a knee in the presence of their master general, and as they did, so too did his Southern comrades, and he grimaced. He'd been getting quite good at knocking this bowing shit from them these last few weeks.

"Erroh, Erroh, Erroh."

All around them, the warriors from both factions dropped to a knee. There soon began a Southern chant of his name, and at this, Lea finally looked up from her kills, and she was everything to him. She did not kneel, and that was how it should be.

Alive, alive, alive.

She's alive and fighting.

"My love," he cried, and she did not reply. In shock, no doubt, from her actions. Scrambling through his followers, all clad in grey and black, he broke across the line of kneeling sycophants and stumbled towards her. Then he ran, and she stood proud to meet him. He wanted her so badly. He couldn't believe it. But he did believe it. Because she was Lea. Perfect, heroic Lea. She could not burn. She could only survive and be better.

You've no idea what I've been through.

He reached for her, and she drew back, pointing her finger accusingly. Her face was contorted with rage, her eyes were slits, and he hesitated.

"Don't touch me, Erroh," she hissed, and her tone was a sharp contrast from the one he'd always known. He knew her voice, even when contorted by rage and tragedy, but he also knew her chosen tone. This was different. "Not ever again."

"What?"

68

HAPPY FAMILIES

The knock shook Emir shook from his daydreaming. *Is it that late already?* he wondered, and knew it was. The knock came again, and he jumped, recovered, and stood up from his seat in the kitchen. A third knock came, and he took a breath. One more knock, always at dusk, same time, same thing every day. The unwanted guest, overstaying his welcome again and again and again. A demented loop of time repeating itself.

Insanity.

He wondered if there was a life after this one ended. Something beyond the darkness where the dead trod. Where a lost soul endured the same torments repeatedly, like he had to do each fuken night with their guest. He'd been beyond the dark and returned with nothing. No fuken light, no fuken warmth. No memory of anything reassuring.

"And there's the fourth," Roja muttered as the offending knock heralded the click of a lock, the turning of a handle, the heavy creak of a door opening and the low, thumping step of an unwelcome god.

"Are ye both decent?" a thunderous voice cried, and Roja sighed loudly.

"We are," Emir replied. Frustrated, he shook his head, and the beast neared them from the hallway beyond. Every day the bastard asked this question, and every day Emir replied in kind, offering entrance to the brute who ruled the world. With another sigh, Roja returned to the stove and the busy stirring of delicious brew. These last few weeks, she'd become quite the culinary expert, the only thing Emir enjoyed in this prison. At least they ate well.

Drank well too.

"I bring gifts," Uden offered, stepping through the doorway. In his hands was a basket of wine bottles. Red, dusty, old. Beside them lay a fresh loaf of honey cake. Whenever Uden brought honey cake, he was in no good mood. It was terrible recognising his habits, yet here was Emir doing just that, wondering what irked the false god enough that he desired honey cake this evening and how it would affect everyone else's mood.

In Uden's mind, he was family to Roja, regardless of her protestations, irrespective of her knowledge of her lineage. Still, if it kept her safe, kept them both safe, that was something at least.

"Honey cake?" Roja asked, caring little about concealing the disdain in her voice. Uden didn't mind. He smiled and placed it on the table. He took his usual seat, and Emir began setting his place.

"It was a trying day, little one," Uden offered, and extended the first bottle of wine to Emir, who promptly popped it open. They already had plenty of wine in their extravagant prison, but Uden would consider it rude of them to refuse his gifts. Uden was learning to be a polite guest, as they were learning to be gracious hosts. Admittedly, these practices took work. Being little more than a plaything for one so fierce was a sobering, belittling thing, but Uden was a man of his word so far. It had been weeks since Emir's "escape attempt," and still, Uden had not pressed the matter of his poison concoction. It was a fair deal. They made no attempt on Uden's life nor any attempt to escape from the city in exchange for such mercy.

Uden nodded in appreciation as Emir filled his glass, Roja's, and his own. He sniffed the air, and a small smile appeared on his lips.

"What occurred?" Roja asked, stirring the bean and meat stew. Emir loved this particular dish. As did Uden; he'd asked for it several times, and Roja, playing her part, had always done what was needed.

"Just worrying words from the arth, superstitions of demons, a few groups slaughtered," he said, drinking deeply, and Emir immediately refilled his goblet. The quicker Uden drank, the sooner his ramblings would turn to those of a lonely old man. Regretful, melancholic, lost. Mostly, though, by the second bottle, he was ready to slip back out into the evening air. Were Emir capable, he'd have started with a glass of sine to send the bastard on his way right quick.

"So, our people don't go into the darkness without a fight?" Roja asked. She could play the cold prisoner far more than Emir ever could. She stepped away from the stew pot for a moment. Few people were better at tearing shards of information from a stubborn soul than Roja. From his time battling her in the city, he knew that better than most.

"But they will go into darkness," the god snapped, and offered a delicately raised hand in apology almost immediately. Emir could see the furnace of rage festering deep within. He'd seen broken spirits before, and Uden's was more damaged than most. Emir felt revulsion and wary curiosity about what deranged thoughts swam in Uden's mind. What had led him to proclaim himself a god? What horrors had he endured to make him behave as he did? Was there a key to locking and unlocking the gates of sanity? Was there any way to cure him of his cruelty? Admittedly, he didn't believe he could influence Uden's thoughts or actions, but Emir would bet a year's worth of ale that a less-deranged brute would be a far better thing for this world.

Roja spooned out Emir's plate first, then her own, before tending to Uden. It was bad-mannered, but Uden said little. Instead, he bowed his head and waited for her to sit with them. Just three fiends at a table, playing at friendship. Emir offered some bread, freshly baked by his own hand. He was getting quite good at baking. It was the added salt to counter the excessive dollops of honey, he said, that made it good. Uden did not trust him yet in the medical theatre. It was something pathetic to do. Still, he liked his bread. Emir enjoyed both Uden's and Roja's reactions to the bread as well. He offered some butter to his eating companions. Buttered bread with this meal was just the best.

I have to get out of here.

In between mouthfuls, Uden told them of his latest reports from the city, from the skirmishes in the Wastes, and this interested Roja most. She asked questions, offered thoughts and suggested subtle mercy, and only at this time did apparent niece and nephew appear genial. It wouldn't last, though, for every veneer was eventually removed, every delusion crumbled. He would look at her one day and realise his own mistake. She had no uncle named Uden and knew her family tree well.

They battled wits for over an hour every evening, and Emir could only look on without offering any great opinions. Emir frequently suggested she play her part more warmly to curry favour, but Roja could not do this as masterfully as Emir. She was too stubborn in her hatred. Too dignified in her political manoeuvres. Perhaps that was what had lost her the city leadership. Emir might have suggested such a notion, but was wary of the fiery consequences.

After dinner, they drank a bit longer until the sweet cakes were served. Roja had the good sense to serve them with creamed strawberries, which greatly pleased their guest. Usually, once he was sufficiently fed and watered, Uden changed the topic to less significant things, and his hosts listened, for there was little else to do. His tales of his life were interesting, at least, as were the observations he gladly shared at the table. He was charming and darkly witty, and were Emir not suppressing his desire to plunge a blade through his other eye most of the time, he might have admitted Uden was a pleasant dinner guest. As it was, he could never forget that Uden had taken everything from Emir, barring the redhead. The wretched healer would do everything to keep it that way.

As usual, when the hour was late, and Roja could take no more, she excused herself, feigning tiredness, and Uden stood up to allow her to leave.

"Good night, little one," he offered, kissing her once upon the forehead as any close family member would. Emir always watched her knuckles turn white for a moment before she smiled weakly and disappeared upstairs to her bedding, where she would wait for Emir to return once the last bottle of wine was consumed. This last hour was the worst, for this was when Emir's tongue was loosest. When grief almost surfaced and tore his words to shreds.

Still, though, most nights were without event.

"Another round," Emir declared, refilling Uden's glass and then his own.

"At least one more before the road," Uden said, taking up his wine and watching it settle in the light of flickering flames from the fireplace. "She has not yet warmed to me," he said in a strange voice, and Emir held his pour for a breath as a terrible shiver ran down his back.

"She is still grieving this life," Emir countered.

Uden leaned across the table. He could have taken Emir's collar and pulled him clear from his seat. Instead, he just whispered, "I'm no fool, healer. I know how you both feel about me."

"We are prisoners, but we appreciate the generosity," countered Emir. This was not a lie, precisely, but an ever-so-delicate curving of the truth.

"You will both care for me eventually, friend," the behemoth said gently, and indeed, his whispered words were like a drummer's beat upon skin. "That is what families do."

"Aye, perhaps so," said Emir evenly. His heart began to settle; he would need Roja to put in more effort from now on, pride be damned.

"I know none of this is real," Uden said, draining his glass, and Emir immediately refilled it. "But it is a reminder, a taste of normal; it is a human thing." He looked at his hands as though seeing them for the first time. His one eye was glazed over ever so, his words slightly slurred. Emir knew that level of drunkenness: it sneaked up from the dark and took you.

Uden suddenly turned to Emir, shot out his arm and grabbed his shoulder. "Sometimes, I think about my blood coursing through you." He tightened his grip, and Emir's wrist began to itch. "I wonder if I took some of your blood into me. I wonder did it taint my mind, ever so."

"I have some rightly shitty blood," Emir countered before he could stop himself, and the god laughed loudly before catching himself lest he disturb Roja's rest. He raised his finger to his lips and shushed drunkenly.

Despite himself, Emir laughed. It was the first time both men had shared a laugh in the many hours they'd spent conversing. Emir knew the threat of warming to such a brute, though. Knew it occurred among prisoners, but how many prisoners had as much hate as he did stored deep within?

They killed Aireys in his name.

"I should leave," Uden said, tipping a little more wine into Emir's glass—only a little, just enough to keep the conversation moving. "I have so many people to kill come the morning," he jested.

"I suppose I should get you a little drunker, so," Emir countered, and, taking the glass, nodded in appreciation. It was a precarious act, a deadly game, but he would now do anything in the world to save his own life, and hers. It wasn't much to bring to the world, but it was all he had.

"Tell me again of your brave friend Stefan," Uden said thoughtfully. His eye fell upon the long knife lying beside the remains of the honey cake. He glanced up at Emir, and for a moment, Emir wondered if the brute wasn't looking for an excuse, any excuse at all, to kill him and be done with it. Emir swallowed the seething anger as swiftly as it surfaced. A drunken brute might not even notice it at all. "I have so many sins; I have so many thoughts," Uden added after a moment.

"Would you like another slice of cake?" Emir asked. He slid the plate across, knife and all. "For the road."

Uden smiled sadly and declined, and Emir told the brute about the first time he and Stefan had shared camaraderie on the road from Keri. Uden listened wistfully, and Emir counted the moments until the fiend would leave.

One tale was not enough, though, for Uden asked more of Stefan, of his friend's love for Aurora Borealis, and the colour drained from his face upon hearing Emir's description of their dalliance. It had been a small matter, but, regardless, Uden drank the end of the bottle and, after a time, rose to leave.

"You welcome me in, despite my actions. Despite your hate," Uden said at the doorway.

"Aye."

"You are a fine man. You would be a good fit too, and you have my blessings."

He turned to leave, but Emir needed clarification. "What do you mean?"

Uden smiled, which was terrifying, especially when it was genuine. He pointed to the room above their heads where Roja lay in silken sheets waiting for Emir. "It was an old tradition for a suitor to ask the father for the lady's hand," Uden said. "You have only to ask, and I will gladly lead her down the aisle."

Emir knew of marriages—an archaic thing with much ceremony, and certainly not for him. Besides, an Alpha never married. Alphas culled and mated.

Uden rummaged in his pockets and smiled again as he found what he was looking for. He drew out a little pouch and opened it to reveal a glistening ring of white gold. At its centre was a dazzling sapphire jewel surrounded by many smaller diamonds. The god held it in the light, and it shimmered. "This was Roja's mother's wedded ring. I cut it myself." He tossed the ring across to Emir, who miraculously caught it with clumsy hands. "Take her for a walk beneath the stars; ask her for her hand."

"I do not understand," hissed Emir.

"You are a fine couple, so you should become mated."

"I do not understand."

"Wedding unions can be a wonderful thing," Uden said. His eye was turned away, thinking of something far beyond this elegant kitchen in the most prominent house in the city. "Good for families, too."

Emir still did not understand. "I do not understand," he said again.

"Good night, friend," the brute said and, upon wobbly feet, slipped out into the night towards wherever a god needed to sleep, leaving a drunken wretch of a man behind him.

Sitting down at the table, Emir was unsettled and confused. He did not know how to play this game or how to find a way out of it. Emir understood mating; understood love. However, Roja was a goddess, an Alpha of Spark City, and he was a lowly healer. Wretched and all.

"What the fuk do I do?" he asked the silence in the room. Holding up the ring, he examined it more closely and thought it fetching. He'd seen beautiful rings in his time, but this was special. He popped it onto his little finger and watched the shimmering flashes as it caught the light. "I am no Alpha." It was true; he wasn't, and deep down, Roja still believed in the city ways. She might feign polite conversation for a mad god, but she would not openly declare herself to another outside of a Culling. Would she? The silence and the ring had no answer for that worry.

Emir had never felt more unsure of what to do. "What if she said no?"

"What if I said yes?" Roja said from the doorway, and fear came upon him.

69

QUEEN OF ADAWAN

"Discipline carries us through," Elise screamed. A shrill scream to rise above all other dissenting voices, thundering drums, soul-crushing horns. She took hold of Ulrik by the scruff of his shirt and screamed "discipline" again. He didn't react in disagreement; now was not the moment to do so. Instead, he took her manhandling and nodded in agreement. Most of his bruises had cleared more quickly than hers, but it was a small matter. She shoved him roughly and spun back around to meet the eyes of every general present, for there were many. A dozen in all. All armed to the teeth, all breathing heavily beneath their heavy armour. And their mouths were wet, and such a thing in this heat was valuable.

"They will come in thousands, and we will hold," she warned, and a few more heads nodded in agreement. If there had been any doubts about her leadership, they had been swiftly lost in the last few days before the invasion. She had taken the crown; more than that, she had stolen it fairly and proven prudence bested brawn. The invading Hunt numbered at least eight thousand. The defenders were closer to three thousand, all battle-worn but including older bandits and youth with few crimes to their name. The odds were hardly fair.

"We will hold!"

She had done nothing these last weeks but think on battles. Running up and down the eternal steps, mentally playing out the skirmishes to come. Battering her punching bag and overthinking the weaknesses and strengths of each line of defence. An agonising obsession that took most of her energy. It was a minor miracle she'd had the power to take the throne for herself. So now, on the eve of battle, she only had to put them to task. However they came, they would be prepared, and they would hold.

The time for challenges and arguments had passed. Those meetings had occurred days before. She had laid out every possible plan, listened to their thoughts, and argued all counterpoints reasonably. Every general had left the table in agreement with her plan. They were content to stick to the tactics for whatever attacks they faced. She looked around and saw fear and determination, and was pleased. They knew their parts to play. They knew their actions when the Hunt came thundering.

"We hold through discipline," she roared again, and this time, she preyed on Bison, shoving him brutally from his seat on a barrel and almost knocking him over. He took the shove and growled in approval, then stood tall to meet her. Around them, there were more nods, more grunts of acceptance. She was their queen now; her word was gospel, and her will would be followed. "Do you hear me, big man?" she demanded, grabbing his shoulders before slapping him across the chest, and he gripped her shoulder fiercely.

"We fuken hold," he cried, and they roared in unison, and she spun away, striking her fist against her heavy breastplate. They were all in this together. The scales of leadership had been tested, and she stood above them. She only needed to psych them up for some savagery.

Around them, in the ramparts beyond, a few hundred listened where they could. It was a hard thing considering their watch, the drumming that beat through their bodies, and the blowing horns playing their foreboding wail of death. Elise stormed among her generals, thumping her armour to the beat of their drums, and the gathered crowd began to drum along with her. Stamping, barking, striking anything that made noise. She was a master at stirring any man to fire, but at war, she was divine. She left her generals behind, left them to spread out among their defenders with a stirring in their blood and a craving for blood in their hearts.

She strode forward and met the eye of every beautiful bastard bandit along the way, showing her lack of fear and her desire for murder. If they weren't impressed with her brightly polished armour, then her massive halberd, dragging behind her, completed the task. They knew the tales; they knew her legend and were eager to see her actions, keen to see her lead them towards victory.

"We hold!"

Stopping below a massive tower, she climbed the ladder to look at the gathered Southern invaders. Many thousands, all set at camp, preparing themselves for a long siege. Far enough away that only the right sort of catapult could bombard them to oblivion as they slept, but close enough that she could see their banners, see their garrisons, see them prepare for a fateful march across terrible, hostile terrain.

Around her, a gathering of archers were in muted conversation. Discussing the coming battle, she thought with a frown.

"You fukers look ready to shit yourselves," she said, and they sniggered uneasily. "Don't put it to waste. When you do the deed, lace your arrows with whatever horrors you find in your nether regions." They began to laugh, and she gestured with one of her own arrows: a slight dipping motion followed by a swirling technique followed by a swift removal of said arrow tip. "The trick is firing shit arrows before the foulness makes you throw up." They thought this advice excellent. She wasn't done. Sometimes good cheer carried warriors to immortality. Or at least allowed them to die grinning. There were worse ways to go. "I like to cover a bit of the shaft when I fire my shit arrows, so the poor bastards in the healing bays trying to pull them free are treated to the shit as well."

She laughed with them and enjoyed the jests they offered, for a time, until her mind returned to preparation. Adawan's primary defences were facing the camped attackers. And why wouldn't they be? She expected the front of Adawan to take the brunt of the assault. She might have been wary if the Southerners were wiser in their behaviours and movements. However, these fiends had shown little tactical acumen from the first town they'd flailed. They were terrifying; they were a rolling machine and more significant in number, but rarely had numbers alone won a war. She remembered her son's recollections of Keri. She had been proud then and was proud now. He had shown the way for the defenders to follow, and follow she would. Be wary of the flanks but expect them head on and cut them to ribbons. This war should have ended beneath a Ranger banner. They should have fallen to lesser numbers but wilier tactics. Betrayal had robbed them of that victory, but now, she would do her mate's legacy proud. Then she would tear the fuken factions apart, seeking out the bringer of so much death and destruction.

"Calm yourself; look at the numbers before you. Let fear take you."

Magnus's words. Long ago, on the eve of battle. A fine thing always to be aggressive but also careful. Especially in the moments before. She leaned out over the balcony and stared at the gathering storm, and allowed her stomach to churn in unease. She did this because this was

The Actions of Gods

what Magnus did; she had been a willing apprentice. Then she had become his equal. Sometimes she believed herself greater. Regardless, she remembered his wise words. Even so many years later.

"Spot the dip of a pebble and its ranging ripples."

She looked for the pebble. For the thing she hadn't prepared herself for. It was something to do while absently counting their numbers. It was all about numbers. That was fine. She would rather be tucked in behind defences, with a wet mouth and a plan of attack. Were there a need to hold these lands, the enemy might have thinned out her line of fortifications and attacked from either flank or, worse, torn through from their rear and set Adawan ablaze while they struggled to turn around and shuffle down towards the mine. But the mine had no value, did it? This lesser sanctuary in the middle of a lifeless desert was no tactical vantage point, no matter how many barrels of salt it offered. Nor was it a launching platform to the east beyond. Instead, Adawan was a defiant place to be crushed. They were an army to be met.

The absent gods agreed.

Perhaps that was why they favoured her ever so.

She did not know how long she stared quietly at the gathered brutes seeking out a chink in Adawan's defences, but all at once she sensed them stirring; a ripple of movement like a catching fire flickered and rolled through the Southern camp. The horns fell silent, and she knew the moment was at hand. Desperate panic surged through her for a breath, and she swallowed it deep down. She gripped her halberd tightly lest her hands shake, and she watched them gather, seeking blood.

"Not this fine day," she warned under her breath. It was the one warning she would offer. After this, she would show no more—nor mercy, either.

"They come?" asked Ulrik from beside her.

"They're preparing to."

"If we fall, this is all on you," he jested softly, gripping her shoulder. His eyes were upon the roving soldiers clustering together, lining up, answering guttural Southern orders. As they did so, like any good defensive army, Adawan, too, was preparing. All along the battlements, her defenders went to task, readying themselves for horror. Weapons were gripped, armour clasped and tightened. Arrows and bolts removed, notched, but not drawn. Not yet. She might have preferred a fine, experienced army built for discipline and brutality at these gates, but truthfully, in these last few months, she'd grown to appreciate the stubborn steel flowing through these bastards' veins. They feared death but had not once allowed that fear to take their nerve. Such a thing was rare enough in an untested soldier. These bandits lived a life on the edge, forever within a breath of slipping over into the darkness, all for the price of a pilfered cart, a load of illegal contraband, or a few stolen bread loaves. When the thunder came, she knew they would hold—all of them.

"I'm sorry," she said after a time, and Ulrik laughed humourlessly. She'd apologised more than once for her betrayal and to win back his favour. Why? Because she desired honour, she desired loyalty—more than she had shown, at least—but mostly because he was a friend of sorts. A strange thing indeed.

"It was never truly my throne," he said. "Besides, I miss the rush of the Wastes and the call of the road. Should we survive this, I will enjoy such things once more."

"We will survive this, most of us," she countered quickly, looking down through her defenders, sensing their trepidation. Their hushed conversation had now died away to a thoughtful silence. Many held trinkets and pendants, kissing them, whispering to their gods, and why not? She couldn't imagine any god not being present upon a battlefield, not to influence the battle, but for entertainment. Humankind was gloriously entertaining in its actions. Gods could learn much from them, she imagined. Absent or no.

"How will they come, do you think?" he asked. That was the golden piece of the question. Those who predicted the tactics of any battle would most likely emerge the victor. Still, even now, it was anyone's guess.

"Couldn't rightly tell you, but we will hold." An acceptable, reassuring answer, and her archers nodded absently before returning to their prayers.

"They could come up through the middle, cavalry first."

It was a fine observation. One that would serve them well. "That would be expected," she agreed, watching the numbers, counting, searching for signs. Riders? Archers? Infantry? She was ready for all.

"Or else, they might come at us in numbers, infantry roaring, thundering through, washing over us like a breaking wave." There was no panic in his tone. He was merely thinking aloud, saying what most warriors tended to be thinking at this moment.

"Aye, could be that too," she agreed, still watching. Riders began to emerge now, parts of their armour shimmering in the sun above their brethren's dull black and grey.

"I don't think they've enough archers or crossbow wielders to reach us. We have the wind at our backs; more than that, we have the sun behind us," he said, and she agreed. Archers would have been a foolish first wave of attack. The defenders hid behind defensive blockades, while getting into range offered the attackers little cover, and such things changed battles. More than that, rows of markers were laid out in the burning sands, a hundred feet from their line, to mark the spot that the defenders could easily fire from. That last hundred feet to Adawan would be death to many.

A long walk.

"Shouldn't you be setting yourself up?" she asked, but Ulrik seemed happy to hover beside her, even as the clustered soldiers spread out along the line in a terrifying show of force.

"What if they all come at once?" he said thoughtfully, and a cold stirring ran through her body.

"Then this battle will cost us. But it will cost them tenfold."

"And we will hold?"

"Whichever way they come, we will hold, triumph, and change this war."

70

BLINDING STORM

Something is wrong.

The breeze was cutting, but Mea strode from her room, ignoring it. With Jeroen beside her, she felt stronger, felt braver. Only a little, but enough to feign leadership. Shadows danced a darkened jig around her as one by one, the torches sputtered away to darkness. It felt wrong. The wind gusted, lifting her hair, cutting through her clothing, trying to take her warmth. Strong enough to take the flame from torches? she pondered.

"Why is it so dark?" Jeroen muttered, and she could hear his apprehension. The stirring of panic too. She could barely make out his features, but his jaw was clenched, and instinctively, she wanted to return to bed, wrap up in warmth, wrap herself around him. But instead of turning tail and retreating to safety, Mea marched onwards, and Jeroen matched her every step.

A few large galleons over, she could see a tremendous reassuring glow, and she marched towards it like a storm-inflicted barge towards a welcome harbour. She could see Melinda and a few similar Alphalines on watch. A dozen in all, armoured carelessly with gowns of silk beneath. They took their watch, but were engaged in conversation, giggling, jesting and being youthful. Mea couldn't be sure they weren't drunk, and strangely, at that moment, the taste of ale on her lips in the company of cheerful goddesses seemed like a fine thing.

"Oh fuk... ouch... wait a moment, my love," Jeroen cried after a loud thump. She turned to see him sitting upon the deck, nursing an aching ankle. She glanced at his sheepish smile for just a breath as another torch behind him fell to darkness. "Some fuk left a bucket in my path," he muttered, kicking the offending iron piece from their path.

"Bold bucket," she scolded, sitting down beside him. It was something to do in the dark in the middle of a gale, with the world getting darker and darker and a perpetual feeling of doom taking hold.

"Aye, it didn't even have a proper handle on it and all. What type of bucket has that type of handle?" he said in mock outrage, swinging his good leg at the piece and missing dreadfully.

"Fuk that bold bucket," she mocked, and strangely, the unease lessened for a breath. If there was one thing she'd learned in life, it was that everything was more manageable if one took a moment to laugh at one's misfortune now and then. Or one's mate, at that.

"I have a terrible feeling," he said after a breath.

"Me too," she whispered, and for a moment, they took each other's hands as another torch was extinguished, and they found themselves in almost pure darkness.

We aren't alone.

From all sides, there came footsteps, and Mea was suddenly grateful for the shadow they found themselves in. Swiftly, Jeroen climbed to his feet, dragging his shield from his back as he did.

"Who goes there?" he demanded, but no reply came. Instead, they heard further shuffling of boots on the decks across from them. That feeling of unease came upon her again. Tearing and ripping at her mind. The kind of apprehension only a fool would ignore. She was blind and hunted, and everything was wrong.

Shut up, Jeroen. Let us flee.

She wanted to be free of this place, near the lights and surrounded by comrades with weapons.

By chance, she caught sight of a figure emerging from the darkness a few dozen feet away, and instinctively, Mea reached for her sword. Barefoot and soaking wet, the fiend sprinted soundlessly across the wooden deck. He did not grunt, warn, challenge or terrify. He ran at them as though the dark air had created him, which was disturbing.

"Keep back," she cried, stepping away.

Jeroen didn't hesitate. Stepping before her, he raised his shield as the cur raised a short blade.

"He has a weapon," she called, and that glowing light and her companions seemed a thousand miles away.

Jeroen was no master with the shield, but he was elite. Holding the weapon low as the fiend charged down upon him, the broken Alpha suddenly leapt forward instead of awaiting the first blow, striking the cur across the face, spinning away and then whirling and striking him a second time. Swiftly after, a third strike with both hands clenched tightly. He was smooth, and despite her fear, she was impressed. She heard the blade fall and the further shuffling of feet. She heard a scream from somewhere in the darkness, followed by the unmistakable sound of a body falling heavily to the deck. Turning back, she saw Jeroen leap upon their assailant's chest; ignoring his struggling arms, Jeroen repeatedly drove the shield into his face until he broke skin, smashed bone, and splattered the contents of the man's skull to a bloody ruin. All within the space of a few breaths too.

"We are boarded," he hissed, climbing away from the ruin and stepping beside his mate. Without warning, a flame appeared in the darkness. Blinding and wavering, illuminating the dead body, illuminating Mea's unpreparedness, illuminating a walking horror. A Wolf shuffled from the night as though drunk, clutching a torch in his hand; he held his throat where a dagger protruded, spilling blood all over his chest plate.

We all die this night.

"It's okay, boy," Jeroen cried, running towards the Wolf, but before he could reach him, another figure appeared from behind the waving flame and recovered its blade from the dying man's throat. There was a brief struggle before the fiend stabbed the Black Guard, over and over again, and left him to fall upon the torch and quench its light in crimson, and she was blind again. Jeroen did not hesitate: he charged upon the attacker, and Mea, too shaken to move, could only watch as the world around her fell apart.

I have failed us again.

She felt the panic take her. For a frantic moment, she wondered was she asleep and if this was just a restless dream from which Jeroen would wake her. And hold her. Kiss her. Save her. Really, though, she knew this was her life. Her death too. It was too much. She felt her limbs shudder under the sway of the boats beneath her feet. Felt everything take her. This blindness was a step too far. She was broken. She probably always had been, ever since taking the city as her own.

It is all my fault.

She collapsed upon the deck and could not move. She wanted to lie here and be done with it all. She could not breathe, lead, or save them all from certain death. Flashes of her life flickered in her mind, different moments in a chaotic procession. She searched each image for something familiar, an antidote to the panic she felt now, an answer to save her, to get her moving. Instead, she felt her heart hammering in her chest as it neared its frenzied last beat. And there was suddenly a blade in her hand, but she had no strength to wield it. She recognised its grip as her own. She'd never imagined it could be so heavy. Distantly, she saw the glow of the females' light, and for a moment, she considered crawling towards it. With a will guided by a force not her own, she rolled onto her belly and then rose to all fours. Holding the blade in front of her to guide her way, she crept towards the light. She tried to call out, but nothing came from her throat, and she wondered if it was her own throat that had been cut. She heard roaring. Familiar roaring. A male voice, beautiful and barbaric as it killed. She longed to rush towards it but she could only crawl because she was no longer Mea of the city; she was a waif, broken at this moment. This last, pitiful moment.

"Come to me, Mea," her mate cried, and the sound of his voice shook her from her stupor for a breath, but all around her came the hammering of feet. Little cracks of light struck her eyes as comrades emerged from the lower parts of the barges.

And then something terrible happened.

She saw the females fall first. Melinda shook suddenly and then collapsed away from the barrel she'd sat upon. Her body was covered in arrows. A terrible death. But at least quick. Shocked by the sudden thud of her body on the deck, her comrades turned to look, and then they, too, fell to the ground, bleeding, squirming and dying.

"Mea!"

Without warning, there came the unmistakable *thunk* of an arrow upon wood, and Mea gripped herself and awaited a rain of death from a darkened sky. All around her, arrows and bolts struck the deck, the buildings and the innocent. The night came alive with wet screams of horror as wave after wave of projectiles came sailing down upon them.

"Mea!"

She could not rise, could only curl up and cower and know this was the end; truly, Mea was disgusted with herself. She'd felt fear, and this was not it. This was something else entirely. This was soul-tearing and mind-cracking, and she was alone in the world and in the dark; she had led them all to death. More and more volleys dashed down upon Boat Town, and there was nothing to be done but give up and die.

"Mea!" the voice cried again, and she was too lost to answer. This was one step too far. She saw the last female fall. The young girl had been struck enough times that her leather armour had torn free of her shoulder, leaving nothing but shredded flesh beneath. Three or four arrows had punctured every limb, but the girl had continued to crawl towards the safety of the darkness only for a lone arrow to pin her head to the deck, and Mea thought it a terrible waste of life. A terrible waste of resources too. There were only so many Alphas they could call upon, after all.

"Mea!"

A jagged shard of pain made her cry out as an arrow struck her leg. As she turned to pull it free, she caught sight of an eerie brightness billowing up into the night. Dreadful balls of flame as large as barrels were careening into the air, as though seeking out a less watery grave.

She'd seen such a thing before. Many years earlier, one dark night, a great sphere of fire had cut the sky open and landed deep in the forest no more than a mile from the estate she shared with Jeroen. She'd never heard such a roar as that fireball made, and the following day she had been shocked to discover the massive scorched crater, spanning a few dozen feet across. Jeroen had been convinced it was a warning from the absent gods, but she had known it was merely a shard of a shattered moon as it slowly prepared the world for its inevitable return. Everyone had thoughts on such unknown things. She wondered, had the gods known that these flaming orbs would come at the end of her life? Had they sent her a sign those many years ago that this was the last thing her eyes would gaze upon?

But then her head cleared and she watched the balls of flame, and knew that these were no spheres gifted by the shattered moon. These were far less impressive but ultimately more devastating, for they only targeted Boat Town.

With a terrible crack, a sphere crashed beside her and bounced over her head, and she felt the terrible heat as it lifted over her and slammed against an open doorway, setting the wood alight. Further down the decks, she saw many more such barrels of flame hit and break and burn, and within moments, the darkness surrendered its hold to the burning light of death.

Surrender.

She tried to squirm away like a dying Alpha, but the arrow embedded in her leg held her fast. She accepted her pitiful fate, and the sky suddenly turned to day as a thousand fireflies appeared above her head.

They landed all around her, and she watched as too many comrades took burning arrows to the heart, throat, chest and more. She saw them die around her, and she wailed not for the pain but for the sorrow of those let loose from the hands of evil. She rolled to her side and fought the agony that threatened to take her sanity. She risked a glance at the waters below and saw the attackers' vessels alight with fire, the rows of warriors reloading their bows. She looked further, to the far edge of the water, where more attackers were reloading a dozen trebuchets with barrels, setting them alight and preparing them for firing. Lastly, she looked to a long line of rafts laden with warriors waiting to board unobstructed.

"Fuk you," she roared to the one-eyed god who likely stood among the attackers, grinning and hating. "Fuk you," she cried a second time and fought the panic, the fear, the sorrow. She took a smoky breath and looked to her people and their suffering, and oh, she hated the attackers. Hated them with every speck of her being. If not for taking her will, then for their cruelty. Before she could stop herself, she reached out and snapped the arrow free from her leg, but left the main shaft embedded in her flesh like a cork. She would bleed, but not dry, and that was enough for now.

With all her will, she climbed to her knees and then to her shaky feet just as another vile assassin appeared ahead of her. Disorientated, he spun around, looking for a victim, and set his eyes upon her. Only then did she notice he had taken an arrow from his comrades, clean through the thigh, a deep and painful wound, no doubt. The cur was as caught in this terrible violent moment as she was. Crazed and shouting guttural curses at her alone, he charged at her with dagger raised.

"To the fires with you," she roared, meeting the charge, pain be damned. Ducking beneath his blow, she ripped the protruding arrow free of his leg, and he howled as she did. She enjoyed this more than she imagined she would. Not as much as plunging her sword through fabric into flesh, though. That deed brought her near delirium. "We are not done," she howled, pulling her blade free of his flesh as more defenders appeared from below deck, seeking a fight but fearing the worst. "We stand," she cried out to any who might hear. Any who might have been lying upon the deck, broken and lost, needing a leader. She cried out because this was her calling, her duty. And soon enough, a few figures dressed in black, chainmail, leather and gowns appeared beside her.

"What do we do?" an Alpha cried in her ear.

"Kill them all," she demanded, and it was a fine suggestion, for many needed killing. Most of these were down below in the rippling water, balancing upon rafts as they set alight another volley and let loose.

"Cover," she heard a voice cry. It might have been Doran's.

Regardless, through the smoke she saw the arrow that would kill her. A dozen or so arrows, if truth be told. She tried to dodge the incoming strike, but her reactions were too slow, her fate too inevitable.

And then he was beside her.

With shield raised, he gripped her and dragged her from the arrows' path. He screamed in pain as he took a few of them upon his wooden shield, then fell against an open doorway and stumbled into the darkness within, pulling her with him. For a breath, she felt safe again in his arms as he carefully checked her for further injuries.

"I am fine, my love," she whispered, and Jeroen hesitated for a breath before kicking the door shut behind them, and for a brief, dark moment, they were away from the devastation.

"All is lost," he cried in panic. He slithered away, gasping, and locked the door. Already she could smell the burning from the roof above. Could hear the crackle too. This would be a fine bastion only if a rainstorm were to erupt around them.

"We can still go out with a fight," she said coldly. She remembered being lost, having her soul torn into pieces. Now, though, she was enraged. She was Alpha. She was queen bitch of the city. She was Mea. She eased herself to her feet for the second time in a dozen breaths. Much had occurred in between each one.

"I will follow," he whimpered, and she knew the toll that war and death had inflicted upon her love. She moved to the door, wincing with each step. Only a few more painful steps would be required before the end of her life. She could take the pain until then.

"Wherever you go," he rasped.

She still held her blade. It felt less heavy than before. Effortlessly, she shifted the lock, kicked the door open and gazed upon her heroic comrades out there among blade, fire and arrow. She thought them brave, beautiful and brutal. She was certain that this was their end and vowed that she would lead them as best she could.

"I love you, Jeroen," she whispered, and he stood with her, his body tense and ready, his bloody shield quivering, knowing these were his last moments.

"I love you, Mea. Let us step into the darkness together."

They charged out into the night.

71

ASSAULT ON ADAWAN

Elise watched with satisfaction as the battle unfolded around her. The oak-roofed platform she found herself on was twenty feet above the ground. It was spacious, with a waist-high railing that offered protection from wayward bolts and arrows. Six such platforms were erected around the front of Adawan's defences, all full of archers, all ready to face the oncoming attackers. A dozen more stood along each flank of Adawan, though these had fewer archers aboard. A warrior might have felt lucky to be dispatched along the edge, for these were the safer posts, unlikely to see much action. As it was, the oldest and the untested stood watch while the main forces endured brutality.

Thousands of southern soldiers jogged towards the defences as she expected. All menacing, all screaming, all very predictable. Like rats seeking shelter from the burning sun. Only then did she notice the defenders' drumming had fallen silent, and she was furious. The Southerners had stepped onto their territory.

"Where are my fuken drummers?" she demanded, leaning out over the balcony, and almost immediately, the drumming recommenced, and she beat her breastplate in time. Before she realised it, she was howling wildly. It was a terrifying thing, and voices screamed along with her demented descant. Desperate, derisive and demanding death. It was contagious. A few climbed atop the ramparts and struck their armour as she did, and soon there came a defiant roar like a battle hymn from an ill-fated gathering of legends, and she was frenzied. She wanted to leap from this platform, weapon in hand, and take the fight to them alone. The rest could follow—those who most wanted to kill.

Discipline.

She grinned, screamed again and dropped back in beside her screaming allies. They cheered, for in the few moments they'd stood with her, they'd already learned the art of leadership better than they ever could have done in a drill.

Discipline.

She played the mantra in her mind, countering the frenzy she felt. Without discipline, the Hunt would surge in and destroy them. She had little intention of dying today.

As though reading her mind, Bison leapt free of his defences, and a hundred brave archers leapt with him. He sprinted out into the sand, and she held her breath. It was his idea to leave the safety of cover and, having convinced her of the necessity of this, he was playing his part.

Her archer comrades were impressed. They exclaimed colourfully what a few thousand others were likely thinking in that moment.

"Mad fukers."

"They're dead."

"Look at the fuken speed of them."

"They'll never make it back."

"Fuken legends, the lot of them."

"They're taking our kills."

She smiled, watching them sprint to the first marker, where they spread out into two lines of fifty.

Discipline.

Bison walked out beyond the two lines. He held no bow, not even a shield. He stood there howling guttural tones in time with the drums, challenging the charging army to a fight, and he was impressive. For a time, they did nothing but kneel and hold their bows ready until the thundering warriors were within a hundred and fifty feet of their line. Ten feet short of the second marker, Bison, feeling the wind at his back, raised his arm high before dropping swiftly to the ground. Fifty arrows shot high over his head, carried in the wind, and descended towards the charging attackers. Immediately, he raised his hand again and dropped it, and the second line of archers fired. Elise thought it was the perfect technique. Especially when he drew his hand high again for a third time and those in the first line, who had already reloaded, released.

Aye, she thought, a hundred arrows was a fierce thing to face in a couple of breaths, but a continual volley of arrows fifty at a time was something else entirely, and this is precisely what the Southerners faced in the first few moments of the tremendous Adawan invasion.

The first line of attackers did not realise the defenders' tactics. They raised their shields mid-step as the arrows hit. Instinctively, they lowered them to see the path ahead, and many met their end in the second and third volleys that quickly followed. Those who realised the mistake immediately slowed and dug in, and were then mowed down by their compatriots, who charged mindlessly onward, pushing through them, crushing them into the sand as they passed.

An outstanding tactic indeed, thought Elise, watching Bison deliver wave after wave down upon their victims. Tragically, only a hundred hardened archers had volunteered for this defence. Perhaps had every archer in the defending army joined him here, out in the sands, the win would have been assured in the first assault.

She thought of Magnus standing triumphantly over the battlefield as the Rangers decimated an invading force and felt that familiar pang in her heart. Instead of allowing her tears to fall, however, she concentrated on one of the Southerners, who charged forward with arrows protruding from his shield. Around him, his comrades fell, and she imagined him feeling both terror and hope, and she wanted him to fall. She thought him brave, and she hated him. She thought of Magnus again and dedicated this nameless brute's pain to her mate, wherever he was. Wave after wave fell around the Southerner, and still, he charged, and for a terrible moment, she thought he would survive—until a lone arrow took his throat. He died badly. He spun as though upon a dance floor, spitting blood upon his passing comrades. She wondered if he was attempting to retreat, whether the stain on the front of his pants was piss or seeping blood. Regardless, he fell clutching his throat, and though she couldn't be sure, she believed a charging Southerner crushed his skull as he ran him down. She thought it a fitting end and felt a little better.

The Southern leaders must have seen the devastation occurring in the leading ranks of the foot soldiers, for the large Southern mounts and their impressive Riders suddenly appeared, pushing through the breaks in the lines. It took only a few moments for the Riders to gather, cluster, and charge. There were hundreds in total, and it was an impressive sight.

Around her, she heard a few gasps as the Riders raced down upon the hundred archers.

"Oh, they are fuked now," a voice beside her said.

"Best retreat," another voice said. Others agreed.

"Rightly fuken quickly, too."

"They're not moving."

"I'd be fuken running right back now."

"Why aren't they moving?"

"You have done your bit, lads. Come on home."

She thought they had too, but Bison was his own general with his own thoughts. He ordered the archers to continue firing.

"Come on, Bison," Elise hissed to the wind. She could see the mounts' alarming pace. Could see the distance disappearing to nothing beneath their charge. Then, once more, Bison calmly raised his hands and dropped, ordering another delivery of devastation to those charging.

The defenders were smooth and assured, and many Southerners fell. They held their nerve even when the Riders gathered pace. Still, the crowd wailed, the drums beat and the arrows flew. Again and again, without a break. They were impressive, heroic, foolish and disciplined. At that moment, she wondered if a little less discipline might suit their cause better. A hundred archers slaughtered in the first assault was a costly loss. She was a breath from dropping to the sands again, not to kill but to order the defenders back.

"Get back, you fools," she roared, and she was not alone, and still they attempted to empty their deep quivers into their attackers. "Flee!"

Bison could likely see the Riders' faces when he spun around and fled. With him, there came one last volley. Straight into the ranks of Riders, as planned.

It was not enough to stop them nor even dent the numbers impressively, but it was a fine last blow as a dozen or more fell from their mounts in a ruin.

Run, you crazy fukers.

They did run. They raced back towards the defences, and the cavalry spikes at the front of the ramparts. Really, though, they ran towards their waiting comrades who were eager to join the killing. And the Riders were behind them. Sprinting across the desert, those nearest drew their swords; those furthest fell into position.

A little further.

Eighty feet from the ramparts, the defenders sprinted, and Elise held her breath. She wondered how well Bison knew the pace of mounts upon even, solid ground. How well he knew the pace upon ground that was downright impossible to traverse at speed. She wondered had he fooled himself and doomed all those under his leadership. But she soon realised he had played his part to perfection.

From a distance, the uniform colour of the sand disguised any treacherous footholds, and as hoped, the attackers noticed nothing amiss until they were right up close. Were the brutes not upon galloping mounts, they might have noticed the subtle changes in the ground beneath them.

A long trench had been cut into the ground, only a foot in depth. A foot behind it was another similar channel, and beyond that, a few dozen more. All had been painstakingly dug by an army of impatient defenders with little to do but wait for the oncoming invasion. Atop the parapet, Elise smiled in anticipation.

Suddenly, as the ground began to sag beneath them, the mounts struggled as they sought a foothold. Some fell, taking their masters. Others reared, sending their masters to a crushing death beneath the charge. Moments later, all of them slowed to a saunter, and it was perfect.

Didn't even need to use anti-cavalry spikes.

Once more, she thought of Magnus. "Kill them all," she commanded, but her voice was lost to the many thousands already screaming their hate. Hundreds of her warriors rushed forward, sending waves of arrows down upon their helpless targets. Dozens of the leading Riders fell in the first volley, which was only the beginning. Many of the leading mounts, all wild with fear and some of them injured, scattered now, sending the attackers into disarray. The screams, both of the dying and of their killers, could be heard above the drumming, and Elise was proud. Beside her, the archers fired, too, and they were joyous in their murder, cursing their rarely missed shots, whooping and hollering with every success. It was a delightful sound.

But this bloodbath could not last. All too soon, the Riders formed up again. For just a breath, she wondered could they break rank and charge down either flank, hoping to find a way inside. They would face only Adawan's cavalry, waiting at the lip of the mine, listening for their call to charge. Instead, they turned to the defences head on, which pleased Elise.

She heard their leaders barking orders in their foreign tongue beneath the hail of arrows and the frenzy of drumming and hatred. Were they to retreat, the battle would be over. That would, of course, be the wiser move, allowing them to conserve numbers, lick their wounds and attack again with renewed strength. A braver, foolish move was pushing to break the line from so close, and that is what they did.

"They're charging on us," an archer muttered, and she saw it too.

Heroic and costly.

They clustered and charged towards the centre of the defences like a massive battering ram. Focusing all their numbers on one section, they raised their shields, dipped their heads and prepared to sacrificed their lives, and it was a fine sight for the absent gods watching on, savouring the brutality.

She could have ordered the defenders to dig in, fire at will, and do anything they could to survive the breaching, but she knew it was impossible to stop. Below, she could see a hundred bandits bracing themselves, knowing the end was upon them, and she howled her war cry. Again, she was not alone.

Though the arrows rained down, there was no stopping them, and with a dreadful crash of a thousand pieces of iron striking timber, they reached the wooden ramparts and broke through. Many attackers died, but so did many brave defenders, who met their aggression with ferociousness. The Riders went through swinging blades, breaking bones, slicing flesh, shattering families, and the bandits did all they could to hold, but they failed, and soon enough, the line was broken.

And it was perfect.

Seeing the break in the line, the infantry, discouraged by their agonising march through the desert, found heart and sought easy entrance. An acceptable tactic if they desired to send the defenders fleeing, but no man, woman or child in this sanctuary had a place to escape to. A gap fifty feet wide opened up at the front, and every Southern soldier, no doubt infused with mindless faith and stubborn hate, raised their war cries and turned to sprint after their Rider brethren.

Perhaps, were they to have seen the massacre of every Rider who broke that line, the thousand blades that assailed them from every side, they might not have focused their attacks on such a position. As it was, they charged, and though countless more fell to further arrows every step of the way, they pressed forward over the uneven ground, through the wooden barricades, and over the sand mounds to where the terrified and brutal sword wielders awaited them.

A churning, desperate bottleneck formed, and the crush was terrible. Elise knew the agony of such a thing from that dreadful day in the city a lifetime ago. These were the tactics they'd agonised over for days. These were the moments they'd eagerly awaited.

The six miniature catapults were lit and cranked. She watched Ulrik moving from unit to unit. She could not hear his words, but he appeared calm, controlled and disciplined. Moreover, his little garrisons seemed to be relaxed despite the daunting job ahead of them. Like Bison before, they answered his orders instinctively, having practised these actions for weeks now. He gestured with his arm and dropped to the ground, and with a crack, the first catapult sent its sphere of fire into the sky. There was no second shot for a breath, as every unit watched in silence and prayed to their gods for death and horror. The world slowed as the burning sphere cleared the defensive line, still rising lazily. Elise held her breath, praying that their aim had been true. The ball reached its pinnacle, and she leaned out over the balcony to watch it begin to drop towards its prey.

A sphere of fire was difficult to miss, even in the bright afternoon, and those in its trajectory screamed and fought to escape its awful landing. She was truly glad of the bottleneck and the crush in that moment. The trapped warriors tried to flee and raise their shields, but it was too late. The devastation might have been slight if the thing approaching them were a traditional burning barrel. But Adawan, having a good agreement with a former patron of Spark City, had an abundance of sine to call upon. Not to mention plenty of sand for casting into glass. It didn't take the most skilled glass blower to create these special, deadly spheres of death either.

The glass orb shattered into a million pieces, spilling its burning payload upon the unfortunates below. Dozens fell away from the fire, screaming and flailing at their flaming clothes and hair. Those who didn't die immediately fought the flames by rolling wildly on the ground or emptying water tankards upon themselves. All too soon, there was a second desperate crush, and the defenders at the front began to realise they were done for. She knew they could not hold; it was time for her to move. She grabbed the ladder.

"Keep firing upon those at the rear," she demanded, but her archers were already diligently doing so.

As she climbed down, she caught sight of five more spheres taking flight. With a loud whoosh, they shot over her head and landed on another platoon of attackers, smothering them in a thick layer of unforgiving flame. Countless more died under the barrage, and it was a dreadful, beautiful sight. The stench of seared flesh filled the air. A necessary butchery, she told herself. Their screams rose high into the air, and she might have felt sorrow for them if she had taken a breath. Instead, she stopped partway down the ladder, turned and savoured the carnage, raising her fist in a simple act of defiance before resuming her descent. Reaching the bottom of the ladder, she did not hesitate; she sprinted towards the line, steeling her nerve for the brutality needed in the moments ahead.

Kill them all.

Show no mercy.
Show discipline.
And a little wrath.

All but the most fevered of the Southern mounts cleared the path as she charged through the ramparts with weapon in hand. As she did, warriors gathered behind her. A few steps from the line, she caught sight of Ulrik calmly assisting one of his comrades struggling to light the wick of a glass sphere, and she was heartened by the sight of a hundred more waiting to take flight.

As she came to the rear of the defensive line where the growing chaos was most prevalent, the thundering noise was unnerving. Still, her brave bandit bastards screamed and intimidated, and for a moment, she marvelled at the Southerners still charging despite this dreadful welcome.

"Prepare yourself, defensive line," she demanded, watching the haze of swords raised like nettles in the wind, and she held her halberd out in front of her as dozens of screaming bandit warriors formed up on either side and to her rear. Those standing firm on the line ahead surrendered a foot of land, and the Southern attackers surged in to occupy it.

"Be ready," she warned the line ahead, and though they struck and slashed and bled and died, those with wits and those who'd listened to their generals knew what to expect.

Suddenly, Kaya was beside her with a sword and shield. She was hunched low; her face contorted in a grimace of unrivalled hate. Elise understood; she would never be far from Elise this dreadful day, not out of loyalty alone or a need to protect their queen. Oh, no, Kaya knew Elise would throw herself into the most brutal of skirmishes, and she desired blood as repayment for the life she had lost, and Elise was proud of her.

On Elise's other flank stood Bison, who had left his archers behind to join the dirtiness of close combat. He drew a longsword, and his powerful body twitched with adrenalin and fear. He roared as she did, and Elise felt more alive than she had in a lifetime.

Enjoy these few breaths.

"Fall back," she cried to the defensive line ahead, and her comrades echoed the order. Those farthest forward wasted no time seeking the next strike or pushing back the never-ending mass of attackers. Instead, they retreated backwards in one impressive swell, and those attacking were unprepared. They stumbled, they fell, and they were crushed, and as a gap appeared, Elise led the defenders of Adawan through it as only a goddess could.

Screaming intensely from lungs surging with life, Elise charged over the falling fiends and swung her blade once, taking three lives in one mighty blow. The second blow took three more, and suddenly, the attackers in her way recognised a goddess of war in full flow. More than that, they knew she would not fall and could not be struck down. The nearest dozen attackers tried. They swung their blades, hoping to break her guard and stop her storm, but she was elite. The greatest warrior the city had ever created. A female who had little issue taking on an entire army and sending them running. She spun her deadly double-ended blade and put every ounce of strength into the act. Blood spurted, fresh screams echoed across the battlefield, and many more victims died beneath her fury.

"To the fires with you all," she thundered, charging through the army of death. All she saw were blades and blood. Mostly theirs, although she took a few grazes here, a few glancing blows there.

Were every gathered Southerner to stop, take a breath, and focus on the spinning goddess demon alone, the counterattack would have been but a few moments long. But they cowered beneath her storm, and the defenders, buoyed on by her daring, charged forward. The attackers who had surged and fled the fires behind them stalled and slowly began to give ground. Once this occurred, the whiff of retreat was in the air.

Turning tail to the countless arrows, the flaming spheres of death and the lunatic lone female warrior who might or might not have been a relative of the god of fire, Erroh of Spirk, the Hunt retreated slowly through the devastation. Screaming for mercy and wailing in terror, they tried to escape with their lives from an army that, in fact, they outnumbered. They retreated in a wave, like a sea suddenly drunk dry by an absent god.

Suddenly, Elise realised that there were gaps now in the battlefield and only fleeing backs to stab, and at this, she screamed louder, both in triumph and as an exhortation to a final orgy of ruthlessness. Swinging and killing with every blow, she ran at full speed after the Southerners across the burning sands.

For a moment, she wondered could her people win this battle outright? Could they send the fuks running right back into the South, to the city they should not have held? But then, with the distance to their camp shortening and the next line of archers rounding up and preparing to let loose, she slowed and called for a cease in aggressions. Around her, the many hundreds charging slowed to a walk. Two hundred feet from the camp, they stood in a long line screaming in challenge. Were the Hunt to play their awful horns, they would have sounded hollow after such an attack.

A few Southern archers let loose, but their arrows fell miserably short. For this, they were mocked. After a time, Elise turned her back on them and ambled back up to the defences, taking a moment to slaughter every wounded Southerner she encountered along the way. She was not alone, and as the cries of the injured were snuffed out one by one, a deathly silence descended upon the battlefield, with no sound but the wind playing its knowing, tragic melody.

Beside her, Bison and Kaya walked silently, each panting slightly.

"A good day," Bison offered. He stepped aside now, allowing her to step through the defences first. A deafening roar of triumph rose up from the defenders.

The sound carried in the wind like a brutal arrow or a sphere of fire and struck the attackers as a last deadly blow. No Southern army had ever taken a loss as significant as this in one swift attack.

Welcome to Adawan.
Wipe your feet.

72

RARE OLD TIMES

I *hate you.*
Hate you.
Only you.
Nobody else.

Lea knocked Erroh's hand away and took a step back despite herself. She wished she hadn't stepped back. She wished she'd stared into his beautiful, dark eyes and cut him with her words.

Hate. Hate. Fuken hate.

Green eyes.

"Lea?" he cried, reaching for her because he was an idiot, and that's what idiots did when they didn't know what was happening. They acted; they did not think. Did not question their actions. They only saw treasure and reached for it. "I don't understand."

I hate you; I hate you; I hate you.

In the lonelier moments, she wondered how she might feel if she came face to face with him again. She had feared she would love him still, and this had proven true. She did love him. But she hated him with equal passion. It was all his fault. Everything. Her entire life would have been happier without him. So, she hated and spat and stepped away from him. And the idiot followed after.

"Of course, you don't understand," she said evenly. She showed little emotion. Let him be emotional, she mused, and stepped back again as he stepped nearer. It was a strange dance between the two of them, and Erroh was thoroughly confused, as usual.

Bastard.

He looked around in bewilderment. Around them, his brutish Southerners chanted his name while her Wolves knelt in his honour, and she was dismayed with them. Disgusted. She knew they answered to the master general, but she had led them, kept them alive, and gifted them slaughter. To see them bowed like the Southerners was humiliating. It added to her anger. She wanted to bid them rise. Answer only to her. Instead, Erroh, the legend of the Wastes, strolled into the fuken green, and everyone dipped their head, impossibly impressed with his presence. Of course, they were. And she, the silent little Lea of Spark City, was insignificant.

"Please, Lea," he whimpered, and forced a smile, but she could see the horror on his pale face. Could see it in the stream of silent tears erupting from his beautiful dark eyes. She remembered a similar pathetic tone from a long time ago, when he had hidden among blankets in a little shack, and only little Lea was strong and patient enough to pull him back to life.

Bastard.

She remembered his note. She remembered being the crushed simpleton he'd left behind. No more, she told herself. No more would she be his lesser shadow, taking what limited credit he offered. She was a goddess, a legend, just as fierce as he, but she was also no betrayer of a pledge. She was no breaker of their mating vows. She had done all she was asked, and tenfold after that.

And he still left me behind.

"No, Erroh, do not," she warned.

"What?"

"Just... do... not."

He was panicked. She liked this ever so. "Do not do what? I don't understand. Why are you like this?" he exclaimed, and she almost reacted. Almost screamed in his face, struck him fiercely and condemned him for the bastard he was. Instead, she stepped back again. It was no sound tactic, but coming upon her beloved mate out of nowhere had unsettled her too.

Don't let him kiss you, girl.

He shook his head and wiped his eyes, but the tears kept flowing, and she felt little for his misery. Why should she? His steps had been misguided. His actions had been costly. He had brought ruin upon them, upon the world, and a charming grin would do little to pull him from trouble. She loved him, but they were finished. She knew this now, just as she knew she was the daughter of the greatest bastard of them all. A painful thing indeed. All it took was one's entire world shattering around one's head to understand one's place.

Suddenly, he realised his pleading tone and checked himself. He looked around at the kneeling sycophants and gestured for them to rise, then stepped in closer to her and whispered, and she wasn't prepared for that.

"Talk to me, my love," he said, and his hands shot out and caught her own. They were cold and clammy from the weather. Or else they were always so, and only now, in this moment, did she see his flaws, few as they were.

Do not think him perfect, girl.

"I can barely stomach you," she hissed. Still, she did not break his grip, for she ached for comfort. Ached even more for his touch. His taste, his everything, in a violent act of beauty and desire.

Do not think of him that way, girl.

"What have I done?"

"To the fires with you, bastard," she whispered, so low that only he could hear above the awkward shuffling of both their groups rising to their feet while trying to ignore their parents' arguing.

"Please."

She thought him pathetic. She might have told him as such. Instead, she caught her breath and held her tone. "Walk with me," she ordered, yanking her hands free, and the dutiful idiot followed as she sought refuge in the forest. Behind them, both groups faced each other, unsure if they were allies. She could hear broken conversation from uncertain tongues. Perhaps they congratulated each other. Perhaps they recalled their heroic battle. Perhaps they discussed the finer art of rummaging among their victims' belongings for trinkets and supplies—anything to avoid conversing about Mom and Dad at war somewhere in the forest.

She said nothing for a time and increased her pace into the green. Maintaining calm around her boys was one thing, but she wasn't sure she could be restrained in the forest, where screaming was encouraged.

"Talk to me, my beo," he said when they were deep enough that only the rain could be heard. "I thought you were dead." He was weeping again. "I can't believe it."

She spun around to him. She thought him beautiful. It felt like the beginning for just a breath—the two of them alone in the forest. Him apologising for hurting her. Him apologising without a notion as to how he'd hurt her.

"Do not call me beo," she cried, and again, he was fast. He gripped her tightly and dragged her to his powerful form. Before she realised, his lips were upon hers. Before she could stop herself, their tongues touched, and deep down where she kept her spark for him, a little flame sickened her.

They shared only a breath, and she remembered her love for him. For that breath, she imagined weakening. Imagined allowing him to escape with only a few harsh words. She even relaxed her resistance, and he embraced her tightly. He was warm, powerful, loving, and home.

She drew away and felt the tears stream down her face. Felt them warm in the cold air, and suddenly, his warmth was upon her. She remembered a shared cloak in the rain.

You let him kiss you.
Kiss him again and be done with it.
Take on the world again.
Be in love.
Be happy.
Tell him of your lineage.
Uden.
The Woodin Man
Fuken Uden.
Green eyes.

She broke the kiss. Spectacularly too. Of all the ways to break a kiss, her particular technique was flawless. He never saw it coming. Nor did he see her forehead strike his cheek, but it did. A bird above took flight, terrified hearing such a loud crack. Perhaps the gathered warriors waiting for the arguing couple to return heard it too. It was a fine, disabling strike, and he stumbled away, clutching his face, before tripping on a rock and landing on his rear.

"What the fuk?" he cried. It was a fair question, and she stood over him, wiping her mouth, lest his taste remain upon her lips. She did not want that scent. Never again. Not ever. Definitely not.

"You left me behind."

"I know, and I'm sorry," he said. He still held his cheek; his bleary eyes stared at her. He'd landed in a muddy puddle too. He was pathetic.

And beautiful.

"You left us all, and we suffered for it."

At this, he dropped his head. He probably noticed now that he sat in a puddle. She held herself from kicking him in the chest. Just a little kick. Just a little more pain to inflict. He deserved it. He'd kissed her and almost taken her will.

"I thought I was doing the right thing; I failed, Lea. I failed to kill him, and the city fell."

She knelt beside him. So close that were she to lean forward, she could kiss him, could take away the shame she felt. The pain she felt. His pain too. "They're all dead, Erroh. Every one of them. Lexi, Wynn, Lillium, and little Tye too. And you were nowhere to be found." She could see the words cut through him. He shook, and were there any warmth in her, she might have held her tongue, but she ached too much. Her burden was too heavy. She could have said as much, but he deserved no such release. "Roja, Stefan, Wrek and Ealis." Every name took his breath anew. He dropped his hands and stared at the mud. She hated that she'd loved him. She hated she still loved him. She hated him.

"Please stop. I can't." His tears fell again. Less silently this time, though.

"I had to leave them behind too. Had to fend for myself while you sought fame and immortality against a god."

He nodded his beautiful, pathetic head in agreement, and she knew she'd broken him. She almost felt bad about that too. More so for the war effort and the awkward conversations she'd have with her Wolves upon returning.

"And Nomi?"

"Of course, you ask about the whore," she growled.

"Aye, I did... I'm sorry," he whispered, and just sat in the mud, being wretched. "I failed."

"Nomi still lives," she said after a time, and he nodded weakly. It was a fine thing he made no further questions after her. Lea was likely to spin him a yarn anyway. The truth was, she was probably long lost with the rest of the citizens of the floating city.

"I failed everyone."

"Aye, you did, as usual. I will never forgive you, nor can I look upon you with love or kindness," she said, feeling emptier. Seeing him crushed and broken took some of her anger, but the simple emptiness remained.

"As you wish," he croaked, and the tears streamed freely for a little time more. He would not meet her eyes, would not plead his case. Instead, he formed a fist a few times and relaxed it again before looking around as though waking from a dream. "I think I fell in mud."

"Little point in crying about that," she snapped. "Best you stand up; there is a war to fight. And we'll need warriors with skill." They weren't the kindest words she could muster, but it was better than spitting further venom. She almost expected him to proclaim his defeat at that moment. To whimper and moan about the injustice of it all.

"I'm on my way to Adawan to find more warriors," he said, reaching for her hand. Not for caressing, not begging for forgiveness, or even asking her to take the pain away. She gripped his hands and pulled him to his feet.

"I see you wear black," he said hollowly, staring at the armour she had so proudly donned. He was pale and shaken. She'd never seen him like this. Not even when he was in chains. Or dying from the cold.

"Aye, I have found my place among them. We are out hunting," she said.

"Not anymore, Wolf," he said, and turned from her. She spat on the ground in disgust.

"What do you mean?"

"You will accompany me to Adawan."

"I will not, Erroh. These are my boys; I lead them."

"If you are a Wolf, you will answer to your master general," he snarled, marching away.

"You bastard," she howled, following after. Daring him to turn, to challenge her, to kiss her again, but he didn't. He just marched through the forest, indifferent to the branches snapping and swinging back as he passed.

They said nothing more until, abruptly, he stopped on the outskirts of the dell where she'd saved his life. Gone was the broken, tragic cub who had sat in the mud and taken her torment. In its place was a fractured general delivering orders and finding any way to survive an inevitable overrunning.

"I know who you are, Cordelia."

Green eyes.

She caught the gasp in her chest as he grasped her roughly by the collar. She could see the madness in his weeping eyes. The delirium too. As swiftly as he'd grabbed her, he released her again.

"I can do nothing about your hatred for me," he barked, but she could hear the heartbreak beneath the anger. Could hear the broken soul too. Whatever pain she had endured might well have been endured by him. She could have stopped and taken a breath, asked what fresh traumas took his dreams. Perhaps they matched her own. Instead, she focused on the name he called her by.

"I believe you might take joy in meeting my most trusted ally, though," he said, and set off again.

She did not know what he meant, but she followed after, hating him in silence, and he could only turn and look back at her every now and then, with the gaze of a stranger.

He led her through the tree line, where he stopped and gestured to a Southerner. "He's been looking forward to seeing you, little Lea," Erroh said, and walked away as a familiar-looking brute from the dregs of the South removed his helmet, dropped it in the mud and smiled a wonderful, familiar smile.

She could feel herself quake uncontrollably. Could feel the taste of fire and sadness like never before. Then she felt an extraordinary love for her idol. Her brother. Her best friend. Her forgotten memory. Before she realised it, she was sprinting towards him, and her anguish was forgotten.

73

DESPERATE HOURS

It was strange to wake up with a burning barrel bouncing over one's head, but that was precisely what befell Nomi at some point after midnight. It wasn't just the loud thumping roar as it bounced over, but the searing heat as it landed with a deafening crash against the wall across from her. Her club was in her hands before she climbed free of the rags she called bedding, and illuminated by the flickering flames all around her, Nomi dove up against the nearest wall, trying to stir her senses to alertness.

What the fuk?

Around her, smoke billowed, and the screams of warfare filled the night. She recognised all the signs of a Southern attack, even if it was aboard a Boat Town in the middle of a lake.

"Is there anyone out there?" she cried, but the darkness beyond the flickering flames was all-encompassing. A few drops of seeping oil from the barrel trickled across the deck and set her bedding alight. She could have extinguished the flames. All she had to do was stamp down hard on her pack and the rolled-up shirt she used as a pillow. Everything she had was strewn among the bedding. It wasn't very much. Her place in this wretched sanctuary was beneath a doorway that barely covered her head from the elements. The flames took her pack, and she was mesmerised. All that remained within was a half-eaten loaf of stale bread and an old brush with most bristles missing. Suddenly, she felt an overwhelming desire to leave this burning fire to its task, leap over the edge of the nearest balcony, swim ashore and be done with this war. She hated this place, hated the lonely shell she'd become; she had no friends; she hadn't had a conversation with another in days. She was constantly fearful of attack in the dead of night from the aggressive hands of leering brutes, and she was sick to her stomach of mushroom stew.

Nevertheless, this was her home. Her chosen place. And she would be loyal to the end. The deathly end. That was all right. She was just so drained. A scream brought her to her senses, and she went to task.

Climbing out along the edge of the boat, she caught sight of the invading force and their means of attack. Three rafts, long and wide, floated across from Boat Town. Upon each raft, a dozen Southerners rolled barrels onto a trebuchet, setting them alight and firing them into the night. Further on, four larger rafts were loaded with crossbow wielders and archers. She frowned, looking at these brutes. Few Southerners approved of these tactics, but such was Uden's desperation, apparently, that he had chosen these unsavoury warriors to undertake the assault. Among the archers stood barrels alight with oil. Each archer set their arrow ablaze and let it loose into the night; there was little else they could do.

I die tonight.

She could see a few dozen Wolves spread out along their sanctuary's boundary. Their desperate defence had little effect against the Hunt, who had the wind in their favour to carry their arrows even farther, but they tried their best, even as they were slain. She heard voices bark out orders, attempting to rally the defenders, but with fire catching and the smoke becoming heavier, it was nearly impossible to form any semblance of a defensive line. Then she saw hope. Above the flames, she saw some Wolves attempting to counter the attacks using three ballistae. Standing high above the battlefield on the largest barge in the entire town, she watched as they tried to load the fantastic beasts, even as arrows rained down around them. She could see them turn and aim, but suddenly the three war machines exploded in fire, and Nomi screamed in horror. Such weapons could have fought back the tide.

All is lost.

The Hunt had clearly studied the sanctuary, for without the fear of ballistae sinking their vessels, they focused the rest of their attacks on the more populated sections, raining down volley after volley, both panicking and killing those who reared their heads from the lower decks. They were the lucky ones, for Nomi could see where the doorways were alight with flame, trapping those below. A terrible way to go, she imagined.

The rafts, heavy with Southerners terrified her most. Under cover of the night, below the glow of burning wood and flaming arrows, they crept along the edge of Boat Town, twenty at a time, all silent, all armed to their teeth, all dressed in their warrior's finest. As they slipped aboard, there was no one to stop them. She knew this battle was lost. It was lost the moment the Hunt had lulled them into inaction. She had little blame for Mea. This sanctuary was always going to fall to a well-thought-out attack. It had lasted more months than they had expected.

Flee this place.

With the wind behind her, and the careless bounce of barrels all around her, Nomi charged from shack to shack, hatch to hatch, screaming and kicking, wailing and warning. She met many a slumbering wretch disinterested in warfare; she also met lively, youthful warriors who donned their armour, grabbed their weapons and charged out into the night. For those, she wished she could do more, but there wasn't time. She continued her charge, warning her comrades to awaken and join the fight.

It wasn't until she reached the far edge of Boat Town, with nothing but the peaceful, uninhabited lakeside to gaze upon, that outcast Nomi came upon unlikely fortune, and a strange notion occurred to her. The last ballista stood before her, silhouetted against the night, high upon the tallest galleon in the fleet. It could offer little assistance from where it stood on the far side of the battle, so it was no surprise it remained leaning out over the edge, unloved, unused and undamaged.

"Do not think of it," she warned herself, but she wasn't listening. Behind her, the screams intensified as the battle raged on, and Nomi felt very alone in the world, as usual.

Leave this shithole of a town.

Scrambling up through the levels, she found a rope ladder and began climbing. She didn't know what she was doing, only that she needed to do it. Higher and higher she went. Climbing up and over the aged oaken balcony, she found herself atop the galleon, where the air was clear of smoke and the wind took enough of the screaming that were Nomi to close her eyes, she might have imagined herself asleep beneath her doorway, or out in the Wastes. Or in Raven Rock. With her friends. With those she loved.

"Help me," she told herself, and peered back into the night, seeking comrades to assist with her foolish plan. "Hello," she cried out. "I have a plan!" But there was little movement among the passageways, which were usually filled with wretched Northerners wary of her accent on the best days. Unable to do the massive knots, she swung her club down upon the large rope wrapped tightly around the barge's edge. Knocking at its iron holding, she called out again to those who ignored her. Those who cowered. Those who allowed foolish girls to attempt to fend off the attackers alone. "It will never work." Still nothing. "But it might," she added, and swung again. The edge of the balcony shattered inward as the rope snapped and fell away, and she ran down along the side of the barge, hacking at the dozen similar holding ropes, until the rear of the vessel edged itself away from Boat Town a foot at a time.

"I cannot do this alone," she pleaded, hoping for a dozen fools to join her misdeeds, but the world was at war, and little Nomi of the Arth was alone with nothing but a foolish plan that would most certainly get her killed.

"Come on, Nomi," she screamed to the wind, reaching the last rope, taut and quivering and screeching loudly under the strain. As she freed the final rope, the barge creaked and rumbled as the deck below her feet quaked.

"Fuk, fuk, fukety, fuk, fuk," she said, for Lea sometimes said that when everything was awry. She almost stumbled as the barge, tasting freedom, collided against another barge and veered to the side fiercely enough that she left the ground for a breath before stumbling towards the main sail.

"Fuk."

She knew the theory on barges, for there was little to sustain an active mind aboard a wretched sanctuary. However, she'd never been aboard when they dropped sails and spun with the wind. Pulling at various riggings for a time, she cursed her idiocy, her luck, and her scanty knowledge until one rope came free in her hands, and immediately, a long sail roared to life far above her, flapping with a sound like thunder as it fell with a heavy thud onto a long beam above her head.

This will never work.

The barge surged away from Boat Town for a dozen feet before crashing to a sudden stop and almost capsizing. Again, she was knocked from her feet, and though some distant lights caught her attention, she was drawn to the problem of her shuddering barge.

"Fuk me!" she cried, and spun around the main deck, looking for something to help her, until she caught sight of a chain as thick as her arm, lying taut over the edge. "Fuken anchor!" she cried, and distantly, she heard a different cry of war in the wind, and panic took her.

Sprinting to a winding lever, she began to turn it, her muscles screaming with the strain. She fought the heavy weight until, with a painful jolt, the chain surrendered. It moved only a foot before shuddering and slithering back into the black water with a loud, chinking splash.

She cursed for a little while and withstood another lurch of the barge as the wind took it before summoning the strength to turn the lever an entire revolution, hold it fast, and reposition her stance before turning it farther. Again, the chain fought her, and she screamed in defiance. "Why is nothing easy?"

The wind offered no reply, so she fought the strain until, eventually, the lever began to turn more easily, and with a triumphant squeal of delight, she pulled the anchor free of the water and secured it along the barge's side. "Fuk you," she told it, before setting off towards the grand wheel at the far end of the vessel, fighting the sway of the barge as she went. She knew it rotated a large fin below the water, but that was about it. The barge itself had turned around the anchor's chain several times, and slowly, she turned the grand wheel and felt the lumbering, floating beast answer her commands.

"I have this," she proclaimed to the night, and, once more, thought about following the darkness with her massive new barge and sailing away to safety. With the wind catching the enormous sail, the barge moved far more quickly than she'd expected. Below, the dark water rushed and broke against the body of her galleon, and it was a soothing, beautiful thing. Truthfully, the beast would be challenging to pursue, harder still to climb aboard at speed, such was its massive height. As she gripped the wheel, she thought about Erroh leaving her, about Lea no longer desiring her company, and the sight of her belongings burning away to nothing.

I've taken too much pain.
I'm so exhausted.
I owe them nothing.
I have nothing.
Except for my new barge.

Turning the wheel and easing the vessel back towards Boat Town, Nomi decided to die this night. It was oddly settling. She thought again of Erroh and loved him. Then she thought of Lea, and loved her too. Then she wrapped the chain around the wheel and let it hold the beast on course as it charged forwards.

Swiftly, she slipped down to the massive ballista, still standing unloved and inviting, and dragged the long crate of arrows up beside it.

A dozen shots in all. Carefully, she lifted the first long piece and thought it impressive. It was as heavy as the anchor. She placed it across the crossbow part of the massive weapon and hoped she understood the finer mechanics of what it took to fire this beast into the night. The ballista's lever was far easier to turn than the one that raised the anchor, and desperately, she turned it until the long arrow rolled back and sat waiting for a gentle release.

"Fuk me."

Checking that there was no secret mechanism she needed to release before firing, she found to her relief that the beast moved easily upon its greasy stand, turning and holding to whatever angle she desired. She had no idea how far the arrow would travel, so she chose the nearest target a couple of hundred feet away. She eyed the nearest raft, swarming with archers who had not seen the massive barge looming closer, for they were busy lighting a fresh volley.

"Fuken please..."

She pulled the trigger, and the crack of the machine shook her to her core. She barely saw the arrow take flight, but she saw it land. It missed the raft completely, travelling over it and tearing through another one, impaling three archers, ripping out the supports of the wooden platform they floated on, and sending the rest of the Southerners into the lake.

Many of them struggled and sank in their armour, but she knew many more would swim. It didn't matter. She only needed to stop the brutes from setting fire to the rest of Boat Town. If she did that, she could let others take care of the invaders.

She took a triumphant breath before taking out another long arrow and inserting it into the bow of the projectile. Her forehead was covered in sweat by the time she aimed, and this time, aiming the ballista far lower, she prepared for the recoil and fired.

Her body was winded once again by the shuddering weapon, but she took the pain and, delighted, watched as the arrow struck her chosen target—a lit barrel. It exploded in shards of deadly splinters and flame, spilling oily fire all over the deck and any nearby archers not fast enough to dive into the water.

Swiftly, she reached for a third, and only then did she see the lines of Southerners on the shore of the lake, watching as her barge drifted by. Most were cheering their comrades' success, and a cold hatred came upon her. She lifted the third arrow onto the piece and let off another fine shot, this time taking out another raft of invading soldiers before they could climb aboard her home.

Only then did the enemy's arrows start hitting her barge's deck, and Nomi knew she would be felled soon enough.

She decided nothing would change. Suppressing all terror, she fell into a routine: reaching down, placing an arrow, turning the lever, releasing, and killing. It was her finest moment. Again and again she fired, and she imagined herself as one of those mindless Southern warriors and tried to envision what terror they endured facing Nomi alone on her barge of death. If they believed it was right to burn a heroic woman alive and continue to follow their god's wishes, she would feel no remorse for sending them to Valhal. Or wherever the fuk warriors went when the darkness came.

I will see you all there soon enough.

Arrows continued to strike all around her, and she did not flinch. Instead, she hummed a few notes from a song she'd once sung with her comrades in Raven Rock. A simple enough song with few lyrics, and that suited her just fine.

"Ride home with barrel in tow."

She fired another arrow and it, too, hit its target squarely. The unlucky raft floated briefly as its occupants tried to keep the flimsy wooden poles from separating, but it soon subsided below the water.

"You brought blood!" she bellowed. "You brought death. You brought an end."

She reached for another arrow, and the barge roared and creaked as it struck a raft, crushed it beneath its hull and sent it and its occupants to the bottom. She loaded the arrow, and knew her next target would be an easy strike from this close, even with the crack of projectiles hitting everything around her. She took out one last raft and its cargo of archers, smashing it to pieces—but not before their last deadly volley was unleashed upon her.

"Oh no, oh no, oh no, oh no, oh no," she sang as an arrow sailed towards her ballista and embedded itself in her chest.

She fell back upon the deck in shock and smiled: every arrow of her great machine had been fired. Her chest ached, and she waited for darkness. She thought that she would very much like to meet her sister beyond. She caught her breath, rolled a little to one side, and pulled at the protruding arrow, hoping to hasten her death. Suddenly, there was a deafening rumble below her, and her body lurched forward, jolting her arm. She looked down with astonishment as the arrow came free; it had pierced only her leather armour. Staring at its glittering tip, she laughed softly.

"Not fuken dead yet."

Climbing to her feet, she peered over the edge and discovered what had caused the mighty barge to jolt: it was honouring her with one final act of greatness, it seemed. The last of the enemy's rafts, the ones housing the trebuchets, were directly in the path of her mighty vessel as it surged forward and broke through the Hunt's offensive line. She could only laugh as the Southerners tried desperately to steer their rafts to safety, but this beast was indomitable. With a splintering sound, the first raft was shoved under the water, taking the catapult with it. The second raft disintegrated within a breath and met a watery grave, but the last one resisted bravely until it was driven against the rocky shore of the lake, where it was smashed like a toy.

With a dreadful surge and shudder, Nomi's barge beached itself against the lake's edge, and for a moment she thought she was victorious. But then she heard a growing chorus of shouts and knew her cause was lost. Sprinting to the edge, she looked down to see countless Southerners, like enraged fire ants, clambering up the impressive hull of her once proud barge.

Reaching for her club, Nomi prayed to the absent gods, whatever they were, and waited for the first head to appear over the edge.

"This is a good death," she whispered, and suddenly a little terror crept into her heart, and she begged it not to settle itself. Better to die without fear; better to die in an orgy of savagery, surrounded by the screams of her victims. A fitting end for one as pitiful as her.

"Aren't all heroic deaths good?" a voice from beside her said, and a figure stepped through the smoke and looked over the edge at the climbing ants. She recognised his smooth, cautious tone, but it made no sense. A moment later, another figure appeared. Both were dressed in familiar attire, recognisable even though both were soaked through. It was the eerie masks that threw her off, though. Unnerved her too. A primal part of her believed she was already dead and standing with feral demons. But the demons drew their bloody blades and stood on either side of her, and she felt far less alone in the world.

"It is good to see you alive... friend," the other figure whispered, and Nomi knew that voice, too. Knew her as an ally. And... a friend?

"Let us three kill them all," she said, and set upon the first Southerner to appear from over the edge.

74

SAILING TOWARDS A STORM

Magnus lazed in his bedding as the room rose and dropped ever so. The creaking was less now. All night, the ominous creaking, the alarming rise and fall, had kept him from sleep, and his boys too. But now, all around him—on the bed, on the floor, by the door—his wonderful hounds slept peacefully. He listened to their gentle snores, their sleepy growls, their satisfied sighs as they stretched and arranged themselves into impossible positions no human had ever experienced. Apart from the creaking and the room's roll, there were worse ways to travel.

"Are you decent, Magnus?" a familiar voice called from outside in the hallway. A gentle rap upon the ornately carved door followed, and Magnus stretched, as did his hounds. He was king again, accepted and adored, at least for now. It was perfectly acceptable for the great man to roll over and ignore the duties of a leader for another hour or so.

The room was massive, far too big for a solitary occupant, but he was grateful. The floor was carpeted, perfect for barefoot lazing. Heavy curtains covered small windows on either side of the bed, keeping out the chill. Glass trinkets hung in the corners, and bowls and vases holding dried flowers sat on every surface. Bright oil paintings lined the richly coloured walls, and the beams were of varnished oak, from what he could see. At the far end of the room stood shelves, at least a dozen of them, with a thousand and one books standing neatly upright like soldiers at attention. There was also a comfortable chair to read them in. No doubt, the captain believed in ostentatiousness and luxury. The room certainly suggested wealth, and Magnus wondered how bitter the older man might have been if he'd known he'd be gifting it to the ruler of the Savage Isles.

It's good to be the king.

"I know you are awake. You should be awake. I've been awake for hours. It's almost noon," the voice cried again, and Magnus wanted to silence Padir, but instead, he reached over and pulled the nearest curtain aside and gazed out into the miserable day. The horizon rose and fell as each wave broke and failed to sink the great ship, and Magnus shuddered at such a thought. It would do no good to get this far and then sink on the last leg of the journey. The knock came again, and with it, the turn of the handle as Padir slipped in. The hounds, well used to the little shit, rolled over to show their bellies as he passed and accepted a quick scratch.

Magnus thought it a fine thing that the boy had earned their trust. He turned back to watch the waves, imagined them breaking upon the distant shores where the armada would soon surge towards the shallow, more precarious rivers. Sometimes it was all about conquering the wild, where so many had failed. Few seafarers knew the route from here on to Samara, but Magnus did, or to be more precise, his maps did. Although few believed him, he had made this difficult journey thrice. He couldn't trust his memory after so many years, though. He had also never attempted to lead an armada up the river. Despite this, he was confident he could lead them inland without sinking too many. He'd done more impressive things in his life. Looking away from the water, he breathed deeply, trying to settle his nerves. The sea belonged to the savages. Now, though, who knew what awaited them?

"If I had a room like this, I'd probably stay in here all day, too," the little shit muttered, drawing him from his uneasy thoughts of the voyage ahead.

"Well, you should try to be king next time," Magnus countered, sitting up in the bed and pushing one of his hounds off the silken bedding to the floor. The hound gave a little snort of disapproval, and Magnus smiled. He was a great man, but better with his hounds beside him. They also ensured privacy aboard this vessel—apart from the little shit Padir, that is, who'd learned a thing or two about charming a dozen war hounds.

"They're coming aboard, by the way," he said, and Magnus immediately shot out of bed, grabbing his clothes and armour. It was lovely to laze around in bed, but with his generals aboard, it didn't send the right message. Even from a king.

Swiftly, he donned his clothes, brushed his hair, washed his face and took the steaming cup of tea Padir provided. Last, he placed his crown upon his head and pushed it down until it was tight. He despised the thing, but they were at war, and his generals expected such shows of decorum. He would only have to endure its weight another day, for they neared journey's end. Better to be prepared.

Leaving his hounds to enjoy the freedom of the lavish cabin, he followed his eager squire down through the ship's lower decks to his battle quarters.

Unlike his cabin, his battle quarters were simple and functional. It was easier to focus here, without distraction and comfort. It smelled of the ocean and mould, and it was dimly lit, but for an impressive lamp that rocked gently over a large desk surrounded by a half-dozen chairs. A pile of knotted-up nets lay in one corner, no doubt used for emergency fishing. It would take a poor squire many hours to undo such knots. Should one be needed, however, Magnus would have the perfect candidate.

His maps, notes and battle plans were on the desk. No battle plan mattered, however, until they had landed, journeyed to Spark and discovered the lay of the land, the numbers the faced and the city's standing. Any other man would have gone crazy these last few months without a project to work upon. Magnus liked to think he'd written a formula for every possibility, a plan to counter every possible scenario they discovered. If he had marched across the lands, he would have had scouts to ride ahead, but now pace mattered more than intelligence—and the conservation of supplies. Sometimes it was thunder, thirst and hunger alone that turned a war. Magnus was well aware of such things.

Drawing aside the curtain from the lone porthole to let in some light, he caught sight of two rowboats from different vessels, their oarsmen desperately rowing against the pace set by the lead galleon. He could make out the figure of Tusk standing at the front of the first one, dressed in his finest attire.

"I thought they were aboard," he said, giving Padir a cross look.

"I thought it the swiftest way to get you up, my liege," Padir offered apologetically, and Magnus grinned. The little shit understood him well enough. Who knew it took only a little betrayal, life-saving and savagery in a kingly event to form a bond? Perhaps even a friendship, but he wasn't sure yet. Since his ascension back to the throne, Padir had stood with him every step of the way. As had his generals. And the clans.

Well, most of them.

To the fires with Curroi and his region of the isles.

"Very well. Bring them aboard," Magnus muttered, sitting down to gaze over the map showing the route the vessels would face. A difficult task in daylight, but he aimed to travel through the nights as well. Foolish but needful, despite his generals' arguments. Padir went out to greet the visiting generals, closing the door behind him, and Magnus felt the sobering weight of the crown on his head.

Every few days, his generals braved the waves to board Magnus's ship and converse with him as his council. This day should have been no different from the others, but today Magnus had other things on his mind. At first, he listened to their reports attentively, each one relayed as though he could do anything about the issue at hand. But soon their complaints fell into a mundane sort of rhythm, and Magnus shrugged each time without a decisive reply. He was no mariner; he had little idea how to address the wicked flu that had broken out among seven of the vessels. Magnus had few thoughts on the current stocks of oranges as they lessened at an alarming rate, or why they were necessary at all. He could do nothing about the livestock keepers, who insisted the beasts be allowed a few days of grazing when the ships made landfall, before their final charge. And, no, he couldn't give an exact date upon which they would land in Samara or predict what awaited them. Padir had a further ten points to make, but most were complaints about the food he was forced to endure and how cramped his cabin was. The rest of the generals took him as Magnus did—with a grin and a dismissive shrug. But the little shit had a charm to him, especially among those who had lasted until the trial's end.

Tusk sipped the wine he had been offered and gazed over the maps. His finger fell upon the spot where the land ripped open and the river gushed out into the sea, the very break they were surging towards now. "Within the hour, we will be free of the taste of salt," he muttered, clearly unhappy at the prospect of clear, calm waters to overcome. Some warriors were built for the land. Tusk less so.

Magnus nodded his head, removing his crown as he did. He was loath to carry it a moment longer than needed.

Sloan disagreed. "Unlike some of us, we were not all built for the sea. I will be glad to feel the rock of the boat a little less." Grinning, he clinked glasses with the bigger man. Tusk's barges and boats carried most of this invading army. It was no surprise how well the brute had faced the first night on the water. Magnus imagined the enormous fuk feeling at home in the sea's embrace. Tusk's support had served them well. He represented no clan but he was from a family of wealthy mariners and it had taken the young warrior only a few weeks to sail up along the coast, gathering together the largest armada ever to embark towards war. Only the Rangers had assembled themselves into a march more swiftly.

Sloan, too, had honoured his word and arranged miracles in weaponry, supplies and warriors. He was harsh and brutal, but he commanded the respect of every single fighter who served under his banner. Magnus now considered the grumpy bastard a friend. Something he'd never imagined a few months before. Magnus had little interest in testing said friendship so soon, but his needs trumped such things.

He got to his feet, found a hammer and nails, strode to the farthest, darkest corner, and set to work.

"What are you doing, Magnus?" moaned Padir, who could see perfectly well what he was doing.

Ignoring him, Magnus pounded a short line of nails into the wall, hung the crown upon them and stepped away. The lands towards which they were headed were no place for a savage king, and he would not return displaying his royalty for the world to see.

"You know my legacy. I will wear no crown in the Four Factions, nor will I play as king," he said, and his generals stood quiet. He touched the crown once and kissed it before stepping away to admire his handiwork. "Do you all follow my final words as king of the Isles?"

"What?" cried Padir.

"We do," Teaolor hissed, silencing the boy. Teaolor had regained much of the respect she'd lost these last few weeks among both the five thousand or so warriors aboard and those generals at the table.

Magnus faced them as equals. He dropped to a knee. "I relinquish my crown until this war is done. Do any of you have argument?"

"We do not," said Teaolor firmly, speaking for the generals, who agreed in silence. They had little issue with her answering for them, which pleased Magnus.

"Are you jesting?" cried Padir incredulously.

"Quiet, you," hissed Tusk—a fine suggestion. The boy didn't understand, but that was fine. He was full of the excitement of youth. The boy had not yet realised Magnus was doing precisely what he should have done when he stepped upon these lands.

"This crown is Teaolor's to bear from this moment on. She merely needs to reach out and take it whenever she desires to do so," Magnus said.

Teaolor rose and strode to stand beside her king. "Not until this war is done. You must lead us one last time."

"What?" cried Padir again. He looked at the crown. He looked at Magnus; he looked at Teaolor. He looked back at the crown. He didn't seem to understand. "This is fuken stupid!"

Magnus looked past Teaolor at the rest of his generals. "Do any of you have any argument?"

"I gladly bow to Teaolor," declared Sloan, kneeling before the girl.

"Everything you endured, and you are giving up the crown? Just like that?" Padir cried again. He appeared to be the only one with issues.

"As do I," Tusk said, dropping to a knee. "As does he," he muttered, under his breath, gripping Padir by his belt and forcing him to kneel.

"Fine, fine, so do I. Whatever my word is worth," Padir muttered after a time, and only Teaolor was left standing. She turned to the crown, ran her fingers along it and left it where it stood. When the time was needed, she would take it. Magnus thought this a fine thing indeed.

"Rise, comrades, and drink to my health. And then, let us get back to discussing the turning of this war," she said, and the grand generals of the Savage Isles did as their lead ship broke from its path and turned towards the grand opening where the Great Mother gushed out into the ocean.

"All that for fuken nothing," muttered Padir, watching as the last boat cast away and a half-dozen desperate rowers ferried their generals back to their vessels.

"You seem to have an issue with your new king," Magnus observed. His head felt lighter, though he wondered would he live to see the crowning. He didn't think so.

A fine life lived.

Distracting himself from his morbid thoughts, he looked to the bay as the river grew steadily narrower and narrower, and he wondered, not for the first time, how wise it was leading the vessels down this route without an idea of what was ahead. He could do nothing now, he mused, as the first torches were lit out along the galleon's edges. They would light the way and help the ship avoid the riverbanks, but they would also light the way for the many more who would follow them in single file.

Already he could hear that the sails flapped less as they left the sea breeze behind and moved farther inland. No matter, for the savages and their barges were built for speed.

It's all on me now.

Below, he heard the rumbling of the oars and, saluting the captain who was steering the beast, he made his way below deck where, for many, even in the darkness, the day was only beginning.

"I have no issue with our king, Magnus. I just can't understand why you give the crown away so willingly," Padir said. "You have our support and an army; why let it all go?" he added, and Magnus hissed at him to lower his voice. It wouldn't go well for them if word reached the rest of the armada a few weeks from landing.

His face darkened, and he leaned in close to the little shit. "My time is done. Better that these things be left to the youth."

"And what about me? I've hitched my sail to a sinking barge, Your Highness."

At this, Magnus laughed. "You have earned your place among them, little one. However, should I be lucky enough to live beyond the brutal days to come—and you too, for that matter—you would be welcome to march the next chapter of my days."

"That sounds like a rightly shit time altogether—Wait… wait… what are we doing here?" Padir cried, looking around in misery. "Magnus, what the fuk are we doing here?" They had reached the lower decks, where a few dozen benches had been fastened in rows to the floor. Warriors sat upon them, two apiece, each pair holding the end of a long oar. "Answer me, Magnus?"

Magnus patted a warrior to let him sit in and took hold of the oar's handle. He might sleep like a king, but he would work up a sweat with those he called equal in war.

"A little effort will serve you well in the coming days," Magnus suggested, popping his neck and knee in preparation. He knew the pain to come. But such things bred loyalty. Besides, an hour or two rowing was sure to loosen his body up, break it down, and toughen it again for the coming battles.

"Ah, for fuk's sake," Padir cried, looking towards the doorway behind him as the drummer beat a warning blow, signalling the rowers to take their positions. After a moment, Padir sprang across a few rows and patted the shoulder of another warrior, asking to relieve him. He took a seat beside a gorgeous young redhead.

"Hi, I'm Padir," he said, flashing her a grin. "I presume you already know me from the trials. I lasted until the end as well. Kingly I am," he said in the time between the first and second hammering of the drums, and the girl smiled and pulled the oar with him. Magnus, watching on, laughed to himself and wondered if the young redhead would be afflicted with a terrible case of itching by the week's end. From how she giggled after Padir's next outburst, he imagined she would.

As the oars drove deep into the water and dragged the galleon forward, he smiled and accepted his fate for what it was.

75

AFTER PARTY

Of all the orders Elise had to give, these were the most difficult and the most contested among her generals, and with good cause. This was normally a time for silent contemplation, rest and preparation for the coming battles. Instead, she had insisted they drink to each other's health and the health of their fallen comrades, and her orders were that they do so loudly.

Feigning enthusiasm, Elise walked along the ramparts, watching as the barrels of ale were rolled out and the waiting goblets were filled. The barrels would be rolled away long before midnight struck, long before any brute became so intoxicated that he couldn't stand watch, carry a pike or shove it up the arse of an attacking Southerner.

"I've been to livelier funerals," Ulrik said from beside her, and he was right. There was barely a jest in the air, no music playing, no bodies in motion jigging to a beat. It was a wretched gathering, and nightfall would soon be upon them.

"You've never attended a funeral in the Savage Isles, my friend," Elise retorted. The so-called savages honoured the dead properly; there were tales, there were tears, there were jests, and then there was music. It didn't hurt that every mourner at these events was determined to outdrink every other mourner either. A Savage Isles funeral was the finest celebration in the lands, and looking around at this miserable gathering, she would have liked a couple of thousand of those revellers to kick this party into life.

Looking out into the darkness at the many thousand Southerners still alive and awaiting revenge, she also would have liked a few thousand savages to call upon in the battles ahead. In truth, one beautiful savage would have been enough. She imagined him beside her, matching her step, whispering sage advice, delicately disagreeing with her more ludicrous suggestions. She wanted her Magnus dearly—to dance with him, love him, and breathe for him.

"I have heard such things," Ulrik said, sipping distastefully at his mug of ale. He raised the mug to a gathering of weatherworn defenders around a fire, all looking dreadfully serious. From the blood on their clothing, they'd seen the front advance and lived to tell the tale. Elise, too, knew the awfulness they had endured, and that most of them would carry memories of the horror for the rest of their lives. Those were the warriors you moved to the rear. If they argued, they were valued; if they accepted the demotion, however, they were done with fighting, and best left to their own devices. She raised her mug, and they raised theirs in reply. She might have stopped by them, relived the battle and comforted them with reassuring words of bravery and honour, but were she to do that for one group, she'd have to do it for the rest. So they received a raised mug. Some generals did less for their warriors.

"I think it is time to open the cages," she said when they were a few steps from the tired soldiers. She'd already raised her mug to two more groups in no more than a dozen steps. Distantly, she heard the first notes of a guitar being strummed, and a familiar melody filled the air. This pleased her, for sometimes a little music took despair from the hearts of the wary.

"It is your right," Ulrik said quietly. He stopped to stare out into the darkness.

"You think it a mistake?"

"No, it is good thinking; Wrek is a warrior. He'll stand firm if the Hunt streams over the edge."

"Will you stand beside him?" She couldn't read Ulrik's expression, which was likely why he would not meet her eyes. She knew Ulrik's dispute with Wrek; he had every right to be angered. Still, they needed every leader, and Wrek was very much loved in this place.

"I would even stand with my father and his bastard ways, if that would help us to hold the line. Will I look him in the eyes? Probably not." His tone was peculiar, and Elise suddenly felt cold in her belly. She gripped his shoulder, spun him to face her and was shocked to see the tears glistening in his eyes.

"What are your intentions?" she demanded, and he smiled sadly.

"You fear for him or his comrades?"

She did. It was no good that Tye had linked himself to him. If Ulrik took his vengeance, a blade would not be stopped from cutting Tye. She couldn't do that to Mea.

"I once sent my friends out to kill Wrek. You can never know the torment I suffered for such an order." He hung his head in shame. "My fuken brother. To be slaughtered because of words."

"Will you have him slaughtered still?"

Ulrik met her eyes at this, and though they glistened, they were warm and kind. "You stole my opportunity to have him flailed, killed, burned and buried. You take away my right to banish him from this place."

"I'm sorry, friend, but I did what I needed to do."

"You don't understand, woman. I am grateful; without this burden, I am absolved of my actions."

"You miss him, don't you?"

"I am less without him, and in a rage, I condemned him to death. I have lived with that for a few years. I cannot look at him out of shame, but I will stand beside him until the world ends."

"It is a delicate task releasing him as a prisoner. I would like you to take care of the matter," she said, and he took the order for the gift that it was. With a cough, a wipe of the eyes, he bowed to indicate that it would be done.

By the time she had walked the entire rampart, the hour was late. More than that, her second mug was clouding her vision ever so. The gathered crowd were louder too. Most were on their second or third ales, and that had eased the mood. With only a little argument, the barrels began to be rolled away. However, the songs were getting louder, and were now accompanied by shouting and clapping. If it wasn't for the vacant stare of so many, the stains of crimson along the ramparts, or even the stench of charred Southern skin, it might have felt like a genuine celebration, and not just the taunting of the battered Southerners who nursed their wounds a short distance away.

She looked to the watchtowers above and was pleased to see the keen eyes of sober guards peering into the night, searching for movement. She expected retaliation, and though they would have been better prepared had there been fewer beverages consumed, the majority were battle ready.

Her last stop was at the Wall of the Dead—a newly erected structure overlooking the pit of Adawan. Standing ten feet high and as many feet across, it was whitewashed and illuminated by many a torch. On it, the names of the dead were inscribed in black ink for all to see. There were only seventy or so now, filling barely a quarter of the impressive structure, but it was built for additions. And three more similar walls sat ready to be attached for the future comrades over the coming battles. It was here that the mourners gathered, and indeed, there was no more fitting place for her to be. They wailed and lamented, cried and embraced, and Elise felt herself an outsider among these wretched few.

Still, she drew nearer, and a middle-aged woman approached her. She looked to have lived a tough life, and was hardened and wary. Elise wondered was she a recent inhabitant of this place, or had a life delving in the mine taken her spark? Without warning, the woman took Elise's hand in one of her own, then reared back and struck Elise's cheek with the other. The sharp crack made the mourners turn their heads in alarm. Before Elise could react, could pull away and offer a pathetic apology for her loss, the woman kissed her other cheek and dropped to her knees, crying, at Elise's feet. Elise drew her upright once more, and the two women embraced, and Elise cried with the woman for a while before releasing herself into the embrace of another mourner.

She had not brought this war, nor had she mishandled the defence in any way, but warriors had died under her orders. Eventually, standing alone, she read aloud the first name from the wall. Her voice felt hollow and cold, but it was respectful, and that was all she could offer. She read the second, and around her, the voices fell silent as though she was giving a eulogy. She wondered if hearing their loved ones' names spoken aloud by a legend meant something. It was all she could do, and it was enough. She read, and they listened and loved and lost. When the last name left her lips, they all sat silently, and it was almost too much. She wanted to cough, to talk, to somehow break this enchantment, but instead she remained silent until they allowed her to leave.

"Here," a young voice whispered, and Elise turned. The speaker was a young girl, no older than a child, dressed in full armour, with a blade sheathed and unused. She held a mug of ale taken from the one barrel no warrior dared to drink from nor roll away at midnight. This ale was for the mourning alone. She held out the mug, and Elise took it, and the enchantment was broken. Fresh ales were poured, weeping recommenced, but the mood was less desolate than before, or so it seemed to Elise. Or maybe those thoughts were simply her way of alleviating her guilt.

"Thank you, little one; tell me, what is your name? Who did you lose?"

The girl thought about this for a time. "I lost my best friend, Sari. My only friend. She was brave. She went to defend the front, and they took her," she said as though answering a master in lessons. "I am Elcass," she added and sat down with Elise.

"Tell me some stories of Sari," Elise said, and Elcass smiled sadly and told her tales of her close friend, which broke Elise ever so.

When the girl was finished speaking, Elise thanked her and moved once again among the mourners, listening to their various tales. Around her, the party rose to a complete celebration and eventually died a natural death as the hours drew on and the shattered moon passed across the sky. But not before the damage was done to the morale of the Southerners. No army could hold their heads up after losing in the face of such underwhelming odds. Having to lick their wounds and listen to much revelry must have been an added blow. Come the next battle, Elise vowed, she would ensure they suffered an equal blow and celebrate even more uproariously after that.

Fighting a wave of exhaustion, Elise walked the ramparts one final time. Most warriors lay where they sat. All dressed for war at a moment's notice. She only once or twice came upon a fool who'd emptied their belly in the sand. It was no fun fighting a war with a hangover, no matter what the poets declared. Most of their defenders, however, were relaxed and ready, and this pleased her.

Climbing back up to the tower, where she hoped to snatch an hour or two of sleep, Elise wondered what battles would come and what soldiers she might lose. She worried about every soldier, but mainly Lexi. She could only keep the girl locked away from danger for so long. She was so much like her mother; like her father too. She was young, but Elise could already see the killer in her, as she once had in Erroh. She considered keeping her close for the next assault, but such a thing would distract them both, would work against them should the fighting take a turn.

Wrapping herself in a blanket and little else, Elise leaned against the balcony wall and listened to the silence of a sated camp. Her archers stood firm above her, and this pleased her greatly. Pulling her blanket more snugly around her, closed her eyes. Sleep took her swiftly, and then what seemed like only moments later, she woke to the sound of war and horror.

It started as a clanging bell on a distant watchtower, and suddenly Elise was up and about, wiping her eyes, reaching for her halberd. It was still dark, and as she dropped down the ladder, she heard the clatter of her defenders rousing themselves from a stupor, and she sprinted past them towards the clanging.

It was loud and constant, and the night was clear, without a breeze. She sprinted towards the sound and distantly caught sight of a flicker of light deep in the darkness beyond, on the Southern flank. Those defenders who had risen first charged with her, weapons at the ready. Another group followed behind, preparing their arrows, tightening their armour and readying their barrels of flame.

"Look to the light," she screamed, and a coldness came upon her as she uttered the words. Surely, she was wise enough to see beyond a possible trick on the enemy's part? The flame flickered. It was far away, a solitary light in the vast darkness beyond. Hundreds, nay thousands, were poised now to follow her urging, to break rank and charge out towards the flank of Adawan—all after seeing a single light. All the while, the curs might have set a trap and attacked from the other side.

Then from nowhere, Lexi appeared. Climbing the ladder of the lookout tower, she shouted a warning down to the soldiers.

"Aim for the fire," she screamed, reaffirming Elise's words, and a few archers set off towards the barricades. "Take aim at anything you see moving and let loose, for there are hundreds," she roared.

"Hold," Elise cried, and those who recognised authentic leadership hesitated. Lexi, from above, stared at her with a rage that was usually directed by masters to apprentices or by mothers to daughters. "Light your arrows first," Elise reminded them, and truly, it was a fine idea. The many archers gathered around the nearest barrels and let loose into the night.

"Again," Lexi cried, hoping to assert herself as a leader; she certainly had the tone and tactics. The first volley struck deep into the ranks of phantom invaders, and Elise heard a satisfying chorus of screams and groans. Some arrows struck the ground and died in the suffocating sand, but many stayed their course. A few flaming Southerners ran around a while and collapsed, and Elise knew her daughter had been right. Lexi did not hesitate: she roared, and they followed her orders. In all, a few thousand warriors followed their goddess out through the night towards the phantom attackers.

"Kill them all," Lexi screamed, and they replied. Another volley of a thousand and one arrows and bolts lifted into the night sky, some alight, some as invisible as the darkness, and they too hit their targets. Once again, the night was filled with screams. She moved closer to where the enemy seemed to be, raised her blade and saw nothing but the grim struggles of dying fiends. Around her, the warriors of Adawan, weary but brutal, were fierce. They roared as they charged with her, out through the defences towards the nothingness. For a breath, Elise considered restraint and discipline, but something deep within her told her now was the time for anything but. She led the brutes onward, towards the agonised cries of those taken by arrows.

"Listen to their screams," she shouted, frenzied. Driven by the horrors of the day, she desired to kill in the names of those seventy-odd warriors who had been lost.

Among the flickering flames and the blur of moonlight, she saw the enemy more clearly. Confused and slow—and numbering in their hundreds. Perhaps more. She held her breath, fell silent, and charged the last few feet spinning her blade. Such was the fury of their charge that the Southerners fell back almost as one. She heard their cries of terror, gazed upon their armour-less bodies, and knew she and her warriors had the beating of them.

"Sneaky little fuks," Elise howled, killing with every strike, driving her blades deep into the bastards, slicing, hacking and decapitating. It was brutal, and it was easy. In truth, were it not for the clanging bell or the careless flame of the enemy in the night, the battle could have been more costly for her people. As it was, her defenders were unrelenting in their surging drive. She'd never seen an attacking force so beaten in the first charge, yet these brutes wailed and fled, and Elise was unsatisfied.

Such was the swiftness of their retreat that the defenders did not follow after. Instead, they stood where they were and shouted after their prey, who raced away through the darkness, some still alight and most bleeding. If the infantry were tired from the day and thus gave no chase, the Adawan cavalry were fresh and willing. She grinned as they thundered past—a hundred or more, with torches lit, swords raised and no blood yet on their blades. They thundered eagerly through the defensive line, and were merciless in their hunt. Swinging sword and axe, hammer and pike, they slaughtered the Southerners as they fled, and like before, it was easy.

For a time, Elise followed after them, jogging down towards the fleeing Southerners and their killers, but there was no further need of a goddess. Around her, they cheered, and why not?

Marching back towards the ramparts, Elise came upon the terrified figure of Lexi running back and forth in the field, searching among the fallen. She was screaming, wailing and frightened, and Elise ran to her.

"What is it, little one?"

"Where is he? He pledged he would be fine!" she screamed, and Elise gripped the girl.

"What are you talking about?"

"Where is my Tye? Where is he?"

Elise, still holding the girl tight, looked out among the bodies. There were too many to count. Her stomach clenched, watching her daughter suffer.

"Where is he? *Where is he?*"

76

NEEDFUL LIES

Erroh had felt this lonely before. Long ago, in better times. This was no different, he told himself and wiped his sweat-covered forehead. The green leaves did little to shelter him from the afternoon sun. Thick as they were, Erroh still felt the burn of its rays every few steps. Highwind felt the heat too. Her black neck was warm and dry, and Erroh missed the rains something terrible. With every mile they marched, the air grew warmer and warmer, despite the season. He hadn't remembered it being this hot when they had marched here before, but that march had been a lifetime ago. It felt like a decade had passed since his previous visit to the bandit domain.

Perhaps it was the loneliness that made this trek so dreary and exhausting. That awful loneliness that threatened to tear him apart. It seemed his life was nothing more than a sickening punishment delivered upon him by the absent gods to see how he would break, how soon and how deeply. The jest was upon them; he was already broken. Lea's cruelty had seen to that. Difference was, he would march on. He could take more. He *would* take more.

He picked at the leather reins in his hands absently. It was something to do while lying to himself that he could endure the sins of Lea, whatever they were. It was all he could do to make himself feel better. He thought her cruel; he thought her unfair; he thought it fuken typical. Erroh would never claim to be the most intelligent male where females were concerned, but truly, he thought they had left this shit behind. He'd voiced such an opinion several times these last few days and met the same stoic silence from his mate.

She will open to me when she is ready.
She must.

Perhaps they might have found it easier to talk were they alone. But they were not. More than that, the world relied on his strength.

"The air is getting dryer," he called to the two figures ahead. Drahir turned in his saddle and agreed with a smile. He shrugged after a moment, and Erroh deduced that Drahir's efforts to speak on his behalf were meeting little success. The two figures returned to their muted conversation, which likely wasn't about himself, Erroh reasoned, and he knew the shrewder tactic was staying mute. "It's getting warmer, too," Erroh called out to them. A Wolf muttered something under his breath that might have been agreement, and kicked his mount's ribs as he passed, lest Erroh ask after his words or try to engage him in conversation. Erroh understood the Wolf's reluctance. He and a dozen of Lea's Wolves had been commandeered. He would have taken them all, but supplies were limited. He took who he could and felt perfectly fine about it. Despite her protests, she answered to the master general. She knew better than to challenge him openly, but they knew her feelings. And they followed her. It just made travelling to Adawan a little awkward, is all.

The path they took was secluded and unforgiving. Strangely, his scouts had claimed this region of the world would be heavily laden with Fingers and patrols, yet no other hunting pack had appeared since the slaughter in the glade. Erroh might have been suspicious, but such was his mood; he took it as a gift from the absent gods. It was all he could do. These last two days, he'd forced himself to look on the brighter side of many things. He had hoped things would improve, that Lea would speak more, but she remained aloof. Erroh sighed as he caught a laugh from the siblings ahead.

"Fine, don't reply," he called out, and she reacted this time. He answered her disdainful glare with one of his own, and he waited for a reaction. Instead, she turned back to her brother and continued to discuss matters that most certainly weren't of him.

We need a lovely abandoned town.

It was intoxicating to be around her. For a sad moment, he remembered what it had been like to fall in love with her—a wondrous journey filled with missteps, mistakes and mayhem. He thought of the good times, but also the awful times. His life had been a struggle these last few years, but it had been easier with a lover to call upon for companionship, for a shoulder to cry on. For a whisper in his ear, reassuring him of his actions. He needed her so very much, and she needed him. This, Erroh knew.

Admittedly, he had never imagined himself a jealous man, yet here he was, resenting his second-in-command for the attention "Cordelia" gave him. For two days, they'd been inseparable. Through the long hours in the saddle, as they journeyed east towards Adawan, the siblings had ridden side by side, deep in conversation—not about him, and not for him, either. He'd tried to join in, initially, but her cold words had matched her eyes whenever he spoke of simple things like the road, the turn of weather, and the possibilities of an alliance with bandits.

At night, when the world was quiet and they all sat in front of little fires, he had attempted to win her favour with talk of strategy or simpler things like the return of Shera to her true owner. As before, she offered little but curt coldness, to the point that Erroh, concealing his frustration, had left her to it. Not once did he cry out. Not once did he behave like a wanton cub, too foolish to deny her the space needed to overcome her anger.

She would overcome it. He knew this because the alternative was too harrowing to imagine.

Perhaps I'll speak with her.

Lea found more comfort speaking with Drahir than she did in meeting Erroh's eyes. That said, she struggled to meet her brother's eyes, too, but that was because the memories stirred when she gazed at him. Although not green, they were similar to Wiiden's. Those fuken eyes reminded her of the truth and her shitty heritage. For all her anger, though, she was grateful to remember. She might have said such a thing to Erroh, but the wanton little cub could not fathom what torment she endured. Lea's entire lonely life inside the cold walls of Samara had consisted of years of cruel battles of wills and wits.

Erroh, by contrast, had enjoyed the warmth of a kind family whose only sin was ferociously training their eldest to be the greatest warrior that had ever lived. She had never known this level of jealousy until Drahir had returned to her life. There weren't enough hours in the day to learn of all she had lost. He spoke of their home and filled in many of the missing pieces of her early childhood. He spoke of their fallen brother, Breiga, and Lea allowed herself to mourn the boy she'd never known. He spoke of her mother, wild, cold and murdered. He also spoke of their father, a grizzled, battered war veteran. Then he spoke of the change in his father after a calamity, and Lea listened and learned and, shamefully, felt better for it. These last few days had been a wondrous thing. These conversations had somehow begun to release her from her trauma, and though she fell further from thoughts of Erroh and his warmth, she embraced an unfamiliar feeling of acceptance among kin.

Her Wolves understood it too. They recognised this strange confidence smouldering like wildfire in her soul. It added something steely to her voice. To her fuken walk, too. It was a fine look to her. Being around Erroh, however, had the opposite effect. Whenever she gazed upon her lover, she could see only betrayal, could see only the waif she had once been, overshadowed by a domineering master. She loved him, and she hated him for it. She believed things might be better were he to understand her traumas and leave her to come to terms with her life and legacy. But Erroh could show no restraint. Could never leave things where they lay. Instead, he pushed; instead, he tried to fix her. All because he considered himself the glorious one. The hero. The fuken legend. And she? She was just little Lea, left behind without a second thought.

―――

Erroh could take no more. It was the third morning on the last day before everything changed, and he was sick of the silence shit. Sick of watching the world pass by without having each other for comfort. They were deep into the Adawan desert, a day's march from their salt-stained gates. The spot they'd chosen to make camp was a fine choice: below a looming dune, shaded from the morning sun and protected from the night gusts. Erroh might have liked to leave at dawn, but such was the ill-discipline in his own comrades that they were now forced to march through the blazing heat of the day. He blamed Drahir for the delay. It was not a leader's responsibility to tend to the waking and preparing of soldiers. That shit rested on his second-in-command's plate. Drahir was so taken up with Lea that he had neglected his better judgement.

"We should be on the way now," Erroh grumbled, standing over Drahir, who took the hint swiftly enough.

"I'll see to it, Erroh," his comrade offered, climbing to his feet and leaving Lea alone by the fire.

"You like to give orders, don't you?" she snapped, once Drahir was away from them, barking out orders of his own in his native tongue. The Southerners reacted immediately, and Erroh sat down.

"I have grown into the task of ordering, my love," he said quietly. There was a pot of boiling water over the flames, and she poured some into a cup to make herself a hot tea. She poured a cup for Erroh, too, which he took gratefully. It was the little things.

"Do not call me that anymore," she said.

Erroh sipped his tea. It wasn't very pleasant. "Don't be like that, Lea," he said.

They said nothing for a time, and Erroh found the uncomfortable silence sadly familiar.

"These last few days, all you do is watch me like a craven pup," she said at length.

"I miss you; I do not understand why you treat me like this. Is it Uden? Is that what has unsettled you so?"

Her eyes narrowed. He awaited the storm. A little shouting match would be fine. Even now, around their comrades. Anything to clear the air.

"I do not care what you think of my lineage," she said coldly.

"Well, I forgive your lineage."

Her knuckles whitened, and he reached for her. He spilled some tea as he did, but it was a worthy sacrifice. Her hands were warm, and he took a firm grip on them. "I love you, Lea; let us move on from this." For a breath, he knew she loved him too. Knew she desired to take him in her arms and to kiss and love him. He played his part, and he played it well. He offered a smile. It was a fine smile, and one he knew melted her coldness.

She hated him at this moment. Hated herself a little too. He held her hands and wouldn't let go. She thought of his green eyes, and that hate festered a little more. She realised she could never draw breath free from his grasp. Partly because she loved him, and she always would, but partly because he was everything that destroyed her. She needed freedom from his gaze, from his judgement, from his kindness and from his wrath. Love was a beautiful thing, but it also killed. She could have leapt upon him at that exact moment and kissed him one last time, a gift and a goodbye, but instead, she denied herself such a thing lest she find herself enchanted by his love, the taste of him, and his all-encompassing self.

Fuk you, Erroh.

He looked into her eyes and pledged, "I will never leave you ever again. I will never let you leave without me. I will never let you face the horrors of this world alone. I pledge this all to you, and I will never break my word again." It was a good pledge, and she hated him.

Hate.

Hate.

Fuken hate.

Fuken hate him.

She could see him leaning in to kiss her, and she wanted to cut him, to tear him apart so fully that he'd never retake her hand. And then perhaps she could face him.

Don't.

She released herself from his grip and shoved him away gently. Nothing violent, just enough. "You think so highly of me, don't you?"

"I do, my beo."

"You believe I remained true to you these last few months."

She saw the blood drain from his face, and she almost broke. Almost relented. Almost told him this was but a ploy to seek distance from him. Instead, she watched him break before her like a warrior struck down. She couldn't look away, nor did she deserve such a respite. She imagined hearing those words spoken to her when she'd held him in her hands in the South. She imagined the pain and saw it in front of her eyes. Visions of his kindness struck her, and memories of her happiness flittered away. She imagined him falling back into the sand, curling up and giving in to himself. She imagined the awkward conversation she'd have to have with Drahir, to explain her reasoning and her motives.

"I remained true to you," he gasped.

She hated the pleasure his tone brought. Not to mention his words.

"Will you be all right, Erroh?"

He nodded his head, and tears streamed down his cheeks. He did not weep aloud, and somehow this was better. He climbed heavily to his feet, wiping his eyes and looking around at anything but her.

"I am sorry," she lied, for she wasn't sorry. It was a needful thing, and he deserved it. She thought about slipping away, concealing her own emotions, perhaps climbing atop Shera again and talking with Drahir for a while. Anything but watching her mate break. Instead, his gaze fell upon the horizon, where a dust cloud had kicked up.

"What is that?" she asked. His hands shook, but the tears were subsiding. He drained his mug of tea as though it was something more substantial. As though it didn't burn his throat.

"What is that?" cried Drahir, cupping his hands against the morning sun to gaze at the horizon. He stood in his saddle atop his mount, and

Lea began packing her bags. Gazing every few breaths at the dust cloud, she wondered if it was a terrible sandstorm charging their way.

"It's coming swiftly," her brother added, and Lea felt a rising sense of dread. There was nothing for miles either way. No cover, no shade. Were it a storm, they could retreat or dig in and hope for the best. Were it ground troops charging down upon them, though, there was no place to hide.

"Fuk me," muttered Erroh weakly. He still stood where she'd left him. He looked diminished, and instinctively, she almost took his hand. Instead, she grabbed her belongings and strapped them to Shera's back.

"I think it's cavalry," a Wolf cried.

"Infantry," another Wolf yelled.

"Something, something," a Southern voice shrieked in alarm, and Lea could see them now for herself. Hundreds, no, thousands of Southern warriors sprinting towards them. She climbed atop Shera and considered charging away from the camp, leaving Erroh behind; leaving Drahir too.

"We'll never outrun them," Drahir said. They could see now that there were hundreds of Riders in the pack, and Lea knew this was the end. The ground began to rumble; it portended death. Lea's blade was in her hands. She looked to Erroh, as they all did, and was appalled at how terrible her sense of timing was.

Don't give in, my beo.

"We cannot run; we cannot hide," Erroh called. "Anyone who raises a blade against them will not survive this. All of you are free to flee, but I alone will charge them," he said, and Lea thought them fine words.

77

IT'S NOT YOU

Doran lay back against the bed's headboard. In his arms, the shaking female gripped him tightly. Her voice broke, her tears were plentiful, and he did not think badly of her.

"It is no small thing to lose a child before it comes to term," Celeste whispered, and he agreed. It was a terrible thing to lose a life. Even one that they had not gotten a chance to know. As it was, he was a man, and as such he was charged with strength and assuredness. And every day since, he had been strong for the girl.

"My sisters tell me to live on, but I feel empty," she whispered, and he squeezed her tighter. He felt the same. Sometimes it wasn't easy to go on living, having come so close to parenthood. Were there anyone to talk to on such things, it might have been easier. Having a way to mourn such a thing would have helped too.

He could not see her face; perhaps that was also a fine thing. She snuggled into him, taking what comfort she could, even at the end. And still he did not think badly of her.

"It's okay, my dear," he offered. There wasn't much else to say. For all his agony at being denied parenthood, the loss had shaken Celeste to the core. They had not slept with each other these last few weeks. It was her decision. He was a hot-blooded male, but some things trumped physical connection. They would never sleep with each other again, and he accepted this openly. They had been lovers out of excitement, necessity and convenience. Unintentional parenthood had linked them together.

"Don't cry," he whispered. He wanted to cry, himself, though not because of her cutting words; rather, he wanted to weep for the horrors of the world, for the loss of the life so briefly gifted to him. And, perhaps also her cutting words. Nobody liked rejection, even if she was right.

"I'm sorry, dear Doran. I cannot be with you, not another moment."

"It is okay, my dear."

"We were never meant to be a mated couple, and every time I see you…"

"You remember your loss."

"Our loss."

"Aye, our loss," he whispered, kissing the back of her head. He didn't want to be here anymore. He'd been with her all evening, drawing out her concealed sorrow. Now, at this late hour, he wondered if slipping away and leaving her would be the finer act on his part. She would be fine, no doubt. She would receive support and camaraderie from those she called sisters. He would walk out into the night, march around Boat Town a few times and find solace wherever he felt like resting his head.

He squeezed her tightly once more and eased her quivering form from him. Slipping free of the bed, he stood up and grabbed his armour. He was fully clothed, having climbed in beside her with nothing but gentlemanly thoughts on his mind.

"We would have been fine parents," she said as he clad himself in thick metal. He always felt better with armour on, strapped and tight.

"I will see you soon," he pledged. He kissed her once upon the cheek and then slunk away from further rejection. He thought her beautiful, a good person, if perhaps a little officious. She was perfect for some other male. These thoughts didn't help, especially as he crept from her curtained quarters at the far end of the dormitory, where he met the eyes of far too many watching sisters. He knew females enough to realise they shared gossip. He would be the butt of jokes come dawn, even as they offered sympathy at this moment. A few draped their arms out and touched his hand as he passed. He hadn't expected that. He continued on through the rows of "sleeping" females and didn't look back at Celeste. That seemed like a pathetic manoeuvre— but he couldn't help himself. For a breath, he wondered was his future Cull mate in this room this very moment, watching and sympathising. He snorted to himself, thinking it unlikely.

Before he had reached the far end of the chambers, there was a dreadful hammering on the outer hatch. It was flung open and a head peered in, its owner screaming hysterically. Doran was already running, for he had expected such a moment. Had done for weeks. He was no fan of sitting silently waiting for invasion. However, he was only a foot soldier, and the significant decisions were made by those he answered to.

"Attackers," the voice cried, and was gone again before Doran could reach the hatch and learn what he could. Moments later, though, he stood at the entrance and knew it was bad.

Worse than any journey from the Spark.

Peering out, he saw that the night itself was on fire. Flaming barrels bounced and exploded around the upper decks, igniting a terrible wave of fire. Arrows, like fireflies, lit up the night, and he knew Boat Town was near to falling. He saw figures clambering over the edges, blades at the ready. More of them appeared, screeching and terrifying, from every corner, and there was a sense of approaching death. Beyond the darkness, in the smoky ruin of buildings, he could hear the screams of the dying, and he hesitated. He looked back to the females, who were stirring and dressing, and for just a breath, he thought it unfair. He wanted to step back inside and lock the hatch. To hide away from responsibility. There were only so many of these sudden attacks he could survive. He wondered coldly if this one would be the end of it all. It felt like it.

It's not fair.

"Tonight, we go to war," he roared, and they reacted with further haste. Even the distant form of Celeste, scrambling to attach her armour, roused him. He knew her terror of battle, but her determination to defend her sisters, her city, and even her fuken Boat Town was inspiring. At that moment, he remembered her fondly and swallowed his fear and his hopelessness and returned as Doran of the Wolves.

"Attack in packs," he shouted. "Do not stray out alone. Kill every fuker you see." He thought it fine advice. He stepped forward, leaving behind the weeping of the youngest females, the screeching of the terrified, and the roars of war from those females who foolishly believed battle was a wondrous thing.

He stepped out into the night and hoisted his shield and sword, seeking out his plan of attack, or more likely, his plan of defence. Around him, the females streamed out, graceful and threatening, and charged towards the light a few decks over. To him, they looked like divine goddesses in flight. They immediately met a gathering of Hunt seeking easy victims. Although terrified and underdressed for the occasion, they spread out and glided across the smoky deck, ruthlessly tearing apart the interlopers. And the Southerners discovered how unmatched they truly were.

Leaving the females to their murder, Doran charged across the decks, seeking to stem the fire raining down from the sky. He was not alone, for though the Hunt's initial attack was devastating, already countless Wolves stirred from beneath the decks, and Doran went about setting them to defend the sanctuary. Gathering a dozen archers, he charged towards the vicious ballista, looming above the tallest galleon. Leading his pack, Doran charged through the dark, hazy pathways, killing every invader unfortunate enough to come his way. He felt the tide of war turn, inexorably, as the defenders showed their steel. The waves of invaders flooding over the gunwales into their territory slowed as the Wolves and the Alphas brought the fight to them.

He might even have believed they would hold when he sent half his entourage up to the ballista, while he and the rest went about countering the brutes with their fire arrows. Setting up a counterstrike, he watched with pride as his comrades set and loaded the magnificent weapons with little effort.

"Take out those fuks," he cried as a raft heavy with archers floated below their first volley. "Shoot lower, against the wind," he cried, cursing the gusts.

We can survive this.

He'd never seen a dozen brothers die in a single moment, yet die they did in an explosion of fire. He cursed the brute whose aim was so blessed, for a barrel lit up the night once more, landing and shattering around the ballista. Oil spilled, spread, and caught fire, and he watched his warriors suffer, burn and die as they tried and failed, in clumsy, blind leaps, to clear the lower floating decks and jump to the water below. The ballista caught fire, ignited by the burning bodies, and the screaming was loudest from his own mouth.

We are lost.

Luck alone saved him from the raft of archers, emboldened by the ballista's destruction. A hail of arrows took flight and took out every brother standing the defence with him. As they screamed and died around him, Doran leapt over the nearest edge and dropped to the deck below. He took the landing badly, rolled his ankle and stumbled to the ground, wondering if an arrow would follow, but he was blessed with a momentary reprieve.

"Doran," a familiar voice cried from above.

"Celeste?" he gasped, and she stood above him, covered in blood, her chest heaving, her blade red and shaking.

"Are you okay?" she asked, dropping down the steps and pulling him to his shaky feet. He feigned a grin.

"Heartbroken is all," he jested, picking up his shield and blade from where they had fallen. Heartbroken or no, there was killing to be done.

"We've taken the middle decks back, but too many are coming from the side," she said, and he could see the determination overcoming her fear. "So, what do we do?"

Though he had no right to be, he was proud of her. He was also her leader in battle.

"We need to move along the edge," he told her, "killing those we can, and hope a few archers take out those fukers raining fire on us." It wasn't much of a plan, but his mind was awash with visions of his comrades meeting gruesome ends. She looked terrified. "It will be all right," he assured her. "We are heroes. Follow me and kill any who get behind me."

She nodded her head and clanked her sword against her chest plate. "I'm terrified, my love."

"So am I," he said, and offered her the charming smile of a man who lived on the edge, one that said she was welcome to play too. She must have agreed, for she smiled devilishly in return.

The arrow came from nowhere and struck her cleanly, right in the forehead. She still held the smile, frozen in death, as her body crumpled in a heap on the deck.

"No!" he screamed, falling with her, but the arrow had taken all she was or ever would be. He wailed for her death. He wailed for himself and, perhaps, for the unfairness of it all. It was too much. He had reached a point beyond what his mind could take, and now, all at once, he gave up any desire to live. He was aware of a volley of arrows landing all around them, but he was too numb. He picked up his weapons, knowing it would be the last time, and he didn't care. Whatever faith he'd ever proclaimed to have in the absent gods, he surrendered in that moment.

To the fires with them.

To the fires with me.

Broken and beaten and numb, he climbed out to the upper deck to kill until killed. It was all he had left. Glancing again at her body, still smiling, he said goodbye and charged into the night, seeking his end.

"Come at me," he roared, and the fools took him up on his challenge. The night came alive with his screaming and the clank of metal and wood. He surrendered his body to the fight and waded ferociously in among the brutes. He would have met a swift end in an open skirmish, but choosing side passages with tighter walkways, he could hold his own, and they were no match for his deadly skill. He stopped counting after twenty Southerners fell to his swords. Onward he pushed, with no particular route in mind. He simply sought out victims, and they presented themselves among the smoke and fire. He was not alone either, for he stumbled into many an ally in desperate combat with invaders along his ravaging route. Some Alpha, some Wolf, some civilian. He thought them heroic and fierce, but he cared little, for his mind was on his own path.

Until he encountered Mea. He came upon her and Jeroen standing back to back, battling for their lives, as a few dozen Southerners surrounded them. Jeroen was a wall of defiance. He was devastating with every strike from his sword, and he wielded his shield with a terrible fury. Each corner was dripping in blood where he'd smashed it through the bone and flesh of any fiend who dropped their guard. Countless dead lay at his feet, and he was as serene as though he were practising with sparring blades in a meadow.

Mea was a whirlwind—a pure Primary for these terrible days. With nearly every blow from either hand, she killed. She was a storm of motion, each strike delivered with a curse, and she inspired Doran. Suddenly, he desired more than anything else that she should live, and he charged forward, attacking from the rear those foolish few who dared strike out at his Primary. The world slowed to nothing but the haze of flame and blood. He felt the spray cover his face and the flames warm his skin, but he never stopped killing. More than that, the allies he'd unwittingly led through this nightmare joined the fight, and suddenly, the Hunt were sent bolting from the main decks like the cowards they were. Only when he saw a few of them leap back over the side in panic did he notice the absence of the dreadful arrows. Cruelly, he believed this battle to be turning—and just as quickly he condemned his foolhardiness. He knew better.

And then, a massive ship passed with one female aboard, firing down at the attackers with the last remaining ballista.

You wonderful lunatic.

Suddenly, their numbers were improving, the screams were lessening, and for a brief moment, he saw the water bearers beginning to win the battle against the flames. A lesser man might have collapsed among allies and lamented the dead, but Doran wasn't yet ready to return to the world of the living. He chased off those last few who were scurrying away and found himself above a large raft with a gathering of nasty fuken archers.

"To the fires with me," he cried, and leapt down.

Falling.

Landing.

A little bit of rolling.

He was confident he'd broken his ankles, but the pain inspired him to better things. He rolled among the shocked archers; their hesitation was all it took. Like a spark igniting the world, he climbed above boots, belts and bastard heads. As he did, he spun his blade and felt it cut deep into the flesh of enemy after enemy. He never stopped, and they fell and died. Some pulled daggers and died just as swiftly. A dozen more killed in a few frenzied breaths, and Doran suddenly found himself alone on a dead-laden raft.

"I will kill you all," he cried, seeking further opponents, and then caught sight of the attackers on the far side of the bank, standing motionless with shock. And why wouldn't they? Blood-soaked and rabid, their comrade killer bellowed primordially, seeking new prey. No wonder they offered no cry of challenge nor dared to fire an arrow his way.

"Come at me," he demanded, but the lake that had not so long ago been covered in attackers was now settling, patches of crimson spreading upon its surface. But that wasn't the end of the Southern charge, for like rats, they surged towards the magnificent galleon as it burned and crashed up against the edge of the lake.

"You aren't alone," he cried to the girl atop the sinking vessel. She didn't hear, so he plunged into the water, hoping his weary body would carry him back up to the surface. He need not have worried, for the lake's edge was near enough to allow him to wade, waist-deep, towards the creaking ship. He met a few more fiends at the vessel's rear and swiftly sent them to the darkness, screaming as he did.

Slowly, he made his way to the vessel's side and began climbing up. Only as he neared the gunwale did he realise his dreadful fatigue, but the memory of Celeste's smiling face infused him with strength, and he climbed higher, releasing a primal howl of hatred and disgust.

Finally, he reached the top and dropped over—straight into the nightmare the girl faced. She was not alone, for standing beside her were two fierce warriors, and together they killed the attackers streaming over the side. Doran, gripping his sword and shield, charged down towards them with murder on his mind and a grim acceptance of his own impending death.

"I am with you," he howled, and threw himself into the wave they faced, battering and piercing and slashing. Although they said nothing, they spread out to allow him to be part of their defensive line, and welcomed him to their glorious end.

78

DRUNKEN RAMBLINGS AND REVELATIONS

Roja had never seen the man who claimed to be her uncle behave like this. She wasn't sure it was a good look to him, for he appeared almost human. Almost, but not entirely. She was terrified for her life, but also, she was just mildly curious, like stepping close to a fire and daring to reach out and grab it. As a child, she'd been fearless, and her grandmother had protected her from everything. The kinder thing, of course, might have been letting her get burned now and then. Roja was always frightened as an adult, but damn her curiosity, for she had little else.

"Fuken Boat Town, fuken Boat Town, fuken Adawan, fuken demons," Uden spat, draining his goblet of wine. In front of him lay a half-eaten dinner, a honey cake with a solitary bite taken from it, and two empty bottles of wine. "Fuk them all," he roared, striking one bottle and sending it flying across the room, where it met a desperate end against the far wall. The room, previously electric with energy, fell deathly silent but for the hammering in Roja's heart. "Oh god," he said, leaping to his feet and stumbling over to the shattered glass. "I'm so sorry." He collapsed to his knees and began scooping up the glass, slicing his hand on one of the shards as he swept the glass into a little mound. "I only need a little hand shovel… and a bucket too," he slurred, and Emir leapt up to ease him away from the glass and any further tearing of flesh.

"Easy, Uden, you'll bleed yourself dry."

"You would know all about that," he snapped, allowing the healer to pull him to his feet.

Roja watched the two men stagger back to the table; it was an absurd vision. A curious one too.

"He would," agreed Roja, and Emir dropped his head ever so, and she wanted to take her lover in her arms and comfort him. Oh, the pain he carried, and she had never once told him of her admiration for his strength, his sacrifice. She would, though, before the end. Before Uden tired of this charade and slit their throats.

"I am sorry. This is no way for me to behave," Uden said quietly, and more than ever, the behemoth looked less like the enormous brute who dominated the world and more like the old man he would soon become. Old age sneaked up upon everyone, especially demented madmen claiming to be immortal gods, she mused.

"What angers you?" Emir asked, slipping away to gather his healer's bag before attending to the shards in the god's fingers. "Apart from fuken everything," he jested, as any healer would with a nervous or disgruntled patient. Casually, as though sifting through a meal, Emir began extracting the shards with tweezers, and Uden allowed him to do so, watching him with a curious gaze.

"I should not bring my mood with me into this room. You both deserve better. Family deserves better," Uden slurred, then grimaced as a large piece was pulled out and a stream of blood trickled onto the tablecloth. "I have listened to many voices these past months. Far too many. All silky and reassuring, assertive and deceiving. I should have listened to my own."

Roja's heart began to beat in excitement. "What has you so riled, dear Uden?"

Let it be beautiful.

"Control yourself, my little one; you secretly pray for failure."

"I pray for an end to war. Why keep successes and failures from me?" She looked around the room in frustration. "I cannot affect the world from this place. I cannot learn war movements when no keeper speaks to me. Spark might lay sieged for all I know, and this city is about to fall. For all I know, you have killed all in your wake and now set your eyes upon the Savage Isles or the deep North. Is it so? Have you taken the world?"

Uden frowned in thought. He was loath to let any words slip free that she might digest and cling to. But tonight, something was changed; something had taken him. She wondered about offering more alcohol.

"There has been defiance," he said at length, "and I have split my forces to deal with them." Worry creased his brow. "But it has been challenging."

Roja held her face still lest she give away any emotion, give away her excitement. Emir continued wrapping the god's fingers. However, she saw him hesitate ever so.

"You ask a crude question?" Uden went on. "Very well, little one. I have not taken the world. Perhaps I never will."

"So, there could be peace," Roja exclaimed. She edged closer to the cur and wondered could she cut through his madness as Emir claimed she might. Could she broker peace? It's what Dia might have done were she sitting at this table.

"There will be no peace, not on either side," growled the healer, tending to the last finger before wrapping it in a bandage and leaving the god to admire his handiwork. Roja could have slapped him for interrupting.

"Well said, Emir. That type of honesty is what makes fine generals."

"I was denied the right to be any kind of general by my friends in Keri."

"Aye, Keri," Uden said sadly. Emir had spoken with him of that fallen town more than once. And Uden had allowed him to. Roja could see the redness in the god's eye now, like a man who had spent the day crying. Or else slaving in fiery pits. "I miss my lands; I miss the cold." He momentarily held his hand in the air, examining the bandaging. "Fuken shadows slither around my home while I am gone." Roja thought this a curious thing to say. The world felt still, and she wanted to press him for more, but she remained silent. Within her, there burned a little spark now, one she'd not felt since the world had burned and everything went to hell. She was proud of those warriors out there, still fighting, especially when they caused Uden cruel, regretful nights like this one.

Uden wavered in his seat as if the world weighed upon his shoulders, and Roja imagined she could recover the bread knife in front of her plate. A quick stab through the heart, a vicious tear across the throat, and his blood would spill everywhere. Or a thrust through the open eye, perhaps. Twist the knife around until his body convulsed and died. Easy.

"Is it after midnight? It must be," Uden whispered. He gazed at a painting behind her. A fine image, large and imposing. It showed a starlit sky and a shattered moon overlooking some wild colours in the night. Roja wondered whether he thought the painting was a window. Were he not such a bastard, it might have been funny. He looked around the table for a drink to celebrate the new day, and Emir, the least drunk among them, offered a refill.

"No, no. No more wine," the godly drunkard said, gazing at his injured fingers as though seeing them for the first time, and then it seemed a grand realisation came upon him. He batted the bottle away, reached down to his bag and pulled out a bottle of sine.

"Is it not a little late?" asked Roja, fearing the worst, and fearing the curious eyes of her lover too. She feared Uden at the best of times, but there was a danger to the man tonight, and she had good enough sense not to kill him. Not yet. Perhaps not ever.

Uden spoke slowly and deliberately, as though every word were anguish spoken aloud. "It is early. It is a new day. It is her day. So, we will drink this," he said, popping the cork on the unusual-looking bottle. "It's a rare vintage. A final gift from a dead man," he said, pouring three new glasses. The brute's mood had swiftly turned from melancholy to celebration, and he would not be moved. "I was going to save it for you both on your wedded day, but tonight… today, I wish to celebrate *her*."

"To her," Emir said, raising his glass. Roja could see the flourishing drunkenness in her lover's eyes. Just the smell of the liquid fire brought drunkenness to the surface. She sipped from her own glass, and conceded that it was probably the finest sine she'd had in her life: familiar flavour, but more refined. Less chance of being blinded by good sine like this.

"To her," Roja echoed, though she wasn't sure of whom he spoke. Aurora?

"She was beautiful," Uden said, and to her surprise, Roja watched a tear roll down the brute's cruel face. "She was perfect."

Roja might have asked, but the god looked past her at the painting again. He muttered a few drunken slurs under his breath before catching himself. "A god should never cry." The words seemed to infuse him as much as the sine sought to break him down.

"Humans cry just fine," Emir suggested, clinking his glass against the god's. He turned to meet her eyes, and she realised he was pressing the fiend. Attempting to influence him, to twist his mind away from murder, atrocities and madness. Deep down, Emir claimed, there was humanity in him beneath the madness. For now, they could do nothing in this enforced solitude but sway his thoughts, or try to get a better understanding of his mind. It was the healer in Emir that couldn't be helped. Roja suspected it kept Emir's mind from craziness. Or else… she feared her lover was beginning to warm to their warden. Could a pigeon befriend a cat that clipped its wings and toyed with it for days without killing? Roja suspected not. And she would not be moved. Could not be moved. They were prisoners, he was a bastard murderer, and they were eternally one step away from enraging him enough that they would be slaughtered as they slept.

Uden coughed, drank a little more sine and sniffed away the emotion. She'd seen him master his feelings like this before. She half expected him to speak without a slurring voice now as well, engage in meaningful conversation for a little longer before abruptly retiring for the night, leaving them shaking and contemplating his presence. How many weeks now had he been coming to join them? The rare nights he didn't come to the door now felt like a deviation from normality. Sometimes they did more than talk over a meal. Sometimes they played cards and gambled into the small hours. Those were the worst nights, for they felt deceptively normal. Sometimes she found herself listening intently to his stories of the war; sometimes, despite herself, she laughed at his jests. Sometimes he embraced her and kissed her cheek, which almost felt comforting. When she played with the ring on her finger, he smiled. It was a beautiful ring, the most stunning she'd ever seen, and she hated that she loved it.

"These will be fine celebrations," he said, and shot out his hand to take hers. He was still drunk, and he gripped her a little too tightly, and she recoiled with the pain. "I'm sorry, little one. I'm sorry—these clumsy hands."

"Do not apologise, Uncle," she said, and he smiled again and bowed his head. She couldn't remember when she'd first called him Uncle to his face, but she knew it pleased him, and pleasing him kept them that little bit safer. She had no uncle, after all. Not since the end of the Faction Wars. However, she knew that if she closed her eyes and imagined he were some other impressive older man, she might have found comfort in his presence.

"Do not close your eyes, little one. You have such beautiful eyes, like your father's. But that smile belonged to your mother alone."

She was often shaken when he spoke of her parents. Oh, how she desired to know more of them. He would frequently tell her snippets of stories about them, little gems of information, extraordinary jewelled lies, fabricated by a bastard tongue. She might have asked after them directly, but she would not pander to his mania, would not risk shattering the illusion he wove for her, for them both. He thought of her as family, and that was fine.

"I wonder whether they would have liked me," Emir said dreamily, slurping at his sine, immensely enjoying it.

Uden hammered the table. "They would have hated you," he declared, laughing, and the room appeared to quake. "Stealing the heart of their perfect goddess," he roared, and Emir laughed with him, and Roja started to cry silently. She raised her glass to her lips and covered the sorrow, the terror.

"Aye, I have that effect."

"I'd have fought your corner, wretched healer, and they'd have listened to me," Uden said, and reached across as though to pummel the smaller man, but instead, he squeezed his shoulder, and Emir refilled his glass in reply. "Though I would dearly have liked to have you as a son-in-law, wedded to my Cordelia."

"Who is Cordelia?" Emir asked immediately. Always prying, always seeking a crack in the madness.

Uden raised his glass, and Emir had his answer somewhat. And then he had more. "She was burned alive. To ashes. To nothing. My little Cordelia. Dead and gone. So long ago now." He drained the glass and coughed heartily.

Emir offered the bottle again. Uden grabbed it, drank from the spout and handed it back. When one spoke of trauma, why waste time with glasses and manners? He wavered again in his chair, and Roja wondered would he fall and crack his head on the floor. Perhaps if she shoved him... Stood on his head a couple of times after. Accidents happened. But she knew better. If Uden died, Gemmil would have them killed. She'd only met him a few times, but there was a darkness to him she'd seen only once in an assassin. They would make it a dozen feet from this house before they were taken away, ravaged and murdered. Roja didn't want to die like that. Besides, better the fuker you knew and understood, she supposed. Uden swore Gemmil's desire to wage war was fiercer than his own. That was a terrifying thought.

"My last born, little lost Lea," Uden said, and wept again. Tears of torment shed by a man near to breaking. "She would be as old as you, Roja. She was lost to the flames so long ago. Beautiful, and timid and wonderful."

Lea?

"Thrice I have lost my children. Drahir, my last remaining son, fell to Erroh." He looked at the painting like a man drowning in a current. "I have no legacy left."

"You will be remembered," said Emir earnestly. He played his part well.

Uden shuddered. His voice was barely above a whisper. "Everyone goes away in the end. And my name, Wiiden, died with them. I was no good man. I am a great god, though."

Wait!

What?

She suddenly remembered Seth's concealed records of Lea. They would be difficult to get access to, but Roja knew her way around the city—and how to get around the keeper of the annals. Had she not taken to reading of Lea, and indeed of Lillium, on the eve of the Cull to reassure herself that no ace of queens sat waiting for her should they battle wits? Her mind was awash now with information that had seemed so trivial at the time. Lea had brothers who never culled. That had stood out most to her. That, and her father's name. It was strange the things a girl remembered.

Lea's father was a Wiiden too.

He was from the East, according to the records.

Lea had no Eastern accent.

Lea had been the lowest rung on the ladder. Who would have bothered trying to discover more about her anyway? She had been insignificant, just like any one of a hundred similar females with few relatives who had appeared at the gates over the seasons.

Roja felt herself begin to shake. "Wiiden?" she gasped. It was hardly a rare name, and coincidences occurred over unlikelier things. Easy to miss if one wasn't searching for it. But having it placed right in front of her like this was a dizzying thing. Roja felt many things suddenly fall into place, like a puzzle revealing itself. She had an uncle Wiiden who had passed, according to Dia. According to the records. He'd lost every child in the war, it was said, and she'd never questioned this. Why would she? Yet here, now, like a blurred dream revealing itself, she saw her kin for what they were.

Cordelia and Lea.

No one had ever visited Lea in Samara.

He doesn't know.

She doesn't know.

Her mind spun. She knew some of her family history. Knew a few names, mostly those of people long dead. Knew of a Wiiden among them. An entire family wiped out, like many others in that bloody time. The names of the children had never been mentioned. She couldn't believe it. She tried not to believe it. All this time, she'd had kin running about in the very same building where she'd lived. So many sisters. It had likely been easy for them to fade into the background.

A blackness came around her vision. She almost fell, almost split her head on the floor. Her stomach churned and turned, and Roja's mind broke ever so. All this time, she had never argued with this brute claiming to be a god, claiming to be her kin. She had kept silent out of terror. Kept on his better side; gave him nothing to kill for. She had never once thought any of his ramblings were truth. She wanted to throw up, to flee from this room, screaming her anguish. Uden looked at her for a breath, and she could see how terribly broken he was. She reached for the bottle and drank and offered it to him.

"Your name is Wiiden?" Roja said evenly, for she knew more now, just as she knew a secret unbeknownst to him.

"I do not use that name, little one, not since she burned in the fire."

Emir leaned forward; in his hand was a knife similar to hers. "Your daughter died in a fire? Is that why you burn women?"

Uden now began to shake, just as Roja had. She'd had the sense to hide it, though. Uden would not meet Emir's cutting eyes, and in that moment, she'd never seen Emir look taller, nor seen the savage murdering uncle so humbled. She almost expected Emir to leap across the table and kill him outright; truly, Roja would have helped him. Let them fight their way out of their besieged city with bread knives. Let them flee to Boat Town, wherever the fuk it was.

"I burn the women as an affront to this city. As a threat to your dead Primary, to her archaic ways. We performed such savagery to enrage her."

"Why?" Emir asked coldly. The knife in his hand shook ever so with every word. His grip was secure, though.

Lea is alive and he doesn't know.

And she and I are kin.

"That vile witch desired nothing except that the precious Alpha males and females of this world would furrow, make families and little else. Enforced inbreeding, dressed up as romance, love, honour and duty. Children they were." He looked directly at Roja. "Children you are. Forced into unnatural things in a dangerous fading world."

Roja attempted to gather her thoughts, play her part. Keep her discovery secret. "She loved humanity; she attempted to save the world. I will have no one speak of her in this way," argued Roja weakly. Once more, she drank deeply from the bottle and offered it to her uncle. Her hands did not shake. She could almost imagine sinking a blade into his chest.

She suddenly thought less of Dia. She must have known the truth. Had to have known. Had she falsified the records to hide her sins? And if so, what would secrecy serve? Roja hated her in that moment. Moments passed, though.

She suddenly wondered whether Dia knew of Wiiden's madness. Had she attempted to protect the girl from him? Was it kindness on her grandmother's part? Such thoughts were almost comforting. Better that than thinking ill of her. And then she wondered what else she might have kept from Roja.

"She loved natural order, but she did not love humanity," Uden said. "Forcing her precious daughters to mate with wanton little cubs to create a better species? A pox on her vision. Look at you both." He gestured to the wretched healer and then to the queen bitch of the city. "You both are beautiful and suited for aiding this world. I hope one day to meet your offspring. I hope they water down the bloodlines of Samara and make it a sweeter-tasting brew. It will be a far richer world for it. I hope they have a choice of whom to love, for such things are forbidden within the grand walls of Samara."

"I don't understand," said Emir, but Roja did, and she hated Uden's rational arguments. She couldn't stand agreeing with her uncle on anything, even this. Not when her mind was awash with such revelations.

"I regret many things; I regret the burning of women. But that is the way of war," he slurred, and Roja realised he was near unconsciousness. He stood up and stumbled backwards. Emir dropped his knife and, quick as a flash of electricity, caught the brute and eased him to a long chair before the fire.

"I fear, in honour of Cordelia, I may have drunk too much," Uden whispered, and Roja thought his voice timid and hollow and human. "I have no legacy; I have only you," he muttered, lying back on the long chair and resting his head on a silken cushion.

"Sleep, Uden," whispered Emir, and, pulling a blanket from beside him, he draped it over the behemoth. He looked up and glared at Roja, who now held the bread knife, all long and serrated. She couldn't remember picking it up, only that it was light and deadly sharp. A girl could slide that blade across some unprotected skin and slice life away in a breath. She took a step forward, and he shook his head, and again, Roja feared his unnatural fondness for the bastard. She was certain Uden *was* her blood, and she hated him.

Without warning, Emir was beside her, his hand upon her wrist, his lips upon her own. "Not like this," he whispered, and eased the blade from her grasp. He went and set it on the table. There, he picked up a large jug of cool water and grabbed a steel basin, and left them both by Uden's bedside. Leaving the slumbering god to wake with a nasty hangover and a crick in his neck in the morning, Emir led Roja upstairs, where gently, he slid her clothing free and then his own. They writhed and loved and lost the meaning of time in the joining of their bodies. When neither could offer any more energy, they lay beside each other, watching as dawn gently lit up the window.

"We could have ended the war," she whispered.

"No, my love, we could have killed a man too drunk to defend himself."

"He deserves to die."

"I believe he will die, just not by our hands. Besides, you forgot my pledge," Emir whispered, kissing her hand and looking at her shimmering ring in the rays of dawn.

"Fuken pledges, so many pledges. Which one is this?"

"I pledged not to kill myself," Emir offered, and she ran her fingers along his scars. They were healing, but there would always be a reminder.

"Very well," she whispered, and allowed sleep to take her. But not before visions of her cousin and the secret she knew could crush Uden or tear him from this frenzy came to mind. She might have whispered such a thing to Emir and asked his advice, but she knew well the fool would tell Uden by hour's end. Some secrets were better left unspoken. She only wished she knew whether this was one of them.

79

NEEDLESS HONOUR

It was the fever that took most of her wits, and it had come upon her the moment she stopped travelling. As though her body betrayed her, now that it could. For three days, maybe four, Lexi tossed and turned within her little prison, unable to walk, talk or eat. Her mind raged with feverish visions between waking and slumber. Sometimes, she remembered her mother with her. Holding her, applying eucalyptus beneath her nostrils. Sometimes making her drink fluids, some sweet, some vile, some cold and some warm. There was food too. She remembered the food the most, and sometimes she sat up and chewed and looked around in a daze. Sometimes it was bread, maybe some cheese. She held some of it down sometimes too. Those were the better meals. She also remembered blearily walking around the room, seeking out a chamber pot, and hammering at a locked door, wailing for a glass of wine. She also remembered falling asleep on a chair, singing about a boy she wanted to kiss. She always woke up in bed, drenched in sweat, seeking a rag to clean her nose and inhaling that bitter stench of eucalyptus.

When the fever broke, her chest ached, and her cough was wet and broken, but she had her mind again; her limbs no longer felt like a dozen mounts had crushed them. She also discovered she was not alone.

"They had me sit with you," Aimee whispered. That wasn't true at all. She was lying in bed with her. If the girl feared catching her fever, she showed nothing in her nakedness. Lexi could feel her warmth, could sense her invitation. "Play with me a while." The sheets rested too low on the girl. Her chest was exposed. Moreover, she knew her chest was exposed. She was perfectly proud of what she possessed, and despite herself, Lexi gazed. For a moment. Perhaps two.

"You lunatic," Lexi countered.

After a moment more, the girl stretched and smiled before wrapping herself tighter in the bedsheets, looking impossibly comfortable.

"It could be something to do while everyone else goes to war." She rolled closer, a devilish grin on her face. "I promise I'll be gentle." She spoke as though she were afloat on a sea of dream syrup, and Lexi wasn't sure if she was in possession of her senses.

Lexi sat up swiftly, fought her vision as it darkened, and felt relieved to discover she still wore her nightdress. Mostly. "Where is everyone?" she said, slipping free of the bed, feeling the chill in the air while searching for her clothes. "I feel like spit." She also felt awkward and observed.

"You should stay in bed. Or we could go and find Tye. That would be pleasing times."

Tye!

Visions of her comrade, chained and struggling, flooded her mind, and panic took her. She had to free him. Had to escape this place too. She remembered the desert, the exhaustion, the walk down into this prison too, and dimly, she recalled her mother being alive and leading these bandits. Suddenly, she feared this was all a trick of her mind.

"Where is he? Where is Elise?"

"Kaya and your mother insisted I stay to watch over you in case they died. Tye is resting in a cage with Wrek and... Aurora," Aimee said, and this information seemed familiar. At the time, hearing of Elise's leadership of this massive place had made sense. Now, in the light of candles and with a clearer mind, she wasn't sure how such a thing had come to be.

What will Dad say?

Lexi recovered her clothes and immediately began to strip off her sweat-soaked nightdress. She couldn't remember the last time she'd bathed, save that the mud was gone from her body, but the days of sleeping had left her feeling anything but clean.

"Outstanding," Aimee whispered, and Lexi hesitated for a puzzled breath before pulling her blouse over her chest. Aimee sat upright among the sheets, allowing Lexi to see everything. It wasn't the first time Lexi had seen a naked girl. It was just the first time a naked girl had wanted to be seen by her in such a way. Her heart hammered, and she swiftly grabbed her trousers as Aimee dropped back into the bedsheets with a loud sigh. "Our loss, so."

Absolutely thank the absent gods for that. Absolutely.

Grabbing her boots, armour and sword, Lexi turned to open the door, only to discover to her horror she was locked in with the temptress. "What the fuk?" she cried, pulling and kicking it. She had to escape. She had to free Tye. Wrek too. They were her kin now. She would not leave them behind. Her mother be damned.

"They don't want us precious creatures out in the battle." Finally, Aimee's words cut through the fog in Lexi's mind. A coldness took her. She suddenly feared the thunder of boots from above as soldiers attacked and pillaged. And she, a little damsel, locked in this room.

"I cannot be in here," she said. "I must escape. I have to fight. Or flee. Or fuken something." She hammered at the door, eager for guards to release her. Keen to free herself of temptation. It wasn't completely frowned upon. Not for a female of the city, at least. But she most certainly didn't want to live up to that stereotype.

Most certainly.

She hammered and kicked at the door, but her weakened body was no match for its sturdiness. Instead, she began searching around her mother's quarters for something heavy to bludgeon the bastard thing with. It required only a little leverage and the right amount of pressure to flip it from its hinges. The problem was finding a tool for such a task. As she searched, Aimee slipped out of the bed and began to dress, impossibly slowly, somehow managing to leave her most alluring features bare for as long as possible.

"I can pick that lock, no bother," she said, tightening her belt before gliding up beside the frustrated young Alpha and smoothly picking a clip from her hair.

"We can just break through it," Lexi argued.

"No bother at all," repeated the young bandit.

Lexi watched Aimee sit cross-legged below the lock; the only sounds between breaths were a few colourful curses as her fingers went to massaging the lock's innards. Time seemed to slow as she worked, and Lexi began to lose hope. And then at last, after what felt like an hour, there came a click, another curse, a little yelp of victory, and the door creaked open, and she was free.

"I shouldn't have doubted you," cried Lexi in delight.

"You doubted me?" Aimee muttered, and looked longingly at the bedding. "Are you certain our time couldn't be spent better elsewhere?"

she asked, but Lexi strode away down the corridor without answering. She crept through the underground passageways, following the small torches set into the walls, hoping memory would grant her a route.

After a time, Aimee walked up behind her, her steps casual and careless. "They're down this hallway, in the cells," she said, and Lexi hissed her to silence. "Why go to them?" Aimee said, ignoring her.

"I must free them."

"All of them?"

"Perhaps. Now hush yourself, girl."

It was one thing to escape from imprisonment; it was another thing entirely to release jailed criminals. Innocent as they were.

"I love Wrek, but he was jailed for good reason," Aimee whispered, and for once, the dreamy indifferent tone was gone. She sounded sincere. Her eyes were wide in fear.

"I cannot stay here knowing they are imprisoned. Can you?"

"I am at home here," the girl said. She meant it too. And once more, Lexi realised she didn't understand her. "And I don't want to leave. Not yet."

Lexi hadn't thought of anything beyond finding Tye and freeing him. Truth was, this place was no sanctuary after all. She had never asked her mother for a thing in her life, but as her comrades were chained, she had begged Elise to free them—and was denied that one request.

To the fires with this place, so.

They crept through the darkness towards the prisoners. All the while, Lexi's mind raced, trying to think of a plan beyond simply charging in aimlessly, hoping to knock a guard unconscious. Perhaps she could simply lie to the guards, tell them it had been Elise's decision to free them. But Erroh was far better at deceit. She'd never had the gift. As it turned out, no guard watched over the brightly lit cells.

"All right, ladies," Tye cried from his chamber as they appeared. He stuck his hand through the bars and waved manically.

"We've come to free you," Lexi declared, hurrying to the solitary desk at the room's far end to search for the key. It was a fine wooden desk, with an undershelf and all. The perfect place to leave records of past guests, and an ideal place to rest a key.

"Not me," Aimee pointed out. She wrapped her arms around herself like a chilly wind had taken her. "I'm just watching, is all." Her eyes were upon Ealis in the cage. And Ealis's were upon her. Neither woman could look away until Aimee broke the stare and, leaning in close, whispered in Lexi's ear. "On the wall."

It was a fine grey wall, and a perfect place to hang a key. A few sets of them, in fact, and Lexi took them and went to work on the locks. Tye paced back and forth in his cell, grimacing at every failed attempt, but when the flimsy cage door creaked open, he took hold of Lexi and kissed her.

"That's my girl," he said proudly as he released her.

Lexi, of course, slapped him before turning to Wrek's cage.

Absolutely didn't appreciate that at all. Absolutely.

"Here you go, Wrek," Lexi cried in delight, opening the lock on the first attempt. The door creaked open, but Wrek did not move. He lay in his bed looking up at the ceiling.

"Wrek, brother," Tye cried. He ran in and tried to haul the behemoth to his feet, but managed only to get him sitting up. It was quite an impressive feat given his much smaller size. "Let's get the fuk out of here before your brother returns and kills you."

Wrek smiled and released himself from Tye's grip. "You deserve freedom. I, however, will not flee this place."

"As you wish," Tye said, without much argument. Lexi tried to step into the cell, but the young Alpha stopped her with a firm grip and a silent shake of the head. "Wrek has his reasons for staying."

"But…"

"Trust me, Lexi," he offered, and though she fought back a wave of frustration, she could see his certainty.

"Fine," she said, turning to the silent figure of Aurora Borealis. "I suppose you need rescuing too." The girl remained staring at Aimee, however, and it was Aimee who answered for her.

"Leave her to rot," she whispered, and with a slight tilt of the head, Aurora smiled approvingly.

"You have your vengeance, so," Ealis said dreamily, and Lexi recognised that tone. Ealis bowed to Lexi and then to Tye. "Goodbye, my friends," she said, and lay back down on her cot, wrapping her sheets around her.

Fuk it.

"You all should leave before someone comes and finds you here," Wrek said. He placed his hand on his forehead and then his heart before bowing.

Lexi could have continued to beg Wrek to leave, but instead she followed Tye back out into the cool hallway, where they began to walk swiftly, hoping that they would be mistaken for bandits. After a time, they heard footsteps behind them, and they turned to see Aimee following after them. They met no one else along the way. Lexi's heart was in her mouth as she walked upwards, though, fearful of what lay ahead. A few times she stopped to marvel at the depth of these mines, but each time Aimee shoved her forward gently.

"It takes forever," she offered, and they continued their trek upwards.

Tye would miss his brother of the cage, but he knew better than to argue with him. What sins he carried were for him alone to endure, to pay for. Tye could have spent the entire night arguing otherwise with him, but he knew Wrek was tired. And Wrek was home. This was no place for either himself or Lexi. Erroh would have wanted it this way.

It took only a hundred steps upwards before the first beads of sweat broke out on Tye's forehead. He could see that Lexi, too, was suffering from the exertions of the climb. Aimee alone appeared indifferent to the strain. Perhaps she was built for such marches. Possibly she hadn't spent the last three days locked in a cage, either.

"How much farther?" he asked miserably. He knew it was far. There was still no sign of either light or another living soul, and it was a disturbing thing.

"A few more steps, at least," Aimee offered, and Tye knew she was lying, especially when she sniggered. He did not know what to make of this place, apart from its impressive defences. In truth, he would have willingly stood with these foul fiends and fought off the threat. He preferred freedom, though. Preferred it more than killing the enemy.

Ahead, he caught sight of a bandit strolling down the pathway. She was drunk. Burping loudly to settle her stomach, she wavered and swayed as she walked, each step bringing her dangerously close to the edge. Her face was grim and marred by the smoke and grime of battle. She offered an unconcerned nod as she wandered by, and without saying a word, all three increased their pace lest she be going to check on the prisoners below.

They passed a few more bandits along their route, but strangely, none showed interest, and all were drunk. For a time, Tye wondered if there was no army charging at all. Eventually, they reached the mouth of the mine, where Lexi, panting heavily, drew in close against the wall.

"What now?" she asked. A delicate question and one he'd hoped she'd considered before breaking him out of jail. They could just faintly make out the empty, sandy settlement in the dark. Empty but for a few late-night wandering drunkards.

"You both could come to my quarters, make a woman out of me?" Aimee suggested. She took Tye's hand, then reached for Lexi's too. Her smile was alluring, and Tye realised she meant it.

What the fuk?

"Now is hardly the time," Lexi gasped.

Freedom is essential, but let's not rule anything out.

"Lexi is right," Tye said. It was the most challenging sentence he'd ever said. "There will be time for that after we escape."

"What?" muttered Lexi in horror.

"Please, my beautiful Alphaline friends." The girl's face turned pale. She began to shake before falling to her knees. "I need this. I need to be taken." Gone was the dreamy tone, replaced by one of panic.

"Aimee? What are you talking about?" Lexi said, squeezing her hand. They could be fleeing from this place. Could be halfway to the main gate. Instead, they were looking after a girl who'd been struck down by an attack of fear.

"He's still in me. Whispering his vile words." She tapped the side of her head, where most of the nasty words usually appeared. Then she struck herself fiercely, and Lexi took her in her arms, and none of this made any sense. "Telling me to kill. I don't want him in me."

"There's no one in your mind, little one," Lexi said, hushing the girl to calmness. Tye could only look around and hope no drunken wanderer paid them any heed.

"He wants me pure. Untouched and a killer. A tempest. He promises me the world." She looked back down the way they'd come, her expression terrified. Tye did not know Aimee's relationship with Uden, but from the few words Aurora Borealis had offered, he surmised it had been brutal and cruel.

"You don't need him," Tye said after a moment, then looked at Lexi and gave a slight shrug. It wasn't the finest gathering of words, but it was all he had. "You are better than him."

Aimee looked at him, and he offered a smile. "He did not want me plucked. If my beautiful friends could come to my quarters…"

It was a weak invitation, and Tye thought her beautiful and terrifying; he was intrigued by such an offer, but also understood how trauma sometimes showed itself. He could never take advantage of a person in so much pain. He could see just how savagely unbalanced she was. There were some things a brute never did, not even if she begged for it. He imagined Emir nodding in approving agreement.

"We are not what you need, my beautiful friend," he said, then hushed and kissed her gently.

Lead as Erroh would.

He looked around and suddenly knew exactly what they were going to do. They only needed to steal a handful of supplies. This would not be so hard in a sieged settlement ready for war. Afterwards, they would stroll out into the Adawan desert, sweat for a few days, and lose themselves forever in the green on the other side. Lexi would be beside him, and he knew there was worse company to be had. With Aimee? Well, she was welcomed too, he supposed.

"Out in the green, you will find peace," he said, and gestured to the night. To the barricades between Adawan and sand and the green somewhere beyond. Far from here.

"I won't be coming with you." She was fighting tears—a difficult wrangle. She struggled away from Lexi's comforting grip as though the attack had passed in a breath. "I want to, but I need my people." She looked around as though seeing this place for the first time. "This is my home."

"Come with us," Lexi whispered.

"Kaya is my home; I need my home," she whimpered, before taking hold of Lexi and kissing her passionately. Lexi must have been shaken, for she did not fight her off. And then Aimee licked her cheek and drew away, grinning. "Salty and delicious," she whispered.

"Um… thank you?"

Without warning, she grabbed Tye and kissed him too. He felt her tongue touch his, and oh, for a terrible moment, he imagined writhing with her. And absolutely most certainly not with Lexi as well; he was tempted and felt some stirrings. She drew away, smiling, and suddenly licked him once upon the cheek too, and Tye imagined that tongue at work on all manner of separate body parts. "Sweet and smooth," she said, as though tasting a fine meal. Perhaps that was all he was to her.

"Um… of course I am."

And then, she released herself, met his eyes and then Lexi's. "Live long, my friends; I will love you forever," she promised, before turning away and sprinting out towards the mouth of the cave.

"Bye!" called Lexi, and stood watching her go, as confused as Tye.

"She's not running off to tell everyone we've escaped, is she?" Tye asked, watching her and her impressive rear disappear into the night.

"No… no… I don't think so… Probably not."

"Let's go."

"A fine idea."

They moved through the nearly abandoned camp, stealing what supplies they could without causing any alarm. Tye was unhappy with the armour he purloined, for it was thin leather, but the two swords he stole from an abandoned smith's stores pleased him. He christened them "Bandit" and "Bane" and thought them sharp and well-balanced. He also took a bow, a few quivers and what morsels of food and water he could liberate. His finest find was a bottle of sine to toast freedom with once their feet touched mud and grass. This war was done for him. This bastion had been his final opportunity to add to the war effort. He would live as a nomad. They both would. It wasn't cowardly; he'd done his heroism. It was simply practical.

"We are done with this war, aren't we?" he asked.

"Aye."

"We march to the green, keep our heads down?"

"Aye."

"Live a life free from war and death?"

"Aye," she said, strapping her scabbard tight around her waist.

"Your mother?"

"I choose your freedom, asshole."

"You made a good choice, trollop."

Through the barricades, they crept, and only here were they cautious. There were lines of sleeping warriors, and it was a peculiar thing. As was the stench of ale above the usual stench of waste and humanity. Whatever battle had occurred, there were fine signs that victory had been attained. There was little cheer, however, and why would there be at this late hour? They said little as they made their way through the lines and appeared as simple bandits. Apart from missing sashes upon their garments, who would notice at this late hour? Lexi never stopped searching for her mother. Tye watched her peering at one sleeping form after another, until they finally stepped beneath two towers along the flank of Adawan and skulked out into the cool night.

"Fuken quicker," she whispered, racing ahead of him, away from the dark towards the starlit night far beyond.

"I'm keeping up," he muttered, following after. Away from the glow of safety, away from prison. The path was clear, and with few clouds in the sky and the shattered moon glowing brightly, an Alpha could escape silently, effortlessly, into the desert.

For a time they jogged onward, until Lexi slowed to catch her breath. No eagle eye spotted them; no arrow struck them from behind.

"I think we are free," he offered.

"Miles to run yet."

There was still the outline of the towers and the glow of Adawan torches, but there was little to fear ahead. Across from them, though, they could see the diminished torches of the invading forces. Straining his eyes, Tye saw few attackers. No doubt many hid behind their tents, licking their wounds after a thrashing. That said, he knew the tales of Keri. Knew the stories of a great many battles. Great tactics would delay a battle, but such were the number of carts and tents that he guessed the Southerners outnumbered them easily enough. He wondered whether Lexi saw as he did. Had she left her mother behind without so much as a goodbye? He could have asked her, but some things were better spoken of away from war, away from a change of mind.

He missed his mother. He wished he'd said goodbye.

"I think we can walk a while," she said, and she was right. They were utterly alone in the desert, away from the conflicting armies, walking towards further darkness.

"It's almost beautiful out here," he said, falling into step beside her.

"Beautiful?"

"Aye."

"It is a powerful word. Tell me, you thought Aimee beautiful?"

"Aye. She is."

"She'll probably be dead come the next battle."

"She had her chance, I suppose."

"Beautiful Aimee, dead in the sands with my mother, with Wrek too."

"Are you all right? Leaving so?"

"I do not wish to think of them. I wish to think of beautiful things. Tell me, would you call me beautiful?"

"Perhaps. I don't know. You are pretty. Nice enough rear, too. I try not think of you like that, though. You are Lexi. To be protected. Erroh would kill me. Are you all right leaving this place?"

"Erroh is dead. By the way, I don't think you are beautiful."

"Yes, you do," he protested. "At least a little bit."

"Wynn was beautiful, but he's dead. I would never call you beautiful. I would merely call you available. Your rear is hardly impressive as well," she muttered, but he could see her grin in the night. She was attractive enough. Nothing spectacular, if truth be told. She didn't even wear paint to impress him, either. However, he found her the most interesting person he'd ever spoken to, but he would never dare tell her that. They would never be mated, and if there ever came a day when he would cull with a beautiful female, it would work in his favour if he hadn't broken the daughter of a legend's heart.

"A man could ask for little more."

"Aimee is beautiful, though," Lexi reminded him, and he nodded in the darkness.

"A good kisser too."

"She really was."

They walked towards a mound of boulders in the distance. A fool could pitch a camp among them, sit out the battles and sneak back to plunder the riches left behind. Soon enough, they reached the boulders and then stepped around them, preparing to walk farther into the desert.

And all at once, in the distance, they spied five hundred Southerners, creeping slowly towards Adawan.

"What the flying fuk is that?" she gasped, dropping to her knees. They were back among the mound of boulders. The Southerners moved slowly, clustered and careful, like one sole weasel slithering across the sands in search of prey. They were eerily silent, despite their vast numbers.

"How are they so quiet?" Tye whispered, dropping beside her.

"No armour. Sneaky bastards. One swift charge from that close and they will never be caught before they reach the edges of our defences. Look back to the camp; what do you see?"

"I see nothing."

"Exactly. There isn't even a sentry."

"They're waiting to charge?"

"Probably hiding in their tents, waiting for fuken mayhem to occur. Bastards."

They watched for a time, unable to say a thing. Tye knew, though. She probably knew too.

"Get back to Adawan and warn them," he said, reaching over and removing her arrows from her quiver and stuffing them into his own. He counted forty of them, at least.

"What are you doing?" she cried in horror, and he took her hand and kissed it goodbye.

"I'll be along, but best I keep them here as long as possible."

"Together," she said, her eyes pleading, but he denied her with a curt shake of the head. And why wouldn't he? Erroh had charged him to protect her; sending her away was all he could do. He could not allow these fuks to continue into the darkness unwatched.

"They must be warned."

"I shall never leave you behind."

"I'll be all right."

"You fuken liar."

"There are things greater than us at stake, my dear," he said, and she kissed him. He touched her tongue with his. It was nice. He hadn't expected that. He'd been kissed quite a lot this night by girls he'd never thought of kissing. Not really.

"So now you know what it is to kiss me."

"It wasn't terrible. Salty and delicious."

"Sweet and smooth. It... um... seemed like the thing to do, is all."

"I completely agree." Their eyes met for a breath, and he felt a strange warmth for her he'd never felt before.

"I hate that you are my best friend."

"I hate it too. Goodbye, my dearest Lexi."

He watched her jog off into the night. He watched her rear for as long as he could. It was ungentlemanly, but this was the end of his life. He knew it. He was about to become an Erroh. A fool, brazen enough to face an army alone. After she had disappeared in the darkness, he felt a terrible loneliness, along with regret that he could have spent the night wrapped up in female forms at play. He'd likely have spent himself by now, in truth. Chuckling to himself at his immaturity, he blew an empty kiss to his best friend through chance and returned to watching the throngs of Southerners skulking through the darkness, preparing to flank Adawan.

Setting his pack on the ground, he took a few breaths to calm himself, stop his hands from shaking, and started to weep. He wept for his parents, his friends and everything he'd endured. He thought back on his life and thought it squandered. He'd done fine things, but believed himself capable of greatness. And kindness. And so many other things. Instead, alone in the dark, he was going to die. No heroism. No legacy. No reward. Just the hope of delaying an invasion a handful of moments longer.

That will save more than one life.

He thought on this and wiped the tears away. Knowing whatever he did in the next few breaths would save lives made it worth it. It didn't matter that he'd done nothing of genuine note. Life mattered. And in the end, so did death.

"So be it."

Reaching into his pack, he pulled out the bottle of sine and took a mouthful, steeling himself for death. He needed a second shot, so he drank again. He wanted a third, but dying because he couldn't line up a shot would be an embarrassment.

"To the fires with the Woodin Man," he said softly to himself, then moved out of his hiding place.

He stayed low and trusted their lack of alertness to serve him. Nearing the bastards, he took a breath, thought fondly of those not beside him and drew his bow. The arrow was silent, and he knew it wouldn't miss. He didn't wait for the scream. He drew a second arrow, released, then a third, released, and began running. He had no route planned, apart from moving along the edge of their ranks. Thirty feet from where he'd started, he slid to his knees, drawing an arrow and firing once more into the group of Southerners. Archery had never been his talent, but it was a small matter. He released a second arrow and hesitated for a moment. In the darkness, he spotted confusion, saw figures bent over and stumbling. He could also hear their screaming, and it pleased him. He thought it a fine melody to hear before he died.

Be brave, Tye.

Sprinting again towards their base, he dared a strike from a running position, but the arrow fell near his foot, and the bowstring snapped back, stinging his fingers something terrible.

At least, in the dark, nobody saw that.

He left the arrow where it lay and ran a few feet more before dropping to his knees, firing again into another section. His eyes followed its trajectory and he watched as a Southerner fell silently with an arrow protruding from his head. Two more arrows released, and he became giddy, knowing he still lived and that the Hunt had not found the killer in their midst. He could have killed them all with enough arrows and enough time. As it was, he knew he was but a breath from discovery. As another Southerner fell, he charged away across the sand, taking a wild, unpredictable route. His feet carried him more swiftly than he'd thought possible. Still, no arrows felled him, and he began to believe.

I can be great.

His movements became routine now as he continued his campaign to delay their advancement. All he needed to do was to fire swiftly and then move silently on; it worked spectacularly. He circled them like a wolf—

one lone Alpha, flexing his muscles, finding his own measure. With ten arrows remaining, he found himself back among the rocks where he'd kissed his best friend goodbye. Dipping behind them and listening to the cries, the orders and the threats, he made one more decision that would most certainly end his life.

Dipping low and recovering the bottle of sine, he poured another healthy amount down his throat. Fighting a cough, he tore a strip of fabric from his favourite shirt and drenched it in sine. It was a terrible waste of sine, he thought, pouring a fresh shot down his throat, and then a third, and then a fourth. He did this because he was an idiot. But also because it was the end. He could hear them more clearly now. They were coming closer, and he suddenly needed to relieve himself. It might have been fear.

Be great.

He decided to be great, even as a warm, comforted feeling came upon him, and he felt less alone, as though distant, fallen warriors were watching from another realm, waiting to welcome him home. It was a welcome warmth against the bitter, chilly night. There was the flash of a spark as he lit the sine-soaked fabric, blowing gently on it, coaxing the flame. Then, stuffing the unlit end into the bottle of sine, he stood on shaky feet, holding the bottle low, to one side. Distantly, he heard the clang of metal, and he realised his best friend had reached the ramparts and warned the defenders.

"You are all so fuken fuked," he slurred, popping up from behind the largest boulder. He half expected to take a few arrows in his chest as he stood highlighted against the night sky. "My girl will kill all you fuken bastards when she finds my body." He didn't think they knew who she was, but it didn't matter. *He* knew. He hurled the burning sphere of glass and watched as it arced through the darkness like a shooting star. His aim was true, and it landed among them with a whoosh, spilling its flaming cargo and splashing the Southerners with liquid fire. "Lexi is coming for you!" he roared, and brandished his bow and last few arrows.

Those who were not engulfed in flame charged him. He fired swiftly into their ranks, mocking them and laughing at their every step. A few of them died, and the rest of them drew nearer, and he held his nerve. They did not carry bows and arrows, he noticed almost calmly. Instead, they carried blades.

"Perfect," he cried, dropping his bow and drawing his two new blades from his back.

He did this because it is what idols did.

They came at him full speed, shoulder to shoulder. Although his body was numbed and his mind lost to a bit of delirium, he charged towards them, through them. His blades never stopped. He felt their blades strike his own flesh, yet he did not fall. In the darkness, he rolled deep into the Hunt, waiting for death, thinking of those he loved and also of murder, for he was murdering them. They must have feared this lunatic laughing and attacking, for they did not swamp him as they should have. Instead, they hesitated, and he made them pay—at least for a few breaths, until at last they did overpower him, surrounding him and raising their blades as one.

And this was the end of Tye.

And he had done his best.

And he had been outstanding.

And then they screamed in horror.

All around him, the Southerners fell away without delivering a blow, and Tye was thoroughly confused. And then, in the last glimmer of the dying fires, he saw the arrows, scores and scores of them, whistling through the air. Felt the blood of his attackers spray over his flesh, heard their screams of rage and surprise. Volley after volley struck, and more Southerners fell, and he laughed aloud in triumph.

"I told you she would kill you all," he roared, and as another wave of arrows fell around him, he waded into them, hacking, slashing, lunging, decapitating. He was a dancing, drunken blur, and it was easy. He was a god. He felt incredible; he felt invincible.

And the absent gods thought so too.

At least for now.

The Southerners began to retreat beneath his madness and the deadly hail of arrows. He followed after for a time, roaring and slashing. Even as he heard the bandits approach, seeking blood, he lost count of those he killed. Finally, when his sword took the life of his last victim, he dropped to his knees, watching the remaining Southerners cowering in the face of his defiance. Suddenly, he felt the ache of his exertions; his breathing was heavy and laboured. A terrible exhaustion took him and for a moment, he wondered was he actually half dead? Had a stray, friendly arrow pierced his back without him noticing? He could have checked for injury but his arms were heavy, so instead, he caught his breath as his comrades charged past him, screaming their defiance, and he realised he was just fine.

The rest of the slaughter moved on without him, and all was quiet and he found himself among the dead. He thought about feigning death, about crawling away while there were no eyes upon him, but until he found his closest friend again, he would not flee. A caged life wasn't the worst end. At least they fed and watered him. There were worse fates.

And then, she was there. "Tye," she screamed, and fell upon him, and he smelled her delicious scent, felt her arms take him and embrace him, half suffocating him. "Oh, my stupid wonderful, Tye," she cried again, and he could only hang limply in her arms. "You did it," she whispered, and he could tell she was weeping. He might have reassured her that he'd never been worried, but he was too exhausted.

"Return me to my bed," he whispered weakly, as more arms took hold and lifted him to his feet. "I fear I had too much to drink."

80

THE GROWING LEGENDS OF DEMONS

At first, Kovak had been grateful for Uden's knowledge, foresight and leadership. At first, he'd gladly taken up arms in the South's name, but the long march and waiting had chipped away at his patience and his taste for war. Kovak felt old, wet and defenceless. He could not see his brothers or sisters of war either. He'd lost them in the swim across. That miserable, freezing swim where he'd been certain a set of Northern eyes would pick him out and end his life mid-stroke. Yet, somehow, he'd survived.

He looked down to the long line of rafts edging out towards the banks of this Boat Town, and he regretted not taking that point of attack. They were an impressive floating bridge, and he resented those comrades upon them with their armour and weapons, all marching impressively, their blades shimmering in the flames.

Kovak's solitary blade barely shimmered, for it was a petty thing. It was little comfort that he'd slain two dim-witted Northerners aboard their floating village. Aboard this monstrosity, he felt the deck heave up and down, and he decided he would very much like to see it sunk this very night.

Hardly the time, though, is there?

Looking back into the darkness beyond, he spotted the lights heralding terrible things. They were closer now than when he'd clambered up out of the water. Little terrifying lights, creeping along in the night as though they knew the Hunt's game. He drew away from them and, staying low, followed the wind through the ramparts of this unsightly floating menace. He wondered whether they would find victory swiftly this night. Or was this another ill-fated manoeuvre by his once infallible leader?

His god.

Around him, the screams of war filled the air. Once, he would have appreciated such a tune and taken heart from it. But Kovak was tired and wet, and he had a terrible feeling. He'd had it since they decided upon this sudden attack. He had been against all the delays in the first days, but now, attacking like this, out of panic, was no attack at all. Their scouts knew it. Therefore, he knew it. Their leader, however, knew something else entirely.

"A pox upon your entire house, Uden," he whispered to the wind, his comrades and the flickering lights in the river moving ever closer. Kovak knew better. Kovak always knew better. It was ages now since he'd bothered offering his thoughts under this regime. The more imaginative act would be to retreat to the city. They still had the numbers, and they had a great big wall to keep any manner of Northern fuks from defeating them. Instead, Uden had sacrificed them all this miserable night.

He shuffled below the upper decks, his damp clothing clinging uncomfortably to his skin, and kept carefully to the shadows. Above, both sides went to thrashing each other senselessly, and he wanted no part of it. Not since he'd gazed upon the demons only moments before. He had been creeping along, minding his own business—up to a little murder—when he had seen the two attackers slip soundlessly aboard. He did not know how they had stayed afloat, weighed down by such heavy armour, but they did. It was a demonic thing.

Emerging from the black water with swords glistening in the night, they were terrifying. They did not creep as he did. Instead, they were loud in every movement, their frightening visages grinning and threatening, a warning to lesser warriors to drop their blades and slink away in cowardice. Kovak cowered, but instead of fleeing, he followed. Why? Because despite the terror, he knew that what came next would be a tale worth telling, a legend for future generations.

They climbed up through the levels without a word. They took mere moments to recognise the threats, seek out prey, and then go to war, which he found incredible. They moved as a blur through the night. Side by side, they marched and hunted and killed. He watched a dozen of his comrades slaughtered in the first few moments. He could have tried to help them, but he knew better, and they should have known better too. They should have seen the grisly, demented faces and turned, fled, or dropped to their knees. Or worse, cowered in the dark, watching, too curious to leave the demons to it.

Around him, he watched the turning of the tide, and he believed it revolved upon the attackers' appearance. Where once there had been fire, arrows and terror, now there was only defiance. When not tearing the living from this world, the two demons battered at burning hatches, pulling wretches from the decks below. They gathered comrades and drove through the attackers, and Kovak saw their influence. Those terrified Northerners picked up blades and shields and began to push them back.

Do you see this, Uden?

He watched other warriors, some without hair, charging from the other sections. Leading and roaring, no doubt touched by the same enchantment the demons had wrought upon the others. Further towards their devastation he crept, avoiding the light, avoiding the horrors, avoiding better judgement. In truth, they were a marvel, and Kovak was awestruck. He should have fled and broken their enchantment, but he could not look away. He hated them, admired them, and knew this battle was lost. If only his foolish comrades could see as he did.

After a time, with countless dead from their beautiful, bloody blades, the pair reached the far end of the vessels and stared out across the waters to the invading forces, too blinded by smoke and zeal as they pushed onward towards doom.

"Retreat, you fools," he told the wind, but his many comrades marched heedless along the line of rafts, two by two, eager to pillage the burning remnants.

Kovak held his breath as both demons conversed in demonic language before they dropped over the ledge to the raft below and went to war once more. "You had your chance," he added to nobody as his comrades, shocked by the sudden appearance of two demons from above, were all too slow to react. A dozen fell in the first few breaths, and Kovak recognised the tales as accurate. They moved in unison, never stopping, never taking a step back, and those they faced in a neat little line could only fall as the duo marched relentlessly through.

Screams filled the night, though this time with a Southern flavour, and Kovak could only watch, cowering and gazing and living. Was that not how stories continued—told by those who watched historical horrors and lived to spread word, to warn of horrors yet to come, of the terrors still to be faced? He thought like that because it made him feel better.

The wet cries of dying panic were lessening above him, where his comrades still fought and died, replaced now by the primal screams of the victorious defenders who pushed back the tide. Slipping over the balcony's edge, Kovak stayed low and dropped to the level just above the water. Even in the darkness, he could see patches of crimson where the water should have been clear. He still held his dagger in his shaking hands, and he reached down and sheathed it. He craved no further bloodshed this night. He longed only for the telling of a tale.

And then things worsened. With no space to manoeuvre, his comrades upon the floating bridge of rafts were slaughtered easily, and the swell of fighters boarding the island of barges was ultimately held.

Two against thousands.

Only after twenty or thirty further defenders had been slaughtered and half the length of the bridge had been reclaimed did the Hunt's leadership finally spot the devastation. Taking a savage decision that should have been made in the first few moments of their appearance, they instructed the archers to bring their rafts alongside and kill the interlopers at the cost of a few dozen of their own.

They did not fire immediately, however, for a large galleon took their attention, and truly, Kovak knew this was the beginning of the end. Of this battle, but also of the South. They fired as quickly as they could, but the archers failed to hold the ship's charge or, indeed, its strike.

If the demons realised the ship's sacrifice, they gave little indication, instead continuing in their mission to kill every Southerner they faced. The galleon's arrows took out the raft of archers and another after that, but even as they set the beast alight, it kept sailing forward, decimating everything in its path.

When the unstoppable vessel crashed up alongside the bridge, Kovak leaned out over the water and steeled himself for the cold drop. As he did, he watched the demons, denied their victims, clamber aboard the devastating vessel as it passed. Like rats, they climbed up towards its upper deck even as it crashed violently against the bank on the far side of the river. He hoped they died, but he knew better. Demons could only be killed by other demons. Or gods, for that matter.

He looked back over the edge; he had seen enough to fill a lifetime of tales. He dropped into the water as quietly as he could, gasping in its icy embrace. Still, as freezing as it was, it was no colder than standing upon a windy battlefield in damp clothes, watching horrors unfold. He bobbed in the water and was grateful he carried no heavy armour, for he was no demon capable of swimming with such a burden.

And then the battle took a last unexpected turn, and Kovak, eager to escape the coming army, swam swiftly away from the island of boats towards the open water. When he judged that he had reached a safe distance, he turned and, treading water, gazed back to the vessel's top to see the inevitable end of the demons, who now faced thousands of Southerners eager for vengeance.

They are more.

Aghast and shaken, he floated and watched in horror as the demons became more. Four warriors in total. They stood atop the ship's main deck, slaughtering all who crept over, and for a terrible time, like they had done upon the bridge, it appeared they might hold the Southerners.

"Kill them," Kovak whispered to the wind and his comrades swarming the vessel, and he wondered whether Uden gazed upon the battle as he did. He hoped not, such was Kovak's cowardice. Turning and swimming against the tide, he reached the far edge of less hostile territory just in time to see the extraordinary breaking of the galleon.

"Burn them," he whispered into the night, urging on the fires that devoured the offending ship from below. He watched the four attackers shatter under the waves of warriors, the burning of the deck, and the wrath of good fortune.

"Burn," he hissed as the deck broke and one warrior and one demon fell into the fire below, no doubt meeting a terrible end. He grinned as he pulled himself ashore and hauled himself up onto the muddy bank. There was no time to warm himself by a fire or find dry clothing. Instead, he marched through the desolated campsite, grabbing what supplies he could and finding a mount worthy of a night charge. He could have joined his comrades, but he had no fight left in him. Nor did he have the faith anymore. It was terrible to lose faith; it was a far worse thing in the middle of a war.

When he had scavenged what he needed, a savage horde of warriors had already landed. From a hundred different vessels they appeared from the darkness, and their war cries filled the night. The world shook as thousands of fighters surged forth. Some made land at the island of barges; many others made land where the Hunt was most plentiful. Already the shrill cries of steel on steel echoed through the night, and Kovak desired none of this. He was too tired, too old, too fuken wet.

"To the fires with you all," he declared, climbing up on his mount as two large armies went to war over a few anchored boats. After that, there would be the matter of the city, but Kovak desired nothing. He gently kicked his mount in the ribs and took off into the night. Not towards the city or his god, but instead, towards the South, where his tales could be heard. "This war is lost," he said to himself, turning once more to gaze at the end of the Southern charge and glean one more tale.

The absent gods might have agreed. They might also have warned of terrible events to come, for all things must end.

81

THE COMING OF SAVAGES

Mea drove through the brutes, hacking into them where she could. The night became nothing more than a haze of blades, blood and brutality. She knew herself to be a fierce fighter but had never thought herself capable of such ferocity. Yet here she was, facing an endless horde, killing all who came at her. Her body was weary, her breath was laboured, every limb was heavy, her body ached, and she wondered, mid-kill, might she suffer this feeling everlastingly when the final blow came? Was that life in the darkness? Knowing Jeroen stood beside her was a comfort. Knowing he would be dead beside her was a comfort too. She hoped they would be buried together, their two broken bodies, wrapped around each other for eternity. Such morbid thoughts. And why wouldn't they be at the end of her life?

"To the fires with you," Jeroen wailed, and for a breath, she saw him move as she did, though more aggressively, like a demon or a deity. In the fire's light, his face was a grimace of anguish and horror. More so than hers. His was a deeper, frenzied appearance. Had she a moment, she would have liked to take him in her arms again and comfort him. And be comforted by him too. Only now, at the end, she realised she had never shown him how very much she loved him. She wondered if he knew he was her everything. All those arguments, all that distance, all those tears, all those missed moments. She wanted to slow the world, turn back the days, relive her entire life with him all over again, and it would be perfect this time. More perfect than before. She wanted their life back. The life they'd had before they tried to elevate themselves. Back before the city fell. Back before the entire world ended. She felt the tears in her eyes, even as she fell upon her next victim, slicing his throat with an easy strike before lunging forward and putting her blade through his heart.

"I want it all back," she whimpered, and this sorrow was for her alone, even as she charged along the pathways seeking out her next victims. It took only a breath to find each one, for, like rats, they appeared from everywhere, scurrying towards both Alphas, seeking murder—and were murdered for their troubles. Dimly, she became aware of the turning tide. Little moments, like allies appearing through the smoke, tearing at the invaders with whatever weapons they had on hand. Little signs, like the glorious sight of a few hundred Alpha females at war. They tore through the night, joined by kinship, answering to no orders but their own, and they were formidable.

"I want it all back," she cried, louder now, and Jeroen was beside her to hear. He said little, and that was fine. He was beautiful and flawless, and she loved him with all her essence, for he was hers and hers alone. He was her perfect dancing partner; he moved with her, matching her swaying gracefulness, swinging with shield and sword in unison, ducking away from her grander manoeuvres, stepping closer to guard her flank. Truly, it was a fine way to die, and she waited and waited.

And fuken waited.

And then she saw them. Dark shadows armed with flapping fire, stepping out of the very darkness, and for a breath, her heart broke, her will surrendered and her blade dropped by her side. Her victim fell too, and for a moment, the waving battlefield settled as their vanquishers spotted the terrible floating shapes emerging from the night.

"I have failed," she cried.

"No, my love. Look at their flags."

―――

To be an expendable figure in a precious moment was a worrying thing. To consider one's self without grandness was a thought reserved for the deepest recesses of the soul. Such ideas led nowhere good. To some, he was the personification of wisdom. To others, he was a name lost to history. But he had a name; he had a wisdom to him. As did every single person in the world, of course; every single person who was born and died, from the ancient times to the times yet to come. Be they a peasant with hopes and dreams and grand delusions of comfort to come; or be they royalty, their greatness earned through fierce feats and glory.

The Actions of Gods

Moments came, and lives were lived. And no one truly understood anything else but their mind.

All things end.

Such sentiments are worrying, thought the king, moving easily with the sway of the boat, the rhythm of the oars. It was a pleasant thing, moving with the rocking of the deck, and something he'd never appreciated until now. Until this late, late hour.

In the water's hold, aboard this little craft, he was safe—more than safe, really. So, too, were the thousands of wild warrior savages he called upon. Up to this point, this very last moment, he had carried a crushing burden of guilt for the lives that could be lost, would be lost. He had taken that guilt with him through the trials, and it had almost crippled him. But now, that guilt was slowly finding its place, away from his mind and soul. That, too, was a worrying thing. No leader should be guiltless, but tonight the savage king felt young and beyond reproach. He looked to his comrades and thought they worried as he should have. Their brows were creased in silent thought, their knuckles white on clenched fingers. The floorboards beneath them were likely dented from the ceaseless, uneasy tapping of a thousand feet.

His scouts had briefed him about the floating town, flying Samaran banners, just waiting for reinforcing. How such a thing had come to be was no great puzzle: there was a river, many city barges, and a massive invading Southern army. It made sense, absurdly. What worried him more was his scout's words of movements.

Standing atop the deck with his closest allies surrounding him, he took deep, calming breaths and played the history of his once beloved army in his mind. He played the memory of their great fall once more, as he had done many times these last few days, ever since his scouts had spoken of the peculiar happenings in the river ahead. Or the lake ahead, more accurately. But now that they were only a day away from the strange floating sanctuary, the king was in no mood to delay or hold the charge. To be cautious. He looked at the map and the crudely figured piece in the deep blue, surrounded by so many attackers.

Not all, though.

Aye, though many Southerners besieged this strange gathering of boats, they were no match for the eager Islanders, just raring for a fight. Just raring to surprise the bastards.

And kill them all.

"Should we not wait until dawn? What's another night?" the hulking warrior general argued. He wasn't looking at the map flapping fiercely in the night, despite the weights keeping the piece secured to the table. Instead, the massive brute stared into the darkness beyond, at the distant lights. The growing lights. A coward might have thought him likeminded, desiring a further night's peace over driving on to the sanctuary. The king, however, believed him simply unenthusiastic about stepping off the barges. The behemoth had been born to the sea. He likely hoped there was a battle to be waged across the waters, and perhaps, at the city, there would be, should it have fallen.

Panic took the king for a breath, and he inhaled slowly, allowing it to centre his excitement.

Can what is lost be retaken?

"Better we get this done and dusted," the sly general argued, clapping the larger man on the back and watching the darkness as he did. He wasn't even limping anymore, despite the bandaging holding his knee in place. He might have been in pain but hid it in every step, much like the savage king did his own wounds. Sometimes there was just pain. Sometimes it could be controlled.

"Those Southern fuks will have watched us these last few weeks," the general growled. "Better we not delay."

It was a fine suggestion, and the king was glad of his input. He remembered hating him once. A long time ago. Now, he appreciated his cutting truths.

"I'm so fuken tired," the boy muttered. He was clad in armour; a sword in a leather scabbard clung lazily to his waist. He stretched and yawned, and the king could only mutter under his breath that the child was still among them, still offering his thoughts, still avoiding any word of work or battle. By the end of this night, he would be no boy. He would be a killer. Or else dead. Perhaps both. "I hate to go to war having not slept."

Another general, a rat-fuk from an unsavoury part of the Isles, could have stood on the deck with them. His army could have been sailing alongside, guaranteeing more significant successes, but the rat was nowhere to be found. More than that, they did not speak his name or lament his absence.

"Plenty of time to sleep if you get stabbed," the last general suggested, and there was uneasy laughter. She stood beside her king, and he was mesmerised by her. They all were. If nothing else, she had grown into the role these last few weeks. She rarely left this royal vessel, instead agonising over permutations of battle they might face. Kingly things, really, and she would be a fine king. "Well, it looks like they are expecting us," she hissed suddenly, and in the distance, a flame rose high into the night, and the king immediately knew his misstep.

His scouts had told him of vast numbers, impressive and patient. All camped and subdued. Perhaps had they slowed their charge. Settled a few miles up the river, they might not have prompted the attackers to action. As it was, this night was almost perfect for an invasion.

The future king looked at her liege and he could see her thoughts. They were at war this very moment. They hadn't arrived on time. "Swifter the charge," she roared, and the king agreed. He stepped to the front of the vessel and felt the order take effect. The black water churned as, deep below, the drumming intensified, and the roar of oar upon water drove them forward, away from the armada, leading the charge towards battle.

"It is time," the king roared, and tightened his belt. He checked his armour and, leaning out into the windy dark, embraced a terrible desire to fight, kill, wreak havoc, and win this night, if not for history or memory, then for the moment itself.

A wonderful, worrying moment at that.

Lillium had never felt more alive than she did now, at the end of her life. She knew this was the end because there was no way out of this dreadful final stand. But even moments like these passed. She moved past the Southern whore and met the first line of Southerners as they flooded up over the guardrail, and she was a torrent of wrath and rage. Built for this war, she moved with the violence, and the world slowed around her. Blades that neared her were knocked away and met with counters as though each blow offended her personally. Limbs were severed, crimson sprayed high, bodies fell away and her tally became legendary. Is this not how wars were fought? she mused, mid-kill. Countless dreadful acts of murder, all in the name of righteousness?

I am death to many.

Until this moment, she hadn't cared about reasoning. She had desired only a target, a vessel upon which to vent her anger, an increase in the number of dead. A slow stemming of the tide against an eternal ocean, if only for a few steps upon dryer land. She was rhythmic, and she was precise. She was Alpha, and she was divine. She was Lillium of the Blue, ready to die, but more than that, she was prepared to kill them all.

It is all I am.

In truth, not every blow was a killing blow, but it may as well have been. She stabbed through leather, through armour, into flesh, rightly fuken deep too, sending her attackers careening back down to the depths below. Few could survive a fall under these circumstances. Those who did were out of the fight, and that meant certain death. Behind her beautiful, grinning mask, she laughed in a frenzy for a savage moment and met every Southern fuker with as little mercy as possible. The roaring night became little more than the screaming of the dying and the falling. And she screamed defiantly with every blow.

I am ready.

Killing in blood was a fine end. Far more meaningful than dying alone, surrounded by little ones weeping and clawing for her last words, awaiting her last breath. She believed she'd wanted such a fate a lifetime ago, but she had lost her love of life in the dark, where vile fiends ravaged and were made to pay.

A Southerner crawled past her feet, startling her from her reverie. He was whimpering, and his hands slipped upon the crimson deck. He sought the edge from where he'd emerged—attempting a pathetic retreat from their line of defiance. Blood was seeping from his broken form. He'd tried to live, despite the injuries. She hesitated for only a moment. Suddenly, a great hammer came down upon him, and his head exploded like crushed, watery fruit under a vindictive fist, and it was a ghastly sight as blood splashed up and covered her mask. She watched the body quiver for a breath as its limbs struggled to fight on, escape, and move, because falling still was the end.

Life and struggle can be beautiful.

She could not draw her eyes from the Southerner. From the Southern body. From the human dying at her feet. She willed him some mercy, even as his whorish Southern vanquisher kicked him aside and hammered at the next warrior climbing onto the deck.

Fall still, warrior; your battle is done.

Still, the dying man shook, and she made out the blond hair, matted with skull, brain, blood and death, and she froze for just a breath longer. Flashes of her first victim struck her like a hammer upon flesh. She had hated her attacker that night far less than this man, who was unaware he was finished.

"Sleep, warrior," she called out, even as Doran swept past her, forsaking his weapons and using his tremendous strength to heft three unfortunate warriors back over the edge while she had been distracted.

"We will all sleep tonight," he roared, before stabbing down at the countless numbers clambering up towards them. "But let's stay awake longer, yeah?"

She thought them fine words, despite her hesitation. She thought on them and desired less to die, just a bit. She did not know why.

Had she come to this realisation quicker, she might not have met the blade's tip so swiftly, but meet it she did. Doran couldn't get to her in time, and the blade pierced her and sent her falling back.

Only Nomi saved her. It was a strange thing to see the Southern whore tending to her duty, hammering her vanquisher away. Only then did Lillium, dying, realise how doomed they all were. For there came a flash as bright as day, as fire, fed by the ample fuel in the lower decks, suddenly bloomed around them.

This is the end.

She could see the blood on her, but could not quite feel the pain. The ground suddenly shifted, and she found herself rolling. The world spun as the galleon broke apart, and such was the force she was thrown over a great, fiery drop. Incredibly, a hand took hold of her, and she swung for a brief moment in space. Injured and dizzy, scared and relieved, she hung above the raging fires in the decks below.

It was Nomi again who saved her. She lay flat on the tilting deck, stretched out and sliding ever slowly forward, pulled by Lillium's weight. Lillium could see the impressive strength but also the terrible fading strain in the girl's agonised grimace.

"Climb," Nomi shouted, and Lillium could see the world shift, the galleon collapsing, and she was dragging the girl with her. The smoke took both their breaths; it stung their eyes and blinded them with tears. Nomi redoubled her efforts as she fought for Lillium's life. Fought harder than anyone else ever had. But their slow slide towards the fire continued, inch by inevitable inch.

"Climb," Nomi cried a second time, desperately, and Lillium thought her heroic, stretched out, with her legs wrapped tight around the rail, hoping somehow to pull her back. If Lillium could, she would have climbed, but her body was too heavy, her limbs too shattered by exhaustion. She looked to the screaming girl fighting for her life and was grateful. So fuken grateful. Were she able to, she would have whispered her admiration and begged her forgiveness for every time she'd thought less of her. But instead, she summoned her strength for the end.

Suddenly the hand holding onto hers began to slip. She could hear Nomi begging her to hold on, for their comrades to help. There was a heroic plea in her tone, but now Lillium loosened her grasp completely.

"Let me go," she called to the girl, looking down at the burning fire beneath her. A terrible end, she thought, and hoped for a quick death.

"Please," Nomi begged, but their hands separated.

I don't want to die.

She fell into the flames.

The invading armada reached the shores and did not hesitate. At the front of the lead vessel, Magnus roared as any king should have in the final moments before an entire nation entered a war. He yelled, and they listened. They howled in reply, as though missing out on kills was a torment. It was savage and beautiful and fitting of their heritage and culture. They were Southerners born and bred, and ready for warring, but the savages were something else entirely. They leapt down the gangplanks and splashed through the waist-high water, howling their menace, and charged ashore in one terrifying wave of primal rage.

The Southerners emerged from the trees to meet them. Disjointed and without purpose, they turned their gaze from the burning floating sanctuary to an army hungry for battle. Although the defenders had the higher ground, they were without purpose; more than that, they were without discipline or a defensive position. They roared, and they were many. They had rightly sharp blades too, but they had never met savages born for war and honour. It was hardly a fair fight at all. Illuminated by the night's fires and the large lanterns burning along each edge of every barge, both factions went to war as though it were a murky dawn. Three hulking warriors bearing great battle Clieves led the line, and they led it well for all to follow. Their route was kept clear; their armour was heaviest, their weapons sharpest. They met the wary Southerners first, and it was brutal. For just a breath, King Magnus, with no crown, watched the three massive warriors, with no shield bearers to assist them, wade into the waves of defenders and keep going. Their strikes were efficient and emotionless, and their blades were quickly smeared in crimson. It took only a few dozen deaths and fewer breaths for the Southerners to turn tail, attempting to flee their strikes. He thought of a lone warrior upon a battlefield as a wave of cowards ran past. He thought of heroism and unfairness, and his heart hammered, not in weakness, not in struggle, but in triumph.

Around him, his generals leapt into the war, but Magnus held himself back and stayed aboard, at least for a time. Surrounding him were his battle hounds, raring and snapping and desperate to join the fray. He looked across to a couple of barges making dock at the floating town, and through the smoke and the gloom he could see friendly warriors greeting them, grasping them, marching with them back through the night towards the curs who attempted to invade. For just a moment, he might have felt a pang of guilt for the fact that it was, after all, his army's appearance that had set these events in motion, but watching his savages turn the tide of battle soon quenched such thoughts.

"Kill them all!" he demanded, and those not yet ashore roared in frustration and desire. It was no small wonder they were considered savages. He himself believed them a most enlightened people, of course; scholars as well. But come a fight, they were primal and beautiful. A good death was their true religion. Following their savage king's warmonger ways was simply the practice of such faith. He moved with the crowd, his sword drawn, quivering in excitement. The savages had landed, and the South would meet some fresh defiance.

―――

Wynn watched the flapping flags of the savages in disbelief as they neared the edge, lowered their gangplanks, and let themselves loose upon the unprepared Southerners. He let out a whoop of excitement, but his enthusiasm was drowned in the screams of his victims. So many victims.

Not enough.

Beside him, his comrades struck and slaughtered and somehow held the line against wave after wave of surging rats. So many lives were lost around them; around him too. There was a numbness that came with such barbarism: a strange thing, but a thing appreciated.

He imagined speaking with Lillium after the battle, knowing she would likely approve of such detachment. Was she herself not the definition of cold and murderous detachment? And did that make her any less of a good person? He didn't know; he didn't care. He had stepped into this battle knowing he would die, and now, there came a miraculous landfall from nowhere. He might die the following day, but he would live that last day as a good day. And were he given more days after that, he would live every one of them to its fullest. For too long, he'd hidden his own fears and regrets. He'd fuked up his life, but he'd lived a good and important one. That was more than most people could say.

The deck shook under his feet, and he almost went over the side into the black nothing below, where a thousand blades waited to end his life. The brute he was killing held his struggles for a moment as both reset their balance and found better footing before commencing their desperate battle, which ended a few moments later when the Southerner, bleeding and screaming, fell headfirst to the ground below. Only then could Wynn marvel at the gush of savages charging up from the riverbank and fanning out into the night, descending upon the Southerners, slaying them as violently as the tales had foretold.

He searched among them for Magnus. For why else would such lunatics appear to turn the tide against the night? For an entire breath, he gazed at them, marvelling at their beauty as they tore and struck and killed and drove through line after line of Southerners. Aye, they were not invincible. They bled, fell, and cried out as death took them, but the Southerners suffered more.

"Look to the night," he cried, and pointed to the reinforcements, to hope. Only then did he realise it was only he standing the line now. Almost tripping upon a quivering body, he spun around to see the bald Doran scrambling down towards Nomi, who appeared to have been felled by a brute. The ship was ablaze, the smoke was overpowering, the deck had shattered, and he stood upon a burning pyre, but more than that, he had left her behind.

"But they have come," he whispered, and the terror took him. Distraction had taken his concentration and had made him fail the line. He realised, as Nomi screamed, that his former mate, his closest friend, had fallen to the fires.

I failed you at the end.

He caught sight of Doran scrambling for Nomi. He reached for her, even as the deck shuddered again, and suddenly, she was gone too, dropped into the furnace below, and Wynn was broken. He could have screamed for their deaths and charged after Doran, who lay over the hole of fire, wailing in anger. Instead, Wynn turned back towards the edge and the few curs attempting to climb over.

One last charge.

In one savage swipe, he took three from the top before climbing over the edge and looking to the brutes below. They were caught between the charging savages and the arduous climb back up to tear at the last defiant warrior. He took the decision from them. Carelessly, he dropped to the blackness below, landing upon unprepared attackers as he did. He had a plan. A stupid plan. He cared little if it worked.

He earned enough room to swing his blades, and that was all it took.

Through their confusion, terror, and smoky vision, he tore them asunder, spinning like a whirlpool in a savage storm. He moved through the dim light like a demon of fire, and they fled from him, and he killed them for it. They scampered away from the galleon; they rushed out from the charging savages, fled their camp, and yelled as they did. He screamed with them and did not give up the fight. Instead, he attacked, murdered and wailed aloud. He fell upon them and gave everything he had. Perhaps, had they the will, they might have collectively spun and attacked. Sent a few hundred blade tips his way. Had they done so, they might have found courage in their numbers. Might have gathered a line of their own and held him at bay. But they cowered; they retreated. They left their machines of war behind as well.

Wynn, behind his demented mask, joined with the savages. Seeking out murder among the trees he charged with them, until eventually, when exhaustion rendered him incapable of any further step or blow, he collapsed, gasping and weeping in the dark. Removing his mask, he dared not look back to the blazing fires of his friends' pyre. He could only look away like the coward he had once been.

And then, suddenly, he was no longer alone. A pack of hounds surrounded him. Their hissing and snapping were both terrifying and reassuring. He knew those boys, and they knew him. With the screams fading in the night, he succumbed to the licks of his master general's hounds. When a figure approached him, he already knew who greeted him.

"You still live," Wynn whispered.

"I am eternal," Magnus declared, pulling him to his feet.

Nomi watched in horror as Lillium struck a jutting beam on her dreadful fall to the bottom of the wrecked ship. The demonic girl fell silent and landed face down in a torrent of water gushing in from below. A crushing terror took Nomi, and she froze. But only for a breath. A last breath, perhaps. It was all she could do. She heard the bald Alpha scream after her, but it didn't matter. The fall was swift. More elegant than Lillium's. Perhaps knowing a softer landing awaited her helped. Through the flame she dropped, feeling heat and sparks as they touched her naked skin and took light upon her flowing locks before being extinguished in the water below. It was no easy landing, and Nomi hit hard enough to wind herself and nearly knock herself unconscious.

"Lillium," she gasped, fighting to stay afloat in her armour. Above her, the night was a furnace of burning light and smoky death. Around her, though, was simply warmth and a thundering sound. Fleetingly, she wondered whether it was actually safer to be here, inside this burning furnace. She cried for Doran to drop down with her, but he was already gone from the edge, no doubt surrendering her and Lillium to death, no doubt venting his wrath on her former people. "Wake up," she cried, wading clumsily over to the unconscious girl. For a terrible moment, she worried Lillium had died in the fall, or from blood loss from the blade to her shoulder, or by breaking her neck on the way down.

Heroes don't die this way.

She could hear the roar of war on the other side of the burning hull, and it sounded louder still from within this smouldering tomb. Whoever remained was giving a fair fight.

We are still fighting, too.

"Come on," she demanded, gripping Lillium and rolling her over before lifting the mask from her face and shaking her fiercely lest there be water in her lungs. "Wake up!"

Lillium stirred ever so, and Nomi held her above the water as it gushed in around them like a violent waterfall, and only then did she realise how swiftly the hull was surrendering to the rising water. Above them, the failing ship began to break up, piece by piece, with loud, ominous booms, and she saw significant cracks appearing along each side, and she willed Wynn and Doran to flee the deck lest it crumble and crush them all.

"We have to go," she pleaded, and Lillium slipped below the bobbing water and she dragged her back above. "I can't get you out of here like this." She was terrified of drowning, but she could not leave Lillium behind.

"Wake the fuk up!"

They were sufficient words, and the girl struggled in her arms like a drunk suddenly pulled from a deep slumber. Barely conscious, she was helpless, and Nomi, taking a breath, wrapped her arm around the girl and edged to the side where the vessel had struck land and broken open. Although she knew the dangers faced by one woken after a blow to the head, she threw caution to the wind and slapped her once across the face, and Lillium reacted ever so. She blinked her eyes open for a breath, but Nomi knew her to be barely capable.

"Fine, I'll do it myself. Take a fuken breath," she cried to her comrade, to herself too, before dragging the girl beneath the surface, out towards the gap, out away from the failing galleon, out into savage waters where the war still raged. It was no easy task, and Lillium's dead weight tested her every stroke.

But her burning lungs and aching limbs obeyed her wishes. She'd always claimed to be a great swimmer; this terrible task was the ultimate test. She glided and pulled and somehow broke clear into cooler water, and as they cleared the galleon, the burden in her grip suddenly lurched and fought before wrapping its arms around her tightly.

Lillium struggled and gasped, which was a good thing, even when the girl took hold of her and tried pulling her down to the dark. Nomi recognised the desperation of the drowning girl, and knew well the strength that the drowning unleashed upon those who rescued them. Holding her breath, choosing her moves, she drove her foot deep into Lillium's stomach, freeing herself before pulling at the girl's fine locks until she screamed and released her grip, and Nomi pulled her back above the water, just as her feet touched the edge of the shore.

"Easy, my friend," she cried, slapping her again to nullify her panicked instincts. It was a fine strike, for it calmed the girl, and she settled and, leaning on Nomi, fell against the edge of the water as a thousand strange warriors appeared from the dark and sought out the Southern threat.

"Nomi?"

"Are you well, my friend?"

"I fell. I was dead. Am I dead?"

"We are still fighting."

"You... saved me?"

"Of course I did."

For a few breaths, both warriors lay by the water gasping for air, recovering their will, watching the dead float by and the rest face off against a strange army.

"Magnus has returned," Lillium said feverishly, and struggled to rise. Nomi could see the renewed spark in her eyes. She was coherent and ready to go to war. There was just the small matter of her injury holding her back. This, too, didn't faze her for very long. Stuffing a shard of cloth from her shirt into the offending hole, she cursed. "We need to join these mad fuks and kill them all." With a will Nomi hadn't expected, the Alpha climbed to her feet, waded into a group of fallen warriors, and began rummaging through their clothing. "We need weapons," she muttered, and Nomi thought her as impressive as Lea.

Around them, a tide of warriors from the decks of countless barges streamed ashore. They howled like the clans of her people, desperate for a righteous war. They fought and died and never surrendered a foot of territory. She watched her people beaten back, and Nomi thought them incredible. Suddenly being part of this charge felt significant.

Scrambling alongside Lillium, she recovered an axe from a dead Southerner. It was a fine, double-edged weapon; its dual blades resembled a beautiful, bloody butterfly, and she fell in love immediately. Hoisting it aloft, she felt its weight and loved it even more. Beside her, Lillium, still feeling the effect of the wound, could only recover a crossbow, and she cursed her luck. She eyed Nomi enviously before slipping the demonic mask back over her face.

Near broken and battered, they scrambled from the river's edge into the darkened forest, alive with the sounds of fighting and slaughter. "I will cover you," Nomi pledged, matching the hobbling girl's lesser pace.

It didn't take long to come upon three Southerners too foolish to retreat with their comrades. They charged from the cover of the treeline, screaming vile curses and viler threats. Lillium killed the closest with a shot through the eyes. As his remaining comrades charged down towards her, she calmly reloaded, no doubt believing Nomi's pledge.

"I cannot remember how many I have killed," she said, casually flicking damp hair from her face as she placed another bolt. Nomi could not remember her tally either, but that was fine: as long as it was more than the lives she had taken while marching with the Hunt.

Nomi met the nearest fiend with her new weapon, and it was easy. Her axe broke effortlessly through his defence, shattering his feeble blade and embedding itself in his chest. She watched as he gasped, struggled and died. She turned to face the last man, but he was already kneeling, clutching his throat where Lillium's bolt had penetrated.

"But for these next few moments, I am beating you two to one, friend," Lillium declared, ripping the bolt free and looking into the night towards her next targets.

Around them, there were signs of retreat as Southerners fled the savage newcomers, and Nomi couldn't believe such a miraculous thing. When the distant horn of retreat filled the air, she was elated, and suddenly her belief in victory in this terrible war reared its weary head. She gripped Lillium's shoulder.

"This battle is done; let us call it eight apiece."

Lillium held a shot with her crossbow for a moment, and Nomi looked into the night at a warrior watching atop a great steed a terrific distance away. Lillium lifted her crossbow high. "I dislike draws," she whispered, and released. The bolt was invisible to the eye, its deadly strike soundless in the night. The cur shook as it took him through the heart. He gripped at the bolt clumsily and fell from his mount, which ambled off into the night, oblivious to its rider's fate. "I win."

"For tonight, you do," Nomi conceded, gripping the injured girl under the arm and leading her back towards the light of victory, comrades and belief.

Doran remained upon the deck when everyone left him behind, for he had no better idea what to do. He could only fight and kill and wait to die or live. Whichever occurred first. His stomach churned, his back ached, his knees buckled, and he surrendered to exhaustion.

Watching the roving savages charge through the Southerners, he could feel no joy; no triumph either. He only felt sorrowful, the type of sorrow that can break a man or woman in the dark of night, when everyone else has gone. Stripped from a burning deck. Torn apart in the middle of a battlefield, killed mid-conversation by a cruel arrow when seeking solace. He looked at his ruined hand, hidden behind the clawed contraption that gave the appearance of a deathly grip. He was less of a man than he had once been, even less now.

He watched the masked figure of Wynn tear out into the darkness in search of death, and he admired the boy. He looked to the night and felt strangely elated, seeing Lillium and Nomi draw ashore. He thought Lillium was as beautiful as always, even hidden behind that ghastly mask. Perhaps, had he energy, he might have called out to her. Might even have told her his feelings about the mask. Instead, he watched her hobble up towards the trees, killing as she went, and he was in awe of her. But there was also a melancholy in watching her from so far behind.

Everyone leaves me behind.

Though their legacy remained, the brutes had stopped streaming over the galleon's edge. The cracked edge was covered in blood and other bodily matter. It had been a mighty stand, but Doran was weaker in the soul than he'd ever thought. He was ready to be done with this war. Along with the miraculous arrival of the savages had come his responsibility for this cursed gathering of vessels.

The deck suddenly shook violently around him, and beneath the smoke and growing flame, he could see the rats of the South scurry away like the vile vermin they were. The deck shifted again; he heard the terrible breaking of support beams, and he felt his stomach lurch, felt his lungs struggle against the smoke, yet still, Doran did not shift with it. Instead, he contemplated, for a smoky breath, standing his ground and going down with the burning ship.

Do not do this.

He heard Celeste's voice in his mind, and he was ashamed of his desire. He knew it to be his mind, willing him to step over and save himself to kill again. He watched for a bit longer, though. Perhaps, if he watched long enough, the deck would collapse, and he would burn away and be lost to the annals of time. Forgotten by most.

"Do not do this," he growled, and spoken aloud, the words made a good argument. Despite his size, he slipped over the edge gracefully and, ducking low, dropped to the ground below, breaking his fall on the many dead bodies at the bottom.

Winded and shaking, he looked to the night and listened to the war cries as the first melodies of victory were rung out. Only then did he see the emergence of his Wolves from across the sanctuary, haggard and battered but willing to continue their fight. He fell among them as the savages, accepting these Wolfen legends as comrades, patted backs, cheered the death of the Southerners, and met as one army under a master general, fierce enough to lead them.

Living is the best revenge.

For now.

It was her voice again, and he wondered briefly was it a final message from the dark beyond. A letter of love from a female who'd never loved him.

He walked to the riverbank. He could make out the burning sanctuary in the gloom, surrendering to the fire eaters as they went to task. He might have felt pride at their actions, but this solitary misery was for him alone. Sitting down in the water, he weakly washed the ruin from his body. He could hear the distant voice of Magnus the Warmonger, barking orders. More than that, he could see Mea upon the edge of Boat Town, rallying her people as only a goddess could. He felt a little spark of warmth for the world, but looking back to the darker depths of Boat Town and to where the mother of his unborn child had fallen, he broke a little.

Dipping his face in the water, he felt the silent tears course through his body and allowed them. Out here, in the dark water, surrounded by growing revelry, who would notice a balding brute as he succumbed to the unfairness of his life?

He came up for air, and she was upon him. He fought her hold for a breath, but there was a gentle cooing, and he looked to a pair of demented eyes, staring at him through a mask.

"Everything is all right, hero," she said, and at that moment, he almost loved her. He gripped Lillium's arm lest she draw away and take her warmth with her.

"I can't…"

"Shush, comrade. Let yourself be free of this," she whispered, and embraced him fully as she sat with him, rocking him gently in the water like a mother with a newborn.

He felt pathetic for his weakness, but somehow, he knew she understood better than most.

"We can stay here all night," she reassured him. He'd never heard her use such a kind tone, and he welcomed it. More than that, the tears continued to flow, and after a time, when the rocking had soothed him to stillness, he whispered to her of Celeste's passing and his unborn child.

After a time, she removed the mask, kissed him once upon the lips, and placed her forehead to his. He was no craven fool believing her to be tempting him. He knew it to be kindness, and for just a moment, he felt that spark stir, felt himself stronger. A lesser and a sadder man from now on, but strong enough now to break the embrace and stand with her, to rise up out of the water.

Mea stood out along the edge of Boat Town, watching those she called allies tearing their near-conquerors apart. Around her, the wailing of those left behind by the dead was terrible, like beasts braying in the night. No more awful sound had ever been uttered. She wanted to lament with them. She had lost friends this night, and comrades of war too. Mostly, though, she'd lost strangers who had fought under her banner, and somehow this was even more tragic.

She gazed at Magnus in all his magnificence. The godly brute who had escaped the worst clutches of inevitability only to return with tenfold the violence. She felt like no leader this night, even though they rallied around her, weeping, praising, seeking answers, seeking guidance. Nevertheless, she instinctively answered their questions. Her words fell from her lips like any politician's, and they came naturally. She was impressive and reassuring, and she hated herself for it. All her life, she had craved leadership. Believed herself capable and noble. That wasn't enough, though. She had failed, as had Dia before her.

"It's all right, little one," Mea said, dropping to her knees by the little female. The girl wailed for Melinda. Torn and dead and ruined, her lifeless body still pinned to the deck. The little one had been watched over by the dead Alphaline, and indeed, her passing was a tragedy. Admittedly, it was also one fewer dissenting voice, and a reminder how costly and easy the loss of any Alphalines was to a stray arrow or a dozen. Still, Mea would have taken a thousand more dissenters to have the girl and at least a dozen of her comrades restored to life.

The girl leapt into Mea's arms, and Mea held her until the wailing had passed, after which Mea left her to mourn alone. She had other duties, but more than that, she needed to walk this horror away. Dropping her sword, for she feared no further attack while she moved among so many allies, she walked along the edge of Boat Town, watching the night, watching the settling of victory. Those she passed held their suffering for a time to gaze up in awe, with worshipping eyes, grateful to her for leading them to victory, and she felt herself a fraud.

No one else will do it.

Eventually, at the southernmost edge, where the fighting had been heaviest, she caught sight of her beautiful mate standing alone on the deck below the growing revelry. He still held his sword and shield, which he'd used so expertly through the terrible savagery. He had fought until the last savage was sent scurrying from their territory. He hadn't faced the crowd; she thought it a pleasing strategy.

"My love," she called, and he flinched for a breath. "My love, we survived," she whispered, coming up beside him.

He tried to speak but failed, and once again looked back out into the night towards the savages celebrating and preparing for their next march. "I… can't… feel…" he stammered, and then began to shake uncontrollably.

Oh, please, no.

Had he been struck?

She checked him for injury. Checked for a blade. Checked for anything. He shook as though his body had lost the run of itself, and she could hear the cheering behind her. "Where are you struck?" she cried, and desperately sought out the injury. She called for a healer, but her voice was weak.

"I can't take this," he gasped, and fell into her arms. His eyes rolled back in his head, and she thought him to be falling unconscious. "I…

too... much. It's too much." She didn't understand. He convulsed and shook, and she wrapped herself around him as though taking the invisible injury from him. "I lived a life before this," he whimpered, and for a moment, she wondered whether his mind was broken.

"You can live, my darling. Come back to me." Her voice cracked, her arms ached from containing his struggles, and suddenly, he fell still. He dropped his blade; his sword, too. They clattered loudly onto the deck, and she jumped, as did he. And then he calmed. His breathing became deeper and stronger. "Come back to me."

"I... will, my love," he whispered, and curled up and shook a little, though less violently than before, and only then did she realise the strength of her mate. Broken, scared, lost, yet still he fought, still, he stood, still he did the right thing, until the moment had passed. This was no life for a warrior, she thought, for one as deeply wounded in the soul as this man was.

"I will pull you from this horror, my love," she promised.

"Thank you," he gasped, and she could hear his voice strengthening as he pushed the terror further down. Not gone. Just away, to lie in wait. She had never uttered truer words in her life. Only now, in this moment, did she understand love and companionship. Only now did she understand the sacrifice required of any Primary.

"We will survive this horror. We will step away from this world. We will find ourselves once more. We will never be apart again," she pledged.

It was a fine pledge.

The absent gods agreed.

Kovak watched the turn with morbid interest. His better judgement suggested he turn and flee as the battle neared its end, and these mysterious, savage warriors slowed their charge and savoured their victory. He caught sight of two women struggling through the trees towards him. They looked battered and beaten, and still, they charged, and he thought this most curious and worrying.

He considered charging down through the trees with sword raised and murder on his mind. Another part of his mind suggested he flee and warn the others of this horror. "Mercy it is," he muttered, deciding against killing the two warriors. No sooner had he uttered the words than he saw one of the girls raise a crossbow. "Too far, little one," he mocked, and, gripping his mount's reins, he turned to leave when a bolt embedded itself in his chest.

"Not like this," he argued with the wind, with the fates of chance, with his fuken god, if the cur was watching from his unsteady seat in the city. He received no reply. He only felt pain and a terrible weakness come upon him. A final, terrible exhaustion took him as he fell from his mount, and though he tried to stir himself, he realised his limbs were no longer obeying him. "To the fires with this," he gasped, and closed his eyes in death.

82

SWIFT GOODBYE

Her name was Aurora, and she liked to kill. Sometimes she liked to eat her kill too. But not today. Not like this. Her eyes burned as they stared at the ceiling above her perfect head. Burned and teared up as she tried desperately not to blink. Not to miss a moment of the struggle. She did not like the sheets she lay in. These sheets were unworthy of her. Still, this was her penance, she supposed, although she needed penance like she needed a knife in the belly. Or the back. Oh, yes, the back would be delicious. To never see it coming and feel the surprise. And the ripping pain too. It's what she was worthy of.

Among these sheets, where she stared and thought about dying, she ignored the brothers as best she could. It was a tricky thing, for their voices were so loud, booming, imposing and impressive, the two of them at odds with each other. Ealis would have cared about such things, but Aurora didn't. She cared only about keeping her eyes on the dangling spider above her. There was beauty in such things.

Both behemoths muttered to each other for a time, but she no longer cared. It was time to leave this sieged settlement and disappear to nothing. Her place was no longer among these outcasts, these heroes, these legends. Hers was a different calling in the city.

Once, back in the cursed town, she had considered Wrek a friend. Not here. Not with his family around, and that was fine. Family was precarious, she supposed. She imagined. The closest family she had was Tempest. Or Aimee. And neither of them desired to call Ealis or Aurora family. Best to go. To rid them of her presence. Better that way.

The spider took a wrong turn and neared some smooth sandstone. She held her breath. She fought the urge to blink.

Don't go that way. Anywhere but that way.

"I'm sorry, Aurora," Wrek muttered apologetically, and she shrugged carefully in her bedding. She could see the brute standing at the doorway. Everyone left behind little Aurora, Fyre of the Night, and that, too, was fine. She had grander schemes. "I will request you be released."

It was a weak offer, and she finally blinked. The stinging eased, but only a little. She did not look his way, nor would she. He and the rest of their comrades had denied her a chance to redeem herself, to fight in a desperate war against insurmountable odds. Their actions were their own, and hers were her own, too.

The spider struggled, he dangled, and her heart skipped a beat in excitement, "Oh, please," she willed the arachnid, and it must have heard her in its mind. It dropped a foot from the web, looking for an easier path to wherever it journeyed.

Back to your babies?

So you can feast on them?

She squirmed a little in her bedding and enjoyed how badly her body reeked. The wash basin and towel remained unused in the corner. Uden would desire her less in such a state, which pleased her. She heard Wrek leave, which pleased her too, and the spider dropped a little more. It hung closer, and she could see its dangling legs right above her. Could see the skull markings upon its bulbous body, and she thought it most attractive.

Delicious.

She knew her time in this place was drawing to a close. She knew the woman as Kaya, and indeed, she was a crafty bitch. Vicious too. Truthfully, falling to a midnight assassination at the hands of this warrior would be an acceptable death in itself. Perhaps a knife through the back. She could see it in Kaya's eyes when she'd attacked her at the gates of Adawan. Ealis had often wondered would their paths cross again, and she had hoped they would. The woman deserved her vengeance.

Above her, the beastie spun upon its strand, and she willed it to fall. She opened her mouth and raised her godly head to meet it halfway. "Fall into me, little one," she whispered, and the arachnid continued to drop. And Aurora continued to wait.

The flickering torch illuminating this dreadful cell began to fail as she did, and she thought it a portent of beautiful things. Wonderful, glorious things happened in the dark. She licked her lips and willed her companion to fall a little more. Just a smidgen. She imagined that silken strand just creaking and snapping. She imagined her little friend screaming silently as it dropped the last foot. She wondered, if she opened her mouth wide enough, would it fall in, down her throat and drown in her belly? That would be beautiful.

She had always thought spiders were delightful things. She wondered whether it deserved such a fate. And then, a hand's length above her luscious lips, the spider dropped and landed upon her smile. She kept her mouth closed. She called it mercy. She felt the magnificent arachnid scramble across her beautiful face, seeking leverage, seeking a way to kill her, and she wished it well, allowing it to slip down her cheek, along her chin, down around her neck where it lost itself, no doubt happily, in her luscious hair.

"It's time to leave this place," she said aloud to the gods that listened, to the wind that could never breach this awful place, to her little arachnid companion.

Shaking her hair a few times, she slipped from her bedding, stood, and turned to attack the edge of her bed. It was old and rickety, and a few swift kicks knocked one of the metal legs free. She swiftly gathered up her bed sheets, and after a cursory glance out into the corridor for the guards, she wrapped the sheets around two bars and, wrapping them over once more, placed the metal bed leg between them and began spinning it as though raising an anchor from a galleon. Within a breath, the sheets were taut, and she kept twisting.

It wasn't the most secure prison cell at all. Ironic, she thought, considering the inhabitants of this place. Soon enough, she heard the groaning of weak, bending steel.

"Take it," she gushed to the metal, as though it were a lover she demanded more from. And the bars answered her will; they creaked and bent, and then, with a gentle shoulder nudge, she popped them out of their sockets in the weak rock salt.

Easy.

Catching the pieces, lest their echo wake the soon-to-be dead, she left them by her bed before gathering what clothes she had. Her belongings were gone but for an innocent canister attached to her belt. And such a thing was crucial. Had she not kept it safe throughout these last few horrible weeks? She stroked the canister and dared not open it or drink from it. It was the last of Emir's foul serum, taken from her comrades in Raven Rock, kept free of Uden's touch as a parting gift. Now it would be one other gift.

"Hello? I need water," she said to the gloom and received no reply. Struggling between the bars, she wondered had she put on a bit of weight, before taking a deep breath and slipping through from cage to freedom.

Real fuken easy.

She sprinted through the dark hallways, following her route from memory, avoiding any wandering bandits; she reached the grand stairs and kept running. She was elated, free, hopeful, and hungry too. All of these feelings and sensations were wonderful. She only had to catch herself counting every few hundred steps or so, and though the going was tough, she dared not slow, dared not get distracted, until she won the race for her fate at the top of the steps, where she stopped for a moment and stared out into the bright night.

Moving on again, she slunk through the shadows like a rat seeking nourishment. She could hear the roar of war in the distance and was drawn to it. A beautiful beat to dance to, to kill to. She wanted a little death; a little drumming too. Quietly, she slipped through the barricades out into the darkness towards devastation; it was easy.

Glorious.

Her steps were swift, her trail easy to follow. She could see many figures celebrating and standing over the dead, which pleased her. She slipped through the darkness, away from the victorious, out towards the other grounds where the deceased lay. Two armies had met while she lay in her bedding, caged and denied. She imagined beautiful visions of the carnage and tried to savour the smell of burnt flesh. It was the finer part of her day.

Keeping her beautiful eyes to the ground, she stayed low as she moved through the Southern camp where the dead still lay. Scouring each body for treasures, she found much success. She stole some grey Southern garments, ripping and tearing them away from the broken flesh of their wearers. She recovered two blades and a crossbow too. Around her waist she slung a quiver brim-full of new bolts—everything a goddess would ever need.

"Thank you," she whispered to the dead bodies, and slipped far wide of the battle, out towards the rear of the camp. Feeling wonderfully decadent in her new outfit, Aurora Borealis, born in blood and vengeance, slipped from one army to another. She felt at ease among them, and for a breath, she wondered how easy it might be to twist herself back into power.

They stole me, Uden, but I came back to you.

She imagined such a reunion and, for a terrible moment, enjoyed the abuse he would heap upon her. She might deserve it, too—not for her crimes against Uden but for her crimes against the others. Oh, she had committed crimes. A thousand victims flashed in her mind and formed one terrible beauty: a redhead, bent over, shot a second time.

Shaking away the thoughts, Aurora marched deeper into hostile territory. She recognised this setting all too well: their hushed tones, their anguished outbursts, the way they ate and furrowed—the latter she imagined from the low groaning in many nearby tents. They were half-beaten, but a goddess like her could have rallied them to a fine counterattack. For only a breath did she imagine it could have been her leading this massive group. Such an honour would have been worthy of her greatness. And the final taking of her soul too.

She counted thousands as she walked through the camp. Many thousands. Or at least a healthy number of thousands. A girl could go a little mad trying to count the ways to kill so many. Aurora wished she had more gifts to assist her with such a task.

This is all I have, and it is beautiful and foolish.

She saw that there were many large water carts lined up at the centre of this massive army. The days were hot; she understood the need for abundant water, though as she counted the wooden behemoths, she wondered if there was enough water to last a week. Did the rest of the warriors count the water carts as she did? She licked her lips and slipped behind the nearest cart, and, silent as the dawn, she climbed up and crept along its top until she came to the sealing cap. Looking around for any passing guard, she lifted it and quietly slid it across a half foot. Below, she could hear the slosh of water, quivering slightly and waiting to be drunk. Taking out her canister of Emir's vile serum, she popped the cork and poured a mouthful into the water tank before returning both caps.

Footsteps.

Truthfully, she knew little of the potency of such a serum, but in better times, when they had been friends, and she had queried, Emir had promised it took less than a drop in a barrel of spring water to contaminate it.

Closer now.

She looked over the edge of the tank and then dropped soundlessly upon a patrolling guard. The younger warrior struggled for a breath, but Aurora slid her dagger through his throat. The felled man tried to scream, but could only bleed silently in the grass. When he was spent, Aurora dragged the broken body towards a nearby empty tent. The owner, no doubt felled in an earlier skirmish, had left their life's belongings where they lay. Ealis might have spent the night sifting through them, getting to know this fallen hero and feeling fine about it, but she had other things to distract her. Pressing tasks to be completed. Great havoc to be wreaked.

"Enough of this delay," she whispered, dumping her burden and slipping free of the tent. She moved to the next cart, climbing to its top as before and dripping more of Emir's solution into the water.

Wonderfully easy.

She did not know how long it took her to contaminate all of the carts, but long before dawn, she dropped the poisonous canister with its last few toxic drops into the final water cart and dropped to the ground. She dragged a fourth and final body back to the tent and left her to lay with the rest of the dead.

"Four is a good number, my wandering friends," she whispered, and slipped free of the tent, buckling it closed as she did.

Walking away back through the camp, she hummed a few notes under her breath. No warrior noticed her, not even when she recovered a fine mount and walked it to the edge of the camp.

"I will call you Orin," she told her mount, and climbed atop the magnificent beast.

She moved through the camp without causing any alarm. She heard the first panicked cries only as she broke clear of the base. "Is this a gift?" she whispered to the fine beast upon finding the water tankard attached to the saddle. It was half full. "Enough for the journey to come," she declared, bringing her horse to trot. "Going to the city," she sang as the dawn's first rays broke over the horizon. Her voice was both terrible and wonderful. "Going to get me my family," she sang, and felt marvellous and terrified, and it was magnificent knowing her death was but a few days away.

83

EDGING THE SIEGE

The two brothers sat along the slope, looking out across the open stretch of the battlefield. Two giants among mortals. Each bearded, battered and brutal in his own way. Any fool wandering by could see the uncomfortable silence between them. And why wouldn't they be uncomfortable? They had been best friends once, but they were also family; there was no tighter bond, not even among some mated Alphas. Such cruel splits were the hardest to recover from, even if they were humbled, battle-worn, regretful, and lonely for camaraderie. The dawn was beginning to birth the day, the heat already warming their grizzled faces. In their hands, they each held a tankard of water. With little else to do, they sipped more than needed, even with the growing heat.

"It must have been some battle," Wrek said after a time. It was all he could think of to break the silence. He did not meet his brother's eyes. He was not ready to do so, and, strangely, Ulrik wouldn't meet his either. There were better companions to share the dawn with, yet Wrek would be beside no other on this last day. Not with words left unsaid. Years' worth of words.

Where to start?

"It was, brother. Brutal. I haven't forgotten the things I saw. Nor will I ever."

Wrek could only nod in agreement. He'd seen horrors that he could never shake free, but could not speak of them yet. Instead, he looked across to the foreign invaders and wondered about their mysterious stillness. They'd not stirred for a day, a night and a morning now. Not since Tye had sent them running in the middle of the night.

Wrek wondered whether there might be no further battles. Might Adawan have held itself against possible numbers? But hope was a dangerous thing. A part of him relished the idea of staying behind these sandbanks and stakes, digging in and retiring from this life. Another part of him feared for the reinforcements that would appear on the horizon and wash up and over these fine leaking walls in one empowering charge. A third part desired a counter-charge, while the Southerners hesitated. He licked his lips and savoured their wetness. A rare thing in these sands. And a poignant reminder of the Southerners, who called upon lesser reserves. Such things as water and food changed the course of wars.

"There will be memorable things to come," Wrek said.

"I reckon we will remember them together," Ulrik offered softly.

It was a comforting thought, and for just a breath, it felt like brotherhood. Wrek ached to tell his older brother about his time away from this place. To speak of the hardships, joys, and adventures too. Brothers of blood and of the road were inclined to discuss such things when returning as equals.

He remembered the surprise on Ulrik's face, from behind his cell door, seeing him forsake freedom in exchange for honour and attempted contrition. It was a good start. Sitting on the edge of battle awaiting invasion helped also. For a moment, Wrek pondered how fine it was to make a mistake and be forgiven. He dared a glance at Ulrik and almost smiled. Almost, but not quite. Not yet.

Ulrik leaned in close now. "I heard you held the city by the throat for a time and lost it all." He turned and stared at Wrek, and there was kindness in those cold, worn eyes. Warmth in his mocking too.

"Got replaced, I did," Wrek admitted.

"By that little shit Sigi, too."

"You heard that?"

"Aye. Had a little dealing with him. Paid me to… keep Elise in check. Keep her… safe. Fuker had no clue who she was. He did it for his mate-in-waiting or some shit. I just took payment, and I am lesser for it."

Wrek couldn't help it. It was the sibling in him. "I heard you got beaten up by a girl."

"There are worse fates," Ulrik countered, but he held that grin. She had been no girl. She was a goddess. "At least I wasn't alone. Bison took a right beating too."

"By a girl."

"Aye, by a fuken girl with a devastating strike." They laughed, and it reminded Wrek of the camaraderie out in the Wastes in better times.

"You don't resent what occurred?" Wrek asked softly.

"I resent many things, but things occurred as they did. I call it the actions of absent gods."

"Well, for what it's worth, I think this a fine army you amassed," Wrek said.

"I was impressive, at least for a time," Ulrik said, turning back to watch the opposite camp. His water was never too far from his lips. "Lost it all, and I'm better for it," he said, and chuckled at his misfortune. It felt like they hadn't been at odds with each other for so long.

"It was only when I had it all that I began to see things differently," Wrek admitted. He took a long, deep breath. "I'm sorry," he whispered.

Ulrik nodded. It was not acceptance. Nor was it condemnation. It was something, though, and that was enough.

"So, what now, little Wreckless? Will you wage war? Will you take back what Sigi took?"

"I will stand by your side if you will have me."

"It is good to have a brother again. I desired to lose no more. Two lost is many."

"Aye."

They sat for a time and watched the dawn. Listened to their comrades rouse themselves for war. After a time, Ulrik pulled a tankard from his belt. He drank from it, and Wrek recognised the smell of Sigi's brew. He'd have drained that tankard a year ago to face the day, and the coming storm too. Ulrik offered the tankard to him, but he declined. Sometimes, alcohol was not the answer to everything.

"Drink with me, brother," Ulrik insisted, and Wrek begrudgingly drank a mouthful, sharing in camaraderie.

"So, did you meet anyone special in your travels?" Ulrik asked.

"Aye, someone. I do not know her fate."

"I'm sorry to hear that, brother," Ulrik said, sealing the tankard for after victory.

"And you?" Wrek asked, looking around them. "Are you... with a lover that I might know as a comrade?" It wasn't the most convincing attempt, but it was an attempt. Years late in the making. Ulrik suddenly squeezed his eyes shut as though taken with a powerful headache. He shuddered and gasped for just a breath.

"Thank you for asking," he whispered.

The drums of war suddenly erupted around them. In the camp below, those not already stirring roused themselves immediately and stood up, drawing their swords, awaiting the inevitable attack. Each brother might have said more, embraced and spoken of regretful things. Instead, they stood and looked to the sands for any worrying sign of an invading force.

———

Lexi wanted to stretch. She tried to shove away her burden, take a breath, and enjoy the relief. Instead, she allowed her best friend to slumber with his greasy hair against her cheek as he used her for a pillow. The hour was early, far too early. Closer-to-dawn early. The worst type of early. A terrible earliness when one hadn't slept through the night. Her eyes burned, and her stomach churned. The desire for sleep had come upon her far too late. It was her fault. It wasn't the first time sleeplessness had come for her on the eve of something important. Sometimes, needing to sleep was enough to keep her awake. A foolish affliction. Her mind had raced these last few hours with happy, hopeful, fantastical thoughts. Oh, to have taken this night to sleep just one hour. Enough to take the creaking from her bones. The panic from her heart.

Though she had been offered better bedding in the depths of the salt mine, she had refused. She did not trust her mother to keep her door unlocked, no matter what the older Alphaline had pledged upon seeing her and Tye's involvement in their defence. Besides, she needed to feel part of this army without the undeserved privileges. She was but one sleepless damsel among the other thousand dozing comrades, spread out, snoring weakly on any surface they'd been able to find.

With tear-filled eyes, she gazed at a soldier standing upright, leaning against a long artillery pole with arms folded, snoring away, and thought the very skill of sleeping to be an unappreciated art. She stirred in her uncomfortable bedding, which was little more than sand, a cloak and a heavy pack, and felt her friend's hand shift and slide slowly down her chest as he adapted to her position before continuing to snore. He would never know he touched such a sacred gift. She felt his warmth against her, and it was comforting—although it would take more than a desperate kiss in a passionate goodbye for her to answer his charms, beautiful as he was. Annoyingly beautiful at that.

A guard on patrol stumbled by, carelessly kicking her burden's foot as he passed.

Oh, for fuk's sake.

To the boy's credit, he was uniquely calm in his stirring. While most Alphas might have shaken awake, reached for a blade and sought out murder and death, he merely stirred and stretched, had a good long moan, and blinked his bleary eyes as his senses returned.

She'd enjoyed the silence. She worried he'd notice the dark circles under her eyes, that he'd realise what had occurred as he slept and know that she'd left him to suffer it alone. She hated that he knew her so well. She still wasn't used to such companionships. She feared for the future.

"I slept terribly," he muttered, wiping sleep from his eyes.

"Aye, me too."

He hesitated, studying her face. "Liar. You'll be slow should there be fighting today." Of course, there would be fighting. The curs had delayed attacking an entire day. But to wait longer was a foolish thing. She'd counted those water tanks. It didn't take a great mind to imagine how swiftly the tanks would drain once the parched soldiers fell upon them. At that, she reached for her own tankard. It was no substitute for a fine meal, but still a decent start to the day. She drank, then offered it to Tye, who remained wrapped in her warmth, enjoying the morning, despite the feeling of war in the air.

"There's a cloud up there," he said, ignoring her. "Look at it. All cottony and pure. It looks like a rabbit. Doesn't it look like a rabbit?" He pointed to a fat cloud floating a great distance above them, alone and fragile against the clear morning sky. She imagined a fool wandering these sands, following the cloud, hoping for an impossible bit of rain.

"It looks like nothing, idiot. Tell me, how can you be so relaxed on such a day?" She shoved him away. She was in no mood for Tye in full flow this morning. She desired sombreness and cautious conversation.

"Because I think this is the last day, though not *our* last day," he said, yawning. A terrible yawn. She yawned with him. Her insides churned again, and she wanted to sleep so very much. He edged up beside her, wrapped his hands around her head and began to massage it, trying to calm her thoughts. She felt shivers; she wanted him to stop; she wanted to argue; she wanted to sleep.

"How would you know? And also, stop touching me," she whispered, pushing him away gently. Wonderfully, he ignored her and began to tap his rough fingers against her crown, and she could feel sleep coming. She should have woken him sooner. That said, she wouldn't have been able to sleep, would she? And then it would just have been awkward for them both. Her mind raced, and she concentrated on nothing but the tapping reverberating through her head, and soon sleep began to beckon her once more. A little rest before the battle was all she needed.

"Can you not feel it, dear friend?" he said softly. "We are part of something greater, but we are not legend. Not yet."

She frowned and wondered about these words.

"We are destined for greatness. This I know."

It was a wonderful lie, and she wanted to believe him. "Idiot."

He laughed, and it was a settling thing. Even with those slumbering warriors around them rousing, she fell further towards sleep, which was excellent. He was skilled at many things; putting her to sleep was his most cherished gift. She was far too much like Roja, and he? He was nothing like Emir, but he had likely learned the drunken fiend's skills at delivering slumber.

"Where will you go when we win?" he asked soothingly.

She had not thought of that; had not thought of surviving either. "Back home, to the city," she said, and felt herself let go, almost.

"Ah, very good; I want to travel the road. I am due a wander. I desire the deep north. You could come too?"

"No, thank you," she whispered, barely conscious now.

"I might travel the seas and come upon the savages. Declare myself king and all while I'm there."

She wanted to laugh. To ask more. But instead, she sighed wistfully.

"Or I could always stay around these lands a while… if I could find my family, that is."

"You could visit me in the city," she said, curling up against his chest.

"I could Cull and all. I've lived out in the Wastes longer than most other Alphas. Perhaps if I found a mate there, she and I could do everything."

"Many females would desire such a thing."

"Many?"

"Once you grow into your clothes a little more. At least where it counts…"

At that, she fell asleep.

She did not know how long he continued to massage her head, for when a great drumming erupted, she sat up, shocked, reaching for her blade, and he was beside her, reaching for his own. As tired as she was, the brief time she'd slept had infused her. A deeper sleep could wait longer. She was Alpha; she was ready for war.

"They are beating our anthem," he snarled.

"Let us play our meagre part in something greater."

Admittedly, it was a perfect distraction for those too energised to sleep a moment longer. And Kaya was happy to accept the challenge from her young comrade. Now, though, as dawn burned away the night, her mouth was dry, her body was aching, and her skin was coated in a veneer of sweat.

"You are changed, little one," Kaya gasped, moving across the sparring ring with her blade held out in front of her, her legs set correctly, making herself as challenging to hit as possible. Her far smaller opponent spun around the sandy ground, eyes wide and wild in excitement, unbroken by any battering she'd received. There was barely a drop of perspiration on her, either. That was the advantage of youth, Kaya supposed.

Aimee swept forward, her blades dazzling and brutal in the morning air. She screamed as she attacked, a primal wail, and Kaya wondered about the agony she'd endured. When pressed, she still would not speak of horrors beyond the fall of Raven Rock. In time, she might reveal why she had returned with the witch who'd taken everything from Kaya.

In time.

Though the girl was quiet and uncomfortable in conversation, when fighting she came alive and seemed far more like the determined child she had been so long ago.

Not long enough for her to be this far changed.

As she had a dozen times throughout this bout, Kaya retreated beneath Aimee's attack. The girl didn't care about Kaya's wooden sparring blade in her sightlines. She sought out the kill every time. All too swiftly, each engagement ended the same way. Kaya, a master at defence, met each of her strikes and ultimately finished her with a deathly blow, but not before suffering a killing strike to herself every time. The crack of wood, the sound of wailing and a series of frustrated shrieks filled the morning, eclipsing the collective rumble of the few thousand warriors.

"Changed? Ha—I am who I am," said Aimee, retreating momentarily from the hostilities. Only then did Kaya see how tired she was. She gasped for air, dropping her hands by her side and barely keeping her weapon in her grip. Kaya lowered her own blade to gather her breath, and the younger girl was upon her. Blade through the chest, through the heart. A killing blow, and Aimee shrieked in delight before retreating and gesturing to Kaya to continue this battle.

"Your skills are different to those we once trained for," Kaya muttered, nursing the sting where the girl had struck her. "You seem to have lost your appetite for defence."

It was a fair criticism, and well deserved too. The girl shrugged. "If I meet you in sparring on an equal footing, you'll defeat me. At least I can kill as I die. There are worse fates."

Kaya fought the pang of sorrow that rose up in her. She could have dropped to her knees and wept again for the girl and for those she loved and had lost. This creature was Aimee, but also a cruel vestige of that shining light she had been. The sneaky little shit who had loved life and all its gifts. The little goddess who had added the finest golden touch to every endeavour, and a future master of the road, possibly a future leader of the settlement. Or, greater yet, Kaya's replacement when her teachings became too disheartening. A bandit was always inclined to keep themselves alive at any cost, yet this fierce creature was willing to sacrifice herself in a breath. Kaya had never trained her to fight like that.

What became of you, little one?

Kaya knew many steps were needed to find the girl again, and she was wise enough to take each step carefully, slowly. If not here, then at a place of Aimee's choosing. This was a selfish gift on her part, for Kaya wasn't ready to return to Raven Rock.

"Might I meet the girl in battle?" Bison called. He stood outside the sparring ring, and Kaya fought back a grin. She also flicked a few strands of hair behind her ear. She didn't know why she did that, only that Elise was a lesser woman, she thought, for turning down this dangerous brute's advances.

Since his defeat, he'd kept his eyes on Kaya these last few days. At first, she believed him interested in venting his wrath on an easier target. Now, though, she suspected he was interested in her. And why wouldn't he be? She was still alluring, and there was the small matter of her holding the legacy of Raven Rock. Should she desire it? Raven Rock was no simple fallen town in the middle of the Wastes. It still stood and would stand long after she passed. It was a republic and a place of power for any bandit weary of sand in his boots. There were lesser reasons to charm a maid like her.

The Actions of Gods

She noticed he was topless again, his muscles rippled and imposing. Although she and Aimee had attracted a few spectators with their early morning sparring, his arrival brought a crowd, and Kaya, smiling her most disarming smile, surrendered the ring to the newcomer.

"Of course you can," Aimee said, darting towards him and meeting his blocked blades before sliding along the ground, ducking beneath his careless swipe, and delivering a killing blow to his perfectly chiselled chest, all at the expense of a nasty graze from the unforgiving sand.

The behemoth laughed as the petite girl danced around him, and for a breath, Kaya wanted to lock the girl away, protect her, tear her from this life. But even though she was a child, she had seen a world Kaya wasn't arrogant enough to believe she could understand. The best she could do was stay as close to the girl as possible, offer what words she could and hope she returned to herself again. It wasn't fair, but those were the cards she'd been dealt.

As Aimee danced in for a second killing blow, Bison shot his hand out and took the girl by her throat. A simple enough hold, easily broken, and one Kaya had trained Aimee to counter.

Instead, the girl screamed and dropped her blade. She did not fight; she hung limp, and Bison, shaken at her sudden change, released his grip and caught her in his strong hands as she fell. For only a breath did the girl shake and appear her age, and Kaya ran to her. Swiftly, though, she drew away from the larger man, her hand falling to a dagger at her waist for a breath before she regained her better senses.

"Good win," Aimee hissed, and he bowed slowly in deference, and Kaya was further charmed by this right fuken bastard.

"I think we should save it for the enemy," Kaya declared as great drumming filled the air.

"We are being attacked," cried Aimee. There was no fear anymore, no hesitation. She stood proud, looking towards the sound as those around them prepared for war. Her eyes were alight once more, and as Kaya watched, she became once more the feral assassin the South had trained her to become.

"Let us send them running," Bison roared, and Aimee approved.

Kristov clutched his belly and fought the urge to throw up. Throughout the night, he'd thrown up countless times; the last few hours, though, he'd settled somewhat. He inhaled deeply and fought the urge to retch from the stench. He might have stepped out into the dawn's early breeze, but the entire camp carried a similar aroma. Instead, he held his stomach and clenched his bowels to prevent them from releasing again and prayed to his one-eyed god that relief would come upon him this terrible day.

This is the cost of leadership.

"Attacked by the goddess of scorn and death," he muttered to no one, not even a lover in his lavish leader's bedding. Not that he could have done anything. Not that any woman would have wanted to lie with him, lest they catch the plague. "Plague," he hissed, staring at the water in the goblet before him. His mouth was dry. A terrible dry. The type of dryness that led to death in this savage desert. He clutched himself, fought a shudder, and tried not to think of the water goblet. There was a curse upon the water, though it looked crystal clear. It hadn't taken long for the first few soldiers to fall to the poisoned water.

You have to drink.

He could hear the moan of a general in the tent next door. How many generals had suffered the torment as he had? It was not death; it was debilitating horror and a slow, painful wait for this affliction either to pass or to worsen. He ran his fingers along the rim of the goblet, and he desired this water most. He'd boiled it twice before. They all had. It didn't stop the affliction; it merely slowed it. His stomach jerked potently. He knew that were there even a drop of fluid in his belly, it would be thrown up.

"To the fires with me," he muttered, taking that fuken goblet and sipping its life-giving ambrosia. He felt his body's desire. He wanted that water more than he'd ever wanted the ecstasy of spending himself in a willing, wanton woman. He loved this water, even as it seduced and killed him.

More.

He took more, and for a moment, he felt better. The terrible burn of bile was no longer biting at his throat, ripping it to shreds, taking his voice too. Distantly, he heard a hammering, and his head ached with every beat. Like the worst hangover from a glorious night's endeavours, he desired that hammering to fuk right off and let him recover.

To distract himself from the headache and the fire stirring in his belly, he looked at the hourly reports. Runners had been busy this last day and a night, taking note of those who were still fit. Those who had cherished their water rationing more than their comfort. Those who had looked around this plagued camp and instantly known the cause.

The Actions of Gods

He could barely focus on the numbers scribbled on the little piece of parchment. So many, so fuken many, and it was all on Kristov. He'd feared it was the work of the fabled demons, but witnesses claimed they saw a flash of a beautiful girl with godly eyes around the carts. Kristov was no fool; he knew Aurora's desire to take his army. Was she truly capable of such betrayal, though? Kristov knew well the fate of Orin. But that had been one general alone.

This was something else entirely.

The drumming grew, and a cold chill ran down his spine. They were marching drums. Drums that beat against his will. Drums ordered by another general, no doubt clamouring to lead those healthy enough to fight. With the intake of water, his wits began to return. Struggling to his feet, downing the last drops from the poisoned goblet, he stumbled out through the tent to face the burning rays of dawn.

The camp was subdued. Tents were closed tightly against the horrors within. Those not succumbing to the poisoning were dejected and wary. Those fit and fighting-ready were bleary-eyed, dehydrated, and nearly collapsed from their discipline. He could see the desperation in their faces even as terrible things drew in around them, and they were too battered to heed such noises. The numbers he'd read upon the parchment shattered his confidence, reaffirmed his misery and guaranteed his fate. A third of an army left to call upon was a travesty.

"Who beats the drums of war?" a soldier muttered. He was staring blankly at the fire. His face was pale. If the plague hadn't struck him down already, it would in the next hour. He wouldn't be alone, either. It took only a day without water in this heat to dry out completely. It was nearly impossible to stop any of them from quenching their thirst. It was only after the relief passed that the realisation took them.

He knew what the noise was.

A few other generals, waiting by similar campfires, immediately stood at attention. Some unsteadily. He wanted to rally them, to declare one last epic charge into the sands, towards the cursed bandit sanctuary. Towards their eternal flow of water. He licked his lips, wavered a bit and stumbled to his knees. His insides churned angrily.

"Sir, are you all right?"

"I have not ordered an attack," he gasped, and his voice was weak and broken. They tried to help him rise, and he waved away their grubby hands. The hammering increased; he could hear the guards sounding their alarms. His beaten generals only had to look ahead to the camp's borders, to the makers of such commotion. "To arms," he cried, and those generals with notions about victory immediately drew their blades, for that is what any fine general did; he was grateful for them. "For we are about to fall," he roared, and only then did they rouse themselves from their stupor and make the terrible realisation.

A goddess of death and scorn had taken their will and fight. And now, everything was lost.

Elise drained the last of her water and immediately refilled her cup at the nearest barrel. The young runners had done their duty long before dawn; the barrel was cool and full to the brim. Plenty of water, plenty of time to hold out. She thought she would be more tired than she was, but truthfully, war brought out the best in her. Admittedly, she'd felt a little tight in the chest the night before. Who knew that a few hours of sleep, deep in this magnificent settlement's belly, was all it took to heal her ever so? She took a deep breath and thanked the absent gods for another day granted.

It is time.

Her armour clinked loudly as she walked. It was comforting, just like the prospect of turning this war. Her mood darkened at that thought. It didn't take too long to go to that dark place of not knowing what move to make. She'd had a simple plan: dig in, hold the fuks until they were scattered, and charge right through them. Problem was, her tactics had been too impressive, hadn't they? Those fuks hadn't come attacking following their midnight rambling butchering at all.

She was proud of her army. She was proud of their heroism, their aptitude for horror and their control of that vile affliction known as sorrow. These were her people, and as she took more deep breaths, she knew she was content to die here. Eventually.

Certainly not today.

There was too little threat in the air, and as she gazed at those she passed her eyes fell upon her youngest. Asleep, wrapped up in the arms of Tye. Elise muttered a curse under her breath. If she showed any disapproval of her relationship with the young Alpha male, they would likely be wedded by the end of the day. Or worse, absconded like before. She liked Tye. He was a true-born Alpha, but he was trouble, and her beautiful daughter was far too much like her mother. A deadly combination, no doubt. She watched him massage her head and wrap his other arm around her against the dawn breeze, and her mood dropped further.

Too young.
Too wild.
Not yet.

Let there be love down the road, out on the road, away from wartime. Let her endure her Cull. She'd been robbed of many things, but a mother could still wish for a daughter's city entitlements. She spun away from the sleeping girl, cursing once more. She had only just found her again, and had nearly lost her as swiftly. Gifting her freedom was all she could do to keep her near, even if she stayed in the arms of this troublesome cub.

Please, not yet.

She continued to move through the camp, and the crack of blades drew her from thoughts of her impressive daughter. With waiting came boredom. A full day in unsettling calm was terrible for morale. Crushing for the losing army, but damaging for the victorious also. Walking back towards the noise of a skirmish, she gazed thoughtfully at the enemy camp and hated their hesitation. Even scouts with keen eyes could only guess their plans, and so far, they appeared to be little more than a camp licking their wounds, awaiting reinforcements.

It is time.

Standing atop a mound of salty dirt, she could see over the gathering crowd to the women at war. She was unsure about the child Aimee, except that she was dangerous. A little younger than her daughter in seasons, but she had lived twice the life. Elise knew how she spoke, how she shied like a hound from a disapproving master. The attention Kaya had given the girl since her arrival irked Elise somewhat, for there were duties to be performed, and she needed her right hand at her side at all times. Kaya had argued against such obligation and instead played the part of protective mother over her own little cub.

She watched the girl, and a coldness came upon her. She moved well, eerily so. Better than Lexi, no doubt. The only person she'd ever seen so single-minded in battle was Erroh. While Elise's preference was very much offensive swordplay, this girl was reckless; she sacrificed herself again and again for a killing blow. Elise wanted to like the girl, she really did, and perhaps, when victory came and they still stood breathing, she might warm to her, but she had gazed into the girl's eyes and seen a soulless creature staring right back at her. She had said as much to Kaya, who agreed. So it was a strange thing to see her still attempting to pull humanity from her.

Elise watched for a while until Bison appeared, and then she had seen enough; he would batter the young girl, no doubt, and she found such a thing distasteful. She resumed her journey through the camp, down towards the edges of battle, where she came upon Wrek and Ulrik. By then, her mood had darkened even more. In the beginning, they'd had the fuks on the run. They only needed to throw caution to the wind, offer a deathly, costly charge, and win the battles outright. Instead, she had hidden and protected those she loved dearly, as well as those she had come to care for deeply. Now, she was determined to protect those she respected and did not know.

It's time.

"Wield what weapons you have," she imagined her mate whispering in her ear. She looked at the warring brothers, sitting together now, smiling, conversing. All fuken calm. They had lost momentum and rested languidly while the Southern fuks recovered, worked on deadly plans, and plotted victory.

Suddenly, her heart began to beat; suddenly, she desired a charge. Desired to hear the wrath of war. To clash blades, spill blood, throw caution to the wind and reap the benefits. Aye, they were safer behind these walls, these natural and unnatural defences. They were safe and secure—and lessening their advantage. A cold fury rose in her, and she embraced it. What if the entire Southern army appeared on the horizon? What then? No manner of clever defending could win the day.

It's fuken time.

She marched along the battlements, kicking at those who still slept. Suddenly, she could take no more hesitation. No more delay. No more safety, either. It was time to be daring, to be a goddess.

"Get up," she hissed and began running. Her halberd, which had rested easily in her arm, was now raised, and she wanted to punish. "Beat the rhythm of war," she cried to a gathering of drummers. Around her rang the clatter of warriors gathering their weapons. She had no desire for plans. For argument. It was a short charge to the nearest massacre, and she desired to lead it.

Behind her, the drums beat; they matched her excitement and desperation. All eyes were upon her, although she cared for no speech or gathering of generals or loved ones. The time of hesitation was gone.

"We fight," she roared, and those who ran grew in numbers. She broke from along the barricades out through the sands, and with her charged the swelling ranks of soldiers who only moments before had been feeble and gelded by hesitation. "Kill them all," she demanded, and a thousand voices behind her roared, and a thousand more behind them. This was the legend of wild Elise. This was the legend she'd carried for decades gone. Older now, but just as reckless. It was delicious.

She charged into battle with comrades she did not know, whose only sin was rising quicker than the others. Their honour was in matching her pace, spreading out and understanding their risk in a front line; in knowing their duty too. Her loved and dear ones were far behind her now, but she knew that, in time, they would charge too. Nothing could be done, and if this was the end of her life, it was a fine last sprint.

The heroic warriors of Adawan swept over the walls of the Southerners, and they could not be diminished. Led by Elise, they were brutal, and the Hunt were helpless in the face of this unexpected attack. Perhaps, were the generals fit enough to bark out defensive orders, the tale might have been different, but the generals had greater rations than the others: they had drunk deeply of the poisoned water, and they were among the sickest as the end came upon them all.

Those who could stand upright put up a brave fight, but they answered their own instincts, not their leaders' calls. They marched in a haphazard line, defying the inevitable, hoping to silence the drums, to hold back the breaching savages. To live to see dusk. A few dozen archers even managed to fire off a few volleys into the oncoming thousands, but those they struck were few.

With the drumming urging on their every charge, the bandit army, led by a goddess of death, broke through the first line of fit Southerners and kept going. There was no order to their assault. They smashed through the defenders without mercy; sprays of blood filled the air, limbs were hacked away and strewn about, and bodies fell on all sides as the rushing army continued its relentless advance. They hacked and slashed and bled and killed, and the Southerners attacked desperately, but like an avalanche, there was no stopping this onslaught.

Led by a screaming witch who spun a double-bladed halberd, the attackers followed a few steps behind her, and there was no threat to her dominance. It did not take long for the Southerners to realise those she preyed upon were killed swiftly.

Those weak few who scrambled from their tents, half-dressed and covered in filth, screamed, vomited and relieved themselves even as they tried to raise a blade, and such was the mercilessness of the enemy that even they were slaughtered, their bodies messily strewn upon the ground to lie in their own waste.

Those unable to climb from their bedding were left where they were. It was a small matter to be merciful in such cases, Elise insisted, and her warriors obeyed. Onwards through the rancid tents she led her maniacs, all screaming, all charging, all killing, and her legacy received another chapter all to herself.

She did not realise the moment the tide turned fully, such was the swiftness of the attack, but as they charged through the camp, Elise knew victory was theirs. More than that, she knew wars were won and lost on the basis of similar massacres. Magnus would undoubtedly agree.

Those with mounts ready and saddled for a charge fled first. Out through the horror, away from this fallen camp, out into the sands of Adawan they raced as though pursued by demons. The foot soldiers left behind soon realised the dreadfulness of this attack. Turning with the Riders, they sprinted from their camp, from their supplies, from their vanquishers.

She did not know which general blew the horn first, but as its dull drone played out across the horror, the rest of the Hunt, still engaged in battle, lost all will to fight. Some dropped their weapons, some fell to their knees in subservience; many though, sprinted for the sands, hoping no blade would lance them as they ran.

For a precious moment, Elise slowed and stopped her solitary assault to gaze across the edge of the camp at the fleeing army. Around her, there came the sounds of cheering, mocking and excitement, and truly, watching them for a moment, she wondered if this was enough. And then her daring and better sense took her.

"What are you cheering for?" she demanded, spinning around to those she led. Among them were giant brothers, rogue suffering bandit confidants, and wild energetic Alphalines. "This battle is not yet done." Leaving a grateful few to deal with the surrendering Southerners, she jogged off into the sand, and with her came a few thousand zealots all believing in the goddess of war, all eager to defeat the fleeing threat.

84

VIOLENT REUNION

Is this the end?
    Do I care?
Am I worthy to lead?

Erroh was as broken as he'd ever remembered being. Although his body ached from the march and the exertions, the desperate sadness tore him asunder. Gripping the reins lest he fall from Highwind and surrender to his anguish, he gritted his teeth and kicked his magnificent beast towards certain death. The sand billowed up from those he attacked and rose behind the fiends charging directly towards him. Behind these curs, a thousand foot soldiers charged, which was terrifying. He'd have preferred the sands to conceal them a moment longer. A few hundred Riders were daunting enough, but these numbers made his blood run cold.

I do not care.

That was no truth, for Erroh did care. He wanted to live despite the terrible anguish he suffered. Aye, this day was far worse than any he'd endured before it, for only a man whose mate had strayed could know such horror. She brought her horse alongside his. He might have gazed at her a moment with silent love as they raged into war, but he could not face her or look favourably upon her perfect form, not without imagining her at play with another, flesh grinding against flesh, moaning as they spent themselves. And he wanted to throw up upon himself.

"To the fires with you all," he roared, drawing his blades. He thought them fine last words. Were any to survive this dreadful slaughter, he wondered, would they remember them? Would they claim to have been inspired by them? Truthfully, they were hollow words, taken from a hollow young Alpha. To the fires with his mate and her lover. To the fires with the absent gods too. They were truer words, but not words to define his memory.

"Kill them all," Lea roared, and Erroh thought them good words too, although he'd never show it. He'd never look at her either. Her cutting, killing blow would stay with him forever. However long that might be. He had never considered her lineage a deliberate betrayal and could have forgiven her for almost anything. However, those words intended to maim and ruin were not from the goddess he had once cherished.

Once.

But no more.

Not like before.

The pace increased, and the sands below became a burning blur. The wind rushed in his ears, and he kicked Highwind again and willed her not to fall in the battle. Willed her to carry him first into death too. He hoped he wouldn't see it coming. He hoped that, as he died, he might decapitate his killer as his final act. That would be a good death. He hoped she saw him fall first. Perhaps as he was gutted and felled, she might realise her cruelty, might carry some of that ache into the darkness.

He also hoped she lived beyond this day.

The Southerners were unmoving in their desperate charge. The world slowed as they neared, and distantly, Erroh could see the remains of a camp, washed over by a swarm of invaders. For just a moment, he considered his actions, considered attempting to dig in and survive the onslaught in the hope the trailing army would continue their deathly charge. It was a foolish notion. The die was cast, and the cards were dealt. He could see the whites of the eyes of those he would meet.

She tried to push up ahead of him. Her screams rose above the wind and thunder. Erroh hated Lea in that moment, hated her arrogance, her desire to best him. Suicidal dashes were his forte, were they not? He might have hissed her away and let her and her boys take the lead. Might have let her lover die in the melee while he was at it. That would cancel it out, he mused, and he kicked his beast hard and leaned into the race a few breaths from the end.

Nearer now, so fuken close. The open land was black with the rushing of Riders. They came not in a disciplined, cutting shard like Erroh and his doomed comrades, but instead, they charged as an uncoordinated beast, which was unusual.

He screamed once more. One last deafening roar to the gods, to those he led and those he challenged. His comrades roared with him, and then they clashed. There was the ear-splitting scream of metal on metal and the wet thump of blades through flesh. The awful rumble of terrible things as they charged past.

Charged through.

The world slowed, and Erroh's arms became free of anguish and hurt. They became a warrior's arms once more. They behaved as he commanded. They moved as a blur. With thighs dug in against his magnificent warhorse, using only grim determination and brute force to stay upright, he tore and swung from both sides.

Live this last moment well.

He did not think about his actions; he relaxed into this death ride and allowed his wits and reflexes to deflect and counter and kill. Without choosing his victims or relying on accuracy, he merely swung without remorse. He felt the spray of blood against his skin—warm, wet and terrible. He plunged and killed and maimed and missed. All the while, in a few awful breaths, they charged through the racing Southern Riders, and horribly, he imagined himself surviving this battle like so many before. He was unscathed, touched by the gods—until a flailing hammer struck him along his ribs.

Pain.

Like once before.

He felt his ribs break. Or something akin to it. He also felt weightless, and he screamed in frustration and terror as he was felled. The ground tilted below him, and he was stretched and floating above it, flying like a god of fire over a battlefield. He wished the world hadn't slowed as he twisted and turned in the air, and the ground rushed up to meet him, and he had only the pain of his shattered ribs to help him keep his wits before he struck the burning sands.

More pain.

Spinning.

A little bit of tearing.

He rolled and broke, and around him, hooves trampled. Some Southern, some those of his comrades. He caught sight of her, far above, still seated upon her mount. Their eyes might have met, but for the sand he kicked up. She did not hesitate. She did not think. She continued her charge, leaving him battered and beaten behind, food for crows. A river of thundering mounts, racing towards freedom, and little cub Erroh, left behind by his love.

Forever.

He gasped in agony and tried to rise. His chest felt caved in, and he was back in the city for a moment, alone, beaten and bullied.

Get up.

He fought determinedly, even as he squirmed on the ground, coughing heavily, scrambling for breath and balance. Eventually, with the thunder around him, he scrambled to his knees and recovered his fallen blades, strewn on either side of him. With the feel of steel in his gloved grip, he felt alive once more. These were his tools of war; these were things he counted on. These were things he trusted. These didn't play with other sweaty hands. They remained faithful.

He straightened, swung at a trailing Rider, and missed. He fell back in the sand once more, and still Lea did not return for him. Instead, far off in the distance now, she and her comrades charged through the desert towards the sprinting army.

Lead.

He wanted to collapse in pain, yield this battle and shuffle away to nurse his aches in the dark. Instead, he began to run towards the enemy with all his will. It was a shorter distance than he expected. His left side ached, each breath suggesting something tearing deep within. Still, he ran far ahead of his comrades and drove deep into the rushing army as one violent unit. He might have been proud of his Southerners and her Wolves, but he could only feel left behind. The screams of fighting erupted again, and once again Erroh felt himself late to this grand event.

Their splendid charge served well the army routing the Southerners. While the Riders charged at their usual pace, the foot soldiers were slower, some moving at barely above a jog. As Lea's Riders struck from the front, so too did the attackers strike from the back, and Erroh was too far away to be the catalyst.

With lungs burning, he watched Lea's group trample and destroy all they encountered, and they fled away from her charge as though all desire for war had left them. It was barely a fair fight. Still, he continued his desperate sprint across the desert, desperately seeking to recover Highwind. Alas, only as he reached the battle did he see the beast upon a dune, looking uninterested in his plight. He might have screamed in agony and grabbed her attention; however, she had little interest in being part of this battle. Not this day, at least.

When he drew his swords again and stumbled towards his first intended victim, Erroh thought it peculiar how emotionlessly the enemy warred. He considered them traditionally fierce and brave, although lesser in skill. And normally they fought with passion, whereas now, they appeared as though a plague of disinterest had taken them.

Shoving away any unhelpful thoughts of mercy, he stormed through them, and felt grand about being in the midst of battle once more. Driving deep, alone and outnumbered, such was his speed and skill that he suffered no killing blow until, from nowhere, a vision suggested he had died after all.

Mommy?

He couldn't believe his eyes. Wouldn't believe it. He held his swing on a stumbling, wounded warrior who scrambled away from the killing blow. Erroh could have followed after, added to his incalculable number, but instead, he watched Elise at war, and she was spectacular.

She tore through them, halberd spinning and cutting steadily, her slight figure imposing and incredible. Those she hunted screamed in terror, and the fear spread like wildfire in a brush. In his youth, he had watched in awe as she donned her warrior skin and practised battle manoeuvres against invisible opponents. Even then, as a child, he had been impressed. As a walking legend now, he was even more in awe of his warrior mother.

Admittedly, he had questioned the stories his father had told him about her prowess; it was, of course, a natural thing to query such prideful boasts. But now he knew once and for all that the tales were true: she never stopped running at the curs and showed no restraint, either. Barely breaking a sweat, she took the heads off those who stood desperately to defend, and she was elegant and graceful, and lethal.

Around her, her bandit brethren were inspired. And who wouldn't be? They roared and charged and killed. Their blades swung as hers did, their daring keeping them in a line with their ferocious leader. Few of them fell, despite their lesser numbers, and Erroh, darting between them, began to run towards kin. Towards love, towards reassurance. It had taken long enough.

She saw him at the very end, just as the army gave up their pride. Hundreds of Southerners, all as one, conceding their loss, fell on their knees submissively and cried out for mercy. A few bent to the ground, throwing up the contents of their stomachs; such was the terror they faced.

She was brandishing her blade above a humbled victim when she turned and saw him approaching. She let out a terrible, keening wail and dropped her blade. Her bandits took this as a signal for mercy and did not finish off the curs, tempted as they were.

Erroh ran to her, picking his way through the dead, dying and defeated. Months of sorrow and anguish were lost to a miracle. They embraced, and she was love. She was home.

"My boy," she cried, and her voice was like a balm to his soul. He dared not wake from this cruel dream lest the truth reveal itself. She was godly. He knew it now. Back from the dead. A broken waif no more.

Through tear-filled eyes, he caught sight of Lea. She was upon her mount, no great distance from him. She stared at them both, in jealousy, in hatred.

"I missed you so very much, little one," Elise whispered, and he was safe and relieved. His legendary mother had come to save the day. To take the wretchedness from him. To take the responsibilities. His heroic Ranger mother, back from the dead. The world would bend to her will as before, and the little cub Erroh would be by her side every step of the way.

He couldn't have been further from the truth of things to come.

85

WEDDED DAY

Roja looked at herself in the mirror and began to weep. Terrible tears. Of joy, of regret, of fear, or fuken everything. She wore white today. She hadn't worn white in a lifetime. It had never suited her. Today, though, her minders insisted tradition must be followed.

A hand attended to her hair, adjusting a curl, balancing the cut. Another set of hands completed the darning of the hem in her silken gown. A third hand held out her goblet of wine. White wine only. No red tonight. The last hand offered a plate of strawberries with pieces of dry honey cake in the centre.

These Southern women spoke excitedly among each other as though this were the year's social event. Mostly in her tongue too. But not once did they talk directly to her. And that was fine. While today they were her maidens, attentive and complimentary, she was still very much a prisoner. Her stomach churned suddenly, and they comforted her. One of them offered her a rag to clear her nose and dry her tears. Tradition was a cruel bitch, and this fine morning, it was the worst.

The previous night, for the first time since she had recovered, Emir had not slept beside her. She had never known before this how much she needed her lover to soothe her. To reassure her when panic overcame her. Again, she felt herself start with fear and alarm, and suddenly a honey cake was in her hand.

Perfect.

When she wasn't stuffing cake into her mouth, she looked quite the sight in the mirror. The women knew it too, though they said little on the matter. She wished Silvia and Lexi were here with her for just a moment. More tears threatened, but she fought them off mightily.

Get through this nightmare.

She did not know why she and Emir played the part, but they did. It was a shrewd move to please her demented and very much broken uncle, but still, the sight of her own grandness shouldn't have affected her as it did. She felt gorgeous. She felt this day was for her alone.

Wanting to please Emir with her grace shouldn't have mattered as much as it did, but she couldn't help herself. In the same way, she shouldn't have paid so much attention to who would attend. Or how many courses would be served. Or what choices of food there would be. She'd scarcely believed it to hear herself passionately discussing the tunes that would be played, pieces that both she and her guests might recognise. She cared for these petty matters more than she had to. It was a distraction, if nothing else, because learning what had occurred beyond the gates was more difficult than ever. She knew things had taken a turn, but she couldn't say in which direction, or how bad things were. There were reasons to be hopeful, though, even if hope was treacherous.

Believe in Erroh.

They offered her another cake, and she shook her head. There was a limit to what she could get away with in this spectacular gown. It would be unfortunate to burst such impressive seams during the service. The ripping of her dress would come afterwards, when Emir consummated their commitment.

"Beautiful," a maid offered in broken speech, and she smiled in agreement. It was a fair comment. Her companions had done a fine job of making her the best little bride she could be.

All part of the act.

After a time, when there were only so many alterations they could make, and two more glasses had been drained, she was ready to face the world.

He knocked on the door, and her heart began to beat at the familiar sound. He entered and gasped, and her maids stepped away from his godly gaze as though commanded into silence.

"You look beautiful, my dear," he murmured, and she dared a smile.

"I do, don't I?"

"Our boy is waiting; we shouldn't torment him any longer than need be," the god said, offering his hand, which she took. And away they went together, out through the bedroom, down the hallway and out into the streets where a dozen of his trusted guards joined them to escort her.

The Actions of Gods

They marched on parade: a god and his goddess niece. Divinity in a gown. Were it not so bizarre, it might have been hilarious. As it was, she matched his impressive stride through the ramshackle streets, under the gaze of the war-weary Southern inhabitants. The world froze as they passed; every Southern eye was lowered, every head bowed. She met some smiles along the way, but Uden offered nothing. He merely marched her along as though this mission was his finest act.

The city looked different from before. Drained of all colour, it resembled less a vibrant source of life and energy and more the wretched remains of a prison for the condemned. This was the face of war, up close, and she was radiant before it.

At the Cull, he finally stopped and, standing outside the hallowed hall, ensured one final time that everyone was prepared, the right song was to be sung, and the groom was willing and upright.

"It is time," Uden said at last, and, taking her hand, kissed her lightly upon the cheek. "I have done my part for family," he said wistfully, half to himself, or perhaps to kin long lost. She might have asked, but the great oak doors opened to the tune of a song she'd known all her life. A fitting tale of love and the living of life. A natural thing, really, and fitting for the moment.

"Reach over to her; she's holding her breath; she's holding it just like you," a singer high in the rafters serenaded, and she almost broke. Despite herself, she was moved by the moment. There were no more than a dozen gathered guests. Generals mostly, certainly no one she cared for. All but one, that is, and his back was turned. Waiting and shivering, no doubt.

"Reach over to her; she's holding her breath; she's holding it just like you," the singer crooned again.

She could have sung along, but that would have broken her concentration, taken too much strength. She kept on watching him; he stood away from all others, dressed in garments of silk and leather, opposite to his usual appearance. His hair was perfectly groomed; she was not used to seeing his hair this way. She wanted to reach over and ruffle it. She also wanted to leap upon him, for she'd missed him this last night. Besides, it was a fabulous haircut.

"Reach over to her; she's holding her breath. Before it's too late."

She needed him to turn around. To face her. To see her beauty. This room was fated to end her life as a free female of the city. She'd always known it would be this way; had always feared the Culling too. But to step in here, to endure this event, was something else entirely. She needed him to look at her. To know how much she loved him, to tell him without words that she was his for life and beyond. All in silence, all in a glance. Even if it was all just an act for the sake of a demented, broken old man.

Roja held her breath. She saw a well-dressed fiend lean in and tell him of her arrival. She saw Emir nod his head and remain staring ahead. She needed him now more than ever. Before it was too late. The song was about to end; she knew it, as the singer did. She stepped closer and almost reached for him.

"Hello, he says," the singer whispered as the song finished, and at last Emir turned and mouthed a word of surprise and elation, for her and her alone. She stepped up to her husband-to-be, and they kissed delicately and smiled, and she could see the tears in his eyes. Crying was an archaic and indecorous action by many in the factions, no more so than in the city, but in that moment, it didn't matter. What mattered was Emir alone. The boy she'd loved her entire life. At that moment, she remembered him upon his rock those many years ago, and a tear slid down her cheek.

It was Uden who presided over events. He was no holy man, but most wedded vows needed no sacred guest. She had expected outlandish godly claims of family, loyalty and war, but instead, he was quieter than usual in these hallowed halls; he spoke of love and loss, but also of the importance of kindness and soulmates.

Were she to close her eyes, she might have imagined a beautiful event surrounded by loved ones. Nonetheless, it felt like a joyous occasion, like the one he'd promised, and she smiled as she took her vows and Emir took his own. He was shaken and pale, but she thought he had never looked happier in his miserable life.

Misery in love.

When the ceremony ended, rapturous applause erupted around them, and the Woodin Man's softness gave way once more to bravado and leadership. Before the wedded couple could gather their nerves, they were whisked away side by side by excitable guests playing the role of loved ones and delivered to a great pavilion erected in their honour in the arena.

There were hundreds gathered in the stands, away from the main gathering, and Roja was amazed at the lavish feasts spread out for the elusive few among the sands. The elite few. That wasn't to say the guests watching on weren't draining barrels of sine long left behind.

Before taking his seat, Uden raised a glass to all in attendance, and there was a hearty roar of approval. Emir sat beside Roja at a long oak table at the centre of the tent, beneath the warmth of two torches that had been lit against the afternoon chill. It was cosy and perfect, even if they feasted with fiends.

"To the happy couple," declared Seth, sitting at the far end. He raised his goblet of sine, and the guests raised their glasses.

"To the happy us?" Emir said to her quietly. He looked as bewildered and bemused as she did. He sipped his sine slowly, perhaps wary of becoming too inebriated and missing out on the festivities. She drained hers, and her goblet was refilled immediately by one of her maids.

"I love you," Roja said, squeezing his hand for the tenth time that hour. She couldn't keep her hands off him, though she did not know why. Perhaps it was the occasion; perhaps the dreadful knowledge that they were doomed to be together forever—to take no other lovers.

Just him. Just fuken him.

Perfect.

She smiled in delirious joy at such a thought and kissed him again. He even lowered his glass as she did. That was love.

In the distance, a sound like thunder erupted, low and menacing. As if in reply, the musicians began to play the fine songs she had chosen. The crowd drank and danced upon the stadium stands, and only then did she dare look up to where she'd lost Dia that sunny day. She thought it fitting in a way. Perhaps Dia still haunted these sands. Still watched after her.

"He makes me happy," she whispered to those watching on.

Though they were among enemies, it was a riotous night and a memorable one, despite the alcohol consumed, despite the thunder. Grand speeches were made to the gathered crowd, the loyal guests and the special couple—fine, fighting words about love with a hint of Southern defiance, which occasioned much cheering. More than once, Uden sat with them both and offered sage words of love and loyalty before falling still each time as though lost in thought. Finally, as the hour grew late and the revellers grew tired, seeking a respite, Emir called Uden to sit with them one last time.

"Thank you, Uncle," Emir said, and the god smiled sadly before offering him a gentle embrace. On another night, in another world, it might have been moving. As it was, this was a special night, and thus it was necessary to avoid his ire.

"It was a night we needed," the god whispered, and Roja took his hand and played the part.

"Our family has grown much this night, Uncle; thank you for this," she offered. It was as genuine as she could be.

"Perhaps, after tonight, it might grow a little more," he suggested, laughing loudly at his own wit. He bowed and then got to his feet and went to speak with Gemmil. Emir and Roja rose as well, and their guardians stood at attention. Hand in hand, the newlyweds were led from the arena through the streets to their elegant marital bed, and Roja was grateful to be away from it all to spend her time alone with her husband. Her fuken husband.

Only after the door was locked behind them in their homestead did they embrace and kiss with the passion they had withheld all day. Gripping her tightly, he pulled her up the stairs almost at a sprint, and she was willingly pulled along, giggling at his desire and her own. Giddy at the thought of formally consummating their vows.

"I was no good sleeping here without you last night," he said, stopping outside their chambers. His hands explored her dress, seeking out its weaknesses. She wanted him to rip it off.

"I am always lost without you, oh husband dear," she whispered, pulling at his trousers. A fuken belt was knotted tightly around his waist. She had a blade on her dresser that could rectify such a problem.

"My beautiful wife," he murmured, kicking the door open before dragging her through, ripping at her garments.

"Ah, good," the killer said from behind them as the door was kicked closed just as violently. Roja spun in horror to see the figure move swiftly towards them, weapon in hand and murder on their mind. "I was worried you would be too drunk to see me coming."

"Wait, don't," Emir cried, stepping before his bride.

"Oh, please, no," Roja screamed as the assassin fell upon them both.

86

CHOOSE A SIDE

Magnus held the hound as it struggled. He did not like this part of war. In the guilt he felt. The wound was deep. Along the side. Enough to hinder, to slow, but not to kill.

"It's okay, boy," he said, hushing it, but the massive hound continued to struggle in his grasp. Another savage assisted, holding the hound by the hind legs, while another held a thick collar around its snapping mouth. "Be still, little one," Magnus insisted as the hound fought their grip. Magnus was no skilled healer. Nor was he a cruel master. The two days since the battle, he'd tended to the beast with wrappings and ointments. But the wound, delivered by a dead man, no doubt, had not healed and sealed as he would have liked. The hour was late, and there was much to be done. He could not leave the beast behind. Could not leave it to fend for itself either. So he turned to surgery.

With a regretful plunge of his blade, he broke the beast's skin, and it howled and struggled. He took a length of thin thread and stitched it back and forth across the wound, all the while fighting the movement of the hound raging against his work. His pack, chained and watching with worried gazes, whined and growled at their brother's misfortune. They did not know; they could not know; they could only trust their master's actions. And worry for their brother.

"Hold still," grunted one of the hound handlers. The beast fought with a snapping bite as Magnus broke through the last piece of skin, pulled the thread taut, and closed the gap in the furry flesh. The beast howled once more, followed by a whimper, and Magnus grunted as he stitched the knot around the wound and slit the thread. A quick and awkward procedure, but the hound was tended to better than before. He leaned across and applied a little salve to the wound lest there be further infection, before wrapping his work with clean bandaging. His hounds were as vital to him as any warrior on the battlefield; they would be treated as such even if they didn't know it.

Eventually, the beast calmed, and Magnus lay across it, holding it steady. "Wash yourselves of his scent, so the pack don't go hunting you," Magnus muttered to his assistants. It was a half-jest but also a warning. He knew how dangerous his battle hounds were to anyone they perceived had hurt one of their number. The helpers released their hold, and the settled hound immediately fought to stand, but Magnus's weight countered him until the two men had disappeared from sight. Off to the river, no doubt, with some soap. Magnus could prevent the beast from opening his own throat, but there was likely little he could do to stop it from venting its wrath on either man.

"Easy, little one," he hushed, moving away, and the hound bounced to his feet, sniffing and growling. He turned to attack, and Magnus met his challenge, taking the scruff of its neck and gripping hard a reminder. The beast could growl, but little more. "Enough, or I'll do it again, you fuker," he roared in the animal's face before shoving him away. After a moment, the hound dropped his head, and Magnus patted him gently. "Good boy. I'll have you fighting fit in a couple of days," he promised, and it was a fine pledge.

His hound bounded back to the rest of the pack, and Magnus, watching him go, was satisfied with his healing. Even one missing from the pack made them vastly weaker. Better to have the full array of sharp teeth to call upon.

Whatever had occurred in the defence of Boat Town, the Hunt had begun to retreat to Spark City, leaving their war machines and supplies behind. Magnus gladly helped himself to the abandoned booty. Around him, the movement was regrouping, with the unmistakable energy of a rolling army, preparing to march for war. The preparations were nowhere more evident than along the great bridge the Southerners had kindly provided to Boat Town.

Farmers, peasants, wretches, labourers, young, old, and everything in between were streaming from the unique stronghold. Their tearful goodbyes were the worst—all were desperate to keep their loved ones from war, yet desperate to fight, to stand against the awful tyranny that threatened to wipe everything out. All of them were animated and emotional. It was bad for the morale of an army, of course, but good for the soul. They were the braver ones, he thought, simple labourers without skill of war to their name, yet here they were, offering to march towards doom, stand against the night, and attempt to turn the tide of events, not just in the Four Factions but in the regions beyond, regions to which most of them had never before travelled.

Magnus's trained savages made fine bulwarks against the torrents of war, but they still were no match for the thousands more the Woodin Man called upon. They needed all the help they could get. The citizens marched past him, all nervous—at least a thousand in all, according to Mea, and she knew every warrior counted. Skilled or no.

"Brave warriors, the lot of ya," he offered to a group passing. For a moment, they thought him to be mocking them, but then they recognised him, realised his words were genuine and walked a little prouder. There would be a lot of such gestures needed in the days ahead before the fighting began. With the right inspiration, a true leader could make the most diminutive warrior feel ten feet tall. It could make them feel less wretched running head first into a wall of sharpened blades.

He caught sight of Mea upon the deck, overlooking the grand exodus, and admired her. More so than Dia, he realised with a start. It seemed that the test of leadership had taken her spirit. Any warrior could see she was too wise to be a leader. She sought the goodness in people; she hoped for the best. Seeking and hoping were a human touch, and a leader needed to be a rightly vicious witch. She was also too humble to realise her worth to this effort, to know that she alone had saved the world and held out long enough to turn the tide. While most would take such an act as a point of merit, she dwelt only on her mistakes. He knew this because she spoke with him as Dia never had. Listened where she never had, either. Surrendered leadership, too. Not just for the city but for the war. For the sake of better days to come. And why wouldn't she offer leadership? Was he not the greatest warmonger ever to live?

A lifetime ago.

He smirked to himself, for that was all a doomed man could ever do. Leadership was there for those with vitality. Those with the desire to commit horrors. Those who stood out brightest against the rest. Magnus was not the man he once was. Age had taken its toll. He was simply available. The last fuk capable, he supposed. Not necessarily the best.

He grinned at his self-doubts. Perhaps he was too good and humble to realise his value as Mea did. Perhaps whispering of his own weaknesses in her ear was all it would take to help her reaffirm her worth.

Beside her, watching quietly, was Jeroen. Magnus could barely face the man now, such was his shame. He had tried to approach him with words of gratitude, or perhaps apology, but to no avail. He stepped up beside him and, once again, blurted out an incomprehensible litany of excuses as to why he had left him behind and why he had not sought him out. Jeroen merely nodded, and Magnus could see the strain on him. War affected people differently. Imprisonment could ruin a man. He could see Jeroen was closer to breaking than he had ever been; Magnus wondered, was he even fit to fight? Regardless, Jeroen would march with his mate, and that was something.

Leaving Jeroen's side and walking up through the gathered soldiers who dared not mingle with the savage warriors, Magnus surveyed his lost son's comrades. They were at war with words, now, deciding the world's fate for themselves.

"We march within the hour," he told them. His savages and their generals already knew their orders, of course, but these generals were his son's. He believed they waited for orders. He believed they waited for someone to tell them what to do.

At the table of generals were three others, one of whom Magnus had little time for. The other two he considered near family, despite their many issues. They stood apart. They always had. When hidden behind masks they were impressive and Magnus approved, for he'd never seen either one capable of such violence as he had witnessed upon landfall. If all it took was wearing unsavoury masks to become bloodthirsty, he might have had five thousand forged there and then.

Their table was little more than a barrel, covered in maps—a Magnus-style table. Their arguments fell silent as he approached, and he appreciated such reverence. In the time since he'd last seen them, all of them seemed to have grown weary and older. Warrior faces with warrior gazes. Still, his son could have chosen no better generals.

All but the one, of course.

He did not meet the eyes of the Southern whore. Instead, he looked at the girl beside her: Lillium, Erroh's second. Even now, despite the world being on the edge of collapse, Magnus knew his place, knew to choose his words carefully. Not to pay homage to her would be an affront to the chain of command. In Erroh's absence, she was the rightful leader of whatever remained of the outcast Wolves. She was no leader, though. Any fool could see that—even her.

"What say you?" he asked. She played with the mask in her hands. He might have been better asking the question when she donned it.

Magnus knew the price of trauma. Whatever she needed to do was pleasing in his eyes.

"You are the muscle in this war once more, Magnus. I have little interest in leading. I will do so only if Erroh orders me to. You have my blade and that of any who follow me."

There might have been more to say, but she bowed instead. She fingered the mask a little more, and he smiled. He had expected no challenge—had hoped for one, though. But the girl could read the situation: there was little point in splitting what forces they had.

There were too many sides in this fight as it was. The Savage Isles knew well the cost of such division. The other generals looked at her in silence, and Magnus shook his head in approval and turned to the battered Doran.

"Have your Wolves met up with the wretches from the floating city? Best keep them apart from the hunting packs of my savages," Magnus said, watching the younger man. He looked better than he had the previous day. Magnus had learned of his loss. A lesser man might have forsaken his duty as his men buried their dead. A greater man might have, too. As it was, Doran had answered all that was asked of him. Mea had done well in keeping his loyalty, allowing him freedom. Magnus would afford him the same honours. He would merely point him and his chosen Wolves towards the city and let them thrash it out. And the wretches who followed after, well, let them learn from his fiends.

"Aye, sir, can I ask of the prisoners?" Doran countered. It was a delicate, worrying question and one he had thought long on. Four hundred or more had surrendered to the invading defenders in the rush. They had hoped for mercy over retreating to the city. A wary warrior might think such behaviour was a tactic in itself. "I do not think they should be harmed."

"I agree," said Lillium.

"As do I," offered Wynn. "They surrendered and pledged to fight."

Magnus had been here before. He'd seen this argument on a lesser scale, one weighted less in favour of mercy, too.

"We are that desperate for soldiers?" Magnus asked.

"Sir, when we march on the city, I suggest we separate them from the rest, send them in ahead of everyone else," Wynn said. It was a cold proposal. Again, the old master general was impressed.

"Are you volunteering?" Magnus countered. It was easy to sacrifice one's self; easier to sacrifice those who could be enemies.

"Aye, sir," he said without hesitation.

"I will lead," Nomi muttered. She pointed at the map, rolled her fingers along the markings indicating their route, and tapped at the city.

"You are not welcome at this table," Magnus said with just the right amount of disdain to put her in her place.

"I will fight for my friends: I will lead the Southern Hunt. They will listen to me… old man." She did not meet his eyes. She shrugged. Despite himself, he was impressed with her confidence. War made and destroyed so many. He stood at a table with those who would not run in terror or greed. He had never realised how critical such traits would be.

"'Old man'?"

Wynn, sensing a storm growing at the table, stood between them. "I will gladly ride with Nomi in the first wave. It's probably death. But a fine death."

Magnus stared coldly at Nomi, who finally met his eyes. If she was intimidated, she showed little in her pretty face. No, not pretty. She was gorgeous. What irritated him most was that she didn't seem to realise how attractive she was, or to care. Such things were commendable, and he disliked that about her as well.

Behind her, he saw the movement of Riders approaching—two solitary figures dressed in Wolves' armour. For a moment, there was a stirring as they came, and he worried they were Riders bearing terrible news.

"Very old. Not like Erroh at all," she said, and Magnus stood up to her and grabbed her throat. Best to see the measure of any general he called upon, he thought. He half expected her to cower. In fairness, he loomed over her, and his grip was tight and cruel.

"Fuk you," she gasped, twisting his wrist and swinging fiercely with her free hand, landing a fine strike to his gut. Winded, he released his grip and fell away. For a moment, he expected a follow-through—a second fierce strike to send him to his knees.

Instead, she dropped her fist to her side and turned back to the table, point made. She was no pushover, nor was she interested in engaging in violent skirmishes for the small matter of poorly chosen words.

His generals made no move to either calm her or assist her. Perhaps they saw what he should have seen sooner, what Erroh had seen a long time ago.

"I see why he is fond of you, Nomi," Magnus said, standing beside her, following the route with his finger. "I may have misspoken," he said, and she nodded in agreement.

"As Wynn rides with the Southerners, I would ride with Doran into battle," Lillium said. The bald Alpha nodded, and Wynn stared at her for only a breath. He offered a bow and little more, and only at that moment did Magnus understand how far a distance lay between them. More than that, neither seemed to mind. Perhaps there were couplings grown rotten that couldn't be repaired.

"As you wish," Magnus said. "We must rush, appear on the horizon and catch them in one fell swoop." He looked at the Southern girl. "The Southerners take the centre; they charge first. My savages will follow after. The rest will flank."

"Sounds like a plan," said Lillium.

"Simple enough," Nomi agreed.

"It will work," offered Magnus hollowly. He was distracted once again by the approaching Riders. Under armed guard, they were drawing closer to the table. His savages looked suspicious, but Magnus recognised one of the approaching men. Darian was his name; a nice enough man, though a little dim. He carried parchment; his face was animated in excitement. And why wouldn't he be excited? There was an additional army to call upon.

"What word from Aymon?" Doran cried, running from the table. He looked like a man unprepared for more dreadful news. "Is there word of a march?"

"No, sir. I bring news from Master General Erroh, and"—he looked to Magnus—"Elise, the bandit queen of Adawan."

"What? What did you say?" cried Magnus disbelievingly. He ran to the man, gripping his shirt. "They live?"

"Sir, they march on Spark City with near five thousand."

Magnus's knees went weak. Only Nomi caught him as he stumbled. Such was the shock that for a moment he was sure that he was dead, and they were to appear to him in the afterlife. "It can't be," he gasped, but he knew it was possible. His son the hero, his mate, the legend.

"Tell us everything," demanded Doran, gripping the shoulders of both messengers. Magnus could feel it now. Could feel the change in the air and the stirrings of hope. He looked around at all his generals. His son's generals. They could feel it, too: a certainty that the end was just a breath away.

They were right.

87

CHOOSE IT GOOD

"What did you do, Erroh?" Elise asked. She had that face on her. That same disapproving face that only mothers wore. Without words, she warned against lying. Throughout his entire life, he'd rarely been able to deceive her. His father? Now that was something else entirely. It was a fair question. Admittedly, he'd done quite a lot to Lea throughout their courtship, love, separation and reconciliation. But this time, he wasn't sure what he had done wrong, or why he had earned her indignation.

"I did nothing."

It was no lie. Nevertheless, Elise sniffed the hazy afternoon air. He couldn't believe she was still drawing breath, still fighting. Similarly shocking was coming upon his comrades from Raven Rock. To share an embrace with Wrek and especially Tye had been a wonderful thing. The greatest surprise, however, was discovering Lexi alive and fearsome. He might have argued about her donning armour and walking with her companions, but he'd also taken a hand in moulding her into an excellent warrior. To deny her the right to fight would be a disservice to her, and to their cause. Painful and terrifying as the prospect was. They all had long since reunited, and it had been a glorious time, glorious enough that he had almost forgotten his agony. But all things ended, did they not?

"They do," whispered the absent gods in his mind.

"What did you do?" Elise demanded again from her seat in the saddle alongside him. Ahead of them lay burning sands, flickering and dancing in the heat. Beyond that, the subtle lie of glistening water remained ever distant. Then, he knew, came the green—and certain death at the city of light.

Behind them was the reassuring rumble of the thousands of soldiers who followed their lead, and he looked back, surveying them with pride and amazement. They rode as a united battalion, clinking and grumbling, praying and despairing and being human. Despite their better bandit nature, they were at war partly because of Elise's word and partly because of Erroh's presence.

"Very well, Mother. I may have mis-stepped," he said, turning back to Elise. He spoke of Lea's reasoning, and she replied with deep sighs. He'd not heard his mother breathing like this for years. He thought it almost miraculous. Almost the work of the absent gods. She'd said it was the salt air, and Erroh wondered about Emir's thoughts on such a thing. For a breath, he missed his fallen friend. Only a breath, though, for they were on the move, and these sorts of musings were of no use to a master general.

Though they rode side by side, his mount was a foot ahead of hers. She had insisted it be so, claiming none would follow her into war as they followed him. She had pledged herself to him, and it was a sobering thing. He had wanted to be sheltered by her, but she would not relent, nor let him relinquish either. She was a general in this final war and nothing else. Erroh wondered why, but suspected she did not believe she would live to see its end.

"Aye, you have hurt her. Earn her favour once more," Elise said after a time, and Erroh wanted to follow her advice, but that ship had sunk long ago. Although bitter and harrowing, these last few days apart from his mate had afforded him a certain numbness. He looked back at Lea now, talking quietly with her brother, a scowl upon her face. That was not the girl he'd fallen for, nor the woman he'd pledged to love forever. He snarled and hated her for the agony he suffered every time he glanced her way. He could take it no more.

"She bedded another," he told Elise. "How can I step back to that?"

"Oh." Elise looked back to his absent mate. She looked perplexed, as though she didn't believe her daughter-in-law capable of infidelity. She formed a fist and then allowed it to drop down to her side. A mother crossed was a potent thing, and just for a breath, Erroh wondered if he shouldn't have revealed such a crime. "I see."

"Aye."

"Are you sure?" she asked after a time.

"Aye. In her own words, she told me."

"I see."

"My crimes were committed for love," he muttered.

"She thought you dead; she didn't know." Elise looked unhappy. Confused as well. "Did she weep at your feet? Beg forgiveness?" There was a coldness in how she asked the question.

"She screamed it in my face."

"It makes so little sense."

But of course it made perfect sense to Erroh: learning of her lineage had sent her over the edge, and she had sought comfort where she could. It was awful, tragic, but he understood it. "I upset her greatly," he said evenly, "and she could not forgive."

"I see."

Elise thought on this a while, silent as their mounts struggled on the sandy surface. There was little the older woman could say that would make him feel better. He was no little cub, not anymore. And Lea was no cub either. She was a cruel witch who'd been unable to keep her hands off some foul brute.

Never trust a Wolf.

"Were I to have slept with another and had to face your father… I would have done so with tears in my eyes, with regret in my words. I'd have said it softly, even if I loved another. I would not punish as she did. Perhaps there is more at play."

"Your words sound hollow, Mother."

"Aye, perhaps they are; I'm sorry, my cub. You don't deserve this."

"Perhaps I do."

At nightfall, when the massive army set up camp below the clear night sky, Erroh went to Lea's tent and found her alone. He hated the relief he felt that he had not come upon her in rapture with another young bull. Instead, she was sharpening her blades in the light of a little campfire. Drahir sat with her. He offered a bow as Erroh appeared, and immediately looked uncomfortably back and forth between the two.

"I half expected you to have different company," Erroh muttered, sitting opposite his mate. His unfaithful mate. She shrugged and continued to sharpen her blade.

"I am glad you have found your family," she said. She did not meet his eyes; perhaps she thought of her family. Resurrected from the dead. From a fire.

"We have come far together, haven't we, Lea?"

"Aye, Erroh, we have."

"It's almost done."

"Aye, it is."

"I will not have you by my side another day," he said, and she stopped sharpening her blade.

"You would keep me from fighting for the city?" she said. Of course, she did. "You have no right, Erroh. I have earned my place in war."

He wanted to grip her shoulders. To scream in her face. To weep and demand she understand his agony. And tell her of the hurt she had caused. Instead, he bit the inside of his cheek.

"I cannot stand the sight of you, my beo. And to have you out of my sight will be a blessing. However, my feelings are of little relevance. I will have you do your duty: ride ahead with your Wolves, gather your comrades and join us in war." He spread out a map in the sand. "In five days, we will meet and march on the city as one army. Do not delay." He could see the festering anger in her beautiful features and said no more to her. Instead, he turned to Drahir and ordered the Southerner from his sight. Drahir had his orders too. It was best he made a movement on them rightly swiftly.

"As you wish, brother," Drahir said, climbing to his feet. "Goodbye, Cordelia," he said, turning to Lea. "When we meet again, may the world turn in our favour." With that, he bowed and retreated into the night, where his booming voice alerted his Southern comrades of their revised plans.

"You split us up for pleasure?" she hissed, and he recognised this female all too well. She was about to begin a war of words that he had no chance of winning.

"Grow up, child," he snapped, getting to his feet and turning to leave her before she could counter. She could spend the evening mulling his supposed pettiness all she wanted. The savvy move would be to follow Drahir's example and set off this night. Whether or not they did that was down to her.

He stormed away from the campfire, trying not to imagine what would become of her under the Wolves' rule. Erroh could have ordered her to stand beside him, anger or not. Instead, he returned her to her precious pack, back to duty—back to her lover, too, most likely. His stomach turned on itself, and he spat in the sand.

"To the fires with you, Cordelia," he muttered.

Lea had gathered together all her comrades by midnight, despite their irritation. They dared not argue, and why should they. They knew her mood well enough to know that they were likely to earn her ire. Sometimes a girl just had to scream. Her heart beat in excitement, as it had from the moment they had seen the army in ruin. Her thoughts were a blur of fury and fear. Not for dying, for she did not believe she would die—that is, not until she killed her bastard father and rid the world of his terror. Oh no, this fear was for her choices. Thrice, she had almost returned to Erroh to scream at him that little more, to put him in his place. To punish him for sending her away. For refusing to march into war with her. In truth, she had hoped he would be beside her in the end, lest he fall.

When he falls.

Her stomach churned as she secured the saddle on Shera. The beast took umbrage at being bothered at this late hour when it should have been resting for the march at dawn. "Shush, little one. Just a little run at night is all." She didn't want to leave. She thought back to her encounter with Erroh; there had been a certain beauty in seeing his anguish. It was no acceptable way to behave, but she couldn't help feeling like this.

It helped her not to love him.

She suddenly remembered seeing him falling from Highwind and believing him dead. Her hands began to shake uncontrollably as she fastened the saddle in place. Somehow, she knew when it did happen, when he did actually die, she would never be the same again. More than that, she knew she could never forgive herself.

Mostly, though, she knew she would be able to live with that burden of guilt. She was not destined to a happy life. Or a life at all, perhaps, after this cursed war.

"I see you are riding out," Elise said from behind her, and she jumped with fright.

"Aye, Mydame, I am." She tried to keep the coldness from her tone. She adored Elise, adored her legacy. Still, though, she was no great fan of her kin.

"My boy is a great man. Surely you see that?"

"I see it better than most," Lea offered. She did see him for all his greatness, and a curse upon him for it.

"This pleases me, for he must be at his best. Usually, with you by his side, he is better than that. Any fine mate is allowed to fight, particularly in wartime." She eyed Lea peculiarly and stepped closer, not like a hunter, but like a healer upon an infected patient. Interested, and prepared to draw blood.

"This is more than a mere fight between warring mates, Mydame, and I'll have you cease this prying," Lea snapped, stepping up close to meet the older Alpha face to face. She could feel the energy burning off this creature. To her amazement, Elise was now a far more potent entity, nothing like the invalid she had once been. Still, Lea was no delicate walking waif herself, not anymore.

Elise grinned at her anger. "What happened to you in the Wastes, little one, that you must spit such vitriol? That every movement is taken with purest venom? Was it my Erroh? Did he cut you so cruelly that I stand before a shadow of a thing?" She smiled sadly now. "A potent shadow, but a shadow nonetheless."

"You do not know me, Elise," Lea argued weakly, and almost screamed in frustration. The effect the legend had on her was intoxicating.

"I certainly did not believe you would stray," she said, getting to the point. Lea held her gaze, but inwardly burned with shame for her deceit, though she did not know why. She could feel the woman scrutinising her, seeking the truth, and Lea's face flushed. She looked away. "But I know anger, those felled by it. You, my girl, are crushed like fruit upon a fist."

She *was* angry; she wanted to scream the horror of her legacy. The shame, the shame, the terrible fuken shame of her bloodline's terrible atrocities. She wanted to weep in the older female's arms and reveal her terror of what she was capable of. Mostly, though, she wanted to tell the legend that she was not worthy of Erroh, for all his sanctimonious bravado. She was no longer Lea of Samara. That witch had died the moment Erroh had abandoned her.

Left me alone.

"I said what I must," she whispered.

"And what exactly needed to be said?" Elise said softly, moving closer now, and Lea crumbled beneath her gaze. "You lied, didn't you?"

"I… um… Leave me be."

Elise grabbed her roughly, shaking her ever so. She was deceptively strong. "Hate can be a gift. Hate can carry you far. But direct your hate at one who deserves it. Even if it is yourself." She released Lea, shoving her away gently. "Even if it tears you asunder. Choose that gift and see the path for what it is."

With that, she spun away and stalked off through the encampment, leaving Lea shaken. Elise did not know her well, but still, she clearly knew her enough to see through her lies, see her weakness for what it was. She did not know how, only that she did. For a breath, Lea considered following her mother-in-law, pleading for her silence, threatening her, pledging her fealty, or somewhere between. Instead, she stayed where she was and let her walk away. Words were words. Nothing mattered anyway.

Nothing matters but green eyes.

She immediately began to settle.

"Come on, Shera, we are riding this night," she whispered to the beast, placing her foot in the stirrup and swinging herself up into the saddle. Kicking Shera gently, she set off through the encampment, where Wolves waited for her upon horses of their own, their torches lit.

"Time is short. We must ride like the wind," she declared, halting before them. She knew Drahir would do the same thing with his own comrades. She also knew that Erroh would not wait for her while he rode into war.

She could not be left behind again.

88

GATHERING OF TOO FEW

Were Magnus able to, he might have led from the rear of the marching army, berating and challenging every warrior ahead as he did; such was his impatience. Keeping them frenzied and moving was his obsession, for he'd never been so desperate to reach camp. Moving steadily through the deep forest on the gnarled, rooted paths, dodging clinging briars and invisible menaces, Magnus had never been prouder. His son was out there somewhere.

He looked behind him, watching his warriors' exhausted faces, and guilt came upon him for the effort he was forcing them to make. Upon hearing of Erroh's plans, he'd doubled the intended pace of his army's march, allowing them to stop only when exhaustion took them. He could see they were close to breaking, arguing, revolting. They wouldn't, of course, but soldiers liked to threaten.

"Only a bit to go," he insisted loudly, bringing his mount to a stop and letting the warriors march past. He allowed himself to appear imposing above them; assured too. Sometimes a leader needed to remind them of his grandness. If they were reassured in the march, it helped in the heat of battle when panic struck and the desire to take flight took hold. He was confident that none of them would flee. Such cowardice was frowned upon, thanks to their belief in the afterlife beyond. Magnus cared little for such thoughts but approved of his warriors having faith, for it held them in battle.

"Of course there is," someone muttered among the marching lunatics.

"Sure, would I betray any of you?" he jested loudly, and they laughed at such a notion. There was nothing wrong with a little self-deprecating and most un-kingly jesting, after all.

Truthfully, though, any steps taken through the forest at such a late hour, by almost anyone at all, would be accompanied by cursing, cracking, stumbling and muttering. Hardly the finest preparation for an invading force, but according to the messenger, there was little need for silence and more need of haste. He thought again of his kin, his master general, his legendary offspring.

"As you wish," he whispered to himself, and thanked the fates of war for Erroh. And for his darling Lexi too. He wasn't used to smiling these days, yet here he was, watching an army chase the daylight across hostile territory, dragging all manner of war machines along with them, and he with a smile from ear to ear. Only a father's love could have sown such a smile. Truthfully, though, until he saw Lexi in all her grandness and discovered her untarnished and healthy, he might always suspect this to be a daring trap to lure him in. He shook those unhelpful thoughts away. Deep down, he knew they were both alive, for they were from the blood of the two greatest warriors ever to walk these lands.

His heart skipped a beat thinking of Elise. Discovering her still alive and fighting had brought him tremendous joy. He did not know what treatment had delivered her this time, only that as much as he had been overjoyed to discover his children still alive, his love for his mate was a different kind of joy. His kin could wait, but from the moment he'd learned of her wellness, every further hour apart had been painful. He had never felt this excited as a child, awaiting a grand gift hidden beneath ribbons and silk. He had never realised how much he needed her until he had lost her. Until he had found her again.

Magnus shook his head and wiped some dust from his eyes lest those passing comrades think him weak. "Almost there," he muttered, and they muttered in reply as they passed. He only moved on once the war machines began rolling along towards him. He knew these beasts and their deadliness against stone. Putting the Boat Town carpenters and smiths to work repairing them within an hour of their great sinking had been a brilliant manoeuvre by Mea. Perhaps there was still some fight in her, he mused.

They marched for hours, until twilight came upon them and the shattered moon lit up the night in all its violence. They persevered with the aid of torches until they neared a prominent slope where the trees thinned and the river filtered down towards a tremendous open expanse overlooked by a massive grey wall of suffocating darkness.

The Actions of Gods

"They didn't even put the lights on," Doran grumbled as he brought his mount alongside Magnus's.

"Not even a fuken torch to welcome us," Magnus said in reply.

The city looked the worst he'd seen it in decades. Without the stream of lights upon its wall, it appeared as nothing more than an ugly block against the night sky. He'd expected thousands, dug in and camped, watching the newcomers move across the crest above the city. Instead, he saw only a few guards in shaded wall towers above the ruined wooden gates. A fool might think the city abandoned, or better still, under Primary rule. Instead, Magnus knew, they hid behind the wall, licking their wounds, waiting to strike. He suspected there would be no attack this night, nor one tomorrow. They would stay until they had all their numbers clustered together; they would certainly not move at night, when they were at a slight disadvantage. So Magnus could do little but offer a thoughtful gaze to the city before following his soldiers up across the hill towards the meeting place of his family.

"Looks like we are the first to arrive at this shindig," Doran declared, dropping from his mount before ordering his Wolves and Boat Town volunteers to erect a camp. It was a pleasing, open space with plenty of grassland to make their own. Adequate water source too. Magnus could only stare into the darkness beyond, curse his swift pace and hope those he loved would be along for the most violent clashes the Four Factions would ever see.

Lea rode in between her two generals. She was a general too, of course. But really, she was more than that. The Wolves followed her unhesitatingly, and Aymon, to his credit, allowed her to lead them. Azel was happy in his own choice to watch and listen as the Alphas discussed tactics, routes and possible outcomes. Erroh had given her five days to prepare her Wolves, and they had not disappointed her. On the fourth day, they were ahead of the pack, ahead of all others. Chasing the pace, reaching their destination ahead of her lover. It was a petty act on her part, but she insisted upon it.

On the last morning, they were barely a dozen miles from Samara, and now, as the fresh droplets of rain brushed against her face, they neared the crest above the Spark, where death most certainly awaited them. Returning here less as an outcast and more as a conquering Wolf was strange. It was also strange to find it less her home and more a bastion of death. She felt a terrible sorrow come upon her. She could see the damage done to the walls, the gates. They needed to be more adequately repaired and made suitable for holding back the enemy. The sorrow soon passed to hate. Hate was a constant in her life, a reassuring friend. If nothing else, she could hate when scared, lonely, and without hope or anger. Then life had more purpose.

"Looks like we are late," Azel remarked, slowing his mount alongside hers and drawing her from her imaginings. Her comrade's eyes were not upon the daunting shadow of the city of light or the many burned-out war machines littering the landscape below them, but instead on the camp set up on the far side of the valley. For a moment, she thought it the remnants of Boat Town, slaughtered by the Southerners; such was the unfamiliarity of the banners, the colour of their armour, the appearance of an army assured of itself.

Magnus has returned.

"Who are they?" Aymon wondered warily. It was a fair question.

Behind the trio of generals, their Riders continued to trot along the path towards their meeting place. Erroh's meeting place. She tightened her grip on the reins, turned and searched for him among the gathering masses and their thousand and one tents.

"I smell a terrible trap," Azel said uneasily, and she almost smiled. She considered him an honourable comrade of the road, but he could not look beyond anything but deleterious things. It was an Alpha trait.

"I think it's the savages come to fight," she said, eyeing the emerald banner that was larger than all the others. There was a royal touch to it.

"Allies?" Aymon wondered.

Only then, with their Riders trundling along the crest of the valley, did the gathered army react to their arrival. They began to hurry around their camp, drawing weapons and gathering into formation, their movements unlike those of any Southern finger she'd witnessed. She looked to the city wall and the guards patrolling her upper battlements. They flew the banners of Uden, red and black and rightly fuken nasty, but the gathering of so many flags suggested savages.

She had no banner herself. Not even Erroh's.

"Let us greet them so," Azel muttered, and they broke ahead of their comrades, moving down towards the army so they might ensure peace and find assurances in the company too.

Suddenly, Aymon broke away from them, and from the marching Wolves. Once he was free from the masses, he dropped swiftly to the ground. From the other side came a bald brute who, likewise, dropped from his mount. The two met halfway, and their embrace settled tensions on both sides. A few eager eyes from behind the city gates might have worried ever so. While it was slight wariness watching a lesser army set camp, it was worrisome to see reinforcements appearing.

Dropping from her horse, Lea walked Shera the last few steps. She could see families at joy, at sorrow, and she wanted little of it. Instead, she looked to the city again and wondered was her father behind these hallowed, ruined gates. Was he watching with his green eyes?

Green eye.

She did not hear the assault, but she felt every crushing blow.

"Lea," the demon cried, wrapping its talons around her, and Lea almost fought herself clear—and then she saw the flash of bright blue in the morning air. "Oh, fuk me," the demon added, removing its leering mask.

"Lilli?" She looked like herself. Different from how she'd looked in Raven Rock, different from how she'd looked in the city too, but somehow familiar. Her long blue hair shimmered in the sunshine, and it was a good look to her, despite the scruffy appearance of her armour and leather garments. Lea knew she should have been ecstatic that her friend lived, but a wave of cold anger took her as though her mate stood before her, professing his love. She couldn't fight off the second assault from her oldest friend, such was Lillium's brute aggressive embrace, so instead she controlled her anger.

One, two, three.

"I can't believe you are alive—*couldn't* believe it," the girl wailed, and Lea was unmoved by her emotion. Nevertheless, she clung to her friend, for that was all she could think to do. However, her eyes were upon the city, and it settled her somewhat. She was so close to facing him, so close to revealing her shame. It was enough to settle any broken spirit. Make a girl smile at the appropriate time too.

Four, five, six.

"I am not yet done," Lea whispered. She smiled, and it felt better to smile. Easier not counting too. She resented Lillium, though she did not know why. If Lillium suspected her of any such thoughts, she made no show. Instead, she took her friend by the cuff of her shirt and dragged her back towards the camp. She behaved as though they were excitable goddesses of the city come Culling season, and Lea allowed her. "Where is Erroh?" she asked.

"He didn't march with you?" Lillium exclaimed. "He has not arrived. We must talk of many things. I must know what became of you after

Raven Rock," she cried excitedly, but Lea kept looking back to the city walls. She wanted to storm them alone, this very day. She also wanted an army at her back when she did. She didn't know what she wanted, but beating Erroh to the city greatly pleased her, as did not missing the greatest battle in the history of the Four Factions.

It was the little things.

"Lea," came a familiar voice, and she gazed towards the unmistakable form of a Southern whore bursting through the crowd like an excitable… whore. Strangely, Lea felt a trickle of warmth for the girl. However, she did not know why. Nor why she felt no irritation at her interrupting her reunion with her oldest friend. As Nomi bounded up to her like a diligent, loyal hound, she accepted the hug more openly than Lillium's. For just a moment, Lea took comfort in Nomi's reassuring presence, and this shook her.

What have I become, my dearest friend?

"Where is Erroh?" the Southern girl whispered, and Lea tensed. It was always all about Erroh. The entire world turned to the beat of his fuken drum.

"He is late," Cordelia hissed.

———

Elise rubbed at her chest absently. She could feel it like a creeping spectre in the middle of the night. Scratching and clawing, waiting to take hold again. She spat in the grass as she led her horse the last few steps. She'd been here before, returning to the city with a weight upon her chest. Last time, she'd not remembered the steps; now, fragile as her chest was, she was still able. Willing too. Beside her, Erroh, walking with thoughts of his own, fell still, and she walked on without him. His thoughts were his own, his gaze upon the city, and why not? She knew well what drove him. She was no longer the splendid ace of queens upon the deck. Hers was a lesser part in these last few days. She coughed again and felt a little break in her chest; precious air filtered into her lungs, and she was grateful for the relief. She had little desire to seek out some of Emir's eucalyptus remedies. That would come in time, after the war, after her final battle.

"Going to the city," she sang, then thought better of it. Better to focus on her breath, she mused. "There's a man I must see," she finished, despite herself. She missed singing. She hadn't sung in so very long. An incredible thing it was to fall out of passion with something so natural.

She wished she was back in Adawan, among the salt, with the sound of song echoing throughout the cave. Instead, she was home, and a coldness came upon her. She had seen this city this dark before, but tonight, at this late hour, there was an ominous aspect to the sight. She saw the looming walls for what they were now. No longer bright walls of light, inviting all to their tender touch. Now she saw indomitable walls with no siege engines to their name.

Lift your dress, Samara, so we might see what lies beneath.

If Erroh noticed her walk on, he said nothing, and that was fine. He had become quieter these last few days. He spoke little more of Lea's behaviours, instead choosing to focus on the battles to come and the horrors that would accompany them. She supposed such were the weights of leadership; she was an exemplary leader, though like any good leader she was grateful to be relieved of the burden. At first, she had been able to see the child in him, awaiting his mother's comforting words. More than that, in his words, she had seen how desperate he was to relinquish his leadership. It was a hard thing to ignore her son's subtle hints, but this war was not of her making. She was but an elder waif with weakening lungs.

In Adawan, it was different. There, she'd had breath and grace and resolve. With the coming of Wolves and Samarans, though, alongside her weakened health, it was better to leave him to find his way. In truth, though, Erroh was the greatest of her and Magnus's finer traits. She could see it in his sorrow and the strength he hid it behind. Like any mother, she had always thought him an honourable cub. Now, though, with him grown to manhood, she was so fuken proud of him. She might have said as much, but such things were better left unspoken when he behaved as impressively as he did. Better to say such things at the end of the world when there was nothing left but empty pledges and offers of approval. For now, leading this group and gathering his lesser warriors into a mighty fighting force was impressive enough.

"Will you come walk with us the last few steps?" she called to him, and he stared for a breath more before glancing her way. In the light, he looked more like Magnus than ever. A fine compliment. And such a wonderful reminder was also a cutting thing.

"Go on without me," he called, and looked back to the city, no doubt formulating plans to draw the Woodin Man from the stronghold. She looked to their numbers, to the gathered army, and though she was impressed with their march, they had not faced armies en route and had little opportunity to thin their Southern herd a little more.

"Don't be long, Erroh," she called, but he was lost to imaginings and that too was fine. He looked impressive, standing at the crest of the hill as the two armies gathered, watching the city like an eagle upon a stoop.

She marched on, absently counting her steps, absently counting the tents erected at their meeting spot. She could see Erroh's lead Riders approaching the settled army and commencing the welcoming rituals. And why wouldn't they be received? Did Elise's bandits not signify the final arrival that would herald much death and horror?

So many have come.

So many will die.

Though Erroh's Southerners had not yet appeared, they too were part of this fight. She looked to the dark forest beyond and reassured herself they would appear, for Erroh believed as much. She imagined she would fall, too, for she would fight like a goddess for as long as she could. For years she had thought herself incapable of warfare. This opportunity to turn the tide once more was a gift from the absent gods, and she would repay it with fine entertainment. They would demand blood, and she would give it her all until she was bled dry. She felt a coldness run through her, and like a thousand times before, she ignored it and focused on the gathering of many, but still too few.

Ahead, she could hear voices of excitement, exhilaration and feigned bravado, too, as allies met and were welcomed, and she increased her pace to be among the first few.

I know those banners.

For a moment, her stomach churned. In excitement, in disbelief. In terrible, cutting hope. She looked past the city flags and the banners of the Wolves to less familiar banners, from distant lands, from savage places.

It can't be.

She stared into the gathering of warriors; she saw how their armour differed from what she had expected. Her eyes darted from warrior to warrior as they emerged from tents, from campfires. From everywhere.

Oh please.

She looked upon one larger tent, grander and more regal than the others. She recognised that emerald banner, and prayed to the gods for one more kiss from him. One more embrace. One more fuken word. The tent flapped a little, and she was running, her mount left behind. Her bandits took little notice as she sprinted past them, moving quickly despite her weakness that dared not creep to the surface. She saw a figure step free of the tent. He was tall, imposing, impossibly perfect, for her and her alone. Her limbs were lithe, her speed impressive, and she caught sight of him and knew this miracle as truth. She was already weeping, as she had with her children before. But this was different. This was a certainty returned to her.

"Magnus," she cried, and her heart leapt. She called him again, and he followed her voice. He looked through the arriving crowd, but no one else was around—no comrades, kin or enemies.

"Elise?"

He dropped to a knee in shock, and she ran to him. Her heart hammered, and her mind reeled; she wanted nothing more than to hold this joyous moment still for eternity before they turned to war, death and similar inevitabilities. She also needed this moment to speed itself along, to reach her man quicker. He must have thought so, too, for his strength returned to his limbs, and he rose and ran towards her—a fantastic, impressive brute of a man, all for her and no one else.

Except on birthdays.

Among the gathering of Wolves, savages and refugees they collided, and unlike so many things in this world, it was perfect. He wrapped his arms around her as she leapt upon him, and they fell in the dewy grass and allowed soldiers to march on without regard. They kissed, loved, cried, and for just a breath, everything was well in the world again.

———

Erroh was struck fiercely by the massive, dark structure standing against the starlit sky. He had almost expected to see the city glow brightly in the night, like an amusing jest of Uden. Instead, the brute allowed her to sit in perpetual darkness, and she looked like a bulging cyst upon the natural land. She was no longer hiding behind electric light. He could see Samara in all her ugliness.

"Is this what we fight for?" he muttered to the wind. The wind offered little thought on the matter. He looked at the gathering army and ground his teeth. In truth, there were many warriors, but unlike before, there was no way to draw out the Southerners from within. His mind was awash with thoughts, each more desperate than the last. He'd been here before, contemplating an impossible task with only him and Lea and a gathering of heroes to defeat. It had never been about winning back then, and such was the case here, too. As once before in Keri, his grand victory lay in delaying the march. His task was to draw out the fuks into a ground war. More than that, he needed to draw out Uden himself. He wasn't naïve enough to believe Uden's death alone would end the war, but it would go a long way to stirring victory.

"I see you, Uden," Erroh mocked. The soldiers marching past paid little attention, and why would they? He was but a trembling cub, hiding behind a show of bravado. Upon his grand horse Highwind, they saw a heroic brute surveying his destiny, seeking greatness. In truth, he was far less than that. He held Highwind's reins tightly, lest his shaking hands reveal his terror and misery, and looked to the camps beyond. He saw Lea's Wolves among them, and although he felt relief at her arrival, he was cut anew by her sins against him. Even now, days on from her words, he found no solace. Nor would he ever. He felt the horror, his mouth became wet, and strength left him. He imagined her with another, pleasuring another, spending herself in another's arms in naked rapture, and it nearly took him as it had a thousand times before, a jealousy so vibrant and fierce and red that it was all he could do not to scream out and weep and rage and attack. He looked back to the city and hated it. He hated Uden more, and partly he hated himself—for his actions, for his miserable fate that had brought him to this horrible end, and oh, this was the end. He knew it like he knew the wind blew, like he knew the sound of thunder brought terrible things. He would die at the hands of Uden. But he would kill the fuker too. That was a fitting end to any tale. To any legend. An acceptable death and nothing but exemplary deeds left for those who would come after.

His only other hope was that Lea would watch him die and regret her choices, too. It was petty, it was unbecoming, but it was honest. He could be a legend, but also, he could be utterly pathetic.

Drawing himself away from the city and his inevitable fate, Erroh turned and stared across the land at the gathering of legends. This was his making, he mused, and with his pride, would come a terrible death for those who trusted him to save them. He looked at their similar determined, hopeful faces as they all counted those allies they had just formed up with. Admittedly, there were far more than he expected, yet still too few. It was a small matter, though. He only needed to drag Uden into battle, and that would be that.

I'll be ready for his skill this time too.

Erroh grinned at the thought. He'd thought like this before, of course, believed himself capable of killing Uden. An acceptable ignorance, he supposed, for knowing his true inadequacies was as sobering as thinking about his mate's activities.

Stop thinking of her that way, idiot.

He thought it good advice, and the absent gods thought so too. These were their words, after all. He could have looked among the gathering Wolves for his mate, but he had no stomach for such self-inflicted agonies. Instead, it was Elise's cries that drew a distracted smile. As was seeing his father, alive and well and running, as though he had no limp.

For a moment, he froze this wonderful moment in time, even as Lexi raced past him screaming her father's name. And somehow, for a breath, he was a cub again, watching his hero, magnificent and unbeatable, seeking his approval, terrified to veer from his path.

"These tracks are my own," he whispered and, following the rest of the soldiers, made his way across the crest of the hill above the unwelcoming city, towards his family, to enjoy a brief few moments before the world shook and Erroh, the legend, went to war.

Alone.

89

LONG GOODBYE

Her name was Aurora, and she liked to kill. And very soon, she would take her last victim. She knew this, for she was tired of this world, this city, this agony. She had decided to leave. But not until she had made one final gift. To a god. From a goddess.

"Away you go," she whispered to her exhausted mount as it wandered slowly around among the trees. She had little need of the beast now that she was marching into this cesspit of a city with the unlikelihood of ever leaving. The mount appeared unsure what to do, free of its saddle and pack. "You are free." She pointed to freedom somewhere beyond the thick canopy of green. "Go before I decide to eat you," she snapped, and the mount went on its way, albeit slowly. She felt for the foolish creature. No doubt, having spent no solitary day free since its birth, it relied on humankind to feed and tend to it. It would struggle out in the great world, as did many things. But those who were worthy rose above like fyreflies in the night—for a short time, granted, but beautiful and unchained nonetheless.

Hidden among the trees, she watched the army retreating towards Samara. She knew them as former comrades but not their intentions nor where they withdrew from. They looked jaded and battered. A massive number, too, and she wondered what horrors they'd faced to send them scurrying to the city without shame.

Slipping free of her hiding place, she skulked through the darkness, counting her steps as she did. Swift, even steps, drawing her ever nearer to their wretched, defeated march. With dipped head and slumped shoulders, her eyes hidden behind cracked spectacles and hair tight in an unattractive bun, she played the ever-insignificant soldier perfectly. Effortlessly, she slipped in among the hundreds streaming through the creaking gates as though it was no small thing to singlehandedly invade a city.

There was a dreadful energy to this place, as though death walked freely, and those within accepted the guest openly. It felt less a triumphant bastion of supremacy and more a sanctuary for the weary and weeping. They gathered where the market once stood, and Ealis was horrified. Gone was the vibrant, burning city of life, replaced instead with charred walls and streets filled with debris. She remembered disliking this place when she had hunted long before, but now, under Uden's leadership, his touch, his poisoning, it had fallen to dire ruin.

The retreating army were tended to by lines of helpful comrades, fresher and without the weariness of war. They would face such strife soon enough, she imagined. For now, though, they greeted the shamed soldiers with hot beverages and blankets. Aurora might have been tempted to take a loaf of bread, such was her hunger, but no such things were offered. Instead, as quickly as she'd joined their mass influx, she slipped free down a side alley, using night as her only companion in this city of enemies.

She was ready to say goodbye. But first, there was a hunt to complete. One final act she had to tend to. And then, afterwards, a sweet goodbye. Her soul stirred at such notions; among the shadows, she allowed her mind to shift, her heart to beat wildly and her mouth to fill with saliva.

The first night was the most difficult. Slipping from house to house, seeking shelter and food, she felt wretched, for such things were below her. Long after dawn, she found herself a little unused abode. A locked door, shaded windows, a bed and little more. It was a perfect start, for a goddess could find anything she needed after this; she only had to ask the right way—and Aurora Borealis could ask every question every way imaginable.

As armies gathered outside the city, she went to work building herself a right little life. Perhaps, were she inclined, she could have waited out this entire war, and no one would have been the wiser. Not even Uden and his cursed eye. Her dwelling became one of the finer hovels in the city. She stole for herself fine treasures and finer weapons. More than that, she stole with a dazzling smile, and some lucky victims were charmed as they surrendered their riches to her. She thought it a fair price.

Days passed, and somehow, she kept herself from losing her nerve and the scent. Every morning, she rose early and walked this wretched, sieged city. Keeping to the side streets, hiding beneath a hooded cloak and avoiding the generals where possible, she learned the feeling of the city and the mood of the soldiers within as they endured the war.

For those lucky few who went to war.

She listened intently to the collective drawl from those within this dreadful place between the bouts of battle and retreat and loss and brutality. Aye, some still believed. Still desired for the great fires to burn away the tainted. Those fools offered little of interest. But further in, among the ranks of warriors, she sniffed out a little dissent. She learned of their boredom, fears and longings for things more extraordinary than their share. Their fortress. Their prison. Many spoke openly of distaste for Uden. They called him cowardly; they called him cautious; they called him seething. Were she his lover still, she might have hunted down every vocal renegade, followed them to their shacks or tents near the front gates and slit their throats as they slept. Fewer mouths to feed and all that. But Aurora did none of that. Instead, she smiled and charmed, stole and survived, and learned everything she could about her prey.

And Uden saw none of it.

She watched from the walls the actions of armies. She saw them at their worst, when the screams reached her at her lookout high above, but also when they were settled and peaceful and all that remained were the dead strewn in the fields below. Too few battles, yet so many dead. So many bodies covered in blood. So much blood that were she to drop down, she might have fallen into a deep crimson pool. Imagining that drop, she had visions of Erroh falling from such a height and surviving, and her mouth watered again, for she craved him. Not as a lover at all; she had tasted godliness and stepped far from it. Instead, Aurora contented herself with worship from afar, like any pure zealot. And she would follow his godly will as though he had commanded it himself.

Away from the wall, down in the shadowy streets, she learned the location of her quarry from an unfortunate general unfamiliar with her legend. It wasn't hard to pry the information from his grateful lips. Nor was it hard to conceal his body after. She knew her quarry was living it up when she saw their mansion in the heart of the city late in the night. Fit for a god or a queen. However, after many hours watching for signs of her prize, she reckoned this lavish estate to be little more than a frustrating prison. In those same shadows, she stumbled upon a plan. A brutal plan. A plan worthy of a goddess determined to finish a task she'd set so long ago. Red hair came to mind, and Aurora knew, as she knew the counting of steps, that she would be victorious.

From another wanton general, drunken and clumsy and altogether too grabby, she learned the more intimate details of a grand wedding, and her mind became awash with glorious visions of blood upon the sand and the screaming of her victims. Licking her lips, she mapped out her route, sharpened her finer blades and dared to wonder about a little savage murder.

On the last day, she donned her finest stolen garments, painted her face wonderfully and wrapped her hair up intricately in a style she had never worn before. The spectacles remained, however. It wasn't difficult to present herself as a dignified wedding guest. No more than a dozen feet from her god Uden, she concealed herself in the side passage of the Cull, among the other notable guests, as Uden welcomed his niece to womanhood by way of a drunken healer husband. She'd slithered into more precarious places in her time with less lavish garments upon her, but truly, it was wonderfully terrifying to stand so close to the fire.

Admittedly, she might have been wiser to watch from afar, but she couldn't help herself. Ealis feasted her eyes upon the goddess in the white gown as she spoke her vows, loved her man, and earned the heavenly gaze of Uden. And Emir's shy words of commitment might have brought a smile to her face; such was his terrible discomfort. She mostly listened as Uden spoke kindly of loving things, and she barely recognised him anymore. He was diminished, tired and older. She still felt stirrings for him, for he was still the most potent fiend in the room.

Aurora did everything to avoid his godly gaze until the service was concluded with a delicate yet passionate kiss between the two lovers, much to the reserved approval of the audience. She followed the wedding party down through the streets and thought it a rather amusing thing that as the city remained sieged, as the god was called out to war alone, as the Southerners thought less of his actions, they still bowed, they still adored Uden as though he were formidable. As though he were a god. As though his mind were upon proper things. He revealed weakness in his love for Roja, a depth of love she'd never seen. A love she might have wanted once. Such a thing might infuriate a girl if she counted the blessings that had brought her to this life.

Tamping down her feelings, she followed as a guest, feigning a humble smile, engaging in whatever inane conversation her guests-in-arms offered as though it were a glistening thing to be respected. She played the meek follower just right, until they reached the arena where the guests were tended to and the rest were sent to observe and approve from a distance.

As the city shook from bombardment like an awful thunderstorm, Aurora sat upon the stands with countless unworthy others and watched the generals celebrate this fabulous day, and she was disgusted. She allowed herself one glass of sine early in the evening before leaving the party early to attend to duties leading to her inevitable death.

It wasn't a long distance, and she covered it swiftly. Waiting and studying the guards' movements took her longer than she'd have preferred, but she accomplished her task with guile and swiftness, and, most importantly, the cover of the shadows. Three guards, all killed in sudden, silent violence. Admittedly, she might have eluded their notice as she gained entry, but three fewer guards to deal with in the aftermath could be the difference between victory and defeat. Besides, it was something to do while waiting. She would have preferred to kill four in total, as it made finer sense in her mind. Still, three was enough, she supposed, and concealing their bodies in a large bunker beneath mounds of coal took no longer than an hour. With only the unpleasant black dust marring her fingers, she slipped into the residence through the top floor, where washing her hands with soap and water removed the coal, leaving a fresh aroma of roses in its absence.

Wonderful.

She was not bored waiting for the newlyweds to return home to consummate their vows. She made a pleasing sandwich of cheese and salted meat, with just the right amount of mustard too. She thought it a fine last meal and wondered if Roja or Emir would notice their absence once they returned.

Long after midnight, they arrived home, bumbling, drunken and careless. She listened with glee and a little relief that the task was finally at hand. They burst through the bedroom door where she lay in ambush, and she was delighted. As she stepped out and introduced herself, the faces of the beautiful, drunken lovers turned from joy to horror. Emir leapt in front of his bride, begging for mercy, and Aurora thought it a wonderful gesture, even as she tried to calm her quarry, lest they alert whatever guards remained out on the street. She tried to cover Roja's mouth lest she scream, and barely missed the swipe of dagger in the redhead's grip.

"I mean you no harm," Aurora cried, slipping quickly away from the second strike before gripping the redhead's wrist and slapping the blade away. It spun away into a corner, and Aurora raised her hands, all empty of weapons, and stepped away, doing her best to appear as non-assassin as possible. "I'm here to rescue you."

To her dismay, the sight of Roja brought forth a wave of crippling guilt for the agony she had caused. She wanted to drop to her knees, to beg for forgiveness. To explain his terrible grip upon her mind. To offer her life in reply. But not yet. Not until her deed was done.

"Why are you here?" demanded Emir, reaching for the blade. Then, after a moment, he decided it was better in the hands of his wife.

"Atoning for my crimes, unless you would rather stay in this city as it burns."

"Burns?" Roja demanded. Even inebriated, with hair dishevelled after being pinned up for so long, Aurora thought her the most beautiful goddess—after herself, of course.

"Your people wait for you on the other side of the wall, and I know the way free," she whispered. It was her gift. It was all she had.

It took longer than Aurora would have preferred to convince the drunken newlyweds of her intentions, perhaps because she had to keep repeating what she said. Eventually, as fear brought them closer to sobriety, they trusted her enough to take their chance. They wandered drunkenly after her, having covered their lavish wedding outfits in heavy cloaks, answering her silent orders more or less effectively, while she tended to the guards outside their prison. Eventually, with three new victims for the night, which made it six, an acceptably equal number, Aurora led them quietly away towards freedom.

With the shattered moon as their guide, the trio glided from street to street, carefully avoiding questioning guards or keen-eyed generals. Instead, they played the part of Southern veterans merely walking the night streets, albeit with dipped heads and low, muffled voices. She knew the route and how quiet it would be at this late hour.

They spoke little on their journey, and this suited Aurora. For all her wily actions and assuredness at dragging the truth out of unwitting victims, she still had not mastered the art of contrition beyond holding sorrowful thoughts in her mind. Where could she even begin? Leading them to safety was a fine place to start, she supposed. She kept telling herself this every few steps as the night drew in. The path looked clear, and, most importantly, they neared escape.

Their escape.

Beneath the gates at the rear of the sparkless city, they reached the lone guard house dug into the wall rearing out over the water. It was all that stood in their way. Her mind was awash with dizzying thoughts of redemption. They were close. So fuken close that she could taste freedom on her quivering tongue. It was almost honey glazed.

Along the grand pier, where a thousand and one ships might have launched, they shuffled up to the gates. There, she dropped to her knees and went to work picking a massive lock that secured a set of chains over the entrance.

She was no master of the lock, but she was gifted enough. It was a skill she'd learned not from her god but from her life before. A life in which she hadn't practised nearly enough. Thrice she'd practised breaking these locks, and thrice she'd known success in a few breaths alone. But now, perhaps with the cool air, in the frenzy of immediacy, her fingers slipped ever so. The chains rattled a few times, and she swore she heard a guard in the tower above curse as he went to seek out the noise.

"I'm just the wind," she whispered to the light a few dozen feet above. She willed the occupants within to think as much, and mercifully, no head appeared out the window, wondering why three figures were hunched low, acting all shady and mysterious.

"Can you break it?" Emir hissed. He, too, looked to the light above and the slow-moving shadows within. Before she could reassure him, the click answered for her. "Oh, I suppose you can," he said, helping her lay the chain quietly on the stony ground.

"Through these gates, down through the abandoned shacks, and swim across the mother, and you will be free of here," Aurora whispered, sliding the gate open to allow them through.

"You aren't coming?" Emir asked, leading the way, brushing past her. If he cared for her reply, he never pushed for it. Instead, he sought the other side, leaving Roja and Aurora alone.

"I am sorry for what I did," Ealis whispered, turning to Roja. She wanted to take her friend's hand, capture the words that streamed around her mind like a howling tempest, and gift them to her. She wanted to pledge fealty, beg forgiveness and tell her she looked most beautiful today. Instead, she stared dumbly at the ground and wondered what the gravel tasted like. It was something to do when apologising for an impossible act of betrayal.

"You opened the gates on us in Raven Rock."

The memory of that sin stung as much as killing an old defenceless Alpha in the dead of night. It stung as much as killing a king and his beautiful son. It stung as much as hunting an old Ranger to his doom. It stung as much as betraying a lover to his slaughter. It stung as much as watching her friend fall with two crossbow bolts embedded in her stomach.

"I was wrong," Aurora countered weakly, and Roja shook ever so slightly. She looked out to the gate where she could see Emir moving, hunched low, seeking a route through the hovels towards freedom. "I can never make up for my actions, no matter what I try. But know this: I will undo what evils I have done." It wasn't much of a speech, and Roja looked far from convinced.

"So, you will stay hidden behind these walls until the war is done?"

"I will do what I must." Truthfully, she had quite the deeds to accomplish this very night.

Suddenly Roja reached out for her and dragged her into an embrace, and for a moment, Ealis rose above it all and nearly cried. Nearly fell apart into a thousand pieces as well. She fought this gesture even as she allowed the girl to embrace her tightly and offer a solitary kiss on the cheek. She had considered her a friend once. Perhaps Roja had seen the tremendous hold Uden could have upon anyone. Perhaps she saw Ealis for the broken pieces she was.

Her back exploded in agony, and she slipped from the girl's grip, falling to her knees and then collapsing to the ground. She could barely breathe, such was the pain. And Roja stood over her, cocking her head to the side as though she were an insect beneath her foot.

"I will do what I must," Roja hissed, and the terrible coldness wrapped in hatred was evident now. Aurora struggled and felt the blade where it had pierced. She had endured wounds before, but never this deep, never this mortal. She gasped and held her tongue lest the guards look out and undo her last act. "Fuken bleed, you whore," Roja said, and stomped down once upon Aurora's beautiful face. It must have been a heavy stomp, for Aurora imagined she could hear bones break, and fresh suffering took her. She lay there, dying and awaiting one further strike. One last kick to crush her head to mush. She wondered if she had done enough to escape the darkness or if her soul was long lost to the next world.

"Goodbye, dear friend," Ealis said, and spat a back tooth free from her mouth. An unhealthy amount of blood spilled free, and she could only blink and allow herself to breathe her last breaths, tasting the ground as she did.

It was bitter.

"May the wind be at your back," Roja snarled, and spun around to follow after Emir, and Ealis was left to die alone in the middle of insignificance.

Her name was Aurora, and she liked to die. She knew this because she was very good at it. She did not know how long she lay on the ground with a dagger in her back, except that her will alone drove her to move. A few steps. Before she died.

Summoning whatever reserves she had, she climbed to her feet and, careful not to pull the offending blade free lest she bleed herself dry too swiftly, struggled away from the harbour back towards the city centre.

Every step was anguish, yet somehow, without spilling all of herself, she stumbled deep into Samara's heart and came upon his domain. It was the grandest house in the city. It hadn't been too difficult to locate, though Uden had been a perilous prey to seek out.

She did not know how she killed his six Azier guards, only that she did so in a blurred vision of wrist bolts and daggers and impossible luck. She wasn't silent in her undertaking, and that was fine. She only had to reach his room and slit his throat. Injured or no, she would do it. A singlemindedness took her, and she used all the hate of her twisted life to break through that stubborn front door, march up those sixteen steep steps, and seek him out, just twenty paces from the landing in the grandest room of the house.

"Where are you, my love?" she mocked, her voice slurred and distant. Her vision was even darker than usual in this light. She met one more guard outside his doorway, and this fight was no simple task. The young cur was swift and heroic. He charged her before she could fire off a bolt, hoisting her high and crashing against the far bedroom wall. Such pain took her that she almost wailed for mercy, but instead, she drew that dagger from her back, condemning herself as she did, before driving it through his exposed throat three times, and then a fourth, and then he went still. And then, wrapped in another man's embrace, she looked up to see her weary, drunken false god outside his bedroom.

"What has become of you?" he snarled, but she could see his shock, his fear.

"I come on behalf of the true god, Erroh. If you will not face him, I will do his will. His actions occur through me, Uden," she gasped, knowing her breathing had few rounds left. She pulled herself free of her victim and held the dagger aloft, and Uden stood shirtless, watching her. Although he was fresher, still, she knew she would take him. She was born in blood, and she would die in it. Drown in his blood too.

Drown in it.

"You are to die, little one. Shut those beautiful eyes so they won't see it coming," he whispered, and it was a seductive roar.

She detested him. Her hate gave her further dying defiance. If nothing else, her eyes would be open to spite him when they lost their light. She sprinted at him, waving the dagger with all her might. Just a few steps to reach him. She expected him to recoil, seek protection and meet her attack as he had done a thousand times before. Instead, he watched her body crash against the wall, half a dozen steps short of her destination. She dropped the dagger. Heard it clatter at her feet. She felt cold as her knees buckled, and only then did she realise her fate.

"I hate you," she gasped, and thought them cutting words, even as she fell. Aurora had truly failed.

"Born in blood," he whispered as he caught her. She finally wailed, broke, and gave up. "Not long now. Unless I tend to you," he warned, and she knew his words were cruel. She needed to kill him, to hurt him. To fuken scratch him. Instead, she was drained. So very tired, and she felt herself plummet from a cliff, and the only remedy was to sleep away the terrible journey.

"I killed Roja tonight," she lied, and it was a pleasing lie. She could see it on his face. The sudden terror that a creature of his creation would tear apart his only kin. "She looked beautiful, and I spilled her dry, all over her white wedded dress."

He dragged her to him, lifted her high so that she felt as though she were flying. She heard him threaten her and challenge and demand, and Aurora decided to close her eyes so she wouldn't see his terrible and fatal last act upon her.

She cared little for whatever it might be.

90

CLAIMED

It was a fine tent, in truth. Large, heavy and built for withstanding fierce storms and the sun's burning rays. A master general's tent, no doubt, and Erroh had little interest in being in it a moment longer than he needed.

"You are insane," argued Nomi, and he almost smiled. She alone had issue with Erroh brokering peace with the Southerners. She claimed it wasn't the peace talks; it was more the small matter of Erroh alone attending such a thing. She argued that she should be allowed to stand with him. She argued longer than any other at the table, and indeed, he was humbled by her dedication.

"I won't be alone for long," he assured her, looking around the room to the others in attendance. His generals, his allies, his loved ones, most of them. "You'll see my signal, and you fuks come running." He tapped the detailed map of Spark's potential battleground upon the table in the middle of the impressive tent to emphasise his point and reaffirm that they knew where they needed to be. His generals nodded in silence at his orders. He thought them well constructed. Intricate. And just about reckless enough to work. His generals did, too, apart from Lea.

"We'll be along right swiftly, Master General," ensured Magnus. A good thing, too, considering any delay might result in him losing his head. Then where would their plans be?

He did not bother to look at his mate. Her silence on the matter spoke loud enough. She would fight, and that would be enough, he supposed. He wondered if she would come to him on the eve of battle and ask forgiveness. Instead, she had remained among the tents of the Wolves, no doubt pleasuring those who needed it before going into battle. He ignored the crushing visions in his mind. The same thoughts churned his stomach so fiercely that he thought he might throw up. Instead, he thought when best he might offer a final kiss and be done with this awful torment.

Not yet.

But soon.

"It is time we go to war, my brave comrades," he said, and they waited for more. Waited for a few stirring words. But he had none. He thought each of them hardened and ready. Theirs was to inspire those beneath them. If they required Erroh's ill-thought bravado to carry them into war, they did not belong at this table, in this impressive tent offering a voice.

They watched in grim silence as he stepped out into the rainy morning. He heard a few muted wishes of good fortune upon him but ignored them. It was all in the hands of the absent gods anyway, wherever the fuk they were. Marching through the camp as his generals surged out behind him, eager to tend to task lest they let the entire world down due to sluggishness, he wondered were they as enthusiastic as he was to get to war.

The previous night had been one of joy shared among many comrades. The gathering of all forces was beautiful for those who needed it, but something Erroh had little passion for. Aye, he had embraced his father, his friends too. He had sat for a time and listened to their tales, but his mind was elsewhere. There had been no grand gathering, no sharing of food and alcohol, for only a fool celebrated on the eve of battle. As night set in, Erroh had taken a bed in a small tent far from the gathered few, where he had slept well. A fine thing, for he imagined he'd sleep little the next few days. Or else he'd sleep for a long time after tasting a blade's tip. He might have spoken with Lea of such things, but she had been as cold to him as before, and despite himself, he was growing accustomed to her silent vitriol. It had been an unremarkable night, and he had risen fresh and renewed and ready for the horror to come.

Stopping to drink from a barrel, he allowed the rain to wash over his grizzled features and wondered if he should have taken a moment to bathe and shave before the end. He decided against it, then went to his tent and recovered his armour and weapons before praying to the absent gods that Uden would answer him and come visiting.

Come out and fight me, Uden.

Long ago, Erroh had believed in little more than winning, but violent humbling was sobering, as was learning his shortcomings. Once, he'd thought himself the greatest swordsman ever to live, but really, that title belonged to the brute he called out. Yet here he was, trying his hardest to get that bastard to attend a simple game of death.

Is dying a worthy sacrifice for the war?

Of course it was, when the words were spoken aloud. However, it was a dreadful, sobering thing to think it, here, alone, where no one could argue against his instinct for survival.

Just you.

Just fuken you.

Finding a sheet, he wrapped it around a long wooden pike to form a flag and began his solitary pilgrimage down to the Spark. He could feel his comrades' many stares. Those he loved, those he'd never met. Moving away from the relative safety of the camp, he marched on the city. It was a long walk, filled with a milliard of regretful thoughts and memories. When he reached the humming hydro machines, long silent and whose mechanics he knew little of, he thought of his first visit to this awful place, and a tremendous sorrow came upon him. If that little cub could have known the events that would take place since then or have learned that he alone would fight for the city, he would never have believed it.

Come out and fight me like a man.

Not a fuken god.

"Oh, Spark, you have broken and twisted me. Yet, here I am," he warned, looking to her dark walls. Further sorrow came upon him as he continued trudging through the abandoned Ranger camp, tainted by time, battle and Southern encampment; little remained now but memories. He thought fondly of a grand gathering here right before the end. Before Dia. Before imprisonment. Before finding brothers in the dark. "You, who hated and beat me, yet still, I fight for you, bitch," he mocked, and, drawing his sword, he slit his palm along its edge. He fought the pain grimly, knowing it would be little to the wounds he would receive.

"And so it begins," he whispered, wiping his hand on the white flag, smearing the piece with crimson, before leaving himself to bleed and waving the flag high in the foggy morning.

"Uden!" he roared, gazing at the distant Southern warriors upon the walls, wondering if they recognised him. Did their false god? "I see you!" he mocked, and grinned. He swallowed his horror, swallowed his fears, swallowed his mercy too. He assumed the stance of a warrior and beckoned the Southern god to come play.

For a time, nothing happened, and Erroh thought fondly of Jeremiah of Keri. He wondered whether he watched from the darkness beyond with a glass of crimson wine and good company. Erroh hoped as much. That would be nice. The bloodied white flag continued to wave, and Erroh continued to call out Uden. He mocked him, threatened him, demanded and demeaned him in their savage tongue; in his own too.

And then something did happen, and Erroh's arms began to itch, such a terrible itch that he almost stopped waving that flag of white and blood. The gates began to creak open with a terrible scream of metal twisting, and Erroh wondered could they take the force of many volleys of stone, should it come to that?

Feel nothing.

Play the part.

"Uden!" Erroh roared as twelve figures emerged from the gates, dressed in their finest armour. Uden's generals, no doubt, come to talk with the foolish cub making a scene at the front. He suddenly felt like the most watched prey in a hunter's tournament. All sides waited. For peace? For war? For friendly accord? Unlikely.

"Where is the coward Uden?" he commanded, ensuring no fiend hid a missing eye behind an impressive face plate, but these were no gods; no false gods, either. They were members of the regiment, no doubt arriving to outnumber him and send a message. That was fine. The odds were acceptable, and Erroh was in no mood to let Jeremiah's sacrifice go unanswered.

The tall brute who spoke for the god led his companions, and the world slowed, and he called out the inevitable truth. Of course, it would take more than a few loosely chosen words, a little petulance and no sign of force whatsoever for a god to grace Erroh with his presence.

"Uden will not speak with—"

It was all Erroh needed to hear. Had the generals taken a moment to notice Erroh's flag, they might have seen the weapon upon which it was mounted. With a subtle twist and a mighty lunge, he drove the anti-cavalry tip through the speaker's face mid-reply and kept pushing it until it ripped right through him and speared one of his comrades behind him. A terrible way to die, no doubt, and a shameful act on his part.

Did you see that, Jeremiah?

It only took a breath for Erroh to draw his swords as the dead men shuddered and fell, shocking the rest of the men to stillness. Ten against one was a fairer battle, and one Erroh dared to play a hand with. He leapt forward, slicing with Mercy and Vengeance, with arms swept wide like the figure upon the holy man's totem. It didn't matter if he killed; cutting deep and taking them from the fight for a few breaths mattered. He drove into the fiends, slashing and tearing, and it was easy, for it was dishonourable. And that was fine, for they had started it in a little lost town long ago before all this began.

He drew away, spinning his blades, and only then did they draw their swords, but the damage was done. Three more lay dead, and another two were scrambling away with grievous injuries, howling their terror, and Erroh wondered whether their god had foreseen such stupidity. Such wonderful recklessness.

Kill them all.

It was a fine plan, and instead of retreating, he charged forward, engaging the nearest in a desperate duel. Blades clattered and clashed, and his opponent was impossibly fast and wonderfully skilled, but he was no match for a crazed Alpha trying to send a message. Erroh took the cur apart. It took a few breaths longer than needed and was perhaps a little ostentatious but practical, he supposed. He severed one of the man's arms at the wrist. The hand bounced to the ground and the generals stared at it in horror. The man screamed, and Erroh sent Vengeance through his heart, killing him instantly.

He did not allow the rest of them to form up on him, and they were too shaken to attempt any proper, disciplined approach. That wasn't to say they weren't highly skilled. In that moment, he wondered, were they the finest warriors Uden called upon? It was possible, such was their skill as they met and drove back his attacks before forming their own, only to meet his defiant defence. Bodies tripped and stumbled around him, trying to kill, and they never spotted their fatal flaw. Perhaps, were they accustomed to fighting in a group as this, they would have slain him, but as it was, each got in the other's way, and as he cut and tore, they fell away in sprays of crimson and murder, and it was easy.

To anyone watching, he looked a sight, singlehandedly tearing a dozen warriors apart. Anyone who blinked might have missed the entire thing. As it was, Erroh displayed skill he never thought himself capable of and won the day, or, better yet, won the first skirmish of Spark City.

The last warrior fell to a brazen spinning of blades before Erroh leaned in and slashed him below his guard, through his leather armour and across the belly, then held the blade inside him as he collapsed to his knees. He struggled, but Erroh raised his sword and held him aloft before slowly ripping his insides free with a gruesome cut. The man died screaming; though it was a shameful deed, it was a necessary cruelty, Erroh told himself, trying to excuse his indifference to such murder.

Feel nothing.

Play the part.

Kicking the body away, he turned to stabbing those who still took breath—a grisly task. One fiend feigned death; he hadn't been cut as severely as the others. He lay still with eyes tightly shut, and he was a pitiful sight. Were it another day, Erroh might have allowed him his ruse. Might have let him live this day. As it was, Erroh needed to intimidate, be cruel, and call out a god hidden behind an indomitable wall. He finished off the remaining defenders before turning to the fiend, then dragged him up and battered him with a gloved fist as he screamed for mercy in both tongues.

"Silence, cur," Erroh roared, but the man argued.

"Please."

"You will not live through this," Erroh whispered.

"Mercy."

"And it will be agony," he said. It was a simple bit of bad luck on the man's part that he'd not been killed outright, and that he'd chosen cowardice to sneak away from Erroh's blade. It was a small matter. His fate had been sealed the moment Uden had decided not to come out with him.

"Do not kill me."

"Call out for your god," Erroh demanded, and the man dropped his head in defiance, and Erroh gripped his hair, held him tightly and held Vengeance to his throat. Still the man said nothing, so Erroh pressed the blade into his skin, slowly and painfully. The man squirmed and wailed and as warm blood began to stream down his neck, he broke and gave way to pure survival instinct.

"Uden!" the doomed man roared, and Erroh paused for a breath. For only a breath.

"Louder," Erroh said soothingly, and the wailing man cried out for his god again and again, to no avail. As Erroh continued to inflict the dreadful cutting, his cries became more manic, more pitiful until suddenly, with a wet gurgle, he died. Erroh continued cutting for a time until the head was sheared free, then held it aloft and allowed drops of blood to cover him.

I am sorry.

It was brutal, awful, but he was not yet finished. He dropped the head on the dirt and then stamped upon it a dozen times until nothing remained; he knew this tale of horror would spread throughout the city. He hoped it would. He knew it would spread among his allies, too, but that was the cost of intimidation. That was the cost of claiming a god for war.

Come out and settle this, Uden.

Distantly, he heard the shaken city defenders call out orders and, raising his blades, prepared for the next volley of violence to fall upon him.

91

COME OUT AND FIGHT

Horrified and disgusted, the defenders answered their Southern masters and drew their bolts and arrows. If Uden had ever ordered against slaying Erroh, they ignored such a thing now, and let loose and rained down all manner of hell upon the false god.

Erroh watched dispassionately as each bolt and arrow rose up, caught in the wind and dropped to the ground. The nearest landed twenty feet short of where he stood, and for a breath, he was grateful for Lea's suggestion of the distance he would need to stand upon safely. He raised his blades mockingly, goading them to try again, and the Southerners took the bait and fired freely. Once more, the air was filled with projectiles. A few ricocheted off the ground and bounced near him, but none came close. He played the part of a god for a few outstanding breaths, inviting and intimidating, demanding and daring any fiend to strike him down, and try they did. The sky darkened with the incoming swarms of arrows and bolts, but still, none came close. Finally, the siege tapered off until only a dozen or so were still firing at him, and at this, he took a risk.

Stepping nearer, watching the sky, not daring to blink, he moved into the path of a solitary shot and struck it out of the sky as though it were an irritating mosquito. He leapt forward another few feet and struck another arrow in half with Mercy, roaring boldly as he did so, before striking another and stepping away slowly. A fresh wave took flight, but these too landed short of their intended target.

"Uden!" he demanded, clattering his blades together as he stood over the dead. "Face me, coward." Still, no single-eyed madman appeared to meet him, accept his challenge and mock him in return. Instead, from behind the gates, Erroh heard the hum of movement. Lots of movement. Possibly more movement than he'd ever heard in his life.

With a screeching creak, the great gates opened again, slowly. Then, like a gash spilling seeping crimson, the enemy streamed out in their barbaric hundreds, and Erroh took a step back despite himself. Just one solitary step, before he remembered his ruse, his bravado. Behind the hundreds must have been thousands, and they poured out in pursuit of one solitary warrior. Desperately, he looked for signs of the colossal brute who should have been leading. Upon a massive war mount, no doubt, in his finest flamboyant armour. Something impressive and godly. His belly churned, sick with disappointment. It would have been a fairer fight with the god. His entire army could have joined in then.

Show them the actions of a god.

He looked behind him at his allies, now charging down from their solitary line to join the massacre. Aye, they were outnumbered almost three times over, but the Southerners were a different type of careless. Arrogance won many great things, but lost many more. He prayed they were arrogant enough to believe they did not need to send the entire Southern nation down on him. On them all. He heard the thunder of their feet as they charged through the entrance, down past the hovels, towards Erroh alone.

He held out his blades, widened his stance and fell to silence. He closed his eyes and imagined himself in the rain on a lighter day.

Be great.

He took a step forward. He heard them draw near, and his arms began to itch. He drew from deep inside him the savage that lurked. The fearless, careless, laughing lunatic that stood firm against impossible odds. He also sought out the luck that had kept him alive this long.

Behind him, he heard his allies drawing near; they had been sprinting his way from the moment the gates opened in a desperate race to reach their master general before an entire city took him down. They would be late, he knew. Just a few breaths was all. A small matter on any other day, but with a couple of thousand swords pointed his way, well, an early arrival would have been better.

"Coward," he roared to the oncoming army, to the god most likely watching from the shadows behind the gate or concealed beneath a heavy cloak on top of the wall.

He thought it a fine last word, mocking their god, and then the Hunt fell upon him, and Erroh went to war. He did not stop moving as they came upon him. A long first line, at least twenty in all, all seeking to plunge a blade into the anointed one. The demonic one. The false god. Whatever they thought of him meant little in the end. These twenty were his alone, and he had no chance.

Their blades neared, the world slowed to near stillness, and Erroh moved freely within their treacherous path. Choosing not to counter, he concentrated on defending against each attack as they came from all angles. His body was a blur, and he dared not let his mind wander beyond the tips of the blades in front of him, beside him, swiping across his chest, lunging in towards his bowels; wherever, really.

The roar of so many charging across the battlefield was lost in the scream of metal as Erroh's blades performed admirably in his grandest defence. Spinning and retreating towards those he would call allies, he feared how easily a slight mistake, a casual clumsy stumble or a misguided parry could end it all. He thought of Tye and continued to defend, waiting for the moment when he wasn't alone. When he could reveal himself to those who hunted.

Be greater.

Distantly, or perhaps beside him, there came louder screams of war uttered by warriors in the moments before a great clash. To ward off, to threaten, to reaffirm too. Poets and storytellers might unwittingly lie in their description of authentic war cries, for only upon the field of battle amid war could their melancholic challenge truly be heard, and around him, they rose and clashed and brandished their blades.

He knew this defiant line as an impressive one. Only days before they had sworn to fight for Uden, they fought for Erroh now, and he was glad of them, even if they could offer little more than their deaths to the battle. The numbers from the city swelled, and Erroh could see no end. Not even the coming of savages, eager to earn their legends, could slow the numbers marching forth, seeking Erroh, seeking every one of them.

With his comrades beside him, Erroh began to beat back his attackers. Soon after that, he began to kill them too. His blades never stopped, and he pushed to be quicker, more efficient in killing. Swinging and ducking, stabbing and slipping, he charged from one enemy to the next, killing where he could, maiming where he couldn't—making a break in the fierce eternal line.

He looked at that fuken gate, and it was ruining his day. There was no end to the stream of defenders emerging; it seemed Uden had little difficulty in sending his entire force out into the battlefield without testing the strength of their adversaries. A foolish, arrogant move—but one that could win the day, after all.

His comrades fought, screamed and died, leaving him to be pushed back. He swallowed panic and horror and, instead, threw himself wholly into battle, fearing only briefly that he himself might be the first costly casualty in this war.

And then he was no longer alone. They came as one force, striking, killing, and being as efficient as he. Two figures in all. Wading through the melee, working towards one goal.

With a mighty battle axe that appeared forged for her alone, Nomi wielded devastation with every decapitating blow. She waded through the Hunt from his right. Already covered in blood and less appealing things, she roared her own battle cry with every strike, even if it took all her strength. In that moment, he loved her. Not only as a friend, but not as a lover either. Something more significant. Were the moment to fall to stillness, he might have grabbed her and kissed her. Or just embraced her. Lea's wrath be damned.

To his left was the demented demon he knew better as Wynn. With his tight ponytail whipping out with every strike, he appeared as impressive as when they had first met. Truthfully, the cub had grown to become the Alphaline male the world required. With every strike, he made a kill. Erroh knew this because he whooped in excitement every time a Southerner lay in ruin at his feet before speedily tackling his next victim. There were many whoops in those first few moments, and it was incredible to know a skilled lunatic like himself stood upon this battlefield with him.

As impressive as the trio were, the army they brought to the fight was far less skilled. They roared and battled but collapsed under the numbers, far sooner than Erroh would have liked but as swiftly as he'd planned for. They were the tip of the attack and little more. Any doubts Magnus and Elise might have had regarding their new loyalty was swiftly lost, although the price was costly. Daring a quick glance back up to the crest of the hill where thousands of savages were placed, it pleased him to see Magnus charging down, drawing ever nearer. The bandits of Adawan charged alongside him, though their task was a little different. Armed with bows, they answered Elise's orders and, in one fluid motion, let loose a thousand arrows that landed deep within the surging numbers of Southerners still emerging from the city gates.

Close those gates.

Though the arrows struck, there came no sign of the torrent drying

The Actions of Gods

up, and Erroh, Nomi and Wynn, though fierce and impressive, were driven back suddenly from the masses converging, spreading out, and threatening to surround them. To suffocate. To snuff out swiftly.

"On us," he roared to any comrade as they gathered close. He thought them fierce, brave, but ultimately doomed. Nomi and Wynn screamed as he did, dragging what warriors they could back into a tight unit, hoping to contain the Southern march. Desperation drew them to this gathering, for in moments, there were a dozen, and then fifty and double that after. Each Southern ally called for their comrades, tucking in, holding and delaying, and defying the inevitable tidal wave threatening to kill them.

Those with shields surrendered any thoughts of attacking and protected themselves and their comrades as movement lessened and fewer fell, and for a moment, Erroh thought of the crush in the arena, but only for a breath. This chaos was far more contained.

"A good day to die," cried Wynn deliriously, knocking away a fiend seeking to get under his guard. Far above, he could see the charge of Magnus and Elise, and he wondered, for all his meticulous planning, had he fruitlessly condemned them all in the first attack? The blame lay not on the charging reinforcements for being late, but more upon the dreadful numbers pummelling his gathered few quicker than he thought.

This is the end of it all.

It was strange to think that there would be no escape from this skirmish. Still, he fought, as did his comrades, but the gate never closed, the numbers continued to surge, and their little clustered group began to falter under the onslaught.

"We will be avenged," Erroh cried to those around him—a final few words to reassure them as they stepped into the darkness.

And then there came the sound of devastating cavalry in his ears, and the world shook something terrible.

92

CORDELIA'S DEFIANCE

"Close, you fukers," Lea hissed from far away. She sat atop her mount surrounded by her comrades of the black, those she trusted the most, those she loved, those she led. Beside her, Aymon watched as she did, cursing every breath or two. Nothing loud, nothing disheartening to any Wolf listening, just a curse for them alone.

"They just keep coming," Azel muttered. He was counting them by the dozen. A disheartening thing to see from so far. She could see their Southerners going to war, and she thought it peculiar how easily they had changed allegiances. She would die under the banner of Samara. The Wolves' banner too.

And Erroh's?

The Southerners clung to whatever power moved with longest strides. She supposed there wasn't much else to cling to in such unforgiving lands. It was not surprising that her father had risen to power as he did, and that Erroh had amassed the support.

"Thousands," agreed Aymon before spitting distastefully into the grass, and she nodded in agreement. Thousands of similar-looking brutes were killing a few hundred in a terrifying show of force. They had expected an approach similar to Keri's, and had in fact hoped for it. A few paltry attacks to thin out the numbers, to test the strength of the Northern alliances. This was far worse. She looked warily to the far forest and wondered whether the moment had arrived in the first clash of swords.

Not yet.

"Too many," Lea said quietly, and her mind reeled. She could see

Erroh fighting down below. Truthfully, her eyes had never left him. She did not know why. Learning of his passing would have been easier than seeing it occur. She felt a suffocating grip take her chest, and she did not know why either. To be this helpless was dreadful; to be ordered to be this vulnerable was another thing entirely.

She brought her horse around to view the Wolves she commanded. They looked at her for leadership as she looked at them for allegiance. Aymon did too. He released his grip more and more every day, not because of Erroh's words but because of his own better judgement. Few people in the world saw her greatness. Or, more accurately, saw the greatness she could attain. While Erroh doubted his every move, she would not.

"Too many," she repeated, tightening her grip on her horse's reins, calming her beating heart, and allowing her mind to become cold and calculating.

"Run quicker, fools," Azel muttered, watching the grand numbers of savages charge towards the melee.

She knew Erroh would suffer for it, for she understood war as her father once had. She knew this because she was mated to one of the finest warmongers ever to have lived, and she would surpass him.

"They'll not reach them in time," Aymon said, pulling at his long hair. She could see his thinking, could see his actions. He only needed to release the words, and many would die.

Close that fuken gate.

The gates were crowded with Southerners emerging, slowed now by the many ahead, and it was a dreadful spectacle.

"They were built for this," Aymon said of the savages, and he was correct. They howled and screamed deliriously; their voices became a demented wall of mania, with a sound far more cutting than war horns. They desired war as though it was their right, and as terrifying as the Southerners were, she wondered what horrors might have occurred had the Savage Isles turned their attentions to invasion instead of enjoying their peaceful years under Magnus's rule.

Alongside the thousands charging to save Erroh, she saw three fiends in savage Clieve running with them. She imagined gleefully the devastation they would inflict, but it would be all for nothing. Erroh would be dead, and she wasn't sure the world could suffer a blow as brutal as this.

Not yet.

She brought Shera forward again. She could take no more. She could not allow Erroh to fall without at least attempting to pull him from the fire.

As usual.

At that moment, she cared little for his rage and arguments. For his insufferable criticisms of her tactics. Aye, his own judgements were sound, despite the terrible luck. Who would have expected the South to charge so brazenly into an obvious ambush and hope their numbers supported their recklessness?

Dad did.

It was a small matter. As it was, Uden had little regard for the lives of his warriors because that fuken gate wasn't closing. But Lea had a plan. A simple plan that would really need to fuken work.

Aymon made no order, so she did—the final act of defiance to claim her place at the top of the ladder. "Follow me, fiends," she roared, kicking Shera in the ribs and charging out across the crest of the hill. She commanded her Wolves to gather with her, and they did. Swiftly too; she would have it no other way. Three hundred upon horseback, most with long sharp pikes, ready to inflict death and destruction. They were the largest cavalry unit remaining in the Four Factions, by her reckoning. And on a whim, she would lead them into war far earlier than expected.

He will hate me more for this.

"Faster," she roared back to her comrades as they drew wide of the city and galloped past the racing savages, past the bandits who continued to fire volley after volley into the emerging Southerners. She caught sight of Elise among them, sprinting with her halberd, no doubt seeing the turning of the battle. Despite her age and health issues, she sped ahead of her comrades. A mother's protectiveness driving each step. Too far away.

Don't worry, Elise; I have this.

"Don't stop," she demanded of her boys, and Aymon roared in agreement. Azel, beside him, was already drawing an arrow. Digging her knees against Shera's mighty ribs, Lea drew her bow and, with it, eight arrows. Although the movement of her mount sent her waving and shaking, she compensated, her eyes narrowing in hate as she charged below the shadow of the eternal city.

Her Wolves were magnificent on either side as their mounts carried them towards the impossible numbers of the enemy. They held out their pikes as they charged forward, and distantly, she heard the screams of the dying and the clash of metal upon metal. She drew her first arrow and released and drew again killing two distant fools. Admittedly, accuracy was unimportant given the amount of flesh on offer to be pierced. Three or four more kills, and her arm became a blur of movement as she drew and released over and over again. Ahead of her, there formed a little break in the crowd where her arrows struck, and turning in her saddle, she fired eight arrows directly into the fiends surging through the gates.

Azel fired as she did, though at a quarter the speed, such was his ability. There were screams, panic and a crush of frenzied bodies, but she could look no more, for her line of Riders was now driving into those attacking her beo.

Beo.

They rode with their pikes stuck out in front of them, and they were truly awesome. Holding tight, they pierced, bludgeoned and impaled many as they passed. Wrapped tightly in sturdy leather, their mounts drove those killing spikes wonderfully, and Lea waded into this butchery, hacking brutally with dual blades as she charged through.

Kill them all.

The world slowed, and all that remained was the mayhem of a thousand warriors being trampled by fewer riders, and the screams were piercing and haunting. She watched bones break and heads being crushed to mulch; she saw warriors pierced and held high in the air where they died and lay motionless at the tips of pikes, striking their Southern comrades until their bodies were ripped clear or the pikes broke under the weight.

Around her flew splashes of blood and horror, and she had never seen such a terrible sight. Still, she roared at Shera to continue her incredible charge over the doomed Hunt. She screamed triumphantly and thought less of green eyes for a moment, until suddenly, they had breached and broken the Southern line and found themselves on the other side of the gates and the battle itself.

The effect was immediate. There came a break in the Hunt streaming out from the city. If nothing else, it allowed the gathered allies to take advantage of the hesitation and crush home their sudden advantage.

Yet still, the gates remained open.

Looking around, she saw the cost of her selfish drive. Dozens had been lost in the charge. She could see riderless mounts wandering among the Southerners, no doubt seeking out their masters who had fallen to a terrible end.

I killed them.

"We are not done," she told her companions. "We charge until the gates are closed," she roared and they roared with her as she made a second terrible charge back towards the Hunt. Those who'd lost their pikes pulled their swords free. They were fierce and heroic, knowing this second charge would be more costly than the first.

This is all my fault.

She felt the terrible weight of guilt for the pain her actions caused, yet still, she drew her bow and fired as swiftly as before. She was not alone. The bandits nearing the battle fired what they could, and the sight of arrows raining down on the archway was extraordinary. She fired until her quiver was empty, and then, grabbing her blades, she trusted Shera to carry her through again.

This might be the end.

She swallowed her fear and thought more fondly of Southern death and destruction. Such things were a comfort. Her Wolves formed around her as they charged; the going was harder than before. The Southerners put up a sterner fight without the poles to drive through. She held her breath as they fell upon the brutes, smashing, cutting, ravaging, dying.

She heard Shera whinny in panic as the Southern rush fell below her. Their screams were louder now, as were those of her comrades, as many met their doom upon this devastation. Still, she dove through the sea of hate, killing, crushing and slicing mercilessly.

Perhaps the arrival of the bandits and savages put the city to motion, for above the roar of war, she heard the great shrieking of metal as the gates began to close. She thundered on through the crush of humans, seeking the edge, seeking a breath, seeking victory. She caught sight of the savage allies tearing through the Hunt and surging up around what remained of Erroh's forces, and then suddenly, the line thinned. She was through, with her skin intact.

Around her, many of her comrades still charged. Battered, exhausted, but many still alive. She absently began to count the missing and wondered about a third charge when the Southerners suddenly broke the line. They fled from Magnus and Elise, wide of the city, down through the wretches' hovels or out towards the far woods where they would meet an end, no doubt. Their fight lost, their banner challenged, it was a spectacular turn for the gathered factions. Some dropped to their knees in surrender. She wondered for a cruel moment if they might win after all.

Those remaining loyal retreated towards the gates as they closed, regardless of who was through. There came a terrible collective squeal as dozens were crushed in the process. Limbs were severed, heads were smashed, bodies halved, and Lea could only stare in horror, marvelling that they chose that fate over disloyalty to a mad god. She thought it was

The Actions of Gods

a terrible way to die as the gates closed on the zealots, leaving many stranded on the other side. Those left behind, however, were reluctant to go quietly into the dark; they fought their last, and the gates of Spark City soon turned a terrible shade of crimson.

Only with the gates shut did the archers above dare to fire down upon the attackers. They managed a few volleys before the bandits, seeing easier kills, fired wave after wave upon them and killed them all within a few breaths. Dissatisfied, with no further targets, they fired their weapons high into the sky, up and over the main gates, raining destruction down on those bastards behind them, and Lea wondered at the terrible luck of escaping this slaughter only to be taken by a stray arrow.

All too swiftly, the battle was won, and only then did Lea seek out Erroh. A cold feeling settled in her gut for a moment, for she saw Wynn first, then Nomi among the gathering, but Erroh was missing. The coldness turned to fear, then to something else. Something cutting that threatened to take her from the saddle. To leave her curled up in a ball on the wet ground.

Green eyes.

And then she saw him. Far ahead, among the savages, cutting and killing and very much alive, and she hated him for it. Always taking the legend for his own, always being reckless while the world worried about him.

"That was incredible," Azel said, drawing up beside her. There was a fine slash across his chest where a brute had tried to cut him, but the wound was shallow. He wore a grin despite the sorrow in his eyes. Beside him sat Aymon, as untouched as she but for a weary gaze of dismay.

"He'll take all the credit," Lea muttered.

"He might deserve it too," Aymon jested.

For just a moment, the skirmish fell still. The victorious retreated as one, back towards their line, having dealt a devastating blow to Uden in the first battle. They carried their dead with them.

Lea, Aymon and Azel joined the rest of their comrades, collecting their heroic but very much dead brothers from where they had fallen. It was sobering to lay a body on her mount and walk her back to camp. A heavier thing was in knowing it was all her fault. It was a small matter they had died turning the battle. They would have preferred to be alive.

Aymon offered a simple pat on the back as she walked. It wasn't a lot, but she took it gladly.

The toast of the day was to Erroh, and though they stood ready for a counter-charge from the Hunt, there came none. And it was reassuring to know that despite the losses, they had sent a message of threat to their one-eyed adversary.

They did not drink heavily that night, but most shared a bottle of sine with their nearest comrades. After living for so long in fear, in retreat, and having lost everything, the South had finally shown its hesitation, and the remaining factions were better for it. There was no great revelry, no music either, for there was mourning to do, and all were worried about the battles to come.

Lea could not join her comrades after her actions. She could not face the thought of their harsh, cutting words. Could not gaze at faces around the campfires and contemplate their absent comrades, either.

When Erroh came for her, she was unprepared. Sitting at the campfire outside her tent, she watched as he approached cautiously. He was no longer covered in blood; no longer was he playing the part of lunatic warmonger. He appeared human, and it was a better look to him. She steeled herself for his outrage. For his criticism that she'd charged too soon. That she'd gotten in his way. Her knuckles whitened, and she hated him. And herself, too, because he might be right. She replayed her choices in her head for the hundredth time and wondered whether the savages might have broken the Southerners' will as she had.

"What you did today was rash."

"Aye, of course it was."

"It turned the battle when it had all but slipped away. You were incredible."

"It needed to be done," she said evenly, but she quivered with anger. He nodded as he agreed with her, which was just as bad.

"Thank you, Lea. I would be dead now, but for your swift actions."

A terrible wrath came upon her like never before. She thought him so fuken smug, standing before her, taking just a little pleasure in her trauma.

"And thank your comrades," he went on. "They were magnificent. And… I'm sorry for your losses. A terrible, needful thing in war. All of them were heroes."

She spat in his face. A glob of spittle struck his cheek. He recoiled for a moment before wiping it off. She could see his disgust, could see his hatred, and that was fine. She didn't care for his words, didn't care for him. She hated the relief she'd felt when seeing him alive; it was all-consuming. "They were my friends."

He nodded like a politician. She'd hoped he'd strike her. Scream in her face. Punish her. Instead, he bowed slowly, tapped his heart three times and walked away, leaving her cold and alone, and her only comfort in this world was thinking of green eyes and tearing into flesh.

93

QUIET TIMES BY THE FLAMES

Erroh was shaken, though he dared not show it. He trudged away from his mate with a heavy heart. Compulsively wiping his face, he walked almost blindly. Sometimes he liked to walk. To clear his thoughts, find reasoning in certain things, and come upon answers to stubborn questions. He thought it better to be away from her instead of remaining to share his thoughts. Argue with her. Demand to know the reasoning behind her actions. Also, he wanted to spit in her face so she might feel as worthless as he.

Great master general I am.

It was a terrible thing to mishandle his relationship as he did. Again, he thought of a final kiss. She'd probably bite his tongue off in the act. He was lost upon her precarious path. He'd tried everything. He'd banished her away, he'd kept her close, he'd come at her with love and warmth, he'd come at her demanding answers, he'd come at her critiquing, he'd come at her complimenting, he'd come at her shouting his venom, he'd come at her begging for forgiveness, but no matter what he did, he was wrong in her eyes. Admittedly, he probably was to blame because it usually was his fault. Still, though, he couldn't help but sense he wasn't the only cause of her terrible anger. Regardless, no matter what he did, he couldn't escape from her fiery gaze.

Let her bite and be done with it.

Erroh walked through the camp seeking answers too distant and twisted to grasp. He felt utterly lost, though he didn't know why. Indeed, there was an intriguing energy in the air this night. Most warriors he passed walked with renewed energy, as opposed to before, for as costly as the day had been, there was renewed hope. Belief in him, too, he imagined, and fought that fuken panic right where it festered. Nothing like the sight of a victorious butchering to boost morale, he thought wearily.

While the city remained in darkness, nursing her wounds, the allied factions came together in muted celebration. Erroh wouldn't condemn a warrior for partaking in a beverage or two. There was no music; there was no boisterous celebration. Instead, many talked excitedly among themselves about the battles to come, the crushing blows they would mete out to their foes. They raised their glasses as he walked among them, and he offered a bow each time. He would take no alcohol, not yet. Not until the day had called for one.

Few of the savages partook of alcohol, and this surprised him. They had better reason to celebrate than most. Despite greedily waging war, they had lost few comrades. In truth, he'd never seen a more efficient gathering of warriors in flight. However, it was hard not to be grateful for them for more reasons than their warmongering. It was their buoyant energy, which elevated those around them. Not to mention, away from bloodshed, their cheer was wonderfully contagious. Although the allied factions were segregated from each other in their camps, they moved freely among the other allied groups, introducing themselves and making friends, and challenging each other to tests of will, skill and wit. They did so with muted camaraderie, but it was appreciated. He had heard from his father of such ways, and it was a wonderful thing to see for himself. He imagined were they to know victory, their celebrations would be wild indeed.

He came upon his father, who cut a frustrated figure as he and a dozen others worked the siege machinations. There were four massive beasts in all, and they lay in four separate states of readiness. Every carpenter and mechanic was hard at work attempting to come to terms with the monsters, and truthfully, Erroh couldn't understand the finer mechanics either. It was more than counterweight, he imagined. Although the machines were unprepared for war, there still sat mounds of boulders, ready to be fired in anger. How they even hoisted the piles upon the levers and into the baskets, Erroh couldn't say, and judging by the arguments Magnus was having with the others, they couldn't either. The two ballistae, however, made for no such discussions. They stood ready, weighed down and sturdy, but Erroh wondered how effective their arrows would be against stone. There was talk of placing fire upon each tip, but he still needed convincing, despite learning of their effectiveness in Boat Town. He marvelled at the thought of such a ludicrous place and vowed to see it for himself someday, after the city had fallen and he'd taken Uden's head, burned his remains.

No problem.

Leaving the great machines to their stubborn secrets, Erroh continued to walk among his fighters, smiling, bowing where he could. All the while, he couldn't help shake the fear for each of their fates this night. They trusted him to carry them to victory. More than that, they trusted him to keep them alive. They weren't to know that neither scenario was likely. As he walked, he deliberately avoided his generals and friends, for fear of souring their better mood. For a time, he watched Wrek, Nomi, Lillium, Doran and Wynn play cards among themselves, and it was a settling thing. He couldn't make out their words, but from here, in the dark, it sounded like the place to be. Were it not for a distant cry of outrage from deep within the centre of the camp, he might have joined them for a few hands. But the roar filled the night, and Erroh's heart sank.

This is on me.

Though many had fled as the gates closed, others had surrendered. Those immediately pledging to a greater warrior was becoming easier apparently. A hopeful fool might well believe the iron grip of the Woodin Man was slipping ever so. His father had long spoken of the perilousness of morale. This was nowhere more so than in battle, but morale could also vanish when greater opportunities came along. Hiding behind a city of darkness in hostile lands was a fine cure for optimistic thinking. That wasn't to say Erroh was inclined to welcome any fresh recruits into their army just yet. Who was to say there wouldn't be a few carefully placed fiends among the new allies? So, under guard, they were fed, rested and left to ponder their loyalty. It was good enough for them, for the moment at least.

The shrill cries increased, and Erroh was drawn to the sound out of duty, horrible as it was. For there were a few who fought beyond the bitter end. Fierce brutes who, despite inevitable defeat, continued to battle in Uden's name. These fiends were most impressive. No more so than this general, a woman whose shouts of fanatical challenge were a cutting thing indeed.

He saw her, in the darkness. As old as Uden and nearly as impressive. She claimed to be a general, and given her commanding voice, Erroh had little doubt. Truthfully, if she had been present on the night of his fight with the god, Erroh couldn't remember her. It was a small matter now.

"Cowards, all of you," she roared to her fellow prisoners and her steely voice was rich and arresting—this was a woman used to giving orders. Even chained to a tree, with fiends all around her threatening to take her tongue, she showed little fear. Instead, she called out across the camp for retribution and warned against his wrath, and it did little for their new comrades. "He sees all; he will punish all."

Erroh stepped from the darkness towards the woman. She was taller than Erroh and could punch harder. In battle, she'd taken his strike well enough, but not his second gloved fist to her chin. It would be a shame to cast such a warrior away into the darkness. Erroh could see the frustration in her watching guards as she cried out. It was a miracle that she hadn't been gagged or battered unconscious.

"I'm not sure he sees all too well with one eye," Erroh said, and mid-yell, she fell silent to stare at him in disgust.

"His human part was struck down, but he is godly."

"Well, so am I."

She didn't like that. Not one little bit. She struggled in her bindings, and Erroh imagined she would give up her life to attempt one strike more on him.

"You are a beast of the night, a demon of fire. A lesser god, by Uden's glorious tongue," she spat at him. Her tone was smooth and familiar, and she spoke without a hint of accent at all. Were Erroh to guess, he would imagine her educated by many a book.

"But I am a god?" he challenged.

"Release me, and let us see how godly you are."

Erroh stood close to her. Enough that only she could hear his voice. "I would release you if you yielded."

"I would never pledge myself to a fiend like you." She was definite, determined, and even as she doomed herself, he admired her courage. The Southerners were fickle in their leadership. It was a rarity to see them remain loyal. Only Drahir had raged against his fealty, and only then because of Erroh's mate.

Drahir.

He looked away into the darkness to where Drahir and his comrades would arrive—needed to arrive. For only a breath did he imagine his brother-in-law turning tail in war. For only a breath.

Her keepers watched them both, no doubt, hoping he would take that moment to put her to death and leave them to a more leisurely night guarding a docile few. The females of the city would be outraged, though. They were hurting from the horrors of Boat Town, and Erroh knew they desired to punish any who still marched for Uden. A lesser man might have given this general to the females and allowed their wrath to entertain the masses, or at least themselves. Some cruelties were necessary for war. Sometimes a master general should commit terrible things for the greater good.

It was a dreadful thing, really, to make excuses, for there were none.

"You will die if you do not," Erroh told her quietly, standing face to face with her. Trying to read the madness behind those eyes. He couldn't tell how mad she was at all. He'd been friends with a mad woman for far too long and never seen through her. Still, she appeared coherent and controlled, and somehow that made it worse.

"I should have died in the gates following his orders." She was so coldly definite, Erroh knew he could never tempt her to his side. Twist her mind to serve his well-being. He almost considered drawing his blade, plunging it deep into her a few times. Better for her, better for him. Better for their war effort, though? His fingers twitched. He knew the damage she could inflict upon those he called allies.

Yet still, he could not kill her in such a way. Better her death mean something. If not for her benefit, then for the benefit of her comrades behind the gates, unsure of their call in this world. He thought again of her heroism at the gate. As the savages had moved in around her, she had fought valiantly, knocking away every strike. Even Erroh's for a time, until with only a shield to call upon, she had fought as though there was hope. Undoubtedly, Uden had chosen well to enlist her as a general.

"And if we released you into the Wastes, would you return home?" Erroh pleaded.

"I will offer no such agreement. I am to die. Better it be at the hands of a lesser god, as well," she hissed.

"You will die, but not by my hand."

"Very well, cur. You have not even asked my name."

"Nor do I desire to know it. I want no familiarity with one whose fate is so tainted," he said.

She spat in his face, and he recoiled from her venom. He stepped away and fought down an anger most violent. She sneered in glee, and he hated her at that moment. Yet still, he admired her nerve and knew she did not deserve her fate.

"Give her all she needs this night. Every rich food we can offer," Erroh said to her keepers, and wiped saliva from his face for the second time in an hour. "Give her all the sine she desires. Fuken force it down her throat if it will silence her for a time."

"Cowards, all of you," she howled, and laughed manically.

Erroh turned to leave, and hesitated. He gestured to a keeper. A wary one ready to knock her out. "Summon a healer. Ensure she takes some potent tonic to dull the pain."

"What pain?"

"The pain to come," Erroh muttered, truly hating what he had become.

94

COMMITTING THE GREATEST SIN, A LITTLE TASTE OF VENGEFUL SCORNING, AND VISITS FROM NEW FRIENDS

The torch flickered in Shinaid's eye line. It wavered in the bitter noon wind, and she wondered if it would blow out. That would be a little awkward. A little embarrassing too. She had been given one task, and she supposed that failing in front of so many would be a story to tell. She shuddered, knowing she'd never tell the tale. Today would be the last day of her life. She was terrified, and the torch quivered ever so in her grip. She was frightened but determined, and was that not the way of an Alpha? Was that not why she and her many sisters had trained their entire lives?

She took that fear and swallowed it whole. It was all she could do. Above her, the afternoon sky was eerily dark, as though the absent gods were preparing to punish her when she went to task. She did not know how she felt about the absent gods. Her entire life, she'd never truly believed, never wanted to. Never needed to. She had accepted her place in the world for what it was and dealt with the blows and the better days as her lot in life.

There was serenity in such thinking. However, there was nothing like introducing brutality and hardship to make one question one's lack of belief. She'd felt the presence of the absent gods the day Dia was slaughtered. Felt their glee like a whisper in the mind. She might have felt them walk with her as she was ordered aboard an unimpressive vessel and made to sail away from all she'd ever known. She had most certainly felt them at her side, watching absently, as she went to war defending Boat Town when all around her were felled.

Visions of her Alphaline sisters filled her mind, all pinned and destroyed by dozens of arrows. She had been one of the few left untouched and vengeful. She'd taken lives that night, both alone and with her gathered sisters. She had walked a vengeful path that had led to the forest, where she had witnessed the coming of the divine savages. Was that not the work of absent gods? She looked back up the ridge to where most of those warrior kings stood, and wished they were with her now. How easily the lies of their barbarity spread when there was so much more to their ways. A girl could learn some of them too. Could rightly take a fuken vessel and sail to those lands and see for herself.

It was just a shame these grand desires could never be realised, for today she would die.

"Uden," the prisoner cried, and anger stirred within Shinaid something fierce. She took that anger and held it close lest she diminish and cower. The prisoner continued to cry out, and it was a wonderful thing. Despite the large number gathered here, there was a knowing, poignant silence. Every fiend was entitled to their final words. Few were heard by so many.

Distantly, she could see the Hunt upon the walls, staring in grim silence. She wondered whether the woman's voice carried that far in the wind. She thought so; otherwise, why allow her to cry out as she did?

Orders.

The wind caught Shinaid's hair and near blinded her for a moment. It looked fantastic today. She had seen to it since being given the order by beautiful Erroh, master general of the remaining factions, the night before. He'd come upon her by her campsite, his words kind and reassuring, his orders severe and cutting. Truthfully, she hadn't expected anyone to speak of her Boat Town feats that awful night, but he spoke highly of her deeds as though he'd been there. She could only play the humbled warrior, knowing his legacy. And she would do his will, for any good soldier would do that. Cruel and awful and potently necessary as it was.

Brushing bright green hair from her face, she kept that flame steady. She could allow her hair to flow only until the battle began, after which she would tie it back. With stripes of blue, orange, red, purple and plenty of green, she looked like a rainbow in motion, and were she able to fight with her hair down, she would look incredible—until she was covered in deep red, of course. So no, she would tie her hair when the moment came. Another necessary act of cruelty on her part.

She looked to the woods beyond and trusted beautiful Erroh. She'd always thought him beautiful. Many of her sisters did too. His name, though once cursed and ridiculed, was now considered sacrosanct. Shinaid might have argued about how swiftly her sisters had taken to him, but what was the point in a needless argument? At pressing times, people could believe whatever they liked. Who was she to tell them otherwise? She certainly wasn't going to convince them of her own opinions, no matter how frantic and passionate her counterarguments were. They adored him these last few days, and that was fine. She, herself, had always loved him. Were she older, she could have stood to Cull with him too. What a life that could have been.

Or death?

The smell of flowers touched her nostrils—a wonderful aroma that brought thoughts of camaraderie. Even at the end, a girl wanted to look and smell her best. It wasn't her particular perfume, for she wasn't alone out here on the battlefield. As the remaining factions watched on with bated breath, around her, she saw that every Alpha female of the city old enough to fight was here; they had chosen to do so when asked by their master general.

We wanted this.

How could they not fight? Had they not spoken openly for weeks of their desire to join this war? Nearly two hundred females from the city, all clustered together, with no one to support them, waiting for Uden to open his steel and wooden gates and come out and play.

We needed this.

Every one was dressed in her finest silken gown. Even though these were worn beneath the thick leather armour, they still were an explosion of colour against the dreary day. They, too, had coloured their hair, and their colours were dazzling, vibrant and expressive. In this way, they sent their message of defiance to the one-eyed brute behind the walls. He wanted to burn the women? Well, here they were, the finest of their kind, and the most scorned. They demanded war, and Shinaid was proud to be among them—terrified or not.

"Uden, come for me," the prisoner cried, louder and more slurred than before. Twice, the witch had boldly claimed she had burned a village's worth of women in her better days. She spouted zealous rhetoric for all to hear, even as they wrapped her to that wooden post and swiftly gathered kindling and logs. She had shown no remorse as they doused her in oil and forced the last tonic down her throat. And though this was a dreadful act, it was necessary. By Erroh's word, she was condemned; by Shinaid's hand, she would burn.

Shinaid wished Mea stood with them. She would gladly have

relinquished her leadership role if their Primary had stood with her. It wasn't Mea's right to sacrifice herself, though.

Sacrifice.

For long enough, she'd waited by the prisoner. Long enough that Uden would be informed that one of his prize generals was howling for him. The flame flickered; it was time. Shinaid lowered her torch to the kindling and did the unthinkable. The tinder caught swiftly. Shinaid felt a splash of rain on her cheek for a moment, and she wondered if the absent gods thought less of her now. Stepping away, she watched the fire grow.

"Call for your god, whore," she hissed, but the prisoner merely struggled in her metal bindings, all the while moaning for her Southern deity.

The Hunt must have taken offence, for the gates began to open. Swifter this time. The screech of dry hinges pierced the air, camouflaged by the prisoner's demented cries—they had learned from the previous day's routing, no doubt. Clearly, they had counted the few hundred Alphas and thought them feminine and beatable. They streamed out, fierce and aggressive, and Shinaid sought out the brute Uden among them.

A thousand at least, in no time, came running towards them, and the prisoner began to shriek as her faith was tested, and Shinaid tried to block out her cries. A difficult thing, such was her anguish, vitriol and pitifulness. The prisoner wept; even generals, it seemed, had a limit to the pain they could endure.

Shinaid dropped the torch onto the growing pyre as her sisters spread out around her. There would be no disciplined assault, no tactics to call upon. They would be fierce and unrestrained, and they might win the day, or at least know their measure, having spent a life believing themselves elite.

"We want our home back," Shinaid cried, and they agreed. The Hunt charged down from the gates, screaming impressively. Behind them were hundreds more, but Shinaid saw with surprise that the gates were closing behind the first platoon. There would be no panicked retreat, no crushing, and no chance of a counter-charge. There was a tragic beauty to such singlemindedness, a beauty that matched the determination of she and her sisters.

The nameless prisoner caught fire, and she wailed for Uden; it was awful. Her hair smouldered, and she shook her head wildly, and Shinaid felt for the pain she endured. But not for her.

"This is what *they* felt, whore," she bellowed, and, wrapping her dazzling hair in a neat ponytail, drew her sword and shield. Around her, her sisters did the same, and they marched towards the Hunt, eager to die and kill.

She watched for a moment more as the flames engulfed the Southern general, and though she struggled until the end, there came no respite. No sympathetic blade or arrow to end her horror. Not one fuken female felt for her. And that was fine. If she was who she claimed to be, Uden would understand the horror and might even appear in a fitful rage.

Were that to happen, Shinaid had no doubt, the remaining factions watching from far away would be swift in entering the fray.

As it was, no false god appeared at the gates, and the Alpha females of Spark City took their chance and went to war.

Be incredible.

Shinaid wished she could have been the first to strike down a fiend, but her girls were relentless and wonderfully reckless. They sprinted the last few feet, swinging blades and killing from the first breath. They moved like pure deities, bringing the fight to those who hunted them. They danced through the many blades, never stopping, never hesitating, never delivering mercy, and the Southerners, unprepared for the sudden attack of their lesser opponents, fell to their divine savagery.

Shinaid killed a half dozen in the first few moments, all at the expense of a few scrapes, a tearing of her leather armour around the shoulder blade, and the misplacing of her shield, embedded in the head of a twitching carcass. The battlefield became a brutal melee of screaming and awfulness, and soon, the Alphas found space among the Hunt where they could fully express their violence. They spun, twisted, and destroyed, and it was easy, at least for a time.

"For Dia," she roared, and around her, her sisters squealed, hissed and struck. They killed until they could no longer hold back the tide of attackers. When the first few Alphas fell beneath the mass of swords, those remaining gathered up and plunged their weapons through leather and skin, some gazing back at the forest in hope as they retreated ever so. She understood the speed of war, the way a battle could turn in moments. They could not win, could never win, such were the numbers of their foes. But that never mattered; theirs was to offer a tantalising tease, an invitation to slay true beauty, and prevent their attackers from seeing that their actions were a ruse.

They did not retreat fully; they merely retreated behind the burning pyre, waiting to kill more as they came. And they did come. Hundreds

The Actions of Gods

more, surging away from the cover of the gates, away from Samara's shadow.

And then Drahir of the South announced his arrival with the braying of war horns.

It must have been no easy task bringing his warriors to the edge of the treeline and remaining unnoticed, even in the face of the scene that played out before him. However, they were patient and watched for the women to retreat behind the flames, and displayed little regard for their former comrades.

Then, with a mighty roar of aggression and warning, the Southerners, loyal to Erroh alone, emerged from the forest as one terrifying scourge. Hidden within the woods for days now without light, without warmth, they appeared fresh, fervent and fierce. Charging across the open lands in full sprint, they were impressive, disciplined and numerous. The Hunt hesitated, and Drahir's attackers ignored the city entirely and charged towards their rear.

The Hunt turned and split their forces. Attempting to meet the thundering charge, some raised their blades and were the first to die. The clatter of swords and the thud of falling bodies filled the air, and those chasing the retreating Alphas were caught between meeting this new threat or continuing to hunt their quarry. What had begun as a straightforward assault on a few hundred women became a dreadful ambush.

Kill them all.

The Alpha females took the enemy's hesitation as an opportunity to turn the attack on its head. They held the line and suddenly broke wildly back towards the masses, releasing their anguish from the horrors of Boat Town, from the sacking of Samara, back onto those they knew to be responsible. Shinaid tore back through the Southerners, and her blade became heavy with blood. Many died at her feet or suffered grievous harm, and she never hesitated, never thought less of the murders she committed. She and her sisters battered them and held, just as Drahir's Southerners waded deep into war, killing all in their path. As with any skirmish, it was never-ending once the wave rushed over. The Hunt were crushed in moments. And the gathered factions took the victory for what it was.

Shinaid stood among the dead and felt a ruin. She'd never felt so tired or suffered so many cuts and bruises. A few crimson strands of hair flapped in the wind, and she felt the weight of her deeds. Looking to the pyre and her greatest sin, she bowed once and thanked the absent gods before following her battered companions back towards their camp.

Were Uden to have watched from the wall, he might have wept in horror and rage and despaired at losing another battle as both sides tore the Hunt apart, leaving none alive, leaving none to relent, and leaving none to be burned in his name. Instead, Uden focused on family, beauty and wondrous days.

The moment to answer the false god's call drew ever nearer, and soon the fate of Spark City would be decided once and for all.

95

THE MAKING OF THUNDER

"They're ready, sir," the runner said, and Erroh nodded. His eyes were on the smouldering ruin where the general had perished. Perished? No, murdered by his design. He had become evil, vile, a warmonger of such cruelty they would whisper about him as they did his imposing father. Erroh, the murderer. All hail the king.

As the darkness crept in and the rain began to fall softly, he could only stand on the outskirts of his army's camp and gaze down at the horror of his own doing. The pyre had burned quickly and brightly. The general was but ashes over embers now. Oh, aye, they congratulated him on a perfectly manoeuvred skirmish; they called him a genius for two battles fought and won against more impressive numbers. All of it was for nothing. He had played his cards, and Uden had not emerged from behind his fortress.

Were Uden to emerge this very moment, he wasn't sure how the biggest battle ever fought in the Four Factions would end, but he would gladly have accepted such odds a year ago. Tonight, though, he couldn't help but feel he had failed. He had called Uden out in challenge; the cur had remained hidden.

Here he was, with all cards played and only a dent created in the Woodin Man's massive forces. His mind was awash with frenzied ideas, seeking a way to hold what miserly advantage they had. Some hidden gem never imagined by another general. Schemes fantastical and mundane, pathetic and incredible, spun through his mind, none of which he could call upon with any confidence.

"Sir?" the runner asked, and Erroh nodded again.

"I'll be along. Have them hold until I arrive," he muttered. He looked once more to the pyre, and he thought of Aireys. He wondered would she approve. Had her own end been so cruel that she would not have wished it on another soul, vile as they were?

The absent gods knew her thoughts on the matter, but it wasn't their place to give relief.

"I'm sorry," he whispered to the wind, Aireys, and every woman who had burned in the fires. To the nameless general as well.

He walked through the camp, meeting the eye of every saluting warrior and bowing in reply. They treated him with reverence for his actions, which was a humbling, depressing thing. He thought of the Keri warriors and recognised those smiling faces in every soldier he passed now. He had let those fine warriors down, even as they outdid themselves. He would let all these nameless comrades down just as violently.

And I'll somehow survive this.

He sneered to himself, for he knew better. His hour was nearly up. His deck was to be shuffled no more than once again. He was tired down to the depths of his soul, and the absent gods in the darkness likely knew it too. He was too young to feel this old. He was no Magnus, despite what they whispered. Were he to weep, he might lose himself completely, crawl away into the night and wonder what other terrible cruelty he was capable of. Instead, he made his way to where they tended to the impressive weapons of war, holding himself against the desolation he'd felt when they lit that fuken pyre in his name.

And you burned her alive.

He saw Nomi stretched over one of the powerful ballistae, tending to its sight with a little wood knife. Nobody seemed to have a significant issue with the Southern girl, and he marvelled at how far she had come. Drahir stood with her, asking questions, attempting to understand the great weapon. Erroh offered a wave, but she was too engrossed in her activities. Erroh could barely fire a crossbow, let alone a monster as impressive as that.

Long pikes with glass balls smelted onto their barbed ends lay at her feet. He thought such a thing impractical, but he wouldn't argue against those with better understanding. Besides, it was the enormous trebuchet that garnered most of his attention.

His father was back among the engineers, he noted, looking ten years younger than before. He was positively giddy, occasionally jesting, eagerly barking orders at those attaching the boulders to the mighty basket. Erroh watched for a time as they drew the beast back, tightening the long arm that would catapult the boulder into the city, and once more, he marvelled at the destructive nature to humankind. These fine weapons were from beyond the time of the ancients. They had been history long before the fires took the world, yet their legacy continued after so many generations.

"We are ready, Master General," Magnus cried, pointing to the lever. The beast appeared to quiver under a strain, and Erroh, staring deep into the city, imagined no beast could throw a rock that far.

He thought of the assault on Samara and the terror endured by those within its walls. He remembered the terrible feeling of helplessness as the world crashed down around him, and his inner warmonger reared its head in a near chuckle. No manic laugh. Not yet.

"You are sure this contraption is ready?" Erroh asked, much to the disapproval of the dozen engineers around his father. It was more than a contraption. He was suddenly struck by the differences among the engineers: some were savage, some Southern, some from the North. They had come together to destroy, and he thought it wonderfully typical and predictable. Sometimes all it took was a little war and death to unite disparate peoples.

Erroh folded his arms, and Magnus took it as permission to fire. He pulled a lever with a grunt, and a great swishing sound filled the air. The ground rumbled for an instant, and then, with a deafening crack, the arm raised, the basket released, and the boulder flew out into the night.

"Look at it go," a voice cried in excitement.

"Keep going, you bitch," another roared.

"Come on!"

The missile hung in the air far longer than Erroh would have thought possible, and beneath the whoops of excitement, Erroh willed it to smash the Hunt beyond. It was no genius tactic, but it would undoubtedly add to the strain the city was already feeling. Who knew, it might crash right through the Woodin Man's house, killing him, and that would be that.

It didn't hit the Woodin Man's house.

"Fuk me," moaned Magnus, seeing the boulder land short of the gates with a massive crash before bouncing and rolling onwards until it collided ineffectually against them. It was a loud enough noise, but a crushing waste of ammunition nonetheless.

Maybe Uden will come out to see who's knocking at the door.

Erroh looked to the great mounds of boulders they were already beginning to choose for their next strike. There were many. Nevertheless. "Perhaps someone could walk on down there and get that rock back for us," he mocked, but Magnus was already barking orders about angles and degrees, doing his best not to meet the eyes of his eldest.

For a while, Erroh watched the engineers at work preparing the next strike. If nothing else, it helped him to enjoy the discomfort his father would feel at having failed so spectacularly. Erroh was in no joyous mood, but sometimes a boy had to take a moment and appreciate the spectacle of a determined, flustered father at work. Sometimes a cub could hold a stern, critical gaze like a master upon his own master for his entertainment. It was a fine distraction from his own darker thoughts.

Watching.

Waiting.

Silently disapproving.

"Ah, just fuken fire it," Magnus roared suddenly, and the machine came to life with a deathly scream, and another boulder shot so high into the night that Erroh lost sight of it for a breath. There were no cheers, only silent excitement, and Erroh found himself excited too. And then it fell to earth again, clipping the top of the gate, smashing wood and metal, before dipping behind the wall, where he liked to think it would crush some thoroughly confused fiends below.

"Masterful," Erroh said, clapping each engineer on the back as they loaded another. "Well done," Erroh offered to Magnus, whose eyes were bright with excitement.

"I suggest we keep those fukers awake all night," Magnus advised, and Erroh committed the order, much to his pleasure.

Turning to leave, he watched Nomi barking orders of her own to the engineers preparing her weapon. They lit the oil within the glass tip and immediately raised the weapon high into the night. Then, with a far less angry release, they watched the burning projectile sail away into the night.

"Pretty," Nomi said, walking up beside Erroh. They watched as the arrow landed deep within the walls, among the buildings, where Erroh imagined an explosion of flame suddenly gifting the Southerners a last burst of light so they might see their demise. It shouldn't have pleased him as it did. There was a cold, terrible reassurance to such warfare.

Destroying what we fight for.

"They are impressive," he said. "Do we have enough to fire all night?"

"Enough to last a time," she said, taking his hand. "Come, Erroh, you need some peace among friends," she said kindly, and he allowed her to lead him away from the machines of war raining down death and misery on the faceless enemy.

96

RESPITE OF THE GUILTY

Nomi led Erroh through the camp to a little fire where his generals sat enjoying a game of cards. Lea sat with them, a scowl on her face, no doubt reserved for him alone. Beside her, Lillium matched her bet. As did Doran, who cursed under his breath as he did. Wrek thought for a while, watching Lea's face for signs of deceit or truth. Eventually, having the larger share of pieces, he played. Wynn was silent but for the folding of his hand, although he did mumble something about his dismal luck. Erroh sat down between Tye and Lexi, who added their pieces to the growing mound.

The round ended with a notable victory for Lea, who gladly scooped up the pieces. She smiled momentarily before scowling back at her freshly drawn hand. She immediately made a bid, despite it not being her call at all.

Erroh and Nomi were dealt in, upon which Erroh immediately folded and allowed the rest of the hands to play. Even saying little, he found a sense of peace among them. Not a great deal, but enough to ease his mood ever so. After a time, Magnus joined them and played as recklessly as Lea. His concentration wasn't on the game, which was no surprise. He was preoccupied with the boulders, as were most of those present. Every ear was tuned to the cursing and calling and cheering as each boulder flew into the night, to the sounds of distant thumping as each one landed; after a while, it became a surreal routine.

Nomi, for her part, was attuned to the great arrows being launched towards the city walls.

"Ooh, pretty," she would say softly as each one lit up the night, and each time she did, the others would mock her. Truthfully though, they were a sight.

As with any good game, the hours passed easily away, and it was pleasant, even if Erroh's heart was heavy, for his mind still failed to gather any semblance of a plan. His generals must have taken pity on him, he realised. On more than one occasion, he knew himself outplayed by a bet yet still beat whomever he faced. On any other day, he might have challenged their misguided charity, but Erroh was tired, in his soul, in his mind, and he took the wins without his usual mocking bravado. Truthfully, there was no place Erroh would have preferred to be at this late hour.

After a time, it was Wynn who spoke up and cut through his weariness. "You look like you carry the world upon your shoulders, brother. You are bringing down the mood for the rest of us utter legends of war," he said, matching Erroh's bet and showing his cards, and all eyes fell upon the little cub playing as king.

Erroh mustered his last reserves of bravado and charisma, all the things needed to lead, even at quieter times in the middle of the night when looking at one's soul was precarious.

"That is the cost of being as impressive as I am," Erroh countered, throwing down his hand. He'd earned that hand and earned that win too. Probably the first time this night. Before he could celebrate, Tye dropped his hand down, taking the round. "Oh, you little shit. I never saw that coming," Erroh barked, shoving the child away.

Not a child. A young man.

Everyone had grown so much in so little time.

"What ails you, Erroh?" Magnus asked. His eyes were warm. It was a strange thing to see him stare at him as a father would. Should. Erroh was unprepared and grateful.

Fuker.

"I am at a loss in this grand siege, Father. I do not know why Uden has not emerged," he confessed, throwing his cards down in frustration. This was no meeting of generals, he realised. This was a meeting of friends. There were no answers. There were no tactics to discuss. But there may as well be honesty.

"Well, you have certainly tempted him enough," Magnus said.

"Who hides behind a wall after such defeats?" Lillium wondered in disgust. She spat in the dirt.

"A brute with a plan," Lea said evenly.

Wynn leaned into Erroh. "None of this is your fault," he said casually. So casually, he almost sounded believable. Distantly, a firefly took flight and likely struck some hapless Southerner far behind the wall, and Erroh didn't know what to say. His wretched will was near spent, his heart shattered by too much. They could see it now too. Why else would they treat him as they did? Why else would Wynn speak with such kindness that Erroh wanted to lay his head down and weep?

"Things might have been different had I been greater," Erroh offered. Each word was heavy and laced with depthless guilt. It was all his fault. He had failed them all again and again. Yet still, they looked to him, and he had no idea what to do.

"You think Uden took Spark because of your actions?" Lea asked evenly. It was the only thing she'd said the entire night.

"Perhaps," Erroh answered the table. Not just Lea. He couldn't face her. Wouldn't face her. Not until the end.

Wynn sniggered, picked up the cards and shuffled them. "If it's anyone's fault, I would blame Dia." The table gasped ever so. "Was it not she who insisted you travel south?" He looked around them mischievously. "Sending a little shit like you south would always end in trouble." He grasped Erroh's shoulder in mock reassurance. "Were it me, I'd have charmed Uden into peace. Or else killed him quick enough." He began to deal. "Who takes a fuken eye anyway?"

Erroh smiled. The others snickered—a delightful sound.

"It was my fault," Nomi said suddenly. "If I had just let you die. No eye taken, no fuken march of the Woodin Man." She examined her cards and then threw them down in defeat. It wasn't her bet, so she lost little in this hand.

"Aye, it is your fault, Nomi," agreed Erroh, taking his cards and feeling a little better about himself. About his choice of generals too. They would help lighten his mood if nothing else, even if he led them all to failure.

"It is all on me," Tye announced to the table. He threw some pieces into the pot, daring anyone to bet. "If I was better at charming Lea, I could have made her my own." He eyed Erroh's mate and offered his most suggestive wink. It wasn't impressive, but he earned a smile from her. "I could have left Erroh an awful wretch, left him to wander the Wastes. He'd never have made it south."

Lea agreed. "A terrible shame, my little stallion. Next time, try harder."

"Thank the absent gods. I'm not the only one who is to blame," Lexi said, matching Tye's bet because fuk him. "I should have told him to chase after Silvia. He would have ended up with a slit throat as he slept some night in the Wastes long before reaching Keri… I hate that bitch; I hope she's dead."

The table laughed at the sudden impressive vitriol from one so diminutive.

"So it's your fault he ended up with me?" Lea asked nastily. She was grinning, though. That was something, he supposed.

"You stole him for your own. I'd have preferred to see Roja with him… or Lillium… or maybe Silvia," Lexi countered, also grinning. For just a breath, Erroh imagined he heard a slight threat in his little sister's words. It was lost beneath the laughter at the table.

Lillium took her turn. She grabbed Erroh's hand in hers and flashed her most dazzling smile. "I should have taken you as my own, my future lover." She kissed his hand and pressed it to her forehead. "We would have beaten them back at Keri. Gone on and killed that Woodin fuk outright, as well."

"I'm right here, Lillium. I'm right fuken here," Wynn said with a laugh, trying to separate their hands. A futile gesture, for Lillium simply held on more tightly. She reassured Erroh of her unwavering support in that simple, humorous gesture, and he was grateful. But Wynn wasn't done humiliating himself. "I mean, that night, when you kissed him first in the tavern? I fuken knew you were after him."

"You did what?" Lea asked evenly, but Lillium just shrugged noncommittally. It was a strange thing to see the mood rise; Erroh's mood rose along with the others'. He liked to play the part of the fool for others' entertainment; it played well with morale, and made him feel far better than before.

"We all know it was my fault," Magnus declared. "Had I not had so many drinks that night, I might never have taken Elise to bed. Fuken travesty that was," the old legend mocked. The gathering agreed. They didn't even notice as another sphere of fire lit up the night, flew in low and embedded itself deep within the city walls, sending sparks and flame into the air. Their attention was on the camaraderie between them now, for deep down, they all knew there was an energy in the air, a sense of terrible things to come. They just didn't know how soon.

"You are all fukers," Erroh countered, and drew his cards. "But it's a relief to know it wasn't entirely me who led us to this place."

"Hey," Doran interrupted. His face was grave. He looked at his cards in his misshapen grip before tossing them to the table. "Truly, the blame lies with me. I knew I should have killed him the day I battered him in the Cull. I fuken knew it. Also, I should have killed him in the sands as well."

The gathering fell silent in the face of such passion.

Erroh countered. "It wouldn't have mattered if you killed me in the sands; the damage had already been done. Uden was already marching."

"I know that, Erroh. We all know that. I just think it would have made me feel a lot better if I'd also killed you back then." He grinned manically, and the table erupted in laughter. Erroh thought on the miles he'd walked these last few years. He marvelled again at how strange it was that war brought out the best in petty enemies.

Wynn would not be outdone. "Remember that party, Doran? And that fuken barrel?"

"I should have killed you back then too. All you fukers," countered Doran.

"No, I would have killed *you*," argued Wynn passionately.

"I demand a rematch. Blades or fists? Whichever, really. Um… probably not fists…"

"You have my word, brother," Wynn said, laughing.

The gathering went back and forth, arguing and boasting, challenging and threatening, in a show of good-natured Alphaline behaviour. Only Lea resisted the jesting. She threw in her last pieces on a terrible bet and retired from the table. But not before stopping by Erroh and whispering, "This *is* all your fault," before slipping away into the night, leaving Erroh a little winded. Truthfully, such a cutting remark from her a few days prior might have thrown him further than it did now. As it was, he was used to her anger, her cruelty.

If Tye heard her words, he showed little interest, for he was laughing to himself. "Hey, Erroh, tell that tale about the cards again. The one about the big brute and the cheating," he said, nudging Wrek in the ribs. "It's hilarious; you must hear it," he added.

———

Lea didn't hear Lillium's approach, such was her distraction. She stared at the city in the darkness and hated Uden with all she had—resented him as well. For his actions, for her miserable life. For leaving her alone and forgotten. Little Lea of the city, shuffling through the hallways, never knowing any better.

Truly, she wanted him dead. Wanted him punished. She also wanted to know why he had never come for her. Why he had burned the world and not once attempted to meet her. Mostly, she was grateful he never had. Who knew what influence he might have had upon her at such a young age? Especially in those early years, when staying afloat among so many sisters had been so dreadful. Now, she mostly wanted to look him in the eye and cut his fuken heart out, howling as she did.

"What is your problem?" Lillium cried, grabbing her roughly from behind and shoving her forward so hard that she nearly stumbled. Lea had surpassed Lillium in archery all their lives, but Lillium had always been the taller, faster, stronger fist-fighter. This show of force was nothing unusual.

"Fuk off, Lillium. Leave me be," Lea countered, shoving her friend away. The taller Alpha rolled with the punch, took hold of Lea's wrist and spun her ever so. Some arguments required greater force, and Lea had rarely seen Lillium as mad as she was now.

"You haven't said a fuken word to me these last few days. You shun those who care for you; you display open revulsion for our master general."

"I have reasons of my own," Lea snapped. Her hand was a fist, her anger overflowing. Lillium was still a child, for all her deeds. Still naïve and passionate and rightly fuken righteous. Lea could see through her bravado. Always had. Always would.

"Piss on your reasons. You cut into Erroh when any fool could see he needs our support."

"Have you wondered how much better we might be if we did not rely on him? Did you not listen to every word he spouts? He's a fuken liar." Lea leapt towards Lillium, swinging fiercely at her. Lillium merely stepped wide of the blow, clipping Lea across the head as she sent her careening into the muddy grass.

"Where is my friend?" Lillium asked sadly.

"Help me up, will you?" Lea asked. She reached for her friend, who was deceived by the ruse. Lea snaked her arm around Lillium's, pulling her to the ground, wrapping her legs around the taller girl like a serpent with a careless shrew. "You think you are perfect because you dye your hair all vibrant? Is that all it took? Is that all it took to feel good about yourself, you fuken whore?" she shouted, squeezing Lillium, trying to break her arm, trying to defeat her. Trying to inflict what agony she could. Anything. All of it. She did not know why.

Lillium squirmed, her body as lithe as though her limbs were designed for this violence. She slipped from Lea's careless grasp within a breath before rolling away and climbing to her feet. She was calm, annoyingly calm. And controlled too. Lea rose and stumbled after her and was immediately twisted into a vicious hold and spun, heels over head, painfully back onto the ground. Lillium straddled her, pinned her knees and slapped her across the face.

"Why do you jeopardise the entire world?" she demanded.

"What do you mean?"

"You kill him with your words every fuken day."

"Fuk off."

"Why must he be so punished? What did he do, Lea?"

"He left me; he punished me; he tormented me."

"You are no victim; why play at being such a thing?"

"You have no idea what I have endured."

Lillium slapped her again across the face, a stinging blow, and Lea tried to fight free again, but Lillium was in control. Worse than that, Lea wasn't. She wanted to burn the world; she wanted to punish everything. She wanted hate and anger. She did not know why.

"I endured horrors, but it never crushed my spirit as it crushed yours. I carry my horror, and I use it," Lillium said calmly. All too calmly. Really fuken annoyingly calmly.

Without warning, Lillium rolled away, and Lea leapt to her feet and immediately drew her blade. A breath after that, she dropped it in horror. "I could never hurt you willingly," she whispered, recoiling from the blade.

Using her foot, Lillium flicked it into her hand before spinning it around like Erroh before offering it back to her best friend. "Do not lose Erroh as I lost Wynn."

"It is completely different."

Lillium took Lea's quivering hand and eased the blade back into its scabbard. "Hate that which should be hated."

"I have done such terrible things to him."

"As terrible as what he did to you?"

A terrible horror came upon Lea, and in that breath, she understood what she had done. For just a moment, the anger fell away, and she thought of that fool that she loved with all her heart, for always.

Green eyes.

Green eyes.

Remember?

"Who have I become?" Lea whispered.

"Someone at the precipice. Come back to us; come back to me. And perhaps, come back to him."

The Actions of Gods

Lillium stepped away, leaving Lea shaken. She looked at her with less anger than before, but warmth was such a fleeting thing. This Lea knew, even as she knew she would soon revile Erroh for leaving her behind to face her father as the world fell apart around her.

Around them all.

"Perhaps we should return to the game," Lea said weakly. She didn't want to. She wanted distraction. She wanted sorrow. She wanted to run away into the night and weep until dawn. She could not face Erroh, could not bear the thought of looking upon him and imagining the torment she'd delivered. But there was also the horror he had inflicted upon her. She imagined a final kiss, and her stomach turned.

And then the cries of alarm distracted them from any further uncomfortable conversations.

97

STIRRING OF A GOD

He had felt this way before. Once in his life. Back then, during the great time before. At the end of his human life. When he could take no more. Back when he'd roamed the world as a man, before the pain became too much. He had vowed never to return, yet Uden had returned to the arth too casually. Hadn't he? Played at bitter, beautiful things. He knew it now, as he had known to leave so long ago. A terrible place, this realm, he thought, and hated it. Hated himself for allowing himself to be human.

Hated. Hated. Hated.

He struggled away from the cells, leaving those that wondered after him far behind. Slamming the door, he stumbled out into the night, looked up at the stars, and cursed them and his misery. Then he cursed the shard of fire that flew overhead. Coming to get him, no doubt, he thought, and drew his eye back to the darkened streets where no god should walk at this late hour.

"I can smell her still," he muttered, and, in the dazzling shattered moonlight, saw the blood upon his hands, his shirt. A thousand other places, no doubt. She had been born in blood and would die in blood too. That was the way of so many. "Not enough," he roared. Around him, his guards shifted uneasily, watching him. Wary and cautious, they flanked his every move lest he collapse and show his inner human a little too much.

He thought back on her dying words. Her final words. No healer would be able to pull her back from the dark, no matter how many of his protégés went to task repairing her. It didn't matter. He hadn't wanted her to live. But he couldn't watch her die. He was a father of sorts and deserved never to see his beloved die before him. He'd seen that before, the human part of him at least.

"Light the way," he demanded of his guards. Then, shoving the torchbearer forward, he shouted, "To their house. To my beautiful family's house."

He roared aloud as they marched through the night, and they did not hesitate or argue. "To arms, my comrades, my people, my children." His voice echoed in the night, and candles were lit in many a household as he passed. "We go to war this night," he roared repeatedly, and they listened, for he was still a god, and they were his flock. "Spread the word, my beautiful things; spread it and arm yourselves." Around them in the darkened night began the stirrings of movement as warriors sprinted from door to door, bringing word of a divine battle. There were cheers, there were curses, and there were gasps. He even heard doors slammed in rejection. Those were the households he would hunt first after the fall of the world.

"My lord, perhaps we should wait until dawn," ventured a young guard. Uden thought him brave for arguing his point, for challenging him in front of so many. He dashed the boy's head against a wall and kept walking. There was a yelp and a dull, heavy thud. The boy would survive. Probably. It was a small matter. What mattered was finding his kin alive and well. However, were Aurora to be truthful in her words of murdering Roja, the factions would pay this very night. Erroh would pay too. Everything the boy loved and represented would be destroyed this night. He called a god out? A god would answer.

"My master, what is happening?" Gemmil said from the shadows. He had dressed hastily and still bore the signs of a man suddenly woken at the call of war. "What are you doing?"

"Terrible things are afoot, Gemmil. It ends tonight," he growled, and Gemmil, as brave as that young, unconscious guard, stepped in the god's way and held him fast.

His eyes were cold and calculating. Uden could see his unhappiness at such timing. Gemmil had spoken for days of Erroh's actions, of his taunting. He knew Uden well enough to know some spark would eventually light him to action. He shouldn't have spoken with such surprise.

"We aren't ready," Gemmil insisted, and Uden shoved him away. He cared little for the man's apprehension. Sometimes there was a time to be careful. Other times, a god was right to wake up an entire city after the witching hour to finish a fight.

"Get them ready," he demanded, then bowed magnificently before barking orders to all in the vicinity like any fine general. He knew his place.

Uden could have assisted him, roared more and challenged him to follow, but instead, he turned away and followed his torchbearer. He was still wary of what he would find, praying his whore of a lover was lying at the end. He suddenly thought of the ruined Aurora in his arms, dying, bleeding, fading and hating.

She lied about Roja's fate.

Above him, another shard of light lit the night, not from the shattered moon but made by the hands of men. He watched it careen through the air, strike a tower and come alive in fire, and he thought it beautiful and fitting. It enraged him further, as did the thunder from various parts of the city where the tainted curs brought his great war machines back to life. He would admit only to those closest to him that it was costly to lose such beasts, but even they would not make him stir from his city. Not even the sight of demolished houses with families dead within them would stir him. Not even seeing the route blocked by debris and gathered Southerners wailing at their losses. He stirred this night only because hers was the last challenge he could accept.

He took a different path, away from the falling boulders and the shards of fire, and finally he rounded the corner to see the ruin awaiting him; it was truly awful. There was no need for torches to guide his way now. A crowd was gathered—no doubt drawn to the terrible sight of death.

He went weak at the knees, and he was a man again. Watching the fire take their house, he wailed for little Cordelia, burning to nothing within.

In the blaze, he could see the massive bolt plunged right through the upper bedroom window, where his kin, asleep or at play, would never have had a chance. It had probably lanced them where they lay, spilled its burning contents all over their perfect bodies. Already the room was collapsing onto the floor below, and it was a pyre fit for gods. It didn't matter. He fell to his knees and roared like he had done only once before. He saw brave comrades attempt to fight the flames, but it was a futile gesture with so few buckets.

"Let them burn, let my family burn," he cried out, and his Azier guards were around him, protecting the people from seeing his agony, from seeing his humanity. He felt the world take hold and crush him. It came in the form of a young Alpha who had played his part in bringing about his ascension, but also in crushing him. He did not know how long he knelt, watching the flames, only that around him, they prepared for war as he commanded. Platoons of warriors marched past, and he thought them fine tools for his wrath. He did not remember calling for his armour and swords, but they were presented to him, and instinctively, he dressed and armed himself and felt fuken fierce.

Before dawn, he summoned the will to draw blood. Placing his hand upon his heart, he bowed with finality to the burning ruin of Roja and Emir. They lay either as raging embers within the ruins of the house or slain somewhere else by her hand, which was too much.

He drew his blades and marched through the city. All around him, the streets were emptying. Everyone was invited to the end of the world, and most were attending. With every step, he thought less of his shortcomings and more of his godliness. He became wrath, he became mercilessness, he became Uden the Woodin Man, marching out to bring death to the defiant, tainted few.

He met them at the gates, and they were patient and alert. He grinned as he marched through them—thousands in number, far greater than any number in the fields beyond.

"Today, we kill," he roared, and they cheered, even as a boulder sailed over their heads and crashed far away, no doubt taking out another home or tower. The crowd looked to the noise, and this displeased him greatly.

"Look at me!" he demanded. "Look at me, and know those few are unworthy of our kind." He marched among them. Among generals, confidants and strangers. He looked at them all as lesser brothers and sisters. Beautiful and destructive and perfect.

"I will not fall this bloody day, and neither will you. Believe in Valhal, and it waits for you in the great journey after."

They cheered again, and he reached the gates. He was impressive in this light. He knew he was. He could see Gemmil and Seth side by side, concern and excitement on their grizzled faces. They alone had brought the world to this point. For this, he was grateful, but it was time for Uden to carry them the last mile.

"They burn our generals, rape our kind; they slither their way through this skirmish like the serpents they are." They reacted with hate and urgency to such vileness as any warriors should. He could see how dearly they needed to believe his words, how they required meaning for themselves.

"I will finish these tainted curs where they stand, and you, my beautiful brothers and sisters, are my tools of ire. Most people never live a life of significance, but this brutal morning will be spoken about for millennia. I love you all, care for you all, and see you all. We will know victory this day as the god of fire falls in ruin…"

A strong finish. They needed hope; they needed repayment for the tremendous sacrifice they had made.

"A new age begins, of your making, in my light, in our ways. I see it with my one eye."

They cheered. They wanted to see it, too.

"Can you see the beauty of the days to come?"

They could see it. They roared, they demanded.

And he would deliver.

He gestured for the gates to part, and as the great shrieking filled the air, he clattered his sword against his breastplate. He stamped the ground in primal defiance, and they copied his gestures, and soon the thousands drew thunder of their own, roaring, daring, believing.

The gates creaked wide open, and he could see the gathered armies distantly. He spun around and roared, "They are so few?"

The crowd erupted in manic laughter and jeering. They stepped forward like hounds on leashes, desperate to do his savage deeds. Desperate to be released. He was happy to hold and release them, and to tear apart all who defied him.

"Where is the army I was promised?" he demanded, stepping out into the night with ten thousand shadowed warriors in pursuit. He could see them. Stirring and preparing. All too few. All too unprepared. He looked at the shattered moon burning itself and thought it was lively. Ready to spit all manner of fire upon the Arth. Let it gaze upon the horrors to come this night. Let the entire world shake as the true god of this world marched and waged his war. He stood out beneath the gates and bellowed his arrival in a terrible war cry, and they answered with their own, with their charge. And he, with his guards, charged with them, seeking death, punishment and victory.

And the factions, waking to the terrible sounds of war, were dreadfully unprepared for this savage attack in the final battle in the last fight for Spark City.

98

FINAL EXCERPTS FROM THE DESKS OF WEASELS

Equinox 125th
    Dearest Gemmil,
    I write this with haste and with tears in my eyes, not of sorrow but of terrible, terrible anger. I'm surprised you might even read my words, such is the appalling tremble in my hands as I write this. You bastard. You vile cur of a beast. A pox upon your house for what you ask of me. You speak of murder so cavalierly, as though it were nothing. You speak of butchering innocent beauty as though it were even less. You were her chosen uncle in all but blood. Is the cold so brutal that your heart and better judgement have frozen? Are you that far gone that killing a child is merely one more task to be handled? You speak of love for a friend, and then plot and murder... another of his children. This one, from a thousand miles away. I would suggest if you want the deed done, you commit the act yourself. I fear, dearest friend, that you would make that journey alone. Are you so very twisted that you would choose your closest comrade's trauma as your vessel for violence? For your sick desire to gain power? Look at Wiiden. Look into his eyes and tell me you believe killing little Cordelia is the finer task. How far you have come these decades. How far you have fallen away too. I am disgusted to read of such things.
    Little Lea will remain in Samara under my distant protection. Truthfully, keeping her from Wiiden's madness will not be difficult. Nor will it be difficult to smooth away what truths she remembers. A child is an astonishing thing for keeping long-forgotten secrets. Among so many sisters in the city, she will fade into the background as though she is

unimportant. A tragedy for her lineage but better than the harsher risk. And as for her surviving kin?

Kin used to mean something to me. No more. You have tarnished any such belief. She will know nothing of Roja, and Roja nothing of her. An easy task when I control the records. I give you ample reason to calm your plans for her. I am no saintly man, but I will do what good I must. Although I hate this place and all who reside in it, I will honour Wiiden. Until his madness is lost. Until he can learn of her survival. And if that never happens, well, so be it. What will matter is her life will be saved. Know this, though, "friend": should something ill come of her, Wiiden will soon learn of our deceits. I will be safe behind these fuken walls. I might even survive until he brings his wrath upon the whole place. But you, brother, will be dead long before Wiiden marches.

Do not contact me again.
–Seth.

Equinox 76th

Dearest Seth,

You wise old comrade. How long has it been? A year? Two? How many letters have I written? At least a hundred. It feels like a hundred. Did you read any of them? Did you enjoy my arrogance, my arguments, my petty reasoning? Did you learn of our marches across these frozen lands? Did you care? Did you send hunting packs after me? They would have been deserved. I want you to know that. Whatever foulness you planned, or plan, is what I deserve.

Fuk. It is late here. It is late, and I am tired, morose and lost despite the world improving.

Fuk.

I sat and reread these last few sentences back over again and again. My mind is broken. Will this reach you? Will you forgive an angry old man who mis-stepped? You can tell by how few assassins have knocked on your door this past year that I bear you no ill will. As for the girl, I will leave the matter to your better judgement.

In truth, I read your last message daily—a timely reminder of the blood on my hands. Whenever I feel I am getting ahead of myself, I receive that little taste of humility, as I've said in every letter before. You were right, dear brother. And I was wrong. A thousand times over. Were you in front of me, I would drop to my knees and weep for the loneliness. But also for the wretched sorrow I feel.

I have seen terrible acts these last few years at march—dreadful, awful acts. Women burned, and children lanced upon pikes. Their squeals. Their desolation. Their gruesome ends. All for the benefit of building something more significant, and I am tired, brother. I miss my friend. I miss our times. I will give you the world if you reply. I will hold whatever debt there is complete, should you write back.

For we also need you. If you read no other letter, know this: we need your efforts again. I will do whatever it takes, but for now, think of what we lived through and offer me one chance to work again with you. This will be my last letter ever, brother. I hope it finds you and finds you willing to listen and forgive. For things are coming, brother. In Uden we trust.

Yours faithfully,
Gemmil.

———

Equinox 65th
   What is it you wish of me?
   Yours,
   Seth

———

Equinox 123rd
   Dearest Seth,
   I had lost hope, but to receive your reply was a blessing. You ask a simple question. My reply is this: I desire only your friendship again. Let me earn your trust once more, brother.
   Yours,
   Gemmil.

———

Solstice 52nd
   Perhaps, out of necessity, I resume contact with you, old friend. 'Old friend.' Are we friends? Perhaps. Have I forgiven your deeds? That is a challenging question to answer. I'm older now and think less about this

cursed place and my part in it. I, who have lived a sanitary life behind these walls while my brothers strive for war, deep in the Wastes. How quick I am to judge. Even barbaric actions. Was it not I who begged your forgiveness once upon a time? Was it not you who allowed me to creep back into this world? A world where I believed I mattered. These last years have given me much to think about.

My station in Samara is far below what it once was. I exist within these walls, barely a footnote in a withered old woman's eyes.

A long time ago, you asked me for written documents of every Alpha family to come through this city. I can only imagine what you intend to do with such a prize. Rest assured, with Magnus gelded and no movement in the Savage Isles, I can only imagine what dangers lie in an army of Alphalines all rearing for a fight.

Enclosed within is what you desire. I do this out of necessity, for my gains. This cold place with its humming walls is no home, and I am barely alive. I am without hope. But I clear all my debts should I decide to leave. The hour is late, and I must sleep.

Goodbye, old comrade, friend, brother.
Seth.

Solstice 102nd
Dearest Seth,
Your message both warmed and terrified me ever so. It did for our godly brother too. Aye, godly. He plays the part of a god, and he is imperious. For a time now, he has called himself by a different name. A terrifying name. Uden. Why does he answer to another name,? I hear you ask. Because he is capable of all things under this banner, and I will follow him. You were right to keep the child alive. Tell me about her so I might know her. Tell me of Roja too. Uden talks of his forgotten niece most frequently. It is one of the few warmths he clings to in the dark nights. That and a girl. A vicious girl. A witch so capable of greatness it is blinding. A youthful witch who might also burn down the entire South for the sheer joy of it. You saw a truth a long time ago that, in my desperation, I could not see. In my need to destroy, I was blind too. The child Cordelia might well pull Uden back from the brink... should there ever be need of that. You always claimed knowledge was greater than any power, and I trust your better judgement. We are on the move again

but have come upon a new stronghold deep in the South. The South is close to bending to our will.

Were I to tell you of a swifter way for us to communicate, would that give you hope? Were we able to better plot out the city's downfall, might that offer confidence?

Write again swiftly, my brother.
In Uden we trust.
Yours,
Gemmil.

Equinox 77th

Dearest Gemmil,

I hate these fuken birds. They hate me more. The smell. The fuken noise. Worse than a hum, they are. Yet still, I am grateful for them. And for the advantage they bring. I still don't understand how you trained them or how yours flew to me, but I am grateful for these last few months. Knowing I am a few words away and no longer relying on riders. I shall send a second pigeon along soon, with word of a more recent Culling. A fine firebrand. A right threat. Something to be dealt with.

Speaking of, tell me more of this underling of Udin's. I wish to meet her now that she is out in the world, killing. Doing our better deeds, as you claimed. It eases the pain of my place here, you know. Have I said that recently? Knowing we creep beneath Dia's gaze is a soothing thing. Knowing that every season she frets more and more about fewer Alphalines is ambrosia to this aged tongue. Oh, aye, it is quite the task, keeping an eye upon such movements, but a task worthy of my many hours. It keeps me young, but honestly, I feel old. It may be because I am struck down with such an affliction.

Oh, listen to me ramble as though this parchment has no end.

As I write this, I sit below a flickering light, sifting through missives from across the reaches of the Four Factions. So many higherlines. I hear their worries. I acknowledge their threats. I answer for Dia. It is a rewarding task to send them not a saviour but a roving Southern group or a young witch at night. In many ways, I sign their death warrants once more. But there is one foul settlement we must tend to before we march—a bandit's lair, a formidable place. If any settlement might get wind of terrible things in motion, it is Raven Rock, but that might come in time anyway.

Our friend might wonder after his daughter. She has turned into a proper little miss. Honestly, I feel little warmth for her. She has become just like the rest. I do not wish to see her dead, though. She has come of age. She might well Cull next season.

Roja should have Culled this season. Instead, she went against Dia's better wishes. The arguments echoed through the city. She has her lineage in her blood. You might tell Udin such a thing. It might warm his heart.

I ask you this, dear comrade: after so many years, I wonder, have you amassed enough? Are you ready to creep down and take what should have been ours long ago? I ask, for again, I look in a mirror and see a broken old man looking back.

I always do like to end these messages on a bright note.
Be well, brother.
In Udin we trust.
Seth.

Equinox 96th
  Dearest Seth,
  Perilous times are coming, my old friend. Already the first of many are entrenched deep within the factions. We spare none, and our sins are plentiful, but that is the cost of our grandness. The witch Aurora has outdone herself again. Wretched, vile, and dangerous as she is. You speak of the settlement called Raven Rock? That is some memory I thought was long lost. In reply, the deed will be done. Let bandits whine and worry about a sacking. They will hardly turn to Samara for help.

  <u>Uden's</u> zealots are whipped up into a frenzy. The South waits to march, to repay the North for its bastard ways. For its mistreatment. Admittedly, there are whispers of dissent, and <u>Uden</u> is obsessed with such few voices, but it is mere distraction. He knows the time is upon us. Rest assured, brother, we all feel the years. Ours have brought a few additional scars. Yours brought the horror of enduring Dia as long as you did. I am eager to march into greatness.

  I read of little Cordelia, and it shook me to learn that she has come of age. Perhaps a fine young Alpha bastard might take her heart, and then off with them to furrow and make further cubs. Perhaps no Aurora will appear at their door like she did with the others.

Uden speaks fondly of Roja. The excitement of seeing her again brings a spark to his eyes. Keep her safe in the months ahead. If there is one Alpha he would care to gaze upon, it is her. It is the most human side to him too.

Be safe, my old friend; avoid mirrors and humming things.

In Uden we trust.

Yours Gemmil.

———

Solstice 54th

Dear Gemmil,

I am writing this letter in a cold panic. For a time now, I have agonised over revealing the news of Lea. She has mated with another. A marching threat to come, for it is Magnus's child with whom she has mated. I do not know how such a thing occurred. Truthfully, he is probably no menace to the Four Factions or beyond. I can only presume Magnus diverted all his skills into the act of warmongering over instruction. Perhaps I concealed Lea all too well these years, and she believed herself unworthy of none so spectacular. The damage is done, and the die is cast. More than that, Dia has commanded they venture south to speak with you in Little Rose. They come with word of our actions, though little has changed to suggest Dia suspects anything more than roving warlords. I play my dutiful part, and the wench trusts everything I say. While the onus is very much on you, I would have you keep both young Alphalines safe and well, and ultimately ignorant, and return them so they might slip away to their insignificant lives. If not for Lea's lineage, then for keeping that slumbering behemoth in the east.

At least for now.

I beg you, brother, give me your word that they will come to no harm so that I might continue to keep Dia's watchful careless eye over the South. At least for another season longer.

In ~~Udin~~ UDEN we trust.

Yours, Seth.

———

Solstice 62nd

Dearest Seth,

I give you my word. No harm shall come to the little Alphalines. I shall meet with them in Little Rose, should they survive the journey down here. More than that, brother, I pledge when we meet, I will treat them as family, allay their fears and send them on their way, as I have done with every single Alphaline that queen bitch of the city has sent my way.

It is a small matter.

And besides, two little insignificant Alphalines, newly mated, with hormones aplenty?

Honestly, how much trouble could either of them cause us, anyway...

99

THE BATTLE FOR SPARK CITY

"You fuken asshole. I knew it. I fuken knew it," roared Wrek. His outburst filled the air, but few were paying attention. Those who were might have found it funny to see the great behemoth enraged with their master general, who cowered behind any who would protect him.

"That was you?" countered Erroh. Lillium stood between them both; Wynn stood a little further off, holding back Wrek. He laughed at the snarling general even as he held him from throttling the much smaller Alpha.

"Aye, that was fuken me. I fuken knew I recognised you from somewhere, and I couldn't fuken place you." He struggled and swung wildly at Erroh, who laughed wonderfully at the sudden outburst. And why wouldn't he? This just added to an already excellent story. "You little shit. I ought to brain you, here and now," he roared.

Tye was delighted; apparently, taking full accidental credit for this mayhem was an excellent end to the evening. "He's told that story so many times, I'm surprised he never once said it to you," the young Alpha declared, stepping towards the raging Wrek, who failed to see the humour in everything but his eyes. To be fair, and to the betterment of the evening, he'd waited for Erroh to tell the tale in full before leaping to his feet, playing wonderfully at being outraged. If their camaraderie did nothing more than raise morale among the group, this outburst merely added to it.

"Up and down the Four Factions, to anybody who would listen," Erroh cried, and couldn't help but laugh at his friend's misfortune. "In my memory, you were taller." This gloriously enraged Wrek further, and the players laughed along with his mock fury. Truthfully, there had always been a familiarity to the big man. Erroh could see it now. Not just the similarity to Quig. "I offer an apology," Erroh offered, bowing with just the right amount of mockery, and the brute was not best pleased.

"Do you know what fuken Sigi used to call me?"

"I can't imagine."

"The fuken ace of queens."

"That's a great nickname."

"Not the way he said it," countered Wrek. "Fuker used to call me that sometimes when no one was around. To put me in my place. To remind me of my foolishness," Wrek said, holding his struggles for a moment as though lost in a bitter, better memory. And then he charged again. "And it was you who fuken made me look the fool, making me think a blade killed me, and you with your fuken cheating queen of aces up your grubby fuken sleeves. I bet you have some cards there, don't ya?" he roared, breaking the grip, slipping past Erroh's defence and lifting him high as though he was going to throw him right into the fire. "Fuken don't ya?"

"All right, all right, I yield," yelled Erroh, laughing.

"Yer fuken right, you yield," snarled Wrek, and as he did, some spittle took flight and struck Erroh's cheek. "Ah, shit, I'm after spitting on you," he cried, dropping the performance and dumping Erroh to his feet. He immediately went to remove the offending spittle, but Erroh was already away from him, wiping it off.

"It isn't the first time that's happened. Although that one was at least deserved," Erroh countered. "I will tell that tale no more," he offered sincerely.

Wrek leaned in close. "Don't be ridiculous; it's a good story to warm listeners to your ways. Those that want to know more are welcome. Those that think less? Fuk them."

"It's only a story," offered Erroh, shrugging. He thought of that event with a clearer mind. How long had it been? How different was he now? Though he had been careless and unimpressive, there was a simple happiness he had enjoyed in those times.

Better times?

Probably not.

Suddenly, from the outskirts of the camp there came cries of alarm, and Erroh snapped himself from that little cub and became the warrior legend they needed. More and more voices emerged, and Erroh and his comrades ran towards the alarms. For a breath, he wondered was this the end. Was this the battle to end all battles?

It wasn't.

He came upon a crowd gathered around two figures appearing scruffy, lost, ruined and broken. They might have also appeared glamourous, joyous and triumphant.

"It can't be," he cried, and his knees were weak at seeing his old friend, soaked and shivering, accepting hugs from the gathered Wolves. They remembered his healing hands; they remembered his impressiveness. They paid homage. Beside him stood Roja, shimmering, despite her dress clinging tightly to her body in the freezing air. She beamed a dazzling smile and fell upon the nearest Wolf, Lea, who accepted the hug carefully.

"My boy," cried Wrek, charging past, tearing through the Wolves as though he were clearing a room in a busy tavern, grabbing the wretched Emir and hoisting him aloft as though he were an Alpha accused of some terrible mischief. They weren't alone, for the wretches from the hovels took Emir as their own while the Alpha females took Roja, and despite the threat in the air, despite the late hour, despite knowing doom was upon them all, there was a wondrous joy at their return.

Before long, all the outcasts were upon the duo, hugging and crying, and for a breath, Erroh enjoyed the levity. He pushed in among them, hugging and exclaiming, and it felt wonderful. Although no sine was offered, no music played, no beat to dance to, it almost felt like a party—a grand gathering of those doomed few in the middle of the Wastes, celebrating without care.

Eventually, when the frenzy simmered down, most went their own way, seeking rest for the night ahead. Erroh sat with his two comrades until near dawn. Listening to their tales was as sobering as learning of their wedded day. He could see their tiredness, despite their enthusiasm to stay awake until after dawn. Eventually, fatigue got the better of them. With the newlyweds having been given a tent so they might consummate the marriage, Erroh returned to the fireside and lay down in its warmth.

"A good day," he mused, feeling the sleep come upon him. Around him, the warriors were still and settled, and he thought them the smarter fiends.

Suddenly, the gates shrieked their piercing cry, alerting the world of terrible things to come. He shot awake, sitting up as the darkness filled with sounds like the cries of a beast of prey, and far below in the city there appeared flaming torches aplenty.

"Wake up," Erroh cried, even as voices around him spoke of threats in the wind. He couldn't keep his eyes from the gates as they opened wide, and beneath the streams of burning light, there watched thousands. "Everybody," he cried, and had already begun to tighten his armour before wrapping his blades in black bandanas to his wrists. His heart hammered, and a terrible sinking feeling came upon him. Death loomed close now; any fool watching the gates knew the dreadful trials to come.

He could hear his comrades around him, all strangers, stir and struggle from their bedding out into the cold air of the early morning, desperation driving their movements, panic tearing at their will and better judgement. He wondered might some run in fear. An easy thing in the dark. Who would know?

They would know.

Far down, he watched a prominent figure standing near the gates of the city, roaring and ordering and riling up this gathered army. Without warning, they rushed out through the gates like a terrible wave, up towards the unprepared army. He knew it to be Uden. He knew it like he knew the turn of the wind, like the turn of a battle.

What did I expect would happen?

I never expected this.

"Prepare yourselves," he cried, and his voice was lost to the screams, the frenzy, the horror. Around him, they made no move to fall in line, and how would they? Most were still undressed, bleary-eyed, looking for anything in the world but orders and war. This was a time of slumber and relief. This Woodin Man fuk was taking them from it.

Erroh looked around for his generals. For those he trusted more than anyone in the world. He knew he could lead a group, gather their terror and fuel it into desperation and violence. Still, as warriors scurried around him, there appeared no general to assist him, so he roared for himself and began to march towards the oncoming army.

Thousands were charging out from the city without respite. He imagined them outnumbering his forces three or four times over, which was humbling. "On me," he demanded, and a few gathered their swords and shields and fell into marching with him. More followed, desperation giving way to discipline, and though he did not know these savages, these Wolves, these wretches, these Southerners, these citizens, he thought them heroic.

"We few might die this night," he roared. He didn't know how many heard him cry out amidst the rumble of the charge and the roar before the end. It didn't matter. In a few breaths, a few hundred had gathered around him, marched with him, and prepared to die. "Others might live on and know we played our part."

His pace increased while the snarling Hunt from the South moved towards this little pack as though they smelled the false god of fire.

"Do not slip away without a sound. Tear and cut and kill and bleed. Never fuken stop. Not until the path ahead is clear. Look to your brother and sister either side of you and kill with them, kill for them." He didn't even know what he was saying. He didn't care. He'd never been great for speeches anyway. But he could wield a blade just fine.

He roared loudly, and across from him on either side, he could see the desperate warriors sprinting to join this last heroic line. Ever so slowly, spreading out, swords aplenty.

"I've never fled from a battle, friends. I've only run headlong into them, and this glorious day, you will too," he shouted, and began to run. Swiftly at first, and then a full sprint. With blades out and swinging, he heard them roar behind, heard them sprint with him. Once more, before the end, before the clash, before he sought out Uden, Erroh looked into the gathered doomed comrades, saw no familiar face, and thought, was this a dream? If so, it would be a typical, miserable dream suggesting his weariness with solitude. As it was, he was very much awake and would remain so before he slept eternally.

Alone.

"Kill them all!"

They roared his words in reply. They echoed across the valley as triumphantly as a song about a brigand on the eve of battle. "Kill them all, kill them all," the words boomed, and he was proud, and for a moment, he was less afraid. He sought out Uden in the mass of terrible things twenty feet ahead, snapping and swinging, and said goodbye to the world.

Screaming.
Swinging.
Dying.
Bleeding.
Losing.

The world slowed as he crashed into an opponent and another after that, and many more after that. He saw nothing but shapes and flashes of light as torchbearers neared and died around him, and he was cold and cruel. He dared few aggressive attacks instead, using his skills to parry and counter, avoiding a likely blade to the belly or an axe to the head. He screamed without drawing breath at every cur he felled, and they were many. Around him, his comrades died, and he felt everyone's passing as he gazed upon their broken bodies. He felt his victims' loss as well, and it was terrible.

He cursed and challenged, he roared, and he sought out Uden with every cry. He demanded the brute, for every moment the man lived was a moment longer that his kin, comrades, loved ones and warriors faced ruination.

Kill them all.

He did not know how long he killed nor how many of the original line stood with him. Only that every breath was a life of its own. A short one, admittedly, made shorter by the killing, but in the end, he finally appreciated what he had, what he could lose. As the world slowed to nothing, he could see as far as a one-eyed god might claim. He dared a gaze around and saw the entire valley swarming with warriors, both Southern and not. They fought and died around him, and it was a terrible sight.

This is the end.
This is the fuken end.
I am ready.

He called for Uden once more, and far from him, charging through the violence, a marching god surged and glided and killed.

This is the end.

The absent gods agreed, for they had seen this end long before. They moved what they could, pushed even further—manipulated for their pleasure, for their story to be told. For those who would come after to listen and love and demand more. They twisted and shaped and played their final miraculous part. They smiled amongst themselves as they did. Watching from above. Within this world but never setting foot in it. They took that shard from the shattered moon, for that, too, was their making. All for this dreadful moment.

The shard eased itself lower, catching fire as it did. Years in the coming. Moments in the reckoning. No monstrous fragment of deathly things to swallow the world in fire. Oh no, this piece was for a god alone. A lesser god, but a god regardless. The shard seared the dark sky. Burning the dawn as it followed in its wake. It tore across oceans, across lands untouched by but a few; it pierced the air and soared down upon its final resting place—a small shard, shattering in the fire, spitting as it did.

It tore the sky apart.

It lit up the battlefield.

They did it for Erroh because they loved him, even in the end.

Eased a little wider by an absent hand, the shattered piece struck the gates of Spark City and smashed them apart into a million shards of wood and metal, killing hundreds in a fiery blast that warmed the face of the fire god Erroh himself and shaped the flow of the battle ever so.

But not enough to end it.

For a one-eyed god went to war killing beauty before facing his greatest nemesis.

And the absent gods stepped away, their efforts tended to—for this dreadful dawn at least.

100

FINAL FIGHT

She did not know how she came to this place, yet here she was, in the heart of war, chaos and misery, amidst the killing of her kind. Mea stumbled shakily through the night. Every which way she looked brought fresh scenes of mayhem and violence. The drawing together of many warriors, the clashing of the disheartened, the end of it all, and it was all her fault. All who trusted her, all who fought for her, would be dead by dawn.

I should have expected this.

Jeroen marched with her. His clumsy fingers wrapped the leather armour around her chest as she strode, despite her protestations. No armour would save her this night. Let the fukers pierce her right through and be done with it. Let her go from this world in a state of near undress. It was what she deserved.

"Just fuken hold your step a moment, my love," he gasped, pulling on the straps as best he could with such interference. He was dedicated. In that moment, she loved him for his loyalty, his attentiveness. He looked out for her alone when a man of his might and measure was better suited to leading any who would follow. She might have cast him away from her, as was the responsibility of a Primary, but she wanted him near, wanted his strength. Even if all he did was quietly fuss over her protection. A good mate. A cherished mate.

"I will need no armour; I will be among generals," she snapped, but he wouldn't release her, wouldn't stop wrapping the buttons, tightening the clasps, and she allowed him.

"Everything falls this night, my love," he said, attaching the last piece and pulling at her to ensure it held. It was heavier armour than she'd have liked. Heavy and black and Wolfen, and she struggled to breathe in it. It didn't match her night garments at all. A better-prepared Primary might have slept in armour for such an occasion. Dia would not have done so, however, so neither would Mea.

I fail again.

"We might live this night," she argued weakly, but he was right. It took no genius of war to see where and why they failed. It was a cruel and unexpected tactic on the part of the enemy, attacking so early that most were asleep. The darkness concealed them. Not to mention, it made it that little bit fuken harder to gather suitable defences to meet the largest marching army ever assembled.

Fail, fail, fail.

Perhaps, on the first night, they might have been better prepared for such a dishonourable assault. But the battles they had won so easily had softened them, lulled too many into sleeping more deeply, into sleeping out of armour. Some even stumbled around in the wee hours, still drunk from the evening's activities. Even now, watching so many brave soldiers struggle wearily from their beds, blurry with fatigue and uncertainty, she believed the gathered Factions had already been routed. This battle was but a few moments from becoming a slaughter.

"Gather the Alpha females," Jeroen cried, looking into the distance where a thin line of warriors were giving what fight they could against impossible numbers, and she thought them heroic.

She could not think, find her nerve, or find a way out of this. Around her, the night was pierced with screams of panic, fear and death. Beyond that, there was the crashing of blades, the cries of dying warriors, the thundering and whinnying of mounts, and the end of it all. Yet still, somehow, through the horror, she heard the howling laments of hounds who knew well there would be no sweet ending to this tale.

Jeroen led her through the crush of bodies, seeking war, denying cowardice. She could see their terror and confusion and tried to conceal her fear.

She called for numbers to rally, as did he, yet their voices were lost in the ruckus. Perhaps they heard her; perhaps they ignored her; perhaps they thought her a failure.

She saw dozens fleeing from war, skipping off into the night, no doubt to boast of how they'd fought bravely at the end and only luck had saved them. Had Jeroen fled with them, she might have followed. Not out of cowardice but as a means to gather, rebuild and get through it all without this being the end, but really, this was the end. And Jeroen, who had more reason to be fearful, would never flee, nor would she. Nor would she order such a thing.

"They fight bravely," Jeroen said, slowing to look at the line of warriors fighting, giving their all, slowing the tide where they could. So many, lost in the dimness… She thought them incredible. She could see how Jeroen did too, and she nearly ordered him from her again.

"But it's not enough to halt the rush," she argued, and she was right, for despite the width of the line they held, the plentiful Hunt slipped past them on both flanks. They did so in the thousands and, breaking from their regiments altogether, surged up the slope towards the camp, screaming and killing and terrifying like a cancer. There were too many to slow, to stop. They came from everywhere, and there was nothing they could do, and Mea stood frozen for a breath, much to Jeroen's exasperation.

"We must add to it," he cried, looking around. She could see the fear in his eyes. They were a couple built for farming and little more. Their rising star had led too many to depend on them.

I reached too far.

"We have brought this doom upon the world, my love," she whispered, and somehow, he heard her. He was beside her once more, dragging her up the slope towards the tents of the females. Those fighting few who might offer something more. They would not flee, would not scatter either. Distantly, in the dark, she could see them gathered. They only needed to be led.

"Enough of this, Mea," he commanded, shaking her as though she could not wake from a terrible dream. "Where are you?" he cried. She didn't know where she was. She didn't know what he meant. "What have they done with you?"

"I don't know." He shook as she did, but there was a frenzy in his eyes. A warrior's eyes, and she wanted to answer him appropriately. To shake herself from this terror. "Come back to me," he demanded.

"I have failed."

"You have stood firm," he roared with such venom she almost came to her better senses in that moment. Instead, she followed him towards the Alpha females, even as they rushed to meet the first smattering of Hunt, who broke through the edge of the camp and poured in. "Fight with them," he roared. It was good advice, and she agreed. She gripped her blade, her pace increased, and she walked straight into the ambush from the flank. He couldn't have seen it. His focus was on inspiring her, and she felt once again like a failure. But at least she had some fight in her.

"To the fires with you, curs," she roared, and those nearest heard her and rallied. A dozen Hunt surrounded her and Jeroen, and she was not scared. She was determined. She charged into them, spinning her dual blades like her mate, and swiftly, they earned a reprieve. She did not know if the females knew their queen was surrounded, but it was a small matter. As she drew blood, all her doubts fell away. He stood with her, thrashing with shield and sword, knocking them away, even as more thundered forward.

"Come at me," he roared, and he was furious and impressive, and she matched his wrath. She took the horrors of the past—his absence, her dreadful lonely rise—and put them into every strike. "You have nothing," he challenged, and they were suddenly hesitant. He was a tempest of unbridled force, tearing through them, putting all to the blade as he was born to do. With a start, she realised she had never truly appreciated the warrior he'd always been, but she saw it now and loved him for it. They were just two Alphalines, bringing war to unconquerable foes.

"I will kill you all," she roared, matching his step, complimenting his every movement. He took her renewed belief and used it for himself, howling triumphantly. Constantly pushing forward, they flowed majestically through wave after wave of Southern curs, and had there been no change in the tide, they alone might have won the day for Samara.

Time became nothing but the clashing of blades and the killing. The Alpha females, seeing her attacked, fell upon her aggressors and tore them asunder. But the fates had different thoughts on victory. There was always a point at which any good battle turned, and the final battle for Spark City was no different. Among the crushing charge of so many, it was easy to miss a few fiends slipping in among the shadows. Dodging between the tents, keeping their heads low, seeking a kill before their own demise, the three crossbow wielders made their way in among the enemy, unnoticed in the battle raging around them.

Mea discovered a gap in the Southern assault and, emboldened by the advantage, she sprinted towards the crest of the slope, leading the females with her, only to come upon the three fiends, loaded and aiming. She heard Jeroen scream from behind her, but it was too late. They released upon her. She was quick. Fuk, she was faster than they could have imagined. She spun away from the first bolt; it clipped her as it passed and bounced harmlessly into the air, then it dropped, spent, upon the body of her previous victim. The second bolt she split with her blade, taking it from its path with a fierce slice. The third, however, took her in the chest, cutting through her heavy armour, through her shimmering bed gown, through skin and more, and she was felled.

Her attackers met a grisly end as the females fell upon them, cutting them limb from limb. They were dead long before Mea fell to the muddy ground, grasping the deadly bolt as her breath began to falter.

"No, god, please no," moaned Jeroen, falling beside her. Around them, there wailed the Alpha females, and she was a failure. She grasped his hand as the pain took her. "I need a healer," he cried out, but she knew no healer in the Four Factions was skilled enough to save her. She shuddered and began to quiver. She did not want to die, did not want to cry out either. She tried to be brave, to be the leader they could avenge—a difficult thing as the agony took hold and tore deep.

She looked to Jeroen, fierce and beautiful and unshackled. "Do not watch me die, my love," she whispered, and it was an order, and he refused her, tears spilling down his cheeks as he shook his head defiantly.

"I will wait by your side until you can walk," he argued, and took her hand and squeezed tightly. A little too tightly. It hurt her fingers ever so. She might have said so but loved him enough to take the pain.

"They've taken everything from us," she whispered, and he drew closer and shuddered and shook his head, and she loved him. "Make them pay," she demanded, freeing her hand from his grasp and shoving him away gently, with all her strength.

"I cannot live without you," he cried, but she was determined. This battle was greater than all of them. Even a Primary, even a dying mate. It was a mercy, and it was leadership, and it was cruelty most evil. But also, it was a necessity.

"Avenge me until you fall." She thought them awful words, but he was a god of war, and she would not deny the Factions his presence. "Be great, my love. Do this one act for me," she begged but, he would not budge, so she gripped his shirt, pulled herself to him, and screamed in his face. "Do this for me, and I will meet you on the other side."

He kissed her once upon the lips, and his breath was bitter and reassuring and lovely, and he released himself from her grasp as a broken man but also an inspired killer, and they dragged her away from him. The females lifted her high upon their shoulders, and she thought how wonderful it would be to die afloat in the hands of her daughters. If

Jeroen cried out for her, she never heard. Instead, she fought the call of sleep and the settling of pain.

"You cannot do this here," Roja cried, but Emir wasn't listening. Of course, he wasn't. He never listened. Not to anyone, not when he was right. She hated that he was partly right. It still didn't change matters.

"I will do what I must," he argued, leaving her to watch the night of a million movements around them as he rummaged through his stolen healer's bag for any tools suitable for the task. The Wolf at his knees was cut deep; he coughed blood, howled like a slaughtered lamb and struggled against Emir's weight as he held him down. "Shush, my friend. I want you back fighting in the next hour." Fine healer's words, and Roja wondered had his bedside manner improved by watching her. Probably not. Sometimes he had no words, and sometimes he had the exact words to say. The doomed man held his tongue and stopped struggling, even as he and a dozen comrades around him passed away.

A Southern fiend came from the dark; he ran past Emir for a few steps before realising the simple target. Perhaps he had not expected to see open surgery occurring in the field; his eyes weren't the best in the dim light. Regardless, before he could smite Emir, Roja was upon him, stabbing and killing him in a few breaths before leaving him leaking crimson in the darkness. This was her call in this awfulness—standing guard, trying to kill them all, while her husband wanted to save them all.

Husband.

If Emir realised her actions or was grateful for them, he said nothing. Instead, he demanded his next patient fight to live and climb to his feet and grab a sword. His arguments were convincing. Roja almost believed them, as his patient did, even if his wounds were too severe, his blood loss too great.

"This is no place," she argued softly, for she could see the brave warrior slipping away, despite Emir's efforts to hide the sight from her.

"There are no bad places to save a life," he countered, but his voice was as hollow as the argument. The man, torn open and spilling his innards, struggled ever so and fell still, and Emir shook as he left the dead man where he lay.

"Fuk me," he growled, slapping his hands in the mud. She could see this torment was his private nightmare. How many had he attempted to save since the attack began? At least a half-dozen, some minor, some major, yet the curses were upon him. He'd said as much, and he said it again now. "Every fuken one of them lost," he moaned, and she dragged him away from the ruined body.

"We can do better in the healer's bay, my love," she argued, and he allowed her to pull him towards the brightly lit tent at the centre of the camp, away from the violence and the dark where a careless nick could end a life. "See, Emir, you can tend to the desperate in here," she said. Their previous visit had been a joyous thing, having survived the trek through the hovels and out across the Great Mother, where they'd swum to freedom, only to meet the end of it all before dawn struck.

"This is all our fault," he mumbled, stepping into the tent where the dying and helpless remained.

"It is," she agreed, and a heaviness came upon her, such was her guilt that, despite the attack, she was still glad they were free of the city and Uden's hold upon them. Better to die free than a prisoner to a madman. Or a mad uncle.

"What the fuk?" Emir cried, looking around. There were no healers within the large tent. A dozen beds held battered warriors, leaving a dozen more empty. That would change soon enough. Emir's hesitation was momentary; he began checking on the patients. "Who's alive and able to fight? And willing to give up their bed?" he cried, separating the empty beds from those taken before sprinting to the far end of the tent where every conceivable medicine and surgical utensil was stored. "I need you all to get the fuk out of here," he cried to those shuffling few sporting slings or hobbling on crutches. With a wave of his hand, he sent them back into the night to die or to add some effort to the fight.

"What can I do, my love?" she asked, looking around in despair. She could assist, could help with surgery, but there was a war to be fought, but she also didn't want to leave his side, but also, the rumble of threat was nearing, but also, she was married, and that made her mind spin even though they hadn't consummated their wedded vows. She did not know what to do. "Tell me what to do."

"I need more healers; I need more patients," he cried, looking through the scribbled notes on the current patients. He looked as lost as she felt, but also, he looked in control, and she loved him, and she would live through this night and consummate their wedding and be married and be blissfully happy. And they would not die. They most certainly would not die. They would not perish. No matter the grave circumstances to come.

No matter what.

The Actions of Gods

She might have stayed a little longer, but she did as he asked instead. She ran into the night, seeking those in need, seeking those who could help. She just hadn't a clue how to accomplish these simple tasks.

Think, girl.

Despite the shattered moon above, despite the many flaming torches illuminating the camp, she found it difficult to gather her wits, such was her exhaustion and the rush of adrenaline. She still wore her wedding gown, although it was torn and muddy and damp from the previous day's endeavours. She thought herself still beautiful, despite it all. She clung to these semi-coherent thoughts lest the guilt of this attack retake her.

She killed a few as she stumbled through the camp. Careless Southerners, foolish enough to charge her when she was alone and not in a crowd. She killed and moved on as though it were nothing. In her mind, she counted her kills. Eventually, with her body coated in a veneer of sweat, she came upon her sisters of the city, gathering, riled up, preparing to fight. She called for them, and, strangely, a girl she knew as Shinaid brought them to settle.

"Where are the healers?" Roja cried, and the girl pointed to a group of men gathered over a fallen sister, and a fit of terrible anger took Roja. Every sister's life was worth a little more, but to sacrifice so many for one life was no small thing, she thought angrily—until she saw Mea dying and ruined among the desperate healing hands.

"Get her to the healing bay," Roja roared as only a queen bitch of the city could, and her sisters immediately fell still. "Do not hesitate, lest we lose another Mydame," she shouted, and seeing that ruin of a chest, she gripped her own chest, knowing little could save her.

It didn't matter. What mattered was putting the healers to task and, more so, rallying the Alpha females, who were too shaken to understand their importance in this terrible battle. Gathered so close and becoming a menacing battalion, they could offer a point of defence for any allies seeking a staging point to defend, to attack from. Their shimmering outfits, their glamourous hair, would act as a beacon against the milliard of browns, blacks and greys of the night. It wasn't much, but it was all she could think of.

She ordered them to gather, and the Alphalines hesitated for only a breath before a half-dozen hoisted Mea up and carried her towards the distant tent. "You few," she cried, stopping four of the bewildered healers and pointing to a dozen sisters eyeing the battle with relish and glee. She knew that unforgiving gaze. Simply having them wait for war was no good when they had a little vengeance on their mind. They only needed a push in the right direction. "Go out into the night and drag back any who need healing," she commanded. "And you, my stunning creatures, protect them," she ordered, and for a breath, she was the queen bitch of the city, not voted out, not wanted for treacherous things. They looked for her leadership and answered.

"What will you do?" Shinaid asked indifferently, gathering a few stragglers around her, watching a few dozen Southerners move closer, drawn to their colours like insects in a warmer season's meadow. She notched an arrow and directed her comrades towards the charging fools. Her eyes never left Roja, as though she'd decided in that moment that she was, after all, to be trusted and honoured. It was a small matter.

"I will be with my husband," Roja muttered, following after the healers.

"As you wish, Mydame," Shinaid said before releasing her arrow. A few dozen sisters followed her lead before reloading and waiting for the next wave of Hunt to test their luck.

Satisfied with her orders, Roja sprinted back through the night towards the tent. It was a safer journey this time, with an army of Alphalines drawing in many of the nearing Hunt. She thought she would return to a healer's bay alive with the energy of her husband's passion and brilliance.

Instead, she returned to horror.

Emir went around the cots tending to the injured. Most were stable, but few were conscious. Most were asleep, no doubt dreaming whimsical dreams from the sweet syrup. Despite the roar of battle from beyond the tent's entrance, he found this place to be quiet and soothing. Truthfully, his senses settled when the stench of cleansing alcohol and eucalyptus, among a thousand other medical aromas, struck him. Here, he could wage his war, could make a difference. He found peace in the demands of those lying upright in their bedding, crying out for a saviour, reassurance and kind deceit.

I can't lose every one of them in here.

Checking the breathing of his nearest patient, a large brute with scared eyes and a drunken gaze, he heard the wet sound of fluid in the man's lungs. He listened to the patient's stressed heart a moment until, to his horror, the man suddenly began to retch and spit blood. Emir immediately turned him onto his side, attempting to drain the fluid from

The Actions of Gods

his mouth, but as swiftly as it happened, his body quivered and he fell deathly still. Emir tried to strike the man's chest, to breathe life back into him. He pumped and attacked, but the body merely moved with his actions and made no attempt to answer his demands. Eventually, he fell away from the dead body, shaken and weary.

"By my cursed hand," he whimpered quietly, lest any other patients hear of his deathly touch this horrible night.

Another spare bed.

Horrified, he pulled the man from his deathbed and dragged him out into the night. It was cruel and vile, but he *would* need the extra cot.

"That wasn't my fault," he whispered to the gods, to himself, to nothing more than the wind. It didn't make him feel any better.

He almost looked into the night, down to the edges of the camp where the fighting was at its worst, but he couldn't bear to see what atrocities were occurring, lest he be tempted to grab his stolen healer's bag and sprint straight into death, with blind intentions of honour and heroism.

Instead, he attended to the next patient. The fiend rolled from his bedding and collapsed with a dreadful wheezing gasp as Emir tried to check his pulse and attempted to administer a herbal tonic to thin the blood; the man looked past him, though, and whispered in a foreign tongue before reaching out to nobody in the beyond and then falling still.

"Oh, please, stop dying," he cried, and cursed the absent gods for the deaths at his hands this night, and the absent gods offered little in reply. Their eyes might have been on more violent things.

He turned to a third injured warrior. She was young. At least as young as he. Beautiful and meek, and familiar too. He'd seen her in the hovels a lifetime ago. She could not speak. Her eyes were glazed over, but as he checked what vital signs she had, she began to convulse from some unknown trauma. He froze briefly before slapping his face and checking to see why she struggled. It did not take long to see the swelling along her throat. Reaching for his instruments, he cut swiftly into her neck and slid a little tube through the incision, and a little air released itself. She immediately began to breathe easily, and he went about easing her airways before sealing the flesh he'd severed. With shaking hands that settled as he touched skin, Emir eased her from danger and, settling her back in her bedding, urged her body to sleep away the trauma.

That done, he took a moment to look around and be grateful to the absent gods for his less acid touch with this patient.

Perhaps I am not cursed.

Having broken the terrible trend, he went to work at the rear of the tent, concocting serums and ointments for the casualties to come. So preoccupied was he with his endeavours, he never heard the rush of violence outside the tent's entrance, nor did he hear the wet, dying cries, nor did he notice the three fiends enter the tent and then stop, staring about them, contemplating their next savagery, until it was far too late.

"Oh, please no," a warrior cried from his bed, and Emir spun around in time to see one of the Southerners hack the man to pieces with a heavy war axe, all to the glee of his two accomplices. The trio then turned their attention to the rest of the defenceless patients, rushing from bed to bed, plunging their blades into flesh, and Emir wailed louder than those few screaming for mercy. They fought back with what strength they could muster; some tried to climb from the beds, but they were easy prey, and in a dreadful few breaths, nearly all were slain, and it was too much.

"You cannot do this," Emir cried in horror, and the trio hesitated, watching with amusement as he ran to them, armed with little more than a bottle of methylated spirits. "I am Emir, blessed by Uden," he added as their leader stood over the girl Emir had just saved. She looked dreamily around the blood-stained room, unaware of the danger. "Please," he screamed, but the cur drove the axe down upon her head, cleaving her from this world, and it was all too much.

The world slowed as Emir charged them, grabbing a wooden stool as he did. Three steps more, and he swung his makeshift weapon against steel and connected, knocking the weapon aside. He shattered their leader's face before dodging the second blade and smashing the bottle in that bastard's face. The third attacker, shaken by the diminutive healer's violence, turned for the door, and Emir was upon him. Leaping on his back, wrapping his arms around the murderer's neck, he choked the breath from him, hating him as he squeezed ever tighter. The Southerner struggled desperately, but it was too easy. Emir held the fuk until he fought his finest last struggle and departed from this world. Still, he would not let go, even when he heard the screaming of his wounded victims as they tried in vain to rise. Squeezing one last time and ensuring the brute soiled himself in death, he turned on the southerner's comrades and, with his scalpel, slit their throats. The blinded fiend screamed loudest as he died; the leader barely squirmed as Emir stood on his ruined throat and crushed the life out of him. It felt good murdering the last, and Emir felt no shame.

Leaving the dead where they lay, he checked every remaining patient

The Actions of Gods

and, to his misery, found each of them dead.

"I am cursed," he cried, dropping to his knees, thinking of vile serums and foolish youthful experimenting. He wept until his wife came for him, bearing with her a victim so important he almost shattered.

I will slaughter her too.

They placed her upon a bed, and she moaned weakly, and he could not rise, even when the healers, knowing his legend, looked to him for instruction.

"Get up, Emir," Roja commanded, though there was a softness beneath the tone. She looked around her at the devastation that had just occurred. He wanted to crawl into the dark and drink away this life. Smile dreamily as an axe hung above his head.

"All I touch is ruined," he whimpered, and Roja pulled him to his feet, slapping him gently across the face.

"You are her only chance."

He looked to the woman's ruined chest as they tore her armour free, leaving the bolt exposed. Around them, a dozen faceless warriors stood watching. One was more distant and grief-stricken than the rest, and Emir didn't want the rest of them here. He didn't want her shame on display for all to see; he knew she didn't want them to see him either. "Stand watch and keep this fuken tent safe," he ordered, turning to the Primary and stroking her cheek absently.

"I will work with you," Roja said, but he was already examining the wound.

"Sorry, Mea," Emir muttered as he examined her. Mea's groans were nearly inaudible, but they were there. The wretched healer slapped his cheeks sharply and shook his head to rouse himself. He inhaled a few deep breaths, and the youngest-ever master healer of Spark City went to work salvaging his soul, restoring his faith and earning his legend and his next glass of sine. This great woman was not yet lost to the night.

Tye was terrified. The most terrified he had ever been. He was afraid he might soil his trousers. He wished he had taken some sine. He wished he alone faced an army with a bow, arrows, and the cover of darkness. What he had was a comrade in arms, as desperate and as terrified as he was, fighting and killing and trying to stay alive, despite the inevitability. He could see the open gates from here. Could see the terrible numbers still streaming up to the camp. They were unending, these dreadful grey warriors filled with hate, roaring and charging and killing. Around them lay the dead, and it was an awful thing. A dozen warriors from all regions had fallen beside him already, and yet somehow, he still took breath. They still took breath.

"What the fuk are we doing?" Lexi cried. He couldn't see her, but he felt her movements and the motion of the battle. She clung to life as he did, and for all her youth and terror, she was elite when mixed with his sway of combat, timing and manoeuvres. Back to back they fought, and never mis-stepped. Never slowing, never letting the other down. They fought majestically despite being surrounded, despite being a hair's breadth away from death, despite being one thrust away from a gutting. Ever moving, ever spinning, ever complementing each other, they fought for unlikely life, even as the Hunt kept coming, kept hunting, kept nearing.

"Surviving," he replied, deflecting a blow with his left hand and holding the fuker in place before sending his right sword through the woman's unprotected face. She screamed as he pulled away, even as her brains were already spilling free. She might have been pretty; he'd put an end to that.

I cannot do this.

He wanted to weep aloud, to give in. But not with Lexi beside him. Besides, it was fine to die with a best friend by one's side; he told himself, mid-kill. It eased the terror ever so. He felt her turn left, and he went with her, ever aware of her steps as she was of his. They moved back up towards the top of the slope. He wanted to hear her voice among the screaming. There was a comfort in her words. He listened for her retort, even if it was screamed in panic and fright.

"This is rightly fuked," she announced, and he agreed. It was rightly fuked. Everyone around them was dying. He didn't know how many were left. How many comrades? How many of his friends and loved ones? He imagined his father and mother dead. Side by side. Hand in hand. Ruined and unmoving forever. He shook away that vision. He thought of Erroh, no doubt in the middle of the first defending wave. He believed him dead by now too. Gutted like a swine. Would he have screamed? He tried to shut off such thoughts; they were of no use in battle.

"I think we are rightly fuked," he offered as a fiend knocked her against him and she collided with his back. He dared a glance behind him, and she made the bastard pay with a strike across the neck that silenced his scream.

The Actions of Gods

"Don't fuken die on me," she warned.

"I won't," he promised. He thought it was a good pledge.

"Good, cos then *I'll* be fuken dead."

"I'll try harder so," he shouted. It was meant as a joke, a distracting few words, as four blades were drawn upon him, swinging and stabbing. Only luck and incredible reflexes saved him. He didn't kill all of them, but at least he took them from the fight. That was something, at least.

"Well, if you can, I'd... appreciate it... if... ouch... uh... that fuken hurt... you fuken cur."

"What happened?" he cried desperately as she hesitated. All around them, the Southerners neared, ventured a little closer. He wondered was this the end. Was she already felled? Was he next?

"Small case of getting stabbed," she muttered, and he looked again, but she was already flowing through the battle, oblivious to the wound.

"Are you fuked?"

"Nah, he just stabbed me from the ground as I stepped over him."

"Shitty bit of honour on his part there."

"Aye, it's all right; I stamped him to fuken mush, so we are even."

"So now what?"

"Perhaps a hasty retreat back to the light?" she said quietly. Not for tactical purposes, but to save face. It had been her choice to charge so recklessly into this battle. She had told him not to follow, but she knew he would. And he had. Right fuken deep down into the crowd where the fighting was at its worst. Where a hasty retreat was the more intelligent move.

"Follow my step," he said, and she did. Swinging and circling and breaking for better ground, both young Alphalines fled an invisible defensive line of their own making from the dimness of the middle battlefield, back towards the gathered Faction's base camp. It was no less dangerous there, but there was more light to kill by, at least, and less chance of a cur stabbing you as you walked past them. They aimed for the distant bursts of colour, the sight of flashing blades, silken gowns and vibrant hair.

Despite the numbers and threat, they made it back up to the camp. The problem was the thousand or so Southerners that had the same idea.

Just as fuked.

If truth be told, were the Factions to have faced such a charge at a reasonable hour with light as an ally, they might have had a chance. As it was, despite their heroism, he could see the numbers and it was crushing. He felt helpless to do anything but survive and keep Lexi alive.

If he accomplished that last feat alone, his life would have been well lived.

"This is better up here," Lexi lied, drawing up beside him. She examined the minor slice along her arm where the cur had sneaked the attack. It was barely visible, and a surge of relief took him. For a breath, he almost felt hope.

"'Course it is. It was my idea."

"It was *mine*," she declared pompously.

"No, it wasn't; it was mine," he argued.

"If they ask, I'll say it was mine." She sounded so confident.

"What are you talking about?" he cried in puzzlement, and she laughed deliriously.

"I mean, who would believe you?" she mocked.

They could easily fight side by side without the threat of being completely surrounded: a better, more violent proposition. Within the mayhem among the tents, there were stirrings of defiance. Perhaps it was the torches that emboldened them; perhaps the vision of Alpha females at war in their finest. For a breath, he believed they could stem the tide. If only for long enough that they could form a proper defensive line.

"Now that we are here, I think we should…" Her voice trailed off suddenly, and he feared she had been stabbed again. He froze then, seeing what she gazed upon.

The gathering of females rushed past carrying his mother, and he was shaken seeing her in such a way. "Momma?" he moaned, and Lexi, beside him, gasped as he did. "Momma?" he cried again as they carried her towards the healer's bay.

Where is Dad?

"A crossbow bolt," Lexi said. She lowered her blade; the world went still. She looked past him to the brewing battle, and something caught her attention. Some advantage, some horror. Some moment. He could have asked; he could have looked; he could have had her back. But instead, he could only look at the blood upon the females carrying Mea to the healer's tent. He needed her. He hadn't told her he loved her. Even when they'd embraced after being so long apart, there had been a coldness between them. Not on her part, for she had wept, but he had remained himself.

I need to tell her I love her.

"We have to go to her," he said, breaking their line of two.

"We have to fight, Tye. We have to fight."

She doesn't know I love her.

The Actions of Gods

He shook his head. He wanted his mother. He wanted her to live. He wanted her to tell him she was proud, that his father would be along, that he wanted to go home. He wanted none of this. "We will, but I must see her," he snapped. "Please, come with me for the end," he pleaded, but she did not reply. "I need this," he cried, setting off after them. "There is plenty more battle to be had."

He was in a panic. He wanted to run. He wanted to hear Lexi's reassuring words, telling him his mother would be okay. But then he saw Lexi was gone. Away from him. Leaving him alone to face this horror.

"Lexi," he cried out into the night. He searched for the girl among the struggling warriors on either side. He cried out for her again, but his feet carried him towards the tent, his mother, and the light. "I'm coming, Momma."

He could see guards standing outside the tent. If nothing else, he could stand watch over her. Even if she didn't know, he would. It wasn't much, but it was all he had. He looked back into the night of ten thousand deaths and whispered a prayer for Lexi, who had left him behind. He began to sob silently but gave nothing away, stepping through the tent opening to the chaos within. There were so many wounded. For a moment, he gazed in horror at her terrible injuries. He heard orders, but mostly, he saw Emir at task and he believed. Taking a post by the doorway, he readied himself for any bastard foolish enough to attack his ailing mother this night.

I love you, Momma.

She couldn't help herself even if she knew how cruel her actions were. In her defence, she was thinking of the greater things. And only partly of herself. She had seen Tye's face as they carried Mea past. The fight had left him. She could hear it in his tone, and fuk it, but she slipped away from his blank gaze and hated herself for it.

He will never forgive me for this sin.

Leaving him behind without a word was the only mercy she could offer her diligent guardian, her closest friend, her Tye. Truthfully, had he begged her to stay with him, she might have, and she knew in her heart that such selfishness on her part would have meant little to this battle, nay, this entire war. Through the skirmishing warriors she sprinted, stopping after a time to look behind her and make sure he was not in pursuit. To her relief and slight sorrow, she saw him standing there, calling out for her, like a parent for his children. Despite the roars, screams and the beating of her heart, she could make out her name, and it was cutting.

"I'm so sorry, my dearest Tye," she whispered, leaving him behind to face the night. Perhaps, had she not caught sight of Magnus charging across the battlefield towards the heaviest numbers a moment before, she might have stayed with Tye. But her father was hard to miss, and an enraged Magnus was an even fiercer thing than her broken companion.

She suddenly felt her age again; she needed her father's strength. Needed his protection. Gripping her sword, she moved through the battle, following in her father's footsteps, hoping to see him or her mother. She was no longer terrified; she was, instead, determined no bolt would pierce her heart, no blade would slice her throat. No sword from a creeping cur in the grass would touch her. The world slowed as she charged down towards her likely death. She struck at Southerners as she passed, sometimes with enough skill to kill or maim and other times, with just enough force to distract them from the battle. She counted a dozen strikes and a dozen felled fiends, and it was impressive. Greater than Erroh's skill at this age, for certain.

Be great.

Through the awful dark she sprinted, killing and slashing, seeking the large group of savages at war with the greater masses, listening for the howling of hounds too. Further into the mire of Southern hate she waded, and only through bad luck did she catch sight of Wrek. Bad luck, for it likely doomed her. She saw him high upon a lone cart, surrounded and dominant, and she thought it magnificent to see such an imposing, impressive outcast lording it over the battlefield, bringing devastation upon any who neared. He was godly, and she was drawn to him.

This is not your fight.

Upon the cart, a body lay at his feet, unmoving, and he stood over it protectively, swinging a great battle scythe with such violence he almost kept the numbers from swamping him. Almost, but not entirely, for there were too many for even one as impressive as he. Back and forth, he swung that deadly weapon like a Clieve, and Southerners fell around him. So many. But not enough.

Foolish.

She ran past him and carried on for a few breaths before common sense got the better of her. Before she realised that leaving a friend behind to die was a grievous act. Before she allowed her selfish motives to override her honour.

The Actions of Gods

This isn't your fuken fight.

She lost sight of Magnus as he stepped further away, and she screamed in frustration, in terror and in resignation.

She was small. Smaller than most girls her age. Far smaller than Erroh had been at this age too. She'd always hated her unimpressive frame, but in this moment, she was grateful for it. Slipping unnoticed through struggles she had little part of, she emerged among his Southern vanquishers and was merciless.

"Come on, you fuks," cried Wrek, slipping in the blood of those he killed while somehow remaining upright. "I'm not even Alpha," he challenged, and if they understood, they made no shift in their tactics. They continued to charge him, seeking to get in blows of their own beneath the swing of his savage weapon, aiming to land one deadly strike upon this magnificent monster.

Some Southerners, watching this behemoth, fled, such was their terror at seeing a ghost taking up arms once more. Those who had never fought in Keri were just as fearful but did not flee.

Those were the ones who died.

When they finally took hold of his swinging arm, at the expense of a half-dozen more fatalities, Lexi took her chance. She moved as a blur among them, all small and precise. She picked her strikes and dared not waver. Nor did she deviate from her actions. She plunged from among them, and they never saw her, such was the frenzy, the spraying blood, the darkened night and the drunken haze of massacre.

Before long, and with a further handful of Southerners either felled or falling, she broke their line and leapt upon the cart with Wrek, breaking their hold and giving him the impetus to continue his single-handed assault on the entire army. Buoyed on by this victory, she moved behind him, knocking away blows towards his rear guard, punishing any who tried to kill her outcast comrade.

She did not know how long they stood upon this cart battering away the ocean of Hunt surrounding them, save that, soon, their attackers lost the will to keep attacking this unlikely higher ground. Many turned tail, chasing easier prey instead. During the slight reprieve, Wrek dropped to a brute who lay on the ground and went to him.

"Come on, you fuk, up on your feet," he demanded, but the large bandit groaned in argument. She looked to the night, the raging battles beyond and the pull of her own need to be among her kin. A dreadful pull, indeed. "Will you help me with him?" Wrek asked, wrapping a sash from his arm around the head of his large comrade, and Lexi could taste the turning of the battle for the worse. She could feel it like beasts felt the rain. It was coming, and suddenly, it seemed very important she be away from here.

"I cannot," she said, and dropped from the cart. Only then did she realise how exhausted she was. She was panting; her limbs felt heavy. She considered lying on the ground for a while, getting her breath, missing Tye, and stabbing a few Southerners as they passed by. Instead, she left Wrek behind and dashed into the night, seeking out her family, knowing it was her last march.

"Where are you going?" Wrek cried out, but the girl's face was a mask of delirium. The war had taken her mind, no doubt. He'd seen that face a thousand times on many a patron attempting entrance into one of his taverns late at night when returning home was the better decision. Usually, he'd send them on their way. Those he allowed in were frequently too drunk to do little more than fall asleep in a corner. "Stay and help me," he added, but she looked set on her path. He worried after Tye for a moment, and then shoved that terrible thought away as swiftly as it came upon him.

"Be safe, little one," Wrek called out, wondering if he could have done more to keep her near. If not for Ulrik's sake, then for her own safety. But he had enough doubts as it was.

When the gates had opened, they both had been sitting in the darkness smoking a little tobacco weed. His mind had been pleasantly dizzy, but the violence had ended that happy high. He began to shake now, thinking of the terrible deeds he and his brother had inflicted upon those who charged upon them at first. Between then and now, they had nearly made it back towards their greater allies among the temporary barricade.

They had been brothers again, facing all who challenged them, battering the bastards back with brutal brilliance. He'd forgotten what it was to stare down death with Ulrik by his side, and now, among the horror, the misery and the cruel awfulness, he found a wave of peace that had been years in the making. All it took was the world's end. He felt tears stream from his eyes and decided it was simply blood, one of the many sprays of crimson upon him.

"It's just you and me again, brother," he whispered, and the silent body made no reply. It lay where it was felled. There was little blood, and no dent in his skull where the hammer had struck him. He told himself a healer could return consciousness to him and stitch up the gash, but that might have been denial. He thought of his saviour Lexi, wandering through the battle, and he wondered was he as stunned as she.

He placed his ear to Ulrik's mouth and felt the air; he listened to his chest and found a steady beat. That was enough for Wrek. "Can you not wake?" he asked, and his brother answered with silence. "Can you not walk these last few steps with me?" he demanded, and his brother answered with indifferent unconsciousness.

Around him, the flow of the battle was changing again, as it should do when two armies clashed in anything but an open plain. He wondered if the flow of violence would come back around to them. Far ahead, he saw the camp and the impossible numbers in between. He was a simple man with no plan. Nevertheless, waiting by this cart was an invitation to death, especially once dawn struck.

"Come on then, so," he muttered and looked at the massive battle scythe in his hands and marvelled at its appearance. He had suffered no doubts about that weapon. The fiend who'd come at him hadn't any skill in wielding such a piece. Wrek had put the beast to some fine work once he held it in his blood-soaked hands. He might have killed them all with such a weapon, but at a terrible cost. With a heavy heart, he kissed the handle, placed it to his forehead and christened it "Gull's Wrath" before tossing it aside in the grass. He might scour the ground for it later on, if he lived through this night. As for now, he sacrificed his life, and countless Southerners' deaths for his brother, and it was no difficult choice.

"You fuker," he cried, dragging Ulrik's body from the cart, easing him to the muddy ground where, in the darkness, he looked dead. "You aren't dead; you're just making me earn it," he hissed, dragging him from the cover by his feet, and it was a miserable slog. Within a few feet, a fiend came upon him with blade and sword at the ready. It was an easy kill, but the cur was overconfident. He lunged forward, and Wrek, well used to the skills and speed of Alphalines, took that fuken blade from him with a side kick to the wrist before falling on him and stabbing him until he died. For a moment, he lay there as the cur bled all over him before summoning his strength for one colossal last act that would kill him, no doubt.

Hauling Ulrik across his shoulders and lifting with his knees, he hoisted the larger brute and miraculously did not stumble. Holding him, he swayed around the battlefield, seeking a finer place to escape to. And distantly, he saw his kind, and then he was running.

Leave him.

I can't do this.

He'll never know.

"Aye, he'll never know because he'll be dead," Wrek roared aloud, arguing and defeating that lesser part of him that knew this was the end. "Just keep fuken going." Every step was agony, laboured and precarious. He ran as fast as his aching knees could take him, and he knew his pace to be no swifter than a leisurely jog. Around him, warriors fought and mutilated and killed and died, and he ignored them, focused only on the distant gathering of carts and his kind who prepared for invasion, as only they could.

His thoughts were of Lara when the pace became too much. Soft, wonderful thoughts, tinged with harrowing sorrow. He thought of her all the time. He imagined her scent. Her laugh in his ear. He pictured her smile, and he loved her. "Are you with me?" he asked those in the darkness beyond. Most days, he spoke to her. Spoke of his fears and doubts. She never replied. Never gave him a sign that she watched after him or waited for him. Every other day, he imagined her in the darkness with the one she'd called Quig.

Truly, though, he hoped she might not have faded into the dark when the city fell. That one day, she would appear at his door, ready to weep, to laugh, to put on an apron and get to work running his tavern. "I miss you, my love," he cried out, forcing his aching body to continue this dreadful last pilgrimage.

Redeem yourself.

Nearer the blockade, he picked up his pace, and his body stumbled with every step, and above him, Ulrik groaned with the violent shuddering. "Nearly there, brother," he cried, but then he threw himself upon the absent gods' mercy. For ahead of him appeared a trio of Southern crossbow wielders laying siege upon the blockade. Seeing this behemoth charge them must have shaken them, for he was an easy kill, yet as they all, in unison, let loose their bolts, not a one went through his unprotected head.

"Ah, fuk yas," he cried, as he spun away from them. One went through Ulrik's leg, one through Wrek's hand, and another through his rear as he attempted to dodge the strikes. He didn't stop running, despite the pain. For a time, at least.

The three crossbow wielders reloaded and aimed. They were closer now, so that no manner of fear would sway their strikes, so he did the only thing he could do. With the last of his strength, he cast away his burden. It was a fine throw, using his momentum to launch from powerful knees and arms the size of tree trunks. "Here," he roared as his brotherly burden took flight and landed upon the trio, and Wrek fell after them, pummelling, kicking, biting and tearing. He battered with everything he had and left them a bloody dead mess. Then, pulling at his brother, he tried to rise.

"What the fuk, Wrek?" Ulrik hissed in a hazy voice. Hazy but living.

"I never left you, brother," he gasped, and dropped beside him. The blockade was too far, and his limbs were so weighty. He felt himself fall unconscious. It was terrible thing to collapse like this, at the worst time. He fought it, but his vision darkened and he gasped for breath.

"I knew you never would," his brother said, gripping his shoulder. "Why are there bolts stuck in us?"

There came familiar voices around them, but Wrek was too tired to fend them off. He slipped into darkness and barely felt the pull of foreign hands dragging him towards the murky bellows of this dreadful ocean of death.

"Grab his legs, Aimee. Right, fuken there. Kaya… Kaya… are you listening? You grab his arms. That's it," Bison said to his two comrades. "Here, I'll grab the other fuk; he's barely conscious. Wake up, brute," he added, but to no avail. Around them charged Southerners, blinded by the blockade, overwhelmed by the night, and Bison took advantage. No one would tell of his bravery or honour, but that was fine; that was the way of their kind. Admittedly, seeing the monstrous brothers felled as they had been would serve his greater purposes should he survive the war. It certainly would have helped him take his crown in the mighty Adawan, but as it was, he couldn't leave the fuks lying so close to the blockade wall and consider himself a man of any measure. So, he did what only two others were foolish enough to do. He slipped down from his elevated platform atop one of their carts and now, among the enemy, only partly regretted his actions.

Bandit archers covered their recovery, and he was thankful for their discipline, even in this horror. "He's so heavy," cried Aimee, mid-struggle, and Bison knocked her aside, grabbing Wrek's leg and pulling it and Ulrik towards salvation.

"Big bastards, all right," he roared, challenging himself to fail while also urging the two men to wake and rise to carry themselves. Instead, they remained stunned and unmoving. Embarrassed by her weakness, Aimee marched vigilantly beside him, daring any fool to attack. A few did, a few fell thereafter, and Bison grunted what praise he could. He needed to drag them only a few feet nearer to the wall, where a few others waited to drop down and relieve him of his burden.

"Come on, get them up," he ordered, ensuring Aimee slipped up first. He did so because Kaya would go only after she was safe. It certainly wasn't Kaya who had leapt down first at his utterings. She'd merely followed her protégé. He did not like the child. Not one little bit. He did not like the way she stared through everyone she faced. And talking with her was unpleasant and unsettling too. She always appeared to be cutting him silently with her eyes, just to see his entrails.

Does not know her place.

In those moments, though, he was grateful for her bravery. "Watch his head," he snarled as a dozen hands dragged Ulrik over the top. The last thing he needed was for him to die due to dropping his head against the edge of a cart as they carried him over. He could see a welt under the loose bandaging on his side where some fiend had pummelled him. "For fuk's sake, be careful with him."

Climbing back up over the blockade was the worst moment. Confident he would receive a blade or bolt in the back, he scrambled over the cart. It was no massive undertaking, no grand mountain to be bested. It was only a few feet in height, but in this dreadful battle against the rushing killers, it felt as high as a solid stone wall.

Dropping down on the other side to relative safety, he watched as a handful of bandits climbed back up to cover the gap. They lined up along the ledge, firing arrows, shielding the rest from strikes, cutting the many fiends as they swarmed over the impromptu stronghold. A fine fortress of bandit design, swift to erect, adequate to hold.

For a while, at least.

"A fine thing," he offered Kaya and Aimee. The young girl shrugged indifferently at his praise, but he could see the grin she hid. Even unsettling little witches like her desired recognition. Around them, what healers they had tended to the former leaders of their kingdom, and Bison, beaten and forgotten, was not praised or acknowledged. It was a small matter, he supposed.

Constructed from no less than a few dozen carts in all, overturned and wedged tight against the next, it was no masterful creation but the same type of wall he'd made many a time throughout his life, wandering the Wastes. Within the fortress, there was the roar of war, and it was a chilling thing. A reminder of how unlikely survival would be. When the gates of Spark had opened, they'd turned to primal behaviours. Even in the dark, the many bandits went to task, grabbing what carts they owned or had borrowed and putting them to use.

Aye, the savages and Southerners and those from Boat Town watched on and armed themselves, but they did not offer help, which was fine. All were welcome regardless, and as the turning of the battle occurred almost instantly, and the last few carts were dragged into place by the hundreds, they were gifted sanctuary, and many swiftly took it. They were expected to fight from within, but that was far better than standing without protection in the middle of the battlefield, where luck mattered far more than skill.

"Will they live?" he asked a healer tending to the arrows. He was a Wolf by his attire. At any other time, they would have been enemies, yet here he knelt, fighting to keep bandit royalty alive.

The man shrugged before pulling an arrow free, and Wrek yelled aloud before swinging at him and missing.

"Um, this one will."

"Well, wrap him up so he might fight and die with a sword in his hand," Bison ordered, leaving the former leader to recovery or death. Whichever, really.

Fuker will be back up soon, countering my leadership.

He had been the leader of this place ever since their grand leader chose heroism over practicality. Regardless, he behaved as any leader should. Offering what orders he could, meeting problems to be countered. Few argued with his words. It might have been the stern gaze he offered when delivering said orders. Leaving the royalty to their recovery, Bison walked the thin line of defiance, seeking weaknesses, and there were many. Still, there were enough warriors of all breeds, keen to climb atop those overturned carts and batter back whoever reared their heads.

He tried to ignore the piercing cries of horror on the far side of the blockade, lest they take his will, but there was little to be done against such a wall of deathly noises. Warriors fell above him as he walked, while others were battered back, wholly pulled from the wall, and those sights were the worst.

Now and then, a few Southerners broke the line completely and spilled out over the top, landing on the other side; they never lasted more than a few breaths before falling to dozens of blades. Such defiance might have given a man hope, but Bison knew better. He looked to the stars above and counted them absently. It was something to do while wondering if the coming of dawn would bring a reprieve from the fighting. Would it give his people hope? Or would the light simply illuminate the true nature of the numbers they faced?

Suddenly, there came a roar as a cart was knocked from its place in the line as a swell of a hundred Southerners charged it. Calling his warriors to the breach, Bison sprinted towards the fiends attempting to slip through the small gap. Perhaps, had the entire army been aware of the breach, they would have fallen there and then, but the bandits, used to facing such challenges, met the swell and beat it back. All the while, a few dozen warriors dropped their weapons to shove the cart back into place. With a joint heave and a roar of triumph, they closed the gap. It was smooth, instinctive; it was a pleasing, bandit thing.

But their confidence did not last, for upon the other length of wall, a large gathering scaled the edge. Bison saw it first.

"Get over here," he roared, sprinting towards the breach as it filled up with bastard Southerners who held the precipice, attempting to secure a route with all the reinforcements they would ever need. "On me," he cried, but the numbers were too great. All around, the enemy gushed over the top. Most were beaten back, but for this rogue channel. The Hunt roared in defiance, and their comrades rushed up after them, keen to take the blockade. Eager to kill them all.

And Aimee was suddenly up there with them. Among them. Challenging them. For a breath, Bison felt defenceless and helpless as the diminutive girl raced along the top, hopping from cart to cart with flashing blades in each hand. She was emotionless as she met her first victim, slipping away from a careless strike and sending her sword's tip through his throat as though it were a small thing. She hesitated for only a breath as his blood covered her face before twisting, shoving him aside and charging the next.

Behind her raced Kaya, while Bison was already charging headlong from the other side.

He leapt high, reached the top and charged at the first fiend, shoving him back and slicing through his guard before kicking him back over. "No mercy," he roared, hoping his voice rose above all others. It didn't matter, for by the time any assisted him, the battle would be done, and more importantly, he'd be dead.

On the far side, he saw Kaya meet a Southern fiend and battle him for a few exhausting breaths before cutting deep into his heart. Ahead of her, though, danced a child, and she was incredible. Spinning and cutting, gliding as though upon ice, she tore through that top line of invaders and for a moment, Bison believed them capable of holding out.

At least for a time.

The allied Factions were not the only army with skilled fighters, and one such behemoth, who stood taller than Bison, appeared between them. Shoving aside his comrades, he set his eyes on the girl.

"Leave her be," roared Bison from across the distance. Casting aside a fiend of his own, he moved along the edge, seeking to save the girl, for he knew this cur to be her killer, much as he knew him to be his own. Aimee was indifferent to the greater brute. She continued to kill, to drive forward, slaying all in her way as though it were no impressive feat, and Bison felt too old, too slow, too far away, to save her, to warn her. He shouldn't have cared for her, yet somehow, he did. "Aimee, look out."

Though Aimee likely never heard his warning, Kaya did, for she slipped past her younger companion, battling her way through, and before too long she stood to face the behemoth. Bison knocked three attackers from in front of him, attempting to reach her before it was too late.

Save her.

The massive Southerner stood over her with a mighty battle axe. He swung once, and she ducked and attempted a counter, only to strike his heavy armour and lose her blade in the process. He heard her curse. Heard Aimee squeal in horror at her companion's fate.

Save her.

Bison had never believed himself an agile person. That didn't stop him from trying to fly, and fly he did. Leaping high, using the bulk of a bettered opponent as leverage, he cleared a cart and fell heavily against the massive Southerner, knocking them both clear of the ledge.

A fitting end, he thought, falling in a heap on the outside of the blockade where death awaited. Above, he saw Aimee and Kaya scream in horror. With his last move, he gestured them to halt, leave him to die, and save themselves. He'd never believed in much, apart from a gut feeling here and there. And he wondered if either girl might play a significant part in the world beyond the war. It was a comforting thought as his killer climbed to his feet, drew up his battle axe and stood over him, swinging.

An unimpressive life that should have been more.

He did not close his eyes; he cursed the fate of the bastard who slew him. With the girls' voices ringing in his ears, he saw it all. The massive arrow pierced the brute through the chest, its momentum sending his dead body flying thirty feet away to topple another half-dozen unsuspecting warriors. They lay dead in a gory, broken mess, and Bison still lived.

Scrambling to his feet, he climbed back up the blockade and looked across to his saviour, an attractive blonde who offered a casual wave before reloading her massive ballista and turning it back towards the melee down at the wall.

"Are you okay?" Aimee asked, helping him back over. They reclaimed the line just as another gap appeared a little ways across.

"I am fine. Come on, little one. We have work to be doing," he snarled, and she followed his lead as they held this bastard's bandit bastion until the break of dawn. After that, they could face whatever nightmare it brought.

Nomi was unprepared for the respect she was receiving; even the bandits, who made an island for themselves among the breaking waves, answered to her above most others. This was due to Erroh's legacy, no doubt. As she pulled back on the trigger and fired another bolt into the night, killing at least four brutes before they knew they were hit, she mused about her journey to this moment on a path taken by godly suggestion.

"What the fuk is that noise?" cried Drahir, who was close beside her. Too fuken close. He smelled of the march, sweat and a dozen other stenches. Many were from his mouth. She considered offering the cur a eucal twig to chew on should he survive this night. She didn't mind sharing; she had good teeth, pleasant breath and plenty of fragrant twigs in a little pouch in her satchel. She was also confident she would survive this night; whether he lived or died was another thing. "Can you hear it?"

He reloaded another massive bolt as she tested her sights and eased the huge weapon a few feet to the right, down towards the gate, where Erroh stood waiting for Uden, no doubt. She would be there soon. She only needed to fire her last arrow. Any moment now.

She couldn't hear what he could. Perhaps it was the entire army all around them making such a racket. "Of course, I hear it," she lied, and began to wind the draw on the weapon, or whatever the engineers called it. It was a small matter. She was the finest wielder of this beast. Like an extension of her battle club, or now battle axe, she just knew where to aim it, how to angle it and how to release the killing blow.

"Where is it coming from?" Drahir said. His fingers lingered over the bolt momentarily, and she wrapped them with her fist. "Wake up. Our comrades are dying out there."

She could never have imagined she would find herself standing upon an elevated cart in the middle of a transient blockade, yet here she was, with only Drahir as company, bringing dreadful wrath upon the Hunt. She would have preferred to be with Erroh and Lea at the end. Well, at the end of the battle, that was. She knew it in her bones this night was still to be won. She'd felt it when the gates opened and she'd been among the bandits securing the ballista to a cart. She imagined with a dozen horses and a keen rider, she'd have raced along the edges of the battle, firing deep into the attackers, but alas, she was protected and secure, with her shadow assisting every which way he could.

"Sorry, Nomi, sorry," he said in their shared language. She did not hate having a comrade to speak to, one with whom words came just a little easier. He must have felt the same. He hadn't left her alone the last few days. Even when blades clashed, he denied himself the battle, the honour of standing with Erroh or Lea. He stayed with little old Nomi, insignificant to the last.

"Bah. Concentrate, idiot," she snapped, but she could hear it now—a piercing whistling from somewhere around her. Above? Or behind? Distant, like thunder. She released the projectile, and it skimmed the heads of a hundred Southerners before it dipped and tore asunder many unsuspecting fiends, and she grinned in delight. This beat the fuk out of firing little shards of fire at the city. This type of killing was more intimate, and as she took life after life, she thought of her sister and Uden, and she wanted to leap into the battle, find Erroh and Lea, and fuken kill them all.

And then a giant shard of light lit up the night and flew loudly above their heads, and she froze in shock, disbelief and excitement. "Erroh brings fire," she whispered to the absent gods, though she had no idea to whom she was speaking.

They knew who she was, though.

"What is that?" Drahir cried as the shard lit up the battlefield before striking the gates of Spark and shattering them into a million pieces. The battlefield fell still. Apart from the hundreds who weren't killed or maimed, who scrambled away from the great crater where gates once stood, Nomi marvelled at her Erroh's effect upon unnatural things. She looked across the battlefield, and the armies stood dumbly for a breath, and there was serenity until, as with anything human, violence broke through once again. It spread like a ripple upon a near-frozen lake, and the fighting recommenced. However, shaken by such a vision, many Southerners hesitated in their attack. Many fled the battle in fear, not towards the city either, but out into the darkness where shards of fire were less likely to immolate them where they stood and sinned.

"The end of all things," Nomi said, releasing her hold on the great weapon, and it clunked loudly as its nose dropped forward into a settled position. There were no other bolts to fire, and she ached from the constant work. Sweat covered her body. She was a near-spent force, and she was still not done fighting. At her feet lay her battle axe. It was near time to war one last time.

Seeing a slowing of the violence, Drahir took advantage of the lull. "Check the carts for more ammunition," he called to a few young warriors tasked with serving two of Erroh's generals. They immediately went to work, rummaging through the overturned remains of the many surrounding carts. Nomi watched them. When she had first taken hold of the beast and attacked the city, there had been at least three carts full of long bolts. She'd wasted few of those shots, and her kills had been many.

Around her, the battle began to rage once more, but she felt the turning in that godly sphere of fire. As though to add to her faith in things she didn't understand or care about, the first rays of dawn lit up the battlefield far more significantly than any sphere of fire, and Nomi grinned knowingly.

"What are they doing?" muttered Drahir to himself, looking at the runners tending to the carts, rummaging for anything worth firing. She saw one holding a broom momentarily, examining it, before casting the piece away.

"Desperate times," Nomi whispered. With the growing dawn, her belief in the Factions grew. With renewed vigour, they struck harder, perhaps believing they could hold off the onslaught, but Nomi knew better: they would be overrun within the hour. She stepped away from the ballista. Her limbs still ached, her breath was still short, but the turning would be at the smouldering gates, and she intended to be part of it.

As the sun climbed higher, any fool could see it would be a beautiful day without a cloud in the sky. A zealot might have called it an omen; a tragic legend might have called it an excellent morning to die. Nomi stood aloft the cart, summoning the strength to leap into death.

The Actions of Gods

Distantly, she saw a colourful gathering flocking around the healer's tent. The Alphas of the city stood firm. She could see the hundreds of Hunt who'd fallen at this defining spot. She could also see better how many Southerners had perished attempting to storm the blockade.

An immense grin played across her face. There was still defiance—more defiance than she'd expected. Further down, she saw the struggles of the third defiant group in which Erroh marched, where Magnus followed, and there, too, stood a mass of allies giving fight to the Hunt, despite their lesser numbers.

And then she saw a fourth group charging down upon the blockade—fifty or so Wolves, led by a bald Alpha she knew as Doran—and her heart was lightened by the vision. They drove through the curs, still attempting to claim the bandits' sanctuary, and they kept going.

"We found no bolts," a voice from below cried, and she cursed under her breath. A few bolts would have assisted their mighty charge. A small matter, she supposed, such was their tremendous violence. Doran was fierce, and his comrades seemed likewise. And then she saw another with him. A taller Alpha. Older, aye, but an Alpha, nevertheless. She knew him to be Jeroen, and he was magnificent. Cutting through the bastards, he resembled Erroh in flight, yet with less caution and more grandness.

"But we found something else extraordinary," the voice called, and she looked down at the three strange armoured outfits lying in the mud. Each heavy piece was intricately smelted together, with long blades attached along the sides. She'd never seen such things, but Erroh had spoken of them; she wondered if they were part of his father's collection.

"Make a gate," she cried as the Wolves neared. They'd come this far; it would be rude not to invite them in. With arguments and careful planning, and by waiting until the last moment, twenty warriors quickly slid open a gap wide enough for the charging Wolves to slip through without breaking stride. They were fine orders, and they were the last she gave, for as the gate shut again and the Southerners were distracted, Nomi slipped down from the cart and made her way out into the battlefield to be with Erroh and Lea at the end.

"You are incredible," Drahir hissed, dropping beside her.

"I know," she said, shrugging, before charging headfirst towards the war's end.

It was the great shard of fire that gave the Wolves hope they might live through the night. In that first blush of daylight, Doran had looked out across the battlefield to the Factions still standing firm, giving the Southerners a taste of defiance. He had looked to the top of the allied Factions and the defence they had formed. And to the colourful figures in silk and shimmering hair, that had never ventured into the battlefield, and that was fine; the battle had come to them, and they had stayed firm.

For a time, he had considered leading his smattering of soldiers up to battle with them, but that felt like defeat, or at least retreat. His comrade in arms had agreed as well. A somewhat dishevelled and unrelenting Jeroen had appeared as one of the first at the terrible beginning when he had gathered whom he could to his gang and somehow stayed alive. They two had roared and fought and gathered Wolves desperate to survive, desperate to beat back the tide. Only under Jeroen's raging had they turned from defenders to attackers.

Jeroen mocked the Wolves' skill, their loyalty, their very honour, and he did so while tearing apart every reckless Southerner too foolish to stay clear of his dazzling blade. He fought with an infirmity, as Doran did, and he was far better than any warrior on the battlefield. It had been impossible not to be inspired or to match his frenzied pace.

With the destruction of the gates, they gazed across the open field of horror and saw the grand blockade standing firm against terrible numbers. It had attracted more Southern forces than any small group ever could, and Doran had wondered how it would feel to be upon the walls, elevated, holding back impossible swarms.

Jeroen must have wondered the same thing. "That's where we need to be," he had roared, and it had seemed like a good idea at the time. That wasn't to say that persuading a gathering of fifty-odd warriors in black to traipse across the entire battlefield was easy. To any casual observer, they must have looked like a strange, magnificent thing, shuffling along, supporting each other, killing everyone who stood in their way. They tucked in tight, swinging blades and shields as they went, knocking back their assailants, until they reached the blockade and were welcomed inside.

As they collapsed in the mud on the other side, they discovered that the roar of war was different here. That wasn't to say it wasn't an unsettling thing, knowing more significant numbers were drawing closer, yet still, Doran took the reprieve for what it was. Jeroen, on the other hand, did not. Although he was as fatigued as the rest, he paced back and forth, unsure what to do next. They looked to him, though, and Doran could sense a stirring in them. He stood up first.

"Take a breath, my friend, and we will fight."

Jeroen climbed on top of the nearest cart and dared any crossbow wielder to take a shot by leaning out, gazing towards the healer's tent. He was grinning. "If the Primary was dead, they would not be up there, dug in, inviting so many to attack."

"Mea is built of sturdy things," Doran suggested, and this pleased Jeroen, who nodded as though in a trance.

"This is only a reprieve," Jeroen warned, looking away at the clashes in the distance. In the early morning light, it was difficult to see where the Factions started and where the Hunt ended, such was the melee. "But I feel that is where we need to be now. I feel moved by invisible hands," he said strangely, and Doran nodded in defeat. They had a greater chance of surviving longer in this place, but they could do little to turn the tide of war hidden behind a blockade like this, especially when a thousand comrades stood in the thick of it. Aye, near the burning gates was the place to be now.

"As you wish, friend," Doran said. He offered a canister of water to the taller and far hairier man, as much to refresh him as to allow them all a few moments more to rest.

Jeroen took no water; his eyes were upon the muddy ground below them where the strange objects lay. "What the fuk are those?"

Doran had only once seen such pieces, and recognised the advantage they might bring. Jeroen must have, too, for he dropped down and began examining the mechanisms, shoving aside a few young bandits perplexed by shiny things. He looked suddenly alive, almost giddy.

"Where are the owners?" Doran asked, knowing well his comrade's foolish intention. Such beasts required mastery long before they could be used on the field of battle. Only a fool donned these machines without training, no matter the desperation.

"I see no owners," muttered Jeroen. There was a dangerous glint in the fiend's eyes. The first of the beautiful pieces was painted in a dark green, another in a rich red, and the third was bright steel, unpolished and less fetching, yet still just as dangerous. It was larger than the other two pieces. Only a behemoth could carry such armour into war.

For a breath, Jeroen stared at the pieces before settling on the red monster, where he began testing the counterweights and the mechanisms and appearing thoroughly satisfied with what he discovered. This machine was far lighter than Magnus's monstrous weapons. With its smaller, thinner blades, there would be far more manoeuvrability. "I mean, they are just lying here…"

"Have you ever worn one before?" Doran asked, taking hold of the green piece. It was heavy, daunting, and he feared his infirmities would impede his ability to use it.

Jeroen showed his comrade his ruin of a hand; it matched Doran's. He wedged his ruined hand into the metal channel holding the long blade and moved it easily enough. "These were built for us, brother," he cried delightedly.

"This is a mistake," Doran argued, taking hold of his own piece and beginning to strap it to his body.

"I'll take the large one," a dreamy voice declared. Doran was shocked to see the unsteady figure of Wrek shuffling towards them. His hand was bandaged, as was his rear. His body was covered in blood, and he looked dazed. Still, no fool dared stop him from strapping the armour to his massive frame.

They spent little time becoming familiar with the weapons. A few steps, a few tests of the weight, and Doran was amazed at how well they answered his commands.

"I don't know where we are going, but I'd like to kill as many as we can along the way," Wrek said. His eyes were sharp, his movements better, and suddenly, Doran felt less afraid than before. His eyes were upon the gathering far down the battlefield and the flashes of blue that appeared among the melee. He could see her.

"Let's kill them all," Doran roared, and behind him, his Wolves roared. Jeroen sprinted into the field, eager to fight, kill and lead.

"To the fires with them all," Wrek roared, following after Doran to where they would claim the battle as their own.

It wasn't only hate that fuelled Jeroen at the end, but the feeling was ever-present. With every kill he took, he put his anguish into every bloody strike and emptied himself of bitterness. He was only half the warrior he was with sword and shield, but he was still fierce and considered himself superior to any other on the battlefield. Although devastating, he was crippled. Felt it too. Defending more than he would have wished. Countering far too often when a second blade would have killed in the first spinning attack. These foul brutes humbled him, and he hated them for it. Until they died, and then he felt nothing for them at all.

His mind was awash with such fresh anger that it threatened to take him completely. His heart broke for his mate. He grieved not only for her suffering but also for his own. To be denied the right to stand with her as she fell was an order most cruel, and were he a lesser male, he might have rejected her wishes out of selfishness alone. As it was, he honoured her the only way he could—by killing in her name. Were she to have fallen, she would watch on from the darkness the acts of barbarism he committed in her name. She would be proud. That was something, he supposed.

It's all I have left.

Looking upon the horrors, he thought fondly of his son. If he could have asked the absent gods for one other gift, he might have asked them to take his son a thousand miles away from here, untouched, unaware of this awfulness. Instead, he wondered if he was out there in the night, acting like the wild legend Jeroen knew him capable of being. Last of all, he would have liked his son to see him at war once in his life, doing something more than fending off careless bandits upon their lands.

I was born for this moment.

Standing with his adopted brothers of war, he felt different. Wrapped snugly beneath this heavy uniform of metal and counterbalances, he took that anger and put it to use. Using both arms was a blessing. He'd never known how much he'd missed that until this moment. Despite the tremendous weight, the mechanism answered his every subtle movement. He'd never imagined the pieces were so impressive, even standing alongside Magnus. He had never once tried the mechanism out of curiosity; he had never imagined himself worthy of such fabled weapons. Yet here he stood, angry and legendary, killing them all. With the smaller blades, he needed no shield bearer. That wasn't to say he'd have not preferred a few more soldiers flanking him on either side, knocking away fiends that cut below his sightlines. It was a small matter, though, for the armour he wore covered far more than Magnus's crude pieces ever had.

Twice, a cur slipped beneath the devastating blades, struck at his heart with a sharp edge and met nothing but Jeroen's momentum. Both blades slid off the smooth metal, leaving the attacker open to an effortless dispatch. Shrewder Southerners took the fight from a distance and attempted to strike down the trio with volleys of bolts, and Jeroen found himself laughing from behind the shield of his helmet as they bounced harmlessly off the unmarked surface.

Doran was cold and menacing in his attacks, frequently stepping wide of their incredible line of death to chase down a fiend who neared. His energy was boundless, and Jeroen thought him a perfect fit for Mea's war council. He might have said it to him after the battle of Boat Town, but Jeroen had been unable to speak with any other but Mea. When this night ended, and the banners of victory were waved, he might take the young Wolf aside and bow in respect to him.

On his other side, Wrek was clumsy in his larger piece. That wasn't to say he wasn't the most devastating thing on the battlefield. Every slice he made cut and mutilated many, and with every attack, he screamed in delight as though this were a battle of wits to unsettle the opponent. He screamed in their faces, and many of his insults were spoken in the Southern tongue, which he'd no doubt learned for such an occasion.

And Jeroen? Well, he was divine. He almost forgot the lost feeling in his hand. He no longer felt the lesser warrior he believed himself to be. He kept Mea in his heart, and he killed any who neared, and he was divine.

Though neither said it, they followed Jeroen like children mimicking a schoolmaster. As he moved, both Wrek and Doran charged a few feet across, cutting any he missed and, more than that, challenging from either side. They were the purest, most deadly line of defiance, and had the Woodin Man gazed upon their wrath, he might well have focused all he had on taking them from the battle.

Behind them, to Jeroen's surprise, followed most of the Wolves he and Doran had gathered. He'd expected them to stay behind the cover of the blockade holding a solid position. Instead, they threw themselves into war, trusting Jeroen to lead them to glory, victory and survival. They were a tiny army among greater evils, and they were fierce.

As before, they tucked in close to each other, cleaving a way through the battle. They sent waves of retreat ahead of them wherever they marched, and truthfully, Jeroen regretted the wasted hours he'd spent cursing every wolfen one of them. Whatever shame they brought upon themselves that awful day, when greed had coerced honour from their actions, was redeemed in Jeroen's eyes. The books of history would say they had fled that day; but this fine morning, they stood ready and faced down impossible numbers when fleeing would have been the smarter choice.

He wondered what a sight they must have looked, taking all the Southerners had and marching through them, cutting, slicing, decapitating. Were there another dozen such armoured warriors in the battle and two hundred more Wolves as heroic as these, this war would

The Actions of Gods

have turned most swiftly. As it was, no matter how fierce they were there was a limit to their dominance. Eventually, either they would be overrun by sheer numbers alone, or exhaustion would offer the Southerners an opportunity.

Until then, Jeroen took that hate and drove forward into the masses, seeking allies, better opportunities, and his hero Magnus.

And after a time, they found him.

"They have nothing," he roared, and they yelled with him. Onwards they battled, and among the frenzied storm of blades and death was the unmistakable sight of Magnus in full flight. Although he wore no Clieve, he was impossible to miss. Gathered around him were allies of all Factions, fighting fiercely for their lives in the deepest thicket of violence on the battlefield.

"It is time to turn this war," roared Jeroen, believing his own bravado. His comrades shouted in agreement, and Jeroen thought there were no finer legends to call upon, at the end of his life, as, distantly, he saw a godly fiend larger than all around him, tearing apart those he called comrades.

Magnus had never seen such disarray in his life. He stood outside his tent, watching his armies scatter and run in unhelpful directions. Were they one fighting force, beaten into discipline, trained to think for a breath before going to war, there might have been a greater chance. As it was, for all the grandness of the gathered armies, it took only a little confusion to breed full-on panic.

Too many leaders, he thought bitterly, but found no fault in his son's leadership. He was proud of his cub's aptitude for war. It was simply bad luck. The South had chosen this unlikely hour to set upon them. The runner who'd informed him of the opening of the gates had long since fled, too, leaving him and Elise to consider their actions. Strapping the last buckle in her armour, she stood beside him, watching.

"I have a bad feeling this night," he said. He calmed his rapidly beating heart, settled his shaking hands, and donned his veneer of violence. He did so more easily than he expected, perhaps out of necessity.

"Many will die," she whispered. He could see her calm herself also as she began to stretch. At his feet, his hounds held firm. They did not know the reason for the mayhem, but they knew their master forbade them to erupt unless it was called for. They offered a few little murmurs of disapproval, but were the calmer minds in this terrible beginning.

"Not us, though," Elise said with strength. She hoisted her halberd aloft and tested the edge. All the while, her eyes darted from side to side, watching, scrutinising, formulating.

"I want you by my side," he muttered, drawing his swords. He felt naked without his Clieve, but nothing could be done. With the Clieve, he was a god; with his blades, he was still a master. With her beside him, though, they were unstoppable, no matter the weapons.

"I'll find you, my love," she said before kissing him once upon the lips and spinning around to venture into the turmoil. "I'll want another kiss." He tried to argue. Tried to demand she stay by him. Instead, he loved her in silence and watched her for a breath, wondering why it seemed important to remember this moment. He tried to shake off the unsettling thought, but it wouldn't shift. She marched like it was her last battle. It felt like her last. It felt like his final battle as well.

Distantly, he could see the army gathering, could see a brave group of warriors charge to meet them, and he thought them heroes. Doomed, but heroes, nonetheless. He wanted to be with them, but he was only a man. Better to gather what forces he could.

"It's time to go to war, my boys," he called, seeking out his savages for one delicious last battle before the end.

Elise's heart broke at leaving her man behind, but she was no longer Elise of the city: she was of Adawan, and she understood her calling. She could not allow selfishness to rule her heart. She clambered across the muddy ground towards the bandit camp, calling for her allies, calling for a gathering, calling for them to fall in behind her so they might fight. Although she called out for her generals, her mind rushed with prayers, demands, challenges and pleading, all for the absent gods to deliver her children through this night. She offered herself up in exchange, and though she didn't know it, the absent gods listened to every word and thought on such things.

Sprinting to the campsite, hoping to slow any great flight of bandits, she was taken aback by their actions. As thousands around them prepared in confusion, the bandits went to task, erecting a grand little barricade of defences. Bison led the defence, and she was impressed. They took what they needed at the expense of nobody they cared for, worked as tightly as any regimented army and swiftly built themselves a right little defensive post.

Unsure of what to do, she dove among them and began helping to heave the heavy carts into place. She could offer only muscle to the endeavour, but she tried her best. Truthfully, as the first screams of violence erupted, she half expected them to lose heart, take flight and turn to whatever desperate measures that came to mind. Instead, they were unaffected, as though constructing a camp in the middle of a solstice evening, without many cares.

"More over here," Bison roared, and three hundred bandits turned to his orders, heaving and pulling, building and fortifying, and she was amazed how easily they obeyed. Soon, a grand blockade covered the battlefield, and they climbed to the top with arrows and blades, preparing for the coming storm. "Reinforce there," Bison ordered, and his voice was gospel. He marched along the makeshift ramparts, inspecting gaps and demanding whatever they needed to seal them, and once again, she thought them fine, hardened warriors.

"Will it hold?" she asked, approaching the brute.

"We will hold longer than most; more than that, we are a bastion should those who fight be routed. We might not live this night, but will hold until dawn."

"You are magnificent," she offered, and he bowed.

"You will hold with us," he said, and she shook her head.

"This is not where I will fall, friend." He looked confused, as though the thought of stepping away from this bandit fortress was madness. But she was not needed here as she was by her mate's side. She clasped her halberd and smiled her most dazzling smile. If nothing else, as she stepped into war, she would show the depth of her fearlessness. "I belong out among the horror, cutting and killing," she said. Her bandits were taken care of; she was called to join the rush of battle where she could dance one last time, not to cower behind a fortress where no goddess could hear the music play.

He might have argued, might have called her a lunatic. But he could see the determination in her eyes. He also might have imagined her death and his survival, a more leisurely ascent to the throne. Regardless, he embraced her, stole a kiss upon her lips that she only mildly fought off, purely to antagonise her mate with afterwards, and left her to chase death.

As they filled the last gap, she slipped off into the night, seeking the savages, seeking her mate. For a frozen moment, she worried she had erred. That she might not find him again. But as swiftly as that terror took her, she heard him, heard his call.

She wasn't the only one.

Magnus missed his Rangers more now than at any moment before. If nothing else, he missed their ability to be precisely where they were supposed to be at such a time. He stormed through the night seeking out his comrades. A difficult task, considering the social behaviours of his savages: many were strewn throughout all camps. He marched through each line of tents, calling out for his subjects, but had little luck given the growing volume of war and panic. Not from his warriors, admittedly, but from those unprepared for such an attack.

It was sheer luck that he came upon his generals from the Savage Isles, clustered among a gathering of agitated warriors, all offering suggestions. They latched onto him like a pack of hounds would cling to a master ready to untether their leashes.

Tell us who to kill.

Because we'll fuken kill them all.

He thought on this for a breath, and they circled him, armed and armoured, seeking orders, seeking a march. A lesser warrior might have taken what he could, but he expected more from those he led. They were not Rangers, but they were fierce.

"Half our forces are already charging down to fight at the gates," Sloan told him, and Magnus could see little fear in the man. Instead, he carried that same grim look he'd had during the trials when he was humbled and limping; he'd continued regardless. There was such a deceiving measure to that man; it was incredible.

"They're the smarter ones," Tusk argued. He looked ready to join them. It was unnatural to delay when there was a good fight to be had. It was no matter they were massively outnumbered. It would just make the stories sweeter when they emerged victorious.

"The dead ones, too," said Padir. Magnus was impressed he'd stayed this long. He was as far from a savage as any fiend could get. He could fight but would have happily chosen a life without violence or honour. But with plenty of cakes. His eyes were upon the unlit regions in the forests beyond. A young rat could creep far into that darkness and emerge somewhere in the east; a quick trip upon a barge and he'd be done with it. "Never mind. We'll all be dead soon enough." He looked back to the battle, and Magnus was impressed once more.

Were Curroi here, he might have summoned his warriors to charge with them. But he wasn't here, and the Factions were lesser for it.

"We will march soon enough, little one; just a shame there aren't more of us," Teaolor said. She stood looking at the gates as though it was her destiny, as though she were a king on the eve of greatness or folly, and only for a moment did Magnus wonder if she was regretting her choice to fight. "We'll just have to kill more than expected."

"Isn't that always the way," Gregor said quietly. He stood with his royal guard. They surrounded Teaolor, and this pleased Magnus. The warrior knew his place, and he knew her importance was far more than that of the old king ready to march into war for the last time.

"We will take this night," Magnus said, and they approved. He looked at their numbers, and they were paltry. Hardly a hunting pack at all.

A hunting pack.

It seemed so simple. So unlikely. He turned to his boys at his feet, agitated and ready to explode. Their voices would carry. Their rallying cry might echo across the entire battlefield.

"Sing for me," he snarled, and they knew his words. They erupted in primal howling, and it was piercing from so many. They challenged the world, whatever that might be, and he roared at them to continue their cry. And those out in the darkness recognised the howl for the beacon it was.

They began to form up almost immediately, following the pack, answering their king one last time. Like a frenzied hive of insects, they swarmed Magnus, roaring and demanding violence, and he responded to their demands. With his howling army, they gathered and marched, and Magnus led them through the dark towards the Southerners at war.

Elise followed the shrill cries, and she wasn't alone. They made way for her, for they knew her importance. They knew her threat, and she was with him before the first blades clashed. He almost broke his veneer of cold killer as she appeared beside him. They shared no words, only a cold knowing as they had done in many battles. Silent words that only a blissful couple could understand.

He asked her if she was ready to fight, and she was.

She challenged him to keep up, and he dared not defy her.

Ahead, the Southerners marched and clashed; there was blood in the air. She swallowed her fear and became a legendary goddess at the end of her life. Eventually, she spoke. To him and him alone. "I never thought I would live to fight this last war."

"I will be beside you always," he said softly, and she loved him. She held that love and tried to impress him as she had many times before. And the absent gods watched these creatures so close to godliness with wonderment.

"You'll have to run so," she said, and darted ahead of him. She was always the swifter of the two and took full advantage. She cleared the way and, screaming, challenged the entire South to a fight.

Those who knew little of her legacy might have wondered why this solitary woman, older than most of the others, led the way, but they soon learned. She did not stop. She dropped at their feet, cartwheeling and driving through them, all the while holding her blade tightly, connecting with flesh, before announcing herself spectacularly, as those she struck fell away in confusion and horror, to die a few breaths later.

Her body was a blur. She charged head-on before leaping suddenly to the side, causing further surprise, spinning her blade furiously and trusting instinct alone before twisting to another angle, circling again and tearing into countless victims. She needed no such weapon as the Clieve. She herself was the weapon. Agile and unlikely. No blade neared her, and as usual, it was easy. She spun, cut, killed, and laughed wildly.

"Kill them all," she demanded of Magnus and his army as they charged along in her ruinous wake, destroying any too surprised to do anything more than die at the hands of superior warriors.

She dove deeper into their numbers, teasing a strike here and there, and they grazed her, as in any good battle, and she took the strikes without slowing. Instead, spinning, dodging and vaulting around the battlefield, unsettling all who tried to plunge their blades in. For when they did deliver a killing blow, she simply wasn't there. Many escaped, open-mouthed with surprise. Others received a dreadful slice from her massive halberd as she skipped away, and for a stolen breath, no longer choked by some awful disease, she was a goddess.

He almost smiled as she waged war alone, for in this light, she was as vibrant and youthful as the queen who had near gutted him on more than one occasion. He'd seen that devastation from both sides; he knew the frustration of attempting to pin her down, missing her strikes, the joy of making a hit.

"Kill them all," he roared, and his army amassed around him, around them all. They knew their foe; they had their numbers; it was a fine last order to give as a king, and with that, he became nothing more than a pauper chasing after his wild mate. She was swift and brutal, but he was all-powerful. He barraged through any who stood up to him, and as swiftly as she was away from him, they were back beside each other, in love, killing and winning.

The battlefield turned to Southern crimson, and the killing never stopped. At least the two warmongers did not stop, even when a flaming sphere struck the city gates and gave the superstitious Southerners a moment's pause. Not long enough to surrender, but enough to allow them to see the fragility of blind faith.

Magnus and Elise, surrounded by their war hounds, who savaged any not fully felled in their wake, turned an entire army on its heels. Not in surrender, but just back towards the burning gates to recoup, gather forces and seek leadership. They fled, and many were slain for their acts. The South had dominated this battle long enough, but the savages held the tide and sought out more.

And they weren't alone.

There charged three Clieve bearers and an army of Wolves from the flanks, snapping and biting. They surged into the Southerners on the precipice of fleeing, and Magnus, sensing a grander moment than his own, called on all around him to gather their shields. Surrendering his blades, he took a shield and drove in alongside the lead warrior. They moved and swayed, and the cur was as skilled in the great machines as he. Elise matched his stance. Standing firm, she covered her man, lest a brute sneak in, and together they battered back the Southerners, who recoiled from this sudden charge.

But they also recoiled from the presence of two demons, who alone brought about the end of it all.

Lillium had twelve arrows left. Twelve shots to turn the tide of war against impossible numbers. Twelve shots to make before she died. With the twelfth, she took aim, followed the breeze's gentle whisper and released across the mass of struggling warriors. The arrow was pure and true. It took a massive cur no less than fifty feet from where she stood upon the abandoned cart. It was no killing blow, such was his armour, but it took him in the shoulder and gifted his savage opponent the chance to kill him. She imagined he did this swiftly while the brute fumbled with the arrow. Lillium did not delay to gaze upon her strike. Instead, she aimed again.

Her eleventh arrow was taken at pace. Not her at pace, for she was smooth, secure, and still upon the cart. Beside her, behind her, around her, she felt Wynn's presence, covering her rear, knocking back any who neared with blade or shield, deflecting any bolt or arrow, shield or sword. Predictable Wynn, ever loyal, ever diligent. Her demon in tow. Her friend. That was enough for her.

The arrow released and cut the hair of three Southerners before it took its quarry, a female charging Lea from outside her line of sight. An easy thing to miss, what with the heavy helmet her best friend donned for this battle. Through the slit in Lillium's demonic visage, she watched the girl fall long before she reached Lea and smiled in satisfaction.

Her tenth, ninth and eight shots were taken swiftly in just as many breaths. Three Southerners attempted to dethrone her, and she made them pay for the gall. She watched them fall, spitting blood, crying out for loved ones or gods, and she regretted not having a thousand more arrows to add a few more dead to her tally and sway the mood in this battle.

It was a small matter. Although she wanted to kill them all, there were plenty to go around.

The seventh arrow was a gift to Erroh. Among the throng of killers, he fought valiantly, covered in blood and cuts; she watched his mesmerising movement for a moment before sending an arrow through the throat of a bastard sneaking up behind him. Admittedly, of the arrows spent, while this was most important, there was every chance Erroh would have spun away from danger or, indeed, turned into it and gutted the cur for his blatant arrogance, believing himself capable of killing a god. Aye, a god. If not a traditional blessing upon lesser mortals' gods, then a god among warriors. Her god of war.

Lea's god of war.

Her sixth arrow was closer to her home and her heart. To Wynn's as well. From nowhere, the fiend appeared, swinging his weapon carelessly, and only a delayed curse from her former lover as he fought off another attacker alerted her to his threat. The arrow released and went deep into his eye as he charged. He screamed piercingly as he fell away from their

The Actions of Gods

cart, clawing at the air, and she hesitated, waiting for Wynn's approval. She received only a grunt of gratitude, and his indifference irked her somewhat, though she did not know why. Perhaps she enjoyed his approval more than she'd care to admit, even after all they'd been through.

"That was a fine shot," he said after a breath.

"Of course it was."

Notching her fifth arrow, she caught sight of a monster and held her strike for a moment. He swung two swords and killed with every blow. He was Alpha in everything but honour. She recognised Uden from the stories and descriptions and was drawn to him. Surrounded by countless guards, he was never taken by surprise; instead, he met every warrior face-on and defeated them with a few swift blows.

"He's terrifying," Wynn said from beside her. They were frozen in fear, anticipation and excitement for just a breath. "We can kill him."

"Aye, we fuken can!" she howled, releasing the fifth arrow into one of his guards and felling him before he knew he was done. She drew another arrow, stepping across the cart to face the behemoth.

The fourth arrow let loose and immediately collided with a swinging axe, sending the projectile careening into a group of allies, striking a comrade through the knee. A cold panic took her as she watched the man fall, injured. "What have I done?" The absent gods made no reply.

Her third arrow felled the fiend attacking her previous tragic victim. She watched him stumble and fall, all the while willing her comrade to rise and fight despite the injury. He never did.

"Make up for it," brave, loyal Wynn cried from behind his mask, and she shook herself away from the accident. She leapt from the cart, taking aim with her second to last arrow, before releasing point blank, felling another of his guards, leaving a gap wide enough to slip on through and challenge him.

We can do this.

The last arrow she left for Uden alone. How sweet to deny the fuker an opportunity to die a true hero's death. Better to bleed from a little piece of sharpened wood than from the blade after an epic battle worthy of a great tale. Drawing a breath, reaching back and ensuring his forehead was open for the taking, she released, and was cursed with a brutal kill. The guard crossed into her path and took the arrow through the nose. It passed into his brain, and stumbling, spluttering, he fell against Uden and died in awful convulsions.

The god looked upon her and snarled; he raised his blades at them both in challenge. "Demons," he roared, and all around them parted. Uden's guards fanned out, keeping her comrades at bay. An arena fit for gods appeared, and she was invited to enter. In her ears, she heard the cries of her comrades—Magnus, Erroh, Elise, Lea, and any others who believed her fated to fail. It didn't matter; she raced down upon Uden, dropping her bow, drawing her blades, determined to tear him apart and end the war.

Wynn was too slow getting to Lillium. This was nothing new. He leapt from the cart after her, hoping to reach the terrifying god before he slew his former lover. One of Uden's many guards blocked his way. Their blades clashed violently. He was no match for the young Alphaline, but Wynn, with an eye to the mad god, took longer than he would like to defeat the cur. When he did penetrate his rough leather armour, another guard was upon him, no doubt seeing his demonic threat, avenging those he'd already slain.

Beyond, he could see Lillium at war with the behemoth, and he'd never seen a more domineering threat. She was brave; she was fierce. If she regretted this bout, she never showed it, and he was so very proud. She leapt towards Uden, swinging both blades, and she was a dazzling blue in the morning's glare.

"To the fires with you," Wynn cried, knocking the second guard away before plunging both blades through his undefended torso. Wynn understood it to be a dreadful way to die. Regardless, he felt little for the bastard, kicking him aside and running towards the two legends in this fleeting arena.

From the mouths of new Southern comrades brave enough to approach the campfire, Wynn had learned the legend of demons among the Hunt. A wonderful thing to be part of folklore, he mused. And Uden must have been well aware of the tales, for he did not face her directly. Did not meet her in the expected open warfare. Instead, he spun to the side with impossible speed, parrying her strikes and sending her reeling to the mud. He roared something incomprehensible to any Southerners not engaged in battle, those with a moment to be educated.

For a breath, Lillium looked a pathetic sight. Within a further breath, she was upon her feet again, attacking, and she was fiercer than before. She ducked and weaved around him, more cautious, with both her blades meeting his blur of violence and holding him back. And then, with a dreadful sinking feeling, Wynn realised she was no match for him. She was little more than pantomime for any who watched. Only a brazen brute could do such a thing.

Running.

Wynn's limbs felt impossibly heavy. He had never been there for her. Not at her worst moments or her best. He had let her down again and again. Their blades clashed, and Uden drew blood across her upper chest. She slipped away from the strike, but he was on her again, pummelling her with the grip of his mighty swords along the side of her head where the facemask could do little dampening, dazing her, preparing her, finishing her. Still, she fought, all to the symphony of screaming comrades seeing the end, and there was nothing they could do.

Her blue hair whipped back as her head was struck again and she was dazed momentarily, and he plunged his blade towards her heart—a killing blow.

And Wynn was bedside her. He knew his place; it was right here.

I have this, Lillium.

He took the strike from the side and tried to roll with it. A difficult thing, really, but he did not die in that moment. Instead, he moved away and met the god's frustrated blade with his own. Scrambling, he felt the rip in his stomach where the sword had pierced his armour and sliced into the flesh.

He could hear fresh screams from his beaten former mate in the mud, trying to rise, trying to save him, and he held her warmth in his mind. Knowing Uden was upon him, it was something to do: swinging, striking, defeating.

It was a strange, wonderful thing not to fear death. He concerned himself with the straightforward task of covering Lillium until she could slip away from the battle. If nothing else, he could do one thing right, now, at the end, for all his sins and missteps. It was no proclamation of love; it was far greater than that.

He was hunted for a time. Uden was graceful, terrifying and mighty in every strike, and Wynn gave himself to the battle, simply deflecting blow after blow. His life became nothing more than watching each tip near him. He considered it a life better lived. Time became nothing, despite the pain. He swallowed it all and showed the world his nerve and determination.

"You are no god," Wynn spat, deflecting a careless strike before ducking the follow-up that went wide. Without warning, Wynn leapt forward, plunging his blades, and met success. It was a lesser strike, but he penetrated flesh. Drawing away, the mad god howled in agony and frustration, which was also a satisfying thing. Wynn dared a glance at Lillium and saw her surrounded by allies. His task was completed.

"You bleed far too much for a demon," Uden muttered, drawing upon the injured Alphaline more slowly than before. Despite the pain, despite his sudden fatigue, Wynn was at peace.

"I have plenty more to spill all over you, cur," he snarled, but he was spent. The god fell upon him, swinging, and his reflexes were too slow. He blocked but far too weakly, and the blade slid up his own and dove deep into his belly. Uden dragged the edge fiercely across the flesh, gutting him fully and bringing him to his knees. Still, Wynn swung wildly, missing, even as he bled himself upon the god's boots.

"Impressive," his killer offered before shoving him to the ground and moving on to his next victim.

His body shook; the pain took him, and Wynn pulled the mask from his face and left it in the mud. Beyond the pain, he could feel a warmth. He wondered if it was his blood soaking him through. Around him, the battle waged, but he was still now, settled in his death. His stomach only ached a little; his limbs merely felt heavy.

Suddenly, she was in his line of sight. Distant and beautiful. Tearing her mask free, she leaned down and kissed him and drew back with blood upon her lips. She didn't seem to notice, so he tried to wipe the blood free, but his hands were wet, leaving a distasteful red smear.

"I made it worse," he gasped. He struggled a little as he felt a tiredness come upon him. A wonderful sleep, calling for him alone. "I'm sorry I made it worse."

"You were perfect," she whispered in his ear, but he didn't mind. He didn't need to hear her words at the end. He only needed to look to the beautiful darkness beyond. "I love you, Wynn," she cried, and she was distant, and that was fine. Around her, he saw familiar faces, and he smiled and looked beyond to the figures approaching.

"What are you doing here?" he asked of those who came for him. He knew them, but it made little sense. "Am I home?" he asked, and the rush of war was distant, as was her warmth and her tears, her wailing and his regret for them both. It suddenly didn't matter now.

"You are, my wonderful boy, and I'm so very proud of you," Marvel whispered, taking his hand and leading him away from the world.

101

THE FALL OF LEA

"Oh, fuk me," Erroh cried, stumbling in the slippery mud and nearly toppling over the brute he fought. Only luck saved him in that moment. Erroh had been a fine believer in the creed of luck, and this moment added to his faith. Slipping below the slash that should have gutted him, he leapt forward and, wrapping his arms around the Southerner, wrestled him to the ground, driving his forehead against his opponent's nose a few times, drawing blood, drawing a breath, drawing a chance. Pinning him with his knees, Erroh thrust his sword down upon the cur's neck, slicing through it and killing him messily. It took more from him than he expected.

"Fuk you," he cried to the quivering man, hating that killing was his only gift to the world, before falling away from his victim and lying beside him for a moment.

He'd never known exhaustion such as this. His limbs felt as though they were dipped in molten lead and left to harden in an icy lake. His body was covered in countless grazes; blood seeped from his wounds with an aching so fierce he doubted he'd ever know relief again. He was tired; he was near the end. He wanted to lie in the mud, surrounded by thundering boots as they clashed and fell around him. He wasn't alone down here either. Around him were dead comrades and dead enemies too. All of them human and beautiful and capable of great things in life. But no more. They were no different from him. They had woken up this morning with ideas and dreams in their heart. Hope, too. Now they merely added to the fertility of this field. He imagined there would be quite the growth in these parts in ten years. Regardless of the battle, life would go on. Nothing would change.

Get up, Erroh.

It was fine advice, and he ignored his better nature. He looked beyond and saw the Woodin Man, farther from him than ever. Erroh's voice was raw and parched from screaming his name, challenging the cur to a battle and begging him to turn and look around and make way for the false god of Spirk to present himself. He was also deathly thirsty, and Erroh wondered if that was because of the leaking of his blood. He did not like being thirsty. He hated the thought of slipping into the darkness with such a thirst on him. What if that was how life was beyond the darkness? If the last moment's experience was carried forward forever and ever? Eternity with a parched tongue was no fine thing at all. Better to stay here and sleep.

Get up, Erroh.

"I can't," he whispered to the wind. To himself too. He was tired in the soul. It was too much. This last charge had been a step too far. There had been too many kills to his name. He was but a human.

Around him, in the mud where he belonged, he could hear the turning of the battle. The turning of the war. He was a failure. He'd tried. The absent gods knew he had tried his best. But there was a limit to the amount of bloodletting any force could sustain. He gasped for air; his arms spread out in a V. It felt like hours had passed since that wretched gate had opened, spilling death out all over the world. He'd stood as long as he could and raged as hard as he could, but there came a moment when every human broke in two. For him, it had been a slip in the mud. Even then, he had been killing.

He felt so lonely at the end of it all. Surrounded by comrades, none with a name he could recall, he missed those he cared for, loved, and warred with. Were they at his side, it wouldn't have hurt as much. They could have carried him; he could have carried them.

"A curse upon me," he muttered, turning on his side. He feared no axe or blade piercing him where he lay. There were no spare weapons now to kill a defenceless fiend on the ground. He could have stayed for an hour or more watching the war turn around him and been relatively safe. It was a wretched thought, and he stirred against it. Beside him, his victim shook his last, and Erroh felt even more lonely. Still, they dashed their bodies against each other, giving no ground, dying loudly and proudly. He did not know them but was proud to be among them.

Do not leave them to their fates alone.

His better senses were right. And slowly, taking a breath, Erroh, the leader of the gathered Factions, climbed to his feet again. Distantly, he could still see Uden, and despite having little vigour, he began to make his way towards the fuk, knowing he would need to cleave through a couple of hundred Southerners to reach him.

"So be it," he roared, facing the mass of Southerners ahead of him. They still surged from the gate, though slower than before. Perhaps the terrifying ball of flame had dampened their enthusiasm for battle; perhaps they were already upon the battlefield, and the entire South had come to fight.

"With me," he cried in a wretched voice, like a child's whisper in a depthless cave, but they heard him and swayed with him. They still held a line against nothing and tried to step forward despite the terrible odds.

I don't know where I'm going, but I know the way.

They had no path, they saw no end, yet still, they fought, and Erroh fought for them. Despite the agony and the crushing fatigue, he still attacked. His arms were a blur as he roared at those he faced once more. Even near the end, he would play the part of wild lunatic for as long as he could.

It wasn't for very long at all.

Suddenly, a wave of thundering Southern bodies drew in from the flanks, and Erroh was almost knocked to his feet again as they pushed past in their hundreds. Ahead of them strode three metal-clad figures of grandness. Around him, his comrades cheered at the coming of the Clieve. The three warriors were reckless and fearless, and they charged swiftly as the flank collapsed upon itself. Their march brought them nowhere near Uden, but their presence created space that was not there before.

Erroh did not hesitate. He sprinted through the gaps, slicing and tearing on either side as he did, to fall among the brutes' slaughter. All fatigue was lost in the opportunity of turning this tide, and for a cruel moment, Erroh believed, but more than that, he took advantage.

The barbaric trio were not alone, for dozens of Wolves fought alongside them. He thought that such a charge might weaken their resolve, tempt them to surrender to foolish hope. Wars turned on such things as this.

"You are still alive," cried a voice from beside him. It was enough to take his concentration. A fatal thing, but such was the turning of the battle. He turned to offer a smile to his father, who shielded the brutes as they charged.

"I'm only getting started," Erroh lied deliriously, stepping alongside his master, matching his movement, slaying any who stood against them.

"Your mother will be delighted," Magnus said, knocking a Southerner to the ground before driving his shield down on her three times and leaving her dead, all without breaking his stride. Erroh looked beyond to Elise, who took the war by the scruff and struck it until it did her bidding.

He almost stumbled as he watched her glide through the menace, never faltering, never slipping, just killing. For a humble moment, he realised the skill level required to match them.

Upon seeing him fight, she gave him a smile she had saved for him alone, and immediately dug in behind Erroh, protecting her boys from fiends that sought a treacherous assault. Around them, the gaps widened as they earned a breath and gained a little grace in their march. They became a line of devastation, singlehandedly holding the war in their fingers.

"Father," a female voice cried, and a figure slipped between Magnus and Elise. Lexi was covered in blood; her eyes were wide; her grin was dangerous. "Hi, Mom. Hi, Erroh," she added dreamily. Her swords were dripping in blood, and without breaking a sweat, she turned on an approaching Southerner and dispatched him swiftly, and Erroh felt that astonishing burn of pride. Had he not refined her skills? Had he not shown her the way of violence in Raven Rock? Had he not shown his little sister how to survive in this terrible world?

Magnus dropped his shield and hugged her before ordering her behind Erroh and himself. A father's protection, no doubt. For a cold moment, Erroh wondered after Tye. He couldn't imagine he had left her in this battle, not after the pledge that Erroh had drawn from him. He shook those thoughts away immediately. That was a fine way to lose concentration. He had his family alive. He had more reason to stay fighting, stay killing, stay living.

Nomi never announced herself; she merely appeared among them. Swinging her axe like a light piece of wood, she stole in around Erroh, saving one blood-soaked smile for him when their eyes met. In that moment, he loved her as he always had. She was family most welcome too.

Beside her, the battered form of Drahir just about kept up. With a bolt protruding from his shoulder, he was still impressive. Blood streamed down every time he swung his blade. He screamed aloud every time he killed, but never stopped, never gave up on covering Nomi.

Erroh tried not to burn a little with jealousy at his behaviour. He had stolen days from him and Lea, and now, he attempted to steal Nomi. A lesser man might have resented him. Might have left him to his fate. As it was, a cur stole up behind him, and Erroh did not hesitate to stab the bastard through the stomach and felt far better about himself.

For a moment, Erroh no longer felt alone at all.

And then Lea was beside him.

This long night was turning to morning, and Lea had never felt as wretched as this. For too long, she had moved with the masses seeking out some grand thing. Some treasure to complete her, something that seemed important, yet she could not put her finger upon it. She had seen her Wolves at war and had driven through the Hunt without them. She desired no responsibilities, no distractions; she wanted her treasure after feeling so lost for so long.

She thought it was Erroh she sought. She hoped it would be Erroh, but it was not. It was a fit of dreadful, terrible anger that carried her, and it wasn't anger directed at her mate. As countless warriors fell around her throughout the battle, she was not scared; she was merely frustrated. An invisible hand guided her, and she allowed this energy to direct her through the fighting. She did not question her step or the brutality she dealt with. She did not fear the waves driving up upon her, for she was not destined to die this night.

At least not until dawn.

She watched the sky and saw the shattered moon's meteorite tear up the atmosphere and more. She followed the trail of flame, even as it struck the gates. She cared little for the destruction. Such an event was no mere impossibility; it was merely unlikely. It wasn't the first such shard she'd seen. Regardless, she was fatigued and delirious enough to follow that trail and seek her treasure.

Through waves of warring fiends she waded, slicing, cutting and killing as though it were no terrible thing at all, until finally, with dawn warming her rear, she came upon her mate at war.

She thought him beautiful and heroic, yet still, she could not give herself to him. He was surrounded by those who loved him most—his family, who nurtured and supported him—and for only a few breaths she was furious that he had such a thing to call upon. She said nothing; she offered less; she merely stood with him for a time, killing as they always had.

Until she saw Uden among the Hunt.

Her heart rose and broke in the same breath.

I must kill you.

Tremendous hate took her. A burning rage that gifted her strength and determination. A lifetime of sorrow, anger and terror all erupted, and with Erroh by her side and a pack of feral warriors breaking the way for them to charge, she aimed towards the god, determined to end the war once and for all…

Until Lillium stood to face her father, and Lea screamed in horror. She sprinted forward before she could help herself, leaving Erroh behind and ignoring any fiends she passed. Not to save her friend but to ensure the witch didn't deny her the opportunity to fight, kill or scream at him.

To her horror, the world slowed, and her steps became heavy as she watched Lillium struggle with the mad god. Lillium was heroic, even when he bested her, and Lea screamed out for her friend, and she was too far away.

Her race was lost. Her steps too slow, the distance too great. But she tried. She screamed only once more, seeing Wynn fall. She thought he died well. A strange thing to think of her friend that way. She couldn't see beyond the green eyes.

Green eye.

She left Wynn where he dropped. She sprinted past him as Lillium wailed for his murder, and she could not stop to cover her friend, could not even mourn herself.

Her eyes were upon Uden the Woodin Man, the vile warmonger, her kin. She couldn't help herself, didn't want to help herself. She wanted to release her anger upon him, strike him down. But also, she wanted to look into his eye before he died, before she died too. She wanted to know him for just a breath and then kill him. His guards did not stop her, nor would they. They were taken up with trying to fend off her mate and his entire fuken clan. She, little Lea of the city, was an unimpressive thing among such giants, so they allowed her to charge their god, and she was lesser for it.

Typically, her scream alerted him, and he met her strikes lazily. Her flashing blades danced around him, picking at his defence, slicing ever closer, and she could feel a victory for herself—for a few breaths, at least. Maybe three or so.

"Come at me," he hissed, and his words cut through her. She knew that voice, and it was so much worse up close, on the precipice of death. She swung everything into her attacks, and the success she believed she had in the first few strikes was taken away in a counterblow so fierce her arms shook. He was far taller than she, yet although she was quicker, her speed was insignificant to him. He was a blur as he spun around her, knocking the blades away and seeking an easy kill, and she was suddenly terrified.

Distantly, she could hear the cry of Erroh demanding to fight. But there were so many in between them. So many. Too many. Erroh couldn't save her. This arena was for her and a god alone.

Green eyes.

He sneered as he killed her, choosing his steps carefully and deliberately. She couldn't match his pace, and for a breath, she admired Erroh for standing with this fiend as he had. Perhaps it was this exact thought that saved her life. Slipping away from him, she surrendered her aggression and dug in defensively as Erroh might have. She watched Uden's shoulders and less his dreadful emerald eye, as it held only deceit. He was far quicker than she, but he announced his strikes ever so. Not enough to help her stay alive, but enough to allow her to hold on longer, until better warriors came for his head.

I am not enough.

She was incredible. Erroh might have thought as much had he been watching. She took Uden's strikes and, gritting her teeth, gave little away, offering even less to take advantage of. Around them, the roar of war was at its loudest, but Lea could hear only Erroh's distant cries for her and the swish of Uden's blade, nearing and missing.

She could hear her breath too, hear that she was gasping heavily.

"Damn you, whore," he roared, drawing away for a moment, dropping his defence, inviting a strike. An easy ploy, she mused, refusing to take the bait. As suddenly as it had appeared, the crack in his defence closed up and he slipped away, breathing hard.

Again, he came at her, and he was controlled and smooth and showed little. She held him off at the surrendering of only a few steps' retreat. As she did, he stumbled and leapt away lest she cut him, and only then did she see the exhaustion in his tired face. An older face too. He was mighty and godly, but he was a man with few reserves left. As tired as she was fighting throughout the night, so too would he be.

She dared not reply, to give him any suggestion of her lineage, of who she truly was. She'd never gone into battle with such a heavy helmet before, but now she realised it disguised her well. It didn't matter that it was lunacy. It kept him from recognising her.

"You fight well," he gasped, and a few guards, not battling for their lives and his, looked up at his startling admission of weakness. "But I will best you," he hissed, sounding so tired, so weak, and so very human. He charged at her, and she could only parry his blows, even when he dropped his guard to slip away from her, cursing her as he did, and suddenly she started to believe she could win this. He was a near-perfect warrior, even with one eye. But there were weaknesses to be found in every fiend. Had she not spent a great deal of time attempting to best a master like Erroh?

She suddenly charged at him, and he deflected her away. She offered no killing blow, and neither did he. Instead, he appeared relieved to be away from her when she drew back to hunt him down. "Near godly," he wheezed, and she knew this exhaustion was a trick.

It's a fuken trick.

He came at her again, and she affected a carelessness in her defences, drawing him in, attempting to unseat him. In the blink of an eye, it was there. An easy strike below his arching right sword. She knew it was a trick. It had to be a trick.

It was a trick.

His fist shot out, gripping his sword, and he hammered her helm along the side, and the strike blinded her. With his other hand, he drove the grip at her head again, and it was as though a brute had kicked her. The world went dark as the helmet slipped, and she fell backwards, ripping the offending piece away, only to receive a full punch from him upon the face.

Fuk.

She fell backwards; her head whipped back, and her hair covered her eyes. Landing painfully, he stood above her, and it was the end. Her swords were gone, her arms were outstretched, her body was reeling.

Not like this.

"You will not be remembered," he mumbled, standing over her, and she looked into his eye, into his fuken soul.

"Can you see me, Father?" she asked softly, and he hesitated.

"What?" He dropped down beside her, and she felt the world darken.

Her senses were a ruin, and she wanted Erroh to save her as he said he would.

"I see you, Father," she whispered, and he looked into her eyes, into her fuken soul.

"Cordelia?" he whimpered.

"Did you ever love me?" she gasped, and he turned pale at her words.

"This cannot be," he wailed, and then slipped away from her like a spirit had formed in front of his eye. His green, human eye.

"My name is Lea," she cried, but he was already retreating from her, and she fell unconscious.

Uden slipped away from the battle, and his retreat was the final deathly blow to the Southerners' unholy war. His most loyal guards dug in around him, prepared for such an unlikely eventuality. They dragged him away, despite his half-hearted attempts to stand, and carried him far from his daughter, through the ranks of weakening Southerners, towards a group of prepared mounts up to the task of a nasty trek across open, hostile territory.

He retreated, not to the city, but towards the South. Flanked by his protectors, he mounted his horse and charged through the hostiles, out through the forest, urging his mount to the fastest pace she could manage.

Unable to speak, Uden shook uncontrollably for the first few hours upon the saddle. He was accompanied by his two most trusted survivors, who knew the route; they watched him warily as they rode. They charged with the wind against the dawn, and the road was clear. Such was the threat of their numbers.

There was no grand call of the horns to signal this retreat. Nor was there a grand announcement of victory. Truthfully, there was a state of confusion in the Southerners as word spread of their god's retreat. If the sphere of fire had made them doubt their actions, Uden's apparent cowardice deterred the remaining Southerners from warring a moment longer.

Many dropped their blades and then fell to their knees in shock. Without the Woodin Man, they still outnumbered the Factions, but no manner of stubborn generals could stem the tide of retreat. They bent the knee to Erroh, the bringer of lightning and fire, and they called for mercy. It was no small thing to have an entire nation surrender itself to one man, and were Erroh aware of this, he might have lost his breath at such a sight.

Instead, he was beside Lea, willing her to wake up and see what her actions had done for the world.

102

AFTER THE END OF IT ALL

"What the fuk?" Emir cried, jerking awake, much to the mirth of his wife. She sat on their bed with a steaming cup of cofe in her hand, giving him a dazzling smile. She was stunning and perfect, and he squirmed in the bedclothes. He had fought her every step of the way to sleep. Now that he had slept, he had little interest in returning to the cold bloody world.

Wife.

"Good morning to you too, idiot," she said softly, offering the mug.

"Is there alcohol in it?"

She shook her head; it was a tragedy. He could feel the hangover that had been brewing since the wedded day and the night after that. "Take it, anyway. It'll set you up for the hours ahead."

"We won the war. Surely that's cause for great cheer. For a respite. For a fantastic party. For alcohol."

"Celebrations are still going on, since the last Southerner dropped to a knee, my love. Were you not sleeping off your hangover, you might have come along."

"I just want the booze, not the celebration… Not yet." As alertness came upon him, so did the sorrow of what had occurred. His hands felt tired; bloody too. And inadequate. He'd saved lives, but nowhere near enough. Nowhere near what he was capable of. He felt like a failure, and the world was less for it. She smiled sadly as he climbed out of bed.

"Aye, it feels an unnatural thing. We lost many comrades at the end." She stared at a corner in their shared tent for a breath. "Sisters."

"A brother too," Emir said, reliving the terrible moment he had learned of his friend's passing. More than a mere friend. Their bond was one of darkness and brotherhood. He suddenly wanted to be with Erroh. He didn't know why, only that Erroh would feel the loss as he did.

Emerging from the tent, he looked out across the dreadful marred landscape that had once been fields of golden crops, now drenched in red. Grieving families and friends were walking the field where their loved ones had fallen. Their wails rose and fell in a dreadful melody never spoken of in bards' tales. This song would continue with every group of Boat Town wanderers who returned to the city only to be crushed when they learned the cost of liberation. Desperate for joy, for hope, only to come upon the lined-up dead, rotting and gone forever.

The unclaimed bodies and the mourners weren't the only ones on the battlefield, however. They were joined by the Southerners who had surrendered so swiftly. Theirs was a different torment. For although they dropped to their knees, who did they serve? He'd heard whispers of dreadful penalties to be placed upon them and their Factions. And why not? Aye, they had followed their master; they had killed all in their path. They deserved what they got. For now, though, the rumours they would be marched back south were welcome. The sooner they were gone, the better. He could see their listless faces; most were still wearing the armour they'd donned and were living off pitiful scraps from the handful of carts nearly empty of rations and supplies. They were wretched, and he cursed them. But also, he knew the agony of such a station in this city.

Just send them away, Mea.

"All that life lost, all for nothing," he spat, and she leaned her head upon his shoulder. "They sit defeated, and now we must care for them."

"This is the way of humankind. Little will change; they will march home, stir a little and return in a few decades," she countered, well aware of the evils of humankind. "And if not them, then some other wretches with some other grievance." These were fair points, though unwelcome. So there would be a few decades of peace to look forward to, but war would never be too far away. He desired some peace. He wasn't alone.

Everyone was tired and broken from the violence and bloodshed on both sides. At the same time, many of the Hunt's generals had been killed, while the rest had bent a knee to the Primary or Erroh. However, the rumours of Uden's escape were spreading like wildfire. He'd expected a counterattack, a great hunt for the fiend, but instead, Uden was allowed to flee without facing a hanging rope. What was the cost of

The Actions of Gods

continuing a war that was already won? Uden would pay, this Emir knew. Perhaps once the dust settled. Perhaps.

"This place is a curse," he muttered, drinking his cofe and resenting its lack of a kick. Perhaps later, among the savages and their revelry, he might find the desire to celebrate. To get drunk. Among his kind. He'd always known he had savage blood in him, though it wasn't something his family had spoken of extensively. He had picked up his unique accent from his parents, and now hearing their tones in celebration was almost comforting. Perhaps he might someday visit the place once and for all, but he knew it was unlikely. He had more substantial worries to attend to.

A thousand miles in the opposite direction.

"Aye, a curse, but it is home, my love."

"It's no home of mine," he said sharply. His eyes were on the gates, the smouldering, charred carcass of a beast that had once been so unwelcoming. He mused that he wouldn't need to get into a fight with a goddess at all now to get through those gates.

"We'll make it your home," she whispered, tugging at his shirt. "Come on, my love; it is time to tend to your duties."

Emir was too weary to argue, though he should have. Better to speak now than hold his peace. His longings were of his home. Just not in Samara. Certainly not in the Savage Isles, either. His jaded thoughts were with a little fallen town waiting to be inhabited again.

They walked from their tent deep into the camp. Roja had commanded most of his energies be focussed on Mea, but nothing could stop him from checking in on another close friend who had suffered another close call.

"Good evening," he mumbled, stepping into the tent where an exhausted, blood-covered Erroh sat, watching a sleeping Lea. He looked like he'd been crying. Opposite him, sitting cross-legged, was Lillium. She had definitely been crying.

"How is Mea—how is the Primary?" Erroh asked, correcting himself.

Her armour had taken much of the bolt. The rest of the wound was superficial. Although no bolt was ever a little thing, she was made of tougher stuff, and he'd already concocted a delicate serum to counter any infection. Indeed, he resented that she had been his one patient for most of the hours when countless people cried out for relief, help and deliverance. It was a needful thing apparently.

Eventually, he had taken the surrendering Southern healers who had learned under his tutelage and put them to work dealing with the masses. They had been eager to please their master, and they had not let him down, and, admittedly, watching them work had made him proud. Roja had mused he would make a fine master healer, for he was "gifted at instruction to the youth." An appealing offer, no doubt, but his heart was on the road.

"Mea keeps trying to get out of bed, barking orders, demanding all she can," Roja said, and Erroh visibly relaxed.

Lillium wiped her eyes. "Same with Lea."

"Is she still collapsing?" He knew the dangers of a few heavy blows to the head. Her colour had improved, which was a good sign, but until her body tended to itself, there was little he could do with such an injury. He was skilled, but not enough to cut into her skull and go rooting around the swelling.

"She said the pain has lessened. She can sit up for a time without getting dizzy. She even managed a few steps earlier. Mostly, though, she is sleeping," Erroh offered.

"That is good," Emir said, patting his friend's shoulder. Seeing Erroh's frazzled gaze, he thought better of talking about Wynn's demise with him just now. There would be time later to mourn with his brother. So, instead, he just inspected the cool wrapping around Lea's head. He had seen such blows take a person's life a day after the injury, but her improvement was very positive. "And she speaks perfectly?"

"She's a little shaken, but her tongue is not slurred, nor is she speaking in riddles," Lillium offered, for he'd warned her of more worrying signs.

"Aren't we all? Shaken, I mean. I will stop by a little later," he offered.

Roja stepped forward and addressed Lillium. "Lea will be fine; she is far too important to this world," she said, and Emir thought them fine words. He turned to leave, so that he could prepare for the midnight watch over the injured, and she followed him out into the evening.

"You heard Emir; she is healing nicely, Erroh," Lillium insisted. She said it with enough conviction that she believed it herself. He smiled sadly and stared back at his mate. For many hours they sat in near silence but for broken discussion of their deeds, victory, and Wynn. Those were the toughest conversations and most welcomed at this time. There were few words Erroh could offer to take away the pain, and Lillium could offer him none to express how deeply she was torn by Wynn's passing, but still, what they shared was welcome. Erroh insisted she stayed close, not for his sake but for her own. It would be easier for her to sit in the darkened room with a man she loved and admired, watching over her closest friend, than to participate in the growing revelries, drinking and singing, knowing Wynn was denied such a night.

"It would be a tragedy to come this far and have her fall at the end," he offered, and she smiled weakly.

A tragedy indeed.

"I'm sorry; I didn't mean it like that."

"It's fine, dear Erroh; it was a good day for him. There are worse ways to step into the dark." She had seen so many far worse. Now she was too tired to fight anymore. Too broken to hunt his killer. For now.

"Will you let me come with you?" he asked, and she could hear him near breaking again.

Still, she denied her master general. Her friend. His friend. "I wish to do it myself," she whispered. She did this out of duty but also out of penance. She deserved it. Erroh had more argument to offer, but it was her decision. In truth, it was also for Erroh's sake she kept this task to herself. He suffered enough as it was. He would only blame himself, seeing the broken body of Wynn. Would only drop his head and lament his choices. As much as it hurt, as much as he might need to weep for his friend over a grave, tonight was a night for action. But it was also a night for levity. Their master general would do well to remember such a thing.

"As you wish," he said, looking back at Lea, who was stirring in her bedding. After a time, she blinked her eyes open wearily and sat up.

"You are still here," Lea said with little warmth. She stared at Erroh, and Lillium knew it was not the time to interfere. She'd told her part to the girl. Let her take whatever path she wanted now. A friend could only do so much. A grieving friend even less.

"Aye, we are," said Erroh, shifting in his seat and moving farther from her.

"You need to continue resting," Lillium said, standing up and leaving them to their uncomfortable silence. Although there was a coldness in Lea, there was an equal coldness in Erroh when he spoke of Lea. He sat with her out of duty because that was the Alpha mate in him; it was what Wynn would have done. Her stomach clenched unexpectedly as though she'd been struck.

"I need to be away from here; I need my horse," muttered Lea, making another feeble attempt to rise while avoiding Erroh's glare. She took her failure to defeat Uden as hard as Lillium did—a strange thing, considering Lea had been his last victim before he fled with such cowardice.

"Take care, Lea," Lillium said, slipping into the cool night air. Lillium knew the true extent of the trauma had not taken her yet, but with every passing hour, it drew nearer. Right now, though, there was a numbness that took her heart and held her steady. It wouldn't last—this she knew. It would all crumble around her, and she would feel the agony for what it was. Would suffer the crushing guilt for how she had treated him, too.

Do not think of this.

She did think on these matters, however. On all her acts of cruelty in particular, for they were as numerous as her acts of kindness. A bad coupling, no doubt. A better friendship. She wondered might things have been better had she apologised for her part. She wondered, was there any way she could have apologised? Probably not in life. In death, though, she wanted to be forgiven for all the pain she had caused, much like she forgave every shard of pain he had brought down upon her.

Think of better things.

She thought it fine advice to ignore. With a heavy heart, she made her way through the camp, keeping her head low, for she did not want to share her misery or take any of theirs upon herself. She came upon the cart he lay in and froze for a breath. It was a terrible thing to tend to the dead, and she hadn't realised how much it would hurt to do it alone. She almost considered delaying this awfulness and asking Erroh and the rest of the Outcasts to attend after all. Wynn might have liked that. But this was her penance; this was what she deserved. She picked up the shovel standing alongside the cart and slipped it in beside her dead mate's body.

"Hello, demon," Nomi called from behind Lillium, and the girl recoiled. "I'm sorry; I thought you saw me approach." She could see what Lillium intended, for she knew what rested within the cart. No warrior should have been laid to rest alone. No friend should tend to the task alone, either. Without invitation, she climbed up on the cart beside her. Looking back at his frozen body, she shuddered. Wynn had been torn apart, gutted and ruined, and Nomi lamented the loss just as much as her Outcast comrades.

"I was going to tend to him myself," Lillium mumbled, and Nomi rested her arm on her quaking shoulders as Lillium wept silently. "But

I'll take the company," she said, urging the horse forward slowly. Together, they journeyed into the dark forest where he belonged, all concealed in natural things.

"Why do you do this alone?" Nomi asked after a time. It was some question. A cutting question.

"Tonight is no night for morbid ritual. Tonight is a time to be grateful for survival. For victory. People need this. You and the rest of the generals need this night too. Wynn would have demanded it."

Lulled by the gentle sway of the cart, Nomi thought hard on her words. She could see her fragile friend was close to shattering. "Perhaps, but why not wait until tomorrow?"

"I cannot stand the thought of him lying in this cart, rotting away. I need to do this. It is my right; it is my duty," she whispered, and began to weep again. "It is my penance."

They travelled silently for a time, but as they passed the last of the tents, Drahir appeared. He had spent his time among the Southerners all wretched day. Nomi had watched from the outskirts, daring to do little more than walk among them with her head bowed. He, however, had gone to task, offering what aid and supplies he could find and delivering them by the cartload to the humbled army. He never stopped walking among them, offering reassuring words, setting them at ease as much as he could. Strangely, many listened to him. Perhaps, in Drahir, they saw the shaded image of Uden among them, stirring them for the future. Or else they saw the sins of his father, who'd escaped without retribution.

Such a thought was abhorrent to Nomi, but hers was not to demand the sacrifice of a madman for her vengeance when greater political things were at play. Aye, there wasn't a day when she hadn't thought of her treatment, gazed upon her scars, or thought of little Mish, but her desires paled when she thought of those who'd lost more than she. She was satisfied with her lot in life. Perhaps, in time, so too would her people be when they returned to the South.

Drahir jogged alongside, grinning, and Nomi dismissed him with a glare. "Not now, Drahir," she snapped, and Lillium looked away from him lest she display her tears for the Southerner to see.

Since Drahir had first started talking with her, he hadn't left her side. He was like a little pup, eager for her praise. She wondered had he listened to Erroh a little too much about love and one's for life. He wasn't unattractive, but her mind was on more substantial things. She was no longer part of the Hunt; she no longer followed their ways.

Absently, she rubbed her belly and felt an emptiness she hadn't felt in quite a time. She wasn't confident about what to do with herself now that the war was over. She would most certainly return to the South. It had been too long since she'd tasted the chill of that unforgiving place. It was strange what a little bit of peace could do to the mind.

Drahir pledged that her name would be revered among her people. That her voice would be listened to. The lover of Erroh and the mother of the South, he claimed they whispered in the wind. She was disinclined to believe such a thing, but her people were hurt. They had endured decades of hurt, long before Uden came to power. If her name carried weight, who was she to step away when she could ease some of that pain? That was the finest of reasons to leave with the rest of the South on their lonely, bitter return home.

"He likes you," Lillium said, sniffing, before slowing near the treeline.

"He's unimpressive." Nomi had seen his fierceness; he had never recoiled or taken a step back in battle. He'd answered her orders as though they were Erroh's and had gone to task each time, killing any around him. Such things were impressive indeed. She just thought him capable of more than merely standing with her, protecting her. He suffered an affliction of the vision, no doubt. Short-sightedness. She wondered if he was besotted with her rear. It must have been her rear, for little old Nomi of the South was hardly worth anything. To allow him to suffocate her with his presence would be a disservice to him, to the South. To someone claiming to matter.

The two friends dropped from the cart, and a stillness came upon the world. No insect or creature stirred, for they must have known the terrible task at hand. Carefully, with Nomi taking the brunt of the weight, they eased Wynn's body from the cart and carefully carried him into the trees. There it was nearly pitch-black, but for the light of the shattered moon guiding their steps.

"Here is good," Lillium said after a time, lowering him carefully to the ground. "Concealed, but with a nice view of the city when the lights are on," she whispered, and Nomi looked through the thick undergrowth to the shadowed monstrosity far across the valley. She supposed it was a decent view. She began digging into the soft earth with the shovel. Lillium attempted to take the tool from her grip, but with a shake of the head, Nomi denied her. It was not for her to bury her lover, former or not.

Within a few hours, the deed was done, and they placed his body into the deep hole. Nomi immediately began to cover him up.

The Actions of Gods

"I'm sorry, Wynn," Lillium whispered as the dirt covered his head. "I'm so, so sorry."

Nomi continued for a time, heaving the dirt down and covering him. She felt her tears slip free, and she felt like a thief taking away from her friend's grief. Eventually, with the ground smoothed out, Nomi left Lillium to weep alone. But not before embracing her once and bidding her gaze upon the night above. "He's gone from here," Nomi whispered, and looked at the beauty of the night sky. "Look to the stars and speak with him then."

"Perhaps so," Lillium whispered, falling to her knees by the grave. She inscribed his name and heroic deeds on a large rock. She slid it across the top of the grave, and Nomi thought it a fitting, beautiful end to a tremendous warrior. And a friend. With a delicate bow she left her friend where she knelt. Some tears needed to be shed privately. Nomi would cry again for Wynn, no doubt. But Lillium was correct. Tonight was a night for celebrations.

Stepping away from the woods, she returned to the camps, listening to the low rumble of celebration. She smiled sadly and wondered if Lea would rise, join in and play her part in the festivities. Would Erroh be there too?

"I was waiting for you," a Southern voice called in her tongue, and she knew it to be her shadow.

Drahir had been lost these last few days, unsure of his place beyond the war. He had belonged by Erroh's side for a time, but the gathering of his comrades had brought only casual indifference from his master general. To be fair, the boy carried the world upon his shoulders and held it better than most. It was a weight Drahir had once desired. Not now. Seeing his father flee like a coward had been the final strike that shook him. It was no small thing to realise an entire life had been lived for nothing. He had always sought out power for himself, a trait passed down from his bastard father, no doubt. Seeing Lea act as she did with her lot was also sobering. He had never understood the notion of happiness beyond striving for greatness, beyond challenging, rising, killing and victory.

In Nomi, he saw something else entirely. There was such threat to her, and such warmth; he was taken with her more than he had ever been with any woman before. She didn't appear to reciprocate or be impressed with him, but this intrigued Drahir a little more.

Truthfully, it wasn't her appearance that drew him to her, though she was incredibly alluring; it was her power over her people. They whispered her name as they did Erroh's. It was no small thing to be revered by a nation, yet, there she was, unperturbed by it and uninterested in such things. A man could do a lot worse than learn from such a woman. So could an entire Faction, too.

For the first time in his wretched life, Drahir chose to follow another without the threat of violence, without the promise of reward. He wasn't sure where this path would take him, but he was determined to be by her side. More than that, to place her upon his shoulders so the world could see her that much more easily. He mused that desiring to put someone else into power was a step towards betterment. It was certainly better than watching from afar as his father tore the world asunder.

"Why do you haunt me?" Nomi snapped, and he grinned despite the slight. He was a willing and stubborn acolyte; he could outlast her dislike of him. More than that, he could serve her even if she had no idea of her value.

"Will you walk with me a time?" he asked in their tongue. She was usually a lot nicer when she spoke in her native tongue. He also thought she had an attractive tongue. He'd said as much; she hadn't seemed to care.

Muttering under her breath, she walked with him back through the camp. He loved her hair. It never seemed out of place, no matter the grime or gore upon her.

"Why are you looking at my hair?"

"It's fine hair."

"I know; I brushed it." He enjoyed this easy conversation, though he did not know why. It should have irritated him.

"So, will you come to my bed tonight?" he asked. He'd asked such a question a thousand times before of other women, with tremendous success. It was a mere formality between Southerners. He had taken no lover in such a long time. He hated that fact, but this was how the Northern Faction played, and furrowing with her would be worth the alluring frustration.

"Stop asking me," she muttered, as she had before.

"As you desire, my dear."

She didn't seem convinced, and he determined to wait at least a day until he asked again, no matter how powerful his urges. For a time, they walked through the camp, watching the growing revelry, watching the misery. It was a strange thing to be among both things at once, yet here they were. As they walked, they spoke of lesser things; he was always a step to the side and a half step behind. They reached the edge of the battlefield, where their people remained for now.

Until we march home.

Truthfully, he was wary of such a march. Not the preparation, for they were an itinerant race, willing to gather and trudge at a moment's notice; finding supplies and food along the way as they did. It was returning to their frozen homeland that worried him so. His father was crippled by grief over Cordelia's appearance, but how long would that shock last before he stirred again? Not only that, but there was the sobering thought of returning with such a defeat as their legacy. A race would struggle to rebuild after that.

We had it all, and now we must freeze in the South again.

His people needed something more. Someone more.

"What now?" she asked, looking at the thousands of Southerners stretched out in the blood-soaked grass and mud, waiting for a king, a leader, or someone else to tell them what to do. How to behave. They were a defeated army with little fight left, watched over by a handful of Wolves. They were humbled, and it was the most sobering thing of all.

"Talk to them; they need someone to reassure them."

"What are you talking about?"

"You are Nomi of the South, chosen by Erroh; they know you," he said, and she laughed. If she'd looked to the nearest group, she might have seen how they sat silently, watching her, waiting to be led.

"I am unimportant."

"Not to me, not to them," Drahir said, gripping her shoulder, looking into her devastatingly beautiful eyes. "Please, just walk among them, tell them all will be well, tell them the South beckons."

"I know none of this," she argued, but her eyes were sparkling with intrigue—such pretty eyes.

"Will you watch over them if asked?"

"Of course. I still love the South."

"Go speak with your kin," he urged, and bowed theatrically so that anyone watching might know she was the one they spoke of, the one that he pledged for. "And I will be by your side, my queen," he whispered.

He might have failed as a leader of the Hunt, but that wasn't to say he could not offer support to those who came after. His father would have hated being in such a position. This intrigued him most of all.

Doran looked on as Nomi walked among the Southerners, speaking quietly with them in her language. He might have seen such a thing as worrisome long ago and sought to question her motives. But now, he had learned the value of recognising his shortcomings, judgements and cruelties. He was no old man, but he felt older, wiser and more compassionate. However, he was worried this night. Not all his surviving brothers had returned to gather up. Aymon, his lover Azel, and a dozen others had not appeared since the fleeing of the mad god. A worrying thing, mused Doran, thinking of Aymon's stubborn dedication. It wasn't enough to rout the army. That said, Doran wondered if Aymon was right, and charging after the god was the better decision. In contrast, all the others had gladly accepted peace without further bloodshed.

Where are you, old friend?

Perhaps you've gone hunting our old Wolfen leader while you are at it?

To the fires with you, Dane.

It was a terrible thing that Aymon hadn't offered him the chance to ride with them. Two lunatic Alpha males were better than one in a fight, any day.

Truthfully, though, while Aymon walked one path, he took another. Doran would not have taken up the cause with him. It was just a little galling that his comrade had not waited for him. How many times had Doran sacrificed his own betterment for his unsettled friend's sake?

Fuken typical.

He could feel the anger rise, and he allowed it. Allowed his sadness to fuel thoughts of a little vengeance. "I deserved better," he muttered to the wind, feeling no shame. Anger or no, he still hoped to come upon his friend again. If not for the chance to strike him, then for a chance to hug him in relief that he'd survived these terrible times.

I'll never see him again.

He distracted himself from these lamenting thoughts by watching Nomi walking among the Southerners, and truthfully, she appeared to bring a strange serenity to them, like the utterings of a god over a flock of tragic zealots. He did not hate them anymore. He wasn't sure he'd ever truly hated them, away from the red mist of battle. He knew them to be human. He knew them to be deserving of humane treatment too.

Fifty of his comrades watched over them now, but there was no need to stand guard. They were docile, and it was a beautiful thing. The city offered what food stores they could, and they kept their mouths wet with fresh water. They required no chains either. Once Mea recovered, he imagined amnesty would be in the air. He'd argue for it. Alas, he was but one Alpha in this war—hardly likely to sway her opinion.

Still, though.

Nomi offered a smile as she passed, but her eyes were wet with tears after hearing the tales of those who had fought and yielded. It was no small thing to be among a routed army, Doran remembered. He bowed slightly and decided he'd had quite enough of watching over the prisoners.

Prisoners?

He nearly laughed at the thought. He watched over the remains of a nation, beaten down and humbled.

"I will take my leave," he muttered to a Wolf sitting nearby who was currently engaging in broken conversation with a rather attractive Southerner. They looked taken with each other, and not for the first time did Doran wonder just how passionately the South had actually desired this march in the first place. "I need a fuken drink."

The Wolf waved him away and returned to describing the finer details of catching fish in his hometown. The Southern girl appeared riveted.

Continuing on through the battlefield, he met many glances and a few bows but little anger. It was strange, he mused; they took defeat better than he could have imagined. It was a relief; it was simply part of their upbringing to gather closer to the stronger clans, as though this was little more than an arranged coupling. He thought about this and decided it was a healthy way of warring. Better than prisoners and executions too.

Distantly, he could hear the sounds of music and a gathering of people enjoying better times. Although he was in no great mood for a celebration, he desired a drink, good cheer, and distraction. Distantly, he caught sight of Lillium dropping down from a cart, and he immediately changed direction. She, of all his generals, understood the agony of loss. And after a few drinks, he might have liked to share a tear or two with someone needing similar things.

She didn't flee when he approached; to his astonishment, she leapt into his arms and sobbed uncontrollably. Doran held her, hushing her without words, until eventually, she drew away from him, looking embarrassed at the wet patches on his shoulder.

"Thank you, Doran," she whimpered, and his heart broke in agony. He wished he had the words to take the pain. He was no good with words, or with females for that matter.

"Perhaps you might walk with me to the celebrations and tell me every story you can of the legend Wynn," he whispered, and she wiped further tears from her beautiful face as she nodded and followed his lead.

Towards the far side of the camp where the savages reigned, the gathering was reaching its zenith—due in no small way to the reserves of sine recovered from the city as the grand retaking began.

Throughout, there was laughter and song, mocking and revelry, and immediately, far from the sombreness of the Southern prisoners, Doran began to feel better in himself. There was even Wrek upon a cart, pouring out sine after sine, ale after ale, to any who wanted it. Doran waved across at him, but the behemoth was too busy.

He would have called for him, but Doran was suddenly distracted by a venomous Alpha male looking for blood.

"Everyone likes you now, but I still think you are a fuken asshole," the Alpha cried hysterically.

"No, no, that's fuken wrong," Tye hissed. "I *know* you are a fuken asshole." Unsurprisingly, the little cub was drunk. It seemed like the thing to do. It was either that or fall apart. He didn't want to fall apart. He wanted to keep going. He wanted to start a fight. He needed to keep fighting. He wanted it to end.

So, he swung at the bald bastard Alpha male and was lesser for it. In truth, he had no real issue with Doran, but he had to attack someone. So, the hulking brute was as good as any victim, he supposed. Problem was, Doran was quick. Quicker than he'd expected.

Looking back, Tye might have picked a better opponent if he had thought on the matter a moment longer. As it was, Doran dodged his strike and countered with a jab of his own. It was a light strike that buckled Tye's shaky knees. He collapsed onto his rear, where he sat momentarily, trying to comprehend his actions and remember where the war hammer had struck him from. Dragging himself to his unsteady feet, he gestured for his opponent to wait as he tended to the mud patches on the seat of his pants. "They'll call me Shitpants," he muttered.

"What are you doing, Tye?" Lillium hissed. She did not attempt to block his way, nor Doran's either.

"Enough of this shit, boy," Doran warned, as Tye, leaving his marred garments, attempted a wild, arcing kick. It came up short, and the young Alpha jarred his knee something awful. It didn't matter. He didn't stop coming. He spun around the brute, jabbed for himself and landed a strike upon Doran's clean-shaven chin. It was like striking a marble wall.

"What the fuk?" he cried, leaping away and grabbing his throbbing hand.

At this, Doran slapped him open-palmed across the face. With the same hand, he slapped him across the other cheek, a humiliating blow, before stepping away, leaving him to his embarrassment.

"If you can't best a one-handed man in a fight, perhaps a change of approach is needed," Doran said evenly. It was a threat, a jest, and were Tye drunker, younger, he might have reached for his blade. As it was, he finally met the older Alpha's eyes and realised his drunken misstep.

"I'm lost," he muttered, and collapsed in the mud. His head spun, and Doran dropped to a knee beside him.

"You carry much horror, don't you?"

"Fuk off. I carry enough that I can take."

"I, too, made mistakes," Doran said, and Tye hated how rational and gentle the brute sounded. "All Alphas do. Best we can do is learn from them."

"You aren't my father; you aren't Erroh; you aren't my master. Why are you talking to me as though you are a master? You are just a fuk."

Doran laughed, as did Lillium. Hearing Lillium's laughter was a welcome, sobering tonic. "I may be such a thing. Though, I'm not sure I'm the one you are mad with."

"I'm mad with everyone," Tye blurted out before he could stop himself. He wasn't mad at everyone. Just a few people was all. The Southerners who had attacked his mother. And whoever had killed Wynn. Some comrades too. A pretty comrade, to be exact.

"What can I do to stop you from being mad at me?" Doran asked, stepping away and pulling him to his feet. He braced himself for another onslaught, and Tye hated how charmingly disarming he was.

"You nearly killed Erroh; I fuken knew about that," Tye mumbled, but they were drunken ramblings. The fuker was right; he was only mad at Lexi for leaving him when he needed her most. It was no small matter to be betrayed like that, regardless of the reasons.

Fuken females.

"Alphas don't play well," Lillium argued, and he nodded his head. They didn't. Although, for a time in Raven Rock, they had.

A flood of sorrow overcame him, and he embraced Lillium, weeping. "I'm sorry. I shouldn't have done that. I don't know what I'm doing. I never do. And I get so scared. And it was terrible," he babbled, and she said nothing but hushed him to calm.

When he drew away, Doran was smiling. "You nearly took my head off," he offered, holding his chin. A fine thing to hear. Especially from a master. "This time next year, I reckon you'd have me beaten outright."

"Perhaps we will see then," Tye said, slipping away from Lillium and feeling ashamed of his actions. He offered a bow to the Alphaline he'd assaulted. It was the best he could do.

Doran grinning, bowed in return, and for a breath Tye felt a little better. "Until then, drink more and fight less, little cub," Doran offered, and Tye nodded in agreement, although he knew he had one other fight in him this evening.

"Aye, sir, maybe I will," he said, pulling himself away.

I'm an idiot.

He stumbled through the gathered groups of revellers, and it was a blur. He had spent hours before, drinking among them, enjoying their banter, marvelling at their acceptance of war, death, and anything in between. He'd pledged to many along the way that he would gladly sail to their beautiful country and see its brutal beauty after walking the road. But only after he had spent a little time with his family.

Mea had given him a pledge that cut through the armour of most of his anger. In a few words, she had promised him something he'd no idea he'd craved. He wanted his mother back; he wanted his family back. Such things should have eased the anger from him. And perhaps they did.

Looking around the gathering, though, he spied the main reason for his rage this night: Alexis, though she hated being called that, stood there glamorous and timid, as though she weren't a goddess in the making. He watched her get a drink. He suddenly wanted a drink too.

Lexi drank heartily, even though she knew this beverage would put her over the edge. The world was spinning, her stomach churning the few morsels of honey bread she'd toasted. It was a small matter. She wanted to forget everything. The blood, the horror, her cruelty, her victims. It was no small thing to have so many deaths on her hands. So she drank and tried to forget.

To my beautiful Wynn.

"There you are," she said drunkenly, catching sight of Tye. He had not spoken to her all day. Not since the end of the war.

The Actions of Gods

The end of the war.

She wandered over to him, hands outstretched, head tipping from side to side. "Catch me," she mumbled, and fell against him and immediately slid to her knees. It hurt. It was embarrassing, and a flash of anger took her. "Did you not hear me?"

"I heard you."

"Well, I fuken fell over."

"You did." He sounded as drunk as she. That was fine. She could stumble around with him and drink until dawn. Then she could cry. Then throw up. And he'd be there to hold her hair.

"I knew you were alive, but I didn't see you all day. We could have talked—could have talked about Wynn. I was there. It was terrible."

"I would say it was."

"Why are you looking at me like that?" She wavered a little as she climbed to her feet. She leaned against a cart brimming with massive barrels of sine, all ready to be consumed. He was staring through her. She didn't like that gaze. Not one little bit.

"I'm not looking at you in any way, Alexis."

"You fuken are, and don't fuken call me that."

"Well, I'm sorry you were in the midst of the battle. I'm sorry you were alone. I'm fuken sorry I wasn't there. I'm sorry you weren't fuken beside me."

She looked at him for a moment. She didn't think he was sorry at all. "Fuk off."

"Fine, I will," he snarled, and stumbled away, knocking into a group of revellers as he did. "Sorry, sorry," he muttered, trying to hold on to some dignity.

He is sorry for them.

She chased after him. Mad, alarmed, clumsy. "Wait, idiot, I didn't mean that," she slurred, and, stumbling past the same group, knocked a few beverages from similarly drunken hands. It was near enough to cause a riot. "Sorry, sorry, friends," she called. The savages were delighted with her drunkenness and took no offence. It was one of the finer traits of their kind. Or else they knew her lineage. Wasn't she technically their royal princess? Thinking more on it, simply being a relative gave her no divine right to leadership. That was how things became rightly fuked.

"Are you upset about when I left you? So you could be with your mother? Fuk off. I wasn't out of the fight. I still had some warring to do."

That stumped him rightly, and she smiled smugly. She even leaned against an empty barrel of sine with a bit of arrogance. Sometimes winning an argument was the finest feeling in the world. Sometimes, when she had nothing else, winning an argument was enough.

"Whatever your reasons, you left me when I needed you most," he murmured, and she could hear the pain in his slurred words. He looked ready to cry. She didn't want him to cry. She loved the fuker. He meant the world to her.

"I needed to go," she said weakly, and he shook his head as though he expected as much. She hated that he expected that.

"You did what you had to do."

"I am sorry, my dear friend."

"I'm going to go check on Mom and Dad," he said, looking away.

"Can I come too?"

"No, it's fine. Enjoy this celebration. We deserve it."

"We can talk when things have calmed down," she said, gliding up to him, taking his grubby hands in hers.

"We might, but I'm not staying here long."

She didn't like this at all. "What do you mean?"

"I think I need a little time." He looked to the darkness. "I think I need to see the road a little."

In that moment, she could see the incredible man he had become. She could see him walking the road, learning to be an even greater Alphaline, while she would lie languidly in the city, where her life would resume, and stay until she was chosen.

She suddenly wanted to leave with him. Wanted to face the world as equals. To become the best little Alphas they could be. Away from the city, away from everything she had known. He didn't ask her to come, though, even when she asked silently with her eyes.

"Ask me to walk the Wastes with you?" she asked. She wanted to see his eyes sparkle in delight.

"So you can leave me again should you find something of greater interest?"

"Well, perhaps," she said, laughing. He turned away, seeking an escape. "Hey, where are you going?" she cried. She was annoyed at him for not asking, and for not answering correctly either. Fuk him.

"Goodbye, Lexi. Live well, my friend," he muttered.

No, no, no, this isn't goodbye.

She ran after him; her mind was awash with thoughts and frustrations. She didn't want him to be mad. She wanted to celebrate with him. She wanted to march the road with him. She wanted more than this. "Will we walk together?" she cried. He was marching at pace, and she was running. Desperate and stumbling too.

He spun on her, grabbed her shoulders with a firm grip, looked her in the eyes, and she wavered drunkenly. Perhaps it was him. "We were a good team. I treasured every moment, but I fulfilled my oath to Erroh."

"What are you saying?" she demanded. She could feel tears coming. She didn't know why. This wasn't fair.

"Goodbye, dear friend; I will see you soon."

With that, he left her behind, and she could only watch him wander into the night. She knew she had hurt him, though not to that extent. She wanted to scream at him. To cry out for him. "Goodbye, Tye. I will see you soon." Her voice sounded hollow. He didn't wave back. He never looked back either, and she stood for too long watching him disappear from her life. She wiped the tears away, knowing their companionship had ended in a drunken whisper.

Not knowing what else to do, she wandered back to her parents' tent, where, drunken and stumbling, she fell into her mother's arms and wept.

"Well, fuken good riddance, so," muttered Magnus, and Elise shushed him to silence. She grasped her daughter and took her affection openly.

"It hurts," Lexi muttered. Her first love had broken her heart, and Elise could only hush her for a time until she began to doze. Then, with her mate's help, she lifted her into their bed.

"So does this mean I can find another suitable bed companion for the night?" Magnus asked brazenly. He dazzled her with a smile, and for a moment, Elise nearly considered it. It was his last night without a crown. Better to go out with a bang, she supposed. Not only would it give her peace from his drunken snoring, but it would also help her to get on his better side. There were things afoot that might dampen his lust for her.

"Behave, you old fool," she warned softly, then took his hand, kissed him and led him out to the revelries.

"Aye, I suppose not," he said, laughing. She loved seeing his face free of the torment of strain. For too long, he'd carried the world on his back. It wasn't he who had donned the Clieve, though. It wasn't he who had turned the tide, even if he had played his part. Tonight, Magnus understood that he had finally played his role in history. A lesser man might have regretted such a thing. Might have held desperately onto power. That had never been his goal, though. He'd craved peace and civility, although he hadn't been able to accomplish it. His son had. It was a fine thing to see Magnus's pride in such a thing. And she was as proud as he was.

Proud and driven. She still had deeds to be done, but she could not speak them aloud. "Come, let's get ourselves another drink." Leaving his hounds to sit and watch over their drunken ruin of a daughter, they returned to the gathering for a nightcap that could last until dawn. She led him through the crowd, which parted in their wake. Southerners, bandits, savages all stepped aside to let their legend pass. This type of respect was a fine thing to have earned before retiring, she supposed.

Retire?

"So little Lexi doesn't want to wait in the city for a man to take her?" Magnus muttered, and Elise hugged him gently.

"You love the idea of her out there in the Wastes?"

"Do you remember the little shit Erroh was before he walked the world?"

"A fine point," she offered. "And besides, there's less chance there of her becoming a prize calf to be culled."

"I know what goes through the minds of young men."

"She's too much like me," Elise offered. It was a compelling argument.

"Oh, fuk me, I hope not. Let's take her home, strap her to a post and never let her leave us again."

Home.

They neared a gathering of Magnus's generals, and she pulled him aside to a bench. It was currently occupied by a dozen revelling bandits mocking each other's accents, manhoods, chest size and rears to all who would listen. Her softly spoken orders cut through their camaraderie like a pickpocket's knife through a leather purse.

"Leave us."

Within a breath, they were alone, and she sat on the bench and dragged him down to eye level.

Home.

"Can you hear my lungs' deathly rattle?" she asked, and his face darkened.

"What do you mean? I haven't heard it since you arrived here."

"Adawan is my bastion, my love."

"And you are the queen of that place."

"You will not have royalty in this family," she argued, and he smiled as though he knew this and all her fears besides. He reached for her and kissed her cheek.

"So, I am not free to find a beauty to ease my pain this night?"

"Magnus, you fuk, I'm serious. I cannot leave Adawan. I can breathe in that place."

Magnus kissed her again, and fuk him, but he was charming, even when acting the cad.

"You think for a moment I haven't questioned Emir on such things? He was barely finished stitching up Mea, and the trumpets of victory were still blaring, but there I was, questioning that genius about your health. He offered several suggestions, but mostly he muttered something about the salt mines helping your chest."

"Aye, so you see."

"We could always seek out a salt mine nearer to the east."

"Perhaps in time, if I decide to relinquish my leadership," Elise said and hesitated. "Would you deny me this earned crown now, though?" She added carefully.

"Would you have me by your side? As your lover in waiting?"

Her heart beat in excitement. "Would you live in Adawan?"

He gripped her hands tightly, his eyes sincere. "You are the only person that has ever known me. All I want is to slip away from history, my love. You offer me a place behind you, the chance to live in the shadows doing little more than offer you advice?" He peered into her soul, and she loved him anew. "Not advice to be taken either, mind, yet still, I will retire a happy man."

"You would do this for me?"

"I would burn the world for you, fight wars in your name, kill everyone in your honour, but more than that, I would live a quieter life with you."

"It might not be peaceful, but we will have each other."

"A man could die happily with such things."

She kissed him and whispered in his ear. "Happy birthday, my love."

"But it's not… Oh…"

Magnus watched Elise move among her bandits for a while and was glad of his words. Seeing her face light up in such a way was glorious. Although each was as impressive as the other, his name carried greater weight. It was time for her to make a path for herself without the burden of an affliction preventing her star from rising. Aye, he was anxious for the future, and while he loved his home, it was nothing without her.

He grinned, thinking of his retirement among such fiends. It would be interesting, as would the sight of Elise putting manners on the brutes. Truthfully, it would not harm the rebuilding of Spark to have Elise as so close an ally. Nor would it damage the civilising of this place, Adawan, he'd heard so much about. With the growing of Boat Town, there was also no harm in humanity spreading further into the Wastes. And Magnus would be there to see it all—better that than hiding away in the east as he had done.

I have no kingdom to keep an eye on, either.

He smiled again and felt the weight upon his brow lift a little.

"Speak to us, Magnus," Teaolor cried from among the gathering. She was king now, but until she set sail, this victory was his, and this kingdom was his too. Around her, his savage generals cheered in agreement, and their sincerity moved him. He considered them magnificent warriors, born for war but wise enough to watch over his savage, beautiful lands. More than that, they would be bonded in battle under Teaolor's rule. Some things were priceless. He thought momentarily about the trials and felt weary in his bones. He'd miss none of that.

They cheered and demanded until he finally climbed atop a bench with a glass of sine in his hand. His voice echoed across the savage gathering and all the Factions, who listened intently.

"These days were brutal, beautiful days, and there were no greater warriors to stand with at the end."

They loved this; they cheered loudly.

"Perhaps, if Curroi and his clan had stood with us, we might have lost fewer kin."

The crowd booed for the absence of the cur, and Magnus grinned. Let the annals of time show his cowardice.

"However, our people still marched to the aid of allies in dire need. Our people showed a deeper mercy than has ever been known, and they did it with nerve, steel and honour. No greater feat has ever been accomplished."

They agreed. They let him know.

"And I have never been prouder to bleed with such legends this last time."

They knew this, and they applauded.

"My time is gone." He looked to Teaolor and raised his glass. "But a king, greater than me, shall soon rise… To Teaolor," he roared, and the crowd cheered loudest. Even the bandits joined in, even the victorious Southerners. The crowd cheered her name over and over as Magnus at last stepped away from leadership and responsibility with a victorious whisper.

"That was perfect," Elise said, kissing him. She was eager to enjoy the festivities, as was Magnus. But only when he presented himself to the Primary so she could learn of his intentions. It was no small thing to know that a leader of a terrifying force was stepping down, to be replaced by a younger warrior eager to step out of a godly shadow, keen to stamp their authority on their legacy.

She took it rather well.

Mea sat up in her bed, scratching at her bandaged wound. It wasn't itchy; it was merely the idea of the thing. It was something to do while listening to a legend admit his demise. She thought it a shame and a worry that the Savage Isles might be ruled by another with possible ideas of invasion, having seen the fragility of their forces as she had. Mea didn't care anymore. She should have been out of bed, scrambling to the gathering, honouring this Teaolor with all the plaudits due to her while still showing her teeth. Instead, she squirmed beneath her covers and allowed the great man to deliver his sermon.

When he had finished, she did her duties. She praised his heroism, spoke highly of the debt the city could never repay, and offered him a reward for his actions before providing her admission to him alone, one that he pledged not to speak of. Knowing her value was lessened, he stayed longer than needed, speaking warmly with her and Jeroen, thanking them for their duty and heroism, before offering a bow and retiring to the celebrations.

It was only after Roja returned that she felt better about herself.

"Is the task done?"

"Aye, it is," said Roja, smiling. She wore a look of relief that matched Mea's own. This war had taken so much from them both. Here they sat in a haven of a healer's making, surrendering what responsibilities they could. Mea most of all. And Roja? Well, she took on precisely what she could, and Mea was grateful to her for her sacrifices and responsibilities.

"You look tired, little one," Mea said, and Roja smiled sadly.

"There is much to do, and I am not sure my heart is in it."

"You have served the city and your people better than most; you have earned whatever you desire." She took Roja's hand, as any Primary would with a diligent servant seeking reassurance. It was the mother in her.

"I fear Emir desires a path away from the city lights."

"I know the cost of a mating where both look upon differing things; you cannot have it both ways."

"I love the city, but I love my husband. One is duty; the other is happiness."

"So, you have made up your mind?" Mea asked. She wasn't worried about the young female's actions at all. She would make the right choice in the end. The smarter ones always did.

"It changes by the moment. Mostly, when I am not around him."

"Your husband is a good man," Mea offered, and again Roja smiled sadly.

"He would be worth giving up the entire city," she whispered, lest Emir be listening from outside the tent, giggling at her devotion.

"I know mine is," Mea said. "Though it took me far too long to realise it."

103

KINGLY WAYS

Massey was tired. The type of tiredness that came with being old. She felt ancient this dreadful, sunny morning. Not because of her years, though they were many, but because of the thoughts running through her mind. It wasn't every day a broken Alphaline considered actions of such importance that they would change the world's future.

On the surface, she was similar to every other wretch from Boat Town who had streamed back into Samara in the days after the great victory, but underneath, there was more. A spark of excitement, a mind brimming with ideas for the future. Something unbefitting one who appeared as jaded and ruined as she. She had little interest in the revelry occurring in the city now, though she was grateful for the change in mood. Gone was the feeling of despair and terror, replaced now with a foolish sense of optimism. War was finished, they said, but she knew better. She'd seen enough in her years. Humanity was capable of beauty, love, kindness and mercy, but it was also driven by the desire for advancement. It was a shame that war walked hand in hand with such a thing. And war was always in the wind.

These last two decades had been a success, but such was the fragility of the lands, it could have never worked in the long run. And she had thought on this conundrum all those miserable days and nights in the floating fortress. It was all she could do with a body so old and jaded that only the mind could offer solace. In thoughts she had hidden, and in thoughts she had come upon better things.

A balance of things, to be precise.

Righting the wrongs of humanity was a welcome distraction as she stepped beneath the battered remains of the gates into the ruined city beyond. She had nearly stayed behind to protect her library, even as the fires burned in Samara's heart on the last day. She patted the sword at her side. She was no warrior anymore, but she might have lasted a while before the Hunt roared through her front door, waving their blades and their ignorance in her face. Instead, she had fled a mad god, knowing well the knowledge left behind was far more important than her paltry existence.

Human.

She wasn't used to seeing the city so bereft of life. She had been one of the first to return; such was her station. Soon enough, it would fill up again, the world would turn, and people would behave as they had done before. Mistakes would be made once more.

For now, though, it was nearer to a graveyard. All around her were debris and death, and only now did she truly regret not seeing the grand retaking of Samara. To be able to say she was there. Warriors made dreadful bards. Better a wily old female to recount the details for future generations so they might learn. Brave were those who fought; brave, too, were those who observed and remembered. She should have been here, she thought shamefully.

She wasn't used to hearing her feet echo so clearly on the cold stone. She felt a right old wretch shuffling along these quiet streets; those she passed likely didn't recognise her. Aye, to some, she was an ageing librarian with thoughts above her station, but to a few others, who knew her potential, she was known to be a proven Alphaline of this city. Proud and selfless in the service of humanity. She was Massey of Samara, but she was so much more.

With ideas.

She did not visit her home first, for there was little comfort in the thought of the wreckage it had likely become. It was towards her library that she shuffled along, warmed by her thoughts, chilled by the sights she passed. Crushed bodies. Timeless walls scorched to black. Sturdy buildings cracked or ground completely to dust. Many taverns had survived, however, and were she not so bitter, she might have laughed at the absurdity. Given the empty barrels she'd passed upon the bloody battlefield, she doubted any surviving tavern would be opened soon. She thought of that bastard Sigi and hoped he had met his end somewhere in the Wastes. She considered this cur more to blame than any other.

Eventually, she turned the corner of the side street leading to her library and fell to her knees in disbelief. The entire side street had been

The Actions of Gods

battered as though a god had reached down from the heavens and crushed each structure to nothing. Each neighbouring building had also been destroyed, leaving nothing but shells of what they had once been.

However, whatever horrors had taken those buildings had swept past her treasure without harm. More than that, some Southerners had apparently seen that the building survived whatever attacks it faced. Mounds of rubble from other structures had been placed along each side, masterfully stacked and supported and layered high into the sky on all sides, protecting it from bombardment. The windows and doors were bricked up as though the building were a shell for the ages, and she wept tears of gratitude that some fiend had seen the value in her vision.

It took her time to rally enough wandering Wolves to assist in breaking through the bricked-up entrance. Once the transient wall had finally collapsed under the strain of their blows, she slipped past their hammers and pick-axes like a child eager for treasures. In better days, her door handle had stuck in its lock. But now, after such a time, hidden away, it took all her weight to shift it enough to break through.

"Come back to me in a few hours," she ordered the Wolves, upon granting herself entrance. Their tasks were not done for the day. Nor were hers. She had much to do, but couldn't help checking on her beloved library before tending to the world's changing.

Instinctively she flicked the light switches a couple of times, although she knew full well there was no electricity. Then, with a quivering hand, she lit a candle and ventured through her sanctuary in search of her riches. She first came upon her printing press, pristine but for a few layers of dust and a cobweb or two. "How safe you must have been while so many Southerners were crushed and burned," she whispered, blowing at a spider escaping her presence. She ran her excited fingers along the surface of the press, caressing it fondly.

She then ventured further into the building to where the capsules were displayed, and to her shock, she came upon her collection, clean, immaculate and apparently read quite recently. She turned away from these captivating gifts from the world before, and then wept aloud at the sight of the wall at the far end of her library.

Painted upon it in delicate, neat writing was a single sentence:
Knowledge brings about the turn of gods.

It was an entire wall of time capsules, and she had them all to herself. Some skilled master had chiselled a hole in the wall for each piece; it was a miracle. She ran her fingers along them where they rested, and then, almost holding her breath, unscrewed one of the little capsules, extracted the scroll within it, and began reading from the ramblings of a girl who had died hundreds of years before. Her heart beat in such excitement that she knew if it fell still suddenly, she would have died happy.

No, not yet. Not until you find balance.

The thought shook her from the joys of this discovery back to her duty, to what she needed to do to reshape the world for the betterment of humanity. She lit a few more candles, sat down at a table and began to put her thoughts down on paper, her legacy for the many who might speak for humanity in the future. She did not expect all to listen to an old Alpha and her imaginings, but enough would, and that would be all it took.

"If Magnus can do it, then so can I," she whispered to the wind, the dead in the room and the many who'd fallen in battle.

For hours she scrolled the requests calling upon the names she gleamed from every Faction near and far. But not from any lands beyond, for they were not invited to know their ways. Not yet.

When the Wolves returned, she instructed them to deliver each missive under strict secrecy. Left alone, she turned back to the wall of forgotten gems and began to scroll through them once more, reading, learning, weeping, and giving thanks to the vile Southern cur who had seen to the keeping of this place and had protected this collection. She looked to the words on the wall again and again until exhaustion took her mid-sentence. She curled up on the floor of her library and slept until morning.

―――

She was not nervous entering the arena of wits, though she should have been. Perhaps it was the advantage of age and her indifference to embarrassment. She strolled through the Cull, through the aged old doors, into the freezing room, which was far warmer than usual.

They all came.

For the second time in as many days, Massey was shaken by people's actions. She walked through the gathering on the upper floor, looked from the ledge to those around her, and those below, and counted over a hundred in attendance, all of whom she deemed to be worthy of hearing her thoughts. They fell silent as she walked to the centre of the room, her eyes falling upon legend after legend, warrior after warrior. From Alpha to Wolf, from wretch to bandit.

The Actions of Gods

She stepped up to the podium and as she prepared to speak, she looked around at the expectant crowd. Perhaps they had come to support her after all, rather than condemn her foolishness? Her eyes fell upon the behemoth Magnus leaning against the far wall, surrounded by his clan and comrades. That in itself was a good omen for the day. He had forbidden such actions before; to see him here was a victory that she aimed to twist to her benefit.

Her eyes fell next upon Roja, standing nearby, scrutinising this deranged old woman who dared to challenge the majesty of the Primary. She then looked at the wretches, eager for a change, at Wolves wary of change, at bandits intrigued to be considered, and at some Southerners, clearly feeling blessed to be in this place.

"My friends, comrades, my allies, I stand before you with eyes open to the flaws in our nation. I have scribed my thoughts about the matter, and my opinions about what needs to be done to rectify these problems."

There were murmurs of distaste from above. She had expected as much. Were she a mere lowly female of the city, she would have been roared out of here by now. As it was, the rumours of a new Primary provided a perfect opportunity for open discussions of such things. She looked to Mea, standing at her own podium, staring in silence. She offered no argument, sent no guards to take Massey from the room either. This, too, was a good omen.

"This world needs balance."

She let her voice echo above the dissent.

"Balance!" she roared again, and they fell still and listened.

"Magnus once declared no solitary royal fist should rule these lands, and in part, he was right."

The crowd held their breath. Magnus stepped away from the wall. His son stood beside him, silencing him lest he create a scene. That was fine. They were all ears now, listening more keenly than she expected.

"But under the Primary, our lands have been shaken these last few years. Unbalanced. Torn asunder in the name of the betterment of Alphalines and little beyond." She looked around. "It wasn't Alphalines alone who stirred this war, however; nor was it Alphalines alone who ended it."

At this, there were nods of agreement.

Here it is.

She took a breath; she waited for outrage. She had written these words, more or less, into each of the scrolls delivered, but to say it aloud was something else entirely. "We need a Primary, and we need a king to counter her rule. These two must work together to bring about a balance in this unsteady world."

She raised her hands as though calming opposing forces, then brought them together and clasped them in front of her chest.

"I challenge each of you here today to find someone who will serve as a worthy balance to the Primary."

And that was it. Her attempt at democratic voting in a monarchy. She stepped away and dropped her hands. There were looks of horror, the sound of curses; there were raised voices rising above others as the Factions went to war using cutting words alone. Some called her words heresy; some called them enlightened. They demanded this vote; they demanded the head of this old woman. All the while, Massey remained calm; she eyed Mea and silently hoped the younger woman would see the advantage.

Unless the rumours were a ruse and she wishes to remain Primary.

"Perhaps," Mea said, rapping her hand upon the podium, bringing silence to the room. "Perhaps what Massey proposes… could be discussed more."

There were further outcries, and once more the room vibrated with the racket. They fought, argued and drummed their feet on the floor, but it was all for nothing, for Mea's words had condemned the move to action. Massey offered a bow and a smile as the volcanic turmoil erupted around her. As the Four Factions looked to the future and an age of purest balance.

104

VOTE

Emir was amazed at the mayhem. He wasn't the only one. That wasn't to say he wasn't happy. On the contrary, being among such havoc without his life and innocence on the line was excellent. He listened to the suggestions, considered the discussions, grinned at the outrage. He was no longer the centre of attention, and the room felt smaller. Perhaps it was because he'd come so far since that time. Regardless, after so many hours of a hundred sweaty patrons going back and forth, arguing over every detail, the place had turned into a rightly nasty furnace of body heat.

The gathering was a turmoil of democratic hysteria. He thought that a fitting term. With no voice apart from Massey's filtering through, it was a sight to behold. It was almost like the last night of the Puk in Keri.

To the Puk.

Truthfully, despite the mayhem, Emir could sense the tremendous energy in the room. It was incredible. It was electric. It was growing.

It.

He needed to see *it*. He didn't know what *it* was, but *it* seemed necessary. Historic. Or world-shattering. Looking around at the females of the city who had taken the upper tier, he could see their outrage was most volatile of all. And why wouldn't it be? Had the greatest of their kind not been openly challenged for the entire world to see? Had their Primary not only accepted Massey's challenge but also welcomed it with open arms?

He wondered whether Mea suffered the dreadful weight of leadership as he did. Perhaps this was why she had gladly relinquished her power in favour of a fairer voice. From what he'd seen and heard of her actions, Mea had been a strong leader, despite having her knees taken out in the first volley of the war. After that, she'd taken strike after strike, and really, they would not be here today were it not for her.

No good deed left unpunished.

He wondered, though, might the South have risen if a more robust hand had taken charge a couple of decades ago? He looked around the room to Magnus, who stood quietly among his kin. They might have been calming him down. They might have been suggesting it was Magnus who should rule. He would have had Emir's vote, wretched as it was.

And then Emir realised he wasn't alone in surveying the room. As Massey spoke openly of the benefits of a more balanced world, and truly, she did offer some intrigue, fewer and fewer shouted aloud against it. Those in the lower levels, of course.

Around him, a few groups clustered together, muttering about political gain, and he thought it wonderfully human. He could see it on their faces—their desire for power, or to be standing next to greatness, climbing towards the next step. It didn't matter the region or the bloodline. Human was human, and Emir took great pleasure in caring little for such things.

Massey barked out orders as to how voting would occur, but Emir took little interest. He was too busy wondering who might step forward and challenge Magnus. His gaze found Erroh, and he thought him a suitable candidate, despite his age.

"So, who will pledge?" Massey asked suddenly. There were only a hundred present, yet all stood as though they were up to the task. Well, those with manhood between their legs. He imagined that was the result Massey had in mind. He wasn't going to start that debate, though. This was no savage land, after all.

"Who speaks for a worthy… candidate?" She played that last word out slowly so all would understand. It was one thing to suggest a leader; it was another for the masses to accept that suggestion. Aye, she'd mentioned that a majority was also required. Only in those few breaths did Emir suspect she wasn't sure how best to tally this vote.

Let them all out into the arena to beat the ever-living shit out of each other until one remains.

He doubted it would come to that. Were it to do so, he'd have his money on Magnus or Wrek. Or Erroh. If anybody could find a way to win, it would be his close friend. Only then did Emir really look to his

The Actions of Gods

brother of the dark, who was arguing with Lillium in a whisper. Edging closer to them, he heard Erroh's pleas and orders to her that he not be nominated. Elise watched on with intrigue, Magnus with casual indifference. His mind might have been on other things.

King Erroh.

Emir also thought about this and wondered who wouldn't vote for the boy. Aye, he was young, wild, reckless and... heroic. The things any king should be. Not an unimpressive vessel, and after all, he had been born into the role. Erroh could grow into it. More than that, he *would* grow into it.

"Fuken *no*," Erroh hissed, grabbing Lillium by the shoulders.

"If it isn't me who nominates you, who else would you have?" she argued, knowing that only Magnus was more suitable.

Nearby, a young woman nominated a wretch from Boat Town, and Emir grinned, seeing the shock on Holt's face at the suggestion. Emir clapped aloud before he could stop himself. He wasn't alone. Even Mea approved with a delicate nod. But there was no majority, nor was there any sign of it. Most did not know anything of the man's goodness, heart and struggles; perhaps, this made him a fine choice, a delicate balance to the narrow-mindedness of the city these past decades.

Suddenly, Roja stepped forward, her voice grand and regal and cutting. The room fell still. "You know him as the wretched healer, but he is already a king among our kind. I pledge Emir," she declared, and the room erupted into a terrible ruckus, and Emir fell backwards against some faceless comrade who held him aloft and eased him back to his feet as though he were royalty. He looked to Holt and the two exchanged bewildered stares.

"What the fuk?" he hissed to Roja, but she ignored him, instead looking to every female Alpha above who did not applaud—and there were many.

King fuken Emir.

Emir was suddenly not enjoying himself at all, even as those around him cheered wildly, including many Wolves. Near half the room was cheering, and it was a sobering thing to be considered a king. Not that he wanted it in any way. He thought of Keri, he thought of the quiet little haven slipping away, and he almost wailed at the horror. Taking control of a small town could never have prepared him for a task as great as this, especially as he had no desire to rule. He thought about trying to flee. It would be easy. Out the door, grab a horse, into the Wastes, and never look back.

Roja won't follow you.

A sobering thought, he mused miserably, and kept his expression neutral lest he fall apart.

Elise thought all of this was wonderful, he noticed gloomily. As so many reeled in horror and surprise, she applauded and whooped as though it were the arena. Her eagerness was contagious, for the enthusiasm grew in the old room, and for a breath, Emir wondered if it was more for the shows of bravado and the idea of bringing about change than a genuine desire for balance. Regardless, he was fuked. He knew it in his bones.

"I pledge for Doran," Wrek said, and his voice carried far. Even the females above met this pledge with less coldness than they had the others.

"You fuk," Doran cried, shaking his head at Wrek. He waved his uninjured hand to the females above. He bowed to the wretches from Boat Town, and they reciprocated, and Emir's heart leapt at his growing popularity. "I was going to nominate you, Wrek," he mocked, pointing to the behemoth who'd put forward his name.

"I'm no king," Wrek argued. He looked genuinely pleased to remove himself from the running. A few argued for his name, but he shot them one of his special glares, and they fell silent mid-proposition.

As the room churned in uneasy debate and furious arguments that this madness had gone far enough, all eyes fell upon Erroh and his companion. And his companion beyond that.

"No, Lillium, do not," Erroh warned, loud enough that all would hear, before meeting the eyes of every brave warrior and delivering a silent warning that he would play no part in these proceedings. Beside him, his father eyed those with similar thoughts on the matter. Although he'd forbidden such a thing twenty years before, neither father nor son would interfere today. This tacit support was as fierce as Mea's acceptance.

A few more names were thrown out haphazardly for a time, but they garnered little interest. Those mentioned, having learned achingly the measure of their popularity among their peers, crept behind the nearest participants and pretended they were not part of this.

"Have we any more names to pledge?" Massey asked when the room began to fall silent once again.

There was a last round of mutterings, curses, laughter, threats, outrage and praise among the clustered groups, yet no further names were brought forward, and Emir's heart began to sink. He'd have preferred to be laughed away, but the cheers had been too many. More than that, he knew he was the only warrior with the gift of life to offer. He had saved Mea and a thousand others. He knew the city; he was wedded to royalty. He had fought battles and led refugees.

Oh, please, no.

"In that case, I shall pledge one name myself. I pledge a true ruler, a mighty force in both war and peacetime. A friend, honourable and heroic. Under his rule, there will be no war." She looked at Erroh briefly and smiled ruefully at the man beside him. "I pledge Magnus."

There was mayhem again.

For a few more hours, they debated and argued and debated some more. All with a vote appeared to have suddenly found their voices. Those who had been pledged stood in stony silence as their peers argued their fates around them. The only agreement was that a high majority was needed, and truthfully, only Magnus came close to that number when the first round of votes was tallied up. By then, it was late in the day, and to Emir's horror, Massey announced there would be no further voting until dawn the following morning.

It was only then that Emir discovered feeling in his fingertips once again. He did not meet the eyes of Roja, nor did she attempt to speak with him. Perhaps she understood his anger at her having pledged him. Nothing good ever came of such a thing. More than that, she knew well his intentions to return to Keri. However, a wife would not be bested without a fight, it would appear.

Erroh stormed out first, followed by his kingly father, dismayed at this turn of events. The crowds allowed the other candidates to leave after that, and Emir stormed out with them. He heard Roja call for him but dared not turn to her. Not in front of the world. Better to slip away unnoticed and try to forget his failed attempt at becoming regal.

105

SECOND-LAST DAY

"And just what feats have you performed to think yourself worthy of such a position?" a voice from the rafters asked the unfortunate Holt. The old man shuffled uneasily. Emir thought he held himself well, though, despite the questioning. It was a dreadful thing to be on display like this, yet here they were.

"I've done my part for those in Boat Town. Dug into the mud and scrounged for survival." He looked to Mea. "I've seen horrors and endured torments, yet here I am for all to see. If that isn't enough, then so be it," he replied, and indeed, with his old cracked voice full of integrity, it was hard not to respect the man for the subtle strength he suggested.

Almost immediately, another voice from the floor of the Cull demanded a reply to another precarious question, and Emir, standing beside him, could only admire how untroubled he was, enduring the second and hopefully final day of voting as it transpired. Holt replied quickly, and the questioner and many others seemed pleased with the answer. Although less fascinating than the others, Holt was doing well with this performance. For a jaded moment, Emir wondered if he himself might finally be free of this shit.

There were a few uttered mumbles among those gathered of his replies. Holt would have a reprieve, just as Emir, too, had his reprieve, at least for now.

"Doran, do you not think yourself a little young for such a role?" Again, the question came from the upper reaches of the Cull, where the females stood. They asked the most cutting questions, which was an interesting show of acceptance for this new leadership. There was anger, but less than before.

Emir looked and saw Roja standing proudly among them, watching him keenly. She appeared to be ecstatic at his standing in this race. He loved her with all his heart, but he'd never been angrier with her. Not even upon meeting her for the first time.

"Aye, I'm probably a little bald for it too," Doran said. "The crown will sit awkwardly upon my misshapen head." The bald brute was charming and funny. He took this questioning easily enough, as though he'd experienced similar cutting queries. Regardless, with a grin and an arrogance befitting a king, he answered everything with wit but also with a certain cold intelligence. Emir could see he played the fool rightly enough, but more than that, he wanted people to know he played it. Only a fool or an intelligent man, comfortable in his own skin, would use this sort of tactic. "But I'll rule with an iron fist," he added, hoisting his misshapen hand aloft, and there were some sniggers. "Perhaps with this thing, I'll be no brute," he muttered thoughtfully, and many of the females approved. Emir wasn't sure why he was so popular among the city's females, but they seemed to like his words better than those of the others. Better than Emir's as well. He didn't know why he cared for such things, but he did.

The candidates stood side by side this day, surrounded by comrades, allies and begrudgers. It was strange to be on show, yet here he was, singing for his food, his sine, and his very life.

More questions were thrown Doran's way. Many asked after his ruthlessness, and his history of violence, and he answered them all without pause, and again they thought him impressive. Emir couldn't warm to him, though. Had Doran had his way in the arena, Emir would be dead by now. Things had changed since then, but it was tough to forgive, and Doran hadn't even apologised.

The bald brute bowed and stood back from the other candidates. Once more, he'd displayed wit and charm, and once more the females had shown their appreciation, as had the different Factions in the room as well.

Last of all, the crowd turned its attention to Magnus. The questions for him were delivered with a certain tentativeness, especially those of the Alpha females in the gallery. Perhaps they knew the story of how he had leapt up and intimidated the Primary. As questions were thrown his way, he answered each with the skill of a man completely uninterested in the role altogether.

"Will you bring in an age of enlightenment? Or will you seek new lands to have dominion over?" asked a man on the main floor.

"Probably neither," he replied, and eyed the man coldly. Unblinking, he waited patiently for further follow-ups, and Emir could think of no better man for the job, despite his rejection of the title twenty-odd years before.

There was no follow-up question, and Magnus sighed loudly for any and all to hear. Even as he showed disinterest, he was impressive. Even as a lowly general, he was kingly. They all knew his legend. Most had seen it with their own eyes. He was a wise old brute, but he was restrained, and really, what lunatic would dare start another war with Magnus upon the throne? Emir was but a day from demanding that his followers vote for the best of them all. Perhaps that was Magnus.

Perhaps.

"Why should we vote for you?" an elderly female asked. It might have been Massey, no doubt trying to stir some spirit of competition in him. And perhaps, were Magnus genuinely interested, he might have played his part, argued his value and declared why he was the most suitable candidate among the youthful and inexperienced. He was the king of the Savage Isles, and there hadn't been a war there since right before the Faction Wars. Instead, he just shrugged as though he'd been asked what beverage he'd enjoy at lunch.

"Lack of a better candidate?"

There were a few sniggers, as well as a murmur of outrage from the females above. They were entitled to their anger. Magnus openly mocked them, despite their better behaviour today. Despite the part they'd played in the surrender of power. After a breath, he raised his hand against the rage. He must have realised his error, for his voice was passionate. "Forgive an old man his petulance. I have just fought a war. I find such a debate tedious at best."

It was an apology of sorts. It was also a cutting comeback, and many agreed.

And then they started to ask Emir questions, terrible questions about his history. About Dia, about her death and about his apparent guilt in the affair. Someone asked about his imprisonment in the dark.

With my brothers.

And Emir stumbled through each answer as though this were an exam to become a master healer that he had failed to study for. Somehow, though, his replies were genuine and humble and he saw many heads nodding in agreement with him. The nods came from all quarters, but mostly from above, which was a worry. He remembered that Roja had not come home the night before, and this morning she had looked jaded and all spoken out, and he realised now that she'd spent the time politicking among the city females on his behalf. She desired his successes far more than she'd ever wanted leadership. Admittedly, there was beauty in her unwavering support of him. In her belief that he could become someone greater.

Really, though, this was just a different tactic to keep him with her.

They had not fought over this matter yet, but there was a desperate argument brewing, he knew. He could feel it even as the questions cut further. Even as he stumbled awkwardly over his answers, yet somehow continued to talk until he'd managed to supply the information requested of him. He cringed when he accidentally offered a little of his charm; Roja's smile beamed brightest in those moments.

Around and around the questions went. The hour became late, and still no clear winner emerged. Magnus's position remained steady. Holt had slipped further behind, while, to his dismay, Emir moved above Doran. Aye, he was still a mile from Magnus, but close enough to give Roja reason to canvas that little bit harder and for Emir to begin to fear that he might actually win.

Only Erroh appeared unhappy with this turn of events. As the voting reached its conclusion and still no leader had been chosen, he was heard to mutter loudly about Southern events, Woodin men, and delays. Only his mother hushed him, which was curious. He stormed first from the room, leaving the rest to follow.

"Emir, wait a while," Roja called from above, and a coldness ran down his spine. There was electricity in her eyes and argument in the air. "I'll be right down to you."

106

BROKEN GIRL

"You did well, my love," Roja said, grasping him and kissing him lightly. Around them, the last of the crowd was leaving through the main door. Some had departed earlier using the smaller door Roja had appeared from, and she led him through this door.

He did not reply, for he knew he'd answered the questions well enough, and a terrible sinking feeling had taken him. This would be no explosive climb to the top, but a slow crawl, step by step, until the crown was placed upon his sweaty head. For all her skills as a failed Primary in waiting, she was a fine politician altogether, and Emir was irked at her manoeuvring. He wanted to tell her as much, to take her in his arms and lead her away from the city. She wanted to shirk the very responsibility she believed him capable of carrying.

Perhaps only for a few years.

He shook that thought from his mind. Aireys had asked something similar. "Just to the city," he'd been charged with. How long had he kept the wretches under his watch? Roja knew precisely what she was doing, for she knew exactly the type of man he was and to what lengths he would go to keep those who followed him from harm. And now, as she led him through the dark corridors of the Alphaline tower, he began to seethe.

"I'm so proud of you, my love. They were eating from your hands by the end," she gushed, while never breaking stride, and he could only follow her trailing dress as she marched through the darkened corridors, down flights of stairs, out through doors. He imagined Aireys had been proud, too, when he'd taken the leadership and left her behind. So fuken proud.

"Fuk this. I can't do it," he said suddenly, stepping away from her and out into the streets, where the unusual warmth of the day struck him. He looked around. He knew this area. Although the last time he'd taken this path, he'd hidden himself in the darkness and walked from the other direction.

"What is it, my love?" she asked, stroking his chin, dazzling him with her smile. Such a lovely smile. It was always loveliest before he tore it from her.

"It's all falling into place wonderfully, isn't it?" he challenged.

"Aye, it is," she said carefully. "Wait—what do you mean?" That smile faltered, and that was fine.

"You think I'm an idiot."

She broke out into a mocking laugh and walked away, and he could only follow, could only increase his pace to keep up with her long strides. "You are so many things, but you are no idiot," she said. "You are still unsure of this title, I see." She sounded almost disappointed. Fuk that.

"Oh, aye, that I am. But it's not just my title. You have greater plans afoot. A right powerful couple we will be."

"We already are," she said.

They were walking more quickly now. He could tell where they were going, though he had no idea why they were returning to the jail. No Southerners were held there. Their sins were forgiven and they were readying themselves to leave. He'd seen them that morning, preparing for a long and defeated march. He had his eyes on joining such a trek as well. Not with them, though. His would be a fine march. A last parade, in fact, with those for whom he had accepted the responsibility of watching over.

"What are you talking about, my far from idiotic love?" she said, turning to look at him.

He grabbed her by the arm. A little harder than he'd have liked, but enough to stop her, keep her in place, stop her from leading him so ruthlessly to the jail. "The rumours are true of Mea stepping away, aren't they?"

He expected a lie. A distracting clash of words to set him on edge. She was nothing if not dedicated to her Primary. Her predecessor. Oh, yes, he knew very well her intention to reclaim her throne.

Instead, her face paled ever so. She looked around the street for eager ears and found none. "It is true: Mea has decided to stand down, and a female has been chosen, though there is no announcement as yet."

"Why wouldn't you tell me sooner?" he snarled, and she shoved him lest he shout the words aloud and make public the rumour.

"Lower your voice, idiot."

"Fuk you."

She sighed heavily and, setting off again, gestured him to follow, speaking quietly. "These matters are for Mea to divulge. It is not my place." She took his hand as she walked. A smooth move to calm him, but also a way of taking control of him quickly were he to blurt out privileged knowledge to the masses.

"You could have told me you would become Primary," he hissed, and this time, she stopped and peered at him peculiarly.

"You think I am suitable for such a title?"

"Who else?"

"It is not I who will rule, nor do I desire such a role," she said softly, and he could have kissed her.

"So there is no reason for you to stay in this place?" he said, careful to keep his voice low.

"I want to be with you in Keri, my love. I desire no finer life for me, for you, for our family, but look around, my love; look at the ruin my uncle has brought upon Samara."

He did so, and could now clearly see signs of Uden's actions on every street. Debris from buildings. Dried blood along the paths. Scorch marks upon ancient walls. It had fallen to ruin. It could have done with some help, he thought miserably. Even from a diligent queen bitch of the city with no significant title.

Stopping outside the jail, Roja saw the weariness in Emir's beautiful eyes, and it cut her dearly. She knew he desired to leave this cursed place more than she did. To slip away into anonymity in a forgotten little town called Keri. And why wouldn't he? More than that, why didn't he deserve to have such a thing? Truthfully, she no longer wanted to be in this city either. Her heart was barely in this place anymore. She was tired of responsibility. Tired of these walls. She'd had a taste of peace and happiness in Raven Rock. She craved a life away from the workings of this city. And more than that, she wanted to live quietly and happily with her healer husband in a little town of wretched legends.

It wasn't fair.

And it wasn't her place to question her duty.

"It isn't your fault," Emir countered, and she squeezed his hand. She wanted to yield. She was tempted to yield. They would be but a few hundred people escaping in a long trail of carts, with a few packs and a couple of horses. She only had to say yes. She only had to give up on her grandmother's legacy, the dream of Samara, and everything she understood.

"It is my duty," she whispered through clenched teeth, and he took it as a challenge. But really, it was merely her frustration over never being able to admit her desires.

"So you trick the world into selecting me as king just to keep me in Samara?"

Her stomach turned. It wasn't like that at all. Not really. Was it?

"No, my love. This world needs a kind, strong man. A better man than ever."

"One who is forced to stay here with you?"

"Will you not stay with me?" she asked, feeling a crushing sorrow. Was this a step too far? Was it too much for him, for her?

"Will you not come with me to Keri?"

I will, she almost said. But instead, she fell silent and rapped upon the jail door, knowing things were about to get worse.

Once they were granted entry by a stern-looking Wolf whose name she couldn't remember, she led her husband through the darkened corridor. He froze momentarily outside the last doorway.

"What the fuk is this?" he whispered, and she heard the quiver in his voice.

"It's fine, my love; there is light within," she replied softly, opening the bars. Inside, she knew, lay the ruin of their former comrade.

It wasn't guilt Roja suffered when thinking of her actions towards Ealis. What she had done had been a needful act of vengeance on her part, yet still, she felt a stirring of shame for her assault. Emir had never questioned why she had stayed behind while he ventured ahead on the outskirts of the hovels, although he might have noticed the blood spatter on her gown and ignored it. It had been two days now since she'd learned of the girl. Two days of wondering what to do.

"What happened to her?" he demanded.

Ealis lay on her stomach on her cot. Her shirt had been ripped open so that the stitches on her back could heal in the air. Roja was no master healer, but recognised that someone had done a fine job of tending to a near-mortal wound.

"I did this," Roja said, as her beautiful husband slipped past her into the cell and unlocked the chain around Ealis's neck. Ealis barely moved. She inhaled slightly, seeing Emir; she sighed as the chain around her neck slipped away. She barely took breath, barely blinked either. She merely lay there as she had since she was found. "I needed to. After what she did."

"Aye, a blade to the back. While I scampered on ahead?" he muttered, standing over the girl, inspecting her wounds, checking her heartbeat. "Are you well, Ealis?" he asked softly, but the wounded waif did nothing but stare into nothing. He turned to Roja. "What is wrong with her?"

A lot.

"The healers who tended to her believe she is in some shock."

"The healers?"

"I didn't want to tell you."

"So, you allowed her to be tended by amateurs."

"Well, she deserves what she gets," Roja snapped, rubbing her chest absently.

"And now she deserves to be free of these chains."

"She's dangerous."

He shook his head, held his finger across her eyes, moved it a little and looked to Roja. "Her mind is broken. The state she is in is not from any knife wound. Something terrible befell her after you stabbed her."

He bent and whispered in Ealis's ear. "Did someone do something awful to you?"

The girl made no reply, of course, and Roja felt herself redden with shame, not for the attack but for her haste in bringing Emir here. The wounds themselves were healing, but who knew what acts of depravity might have occurred in the meantime? Was her uncle a forgiving man for freeing his niece and nephew-in-law? Her shame grew a little more.

"You are safe now, little one," Emir assured her, and went to wipe the blood from the many smaller wounds on her uncovered back.

"Will she live?" Roja asked, after a time, watching him spoon-feed a little cold soup to the girl. That was something positive, at least. For all his self-doubt, he could renew life where nothing but rot and decay were present. And she wanted the entire world to see his gifts.

"Aye, she will, but whatever she endured must be unimaginable. I've seen vacant stares in my time. This one is different. This girl is completely lost." He turned to Ealis and, for a moment, considered reattaching the chains before stepping out of the cell and sliding the door closed. "I'll come to see you tomorrow, Ealis; perhaps we might talk of such matters," he offered, but the girl was still. Were Roja to guess, she might have imagined she was ready to die. Simply waiting for the moment her heart gave out.

"Let's go home, my love," she whispered, leading him from the cells out into the chilly evening.

"Home?" he muttered, but followed after. And though it hurt, she knew she would convince him to stay. More than that, the world would benefit greatly from a man like him. Such thoughts kept her warm. Such ideas made living in this city bearable. But such reflections led to a darker, colder belief. She had a sudden vision of him with his wretches upon a cart, leaving her behind, abandoning her to her duty among the glowing lights of her prison.

And I will watch him go.

107

BETTER MUSINGS

Lea no longer thought of green eyes. Not of one green eye, either. Whatever enchantment had taken her that day in Raven Rock was gone, replaced by a terrible guilt. Not for her actions, for they were many, but for her very existence. She thought of her father's expression of horror as she'd revealed herself. His only response was to flee from battle, flee the war under a cloud of ridicule. And she, a battered ruin, could only watch him end the war on her behalf.

And she'd watched him start it too.

Her head spun, not from any affliction but from memories of the horror. Knowing she was responsible for such atrocities was a thought that could take her sanity. She wanted to hate those who kept the truth from her, which had, after all, allowed these horrors to unfold. But really, she had lived a better life than she had under his watch and was mostly grateful for it. Mostly.

Gratitude didn't stop the hate, though. She rolled around in her sweaty bedsheets for a while and hated everything. Her father, her people, herself. And Erroh? Perhaps not. Perhaps there was still some part of him that wanted to pull her from the murky waters—wanted to mend her fractured soul. Hold her, tell her everything would be all right.

She looked to the roof of her tent and despised its cloth finish. She wanted to stare up at the stars above. She wanted to feel the air in her hair as she stretched out. She wanted to be in the Wastes for a time, anywhere but here. Her stomach churned as she considered her choices. Her future. Miserable and fitting.

She could smell herself in this tiny room and was disgusted with it.

The Actions of Gods

Only in confinement could she smell as she did now. She missed the rush of water, taking her breath, removing her stench. She wanted the wind to dry her hair, not the smoky, fetid warmth of a bed, at least for now.

She listened to the night, and realised that the camp was quieter—there was less frenzied celebration, less of the weeping that dragged her down to the murk. People died, people mourned, and people took to marching again. This was their way. Someday, her father's sins and her own would be forgotten forever.

Her head no longer spun when she walked; the ache was gone to nothing and, blissfully, no dream syrup flooded her veins. That didn't stop her from having dreams beyond her immediate future.

Fuk the future.

She wondered what it would be like to stare at a stone ceiling again. She wondered if it would engulf her with terrible claustrophobia. She almost threw up on herself, and forced herself to think less on the tent's shitty roof and more on her shortcomings. Such things were more of a comfort to her than the false platitudes she knew would come.

"Fuk this," she muttered, sitting up in her bedding and reaching for her journal. She read through her last few scribbled lines for a few casual moments. They had been written in a time of torment, when she had been lost and angry and vengeful. Cruel and cutting too. Her current torment was a different beast altogether. Now, she knew herself that little bit better. She was not the fierce warrior she had once thought herself to be. She was not the greatest swordsperson ever to march the Wastes, either. Uden had removed that illusion from her easily enough. More than that, to know her mate had stood with him twice and escaped with fewer injuries than she had was a sobering thought.

Erroh.

She tried to suppress thoughts of her beautiful mate. It was a difficult thing, for he slipped into her thoughts more and more the longer she lay recovering. Now that she'd regained her senses, he wouldn't be around as much, she imagined. Only in that moment did she realise how little she thought of him—and how unfair that was. He had watched over her as she slept, had he not? He had done so because he loved her. What other reason could there be?

She thought about this and began to scribe in her journal. Each word was carefully chosen, though there were few. It took her some time. The words did not flow, and she wept aloud as she wrote, but no one would hear her inside the safety of her tent. It was something she needed to do.

The world turned around her, but she could not leave matters as they were.

Eventually, with the note finished, she tore the sheet from her journal, and folding it in half and scribing his name upon the outside, she rose and placed it on the desk where he would find it.

Dressing quickly, strapping her boots tightly lest her nerve betray her, Lea grabbed what belongings she needed and stuffed them into her pack before slipping free from her tent and its unimpressive roof into the cold night. Outside, she did not smell her own scent as powerfully. Or else the stench of the surrounding tents concealed her odour—another reason to be free of the place, no doubt.

"I'm doing this again," she whispered to the wind of her desire to be alone. She knew she was wrong. But if she didn't leave now, she'd never be able to escape. She might have gathered her comrades, her outcasts, but this journey was hers alone to take. Perhaps if she were to find what she needed, then she might find herself again. Find Erroh, too, though that was unlikely. Her heart ached, and her will was tested, but stubborn determination won. It always had.

With her hood up and her shoulders slouched, she ventured through the camp until she came upon Shera, loose and at leisure among a dozen other mounts. No fool stopped her prepare the beast, nor did Shera fight her hold as she led the magnificent animal from the paddocks, away from the light of the camp.

"Goodbye, my love," she whispered. She knew of the rumours stirring in the winds, whispers of a king to match the Primary. She was both disgusted and relieved at the idea of such a thing. She'd heard the word "balance" thrown around. Lea was sceptical of such notions, but it was a small matter to worry about on another day. Everything was about to change, and she wasn't quite ready to be part of that world. Not yet.

"Come on, my girl," she whispered, climbing upon Shera and riding slowly to the crest of the hill, where little Lea of Samara could gaze one last time at the city and everything she had ever known.

"I'm sorry," she whispered to the wind, her duty, her comrades, her brother. Mostly, though, to Erroh. This last step, delivered with a kiss, would be the end of them. It shouldn't have been this easy to slip away, but who could stop her?

She looked to the south and kicked her beast gently in the ribs as she followed the shattered moon's light down the path towards her destiny. Alone.

The Actions of Gods

"Hey, brother... I... um... don't know what to say," Erroh said. It wasn't the finest conversational opening, but he'd never once been accused of having a silver tongue. He held a stick in his hand. It wasn't an impressive stick. Unsure of what to say, what to do with his hands, he snapped a bit off the end and threw away the offending piece. His brother had not replied, nor would he ever.

"I'm feeling a little lost these days, Wynn." He snickered at the absurdity of talking with the dead, yet here he was, sitting cross-legged at the grave of his friend, asking him for guidance. "I'm sure you have it far worse," he added, and continued to laugh. He was almost going to cry as well, but Wynn wouldn't have wanted that. He snapped another piece of stick free and tossed it away. It rebounded off a low-hanging tree branch and struck the rock where Wynn's name was scrawled. "Oh, shit—sorry," he said, throwing both pieces away. "Can't have your shiny new grave getting messy too soon." He looked around and felt the loss anew. His friend deserved a grander grave than this place, hidden away in the forest where time would soon conceal everything he'd ever been.

"It's fine, Erroh; it's a nice stick."

"And a fine grave too."

It wasn't Wynn replying at all. It was his sorrow forming the words in his mind. It would say only things he wanted to hear.

"Things like it wasn't your fault I'm dead?"

"Exactly, brother," Erroh said, and felt momentarily better about himself. He wiped his eyes and gazed at the sun hidden above the canopy. "Though it was partly my fault, you know."

He heard no reply in his mind. Nor was there one coming. Some things were better left unsaid, after all.

"I think you might have made a good king," Erroh said, and the stirrings of anger began to form. Wynn would have been angry too. The world turned on its merry way as he lay rotting in the ground. His killer had escaped to the South, and they had argued over kingly things, and it disgusted Erroh, for that was the way of things. Apart from journeying there himself one day with a sword in his hand and assassination on his mind, there was nothing he could do. And perhaps that was something he would be part of. For now, though, few warriors desired another march, war crimes were forgotten, and peace was to reign. And Uden, the Woodin Man, was allowed to flee like a coward.

"And you?"

"I'd make no suitable king, nor would I allow any brave fool to nominate me."

Erroh sniffed the morning air again. It was later than he'd expected. "They're going to be calling for another vote soon, and I should probably be there," he muttered unhappily. "Fuken fools argue over leadership while that animal flees, escapes to the South, where he will gather an army once more." He shook his head. He hadn't meant to bring up Uden that way. It was probably a sore subject with his dead friend. Regardless. "This kingly vote is something they cling to instead of facing the reality of war. Changing things will make it better, they say," he said, sneering. He wanted to find another stick or a rock to cast deep into the forest. "It might be Emir, you know. Could be Dad. I don't think either one wants it. Why would anyone want such a shackle?" Erroh shook his head. "I'm sorry. None of this matters, I suppose." His comrade didn't want to hear of such petty things. Maybe his comrade wasn't hearing any of this at all. That terrible sadness came upon Erroh once more. He didn't want to believe a thing of such extraordinary and tragic magnitude, the idea that he'd never speak with Wynn again. He wanted to speak with his friend again. He did. He didn't want it to be the end at all.

"I'm here, remember, and this is most certainly not your mind answering for me."

"I can't believe you died, brother," he said before he caught himself, and the tears fell freely. A beautiful, awful release, and he felt both better and pathetic at that moment. Eventually, he felt simply better and thought he could continue the conversation. "Do not worry; I'll look after Lillium for you, brother, I promise."

This was only half a lie. He was trying. He really was. She was a shadow of the goddess she had been. A lesser fool might have suggested she don that demonic mask again, as Wynn had once done when seeking courage. He thought they would have formulated grand plans of retribution by now. Pledged in blood, they would tear Uden apart, but the truth was, she looked to have lost the fight. He wasn't going to place such a burden on her when she already looked fit to break. She was tired, and she had earned her rest. He had bidden her tend to duties befitting a first general after a war and little more. It was all he could think of doing. "Every day, she weeps. She loved you in the end, you know."

"I never stopped loving her."

I know.

"It's time to go, brother. I'll be around again soon. Don't go anywhere," he joked, and imagined the mocking laughter from his brother of the dark. Sometimes in the darkness, only humour could get anyone through.

Deciding to check in on Lea before walking to the Cull, Erroh called for her outside the tent and received no reply. Daring a glance inside in case she was sleeping, he was puzzled to see her bed empty and her belongings missing. That confusion was swiftly replaced by a terrible coldness when he saw his name upon a folded note. He snatched it up and opened it, and the coldness became a simmering fire the more he read.

Dearest Erroh, my beo,
I cannot stay here a moment longer. It is late in the night, and I cannot sleep. I see the world continuing to turn after such horror, and I learn you all fight over leadership. That is the way of humanity. Perhaps I am a child to desire less of this; perhaps I am more than that. I look to the South, and I see my father waiting. Not for love, not for comfort, but for a terrible vengeance. On both our parts. I fear the reason he marched. I think you do, too. I fear, some night years from now, hearing the rapping upon our door from a brute seeking me out; seeking you too. I cannot sleep another night knowing there are actions left undone. Your war is done, and your oaths are answered, but I am still lost and angry.
This time, I leave you behind.
Goodbye, my dearest Erroh.

Erroh read the letter three times, each time becoming angrier and angrier. With her, with himself. With his hesitation. He tried to count to ten.
One, two, fuk it.
He kicked over the bedside locker. It was the most breakable thing he could find. He turned on her bedding and began tearing the sheets and blankets free, throwing them viciously against the far wall, where they suffered no damage apart from a few extra creases. He stormed out of the tent and immediately considered climbing upon his mount and chasing her down. It didn't matter that she was right. It didn't matter that he wanted to march down south with every beaten Southerner and an army of his own. What mattered was an end to marches. Peace in the Four Factions and all that shit. He knew this because his father

knew it, and he rarely disagreed on matters of which he had little understanding.

Yet still.

Around him, he saw comrades walking down towards the shattered gates to commence the onslaught on candidates who desired little part in such kingly appointments. He looked to the south and imagined Lea free of this shit, riding with the wind in her hair, leaving him behind, refusing to talk with him again, and perhaps in that moment, he finally realised they would not survive this mating.

Dropping his head and shuffling forward with feet desperate to turn the other way, Erroh marched with his comrades towards the Cull, without any idea he was about to make the greatest mistake of his life, one that would change the entire Four Factions in one fell swoop.

108

OH, ERROH

Erroh had never taken a moment to look around and truly understand his lack of importance. Seeing the world around one's self twist and turn without one's fingers in the spin was a human thing. He was without ideas, without a place. Without kin or hope. Everyone was leaving or moving on; he was stuck where he had been so long ago. Some people found comfort in nothing changing. Erroh wasn't used to such things at all. He wasn't used to stillness. He'd forgotten what it was to desire peace. Fuk it; he'd forgotten what it was to live in peace. He felt older than his time. And he felt alone. And he felt betrayed. And he felt unfulfilled.

However, the mass movement of a few thousand Southerners took his attention from such devastating reflection. They were preparing, as he knew they would be. Still, though, to see it happen was also a sobering thing. Although it was time to tend to political business, the sight of so many readying for departure was enough to stop him in his tracks. They were regimented in their packing, in their preparation. Like little worker ants, toiling for the betterment of a nation. Although not like one great army at all.

Many separate Fingers were individually preparing to march, and he wondered would the nation separate once again. Would the Fingers turn to clans, spreading out, warring among each other in the years ahead? Such a thing would be dreadful but also beneficial towards peace for the rest of the Factions.

I do not want this.

The Southerners tended to matters with the efficiency of wanderers familiar with marching in large numbers. He'd known this march would occur, and truthfully, while he had grown fond of the fierce Hunt who had surrendered and followed him, he would be glad of their absence. They were a means to end this cursed war, but they were not welcome in this part of the world—at least now, while the wounds were still open, while resentment was still so strong. It wouldn't take time for that resentment to turn to anger. Every day, more and more returned from Boat Town. The first thing these returning refugees gazed upon was their humbled vanquishers. It would take only a few fools to stir violence and a few hundred more to continue the advantage. Wars had started over lesser things. The South had lost, and there would be ramifications, no doubt, for whoever led the region after, but for now, Mea's decision to remove them from their place of conquest was the best course of action.

Punish them when they are in their territory.

Truthfully, Erroh would have been more inclined to work with the South instead of punishing an already beaten beast. He'd seen the South for itself and had wondered what some adequate trade routes and fewer sanctions for the sins of their predecessors might do to help those frozen lands prosper. And if not prosper, then at least improve the living conditions of the Southerners enough that they wouldn't resent the warmer climates with greener fields.

"Good riddance to them," said Lillium from behind him. He hadn't heard her approach. His mind had been upon kingly things like kindness and charity.

"Better for the world," Erroh noted, but he wouldn't argue. She had more reason to be bitter than he did. He thought of Uden down in the South, and his anger returned. He knew he shouldn't have asked, but perhaps it was better to ask than let her feel as he did. "If you could, would you march south searching for Uden?" He thought of Lea. He thought of his outcasts marching one last time.

"I'm so weary, Erroh."

"You would leave Wynn's death unavenged?"

"Wynn deserves what vengeance we can give him," she said wistfully, looking back to the forest where her mate lay still. "And someday, when I can draw a sword again, I will march with you."

He could see the agony in her. He could see that she needed to be pulled from her misery, and he was incapable of doing so. She would rule the Wolves in his absence, though, and perhaps that was a finer tonic for her affliction of the soul. He hoped.

The Actions of Gods

"Why not now?" Erroh fought the anger in his voice. The anger was for Lea, not for her friend, who likely knew of her departure. Still, arguing about it was a small matter. She looked ready to break. Only her vibrant hair suggested the residual strength within. He'd seen this in many people since the final battle. A desire to rest, to forgive. To let murderers walk free. They had allowed the Southerners mercy. Did that include the barbaric butcher behind it all too? Sometimes the power of forgiveness was a most human thing. Sometimes it was a damning thing.

"Perhaps tomorrow I will wake up and have the taste for blood. Perhaps then I will do something worthy of Wynn's memory. My heart is broken, Erroh; I'm not like you anymore. I wish I were. I wish I had the strength to face that monster, but I do not. All that killing has taken its toll."

"Are you done, then? Ready to retire from war?"

"No, I will answer to my king and to you, my dearest master general. If you command me to war, I will raise my blade."

"Perhaps tomorrow I would ask such a thing, but not today," he said, embracing her. As much as he understood her need for revenge, he also understood her need to be silent for a time. She had been incredible, ferocious and heroic, but there was a limit to what anyone could take. For all the horrors, she had lasted longer than most.

"Thank you, my friend," she said, kissing him upon the lips before pulling away. "It should be you," she whispered.

"What do you mean?"

"You know what I mean. Now don't be late," she said, pointing to the city before bowing magnificently, leaving him to stand watching the Southerners for a little time. His mind was awash with thoughts of desolation and loneliness. Most of them circled around the vision of a diminutive girl with a roar and a strength beyond all. And he knew what he had to do. He was tired of the world revolving around his actions. The world desired peace; well, so be it. He would play his part in his own destiny. Let the fuken world do its thing. Let them squabble all they liked. It would be a wonderful thing to be free of this. He was no longer a master general. He was free to step into the Wastes. Seek out his mate. Kiss her one last time. And kill a god.

"Did you think I would leave without saying goodbye?"

He spun towards that familiar feminine voice to meet a warm, tragic smile. A smile that suggested separation was upon them both after everything.

Not you too.

"You are leaving?" he cried in disbelief.

Nomi kept that smile, but her eyes betrayed the true depth of her sorrow. In all the emotion of the last few days, he hadn't even asked about her intentions. For a breath, his anger gave way to the shame that he'd forgotten his close comrade. His Nomi.

"I miss the cold," she whispered, sliding away from her companion to embrace Erroh. She placed her forehead against his and held there for a time. He could smell her familiar aroma, and though she stood before him, he missed her already. He couldn't take this betrayal from one so loyal and kind. But he dared not stand in her way; she deserved more than she had received. She was incredible.

"What of the king?" he asked. She had a vote. A meaningful vote too. Few in the South had votes, but her voice carried as far as Massey's ears. Further than Lea's had, at least, for Lea had not received an invitation to the dreadful event at all. "You have to vote. It affects you. It affects the whole world." He could feel himself quake, and she wept silently in his arms. A tear of his own spilled free and then another, and he allowed them. Lea's leaving had torn him asunder, but Nomi's desertion was just as cutting.

For one thing, he had not repaid the debt he owed her. Such things mattered. As did thanking her for the world, her heroism and her kindness. A significant debt indeed.

"Bah, not for me. I have enough to worry about," she said, pulling away, then swiftly hugging him again as though it was their last. It could be. It was a distance to Conlon, and he aimed to pass it by.

"Lea has left too," he blurted out. He didn't know why. It seemed she'd need to know.

"I know; I read the letter."

"Oh."

He took hold of her again and gazed into her lovely eyes like it was the last time. In that moment, he was jealous of Drahir's infatuation. To choose a girl as incredible, as fierce as she was. If not to love, then simply to be around. "There are no words of gratitude I can offer for all you have done."

She smiled sadly. "I love you, my Erroh. I always will. I will vote only for a king I desire." She hesitated, struggling to find the words. "It should be you," she said softly, prodding his chest with her finger.

"It should be," agreed Drahir from beside her. He'd had the discretion to remain quiet until now. The large man leaned forward. "I would follow you, brother," he said softly, before bowing at Erroh's feet. "Though I, like my kind, choose to follow another." He looked to Nomi as he bowed to the gatherer of armies.

"Do not bow. We are… family," Erroh said, for he had nothing else. It was true in part, for now.

"I will see you, no doubt," Drahir said, accepting Erroh's embrace—a strange thing between warriors tainted by Uden.

"Be safe, my comrades; it's a long walk," he said, and felt sorrow give away to devastation. He was better with Nomi in his life. He always had been.

Erroh turned to walk away, and Drahir called out to him. "Though I would follow you, brother, so would the South. But my frozen lands have followed my warmongering father for too many years. Perhaps it is time we allowed a mother to watch over us." And in that moment, Erroh understood what Drahir saw in the girl. What Erroh had always seen but had yet to speak of.

"Perhaps so," Erroh said, and Drahir turned away to tend to a thousand tasks Erroh had little understanding of.

"Perhaps I will find a one for life, like Erroh and Lea," Nomi offered, and that hopeful smile almost winded him.

"You would be fine, Mother," Erroh said in her language.

She placed her hand to her heart, smiled a final time and turned away to tend to the procession as it prepared for its march.

Broken-hearted and furious with those closest to him, Erroh stormed through the city, eager to become a wrathful furnace by the time he arrived at the Cull. The walk was a long enough trek, however, and by the time he stepped through the oak doors for the last time, his temper was already cooling, his reason already returning.

For the first vote of the day, at least.

As before, the votes were cast and counted, and, once again, there was no pure winner, and Erroh muttered a curse loudly under his breath that he barely kept from being a shout. Such was the growing respect for this process that his outburst was gazed upon with disdain by far too many people. Erroh didn't care. He just shrugged rudely as Massey called for the candidates to state their cases for all to hear, and Erroh thought it was a stupid practice. He wished Wynn was with him, laughing along with this idiocy, adding his curses to the madness and becoming far too emotional in the same breath.

"Say what you feel."

"Not yet," he whispered as the first candidate began to state his case. He spoke of the need for peace, strength and commerce, and was truly impressive.

As was the next candidate, who, jesting lightly, stated his accomplishments as a leader in wartime. Only once did he offer a terrifying suggestion that war was in the wind, as always. Better to have a strong and hardened warrior at the helm, he asserted, and Erroh thought him convincing.

The third was a brother who squirmed with discomfort, and his humble passion won many a cynic over to the importance of goodness. As before, Erroh would vote for the wretched one.

Last to speak was a legend who offered little, and this angered Erroh. He agreed with the idea of no king holding dominion over the land, yet still, were Magnus to lay his hand over the world, perhaps he could undo some of the savagery through better deeds. A king should never desire the title, but gifted the honour, he should indeed honour those who had bestowed it upon him. Every time Magnus shrugged off his importance, it was a cruelty in itself.

This is all madness.

And then they took a vote, and nothing changed.

Complete fuken madness.

The room began to spin as his anger took his better judgement. He tried to distract himself, but nothing calmed him down. The world was turning, and Massey was suggesting that perhaps a candidate should step away in a sacrifice for the betterment of them all, and Erroh could take no more. He thought of a bottle smashing against the wall below the podium. Sometimes, he couldn't help himself.

"Enough of this shit," he roared, brushing aside all four candidates and addressing the room. He might not have addressed the crowd as he did if he had thought on the matter a little more. But address them he did.

And the world was forever changed.

"All you fuks stand here with your prejudice against all of these fine comrades," he snarled, and the room fell silent.

"To the beautiful queen females of this room, I command you to recognise each of these males for who they are. You need a king who will respect, challenge, but not fear you," he spat, and pointed to the women up in the gallery, who watched with cruel, condemning eyes as he challenged them. "Look at them, and choose better than you have done before," he roared, his voice echoing to the rafters above.

"To all of you wretches who have endured such horror, look upon these four humble servants and see that they have tasted the life of outcasts as you have. A king should know their place in both silk and gold, and in the hovels, mud, and blood."

He spun around and grabbed at a nearby Wolf in the crowd. "I know how the Wolves vote, for they attack only in packs." The crowd were mesmerised as he held the Wolf by the scruff of the neck. "A king should be a warrior. A king should know the horror of war and blood, and they should know of fuken mercy. Can any of you declare four better candidates?"

He dropped his voice and released the Wolf.

"There are few Southerners here left to vote," he went on. "Theirs is a life of strife and cruelty. They deserve a merciful king who can forgive the sins of a madman."

Suddenly, Erroh felt empty; he felt the entire room hanging on his words, ready to shout him down, tear him apart, and why not? He was not part of this spinning world anymore.

"Just pick any of these legends, and I promise you, you will feel safer in a better regime," he whispered before turning to his mother and father, who watched on with equal parts amusement and bewilderment. "I must leave, for there are greater matters to take care of," he said, and as his last words reverberated through the room, he slipped away from the watching eyes, the silent criticisms, the mocking glares. His parents knew this was goodbye. It was easier this way.

He should have left a note.

He slid out the door and closed it behind him, and there was silence for a time until the roar of outrage reverberated through the Cull. Erroh listened from the other side of the door, and his heart sank as he realised his words had meant little to the gathering. He turned away then and marched from the Cull, making his way through the city to where his tent stood. There, he gathered what belongings and supplies he needed before recovering Highwind.

He stopped only once more, to explain his actions to his peaceful brother, before riding away into the darkness, away from Spark City. But despite himself, at the crest of the hill he turned around once more to gaze at her ugly walls and hated her so.

"You broke my heart, you fuken bitch," he whispered to the city, knowing well he had little intention, or chance, of stepping across her borders ever again.

109

RECAPPING LESSER LEADERS, AN UNEXPECTED REVELATION, A WONDERFUL MOMENT AND THE SUDDEN END TO SOMETHING BEAUTIFUL

"Fuk, can you believe that just happened?" Wrek cried, storming along the street. Emir couldn't. Nobody could have seen such a thing, apart from the absent gods. A great weight was lifted. That's all that mattered for now. That, and swiftly escaping from the Cull and the madness within.

"It's a fuken miracle," Emir agreed, quickening his pace and hoping his comrade would match it. Around a corner, down an alley, and across another street, and finally he began to relax ever so.

"King Erroh."

"Aye, seems rather unlikely."

Magnus had been the first to speak once Erroh had stormed away from the Cull. In the deathly silence, as those present considered the vote, he had stepped forward and declared loudly, "I nominate Erroh as king." Somehow the room fell even more silent after a collective gasp, and then it exploded more loudly than ever.

Emir tripped up, crossing an uneven bit of path, and nearly twisted his ankle, stumbling awkwardly. He could only laugh at his clumsiness as Wrek stood over him.

"You seem rather happy, considering you've just lost out on such a prestigious title," the big man said, offering a hand to the laughing healer and pulling him to his feet.

"This, brother, is the face of relief," Emir countered, and he was relieved. He'd had no idea how relieved he was until the crowd had turned against him.

It had started with the Primary.

"Yes," she'd shouted, and her voice set off a roar of approval most impressive, and Emir had looked up to see the desperation in Roja's beautiful eyes as the crown slipped from his grasp. From hers. It was no easy thing to end a marriage, but he had certainly stoked the fires by stepping forward first and declaring that he would vote for such a king, and more than that, he urged those who voted for him to consider Erroh instead. Most of those in attendance had appreciated this sacrifice, and the flow had listed towards the young Alphaline who had stormed from the Cull.

Wrek shook his head. "It was swinging your way, you fool. Even I was considering you." He seemed unhappy with Emir's cavalier attitude. Perhaps he wanted a friend in court. "Now, watch your fuken step," he muttered as they disappeared further into the city. Away from pursuing wives, away from a dreadful end. Emir couldn't think about that; he was blissfully sober but felt the stirrings of delirium from this latest turn of events. He also had a thirst on him, and it was late in the afternoon. He thought of his wife and wondered how long she would hold that title.

He had looked at her as he said the words, and it was cruelty on his part. He regretted it now. Not the act, for that was a godly thing, but for looking into her eyes as he cut her down as though she were a lunatic with two crossbows on her wrists.

"I would have made no good king," Emir said, and Wrek immediately stopped him in his tracks, gripped his shoulders and stared into his eyes. When Wrek looked at a fool like that, it was hard not to listen, to think about the words.

"You would have made a great king, Emir. A great king."

Shivers ran down Emir's back for just a breath. It was a strange thing to imagine that he had value in the world. It was no small thing to be told he was kingly. He shook his head and rejected the thoughts.

"I'd have drunk the kingdom dry, started a war with the South and had my way with every Alphaline female in the Four Factions right before they were sent out to Cull," he mocked.

Wrek grinned, but his eyes were serious. "Every female? Bah—as though your stunning wife would have allowed such a thing to occur. As though she would share you with anyone either," he jested.

"You haven't heard the stories about her," Emir countered.

"Well, so be it. You would have forgiven the South's sins. Even after Keri, even after Aireys and Quig," Wrek said, and Emir's grin wavered ever so. This was a low blow, bringing them up to remind him of his humanity. Of course, he wanted vengeance, but he, too, was a merciful man. If anyone understood the ability of people's allegiances to change, it was Emir. It was so very human, and he *would* forgive the South. He'd had enough of war, as it was.

"Perhaps so," he mumbled as they continued their desperate flight from the Cull.

"You would still probably drink the city dry of all the sine, though."

"The 'drunken good king,' does sound nice, I suppose," Emir agreed, looking back the way they had come, lest Roja be in pursuit.

Once Doran and Holt had cursed loudly in mock agreement, the tide had begun turning swiftly—but the future king was nowhere to be seen. It was a small matter, though. There were loud demands for a vote to be called, and Massey was swift to take control of this emotional madness.

Without debate, bravado or grandstanding, she called out the numbers, and still Emir held more votes than most, although the numbers had dwindled. And then she called Erroh's name, and any fool could see it was the correct decision. As the numbers were read aloud, Emir's heart had felt lighter but heavier too. He could only shy away from his wife, whose look of betrayal was cutting. Erroh's tally was confirmed, and the crowd erupted. He felt the slaps on his back from comrades, strangers and kin, and as swiftly as Emir had been nominated, Erroh was declared King of the Four Factions. An absent king. But a king, nonetheless.

"You know that Erroh will make a better king, though," Emir said after a breath.

"Regardless, it will be a fine end to his impressive tale," Wrek said thoughtfully.

"Perhaps," Emir noted hesitantly.

"Perhaps."

Eventually, with responsibility far behind, they reached the abandoned building that Emir recognised as the finest tavern in the city.

"Are you thirsty?" Wrek asked, easing his shoulder against the locked door and effortlessly breaking through it. The two friends slipped into the tavern where Wrek's great rise with Sigi had begun. Emir allowed the behemoth to stand and take in the dark interior for a moment. Cobwebs had overtaken the place in no time at all. Debris and glass lay strewn everywhere, but some mysterious force had protected it from true devastation.

"Are there any bottles left?"

"There will be some in the back," Wrek said, and as he listened to the sounds of his friend rummaging through all manner of debris, Emir remembered the place in better times. He thought of Roja and missed her dreadfully, but knew it would be better to get used to this feeling.

Perhaps I can visit.

"What are you going to do, now that the city is ours again?" Emir asked, sitting down at the one remaining upright table. He could almost hear the crowd's chatter, feel the night's energy and the beat of the troubadours. "Will you run all the taverns again?"

"With Sigi dead or lost, I imagine a few vengeful people will come looking to take the establishments for themselves," Wrek said as he went to task, and Emir worried they'd come this far only to find no alcohol at all. "Leave them to it, I say, but this beast I will keep for myself," he said, appearing from the back with two bottles of sine and a handful of sheets of paper.

He poured each of them a glass, but his eyes were on the notes, written in awful handwriting.

"What if Erroh never returns?" Emir asked seriously before clinking glasses with the distracted innkeeper.

As the dust settled in the Cull and the calls for their king to be crowned grew louder, Magnus forbade a soul to leave the room, seek out the king, or spread the word. "Better my son completes his task without the support of the Factions behind him. Better he never knows his responsibility in such a thing. Better a Faction does not take offence to an action taken by a king in their territory."

He looked around to ensure people understood the need for peace in political manoeuvrings. "A warrior following his path is less likely to add further insult to a Faction that was already reeling. But were a king to commit petty vengeance? Now that is something else entirely," Magnus stated, and there followed a volley of questions about Erroh's actions; there was even a hint of outrage as people, slighted by such a thing, claimed it was their right to spread word.

Only Mea, still holding equal authority, decreed that Magnus's word be honoured. There was still muttered outrage but it fell silent soon enough. Besides, everyone liked to keep a secret. Only then did Emir realise that Mea had played her own game all along, that she might well have deceived the entire world into agreeing on a shared balance of leadership. Emir was cynical, and he wondered whether she had little intention of stepping away at all. Only then did he realise Roja might have been aware of such a ruse. That no new Primary was incoming at all, that, instead, she would allow time to pass, matters to settle, and only then, continue as though nothing had changed. But with less of a burden upon her aching shoulders.

Whatever her reasoning, the uncrowned king was allowed to go on his merry adventures, unaware of his sudden importance.

"She will eventually find you here," Wrek said, staring at the sheets of paper one last time before dropping to a massive safe behind the counter. "I wonder," he muttered, reading a few numbers on one of the pages, then spinning the dial, twisting it and unlocking it. With a creak, the door to the safe swung open.

"Aye, but hopefully, I'll be drunk by the time she gets here," Emir muttered. He had one card left to play that would hardly win him the game. He was to leave this cursed city with his comrades from Keri. Then, he would return home and ask Roja only once to come with him. He knew full well that she would refuse such a request. He thought it a terrible thing that she would choose a sorrowful life over being with him, that she would choose a stubborn act of dedication to a city she wanted no part of.

He was heartbroken. He knew well she desired to be free of this place, but she would never leave. He would retire to the far end of the world, and she would never once see him again. And if she did visit? Well, he'd never allow her to leave.

Emir knew this, and the absent gods did too. But they would play no part in swaying her decision.

"Fuk the gods," he muttered.

"What was that? Ah, never mind," cried Wrek, appearing with dozens more sheets of paper. "Look at this," he said, spreading them out on the bar. His hands shook; he looked pale and excited, and his eyes were watery. He kept shaking his head, and Emir didn't understand what he was reading.

"I see," Emir offered, looking from sheet to sheet. He didn't see at all.

"They are the deeds to everything," Wrek cried, tapping names written on each page, and Emir nodded.

"Very good," he said.

What's he talking about?

"I thought when we went our separate ways, our partnership was dissolved, but Sigi kept my name on every single one of these documents. Look, right here; I own this tavern. I own this one here. This one too. I own them. I own every single one of them. I… fuk… I own…

the brewery… fuk… the Rat's Nest… the fuken Rat's Nest… All of them."

"Oh, now I see… fuk me… All of them," Emir cried, suddenly understanding.

Then Wrek's face darkened. He picked up a separate bundle of deeds. He held one out to Emir, who looked at it and, with his basic understanding, realised it was the collection of rental agreements that had brought about the end of the city. He dropped the sheet as though it were poison.

"There is blood on these deeds," Emir whispered, and Wrek agreed. "What are you going to do?"

"I am not Sigi; I do not desire to rule as he attempted to do. I will deliver these to the Primary with the condition that they are to be honoured at the lower rate," he said.

"I see," Emir said. He didn't at all, but it seemed a better idea that the Primary or the new king handle the finances, rather than his comrade.

"Aye, that is a better use of such a thing," Wrek said. Tears were flowing from his eyes—of gratitude, of sadness for his lost friend. Or perhaps tears of joy at his wealth. It didn't matter. It was a peculiar thing to gaze upon, and uplifting in a way.

"So, can I have one of your taverns?" Emir asked. It was a joke. But also not a joke.

"I'm not sure I want to be responsible for my best friend's death just yet."

"I'll be a distant owner. You can stand at the door, only let the roughest, nastiest fuks in, and you can send me the profits every month, brother. Or every year, if that suits."

"That sounds like a plan." Wrek laughed.

Emir knew he was leaving soon. He did not know how to say goodbye and could not think of a way to repay his best friend for everything he had done. How could he even find a place to begin? Yet still. "I'd never have made it this far without you, Wrek; you are a godly man."

"We did our best," the big man offered, and in this light, he looked like Quig, and Emir did all he could not to wail and burst into tears for all he'd been through, for the relief and hope.

"To Sigi," Wrek offered.

"Aye, I suppose," Emir said, drinking with him.

"And to King Erroh."

"To the fuken Puk!"

The Actions of Gods

They drank, told stories, marvelled at Wrek's good fortune, reminisced, spoke of those they had loved and lost and even argued over how "Emir's Hole" tavern should best be run. It was wonderful, and it was not the finest part of Wrek's day: no less than an hour after sunset, a feminine shadow appeared at the doorway.

"We are closed for now," Emir called, but she would not be stopped.

"Wrek," she cried, stepping through, and Emir knew that voice. Loved hearing that voice. "My Wrek?"

"Lara?" he cried, slipping drunkenly from his seat, rushing through the ruin of the tavern to catch her and lift her aloft with such delirious happiness that Emir could only stare in dumb joy at his friends' beautiful moment.

They kissed, loved and wept, and Emir refused to move from his seat, knowing this would be the last good night for him in this city. Lara spoke of Boat Town, of the terror, of her faith in Wrek, and of how, only now, she had reached the city only to find it in ruins.

She greeted Emir with love and a sturdy embrace. She wept aloud for Stefan's fate, and Emir lamented with her. She cared little for Wrek's new fortune, but told him that it was a fine thing he would sacrifice the rental agreements, and Emir thought this a wonderful, impressive thing.

As darkness fell over the city, Emir insisted they all retire for the night so they might reunite properly upon the morrow. Insisting he'd "lock up on the way out" was the compelling argument they needed. The two lovers slipped away, gazing into each other's eyes, and Emir thought that a fantastic memory to keep locked away should he never see them again.

It was near midnight when Roja appeared at the doorway. She was not angry, though the tear stains and her ruined makeup were telling, and Emir was nowhere near drunk enough to say those words he needed to say.

"When you and the behemoth slipped away, I knew you would end up in one of the taverns," she said quietly, sitting down in the chair beside him. He remembered a night a long time ago when they had been at odds like this. When friends had danced and the night was alive with fire and harsh words. He poured them each a drink, as she had paid for one then; he marvelled at how many miles they had both travelled since that time. There would be no bards' tales of their love, though, for who would want a story of such sorrow anyway?

"I think we must talk about terrible things," he said softly.

"I think so too," she said, and began to weep.

110

HERE WE GO AGAIN

Lea was in no rush to escape Spark City's territory. At least at the beginning. With every mile travelled, she felt lighter than before. She felt relief with every bird that flew over her head and every slap of a low-hanging branch upon her grinning face. She had a profound sense of release, of liberation. She felt different, somehow, yet also the same as she had once been. Shera was wary of their leisurely pace, sensing that it was inviting to followers.

Lea did not burden herself with too much thinking; she listened to the sounds of the road and was grateful. She would gaze back every few miles and wonder about pursuers, but each time, she saw no signs of charging Alphalines, no gangs of Wolves sent out to hunt her. She was taking this time for *her*. The fuken world could wait. Those who needed to know, knew. Those worrying after her would see her when she returned.

The first night was the most treacherous. The going had been tough, and she had felt keenly the remnants of her injuries. Eventually, near dawn, she had rested for a few hours. Every day since then, she had been careful to keep resting throughout the day, likely more than was strictly needed. Anyone watching her might have thought she was not desperate to hunt down a mad god alone at all.

Alone.

She swiftly fell into a routine. Although she grew tired in the saddle, she practised her swordplay frequently, more out of habit than passion. If shadow-fighting against no enemy in particular was good enough for him, it was good enough for her, even if she could not push herself.

The Actions of Gods

When she stopped to let Shera rest, Lea would spin around whatever transient camp she had made for an hour or so, killing a few dozen invisible warriors. In the first few days, she had to push herself to believe they were there and push harder to try outfighting them, she rarely broke a sweat, and she knew well she wasn't striving to be great, but she persevered. By the fifth night, she could imagine it was him, and at least half the time she won.

Twice a day soon became thrice, and she wondered how long it would take before she found her rhythm. A part of her wondered about avoiding fighting her father altogether. A part of her wondered whether, given the chance, she might draw a blade upon him as they sat down for dinner. Father and daughter and a little killing. Perfect.

At first, she was not lonely, for she enjoyed the quiet, but she felt an absence in her soul in the colder moments and in more peaceful times when she allowed her thoughts to wander. The feeling grew with every day that passed, and became an ache that had her look behind her longingly, hoping to see a storm of rising dust or a handsome figure in black. Looking forward, she met no weary traveller or cursed Southerner and was not surprised. The world had gathered at the city; all were invited. She had the road all to herself, and it was lonely.

Against her better instincts, she allowed her nightly campfires to blaze brightly. Nor did she attempt to conceal her presence, always resting close to the path, where any wanderer might pick up her trail. She took what loneliness she had and pushed it far down, where no one but him could relieve it.

Her days soon became focused on attaining the perfect resting place instead of counting the miles she had ridden. Instead of sticking to the flatter ground closest to the path, she sought the highest point in the land, frequently discovering a grand crest where she could see for miles either way. A place where she could look out and check for riders on the road. It was in these elevated places that, as night fell, she would build a large fire—bright enough to dazzle any nearby creature curious about the interloper. Every night, the fire she built was bigger and brighter; soon, she was spending hours of every day recovering dry wood suitable for burning away the night, lighting up the world and delivering a beacon to any worthy tracker for miles around.

Lighting the fire became the highlight of her day. She would sit near the crackling, waving flames, lost in the fire dance, and whisper to the wind her hopes that he would find her.

He.

These were beautiful, welcome thoughts, and every night she became little lost Lea of the city in need of grander things. She raged against all her strength and allowed humbleness and weakness to take her. She did not cry, for it was no tragic thing to embrace her mistakes; it was no tragedy to need another to fulfil her when she had spent so fuken long being strong.

The loneliness crept up on her, and for once, she accepted it and took it as the gift it was. Raging Lea of the road might not have seen it these past few months; more than that, she would have blamed him for such an affliction. Instead, now, she gripped the reins and took this sorrow for what it was.

Guilt.

———

Erroh should have had Wynn at his side. He might have picked up a scent, might even have found her. As it was, when he had finally picked up a trail, it had already gone cold. He'd given Highwind little reprieve in those first few hours. He'd driven her hard until the dark had spread its veneer across the land. Only then could he admit to himself that all his time on the road, his time in chains, and the months in Raven Rock had added little to his already inept skills at tracking.

Even on the first night, as he sat without flame or sustenance until sleep took him, he had the awful realisation that finding Lea was impossible. Although he hoped she had stayed on the path, he also knew she could have taken any one of a thousand different side routes at any time in the first day alone. He was filled with terror that in his haste to catch up, he had missed where she had set off on a different path. For hours he agonised over such a possibility. From the second day onwards, he kept his eye on the ground, but found it no easier to distinguish between her trail and those of others. It was a torturous thing.

Flailing wildly for a solution, he considered seeking out landmarks to which they had journeyed together. It was madness to believe she might have left him a clue, yet he clung to this thought like a hungry peasant at a king's royal spread.

The days drifted into one endless, slow march through the Wastes in search of an improbable treasure. He discovered a loneliness he hadn't endured in a long, long time and truly missed his comrades and his family. And he missed her, in a way. Not the girl who had left, but the girl who had marched with him. His sleep became infected by visions of horror. Of his family slain at Spark by a one-eyed god at the end of the world. He never dreamt of her, though. The daylight hours were for her alone, but the night was for his nightmares.

On the more frustrating mornings, as he took to the saddle, he gazed back to where he had come from and considered giving up, gathering better hunters than he was and assigning them to the search instead. There was a better chance that they would find her, but surrendering her to the march was something even he wouldn't do. Not even if her heart belonged to another.

Oh, aye, during those long hours in the saddle he thought frequently of her wrapped up in another's arms, and it was a sickening thing. It was no small matter to feel such a betrayal every day yet to still venture forth, seeking a way to help her. Never did he consider abandoning his duty to her. Even if she didn't want it. Besides, if he were to meet the Woodin Man in combat once more, he would need her by his side.

A week into his lonely trek, he woke in the middle of the night. Distantly, a mile or so behind him, in the pitch darkness, he saw a light flickering in the wind. He thought little of it, and a moment later sleep retook him.

The next morning, as he brewed a cup of cofe and prepared himself for the march, he saw the fire again, smaller now. He thought about the wanderer who had lit it, deep in the Wastes as he himself was, and wished them well. It was the first sign of life he'd seen since venturing south. Erroh was used to such solitude, but he liked to imagine the Four Factions taking a collective breath, having endured the war, and spilling out into the land, taking it back; now there was little to fear. He wondered absently if it were a roving group and not just a single wanderer. He feared no bandits; he feared no Hunt. For a peculiar moment, he considered seeking out that light. A foolish thing, he thought, enjoying his first brew and waiting for the sun to rise fully.

To say he thought again of the flame that day would have been a lie, for he drove harder again, with the South as his only thought. Eventually, as night fell, he lit his own fire to stave off the chill, concealing it deep beneath a small cairn of rocks. He had little intention of announcing his whereabouts to the world.

As before, though, he caught sight of that flame again. It was still behind him, but the same distance away, and Erroh thought this peculiar. Only then did he consider it might be her. Immediately, his mind reeled against such idiocy, for she wouldn't be so reckless as to allow anyone to see her so easily. Scolding himself for his foolish optimism, he let his own fire burn down to nothing and fell into a fitful sleep. Come the dawn, he charged as far from that larger fire as he could.

For many more days, he drove ahead as fast as he could go, but each night, he caught sight of that little flickering flame, now smaller and further away. It became no welcome thing at all. It became an obsession. Each day, he drove his beast relentlessly onward, gazing behind him less and less. But as the night drew in, he took to the nearest high point, seeking out the light. He didn't know why he did this.

On the last day, he drove Highwind longer than he would have cared to and crossed a great distance. Eventually, with night fully taking the land, he allowed the beast a reprieve and set camp. To his relief, he saw no other fire in the night, and he relaxed, reassured that no fiend was seeking him out.

For at least an hour, he sat warming himself by his own small blaze. Erroh felt lonelier this night than he had before. His mind raced with unlikely scenarios—that she called to him from a distance and had lit those beacons so he might find her. What had begun as a careless notion soon became irrational speculation and wild regret now that the fire was gone. Now that there could be no answer.

His mind began to whirl with more and more unlikely reasons why it could, indeed, be her, until, sitting bolt upright with horror, he finally realised his error.

He would have done exactly what this mysterious fire-setter was doing, if he were in her shoes and trying to grab his attention.

He did not sleep that night, such were his racing thoughts. More than once, he climbed from his bedding to seek out the light, as though perhaps, in the time he'd rested, she had decided once again to light a bonfire in his honour.

"You are a fuken idiot," Erroh hissed to the night, to the wind, to the entire fuken world, and got no reply.

By noon the following day, he had yet to depart. Instead, he had agonised over what action to take. Eventually, better sense won out, and he took to the road and continued venturing south. He felt wonderful about his decision.

For about an hour.

"Fuk this," he growled turned Highwind on her heels and tore back the way he had come. He knew he was an idiot, but until he discovered the bringer of the light, he could never settle. In truth, he knew he had little chance of finding her on the road ahead. The realisation calmed him somehow.

Eventually, when darkness came, he climbed to the nearest crest and looked out into the night. To his horror, he saw no light, and its absence was like a strike to the gut. Making his bed and wrapping himself up against the cold wind, he fell asleep for a time. He dreamt of mad gods slaying all he loved, and he woke screaming her name. He sat up, his heart racing, and peered into the night, and there it was: that flickering light, like a candle against a tempest. It was barely alive, barely a beacon at all.

He wasted no time; he gathered his belongings and set off towards it, hoping, believing, fuken knowing it was she, calling to him from across the world.

She was a waif, a shadow of herself these days. She knew she had brought it upon herself, and that was fine. She accepted it as a sort of holy penance and punishment. Perhaps the absent gods considered her solitude as the correct way of things. That was fine with her as well. The fire she had lit the previous night was long since burned out. Her body ached from her vigorous workout, and there was no river nearby where she could bathe away the pain. More than that, she was thirsty. With water so plentiful in the first few days, she'd been generous in consuming the life-giving fluid. Now, though, without a sign of a stream, river, lake or brook, she regretted her carelessness.

Looking at her map, she sighed, licked her dry lips and wondered what had become of her. She felt empty now. Bereft of hope and expectation. She had long stopped wondering about him. Instead, her thoughts were with her father some long distance away. Was he still thinking of her? Was he already planning his vengeance? On her? On the world? She pushed these thoughts from her mind, knowing they were likely to sap her energy, take her from the path and send her to despair. Still, she raged against such ideas, so once again, she packed her belongings and took to the road, seeking out water and a distraction from the exhaustion and pain.

"What have I become?" she asked the wind, and it blew coldly in reply, and it seemed fitting.

She urged her beast forward and carried on her solitary trek until, in the late afternoon, she finally came upon a water source deep enough to ease her agonies.

It was the most beautiful thing she'd ever seen. A river, slow-moving and as clear as a potent glass of sine. She was in love, and nearly hummed along to the babble of the gentle, rushing water as it went on its way. She lit no fire; she didn't even consider hunting some quail for supper. Instead, she walked Shera to the riverbank so the beast could drink its fill before she did.

Satisfied that Shera was tended to, Lea leapt into the water with a childish giggle. She went down further than she expected, but she was no feeble urchin, fresh from the city. She took the depth, the cold, the refreshing grip of the water and the thud of her feet against the rocks on the riverbed, and then pushed herself back up. She glided across its surface and nestled against some reeds, stripping her garments free, enjoying the cold against her bare skin.

She did not know how long she lay in the chilled water, only that it shook the life back into her. Grabbing some soap and taking her garments, she gave them all a vigorous scrub before turning the soap upon her skin. Immediately she felt better, losing herself in cleanliness and alertness; she did not hear her hunter steal up on her.

———

He had hoped to reach her camp by dawn, but it was too far. For hours he trekked through the undergrowth in the dark, stabbing himself on every thistle, stumbling on every gnarled root. Fortunately, there were no fallen branches to impale himself upon, and for this he was grateful. As dawn neared and the light of the fire disappeared in the growing light, Erroh tried to close the distance, to no avail.

At noon, with only luck and hope as his companions, he finally came upon the camp and recognised it as hers. Although the fire was long burned out, he recognised the tell-tale signs of the battle she'd fought on the dry ground. He recognised her form, her manoeuvres, and for the first time in many days he felt less alone, less terrified.

He read her story, and he read her direction, and with his head held high, he began to follow Shera's tracks, for they were obvious to him now. He galloped along, careful not to lose her scent until, unbelievably, he came upon her next place of camp and a tremendous weight was lifted from his soul.

Highwind immediately went to Shera, her companion from previous times, leaving Erroh to wander down along the water's edge in search of Lea. It was no difficult task, for he heard the sounds of splashing, the loud scrubbing of fabric against rocks, and he stepped into the open and near scared the life out of her.

"What the fuk?" she cried, crossing her arms over her breasts in fright, and he dared a grin.

"Hello, Lea," he replied evenly.

She relaxed ever so. "Hello, Erroh," she said after a time. She eased her hands away to reveal herself to him. She showed no shame. Nor should she have—had he not seen those breasts a thousand times before? She strode to the riverbank on her perfect, glistening legs and drew up a little away from him, far enough that he couldn't reach for her, but close enough that he could see.

There was no joyful reunion. No tears of joy. There was too great a distance between them. Erroh fought against his jealousies, but he was a hot-blooded male. He imagined her similarly seducing some wanton Wolf and was disgusted with his imaginings. He might have said something in that moment, but instead, he merely thought about how hot it had been in the saddle, despite the time of year. There were only so many warm days like this left, he knew. Also, he cared little about what she gazed upon.

"What are you doing here?" she demanded.

Ignoring her, he began unbuckling his belt, then stripped off his trousers and undergarments, followed by his shirt.

"I came to march with you," he said, standing naked before her. She gazed at his manhood as she had so many times before, and he was indifferent. He dropped into the water and swam into the middle of the river, carefully keeping his distance.

She was silent, watching him, considering his words. He prepared for an explosion of argument or at least a volley of cutting words. But none came. Instead, she watched him bathe, even offering him her soap.

"I hoped you would," she said after a time, and he smiled at the lie it was. If she had wanted him to accompany her, she would have asked him. Would have said goodbye, too.

"Of course, you face an unenviable task, but I will be by your side." He meant it; he really did, but when she smiled in reply, he imagined her gasping as her lover entered her. He kept his face carefully blank, pushing the thoughts away. He moved slowly towards her, as naked as she was, with nothing more but a pledge that he would be with her at the end. He offered her everything but his heart, and he did so without a word spoken. It was better this way. As far as pledges went, this one was better than most.

"Thank you, Erroh," she whispered, and dared a few steps towards him, standing tall in the water so he would be reminded of everything she was. Offering herself and offering a reconciliation without clumsy words or heartfelt apologies. She was incredible, and he couldn't help but be attracted to her. But there was no desire to grasp hold of her and win her back. For all their anger, wrath, love and sorrow, she had stepped away from him first; there was nothing to return to. He knew this now, even as he smiled and accepted the embrace she offered, but pulled himself away when she tried to draw him close as only lovers did.

"There is light left in the day; we can still march a few miles further, Lea," he said evenly.

"Oh, all right," she said, allowing him to step away. She smiled her most tragic smile, and he suppressed his anger. Such things faded in time, and there were miles to walk before they reached the end—plenty of time to accept them. "As you wish, my… beo," she said quietly, and oh, that did sting a little. Climbing from the river, he said nothing more, but his mind reeled once again.

Don't call me that.

111

THE BOAR

He could feel it so fuken near that the taste was on his tongue. His body was a machine of motion, constantly driving forward, and his reward was ever closer. Stewed in gravy for a few hours would be perfect. Some potatoes on the side, slathered in butter. Each step he took was agony, but that was fine; that's how it should have been. A branch caught him unaware, and he stumbled, tripped and rolled a few feet, but he sprang back up as swiftly as he could. Such a delay could cost him everything.

Perhaps roasted upon a spit, coated in salt and pepper, with a few slices of fried and oiled potatoes alongside, as those of the South liked. His mouth watered despite the dryness, and that was fine too. He would savour the wait; such things were vital.

"Are you all right?" Lea cried from behind him, seeing him fall. Her smaller legs were as rushed as his. She kept up. That was enough.

The boar was large and imposing. More than that, it was fast and wily. They'd picked up the tracks a few hours before, and after a painstaking crawl through the undergrowth with weapons in hand, a slight stumble on her part had alerted the beast. A change in the wind had blown their scent directly towards the gigantic creature and sent it sprinting.

"I'm fine," he said evenly, watching her charge past, eager to keep pace with her quarry. The boar must have sensed its slight advantage, for it darted wide once more as it had a dozen times already, eager to find a thick patch of undergrowth to slip into while its hunters with their cumbersome limbs would need to find another way around. "Fuken keep at him."

"As you wish," she cried back deliriously. Erroh could see the hunter was alive and thriving in her, that same killer instinct that had left thousands of quails dead and eaten. She held Baby in one hand, three arrows in the other. Twice she'd gotten close enough to fire an arrow, but the boar was blessed with an almighty amount of luck, for every time she fired, it veered to the side, making a mockery of her accuracy. "Fuken stay straight," she cried as it broke cover and dashed out of the trees, and she wasted another arrow as she sprinted after it.

He imagined the animal lanced and hoisted over a large fire. They could strip it clean, dry and salt the meat they did not eat that night and eat well for the rest of the journey. He wasn't sure he'd enjoy the long process of curing such a monster, however. He wasn't sure she wouldn't prefer a few weeks with him alone. To break him, charm him, ease his heart closer to hers.

Fuk off, Lea.

Aye, in the days after their reunion in the river, Lea had not given up on trying to repair the bond between them. Although she spoke little with him beyond what was necessary, she continued to try to regain his favour. Erroh knew this because he knew her all too well.

Although not as well as you thought.

For a breath, he again imagined another grabbing at her body, tearing her clothes free, and he nearly stopped the chase, almost gave up altogether and left the massive tusked prey to its victory.

Stop thinking of that.

He tasted that boar in his mouth and wanted it more than anything. He imagined severing mighty slabs of meat from its carcass and charring them to a crisp upon a fire. Perhaps a little honey and onion upon the spit to finish the meal?

She took his rejection in the water better than he had expected. She had not pushed the matter, and he had been thankful for that. Instead, she had dried herself across from him, again showing all she had, before sitting down in front of the fire he had built and sharing her food with him. It was a neutral enough gesture, so he accepted the offer.

They spoke little, not of war, not of death, not of loss or love either. But of lesser things. They spoke quietly, fondly, of the road, and the conversation began to flow more easily between them. While their mounts enjoyed their own camaraderie, grazing at the side of the camp, Erroh and Lea found comfort in muted talk and a meal shared.

She had been the first to lie down by the flames, and she opened her blankets to welcome him. Declining was no small thing, but he had suffered far more harrowing torments in his time. She had offered her warmth every night since, without ever querying his refusal, without ever challenging his motives. She accepted his distance. Were he to think on the matter more, he might have accepted, but really, he was comfortable to offer a delicate shake of the head before turning his back to her and seeking sleep and giving in to horrid dreams of death and slaughter.

Every day was similar. They rose early and rode their mounts side by side, watching the road, looking for tracks and scanning the sky for ominous things. He caught her smiling to herself occasionally, and he wondered who the smile was for. He wondered if it was her new lover, who was no doubt unaware she offered herself to Erroh every night. He wondered if it was for Erroh himself, for her attempts to creep back into his heart, one small step at a time. Perhaps it was for herself alone, and he hoped this was the truth. He did not hate her; he could not wish ill upon her, for, once upon a time, they had loved, and that girl still held his heart.

Smile away, Lea, for yourself.

Lea saw where he'd fallen, and for a breath, she thought he'd injured himself. Over his eye appeared a thin line of blood where his head had scraped the ground. She almost dropped down by him to tend to his wound, to show him she cared with actions instead of words. Words she wouldn't share with him yet. That would come in time. This she knew. Just as she knew he was losing his resistance to the offers she made him every night. She was not embarrassed.

On the contrary, she accepted the punishment he delivered upon her. Truthfully, these last few days had been finer than the time with the Wolves. In Erroh, she saw so much more that she'd seen in him before. Notably, the great man he had become. She no longer endured loneliness or hopelessness either.

Her heart still fluttered a little when they spoke of lesser things. She remembered this agony from before. Two young Alphas finding their way towards something beautiful. There would come a time when the words would rear their ugly heads. The agony he held was no doubt similar to the betrayal she had once felt. A feeling that lessened every day she was around him.

She missed another shot. The beast veered away, and she cursed loudly, but she had never been more at ease, like a feline chasing a kill. She savoured these moments; stalking their quarry had heightened her bloodlust more than she'd expected. She marvelled at its massive body, its muscular limbs built for charging and destroying, its terrible tusks, albeit a little misshapen, that could gore her to the bone should the animal turn upon her.

"Come on, Erroh," she howled as he neared her, came alongside and then moved a few steps ahead. He wasn't sprinting full tilt, but he was near his limit. She wasn't as fast, but that he did not leave her behind was a telling thing. She loved this man; she had always loved him and couldn't wait to love him more. But that would come in time, perhaps over the carcass of their quarry, medium rare, a little bloody if need be.

Green eyes.

As swiftly as they appeared in her mind, they were gone. She grinned in triumph. She had come far these last few weeks. Better to take that fuken trauma and recover, become stronger for it. It was either that or capitulate completely, crawl into a corner and wait for the storm to pass, or for someone to pick her up and shield her for the rest of her life.

Fuk that.

He drew back his massive spear and let loose. It was an impressive spear. He'd whittled and sharpened the long piece of wood for days to get it just right. She supposed it was something to do instead of speaking aloud his darker thoughts.

"Not again," he cried as the spear flew far but barely grazed the beast's shadow as it landed in the undergrowth. "And there he goes again," he snarled, ripping the spear from the ground as he passed without missing a step, and she thought him impressive. She wasn't going to say as much. Perhaps, after they lay together, she could whisper her love and pride, and the arousal she felt at witnessing such deeds.

The boar cut wide again and ran mindlessly back through the forest, seeking a reprieve. She would have liked to take a reprieve of her own, such was the pace Erroh had set. He hadn't cursed her clumsiness earlier when they had approached the team of boars in their glade, but she knew it was her fault.

Without warning, the creature suddenly came upon a small crevice in the land, attempted to sidestep and tangled its feet in some gnarled roots. With a squeal of terror and confusion, it reared high into the air and spun around, thrashing madly, before falling directly into the crevice, ending the race.

The Actions of Gods

"What the fuk?" Erroh cried, scrambling to the deep hole to peer down to the panicked animal below.

"That was amazing," Lea cried in delight, standing over the open hole, looking down at the terrified beast, which lay upon a ledge a few feet down. "We are fortunate," she declared, watching the boar charge back and forth along the ridge, getting more panicked as it found no escape but a depthless drop below. "We have you now," she said, gasping as the exertions took her. Erroh gasped as well. It had been a decent hunt with an unusual ending. It was almost a shame, really. Up until the luckless creature had tripped, he wasn't sure how this hunt would go.

She leaned over the side and held Baby aloft. She aimed and released. And missed from a few feet away. Something knocked against her arm, and the arrow struck a rock and careened down to the darkness beyond.

"Why did you do that?" she demanded, turning to Erroh.

"It just seemed a little unfair," Erroh muttered, looking to the helpless boar. It had settled somewhat, despite their presence. Perhaps it knew it was at their mercy; perhaps it was as tired as they were. Perhaps it had simply given up.

"Fuk that. I'm hungry," Lea argued, raising the bow again, and this time Erroh caught her arm as she loaded the shot.

"I said no." She stared at him for a breath. He knew she was ready to argue, to pontificate all the hazy morning, but instead, she unloaded the arrow and returned it to its quiver. He wasn't used to such obedience. He'd expected at least a curse or two. Instead, she looked to the beast below and appeared to see the prey as something else entirely.

"Fine. As you wish, but we can't leave the poor thing to die down there; it is no way to pass."

"What do you propose? A bridge? A ladder? Dig him out?"

She looked around for a time until she spotted a menacing-looking log, thick, rotten, manoeuvrable. "There," she said, and he followed her lead. "This is so fuken stupid," she muttered after a time as they heaved the log towards the open crevice. "You'll probably let it live afterwards, too, won't you?" she grumbled accusingly as the log rolled a few feet, revealing civilisations of insects underneath. "Oh, there are so many," she squealed, but stayed to task as the beasties crept around them, upset at their forced liberation from their home.

"It just seemed wrong to kill it that way," Erroh said, looking at the

945

beast's crooked tusk. Crooked or no, it would devastate. "Truthfully, the war has wiped out so many; it might be time to let them repopulate," he added.

"Like Alphalines," she countered.

"Like humankind."

They worked the log over the edge. With insects now crawling across their hands, they somehow eased the massive log down along the side of the pit and left it at an angle slight enough that a creature, desperate and brave enough, could scramble up and not fall over the side.

"What a waste of a morning."

"It's a small matter," Erroh said, grabbing his spear and walking back towards their camp, a few miles away.

"*You* are a small matter," Lea mocked, following after. Behind them, the trundle of excitable feet upon wavering bark could be heard as the boar dared to rescue itself.

"Perhaps so," Erroh said evenly, setting off through the forest.

Suddenly, there was a cacophony of hooves upon wood, and from the darkness emerged the majestic boar they had just rescued, now in full flight. It stopped momentarily on the path, regarding them, and then darted off into the treeline opposite; a moment after that, it was gone entirely from their lives. Erroh groaned inwardly. At that moment, he would have accepted something as uninspiring as boar soup or stew with little more than a chunk of bread accompanying it.

Their hunt had been a failure, yet strangely, Erroh didn't feel bad. He imagined the animal becoming a legend among its fellow wild beasts. He imagined it mating with many a sow and even more little boarlets filling up the meadows, spreading out, growing and beginning the cycle anew. All because of Erroh's mercy.

"Well fought, little one," he said to the beast, now long gone, and Lea strode by, muttering under her breath.

For a time, they walked in uncomfortable yet also wholly comfortable silence. Erroh enjoyed listening to the natural world, the rush of wind, the hiss of insects and the cackle of mocking crows.

Fuk you, crow.

Lea, on the other hand, was determined to have no part of nature. She stomped through the undergrowth, cursing their luck and "Erroh's nobility."

"Better to be noble than a whore."

He didn't mean to say it, but he also meant to say it. In his defence, it had been on his mind for quite a time.

Lea stopped in her tracks. Immediately, the forest became quieter. "Did you just call me a whore?"

He had. He hadn't been subtle about it.

"These last few days have been pleasant and such. But know this, dear Lea: in every action, I see you perform, in every word you speak, be it kind, be it vicious, be it warm or sorrowful, I think of you as a whore."

She must have believed him, for her face went pale.

"Oh, fuk off, Erroh. You know damn well I never took another lover."

Liar, liar, fuken whore liar, loving another.

He hadn't expected this, but he knew it to be a lie. A better man who had never loved as he had would have felt lighter with such knowledge, but Erroh was a hot-blooded Alphaline. More than that, he was a spurned hot-blooded Alphaline.

"He died in the battle, didn't he?"

"What are you talking about?" she yelled, and he knew he had struck a vein of gold. To the fires with her dead lover, and her as well, while he was at it.

"Were you there when it occurred? Was it your fault? Was it his? Are you carrying his child?" He didn't know where that last question came from, but he didn't care. He needed to know. He wanted him to be dead too.

"You are a piece of shit," she cried, striking Erroh fiercely across the cheek, and he allowed her. He merely looked into her soul and answered the questions in his mind. "I never took another lover. You know me better than that; I could never touch another. It was you, always you," she screamed, and Erroh wondered whether the boar heard her outburst. Did it send the beast sprinting further into the Wastes, or was it still nearby, watching with eagerness to see how this argument would pan out?

He turned away from her. Refusing to become emotional, to show how deeply she'd cut him. How close he was to weeping. How tempted he was to believe her lies. "Don't turn from me!" she demanded, and her voice was close to breaking, and fuk it, but it felt good to hear her as agitated as this.

"Your lies are so finely tuned, they could be played upon an instrument," he said evenly.

She suddenly became desperate. She ran alongside him and grabbed at his arms; she pulled him to her. Her eyes were genuine and terrified, soft and regretful. "It was a lie, my beo," she whispered.

Don't call me that.

"Don't call me that."

She wasn't finished. "No, really, my beo. I needed distance from you. My heart was broken, not by you, but by him." She pointed towards the South as though bringing up her father was an acceptable reason for such cruelty. As was lying to escape the results of her ill-taken actions. "I love you, Erroh; I've only ever loved you."

"Distance from me?" he snarled, shoving her hand away. The pain was fresh. The agony of betrayal was as potent as before. He wanted to die. He wanted to give up there and then. "Well, it worked," he roared, and near broke at her gaze. He shoved her away as she clawed at him, whimpering, tears coursing down her cheeks.

"Please, Erroh," she wailed, and this sudden emotion angered him even more.

"Fuk off, whore," he roared, storming away.

She did not call after him again, but she did follow. Her steps were more hesitant than before, and he heard her sniffle, but he felt little for her. He played her words in his mind, and he could see nothing beyond another lover charming her to his bed, and he was sickened.

112

BREAKING HEARTS

Lea knew she had fuked up everything. Even more than she had ever thought possible. She followed him back to the camp, eager to find words to break through his defiance and drag something more from him. Her mind was awash with thoughts, great thoughts, all the thoughts, and few words. She had never suffered an inability to speak, had never found difficulty in words, but Erroh had shaken her. Until this very moment, she had considered only his betrayal, her own traumas. Admittedly, she had endured more than most, yet still, she realised the damage her cruelty had bestowed upon him. And for what? A little reward on her part? A little grace for herself alone?

She watched him walk and thought he had a fine walk to him. She thought many fine things about him, but none that she would share with him, at least not yet. Strangely, she wished Nomi were here with her now. With them. In the time she had spent with the girl, she had recognised how important she was, how wise beyond her years she was in such matters too. Nomi spoke directly, more so than Lea ever could. She wished she could ask her advice; she wished that Nomi could speak to Erroh on her behalf, break through the shroud of betrayal he wore and see her for who she was. She was no longer Lea of the road, mated to Erroh the beautiful, Erroh the heroic; she was so much more. She wanted to be more.

"Come break my heart," he mocked lightly, recovering some sparring blades from his pack. Her heart leapt in excitement. They had not sparred once on this journey. Such a thing between them was sacrosanct. Such a thing was intimate. She hadn't broached the topic with him before; she had waited for him, and now, with her heart broken, her terror that losing him was a possibility, he offered a gift.

Break his heart? Aye, she would do all she could.

She met him in the middle of the arena, the boundary in their minds. He held out his blades to her, and she held out hers to him. Within a breath, they both charged upon each other, hacking and slashing, seeking a kill, seeking to inflict a little pain. Their bodies became a blur of movement as each gave their all without restraint. It was fantastic and familiar, and Lea moved with the battle, enjoying his threat and her body, ready for whatever tricks he called upon.

"You are sharp," she cried mid-blow, and he did not hear her; he merely spun away from her strikes, seeking a weakness she had little intention of revealing. Immediately, she felt herself pushing harder than she had for months now, since before the fall of Raven Rock. She had been elite in that fallen town. A coldness took her; she wondered if she might have bested her father were she at her best in battle that miserable day? "But I can take you," she added, lunging towards him, clipping his shoulder, and receiving a careless strike to the arm that could have disarmed her were it a real battle.

He grimaced at his success, or else her mistake. She decided it was the strike; what right did he have criticising her, anyway?

She retreated from his swords to regroup, and decided to approach from a different angle. He followed after, his eyes cold and alert; he matched her retreat, waiting to pounce, and for a breath, she missed this terribly, missed *him* terribly. She needed to fight out of her skin to keep up with him, match him, and best him. His style hadn't changed; it was her own. Those months in the saddle with the Wolves had left her better skilled with the bow, but her swordplay was a little rusty, her timing a little loose. No amount of imagining could improve such a thing. To remain a master, one should have a partner. She knew well she'd stepped unprepared into battle with a master. She was far better than anyone else out there, but now she realised that such confidence had led to stagnation. It was a terrible thing to understand that Uden had bested her, not because of her inferior ability alone but because of her hubris.

I did this to myself.

He spun around her, his body taut and controlled as though every muscle agreed to his demands. He played with her without actions or words, using her for his own means, and it was humbling.

She had taken Erroh's opportunity to fight Uden, and the world was lesser for it.

He scored a killing blow with a strike that she saw too late. A nasty crack across the chest took her wind; she fell to her knees as he slid his wooden blade across her unprotected throat, shoved her to the ground and stepped away.

"A fine kill," she muttered, coughing at the irritation the blow caused. He didn't react; he shook his mighty body, popped a tendon in his arm loudly, tested the movement and awaited her attack.

She did not like his silent indifference. Truthfully, she had been here before, but it was never easy gazing upon him, knowing he seethed below the surface, that he was a few steps from rearing like a wild mount and tearing her apart with venomous words. Aye, she might have deserved it this time, but there were only so many times she could apologise. Would apologise. She had said her part, said more than he needed. He would have to hear more, but now was no time to add to the heavy agony between them.

She charged again, and he met her blade, and his counter cut through her defence and delivered another killing blow to her sternum. "Fuk me," she gasped, tripping in the mud. Above them, the day's warmth suddenly gave way to an explosion of rainfall. Without warning, there fell upon them a mighty deluge, and it soaked through her clothes almost instantly, taking her heat and adding to her misery.

"Why aren't you speaking?" she muttered, climbing to her feet, but he stepped forward and shoved her back to the ground. He stood over her and prodded the sparring sword against her forehead like he had pierced her. "Smooth, my beo," she mocked, rolling onto her side in the mud, away from his gaze, away from him, seeking out a blade, eager to get a killing blow. If for no other reason than to demean him as he did her.

He stood ready, and she leapt to her feet and sprinted towards him. At the last moment, she slid in the mud and lunged forward as before, and he was away from her, swift and clean. Quick as lightning, he appeared from behind her and dealt her a cracking blow across her back. She squealed in fright and frustration, and he brought his blade to her chest and her heart and slid it against her.

"Fine. I didn't practice as much as I should have," she said through clenched teeth, her face dripping with rain. He spat on the ground at her feet. At least, that was something. It wasn't much. She didn't appreciate his behaviour. Right or wrong, he was nasty, and it was no good look to him. Distantly, thunder rolled loudly and only then did he look away from her to the north and to the unpleasantness that came with such loud noises.

The rain grew heavier and its chill began to cut through her now. Her hands shook, and she thought of the frozen South and a stain on a map. It wasn't a great distance from here. She wondered if they might take a few days to visit. He once said he'd fallen in love with her in that place.

Come back to me, Erroh.

And then, suddenly, over the roar of the rain, he began to talk. "How much hate must you carry for me, that you would say such things?"

She would not lie to him. Not again. "I carried nothing but hate, my beo; it wasn't for you but for me."

He didn't seem interested in her words; nor did he look moved.

"You are a foul liar. Even here, at the end of it all, you would look into my eyes and lie about dreadful things instead of owning up to your cruelty?"

"Why do you refuse to believe me?"

"Because the Lea I loved would never have cut me so deeply, just to keep me… distant." The anguish flashed across his beautiful face for just a breath, and she reached for him. To hold him, love him, beg forgiveness a thousand times more and convince him her soul and her heart belonged to him alone. Forever, no matter what choices she made.

He shoved her back in the mud, and the look of anguish vanished right fuken away. She could see the piercing hate again now, and was ashamed that she'd twisted him into such a thing.

"Would it have made you happy were I to have stepped away, Erroh? Happy enough that I might earn a final kiss? Would it free you to take another? Is it Nomi you truly want?" She knew she shouldn't have said such words, but in Lea's defence, she, too, was an idiot on occasion. She looked at the ground. "I didn't mean that, not about Nomi; I shouldn't have."

He sighed heavily, and the thunder rolled. This time he did not flinch or become distracted. His eyes were upon her alone. In the mud. Where, she belonged.

"You think you have earned a final kiss?" he roared, with such grief that she shook. "Our lips shall never touch again lest I recognise his taste."

Her heart began to beat rapidly; she couldn't get it to settle, couldn't get it to fall in time. She felt the grip of panic take her; she wanted to reach for him again and say the right things. She wanted Erroh back—her Erroh. Nobody else's. Not ever.

"Can you not see the world through my eyes?" she whimpered,

deploring her tone. Little meagre Lea of the city, without a clue. Without love. Without family. Without anything.

"I tried to," he said, crouching down to study his vanquished opponent, and it was raining, and she was broken-hearted, and the true tragedy of it all was that it was her doing. She had betrayed him with such malice, and she suddenly understood why he was as he was. And she? Well, she demanded more from him. "I did everything to ease your suffering, and I met a punishing goddess of the city." His hands shook as he spoke, and Lea realised his anger could not be sated with words alone.

"I was wrong; you deserved none of it, beo," she cried, and reached for him, and he was away from her, disgusted, pacing around the camp as though he were a caged beast of prey, desperate for release.

"You tore the trust apart. How can I ever know if your words were a lie? How can I ever forgive a person who would lie to devastate me as you did? Better you take another and be done with it."

"I see that now, my love; I couldn't see it before. I was wrong; I was so fuken wrong."

Her breath began to catch in her chest.

"You cannot fix this, Lea," he said quietly, and she barely heard him. Only then did she realise her grip upon him was lost. Her thoughts of his betrayal were nothing in comparison to her own conscious treachery. Some things should never be said, and yet she had screamed them in his face, purely for her own relief. She could see it now, as clear as the water had been in their river. She began to weep uncontrollably—a terrible crying that no other mortal ought to have heard.

She howled her words. They spoke of innocence, of her anger with Erroh for leaving her on the worst day of her life. She cried for a life she had been denied. It didn't matter that it was Erroh alone who listened. She released this torrent of pain upon the world for herself alone. He did not interrupt, even as she lamented for the shadow he cast, for the fact that she had been denied such a legacy because of the actions of others, that she had only walked behind him, never aspiring to be anything but his mate.

He interrupted only once, to ask her about the Wolves, and she wept more, challenging with questions of her own. How could she have chosen foolish desire, to mate with a soldier who was below her? How weak a leader would she be to take a chance with men she commanded into death? He did not believe her fully, but she could see that he was at least thinking on the matter.

She felt terrible panic take her, drag her to darkness. She wailed loud enough that the Woodin Man would have known of their nearing had he not been fighting for his life that very moment.

Lea's words began to fail her as her chest tightened, for she knew nothing in the world would ever be the same again.

I am dying.

Her breath lessened, and the light of the day began to fade as the storm intensified; it seemed hours too soon. She felt herself drowning, and still, she could not stop weeping, begging for a release, until she collapsed in the mud and he was beside her, hushing her, whispering words she couldn't rightly make out. Not that it mattered, for this was the end of the world, and she told him as much.

"You won't be alone at the end of the world," he whispered, and her breath caught and held. She dared a gasp and still couldn't breathe fully, but her sobs began to taper off as she stared into those beautiful eyes, as she listened to him pledge that he would not leave her, at least for now.

It was not a lover's pledge, but it was a fine pledge, and she turned it over and over in her mind until her breath eased, his hold released and he left her to recover in the mud and the rain, where she belonged.

113

AMBUSHED

It was a rightly shitty day to die, thought Aymon, rising from his bed in the middle of the Wastes. He thought as much every morning as he clambered free of his bedding. Sometimes free of his lover's arms as well, but not today. Today he had awakened to the coldness of a lonely bed. The sky was cloudy and miserable, a perfect day to die, but he wouldn't say that aloud, not with the rest of his Wolves so near.

They were almost a dozen in all, all now waking up as he was. He could see them from where he sat in the blankets. Little figures, rousing themselves and preparing for the splendid ambush to come. The sooner the better, he mused. Why put off the inevitable, even if that was death? They couldn't see him, nor would they look to the small site reserved for him and Azel alone. They were accepting of his true self; they never commented, never mocked him behind his back, or so he thought, but he was also careful never to rub his natural acts with his lover in their faces. They were good men, the lot of them; there was no shame in their being uncomfortable with such things. There was no shame in bedding his lover that little further away too. And besides, it was nice to have a little privacy out in the Wastes as they marched towards death.

Stretching, scratching, becoming alert, he dressed swiftly against the brisk morning chill. Their shared fire was still glowing, and upon it was brewing a little mug of cofe. Azel had put it on. He was no cofe drinker himself, but he knew the advantage of keeping his leader in a good mood. It was the little things that warmed Aymon's heart. He'd never told the fuk he loved him because he wasn't sure if it was love. He was a man of the world, but he'd never taken a lover, unlike Azel. Azel was a man of the world and had taken many a lover. It was an intimidating thing, but Aymon never said as much. Truthfully, he was a fine companion, and that was enough in this world.

He could see the rest of his warriors preparing for the day. Theirs was a nervous shuffle, and Aymon could not reassure them, no matter how much confidence they had in the plan. Some of them were going to die today. This Aymon knew.

For the hundred time, he thought again of this wild pursuit across the Wastes and doubted his sanity. All their sanity. The frenzy of battle was long gone in the first few days. But as they followed the Southerners and the barbaric god, they had not slowed, nor had they questioned their decisions.

He thought of Lea and Doran and knew he would miss them this day. He would especially miss Lea's blade, for she was elite. And Doran? Well, he missed that hulking brute something terrible. A pang of regret coursed through him at the thought of his betrayal. No, not betrayal; Doran had done little but abandon his friend to his own calling. It took no fool to see the bald brute was better off among the city's females than remaining with these outcast Wolves. Still, though, were he to die, he might regret not thanking his friend for the kinship of so many years. He owed much to Doran. In a way, his deserting him was a gift in itself.

Aymon looked to a massive rock across from their camp that had shielded them all from the wind's rush as they slept. Azel sat upon it now, far up. His eyes were open, but his face was blank and distant. Wherever he was, there was blood flowing and people dying. Aymon had asked many times about his distant stare and received little more than mutterings about Keri, and Aymon rarely pushed him. Occasionally, though, he would talk of the crush in the arena as the worst moment of his life. Aymon suspected he was there now, swaying with the crowd, trying not to die in the stampede.

Sipping the steaming cofe, Aymon walked to the base of the rock and looked up again to his companion, friend, lover, and many other things. "Thank you for the brew," he whispered, hoping not to startle the young man from his imaginings.

With a start, Azel returned to the rock, to the hunt, to his lover below. "Oh, good morning, sir," he said softly. His face was paler than usual. For a dreadful moment, Aymon imagined Azel had taken a blow during the final battle, and only now was the blood finally seeping from him. "I was away," he said, carefully sliding down to greet his lover.

"It will be today," Aymon said, and Azel smiled sadly. While chasing the Southerner and his twenty-strong entourage had been frantic, the last few days had been taken at a more leisurely pace now that they had caught up with them. They were a few hours' ride ahead of them as it was. Opening the detailed map he'd brought with him, Aymon scrolled briefly through their route and the area where they would ambush the curs before looking to the sky again. It was going to rain.

Sometimes he liked to listen to the rain. It gave him peace. It also soothed his mind with healing thoughts. In battle, it could help them this day. Rain caused distraction, making it harder for the enemy to see where attacks originated. Perhaps the absent gods believed in rewarding curs who'd endured a lifetime of strife.

They did not.

"I am wary of stepping into the darkness today, my love," Azel mumbled. His colour was worse; he would not meet Aymon's eyes, and Aymon suspected his thoughts were not the true reason for this worry. Azel wasn't afraid of dying either. It was the Keri in him. Also, he'd never called him his love before. For a breath, Aymon's thoughts were thrown into chaos.

"We will live through this… Azel," he countered. He could have said 'my love' as well, but he would not throw the words around so casually just because they might all die.

It is a good plan.

There was a great crossing where only one bridge would suffice. With deep treelines on either side, almost a dozen fine Wolves could conceal themselves there and rightly tear the bastards apart from a distance. They would take Uden last. If he died in the process, so be it. If they returned with the brute in chains, there wasn't an honour they wouldn't receive for such a thing; besides, a brute like that deserved to be hanged in view of a thousand and one members of families torn apart by his ugly march.

"Live through this? No, I think not. Yet here we are, preparing to march towards death."

"Would you have me retreat? Would we gather larger numbers?"

Azel laughed bitterly. "That choice was ours, and we never took it." He pointed to the Wolves preparing. "Not a single one fled. Can you name a single warrior who hasn't suffered at the hands of that bastard? No, we want this, even if it is the end."

Perhaps Aymon wanted it too. Possibly seeing the misery was too much for even his cold heart.

Azel dropped his head. "I've done great things in my life and terrible things too. I want to step into the darkness with a cleaner conscience when I die."

"What do you mean?"

"I made no apology for my hatred of Dia, the Primary."

"Aye, you had reason, I suppose. Keri and such," Aymon offered. Azel was quivering. His lover was afraid of nothing, yet here he was, wavering, and it was a worrying thing. "And she was no friend to our kind." That was true.

"When she died, it was a good day. Or it should have been a good day."

Perhaps this was true also. Aymon was no great fan of the old woman, but his pledge to her was one of duty. Some things couldn't be changed; actions couldn't be twisted under every circumstance. Still, for her to die was awful, not to mention the horrors that had followed.

"Stop this," Aymon mumbled. He gripped his lover's shoulder. There was more, and he didn't want to hear, for deep down, suspicions he'd once held were beginning to stir.

With her death, there was most certainly prejudice against his ways lost too. Azel knew all this, for they had spoken of such things before, in the late hours when few were around to listen or offer their thoughts. But there had always been more that Azel wouldn't say. And why didn't Aymon push? A lover will only question some things, lest they learn something terrible, something they are unprepared to know.

"On that day, in the arena, when all were gathered in the Primary's box, they checked Cass for weapons, you know," Azel whispered.

Shut up, shut up.

"What did you do, Azel?" Aymon's stomach turned upon itself. He knew what he had done; he might always have known but denied himself the knowledge. Every Wolf had known there were mysterious circumstances behind the assassination. War had gotten in the way of a proper investigation.

"I have regrets, dear Aymon; I had no idea so many would fall that night, the turn the world would take after. Cass was a good man. A truly great man. I miss him, but he knew what needed to be done, and so did I."

Aymon gripped Azel's shoulder tight enough that Azel flinched. Aymon's free hand became a fist. He needed to punish this beautiful boy. He needed to kill him. It was his duty, what the boy deserved for his crimes.

"You placed the weapon in his hand, didn't you?" Aymon hissed, and

The Actions of Gods

his voice broke with horror, with agony. He struck his lover fiercely in the stomach and brought him to his knees.

"I needed to tell you," Azel gasped, but he did not fight back or try to block the next strike to his face. Aymon's face was contorted with pain and indecision. He dealt the boy another strike, and then placed his massive fingers upon his throat. He needed to kill him, despite the love, despite his need for him in battle. "I am sorry, my love."

Clenching his teeth, Aymon leaned over him, tightening his grip on Azel's throat. When the boy fell limp, he released him, shoving him down in the mud beneath their rock.

"I cannot stand to be around you, cur," he roared, leaving Azel to his misery. Swallowing his torment, Aymon stormed away to the Wolves, his brothers, his comrades and his accompanying murderers. He was empty of hope, of love, of faith. He could only embrace the anger, and any thoughts of slipping away from this battle were swiftly lost.

"We leave now," he roared, and they fell into line, gripping the reins of their mounts as he did. After a time, Azel scurried down to grab his mount, and Aymon, unable to look at him but unwilling to leave a fierce archer behind, delayed long enough to let him join the pack. If his comrades recognised a fight between the lovers, they offered no words, jests or thoughts. They followed their general towards doom, and they did so in silence.

They recognised the terrain from Aymon's map and fell into place swiftly as they arrived, leaving their mounts to roam freely in a nearby glade should the unthinkable occur. Then they waited, still as statues, knowing the afternoon would draw on swiftly. Their eyes were upon the bridge, stretched across the deepest, most unforgiving waters for twenty miles each way. It was a perfect point for an ambush—so obvious, in fact, that it might have been wiser to assume no ambush would occur here.

Hours passed, accompanied by the heavy fall of rain to sap their mood, before the light rumble of mounts could be heard travelling along the path, and Aymon's heart began to beat in excitement and terror. He dared a glance at Azel at the other end of the bridge. He looked upon him with horror, disgust and awful, awful love. He couldn't help himself, as much as he couldn't forgive him. But at the end of his life, with a few breaths left, things seemed ever so different to him.

I love you, Azel.

The Hunt appeared on the far side of the river. They were not charging; they were taking their sweet time, hunched against the coldness of the drizzling rain, the biting wind. Aymon's eyes darted from warrior to warrior, seeking out the Woodin Man. Each of these fiends was fierce and impressive upon the saddle. Their gazes were fixed steadily upon the South; not one noticed the hidden fiends on either side of them as they drew near. Within moments they were halfway across the wooden bridge.

Aymon held his sword tightly; the next few breaths would be welcomed and cherished, for he wondered if they would be his last. And then Azel drew and fired, and the first of the twenty-odd Riders fell from his mount, over the bridge, into the watery grave beyond.

What followed was his plan, exactly as he'd drawn it out. Each of his archers let loose, firing arrow after arrow upon the fiends, and it was beautiful.

But ambushes had the advantage of surprise for only so long, and immediately, the Riders who had not been struck by arrows cleared the bridge and drove their beasts deep into the bushes, seeking their killers. Terrible screams filled the air, and Aymon was upon his feet with sword in his hand; a fierce Alpha, deranged by tragedy, determined to seek solace. He charged the Riders, and he was not alone. Those warriors not crushed by crazed Riders upon frantic mounts went with him and met their death spectacularly at the hands of generals and gods.

This battle was over the moment they struck, and it was a glorious assault on the Wolves' part, but their numbers were not enough, and though Aymon charged mindlessly towards the Southerners around him, his comrades fell.

He killed all who stood in his way, though, and perhaps, had he a couple more warriors at his side, built for skilled swordplay, they might have won out, but as it was, they all died.

Apart from him.

His blade was fierce; it tore at any who neared, even as they cut into him. He pulled every trick, move and form in his arsenal in a blur of movement, but it was all for little.

Azel was the last to be felled. A blade through the heart took him from the fight.

Aymon cut through them all until a blade took him in the gut, and he fell to his knees. Only then did he see the devastation he had wrought: all around him, there lay Southerners. Only three remained alive, but he could only look to his killer, a tall, one-eyed god who leaned over him to study him with curiosity.

Aymon wanted to reach for the cur and tear out his other eye, but instead, he fell back against the edge of the bridge, close to where Azel leaned, watching and dying. The two slumped together, shoulder to shoulder. Uden stood over them. He smirked as Azel's head rested against Aymon's, and he allowed it.

"A fine ambush, Wolf," the god said, and he was impressive and daunting. Aymon could only clutch at the wound that had felled him and wait to see who would sleep first—him or Azel. "I will remember you," he pledged, and drew away from the ambush, tending to his horse as his two comrades joined him.

Aymon tried to call after the mad god, but the brute was already upon his mount, looking ahead to the South. He had pledged to remember him, but Aymon doubted he would do so. Beside him, he felt Azel's head grow heavier as his life seeped away.

"I'm sorry, my love," Azel whispered, and Aymon took his hand and kissed it.

"It's all right; I'm right here with you."

"I'm sorry."

"I love you, Azel," he said, leaning over to kiss the boy once upon the lips, and was gifted his last breath as he did. As a serene Azel slumped away from him to die in the mud of the bridge, Aymon thought it a rightly shitty day to die altogether. He could have climbed to his feet and tried to find a way to tend to his injury. Perhaps, were he to feel like it, he would. For now, though, he decided to sit here and listen to the rain awhile.

114

GOODBYE FOR NOW

Her name was Aurora, and she liked to play her part when everyone was around. All it took was a little discipline. A little staring into the darkness as though nobody was watching and keeping her body still as though it had been broken, as though she were tainted by the unwanted touch of another. Although Uden reviled her, punished her and condemned her to the dark, no fool would have dared defile her body even as she fought for her life.

The outer door slammed heavily as the wretched healer left, and she smiled sadly, for she would never see him again. These last few days, she had grown quite used to him appearing at some ungodly hour, sometimes sober, sometimes drunk, but always with a loose tongue in him. A broken-hearted man with no one left in the world to talk to and the deadliest assassin playing the part of mute victim made for excellent conversation in the shadows.

He spoke of many things as he tended to her wounds, listened to her beating heart, looked her over and wondered loudly what terrible afflictions she suffered below the surface. She could have whispered the truth. She loved Emir as much as she could love any friend, but it was a secret she would take to her grave. Or his. So instead, she listened in contented silence as he tended to her healing, telling her all he knew of the world.

She knew of the king; she thought it beautiful that Erroh would rise that high. She thought it a curious thing, too, that the Primary would share leadership. She could have asked his thoughts on the matter, but that was a most sore subject.

She learned of the goddess Elise leaving with the terrifying Magnus in tow, headed deep into the burning sands of Adawan, and she thought it a fitting end to such legends. Better they live on in memory and die of old age without tainting their perfect legacy.

She learned the Hunt had begun its great trek south with its tail between its legs. She would have loved to watch an entire nation humbled and sent marching; it would have been a sight to see. She wondered who would vie for power now among their brutal kind. She believed Uden's son would be a most suitable and dangerous candidate. She might have taken an active interest and even earned her place among them, but such a fate seemed dull to her. She desired something more interesting.

Like dying. That could be interesting. Or else changing her hair.

He told her of Lexi's departure out into the Wastes, against her family's wishes. Against the city's traditions, as well. A solo trek was a rare thing for a young female, but who would dare stop her? Aurora was proud of the little cub and wished her many silent, extraordinary adventures.

She took in all of this without any sign that his voice was anything other than a series of noises bouncing around inside her empty head. However, she did blink a few times when Emir spoke of Tye and his decision to return to his home to play the part of the young cub he was. She thought it wonderfully typical of the boy, and a warmth spread through her. She thought of those better days when she had slipped towards Stefan with warmth in that same homestead, all the while discovering that Ealis held more sway over her than she'd expected.

She learned of Roja's dedication to the city and Emir's dedication to anything but the city. She listened for many days as the broken wretch told of love, of regret, of harsh, dreadful decisions. It might have made a tear come to her eye, hearing the sorrow in his tone. She nearly turned to gaze at him, but remained still and emotionless, as though his words were powerless to reach her. He said he would leave within the next three days, and she might have liked him to stay a while longer to keep her company, to learn whether Roja would forsake everything rotten to her and go with him, but that was not to be the way of things.

He spoke of the savages, and he spoke fondly of them. For a long while, she listened to his tales of their doings in the battles, their leadership and their approach to the world. He also spoke of their grand departure from Spark in the coming days.

He did not speak of Aimee and Kaya, and she wondered if they would return to Adawan with the many bandits or if they would be the first to slip away and return to Raven Rock. A terrible shame came upon Aurora as she thought of that beautifully cursed place. She thought of her betrayal, of the savagery she had inflicted upon those who had come before. Only when she entertained those thoughts did Aurora squirm ever so in her bedding, enough that Emir hesitated tending to her wounds.

I'm fine; continue the sewing.

Everyone was leaving the city, apart from little old Ealis, and that was fine; she had stayed long enough as it was.

Emir spoke of a thousand other things, which warmed her considerably, for she could imagine she was loved once more. She might have replied, pretended that his healing was returning her mind to her, but she knew that the moment she displayed any sign at all that her wits were about her, the chains would be back around her, and she would spend the rest of her life caged in the dark. Thus, she remained silent and decided it was time to leave. But not before offering him a broken whisper to send him on his way.

"I'm sorry," she rasped, breaking her silence, and his face lit up in delight. She dared not gaze at him lest he see her ruse, lest she reveal it herself. Instead, as he questioned her further, she returned to her act, playing the broken urchin. Realising her recovery would take a few days more, Emir offered a sweet goodbye and little more before disappearing from her life forever.

It is time.

She waited for hours as the darkness drew in upon the land, and the grumble in her belly told her the hour was late. As he had every day, with a clink of the lock her keeper appeared at her cell with a bowl of warm, tasteless gruel. Murder was on her mind as she watched the black-armoured cur slide the door open and set the food by her bedside, but she suppressed that delicious desire.

"Come on, Ealis, time for food. Eat up, lest Emir scream at me again." Usually, he slipped the spoon into her mouth and she did the rest, but today was different. As a parting gift, she would take no lives on her way out. Not even her own. She sat up suddenly as though shocked, and her keeper gasped. "This is different." He didn't know her at all. She wondered if he had been warned of her threat.

"I desire something more," she whispered to the bewildered Wolf. His hesitation was all it took. She dashed the bowl of gruel into his face, blinding him momentarily. Before he could scream, she was behind him.

The Actions of Gods

With a swift strike, she knocked the wind from him before climbing upon his back and wrapping her godly arms around his neck. Just enough to squeeze, not enough to crack. He gasped and clawed at her, rising like a rearing mount; she thought him a brute of a thing, clumsy and monstrous and a dangerous threat.

Easier to just kill.

She fought that urge as she fought the brute. He charged backwards against the cell door, slamming her against the edge of the doorway. He was massive, and she was battered, and she moaned in pleasure as he drove her back repeatedly, and she was in ecstasy. She could feel the strain on her stitching and imagined fresh crimson seeping down her shoulder. It was almost too much.

"That's good," she moaned, responding to his brute strength. "Harder," she cried again, but not loud enough that his comrades would come and play too. She was quite the goddess, but two or three in such an act was too much. She would partake only when she had the advantage.

"Please," he gasped, and she enjoyed this. "I have a boy, a young boy," he wheezed, and she stole a little more of his breath. Her arms burned, and her back was a ruin, but she would not leave him unsated, would not leave herself striving for more either. "You fuken witch."

"Do not call me that," she warned as he fell to his knees, knocking her loose ever so. In that moment, he could have taken her. Her grip loosened, and she heard him hack, gasping for more air. She wrapped herself around him again and stood up, pulling on him with all her weight so that eventually, she began to weaken him. "It's all right; you did well."

The Wolf fell delicately upon her bedding, where she left him to sleep. She took only his keys before locking him away and turning to the outer door.

In truth, neither of the remaining guards could have predicted the appearance of the goddess as she strolled the twelve steps across the room, picking up two wooden battering clubs from the wall in one smooth moment. When their senses caught up with their disbelieving eyes, it was already too late. She met them as they rose, battering them with such ferocity that any wanderers on the other side of the wall might have believed the worst form of torture was occurring within. It wasn't, for she left no scars, just a few broken bones that would quickly mend. She was vicious and precise, and they fell senseless at her feet. Dropping the clubs, she left the unconscious men behind to seek her true escape.

She might have left the city unimpeded, such was the damage to the gates. There were enough mounts to steal or barter for, even at this late hour, but she was tired of the Wastes. Tired of the charge too. She had ideas above her station, and they were wondrous things. She lost count of her steps thrice while seeking out her hovel of riches: she was too busy marvelling at the devastation everywhere around her, and she wondered how near the city had come to falling altogether.

It was a small matter, though. After spending an hour tending to her bathing, beautifying herself and dressing in her finest gown of silken blue, she stuffed what weapons, riches and supplies she could conceal in a little pack and slipped away through the city, down towards the harbour.

"I should have died," she told the wind, as she came upon the spot where Roja had torn her apart. She kissed the ground where the first godly drops of blood had fallen before descending to the quayside and strolling along the row of vessels preparing to embark the following morning.

She sought the finest, largest boat, intending to make it her own. It did not take her long to find the captain of the most immense galleon in the fleet. It was an impressive ship, and, according to the captain, worthy of returning to the Savage Isles with their king aboard.

Aurora was intrigued at the idea of seeing royalty. Offering her own charms and a trinket of gold as a means of payment, she begged the captain to help her escape from this dreadful place where her "father and sisters had all perished under Uden's charge." It was a convincing tale. As was her performance. The tears were plentiful, the shaking was voluntary, the delivering of payment was swift, and as dawn settled, Aurora was gifted with an elegant cabin suitable for a goddess, and she felt right at home. Only when the ship embarked did she return to the top deck, in her new guise as an orphaned waif of good heritage, to stare at the broken city as it disappeared behind them.

"To the Savage Isles," she whispered, and in the distance, beyond the rivers and wild open seas to come, she imagined a beautiful isle of rich green. She also imagined its people quivering slightly at the thought of her coming. "A fine end to me," she whispered to the wind and the absent gods, thoroughly convinced she could live a good, healthy life, worthy of a pious goddess in search of redemption, and slip away from notoriety forever.

The absent gods thought otherwise.

115

CLEANSING WATERS

For weeks, the rain never stopped. Every day was worse than the last, or at least that's how it felt to Lea and Erroh. Their vision was blurred behind an ever-constant wall of glistening, freezing water as it battered them from morning to evening. He'd never imagined there were enough clouds in the sky to carry such showers, but every day he was surprised. The road they travelled became a waterlogged marsh; their mounts were slow and cumbersome, but at least there were no dreadful slopes to master with a cart. Every morning, wrapping his hood and cloak tight, Erroh led the procession south, and every step was difficult. By the third week of near-constant saturation, he was ready to forgo their adventuring for a time in search of an abandoned settlement. Just a few days out of the saddle to dry his clothes and get warmth back into his body.

To be reminded what it was to be a newly mated couple.

Perhaps to fall back in love in a little forgotten town.

As it was, he ignored any promising marks on his map, and they maintained their course upon the road, and aye, it was truly miserable, but also it was fantastic.

Once they had placed everything out for the other to see, they lost the awkwardness, and it was a welcome thing. They were not lovers, but they were something more than simple comrades. When they sat in their saddles and wrapped their arms close to themselves as they travelled, they spoke more than before to distract from the awfulness. Without the need to impress, they could be themselves. She discovered her smile again. No longer did she mutter as though the world was against her; no longer did he despise her every action and ignore her approach.

They became at ease with each other, and strangely, although they trudged towards almost certain death, Erroh was at ease most of the time. He appreciated her wit and charm, and the kindness in her words and actions. It was a wonderful thing to see such things when one was not blinded by lust or love, he realised. More than that, he liked her some of the time. No, that wasn't true at all. He liked her all of the time.

The highlight of his day was sitting in the rain, over the remains of a fire soon to meet a watery end, sharing a mug of cofe with her, and discussing mundane things such as Uden's skill, the path leading to Uden's domain, the tactics of attack, the chances of survival. Also, they talked of greater things like the rain and the fuken mud.

That terrible cloud that had clung to him for so long disappeared in those few weeks, and he had her to thank for it. Not that he was in any way ready to say as much. Not that he was willing to give her hope that things might begin to change. Not that he feared things changing as much as he might once have.

After their argument, he wanted to believe her. Truthfully though, there was something hidden beneath the surface. Something she kept from him, and perhaps, in the beginning, that was what he saw. He might have felt anger at her deceit, but now, he was more tolerant of her choices. More than that, he understood her actions and decisions, even if he thought some were unforgivable. It was a start to better things, he mused.

Lea was blissfully happy these past few weeks and cared little about hiding it. Every day was predictable and wonderful. She might have preferred a little less rain, but with Erroh at her side, she felt better than ever. She became herself once more, and it was beautiful. She did not follow every word he said, nor would she play the humble waif any more than she had during the first days. He enjoyed that she challenged him, disputed her points and swayed him on matters occasionally.

Aye, there had been fierce arguments where both raised their voices. But she never fell silent to please him, and he appreciated it.

Especially when he won some of those arguments.

Days passed in ease and recovery, and she loved it. She found her feet in the Wastes and no longer dreamed of her father. It was Erroh whose dreams were loudest. Only on those nights did she come to his

The Actions of Gods

bed and ease him from his horrors with gentle whispers of reassurance. When he settled, she would whisper in his ear that her heart belonged to him alone, forever, before kissing his forehead and leaving him to sleep. Admittedly, it was a delicate betrayal of their separation, but she would not be stopped, and if a thousand nights passed and she whispered such things so much that he believed her, well, that would be fine too.

They allowed themselves one vice, a far cry from how things had been on the day they'd reunited.

They bathed together when they came upon rivers, and she did not hide herself. Occasionally, he would gaze upon her, and she would allow him without shame. He would look on until he had his fill of her nakedness, not averting his gaze even if the water was fuken freezing. And after a time, she began to return the favour: every time they dropped into the cold waters, she gazed upon his body with evident desire, and he did not deny her. Although these mutual gazes felt like the most noticeable and natural thing in the world, not once did she invite him to her bedding, and he never offered warmth to her.

As wonderful as the travelling was, it was in their sparring that they fell back into a comfortable rut once more. Thrice a day, as much to escape the cold of the ride as to hone their skills, they took to battering the ever-living shit out of each other in the grand sparring arena of the entire Wastes.

Every time, after vigorous pull-ups and push-ups to tighten their muscles even more, they went to war, and the feeling was glorious. Moving as gods with blade and intent, they danced around each other, striking mercilessly, trying to draw blood and succeeding in every skirmish. He was the better warrior, having never lost his edge, but she swiftly caught up to him with her terrifying ability.

They did not plateau either. They continued to push each other. Faster and faster they moved, becoming spinning blurs upon the vast battlefield in preparation for the one final battle against a god.

Their battles also became a welcome release from such treacherous things as desire and love. They took that energy and used it to inflict pain on each other. Each round of sparring soon became a competition as to who would draw the most blood. Lea would laugh as blood spilled from her nose and mouth, ruining her shirt. He would roar in mock triumph, spitting blood from his mouth or wiping at an injury above his eye. They would meet, battle and separate, and both were better for it. Harder and fiercer.

And then, they would pack up and ride for a period before doing it all over again.

Lea became accustomed to the constant feeling of pain. After a time, she didn't think of it as anything more than a reward for bettering herself. Every night, they counted the bruises, the welts, the growing scars, and they laughed as though they were Lea and Erroh of old, falling in love in violence and triumph, and perhaps this is precisely what they were doing.

And through all this, Lea knew this march to be their final one, regardless of whether they survived the battle or not. Yet she didn't care. And, perhaps, neither did he.

On the night before they came upon the town where everything changed, she finally broke and spoke of the one secret she kept to herself. He took it better than she ever expected.

With the rain pouring down upon them, she was close to asking to join him beneath his bedding. Not just from desire. Her cloak's wax was rapidly losing the battle against keeping her and her bedding dry, and beneath the sodden fabric, she shook something awful. Although it might have been her nervousness.

"There is something I must tell you," she said suddenly, sitting up and shifting her bedding nearer to his. Above her, a tree branch creaked under the weight of the rain and shook its burden onto her cloak, and she shivered.

He sat up immediately. "No conversation ever ends well when it begins with those words," he warned. His chest was perfect in the struggling fire's light. For a moment, she imagined climbing right over and depriving him once and for all of his solitary comfort.

Instead, she told him that she was to become Primary.

It was Roja who had come to her in the middle of the night, she told him. She had thought it was a dream at first, but her friend had decreed that Mea could no longer lead the city. She demanded an Alphaline of strength and determination to carry the city through the difficult days. A heroic female who knew the city, knew her guards. Lea had been shaken. She had agreed to the post almost immediately, with one proviso: she required the freedom to seek out Uden without interference. Roja had agreed, and Lea had been shaken at the realisation of what was now a reality.

It was the most prominent position in the world. Little Lea of the city, would stand above all. Aye, sharing it with a king would diminish the power of the throne, but she saw the advantage to balance.

The Actions of Gods

Erroh could only listen on in numb silence.

She confessed to Erroh her terror and finally broke into tears. Erroh climbed away from his annoyingly dry cloak and blankets and knelt beside her, not in anger, jealousy or sorrow, but with pride.

"You will be a strong Primary, dear Lea. You will be strong, heroic, kind and wise."

"Do you believe so?" she cried, grateful for his praise, choosing to believe him. Begging to believe him. "How could I refuse to accept this role?"

"How could anybody refuse? There are greater things at play now, Mydame," he whispered, and she wanted to take hold of him and kiss and love him. "The world tore itself apart while those who had seen more years allowed it. Better that we have a youthful Primary, with proper notions."

"I should have told you sooner."

"I would have made it about me. Likely found reason to argue with you," he said, and, noticing that her hands were shaking, drew her to his bedding.

She wasn't ready for this. She gasped.

"But things change, I suppose," Erroh went on. "I long suspected there was still something you were keeping from me. I suspect only watchful mates can recognise things like this. Regardless, it is good to see you with no cloud above your head anymore," he added as she slipped under the blankets. It was warmer there; dryer too. Mostly, though, she could feel him near, could smell his wonderful aroma. Her Erroh, only hers, nobody else's. She hoped.

"What are you doing, my love?" she whispered, and he shook his head. Not her love at all.

Not yet.

Perhaps not ever again.

"This means nothing, Lea," he warned, but his tone was softer than she expected.

"Are you trying to bed the Primary?"

"I'm sure many will try when you return."

"I will only desire you," she said curtly.

"That's because I am so grand," he mocked, and she giggled.

"Really, my love. Why are you not angry?"

"Being mated to the Primary would be quite the advantage, I suppose," he teased. His face turned a little grave now, a little serious.

She didn't like that at all. "What becomes of your choices has little to do with me. I have no card to play in these matters."

She was stung by the retort. She wanted him to care. She tried not to dwell on it. Tried to tell herself that the next few weeks of marching would allow him to warm that little bit more to her. But she couldn't help herself. His beating heart was close to hers, and his warmth took the cold from her.

"You are part of this, my love. I would give it all up to walk the Wastes with you, hand in hand or side by side. These last few weeks have been the greatest of my life. I love you, Erroh; I need to tell you this tonight. It seems very important you know this." She sounded desperate. She didn't care.

"So, after all these weeks, you still try to win me back?"

"Of course I do, you idiot," she declared. She didn't care if she revealed her cards. She was playing with them on show anyway. "It is no crime to love you as I do. I will not apologise for trying to win your beautiful heart back. You are no fool, Erroh, though you act it, plenty. You know what we have. I will keep this companionship as long as I can."

"So I can never be done with you?" he asked carefully.

"Until you choose another, I will fight for you, whether you like it or not. I expect nothing from you, but do not be so cruel as to deny me my faith in us."

He thought on this a time. A longer time than she would have liked. Eventually, he pulled her tightly to him. "I do not know what the world will lead us to. However, regardless of my heart, you must accept the role of Primary."

"Were your heart to return to me, would you surrender your life on the road? Would you walk around the city as my mate?"

"There is less for me in the east than there was."

"Do not torture me with false pledges, my beo. Do not do it."

"Do not torture me with acts of love, so," he challenged, and kissed her forehead before resting his head on her, closing his eyes and trying to sleep.

Beneath the covers, her heart spun a rhythm, and she could barely contain her hopes, her excitement. It was no pledge of love; it was a mere suggestion that they might walk hand in hand once more. "Good night, Erroh," she whispered.

"Good night, my beo," he whispered.

He called me beo.

116

MUCK RIDGE

It was pure chance that they came upon the small town of Muck Ridge. While setting camp, they discovered some fresh tracks by a river, and curiosity had them follow the trail. It was something to do to break from the monotony of the road for a time. The tracks were easy enough to follow, though the journey over the uneven terrain was difficult. They made their way through thick trees without any specific path, through valleys deeper than most with little more than hoof prints to guide them. Erroh and Lea walked their beasts hesitantly, unsure whether to return to their pilgrimage and forget about these tracks.

Yet still, they were drawn to the possibility of life beyond the ever-constant solitude. They had almost given up when a gust of wind carried the faintest sound to their ears: the hum of humankind in the forest ahead.

A little further on, nestled in a deep valley far below steep, shielding mountains on all sides, they caught sight of delicate wisps of smoke rising and dissipating in the air: a town. Natural things had once protected Keri. Perhaps it was the same for Muck Ridge.

Setting a camp for themselves outside the settlement's territory, they hobbled their mounts in a concealed dell and tentatively made their way through the thick woods to the open town.

"It almost feels like we were here before. Once before, long ago," Lea said, leading the way. She was eager but nervous, and Erroh felt the same familiar stroll he once had. Except for the rushing river streaming through the town, Muck Ridge felt similar to the town that had changed all their fates.

For a terrible moment, Erroh wondered if they were walking right into a Southern stronghold. A fine, foolish end, he mused, and checked the reassuring weight of the weapons upon his back. Of course, they could take on an entire town. Had they not faced down solitary armies more than once?

"Aye, in a different life," Erroh agreed, walking alongside her. His heart was pounding, but no unpleasant banners were on show, no sign that this town had been sacked or was ready for war. On the outskirts lay field after field, each tilled and clear of weeds, although few had crops. It's too late in the season, he mused.

Though smaller, the town's resemblance to Keri was striking. The signs of the ancients were upon every building and roadway, and it had been kept clean and maintained with the same love that had gone into the keeping of Keri. No derelict structures marred its beauty; there were no ravaged areas where fires had burned uncontrollably. The natural green of the Wastes was held at its border.

He could see farmers and labourers going to task, and not a Southern cur among them all. The war was over, but would a town as far down as this be aware of such things?

"We're just simple wanderers of the road," Erroh reminded her, upon seeing a well-dressed man leading a cart towards them. Erroh could see sacks of grain, barrels of wine and many mounds of bread.

"Simple wanderers with finely crafted weapons," Lea countered.

"Well, it's dangerous out on the road. Let them believe that."

For a breath, Erroh wondered if the man with the cart was headed towards other, more distant settlements. He might have asked as the man passed, but he dared not breathe a word. The driver looked like a friendly enough trader; he gave them a gentle nod as though they were indeed simple wanderers of the road with finely crafted weapons. With the echo of his mount's hooves behind them and the growing hum of a peaceful settlement ahead of them, they began to relax ever so.

"War has not touched this place," Lea said wistfully. Her hand touched his for a moment. He felt her sorrow, too, for all they had come through. The world had turned with blood and death and war and horror, and they gazed upon a settlement beautiful and vibrant, brimming with life and unaffected by such horrors. It needed only a sunny day and a little music in the air for it to be like the beginning of the festival of Puk. When joy and good times were the only concerns of the day.

Truthfully, he was not ready to step back into such a place. He did not want to walk among those whose lives were normal, conventional.

Not yet. He looked behind them to the camp hidden in the forest, and he suddenly wanted to turn around and run, with her beside him, to resume their dreary pilgrimage south. He understood anguish; to feel carefree was something he was unprepared for, at least for now.

Be mighty.

"Perhaps we should stay for a drink," he said through gritted teeth, looking to a large tavern on the far end of the cobbled street. He could handle a drink or two—a small step towards normality and fewer nightmares.

"Are you as unsettled as I?" she asked, and he felt a kinship with her in that moment. She was evidently struggling as much as he was.

They passed pristine houses, as they had done once before. Each person they met upon the path offered a kind welcome or a brief suggestion that the weather was about to change, and they wandered as though in a dream, following each other, not daring to believe such a place remained.

"I do not want to stay the night here," Lea said firmly, following him through the tavern doors where they were met by the unmistakable hum of music, chat, cheer and good fortune.

"As you wish," he said, fighting the unease a little more. He'd felt a little like this a lifetime ago. After walking so long on the road without meeting another soul, it was always unsettling returning to civilisation. In that moment, he began to relax anew. His heart began to settle. He began to see beauty in things that did not involve life-or-death victories, and he held on to that thought real fuken tight.

Ordering an ale for each of them, they sat on comfortable bar stools and sought what conversation they could among the locals. The tavern was as grand and pristine as any establishment he'd ever seen. Hardly good for a tavern brawl at all. No sawdust on the floor either. Instead, there was rich red carpet, old but soft, with a thousand stains in every corner. Brightly coloured paintings hung on every wall, and Erroh tried to shake off his discomfort in this comforting place.

The alcohol helped. The ale was cool and bubbly; Erroh closed his eyes and sighed contentedly as the beverage reached his belly. He'd been sober these last few weeks; it was far too long. As eager as they were to escape this strange town, untouched by worry or time, there was nothing better than a beverage to sway his judgement.

"Oh, that is so fuken good," Lea whispered contentedly, and in that moment, he was happy to stay here for a time.

The tavern owner was welcoming and full of words of the wind. He spoke of the problematic season with the rain and the unsatisfactory crops; he spoke of the mayor being discovered in a compromising position with a popular lady of the town down by a tree in the fields. He did not discuss the war beyond accepting that the Factions were "at it again." Erroh didn't argue the point, and neither did Lea. Instead, she focused on a card table and the trio seated at it, battling wits.

"Perhaps a few hands," she suggested, gesturing for Erroh to follow. As she made introductions, Erroh drained his pint, ordered two more, and felt much better about himself as the warmth took him. He almost stumbled as he hopped off the bar stool and approved of the potent brew the tavern offered.

The trio, it turned out, were intriguing companions with whom to while the night away.

Ayden was as young as Erroh, and his eyes fell upon Lea immediately, and it was no surprise. Even with a look of the road to her, she was stunning. That she had applied a coat of paint to her features earlier that morning was even more enticing. Ayden sat beside her and wasted little time asking everything about her, much to the amusement of Erroh. The cur was excellent company altogether. He was witty and charming and appeared a welcoming inhabitant, even if he made himself a little too familiar with Lea's arms as he spoke. And he spoke a great deal. Although he talked of little beyond the communities in this region, his amiable chatter was welcome. His accent held ever-so-delicate hints of the South, but apart from that, he could have resided in Samara itself.

"Are you two wedded?" he asked, and before Erroh could answer, Lea declared, "No, not married, not at all."

This pleased Ayden greatly.

Erroh was slightly irked at her swift reply, but said nothing and showed even less.

Jon, his companion, sitting opposite Erroh and a little older, if not a little sturdier, was as warm and welcoming as Ayden. Leaning towards Lea, he enquired, "So, neither lovers nor family?" Again, Lea answered for both of them with a curt shake of the head, and Ayden took greater pleasure in this.

Built for heavy lifting and enthusiasm, Jon spoke of the crop concerns this season, for they were plenty, and Erroh felt a serenity come upon him at talk of such mundane things. It was far from mundane to Jon, however, and that, too, was wonderful. Erroh asked about farming, about life in a town untouched by war and with little interaction with Samara. Part of him wanted to retire to this place. All it needed was a festival of violence and alcohol, and he'd seek out a home for himself. Alone. Probably. A passion for farming would be required for such a place, which was fine by him.

Beside Erroh sat an incredibly alluring girl called Shinell. Highlighted with the finest paints, she was beautiful. Erroh couldn't tell what made her so striking, but he suspected it was her lips. Sensual lips. Lea's lips were perfect, but Shinell's were better. He didn't say this aloud, but Lea did catch him staring at those lips a few times. He shouldn't have felt that pang of shame, but he did. While Erroh was careful in gazing at her, giving few hints of his attraction, Shinell was the opposite. She wore her interest in Erroh like a blazing yellow dress. Each time she returned from the bar with an ale, she squeezed down closer to Erroh. Her hands were casual and careless. She liked to touch when she spoke, and Erroh was her target. Truthfully, it was a pleasant thing to be pursued, and he played along, enjoying the flirtation, allowing his tongue to be looser, imagining what her tongue might be like too. It was the hot-blooded male in him, and he would not apologise.

On the other hand, Lea allowed Ayden little room to manoeuvre as he attempted to charm her. She played the disinterested wanderer perfectly. As drunk as Ayden became, he never noticed his advances were not reciprocated.

Lea watched the whore falling all over Erroh, and she held her irritation behind a few hidden grimaces and unheard sighs. More than that, she focused on her cards; it was the best she had ever played. Although she'd been apprehensive about this town, the camaraderie and the alcohol helped to relax her, and she began to feel better about being here.

Around them, the tavern began to fill, as it likely did every night, and the cheer was contagious. The troubadours were accomplished enough, but their music lacked the skill found further north where work was more competitive. They riled up the crowd, which added to the night's enjoyment. She felt no need to dance, nor did she feel the need to sing along with the more popular melodies. She would need some sine to partake in such things, and, after so long without drinking, she didn't trust herself to overindulge; she had no desire to behave any differently than the calculated Alpha that she was.

Though she wanted Erroh to behave, she would not allow herself to step between him and Shinell. She had given him her heart; it was down to him to offer something back. A part of her relished the challenge of

Shinell and those lips. The truest love was absolutely not a painted goddess, drunk and flirtatious and an easy furrowing if given a chance.

Right?

She managed not to lose her entire stash of pieces in a loose bet the whole night, and as the hour grew late and the last calls were ordered, she was rather proud of her performance and her behaviour. Truthfully, though she condemned Erroh and Shinell's behaviour that little bit more, she trusted him. Trusted him with those lips.

Those annoyingly beautiful, alluring lips.

They drew near him; they touched his ear too many times when she whispered a jest he hadn't heard the first time. Lea did not like her laugh either. Her entire body bounced when she laughed, heartily and briefly; Lea despised her for the fact that laughing so freely came as easily as it did to her. The girl had clearly never experienced hardship or cruelty.

You wouldn't laugh like that around the city, would you, bitch?

She did not like her outfit either. It showed too much leg; the silks were a little grandiose. And really, everyone in the tavern knew she had an impressive chest; she didn't need to continue reminding them, particularly when she laughed. Lea wasn't aware that Erroh was that witty anyway.

She could have shot Erroh a glare at any point in the evening. A warning, a plea. But she did nothing of the sort. He was free to do whatever he wanted, with whomever he wanted, and though it would break her heart and end their chances, she would not step between them. It was on Erroh to give her something.

Anything.

The music played, drinks were downed; the night grew late and the revellers more drunken. When the patrons began to step out into the cold night, Erroh said he would be leaving soon, and Lea, lightheaded and irritated, made no move to go with him. She continued to deal, and the two young men on either side of her were glad to keep the game going until the very last moments.

"Who would walk me home?" Shinell asked, looking to Erroh.

"I will," Jon said, drawing a card. In truth, he appeared to have little interest in joining the whore goddess in the cold night air.

"I don't want you to walk me home; I want Erroh to. Will you walk me home, Erroh?" she said, sliding up to him, grabbing his arm for the twenty-third time that evening. Lea knew this, for she'd counted every time.

Erroh looked to Lea. He looked drunk and stupid, and she saw the card in her hands begin to quiver from anger. She would not stop him, though. "Whose bet is it?" she asked the remaining players.

"Goodnight, so," Erroh said to the table, and Shinell, giggling, took hold of Erroh's arm and led him from the tavern.

Lea was furious. Her stomach churned the ale they'd drunk all night, and as Jon went all in and took many of her pieces, she held back a scream. Held back the tears as well. She looked to the door as the tavern owner called time on the night, and Ayden, reading her worry completely wrong, slid in beside her as Shinell had with Erroh and ran his hand along her leg.

"Will you walk me home, Lea? It's not far," he said, with all the charm of a cub used to seducing single women. But Lea wasn't single at all. She was mated to her Erroh, who had let her down. Also, she should have fought for him. This she knew.

"Fuk this," she slurred, grabbing her remaining pieces and her bag before stepping away from the table and Ayden's grasp. "I have to get Erroh," she added, and Ayden laughed.

"I would say someone else is getting Erroh by now," the charming fuk declared.

"It was lovely to meet you," Jon said. "They'll be taking the upper path," he added, and she was away from them. Her heart beating, her mind racing, her terror rising. She couldn't leave him with another lover. Couldn't allow him to slip away without a fight.

She fled into the night, and the shock of the cold air on her face almost sent her reeling. Around her, revellers were wandering away in every direction, and she couldn't see which routes they took. Panic took her, and she suppressed visions of those lips tending to his pleasure.

How could he not want to put all manner of things into that mouth?

Around her, there was cheer and drunken declarations, and she took the route Jon had suggested and began to run swiftly up the top path, seeking with keen eyes her love and his whore.

Every step echoed loudly, and she cared little for her appearance as she sprinted through this beautiful town. Eventually, she saw two figures moving in a field behind a tree, and her heart leapt in excitement, relief and fresh terror. It was them, and they were embracing in the dark, engaged in all manner of acts.

He hasn't walked her home at all.

She leapt a waist-high fence and dashed across muddy terrain, caring little for her garments or her behaviour. She began to scream threats to Shinell and her toy, and almost drew her blade when she came upon them, furrowing against a tree. No, that wasn't true; she came upon Erroh pulling his beige trousers back up and buckling his belt, and then she realised Erroh didn't have beige trousers.

"You aren't Erroh?" she cried in relief and horror, and the older lover, with a tight moustache and ill-fitting toupee, cursed her, as did his younger lover, who struggled quickly with her fallen garments.

The interrupted lovers shouted at her in anger and embarrassment, but Lea wasn't listening. She was away again, back across the field, over the fence, running back towards the tavern. She screamed his name in terror. This felt worse than seeing Nomi in the snow. It was a thousand times worse, for he had knowingly stepped from their joining and intentionally broken her heart.

She raced through the town, looking everywhere for a sign of her love, but saw no one familiar. Desperately, she returned to the tavern hoping to coax Jon into leading her to Shinell's house, only to discover, to her horror, that the lights were off and the door closed. She wailed aloud once more and felt the panic retake her.

She wanted to die, scream, kill and hide away. Instead, she wandered the streets looking for Erroh, looking for a sign, looking for anything. Eventually, with the night still and the cold so very cutting, she accepted defeat and traipsed back towards their camp, desperately trying not to imagine what that bitch was doing to Erroh. What he was doing to her. And those fuken lips.

It was the campfire that she noticed first through her drunken, miserable tears.

He was sitting cross-legged in front of the fire, scraping at his golden dagger. He looked beautiful in that light, and she stumbled towards him, weeping in relief.

"I thought you were with her," she cried, falling at his knees.

"I walked her home. She kissed me and went for my manhood, and I left her by the doorway right swiftly."

"You kissed her?"

"She kissed *me*. Mostly. She had sensual lips, but I prefer you. You, Lea. Not your lips, mind. Hers are better, but yours are still perfect." He was positively beaming, and he wrapped her in his arms.

"I was searching for you," she cried, grateful for the warmth. She suddenly cared little for his flirtation, for that bitch's taste of him. For her wandering hands. "I thought I'd lost you, my beo."

"I did not understand why you allowed her upon me as you did."

The Actions of Gods

"I was wrong, Erroh; I was foolish. I sought you out. I ran through the town a few times over seeking you."

"You know, I thought I heard my name and wondered if I had drunk too much. But you will never lose me."

"I think I felt briefly what betrayal you felt," she sobbed, reaching for him, clawing at him. Loving him as only a mate was allowed to do, and he let her. "I'm so sorry; I'll never give you a reason to lose faith in me. I pledge this, Erroh. Be mine. Be mine and no one else's."

"As you wish," he whispered, touching her body as only a mate was allowed to do. More than that, he began to kiss her. A kiss of love, of trust, of promise. Their tongues met. Their breath became each other's; she scrambled upon him as the months of denial rose to the surface.

At last.

"I must have you," she groaned, tearing off what clothing she wore, and he allowed her. She reached for his non-beige trousers and slid them loose as he unbuckled his belt. She couldn't control herself, and neither could he. They tore at each other's bodies, and she moaned as he entered her, and it was perfect. They furrowed roughly at first, wildly and furiously, and she could only scream aloud with pleasure, but as time went on, their actions became gentler, their urges heightened, but the closeness became pure and warm and loving. They stared into each other's eyes as they furrowed, rhythmic and smooth, in perfect unison, and for long enough that their bodies ached in rapturous satisfaction. Eventually, when they had spent themselves, they fell back in the bed together, wrapping up against the chill, gasping and giggling at what they'd done. A perfect, blissful moment before they marched to the end of the world.

"I love you, Erroh."

"I love you, Lea."

117

THE LONG MARCH

They travelled towards death willingly one last time and were truly grateful for each other. As though freshly mated from the Cull, as though they had been lovers for twenty blissful years. The road was difficult, as it always was. The miles disappeared beneath their charge, and side by side, they looked to the South, to the mad god, to family reunions, to vengeance, to honouring pledges. They spoke at length, while riding in the saddle, sitting by the flames; through sparring, through everything else. They learned more about each other than they had ever known before. They cherished each moment, knowing the shadow of Uden's keep would soon come upon them.

"And here we are, riding towards the end… again," Erroh said.

"It has been a great and terrible journey," she said in agreement.

"I'm glad it was with you," he said, looking at her, and she smiled.

"I'm glad every journey after will be with you too."

The mud of the road grew white as they ventured towards the end, and it became treacherous and relentless. They never stopped looking to the sky, tasting the air for signs of snow. They became masters of the South, for they adapted. Lea, skilled at these sorts of treks, chose their routes, and Erroh never questioned her. They rode hard when the land and weather allowed it; they dug in, sheltering their magnificent beasts, when the weather changed and the wind blew its freezing, murderous rage upon them. They took what the frozen South threw at them, and they did so with smiles on their faces. Hand in hand.

"Ah, fuk me, I think it will snow again," she spat, looking to the sky, feeling the change in the air.

"Really? Do you think?" he mocked. He could feel it too.

"I do."

"Was it the fact that it has snowed every day for two weeks that told you this?"

"I am rather skilled at these things," she countered.

"Let us wrap these beasts below those clustered trees over there."

"Sounds like a plan."

Only once did Erroh nearly die. It would have made no great tale. Erroh was never great at crossing rivers, and leading Highwind across a seemingly innocuous crossing, he bounced along from rock to rock, following Lea's lighter, surer footing. She had warned him of the moss, told him not to step on any moss-covered rocks, but his momentum was fierce, and the far bank was that little bit closer, so he stepped upon a moss-covered rock and immediately slipped, not on the moss but on the nasty green algae growing along the edges. As far as falls went, it was rather spectacular. He spun in the air and struck the rock, dazing himself, and was taken by the freezing current. With senses numbed, he travelled further than he would have liked, but she was swiftly beside him, holding his stunned head above the water, pulling him ashore with his clumsy limbs fighting her every step of the way. But it wasn't the fall that near killed him; it was the cold afterwards.

"You are such an idiot," she muttered, rubbing at his chest beneath the warm blankets as it snowed heavily around them.

"And you, my love, are a terrible healer. Now, pass me a few more heated rocks to place under my back; I still feel the cold there."

"You know, there are finer ways to heat our bodies."

"You will make me a cofe? It is late, but I would gladly take a brew."

"After," she whispered, winking.

They furrowed much upon the journey. And not just to keep warm either. They explored each other's bodies, writhing and grinding, devouring, punishing and teasing; these were the more enjoyable moments of their travels. They never left the other unsated, each ensuring their lover enjoyed their gifts as though it were the first time. They furrowed fiercely, made love delicately and lovingly, and sometimes spoke of children when wrapped in each other's sweaty, satisfied arms. Erroh admitted he wouldn't be sure he would make a good father, and Lea suggested a fear of such a thing altogether—particularly going through birth.

"They will have the finest healers in the world tending to you."

"You think so?"

"A Primary with child? They'll never allow you a moment to yourself," he said, both in jest and as a reassuring truth.

"They'll probably have Emir there," she suggested.

"That will be difficult, seeing as he won't be allowed to look up your dress."

"You can tell him what is occurring."

"Me? I won't even be there. I'll be down in the pub celebrating my victory."

"Fine, but that'll be the last child I gift you."

"Us, darling—us. But very well. I'll be waiting with hands out, looking to catch him. Each time. All twelve times. Will it be messy?"

They played cards most evenings. Sometimes, though, drawn to their thoughts, they tended to their own tasks. Lea was never far from Baby, and kept her firm and oiled. She tested her many parts daily and kept her clean of mud, grime and rust.

Erroh, for his part, tended to the broken blade of gold. Glimmering now after the months removing its concealing veneer. He had grand ideas about creating a solid grip for it when they returned. Perhaps out of boar tusk? He cleaned and sharpened the blade and sometimes thought sadly of Stefan; other times, he thought of that beautiful day in Keri before it had all gone to hell.

"That is a piece of shit," she teased, grinning at the blade over his shoulder. He hadn't heard her approach.

"Don't speak ill of Shinell," he countered, defending his newly christened blade. "Besides, she is rather fetching and worth a glorious fortune. Sometimes looking the part is better than being the part."

"If you looked at it the wrong way, it would shatter into pieces."

"Well, don't look at her, then." He stabbed the air. The blade's wrapping of fur and cord had a fine grip to it. The little canister of sticky fluid his father had given him for sealing shut wounds and sticking tight all manner of things had held as Erroh had hoped it would. Still, it was no boar tusk.

"My idiot."

"Your idiot with an expensive blade."

Sometimes, in the darker moments after a hard day in the saddle, when the world was colder and when the threat was ever closer, they spoke of retreat. Sometimes in jest. Sometimes in cutting truths. They were not cowards, nor did they feel their pledge could be revoked. It was no small thing to endure a life as lovely and rewarding as this, knowing there was a set end to such things. They could so easily die when they reached the end. And if only one of them were to die, the other would be left a lonely wretch, forced to live without their mate.

"No one would ever know if we retreated," he said.

"Emir would find out, and then I would be known as a cowardly Primary," she countered. He reached for her across the gap between their mounts and kissed her hand.

"And they would be right."

"Hardly worth keeping that legacy," she said.

"My legacy is assured; perhaps I should just leave you to tend to matters yourself."

"You would probably just get in my way."

"Always," he said softly.

"Always? Wait, were you trying to sound meaningful there?"

"I think I was; I think I wasn't paying attention to what I was saying."

"I do love these conversations."

"May there be many more," he said softly.

"You nailed that sincerity there."

"Aye, I'm glad you noticed. That's what I was aiming for."

They sparred much in that last leg of the journey as they drew nearer to Conlon. Their battles became more frantic, more threatening. Far more violent. Each morning, just after dawn, they tore into each other. Then again at noon, as their mounts rested and ate what grass they could in the white blanket of snow. And again at night, when every skirmish became a near battle to the death as well as a battle of wills.

"Ha, I got you," he roared in triumph. The melee had lasted longer than usual, so great was the skill with which they fought now. Each strike was precise and deadly, each counter and parry controlled and natural. Were Uden to have watched, he would have shuffled his feet and wondered about words over violence. Then he would have attacked anyway, deciding he had the history of their skirmishes favouring him.

"What the fuk are you talking about? That was my kill," she challenged, dropping her blades, inviting argument and assault. Only a fool would have attacked her, such was her irritation. A boy would likely get a kick to the groin for such a deed. He would still argue his case, though.

"Not at all; I had you right there, through the belly. Dead. My kill." It was a compelling argument.

"Aye, and I took your heart. See? Right there. You would bleed out all swift-like. I would not die straight away at all. I'd watch you shit yourself and die, and I'd go sit down in the snow, contemplate deep things for a while." Her tone was definite and severe. She looked straight through him. "Then I'd scoop up my entrails, shove them back in, wrap them in a clean rag, and keep going."

"Um… I'll give you the kill, then… you absolute lunatic."

Sometimes they spoke of the comrades they'd left behind. These were warmer words, for they missed them so. They reminisced about the greater days when the world was falling, when they'd had each other in Raven Rock.

"I think they will go out and make their paths," Erroh suggested.

"They were like children."

"Ah, we all were. We still are. Despite how ancient I feel."

"They won't crumble after this, will they?"

"I'm sure they will struggle, as we all did. For a time."

"I wonder, will we all ever sit at a table again and be merry?"

"I have no doubts. Although no bards will tell the tales. Some things must be shared only by those attending."

"We have enough tales and songs as it is."

They neared Conlon. They knew this, for after so long on their solitary ride without seeing another soul upon the road after the town of Muck Ridge, they finally came upon Riders. From nowhere a dozen appeared, riding swiftly, and both Alphalines believed they were about to be assassinated. But the Riders offered only welcoming waves as they passed. Their attention was on other things, and the two wondered whether news of the cessation of violence had reached the South.

For days more, they travelled towards Conlon. When they reached it, they sat upon their mounts on a hillside and gazed upon its remains; a devastating fire had burned fully a quarter of the town to nothing. They looked for a time and moved on.

They spoke of truer things as the end of their journey drew nearer. In jesting tones, of course, but also from the heart.

"It should be you," Lea said.

"Of course, it should… Also, what should I be?"

"You should be king, Erroh. You should be the one to gather these factions together and help them heal."

"Oh, stop with that shit, my love. I'm no king; I'm barely a functioning Alphaline anymore. Better to leave it in the hands of the capable."

"With me as Primary and you as king, we could change the world. We could do great things."

"A terrible idea."

"Some days, I wish you had allowed Lillium to pledge for you."

"How great a slap to you would it be, were I king? You desire freedom from my shadow. What would sharing the power do to the shade?"

"We could cast equal shadows, my dearest Erroh. Fine shadows."

"Spoken like a true warmonger. But really, do you not think I would impede you, step upon your toes?"

"I feel we could rule well. Justly. Also, I can control you, Erroh, so it would be to my advantage," she mocked.

"And I can argue a point now and then."

"So, it is decided that if we return and Magnus is king, you will challenge him? It would be easy. It was easy before. I imagine he'd hand the crown over to you anyway, out of cowardice. He's good at handing over crowns."

"We both know they are still arguing over the title as we speak. That, or they gave it to Emir. King Emir."

"King Emir," she said wistfully.

"It has a nice ring to it," Erroh agreed thoughtfully.

"It does. But also, it would be great if it was Emir because you could take him easily. Ooh, I could take him easily. I could be both king and Primary. That would be convenient. And who would argue?"

"There will always be people who argue."

It was a beautiful day, one of the finest, but they watched the sunset and knew the last day was close. They marched their mounts to the bottom of Uden's stronghold and knew there could be no return. He could see how pale she was, gazing up to face him, and he took her hand and kissed it.

"Fuk me. I just hope he's up there," she said, and he sniggered.

"I hope so too. It would be a shame to have come this far and not actually die."

"Come on. All things must end."

"All things must end," he whispered in agreement.

118

ALL THINGS MUST END

No army waited for them as they approached the stronghold. This place could have been no further away from the impressive kingdom that he'd come upon that fateful night so long ago. As they passed through the gates, ajar and unattended, he suppressed a cough and swallowed the guilt for his failures. He wasn't the same cub anymore. He would make fewer mistakes, be in greater control, and were Lea unable to do so, he would gladly make the killing blow.

Within, the black and red paint was as daunting as before, though perhaps the harsh Southern weather had allowed it to fade ever so. The courtyard where he had fought for his life was a far cry from the intimidating arena it had once been. Gone was the appearance of a warmonger's stronghold; no more was the furnace lit, and no weapons of every size, shape and style hung on the walls. It was as though this place had been stripped of all that had once made it breathe, and all that remained was a shell.

There was some life within the courtyard, which was something. At the edge of the house lay a mound of carelessly strewn hay. A few untethered mounts grazed upon it, and Erroh had a dreadful feeling that they had come this far for nothing.

Perhaps Uden had been strung up by his minions a hundred or so miles from the city from the sturdiest tree they could find. A godly tree. Hanged for his cowardice, their shame. Or else, perhaps, Aymon and his hunters had tracked him down and killed the fuk outright. An unsatisfying end, admittedly, but perfectly acceptable, he supposed. Were his pledges to allow it, Erroh would gladly have turned from this place

The Actions of Gods

and marched home to Spark with his queen of the world at his side. Savouring a journey as pleasurable as before would be a reward befitting his exploits during the war, he reasoned.

And if Uden were hiding a thousand miles from here in a little shack by a frozen lake, Lea would be vigilant in finding the cur.

As it was, Lea dropped from her mount first and, taking the reins, led her beautiful beast to the hay so that it, too, could dine upon the finest food the South could offer. "Be good, girl; we'll be back in no time at all," she reassured her as Shera chomped greedily on the feed.

"Now, don't let any of the males try anything while we are gone," Erroh warned, leaving his beloved Highwind alongside Shera.

"We have been waiting on you all day," a voice called behind them.

Spinning, they drew their swords, and the old office worker that Erroh had never truly liked stood there. Beside him appeared Uden's butler, helper, or whoever he claimed to be. Erroh couldn't remember their names. It didn't matter.

"Seth?" cried Lea. If he recognised her, he showed nothing on his face. It didn't stop Lea, though. She stepped forward, pointing her blade towards the man. He carried his sword, as did the butler's assistant. Neither looked like the type of master to be feared. It was a small matter. "You knew of my lineage, didn't you?"

He frowned.

"You held the records. You fuken knew." He shrugged his shoulders. "Answer me, damn you."

"I have no idea what you are talking about, little girl," he said after a time. Erroh didn't think that was the right way to speak to an incensed Lea. He wasn't going to say a thing, though.

"Enough of this; Uden is waiting for you within," the butler said. He looked at their drawn blades with distaste. "You can bring your weapons with you if you would prefer."

Erroh didn't like this, but was disinclined to allow Lea to enter without him. Despite his rising fear, he slipped in ahead of her, following the two fiends, who had the temerity to turn their backs on them. They made their way along corridors that were dark despite the brightness of the day.

The house was a shadow of the grand residence it had once been. Erroh dared a glance into the long room where Uden and he had met, eaten, drank and argued. To his surprise and disappointment, no wall of capsules remained, and Erroh felt a twinge of sadness. Little else remained, either. The building was an abandoned husk. Were he to defeat

Uden, he had wanted to take the precious capsules to Samara and place them in the library where they belonged.

He destroyed them.

The thought angered Erroh, and a bit of his growing fear immediately dissipated.

Anger is a gift.

The two hosts led Erroh and Lea up the stairs, and Erroh felt they walked through corridors of the forgotten. Erroh wondered whether the god had left this place the very night he had taken his eye. Perhaps his plan had always been to take Spark City as his own and never return. Perhaps, somewhere among the ruins of Spark City, there rested some of his belongings, his capsules too.

They were led through a door and emerged in the centre of a grand room spanning the near length of the house. Two shrines at either end of the room caught his attention first. A thousand or so little candles illuminated this peaceful place. Lea stepped towards the more brightly lit shrine. Fresh flowers lay at its bottom. They had been picked in honour of a goddess—a fine thing to come upon in this cold place. A painting of a small girl among flames, roughly daubed by a not entirely unskilled hand, clung to the wall high above the candles. It was meant to be worshipped, no doubt.

At the far end lay Erroh's own shrine; Erroh gazed upon it with dismay. While Lea's shrine was a thing of delicate beauty, the opposite was true of Erroh's. It was crude and awful, although his portrait had been made by a more skilled hand. An older hand. It showed a god of fire standing upon a city as it smouldered in ruin. At the top, above the painting, hung a crude crown of decorated silver. It hung loosely from a bent nail that appeared to have been hammered into the wall in a rage—a curious thing. For decoration, Uden, or one of his acolytes, had chosen blood smeared across the painting and the wall in crude, aggressive strokes. Erroh wondered what man, woman or beast had been slain to add to this hideous piece. Three candles illuminated the vile shrine, as dark a red as they could be, and little light emanated from them. Looking a little closer, Erroh couldn't be sure he didn't see mounds of faeces smeared against the wall where the blood had not seeped down, and he was horrified. He envisioned the Woodin Man with a waste bucket, spreading his foul art, cursing Erroh as he did. If he were to strike down Uden, that wall would be the first thing to go.

"Thank you, Seth. Thank you, Gemmil," boomed a voice in front of the fire. Erroh hadn't noticed the man, hunched low in his seat, camouflaged beneath a comforting blanket that blended in with the chair's flowery patterns as he watched the flames.

Erroh and Lea stepped away from their shrines to be near each other. Uden remained in his seat. If Erroh were to guess, he would believe Uden was either injured or slipping from this life. He looked far too human, and it was tempting indeed to commit a little murder upon him while his minions stepped up alongside him on either side of the fireplace.

"Father?" Lea said carefully. That question took a lot from her. She had claimed she wouldn't know how to behave around him. Would she be capable of striking him down?

"You are so beautiful, little Cordelia." He looked at her with the gentle smile of a father upon his daughter's wedded day.

"You come to me, beautiful and brave, and with murder on your mind. I see all. I saw you both from afar, walking to me," he said. His words were gentle, but his voice was like a booming hammer. There was strength in that tone, concealed and controlled. Erroh felt his unease rise as though they had, in fact, planned a murder outright. "And you," he snarled, turning on Erroh, who stared through him in reply. He felt his heart flutter, and he suppressed his fear.

He thought of Wynn.

Fuk this fuker.

And felt much better about himself.

"You come as a king to slay a god? How very savage of you."

King?

What?

There was a snivelling laugh from one of the standing fiends. It might have been Seth.

Lea looked to Erroh in bewilderment, and Uden must have caught their surprise. "Ah, so it is true. The whispers in the wind were that you didn't know. And here I sit, in the presence of a king on his first official business, coming to slay a god." There was more laughter, and Erroh could only gaze at Lea dumbly.

I didn't know.

"I see all. I know all," Uden growled, watching Erroh squirm, watching him try to shake off the shock of learning such a thing and wondering about its truth. Were there to be violence, Uden might have chosen that moment to attack. He didn't; instead, he kept his eye on his daughter. He looked like a skeleton in the fire's light—a lesser fiend than he had once been. War was not kind to the aged, it appeared. "Though all

I had has been taken from me." He looked to Erroh, his face suffused with a burning hatred. Diminished or not, he appeared to gather strength with every breath as the moments passed, and Erroh was rattled something terrible.

Count to ten.
One, two, I'm fuken king.
Three, four, five.
He must be lying.
Five, five, five. Fuk. How can I be king???

"You are my one beautiful creation. For gods can fail too," Uden whispered," looking at Lea once more. He looked to sit up from his chair but hesitated, and Erroh felt Lea begin to shake beside him. "But I can rise again; I can go forth, wiser and fiercer."

"She truly is beautiful," declared Erroh. His words shook Lea to return to herself. Whatever spell her father had upon her was slipping away. Erroh could see the emotions upon her face, the agonies and the horror. She took it well, and he was so proud of her. War was easier than hearing words like this.

"And you, Uden, never knew the man who took my heart," she said sneering. She looked to Seth as though he should have known and told Uden.

"You have come such a long way. Will you not sit at my table? I have the finest foods, even in this battered ruin of a home," Uden said, gesturing to a doorway leading to a dining room. Perhaps, despite the odds, there were all manner of fine foods within. Possibly boar. What struck Erroh was the old man's arm as he pointed. It was as fierce and broad as before. It was hard to see what truly hid beneath that wretched blanket.

"We will never sit at your table, Uden," Lea snapped. She had more to say, but she hesitated as though it occurred to her for the first time. "You speak of Erroh's deserved rise to the throne? But tell me, Uden, did you hear of mine?"

"What are you talking of?"

"I will stand as Primary."

The colour drained from his face, and a grimace of anger quickly rose. His body began to shake.

"That's a lie," Gemmil said. "You can't. You… just can't."

"Believe what you like. For it will not matter soon enough," she hissed.

"You will stand upon the podium as a whore of the city? What have you become, daughter?" Uden roared of this betrayal, and Lea stood ready as the behemoth rose from his seat. His blanket fell away, revealing the massive frame underneath. He wasn't diminished at all. Merely older. "What have you become?"

Though his army had been routed, his entire Faction had slipped from his grasp, his house had crumbled to a decrepit shell, and he had no obvious riches to his name and only two servants to call upon, he still appeared mighty. Reaching down beside the chair, he produced two large blades and raised them in threat and challenge. He was daunting, and in that moment, Erroh knew there would be no hiding for this brute ever again. Uden would gather what strength he had left and unleash his hate upon the city—and upon Lea, no doubt. Fiends like this did not slip away into the dark; fiends like this needed to be put down.

Seth and Gemmil drew their blades, standing firm on either side of Uden, and Erroh stepped back. Not out of fear but as a matter of tactics. Better to keep a bit of space between themselves and these bastards.

Lea thought differently, however, and why wouldn't she? The trauma of facing her father was a terrible thing. She was entitled to crumble into a shell of her own and weep for the unfairness of her life. She was hardly likely to deliver the first strike in anger, but this was precisely what she did, and she was incredible. She had always been incredible, and there was no one else in the world he would have liked at his side at the end of it all.

She leapt forward like a springing insect of the Wastes and fell upon Uden with both blades raised.

The cur was faster than she, but only reflexes saved him. He drew his blades and blocked, but she wouldn't be stopped; she swung at him fiercely, tearing at his defences as Gemmil and Seth moved in on either side, attempting to gut her.

Erroh was never one to leave his mate to face death alone. Mostly. He attacked Seth from the side, slicing his skin and leaving a thin line of blood; distracted by Lea's wrath, the bastard could only block lightly. However, Uden retreated from Lea swiftly, for as mad and hate-filled as he was, he was not ready to slay his daughter.

Gemmil, seeing the gap, slid in and covered his retreat; his eyes were wild, and Erroh recognised a master in that moment. Seth veered away from Erroh as though he had been ordered in silence to kill Lea, leaving the retreating Uden to face Erroh alone. As Lea took the fight to the two servants, Erroh circled Uden, knowing the advantage of surprise was lost. Instead, the recent months of practice and the earlier years of dedication would need to serve him now. He was not scared. His thoughts weren't even of Lea. He could focus only on the monster in his sights.

"How fitting it is at the end of it all. Or the beginning," Uden mocked. Distantly, Erroh heard the clatter of blades as the trio moved down the room, away from the fireplace, towards the shrine of blood. He trusted Lea, trusted her skills, her mind. Her everything.

"You will not be remembered," Erroh warned.

"But you shall be, at least for a time," Uden challenged. He glanced briefly at his comrades, who were at war with his daughter. It was an invitation, but Erroh was no fool. Aggression rarely served him well.

"Fight well," Erroh taunted.

"Go fuk yourself, my liege." Uden charged Erroh, his massive body fiercer moving forward with surprising swiftness. The world slowed, but his strikes did not. Erroh met them, and he was calm, despite the threat. He parried what he could, blocked the rest and offered few counters. He spun away and allowed the fiend to hunt him down. It was no plan, but Erroh knew exhaustion would eventually take its toll on the mad god. Time had passed since they'd met; Erroh was stronger, fiercer and less reckless. Less likely to cough too. Uden, though, was a broken man; he had tasted greatness, held the world as his own, and now was reduced to a skeleton wrapped in a blanket, without anything to call upon but the desire to best his most vocal challenger. They had met twice, and Erroh was greater for it, and Uden was far less—in his mind, in his soul, in his weaker body too.

You should have just killed me that night.

The strikes were furious. Uden roared with every blow, and Erroh fell into himself. He dared not take on the brute in his style of warring. Better he play the part he was determined to play. The blades neared his face, chest and fuken throat, but Erroh was serene in his fighting. More than that, as he slowed his breathing and allowed his heart to beat freely, he was delicate in his defences and retreats.

He saved what energy he could. He made no moves other than what was strictly necessary; he swung back only when he needed to. He took the lessons from every brutal battle he and Lea had ever fought and put them into practice. He vowed to take no death blow in self-sacrifice either. Oh no, he would wait this fuker out, drain him of his ungodly strength and tear him down after. Each time Uden retreated to catch his breath and plan his next move, Erroh would immediately step into range and draw further attacks from the fiend. Gone was the deity who had thrown him through tables, leapt upon him and battered him back with every devastating blow.

Perhaps that brute might still be inside this ageing monster, but Erroh was something else entirely, and he refused to allow him to surface. Erroh was older, wiser and faster, but more than that, he was smarter. He had, after all, taken thrashings at the god's hands and learned from them.

Though he tried to ignore the skirmish at the far end of the room, his eyes were drawn back to the sight of Lea at war, and she was incredible. He could hear her roars of frustration as she held off her attackers, no doubt awaiting the perfect moment to deliver the killing blow. Were Uden to turn and witness this, he might have stared with fatherly pride at her prowess.

As it was, Uden, with his back to her, could only focus on the little cub, and it took all his concentration. Erroh could see the fatigue come all too swiftly upon the behemoth. However, there was still ferocity in his every pounding strike. Maintaining such a pace with respite was possible, but Erroh refused to give him that. Oh, Uden attempted to drop his guard and draw Erroh in, but Erroh was no fool. He struck back at Uden's defence, drawing more energy from him, increasing his frustration, and soon Erroh began to see the first signs of panic.

Panic would bring a swifter end, and Uden seemed to realise this, for he doubled his efforts, hammering wildly at Erroh, hoping to knock him back and move in for the kill, or else to earn a few moments of recovery. As it was, Erroh was at ease, as though he were out in the Wastes with his sparring blades. He fought with a smile upon his face, much to the annoyance of his father-in-law.

You know I have you, Uden.

He merely had to give him a little more time.

It was so easy.

And then something terrible happened that drew Erroh's attention from the battle.

Lea was rattled. No, that wasn't it. Her soul was shattered. Every step she took was taken on unsteady feet. Her arms were weak, and she was sure her grip on her weapons would betray her, send them clattering to the ground, and she would resort to screaming for her beo to save her.

Pathetic.

Seth and Gemmil attempted to surround her, to plunge their blades into her from either side, and she allowed her instinct to take control, but she fought without form, secure footing or deadly intent. She merely existed in this fight, and she was ashamed. She didn't want to die in this unimpressive room, in this freezing part of the world. Many decades from now, she wanted to die surrounded by loved ones, with her old, withered mate wrapped in her arms. She could feel the panic take her; no, she had felt it the moment she'd set eyes upon him.

Only Erroh was her strength now, and out of the corner of her eye she could see Uden hunting him down, pinning him, driving him steadily farther away from her, and it was too much. She spun her blades, knocked her opponents' strikes from her and sought retreat and an opening in their defence that seemed so unlikely. She was not herself; she could not be. His words had rocked her. It didn't matter what they were, only that he had spoken them to her directly. She turned her flagging attention back to the two fiends, who cursed her as they set about killing her, their voices filled with hate. Lea could only gasp as she held them at bay, and she had never been more certain that she would die. She'd never been more certain she didn't want to die either. This was all upon her. Silly Lea, little lost waif of the city. All grown up and lesser for it.

Only the lessons she'd learned in the devastating sparring matches with Erroh kept her alive now: even war had not prepared her for this intimate nightmare of a duel. Once again, she realised how impressive it was that Erroh had survived that fateful night, all alone with Uden to contend with. Or alone upon the top of the city walls with only death as a companion. In war, there were no decisions. There was only the rhythm of murder, and the fiend in front of your blade. It was easier, somehow, and more terrible. But this was something else entirely.

It was Gemmil who struck the fateful blow and Seth who finished her. Gemmil launched himself at her, drawing her blades to meet his solitary blade, and then he ducked and pulled her off balance. It was enough, for immediately Seth was upon her, but not with a sword; he fought with sheer barbarism. He launched his heavier body at her, knocking her fiercely towards the far window.

Glass shattered around her and the wooden panes splintered as she flew through the jagged opening and sailed out into the air.

Falling.

She screamed as she fell free of the window; the ground below raced up to meet her, and she knew it would be a terrible end. Were she to live, the impact would crush her legs, arms and back, and leave her to struggle in agony until Uden, covered in Erroh's blood, came upon her and stamped her from this world.

Gripping her swords as though they were ropes to slow her descent, she allowed her body to spin, hoping either to land as painlessly as possible or to die quickly.

She thought of her failures, her love and her betrayal of Erroh. This day was a betrayal. Not being ready was a betrayal. And she was sorry. She was so fuken sorry. She had never been prepared to fight, and Erroh would die because of it.

———

The absent gods edged her to the left ever so. Just a bit. Just enough. They did this, because they loved her as much as they loved Erroh. They always had.

———

And she landed hard, painfully, and bounced more painfully, and lay stunned in the mound of hay that had been left for the horses. The horses reared back in fright as hay and fragments of glass fountained into the air. She lay there gasping for a moment, with the snorts and whinnies of the startled mounts in her ears, before climbing to her feet—and then stumbling as her ankle gave way.

She heard the clatter of blades far above her and heard Erroh, still fighting, still surviving for her.

"Erroh," she roared, for him to know she lived. To know he wasn't alone and that she would be back beside him in a moment. She bent and examined her ankle; one of the bones was dislocated. She knew this pain, knew how to fix it. Grasping her foot and holding it at just the right angle, she slid the bitch back into place with a sharp pain that near took her consciousness.

She gritted her teeth and controlled the pain, for that was what an Alpha was trained to do, what a Primary should do. What Erroh would have done. And she took it and summoned her hate, summoned her thirst for vengeance. But more than that, she summoned her incredible love for her beautiful mate, who still fought for his life.

She would not leave him, not ever again. Her ankle throbbed, but she tested her weight upon it and it held. Satisfied, she set off at a sprint. Back through the house, up the stairs three at a time, slipping only once.

With a mighty roar, she burst through the doorway, ready to end the battle, the war and her father's dreadful march, once and for all.

Erroh knew Lea was dead. He had seen the size of this house, knew how far up they were. Knew the chances of her walking again or even living after such a fall were slim. He froze for a moment, and a terrible cry of loss and desolation burst from him. And then, to his astonishment, Uden, too, began to wail, his ancient eyes fixed on the smashed window through which his daughter had fallen.

Erroh could barely move; his limbs felt heavy. He gave up in that moment. The fiends who had killed her turned from the window, grinning. Uden turned back to Erroh, and his heartbreak gave way to hate. To murder. He already mourned her death, and he was prepared to inflict pain upon Erroh for it. Erroh wanted to allow him. Wanted to drop to his knees and give up.

Instead, he honoured Lea, honoured Wynn, honoured the young boy in a dead town and everyone who had come after.

As the three charged upon Erroh, he met their strikes, and it was frantic and unfair, and none of it mattered, for she was dead, and soon he would be too. He spun and defended and sought out their weaknesses, but it was futile. Although his opponents were tired and becoming increasingly awkward with every strike, they were simply too many for him, and he was but a cub, outnumbered and distraught.

And then, as he twisted wide of a glancing blow that might have drawn blood, he heard her call for him. Just one word, his name, sung beautifully from below. Whatever agony she was in, whatever injury she had suffered, she still drew breath, and he needed to be with her. And these fiends were all that stood in his way.

Erroh had a plan.

A simple plan.

It wouldn't work.

But it didn't matter.

He cast off his defensive stance and released the full force of his anger upon them as they surrounded him. He let go of restraint and fear and caution. He remembered the mania that had taken him in Keri, and he drew upon it and began to laugh as they closed in. He allowed them. He wasn't worried. He didn't care. He only cared for her, and she still drew breath, and he needed to be with her. Needed it more than ever.

He charged upon them, his body a blur of movement, and they

weren't ready. He tore at them, drawing blood, tearing skin, and laughed with every blow.

"Stop laughing," cried Gemmil as Erroh spun and slit him above his eye.

"You maniac," roared Seth, taking an inch of steel into his shoulder.

"You are a demon," bellowed Uden, and for him, Erroh made a deep slash across his naked chest. A long tear crossing over a previous scar. He roared hysterically, and all three stepped back from this mad fool who drew their blood as though it were a game.

And, like every dreadful, violent skirmish, it ended all too swiftly. From behind them, Lea suddenly appeared, and she was as wild as Erroh. She burst through the doors, screaming for her love, and Erroh cried louder, and it was perfect. He whirled upon Uden and set upon him viciously, while his goddess mate tore into Gemmil and Seth, who were no match for her sudden fury.

It was Seth who died first. He attempted to grapple with her, and she spun past him, twirling her blades out behind him, catching him in the neck and tearing his throat apart as she passed. He did not die immediately; he scrambled around the room, clutching desperately at his comrades, begging them to save him. Blood sprayed every which way, covering Gemmil, who was too busy to notice as Lea gutted him in turn with her blades. To finish, she sent her sword through his mouth and stuck him to the far wall, where he stood struggling and pinned for a precious few moments as he died.

Uden saw none of this. He fell upon Erroh wildly and was torn asunder by the younger Alphaline. Laughing as he did, Erroh plunged a blade into Uden's hand, causing him to drop his sword. This should have ended it, but Uden had one further godly act to carry out upon his nemesis. With his injured hand, he reached out, gripped Mercy and Vengeance at their tips and clenched hard. He screamed as the razor-sharp blades severed his fingers, and the sound distracted Erroh for just enough time to allow him to strike a killing blow at Erroh's undefended side.

The traumas Erroh had suffered served him well now, as the end drew near, fuelling a fresh surge of anger within him. With Lea screaming from so far away, he remembered the tears upon the boy in a fallen town long ago. He remembered Quig and Aireys and Jeremiah and all those warriors, brave and gone. He thought of the punishment of Nomi, the severed head of Mish, the fall of the Rangers, and Wynn's heroic death. He thought of the world's suffering at the hands of this brute. He thought of Lea's horror. Of her shame.

And last, he thought of a night in the city when, with all his companions around him, he had received a gift from a broken man. A man he'd considered an enemy. A man who had at last chosen to learn humility, who had become a friend. A man killed at Uden and Erroh's hands, who hadn't been there to help him.

Champion of Keri.

He drew that expensive, broken blade from his waist and, leaving his swords in the grasp of a mad god, he dove upon him, ducked beneath Uden's strike, and stabbed the blade deep into his side. He fell away from his victim, who gasped, dropped Erroh's swords and collapsed to his knees, staring at the dagger, golden and shimmering, protruding from him, killing him. He pulled it free and godly crimson began to stream— so much blood.

"I am spent, demon," he whispered, and slumped to the floor. Erroh bent and recovered his blades, then stood over Uden and placed them upon his neck. Uden did not resist. He could only stare with one eye, first at Erroh, and then upon his daughter with love and sorrow.

"Make your peace with her," Erroh whispered.

"I am sorry I lost you," Uden said, and Lea bent and placed her lips to his forehead and kissed him goodnight.

"Goodbye, Father."

She looked to Erroh as Uden closed his eye for the last time, and she nodded. All was said. With all his strength, Erroh drew the blade across Uden's neck, severed the god's head cleanly and allowed his body to fall back among the ruin with his comrades.

Lea said nothing. She limped over to her man and kissed him once before fetching a lantern and pouring its oil upon Uden's body.

"Fuken burn my shrine too," Erroh mumbled.

She went over to her shrine and retrieved a candle and the painting. Holding the painting under one arm, she dropped the candle upon his eternally sleeping body and lit a pyre fit for a god.

"It is done," she said, wiping a solitary tear from her eye.

"Are you all right?"

"I will be, my love."

They swiftly scoured the house as the flames took hold, but there was little to be found: no collection of ancient scrolls, no desperate prisoners locked away in the deep below. Everything Uden had ever been, had held precious, was gone. With the crackle of fire rising and the smoke

The Actions of Gods

billowing out through the shattered window above, they walked through the doorway, where Erroh dropped to his knees in gratitude to the absent gods and to her. She knelt with him, and they embraced and kissed and wept ever so. The deed was done. Their tale was written. They had only each other to care for now.

And apparently, the entire world.

There was still enough light left in the day to allow them to ride for a few miles. Suddenly, they wanted nothing more than to flee from this place as swiftly as their mounts would carry them.

"So, what now, my liege?" she asked, taking his hand.

"Whatever we want, Mydame. The world is ours," he said.

119

EPILOGUE

The wretched healer roused himself from his bedding and sucked in deep breaths. He might have stayed longer in these warm silken sheets, but he knew better than to dwell on his thoughts. Best get out of bed, be grateful for what he had and keep marching.

Scrubbing himself with a warm bucket of water, he cleaned himself as he did every day. He doused himself in lavender oil to finish. A perfect tonic to enhance his charms. He wasn't the only former wretch from the hovels who cleaned themselves like this. It was a simple routine and one he relished daily.

He left his house with a steaming cup of cofe and set off down the front walkway. It had been three days since he was last drunk. It might have been four. He was losing count, which was a welcome thing. Without the weight of the world crushing him, it was easier to enjoy alcohol for the right reasons and not to numb himself away to nothing.

"Good morning, Fighting Mongoose," he said to the cat sitting atop the pillar of his house as he left the front gate. He wasn't sure of the cat's name. His previous owner, Stefan, had told him once, but he couldn't remember. "I heard you come in through the back window late last night; what a time you must have had." The beast meowed in reply, and, digging into his pockets, he rewarded the cat with some dried bacon for its trouble.

The cat had left him a gift. He picked up the dead mouse by the tail and inspected the poor thing like it was a delicious meal. "Why, thank you, Fighting Mongoose. I'll enjoy this later," he said, throwing the dead creature as far from his front garden as possible.

The Actions of Gods

They lived a quiet, peaceful life, he and the cat, for Emir had many open windows, freshly stuffed cushions and more than enough morsels of food to keep him fed. And the occasional bacon treat as well.

"I might walk down to the office. There's nobody to treat, but I should do something productive. I'll be home for dinner later, so don't worry."

"Meow."

Every day, he found a new name for the cat. One of these days, one would sit. For now, it was Fighting Mongoose. Tomorrow it might be Killer, given the carcasses appearing at his door daily. Truly, though, he loved the cat and felt Stefan would have wanted him to care for him. It was all he could do.

Leaving the beast to do whatever it liked in the brighter hours, namely inflict brutal murder on the local rodent population, Emir walked along his street, listening to the sound of hammering from nearly every house he passed. It was a glorious time to be a carpenter in Keri, as every household needed new furniture. Emir's pockets were full of pieces from Wrek's frequent deliveries, and his own house was close to being fully refurbished again. He quite liked his new door. It didn't squeak or anything. A man could want for lesser things in life.

He loaned much of his ill-gotten gains to assist with Keri's restoration. He took no profit on the loans either. It was what Aireys would have wanted, so it was what Emir did. Soon enough, he would refuse Wrek's monthly payments. He needed no such kindness, just his friendship. For now, though, rebuilding this fractured town was too important a task to ignore.

He decided against going to the medical office just yet. A convoy had just arrived in the town, and he was in no mood to meet with the newcomers. All of them, he knew, were eager to return to life here and intended to approach the mayor about buying or renting one of the many abandoned houses.

The whole scenario made him squirm with unease. Not the people, mind. Mostly, they were fellow townspeople who had suffered the terrors of the war and the wretchedness of the hovels, just as he had. Mostly. It was just an awful reminder. In fact, he held the deeds to Aireys's house, but he hadn't yet found anyone he trusted enough to rent the place, no matter their wealth. He had decided he would give it only to Wrek, if the cur was willing to travel this far someday, perhaps with a new bride in tow.

That would be nice, he thought, to have friends again.

Quig's estate he had taken for himself, and had given away his old house. It was a good place; a little bigger than his old one, with miles of fields. And why not? Hadn't he almost been king?

Ignoring duty a little longer, hoping one of his regulators would tend to the newcomers, he ventured out to the gap. He walked among the graves of those he had lost, whispered prayers for them under his breath and then spoke aloud of more pleasant things in this world, as though they might hear them from their place in the ground or from a cosy tavern in the afterlife.

In truth, he was happier here than he'd ever been. He was older, but that wasn't necessarily a bad thing. He deeply loved this place, and really, the people of this town loved him dearly. It was just a shame he was so heartbroken without her. He had made the right decision, though. This, he knew. As she served her world, so too did he serve his world, albeit in a far smaller way than she had done.

They wrote to each other frequently, declaring their hearts broken, declaring their love eternal, and it was no lie, but the nights he spent writing those letters were the hardest, and afterwards he usually ended up in the Sickle, drinking until dawn, talking to anyone who would listen about how well little Lin was doing. And his beautiful wife, too. Although he argued against it, he rarely paid for a drink.

It's good to be the king.

To distract himself from love and loss, he visited the town's shrine. This, he did daily, and today, as always, he shed tears of sorrow, but of love and joy too. He gazed upon the painting, perfect and precise upon the wall, hiding the horrors beneath.

His eyes travelled over the artwork, painted with love, telling the tale of those he loved so dearly. Upon the crest of the gap stood Lea, firing arrows of flame. On either side of her were men he knew, though few by name, apart from Azel; he stood at the far side, firing his own arrows with similar fury. Below them stood many similar warriors, ready to defend, all brave heroes of the town.

King Erroh, who was depicted with two blades, wore a grimace of hate and fury upon his face, giving fight to countless warriors. On his left, Quig, with a scythe, brought death upon all who neared. Aireys was on the other side of Erroh, standing dignified and beautiful. Emir reached up now and ran his fingers along her silhouette. As sorrowful as this mural was, it was a beautiful thing, and he wasn't the sole occupant of Keri who viewed this mural daily to give thanks to the heroes who had given everything, including their lives, so that this town would live on.

"Thank you, my heroes," he whispered, kissing his fingers and then touching them to his heart. Feeling lighter now, he walked back to meet with the new arrivals, smiling warmly as he welcomed them. This was, after all, the responsibility of every mayor, and a charge given to him by her. There were worse fates in this world.

She dropped down from the cart and stretched out the pain in her back. For too long, she'd sat doing little but thinking of the world and her choices and the few regrets she had about making this final pilgrimage. She wondered how wild she looked. She wondered if she should wear her hair down. Would he see her red, flowing locks and come running? She could have written. She should have written. Warning him. But her letters were a difficult thing to write, harder still for him to read. She knew that now, but she didn't care. His absence had brought her a duty, certain clarity. Without him, she was nothing. Without him, what passion she had for the city was diminished. She did not fear a life here. She did not fear a life with him. Her husband. Her wretched, wonderful husband. She breathed deeply in the cool, clean air and wondered where he could be. Whom should she ask of his whereabouts? She was alone among many strangers, all busily planning their lives in this place, and it was terrifying but welcome too.

Roja followed the crowd as they sought out officials who would tell them where to go and what they needed to make a life here. She felt excited for the first time in her life. Lighter than ever. And then she saw him on the path above. He was frozen, staring at her as the newcomers filed past him. He didn't seem to notice them at all.

He was smiling for her alone.

She was home.

THE END

HERE ENDS THE SPARK CITY CYCLE.
TO GET THE LATEST UPDATES ON NEW RELEASES IN THIS WORLD, JOIN THE ROBERT J POWER READERS' CLUB AT ROBERTJPOWER.COM

Thank you for reading The Actions of Gods

Word-of-mouth is crucial for any author to succeed and honest reviews of my books help to bring them to the attention of other readers.

If you enjoyed the book, and have 2 minutes to spare, please leave an honest review on Amazon and Goodreads. Even if it's just a sentence or two it would make all the difference and would be very much appreciated.

Thank you.

EXCLUSIVE FREE BOOK FROM ROBERT J POWER

When you join the Robert J Power Readers' Club you'll get the latest news from the Spark City and Dellerin series, free books, exclusive content and new release updates.

You'll also get a short tale exclusive to members - you can't get this anywhere else!

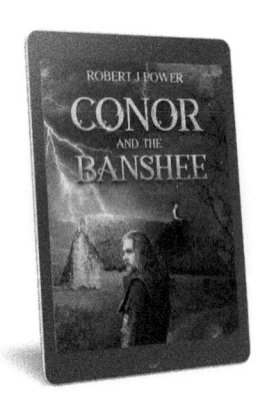

ALSO BY ROBERT J POWER

The Spark City Cycle:
Spark City, Book 1
The March of Magnus, Book 2
The Outcasts, Book 3
The Actions of Gods, Book 4

The Dellerin Tales:
The Lost Tales of Dellerin
The Seven

The Crimson Collection
The Crimson Hunters, Vol I

ACKNOWLEDGMENTS

Thank you Poll and Jill. You'll never know the difference you guys made the last few years. I don't mind that you delicately insist I only write Dellerin tales. Yes, yes, I know it's a better story arc but the fans have spoken. At least for now. Don't worry, I'll get to it.

Paul and Jean for their continual support and gentle prying for a release date. Truthfully, Paul's continual support, and Jean's insane demands for HER finished book. I swear, without this abuse I'd still be on chapter 55. There, it's done, Jean. Are you happy now? Am I welcome back in the house?

Cathbar, the legend of all legends. I've never been more terrified of anyone's opinion more than yours. You were the first Spark City fan that challenged me to work on plots, themes and all that shit. A challenge at 4 am, with too much wine consumed between us all the while debating the intricacies of Erroh's supposed haircut echoing throughout the apartment block. Somehow it all helped. Next round is on me!

Fuken Darian. I give you so much shit mate. Yet still, you call me a friend. Idiot. Also, you are one of the most talented people I've met. A funny fuker too. I don't tell you this in person because that's not the way. So, instead, I hide these compliments in acknowledgements. Who reads them anyway?

Fuken Lcass, my nemesis. I hope this book crushes your latest release. You've probably written another cracking book since I started this paragraph. You are the worst. And also the fuken best. I hate that I'm such a fan of your work. I hate that you are always there with sage advice that helps fix all my career mistakes. I hate you!

Speaking of hate, and the amount of hate my editors must have felt for me as they dove through my absolute dumpster fire of a story and emerged with a script making me look far better than I really am. You guys were amazing. Thank you so fuken much!!!!!!!!

And finally, to the amazing fans who have carried the Spark name far. You guys are the best. Far better than anyone mentioned above. Without you I'd be nothing. Or worse, in a job I fuken hated with an asshole boss who ate raw garlic at lunchtime. Who the fuk does that?? Fuken Jerry, that's who. Fuk you Jerry! Anyway, all things must end and I hope you love this final book as much as I loved writing it. Actually, much more, in fact. Because some days were a right nightmare writing. Regardless, I still love it and I still love you all.

ABOUT THE AUTHOR

Robert J Power is the fantasy author of the Amazon bestselling series, The Spark City Cycle and The Dellerin Tales. When not locked in a dark room with only the daunting laptop screen as a source of light, he fronts Irish rock band, Army of Ed, despite their many attempts to fire him.

Robert lives in Wexford, Ireland with his wife Jan, three rescue dogs and a cat that detests his very existence. Before he found a career in writing, he enjoyed various occupations such as a terrible pizza chef, a video store manager (ask your grandparents), and an irresponsible camp counsellor. Thankfully, none of them stuck.

If you wish to learn of Robert's latest releases, his feelings on The Elder Scrolls, or just how many coffees he consumes a day before the palpitations kick in, visit his website at www.RobertJPower.com where you can join his reader's club. You might even receive some free goodies, hopefully some writing updates, and probably a few nonsensical ramblings.

www.RobertJPower.com

facebook.com/authorrobertjpower
instagram.com/RobertJPower